THE CASTLE OMNIBUS

Also by Steph Swainston
from Gollancz:

The Year of Our War
No Present Like Time
The Modern World
Above the Snowline

THE
CASTLE
OMNIBUS

✦

The Year of Our War
No Present Like Time
The Modern World

STEPH SWAINSTON

GOLLANCZ
LONDON

First published in Great Britain in 2009
by Gollancz
An imprint of the Orion Publishing Group
Orion House, 5 Upper St Martin's Lane,
London WC2H 9EA
An Hachette UK Company

A CIP catalogue record for this book
is available from the British Library

ISBN 978 0 575 09125 2

3 5 7 9 10 8 6 4 2

Typeset by Deltatype Ltd, Birkenhead, Merseyside

Printed and bound in the UK by
CPI Mackays, Chatham ME5 8TD

The Orion Publishing Group's policy is to use papers
that are natural, renewable and recyclable products and
made from wood grown in sustainable forests. The logging
and manufacturing processes are expected to conform to
the environmental regulations of the country of origin.

www.stephswainston.co.uk
www.orionbooks.co.uk

CONTENTS

THE YEAR
OF OUR WAR

✦

TO BRIAN

'Unnatural vices are fathered by our heroism.'

T.S. ELIOT

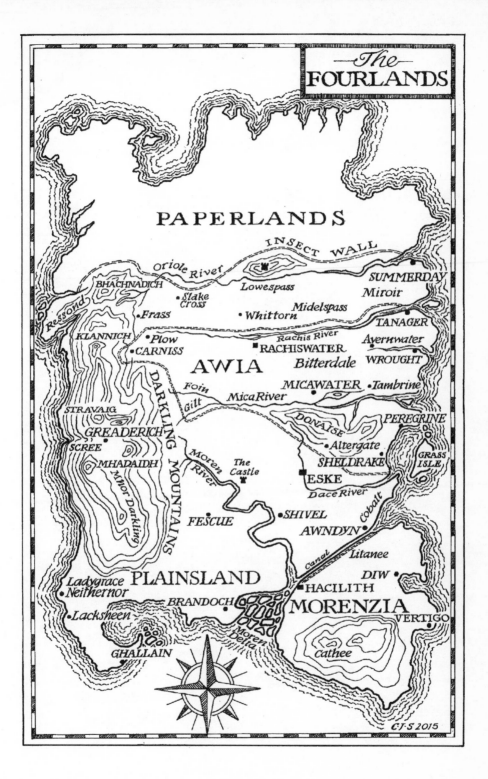

CHAPTER I

As soon as I arrived in Lowespass I bought a newspaper and read it in the shadow of the fortress wall:

Castle Calls for Reinforcements –
Rachiswater Offensive Continues

The Castle has demanded eight thousand fresh troops to be raised from the Plainslands to join the Awian Fyrd on the Lowespass front. Awian soldiers led by King Dunlin Rachiswater have forced the Insects westwards, exposing the remains of Lowespass town, which was lost in the Insect advance last year.

In a joint press conference held on Friday with Comet representing the Castle, King Rachiswater announced that five kilometres of ground had been recovered. He pointed out that this was the first time the Wall had been pushed back in twenty years. His Majesty appealed for 'our brothers of the Plainslands' to send reinforcements so the advance could continue. Comet reported that the Emperor was 'pleased' with the success of the Awian operation.

Lowespass town now presents a dramatic sight, shocking to those who have not seen the works of Insects before. To the scorched walls and timbers – the town was burnt before evacuation – Insects have added their complex of grey paper constructions with pointed roofs resembling houses. The ground is riddled with their tunnels.

Awian losses in the last two weeks were heaviest in the infantry, with one thousand fatalities and as many injured. Five hundred of the cavalry were killed, while the archers, all under Lightning's command, suffered twelve injured. None of the immortals has been harmed, and they continue to encourage the troops. Veterans of the campaign have been promised settlements in newly recovered lands.

Comet said that despite such determined efforts the terror of an Insect swarm appearing remains significant. He reported that the buildings stretch for kilometres behind the Wall. He said, 'Flying over it is like—

I knew my own words, however badly reported, so I flicked to page five, where there was a cartoon with a surprising likeness of Lightning. The cartoon grasped desperately at a beautiful girl who was carrying a guitar. Her figure dissolved like a ghost into little woodcut hearts. The caption underneath read: *Swallow? In your dreams.*

Giggling, I folded the newspaper and shoved it into the back of my belt. I strode away from the fortress wall towards the cliff, hearing the river torrent below. Two strides, and I started running. I forced at the ground, accelerating, faster and faster to the edge of the cliff. Three, two, one. I spread my wings and kicked over the edge as the ground fell away. I turned in a long calm arc down towards the camp.

By day the Lowespass outpost filled the river valley with sound and splendour. Tents covered the ground completely, coloured like scales on a butterfly's wing. Troops patrolled the Insect Wall, covered wagons drawn by exhausted horses rolled in along the rutted road. They unloaded at the fortress, took the wounded away. From the air, carts were the size of matchboxes, parked in a line. Shouts carried from the soldiers at training; those at rest sat in groups on the grass, or in the canvas city, under awnings, around fires. Pennants, which marked fyrd divisions, twisted like vivid tongues on the blunted mountain breeze. They were blue with white eagles for the country of Awia, a scallop shell for Summerday manor, a clenched fist for Hacilith city, stars, ploughs and ships for the Plainslands manors. The Castle's flag was set in the centre of the camp, a red and gold sun-in-splendour. Our symbol of permanence now shines on land reclaimed from the Insects, and soldiers passing beneath it glance up, smiling.

I flew in at midnight, practically blind, trying to remember how deep the valley was. I hurtled down it, balancing on long wings. The river looked like a strand of silver mirror behind the slashed black hillside, and not too far distant I could see the Wall.

Too fast. I'm going too fast.

Good.

Dividing the valley, Lowespass Fortress on its rocky crag soared above me as I dropped. The dark ground was spotted with red, the campfires of the fyrd. Closer still, I could see pale faces surrounding them, but no more. I felt unnerved that Lowespass was populated with silent soldiers. I slowed, flared my wings and landed neatly on a patch of ground not two metres from a cluster of sleeping bags, which yelped.

I made my way on the damp ground between bivouacs and tent pegs to the Castle's pavilion. Lamplight shone in a thin beam from the slit entrance. I stood for a while hearing the chatter coming from within, before remembering that those who listen outside tents rarely hear any good about themselves.

'Welcome back, Comet,' said Dunlin.

'You can call me Jant,' I said. As my eyes got used to the light I saw three men sitting around a thin table, playing cards. The pavilion was so large that the edges were in shadow; the central pole was wound with red and yellow

10

ribbons. I bowed to King Dunlin Rachiswater, and to his brother Staniel, and I said hi to Lightning, the Castle's Archer.

Lightning nodded curtly at me. He was sorting his cards. 'What's the news?'

'Diw won two-nil against Hacilith.'

He gaped. 'Can't you *ever* be serious?'

Dunlin leant forward. 'Have you been successful?'

'Of course. Your Majesty, there are five thousand soldiers on their way from the coast. They'll take a week to ride here. In addition to that, I went to the Castle and spoke with the Emperor, and he greatly favours what we've achieved and backs all the plans you asked me to report—'

'Wait, wait. Didn't we say eight, not five?'

'I can pull another three thousand from Awia if you give me time.' I was slightly ashamed that I had spent the last few days at the Castle visiting my wife rather than working. King Dunlin Rachiswater is the only man I know who has enough stamina to remain at the front for weeks on end without feeling the need for a night with a woman.

He shook his head. 'It has to be the Plainslands. Not Awia. Who'll feed us?'

'My lord, there are few soldiers left at the coast, and most of them are too young. There's no outcry as yet, but I think it's wrong to take so many.'

'If my country of Awia gives all it can, then the Plainslands can too.'

I said, 'If I may venture a criticism, it's your campaign to push the Insects out of land where they're well established which is costing so many lives.'

'So you'd rather remain in a stalemate for another two thousand years?'

I sighed. 'The Castle aims to protect Zascai from the Insects. There's never a shortage of Insects. If you use up the fighting force of one generation, for how long can we guarantee that protection?'

'Immortals are so frustrating sometimes,' he remarked to his brother. 'We can beat the Insects. With eight thousand, we can control their movements. We can support each other!'

I told him, 'I've seen a lot of action, and I think a hot-headed approach is wrong.'

Rachiswater prepared to contest this but Lightning said, 'Your Majesty, don't argue with Comet.'

'Sorry, Jant.'

'No, no. It's my fault. I've flown a long way. I'm a bit tired.'

They fetched a chair for me to sit down at the table, and poured some red wine from a crystal decanter. The drink wasn't good on an empty stomach, and I began to feel very light-headed as the others continued with their card game.

'You look tired,' Lightning said, tone dripping with suspicion. The

Micawater manor insignia on his shoulder caught the lamplight, a similar diamond design on the quiver full of red-flighted arrows dangling from the back of his chair. The arrows were hanging with a little state-of-the-art composite bow: gold-banded horn and polished strips of wood, curved back like pincers. This meant he must have been showing off because in battle he usually uses a longbow. He was a little taller than Dunlin, much broader than Staniel, and more muscular than me.

There was a resemblance between Dunlin and Staniel, but in it Dunlin had taken all the darkness and strength, whereas his younger brother was like a yellow reed.

Dunlin growled, 'I want us to keep our minds on the *campaign*. Especially tomorrow, because it is going to be challenging. Archer, your command is vital.' Lightning didn't say anything.

'And Messenger? Jant …?'

'At your service,' said I. Dunlin filled his glass, raised it, drank a toast to the Emperor. I clinked my glass to his, set it down after the briefest sip. I didn't want him to see my unsteady hand.

Dunlin's expression became thoughtful. 'Out of the immortals apart from your good selves, Tornado, Mist and Ata will join us. Rayne will stay in Lowespass Fortress. There hasn't been such a powerful showing of the Circle for … how long?'

'Just a hundred years,' I said.

Staniel's pale eyes were starry with inward enthusiasm. His skinny hand stroked his little blond goatee. No doubt he planned to write about it later: Staniel Rachiswater fighting fearlessly against the Insects with the aid of the immortals.

In the Awian language immortals are called Eszai. Staniel's poetry portrayed us Eszai as divine and his sturdy brother as a heroic fighter, and so his image shone with a little of our reflected light, but I had never seen him pick up a sword. His responsibility had been to make sure any wounded and food-poisoned returned to the fortress, and that fyrd on their way back to their manors did not linger and become highwaymen. He had delegated those tasks to me at the outset and now remained in the camp, scribbling in his notebook with a fountain pen.

'I have a straight flush in hearts,' said Lightning. 'Gentlemen? Oh dear. Pity. So – I acquire the Rachiswater amphitheatre, and Staniel's library.' He dealt, the red-backed cards pliant in his big hands. 'I stake Micawater Bridge, which as you know is one of the seven wonders of the world, so please treat it kindly. Jant, are you playing?'

'You daft bloody Awians,' I muttered unhappily.

'It's just a bit of fun. I'll let you have your manor back in the morning.'

I declined; I don't see any point in card games. My reactions are faster than the Awians'; if I wanted to win I could cheat by sleight of hand. If I played without cheating, then Dunlin would beat me because he is a better, poker-faced strategist, and Lightning would beat him because Lightning has played cards for fifteen hundred years and can see through any strategy without trying. My thoughts strayed hard to something else. I was beginning to feel shaky, and in case my associates had noticed, I blamed it on fatigue. I stood up, pushing the chair back into damp grass. 'Give me leave to leave?'

'See you at first light,' said the King.

'Sweet dreams,' remarked Lightning.

I found the gentle breeze revitalising. It was the extreme feather's end of the mountains, and, with a little imagination, I could smell the high summits – glaciers and pine behind the reek of campfire cooking and unwashed soldiers. It was only fancy, but knowing that the breeze in Lowespass gusts down from the mountains made me feel nostalgic. I remembered bitterly that nostalgia is another symptom of withdrawal.

I don't have or need my own tent, so I hurried to Lightning Saker Micawater's pavilion where a bundle of chamois-skin blankets just inside the entrance marked my bed. He hadn't touched my maps and clothes, which were still piled as I had left them, though now damp with dew. I managed to light a candle, gathered together my works and took a shot. I soon went to sleep, curled up, racked with hallucinations.

Until golden dawn kicked me awake with big boots.

I yawned and stretched, decongealing. I lay cradled in the blankets, comfortably warm and very relaxed, looking out down Lowespass valley towards the Wall. The vale was filled with blue-grey wood-smoke from a thousand campfires, hanging in horizontal stripes and softening the sunlight. Groups of soldiers were gathering, heading towards the main source of the smoke, where breakfast was being dished out. Food at the front was surprisingly good – it had to be because very few of the General Fyrd wanted to be there and it was better for Castle to tempt them than force them. I watched soldiers striking low green tents, which billowed down and were lashed to carrying poles. I drifted for a while, observing the scene, pleasantly unfocused, and then I thought about how good it would be to take another fix. My needle was lying on an unfolded map. I reached out and as my hand closed round it a boot descended on my wrist.

'No, you don't,' said Lightning. He shoved a couple of folds of crimson scarf over one shoulder, bent down and retrieved spoon, syringe, twist of paper. 'I'll look after these.'

'Oh, no. Honestly. Come on, Saker! Not *again*.'

'Dunlin is calling for us. I need you to talk to Tornado. Up you get.'

13

I should have found Lightning's demeanour inspiring. He wore armour – brass scale lorica made to look like covert feathers – over his chest and down strong arms to the elbow. He had leather trousers laced up the sides, and a Wrought sword at his hip. His scarf, embellished with the Castle insignia, stuck to his wings – which were longer than the modern average – and ruffled the feathers. Other people would have been impressed with such beautiful armour; I simply wondered how much the Wrought craftsmen were making from it, and whether I would see any of the profit.

Feeling rather diminished and dirty, I followed the embroidered sun on his mantle out of the pavilion and through the camp. Faces looked up from turfing ashy fires or pulling backpack cords tight, buckling cuirasses or blowing on hot coffee. The soldiers we met stood up, so that we went in a little wave of startled men standing, then settling down after we passed.

There was a difference between the soldiers of the General Fyrd and the Select Fyrd. The latter were proud of their warrior status, in competition with each other for the attention of governors and immortals; they kept their swords razor keen. They jumped quickly to their feet as we walked by.

Most of the archers were Select Fyrd, as it takes so long to train them; they were waiting by Lightning's pavilion and he nodded at a couple almost familiarly. His goldfish-armour shimmered.

We reached the area of the General Fyrd, soldiers who weren't trained, or new recruits who were much less well-equipped. The main armouries were in Wrought, my wife's manor. On Castle's command they provided every man with shield, broadsword and pike, but the drafted farmers in the General Fyrd could not afford more than this very basic equipment. They were dressed in worsted and muddied denim, hardly a glint of steel apart from ill-fitting battlefield spoils. These men and women shambled to their feet, still holding trays of food. Their camp was carelessly kept, their patched tents stood unevenly. Some tents were simply frames from which mosquito netting hung, weighted at the bottom.

It was one of Tornado's duties to direct the General Fyrd. Tornado was sitting cross-legged on the grass, stripped to the waist, sliding the edge of a battleaxe across a huge whetstone with a sound like sawing. A paunch hung over his cracked belt. At two and a half metres tall he was the biggest and strongest of the Castle's Eszai, unbeaten for one thousand years. He had brown hair shaven very close to the scalp. It looked weird together with the rug of hair growing on his chest and a little on his shoulders. The hair didn't cover pale scars, thick as my finger and long as a span, which criss-crossed his chest and stomach. Slabs of muscle shifted on his sunburnt shoulders as he manipulated the axe. An ancient sunburst tattoo on his forearm undulated as the muscles moved.

Unlike most of the Eszai, Tornado had never owned anything – no lands,

14

and no more wealth than beer money. His reputation hung on risking death in the very thick of the action. If he hadn't faced death so eagerly, so often, he wouldn't be so practised at dealing with it. Tawny and I are similar in that our links to life are more tenuous than people expect.

Tawny's well-chosen girlfriend, Vireo Summerday, was also gigantic. She was scratching her leg by poking a stick through the joints of her plate armour. I couldn't fathom Vireo, she was neither terrified of nor attracted to me. She wouldn't call a spade a spade if she could call it a fucking bastard. Lightning bowed to her; she winked at me.

'Good morning,' said Lightning.

'Yo,' said Tawny. 'All right, Jant?'

'... Considering.'

'I've been ready bloody ages and nothing has happened,' said Tawny. 'When do we get to fight?'

'You will be commanding the Hacilith men and those from Eske.'

'The townies,' I said.

'Nothing changed there then.'

Lightning said, 'When the Insects attack, fall back. There will be shield walls to channel them if necessary. We will drive them into the sixth corral. You should attempt to advance through the Wall. Dunlin believes it possible that we can breach their defences and redeem more land.'

'Whoa! Hang on. You what? Want me to go behind the Wall? No way, little one. I'll be on my own because townies are chickenshit, like you know. They'll run so fast they'll fly, by god! Behind the Wall, like, not bloody likely.'

'It's Dunlin's main aim at the moment,' said Lightning.

'If you thought with yer balls rather than yer heart you'd not let a soft bloody Zascai get in the way of how Eszai have always done stuff.'

'Have we not recently decided to support the King of Awia?'

I interrupted, 'But last time a thousand people died.' If I had been on the field and not unconscious during the skirmish, the Castle might have fared better. Lightning seemed about to make that point, so I decided to keep quiet. Tawny complained for a while but accepted; he doesn't have enough willpower to argue with Lightning.

'Look, Tawny,' I said. 'The Emperor backs Dunlin, so we've got to do it. We can't guess why the Emperor makes such plans. They might come in useful a century from now.'

He respected me; he knew that my experiences have given me calmness, a knowledge that sets me apart from day-to-day concerns. He sensed this, and he admired such steadfastness.

'Whatever you say, Jant.' Tawny poked the bright edge of his axe with a grimy thumbnail. 'But culling Insects should be a waiting game. I'm buggered if I want to stir them up.' He used the axe to steady himself as he stood. I stepped back a little, overawed by his size. He stretched and muscle on muscle tautened under fat.

'Be careful—' Lightning began.

'Get lost, lover-boy,' said Tawny. 'I'm doing my job which is, like, cutting up Insects. I know I'll survive, behind the Wall or underground or anywhere. Dunlin's trying to save civilian lives. It's good that he cares for them, but he's trying *too hard*.' He buckled the axe to his chain belt, plucked at Vireo who had been eavesdropping in the background. In Plainslands he said, 'Let's go, love. Everything round here with wings is crazy.'

'What was that?' Lightning asked. I gave a loose translation; he watched them go. 'Aren't lovers content in their own little worlds?' he said.

In the pavilion, I was left alone while Lightning went to address the archers' ranks and the neat phalanxes of Select Awian infantry. They had blue plumes on their helmets, heraldic creations of carved bone and cuir-bouilli and faience, finely wrought iridium chain mail over their wings. I took the chance to go through all his belongings searching for my drugs. I found a couple of letters that would have been interesting if I hadn't been so feverish. No cat. I called Lightning all the names under the sun. Left a devastated mess behind. Sat down on the grass. Started shaking with an advance on withdrawal – the effect of panic.

Well. Plan B. I found my compass, pressed a button and the silver casing clicked open like a shell. There was a twist of paper inside, ripped from the edge of a map. It's vital to have more than one stash. With a long thumbnail I cut a line of cat on the compass glass, rolled up a five-pound note and snorted it, north-south.

Oh, *yes*.

I let the worries dissolve, one by one, and drop from my mind. Not even immortals are built to take so many misgivings. Wiping my nose on the back of a hand, I considered the forthcoming fight. I was wearing bangles, faded jeans and a cut-off T-shirt which read 'Hacilith Marathon 1974'.

I gazed at the heap of my silver scale armour, a byrnie adorned with smaragd and onyx, a helmet decorated with knot-work, with a high white plume. It matches black-on-silver vambraces. A belt and a sword-hanger, a circular shield; my sword's grip has two snakes wrapped around it. I have pauldrons for my wings, inscribed 'For god and the Empire'. I have latten greaves. I have a black cloak, thin taffeta with a niello silver fastening. I have pinked black leather gauntlets, embossed with Castle's Sun and my sign, the Wheel.

Sod that. I strip my T-shirt off, shove my ice axe in the back of my belt, and consider myself ready to fight anything.

'Jant?' It was Dunlin, and he was looking amazed. I swept a low bow. 'Your Majesty.'

Dunlin said, 'Comet, Tornado is already hacking at the Wall. You must be in the air as soon as possible.' I was irritated until I realised that the true purpose of Dunlin's endless rallying and righteous enthusiasm was to make him feel better. 'What did the Emperor really say?' he asked me. He was shrewder than I gave him credit for.

'San conceded the sagacity of everything you've done,' I said.

'Did he have a message for me?' Dunlin's hand rested on an ornate sword hilt. 'Am I valuable to the Emperor? Am I noticed by him?'

'There isn't time to go into details!'

'Then after the battle, Rhydanne. I know you remember court word-perfect and I have to know.'

'Your wish.' I shrugged. I wanted the bright air, not to be cornered in a tent by the Awian King. I didn't want this man I admired to make reference to my Rhydanne ancestry.

Dunlin regarded me carefully; cleverness would hide in the wrinkles round his eyes. His eyes were grey but not flecked – like silver coins – and he could outstare me, which few can do. He said, 'You must remember to relate my Lord Emperor's opinion of our victory last week, in which Tawny and I were in the melee.' There was a sheen of sweat on his red-brown neck.

His straightforwardness pushed me into telling the truth for once. 'You want to join the Castle Circle, don't you?' I said.

'Good guess, Comet. More than you can ever know.'

'Your Highness. There's nothing I can do.'

He turned, sliding his blade in its scabbard, and with his broad back to me said, 'In a lesser time I might have achieved a place, but not now. Over the years I have seen thirty of you fight and, to give an example, I can't wrestle as well as Tornado, I can't handle a longbow like Lightning and I can't move as fast as you.'

'There hasn't been a new entrant to the Castle for ninety years.'

'Doesn't matter. Lightning says three might come along at once.'

'We value your service in providing a link between the Castle and the common people,' I recited, following him out of the tent.

'Oh yes. Allow us mortals our dream.' All mortals dream, it seems, of joining the Castle Circle. Always pushing for immortality. Always seeking to stop the spin of the wheel of fortune, as it rips through their hands, leaving splinters. How splendid it would be to be eternal, and safe. But at the same time it is daunting to join such a fellowship. The dispositions of the other Eszai are unknown. Make the wrong move, and the pack draws together against you. A new Eszai wouldn't know that the most forbidding are the least dangerous.

17

The best I could manage was, 'Immortality has its disadvantages.' The Awian smiled like he didn't believe me. I told him I'd trade every minute of my long life to own, briefly, his lands and riches. There's no point in being eternal if you're eternally in debt.

'Immortal or not, you can fly,' he said, longingly.

'Well, sometimes pleasure pays.'

'Come on, Jant,' he said, far more cheerfully. 'Let me see you fly!'

The Sun standard's long shadow fell on tent-cleared ground. I heard the battering rams crash against the Wall. Their solid wheels squealed and jarred on the rubble, making the ground shake. Two battering rams, working in tandem. The jangled shouts of Tawny's fyrd got louder after each crash. The tightening sensation in every muscle as my drug kicked in twisted and heightened that already terrible sound.

'I'm going to take a closer look,' I said. I began to jog, in a slight curve, into what little wind there was. Spikes on my boot soles held in the damp grass. I loped, leant forward, started to run. To sprint. I charged downhill, and when I thought I'd reached top speed, I found a little more. A little more, a little more, till it was too fast to breathe.

Speed is a state of bliss.

I forced down half-spread wings. Feathers slapped the ground, but on the next beat I jumped and their downward movement pushed me up. I felt a metre of lift but the effort was agony.

I jump, and I keep going up.

My body took over, my mind dull with pain. Every beat tore at the muscles in my waist. I quickly made it up to a clear height. I looked down and saw tiny people. I started to climb more shallowly, settled into a gradual pace that rowed me upwards, completed the curve into a wide circle so I was above Dunlin. I rejoiced in stretching the full length of my wings. I loved to feel the air-flow as I pulled them down. At the end of a stroke, my fingers, long feathers, touched each other three metres beneath my stomach. I savoured the resistance, which bent the wrists as I threw them back up through the air again. The air felt heavier than Tawny's weights. My wings are like long arms, and flat silver rings on the elongated fingers clacked together as I closed my hand for the upstroke. My weight hung from the small of my back. I kept my real arms crossed over my chest, sometimes spreading them to help with balance.

With great effort I fought my way up to a height where the fyrd had lost all individuality and were just areas of heraldic colour. The General soldiers' ranks were dotted with movement as anxious faces turned up to see me.

Still the battering rams dragged back and surged forward, impacting against the Wall. Surly thermals formed above the Wall; I tried one long enough to get a close look. Five metres tall, the Wall stretched away east and west, a bright white ribbon against the forest canopy; it ran further than I could see from cloud base on a clear day. Close up, the surface was uneven, and it was not built exactly in a straight line – irregularities showed where previous battles had scarred it and where the Insects had encountered difficult ground. Although mostly creamy white, the Wall varied in texture because it was built from anything the Insects could carry or drag.

So it's best not to look too closely. The sweating soldiers on the battering ram had a close view, as the Wall fell apart in fist-sized chunks, like chalk. Hardened Insect spit held it together. It was smooth like ceramic, and sometimes with froth set hard as stone. Inside were chewed tree branches, furniture from ruined villages, armour from old battles. There were also the shells of dead Insects, pieces of tents and weaponry, and children who disappeared many years ago. Here and there a rotting arm or a horse's backbone protruded out, faces could be seen within it, unevenly preserved when the milky saliva set hard. Tawny's fyrd had moved aside the rolls of barbed wire and were hacking at the Wall with hammers. He saw me and waved. I tipped my wings to him.

'Can you see behind the Wall?' he bellowed as the battering ram came to another shuddering halt.

'Oh, yes,' I said.

'How many Insects?' he yelled. Thousands of glossy brown bodies were gathering on the other side of the Wall. Each the size of a man, they clustered at its base, feelers touching. More and more gathered, running out of tunnel mouths, from underground.

'Thousands! They are—' And then they broke through.

Tawny's men drew together. 'Guard!' he roared. A shield wall went up. As Insects began to pour through the breach in their Wall, they met, ricocheted off, crawled up the coloured shields. Tawny's men were shoulder to shoulder and their arms were strong, but the gap between them and the Wall filled quickly with Insects. They rushed over each other, their sword's-length jaws scraping at the painted shields. I flapped upwards for a better view.

The men on one ram were safe. They raised their square shields and retreated until the shield wall absorbed them.

The second team's ram was stuck on some rubble; they wasted a second heaving at it and the Insects went through them like living razors. I saw mandibles close on a forearm and sever it, the blood ceased as another Insect tore his throat open.

I saw two soldiers make a stand, back to back, but when the tide of creatures went over them they simply disappeared.

Tawny from the shield wall hacked off an Insect's antennae; confused, it turned to bite at other Insects.

19

An Insect nibbling at a fallen man got its jaws caught in the gap between breastplate and backplate. Another soldier severed them with an axe, slicing his dead friend's body. He cut the Insect's back legs off with another clean blow. He was a good fighter, but he couldn't stand against the torrent that now flowed between him and the shield wall. He went down chopping and screeching, Insect antennae flickering in his face and claws sliding over his armour. Insects bit into his ankles to the bone. They hauled him, still kicking, to the Wall, where Insects crouched, repairing the breach. They built around the stranded battering ram, which was being covered in fast-hardening froth.

The men felt the pressure on their shields, mouthparts and antennae forced into gaps between them, and they shouted to each other. The Insects made no noise. As it came up to me, the sound of Insect bodies crawling over Insect bodies was a clicking, scratching, rasping. I watched, and flew so slowly I stalled. Panicking, I climbed on a thermal so the shrinking battle-field rotated below.

The men fell back in the centre of their line. As they withdrew, a dent appeared in the shield wall; it grew bigger, curving inwards. Insects surged into the gap. Gradually, Tawny's division split in half, the men walked back and back, cramming together. The manoeuvre created a conduit down which Insects poured, men with shields controlling them on either side. I marvelled at the fyrd's bravery. On the ground men were pressed together, crouching behind their shields, sweating, shouting. Each soldier felt the strength of the man on his right, the man on his left, and the wall held. An Insect antenna caught briefly between one shield and the next. The soldier watched it in terror, his arm in the shield bracket up in front of his face. All his childhood fears were true. The Insect ripped its antenna free and rushed on.

Some Plainslanders with ropes gathered around an overturned Insect; it was thrashing on its back, its soft abdomen showing, compound eyes drab from grass stains. They roped its middle pair of legs together and turned it right side up. The Insect tried to rush at them, but two men were braced with the end of the rope and it simply pulled itself over. It tried this a couple of times before giving up. Its mandibles gnashed and frothed. Confused that it had no freedom of movement, it twisted round and discovered the leash. It closed its jaws around the rope and the soldiers then wound another rope around its jaws, trussed up its back legs and dragged it off the field.

I heard the hollow sound of shell creatures rattling down the wooden tunnel, glancing off the shields. More Insects ran from behind the Wall and the flood went on. Insects, like water, flow downhill. They were directed to the mouth of a long corral.

The enclosure, built by Dunlin's men over the previous months, was made from sharpened wooden posts, set deeply into the ground. It was half a kilometre long, and archers on higher ground sped Insects along down the narrowing valley. I left Tawny's fyrd and flew over Lightning's, gaining height to be above the arrows. Awian archers were an azure splash on the parched yellow ground. They had quivers on their right hips, bare heads and scarcely any armour. They drew only to their cheeks, because the distance to the corral was short, and they shot at a rate of ten flights a minute. Their mechanical repetition impressed me, and I circled above hearing Lightning's voice distorted by distance: 'Notch. Stretch. Loose.'

'Notch. Stretch. Loose.'

Closer – 'Notch! Stretch! Loose!'

Swarms of arrows flew up, reached their greatest height just beneath me, descended on the corral like hail.

Lightning shaded his eyes with a gloved hand and looked around the sky for me. I flew behind the archers' ranks.

'Messenger!' he yelled. 'Comet? Are you there?'

'Yes!' I yelled back.

'Get out of the sun so I can see you!'

'Sorry.'

'Is everything satisfactory?'

'They've nearly all gone past,' I said, circling.

'Are you *sure*?'

'There are very few casualties.'

Lightning looked pleased. He turned back to the two lines of archers. 'Attention! Now to resume! There are arrows left. Notch! Stretch! Loose!'

When they reached the end of the corral, some of the Insects were so full of arrows they looked like leggy hedgehogs. Most were missing limbs or were wounded, dripping yellow liquid. A few had holes in their carapaces where arrows had passed straight through, sometimes catching and hanging in their transparent vestigial wings. Arrows do not kill Insects unless the creature's head is hit directly, with enough force to break the shell. Rather than points, the arrows that Lightning's team shot had broad heads, like blades; they tried to sever limbs and shatter shells. All along the valley enclosure I saw trails of yellow fluid, pieces of glossy carapace. Insects skittered on the ground, some with just one leg left, some with no legs; thoraxes with just the stems of legs attached, bulbous joints with holes where legs should be.

The end of the corral was a palisaded pen, and Insects ran round and round inside, filling it. Still they ran silently while the men howled with effort. Around the fence, the Awian infantry was waiting. Dunlin and his guard were on horseback some distance at the rear. His grey wings trembled.

Some more of the generals – Mist and Ata – were even further back with a division of the Island Fyrd. They were under orders to ride following the soldiers and round up those who ran away in terror, and push them back into the fray. Mist peered at the corrugated wall of the rough corral rising in front of him; stared back towards the gleaming inhuman Wall behind. I saw Mist's stripy charcoal hair and Ata's polished armour under a limp smalt-blue cloak that hung over her saddle's cantle and her horse's butt.

The Awian foot soldiers raised their sarissai to the top of the palisade. These spears were a full seven metres long with crossbars behind the point. They used sarissai to thrust at the Insects that were running around inside the corral. Javelins thrown by another fyrd division reached the centre of the corral. Insects hit by javelins died pinned to the ground.

Too many Insects were dying at one place. The mound of carcasses built up until – so fast I couldn't call out – it grew high enough for Insects climbing it to fall over the top of the palisade and escape. Five were free. Ten. Fifty. A hundred. The first skewered and writhed on the sarissai, then Insects went under the spears, and between them. The Awian spearmen turned and fled. They ran into the men behind, who also turned to run, but Insects cut a path through them, biting, clawing, throwing them aside. Spearmen at the edges who were smart enough to draw broadswords and maces lasted a little longer but two Insects together are more than a match for a man.

'Shit,' I said. 'Oh no. Shit!' I flew through a thermal and had to flutter furiously.

Dunlin from his vantage point saw what was taking place. I streamed down over his cavalry as soldiers lowered their lances, and a hundred spurs set to a hundred flanks at once.

I screamed, 'Rachiswater – Dunlin! Can you hear me? Do what I tell you!' The wind whipped back my words and I got no answer from him at all.

We rarely ride horses against Insects. They normally fear them and will simply shy away. I've seen past battles where horses bolted over lines of infantry. But one of the advantages of having immortal leaders is that we live to learn from our mistakes. Hayl Eske had spent centuries breeding and training the Awian destriers that Dunlin's men now used.

The Insects were covered in human blood as well as their own. They moved fast, close to the ground, their six legs jointed above low bodies. Claws raked on the ground, lifted; the same ground flattened by Dunlin's lancers a second later.

I flew fast enough to overtake the Insects and saw that they were fleeing to the Wall. I wheeled back and tried to tell Dunlin. His helmet visor was down, the blue and argent mantle was tucked into the back of his belt but it billowed. I could see the blue sheen on his chain mail. His guard followed in a wave; on their saddles were fastened long feathers cut from leather, wide ribbons, metal lace.

They went round the side of the corral opposite the archers, and I saw Lightning and those at his side draw their bows and take out the leading

Insects. Lightning's arrow went well home, the Insect died instantly and rolled, then the rest trampled it. The archers would have drawn again but Lightning stayed their hands as Dunlin thundered past.

The lancers crossed the clearing where the battering rams had been, littered with bodies, chewed edges of wounds drying like brown mouths. They went past Tawny's fyrd, who, axes in hand, were standing to seal the mouth of the corral. Tawny's barrier had by now broken up into amorphous groups of men, tan and wine coloured. As Dunlin's lancers passed them shields were raised instinctively. Tawny stood open-mouthed. I circled him; my wings were fucking killing me and this was all going wrong.

'Follow him!' I shouted at Tawny, but that was impossible. Tawny's broadaxe over his shoulder caught the sunlight. He started walking after them, and his soldiers gathered in a crowd around him. They looked so immovable from the air.

Dunlin charged on, over the dead grass.

And then he went through the Wall.

He went through the Wall where Tawny had breached it, and onto the Insect plain. All the soldiers followed, heads bent over horses' necks, braids in horse tails streaming out behind. They knew it was forbidden to cross the Wall but curiosity spurred them. They'd follow Dunlin.

I know why he is doing this. It's bravery, not bravado. He really is determined to beat the Insects and he does want to show the Castle how much can be done. He may have reasons for disobeying my orders, but that's no less reprehensible. I decided all I could do was watch, witness the actions of the King, to relate to the Emperor later. I was shaking with tension.

The riders passed a paper archway half-sunk in the ground. It was the mouth of a tunnel, like a grey hood, standing without support and leading into a smooth passage. A few minutes later, they reached five identical archways in a line between gnawed tree stumps. The Insect group ran down the first of these without breaking pace, and disappeared. Dunlin reined his horse in so rapidly she lost her footing and stumbled to a halt in the tunnel mouth, her eyes showing white with fear. The soldiers stopped in a mass around him, listening to him curse. 'We've damn well lost them after all that.' He stripped off his gauntlets, slapped them on the saddle pommel. 'I don't believe it. Dammit. Shit! Let's get these horses out of the tunnel; they hate the Insect stink.'

One of the soldiers called, 'Your Highness! Can we ride back to the other side of the Wall?'

'If you want, Merganser, you can.' Dunlin stared at him and uncertain laughter stirred amongst the soldiers. They were glancing around, taking in a new landscape where half a kilometre away, an endless sea of paper roofs began. There were hundreds of thousands of identical Insect buildings.

They were pointed pagodas and low halls, like angular fungi. No windows, no doors, just grey paper cells. I flew between them, seeing their laminated surface, rippled and unbroken. I swooped below the height of the Wall, and called again, 'Dunlin, can you hear me? It's—'

'Yes. I can hear you.'

'Come back to the camp. That's an order!'

He ignored me. Nobody had seen the tunnels so close before unless Insects were dragging them there. Dunlin seemed to be rapt. 'I'm going down,' he said. 'Anyone to follow me?'

'No! Rachiswater!' I searched about for a safe place to land and stop him.

'Don't you want to know what's down there?' Dunlin asked his men. 'Let's go!' He drew on his gauntlets, plated with tiny metal squares, and lowered his visor. More than half the men followed his lead and he gave them time to arrange themselves, muster their courage. Merganser backed off, turned around deliberately and began to canter back towards the Wall, which looked just the same on the Insect side.

Dunlin urged his horse forward until he was in the overhang's uneven shadow. A soldier, sword in hand, came to guard him. They looked down into a steep, circular passageway, cut into the brown earth, dark as night.

A cry came from behind them, sound of metal on shell. Swarms of Insects were running from the other tunnels. The Insects moved fast. There were hundreds, the ground was covered. Barbed claws gripped Dunlin's thigh, pulling him from the saddle. With a slash he severed them; they hung on, dripping, and then there were eight more as another two Insects grabbed hold.

No – please god, no! When I got control of myself again I called to Dunlin. With his guard he was fighting for his life, cutting Insects down left and right, a backhand with a long sword, sticking a stiletto knife through the shell heads that came up to the saddle. His heavy horse stepped sideways to crush the Insects gnawing at her hooves. Landing would not be wise. I leant back on the air and, wheeling, left him.

Merganser had almost made it back to the Wall. His black mare swayed on the scorched grass. I unhooked my spurs from my belt and, legs dangling, glided round and landed in front of him. It knocked the breath out of me, but I ran on and he reined in his horse. I could see the creature's eyes beneath her scallop-edged armour. She may have been bred to deal with Insects, but she wasn't keen on Rhydanne and I thought she would rear.

'Merganser,' I panted. 'Get off your horse and give me it. Now. *Quickly!*' Merganser gaped at me and threescore emotions appeared on his face – fear was the first and reverence the last. It was easy to recognise me – who else can fly? – but he found it hard to believe that an Eszai would ever cross his path.

He wriggled from the armoured faring and jumped down. Wordlessly he passed me the reins and stood aside as I scrambled into the high-backed saddle.

He was a slim young man, brown hair knotted at his neck, and he was tall so the stirrups were set at the right height. I waved my feet about until I found them. I plucked the lance from his grasp and held it over my shoulder.

'What should I do, Comet?' he begged.

'Advise you run like buggery.' I jerked the mare's reins left, gave her a hefty kick in the ribs. The smell of Insect blood was strong in the air but she obeyed.

Dunlin pulled his horse round, slashing at brown carapaces and compound eyes. His soldiers were vanishing. They were in a tight group, facing outwards, but they were too few. Insects bit at his horse's legs. She stumbled over them and fell. Jaws half a metre long, jagged and razor sharp, stripped the skin from her ribs immediately, the guts falling out. Dunlin rolled from the saddle, on top of a mashed Insect. Although only the head and thorax was left, it clung to him with two remaining arms, wet with yellow paste.

The time it took to reach him was agony for me. I had been flying so long I still wanted to yaw left, pitch right; and here I was on horseback, stuck with just two dimensions; a gallop is far too slow. Standing in the stirrups I let the horse run over Insects at the edge of the fray. They clung to her straps and I poked them with the lance. I'm no lancer, so I used the chromed weapon as a spear, jabbing at Insect thoraxes, rupturing abdomens, tearing their wings. I soon dropped it and drew my ice axe, which has a long haft and a strong serrated point. I hewed a path, swinging the axe and grunting with effort. The movement was familiar; it was like cutting ice steps in a glacier climb. Insect after Insect fell, headless and coiling.

Dunlin recognised me and moved nearer but there were too many Insects in the way. The fyrd gained strength from seeing me struggle towards them and they fought harder still.

'Get out!' I screamed, waving at the Wall. 'Move!' Their way was blocked by the horde.

I could see Dunlin pressed between bulbous brown bodies. A mandible was in his leg, slicing to the bone. I saw him put his weight on that leg and the chitin tore out. He raised his visor, blinded by brightness, and stabbed ferociously at an Insect clutching his wing.

His sword skittered over its hard thorax plates. The Insect grasped it, losing a claw, put two other claws over the flat of the blade, and twitched it from his grasp. It snapped at his face. Antennae brushed the back of his neck. Insects behind and in front of him brought him down, kneeling, spidery arms pulling. Little cuts sank in, sawing, wherever the Insects could find a

25

gap. Mandibles snipped. Not a man or horse was left standing; the Insects chewed live flesh.

Dunlin turned on his front, visor down, and covered the back of his neck with plated arms. The Insects stripped his wings and then left him. Some ran towards the Wall, and I hoped Tawny had readied his fyrd. Some picked over the carcasses, their heads inside horses' barrel-ribs.

By the King, a single Insect crouched on complex leg-joints. A blow had cracked its carapace across, pushed the shell into a dent from which cream-yellow liquid oozed, running down between black spines. Its snapped antennae hung down like bent wires – still, it sensed me. It opened its jaws and I saw mouthparts whirling like fingers inside. I kicked it, and it struck at my foot. Its jaws gashed my boot open from toe to shin. The crack across its thorax opened wider, and beneath I saw a pale wrinkled membrane, damp with the liquid that was crusting at the edges of the wound. I smashed the ice axe down into its back with so much force that it disappeared to halfway up its hilt. Then I shook it free, my hand dripping. 'Next!' I shouted. 'Who's next?'

Dunlin. The King. Heroically I thought of leaning from the saddle and lifting him onto the destrier's neck. In reality I am not that strong. I grabbed his belt and dragged his body on the ground while the horse shied side-ways. I beat my wings but I still couldn't heave him up. Eventually I had to dismount and tie him to the saddlebow with his own sword belt. It seemed to take a long time, I glanced at the tunnel mouths every second. I became covered in feather fragments and his blood, which was soaking through and turning the chain mail into one big clot. The after-effects of cat and adrenaline grew oppressive. I thought of what it means to die, which raised feelings I didn't understand. 'You're a noble charger,' I sniffled at the mare. 'Black is the proper colour, don't you think? I think his tomb should be black marble. Come on, now let me return you.' The death-scent didn't disturb her, but she was aware of the stickiness as rivers of blood drained down her sides. I talked her into a trot, but the movement jarred Dunlin's corpse. The corpse stirred and murmured. He was alive!

'Rachiswater? My lord?' No answer. I ripped his cloak, bundled it under his head as a cushion. What should I do? Lowespass – the fortress! I wrapped the reins in my hand, pressed a filed spur to the mare's flank. She ran like a Rhydanne.

CHAPTER 2

Fifty kilometres around Lowespass the land is as battle-scarred as Tawny's flesh. Lightning can remember when it was green undulating hills, seamed with darker hedges and patches of woodland; the only graze a pale grey promontory on which Lowespass Fortress would later be built. Now the fortress is over a thousand years old, and its earthworks fill the valley. The moat is made from a redirected river, the outer walls take in the whole crag. The stables and arms depots are entire villages.

This is rampart warfare – Lowespass is sculpted, the ground churned up. There are six corrals, some with multiple entrances and holding pens; palisaded tracks, ditches, mounds, ashlar walls, some with iron spikes. All act to slow the Insect advance, and soldiers are constantly rebuilding them, changing them, as little by little, they are overthrown.

Lightning is familiar with every centimetre of ground. He remembers the construction of even the oldest embankments – five-metre-high ramparts now like lines of molehills, and trenches that are now shallow and grassy. The earth has been dug up and the valley remodelled, not once but again and again, so I think that in Lightning's memory the land itself seems to move – to throw up artificial banks and crease into hillforts, white scars soon sprouting green – to sink artificial pitfalls and flood-land of its own accord.

Fyrd train in the tortured landscape which one generation prepares for the battles of the next. They cull Insects and clear the Paperlands. We call Insect pulp 'paper', but it doesn't have all the properties of paper; it is rigid, inflexible, and the Insect spit that holds the chewed paste together has a fire-retardant effect. Our wooden buildings are burnt when abandoned to stop the Insects chewing them, but Insects use anything they can find; fabric and bone as well. The fyrd wield axes and set patches of pitch-fire to clear Paperlands, but it doesn't burn easily.

Lowespass terrain is like a board game – three-dimensional, in marble and green velvet. This land we've lost to the Insects, and won again, and lost – so many times. Dunlin knew that it was originally farmland, as tranquil and productive as the golden fields of Awia. But I could never make Dunlin appreciate how long ago that was. He was incapable of sensing the vastness of time that had passed since then, although he trod every day along roads that ran through the living rooms of deserted villages and over ramparts raised from the bones of the Fifthland Fyrd. Dunlin was adamant that the land could be occupied peacefully again, if only it was reclaimed. We strive for that, of course, but perhaps if we won, the fyrd's screams and the clash of battle would stay in the Eszai's memories and Lowespass would seem unfamiliar without adversaries.

The Zascai soldiers' concept of the Lowespass front is even more limited than Dunlin's. This is a valley where terrible things happen. Every fable and every childhood threat hangs on the Insects' jaws and the way they move inspires every nightmare.

I see the Lowespass landscape in yet another way. There's bloodshed, sure, but I'm also grabbed by insane joy of freedom when I fly there. The valley alters dramatically for me, but by the hour. Clouds chase over it, cumulus spins into wave-clouds beyond the Wall, but at the moment the western sky is clear and warm. Every morning the sun rises out of a mass of peaks behind peaks stepped like shark's teeth but sharper.

In the Darkling mountains Oriole River starts as a torrent and widens as it flows east through Lowespass, to Midelspass then the coast. At the place where we use the river to undermine the Wall, the Oriole is so fast-flowing that the waterweed looks as if it has been combed. Crayfish live there and, like little Insects, they have fed on dead soldiers' flesh. Then it flows into an earthwork, and at the foot of Fortress Crag the river is channelled twenty metres deep. The Darkling foothills are tamer in Lowespass, the valley is lined with supply roads. Mass graves are covered by woodland but burnt bone fragments rise to the plough. Farmsteads built on latrines of the eighteenth century fyrd are very fertile.

Ramparts and hollows, which make all the difference in a battle, are hard to see from the air because they are often evenly grassed over. I flew low and my shadow flicked over them, changing size. I wished I were not the only one who could see Lowespass from the air. I have tried to design machines that glide so that other people could fly but I have not had much success. I guess that if god wanted us to design gliders, it wouldn't have given us wings.

The door burst open and Staniel paced into my room, Lightning behind him spreading his hands apologetically. Staniel was taken aback by me sitting cross-legged on my bedding, which was on the stone floor, not the bed. The aroma of sandalwood incense and the fact that I was halfway through writing an Imperial report also unnerved him.

He kept his head bowed, gaze fixed on one stone slab. His chest was almost tubular, very narrow, and he covered it with one hand on his breastbone in an act of supplication that was nearly a bow. He faltered, 'Please. Dunlin – how is he?'

'Well ...'

'I have to know how he is! Rayne won't give me any answers!'

'You've seen. He hasn't changed. He's still in the hospital. Rayne is still tending him, and he's still unconscious.'

'He'll wake up, won't he?'

'I've been that wounded and survived.'

'But for a mortal?'

Lightning raised his voice. 'I don't think Jant wants to be disturbed at the moment.'

'Apologies, Comet. But ... Supposedly the Eszai assist us at times of tragedy.'

'What do you want me to do?'

'Dunlin's going to die, isn't he?'

'I don't know. Yes.'

Staniel's clothes were clean and pressed, as befitted his status at all times except after a battle, when he was expected to be as filthy as the rest of us. His long, corn-gold hair was still damp; he had been sitting in the river upstream of the overheated soldiers who crowded the river bank to bank. I had forded the river in a chaos of spray, blood, mane and hooves, and behind me a whispering started that the King was dead.

I was grimy and had a few broken feathers, Lightning's mantle was stained with dust from his ride back, but already Staniel had managed to find black textured silk, the colour of mourning. Buzzard feathers were tangled in his hair, from a thin silver crown set with lapis lazuli. His blue eyes were bloodshot from rubbing them; he looked more tearful than a teenager. Lightning laid a hand on his shoulder, said, 'We don't have to discuss this until the morning, Your Majesty.'

'Stop calling me that! Honestly, Archer.' Staniel twisted the silk tassels of his long sleeves, leaving sweat stains. 'To follow me is disagreeable enough, but then you say, "Your Majesty", "my lord", constantly! How can *you* call *me* "lord"?'

Lightning didn't say anything, but I could sense the intensity of his disapproval directed at the Prince.

I repeated, 'What do you want me to do?'

'Save him.'

'Rayne is doing all she can; she doesn't need my help.' Or respect it. 'What in Darkling do you expect me to do?'

'I don't know ... I just don't know.' He rubbed his face with both hands, because to wake would be the best escape from grief.

The Archer tried again with a tone of complaint: 'There's coffee in the Solar. Genya has laid out some bread and meat. The men have eaten, I don't see why we should fast.'

Staniel started at the name of Genya, like a child who has been told there is a dragon in the drawing room. He was used to me, but had never encountered a female Rhydanne. I had sent couriers to her and had persuaded her to provide food for the exhausted, wounded fyrd.

'Genya ... ' he said, with mixed fascination and repulsion.

Anger flared – I was so weary. I have seen the same emotions on the faces of people meeting me. Often fear and aversion has made city people turn on me with insults at best, then arrows. I fought back in my own way but I have thicker skin than Genya, and she was very violent. 'Careful!' I told Staniel. 'If you trouble her she will scratch your eyes out.'

'We have to keep a vigil for my brother.'

'We'll be more use as commanders if we eat and bloody sleep! My lord.'

'I can't eat.'

'It will help you feel better.'

'Maybe I don't want to feel better.'

Lightning took a deep breath. 'I cannot believe the dynasty of Rachiswater has at its end produced someone as spineless as yourself! This is a terrible situation, of course I admit that, but are you going to stand up and confront it? You're grown from Avernwater, the lineage that held the throne and the walls strong for five hundred years since my line ended. The Rachiswater branch grew so powerful and prolific that it became another tree. I find it hard to accept that one of the leaves on the twigs of the branches of that tree can be so different from the rest. I am not having kin, no matter how distant, shunning the responsibility placed on him by means of birth and tutelage at a time when the whole of Awia needs him. I don't see anything I recognise as Rachiswater in you! Your grandfather Sarcelle would never have cowered in the pavilion the way you have since you came to the front.'

Staniel glanced at me for help. He stood his ground, and I took pity on him because I do not agree with Lightning's notion that men should be compared to each other. Staniel was no warrior – a coward, in fact – but I had noticed his grandiloquence. With time I might turn him into a prosperous diplomat.

I said, 'Calm down, Lightning.'

'No. For example, Staniel has disturbed your rest to ask about His Majesty without bothering to thank you for bringing Dunlin back in the first place. He is so thoroughly—'

'Enough!' I saw that Staniel had begun to tremble with confusion. If his nerves had been frayed before they were ripped to shreds now. I wanted to give him a chance to speak, but stopping Lightning mid-rant is as difficult as halting a bolted destrier. I reached out to Staniel, and he gained composure as he shook my hand, although with another little shudder as my long fingers enclosed his hand completely.

'Yes. Certainly. Yes ... Comet,' he announced. 'Awia commends you greatly for rescuing my brother; it was an act of great courage at no little risk. I have inscribed my profound gratitude in a missive to the Emperor, which unfortunately Lightning won't yet let me despatch; perhaps you could convey it yourself. Thank you also for averting the casualties of those fyrd who would otherwise have been dispatched to retrieve my brother's body.'

If words on paper could be transformed to a token of gratitude in cash I'd be more delighted.

'Where were you?' enquired Lightning.

'Um. Press conference.'

'What?'

'And I also apologise on behalf of Dunlin, that he transgressed your unambiguous orders and rode into the Paperlands.' Staniel stood nervously, his blond wings limp at his back, fading to white at the round ends of the feathers. He had thin gold bands on them, like the rings on his tapering fingers.

I shouldn't listen to Staniel's apologies, and I know the Emperor won't. Dunlin had no excuse; his plight is an example of what happens when Zascai no matter how blue-blooded disobey Eszai on the battlefield. On the other hand, I didn't want to complicate the situation. There was plenty of time to argue in the following months, rather than at the King's deathbed.

'I accept your apologies,' I said. 'But more of this later.'

'Will you come to the Solar?' he asked, and there was a tiny noise out in the corridor.

Staniel froze, mouthed, 'What's that?' I sensed the feeling of intensity caused by another presence.

Someone was listening very quietly, with a concentration that thickened the air. I caught the faintest odour of bracken and alcohol. I leapt across the room, flung the door wide. We ran out into the corridor but there was nobody there.

'Genya,' I said.

Staniel repeated, 'Genya Dara.'

The first time our paths cross in ten years. It's all right, I told myself. Nobody knows.

A crescent moon became brighter as the surrounding sky dimmed. Soldiers' muted conversation drifted through the corridors and courts of square grey Lowespass. The akontistai – javelin men; lancers and archers, sarissai and cavalry alike were waiting for the latest news of Dunlin's progress to be announced.

If I hadn't been so busy, it would have been my duty to walk among the soldiers and talk to them in order to gauge their opinions. Tawny and Staniel were now set to this task, Tawny with the Plainslands Fyrd and Staniel in the Outer Ward. The Outer Ward was a walled grassy enclosure studded with limestone outcrops. The Awian infantry had raised their tents where the soil was deeper, by the thick curtain wall. Most were asleep but some sat in groups talking in subdued voices about their companions who had been left out in the field.

Primroses grew down by the river, and after Slake Crossroads Battle ninety years ago, their yellow flowers had bloomed with pink petals. The soldiers picked these in remembrance of the fyrd who had gone before, because I once wrote it was our blood that stained the flowers, back in nineteen twenty-five. It was strange to see a strong man, weathered and bristly from an outdoor life, with a primrose bloom threaded through the links of his chain mail.

I walked around the keep, trying to dispel a vague feeling that something was missing. It was a sensation, not a conscious thought, but it was very familiar and I knew it was worsening. I would become more and more jumpy, until eventually I would have no other choice but to lock myself in my sparse room and take some more cat. Everywhere I went people asked me how Dunlin was, whether he was still alive, and how long the fyrd may be expected to stay in the cold fortress.

I passed a window left open, and I knew Genya had been here. I could smell her. Pacing along an austere colonnade, which turned sharp corners every hundred metres as it followed the curtain wall, I had the prickly feeling that someone was watching. I called her name and the feeling subsided. Silently, she had gone.

I didn't blame her for wanting to watch from a distance, and I was pleased that she should want to observe me at all. Possibly she was playing a game with her own emotions as well as mine. She was teasing her fear, creeping as close as she could to the edge of the abyss. She was also placing a strong trial on my desire. I kept walking, as she sped through concealed corridors. I imagined her climbing over the ridges of broken-tiled roofs, past cisterns, pantries, cluttered kitchens; running through halls where men looked up in surprise. The image made me growl: *I am an Eszai. This sort of lechery won't do.* But I knew that if I wanted to, I could catch her.

I came to the church, which was part of the main complex inside the imposing walls. As I walked past the glass-panelled door, Ata Dei emerged from the gloom inside. I immediately stopped thinking about Genya; Ata's hair was a beautiful distraction. There was hardly any light in the square church porch, but her hair still shone.

'Hello cat-eyes,' she said, looking through me. I had thought her face to be shaded, but as she strode nearer I saw that the shadow was really a bruise. It covered the bridge of her nose and one eye, swollen from lower lid to cheekbone. The bruise was dark, and pinpoint red showed vivid where the skin had been broken.

'Did you get that in the battle?' I asked.

Her bloodless lips twisted. 'Oh, aye. But it was nothing to do with the Insects. Mist hit me. I wish I didn't need him!'

'Why did he hit you?' I asked warily. I knew better than to get involved in a fight between husband and wife. Anyone caught in the crossfire between Ata and the Sailor fares worse than either of them. Long practice had made their sparring into an art form, and I didn't know the rules.

Ata spat. 'Because Dunlin and his guard rode straight past us. I say, "Let's follow," because it looks to me like he needs back-up, and you're telling Tawny the same thing. Mist says, "No, stay here." He's frankly fucking awkward. He's been alive too long. So I say, "You stupid bastard, I'll do it then," and I'm just about to call the Islanders when he flings out a fist and smacks me in the face.'

'Ow.'

'I tried to stab the dim git but he parried and then I realised the fyrd were watching. I thought you would intercept Dunlin; you were quicker than a curse in a courtroom.'

'I couldn't stop a charge.' Wingless humans, like Ata, and the Awians, who are winged but flightless, will never understand that while I can view the battlefield from the air, I can't control it.

'Aye,' she breathed. 'Well, I hope you're proud of yourself.' I stayed mute until she added, 'Dunlin requested eight thousand troops. If you'd mustered them from the Plainslands rather than the coast like he told you they'd have been here by now. We were short of at least a thousand men this morning, and I doubt the sanity of his plan if we had twice as many.'

I was wary of Ata; her mind set us apart. I'm smart, but not so far-sighted. My best strategy is to stay out of her vicinity. She has a mind like a steel trap – people are either in or out. Those caught in the middle when it springs shut are generally cut in half.

'If you had followed Dunlin, you would have lost the Island Fyrd,' I said.

'Well, I know that there were too few lancers, and Lightning may infer the same. Let us hope the Emperor doesn't guess.'

'I hope you don't inform him.'

She smirked and said, 'What are you doing here, anyway?'

I waved my hands in the air vaguely. 'Organising things.'

She indicated the church door. 'If you're looking for a place to shoot up, this is not it.'

'I'm clean,' I lied automatically. When found out, I suffer intense remorse and indignation – a weird feeling of wanting to crawl and apologise as well as rebel and confront. The danger of being found guilty became a pleasure for me a long time ago, and now I can't quit.

'Aye, right. You're not even walking in a straight line.' She folded her arms, which detracted from the impression of motherly authority it was intended to give because it also gave her an impressive cleavage. I told her she looked wonderful, but she diminished the compliment with a shrug. She put no effort into her appearance but her hair was still mesmerising. She had pure white hair, almost translucent against her tanned skin. Her hair hung straight down her back and over it she wore a maline veil, twisted into a wreath.

'How's the King?' she asked.

'I don't know.'

'For an official response, that is completely crap, Jant Shira. I thought you had more imagination.'

'He's dying.'

'Aye. Mmm. And without children, the royal fool. How will King Staniel repel the Insects? Death by sonnet?'

I giggled, wrapping my arms around my waist, a gesture which Ata scrutinised until I boiled with humiliation. I hopped from foot to foot, feeling slightly strung out.

Ata joined the Castle Circle by marrying the Sailor, becoming immortal four hundred years before me. Those who dislike Mist have said that he proposed to her because he was anxious she would Challenge him for his place in the Circle. By marrying Ata he sated her craving for eternal life, but the wedding also guaranteed that she would be nearby to quarrel with him for the rest of his existence. And like the other Eszai who have joined the Circle through marriage, Ata is dependent on her spouse's continued Circle membership for her immortality.

Ata's shirt was diaphanous, pale blue gauze with a layer of saffron yellow beneath it. What I took to be a skirt was really wide trousers; from her slack leather belt hung a rapier with a basket hilt so fine it was steel filigree. She had been frozen at age thirty-five for six hundred years.

'Watch out, Jant. The last thing the Emperor needs is a translator who's taken so many mind-expanding drugs that he can't fit it back in.'

'Leave me alone.'

Ata shrugged, and did so, saying, 'Your Rhydanne mistress has seen you. She wants to know what you're doing.'

'You've spoken to Genya?' I said, too hastily. She nodded, and walked away.

Rayne had a room on the far side of Lowespass keep, which she ordered to be built within the keep when it was constructed. She tried to keep the room supplied with medicines, gauze and water. When she worked at the front, she stayed in the fortress and the wounded were brought to her.

I thought about Dunlin, and I felt, rather than thought, about cat. It seemed that the best thing to do was pay Rayne a visit, for the sake of the kingdom of Awia and my own state of health.

In the Inner Ward I moved syncopated through sleeping snarls of people. I avoided them, feeling uneasy and empty inside. The hard muscles moved under my skin, my belt pulled across to the very last notch, the stringy flat arms of my wings hugging and rustling against my back.

Boots hand-made in Morenzia clicked on the worn cobbles, the beads in my hair bounced off my backside. Jackdaws sped between the towers, sparks in negative. Good for them, I thought. That reminded me – what am I walking for? It only took a couple of seconds to struggle airborne and join them, and then I quietly let myself into Rayne's room.

Dunlin was lying on a plain bed against the grey wall of the first room, which had no windows and no decoration. Firelight glowed through a nearby doorway, the bustle of servants preparing food and medicines, and soldiers moaning, screaming. I closed the door and noiselessly watched over the King.

The signature of pain in Dunlin's face changed his whole appearance. Lines between his eyebrows and a furrowed forehead made him look fearsome; his body was braced against the pain. His short hair was matted with dried blood, and Rayne had cut it even shorter on one side, to sew up a gash along his neck from earlobe to collarbone. His lips were dry, with blood at the sides of his mouth. The rings had been stripped from his hands, which lay like dead leaves on the cover, and he wore the padded white shirt that lancers have for protection under their armour. Nobility was written in his face there with the pain.

The other thing I noticed was the scent, not of blood but of time. No matter how old people are when death is approaching, there is the smell of age. It clings to clothes and lingers in rooms, an earthy tang which made me whimper. The King's eyes flickered open, drugged and bloodshot.

'Don't move,' I advised, in Awian. 'We thought we lost you, and I'm not sure exactly what Rayne's done.'

'Is ...?'

'Don't try to speak either,' I added softly. 'I can't tell if you can understand me, but you should know that Staniel's beside himself. He's so highly strung he could pass for a Rhydanne. I tried to calm him down. Lightning just intimidates him.'

Dunlin croaked for a bit and then coughed. His square face was dead ashen under a leathery tan.

'I hope the Insects take years to recover,' I said vaguely. 'I'd like to think it was all worth it.'

He coughed until he could speak, managed, 'This is ... *agony*.'

'Yeah,' I said. 'It'll stop soon. You're lucky.'

I leaned closer to hear him as he said, 'I wanted to be immortal,' and a smile played across his face without touching his lips at all. There was a silence. What could I say? I felt a creeping guilt that he will die and I could not. But the world isn't fair; it was only in the Emperor's power to make a man immortal. I contemplated whether to tell him about the Shift. I couldn't stand the risk he might still be capable of ridicule or disbelief.

'This pain ...' Dunlin whispered.

I thought about the trouble I would be in if anyone found out. But who would know? His crusted eyes were fading; he was outwardly oblivious. Blood seeping through the sheet sealed it to the cuts in his sturdy throat, which armour had left unprotected. His wings were fragments of bone with some muscle still clinging. They shocked me.

'There's the Shift ...' I ventured.

'Mm ...?'

'It's another land. Another world, I mean. If you die here, you can stay there.'

'Mm. Really?' There was the smile again, more sardonic than regal. 'How?'

I clicked open my compass, took out the folded paper. 'With this,' I said. Dunlin sighed. He didn't have enough energy left to try to understand. He didn't care.

'It's immortality, of a sort.'

'Then do what you can.'

Lightning might boast of a golden age under Teale Micawater, but I couldn't recall any time when Awia was as well treated and trusted, as under this King. I bit my nail to the quick, stood mournfully feeling like the last of the wine at a funeral. I spoke to Dunlin for a few more minutes and he dictated his will, which I copied word for word onto the sheet.

On a low table by the bedside was a pewter cup, a pitcher of water and a plate with a sponge. Dunlin's ring was there, blue agate set into a silver bevel, engraved with the seal of Rachiswater.

I sniffed at the cup; it was half full of liquid that smelt of cinnamon. I tipped in the powder from the paper wrap, stirred it with a finger, and replaced the cup.

That was compassion, I think. I justified my action by recalling the ending of *The Complete Herbal*, which I owned when I lived in Hacilith: 'It is our duty to correct illness, to alleviate suffering and ease pain; a noble duty.' Rayne wrote that book hundreds of years before I was born.

I don't know whether it is correct to ease pain by hastening death, but at the time it seemed right. He was certain to die, and I wanted it to be with more dignity. I couldn't bear to see the King, who had always been my friend, so altered by agony that he seemed a different person. I told myself that had he been Eszai, he would have survived. If we could have taken him to Rayne's hospital in the Castle, then I could have done more for him, but recently in Lowespass there was a shortage of everything, and the dregs of medicines were god knows how old. I hope I never have to make the choice again, but if so, I would do the same, and I remember leaving him with a light conscience and a smile of goodbye.

Compassion? Regicide? The question is always in my mind and will only be resolved if I am found out. If that happened, I would have to resign my place in the Castle. I'll fall over that hurdle when I come to it.

Only two beds in the next room; on one I recognised an Awian lady who was paper-pale and only stirred when I kissed her hand. The other body was a shallow mess of mandible cuts criss-crossed with bandages. On the floor, lying full length or leaning against the wall, were roughly fifty soldiers. Two tried to stand, but I waved them down again as kindly as I could. I went through to Rayne's private room, slipped past her and she sighed. 'Dunlin's asleep,' I informed her cheerfully.

'At las'. It's good t'see you, snake-eyes.' I hugged her, the soft covering of fat on an old body. She had a long, stained brown satin dress, and a bloodstained apron. Her wrinkled face just reached the level of my chest.

I glanced at the shelves cluttered with little bottles and vials, sticky cordials and spirits, powders and pillboxes. The light was too dim for me to read the browning ink on their ancient labels and as I peered over her shoulder Rayne realised what I was doing and pushed me away. 'No!'

'Please. I really need some cat.' My voice slipped into a hateful whine.

'How is Staniel?' She tried to change the subject.

'Put me together a fix and I'll tell you.'

'Already? Damn i', Jant. I thought you had enough to las' you the res' of the century.'

'What will you trade?' I asked.

Rayne gave me her *you're-not-human-are-you?* look. I dislike being stared at. With feeling I said, 'The Circle is really going to need me tomorrow and I'll be no use by then if I don't have some soon.' A familiar tension was settling around my eyes; my joints and back ached. Soon I would be able to add shivers and nausea, at which point I would probably panic and fly to Hacilith in an injudicious attempt to score some more. 'Can I help you at all? What can I make for the Hospital?'

'More birch bark ointmen'?'

'Done.'

'Aqua absynthii?'

'Done.'

'Papaver?'

'Yes.'

'Moly?'

'Ah— done.'

'An' you can cross my palm wi' silver, as well.' Rayne flashed her scrimshaw grin. I kissed her cheek, dashed across and picked a clear glass bottle from the shelf. The label said: *Scolopendium, 10%.* That's Centipede Leaf Fern, which in Hacilith is called cat. I don't recommend that anyone try it. Behind me, Rayne made small talk but I was too preoccupied to reply. She watched me with professional concern. 'Do y'think i'could be a good way t'die?' she asked dreamily.

'I don't know! I never have!'

'Do y'know there's a spli' second of peace when t'heart stops and before t'brain congeals? Tha's when you no'ice how noisy your body always was. Y'see a las' greying picture frozen through your eyes, and slowly lose comprehension of wha' i'is. Even fas' dying has got t' seem slow.'

I sighed. 'Rayne, this is becoming an obsession.'

'Jant, don' you talk t'me about obsession.'

'I'm an addict, not an obsessive. Please don't talk to me about death.'

I searched through little velvet-lined drawers for a clean glass syringe. I pushed the needle through the seal of the phial and pulled clear liquid back into the barrel. My resistance broke down and the symptoms overwhelmed me. The muscles in my arms twitched, and shivers ran down my back, ruffling my feathers. I settled my wings and folded them in a fluid movement. My hands remained rock steady; I watched them making these precise actions, my mind elsewhere.

Rayne's assistants bustled back and forth outside the door to her room. I paused to calculate how much. Some. More. This is not an exact science.

If I double what I usually take, it should be enough.

I untied a black silk scarf from around my neck. It was fairly ragged, but I twisted it into a tourniquet and looped it round my arm. A vein swelled up underneath. Then I licked my arm and watched distantly as the point dented the skin and broke it. I loosened the makeshift tourniquet and pushed the plunger home. A bead of blood and cat welled up. The shot hit hard. I decided it would be a good idea to lie on the floor.

I smiled, I was happy with the floor. The worn carpet was warm and bits of me were merging into it. Rayne just looked worried. I tried to reassure her but I couldn't manage the shape of the words. Some. More. Way, way too much.

Now I am not my problem. I smiled faintly and fainted, smiling.

I was jolted into the Shift harder than ever before. I was so badly disorientated that I had to stand with my hands over my eyes, thinking: oh god. Oh god, oh god, Jant, you are really going to regret this.

As I lowered my hands the brightness of Epsilon came through. I was standing in the market place. Sweet air was ravaged by the shouts of stall-holders.

There were stalls with sacks of spices, jangling curtains of lazulite jewellery, brass and glass ornaments on striped rugs, pyramids of cloth rolls, incense; stalls with meats and vegetables, and some things which could have been meat or vegetables, half-rotten fruits, cages with live animals in, which flapped and pecked.

There was the sound of hooves as quandries rocketed past along narrow cobbled streets, pulled by teams of four whorses. Humans and some naked Equinnes sat at a round table outside a café, supping wine. Jeopards – leopards with square spots – purred on the City Hall steps or sat hunched beneath stalls waiting for tit-bits. Jeopards ran sleek and fast, but only in straight lines, as they couldn't see curves, which meant that Epsilon citizens had to spend a fair amount of time rescuing them from the fountain.

Two men crouched against a stained white marble wall, behind a blanket spread with bronzes, strass and tombac chains, rings, all cheap stuff. One of them was smoking, and I could smell his apple tobacco, which above all made me believe in the reality of the Shift. I was here, and still alive.

Living dirigibles floated and jostled low in the sky. A fibre-toothed tiger prowled embarrassed through the crowd, receiving gleeful pats and strokes down the length of its striped back. A couple of children looked scared, then pointed and laughed as they realised its teeth were made of string.

I waited for a long time, while people and Constant Shoppers milled about in the market place. Tine strolled up and down, wire baskets on their polished tortoise backs. I watched the archaic and spicy bazaar, where men thumbed dog-eared fortune cards and the edges of second-hand sabres. The market sprawled beneath a gleaming building, a complex of meteoric chromium, concrete, leafy restaurants, and elevators carrying shrieking kids.

I wait, I wait, I wait; and just as I was thinking my plan must have failed, I saw him. I sprinted across the square and took his arm. Dunlin was standing, spear-straight, with his hands over his face, where I had appeared at the edge of the market. At my touch, he jumped in panic. I had made myself more powerfully built, tanned, with a dark pin-stripe suit and some bronze spines in auburn hair. It took a little rearrangement of these improvements before he recognised me. 'Comet?'

'King Rachiswater.'

'What happened?'

'You died. I think you'd better sit down.' I led him across to the little fountain and propped him on its low wall. He was gaping at the noisy market like a fish in thin air. 'Welcome to the Shift,' I said.

He stopped gaping at the market and began to gape at me. 'Remember Lowespass?' I prompted.

He flexed his arms, realising that all the pain had ceased. 'I didn't believe there was an afterlife,' he murmured.

'There isn't.' I smiled. 'It's a human story used to calm frightened children. This is the Shift.' I gestured at the market. 'The Squantum Plaza, in the City of Epsilon.' Dunlin, a paranoid gaze in his eyes, looked at me with an expression that said I had explained precisely nothing. I was afraid what his reaction might be, so I dropped my hand to the hilt of my dagger. 'There's a drug called cat. It's a painkiller. If you take too much, it lets you come here. But I'm afraid that for mortals, it's a one-way trip.'

'I see ... I think. Shira! I'll *never* see Rachis again?'

I bowed my head. There will always be a time when mortals have to die and those left behind them suffer a sense of loss, although they lose only one person from their lives. Dunlin had forfeited everything, and I felt the inconsolable depth of his loss; it even muted the tumult of the market.

'You'll get used to it,' I said. 'Some things are the same. Good company. Food. Women. Insects. I know you'll have questions.'

'That's the understatement of the century.'

'Don't dwell on it. I'll introduce you to someone who can answer.' I indicated some golden biotic buildings on the possibly north side of the Plaza and we began to walk towards them through the crowd and between the stalls. Although still stifling and savannah-bright, the shadows were lengthening to late evening, which seemed strange because when I arrived it was only midday. I couldn't tell the time from these dual suns; I had a watch but it melted.

'You look different,' Dunlin said.

'Yes, well. If you were half Rhydanne, wouldn't you want to change your appearance?'

'Do you mean we can look like whatever we want?'

'No, no. I can because I'm not really here. I'm still in Lowespass and I'm afraid I'll have to return there shortly. You ... can't go back.'

'There's nothing to go back to.'

'My lord.'

Dunlin led me aside into the shade of a paper lantern stall. God, he was strong. 'Did I just hear you say there are Insects here too?' he demanded.

'There are Insects almost everywhere.'

Dunlin ground his teeth, infuriated. 'Who else is here? When do you come here? Why didn't we know?'

I shrugged. 'The Fourlands has locked itself in a darkened room,' I said, with melancholy so profound it could have been rehearsed.

He shook me. 'I'm stranded here, you total bastard! You callous immortal bastard!'

'Let go! I don't have much time left!'

It was evident that Dunlin was stronger than me even here. Physically more powerful, and he was taking to the Shift like a goat to Scree. I had assumed practice would make me more proficient, until I saw the wild light glittering in his eyes. I had never seen anything approaching Dunlin's vitality, especially for a dead man. I began to be a little afraid of him.

At that time, Felicitia was working in Keziah's bar. After landing the King of Awia in the Shift, I thought it was hardly kind to leave him with Felicitia, but Felicitia had the advantage of coming from the same world. I mean, if Dunlin hasn't a life of his own yet, at least he can tag along with someone else's. I couldn't resist introducing them so I asked Dunlin to follow me, through the shopping mall and beyond the Tine's quarter, to the low thatched building of a bar called the Bullock's Bollocks. Dunlin cheered up when he saw the pub, since it looked superficially like a Fourlands inn, and inside I installed him on one of the wooden benches around a scarred table.

I found Felicitia propping up the bar. 'Jant!' he exclaimed, raced across and embraced me. The bar fell over. 'Have a drink, on the house, on the rocks! What would you like?'

'Get off!' Bad memories made my pulse race. 'If you do that again I'll rip you wing from wing!'

'A kiss, at least, for old times' sake.'

'There never were any old times!'

'Oh, not just any old times, those precious hours we spent together in Hacilith, my negligent boy.' He tried to pinch my bum but I was too fast for him.

Dunlin was staring with an expression of bleak despair, his powerful arms crossed over his chest. Before I could compose myself Felicitia was pulling pints of beer for us. He was making the most of his life in the Shift, had sequinned stockings, layered hair, and moved like well-shagged smoke.

'Would you like pizza?' he said.

'No.' I try to eat as little as possible in the Shift, at least since the Tine took over the burger chains.

'Automato sauce and monsterella cheese? Angstchovies?' I shook my head and he sighed dramatically. 'You're so *thin* these days.'

'You should see what I look like in the Fourlands now.'

'Would that I could, my lascivious lad! And who is this?' he exclaimed, pretending to notice Dunlin for the first time.

'Dunlin Rachiswater. The King of Awia.'

Felicitia smirked, realised I was serious. 'Can't be. Tanager's the ruling family,' he said in a stage whisper.

'In your time, but not now.'

'Oh, Jant, my forgetful friend, you never keep me up to date.' He dropped a neat curtsey to Dunlin, who put one hand over his eyes. 'How did a Rachiswater get here?'

'Same way we did. My lord, this is Felicitia Aver-Falconet, from Hacilith. I ... ah ... That's Hacilith two hundred years ago.' Dunlin said nothing, although he must have been aware of Felicitia's gaze on his biceps.

'Jant, is this someone you're setting on me to stop me having a good time? I'm dead and I intend to keep partying.'

'I hoped you'd act as a tour guide,' I admitted.

'Whatever you ask, my beneficent boy.' Felicitia was wearing a white miniskirt and shiny boots which added ten centimetres to his tiny figure. He had a chemise of stretchy lacy material, which clung to his little muscled chest. 'You can come with me *wherever*,' he added to Dunlin.

'The Aver-Falconets are an Awian family,' Dunlin stated.

Felicitia grinned. 'So I am,' he said. He spread little brown wings, stretching the blouse thin as it rode up over them. The feathers were highlighted with silver and cinnabar red.

Dunlin was shocked. 'I wish to return home.'

'Can't be done.' Felicitia minced over and looked him up and down – although more up than down as Felicitia was so short. 'Jant and I go back a long way,' he said. 'Two hundred years! Well, and I've been holding a candle for him all that time. Two hundred years and I never even got my fingers burnt.'

I said, 'This is hardly important at the moment.'

'He's so *shy*. But yes! We should drink! We should celebrate! Keziah – beer for his Kingness. Whisky for the Rhydanne. Pour yourself a tomato juice.'

'Don't mind if I do,' said the Lizard.

'Happy Demise-day, Your Highness.'

'Jant. I should skin you alive.'

The King found himself immersed in raucous camaraderie, while dusk gathered and snow began to build up against the bullseye-paned windows.

I was halfway through explaining the Shift to Dunlin, when the heat-blistered door shuddered open, the bar fell quiet, and my voice rang out loud in the sudden silence. A Tine lumbered in and walked to the bar, creaking the floorboards. Keziah handed him a litre-jug of red juice which he downed in one, received a refill, and seated himself on the table we were using, squashing the ashtray and levering the far end of the table high into the air.

The Tine had transparent plates like flexible glass sewn into his arms and legs, surrounded by thick seams of scar tissue, and at every movement his muscles' pink mass stretched and smeared against them. Blue tattooed dots, the size of pennies, ran in lines over his face; his silver-white hair streaked a wispy blue and purple, starched into long spines; and at least twenty thin silver rings pierced the edge of one ear.

He was easily the biggest creature in the bar, and his arms and legs were knotted muscle-columns, his only clothing a thin blue silk rag wound round his waist. His back was covered by the round, highly polished plates of his oval shell, like a tortoise shell. A crack across it had been badly riveted together, and the bronze studs were turning green with verdigris. Wires crusted with dried lymph, and bound into a bundle with yellow and red tape, ran from under it and disappeared into his spine at the small of his back.

His eyes were pale blue, no differentiation between pupil, iris and sclera. They were fixed on us, as with a deep, ursine voice he grunted, 'More tourists.'

'Let's go,' I said.

'I'm not a tourist,' Dunlin answered, his blood heated by the interruption. I pulled at his sleeve. First thing to learn in the Shift, Tine are dangerous.

'What the fuck're you then?' He squinted down, eyes like azure pebbles. Awia will mean as much to a Tine as the Cult of the Perforated Lung does to us.

'The Sovereign of Awia.'

'Yeah. A tourist. Get lost before I spill your guts.'

No one in the bar had made a sound since the Tine appeared. Silence deepened as every creature surreptitiously listened in on our show. The Tine snarled, showing myriad, laniary teeth.

'Dunlin,' I put in quickly, raising a hand as the Tine reached out. 'Know when to back down or you won't last two minutes. Tine,' I addressed him. 'I'm an immortal. *Deathless*. And I'm protecting him. So just fucking try it, beast.'

The creature lumbered down onto talons and knees. His bulk pushed the table aside as he gravely licked my boot toe with a tattooed tongue. 'Lord. Am Pierce. Am Tine. Drink basilic vein blood, eat spleen, have your testicles for breakfast, tourist. Not that y'have any, hur hur.'

'How did you do that?' said the Sovereign of Awia.

'Immortals don't fit into their creed. So I usually get worshipped – or attacked. Beliefs are stronger here than in the Fourlands, but don't ask what the Tine believe in; you don't want to know. What are you doing here?' I asked the brute.

'Got thrown out of the Aureate,' he rasped. 'The Cult of the Clotted Artery's a heretical sect. No good slaying here; can't make enough for a cut of meat.'

'I'm sorry to hear that,' Dunlin said calmly.

'Do you know you smell of streaky bacon?' said Pierce.

Now that trouble had passed, Felicitia reappeared and started dealing out drinks. I think Dunlin started to relax, although that may have been a bit much to ask. How could I help him further, now he was stranded here with a Lizard, a Tine and a gay Awian? I decided to give him my palace, which I had built over many, many Shifts, a long and painful project.

'The least I can do is give you Sliverkey,' I said. I unpinned my chart from the wall behind the bar and laid it over the table. My outline flickered. I began to feel the pull. With careful timing I said, 'You can have this as well. It took me decades, it's a map of Epsilon. It's the only map of Epsilon.' My outline began to flicker rapidly and started to dissolve. 'Dunlin!' I shouted. 'Goodbye!' We rushed to shake hands, but mine were like smoke and Dunlin reached straight through them.

I looked up with a half-smile and faded out halfway through a bow. Dunlin's last connection with the Fourlands, severed.

CHAPTER 3

I figured that if I could move my little finger I would eventually be able to move my arm, then my whole body and thus be able to stand up. I sent frantic mental messages down my outstretched arm, but the hand – curled up, skeletal and bluish – refused to move. The syringe was still hanging in the crook of my arm, rooted in my bloodstream. I felt as if it had poured another soul into me, an unreal one, leaching out my quick colours, leaving me chemical.

The thought of this angered me so much that I twitched my fucking little finger, then the rest of my hand, my aching arm, and sat up in an unplanned movement that made the room whirl.

Rayne was still sitting in her rocking chair, watching with timeless patience. She called on god avidly on my behalf. I told her to shut up.

She said, 'Jant, tha's not a habi', tha's a suicide attemp'.'

'Actually I have much to live for.'

She said, 'Jant, wha' you used was practic'ly clear.'

'Do you think impure is safer?'

'Perhaps eterni'y's a poor escape from immortali'y.'

'I used to call overdose "eternity",' I agreed. 'But these days it's simply oblivion.'

'Dunlin died.'

Her sombre tone whipped my brittle mood up into fury. 'I know, Rayne! I already bloody know!' I creaked to my feet, the effort making laden blood crash my mind. God's wings. 'I have a job to do.'

'Yes. Go deliver the will. They're meeting in t'Solar. Can y'make i'?'

'If I die will you bury me?'

'Comet?' She sounded concerned.

'Listen, Doctor, he died happy. When he rode behind the Wall he did what he wanted to do. He was in control of his own life. Let me know when you find even one immortal who can honestly say that.'

Rayne spread her brown smile. 'Tha's why we *don'* die,' she said.

When I walked back through the hospital I saw that the King's bed was stripped. Now empty, the pewter cup was still on the side table. There are ways of testing for scolopendium. I dropped the cup out of the window, into the river.

'So we are agreed?'

Mist's voice, 'I back him.'

Ata: 'Aye.'

I insinuated myself into the Solar Room as Staniel said, 'No. I strongly disagree. With all due respect, Archer—'

'Oh, here he is!' Six pairs of eyes met mine, Staniel looked away again.

I said, 'I'm sorry I'm late,' realising that I must look as sick as I felt.

'*At* last. Now we have to go through all this *again*. Where in god's Empire have you been?'

I answered the rhetorical question: 'I've been ill. It was a hard day.' I collapsed into a ladder-backed chair at the foot of the table, my wings tight against it. This furniture had certainly not been crafted in Awia. I looked down the long dining table – transformed into a forum of war.

Mist and Ata sat on my left, with Staniel opposite. Past them on the right were Tawny and Vireo. Candles had been lit to dispel the darkness; it was about one in the morning. A fire in a large stone hearth was reduced to red embers, which with the flickering candle flames cast an ever-changing pattern of shadows over their faces. Coats hung on chair backs; in the last hour Mist had filled a little ashtray to capacity with cigarette butts. I could see another packet in the bag under the table, with a knife, his blue cloak rolled up and a copy of *What Whore* magazine.

There was a carafe of water, which no one had touched, and Genya, presumably, had ordered there to be a whisky jug as well. The night was hot and I could smell the spirit diffusing from the stoppered jar. I helped myself to water, with a very careful sip. It lessened the nausea and I started to feel a little healthier. I was strongly tempted to just put my head down and go to sleep, but I caught Lightning's look. I said, 'Pray continue.'

Lightning had taken control of the meeting, walking around the outside of the table and occasionally getting sullen responses. He said, 'Comet, we will send you back to the Castle, to relate these events to the Emperor.'

'Of course.'

'I'll stay to disband the Plainslands Fyrd, and then I'll follow on to the Castle, so I should meet you there next week.'

'I have business at the coast,' put in Ata. The bruise around her eye was yellowing, making her look even more frightening than usual.

'The Sailor and his wife will leave for Peregrine. But so we do not leave Lowespass undefended, I recommend that Tornado and Vireo, and Staniel remain here with the Awian Fyrd.'

I said, 'That sounds fine to me. I can—'

'No. I do object.' Staniel spoke up. He had been sitting with eyes closed, thin fists clenched in a mass of golden hair, drowning in self-pity. He said, 'My brother ...' His voice was so uneven that he stopped, but couldn't quite pull himself together again.

Vireo said, 'We'll send a cortege tomorrow.'

Staniel said, 'I ... I ...'

'Yes?'

'I would like the Emperor's Messenger to announce the news. Every shop will be shuttered; every flag will be lowered. I would rather not sojourn here; I will depart for Rachiswater tomorrow to arrange the coronation.'

Lightning cut in: 'Patience, my lord. Awia is safe.' He gave a smile that only I saw as condescending. Awia might well be a safe country to Lightning, who owns a little less than one third of it. 'You shouldn't leave Lowespass under Insect threat. The more commanders here, the better. Follow in your brother's footsteps!'

'Comet once said I was no warrior,' Staniel pointed out.

'Would you learn?'

'Need I learn when Tawny and Vireo guard Lowespass? I'll take charge from the Palace which my family built, and then conceivably I will live longer than Dunlin.'

Staniel was suspicious of Lightning's motives. Uncertain of what moves the other lords might make, he wanted to secure his kingdom. It seemed to me that such misgiving was part of Staniel's weakness – an overlord who fears those who answer to him will not be a sound ruler. I also knew that Lightning would rather not have him as King, but the Emperor has made it clear that Eszai should influence the affairs of mortals only lightly, if at all. Our purpose is to help them rather than rule or overawe them. It is a difficult balance for Lightning to maintain; his plans for his manor develop over centuries. He is always more comfortable when Awia has a wise over-lord – one wise enough to know when to leave well alone.

My history is as far removed from the power play of Awia as the slums are from the Palace; it is my responsibility to remind them of the Castle's authority. I addressed Staniel: 'Your Highness, if you wish to leave that is your decision as King, and we must agree to it.'

'Is he, though?' said Lightning softly. 'Castle will take charge if it isn't clear who rules.'

'But it is clear.'

'We don't know Dunlin's will.'

'We do.' I took the folded piece of bed linen from my back pocket and shook it out. 'While you lot were sitting here and bickering, I was doing something useful. Shall I read it?

'"I, Dunlin, leave the manor of Rachiswater and the Kingdom of Awia to my brother and heir Staniel. The fortune is entire for him, for no other and to be split with no other. Signed by my hand this night August 15 2015. Witnessed by Comet Jant Shira and signed by him below."'

I took the ring with its eagle close emblem, and passed it to Staniel, who sat with shoulders bowed. 'You spoke to him?' he asked.

'Yes.'

'What else did he say?'

I shrugged. 'He barely had breath for that, let alone any more.' The will was passed around the table and when it reached Staniel, he examined it carefully. He sat up straight, said, 'Nothing will stop me leaving as soon as daybreak, with an escort of five hundred. Jant, do you agree?'

'As you wish.'

'And Lightning, have you got anything to say?'

'Only that your authority will need practice before it ceases to sound like arrogance.'

Hurriedly I said, 'Lady Vireo, stay here. Tawny, stay with her. Defend Fortress Crag. Keep the Calamus Road clear so we can supply you with food and weapons from Awia.'

Vireo was overjoyed; she had just gained a fortress. 'Thank you! That's to my taste! Jant? Look! That's *her*.'

Genya grasped the top lintel, swung herself through the window and ran a few paces, jumped onto the table and crouched like a spider in the centre. Her arms and legs extended from a swathe of pale green material which encircled her body, and she silently proceeded to unwrap herself, passing the material between her legs and over her shoulder, until it gathered on the table and she was left, a very thin peeled figure. I thought the green fabric was a curtain but she took an edge in each hand and opened it out. It was the Lowespass flag. She had taken the flag down. Genya stalked across the table and left it in a massive bundle in front of Staniel. 'For the Featherback King!'

'Thank you,' said Staniel.

I said, 'Genya. Welcome...'

Mist kicked my ankle. I shook myself and wiped a couple of drops of drool off the tabletop with my shirt sleeve. I put out a hand to her, she strode over and buried her face in my palm, breathed deeply through her nose and mouth, taking my scent. She pushed her face against my palm, the way a cat does when it is urging you to stroke it.

'Genya. Genya. Mmm.' I tried to kiss her but she jumped back. I shuffled in the seat, aware of an increasing pressure against the crotch of my leather jeans – thankfully hidden by the table. 'Can you run?' I murmured.

'Rrrrrrr.' A purr or a growl?

'Excuse me, you two.'

Genya stood up, traversed the table towards the Archer with a single stride, the Insect antennae in her hair waving. She flourished long bare arms at him; he looked rather uneasy.

'I want to know what is going on,' she proclaimed. 'I spit on Insects from the battlements. Insects bite at the walls. What you do is sit in dark halls and talk. What did Dunlin fight for?'

'Listen, Rhydanne—' snarled Lightning, and she was behind him in a flicker of movement, thin hands with nails like daggers caressing his neck.

'What say?' she asked.

'I'm not talking to you until you behave civilly.'

'You talk, Featherback, or I rip your throat!'

'My lady.'

Genya slid back onto the table and sat legs crossed, a wide grin splitting her face. She held her head on one side, a ponytail of frothy black hair cascaded down to her waist. She wore skimpy shorts; all her clothes were minimal because Rhydanne can't feel cold. She liked to make a point of showing this. Her pale, limber legs were wreathed in invisible designs, zigzag flashes and scrollwork. They were ikozemi tattoos, cut using white lead and still poisonous. They only become visible when the skin is flushed, for example by hot water, pleasure, or drunkenness – Genya only ever has the last of these.

Lightning sighed, attempting to mitigate her presence. 'We were discussing—' he began.

'Help me.'

'How?' I asked, nervously. How much would she tell? I wondered if I would be able to stop her if she intended to reveal any secrets. I knew I couldn't hurt her.

Genya crawled across the table on hands and knees, and regarded me quizzically. 'I want to go home,' she said. 'If I run the Insects chase me. So I am trapped here. Jant says he will help me, but how long have I been here? Jay is gone, so why stay? I want to know where is all the snow? This place is so bad. It is hot. The air is thick. It is full of Insects, and now it is full of Featherbacks.'

Staniel removed one hand from a bloodshot eye, said, 'Excuse me ...?'

Genya ignored him. 'This is not like Darkling,' she concluded flightily.

I caught her gaze and said warningly, 'Sister—'

'I am not your sister! If I was your sister I would marry you!'

'This isn't Scree. Please be quiet.'

'You are pathetic, Shira. Insects gnaw us out from where we sit and you would not notice. In Scree this would not happen.'

'That's because there aren't any Insects in Scree,' I muttered, but she caught the comment.

'No,' she agreed lightly. 'There are just mistakes.'

I hissed. It hurts to be reminded that I'm illegitimate, a Shira. Genya's surname was Dara, born within marriage, and in the mountain culture that meant that she could feel superior to me. My hopeless lust turned to anger. A Rhydanne born in wedlock wouldn't associate long with a mistake like me. My childhood of abuse flashed to mind—

'Fucking Dara slut! Slow-runner! Bitch! *Sgiunach!*'

'Goatherd!'

Lightning forced me back into my chair. I pointed a shaking hand at Genya. 'Get this lone wolf bitch out of here or I'll kill her! Tawny, throw her out the window!'

'Don't,' said Lightning, and the conflicting commands rendered Tornado too bewildered to move. I gave Genya a longing look, which wasn't requited.

She strutted on the table, stretching her lean legs, patting Staniel reassuringly on the head.

Staniel gave her the kind of look a child would give a hunting hawk. 'I comprehend,' he said softly, 'that you have had no exemplification of our abilities in recent hostilities and also precious little towards you in the practice of chivalry. It occurs to me that, my lady, since your husband left you as Governor in Lowespass, we have been presumptuous in prevailing upon you. My jurisdiction extends only to *Featherback*-land, but I propose, with the good will of the Eszai, to serve you as we may.'

I had to translate this for Genya, who clapped thin hands in delight. 'I want to go home.'

'Well, a Rhydanne would run away,' remarked Vireo.

'None of that now!' Ata rebuked her.

'Jay shouldn't have gone out riding along the Wall by hisself,' Vireo taunted.

'Fishwife! He killed more Insects than you could count.'

'Hush and hear what Jant says,' said Mist. 'Horse's mouth.'

All eyes were again on me, as if they sensed there was something between Genya and I which it was my duty to end, and end peacefully. I thought for a while, knowing that to Genya, Lowespass was a foreign and frightening place. Vireo and Tawny would certainly not take her into consideration. From living in comfort with her kindly husband, she was alone and confused. From ruling the manor and its solid fortress, she suddenly had nothing at all. It was like being conquered.

Genya discovered the flask of whisky on the table. She plucked out the cork, threw her head back and glugged noisily.

'Sister?' I said. Her green eyes blazed. 'Come down to the stables tomorrow. I'll find a horse for you. Leave the fort to Vireo; I'll let you go home.' I saw her pause, eyes narrowed. 'No tricks, I promise. I'm sorry.'

Ata practically slavered with the desire to know why I was so contrite.

Genya nodded. She unfastened the top button of a thin shirt and pulled

50

out the Lowespass seal, on a dirty string. She bit through the string neatly, and dropped the fat gold ring in Vireo's outstretched hand.

Vireo clutched it, her face glowing with pleasure. After a while Tawny gave her a bear squeeze hug.

'Good horse?' asked Genya, peering up through fine fronds of black hair.

'Yes. And now I need to rest, my sister. We've been awake all night.'

'What!' Staniel spluttered. 'You were asleep for hours.'

'I was awake all night. Just somewhere else.' I pushed my chair back, and was nearly – nearly! – quick enough to catch Genya's hand.

She jumped from tabletop to windowsill, making Mist swear. She fastened her fists in the ivy growing outside, swung herself over the edge and swarmed effortlessly down the wall like a squirrel. At the foot she halted, wreathed in foliage. The courtyard was still so she ducked free, sprinted across and disappeared under a portcullis at the far end.

She trailed a moon shadow rapidly over the tiles of the Inner Ward; muscled, bone-thin and athletic. That's not just the thin of women who aren't fat; there's something essential in her, an animal's constant hunger. Genya is sex on a stick to me, just the stick to everybody else.

The stables of Lowespass Fortress were two long, low buildings. The walkway between them was cobbled and slimy, with a gutter running down the centre into which my boots kept sliding. By the time I reached the stable entrance, a square black mouth in the dark hours before dawn, I was covered in mud and horse shit, and I wouldn't be surprised if it was human shit as well, since the latrines in the fortress are a hundred years out of date and have never worked properly.

The walls were whitewashed stone, roofed with slate. Behind the barn stood Lowespass' Outer Ward, its thick wall topped by a covered passageway. I have spent hours up there, walking along logs painted with pitch and sand to prevent them becoming slippery, looking out over the scenery.

I leant against the doorpost and waited for Genya's arrival.

Each room of the fortress held a handful of men, and many were injured, but the only sound came from behind me, where tethered beasts huffed and coughed. Some sensed my presence and whinnied uneasily, stamping on the strewn floor. A straw fluttered down from the hayracks attached to the stable beams; it brushed my nose. I flicked it away and found that a few more straws had landed in my hair. I removed them swiftly, as my hair is one of my best features.

Soon I will be at the Castle, and I couldn't wait for all the comforts like hot water, clean clothes, customised drugs, my wife. A straw twirled down from the stable. The sky was cut by a long horizontal streak of purple. I watched it turn from dark blue, through violet to wine-red, and it healed as the sun rose, to a pencil line, leaving the sky a pale blue and the walls of the stable clear white.

I waited for Genya. I wanted Genya desperately and I was tormented by the thought I might never see her again. She could lose herself in the mountains, and even if I waited in Scree in a snowstorm she might not come back to the Filigree Spider. Even if I tracked her, above the snowline and in the corries – and I am a good tracker – I might never catch her.

What makes me great also isolates me. Had I been pure Rhydanne, and single, Genya would have married me. Then with the Emperor's consent she would be made part of the immortal Castle Circle. But no, my father was Awian, so with their wings, elongated to a thin Rhydanne build, I can fly, and Genya looks upon me as a freak. In Rhydanne culture early marriages are arranged and the husbands help to raise their children, while the narrow-waisted women recover from the trauma and regain their hunting speed. A newborn Rhydanne is put on the floor – he will be able to stand up. By the end of the day he will walk, and by the end of the week he will be running around uncontrollably.

I fuck my mind up for a little longer with an old, familiar agony: how the Awian trader, rapist, my father, could have managed to catch a Rhydanne girl.

Time does not heal all ills. Some actions can only be seen clearly and understood wholly when viewed through the glass of time. Sick, muddled memories don't fade away but weigh ever more heavily on us as time progresses. They are actions that nobody witnessed, and which I desperately need to confess, but to do so would ruin me. Acts which reappear in nightmares, and that's my punishment.

A stable hand, yawning, disturbed me from my memories. He wore a bright red suede waistcoat slit at the back for his wings. He scuttled by, looked startled when he recognised me, but managed a greeting: 'Good morning, Messenger.'

'It looks like a good morning for flying,' I said. He looked to the metre-long primary feathers at my back. My wings were crossed under my coat, although the bumps at my waist showed the sinewy limbs. The servant had never seen anything like it. He nodded cautiously towards the doorway. 'Want your racehorse ready?'

'No. I want the black mare I rode in yesterday. The charger with the chevronels on its chafron.'

'That's Merganser's horse. From Rachis. Called Charabia.'

'Bring her out and make sure she has excellent tack.'

'Your wish, Comet.'

'I don't care about ornament, but she has to go some distance, so make it sturdy. And let me alone now.' Let me alone to sulk. Still I waited for Genya, scanning the rooftops where she often climbed, wishing for a glacier in the Outer Ward and icicles on the parapets. I waited, I waited, and flinched when a rustle came from just above me. I waited – a giggle – I looked up, and behind the bars of the hayrack were a pair of eyes, vertical pupils, gold as they reflected the sun. Genya was lying full-length in the hayrack. She plucked another straw from her bed and dropped it down on me, giggled, pushing long fingers through the slats. Quickly I grasped a beam and pulled myself up, hoping to lie there with her, but when I climbed in and floundered in the straw she jumped lightly down and paced, tiptoe swift between the stalls, speaking to the chargers.

'Are you good? No, I don't think so. Bad horse, good horse? What about you?' Her body comprised of coat hangers, hanging from thin straight shoulders like her face hung from cheekbones. Paper-white and angular, an origami face, pencil-lead shadowed with lack of sleep.

'My lady! My lady!' I fluttered down. I threw myself at her feet, seized her long, long legs and buried my face in the lace-ups of her boots. She tried to kick me in the nose. I pulled at her leggings but she remained upright with vicious poise.

'I'm sorry about what happened,' I begged. 'Please forgive me. I want to help you.'

She nipped my shoulder violently, the long nails cutting in. I imagined her running and bit my tongue. 'Speak Scree!' she demanded. 'I speak Awian ... not very good.' That would make a mess of my plea, as in Scree there were no words for 'sorry' or 'forgive'. Never trust a language that has no future tense and twenty words for 'drunk'.

'You're safe with me now. What we did was wrong – the Awians would call it wrong anyway. I regret it, and I want to repay you, Genya. Come out to the yard; I help you go back to the mountains.'

'All the horses are spoilt beasts; they bite!'

'I've found one that doesn't seem to mind being ridden by a Rhydanne.'

'Ah – fuck that as well, did you?'

Don't make this hard for me. It's difficult being near you without you making me angry. The cursorial girl was close enough for me to grab, or I could draw my knife and force her to the wall. I was greatly tempted to take her. Damn it, who'd know or care? 'I've seen you catch mice. Don't tempt me to play with you the same way.'

She tossed her hair and stalked out of the stables, ducking under the hayracks.

Staniel's men were gathering in the courtyard and all around was the clink of tack, men fitting saddle straps into buckles, rolling up sleeping bags, rolling fags and chewing on dripping bacon sandwiches.

I saw one sword being examined, but most had left their cleaned weapons in their packs. They were tying little drums, painted gold, amethyst and fuel-blue, to their saddles, plumes and Insect antennae in their hair. The lancers had rolled their colourful caparisons into long bundles and were using them as cushions. Lances had been transformed into pennants, ivory and light blue, embroidered with eagles, with white quills, towers, an appliqué dog with pearl eyes and a sleeping falcon with florid feathers.

A lame man leant on his lance; his friends heaved him into the saddle, his hair still streaked with the blue dye that the most flamboyant wear to fight. A few men chuckled covertly with pleasure at returning to Awia, but most were quiet, bearing Staniel's orders in mind. The black martlet volant was my wife's flag, and I recognised the thickset man who bore it as the warden of Wrought manor, but I couldn't speak to him with Genya treading like a puma at my side.

Genya poked her foot into a stirrup and was astride the horse before it knew what was happening. It kicked, it bucked, and walked round in a little circle, trying to throw her over its head. She clung on to two handfuls of black mane, her forearms like twists of rope, her eyes dancing. The Awian soldiers stopped their preparations and watched, eyes wide and drop-jawed.

I mimicked them. 'Do you want to catch all the flies in Lowespass? Mind your own sodding business!' Genya brought Charabia under control by the simple means of letting it become so knackered it gave up trying to throw her.

'Promise not to eat the horse, Genya ... Well, at least make sure you get back to Darkling first. Here's my compass.'

I showed her the silver device and tried to explain but she just said, 'Pretty!' and shook it to keep the painted disc revolving. I removed it from her talons.

'Keep the sunset at your back,' I said. 'Those hills become the mountains so if you keep going up, you find the trade road which takes you to Scree pueblo.'

Genya grinned maniacally. I took the knife from my boot and passed it to her. If I can't give her my compass she might better understand a knife. 'You could need this, for Insects or thieves. Remember, Insects are too hard to bite. Stab their heads.'

'Yes, Shira.'

I wanted to ask for a kiss but kissing isn't in Genya's repertoire. Instead I took her hand, her pale skin cold to the touch, seeing the even white half-moons on her pointed nails. I will always be able to remember the chill ghost of her skin like marble, and the contrast between it and my wife's warm feathers always makes me feel queasy. I thought, they're too different and yet I want them both, because I am a bit of both and as good as neither.

'All you need is a decent patch of snow to lie in and be as right as Rayne,' I told her.

The gates opened, and Genya urged her unwilling horse forward and through them at a canter. She never looked back, but I knew she was smiling.

Some things are not and can never be yours, no matter how deeply or for how long you know them. I knew I should allow Genya to leave because my lust for her was destructive – although I've never really understood what's wrong with wanting destructive things.

I paid the stable hand generously and went to my room, thinking. In order to be at peace you have to let go of the thing you cherish; you can't move on if you cling to it and even immortals have to develop. Lust for the Rhydanne girl had been holding me back, even as far as the time when I lived like her. I knew it was much better to let her go. So am I at peace? Am I fuck. I cooked up a heavy dose of cat and injected it, enough to Shift.

CHAPTER 4

In the Shift, Keziah was hiding in the Aureate with a hacksaw. We were standing in the shadow of a thick, reflective wall, which stretched up as far as I could see. I was handsome if raw-boned, in black and white, which the wall threw back as different shades of yellow. Keziah never wore clothes. He was a man-sized lizard who walked on strong back legs, stunted forearms hanging down in front. His long snout was full of pointed teeth. The scaly plates of his skin were mottled moss-green and grey. I was desperately trying signs and whispers, to make Keziah come back to his pub.

I had started in Epsilon, looking for Dunlin Rachiswater where I left him in the Bullock's Bollocks bar. He was no longer there, and I heard from the punters that Felicitia had left as well. No one could tell me where they had gone, or why. I then tried my palace at Sliverkey, but it was uninhabited and untidy, as usual. Searching for Keziah, in order to ask him, had brought me to the Aureate.

Keziah was of the opinion that fly-by-night bar staff like Felicitia were worthless drifters. He was better off without them, and Awians in general regardless of how royal. 'They split at daybreak, dude; who knows where they are? Join me and we'll both be rich.'

'This is the Tine's quarter. If they catch us they'll kill us!'

'It's made of solid gold,' Keziah hissed. He turned to see me since his eyes were at the side of his head.

'I know that!'

'So if we cut a piece out we'd—'

'Cut it! Are you mad?'

'Ssh! We'd never have to work again.'

'The pub—'

'Screw the pub; dude, look at this ...' He gestured for me to crouch down and pointed at two jagged saw-marks that ran into the base of the gold wall, carving out a triangular ingot. The cut surfaces were bright, the wedge connected to the wall by half a centimetre thickness at its apex. 'Nearly rich,' whispered Keziah.

'Greedy bastard.' I watched as the hacksaw bit into the wall. He grasped the handle with his hind leg and sawed rapidly. The slice of gold loosened and fell. Keziah caught it in a foreclaw and wrapped it in a piece of cloth, 'Let's go,' he said. We crept to the edge of the wall, and peered round. A group of big Tine were standing there calmly watching us.

Tattoos spotted their pale blue skin, scarred and tanned to indigo. Each

Tine had a flat black shell on his back, pocked with designs and sprouting loops of gold wire. The most immense one had stubby horns grafted on his forehead. Gnarly claws curled into fists. A dozen pairs of pupil-less eyes blinked. A forest of needle-teeth appeared as they all slowly smiled.

Faster reactions than Keziah, I turned and ran. I looked back from the gold cobbled road to see him drop to a fighting stance. He roared.

'Come on!' I yelled.

'Run,' he snarled, showing his terrible teeth. 'You coward!'

The Tine clustered round him, the smallest taller than him, muscles crawling under their blue skin. Keziah kicked the nearest one. His claw opened its stomach. Pink guts spilled out over its belt. Another Tine finished it off and began chewing on its backside.

Keziah lashed out with his tail. He struck the cannibal across the back of the neck, killing it instantly. It slumped over its meal. The lizard evaded another carnivore, bit at it, driving it back. He kicked again, his talon sinking into a belly, where it was caught. Two Tine dashed forward and seized his leg. He teetered and fell over.

I saw the Tine simply pick Keziah up, clawed hands all over him, and twist him apart. Those at his head twisted left. His legs twisted right. There was a series of sounds like strings snapping, then I heard the wet crack as his spine fractured. Tine clamped their teeth in his scaly tail; another began to pick long fangs from his gums. He screamed and thrashed. Blue fingers pushed into his eye sockets, trying to fish one out. His tongue was ripped and Tine fought among themselves for it. They plucked his fingers with gristly sounds and chewed them like twigs.

A Tine took a length of intestine, and squeezed out the contents. Murky slime pattered onto the cobbles. He put one end of the gut to his lips and blew it full of air. He twisted it a few times, held it up. A balloon dog. Tine fell over each other laughing.

Helpless, I kept running; the monsters saw my movement and followed. The gold path shook with their footfalls. They smelt of rotting meat. They couldn't gain ground. They couldn't catch a Rhydanne as shit scared as I was. But they wouldn't give up the chase.

I pounded, slipped and jumped down the gold road. The road narrowed, came to an abrupt bend. This was the knee. Holy buildings with stepped gable ends crowded close on every side. Red gold, white gold. Stench of burnt flesh in the air. Smell of lizard blood and excrement. I set off down the shin of their city.

Shin, calf, the Ankle Plaza. A rounded edifice stood in the centre, full of Tine. They had blue loincloths and thongs round their legs. Their custom was to drop molten gold onto their legs and feet, which set in their skin. It seemed as if they had grown from the golden road, gradually changing to blue. I skidded to a halt in front of them. The Tine chasing me piled in behind. They reached out with transplanted fingers. They made a stinking wall of muscle.

I put a hand to my sword hilt and found that it had gone. I tried to spread my wings but was rooted to the spot. The Tine tensed to rush me.

A skein of voices on my left – 'Shira!' I looked to where a woman was standing – a blonde woman, wrapped in a cloak. There had been no girl there a second ago.

The Tine didn't like her one bit. Forgetting me, they closed in on her and I screamed because I thought they would rip her apart. She threw back the cloak; underneath she was completely naked, and very lovely. The Tine sniggered and licked their chops. As the cloth hit the cobbles her body followed it, disintegrating, flowing down and spreading like the twisted trunk of a tree, then like its roots, running out in thick strands over the floor. The broken facade of her face was last to go. And then silence.

Some Tine went down on one knee. Some backed off. I just kept screaming. Her body became a thick cable of flesh, made from smaller threads. It snaked across the plaza and over to a gold drain covering, where she reassembled into a beautiful girl, and beckoned to me. She raised the grating, although Tawny himself couldn't have budged it, and slipped through.

The Tine began to recover, and looked around for me. I pelted across and followed her down the drain, grazing my wings as I eased through. I retched at the stink.

We were in darkness. Blue arms wedged through the hole and waved about, but they couldn't grab us. A scimitar was poked down. The Tine began to howl. The girl took my arm and we walked a little way along the edge of a deep gold trough, running with blood and dirty water, a few fragments of splintered bone carried along, organs and knots of hair and Insect shells; some other pieces I was glad I couldn't recognise.

'This is the main drain,' said the girl sweetly. 'I advise you not to take a swim.'

'What? Who? Who are you?' I panted.

'This is just a bad dream, Jant,' she said.

'How do you know my fucking name?' I tried to shake free of her grasp; it was impossible.

'You have to go back to the Castle and forget all this,' she said. She spoke Awian perfectly. She had a very mellow voice, very high pitched, and as if lots of voices were speaking together. A couple of gaps appeared in her cheek; with a shifting of flesh they closed again and I suddenly saw that she wasn't solid at all. I peered closer and recoiled with disgust. She was made up of thousands of long, thin worms. Knotted together and constantly moving, they gave the impression of skin. She smiled, or rather, the worms that were her lips parted briefly, and I saw the worms that were her teeth.

'It's a shame to see such a seasoned traveller so lost,' she said.

'Who are you?' I repeated, terrified. I was stuck between this creature and the blood-filled canal. Her faint smile reappeared, as if she had no need of a name, and I was being stupid. She must have come from a very distant place, to be so alien. 'If you think I'm strange,' she said, 'you should see the rest of the court.' She put her hand through her chest and scratched the back of her head.

'Court? What court? The only court is the Castle!'

'The Royal Court is concerned. I think the Tine are not very happy with you,' she said, understating in a studiedly feminine way. Her calm voice stroked me. If she was invisible I'd be in love. 'Never come back to the Aureate. Never talk to the Saurian.'

'Keziah's dead,' I told her. Another faint smile.

I recovered what few shreds of courtesy I could. 'Thank you ... Thank you for saving my life. Maybe in the future I may have the honour of performing the same service for you, my lady. In the meantime, is there anything I can do to repay you, singular or plural?'

'You must go home and stay there.'

'Apart from that!'

'How about a kiss?' she said, sticking out a tongue which unwound into a cluster of worms, and waved at me. The end of the tassel suddenly bloomed red, as all the worms opened their tiny mouths, and stuck their tongues out. I backed away.

The girl laughed and dissolved, writhing down as before and separating out into individual creatures, which squirmed between the cobbles and, clump by clump, plopped into the drain, where they swam away upstream. The last of them merged together to form a floating disembodied arm, which cheerfully waved farewell. I returned the gesture, wondering if she could see me.

I then sat down by the gory canal, and waited to be pulled back. I would have a hangover on my flight to the Castle. When perfectly sober, anticipating a hangover is a bitch. I hated the thought of my useless body lying on the chamber floor, back in cold Lowespass, where the Insects swarmed.

CHAPTER 5

If the Castle had been built in the shape of a sundial, it couldn't have been more accurate. Three o'clock in the afternoon exactly, on a late summer day, a shaft of sunlight pierces the slats in the shutter of the Northwest Tower and slides across my desk. It's done this reliably for hundreds of years; this time it woke me.

I woke with the sun in my eyes, sitting at my desk, my head resting on a stack of smudged papers, post-battle correspondence. That probably meant the wet ink had imprinted in negative across my face. I would have to spend another night writing it out again with the aid of a mirror. I sighed, stretched and yawned.

'You're burning yourself up,' said a warm voice behind me. A cinnamon voice. A scent of vanilla. Tern.

Without looking round I said, 'I didn't know you had come back.'

'I took the coach from Wrought last night. Arrived midnight. You were already ... asleep.'

'And did you have a good time in Wrought, oh piquant one?'

Tern was laying on the chocolate-brown velvet chaise longue, a honey-coloured silk parasol over one shoulder and a paperback novel open on her breast. 'We have to get that fixed,' she said, indicating the broken shutter with a finger spiced with rings and nail varnish. 'Then you can sleep all day.'

This may sound strange but her voice is the main reason I love her. She breathes rounded words like the heady steam from mulled wine or cocoa, word fumes glazed with brandy and syrupy accents. I love languages, and my greatest wish is to be sugar-preserved in Tern's slow voice forever. I gazed at her fondly, warmed by the rogue beam of sunlight. She had a long-sleeved, faded cream dress, mostly lace. Chic, slight and delicate, she looked like icing on the chocolate divan. This is the lady I chose to make immortal, the girl who, to me, is the best in the world. The sweetest in the world, ever. She started spinning the caramel parasol, proud of my attention, just like a child. Her hair was dark, her skin the colour of demerara sugar, soft and warm. Her face was defined by subtle make-up, lips the shade of red that is nearly brown, like sherry; champagne, coffee and liquorice, her eyes. 'My love,' I said, 'you look good enough to eat.'

She glanced deliberately ceiling-wards. 'You're still high,' she accused.

'I'm not. I've given up.'

'Nonsense,' said Tern succinctly. 'My dear, you have more holes in your arms than there are in the roof of Wrought.'

I searched for a way to escape the conversation. Persistence wasn't one of my wife's strengths. I knew from experience that if I bluffed for a while her attention would wander to something else. 'I'll be fine.'

'I worry about you, Jant. Your habit hasn't been this bad since twenty-oh-six.'

Yes, that was the last time I saw Genya. 'It's the memory of the battle, and Rachiswater's death that's made it so bad,' I lied, feeling the pleasant warmth of Tern's sympathy – I know it does me no good, but I love to bask in her attention or concern. I contemplated which hiding places I could use should Tern decide to throw out my hoard of cat. It was rare for her to be so bothered about the fact I indulge occasionally. I thought I owed myself a little pleasure after all I had been through.

'Can I help you come off it?'

'Ah – I'm not ready to quit just yet.'

Tern sighed, she had heard that one before. Prudently I offered, 'I'll cut down. I really mean to. Really.' Tern heard the strain in my voice and relented. The last overdose when I Shifted had truly frightened me, and I was taking less cat because I didn't want to risk accidentally tripping to Epsilon. The Worm-Girl's warning still haunted me – never come back to the Aureate. I didn't want to think about it any longer. Dwelling on the problem made me want more cat, and I was feeling shaky enough as it was.

'Please do, darling. You're skin and bone—' She would have continued but I threw myself on the divan, on top of her, and started trying to fit kisses down the front of her dress. She yelped, giggled. 'Leave me alone! Mmm ... Ow!' I bit her shoulder.

'Come to bed.'

'Mmm. OK. No – there's a note for you.'

I stared at her. More work? 'From whom?'

Tern gestured towards a square of yellow card on the mantelpiece. 'The Archer,' she said.

I tried to stand but Tern wrapped her legs around my waist, a rather neat trick. I poked her belly with the parasol until she freed me. 'Lightning can wait,' she said sulkily.

'Well, if he wants me I should go,' I replied. She tutted. I read Lightning's fastidious copperplate: '*Come and see me as soon as you can. Your reinforcements arrived last night: Governor Swallow Awndyn with her retinue, bound for Lowespass. Owing to Staniel's misfortune she decided to divert to the Castle, for which I am grateful.*' I flipped the card over. '*Although I fully intend to wring your neck for calling Swallow to the Front. LSM.*'

Tern regarded me quizzically. 'You're in trouble.' She had an expression of looking at me over the tops of her spectacles, although she never wears glasses.

'Do I care?' I began to lick her legs hungrily, my mouth full of dress hem. Tern stroked my feathers rhythmically, driving me mad with lust. 'Will you do that thing with your legs again?'

'Like this? Why?'

'Because then I can do *this*.' Tern gasped. Even her yelps were like help-ings of cream gateaux.

Tern tugged at my wing, which extended until she rolled off the bed. I pulled the strong muscles back with a snap.

'Come on, come on. You have to go!'

'Only mortals hurry. Give me another kiss.'

'He's waiting for you!'

'Yes, love. No, wait ...'

'Ready?'

'Wait a minute. I'm missing something here. What did Lightning mean, "Staniel's misfortune"? What the fuck is he talking about? What day is it anyway?'

'Friday.'

'Can't be. It was Friday when I last went to court ... Oh, shit. Not an entire week.'

Tern sighed. She had definite opinions about drug binges that lasted a whole week. She rooted around on the untidy floor for a folded newspaper and passed it to me:

The Wrought Standard is pleased to amend previous reports by bringing you the news that His Majesty King Staniel has reached Rachiswater Palace alive and well after yesterday's disaster. He has not been harmed and has just issued a statement praising his bodyguard (printed in full, page two) who remained with him dutifully during the fast ride back although seven-eighths of the column behind them were killed. A survivor said, 'We came upon the vanguard of our own host cut to pieces and returned with haste, so as to ensure the safety of His Majesty.'

The death toll reached five hundred when Insects beset Staniel's column of soldiers peaceably bringing the body of the previous King home. Insects outnumbering our troops two to one attacked at night while the soldiers were unarmoured on the march and unprepared for such an onslaught. Their bodies have not been found and the casket containing Dunlin's remains has not been recovered, as Staniel has pronounced it too dangerous to venture back into the area. He is, however, mindful of the opprobrium that this acci-dent and loss has brought upon his family.

Many families in Rachiswater and Wrought are in mourning. The whole kingdom shares their grief, which will long endure.

Staniel has not dismissed the survivors, and has also summoned the rest of the Awian Fyrd to protect him in Rachiswater, an unpopular decision as it leaves Calamus Road and the northwest of the country unguarded.

Jant Shira 09.09.15

Shit. No wonder Lightning wants to see me. 'It's impressive,' I said. 'I wrote for the *Standard* without knowing about the fight.'

Tern gave me an antique look. 'You owe me one.'

I looked in a couple of other broadsheets that were lying on the floor among gory Insect dissection textbooks and my chemistry notes. *The Moren Times* just listed what courtiers wore to the coronation, and had good tits on page three, but the *Moderate Intelligencer* had this to say:

Never before has a King raised a host solely to protect himself. We may ask why he has separated from the other manorships in Awia, and how will the smaller manors defend themselves against the Insects? It is the Castle's role to shield Awia but how is it to accomplish this without troops? Why has the Castle not made an official statement? Is the Emperor supporting Staniel, who seems prepared to forsake Lowespass and Tanager? With some notable exceptions, the smaller manors are coming round to the view that Staniel should be deposed and replaced. We look again to the Circle of unusually silent immortals for advice on this issue, while Insects roaming south of the Wall destroy what's left of our cattle and threaten our children.

Kestrel Altergate 10.09.15

'I've got to go,' I said to Tern. I had to find out what Staniel was trying to achieve.

Tern nodded. 'One day we'll have more than a day together,' she said ruefully.

'I'm sorry.' I snorted some more cat, thinking of it as a medicine to stall the onset of my sickness, although it would leave me restless. It's a stupid delusion, I know, because what I call medicine is really the cause of my sickness.

The stifling world outside was hotter than I had thought possible. The sun was a silver coin burning through a white overcast sky, trapping heat beneath the clouds and suffocating the Castle. I stripped off extra clothes as I walked, and by the time I reached Lightning's rooms I was carrying my crowskin coat, a long-sleeved T-shirt, and was verging on indecency.

I have had two hundred years to become familiar with this wing of the Castle, but its grandeur would make anybody feel uncomfortable. I feel I shouldn't be here, but the building also seems gracious – as if the people who do belong here will smile and allow me a little time. In a corridor deep inside the Palace interior of the Castle, black and white tiles were laid to appear three-dimensional. The sides of the Neo-Tealean corridor were open white arches, and I go through one, across an immaculate lawn, into a white building with long, many-paned sash windows.

The brickwork on the lower storey was emphasised, with plain walls above. The windows were set so closely together that the wall was mostly glass, with dark blue velvet drapes. From inside one can see every centimetre of the formal gardens, the square lawns and conical cypress.

Music wandered out onto the lawns. I followed it like a stream to its source, thinking that it was a very pretty harpsichord duet, but when I got to Lightning's rooms I discovered that it was just Swallow, who had found a way of playing both parts of the duet at once.

Lightning was sitting in a chair as near to her as etiquette allowed, with a distant smile on his face, pleased because Swallow was now not only in the same room as him, but she was thrilled with his latest present, a gilt and blue cloisonné harpsichord, with scroll legs, keys of gold and lapis lazuli.

The furniture matched, but with a few modern New Art pieces of enamel and silver. Lightning has always been a collector, and refused to stop although he bemoaned the fact that no artist in the last few hundred years has had any taste. The room's furniture was a record of exclusive trends, from the turn of the first millennium. It was mostly baroque and tortoiseshell but a polished shield with a blue mascle on argent hung on the far wall, with arrows splayed behind. On either side there were ancient oil-painted portraits. Below, a variegated marble fireplace took up most of the wall, winged statues supporting an inlaid mantelpiece. An elegant glass wine decanter stood on a table with a pedestal of polished Carniss granite. Smoked salmon was arranged on a silver tray. Other seafood had legs and shells and looked too much like Insects for comfort. I skirted round it and touched Swallow's green devoré shoulder to wake her from her reverie. The last chord hung in the air for a long, sweet time.

'Hello, Jant,' she said. 'Great make-up.'

I could grow to love some people. 'Governor Awndyn, it's good to see you and I wish the situation was different. Do either of you know what the fuck is happening in Rachis?'

'No,' said Swallow cheerfully. She folded her sheet music, pulled a pencil from behind her ear and began to write more music on the back. In a drunken conversation I once heard Lightning admit it was a shame Swallow keeps her hair short; it was a coppery red like sparks, like strands of silk. She also had thick eyebrows, and freckles all over her face and even down her arms.

Swallow preferred to spend her days practising the piano rather than going riding, and as a result was plump but unfortunately without having big breasts which many well-built women are blessed with. She sat cross-legged on the harpsichord stool, wearing a jacket made of different-coloured squares of velvet. She also wore a dark green beret, which sat at a dapper angle on her ginger hair – such a jaunty angle, in fact, that I found myself braced to catch it, starting forward nervously every time she moved. She wore other stuff as well but it was the motley coat I really noticed, because it was so outrageous.

Lightning stretched his muscular arms and sighed. 'Take a seat,' he advised. I sank into an armchair which all but smothered me. 'The Emperor asked for you this morning. I don't know how you dare stretch his patience. I received a letter from Harrier, my steward, who attended the crowning ceremony. Staniel was so anxious to get into the throne that he couldn't wait for any Eszai to be present, damn him – it's the first coronation I've missed in fifteen hundred years!

'Anyway, naturally Harrier was frightened for Micawater. If Rachis is surrounded by troops to protect it against Insects, what about my house which is only fifty kilometres away? Harrier wanted to know whether an invasion is likely. I have reassured him. I have sent everyone I can find to the front, and further arms to the fortress.'

'You don't want to follow the trend and protect Micawater?' Swallow asked.

'Of course not! If we can't hold the front then the whole thing will fall apart.'

'Staniel wants Rachiswater to be a safe haven,' she added.

'It will be safe all right. It will be a starving island in a sea of Insects. How long will even the best troops hold out with Staniel in command?' Lightning sighed. 'Swallow, I wish I could keep my fyrd for myself but you know we have to work together to save northern Awia from being overrun.'

'I came with two thousand men as reinforcements, I don't see why you can't let me go to the front.'

'No. Not until you become Eszai.'

I took a glass that had evidently been laid out for me, and poured some refreshing white wine. 'The Insects will stay behind their Wall, Saker. There can't be so many.'

'Yes, and they'll push the Wall out and build new Walls and more Walls until we will have lost all Awia. I remember how quickly they used to expand, at the beginning.'

Better change the subject before Lightning starts telling us again about the old heroic days of the founding of the Circle. 'It looks like Staniel's close escape has unsettled him.'

Lightning picked up a letter with a *Top Secret* seal. 'From the tone of this, he is terrified.'

'He spends summers lying in a haystack writing poetry, while Dunlin practised jousting,' said Swallow, citing the popular opinion of Staniel's military prowess without looking up from her sheaves of paper opera.

It may have had something to do with the wine, but I was feeling optimistic. 'Don't worry. He can't keep soldiers at Rachis for long, they've got homes and lovers and a harvest to bring in next month.'

Lightning sounded grim: 'Well, let us hope they would rather cut wheat and bake us bread than sit on their arses in Rachis Park for five pounds a day.'

'He's *paying* them?'

'It seems so, if I don't misread this letter. And as time goes on, and if the crops start dying for lack of attention he'll have to start paying them more and more. The treasury will run dry. If Dunlin was still alive he would die a thousand times to know how his brother is misusing their fortune.'

'Let me go and speak to him.'

'Yes, and we also want to know how Tornado is faring in Lowespass; at least one of us is out there. I should go back ... But San thinks what I'm doing here is more useful for the moment.'

I could not say much in front of Swallow, but I itched to know, 'What *are* you doing here?'

'Simply writing letters and talking to people.'

Swallow put her manuscript down. 'If you're going to court, can I come?'

Our predicament had nothing to do with Awndyn and I told her so, but Lightning said, 'It would help Swallow's petition if she could see the Emperor again. You compered her concert in the Hall, now I would be grateful if you could accompany her into the courtroom.'

I suspected that this whole visit was just a plot so that Swallow could see the Emperor San again. 'Why don't you take her?' I moaned.

'I would hardly be viewed as impartial.'

Swallow had said that if she was accepted into the Circle, she would consider marrying the Archer and not before. It was a clever move, because Lightning now arranges as many audiences with the Emperor as possible. I know that once San's mind is made up on an issue it rarely changes; in fact his opinion defines the issue and in pressing her case Swallow is denying him. San owes his Eszai nothing because he pays us in lifetime, a currency so valuable it leaves no favours outstanding.

Lightning asked me to take Swallow because it meant that he would not lose face if her application should be rejected. I don't fear loss of reputation as much as he does because my reputation has been singed with scandal for a very long time. If I helped Swallow towards success then Lightning might look kindly on me. He might agree to another loan, or at least waive the interest on the two hundred thousand pounds I borrowed in nineteen-thirty.

Lightning first looked after me when I joined the Circle, fresh from Hacilith, knowing nothing about Insects or swordplay, wary but eager to please. He gave me lessons on horse riding and etiquette, as well as letting me run riot in Micawater until I learned the Awian language thoroughly. During that time I became his closest friend and, like Tern, he keeps me on the straight and narrow. I could return the favour by taking Swallow under my wing. I beckoned to her. 'Come on then. Saker, what are your plans?'

'I'm going up to the gallery to watch.'

'I bet you are.'

Swallow said, 'Perhaps I should sing in court. I would be able to melt even the Emperor's heart. He would agree to making me immortal so he could hear perfect concertos for ever.'

She didn't say it boastfully, she said it as fact, and I thought she was probably right but for all I knew the Emperor hated music, or couldn't tell the Eclipse Sonata from a football chant.

'It's harder for me, because there is no Circle Musician for me to Challenge and so displace. Don't the opinions of the other Eszai hold any weight?' she asked.

'None whatsoever,' said Lightning sadly. He had seen Swallow change over the last year: with each disappointment her desire to join the Circle grew, till now there was a determination hard as diamond and brittle as old glass in her, which could exhaust her maiden's spirit, leaving her resentful and still aging.

'Shall we go?' Lightning finished his heart-stoppingly expensive wine in one gulp. Pale with anxiety, Swallow nodded. Lightning once told me that growing wan was as sure an indication of love as blushing was an indication of modesty. As far as I could see Swallow was a frightened girl backed into complicated situations by the rabid dog of her own ambition. I wanted to free her. I could tell she was worried because she wasn't looking directly at me; she was too busy looking inwards, at imagined court scenes. Aware of Lightning's jealous gaze, I hugged her chastely and told her to have courage.

Lightning had told Swallow many times that the struggle to become Eszai could be over immediately, if only she would consent to marry him. A year later she still refused. I needed to find out exactly why she wouldn't marry the Archer, so I could convince her that she was wrong. I can't feel as profoundly as the Archer, thank god, but I did want Swallow to join us. Even with the little I know about music I could tell she was the most talented composer the Fourlands had ever produced, and she was an excellent drinking companion, who could play the guitar so well.

I walked automatically avoiding the uneven floorboards, but Swallow had not been this way before, and she found herself trotting along in an unbecoming fashion in order to keep up. The Archer strode beside her, arrows crackling together in a quiver at his hip.

I wanted to put the cantatrice at her ease. 'Spent all your life in Awndyn?' I asked chattily.

'Apart from last year in Hacilith.'

'Your mother must have been from Diw.'

'Yes. How did you—? Oh. You can pick up my accent. That's amazing!'

I shrugged to show it was no more impressive than her ability to remember every note in every symphony. She wrote two before she was twelve.

The flight feathers of her wings were barred. They were a dark, rust red and had red-brown lines across them, which was very rare. Her wings looked sumptuous, and the rest of her body looked so soft and tender that I wanted to touch her. I quelled the urge and lengthened my stride to put the temptation behind me.

A colonnaded narthex runs around the outside of the courtroom, which is the very centre of the Palace, itself the centre of the Castle, which is the centre of the world. I led Swallow down through carved arches and spiralled columns, to a staircase where Lightning left us, ran up the stairs and vanished through a door leading to the arcade. Stone Insect heads were carved in deep relief on the walls; their obsidian compound eyes polished to hungry black mirrors. Swallow shuddered when she saw them. The stone antennae of these heads were knotted together intricately so that the triangular heads hung in a column like bunches of onions. I once heard that the carvings substituted real trophies brought back by the first Eszai. I expect they were replaced because of the smell, or because courtiers got sick of maggots wriggling out and dropping on them.

Busts and escutcheons were set into the walls, which Swallow examined to see if she could recognise any emblems. 'You won't,' I said. 'This part of the Castle hasn't changed since its founding, and the manorships are different now.'

'Yes. Is Micawater here?'

'No. This was built two thousand years ago.'

Swallow fell silent; she glanced furtively at the faded heraldic paintings on the ceiling – dark gules like old blood, raw umber and green earth. I have researched their delitescent meanings for a hundred years and I am still really none the wiser.

I fretted about the entrance to the courtroom, a huge door of oak so old it is petrified, set with black iron studs. It took all one's weight to move it, and all my weight is not much.

A guard stood by the door, simply and immaculately dressed but dark around the jowls. He held a finely honed spear and had a broadsword buckled at his hip. He saw me and stood to attention, then relaxed when I waved at him.

'Comet.'

'Hello, Lanner. I haven't seen you for ages.'

'Lanner was my father,' said the guard.

'Oh.'

'I am the little lad you used to give sweets to and say, "He'll make a fine soldier one day."'

I nodded, fazed. Mistakes of this kind were happening with increasing frequency.

'My lady?'

'This is Swallow, Lightning's love. She wants to be immortal. She wants another title to replace her unfortunate name.'

He looked Swallow up and down before addressing her. 'You must give up your weapons here.'

Swallow glanced at me. 'I don't have any weapons,' she said plaintively.

'Not even a knife?'

'No!'

The guard grinned at me over the top of Swallow's head. 'You have to leave your jewellery too,' he said.

I explained: 'Zascai aren't allowed to wear gold in the Circle court.' Swallow nodded, thinking it was another rule designed to make people feel small and unimportant.

I said, 'Everybody feels insignificant in front of the Emperor, even Eszai. It is always unwise to hide behind gold trinkets rather than your own solid achievements.'

'And your watch.'

'Why?'

'Because time doesn't exist in the Emperor's presence,' the guard announced.

'Because it's bad manners to look at your watch in court,' I said.

Swallow dug out her pocket watch and handed it over. The sentry walked backwards with his back against the door, to open it. Swallow started forward but I put a hand on her shoulder. 'A word of advice, sister. Don't look up.'

The first thing Swallow did when she stepped inside was look up. She stopped, wide-eyed, entranced, spellbound, and her mouth open. I gave her a firm push and she tore herself away, her shoulders rounded in defence.

'Breathe in and go,' I muttered.

'Shira. It's *massive*.' Her voice was solid awe.

I glanced up, and further up, and the ceiling sucked my gaze into the heights of its arches until I was completely disorientated, feeling as if I was falling upwards. The ceiling was gold and mosaic; huge bosses with churning ships and gyring eagles hung from the pinnacles. There were figures ten times life-size with their cloaks swirling around them like pleated clouds. Oil lamps lighted the ceiling, and candles in gold candelabra illuminated the aisle, on torchères like graceful statues. But once swallowed by the size of the vaulted ceiling, it was difficult to tear my gaze away. I am used to distance but my eyes ached to focus across the vast hall. I looked at the narrow arcade, so dizzyingly distant I had to fight the urge not to spread my wings for safety, and I saw Lightning there, leaning over. I could feel the strength of his apprehension; his will that she *must do well* shone down like a beam.

Swallow swore cautiously. 'By god. Oh, god. How many times could Awndyn fit into this hall?'

'At least you didn't come from a Scree sheiling, sister.'

'Did *god* build this?'

'In a way. I think it asked the Emperor to.'

She began to walk, and as she walked down the scarlet carpet between the thin brass railings I saw her gather gracefulness into herself. Her shoulders went back, her head proudly upright; from somewhere she found an impassive expression and her hands, which had been tapping pizzicato, became still, at her sides. She paced without pause all the way down the Throne Room, past the screen, which Zascai are not allowed beyond.

We walked past beautiful Eszai in stunning clothes, who were sitting in pews along the walls. They whispered to each other as Swallow passed.

We walked past ebony eagles at the ends of the benches; they had opalescent eyes.

Her shadow jumped, grew, jumped and shrank as we walked past the torchères. I wished I had had a chance to look in a mirror before coming in here.

We walked to the steps of the dais where the Emperor sits beneath a sunburst of silk and burnished gold.

Swallow was sensible enough not to look at the Emperor. She knelt, on one knee, and then on both knees, and then her hands touched the floor as well. Her head was bowed. I stood behind her, a hand on her broad shoulder and proclaimed, 'My lord Emperor, I bring Governor Swallow Awndyn from the coast, a mortal who has a message for your attention.'

'Have I heard this claim before?'

'This time last year she was sent away from the court. But since then she's done much, travelled throughout Awia, built an opera house at Awndyn and sung at the Moren Grand.' I recounted a list of Eszai and mortals alike who supported Swallow, a verbal petition that stopped abruptly when I realised the Emperor wasn't in the slightest impressed.

70

'Awndyn,' said San, and at his voice she tensed. 'What is the purpose of my Circle?'

'The most talented person of each occupation is made immortal so that the Fourlands can have a repository of wisdom and expertise, which it needs since god has left us and we are at war.'

'Castle's aim is to protect the Fourlands from the Insects, is it not?'

She nodded and the Emperor continued: 'So how can a musician help us? Your melody turns Insects to stone, is that it?'

I said, 'She can rally the fyrd and I have heard her play marches—'

The Emperor laughed, gratingly. 'Messenger, enough. Next you will have me believing that brave speeches can rouse the rank and file. I think Swallow's presence might even act as a distraction to Eszai who should be fighting. Governor Awndyn, if we were at peace your art might find a place here, but like all arts it is the pastime of mortals, I fear ... If I was to make you immortal, on what grounds would another Musician be able to Challenge you? It would be impossible to judge the best.'

Her soft body pressed against my leg. She shook with restlessness; she had nothing to lose and wished to make the best of the situation in which she was trapped. But I was angry – how could we decide if one activity is more worthwhile than another? I've seen Lightning's tricks with arrows and my flying often verges on acrobatics. For a start, it's impossible to separate the creative arts and the arts of war; they influence each other continually. Creativity is the humanity we're trying to save. If Eszai are war machines we're no better than Insects.

'Even in war, there's space to compose,' Swallow said softly, but the Emperor chose not to hear her.

'I don't wish to endow people with immortality on the strength of their hobbies,' he mused.

'My lord, she is the best of all time.'

The Emperor smiled like a wolf in a children's story. 'Governor Awndyn, I think you have made yourself immortal already. Your music will not die easily.'

'My lord Emperor, I could do much more – I could create forever! If I die the Fourlands would lose my gift.'

'Would your creativity survive becoming immortal? People create in order to leave something of themselves in the world when they die. Immortals do not have that pressure.'

'My lord, only with an immortal lifetime can I express all the music I have inside me.'

'Everyone in the Empire can witness the martial skills of my Circle, but not everyone can appreciate music, and they would criticise your membership.'

71

Swallow's courage failed her; it was impossible for her to argue with the Emperor and she fell silent out of fear that she had said too much already. I thought the virtuoso had a different kind of strength, distinct from mine but equal; those who understood her musical feats would be convinced of her stamina. Many Eszai are jaded and love innovation; some of us, like myself, invent to make our lives easier and to prove we are the best specialists in our various professions. The more confident immortals embrace novelty and would welcome Swallow's continual creation.

San said, 'Do you think music requires an eternal guardian, as Lightning controls the skill of archery? Would it be better if music was left to change and develop as future people wish? I think that your dedication to join the Castle has little to do with music. You confront me with a very selfish determination. Comet asked how he could serve me, but instead you seem to demand eternity.'

'My lord, I'm sorry if I seem hasty. It's the nature of mortals to believe that their time is running out and death is imminent.'

The Emperor's agate eyes softened and he sighed. 'Ah yes,' he said. 'I remember ... Messenger, do you think Awndyn's music would be better loved if she were one day to die?'

I thought of the shields outside the Throne Room, which used to be so important they were fixed in the centre of the Castle, but now nobody knows which divisions of land they represent. I said, 'It isn't the same music if Swallow isn't there to defend and interpret it. When she dies, her work dies too.'

I braced myself, straightened and met his gaze. The Emperor was vulpine, thin-faced, white-haired, his arms in an ivory and gold cloak out over stone armrests. One candle-strength of humour lit his immeasurable eyes.

'How old is she now?'

'Nineteen, my lord.'

'How old have you been for two hundred years, Comet?'

'Twenty-three. But I've grown wiser!'

'Have you? I think it would be a shame to deny the Fourlands the music she would make if she were to grow more mature. When she gains more experience her music will be so improved that the rest of the world will learn from it. I will consider.' San finished, 'I will see you again. This evening I will hear you play.'

Swallow stood and walked backwards a few steps, then turned and left the Hall. In the still space I heard a clatter from the gallery as Lightning raced out to meet her. A couple of Eszai close on the balcony chuckled.

San limited the numbers of people in the Circle. There are fifty immortals, not including the Emperor, or husbands and wives, and there are rarely positions free. It looked like Swallow would have to wait a long time.

'And what shall we do with you?' San asked. It was my turn to drop to one knee, watching the red carpet. 'Take yourself over to Rachiswater and speak with the King. I want to know what he wants, how he plans and how he feels. The last is most important.'

'Yes, my lord.'

'You may remind him that the Circle is still at his disposal.'

There was a weird inflection in the word 'still' which prompted me to ask, 'Would it be better if there was a new King?'

'Comet, you know better than that. The Castle does not have its own fyrd. We have no authority over the King of Awia, nor the Governor of Hacilith, nor any of the governors or lord governors of the manors. We help when they decide to ask us, and we provide advice when they desire it. Otherwise, how will we last for the millennia before god returns?'

'Yes, my lord.'

'If we are seen to be forceful, we would be questioned. It falls to the governors of Awia to decide between them if Staniel should be replaced. Lightning is the only one of them who has made his opinion clear to me. He is concerned that the manors will start fighting between themselves. That would be a disaster.'

'Yes it would.'

'Make sure you bring any news to me first. Not to Lightning; he can be a little overconfident sometimes. And it has been a contretemps for the Castle to be so slow in understanding the situation. Which is your obligation, Comet. I've heard nothing from you, except that which your wife has sent with your name on it.'

'Ah, yes. I—'

'I gather that you needed a rest. I'm interested in knowing how often and for how long you need *to rest* ...' The Emperor left a gap in which I was presumably expected to say something, but even if I had anything to say, I was too scared to speak. 'If this happens again we will remove your title.'

Feigning flippancy I managed, 'I don't have a title.'

'I mean people will stop calling you Comet.'

I dropped a loose hand to my sword hilt and looked up, grazed with worry. The Emperor continued, 'You are only immortal for a while, Comet. I suggest you try to remember why you are lucky enough to have a place here, and imagine what would happen if I called for Challengers against you.'

'My lord. I'm sorry.'

'Remember when you speak to Rachiswater that you address him on our behalf. The Castle's representative. He's afraid of you. Yes. Of course he is. I know you find that amusing but please don't exploit it. Frightened Kings are dangerous.'

CHAPTER 6

The cool smoothness of Rachiswater was calming after the bright autumn morning. The whole Palace was designed to be airy; it was open plan, invaded by its own gardens. Arches and sweeping white walls had elegant, linear decoration, flowing like script.

The Palace was composed of curves, in a garden that featured only circles and spirals. From the air it looked like a long cluster of giant bleached bones in lush downland; even the hills had been sculpted. It was a very modern building, and the hall outside which I waited was completely circular. Every surface was white, the far wall was distant; it was like looking into a vast drum. A balcony hooped the hall, five metres up from floor level, its plain plasterwork picked out in cream. There were no steps inside; one enters from a grand outside staircase.

It was fascinating to fly to Rachiswater from the Castle. I had become lulled by random patterns of the forest canopy. But as I approached the Palace the woodland changed, becoming a little more preened, more cared for. Hunting lodges took the place of villages. The natural forest became neater and neater until it stopped abruptly in a clean-cut border and I was over the geometrical gardens. The Palace rose in front of me, five-storey wings open in a stone embrace. A sudden current played havoc with my steering. I kept head on into it, twisted, stooped. I flew down the curved avenue of trees, so low as to go through the top of the fountain. Straight up and over the roof. Dropped down into a courtyard.

How can I describe flying? You try to describe what it is like to walk.

I jumped up onto a second-floor sill and peered inside, clinging to the masonry tendrils around the window. Some soldiers saw me soaring in; my shadow on the pitch stopped their game of football and sent them running about like guilty children. I had a few minutes before the news reached Staniel and I wanted to watch him.

Staniel sat alone, on the spindly silver throne, which was polished to brilliance. His corn-gold hair was tied back with a taffeta bow; a white shirt with buttons along the tight sleeves showed the gauntness of his arms. His keen pale face was bowed over a tall card table. I watched him move the cards about rapidly: a red five under a black six, a red ace of swords under a black deuce, a black ten under a red soldier. The red soldier went under a black governor, under a red king.

He's playing patience.

Ten minutes later: god, this is boring.

A black five and a red six under a black seven.

I seem to spend a ridiculous amount of time standing on windowsills.

I bet whoever built this window never thought that Comet would use it to spy on the King of Awia. At this point, aren't I supposed to learn some vital and intriguing piece of information?

Swallow once told me that patience allows us to achieve our goals. Unlike her I don't believe that 'talent will out'. The only thing you achieve with patience is a damn long wait.

Exasperated, I hopped through the window and glided down across the panopticon, landing neatly in front of the King. I bowed low, flicking my long hair back and folding my wings. 'My lord, I congratulate you and bring the Emperor's best wishes.'

Staniel jumped, slapped a hand over his heart. 'Don't you ever come in by the bloody door?'

'The Emperor sent me to ask whether the new King of Awia has any requests for the Circle or plans to be made known.'

'I have everything under control,' he said airily.

'Yes, apart from occasional lapses of etiquette.'

Staniel huffed, leant back in the fragile-looking throne and clicked his fingers. A servant appeared almost immediately with a glass of white wine for me on a salver. This country has its good points. 'Tell me about your adventure,' I suggested.

'I barely escaped with my life! So now there are Insects in my province. We encountered a thousand or more; it was a cloudless night and I cannot be in error. They ran along parallel with us, close to the ground like big ants ... Ugh. I hailed my escort; we had no other thought but to flee. They are everywhere! Comet—'

'Jant.'

'Jant, where do they come from?'

I shrugged, hands wrapped around the cold crystal. 'Do you know that once Insects appeared in the slums in Hacilith? Dead Insects have been found on islands far out in the sea. Nobody knows, Your Highness.'

'Perhaps underground.' He shuddered at the thought of caverns festering with Insects below us, waiting to break forth.

'I'm sure Insects are one of the threats that god expected the Fourlands would have to face. That's why it asked the Emperor to be its steward for the lands until it returns. So you should let us deal with them, which I'm afraid we can't do until you grant us troops. Then we will cleanse Rachis of Insects and push them back behind the Wall.'

'If the Castle had been fulfilling its function we wouldn't be in this situation to begin with!'

'I beg to differ.'

'Jant, hear me out. You couldn't save my brother, could you? Castle didn't protect him then, in that battle. I ... Oh, *damn*. No matter how ... how strong he was, Eszai-strong, it didn't avail him against those ... little *butchers*. So what chance have I?'

'I'm sorry I couldn't save Dunlin.'

'He disobeyed your orders, didn't he?'

'That's right.'

'So I must apologise on his behalf as well as mourn him.'

'In the heat of battle, any man might do the same,' I baited.

'Not I, Jant. I aim to benefit from experience. Having clashed with Insects after dark, I know enough never to go beyond Rachis Town again.'

Staniel would be shocked to see the network of scars I carry. I waved the glass around and the frowning servant refilled it. Staniel continued: 'Let the other manors raise more troops. Let Lightning use Micawater, which I have noticed is often spared. Get Hacilith to work for once. I am staying here because if the worst comes to the worst, then the capital will be safe.'

'Is that the answer I must take back to San?'

'Unequivocally. I will dismiss my guard when I am satisfied Rachiswater is safe. Let you immortals prove your worth to me. There is a space in the mausoleum where my brother should lie and I will never forgive the Castle for that. At least you tried, Comet, but where were the others? Mist and Tornado have boasted of slaying that many Insects between them.'

'They were too far away.'

'Then I blame Lightning's inefficient planning.'

'Is there anything else you would like the Emperor to know?'

He thought for a while. 'I am as secure in this Palace as Vireo is in Lowespass.'

'Yes, I am impressed with your defence.'

'The soldiers are one thing, but we also have sufficient supplies.'

'And funds?'

'Not so good, but manageable. I'm the last of my family. The end of the dynasty has come upon us. My family saved and hoarded in case of such an impasse. I am determined to use their accumulated wealth to the best advantage so their endeavours are not in vain ... What are you smirking at?'

'Rachiswater was the smallest manorship when I was born,' I said.

The Awian thought my comment less than useful. 'Try to understand us mortals,' he sneered. 'Time has distorted your viewpoint so much it's useless! For you, Jant, every day is the beginning of a golden age; chance to be playboy of the entire world. To Lightning, the world is broken; the best times ended in eleven-fifty. Even Mist looks like he's been left behind in the last millennium. What is the point of Eszai helping Zascai when they have seen so many of us die that we might as well be ants! How do you *really* think of us? As ants? For god's sake, Jant, I'm just trying to stay alive!'

'I promise you will.'

'Ha! I'd be a sacrifice like my brother in the blink of an eye. While you're assured of eternity! Have you noticed that the Castle walls are even thicker than those of Lowespass Fortress?'

'You have a thousand times more soldiers than there are Eszai,' I said, reassuringly.

I realised I would get no sense out of him while he was so worked up. I only risked making it worse, and I certainly didn't want to raise his resentment against the Circle. It would be best to leave for a while and tell the Emperor what I had learned. Staniel's arrogance was like an addict's, which stems from fear and from the fact one is forced into a more and more extreme position without being able to admit it. I know well the deceit of trying to clothe pain and confusion in mystery and romanticism.

'Let San know I mean no threat to the Circle.'

'Not directly,' I muttered. 'Do I have your permission to return with news at any time?'

'Of course.'

I bowed again and took my leave with a word of farewell. Staniel summoned his glowering servant to accompany me across the circular mosaic and through white passageways to the main gate.

I asked the servant what she thought of the new regime. She kept her head bowed and didn't reply. She was beautiful, slim and brisk. I plucked at her sleeve and when she glanced up I tapped the scarification on my upper arm to show her the wheel that Felicitia had carved there.

'See this? It's the insignia of a Hacilith street gang. I was nothing once, just a homeless stray. Now I'm an Eszai I never get the chance to chat to people, and I really miss it, you don't know how much. Please don't be shy to speak to me, just tell me the truth.'

'We're beat,' she said. 'We really can't feed all these men. I heard His Majesty say he will pay them what he can. Comet – I don't think I should be telling you this.'

'It's all right.'

'Every hour Staniel demands the town wall be built faster and faster. I don't know why. Some say the Emperor is angry with us; we'll have to fight the Circle and that will be the end of us.'

'That won't happen,' I said uncertainly.

'And some say an Insect swarm is massing worse than the year two thousand and four, that will overrun Lakeland Awia and devour us all.'

I returned via Hacilith, where I collected a letter from the Governor addressed to San. I stopped off at every Plainslands manor on the way back – Shivel, Eske and Fescue – in order to reassure them and gather correspondence for the Emperor.

The missive from Hacilith said:

My lord Emperor,

We are gravely concerned about the actions of the Sovereign of Awia who has withheld his men from the Circle's command and is no longer raising troops nor sending them to the front. With deep regret we must inform you that the city of Hacilith and Moren will also no longer raise troops. The far country of Awia is unwilling to guard its lands, so we do not believe that fyrd raised in Moren should be sent to protect it. If the Insect threat is as imminent as King Rachiswater believes then Hacilith requires all its divisions to defend its walls and the other human towns within the borders of Morenzia.

We will reverse our decision when the Sovereign of Awia releases his fyrd, either to be wholly disbanded or placed under the wise dominion of the Circle. We trust he will not be long in making such a decision, and we implore you to send your Messenger to direct his judgement. We humbly and fervently await your answer.

K. Aver-Falconet, Lord Governor of
Hacilith and Morenzia.

The missive from Eske said:

My lord Emperor,

Communication over the Plains is rapid; it's quickly come to my ears that Awia and Hacilith are amassing their own hosts. I find it hard to accept it's because Staniel and Aver-Falconet fear the Insects, when the Castle has always been able to control them. Eske shares one border with Rachiswater, and is only three days' ride from Hacilith so I feel that it's important for our security to keep Eske Fyrd available. Lowespass, the Plainslands, and Morenzia are all human countries and are on excellent terms, but we fear the same is not the case between the Plainslands and Awia. You will remember past instances when Awia expanded its realm forcibly, into the Darkling Mountains, and we would not wish the same to happen to the Plainslands. I beg you impress your authority on Rachiswater and the city for the sake of our safety and co-operation.

C. Eske, Lady Governor

From Fescue:

My lord Emperor,

Your thrice-great Messenger has just explained the situation and has urged me to raise more fyrd. It grieves me to say there *are* no more. The meritorious campaign of Dunlin Rachiswater has depleted our manor and I risk an uprising if I continue to ruin homes and tear men and young women from their families' embrace. Your loyal subject, I await further counsel from the distinguished Circle court, but circumstance forces my hand to add that if Comet does not bring your response within forty-eight hours I will join Eske in reserving my fyrd for this manor alone.

    L. L. F., Governor

When I returned to my Castle room, I scraped off the wax and resealed the letters with care. I used different types of wax and fake seals of the manors which I had crafted over the last hundred years, and which I keep in a locked cabinet. Then I took the letters down to court and presented them to the Emperor, with my report.

An hour later, I found myself leaning against the wall outside the Throne Room, gasping for breath and shivering head to foot, like a burning puppet hanging from hot wires. My legs and wings trembled from extreme exhaustion, and when I rubbed my inflamed eyes I smeared the eyeliner everywhere. Dropping altitude too quickly had given me a nosebleed. Blood. Mascara. Fucking wonderful.

Home, I thought. Sleep, I thought, but I simply stood there trying to work out which way was up so I could attempt to walk.

When I need a fix I get flashes of past. Darkling, Hacilith, Wrought. Bleeding on the battlefield, running from the gangs in the city. I fear I will shake myself apart. May leave sweat stain on the wall like a shadow. Need rest. Need chocolate. Want a solid gold hypodermic and Tern to massage my wings with warm oil.

Shearwater Mist swaggered down from the gallery. 'The Emperor certainly took it out on you,' he observed.

'Uh ... Yeah. Only stopped because he could see I was ... knackered.'

'If I flew seven hundred kilometres I'd be knackered too. Rest. Wicked. We're only bloody human. Flesh. Bone. Rhydanne, in your case.'

'Yeah.' I slid down the wall until I was sitting with my knees bent up in front. Mist's lined face loomed over me, above a rough cloak wound like a chrysalis around his barrel chest. 'No offence,' I slurred, 'but I'm going to be sick.'

'So tired?'

'Need cat ...'

The Sailor plucked me upright and allowed me to lean on him. The most bizarre sight in the Castle – like a rotund crow trying to support a heron – I was so much taller than him I ended up draped over his broad shoulders. He trod on my pinions, I stumbled on the flagstones and eventually we made it to the Hall where he poured rum down me – and into my mouth – and averted his gaze while I shot up some scolopendium.

'God. Oh, god-and-the-long-wait. Ow. Fuck. *Why is the Empire fucking falling apart?*'

'Are you all right now?'

'Oh. Yes.' I giggled abruptly, realised I was being hysterical and stopped.

'The Emperor shouldn't put you through that.'

'Hey, we're immortal. We have a duty to work hard.'

'Hard, yes. To death, no. Candle. Both ends.'

'If San wants a scapegoat it will be me! I'm the most dispensable, Mist. He'll blame it all on me and throw me out of the Circle!'

'That's drug talk. I've heard such from the sailors in Hacilith Dock. Clear conscience?'

'Not really.'

'Nor have any. Comes from living so long.' He sat hunched over his tankard, a well-rolled cigarette in one three-fingered hand.

'Don't tell anyone you saw me in that state, *please*,' I urged. My problem must not become widely known.

Mist shook his leonine head, with an 'it's all right' smile. 'There's been so much happening here lately to distract us that nobody'd notice you. Drop. Ocean. Swallow Awndyn's louder, for instance.'

'Huh?'

Mist drew on his cigarette. 'She threw the biggest tantrum of all time. She was even louder than Ata.' I realised that I had broken my golden rule: preoccupied with my own news I had not asked for the most recent happenings here.

'She destroyed Lightning's harpsi-thingy, you know. Gift horse. Mouth. That thing was worth a ship and a half. Why? Well, waif, you missed a real treat. Swallow had the harpsi-thingy set up right here in the hall and she sang her heart out for two hours solid. Pounded the keys till I thought they would break.'

'What did she sing?'

'Opera, mainly. Some blues. Without accompaniment. The reprise from "Lynnet's Song". Over my head, it was. The Emperor was here. All here; your wife looked gorgeous.' He rolled a cigarette deftly and passed it to me. I declined because smoking is a bad habit.

'Ha! Pot. Kettle. The Emperor listened to Swallow an' he seemed to enjoy it ... It's only the second time I've seen San out of the Courtroom ... He spoke to her afterward. He said her performance was excellent, but he said she couldn't join us. Cat. Pigeons. She was exhausted – she didn't look as foxy as usual. It was after that she went completely crazy. A woman and a ship ever want mending. We could have done with you there to help calm her down. I think she fancies you. Birds. Feather. So now she says she's going to the front—'

'What!'

''S right. She won't listen to Lightning. He's pissed off as you might imagine but he brought it on himself. Heart. Sleeve. He's a fool for love, always has been. The Circle is no stronger than its weakest link.'

'Lightning is not a fool!'

'You never had a father, did you?' Mist asked.

'No ... What's that got to do with it?'

'Grow up, waif. You hang around Lightning like one of his hounds. You'd lick his hand if he let you.'

Nonsense. 'I want to know about Swallow; when is she leaving?'

'Oh, I guess tomorrow – or rather, later today cos it's half midnight. Strike. Iron's hot, she tells me, but I think she just wants to be out of the Castle to escape embarrassment. I've noticed all Lightning's loves look the same. It's because—'

'She'll take her fyrd?'

'Sure. They're getting in the way here. I'm off to Peregrine because Ata has something to discuss with me about our daughter. Absence. Fonder.'

I gave him a look that I expect was mostly green because my pupils were contracted to fine lines. I floated on the drug. 'It's like when Staniel left Lowespass.'

'Yes. Frying pan. Fire. But the foxy redhead is too smart to get in trouble, like the rich sissy did. Chalk. Cheese. No offence but I want the sissy to be King 'cos he won't dare interrupt my trade in Peregrine. It's an ill wind. Bloody Dunlin kept taxing tobacco.' I thought Mist was wrong; Staniel was stupid enough to meddle in anything.

The Emperor and I were the only ones who knew how desperate the situation was. Reading other people's letters brings with it a terrible responsibility.

'Did the Emperor order Swallow not to go?'

'On the contrary, he said it was her choice.'

'Damn it!' I tested my weight on my shaking legs. Result: not good. I had to go to Swallow and stop her riding out. She wouldn't last a minute at the front.

'Where are you going?' asked Mist.

'Have to see her.'

'Don't be daft, waif. Haste. Speed. You're in no fit state to—'

'Don't care. Have to go.' I wobbled to my feet and Mist turned his attention to beer. 'I'm telling you, Jant, rest first. You've been run ragged.'

'Cat keeps me going.'

'No fit state ...'

I made it across the Hall and almost to the door before I passed out. I woke up in bed two days later.

CHAPTER 7

It wasn't difficult to intercept Swallow's band although I had to landfall a couple of times to be sick. They followed the Eske Road north, towards Awia, and the twin columns of horsemen, infantry and baggage train were seven kilometres long. While Swallow and Lightning, riding proudly in the vanguard, passed the half-timbered Eske manor, the tail of her fyrd were still entering the manorship. Those in the middle helped each other traverse the river. When Swallow passed the Quadrivium Cemetery, the middle of the column was bunching together in order to get a long look at the manor, and those at the end were still crossing the river. When Swallow crossed the border into Awia the middle of her column crept past the Cemetery and those at the end straggled to glimpse Eske. She rode past Silk Mill and Donaise, Foin, Slaughterbridge, and the Place de la Première Attaque. They passed through Rachiswater, and held up all the traffic in the town. Lightning craned his neck to catch sight of the Micawater estate wall.

Lightning rode straight-backed on his white horse, red-caparisoned, by Swallow, his armour gleaming like the sun. Often he hung back, reluctant as a dog that's sensed danger. But he had given up arguing with her a long time ago and was now following her for her own protection because he knew she wouldn't see reason. I thought that if he had strength enough to stop following Swallow and let her go alone, after ten kilometres she might have suffered self-doubt, and turned back to join him. But each kept the other going, and they radiated a dangerous courage that rose like warm air. Swallow's hair was copper; she held a guitar on her lap. Her dolphin standard leapt and twined. The fyrd moved with a rustle along the road deep in infinite colours of autumn leaves, sepia brown, russet, rust and gold.

And all the time I hung above them, as high as a kite.

There was nothing I could really do to influence their strange dilemma – Lightning's unrequited love for the musician. Although I had been a confidant to both, I was not intimate enough to break the seal of such a private problem.

Unintentionally attention-seeking, I have taken too much cat on occasion, but I couldn't raise Lightning's wrath when he was obsessed with Swallow. Swallow hasn't noticed me even though I have cheekbones to die for. Adamantine Awndyn has eyes for no man.

I can't divert you with observations and epigrams on the nature of love, because I know so little about it. I decided my disinterest in love was lucky.

I've had lots of relationships, starting with Serin in The Wheel, and ending with Tern, but none have been as intense as Lightning's agony. I have noticed that lovers can be nostalgic for places where they lingered, even grey tram platforms on freezing nights, which makes me think that love is not just blind but blindingly stupid. I do love Tern, but I love within reason and within the bounds of comfort. Lightning's old-fashioned way of loving shakes the roots of his very being.

Lightning first saw her in the opera house in Hacilith. She caused a sensation, a standing ovation, and he heard the news while he was practising archery in the Long Field at Micawater. Immediately, he took his coach to see what all the fuss was about a 'new talent'. The Moren Grand was sold out, but he owned a box so close to the stage he could look directly down on her. When she walked forward into the spotlight and began an aria he was overcome and, leaning out, dropped his programme, which fluttered down slowly, slowly and noisily in the complete silence onto the stage at her feet. He spent the rest of the performance in the dark recesses of the box, head in hands, overwhelmed because her voice was so perfect. He decided to send her red roses, and the floral carnage was such that roses have been rare in Awia since.

Lightning paid me to carry the first letter to her, and I found Swallow backstage in stripy tights and a green velvet shawl. A visit from the Emperor's Messenger frightened her; then when she read the letter she fainted and I had to bring her round with sal volatile.

I flew their correspondence all year. Lightning pressed a letter into my right hand, dropped fifty pounds into my left hand. I stepped over the ledge and off I went. Swallow dropped a note in my right hand, pressed five pounds in my left hand, and off I went. Lightning sipping coffee on the archery field in Micawater, Swallow tapping two-four time on the podium in Awndyn. Lightning in a long brocade coat, Swallow in a tuxedo and tails. Between them, I made a killing on the travel expenses.

Micawater Palace Mews
Saturday 20 June
The Year of Our War 2014

Dearest Swallow,

In your last brief letter you were kind enough to thank me for the gift I sent. It was nothing, a mere trifle. I beg you not to worry about the value of such things when you yourself are so precious to me. You say the difference between Awndyn and Micawater is too great, but I assure you that material wealth matters little. Gold and banknotes are only valuable because we – every one of us – accedes every day in allowing it. We acquiesce in the illusion, but money is simply shaped pieces of metal and paper that we can wisely use to serve us. A small amount can be used as wisely as a fortune when it is the use to which it is put that matters. In terms of your musical prowess you are far richer than I.

Know that I will wait for you and that I can be relied upon. It is good that you want to become immortal on your own worth. As I have said before and you urge me to say again I believe whole-heartedly in your ability, your music haunts me deeply and I speak to the Emperor on your behalf at every available opportunity. I can wait, even, as you say, until you grow old. Eszai who are old forever are more grateful for immortality than the young impudent ones, but they miss their youth and wish they were eternally young.

I can never receive a straight answer from you, you twist and turn like a swallow in flight, but although it pains me to wait, I will. Do you know, heartwood is used on the inside of longbows because it is older and more resilient. As it is hard, it springs back to shape quickly and so can throw an arrow farther. Micawater is the heartwood of Awia, a resilient family with flawless honour. But good bows need sapwood bound to heartwood, to make them more pliable and so shoot true.

I am tormented by wondering how I can prove myself worthy of you. Tell me what you will. Love balances the weights unequally, always forcing a man to love a woman whom no amount of sedulous courtship can win, since she does not entertain reciprocal feelings, not having been fired by love's arrows. Marriage is eternal, and it is mortals who fail it. Only immortals can be truly married, and an immortal can only be truly complete when married.

Don't worry about my Messenger. The first Rhydanne I ever met disturbed me, too. She told my brother how he was to die. For a long time I thought it was a power they all had, but it was simply a coincidence. My brother Shryke was an accomplished hunter; he went riding every day and returned with deer and boar. He enjoyed the amphitheatre where we had bullfighting, and we brought in Insects and whole packs of famished wolves.

A fair would converge every summer on the meadow by the river. My brothers always clamoured to go visit, but Mother always withheld her permission. On this occasion, there were archery tournaments as part of the fair. Mother was both proud of my skill, and keen to remind Awia that our family was worthy of the throne. So I went under the protection of Shryke, my third eldest brother. I remember toffee apples, fire-eaters, iced wine, jugglers and horses racing on a grass track.

The Rhydanne was telling fortunes, using cards like the ones Jant has. She was sitting on the damp grass among all the patched, bright tents and banners. She had a long black skirt, spread out on the grass, and the cards were placed on it. I was uncertain, because she looked so strange, but Shryke was very interested – he lingered near her until people had drifted away, and I wanted to leave, too. He gave her a coin, and she looked at it fiercely, in the flat palm of her long hand. He took it back from her, went and bought a bar of chocolate with it, and presented her with that. She smiled. I expected her teeth to be sharp, like a cat's, but they were quite normal. Then she cut the cards and arranged them, while Shryke stood and watched. She said he would die within the year. She said that an animal would cause his death.

I watched the Rhydanne girl. She knew she was telling the truth. Shryke laughed and dismissed it, boasting that everybody had to die sometime. All the way back he told me that fortune cards didn't work, it was nothing but a game, and anyway only mountain people believed those things. The next day he went to fight leopards in the amphitheatre. Nothing could discourage him from hunting, fishing and falconry; in fact he grew more ambitious, careless, trying to prove that cards are foolish. Celebrations resulting from the archery tournament eclipsed my fears, and soon I forgot all about it.

Mica River cuts through a narrow gorge in the forest near Donaise. Shryke was fond of walking down there with his favourite dog on a lead, and often I went too. It was a great challenge to jump the gorge, it could be done in summer when the river was low. He left one morning and I was in my room, when my cousin came in, tears streaming down her face. I tried to console Martyn but I could not, and she bade me come to court. There we found Shryke's body laid out on a catafalque, and Mother sitting on the throne room floor, wailing, and beating her fists in the air with grief.

The gamekeeper found him in Peregrine, which is twenty kilometres downstream. His limbs were broken, and his skin vivid with bruises from being in the whirlpools. Nothing can survive the rapids there, they even carve holes in rock. Mother said that brigands had killed him but when the faithful dog came back wearing its lead I knew that Shryke had simply tried to jump the gorge. The little dog refused, and so pulled him in.

I never spoke to another Rhydanne after that, until Jant arrived. He has done much since which convinces me that they can't see the future.

My love, while I write it has grown dark and the stars are reflected in the lake. Stars, like people, do not change but very rarely I have seen a bright star bloom among them – like you, Swallow. Write to me, don't deny me a letter; it is deceitful to deny what has been pledged. Your reluctance to love is good because you will be more willing to keep secret what I confide. There have been many women in the past seeking to prey upon Micawater's wealth and the promise of immortality, but I have shunned them because their love is not genuine. Your reluctance marks you as worthy. If I could only succeed in winning your hand, and if just a little of the ardour you show for music could be set aside for love, then I would at last be content.

Yours,
Saker

On receiving this, Swallow wrote to me:

Memo
From: Swallow, the Beach, 02.08.14
To: Comet, Filigree Spider, Scree
Jant – Help me! Help me! The Archer asked me to marry him!! You said I
could treat you like a brother so please help – should I say yes? Can I say
no without insulting him?? He isn't someone I should insult! I want to be
immortal on my own worth, and this sounds more like a demand than a
proposal! I know what my father would have wanted me to say, but I never
took any notice of him when he was alive, so why now? Send your reply to
Awndyn. And, Jant, I know you have the biggest mouth in the Fourlands but
please don't gossip about this. Or else.

Lightning offered her the most fantastic opportunity in the world.
In fifteen hundred years, she was the one. Proud and principled, she was
turning it down. Maybe she didn't understand how untouchable an Archer
Lightning was – his immortality seemed the most secure of us all. She must
know more about what she had done to him. And as Lightning's bride,
Swallow would have plenty of time to convince the Emperor to make her
the Circle's Musician, immortal in her own right. I sent a hasty reply:

> The Filigree Spider inn
> Turbary Track
> Scree
> 27 September 2014

Dear Governor Awndyn,
In answer to your question: say yes. Micawater has held out this long before
asking because he doesn't realise how long a year can seem. Tern has made
me think of things I would never have otherwise considered; so I suggest that
if you do consider yourself to be an adventurer in this life, the very best thing
you can do is accept his belated proposal. In fact, if you want my advice, I'd
like to invite you to Wrought so we can discuss it face to face and over a glass
of whisky.

The Archer is a hunter and a fighter, he is not a successful lover albeit he
has spent centuries practising. He usually keeps his business private but in
the last few days I have seen him shattered with apprehension, which cannot
be assuaged even by vintage port. I thought he had forsaken romance, that
time had made him indurate. I wondered on whom you had set your sights
instead … But now I write to say please accept Lightning's offer; if you do
not you may end him completely. Even in my worst moments I doubt I have
looked so unwell.

If you make your way north on the Coast Road after Cobalt and Peregrine you will reach Wrought manor; wait there. I will come down to meet you. Then we can speak face to face and out of the Archer's way.

I can think of many anecdotes which would sway your appreciation of him one way or the other. If you had seen him with Savory in Morenzia, you would not doubt his tenderness. Unfortunately Savory did not survive. He was married to her, take a look at the scar across his palm. I used to say that she was the fifth race, that there were Awians, Insects, humans, Rhydanne, and Savory. He was in an adolescent storm of passion; I was like a chess player, touching pieces he did not wish to move.

On the other hand, and not to put it lightly, Lightning can be an arrogant and nasty piece of work. He has refused to lend me money when I have been most in need of it, and in dealings of real estate can be absolutely mercenary. Your relationship with him must be all or nothing, clear-cut black and white. I am aware so far that it has been 'nothing' rather than 'all', but now I beg you to reconsider. Surely you should be pleased that he can be bad.

For example, I still haven't forgiven him for what he and Tawny did to me on my stag night. We're talking late December 1892. I held it a week before Tern and I got hitched – it should be the night before but I didn't think that would be particularly wise. Lightning lent me the folly at Micawater to stage it and, since I was famous for giving parties, everybody was there. Everybody male, that is, from four lands, and we had been drinking for two days solid by the time this happened ...

I'd had syllabub for supper, actually I was covered in it, and a bottle of whisky. Well, let us say I was a little intoxicated. Lightning had been planning for this, and said with that scornful smirk we all know so well, 'Do you still think you're the fastest thing in the Fourlands?'

I stutteringly asseverated that indeed I was. He prompted that I didn't sound convinced. It's essential to be convincing because otherwise the next day brings a flood of Challenges from idiots thinking they can outpace me. I climbed onto a table and announced it to all and sundry. Sarcelle Rachiswater smacked his hand on the table gleefully and said, 'Right! Grab him!'

The next thing I know I'm in Tawny's vast grasp, with my face pressed against the table and my wings belted up behind my back. They stripped me, wound a deerskin around my waist, and with a strap under my chin, placed a pair of antlers on my head. They were heavy, twelve-tined, gilded. In exploring them with my hands I dropped the deerskin, to much wild hilarity from those not unconscious or preoccupied with the call-girls.

Lightning stood, gauntleted hands on hips, and said, 'Now you are the king of the forest.'

The best I could manage was: 'Look guys, this isn't amusing.' Sarcelle whimsically slipped a butter knife into my hand. Tawny picked me up over one shoulder and carried me outside, in a ribald procession, into the frosted gardens. The tower clock was striking one, a hunter's moon jaundiced the snow. I stood there, they stepped back and regarded me silently. I said, 'What am I supposed to do now? Piss against trees and eat berries?'

Then from round the stables, came a barking and a baying, the sound of frost being crushed under a hundred scabby paws. They had released the dogs. And you know what Micawater hounds are like: pure-bred and well-trained, evil little killers. Lightning gave me an experimental push, and said, 'I think you'd better run.'

How I ran! I ran deep into the forest, in the semi-darkness, with the pack behind me. I ran till my feet left blood in the prints. I ran wide-eyed and bruised with cold. The antlers kept catching on low branches and jerking my head back – I lost valuable seconds crouching down and struggling with the strap. I went over fences and stiles rapid as prey, heart matching my strides, salt taste in my mouth, every decision the same: run. At the back of my mind, although reduced to instinct, becoming stag, I knew I could do it. I believed with a chance I could outrun twenty dogs. Then I just ran.

Until at length I reached the summit of a rise and looked down on a shallow valley strung with hammock fields. I realised this was Bitterdale; at the far end were the lights of Wrought. Stopping for breath, I heard the snuffling of hounds closing in. They began to howl in excitement. I backed up against a tree which I had no strength to climb. On the edge of Tern's manorship, at the brink of safety, my spirit gave out. I was too exhausted to care any more. I would make a stand.

The dogs were pouring through a gap in the hedge, blurred by the darkness. The first ran towards me, gathering itself to spring. I wondered whether it was possible to shove the butter knife down its throat before I would be teeth and fingernails with the others.

I hissed in a breath. I knew the beast's exultation; I've run down so many deer myself. It closed in, canines, spit and dirty fur.

The dog leapt, and an arrow caught it in mid-air, slamming it down into the snow, where it curled, whimpering, skewered through the shoulder.

The muscled bulk of a white horse galloped between us, and Lightning's hands, one on my wing the other on my backside, lifted me fluidly over the cantle. In the same easy gesture he swung the quiver onto his shoulder, wheeled round and rode through the pack, which scattered. The hunt master, on a scarred charger and with a whip, was following. He made a tight bundle of the dogs and we returned in silence. I don't remember the details of that, except for a bumping, jarring, the world being upside down. I was still drunk; my loose hands brushed the top of every hedge we jumped.

I remember Lightning prising the knife from my grasp, placing a firm hand on my neck for my heartbeat which was calm and cold. He murmured 'Rhydanne ...' with an awe-struck tone.

Lightning fed us with mulled wine and venison until I recovered. They figured that I had run forty kilometres, across Donaise to the outskirts of Wrought, just out of Lightning's manorship. Forty kilometres may not seem impressive when you know I have done a hundred in a day, and three hundred when flying, but under the circumstances ...

Swallow, when I last saw Lightning he was splitting arrows at two hundred paces on the archery field, with lifeless repetition. He's hooked on you: obsessed. Don't say, 'But he doesn't even know me'; he has been alive so long he knows the type of person you are. He can predict all your decisions from his own experience. Perhaps every second century he'll find a strong-willed woman who is worthy enough, otherwise they are a disappointment to him, and those with fewer morals shock him entirely.

So, sister, when the Governor Lord Micawater goes down on bended knee, you say *yes*. I shouldn't have to tell you this; it isn't as if you're Rhydanne. You want to be immortal, don't you? By all the blood of Lowespass, what does it take to get through to you?

Never think that you are young and have plenty of time; you cannot know how soon the end will be. I will gradually let you into secrets that will make your acceptance into the Circle much easier. There are things which the Emperor does not want Zascai to know, and assumes that Eszai are less likely to tell.

Now I should go. Judging from the way clouds are forming and eagles wheeling over Mhadaidh there is some lift to be had there. I am tempted to join them, but I will meet you on the ground, in Wrought in a week's time. Don't forget to bring your guitar.

Failte bhâchna.

Yours with the will of god and the protection of the Circle.

Comet Jant Shira

Messenger and Interpreter for the Sovereign Emperor San

Twenty letters later we are here, in the Rachiswater manorship on the edge of Lowespass. Weather: bracing, even for me. Swallow's fyrd marched until nightfall and then she gave the command to make camp. They had reached the southernmost trenches, and the soldiers set about clearing them out, a very nasty task. While the daylight lasted, they dug around the camp making a square ditch and rampart. Some soldiers were posted along the trenches to keep watch. From the air I could see their round steel helmets in a line as they patrolled the edge.

Broken Insect limbs jutted into the air like machinery; there was a jumble of dirt-coloured skeletons unearthed by the trench-diggers, waiting to be thrown in a mass grave. The trench earth was fetid; sleet pooled in the clay, becoming freezing mud. It stank of sulphur.

I had the feeling I was just keeping pace with the day, only managing the bare essentials until the tiredness wears off and I could tackle the real questions at last. I flew over the encampment, bleary-eyed, incapable of thought, observing the altered landscape that unfolded below. Rachiswater was wreckage. I saw a ruined barn where the fyrd had trapped Insects and burnt them. I saw Insects themselves, tiny in the distance, running across the pale green fields. The perspective was strange – at a distance they looked as small as ants, but they tried to cross a barbed wire fence which I knew to be two metres high, so they must be as large as deer. My first coherent thought of the day – this can't be true. We were at the front with fewer soldiers than ever before, and there were more Insects than ever before.

I focused all attention on the spot where I had to land, and swung in over earthwork and barbed wire, over canvas roofs to the Castle's pavilion. Lightning and Swallow were standing outside, trading opinions. She had a guitar slung over her shoulder, inlaid with mother-of-pearl plaques. I bounded to a halt in front of them.

'Good evening, Jant. Nice flying.'

I struggled to get my breath. 'Ah ... Swallow! Turn round and go back. What do you think you're doing? Saker, you should know better! How many fyrd do you have?'

'Six thousand.'

'How many sodding Insects do you think there are?'

'Is it the Emperor's command?'

'No. Mine.'

Lightning said, 'Swallow, I told you. Listen to Jant.'

'You go if you wish, Eszai. I stay.'

'For a start this isn't the best time of year,' Lightning said.

'So you're scared of a little snow, as well?'

'It's hard to keep a bowstring dry in this bloody weather.'

I shook my wings to dislodge shards of ice, and attempted a conciliatory tone. 'Let's go back to Rachiswater Palace. The soldiers can camp in the park, and I can talk to Staniel and hopefully convince him to help us. Then we can march into Lowespass and reach the fortress. It's foolhardy to try it with just six thousand.'

'There isn't enough time. I've already sent messengers to Eske and the Plainslands manors asking for assistance,' Swallow informed me.

'You have. Good. The Plainslands manors have all refused to send fyrd to Awia, as they don't agree with Staniel's tactics. That's Eske and Hacilith Moren; Swallow, you're on your own.'

Palely, she asked, 'And Tanager?'

'You know what happened to Tanager? She took her fyrd to find the casket of Dunlin's remains which his brother dropped so unceremoniously. She didn't get further than the Lowespass trenches before the Insects ripped into them and they turned back. Half her men were killed there. Eleonora's a brave lady, but she's licking her wounds in Tanager now and gathering new fyrd.'

The Archer let out an exasperated breath. 'We're an Empire. The Empire isn't fragile! It's the most fundamental collaboration! Why are they not working together any more?'

I sighed. If this was outside Lightning's experience what hope did we have? 'Swallow, let's leave ...?'

'No. Let us make an effective contribution.'

'I can tell you're getting older.' Swallow was starting to use those callous efficient words which allow one to deal with the world without thinking about it. She knows how to say 'I'm sorry' when hearing news of a death. In that context, what the fuck does 'I'm sorry' *mean*? She knows how to say 'hard luck', 'good day', 'I'm fine', 'see you next year' – how daring it is for a mortal to anticipate that! The shell is growing, and it hides her. In a few years she won't be thinking or feeling deeply at all, and I am afraid that then her music will cease.

Lightning said, 'I am willing to try to gain the next line of trenches. That is twenty-seven kilometres of land we can ensure is free from dispersed, straggling Insects. It's a small strip of land but it will prove that Castle is still attempting to protect the Empire, regardless of what help is sent. Then we can move, and wait to see if our statement merits any response.'

'That's great, Saker. I knew you were with me.'

'Would that I could always be with you.'

'And I have to prove myself to the Emperor. He said that Eszai are good warriors, well, it is his recurrent theme *a crescendo*. If it will help my cause, I'll show him I can fight.'

I looked at her insouciant body carefully – her wide, freckled face, tip-tilted nose and delicate lips, though she had bitten nails, and muscular legs. 'If your claim to be Eszai is that you are the best musician in the world—'

'And I am.'

'What good does it do you to fight?'

Swallow shrugged. 'Ask the Emperor. It's beyond me.'

I turned away from her and peered into the stripy gloom of the pavilion, palms up, saying, 'No offence, but you are not a warrior. Your father kept you from the field. How arrogant it is! You think you can command where Eleonora failed, and Rachiswater. Eleonora is a skilled swordsman, you are a buxom pianist.'

'Jant, watch your mouth.'

'Saker. Give me my orders for I'm away. I'm not watching your cold, hungry troops turn to pillaging their own country, and fed like titbits to the Insects for the vainglorious lust of some ginger hussy.'

'Jant!'

'He's just frightened,' she said.

'If the Insects kill you, San will have a fat problem taken off his hands. Is the myth of your short life fame enough? I'll put up a statue – maiden armed with guitar against the hordes! Inscription: *More ambition than sense.*' I whipped my sword from its scabbard which was tied upside down between my wings, and prodded the grass between her feet with the point. 'Come, and leave the hard work to the Eszai. One day you'll thank me for saving your life.'

Swallow put out a hand to the Archer, who understood the gesture. He unbuckled the sword belt from round his waist and handed the Wrought sword to her, hilt first. She grasped the hilt and pulled the blade from its jewelled sheath. A few soldiers nearby looked up, interested. 'Guard,' she said.

'Don't be bloody stupid.'

She was furious that I didn't consider her worth fighting. As I turned away she lunged, the blade catching the inside of my leg, slicing through the leather. Bitch! I batted it down; it slid up my sword to the hilt. I parried her next blow easily, and then we were at it in earnest. I was faster than her. I had longer reach. I thrust, the heavier blade turned it. She swung up to my throat, I jumped back. I hacked at her legs three times and she checked each stroke, wincing. She feinted left, left again, and then I lost sight of her sword completely. Where is she? Right? Right. Oh, down there. I dropped the blade low, like a scythe.

I was off-balance, reaching out for nothing. My arms flailed wildly and then I landed on my side in the mud. The breath was knocked out of me as Swallow stamped her flat foot heavily onto my kidneys.

Her sword pressed into my back. 'Is it here?' she asked.

Lightning's voice: 'No. Lower.'

'Here?'

'Ow!' The point cut through my leather jacket.

'Jant? I can push this point though your backbone here. It separates two vertebrae. It doesn't hurt very much but you won't be able to run anywhere ever again.'

'Eeep!'

'Do you fancy that?'

'No! No! Please!'

'Let him go,' said Lightning. Swallow ruffled my scapular feathers, withdrew her sword and I got up with alacrity. She handed it back to Lightning who said, 'Not bad. With practice you'll learn not to look at the blade at all. It's an extension of you. Watch your opponent's reaction.'

'He's been giving me lessons,' Swallow explained, while I pulled bits of mud out of my hair.

I glared at Lightning. 'Why didn't you teach me that trick?'

'I had a feeling that one day a lady would need it to get the better of you.'

'Swallow, I'm sorry.'

'Glad to hear it. Are you with us now?'

'If I must.'

That night a fire was lit in the middle of the compound and the soldiers roasted deer and warmed bread brought in from the villages around Rachiswater. Swallow asked for the venison fat and ate it sloppily with her dagger. I appreciated her appetite, wondered if she was as voracious in bed.

Flying made me hungry, but I was sulking at having underestimated Swallow. Many women are excellent fighters and could beat me; I respect their ability. But Zascai soldiers saw Swallow win; I knew that the story would spread fast and far.

I left while Harrier was handing round cups of wine, and I concealed my supply of cat. I couldn't resist taking a little. Handling it helped me relax, and the ritual focused my mind. Powder lined in the folds of paper, mesmeric candle flame, hiss of liquid, satisfying resistance of solution in the syringe. I was taught about herbs in Hacilith when I was young, and my knowledge can be relied upon when everything else is so vexatious. I am good at it, and it makes me feel safe, but I'd like to be able to stop.

My feeling of inadequacy grew as I dwelt on the Castle's immense depth of time. I thought about all the immortal Messengers before me; the title lives on although the individual might not. Archer, Swordsman, Messenger; the title is important but the person is dispensable. I'm immortal, and the other immortals before me have died, so I shouldn't feel inferior to them, but by my actions I feel I'm letting those worthy people down. I feel I'm letting down the first Comet who joined the Circle at its founding, and at least twenty others that came after him in progression; the last Comet being a cheerful blonde Morenzian woman I beat in a distance race in eighteen-eighteen. There's only ever been one Archer, and he remembers all my predecessors. Indulgently I speculated about who they all were, and how they might have died – displaced by better runners, or injured by the Insects beyond repair.

I had just taken the needle out of my wrist and was dabbing at a spot of blood when Swallow fought her way in through the canvas entrance. I checked that everything was hidden, hoping that she wouldn't notice my drooping eyelids and white lips.

94

'Jant, I'm sorry about earlier.'

'Why? You did well.'

'I showed you up. It was cruel. Everyone could see you were tired.'

Being offered sympathy by a Zascai was worse than being beaten! 'You'll never make an Eszai if you worry about such things,' I said softly.

'If immortals aren't fair, the world will cease to love them,' she answered.

I flapped my hands at her. No one on a rush can bear to sit and suffer truisms. 'Know what the Circle is, sister? Just a way of taking powerful people out of society and herding them all together in the Emperor's care where they can't do any harm ... Of throwing the world's best at the Insects so the world never changes ... Swallow, be clever. Stay and rule Awndyn where San can't clip your wings and command all your potential. We're going to need you free and carefree in twenty years' time.'

'I have no freedom now that I'd lose in the Circle.'

'Mmm.' I lay back on the bearskin and looked up at her. 'You're trying so hard to entrap yourself forever. Mortals are free of the responsibility of ... this ...' I waved floppily at Lightning's stacked sheaves of arrows, bowstaves and armour. 'In many ways I was happier when career-less and clueless in Darkling.'

'I don't want to be forty.'

'Well, I have no answer to that.'

She passed the mother-of-pearl guitar to me. I caressed the beautiful instrument; the pegs were ivory, the strap blue and gold, and Awndyn's insignia was painted on the back. She smiled when she saw how lovingly I held it, not knowing that the clarity of cat made it breathe under my hands. 'Please look after it for me,' she said.

'Why?'

'I won't play another note until I've killed Insects in battle.'

'Oh, Swallow. Why are you doing this?'

'The Empire is forcing me. I'll do whatever it takes to be Eszai.'

'Marry Lightning.'

'You know he'd wear me down. I'm not a river, or a butterfly, or a star, or anything else he says in his letters. I'm not as pure and perfect as any of them, but still more varied than any of them together.'

'Yes you are.' I tapped my nails on the scratchplate, lay with the guitar on my stomach and played a riff.

Swallow yelped. 'It's never made a sound like that before!'

'I'm sorry.'

'No, go on.' She urged me to play the rest of the melody. Although she was surprised that I knew the headstock from the bridge she didn't look down on me. She aimed to learn from everyone. I felt the frets and then played, eyes closed for a while before embarrassment stopped me. She was grinning.

'I made money that way in Hacilith.' I said.

'In the concert hall?'

'Hardly. Busking. One of the Wheel's members taught me. He was called Babitt.'

'Come out and play for me by the fireside.'

'No! Leave me alone.'

Using scolopendium is a very solitary activity and I wouldn't want to appear in public for at least an hour afterwards. But Swallow is persuasive. She simply attributed my condition to exhaustion and said I needed fresh air. She dragged me out to stand by the fire, where soldiers were drinking, cutting roast meat, talking boisterously, laughing more often as Swallow raised their spirits with a song. I played reels and wild czardas while she danced, gleaming and beaming, in front of the fire, and Lightning looked on.

Two hundred years ago in Hacilith the air was dreadful. I remember that I was coughing so badly I dropped my guitar and doubled up, trying to spit. Babitt the dwarf perched up on the black iron railings.

'Put it this way, Shira,' he said eventually. 'I wouldn't give up your night job.' I remember the stench of the seagull oil which he used to set his hair.

I spluttered, 'I can play it! But it would be nice if I could breathe.'

'Felicitia says you've made more money dealing and so you should stick to that. He says he can't feed us. He says there's no money left in our gang.' Babitt scratched at a hairy backside, which his patchwork trousers scarcely covered. I picked up the guitar, began to retune it.

Babitt was pudgy, hairy, short and smug, I was tall and usually bemused; I'm sure we looked well together. We hated each other but Felicitia's word was law. Once I remember he ripped off a pet shop and Babitt called me up one night and said, 'Look, I have two thousand goldfish, what can you do?'

I said, 'Didn't you get the money?'

Patiently he answered, 'Felicitia got the money. I got the goldfish.'

So, anyway, I explained to him that I'd given up dealing, because Peterglass had a contract out for me, and I was sick of having my clientele trail around after me everywhere like the undead. Babitt gave up scratching his arse and started scratching his moustache.

'Felicitia will be angry with you.'

'He could be pretentious at me, is that it?'

I crouched down and began gathering our coins before Babitt could get his hairy hands on them.

'You might not know this, but even Felicitia goes under if I stop dealing,' I added.

96

Babitt grinned, which was not a pretty sight. 'Shira, I know it. You'll never stop pushing cat in Hacilith. You're hooked on the power, which is *worse* than being undead.'

'That's all you know. The whole world will kiss my spurs.' I slammed my hands in deep pockets and slouched off towards Cinder Street. Babitt followed, his eyes at the same level as the guitar across my back. A smell of beer paused us on the steps of the Kentledge pub. We looked at each other, tempted, and eventually gave in. I held the door back while Babitt rolled inside, and dug in my pocket for the handful of grubby coins we'd collected that morning, offered them down in a languid hand for Babitt to translate.

'What are the little round ones with holes?'

'Buttons,' he said.

CHAPTER 8

Hacilith 1818, How Felicitia Died

Thunder in the morning seemed misplaced, storms should only happen at night. Five in the morning, bruise-brown clouds drifted in from the sea and collected over Hacilith, obscuring the dawn. I had been awake all night watching the person who was watching my house.

I don't think she'd seen me, but I knew she had a crossbow because she had been practising on all the cats of the neighbourhood. I was out of the shop by the back door, and reached the street corner in the cover of a flaking brick wall. Crouching in litter and broken glass I glanced back to where the girl was waiting. She turned round and looked straight at me. I ran –

– Along a pavement spotted with chewing gum, over a narrow iron bridge, past the Shackle Sheds. The girl loosed her first arrow and it went far wide. I ducked. It hummed past me and lodged in the slats of a high green fence. I scrabbled over and paused for breath on the other side. The fence was covered in graffiti. The best graffiti was mine.

I ran on through dirty puddles and pigeon shit. She lost me at a block corner. I skidded and swore. She heard and put on speed. Hacilith's thick air caught in my throat, early sunlight reflected on the filthy river. You can't outrun a Rhydanne, I thought, as her second arrow missed my heel by millimetres. Who the fuck are you, anyway? The Bowyers' bitch.

I cut across a rubbish tip. The passageways through the refuse were clear to me but the girl's experience was of the other side of the river and she was wary. Half a kilometre out of her territory and she might as well have been in Scree.

I reached a warehouse by the dockside. Here, rings and iron mushrooms were set into concrete, which narrow boats used to moor and unload. The dock was silted up, derelict; it smelt of salt and decay. The warehouse was the size of three town houses, built of wooden planks now rotten and supported by sandbags. I hammered the fastest-ever secret knock on a smaller door set within the huge sliding gate at the top of a slipway, as the girl emerged, grease in her golden hair.

I slipped inside the warehouse, slammed the door, leant against it, panting. The head of a crossbow bolt splintered wood by my shoulder. I flung open the door and found her five metres away. She hesitated in fumbling a new bolt into the breech. I unfastened the buttons on my shirt and held it open, giving her an excellent view of an excellent naked chest, then slammed the door again and barred it top and bottom.

Thin laughter trickled from the darkness behind me. My arrival had brought something back to life. A weak voice wheezed, 'You're late, goat-shagger.'

In Darkling, things were straightforward. Life in the mountains was simple – I went to bed early, and I was always hungry. Every day was the same; only some days we had more storms, and less food. But Hacilith city draws complication round itself like a cloak. I have a little of the city like pollution in me now. The city supports people who would never have survived in Darkling, for example Felicitia.

'I had to wait till dawn.' I sighed, picking my way into the bleak space of the warehouse. Torrential rain thrashed on the corrugated roof.

'Thought you could see in the dark?'

'No.'

Felicitia Aver-Falconet lay on a mouldering sofa by the side of a low table, the only furniture, in the middle of the pressed earth floor. He was reading by the light of candle stubs, fixed by their own wax to the tabletop.

Aver-Falconet ruled our gang. We were awed by his talk of expensive parties and fashionable society, boastful and offhand. But then, he was the grandson of Hayl Eske who lived at the Castle, and to us the Eszai in his ancestry put him on a par with god. Aver-Falconet had hurt me before, so I hated him. The Wheel he carved into my shoulder has lasted like a brand all my life.

Felicitia devoured my flesh with his eyes. The whites of his eyes were yellowish, and the pupils too high on them, as if they wanted to rise and hide under his eyelids.

'Have you got the drugs?' he asked, anxiously.

'Yeah.'

'Come here and make love to me, oh macilent boy.'

'No!'

'That Wheel on your arm means you belong to me.'

Felicitia wriggled to change position, but couldn't sit up. He had lingered in the gin-shop with me, in the casino with Layce the cardsharp, and eventually malingered in our dockyard base, shooting up every few hours and reading melodramas. I pinched them when he had finished dog-earing the pages, because I had a vague idea that such knowledge might help me if I ever got to the Castle.

'You're lucky, my bagnio boy,' he croaked. I continued to appraise him, his only clothes a stained leather skirt wrapped around well-shaved legs, and an ankle chain with a charm in the shape of a wheel. I knew it would be pure gold. I tingled with avarice.

'Oh, and why's that?'

'That girl is a Eszai-good archer, my ophidian-eyed boy.'

'You know I can fly,' I replied, not without pride. 'And I'm a Eszai-good runner. Layce told me so.' The concept that my ability to run, or fly, or fight could be as good as the Eszai was recurring in my mind with infuriating rapidity. I wanted to join them.

Felicitia hummed affirmatively. 'I suppose you have to run fast to catch the goats,' he mused.

'I have to run fast to get this madness over and done with before my master wakes up. Are you better now?' I asked, with a mildly professional air. Felicitia was a wisp of flesh, a skeleton in make-up. I could see eye sockets, cheekbones, skin coloured blue by innumerable puncture-marks. His skin was pale, his mouth slashed with lipstick and a peroxide streak in dark brown hair. The fire in a makeshift hearth was down to smouldering ash scabs. It was becoming cold, but Felicitia wasn't shivering. He was past shivering; his skin was as cold as the dock water.

'Now? What's "now"?'

'Don't start that again. Either you're better, or you're not. And if you're not, then I don't want to know.'

'Nothing matters but cat, my sweet miscegenation. Not even your indescribable beauty.'

'You're going to die, you know,' I said softly.

'That doesn't matter, my sweet itinerant,' Aver-Falconet assured me. 'I'll live in the Shift. I've been there for days ...'

So you keep telling me. 'It's been *months*,' I said.

'I'm in love with the Shift,' he said simply. Informing me of a luscious secret, his cracked voice dropped to a whisper: 'You can be anything there. Even female.'

I was disgusted. 'What the fuck do you want to be a woman for?'

'For fucking,' said Felicitia, and sighed.

I was unnerved by his power, to break rules I did not know existed. Not regular rules, that were authorised by the Castle or by the Governor; I broke those every day. Felicitia played havoc with the rules of nature.

'There's a market place with jugulars and ferret-eaters and buskers playing pangolins ...'

I giggled. 'That's a scaly kind of animal.'

'No, you're thinking of a peccadillo, my boy.'

Having no fixed point he thought free-form, and came up with plans that shocked us. 'Layce loves you,' I said, biting my lip.

'Huh. You can have her, my avid lad.'

If only I could. She was under my power only because Felicitia was dependent on me. I stayed with him because I knew he wanted more than sensation – he legitimately needed escape; it was the way he was formed. I understood because I was a mountain creature stranded in the city, I despaired of fitting in. He was woman in the body of a man, and had taken to scolopendium as a prescription for frustration. I knew he shouldn't have gone into East Bank with a grain-a-day habit. I would never get him back to the shop.

'I've brought your drugs, but I need the money first.'

'Hooked on it, aren't you?' Felicitia rasped.

'*What?*'

'Hard cash.'

Oh, yes. Definitely. He offered me a key and I swiftly removed his week's pocket money from a little strongbox under the table. I counted the notes three or four times, while Felicitia pursed his painted lips like a bar-room bitch. 'That's a hundred quid,' he snapped. 'What do you spend it on, sex-less?'

'Is it less of a crime if I spend it on books?' I was learning to read Awian, with the notion that it was a Castle language. I was weekly adding to Dotterel's library back at the shop. Felicitia tutted; he thought that spending money on books was the biggest crime of all.

I touched a white square of paper in the left pocket of my fringed leather trousers. 'What if I take the money and run?' I asked, half-jokingly.

Felicitia smoothed his skirt. 'My angelic archer outside is waiting for you. At a word from me, she'll finish you off.'

I didn't understand. 'It's Peterglass of The Bowyers ...' I said. I had assumed Peterglass was sending the assassins because he was a dealer and I was poaching his clientele.

'Yes, but none of them actually hit you,' Felicitia mused. I took an angry step and he gave me a pleading look. He would have loved me to touch him, so I didn't. 'I have been paying Peterglass's archers to ensure they are poor shots. Peterglass doesn't suspect their treachery; he still wants you dead.'

I couldn't believe this. 'Why protect me?'

'Because you make the best cat, my amatory boy. *Obviously*.'

This isn't what I wanted to be! Felicitia and I weren't keeping each other alive; we were keeping each other half-dead. I had become his personal dealer. I wanted to serve Dotterel, run marathons and read books. I wanted Layce, money, freedom, and thought I could gain them by mountain-boy meekness. Cold fury condensed in my mind; there was a faster way.

I bowed and thanked him. I am a great believer in getting my arse-licking over and done with. Then I put my hand into the other pocket, where there was a folded packet identical to the first, which I used when I wanted to rid myself of debtors and freeloaders. I passed it to Aver-Falconet with all due ceremony.

'Cook it for me, would you?' he asked.

'That isn't in the contract!' I didn't want to touch the stuff more than was absolutely necessary. 'It's enough for a week,' I added sweetly.

'Enough for a week. One week! There's enough for a month in me now.'

I loved the chemist's shop, and every morning, when opening the shutters, would gape up at the green and gold lettering above the windows – Dotterel Homais. I hoped one day it would be my name up there – ambitions all confused with those of joining the Castle Circle, which I thought were un-realistic. Perhaps I would keep my master's name up as an honour: Dotterel and Shira.

Thin shelves of glass bottles in the window were filled with coloured water. They gave a riotous display with each rare beam of sunlight. The dispensary smelt of spirits of wine and dusty paper. Some labels on the sprays of plants hanging from the ceiling to dry were in my writing. For the first time I had a feeling of belonging.

As well as my love of niche, I was awed by the novelty of authority. I respected my master. I regarded him as a genius and (because he could speak Scree) as a saviour. The terms of my apprenticeship, which would be complete in a year, were framed in ebony and behind glass, hung in the gallery of my memory. As Felicitia, now lying on his side in order to reach the table, dissolved an alarming quantity of the poison I had sold him, I ran through those rules. Felicitia gave me a wry glance; he didn't understand that words written on paper were sacrosanct.

Word for word my indenture was, to learn the art and mystery of my master's craft for the term of seven years. To neither buy nor sell without the said master's licence. Taverns, inns or alehouses I shall not haunt. At cards, dice, or any other unlawful game I shall not play, nor from the service of my said master day or night absent myself but in all things as an honest and faithful apprentice shall and will demean myself towards my said master and all his during the said term.

That's six of seven years of living a double life, Lord Aver-Falconet. You don't need me to tell you the tension. I've infringed each and every one of those rules even though the contract was written on paper. I knew that if Dotterel had the slightest suspicion of what I was doing I would be homeless again, and a Rhydanne wouldn't survive a week in a workhouse.

'I hope this is good stuff,' Felicitia said, his voice juicy with anticipation. I inclined my head for shame, which he took to be honour. 'The last one Shifted me for a day and a half,' he chuckled. He pushed a needle, still hot from the candle flame, in through his Wheel tattoo. I flinched, and looked away.

He knew something was wrong, and started cursing. Pain turned the curses to screams. Rigid, his back arched, the tendons in his neck standing out, blind eyes bulging.

That's the effect of scolopendium mixed with strychnine. I watched in horror. I could have given him a faster death, but I'd planned a slow reaction to give me time to escape. But I was transfixed, and stared at his clawed convulsions, listened to gasps of agony. Eventually he slid off the divan. I gazed at the blank wall and waited till his varnished fingernails had stopped scraping at the floor. I glanced at him and looked away disgusted. His face was black.

'Felicitia?' I murmured. 'My love?' If it were at all possible for him to return from death to hear that, he would have. I therefore reckoned I was safe. Drenched in Rhydanne superstition, I thought his animated corpse would grab my ankle.

I tried in vain to close his vacant eyes, and my fingers got sticky with mascara.

Closing a dead boy's eyes is supposed to be easy. It was impossible to close his mouth. I stripped off his jewellery. The objects on the table I threw on the fire, getting a little comfort from the brief heat. The novel and the anklet I pocketed.

Jant, you killed one of your own gang. But he wasn't really living anyway. Neither are you. You're Peterglass's prey now. Shit. I have to get out of here.

Wind shaking the walls reminded me of the world outside. Let's go; there's nothing besides remains here. Leaving Felicitia's minute and twisted corpse I ran to the door and risked a glance outside. The crossbow-girl had gone. Another training then kicked in – all that Layce had taught me. The sparse furnishings went on the fire. A tin of paraffin stood by the door; I doused it on the walls, walking round the vast empty building, splashing enough to overcome the rain. Then I stood back and threw what remained onto the pile of furniture. Starved yellow flames sprang up and crackled; within seconds the whole building was alight.

Through a gathering cloud of black smoke I choked my way out, shut the door and touched the Wheel insignia daubed across it. I ran back a safe distance and with juvenile jubilation watched our base rise in flames. My life in Hacilith was ending, the same feeling I experienced when leaving my valley. I was on a knife-edge a hundred times sharper than the icebound cliffs. These are children, by god, and highly dangerous. But how could I explain to my master? Take everything and leave without explaining? Forget him – how in Darkling could I explain it to the *gang*?

Watching the smoke I decided it would be easy to climb on that thermal and fly back to Galt, rather than risk running all the way through East Bank again. I stripped off my shirt and stretched my long wings strung with muscle. The fourth and fifth fingers were joined together, the thumb rigid and un-opposable, the bones swept back into aerodynamic curves, shaped by the stresses of airflow throughout their growth. Right, let's ride Felicitia's funeral pyre home.

'You do and you're dead, darling,' said a voice behind me. I started and looked round. The angelic archer was sitting on a mooring, levelling her little bow at my face. 'How distressing,' she commented. I had to agree, folded my wings to show I wasn't going anywhere, but also to keep them out of harm's way.

'Felicitia?' she asked. She had a shrill voice, which with her pipe-cleaner legs and broomstick arms was that of a child prodigy in the music hall. She was half my height.

'I'm unarmed.'

''Parently you don't have to be armed to leave a trail of fucking destruction. You're coming *with me*.' She spoke loudly, over the fire's roar and hissing molten lead dripping from the warehouse roof. Yellow flame reflected on stagnant green water all along the docks.

'My lady,' I said, images of glory and fortune dissolving before my eyes into a vision firstly of Dotterel shouting for me to bring his breakfast, and secondly of me being nailed to a waterwheel, unable to brew coffee let alone cat. 'Would you let me go for a hundred pounds, which I have right here?' I tapped one pocket hopefully; she giggled.

'No, but I'll have the money as well.' She walked towards me keeping the crossbow bolt pointed sometimes at my eyes, then at my chest, and efficiently relieved me of Aver-Falconet's cash. 'What did you do to him?' she asked.

'Drugs,' I said glumly.

She was unable to keep the excitement from her voice. 'There's another hundred waiting for me at Peterglass's base when I bring you in. Kindly accompany me.' I ignored her terse gesture with the bow. It was delicate enough to be held in one hand and although the point was sharp it didn't look powerful. 'No!' I shouted, feeling the intense heat feed my fury as it was scorching my wings. 'I am going back to Galt. So sod off, flatlander!'

'These are poisoned,' she informed me.

'My master knows the antidote to every poison!'

'There's a grown-up involved?' she shouted, shocked.

'He will be if you don't let me go!'

'An *adult*?'

'My master could end all our games for good.' Winning an award for bravery I took the hand not engaged in stroking the crossbow's hair trigger and patted it soothingly. 'I can almost hear him calling,' I added.

'You're my prisoner!' she shrieked. Rain was bouncing off the shoulders of her leather jacket. Sudden tears of confusion turned her soft-fruit face bright red; strands of wet hair stuck to her round cheeks. The arrow point wavered as her hands shook and I watched it carefully. This girl knew The Bowyers, I knew The Wheel. If we could work together, Hacilith would be ours.

I shrugged, saying, 'By the way, I bet this is worth a million in blackmail.'

'What?'

'The Governor's son, Lord Aver-Falconet – vanished somewhere in the East Bank slums. Murders, drugs, sex. The list is long! I think the gossip column would pay well, but his father would pay better.'

'I'm warning you, cat-eyes ... Um ...'

'Come with me and we'll make a million.' I ventured a smile. 'We'll leave Hacilith. Travel the world. See the Castle, even. That's better than The Bowyers' gang, isn't it?'

'Blackmail ... ?' The blonde girl removed the bolt from her crossbow and stuck it in her wide leather belt. She sniffed and tentatively offered me her hand. 'I'm Serin. Apart from being a wily assassin, I dance at the Campion Vaudeville. You are *still my prisoner*.'

I took this with a pinch of salt. 'I'm Jant,' I said. 'And I can fly.'

Suspicion flickered in her eyes. 'If you trick me I'll hunt you down through all Hacilith. I'd enjoy it—' She jumped, startled as a section of the warehouse collapsed behind us. She threw one arm up to shield her eyes as a tidal wave of glassy heat rolled over us. 'Meet me at The Kentledge at six tonight,' she yelled. 'It has to be six because curtain-up is nine.'

'At six o'clock, my lady,' I said. She executed a perfect curtsey, with a supple chorus girl's grace, and then watched with amazement little short of adoration as I tested the rising air and took off for home.

That's all I'm going to say about my past for the moment, because I keep receiving unhappy letters from the Hacilith Tourist Board.

CHAPTER 9

Lightning was listening to a hasty report from a tired soldier who had plunged over the frosty fields to reach us. I was kneeling to buckle Swallow's hauberk because her fingers were too cold to manage. The time before battle is known as the 'drinking hour', and the men were washing down their breakfast with mouthfuls of rum. There would be no more venison – the deer had been disturbed by our presence, and we were reduced to eating half-cooked salt beef and bread. I saw a cask of wine being hacked open; the frozen wine was broken with an axe, and carried away in baskets and helmets. Planks were laid as pathways through the mud.

The scout's face was reflected in the bracer on Lightning's arm. I addressed him: 'You were with Tanager's fyrd?'

'Yes, Messenger. I've been as far as Lowespass and the villages are empty.' He had a heavy eastern Awian accent and a splendid beard.

'Have you seen the fortress?'

He paused. 'The Insects are building a wall round it.'

'Can't Tawny stop them?'

Lightning related the beginning of the report. 'Vireo and Tawny haven't enough troops to face so many Insects. I think they might run before the wall closes, and come south to meet us. If not they'll be trapped, San help them.'

I knew they had some food supplies, and half a million arrows in the armoury, so if we could reach them we would be able to replenish our own stocks.

The scout bowed his head. 'The valley is full of Insects. They were roused by some men from Rachis who chipped the Wall trying to pull their friend out.'

'It's forbidden to touch the Wall,' I remarked. The scout shrugged as if to say that Castle's rule meant little in Rachiswater now. He said, 'Insects are moving south. They're on their way. They're coming.'

'How many?' I asked, fiddling with Swallow's buckles.

'Many, many Insects.'

'Can't you be a bit more specific than that?'

'Hundreds of thousands.'

I looked up in disbelief.

Three trumpet calls were sounded; at the first every soldier had to pack his gear. Most of the tents were left standing since they were stiff with ice. At the second, the fyrd were to join with their manors, which did not take long as there were only the manors of Awndyn and Micawater. At the third trumpet call the troops took their designated positions, with the banners, and the host began to march.

The fyrd were organised to advance open order, the lines of men being spread out and keeping a good space between them. The scout and a number of archers stayed behind to guard the camp, wagons and trenches. Those who remained behind were mainly soldiers who had seen the Insects recently and I did not want to mix them in with the fresh, spirited troops.

Swallow's horse left hoof prints in the thin sprinkling of snow on the ground; she rode biting chapped bits of skin from her lips and blowing on her frozen fingers. The morning sky was a mixture of pallid colours like the mother-of-pearl guitar. Passing metal-grey clouds dropped wet sleet on us. At the cloud edges a lemon-yellow light came through occasionally in bright patches – then we sighed and stretched and tried to dry off in the sparse sunlight, but the sky was gradually filling with the colour of steel.

10 a.m.: Swallow rode away from an argument with Lightning and myself. She vowed to lead her men into battle and was determined to ride at the head of the rectangle of troops. I explained that if the men had to form a shield square she would simply not be strong enough to survive in the tight crowd. She hated the thought of being a weak link physically, but as she was not built like Vireo, she had to accept it.

Lightning told me that the war had killed Swallow's father, and she believed that he couldn't possibly have died for an unjust cause. So Swallow rode, resolute, behind the first division of infantry, with the cavalry following. The marching lines snaked and contorted as they broke the ice on the frozen fields.

10.30: Lightning took me aside and asked me to watch over Swallow. Misgiving was written clearly on his face. 'Stay with her,' he said. 'Please.'

I clapped his shoulder. 'Yeah, don't worry.'

'Jant, I'm serious. It's agony for me being on the flank; I can't see her half the time.'

I was irritated. Lightning didn't believe in me. 'I swear I'll guard her as closely as you would yourself! From the Insects and the men, should they rebel against wet feet and Insect bites.'

'I'm afraid for her,' he admitted. It wasn't exactly what I wanted to hear. 'When fighting begins you must try to move her out of the way.'

I thought how Swallow had bested me in the duel; her big shoulders seemed more muscular by the minute. 'If fighting happens I'm going to get behind her and plead for protection.'

'I *am* serious.' Strained, Lightning sounded as if he was holding a breaking heart together. I swore strongly I would protect her – surely he knew I was capable? He nodded, placated, and went back to his division.

10.45: Lightning changed the structure of his entire division so he could ride slightly closer to Swallow.

11.00: The men grew more cheery as the marching warmed them. They had permission to speak so bursts of conversation – about swords, axes, and how best to maim Insects – drifted back to us. Some shared tobacco and sips from their hip flasks. They were allowed to change position in an open order march, since men walking in close formation in harsh conditions suffer low morale. We marched into driving flurries of snow, our fronts white as it stuck to us. The soldiers' waxed cloaks flapped; they wore felt scarves wrapped around their faces and carried their shields edge-on to the wind. They leant into the wind and walked, starbursts of flakes driving into their eyes, legs aching from marching against the intermittent gale.

Midday: Marching is repetitive and I, who have studied movement for so long, found the ride soothing, not boring but hypnotic, so that I was calmed, my fear-knotted muscles relaxed and I actually began to enjoy it. Each kilometre we rode was recaptured land, which formed a secure strip behind us. It was not too far now to the Lowespass trenches.

Swallow and I sped up at the foot of each field, forcing our horses to jump the hedge, which the men climbed over or slashed through, before reforming their lines. Swallow kept glancing at her pocket watch. She looked around with a sighing expression, bowed her head and bit her lip. I thought she was missing her guitar, but when I offered it to her she refused: 'Jant, you know what I said. Not until we reach the trenches. Not until I drive the Insects back behind the Wall.'

Eleven thousand feet, two thousand hooves smashed through the ice. Cracked it to shards. Splattered grassy water. Squelched in freezing mud, as we rode on.

2.00: After midday we entered a more hilly landscape, crags and limestone pavements at the tops of the hills. We're nearly there, I told Swallow. At one point Lightning took the lead and Harrier's division moved behind us because the ravine was too narrow for the archers to ride on the flanks.

Several times we saw single Insects running along the road or small groups in the scrubby woodland. None escaped; our men rounded them up and slew them all. The land we left behind was free from man-eaters.

108

I watched my shadow lengthen as the day progressed and still we marched north.

3.00: The Archer came over and said, 'We're losing the light already. We should camp here.'

Swallow disagreed instinctively: 'I would like to reach the end of the ravine. Jant says it opens into Lowespass. We can see the fortress from there. It would give the men a good feeling of achievement.'

'Jant says, Jant says.' Saker flicked his reins angrily. 'The Rhydanne may be happy to blunder around in the dark but I'm not.'

'It's true there's only two hours till nightfall,' I said to Swallow.

'Could we reach Lowespass in half an hour?'

'Yes, but that doesn't leave us much time!'

'We should at least try. How can we camp in this tiny ravine anyway? How could we manoeuvre?'

'You're right,' Lightning conceded. It would be easy to make a shield wall across the gorge, which would prevent the Insects passing, but then we would not be able to use our numbers to defeat them. Lightning knew the archers needed space, and we thought of the massacre that would happen at night if we were caught without room to move. 'We should try to secure the end of the valley. Swallow's quite correct,' he said. After that nothing I could say would convince him that his sweetheart might in any way be wrong.

3.30: We came out of the valley under the last throes of a fantastic sunset, and there before us lay all Lowespass. Seeing the Fortress Crag, the men gave a triumphant yell. Then just as suddenly, they fell silent.

'What *is* that?' Swallow trembled.

'I don't know,' I said. 'It wasn't here before.'

'Saker?'

Lightning was shouting at the men to remain calm. A swathe of infantry sat down in a spiky mass, staring at the view. 'My god, I don't know. *I've* never seen anything like it.'

Next to the fortress, and taller than it, there was a bridge. Half a bridge. It looked unfinished but it dwarfed the crag, arching up into the clear sky. The last rays of sunlight shone between its struts.

'How does it stay up?' breathed Swallow.

'*I don't know.*' Lightning whirled. 'Make camp here! Harrier – I want trenches on each side of the ravine and pavilions up right here.' The men moved obediently, muttering.

'It's Insects,' I said.

'Well it bloody well isn't human hand,' said Harrier.

'*Move!*' Lightning yelled at him.

The ground under the colossal bridge was covered in grey-white Insect buildings. Low, pointed roofs of their cells looked like frozen waves. From the foot of the bridge to the pale horizon was grey paper, with long sections of Insect walls emerging from the mass; walls the Insects had passed that were now redundant, and walls at the edge of their sprawling complex, which they were still constructing. I looked to where the friendly smoke plumes of Whittorn should be, and saw nothing but Insect buildings. The military town had gone. The burnt framework of Pasquin's Tower stuck up from a cluster of walls. Lowespass Fortress itself was ringed with walls.

'Summerday?' I said aloud.

'Who?'

'I hope the Insects haven't made it as far as the coast,' I explained. 'There's thousands of people in Summerday town.'

'How does the bridge stay up?' Swallow repeated.

'It can't be a bridge. It's not leading anywhere!'

It was grey-white like the cells, with thin, twisted struts. They must have been much stronger than they looked. They supported a walkway which curved up for perhaps a kilometre. At a height of two hundred metres the bridge ended abruptly. At that end there were no legs to hold the walkway up. 'It's beautiful,' she said.

Lightning was shaking his head. 'Insects are coming down it.' I squinted into the twilight. He had great eyesight; I couldn't see too well in the jester dusk. I could just make out the familiar low bodies scurrying down the walkway, which was truly vast. Insects were running down the bridge, into their city, but no Insects were moving the other way, towards the apex. My eyes hurt as I tried to spot the point at which they appeared out of the air.

'You could fit four coaches next to each other up there,' he said.

'Shall I go closer?' I spread my wings and my horse reared.

'In the dark? No, Jant, stay here and we'll investigate tomorrow.'

3.50: We had just set camp when the Insects attacked.

3.55: Insects, one and two, cast about them like the lead hounds of the hunt. Then there were suddenly thousands, pouring down the valley, from ruined houses, tunnel openings, the paper cells.

Swallow swore. 'They go on, and on, into the distance.'

'So do we.'

3.57: I screamed at Swallow, 'Put that fucking watch away!'

Lightning was quick: 'Out! Fan out, Select! Full draw! Donaise, central; Bitterdale, wings!'

No time to lose, I ordered the infantry, 'Go forward!'

110

Shield-bearers ran out, dropped to their knees. Their great shields crashed into position, a sixty-metre interlinking line.

The archers darted past, moving forward. Two hundred archers ran off into the darkness on either side to form the wings. The first line shot straight out over the shield-bearers' heads. Two lines behind sent volleys up into the air. Arrows hissed, rained down hard on the Insects' backs three hundred metres away.

Stench of Insect blood began to fill the air, coppery, like old coins. Dim shapes grew clearer as they ran up against the hail of arrows. The stampede moved like a single creature; mandibles dripping septic spit, claws rasping on rock. Their legs razor-tipped, rake-edged, saw-toothed; the shape of every weapon there, adapted for slaughtering. Their antennae were flattened to their heads. They can smell us. Taste us! But I only saw ant heads emerging from the festering night. Paler grey, taking form and colour as they got nearer.

Lightning's voice on the left: 'Slower, Donaise division. Six per minute is all I want.' He appeared next to me. 'I'm saving arrows,' he gasped, 'Half an hour at that rate and we'll have none left.'

Insects battered at the shield wall. The ringing of blows, metal on shell, metal on metal, sounded like a foundry. 'I don't like this,' said Lightning. 'The men haven't eaten. They've been walking all day.'

I ordered a fire to be built at the back. The men passed firebrands from hand to hand until weak points of wavering light lit the mayhem. We held against the Insects, and still more Insects came. We passed water bottles to the shield wall so that the human fortification could drink. They were crouched with all their strength against the shields. The archers were barefoot for grip in the mud. Lightning sent those on the outside to join the brawl and kept the Donaise division shooting. None of us could see where their arrows were going. He sent an order for our horses to be brought close behind us. Our breath hung in the air; it was freezing cold.

'I can't see Harrier's horsemen,' said Swallow. 'I just bloody hope he's still there.'

'He's trustworthy,' said Lightning.

'Yes, but where the fuck is he?'

There was little to see. I raised my lantern to glimpse the chain mail and leather-strap backs of the foot soldiers directly in front. They stood shoulder-to-shoulder five men deep before merging into darkness. I couldn't see the ends of the line either. I heard grunts, shrieks and steady chopping from the shield wall. A scout told me it was crushed and breaking.

'Comet?' Another anxious pale face.

'Yes, Scaup. What's it like down there?'

He pointed. 'That side is breached and Harrier is advancing.'

'I didn't hear anything,' I said to Lightning.

'Comet,' Scaup blinked, 'there's but a handful left.'

I'm the Messenger so I should be down there, among them, to pass on Lightning's orders, but I had promised to protect Swallow.

The shield wall fell in on both sides before I saw it fall in front of me. Lightning and Harrier had already pressed ahead. Insects went over the wall in a wave, crashed into the fyrd behind. Men raised their swords and shields. Some raised their hands instinctively and the Insects sliced their fingers off. Insects continued pouring in. How many were out there? They mangled the shield men, their weight crushing, jaws lacerating those trapped beneath.

I nodded and Scaup shouted, 'At them,' on my left. 'At them!' echoed on my right. A woman's voice: Swallow. Bloodthirsty bitch! Just like Vireo. Why do battles have this ruthless effect on women?

We drove the horses forward all of ten metres before coming up against the crush. Insects clambered towards us over corpses; their shells were wet with melted snow. Guiding my horse with my knees, I tangled with the first Insects. Swallow hewed them with her sword. She smiled. She hacked down at an Insect on her right side, severing its antennae, and then up in a flat arc that cut a compound eye in two. Twenty Insects later her arm was aching and she wasn't smiling so much. I fended off twenty more, before it became clear they would never stop. Scaup's horse stumbled; Insects slashed its belly and dragged it down.

Lightning's armoured white trampled the warm carcass. 'We must go,' he said grimly.

'Then we'd leave the foot soldiers behind!' Swallow protested. Her gauntlet was stained with blood from a gash over the wrist but she appeared not to care. That made Lightning's decision: 'We're leaving, right now. You first – get to Rachis.'

'No.'

'Jant is going. Harrier is going. Swallow – put that shield at your back and follow them.'

'This is my stand—!' She seemed determined to die with the men. Her shout ended in a gasp because I grabbed the reins from her hand, whipped her horse with the end of them, and we lunged away together.

We skittered down the hill into the ravine, scattering stones. We rode blind, the Awndyn cavalry following us. I glanced back to see how many there were; perhaps seven, eight hundred. Had we lost a hundred horse?

Behind them chased the chitin tide of Insects. Lightning was following; I saw him pulling sheaves of arrows from his saddlebag and stuffing them into the quiver.

Cries and thuds reverberated in the ravine as the abandoned infantry fought to the death. The voices thinned quickly, though the noise they made grew in desperation, and then abruptly there was silence.

Scaup had gone. Harrier was missing. I couldn't see any hoof prints on the path. My legs were shaking. I leant over the horse's neck till her mane brushed my cheek. She was spitting foam, running with sweat. Ice had lacerated the skin on her forelegs. Swallow's bay was in worse condition, foam mixed with blood. But Swallow kept a smile on her face that fired my heart. I understood why Lightning loved her.

We fled in the direction we had come. I looked back, calling the men to follow me. We left many Insects behind – our soldiers' corpses distracted them.

'Slower, Jant,' Swallow pleaded.

'Not yet. Soon.'

'You're going to kill this horse.'

I wanted to ride to Awia. We could regroup then; hopefully we would be near Rachis.

At 6 a.m. we passed the border. An hour later we slackened our pace. Swallow's bay was mad with pain. With Lightning between us and the trailing Insects, and the smooth cobbles of Rachiswater road under our hooves. I thought the crisis had passed.

'We left the infantry,' Swallow said. Her face was a mask of guilt.

'Don't think about it. We're not safe ourselves yet.'

'They were in agony. They all died. It's my fault.'

I remembered Lightning saying that all Zascai die, it's just a question of when. I could not comfort her. I was watching a dark shape just left of the road resolve into a mass of Insects. They ran alongside us, and attacked immediately.

Swallow copied my line of sight, and screamed, 'Where the *fuck* are they all coming from? So close to town!'

'This way! The Palace for shelter!'

Swallow urged her dying horse. I led them at a gallop off the road and across levelled grass. We sped along a plantation path and into the gardens of white Rachiswater Palace. We splashed through the edge of the lake.

Mad confusion as we rode. We had no formation. I had no way of making my orders known save yelling. But everybody was shouting. The horses were protesting, the wounded soldiers screaming. The women soldiers howled. Men called to their companions. The air was a cacophony. Swallow gathered a tight group of riders – her rich voice carried well, she commanded attention through sheer volume. But it was terrible – Insects ran among the riders, biting at horses' legs. Men seemed to rush from all directions to the light, towards the Palace walls.

Flickering torchlight shone by the foot of the wall. Yellow torches glowed on the top, reflecting in the lake. The stench of smoke was so strong that I thought the Palace was burning. Then I saw reinforcements marching out, a welcoming party for us. They held long pikes and stood along the foot of the walls. Men crowded into the torchlight, eager to get through the gate, and for the first time I clearly saw their rictus faces. The gate was shut.

'Swallow,' I shouted. 'Stay close!'

'What's happening?' she begged.

I didn't know but I dreaded it. The men held their long spears at rest. The others carried a quickly collected array of torches, candle lanterns and oil lamps. Shadows from the pikes striped the wet grass. A word from the gatehouse – I didn't hear through the tumult – and the pikemen stepped forward. As one, they levelled their staves. Uproar from the Awndyn cavalry, suddenly on the wrong end of the pikes.

I pulled my horse in and she stopped less than a metre from the closest pike.

'No,' screamed Swallow. 'No! This is all wrong!' She shook her sword and shouted at a pikeman, 'You there! What are your orders? What has the King said?'

He stayed impassive.

'Why won't you let us in?' She bit back a sob of frustration.

The soldier made not a sound.

I approached the cylindrical gatehouse. 'Don't worry,' I said. It was a strange misunderstanding, but I could sort it out. I called, 'Comet calls on you in the name of San Emperor, for the will of god and the protection of the Circle.' That was my phrase of command which Messengers present and for immemorial decades before me have used and it has never failed to work before. 'Open these gates!' Nothing happened. I tried again. Nothing happened. 'Staniel?' I called. 'Rachiswater? Come to the parapet and speak to me!'

'You bastard,' said Swallow, but I couldn't tell whether she meant Staniel or me. Where the light was poor, two horses had run onto the spears. That heralded the arrival of Lightning's men. Lightning's archers were hopelessly mixed in with more Insects. More and more Insects arrived. They covered the ground. The Insects got to work biting horses, pulling down men. The horses forced away from the Insects, between the pikes. Unhorsed men found themselves on the ground where they were trampled or gashed. A crowd of unhorsed men grew; they pushed back from the pikes, squeezing the cavalry closer to the Insects.

Lightning saw Swallow's leaf-green livery and forced through the crush to our side. 'I had dire trouble following you,' he said. 'Harrier got bitten.'

'Is Harrier here?' I asked.

'He's somewhere in that mess. Why all the halberds?'

'I don't know.' I watched in horror as an unhorsed man cap-à-pie in white armour grappled against Insects.

'We'll soon put a stop to this,' said Lightning and raised his voice. 'In the name of San Emperor, for god's—'

'I tried that,' I said.

'Open up! Open up *now*! Do you know who I am? Lightning *Micawater*! Comet is here! Governor Awndyn is here! In the name of the *Emperor* let us in!'

'Maybe they think we're attacking them,' I suggested.

'I bloody am now.' Lightning fitted an arrow to bowstring. 'I'm going to shoot them one by one.'

'What good will that do?'

'It'll give us some space.'

'No! They still won't open the gate!'

'Have they forgotten who we *are*?'

'It's because we're mixed with Insects,' Swallow said.

I glanced at her dirty face. 'You're right.' Staniel's fear of Insects was so great he wouldn't risk allowing even one into the Palace courtyard. If that meant men would struggle and die outside his very walls then so be it.

Every second we stayed it became more difficult to leave because we were hemmed in by our own dead and the dead Insects. My horse was treading among the fallen men. Our cavalry pushed into those on the ground, knocking them over and trampling them. The shaggy hooves as big as dinner plates came down on heads and smashed through shields.

Two of our captains were still alive. I waved at them and yelled, 'Go to the edges! That way! No! *That* way! Get Donaise to follow you and head toward the town. Go *slowly*!' I told them to be slow because they would need time to regroup and any fast movement might lead to panic.

There was attrition at the edges of the mass, as well as loud screams from the wounded at the centre. Men at the edges were running away. Men were so terrified they would chance fleeing into the infested park. They threw off their helmets the better to see, flung down swords and they ran like madmen. One ran at full tilt, legs pumping, fisted hands ripping off armour as he went. When one ran, the men on either side gave up and ran as well. Then the ones next to them ran, and within seconds a whole section of the crowd had bolted. They had blank, honest faces without any shame or fear of reprisal.

'Shit.' I realised that those who risked the darkness were certainly doomed. There was no way of stopping them. We would have to pick up the bodies later. But what chance for 'later' if we don't save ourselves?

The captains did their best to move men down the bulwark, easing the crush. Harrier had shouted his division into some sort of order and they seemed to perceive the correct direction for the town. I looked down on this mass of struggling people. Those on foot were at head level with the horses' backs and they were suffocating. The Castle's badge drew them to me, but I could do nothing to protect them. I felt the incredible pressure of bodies on bodies. Men positioned their shields to stop their ribs being crushed.

I moved my horse outwards, but that just pushed the horses behind me more tightly against the Insects. Swallow used her spur against a pikeman's cheek, then kicked his neck as he reeled back. She sobbed uncontrollably. Harrier pointed to Rachis town, raised both hands questioningly, clenching the reins. I wanted the unhorsed men to escape in front of us before the horses followed, but I had to get Swallow out of there.

I felt so powerless that callous indifference took hold, and I was thinking: he must be dead, god, she can't survive, as people fell, wounded, around me.

The Insects were ripping through immobile horses and men. I heard them crackling. I heard the sound of flesh tearing and the horses' screams, louder as Insects chewed their way closer.

My face got spattered with blood when an Insect bit into a horse's heart. Swallow screamed as she was sprayed with blood head to foot. It looked black in the torchlight. She stared in my direction with blind panic, trying to pull her leg up onto her mare's back away from a grasping claw. Then she was gone. Aghast, I saw her foot caught in the stirrup. It flailed in the air. It vanished completely as the Insects pulled her down. The horse stumbled over her.

I heard Lightning bellow through the tumult, yelling something to Harrier. My horse's foreleg gave way as an Insect bit through the tendons. She fell forward and collapsed, spilling me from the saddle. I hit the ground in a burst of pain. I clutched my shoulder, thinking it broken. I saw the underside of a thorax as an Insect jumped and just had time to shield my face. It wrapped four legs round the shield and wouldn't let go. I struggled with its crushing weight and then had to cast the shield aside. I scrabbled for my ice axe in the mud and dispatched the next five Insects with flair.

But behind me, left and right, were Insects, scissoring mandibles, raking spines. It was impossible. Every time I raised my arm one would grab it. They were pulling at my back plate and belt.

I fought my way between close mounds of dead looking for Swallow. The hooves of riderless horses pounded down around me. Swallow. Where's Swallow? Where the fuck is she?

I saw her and called, lost concentration for a second and was knocked flat by an Insect the size of a pony. Its antennae swept my face. I shielded my face with one arm and its mandibles scratched my armour. Inside the serrated jaws another set of mouthparts churned in thick slime. I brought the axe down heavily. It crunched into the thing's top shoulder and embedded in the shell – I couldn't free it.

The Insect's integument was dotted with spiracle holes. I reached down and shoved my fingers in one, tearing the membrane. The Insect kept biting. I was pinned down. I choked. I struggled to hold its face away from mine. Its jointed antennae were swept back out of my reach. Black palps hanging below its jaws slopped across my mouth and neck, tasting my skin. Its hard thorax pressed against my chest, its bulbous abdomen held high.

My face reflected over and over in compound eyes and in three ocelli like buttons on its forehead. Its triangular face pushed into mine, suture lines between the brown plates.

Stiff fringes on sharp forelegs, tarsus feet clawed my neck. A centimetre closer, its mandibles opened to cut my throat. I looked straight into the cogwheel maxillae. My arms shook, screaming pain. This is how it ends, I thought. I braced myself for agony. I let go.

The Insect collapsed onto me, its heavy head smacked into the mud. I yelled, no longer trapped, and slithered from underneath. The Insect lay still. Was it dead? I kicked it, and saw an arrow shaft projecting from the back of its head. The steel point emerged from between its eyes.

Lightning was a hundred metres away, nocking another arrow to string. I cheered him and he frowned. Two deep breaths, then he held his breath. The bodkin point came up from earth to target with precision. He loosed the string and an Insect fell some distance behind me.

It thrilled me to watch the greatest archer ever. As I watched, my confidence returned. I was Eszai, I was powerful, I would fight.

Lightning's horse stood still while he aimed and loosed again, sniping the Insects down in one tight area. Where a ragged shape lay – a red and green shape. Then I realised he was stopping Insects from eating Swallow. I drew my dagger and ran to her. I sliced between sclerites, stabbed through the pedicel waist of an Insect on top of her, kicked it aside and picked her up. Her mail was wet with a shocking amount of blood. Swallow's face was very, very pale.

'Damn you, Jant!' Lightning arrived. 'Don't do that again!'

'This is the mother of all routs—' I stopped because Harrier appeared. He was on a different horse and had a ripped shirt wrapped around his bleeding leg.

Swallow began to wail, her eyes tightly shut and her teeth stained red. 'Harrier?' Lightning asked.

His servant took the hint. 'Pass her up to me.'

I lifted her carefully onto the saddle in front of him; she lolled back against his chest and nearly slid off but I showed him how to hold her.

Lightning put arrows neatly through two more approaching Insects. 'Is she badly hurt?' he asked. 'Will she live? Can she stand a long ride?'

'Yes. Perhaps. To where?'

'My house.'

'We can't ride all the way to Micawater!'

Swallow kicked feebly. I saw a deep wound in her hip, its walls glistening. 'Follow me to the town.'

'Micawater is better ...' Lightning stared.

'I don't want to ride into any more Insects,' said Harrier, who had his hands full.

I said, 'Staniel has fortified Rachis. If they let us in it should be safe.'

Too bruised and exhausted to run, I took charge of a riderless Carniss roan and cantered with them until we reached the main road. Then I urged my horse on and galloped faster. The forest flew by on either side. I tied the reins back. I stood up on the saddle, balancing, and the distressed horse ran even faster. I tilted my wings to get the correct airflow under them, and spread. Three beats and I was up, looking down on Lightning's white and Harrier's sorrel mare.

We travelled without pause and arrived just before daybreak. The half-finished walls were thick, rugged stone not yet faced. The sight was worrying, I thought – Zascai don't trust us any more. The wooden gates stood ajar and a stream of men poured through. I looked down to the dishevelled, silent soldiers already crowding the market place to capacity. The town had an air of unreality, so many people here at dawn. I knew I must find residence for all of them or the situation would become volatile, but I had to help Swallow first.

I flew along the streets at first-floor height with Lightning and Harrier following. I got lost twice; the roads had changed since my last visit, only thirty years ago. With a plan view I found the Grand Place, and led them to the magnificent Spread Eagle Hotel. I settled on the stuccoed balcony and watched Lightning and Harrier dismount.

A cold, chalk-blue quiet, an expectation of the sunrise, made Lightning and his servant talk with muted voices. They took care, as if a sound could cause Swallow to slip away. I glided down as Harrier carried her up elegant steps into the entrance hall.

CHAPTER 10

The hotelier was a short, vigorous man with a paunch, and a duster in his back pocket. He recognised Lightning and I, fixed on the sunburst insignia. We marched into his hotel. Behind us he saw a battle-stained warrior with an injured girl in his arms, dripping blood on the pale pink marble. He was speechless.

It'll be something to tell the children, I thought. 'Give us a room.'

He put a hand over his open mouth.

'You'll be paid,' added Lightning.

The hotelier saw our urgency, and found his tongue. 'Immediately, my lord.' He ran up a New Art staircase – a confection of metalwork swirls and glass petals. Lightning followed grimly as he threw the door open onto a sumptuous cream suite.

'I'll clear the guests from this floor,' said the hotelier. 'The whole building is at my lord's disposal.'

'That's not necessary.' I smiled at him.

'Thank you,' said Lightning. 'We'll call you when we need—'

I looked back but the hotelier had vanished.

I tipped the cream sheets onto the floor so that Harrier could lay Swallow down. I tore the curtains open on their brass rails to let a little of the bruise-blue light into the room.

Lightning threw himself on his knees at the bedside. 'You would tear my heart out,' he murmured. 'It looks bad, doesn't it?' he asked, voice catching. I nodded, checking her over the way Rayne had taught me.

'You can help her?'

'I'm not a surgeon.'

'Please ...'

'I'll do what I can.'

'No ... Another one. Not again. I hope you can do more for my love than Rayne could with Dunlin!'

'Mm, yes. Swallow? Swallow, can you hear me?' She made no response. There were deep gashes in her thighs and belly. They were covered in blood clots, and it took a long time to peel off the torn cloth so I could see how deep they were. One foot was a chewed mess, bones splayed out. I had often seen wounds like that caused by Insects slashing cavalrymen's legs. Harrier was limping from a shallower cut over his knee.

I touched Swallow's forehead and wondered if she had a fever coming on. 'I'm going to need all sorts of things.'

Lightning beckoned to Harrier. 'Anything you want, don't count the cost.'

'I don't think bandages will be enough; I need some clean sheets to tear up. Need gauze, boiling water, liniment from powdered oak bark, tormentil, comfrey – that'll stop the bleeding. For internal bleeding – shepherd's purse and horsetails. Tincture of yarrow and arnica to clean the skin. For pain-killers I'll need aconite, to calm her I need papaver and if she gets a fever I'll need elder in decoction. I also need thread and a knife ...'

Harrier bowed with quick assertion.

'And some scolopendium.'

'Messenger, I won't be able to find that. It's been illegal in this country for years.'

'I know where to find it,' I said.

Rayne's thesis advocates careful observation when treating patients. Over centuries of observation she has discovered that illnesses and infections are caused by dust. I studied her treatise every day when I was an apprentice in Hacilith, and it impressed upon me the fact that even a tiny amount of dirt can induce sickness. Dust is present over everything and very often is invis-ible, so it is important to be rigorous. To clean instruments, Rayne urged the use of hot water, salt water, alcohol and flame.

Lightning lingered until he realised I was stripping Swallow and when I got down to skin level he made a hasty excuse and left me to it. I made sure the room was dust-free and emptied of antiques, and that Swallow's wounds were sewn and dressed before I called him back. There was another problem to deal with.

'Will she live?' he implored.

'This must be our headquarters for a few days until her condition stabilises,' I said.

'Needs must, if we have to rough it,' he replied stoically, kneeling beside the cream satin four-poster.

'During that time, Lightning, we have to gather any surviving Awndyn Fyrd, reward them and send them home. You realise they will hate the Rachiswater pikemen now, and the longer they stay, the more chance they have for retaliation.'

'Leave it to me,' he murmured, peering at Swallow's closed eyes. 'She looks like she's sleeping.'

'She is sleeping. I want a reliable courier to carry my report to the Emperor, another to go to the Governor of Hacilith; and I want fifty horsemen to scout the north of the manorship to see how much damage the Insects caused last night, and where they are now.'

'The Insects trounced us. It is a disaster for her,' said the Archer, venturing to stroke Swallow's hand on the coagulating sheets.

'I'll face the Emperor on her behalf. And I want the tags of all the men who died in Staniel's Palace grounds because I'm going to present him with a list of names.'

'You will look after her, please?' He glanced up.

'I won't move from her side.'

'Then I will do the rest.' He kissed her hand, and stalked out, calling for Harrier.

I wrote to Rayne, who sent me instructions that I followed to the letter, but I sighed six times an hour with despair. What the fuck is a metatarsal and where has it gone? The responsibility was overwhelming, the job was gory. But I kept my doubts to myself, for Lightning's sake.

The hotelier brought my meals to the suite. Nothing could induce him to exchange more than a few words each time. My shape and the musician's blood under my fingernails awed him, and he only told me what he thought I wanted to hear. Harrier kept us informed of the events in the town.

Swallow had not regained consciousness after two weeks at the Spread Eagle. I reluctantly allowed a day's journey to move her to Lightning's Palace in the neighbouring manorship. A white coach with two chestnut horses appeared one morning. God knows what day it was – I was hollowed out and hyper from nights awake watching over her.

Harrier and the hotelier manoeuvred Swallow on a stretcher down wide rose-marble stairs and installed her in the carriage. I knelt beside her to prevent her from moving as the horses walked.

As we entered the portico of Micawater Palace, Lightning visibly began to recover his shattered optimism. Old Eszai are not accustomed to losing, and I could tell it would take him time to recover from the outrage. We placed Swallow on the bed in a dark blue room which overlooked the lake. Checking that the room was clean, I noticed constellations of gold stars painted on the ceiling.

Lightning held the musician's warm, limp hand for hours, kissing each finger individually. I found him still there in the evening; he had not moved at all.

'What will we do about your King?' I asked.

'First Dunlin, now this ... Oh, beloved. Did you think you were immortal already?'

'Hello? Lightning?'

'Is she going to wake up soon?' He was definitely happier with the bold and adventurous Swallow than with the girl who lay prone and had to be nursed.

'Saker,' I tried again with a sympathetic tone. 'We must gain control of the capital. Go and visit Staniel; don't take a large retinue, but make sure you bring him a gift.'

'That waste of time should be apologising to me for the ruin he's caused!'

I bit my tongue on 'I told you so'. 'Praise Staniel highly. Tell him he chose the correct course of action.'

'But—'

'Saker, just imagine how terrified he must be by now, although he may not admit it. I want you to give him all the reassurance you can – as sincerely as you can. If he is convinced of our goodwill it may be easier to influence his next moves.'

'Or stop him making any.'

'No!' I checked that Swallow was still asleep. 'The war has come to Rachiswater. I want Staniel's fyrd to hold the front and stop Insects moving any further south. Offer to join him. Be a loyal subject rather than an immortal advisor, understand? Offer a division of your fyrd for his direct control. Keeping his host together requires money, which I know he lacks. You must seem so satisfied of his claim to the throne that you will offer to lend him funds.'

'Never,' Lightning said, clasping Swallow's hand.

'It's only temporary. I'll put Wrought at his disposal as well.'

'Now I know you're joking. Wrought has no money, and that which you do have is pledged to feed the refugees.'

'We'll supply arms. Your fyrd might need arrows too? If we give Staniel sound and kind advice now he might be more willing to take it in the future.'

'Never.'

I had had a wholesome meal, a hot relaxing shower, and was free from my leathers that I had worn so long they were practically welded to me. I had taken a welcome injection of quite high quality cat and felt wonderful. I was comfortable telling Saker to be the legate for once. 'I'd do it myself but I have to treat her.'

'I don't want to leave her.'

'Harrier will find you if there's any news.'

'Jant, I wish you had been more harmless.'

'Huh?'

'San is now wary of ambitious youth. I knew you came from East Bank Hacilith but your malfeasance became more obvious with time. Your ambition was as strong as Swallow's although it's long since grown decadent. San realised that such zeal could agitate the Circle. He needs no more felons nor makebates, idealists or drug dealers. He can't take the chance that she will turn out the same way – if it wasn't for your misdemeanours San would have made Swallow immortal by now.'

'Hardly fair!'

'Look after her well. And if you take drugs in my Palace again I'll have you locked in this room.'

'I'll try not to.'

'I can't risk the servants finding out. *Please* act like an Eszai.'

If you are an Eszai, then to act like you do is to act like an Eszai. I thought this loudly, but didn't dare say it.

'I shall talk to His Majesty. I didn't spend fifteen centuries preserving Micawater to have it destroyed by Insects now.' He kissed Swallow's hand and replaced it on the sheet.

At the end of the third week Swallow's fever turned to shivering and I knew the crisis was over. I altered her medicine from vulnerary plants to rubifacients and kept the healing stitches clean. Harrier was a great help, as he was far from squeamish and very willing to learn. I had to treat his wounds as well, which he had not bothered to look after.

Harrier was a likeable man, far more relaxed whenever his lord wasn't around. He was private but not secretive, polite but not obsequious, a servant who stood with shoulders squared. He had a house in Donaise, but he lived with his family as wardens in the Palace, and he was clearly proud that Lightning had so favoured them.

King Staniel offered no apology, and kept his guards close at hand. Lightning worked with him to plan trenches and bastions in Rachis Park. The soldiers' imposition caused riots in the town; we had to send them food and wine in order to ease the pressure. The towns of Oscen and Tambrine were destroyed in an Insect attack. A new prohibited zone was created, east to west, from the coast to the foothills of Darkling, which followed Rachis River and the manor estate boundary. The Insects responded by building their own wall, which terrified the civilians. It took a month of fighting for us to slow the Insect advance.

Swallow slept on, unconscious, all that time. At the end of the second month she woke.

'Will she ever walk again?' Lightning pestered me, as we walked through the water gardens to the impromptu infirmary. The gardens were dim and vacant, cut back for the winter; only a few red maples around the lake still gripped leaves.

I said, 'Insects stripped the muscles from her leg. I don't think she'll walk unaided. But she's intent on trying – determined as a human. I don't know if she can bear offspring now; it's unlikely. I haven't told her yet—'

The Archer stopped and stared. 'Swallow can't have children?'

'She was sliced from rib to hip, Lightning, I *haven't* Rayne's expertise. Come on!' Usually unhurried, now Lightning found it hard to walk and be dramatic at the same time.

'Swallow can't have children. Are you sure?'

'I can't tell for certain. But it's far too great a risk.'

'That's terrible! I … She was. We were … The way I see it, she still hasn't got long to live. No Zascai has. What will happen to Awndyn manor?'

I shrugged. 'Swallow's lucky to be alive. She's in a lot of pain, and I'm amazed at her progress. She's happy to still have eight fingers, two thumbs and a guitar. She can sort out the succession of Awndyn later.'

Swallow was propped up on plump white cushions; she gave us a brilliant smile as we entered the golden and sapphirine suite. I loved her courage, and it wasn't lost on Lightning. Dunes of manuscript paper covered the four-poster; slipping off onto the floor, scribble of semi-quavers marching like Insects. She held a jotter, full of torn pages and crossing-out.

Lightning eagerly gathered some of the papers and examined them. He began to laugh sincerely. It's impossible to begrudge or be jealous of genius; you must wish such extreme talent well. Genius sees past the separate circles of darkness in which we live, to the light beyond. Even without words Swallow's music can make the listener laugh; it's because she sees through to the great hilarity on the other side of everything. After her concerts people feel they have been touched by an almighty truth which they yearn to keep forever.

The composer was smiling too. 'Wait till you hear the darkness, the basso continuo power of the battle. You won't laugh then.'

'You must stay here and write it,' Lightning said.

'I kept my vow. Fought the Insects, didn't I? Although it didn't turn out exactly like I'd hoped.'

'Don't fret about Lowespass. Don't dwell on it.' Lightning and I knew that Insects were nightmarish creatures and, after an encounter, they find their way into nightmares permanently. Neither of us wished the terror of Insect dreams on innocent Awndyn. 'You're welcome to stay here as long as you want, until your strength returns. See how lovely the Palace is in spring. When you are ready, I'll ask the Emperor to grant another audience and we can pursue your claim to the Circle again.'

I had been creeping towards the door, thinking it would be kind to leave the couple to their conversation. Swallow said, 'No!' and started laughing. I hastily returned to the bedside.

'What?'

'Forget the claim, Archer.'

'What?'

Swallow paused, glancing at the blue damask canopy, dividing her agony into separate streaks of pain. She was much thinner, from sweating with fever and being unable to eat. In the vast bed, she even appeared dainty, with her millefleurs shawl over a faded print-silk blouse. 'I have a new perspective now. I'm not afraid of death any more. In that battle, and especially after it when I nearly died, I learned something I can't express. I can't even play it, and if I can't express it in music what chance have I in words?'

I suggested that she might at least try.

'I could try, and I might even manage to say something worthwhile, but there's no point in telling you, because you're immortal, and you could never conceive—' She broke off, mirthfully. She was managing to laugh at her experience. She laughed for a long time, with a clear happiness. Her eyes danced with happiness as weightless as it was profound. 'Immortality's pointless compared to what I can do.'

'Die?' said Lightning, with a voice like slate.

'Change. It's important for me not to forget this lesson – I'll bear it in mind always until it becomes a part of me ... All my life I've been knocking at the door, calling to be let in. San's refusal makes him ridiculous. Well, forget it.'

I looked from one to the other – Swallow was far more comfortable than Lightning. If there had been a year-long battle between them, she had won.

'But I still love you.'

Swallow just threw her head back and laughed harder than ever. He stared at her, not knowing what to do, then turned and walked out, slamming the door. I heard doors slamming – bang, bang, bang – all the way down the Long Corridor, which runs the entire length of the front of the Palace.

'Oh dear,' she said. 'I think that's an ending.'

In all, Swallow spent fourteen weeks in bed, in coma, in fever and in recovery. She spent a further week practising hobbling about on two crutches in the confines of the Palace and gardens. She played music and sang, to the limpid lake and empty flowerbeds in which she saw great beauty. Her eyes were bright with tears of wonder; she began trying to put her secret into music. Swallow was right that I didn't understand her, but I knew that no immortal could make music that magnificent.

At the end of November she took the coach back to Awndyn, unescorted. Unfortunately I missed the festivities of her departure, which Lightning insisted on holding. I didn't even see her leave, as throughout the celebrations I was locked in the sapphirine room.

CHAPTER II

To: Comet, for petition to the Emperor
From: Lady Vireo Summerday

12.11.15

Lowespass Fortress

I write to report that my town of Summerday has been evacuated. Families have moved south into Rachiswater. The warriors of Summerday and the entire regions of Lowespass, Midelspass and Miroir have come to Lowespass Fortress.

We do not have enough food. I have already begun to ration. None of us will survive over two weeks in these conditions.

Tornado has groups of fyrd working day and night to stop the Insects completing their wall around the fortress. We are being sealed in. Our efforts continue in vain; yesterday the wall grew fifty metres. While we demolish it on one side Insects build it on the other side of the keep. Their numbers are vast; in half an hour I counted three thousand. We are confined to Fortress Crag as Insects flood the valley. They make no sound except for their shells scraping as they clamber over one another.

Addendum:

Jant, if we could understand the way Insects work we would be much closer to defeating them. They place Walls at the extent of their captured land. It is as if the Walls are not to keep invaders out of the Paperlands but to keep the Insects in. They wall themselves in because they know we are dangerous.

I send my ideas in this letter because it might be my last. I fight every day. Please present my plea to Staniel Rachiswater. We need reinforcements now; I think soldiers from Rachiswater have the best chance of reaching us.

Vireo, Governor of Summerday and Lowespass.

Tornado, his mark: T

I spent the flight home and much of the night when I arrived at the Castle bitterly resenting how I'd been treated in Micawater. I can pick most locks, but the one on the door of the sapphirine room had been crafted by human hand in Hacilith and it was far too difficult to crack.

I had nursed Swallow, the singer who dabbled in warfare. I sent letters to King Staniel via Awian emissaries who were less likely to daunt him. I flew over Insect territory to carry Vireo's despairing letters from Lowespass Fortress. And all the thanks I received was to be locked up like a criminal.

Mist says that when he joined the Circle he was drunk for a decade, so it's possible that mainlining scolopendium may be just a phase of adjustment I have to endure, as I now wake every morning realising I'm two hundred years old and shouldn't be alive. When I'm hooked even Lightning's Palace isn't sacrosanct, and indeed nowhere is special except the warmth of cat, or the Shift hallucinations. I suppose I'm always going to seem like an outsider. When in Scree, I act like an Awian. In Awia, I behave like a Rhydanne, and when I'm in the Palace, I behave badly.

I started using scolopendium when courting Tern – it gave me confidence and energy so I could fly all night to Wrought and vie with her other suitors. Before that, when mortal, I was a dealer. I quickly saw the dirty side of the business and longed to stop trafficking but I couldn't, by then – Felicitia forced me.

Hacilith 1812

I was young when I first encountered The Wheel in Hacilith. Apprentice in Dotterel's pharmacy, I applied my knowledge from the dispensary to the streets. I had been working all night, for several nights, and was on my way to the market to pick up some crisps for breakfast. I took a paddle tram along the main street of Hacilith; they trundle slower than walking pace. From the front of each battered carriage a twisted cable runs, the length of several streets, ending in a hook. Where the trams terminate, all these cables run together, a greasy black web of tensed wire, at about head height. Boys were employed to shunt empty trams up and down the cobbled courtyards of the terminus. They played tightrope on the cables. They fastened the hooks, polished by the wear of a thousand grimy hands, onto the mechanism that pulled them – huge waterwheels standing in mesh cages and spinning slowly under the turbid assault of the Moren River. Many have lost limbs in the Shackle Sheds, but the trams remained more popular than the dreaded eventuality of having to walk into town.

The tram's slow movement was relaxing, a steady pull as the cable wound onto a reel. Soon, I fell asleep. The familiar landmarks of the narrow area I knew peeled away, and stranger sights gathered in the tram's dirty Insect wing windows. We passed the market, most passengers left, and I, oblivious, remained taking up most of the back seat. I often found places in Morenzia to be a little too small, but I had grown used to sleeping on a shelf in the shop's cellar. A tram's back seat was luxury in comparison.

A sudden halt jarred me awake. I rolled from the seat and pressed my nose against the window. Air drenched with the stench of oil, a rattle from the front of the tram as it was unhitched, and then a team of boys laid hands to the brackets on its sides and hauled it under a lintel and into darkness.

I listened to the chanting: 'One, two, three – heave!' as the baroque brass carcass slid along the rails. 'One, two, three – heave!' Grubby lads ran up the steps and started looking under seats for lost property to claim. They stopped in front of me, astonished, all crowding round.

'Who's that?'

'What's that?'

'What're you doin' here?'

'You're not supposed t'be here!'

'Kids that ride to the End of the Line *never leave!*'

'Shut up, Sam.'

I said, 'Please let me go now. I will reward any friend who can show me the way to Galt.' They grinned at my accent, and taut words – although proficient I wasn't familiar enough yet with the language to be sloppy. Smeared faces bobbed like balloons, but they didn't rush to offer help. Instead, the largest one leaned over, forcing me back into the seat. He had red hair poking through his string vest. I could smell oil and onions on his breath. I could hear his brain clicking as it freewheeled. 'I know you,' he said.

Oh no. Please. Not now. 'I don't think so.'

'You're the one Peterglass is looking for. The Bowyers offered twenty quid for the whereabouts of your den.' The crowd froze at the mention of such a healthy sum. 'Fifty quid for your dead body.' They regarded me inquisitively. 'A hundred pounds for you to be brought in, live and whole, so you can be tortured.'

Well, at least I was going to get out of the depot in one piece. 'No. I am afraid you are wrong. I do not know Peterglass. I have never heard of The Bowyers. You must be looking for someone else.'

'Oh yeah. Hundreds of people look like you round here, cat-eyes.'

'Well then it must be one of them.' I stood up and they grabbed me.

I've heard it said that crowds have a fine sense of right and wrong. Crowds made only of children have a fine sense of how many packets of sweets can be bought with a hundred pounds. I was pulled out of the tram, shoved, dragged and kicked over the cobbles while Hairy Shoulders and the older boys went into a huddle. They were all strong; I couldn't push between them, I couldn't see over their sweaty heads. Fists clung to every centimetre of my clothes like weights. In the midst of this gang I was tram-handled out into bright sunlight where they squashed me flat on the ground and sat on my wings.

Hairy Shoulders emerged from the huddle and declared, 'We'll take it to Felicitia. He'll be madder than an Insect if we sell it without showin' him.'

'My name is Jant,' I said indignantly from floor level.

He hauled me up by my T-shirt front. 'You just confessed.'

All the time, curious boys had been peering out from behind trams, slipping between the greasy wires, skipping over the brass rails as they dashed to join the throng. Untended trams were backing up in every direction; a dangerous squealing came from unhooked wires that pulled tighter and tighter. Hairy Shoulders didn't want to attract the attention of anyone over twenty, so he ordered most of the children back inside. Some ran to fetch their bicycles; others kept a firm grasp on me. Their leader hefted his finely carved bike onto his shoulder, encircled my upper arm with his other hand and led me, walking, what seemed like kilometres through the streets of Hacilith, junctions and alleys too many to remember, while a phalanx of orphans marched tightly alongside. Hooting kids on wooden bicycles swooped and raced ahead, and paraded along behind like a comet's tail.

A bicycle propped against the wall of a gin-and-cordial shop suggested much more wealth. The belt strap that drove its wheels was leather, not canvas, and it looked very well kept. It was upright and ebony. The boys poked their admiring fingers into the ornate carvings – horses, falcons and snakes. The seat was a wolf's head. A pink feather boa and satin streamers were tied to the handlebars. The bike was leaning under a sign which read, 'Drunk for a penny. Dead drunk for two pence. Floor space for nothing.'

Twin teenage guards in fyrd-surplus chain mail let us into the pub. We all squeezed through, then the crowd dissipated, leaving Hairy Shoulders and I alone. The room was quite small, with six round tables cluttered with debris of card games, smoking and drinking. The people there were all young, mostly in leather and denim, watching quietly. A fan snapped open and a voice behind it oozed, 'Vance, darling boy, what have you brought us?'

'I am Jant Shira and—'

Vance twisted my arm. 'This is the kid who's been dealing cat in Galt. Lord Aver-Falconet, as you know Peterglass of The Bowyers has offered money for him. I found him...' The voice trailed off into uncertain defiance. Aver-Falconet? That was the Governor's family name. I started to wonder why a backstreet kid would take a pseudonym from the family who must hate us so much.

The fan lowered, revealing a little, heavily made-up face. Lipstick mouthed, 'Really? A Rhydanne, no less! Isn't that totally behind the Wall! I can see why you haven't been caught all this time, unruly child.'

I simply gaped, mind blank and uncomprehending. It was a boy, I could tell that much. But he wore a green gown, and only girls wore dresses. Boys wore trousers. Girls could wear trousers or dresses. But boys never wore dresses. Did that mean he was a girl? Yes? Maybe he was a girl who looked like a boy. Or maybe it was a fancy dress party. I'd read about masquerades, but I thought they were usually more fun than this. Again Hacilith had thrown up something new; every time I regain my poise the city disorientates me. Trams, the sea, money. The crowds, crime, hierarchy. I thought I had grown so used to culture shock I could take these novelties in my stride. But he was the most confusing thing I had seen so far. I couldn't ask my master about this!

'Rhydanne ...?'

I half-spread my disproportionate wings. I knew Morenzians were sluggish people; that's why they needed bikes. I used to go everywhere at a flat sprint, and humans didn't do that. 'Only partly,' I said. 'I can run, and I can fly.'

The boy laughed delicately, then the rest of the room laughed too. 'Fly? No really? I don't believe that!'

Let them not believe it. With a little luck they would throw me off the roof.

'Shira,' he mused. 'By that name you must have been born out of wedlock. Rhydanne are very strict about that. I guess you're an orphan.' I nodded. 'And not married. Oh dear, oh dear, left on the shelf, my vigorous hybrid. I can see why you chose to come to the City.'

'Last year I ran away from Darkling because a landslide crushed my house,' I informed him. My voice had power even then; so factual it made them glance at each other. 'And Eilean Dara within it. She had thrown me out into the storm, so it was her cruelty that saved me. When the storm cleared I flew east until I fell from exhaustion.'

'And now you deal cat?' Smiling redly. 'I find it hard to believe. You must have been here for many years to speak Morenzian so well. Sweet darling, you certainly have Peterglass hopping mad, dealing drugs on his patch. Better quality, much cheaper, and much more prolific than he. Why do you sell such pain and suffering under the guise of pleasure?'

'Junkies would buy cat if I were here or not.' And my merchandise was the safest.

Dotterel had explained finance to me and once I had mastered the bizarre concept, I clung to it and pursued the gain of money with obsessive fervour – my new faith, a very reliable faith. Apprentices were not paid, but night by night I was gleaning what I could from the streets and quays. Surprisingly I had a talent for it. I could talk to anyone; they craved what I gave. I hoarded the crinkled notes in a little tin box. I would stop when the box was full. My aim was to have enough money to escape from Hacilith, or be able to set up my own shop, and marry, be accepted and loved. I was working to improve my life, who can blame me? I was dangerous because although I was good with coins, notes and white powder, life in Darkling had taught me bitter survival rather than affection or remorse.

The busty lady on Aver-Falconet's left took a sip of her gin and rose-hip syrup. 'We have to go soon,' she grumbled. 'Just kill him.'

'Tut, tut, Layce! Have you lost the scent of cash?'

I declared that I only worked for myself and alone. It was a stupid thing to say. Aver-Falconet rose with a rustle, and gestured to Vance. Vance and his lads rushed over and beat the shit out of me. A blow in the stomach and I doubled over. Back of the neck, chin and kneecaps. I managed to gouge the cheek of one of them; he kicked me in the balls. I dropped to the sawdust, curled up. Fuzzy black formed round the edge of my sight. I swallowed bile – please god don't let me be sick in front of all these boys. My lower half vanished in a sea of white flame.

A pair of green high heels minced into my field of vision. 'Oh, my milk-and-water miscreant. What a shame.'

'Piss on it,' called Vance.

'As if wrecking his chances isn't enough.' Aver-Falconet arranged me into a position where I could see the table. He swept the white cloth back, spilling bottles and lanterns. Under the table was a cage. The girl in the cage huddled away from the bars; she was so dirty that the terrified whites of her eyes were shocking as Insect eyes.

'This is the deal,' Aver-Falconet announced. 'Jant Shira, please join us. The Wheel is the ruling gang of Hacilith's East Bank. We offer you protection against Peterglass in return for only three-quarters of the profit you make.'

Still nauseous, I shrugged, shaking my head. I didn't need refuge, usually. Usually I could outrun a coach-and-four.

'If you do not agree with me I will let Serin here go free. She belongs to Peterglass's Bowyers and she will carry a message for us. Peterglass can come here and we will hand you over for an adequate price. I do not think they will let you live very long.'

The blonde girl in the cage soaked in his words. She realised I was an outsider, and was looking at me as curiously as I was at her.

There was a lull in the storm that seethed inside me. I was beaten already, or rather, beaten again. I couldn't fight these boys. Slum children were out of control, people said. They were right. 'Yes ...' I said. 'I know poisons, and the cures to them. Cat is only one of the medicines I make. I can earn two hundred pounds a week for The Wheel if you keep Peterglass off my back.'

'Who'll keep Felicitia off *your* back?' muttered Vance.

Felicitia? This *was* Felicitia Aver-Falconet? I stood up, painfully, and the older boy offered his hand. The fingernails were painted sea-green, with little rhinestones glued to them. A stroke of inspiration – I took his hand, and kissed it. There was a line of pinpoint scars on the back of his hand, reddened and bruised. I began to recognise the signs; he had his own reasons for recruiting me.

The fan flicked open like a peacock's tail to hide his blush.

'If I'd known who you were I would have sworn loyalty at first,' I said. He was the Governor's youngest son, estranged from the family and standing to inherit precisely nothing, but he still had the name. I knew it was important to feign interest in titles.

The room held its breath but Felicitia smiled. 'Don't mention it again.'

'Have you finished?' Layce's rough voice wilted his fan. 'Have we finished with the goat-shagger?'

'Yeah. Ah, yes. Ahem.'

'We have tickets to see Fevvers on the trapeze at the Campion. Like now. Let's move.' Layce's gang set down their glasses, gathered their coats and headed for the door. From outside came the sound of whirring bikes.

Layce took Felicitia's arm but he twisted away and addressed me again: 'Do you want to come with us?'

I stuttered. I'd never been to anything like the Campion before. I was afraid of the bright lights and the sheer number of vibrant people. If you could add together every sound over ten years' time in Darkling it would never make a din as loud as one night's performance in Hacilith. No doubt this would be the first trial of initiation. 'Yes ... Oh, yes – I would love to.'

'Can you ride a bike?'

'I'll meet you there.'

Layce had feathers on the back of her dress, fashionably aping the mainly Awian aristocracy. Her fake feathers were looking a bit worse for wear. Felicitia walked close by, one and a half metres of emerald chiffon sewn with glittering Insect eye facets. Should I be frightened? What does he want? Grown used to accepting, I accepted his hand on my arse.

All this self-pity was making me hungry, which curtailed my introspection. I set to work on Castle correspondence until the quadrangle clock began to chime midnight. By then I was so ravenous I couldn't concentrate on anything so I left for the Great Hall where meals are continuously laid out for the Eszai, visitors and servants.

The Castle was so quiet it seemed unoccupied, which suited me fine. I'm happy on my own until I hear other people enjoying themselves, and have to compare myself to them. If there were no other people I wouldn't feel alone.

CHAPTER 12

The Great Hall was tiled dark red at the servants' end, the colour of dried blood. Rows of pillars down the centre supported a vaulted ceiling. The Hall seemed larger at night as most of the tables had been cleared away. I glimpsed my frosted breath in the moonlight from a tall arched window. A sudden noise stopped me and I listened hard, heart racing.

I stood in the shadow of a red pillar and tried to make out the indistinct voices. Two men at the other end of the Hall were shouting in anger. I edged closer. There was a crash, a chair screeched on the tiling, a metal plate dropped to the floor. Still closer, it resolved into words.

'Well, I thought I would find you here, you bastard.' Petulant and deep, round Awian vowels like overripe fruit. Lightning. The other voice said something with a low sneer.

'Touch Ata again and you're dead,' said Lightning.

'I should have *known* she'd run to you. Port. Storm. When I catch her I'll—'

'You will have to pass me first,' the Archer pointed out. 'Everyone knows she is better than you.' There was a scuffle and another crash. Then nothing.

I couldn't think whether to stay and listen, or make my presence known. Blankness comes when I have to do something, when it's best not to think. For example when facing Insect swarms, or cooking a fix. That's it, I'm leaving. The part of me that charges the Insects or shoots an overdose took control. I dropped my hands to my sides and stepped out into oil lamp glare, stood there blinking.

'Boys,' I said. 'Let's not fight.'

Shearwater Mist was sitting on the edge of the table, leant back, his thick arms among plates of food. Blood was running down his leg from a shallow cut, pooling on the floor. Lightning stood over him with a sword; he had just taken Mist's own rapier from him. He had a quiver of arrows on his back, the embossed strap hanging down, and his flickering shadow on the ochre wall looked like a porcupine. I turned my attention from the suckling roast to Mist's lined face. 'What is this about?' I asked.

'Get lost, waif,' said Shearwater Mist. Lightning thumped him on the shoulder with the sword pommel. An Insect had once bitten through that shoulder, and the Sailor winced.

I edged forward but Lightning pointed the sword at me and sighted down the flat of its blade. 'Mind your own business,' he said.

He's right, it's not my business, and he doesn't want me to make it my business, and I shouldn't be creeping around in the dark anyway.

I closed the space in a couple of strides and grabbed Lightning's free arm. He flicked me away. Mist snarled, looking like a wolfhound. I felt like an alley cat watching lions fight.

'Stop that!' Lightning yelled at Mist.

'You have so much explaining to do, Mica,' Mist shouted back.

'You would be nothing if not for me!'

'Trying to steal it back? Pigs. Fly.' The sneer rolled up one side of Mist's face like paralysis. Lightning seemed itching to hit it.

I sneaked a bottle of plum wine from the table and sat down on a pillar plinth, watching them. Mist hooked the remaining fingers of his left hand under the quiver strap that ran diagonally over Lightning's chest, against his shirt. He tried to drag him closer. I thought the strap would break, and arrows would be all over the floor like pick-up sticks.

Lightning dropped the rapier, drew his own short archer's sword. He pressed it against Mist's neck so the blade ran behind his ear. 'You'll regret this,' he said. Mist tried to kick his knee.

Mist hadn't altered his twisted smile; he looked like a wry shark. Grey hair straggled on his collar, a broad white streak in his hair, which I thought couldn't be natural until I decided that nobody could keep it dyed for so long. His stony eyes were on the Archer.

'I'll tell San,' I declared.

'There are many things I could inform the Emperor about Jant,' Lightning called back. Extortion, our instinct.

'Go ahead,' I muttered.

'Just because you have all the money you think you can do what you like!'

'This concerns honour, not wealth!' Lightning bawled in his face.

'Money is honour,' I remarked irrelevantly, and Mist gave me a genuine smile for a second. Then the sneer was back firmly in place. He grasped Lightning's wrist holding the sword hilt, with his right hand, and squeezed. Lightning flicked the blade and a little trickle of blood ran down from behind Mist's ear. There was a battle of wills, Lightning's brawny arm tensing, the veins standing out on Mist's thick hand. The Archer dropped his sword, and Mist slid off the table with a foot on both blades. He picked the rapier up. I could see white fingerprints around Lightning's wrist; he narrowed his eyes as Mist squared up to him with the weapon.

'Shearwater ... ?' My voice sounded small.

'Get out of here, you inky-fingered waif,' he said menacingly. So I did.

I ran out to the courtyard, icy cobbles sliding under my boots. In the centre of the dark square I spread darker wings and struggled up to my window,

134

where I had left the shutters ajar. I kicked them open and stepped down into a deserted untidy room. The only sound was a steady drip of candle wax onto the floor, where blue stalagmites were growing. 'Tern?' I called. 'Tern! *Tern!* – Governor Wrought! You skinny horse.' A scribbled note by the dead fireplace informed me she had gone to Hacilith. She was asking the Governor to accept the refugees swarming her manorship, with the idea that she could do more for them further south, in the city.

I took a swig of sickly wine, realised I was holding a bottle. A potential weapon. Down in the Hall, I had a weapon all the time without realising. Not a very worthy one, to use against these Awian lords. I giggled.

I only cut someone with broken glass once – that was a rich lord too, back in Hacilith. I left the gin shop in the dark, walking through Galt's stained streets. Eventually I became aware of someone following me. I was so naïve; I had come as far as Cinder Street before the idea crossed my mind. The shop was nearby, the wings of its canopy folded back for the night. I couldn't risk a dash to safety; Felicitia would learn where I lived. Instead, I took a detour, ran round a corner. Outside the Kentledge pub, drunkards had vomited so often the pavement was starting to dissolve. I picked an empty bottle from an overflowing bin, smashed it and lay in wait.

A figure came round the corner, and I jumped for his throat. I pressed the glass to his mouth. If I had twisted it, it would have sliced out his mouth, and the skin around it, like a circle from a pastry cutter.

'Who are you?' I yelled. Fury is the main passion I remember from that age.

'Mmm mm mm!'

'Oh. Bugger.'

I removed the bottle tentatively, my fingers tight enough to break it, and Felicitia regarded me calmly. Blood was running into his mouth from a moustache of little cuts. He smeared his lips together like women do with lipstick, gave a broad red grin. 'Well, my belligerent boy,' he said. 'The East Bank gangs really do need you.'

These are memories of which Lightning and Mist couldn't conceive, and I can't imagine the sort of memories they might have. I crossed to the only clean table and lit the burner under my still, made sure there was enough water and fern in the hopper. This is something I do automatically every time I come into the room. I couldn't calm the older Eszai, I was truly useless. Lightning had always used Mist as a case in point when training me in combat, calling up examples of his foolishness. 'Protect your eyes, fingers, teeth. These things don't grow back. You don't want to live without them, like Mist who caught his hand in an anchor chain, back when he was a *common sailor.*'

I sat down at a writing desk and started transcribing orders, sealing them with the Castle's sunburst crest.

Several letters later – my subconscious had been counting the drops – the tone of their falling into a little glass beaker changed, and I knew I had enough cat to fill a syringe. The needle scratched against the glass as I sucked it up, still warm. I wound a leather bootlace round my arm, and after some messing about, sank it in a major vein.

Tiredness vanished. I went to sit back down at the desk. Cat's a work drug. Sometimes cat is a work drug. With a steady hand, I went back to scripting the commands that San wanted me to send out. After a quarter hour, the peak began to fade, but I resisted taking more. Then I went and topped it up with another shot. Wish I had veins like the Sailor's. I concentrated completely on the letters for a while. I have a theory that everybody in their lifetime gets fifteen minutes of ecstasy. Except me, 'cos I do it every night.

I crashed out of the second high too quickly to manage the distance between my desk and the still. Instead, I sat and stared into space, at the forested windows. Tiredness began to grow on me, unbearably. The glass was iced up in thin fern patterns, like fronds of Scolopendium. They swirled around each other, curving, moving. They curled like girls' downy feathers. I wish Tern were here. The frost plants changed colour slowly, becoming murky grey, then a sharp light blue. I was puzzled. Ice is white. Blue is not white ... Blue things are things like the sky ... During the day ... Daytime. Of course. I had better go to bed.

A hand on my shoulder shook me gently. I realised it had been there for some time. I gathered what little strength I had left and looked round. I found myself eye-to-eye with Lightning's belt buckle. My gaze travelled up to his square face, short hair the colour of burnt sand. He was losing his tan in the Plainslands winter. 'Good morning,' I said, in Scree by accident, then repeated it in Awian. I rubbed at my stubble; I need a wash.

'The door was open. I knocked but you gave no reply. It's cold in here,' he observed. He used my books as stepping stones through the chaos of papers, from *Posteventualism* to *Pharmacopoeia*, *Darkling Linguistics* and *Solution Chemistry* in three apologetic steps.

'Is it? I wouldn't know.'

A glance towards the still, which was dripping away, filling the air with a scent of hot oil and cut grass. 'Oh. Jant? Are you all right?'

A streak of the old fury flickered through me. The idiot was still carrying a quiver over his shoulder. He also wore a circlet, which hid in his hair like a gold worm in hay. 'I'm nothing. It's not fair. This is no time to pursue your sixteenth-century quarrels, Micawater!' I glared at the arrow tops until he swung the quiver from his shoulder and laid it, with a crackle of sticks, on the carpet. The arrow fledgings were dyed bright red, which is the Castle colour, but it also makes them easier to find in the snow, like little drops of blood.

Lightning makes a nervous gesture with his right hand sometimes, subconsciously. The frequency of that gesture shows how worried he is. He makes a fist with his hand, and then slides the tips of his fingers back over his palm, straightening the hand out. I know he does this to feel the deep ridges of a scar. When he was married to Savory, he grasped a sword and drew his hand along it, a quick motion cutting twice to the bone, from each edge of the blade. He loved her and the pale hollow of that scar must be very reassuring to him. It was because of the wound that he lost her, though. Couldn't shoot straight with a hand cut to shreds.

I pushed myself out of the chair, stumbled across to the divan, where I lay curled up, my head on a cool satin cushion. Lightning said, 'I wish to make reparation for what happened last night. You deserve an explanation.'

Did I? I didn't care, really. I wanted a hit. But still I was grateful that he had thought of me. 'I want an apology from Shearwater,' I declared, spreading a wing to form a bony blanket.

'Him? Ha!' Lightning passed a broad hand over his eyes, settled himself in the chair I had just vacated. He looked shattered, actually. 'I hate Shearwater Mist,' he said. 'San help me, I despise him and I always have. Ever since he joined the Circle. Violence is no way to treat a lady. Women are ... Ata is ... The way I feel about her is ... One should never strike a woman.' Yes. They hit you back.

I thought I had made a mess of my life with drugs, but that is nothing to some people's disasters with love. I offered him a broad smile of encouragement. 'Talk,' I said.

'Ata has an idea, to deliver Tornado from Lowespass. She can sail great ships, with fyrd on board, up the river, as close as possible to the base of the crag. We can fight to the Fortress from there, with much lower attrition than if we march by land. You know that Insects don't go into the river. If Mist's caravels could manage it, and I had archers on them ...' Lightning hesitated as he remembered how little I like ships.

'So you back this plan?' I asked.

'I don't know. It is a new way of fighting. I would prefer to rely on our proven strengths ... But I can think of no better way to reach Tornado.'

'Does the Emperor approve?'

'He thought it a great innovation!'

I said, 'Then I don't understand. Why doesn't he order Mist to sail up-river?'

'Mist won't do it. He advises San that the venture is impossible, Oriole River too shallow. They gave San conflicting information. Mist completely refuses to give her authority to try it. Then, right there in the Throne Room,

Ata Challenged him! She said: "Look to your title, Shearwater Mist!" They left the court and he turned on her.

'Ata sought me, for safety. She is still hiding in my room now; she locked the door. She is covered in bruises, Mist beat her; he is a coward and a miser. Ata wants to prove herself a better seafarer than him – and I think she is,' Lightning added loyally.

'What did San say?'

'That Ata has a legitimate Challenge.'

'Yes, but now, of all times!' I picked up a handful of letters. 'Summerday town, gone. Rachis, Tanager, under attack. Insects sighted in Wrought. In Carniss. Insects on the Alula Road. Avernwater wants aid, Sheldrake won't send any. We need Eszai in Awia; she is mad to make a Challenge now.' Mad or brave, I thought; and Mist is equally wrong to force her into it. 'It's a rash act; Mist will divorce her and San will throw her back into the flow of time, and I won't miss her.'

'To hit a distant target one must aim high. I do support her, if she really means to relieve Tornado and the Lowespass Fyrd.'

I was silent as what he said sank in. I examined the letters I had been writing to organise our operations; now everything had changed. I raised an eyebrow. 'The Emperor needs Mist, because with Staniel on the throne, only Peregrine manor will keep you from taking over Awia.' Probably females have nothing to do with it, I thought.

'No! Since Mist owns Peregrine? No! How *dare* you? I suppose you don't know. Listen. There is much you don't know, Jant. Peregrine is my land, as well; the manorship was mine. Mist is no more Awian than you are. His family are lying thieves, they only aspire to what they cannot be.' He sighed, gave me a shrewd look. 'It is hard to talk about the past,' he said. 'So spare me. I had to sell Peregrine manorship in the Bad Years. I didn't want my people to go hungry, and the coast was doing well. Shearwater had ships that brought us supplies. I lost Tambrine, and Donaise was completely deserted. I put vineyards there, where there had been houses, which is how I managed to buy Tambrine back. The Insects destroyed it last month ...

'Shearwater kept Peregrine, although I pleaded for him to return it ... *If you stick that needle in your arm again I'll thrash you!*'

'I, uh, wasn't going to. Would you like a coffee?'

'Please. And light the bloody fire; it's cold as an Insect's backside in here. What I am trying to convey is that the Shearwaters have always been opportunistic parasites without an ounce of morality between them. Thank you. Peregrine Micawater was my eldest brother. There were eight of us, and I had one sister. Peregrine was a traveller, he was a little like you in that way. He was a brilliant archer also. He visited Hacilith, and saw the Emperor's birthplace. He spent most of his time at the coast, where he built a mansion that we called Peregrine. It was under his orders that ships were first built, in order for him to sail between the islands. Previously Awia had no fleet. My brother wished for Awian ships to be the best in the world. Hence we have Awndyn, and the Aver-Falconets, and Shearwater, all owing to the power of ships.

'When Mother died Micawater was willed to Peregrine. I was in the Circle by then but to give the Palace directly to me would have caused some unrest. Besides, I was slightly out of favour with my mother's side of the family. He kept the lands well, although I realise his heart was sold to the ocean. Just like Ata. He added to the Palace as much as he could, because he knew that before he died, he would give it to me. And I could preserve it forever. I saw them all grow old and die or slain by Insects; Shira, you have not had that agony.

'My second eldest brother was still alive. He believed that he was next in line, and he wanted the Palace. Peregrine declined to give it to him. He did not respect Peregrine's wishes, and asked me for it. I refused and we had a terrible row. I said he was responsible for killing my sister. I regret that. His family changed their name.

'Shearwater Mist refused to bring his betrothed with him when he came to the Circle, believing he could have an eternity of young lovers, the selfish bastard. Now he goes through life with none at all, and serve him right!'

Lightning stopped, and gazed at me. He had been on a rush; the past's a drug for him. He did the weird gesture with his arrow hand again, the scar showing like a white ribbon.

I shrugged. 'We should be fighting Insects, and not each other.'

'God, I like you, Jant. So deep and meaningful. Fighting for Ata's cause might be the only way to beat them.'

'You love her, don't you?' I was rolling the sleeve back on my other arm.

'Not properly. It's all right, go ahead. Do it.'

'What?'

'Oh well. You treated Swallow, and you need a rest. Can I stop you?'

'It's more relief than reward,' I said, but Lightning had removed the thrill of guilt. I put the syringe down, still loaded.

He was digging in a pocket of his embroidered red coat. 'I have here a letter from Ata to her husband,' he said, offering me a square envelope addressed with very feminine script. 'I hardly wish to speak to him, so I would be grateful if you would deliver it.'

'Where do I find him? Harcourt?'

'In the Hospital. Rayne is mending his broken ribs.'

'Oh, *Saker!*'

'Nobody draws a sword to me, Comet. You should know that by now.'

Lightning seemed more light-hearted now that he had unburdened himself of a piece of history. He left, full of thanks, asking to see me soon. He thought he had an ally in support of Ata. He strode down the spiral stairs, and away in the direction of the stables. I shut the door, barred it, and began to fill the hopper of my still with fresh water. I had to figure out a way to steam this letter open.

Insects were advancing into Tanager and Wrought manors. Tern told me that the Wrought people were packing and moving out along the coast to Hacilith. I directed ten fyrd divisions to Eleonora Tanager, and sent a letter from the Emperor advising her to move west, and telling her how best to protect the people.

Next, I wondered how I could stop all this talk of caravels and fortunes. I wanted to stop Mist and Ata destroying each other when the Empire needed them both. And I would rather have a blow job from an Insect than go anywhere near a ship.

I sorted out clothes, soap and a massive meal of inoffensive things that I would hopefully be able to keep down, and then went to court, where I discovered that San had no inclination to stop Ata's Challenge. Then I flew to the Simurgh Passage and, hanging on a convenient breeze to the entertainment of quadrangle people, I figured out which windows were Lightning's, and which one of those had the curtains drawn. I landed on its windowsill, and tapped on the glass.

Ata's face appeared disembodied between the curtains. She swept them open and wrestled with the catch. One cheek was swollen and purple; her lower lip was split in the centre, a wide red gash. The face that launched a thousand ships. She was pallid and looked ghostly, but the fire of resentment in her eyes would have fuelled hundreds of phantoms. 'Queen of Ships,' I said, looking with horror at the bruises her makeup could not conceal. 'Did Mist do this to you? I'll kill him myself!'

'Yes, he did, but there's nothing you can do.'

Not face to face, perhaps, but I can put him and his fyrd in a bad position when we next fight Insects. I can talk Rayne into giving him some really nasty potions.

I produced the letter. 'I'm just checking that you still want me to deliver this.'

'Aye,' she said, her mouth twisting.

'I just have a slight feeling – call it a hunch – that you might have been very angry when you wrote it.'

'How—?'

'In fact never since you were a fledgling in gingham have you written such a furious letter.'

'I—'

140

'A letter so sharp you could gut fish with it. A note, succinct, but boiling with such execration and castigation that it would mean conflict between husband and wife, all-out civil war as well as Insect war in Peregrine, havoc and carnage and a fight to the death.'

'Come back when the drugs wear off,' she said.

'So you don't regret it?' I asked. 'You know him well, and you understand the effect that words such as might be contained in this letter would have on him. You're calling his bluff, or mine; that's fine, I only live here—' The platinum blonde reached out and pushed me off the ledge. My spread wings caught like hooks on the steady wind and I hung there, on a level with her teary eyes, slipping the note into my jacket.

'Give him it!' she spat. 'You're afraid of everything! Jant, the Emperor encouraged me. Why is Shearwater being so obstructive? Because it proves I'm a better Sailor! He's a sea trader, doesn't consider the opportunities that being a river rat might bring – I can do both! Frost says it's possible, theoretically on a spring tide. She's the best architectural engineer there is; she uses the river to control Insects, her maps are very reliable.'

'Ata, that means we only have ten days. It'll be hard to mobilise enough fyrd, but I'll try.'

'Nothing will stop me.'

I nodded. 'Ata Dei, I beg you to give me one more command. Would you like me to fly to Grass Isle and ensure the Sute Towers are yours? I can ask Bittern Diw to lay in supplies.'

The ghost gleam in her eyes became searchlight strong. 'Aye.' She beamed. 'I'll never trust you, though. Come back tonight and there'll be letters ready.'

'Can't wait,' I said, angling my wings so I was flung straight up, like a kite. The wall sped away, shrank, and soon I was looking at the moss-green Castle roofs. Now I knew something that the Archer didn't; how dare he say, 'You deserve an explanation'! I had to know more than him about what was going on; it was a heavy habit to feed.

Shearwater Mist was the only man in the Hospital, so he was receiving Rayne's attention in full. I think she was inventing things to do to him. I had been the subject of her experimentation before, with my Rhydanne need for eight-thousand-metre-altitude air and my heart rate that goes down below fifty. I knew how thorough Rayne could be. She showed me where he was, sitting up in a starched white-sheeted bed. Grey eyes watched me woefully; he breathed through a dry, open mouth, little sips like a dying animal. Grey chest hairs like wires poked over the bandages. The bandages were wound around his muscular chest under his white shirt and pale yellow cravat. Rayne must have stood on him to pull them that tight. 'Hello, waif,' he gasped. 'You're looking smart. I should have dressed up. Beggars. Choosers.'

'I'm not staying long,' I said. 'I am here to give you a letter from Ata. She requires no immediate answer.' I handed him the envelope, checked my exits and stood well back. It lay on Mist's injured leg, looking tiny. 'Aren't you going to open it?'

'Jant,' he sighed, 'I'm sorry about last night.'

'Never—'

'That this happened to me. Pride. Fall. Lightning is a quite excellent swordsman. When Rayne lets me leave here I'll confront him again. This time without such an audience. Flies. Shite.'

I was nettled but kept calm. 'On the other hand if you want a neutral go-between, I'd be happy to oblige,' I offered, dodging his sundial nose as he shook his head.

'Horse. Water. You're known for disobedience, and I should think that Lightning has told you his side of the story by now.'

'He has.'

'I hate him. Him and his bloody hunger to call all Awia "Micawater" and leave none for the rest of us. Dog. Manger. The problem is people believe the richer side to every argument. I know I have no support. He's greedy and loud; though I keep stating my case no one listens. Head. Wall.'

'I would preferably describe him as acquisitive not esurient.'

'What?'

'I understand your side to the story. It's far more reasonable than Lightning's.'

'Really?'

'I looked it up. He sold Peregrine to you in the drought of the fifteen-eighties. It seems a fair deal to me. In fact it's despicable to bear a grudge for so long; it's affecting his judgement. Everybody knows how fiercely Lightning conserves Micawater, believing he owes it to his family. I had no family, so I don't understand his need. The other issue doesn't concern me. I'm Rhydanne. We're not fond of prying. What you and Ata do is between yourselves.'

'Yes.' The wedding ring on his index finger, a battered stripe of gold. 'At least I *had* a wife. Bird. Hand.'

I gave him the thin benefit of a cat-eyed stare. He couldn't meet it. When I was in Hacilith I always avoided eye contact. I dropped my gaze to the floor when passing men in the street. I craved obscurity, knowing that they would gape in amazement, or throw names and stones after me. Now, difference seems to be a source of power.

'Can I rely on you to join me against the Insects?'

'Of course, waif. By land, out of Rachiswater. Safety. Numbers.'

I said, 'Now you sound like Staniel.'

'He's a fool but he's a King,' Mist said, regret in his veteran smoker's voice.

'Who's to say he won't be a fool with Eszai behind him? It's our best base to strike north; he has over fifty thousand men in Rachis town. I have the future of my manor in mind. I don't want it to suffer Staniel's displeasure. One hand for yourself and one for the ship, as they say in Diw.'

Mist coughed, and winced. 'Jant, why won't San trust me? Live longest. See most. I told him, about seven metres depth is what you need, and you don't get such margin in a river. An unloaded caravel draws five metres in salt water; loaded, and in fresh water they displace more, of course. San listened to Ata because she's loud, not because she's right. Squeaky wheel. Grease. The Oriole bay's all tide races and sand bars. Ships above five hundred tonnes don't enter, they discharge at Summerday. These are ocean-going caravels, not bloody barges. Book. Cover. They're fouled with weed and all kind of dross; they'll drag in a river current like they had sail underwater. If Ata tries it she'll be beached, drowned or torn to bits by Insects. But, desperate diseases. Desperate remedies; no one will dare Challenge me again.'

I told Mist that was why I was here. Ata seemed very angry with you, I said. I seem to remember she has fyrd in Diw, as well as on Grass Isle at the moment. I finished these musings with a suggestion: 'Should I order her fyrd to Awndyn? I'm sure you would rather not face three thousand Islanders if things get rough.'

Shearwater thought for a while. 'Do it,' he said.

'At your word. Is there anything else?'

'Er. No. Not yet, waif. Thank you.'

I made my way out of the Hospital as his nicotine-stained fingers began tearing at Ata's envelope. I resisted an urge to dash, but found myself walking faster and faster, with ever-longer strides until I reached the relative safety of the bleached white corridor. I paused there, head on one side, and a scream then a stream of abuse and cursing in Plainslands ricocheted down the corridor and burst around me like flame. Sailor's swearing could melt lead.

Shit. Fan. Life is certainly becoming more interesting these days.

CHAPTER 13

Ata left the Castle on horseback. I made sure her journey was fast; she reached the coast two days before her husband. I left her on the quayside at Diw, before a brilliant pink sunset, which melted the massive sky and still ocean together in waxen rose. A boat was prepared for her, five men to row. She stepped down and rested a sixth oar in the lock, saying that she would row with the rest. They splashed out of the harbour and towards a caravel's sharp baroque hulk.

Diw manor belongs to Ata's daughter. She has another two sons who are jewellers, and two who build ships. Originally Ata had five daughters, all of whom married. The five daughters had twenty-five children, of whom ten married. The twenty-five grandchildren had a hundred and twenty-five great-grandchildren. The hundred and twenty-five great-grandchildren had six hundred and twenty-five great-great-grandchildren. After that I stopped counting. Ata put word out that she needed help, gossip ran round her network like a rat in a treadmill, and money started pouring in to Diw.

Some of Mist's children supported him, but he usually paid them little attention. Ata kept in touch with the intricacies of all her generations, and they defended her keenly.

Pink became crimson, then dark and darker purple. I rode failing thermals from Diw to Grass Isle, a black cutout clustered with lights. Ata built a flock of twelve towers there, around the coast, before the Emperor forced her to stop. They were known as the Sute Towers, and each looks out over a separate expanse of ocean. No ship could put in at the Island without falling under the silent watch of those squat sentinels. In this way Ata made the entire island her stronghold, while Mist had simply embellished the port. I soared around the island's circumference, twenty minutes from Towers January to December, sound of breaking surf and stink of burning sea coal. When lights came on in the meeting hall of July Tower I cut short my circuit and landed on a red-tiled roof. From the ridge to the eaves, in through an open window, and I was suddenly in the midst of crowds: servants and sailors knocking each other over in their haste to obey Ata's orders.

At length the sparse hall was empty. Sute was abandoned to a garrison only. Lights were extinguished across Grass Isle, keys turning in locks, doors were being barred. The air of finality was terrifying; Ata was clearing her island for troops. Motionless, I had waited at the window, and now Cyan and her nursemaid were the only civilians left. Ata sighed and slid into a chair behind her candle-lit desk. She suddenly looked old. The bruises on her face were brown and yellow, like a frieze of autumn leaves. Her hair was a white silk shawl, paler than her bronzed skin. She crossed legs in tight blue leather trousers, folded azure slashed sleeves over a waistcoat embroidered with cobalt-blue and ivory plumes. Her shirt pulled tightly over shoulders rounded and upper arms flattened with muscle. She stared into space.

I eyed Cyan's maid, who was sitting on the floor trying to interest the reticent child in an ugly doll. I had always assumed nursemaids to be stern old women, but this one was thin and under thirty, and very attractive.

Ata sighed and leant back in her winged chair. A little bulge of fat showed over the top of her belt. Fat softened the line of her jaw and candlelight accentuated crow's feet around her eyes. The rest of her body was still youthful steel. She could easily beat me in a fair sword-fight. 'You know, Comet,' she said. 'I just can't figure you at all.'

I waited. I use silence as my main defence; flatlanders drown in silence, they find it unbearable. They will say anything, no matter how stupid or recriminating, in order to break it.

'I mean, why are you here anyway?'

Creating debts. 'Awaiting my lady's command.'

'Don't take me for a fool! You're watching the show. Well, I swear you this, the show will be worth watching.' She stood up and walked across the room to Cyan, past the girl, to the window and back. She paced back and forth, saying, 'I've had all I can stand. I'm doing what I should have done six hundred years ago. This is what I was born for! But no – I thought he was right and I was wrong, and in a moment of self-doubt I followed him. Now things will change! My stupid husband waits for instruction from Rachiswater – Staniel is killing Awia with cowardice!

'I should have Challenged Shearwater; by god I *did*, then lost heart. So I married him and sailed with him for six hundred years. Six hundred fucking years! Blood and sand! Sorry, Cyan. Come here, child. I thought joining the Circle by marriage would be as good as having the title myself, but it isn't, of course. Shearwater takes the credit for everything I do and I never had the fucking guts to complain! Those ships still fly the Awian ensign. Not any more! No fucking longer! There will be no pennants on the Castle fleet. My flag will have no emblem. I'll nail his balls to the mast!' She paused. 'I need you, Rhydanne, but I don't know how to play you. You're too damned smart. No loyalty.'

I sat down cross-legged on the window seat. Behind me, a sheer drop to the sea-washed rocks. 'I do admire independence. You say it took you six hundred years to realise what I realised at the age of six. But then, I was put through a harder mill than you.'

'Oh, you were?'

'Yes.'

She crouched down behind the desk, leather creaking, her sword-hanger's gilded chain clinking against the basket hilt. She slid the bottom drawer open and took out a stack of banknotes tied with ribbon. 'Your loyalty is to money?' She gave the ribbon to Cyan for her hair. The sheaf of notes was split in half and counted. 'This is all I have left,' she said, which I didn't believe. 'Take two hundred pounds. It will come in useful next time you go to Hacilith.'

'Ata, I'm not asking for money.'

'I've heard tell you need all you can get.'

I took the battered grey notes from her, riffled through them and shoved them in a frayed coat pocket.

Ata continued, 'Mist is the Castle's Sailor; it's your duty to do what he asks, no matter how much I pay you. You're a wild card. Well, we're all wild cards; every card in the fucking pack is a joker.

'Take Cyan down to the harbour. A boat is waiting. Make sure she is safe at all times, cross from September Tower to Peregrine Quay, where there is a coach. A closed carriage, please – watch for Insects! Deliver her to the nearest place where she will be absolutely safe ...'

'Which is?'

'Micawater Palace.'

I giggled. 'Lightning will never agree to—'

'He already has. If you wish to return you must fly because there will be no sailing between the coast and the island after you leave. Cyan will have the last boat out. Also, there will be no access past the island, Awia will have to manage its affairs and affrays by land.'

I stared at her. She shrugged, hands down on Cyan's chequered shoulders. 'It isn't as bad as all that,' she said. 'There'll be a fee to escort ships taking fyrd to the front.'

'You mean a toll?'

'I mean a fair price for the pilot. The *Ortolan* and another five caravels will enforce it in the south. The sound will be patrolled by four caravels, which will be fast enough to cut down Mist's ship.'

I hadn't been aware she had such resources under her control. Then I realised she had everything that Mist left in Diw – sixty caravels – the *Stormy Petrel* and the *Ortolan* with the greatest weight of sail.

She continued, 'I am afraid that you will take my child to the manor rather than through Peregrine and leave her with Mist. You will not do that, of course, because Lightning expects to receive her – and you want to keep your creditor content.'

'I'm not a bloody nursemaid, Ata.'

'No.' She shrugged. 'You can always refuse.'

'Oh, I'll do it. But San will hear of this.' I slid off the windowsill and

146

offered the girl my hand. Cyan clung to her mother's leather knees. She patted the child's shiny hair – candlelight reflecting in a halo around her head – and whispered something in her ear. Cyan grabbed two bundles of blue skirt, ran to me, stopped just short, and raised a hand solemnly.

'Cyan Dei of Peregrine,' she said, timidly.

Ata winced. 'Of Sute, darling.'

'Of Sute. Pleased-to-meet-you, sir.'

'Jant. At your service and that of Sute.'

'Right,' said Ata briskly, turning away and sitting at the olive leather-topped desk. 'You leave with the tide, so you have five hours. Until then, Rhydanne, make yourself useful – do what you do best. Take yourself down to the Night Jar, and buy all the sailors drinks on my behalf.' She split the sheaf of notes again and handed me roughly a hundred pounds. 'Listen to the gossip; I want to know all their thoughts and fears. I want you to play your fortune cards for them when they ask, and you will predict that every skirmish between my *husband* and myself will end in my favour. Can you do that convincingly?'

'Easily.' I smiled. I bowed to her, shook out my wings, watching Cyan's astonished eyes. I climbed out of the window, and welcomed a waking rush of air. The girl clattered to the window, hands on the sill, and gazed out on my slow glide down to the dark quay.

I can tell by the way the road is becoming smoother that we have almost reached Peregrine. Anxiety grows on me. I say anxiety when I mean fear. The coach stopped briefly to change horses, but I kept the blind down. It is between two and three in the morning and we have been shaken like dice in this tiny black lacquer box all night. My coach has no insignia, the dirty windows are made of veined Insect wings, the flat springs squeal at each corner, every bump in the road. The landscape outside will turn pale grey soon, and we will rush screaming and foam-flecked into another dawn. There will be myths of ghost coaches on this highway.

The ceiling is a canopy of rusty taffeta; the walls are dented plywood. I sit on an uncomfortable leather-covered bench and gaze at the little girl opposite. I find myself wishing she had twenty more years, and that this was Hacilith, not the Awian border. She is lying on the bench, knees pulled up under a long dress, her head resting on my coat. She has a copper ring on her tiny finger, and a wide lace ribbon loosening on a flaxen ponytail. That is all; no coat, no luggage, no spare clothes. I carried her on my shoulders over the fetid beach at midnight, and I am plastered in gritty mud, and sweat from having been in a boat, but at least her white socks are still clean.

'Not a word from you,' I had said, lifting her into the coach. She shrugged, unbuttoned her ankle boots and curled up. 'Aren't you scared?'

'No.'

'Well, you should be.'

The ring was a minute dolphin, which looped her little finger, its tail welded to its snout. She was more interested in it than in the real world. 'Do you know what's happening?' I asked her.

'Yes.'

'Mummy and Daddy are fighting again. Only this time it's for real. This is serious. Cyan Dei, look at me when I'm talking.' I pushed my sunglasses down my nose and glared at her over the tops.

'You're one of them,' she said, 'aren't you?'

'One of who?'

'People who don't die.'

'That's right.'

She gave a contented sigh and put her head down on my coat, evidently deciding she was perfectly safe. She was asleep in minutes. Her trust was touching, which is why I have been watching over her all night.

We sped through Peregrine manorship with the coach blinds anchored tight. I remembered how the gang used to tip coaches over in Hacilith, with a rope strung across the cobbled street. Wheels spun helplessly in the air, we slit open black beetle carapaces with cleavers and swords, pulled out spluttering riches and spilt the horses' hot blood.

A single Insect could scare horses into bolting, and then we would be out of control. On guard, I waited for all this to happen in confused darkness, but we were lucky; no roadblocks, no starving Insect packs, and then we were through.

Cyan woke with the first rays of sun, and stretched along the bench. Splinters caught at her skirt. 'Have we got any food?' she said.

'No.' I pulled a silver hip flask from the top of my boot. 'If you want, you can have some of this.'

Her fingers traced embossed knot-work around the bottle. She seemed to love beautiful things, shiny things. She unscrewed the lid, sniffed. 'What is it?'

'Sloe gin. From the Night Jar.'

Cyan took a sip, seemed to like it. She sipped again and rolled the sticky liquid around her tongue. Definitely Ata's child, I thought. 'Steady, steady. It'll make you sick!'

She pulled the dolphin ring from her finger and offered it to me. 'My father gave me this,' she said, and started coughing. I slapped her on the back. When the girl could breathe again she continued, 'Could you please give it to him? To say that I'm safe and I still love him. Very, very much.'

'Of course I will, Cyan.' I am taking orders from an eight-year-old now.

*

The smooth, shortbread-coloured stone of Micawater Palace glowed in blue daybreak light. Harrier stood on the steps, between fluted columns, in a striped grey waistcoat and narrow trousers, long peach lace cuffs hiding his hands. Ornate gates clanged shut behind us. I lifted the blind so Cyan could see as the aching horses slackened and we scrunched along a long, curved driveway and rocked to a halt in front of the main entrance. I unfastened the coach door, kicked down the folding steps and emerged at last stretching thankfully and measuring the sky; this was a fine morning.

Tackle jangled as two boys rushed to steady the ebony horses and a third to help down the weary driver. A cup of steaming coffee pressed into his hands, he was accompanied into the house. I lifted Cyan from the coach and placed her on the ground. She fell over. The coach drew away promptly. I removed my hip flask from a ruddy hand and stuffed it hurriedly into the top of my boot as Lightning's steward approached.

'Good morning, Comet,' Harrier announced.

'Jant,' I corrected him. 'I trust you're well? How's the Insect bite? No, we've had an awful journey. This is Ata's daughter, please take care of her. I have to be going now.' I rescued my coat as Cyan tried to stand up, hiccuped and sat down again in the gravel. Even her hiccups were slurred.

'Comet, are you sure you will not stay? We have breakfast laid out especially.'

'I don't eat breakfast. In fact, I don't eat. Give Saker my regards. Bye.'

Harrier hauled Cyan to her white sock-feet; she dangled in a bundle from his hand. Puzzled, he tried to walk, but she kept straying out too far to one side, then swaying back and banging against his elegant legs.

I swept my wings through the air in a full beat, realising hopelessly I was too hungry and exhausted to fly back to the Castle immediately. Harrier must have noticed because he foisted the hospitality of his lord's palace on me once again. 'If you wish to rest and wash, the guest rooms are prepared.'

A place to sleep. A place to lie down. Somewhere to shoot up, even. That was an unfortunate thought; a shiver ran through me, pooling the tension unbearably in the joints of my limbs. I gave Harrier a look of helpless pride. 'Please ...' I said.

'Our pleasure.' He took a handful of the back of Cyan's dress and hoisted her effortlessly onto one shoulder, strode under the pediment towards a gleaming entrance hall, the reflection on his polished shoes miniaturising the architecture.

CHAPTER 14

When I arrived back at the Castle I found a note pinned to my door. It was sealed with light blue wax, six numbers only, a map reference. I followed it to where the ocean slides ugly up against the land – Sheldrake harbour, at night and without a breath of wind. It was eerily calm and warm.

Two towns – a real one and a bright reflection in the bay. I saw the reflection first and thought I was upside down. What the fuck is going on? What are all those clouds?

The harbour was burning, the fleet, ablaze. Flames pulsed yellow – smoke plumes were thickening, drifting out to sea.

One of the piers was burning through. I could see figures trapped at the seaward end. They were crushing together, yelling above the roar.

I circled the quayside, saw floating blackened planks and pale corpses jostling in steaming water. Ships' ribs clutched like fingers in the yellow light. Smoke stank of pitch. Mist's flagship was anchored in the centre of the bay, well away from the fire ships, over its own rippled image. I flapped across to it, and a series of pennants went up which read, 'Ata has done this.'

I landed on the raised deck at the stern, unsure whether to cling to the railings and risk going down with the ship if she sinks, or to stand on my own two feet and risk falling over the side and drowning. In reality the *Honeybuzzard* was solid and perfectly safe. How could something so vast and ornate sit on the water, or steer round rocks and evade sea-monsters? How could people build ships this big? How can vessels so huge actually move? The flagship waited at anchor like a thoroughbred.

I gazed at the planks and fidgeted; sweat ran down my wings. Flame from all along the coast glowed orange on the deck.

I recounted, 'Mist, there are four caravels in the Sound. If you sail in the lee of the island you would have to contend with six more. That's all I know. Can I go now?'

'Sail *how*? With the fleet in *ashes*? Look at all my ships! Where has that bitch hidden my daughter?'

'... Micawater Palace. May I leave?'

'How did she get there? Fly? Where is Lightning?'

'Shooting Insects in Rachiswater. Can I please get off this ship?'

Mist had reverted to the Plainslands language, giving the impression he was feeling hunted. He had an expressionless brunette perched on his knee. She wore velvet shorts, and the dimpled flesh of her thigh overhung his leg. Half a cigarette festered in a scallop shell.

The shell ashtray held down one of my maps, which was scrolled out on the deck, paper cracking with age. I caught myself thinking that one tiny error, a miscalculation or omission, would lead to these ships stove in by serried rocks, hundreds drowned and the knowledge never reaching me.

Lord Governor Shearwater was wrapped in a long heavy blue cloak with gold trim, although it wasn't cold. His thick arms knotted around the woman's little waist, his backside on the railings, chin on her shoulder, the gold chain from his stiff cloak collar straining across his broad chest. 'Tell this to San,' he said, pointing at the wrecked harbour. 'See what Ata's done – trying to force me to Lowespass? I've lost forty ships, and who knows how many men! Bad to worse. How could the Emperor let Ata be immortal when she's capable of this destruction? At such a time! She can sit and starve on her paltry island. I'll return to Peregrine and find a way of stopping her for good.'

Speaking of Cyan led me to remember her ring, which had fitted easily on my finger and was presently turning it green. I gave the copper dolphin to Mist. 'The girl asked me to return this.' He looked at it with no recognition in his leathery face, rather scathingly as the ring was a cheap little token.

'Well,' he growled, nipping the fleshy lass's mottled thigh, 'I don't know. There's been so many. Drop. Ocean.' She giggled, lifting her head back to kiss air that smelt of burnt meat.

'No, not a girl. A *little* girl.' I held my hand, palm down, at the level of my knee.

'None of them have ever been that small,' he said defensively. I was obviously wasting my time, but Cyan deserved persistence.

'You don't recognise it?'

'Jant, I've never seen it before. You must be mistaken – one fix too many.'

A powerful arm wound back; he hurled the ring across the deck and over the railing. It dropped into darkness.

As it left his hand I moved. I dived from the rail. Two strong flicks of half-folded wings drove me down faster than falling. I couldn't see the ring. Hull sped up. The water came up, rippled bronze. The ring, a speck. I shot out a hand, snatched it as it hit the water.

I spread my wings, flattened my fall. I skimmed out over the surface of the sea. Tips of flight feathers touched, flicking drops into an arc. Pain flamed in the small of my back. I calmed it by breathing in time with quick wing beats. I kept going and built up speed to gain height and turn steeply.

The ship's hull was metal-clad. The figurehead had pink tits. A red lamp marked the stern. I slipped into a glide between rigging and masts. I came in fast. No wind to land into, so I backed with massive wings streaming the pennants out. The deck came up hard under my feet, jarring both ankles. I ran a few steps with a springy gait to slow down.

I started shaking, the ring tightly clenched in one hand. 'You bastard! Arsehole. Mist, you know I can't swim! Shit.'

The girl had detached herself from his grasp and was gaping at the railings, the paintings on my wings, my Rhydanne eyes, and giving me a look I've come to expect: 'What the fuck *are* you?'

Mist pulled a gold case of cigarettes from a back pocket. He plucked one out and offered it to me. He leant back, the smoke from his cigarette staggering into the air whilst smoke from the burning fleet and the Sheldrake breakwater billowed into cumulus above. I scraped a match and drew hot, constricting air into my lungs thankfully.

Cyan, I thought, you clever girl. I had underestimated her. 'Give the ring to my father,' she had said. Now I have to find out who he is.

CHAPTER 15

The Throne Room carpet was a bright crimson tapestry, a vibrant purple-red. Gold threads formed a swirling design of gold leaves or feathers or waves, which appeared to move. There was also a network of little blue dots but these were actually hallucinations caused by the exertion of flying too fast, and from doing back-flips on the wet roof ridge in order to impress Tern.

The edge of the carpet had a long gold fringe, like girl's hair. I followed it up as it angled over one marble step, a second, a third, but I couldn't follow its shining ascent any longer because the Emperor's throne was on top of the dais and he was watching me intently. It was not good manners to return his gaze. I couldn't because a recent dose of cat was singing in every capillary and if I looked at him, I would get the Fear. Not that the animated carpet was any better, I kept my head bowed and wished that the blue dots would go away.

'I don't think that's all you have to say,' San remarked. Somewhere above me, in a cradle of marble lace and folded samite, he sighed and stretched. I concentrated on a slightly more threadbare patch of carpet where I have kneeled thousands of times before. 'Because,' San prompted, 'I have been reading your letters from the coast. Thank you for your commentary, keeping the Circle so well informed of this unique situation.'

Was that sarcasm? I couldn't decide, so I gave him the same sort of silence as I would any flatlander. Time was nothing to the Emperor; he simply out-silenced me. This could go on for hours.

'My lord?'

'Letter the first, Diw is burning. Second, Sheldrake quay is razed by fire. Third, Awndyn fights a skirmish to protect the ships in her harbour. Additionally a letter from Carmine Dei asking for soldiers to protect Moren port because she doesn't want that to go up in flames as well. Tell me, Comet, does the fleet have any harbours left?'

'My lord, it's more like there is no fleet left.' More silence. 'Ata stole sixty ships from Diw. Those she could not crew she burnt. She sailed them all to join her caravels at Grass Isle. From there, she sent ships to burn the docks and everything at anchor in the rest of Mist's harbours. Awndyn harbour was spared, as Swallow's fyrd defended it. Throughout, Ata suffered no losses. Her ships returned to the island, where she now stays. She moves from tower to tower on the island, which is inviolable. I dispatched her infantry to Awndyn manor; I intend to use them against Insects in Rachiswater until Ata's Challenge is resolved.'

'How is Mist?'

'The last time I saw him, he was preparing to race to Peregrine before Ata could catch him.'

'No. I mean what does Mist have left?'

'Only what was at sea two days ago and escaped. The *Honeybuzzard*, with a loyal crew.'

'That is all?'

'One square-rigger, my lord. Ata has eighty ships – I counted.'

'So Ata is trying to make it impossible for Mist to proceed, or to move anything by sea at all.' The Emperor smiled wolfishly.

'Not trying to, my lord; she has.'

'What does Ata ask of us?'

I searched my memory through a haze of cat which unpleasantly seemed to be hauling me upwards. 'She sends this message, "I wish to replace Shearwater Mist and I will return to the Castle only to become immortal, or I will harry the coast and every ship afloat until the end of my days."'

I paused as the Emperor huffed angrily, and his liver-spotted hand clenched into a fist.

'Ata asked me to report that she regrets people have been killed, but says that would have been avoided if Mist had not been King Staniel's follower. She regrets that Mist lacks the flexibility of thinking, or is not brave enough to seize the opportunity we have to use caravels, the excellent service she is offering to the Castle, my lord.'

His pearl brocade cloak folded awkwardly as the Emperor leant towards me, lamplight reflecting on the white-gold spired crown. 'And the tone?'

Exhilaration. The frustration has forced her to chance things for herself. Now she's free and all the possibilities are crying out at her. 'She's awe-struck by her own determination,' I said.

'Did Mist send a message?'

'I left Mist when the *Honeybuzzard* got underway. His cheerfulness holds together like broken glass which a touch will shatter. He says this: Taking tolls is against the law, not to mention Ata's terrible piracy of coast towns. He begs you and the Circle to agree that she has gone too far. He asks that she be divorced and expelled from the Circle. He said any additional punishment ... Any additional punishment is the Emperor's prerogative. He never asked for help in regaining his ships or his daughter, or his standing.' Eszai never ask for assistance. It would leave the world in doubt that they really are the best.

The hall behind and the space above me to an ornately painted ceiling was vast, boundless space as well as to either side. I could easily fly in such a massive hall, between the slender engraved collections of pillars, through the circuits of galleries lining the turret. All this space concentrated on the

154

Emperor's throne, under a tasselled portico, draped with cloth of gold. The cloth was deeply embroidered, the lavishly intricate Awian crest on one side, on the other the arms of Hacilith Moren. The Plainslands emblem was a white horse rampant, the size of a man, and its cleft silver hooves could just be seen projecting from behind the Emperor's bony shoulder. San asked me, a gnarled finger to pale dry lips, what I thought of Ata's behaviour. I told him it was unthinkable that Eszai should fight each other and not Insects, and he knew I really believed it. I would not support Mist or Ata. I wouldn't say who was less to blame. When I felt brave enough I asked, 'What will the Castle do?'

'Do?' He said, making me feel tiny. 'Why, Comet, we let it run, of course.'

'Yes, my lord,' I said meekly.

'Go and watch them. This is Ata's Challenge to Mist, is it not? How else can we decide who is the superior master mariner? By now she has learnt all his knowledge. Now let us see who has the greater skill. Return often, and tell me everything.'

'Yes, my lord.' I surprised myself by being steady enough to stand, reasonably gracefully. I turned to go.

'Comet, why are there Insects in Awia?'

My silence this time was not on purpose. I simply didn't know what to say – Insects are taking over because we are not slaying them. There are too many to deal with.

'I don't know,' I mumbled.

San put on a show of fury. He slammed his fist on the marble armrest, making the tasselled baldachin tremble.

'*Why* do you not know?' he demanded. As if Insects were anything to do with me. I froze.

He shuffled forward on white cushions, doggedly glaring down. 'Why so many Insects? Tell me! What are they doing that is different from before? What are we doing that is different? Or what are we not doing? Comet ... *Think* about this. Come here tomorrow, first thing. Give me an answer. *I want answers!*'

'I don't—' I began like a boy to say, 'It's not fair,' but San silenced me.

'Think about it. What are you here for? You have an excellent mind. *Use it!* Do you deserve to be immortal? I begin to doubt. Tomorrow, come here and tell me why Lowespass is overrun. Now leave.'

I bowed hastily, eager to escape. This was an impossible request. How was I to know what drove Insects? And how could I watch over Mist and Ata at the same time? I couldn't do it, but Eszai don't admit the impossible.

The Emperor summoned me back and asked me to write a supportive letter to Carmine in Hacilith. I agreed – 'Yes, yes certainly' – in rising confusion. The room started to spin about me. A couple of long braids in my hair had slipped out of my belt and were dragging on the floor. A few of them had even tangled through the bangles on my wings.

Like a white hound baiting a frail feline, San gave me my leave and again called me back. 'You said Ata had enough men to crew ten ships,' he asked innocently. 'Where did she find two thousand sailors? Did she steal them, as well?'

He waited while I deliberated what to recount. There was no way I could avoid the truth, but this was suddenly a question of my own allegiance. I didn't want to involve Saker Micawater in any trouble. That's the mentality I've kept from gangland Hacilith. Anything goes but this – you don't lie, don't cheat, and don't grass on your mates.

'Tell me, Comet,' the Emperor said gently, in complete contrast to yelling about Insects. I was right; he was giving me the Fear.

'Lightning,' I muttered, 'lent her sailors, and archers to protect her island ...'

San gave a loud stage sigh. 'Thought as much,' he admitted.

I had my arms crossed over my stomach, for protection and because cramp was beginning to gather.

'Go and tell Lightning I want to see him,' the Emperor added. 'Immediately, please.'

I walked down the worn length of crimson carpet, at any second expecting to be recalled, and striding faster and faster as I passed the screen. My throat prickled, saliva gushed into my mouth. Two guards held the crested doors back for me and I went through them in a flurry of silk and feathers. I managed to make it out to the terrace before I was sick.

An Insect, well polished and with a faded wreath of flowers round its neck, guarded the door in my tower room. It stood propped against the wall; a couple of chips in red-brown chitin gave it the patina of ancient furniture. Its name was Butterfly, and it was suffering a severe interrogation. I walked round and poked at its hind legs' translucent brown casing. I twiddled an antenna in a ball-and-socket joint, giving it a rakish angle. Butterfly wore a crested rusty breastplate and a sword-hanger with a daisy in it. It had been dressed in various ways over the years and I had even received costumes tailor-made for the creature.

'Butterfly, I have to know where you came from. I'd like to know where you thought you were going. Intended destination, route of journey, length of voyage, time of arrival, and by which maps ... and under whose command. I swear it's more than my life's worth, which is worth a lot, to me at least.' Awians say Insects aren't even sentient, but how can we really know?

'You're living in the Castle, under the rule of an enemy, the supreme

Emperor San, god's Governor of the Fourlands, and you have to obey his every word, like the rest of us poor immortals.'

The statue didn't say anything. I gave it a hug, and went to sit down at my writing desk. Butterfly tipped back against the rough wall. It was a hollow exoskeleton, like a suit of armour. The shell of the first Insect I had ever killed – the first of hundreds – I had cleaned and preserved with varnish. Its barbed abdomen was a hardened, paper-thin bulb, supported by a seam of thorns like vertebrae along the upper side. Serrulate mandible scythes reached to its chest. There were hinges so its thorax could be opened to see the ridged inside surface, like a crab's carapace.

I took the kettle off the fire and poured hot water into two cups of coffee. Tern emerged on cue from behind the curtain, which with a flight of steps separates our round room into semicircles. She rubbed the sleep out of her eyes, saying, 'Jant – Jant, will you please stop the fucking dramatics?'

'Coffee?'

'Hugging Butterfly, how could you?' Tern put out a little hand for it, the fingernails painted bronze. Her white lace negligee, which wound up into a halter round her neck, accentuated rather than hid her pale body. Waves of glossy dark hair prowled round her shoulders, her folded wings made an inviting cleavage at her back.

'I have to find out how to stop the Insects, Kitten,' I said.

'Snogging them won't help.'

'You're gorgeous.' I could smell her musk beneath the peach perfume; she still had traces of cream lipstick and glitter in her hair.

'You are *not* gorgeous,' she said, a trace of anger flirting in her honey voice. 'Staying awake all night!'

'Sorry, my love.'

'Come to bed now,' she said, the anger melting into lasciviousness.

'No time. I need some cat.'

She came and put slender arms round my waist, head on my shoulder, and I held her gently. Her skin was soft.

Tern was very disappointed in me. We didn't really need to speak any more, I felt her emotions forcing mine, like draughts of air when flying. I felt her sadness twist me into hard-heartedness, the only way I could safely go. 'And then I have to return to court, where the Emperor waits for any excuse to be rid of his wayward Messenger, perhaps you too, because kittens like you are too playful for the Circle. I should fly to Rachiswater and see if all your kinsmen have been devoured. Then I must go to the coast and see if Mist and Ata have killed each other yet.'

I won't describe her tears, pleas, or tantrums. What use is Tern's whim against the Emperor's command? But now that I was home she wanted to make me stay.

'I'll leave you,' she threatened. 'I'll go back to Wrought and live there.'
'If you leave me,' I said, 'you have three score years and ten.'

CHAPTER 16

The sea is only noisy when it meets the land. I hated the endless crunch and hiss of little waves curling and spitting at the foot of the cliff. A flapping of banners on the 'Buzzard mimicked it. I could hear the remote sound of sail, whipping the calm air far out to sea. There was no other sound but the slap of water on wood. There wasn't a cloud in the cold sky; I soared above the cliffs being bothered by choughs. With long lazy wing-beats I flew out swiftly, away from the foam and over the foil-blue. The cliff sound receded; movement made a cold flurry on my face. The sun was so bright I had a headache from squinting. A cormorant arrowed along beneath me, its black neck stretched out. I dived and the bird veered away in panic. Then I gained altitude, eager to be away from the surface of the water, the gleaming specks of light. I hate the changefulness of sea.

This was Ata's message to Mist: 'If you surrender *Honeybuzzard* I will see you safely to land in Peregrine. We need never meet again. If you pass my island in that or any other ship she will be lost with all hands.' I wrote it on paper and dropped it in my satchel onto the deck of the *Honeybuzzard* from a great height. I won't land to give a message that dangerous.

Mist read it, sneered and waved a three-fingered hand. 'Tell the Emperor,' he yelled, 'her time's up. Overstepped the line!' I tipped my wings to him and sailed up on a seaward breeze.

I listened to Shearwater addressing his men. He spoke directly to the whole crew. They packed in close to the stern deck's rails to hear him. They were scared and pessimistic but the Eszai's wild cheer was infectious. He punched the air, saying, 'This is the fastest ship built and you are the best crew ever! If you work for me now, then soon you will captain your own ships.' He praised them higher than any immortal ever praised Zascai, and they started grinning and nudging each other. He told them the chain of command and what positions to man. Then he pointed to where I was circling. Grubby faces peered up like stripy fungi in a window box. Mist yelled, 'See? Jant seconds us! The best lookout the *Honeybuzzard* can hope for! Now, all hands. I want speed!'

The sky was clean; a good current blew off the land. I watched from a height. Able crew swarmed on the deck, tending the massive ship. She stirred. She sucked in a dripping anchor on a long wet hawser. She shrugged up a mainsail. The sail descended, flapping, dazzling white. Wind filled it and it swelled, three more unfurled simultaneously. The blue pennant of Peregrine streamed out ahead. The ship dragged in the water, gathered speed and began to slice the waves. Mist was a figure at the stern, shouting something down to the main deck. Men clustered together and hauled on tarred ropes. Sail wound down over the prow. It bellied up in a startling rush of red and yellow, emblazoned with the Castle sun. The ship lurched forward, smoothly gathering speed. Mist poured all his strength onto the wheel, spinning it. I dropped back in the slipstream and watched the rudder turn. He brought the *Honeybuzzard* round in a great arc to get the wind behind her. She lifted. Suddenly she began to race.

I flew round the ship watching from high above. I criss-crossed in front of them, fast and free, damp with the spray from their bow wave. I hovered in the slipstream of cool air escaping from the sail's edge; it was very turbulent but I managed to find a clear space where it was almost effortless to hang, being dragged along by the ship. Cold air bubbled and gushed under my wings, bearing me up. The pain in my stomach muscles that comes from the exertion of beating gradually died away. It was a wonderful ride.

The Zascai on deck sent up a few curious looks, but soon lost interest as I hardly stirred, and besides Mist was keeping them busy. They worked as a well picked team; Mist spoke to them all by name. He struck a match on the compass at the helm. He stood braced, and grinned at his second-in-command. When the weasly Awian went below decks, Mist returned to looking slightly distant and thoughtful. He gazed at the notched horizon. The breeze made his blue cloak flap. The cloak billowed up; I realised he was wearing it to hide the bandages around his cracked ribs.

The wheel on deck was the guide wheel, positioned next to the compass. One man alone did not have the strength to keep such a large ship on course, not even Mist. Below deck, there was a system of gears, to assist the wheel above and hold a direction in even the worst conditions.

The *Honeybuzzard* made good time from its offshore hiding place, in sight of the Cobalt Coast and north past the cliffs at Vertigo and the long strand of beach at Awndyn. An iron cloud hung above Grass Isle, as if the island was reflected in the sky. From my vantage point above the mainsail, I saw the island first. To begin with it looked squashed, but it gradually grew from the ocean and I could see the south-facing Sute Towers of March and April on the coastline before Mist's lookout shrilled, 'Grass Isle!'

There was a commotion on deck as sailors hissed in anxious breaths and scowled at the grey shape. Mist yelled at them. Then he yelled at me. I dropped a little height and hung in the air at the level of the railings. Any lower and I risked getting sucked under and squeezed out in the ship's wake. Mist stalked to the railings and grabbed at the air, as if to pluck me down. I did a quick circuit of the ship and returned. 'Comet,' he said. 'Please help us. You're useless as a fucking figurehead up there.'

'What can I do?' I'm not setting foot on deck.

'You know how hopeless this is. Flogging. Dead horse. We haven't had sight of her yet. The bitch is planning something. Look. Leap. Fly on a few kilometres and tell us what you see.'

I nodded to him, gained height and held my breath for a few strong beats. I sped down a slight descent. Wind roared over my wings. To the crew I must have just disappeared. I looked back and the ship was a toy on immense water.

Behind the island, Ata's fleet was waiting; evenly spaced, lingering with a hunter's silence. Ata had made a net of fifty caravels, anchored facing in the wind's direction. Their prows faced me, and sterns pointed towards the Peregrine coast.

I flew at masthead height along the line and found Ata on the deck of the ship in the centre of her trap. Two comely men were with her. The tassels of her white silk shawl floated on the gusts; she waved brightly, smiling broadly. The vessels were anchored with the width of a ship between them. I glided down the gaps, close to the hollows of the waves, and faces peered over railings and poked over sterns to watch. The ships were clean and scoured; their hulls were smooth. I flew the length of the line, seeing how Ata had made use of shallow water at the coastal side.

A larger carrack, the *Ortolan*, was patrolling the reef on the seaward end of the island. It stood a good chance of catching *Honeybuzzard* if Mist chose to go that way. He would have to sail all around the island, and in its lee, under the blank gaze of April and May, into Ata's net. I didn't see that Mist had any chance at all.

I flew back to Mist and said, 'You don't have any chance at all.'

'What has she done?'

I told him what I had seen and said, 'I'm sorry I can't help. If I were you I would surrender.'

He laughed. 'Skinny waif.'

I said, 'Forget Peregrine. Go to Moren harbour or Ghallain Point, you can provision there; you could prepare properly.'

Mist said, 'There's no time like the present.' He kicked a map lying on the deck to unroll it. 'Come down and have a look at this,' he ordered.

I couldn't land; it was too much for me being this close to a ship. 'No,' I whined.

'Come down! Bloody waif. Bull. Horns.' He lost concentration squinting up at me, swore and glanced back at the compass.

'Ata will sink us if she catches us!' It was my worst fear.

'She won't board us. I can handle this craft better than anyone in the world. Tricks. Trade. I have for decades.'

'Yes, but she has eighty such ships,' I pointed out.

'Cooks. Broth. Come down, Jant, I'm going to prove I'm the fucking best.'

'I'm sorry. I can't.'

'It's beyond me how a nancy boy like you can land such a hot lady as Tern.'

'I've never hit Tern.'

Mist sneered. He never understood how to deal with Ata. Ata's assurance forced him to treat her like a man – I suppose if she was one of his sailors he would have had her flogged around the fleet.

Our argument was beginning to unsettle the Zascai, who were watching me superstitiously. Mist saw this and bellowed curses, ending the argument by sheer power of voice. He clutched his hand to his mouth and bent over the wheel, coughing horrendously. Embarrassed, I watched him cough for more than a minute. He coughed, hacked, spat, wiped his mouth on his cloak. He moaned slightly, hugging bandaged ribs. 'Ah – I should've killed Saker when I had the chance,' he said.

I pulled my wings in and dropped onto the deck. I scrabbled for the hip flask and poured the last of the sloe gin down my throat: Rhydanne courage.

'You know she has some of Lightning's fyrd?' I said.

Mist raised bushy eyebrows; he evidently hadn't known. He shook himself. 'Well, doesn't matter. I'm going to Rachis, via Peregrine, and they can't stop me. Tournament archers, all of them. Micawater shoots at targets; damn it, he shoots at *fruit*.'

One hand on the wheel, he ripped his rapier from its scabbard and stabbed at the map. 'Those caravels, can they chase us? Anchored? Sails lashed? Sticks. Mud.'

Mist's brunette was sitting on the steps between the upper deck and the main deck, sunning herself in the icy air. She regarded me for a while with the Zascai 'I want to look, not buy' expression, gazing intently when she thought I wasn't looking.

I was feeling sick already. I knelt down beside the helm, careful to be facing into the wind, in case I had to take off in a hurry. The folded tops of Mist's leather boots, rough blue trousers tucked into them, and the gilded scrollwork of the helm took up my field of vision. My eyes were watering. I crawled forward and gazed at the crinkled map, dotted with rapier holes. Grass Isle was almond-shaped; it lay close to the mainland, along the coast of Awia. The island was just thirty kilometres long, with a cruel and rocky shoreline. The northern end gave onto unpredictable water and a reef, marked by a lighthouse. To avoid the *Ortolan* we decided to sail around the south side, between the island and the mainland, a very shallow pass at such low tide. Ata's fleet was strung out across the strait.

'They're from here ... to here,' I muttered, tracing a line from September Tower bay to the coast of Peregrine.

Mist peered over his shoulder. 'Good,' he said.

I whimpered, sitting against the baroque carved helm, I preened my wings out and tried to hide my face in the feathers.

I was sitting on the deck of a ship. Shit.

'There's no point in worrying,' he said. 'I know this coast well. Back. Hand.' He kept on in this mode whilst people ran about on the main deck and the plump girl gazed at the swelling waves, and I sat looking into possible death. The cold waves were so smooth and sluggish they looked gelid, practically solidified. One shock could cause the whole sea to freeze. 'I've been sailing this coast since the fifteenth century. My grandfather was a trader too. So don't be so damn scared. Born. Bred. From packing casks and rowing to commanding the Castle's fleet. There's always been caravels on the route from Moren to Peregrine, ever since we bought it off the Archer. That's what made Awia great, and I don't want it to change, but Ata does. Goose. Golden egg. Why couldn't she be happy? She had the best of both worlds. Cake. Eat it.' This wasn't exactly true; Ata wanted all the cakes in the world and to keep them. 'How can she think she's better than me, Jant? How can she Challenge me after all this time?'

A real fucking ship. How did this happen?

His deep voice rattled on: 'I know she wanted to. I'm not stupid. But swept. Carpet; it's not the kind of thing you want to think about.'

Honeybuzzard slowed slightly as we entered the lee of Grass Isle. High cliffs reared up, yellow with lichen and etched with cracks, parading by as Mist steered into a deep channel running parallel to the coast. Peregrine could be seen on the other side, a sweep of pebble beach running down into crystal water. Where the rocks began, the water became dark blue; where we were, it was nearly black. Black and white seabirds swirled and bickered on the cliffs, in shallow caves scooped into the rock and on jagged outposts of stone, splashed white with bird shit and dead fish and strewn with foam and flotsam.

Suddenly the deck tilted viciously. I slid, grabbed at the helm, clinging for life. Waves on the port side came up as far as the railing, our keel ploughed air. I cried in panic, 'What are you doing?'

'Tacking,' Mist said. He had been chain-smoking and giving out orders which I had been too wrapped in fear to hear. I looked up to see the result of one command. The sailors had brought all sorts of objects from below deck, mainly bedding rolls and hammocks, netting and bundles of clothes hastily knotted together. There were planks and buckets, boat hooks and shields. They had piled them along the sides of the ship, wedging them between the railings and lashing them in place to form a thick screen.

'We need some protection from her archers,' Mist explained. Impressed by his ingenuity, I saw him in a new light. He had been swinging the

Honeybuzzard in full canvas and at its full speed between flat submersed rocks and tiny islets.

'Ahoy. There she is!'

From the air, Ata's ships had looked formidable. Now I was at sea level and facing them, our situation seemed much, much worse. They were invulnerable, solid and secure. Four hulks faced us, their sharp wood breastbones paring the waves. On either side the string of identical vessels stretched out, becoming smaller with distance.

The centre ship hoisted a series of flags, which made Mist laugh. 'That's the *Petrel*,' he said. 'She's asking me to surrender. The cheek of that woman! Brazen bloody cheek.'

The brunette squealed. She looked over her shoulder to Mist, who said, 'Starling, darling, why don't you go below for a while and wait in the skylight cabin? *Not* the stern rooms – do you hear? I'll join you when this is over.' She planted her feet in her sandals and scampered away. 'And hang on tight,' Mist added. 'If Ata's body had her mind ... Damn. This ship isn't taut enough! Lengthen the topsail! Don't look at me like I'm crazy – do it! Method. Madness. And I want archers fit for action.'

I could see archers in readiness on every deck. Only the ships directly on either side of us could use them, or they would be shooting over their own decks. We advanced towards the line at a shocking pace. I began to think surely we should be slowing now? Nausea paused me, undecided, then we were too close and I couldn't take off for fear of the bowmen.

'This is suicide!' I shouted.

'Isn't it?' He ignored the *Stormy Petrel* and steered for clear water between two smaller ships. Faces clustered along their lengths became progressively more agitated. There was a hasty argument on one and it began winding its anchor up, drifting slightly sideways and ruining the pattern of the blockade.

I could hear Ata's anger borne on the wind. '*Curlew!* Hold the line. *Hold* the line! *Stay* there!'

'That's it,' breathed Mist. 'Get out of my way.'

We came at them, unwavering, faster and faster with the wind straight behind. 'Have to trim the mainsail.' His fingers were white on the wheel. 'It'll never fit. Damn! I'd like to have some sail left.' All eyes were on him. 'Take it up!' he yelled. 'Take it up, take it up! Lose it!' Sturdy men on the main deck leapt at his word. They hauled on lines that ran up to distant heights in the rigging. The vast white sail flapped for a second, furled, revealing blue sky. The third mast was trimmed, the spritsail went down and we covered clear water in a second before—

The impact slammed me against the railings so hard I was nearly over them. My wings spread reflexively. Mist threw himself against the wheel to steady it. The terrible sound continued. *Honeybuzzard* pushed between the two ships, forcing them apart. The sound was deafening; snapping, rending, scream of planks running against planks. I saw astonished faces at their railings sliding past us. Archers bent bows and loosed straight across our decks. Arrows in a hard flat rain embedded in the *Honeybuzzard*'s side, in our masts, in flesh like thirsty flies. I curled up behind the helm as they cut across the prow.

Our sailors ducked behind their improvised fortification. Arrows thumped into the screen. Two or three men who were not fast enough were thrown back with arrows in their faces.

Mist waved at his archers. 'Shoot at the rigging! The sail!' They had arrows with broad white flights and their points rolled in cloth. They touched the cloth to fire in a brazier and bent their bows, letting fly volley after volley up into the rigging of the ship on our left. The flights caught in the rigging and dripped burning pitch. Ata's rain of arrows ceased abruptly, as all hands were called to quench the sudden flame.

Our momentum carried us through, wood squealing and mouldings snapping, then we were stern to the prow of the starboard ship.

'Watch this,' Mist declared. I clutched the railings. He spun the wheel, holding it at full lock. *Honeybuzzard* slewed round and we slammed against their prow, crushing it. The glass windows and ornate carving at our stern splintered and broke, shining fragments of sculptures and gingerbreads falling twelve metres into black water.

The smaller ship's narrow prow was sheared through. Her bowsprit snapped and she began to tilt forward, yawing away from us as water flooded into the lower decks. Our bowmen let out hoots and catcalls at *Curlew*'s crew not an arm's length away.

The *Curlew*'s deck slid into the waves, spilling people off into our wake. It bellied up and its hull surged sky-wards, copper-coated, slick and dripping. As it rolled its high mast crashed onto the deck of the ship to its right, bringing all the rigging down. Ropes trailing over the side caught at floating planks. Mist started yelling again at his dazed men.

I swore, and kept swearing for fucking ages.

'It'll stop her following me,' said Mist grimly. 'I was fond of that boat. Jant, for god's sake get off the floor.' We had run out of momentum and were sitting there, on the landward side of her net.

My worst fears realised, I couldn't stand. I couldn't watch, was crouched against the helm with hands over my eyes and didn't stop shaking when Mist poked me in the neck with the square toe of his boot. He was exultant, scornful of my fear. He stalked to the top of the steps and looked down at the sailors who were stirring and returning to their stations. 'Get the mainsail up, and let's get out of here!'

Before any of Ata's caravels could break free of the line and chase us, we set the sail and gathered speed for the clear run to Peregrine harbour. Ata must have been standing at the bow of the *Stormy Petrel* because her high voice carried through the roar of the sinking ship. Mist heard her and shuddered, drawing the blue cloak over his bandages.

'After them! No – forget *Curlew*!' A dark-haired man laid his hand on her shoulder to calm her. He asked for boats and ropes to be lowered to men in the water. 'Forget *Curlew*! Raise the foresail!' She screamed at the archers to resume, but her Micawater Fyrd was not accustomed to ships. The situation was too strange, Eszai against each other.

I took a peek through the balustrade to see her leaning over, white silk strands of her shawl sticking to the ship's side. The two men accompanying her now had longbows. She urged them to shoot. She raved like a selfish child. The burly one with bronze-scale armour stepped behind her, shaking his head. This drove Ata into complete fury. 'Are you trying to get in my backside?' she spat. 'Where you came from? Give me that!' She landed a punch on his broad chest, grabbed the bow from him and flexed it, sending an arrow across to us. It lost height and stuck in the *Honeybuzzard*'s belly just above the waterline.

Mist moaned.

'Are you hurt?'

'They're my sons,' he said slowly. 'They both are. Flesh. Blood. It can't be right that she turns my own boys against me. It can't be right, Jant ...'

'None of this is right,' I said.

'They do what she says. Wrapped. Little finger. She's mad, waif. Hasn't she got to be bloody mad? Insult. Injury.' Mist gave control of the wheel to his second-in-command. He coughed stickily for a while, grimacing. 'I'm going below,' he declared. To 'Starling, darling', probably. 'To check the damage.'

'I don't think she'll be damaged,' I said.

'Wha'?'

'Never mind.'

The sailors dragged their comrades' bodies over the deck and down into the hold, knowing that they would be on dry land by the end of the day. I looked behind to see Ata's fleet clustered around heaving water as the *Curlew* sank. I was amazed at how fast it went down. One caravel from the furthest horn of the trap attempted to give chase, but we left it far behind. Mist returned, helped the sailors on the main deck clear up, and then joined me. I was sitting with my legs dangling over the side, feeling the effects of the sloe gin. 'What are you going to do now?'

'Put in at Peregrine quay. Reinforce the harbour. Do repairs.' He shrugged. 'If I can find anyone to help me. If not I'll do it myself. Where there's a will there's a way. I'll pay the crew. I doubt any of them will come back. Bitten. Shy.' He handed me an envelope sealed with pale blue wax and addressed with his unsteady writing. 'Take this to Awndyn,' he ordered.

'What is it?'

'Curiosity. Killed. It looks like a letter. You're the Messenger. So just deliver it, will you?'

I stood up on the railings and unfolded my wings. Awndyn manor was on my way to the Castle. Uppermost in my mind was the fact I had to get back to court and relate these events to the Emperor.

'Shake?' He pressed my hand in a powerful grip. His arms were stocky as well, covered in wiry hair and thick gold chains. I liked Mist; no other Eszai would leave the courtroom for a quick smoke, go out on the terrace and bellow with laughter at my double entendres. I shook his hand with a bizarre feeling of melancholy. Mist must have felt it too, but he bit it back.

'I'd like to know what Ata thinks of me now,' he said, and smiled. 'Bet that took the wind from her sails.' Grey eyes merry in a sea-sand-hard lined face, white twist of hair in a long charcoal frizz, compact wings on his broad back reached like folded grey fans to his belt.

'Shearwater,' I said, 'thanks for letting me through the Castle gate back in eighteen-eighteen.' He knows I owe him that.

'You deserve it, waif. Don't mention it.' But help me now, his tone implored. Trouble was, I didn't know how. I wouldn't be in Ata's confidence after this. All I could do was deliver the letter. I took it from him, said farewell and kicked off. I was seized by the breeze immediately and cast thankfully towards the shore.

CHAPTER 17

To: Comet, for petition to the Emperor
From: King Staniel Rachiswater

Stateroom
Rachiswater Palace
25 November 2015

Emperor eternal,

I wish to present my most fervent apologies for the conflict that occurred outside my gates between the Awndyn cavalry and the Insects, in which six hundred men were killed or fatally wounded. I propose to compensate their families from my treasury, and I will do all in my capacity to mitigate the consequences of this terrible accident.

I am holding my two guard captains at fault for their negligence; their orders were to 'let nothing through'. The Palace gates are too wide for people and Insects to be segregated as they enter, and so my guards resolved to allow neither man nor Insect past, lest the brutes overwhelm the interior of the Palace.

If I had heard the immortals hail us in the Emperor's name, I would undoubtedly have rescinded the captains' decision. But none of my guards heard the call above the clamour. At the time, I was within the deepest part of my Palace, monitoring the situation from the throne room as is proper. I now appreciate that the reports I received were erroneous. In the poor light my watchmen did not identify the Awndyn insignia, nor did they comprehend that immortals were involved. My guard have the notion that there will be repercussions in future but I have assured them that their fears are unfounded; the Castle does not castigate mortals.

Insects continue to wreak havoc in Rachiswater, from my window I observe many in the paths of the parterre, the ha-ha is overflowing with them. No animals survive – only a few cattle were brought in from the fields in time.

Governor Lady Eleonora Tanager has arrived from her manorship in the north of the country, which has been destroyed. It is the worst loss of life and the worst damage yet done to Awia; Tanager Hall has long been one of the jewels of this country. Lady Tanager arrived at the head of a sixteen thousand-strong fyrd guarding a wagon-train concatenation of eight thousand non-fighters who escaped with meagre belongings. They are being lodged with families in my town, as Insects commence to construct Paperlands in their fields.

Lady Tanager is guest in my Palace. She continues to pursue Insects in

Rachiswater, wearing her silver 1910 heirloom armour and surrounded by her lancers. She is a flamboyant individual, to say the least.

I venture to advocate that your travails should focus on the manorship of Tanager so that we may restore her to her rightful place. 'We are loved best where longest known,' as the poet said.

Staniel Rachiswater, King of Awia.

His Majesty's signature and seal.

To: Comet, for petition to the Emperor
From: Lady Vireo Summerday
Lowespass Fortress
25.11.15
How is it that, although I have called for reinforcements and supplies, there are none on the way? We are reduced to four thousand men and the rations are running out. We need supplies *now*.

The Castle has betrayed Lowespass. Tornado is the only man here who does not think the Empire has forsaken us. In my fyrd rumours are rife that the Castle is prepared to let them die, by Insects or worse, of starvation and winter snows. Why are you unable to protect us?

We are completely enclosed. My lord Emperor, I entreat you haste.

Vireo, Governor of Summerday and Lowespass.

Tornado, his mark: T

'Where are the Insects coming from?' The Emperor began to question me again immediately I knelt before him, as if no time had passed at all since my report two days ago. I had spent hours preparing for this audience, but my resolve vanished like straw in San's furnace wrath.

'You don't *know*? But I asked you to *find out*!'

'My lord, I tried. I'm sorry.' No one in the Fourlands knows where the Insects come from. I have asked Eszai, governors and fyrd, and I heard only tales. Rayne said that two thousand years ago the Insects appeared in northern Awia, in an enclave the size of the Throne Room, with a Wall around it, which expanded like flood water.

We all knew this story, but nobody spoke of it in court. When the Insects appeared, the Queen of Pentadrica went to observe their paper enclave. The Insects killed everyone in her cortège. Only a couple of fragmentary documents survive to describe what ensued: half of Pentadrica was settled by Awian refugees fleeing the north, their beautiful towns buried under the Paperlands. Morenzia and the Plainslands fought over the remaining half in the first civil war. San united the countries against the Insects, and was proclaimed Emperor. He was given Pentadrica Palace on which to build the Castle and guard the remaining Fourlands.

'Tell me what you've learned,' San demanded.

'If I may speak candidly, if anyone in the Fourlands has a chance of knowing where Insects come from, it is my lord Emperor.' The Emperor smiled. I sighed and continued: 'Most people say that Insects live underground. If I was to crawl down one of their tunnels I might see warrens and caverns alive with them, passages kilometres long, and chambers large as manor halls where they hide when conquered.'

'And none can substantiate this story?' San said, in an unreadable tone.

'My lord – of course not!'

'I sometimes wonder whether the current members of my Circle work hard enough to justify their immortality.'

Could the Emperor, who spends every day of eternity within the inner sanctum of the Castle, understand the carnage taking place right now throughout the Fourlands? Vexed, I said, 'There are so many Insects that to set foot near the mouth of a tunnel would be suicide. That's how Dunlin died. If I tried it I wouldn't survive long enough to give a report.'

'Yes, Comet.'

'You can tell as much from Vireo's letter.'

'Comet, I am disappointed that the Castle's integrity has split between Mist and Ata, and now you disappoint me as well. How will I recompense our failure to save Lowespass and Awia?' The Emperor left his throne and walked towards the edge of the dais. I looked past him, unable to face the glare in his sky-grey eyes.

I concentrated on the red-gold sunburst behind the Emperor's chair. Four thick columns supported the mosaic ceiling of the alcove behind the throne; one each of porphyry, azurite, haematite and jade. It was less awesome to look at these than at the Emperor himself. If my gaze could wear them away the columns would be thin as matchsticks. 'Mist is on his way to the front. My lord, with a letter Castle-sealed I can force Ata to come to Rachiswater too and save her quarrel until later.'

'Leave Mist and Ata to finish what they've begun. Here is a letter for you to give to Ata. After reading this, she will cease her raids on our harbours. Tell the coastal manors that the Castle has safeguarded them. Then send all the fyrd they have to Rachiswater. I want the front to be solid; I want everyone to appreciate that we will protect Rachis Town.'

'Yes, my lord.'

'Did Vireo Summerday give you letters to deliver to other governors?'

'No.'

'Good. It will be difficult to save the coast, but there must be not one Insect on the Eske road. They would have access to these very walls.

'Send Hayl and his fyrd, the Armourer and all the fyrd he can muster, to Rachiswater. We will concentrate our forces there; I think Staniel will make no objection. Go to all the manors, negotiate with them, I want every mortal who can bear arms out there, every immortal in the Castle to lead them.'

'Shall I stay in Rachiswater as well, my lord?'

'You? I have thought further about you. Recapitulate your account of the Lowespass "bridge".'

Shakily, I described the white bridge, its smooth construction of Insect spit which was so strong it held the weight of the walkway on wire-thin strands, etiolated like a snake's skeleton, stretching from the ground into the sky – where the Insects emerge—

'These creatures destroying the Empire come out of thin air!'

'It's true. Lightning can verify it.'

'Comet. Find a way to stop them.'

I looked at my hands on the floor, in supplication, the long fingerless gloves covering my needle tracks. Bangles were pushed far up on my arms, and there was the rich embroidery of tiny vines on my shirtsleeves. My sword's silver hilt was tight against my hip. How can one man solve the problem that has occupied the whole Castle for millennia? What is San talking about?

'You cracked the language of the Deirn Manuscripts in less than a year. You helped in the Carniss diplomacy. You should enjoy such a task, Comet.'

I didn't answer. None of the Messengers before me would have been given this responsibility. San must want a reason to get rid of me, but of all times why now? Sure, I've been out of my face a lot recently, but that's nothing new. None of the other immortals are treated so badly.

'If you cannot help ...'

I caught my breath. I won't be thrown out of the Circle. San must need me; no one else can fly over the Paperlands to the besieged fortress, and bring letters back. No one else can speak to Zascai so easily.

'... you will be expelled from the Castle. I asked you to think about this! You have not given the question a moment of your time. If the mortals believe the situation is out of the Castle's control, they will band together against us, and then how long will god's Empire last? A matter of months? Weeks? Insects spread through the world and engulf it. You have been irresponsible!'

'My lord.'

'Find out more about the Insects for me, Comet.'

'I'll do all I can.'

'Everyone in the Fourlands talks to each other through you. The Castle depends on it. Your life depends on it.'

I bit at a perfect nail and ruined it.

'You can go now,' said the Emperor. 'I *said*, you can go now.'

*

Wiping sweat from the cords of my neck, I left the court and walked slowly back to my tower. The clock in Great Court was striking midnight. I have had seventy-five thousand midnights, and I looked into a life outside the Castle Circle. What would it be like? Short. There was only fifty years left of my natural life to run. I had grown used to a fast flow of time, the way immortals see it. Fifty years would speed past, and I would watch myself ageing. No, the Emperor couldn't give me age and death back; it was the cruellest threat. I rubbed my hands over my eyes, massaging a withdrawal headache. I would rather die than watch myself ageing, I thought. I ran up the spiral stairs in a dissonance of silver, kicked open the door to our chamber but my overwrought wife wasn't there.

San can't throw me out of the Circle unless the crisis passes, because then he will be missing a Messenger as well as a Sailor. But there was no way to second-guess the Emperor. He had been alive so long, he might already have a plan that doesn't involve me. Facing uncertainty, I felt like a street kid again. I need some cat.

I got down on hands and knees, felt around under the four-poster for my needle case, which I had stuck to the bed slats with tape. Tern hasn't looked here yet; it's too dusty for her, and she can never bend down when fully dressed in whalebone hoops and skirts.

There is a pair of silver candlesticks on the cabinet, elegant and wispy. I unscrew the cold base of one candlestick; it is hollow inside, a glass phial slides out onto the palm of my hand. I sit and watch myself in the dressing-table mirror as I fill the syringe.

I strip off my suit jacket and light an oil lamp the better to see my familiar reflection. I'm used to this fox-face, ebony-black hair, deep-set eyes; I couldn't envisage how I will look if I age. I sketch on my image with imagination, adding lines under green eyes, around my lips, which smile twistedly on one side. I try to picture my pale skin wrinkled, not so tight. I might put on weight like an old Zascai soldier. The thought repulsed me. Please, no, I thought, feeling sick. I spread my wings for the mirror's benefit, ripping my shirt neatly up the back.

If I am dismissed, I'll take the future into my own hands: suicide. I hold up the syringe and tap an air bubble out. Live fast, die young. I made a very strong shot. San is going to expel me from the Circle. The ground under my feet started slipping away and in an avalanche of emotion I turned from the mirror and crawled onto the bed. The Castle towers' moonshadows striped the bedroom like emaciated giants. I do what San says, whatever he asks. San trafficks time; I've been secure for so long I can't leave now. All the successes I've piled up to bring me fame will be nothing; I'll be nothing. My position in the Circle is all I have – to leave is to die, and condemn Tern too.

San knows when I lie. I'll have to face him again and admit I don't know how to defeat the fucking Insects, and that will be my death sentence. I craved Tern's encouragement. Where is she when she's needed?

I deliberated for hours on the Insect threat, as blue-grey silhouettes moved across the room, doubling when bright Tiercel, the morning star, rose.

Asking where Insects come from is not the same as asking how people were made, because at the beginning of the world god didn't create Insects; they appeared later. Unlike Awians or humans, they're present in lots of worlds, as I knew from the times I Shifted ... I looked at the needle and thought, I want to Shift. I want to go under and not wake up for a very long time. This world that causes me so much distress could just fuck off.

I hesitated, realising that I am not welcome in Epsilon either at the moment. Owing to Keziah, the Tine would still be out for my blood. I dwelt guiltily on Keziah's fate. The worm-girl had hinted he might still be alive – Tine prolong their victims in agony, making flesh sculptures till their organs are needed for rituals. Could I help him? Could I save him?

I struggled out of my torn shirt, took the band from my ponytail and used it as a tourniquet. My reflection in the mirror opposite was hunched and strained. Then, as my expression slipped into relaxation, I lay down.

Epsilon, like I'd never left; the market place was as strange as ever. I began to walk through the Constant Shopper's shanty town of stalls, bright striped rugs flapping and racks of crystal beads clattering. The worm-girl's voice was haunting me: 'Never come back to the Aureate.' Why not? Because the Tine will eat me alive. I wandered round Epsilon's market in painful indecision. 'Never come back to the Aureate. Never come back to the Aureate.' My curiosity will be the death of me. I settled feathers that were prickling in the heat.

Cobbled roads ran around the market square's edge, from which further streets led to the quarters of the city. Coaches, rickshaws, and single whorses jogged up and down, sometimes scraping street corners, and bringing down the occasional stall. I walked until the cobbles became gold. Here and there scuff marks showed where people had tried to prise them up. There were scattered bloodstains, and withered hands bitten off at the wrist – people soon learn not to steal Tine gold. Tall buildings slid into Aureate glow around me as I walked on, into the Tine's quarter.

The Transgressor's Forest is the hair of the Tine's quarter. It is especially difficult to reach because the head is a large walled enclosure. Hundreds of creatures were promenading gold dust tracks between the twin Cathedrals of the Eyes, down to the Most Hallowed Nazel Grottoes, whereas the Mouth forms an Endless Chasm surrounded by gold teeth and the Ears are convoluted dishes the true names of which are not revealed to the faithless. I ran, dodged and sometimes flew though this complex, and eventually made it to the high spiked fence of the Transgressor's Forest. Hiding, waiting, in the edge of a bushy gold eyebrow, I watched.

A Tine wandered into view. His saggy blue arms were pouring a flask of thick red-brown liquid into a watering can. I risked a closer look – he was alone, and seemed quite elderly. His clawed feet drew parallel lines in the glittering dust. He had frayed denim shorts, over which a floppy belly bulged. Thin wisps of white hair hung down a massive muscled back, over the vestigial shell that crawled with violet tattoo knot work. As a belt for his shorts, he wore braided optic nerves – the Cult of the Multiple Fracture. At his waist hung a big key ring, on which, instead of keys, were a bunch of ragged fingers. There were slender ladies' fingers, soldiers' thick knuckles, and children's bitten nails. I saw the turquoise digits of other Tine, and the podgy hairy fingers of lardvaarks, all pierced onto the ring. And they were moving, bending, tapping, stroking ... All still alive! The Tine hefted his green watering can, and I stepped out from behind the wall.

Shoulders up and hackles up, the beast growled.

I coughed. 'Excuse me? Perhaps you can help. I'm looking for Keziah the Saurian. He's a grey lizard, about ... so tall, long snout with lots of teeth. Have you seen him at all?'

'Grrrr?'

'You know, I left him four months ago, but I think if he's still alive, he must be here.'

'GRRRRR!'

'Well, if you feel that way, I'll just be going—'

'How *dare* you set foot in the Aureate!' The creature choked in fury. He took a step towards me and I backed off.

'I'm an immortal,' I said, playing the only card fortune dealt me. The Tine gardener was too enraged to be impressed. Dry lips stuck to sharp canines as he snarled.

'What's it worth to let me have a look in there?' I gestured at the gate and blue pebble eyes focused on my hand. 'Oh yes,' I continued, bringing both long hands up with a flourish. 'I was admiring your ... finger collection, and I wondered what it's worth to let me search for my friend in your forest ... ?'

The bristly beast pulled a razor-sharp knife from its belt. I held my hand out. 'After you show me,' I said, teeth gritted, 'Keziah the Saurian.'

The Tine's heavy head nodded. 'He's impaled.'

'What, on a spike?'

'No. In a bucket.'

When I saw them, I was sick. The Tine marched me on, determined not to let me out of his sight among the rows of stinking bodies, the forests of flesh. After all, I owed him a finger. I kept my eyes on the lymph-soaked ground, shuddering. There were rows and rows of canes, irregular against the hot sky. Rows and rows and rows of planted things tied to the canes. Some screamed. The ones that were beyond screaming were worse, because they sighed. And then there were the ones that were beyond sighing, the ones with wet streamers of guts like runners from which new limbs grew. The gardener doused them all with red-brown liquid from his watering can.

We walked underneath a roller coaster made of bone. There were real creatures embalmed on a merry-go-round, and they called out to me through sewn mouths as they spun by.

Still we went deeper, where the smell of rot was salty, too overpowering, and re-formed things with eyes on finger stalks begged to be put out of their agony. Some looked like skinned muscle trees, lumpen and misshapen, and some were skeletal trees in winter, their off-white arms wired to carved wooden posts. Insects kill everything in their path, but Tine are into creative mutilation. The gardener directed me around a clotted bush of digestive organs, bile green and dark purple, and an arterial ornamental garden where sunken things bubbled.

'Keziah?' I called. Why does that tree have so many sets of teeth? 'Keziah! Keziah!'

Eventually, 'You are one *bad* cat.' A voice softened with mortal pain.

'Shit, Keziah, I'm sorry.' I stopped in front of a tall scaly sapling.

'What you doing back here, dude?' the sapling seethed. 'You said you'd stay off the powder.'

'I came to find you.'

'Stunning. Come join the greenery, catch my drift?'

'There are some things I want to know.'

Keziah's peeling face blinked down from a three-metre-high trellis. Cables, ropes and gory tubes held his backbone in place, all covered with strands of dry slime. Keziah's guts were in a bucket, which the Tine drenched liberally with his watering can. The Saurian gasped; a membrane-eyelid flicked over his remaining amber eye. Just suspiring, 'They'll never let you go, now. Not for all the meat in Pangea.' He lisped, because he was missing his bottom jaw, which had been replaced by someone else's.

'Keziah. What is the Royal Court? There was a blonde girl, made of worms. She saved me. When you were ...'

'Ripped apart. Hurt, that did.' His top lip curved up in a grimace.

'Who is she?'

'I can't t—'

'*Who is she?*'

'Bad news, dude. She's a Vermiform. Captain of the Guard ... She works for the King.'

A King in Epsilon, how bizarre. 'Who's that? A Tine?'

Keziah paused and gasped again, looking to the Tine gardener for a little more red water. The gardener was transfixed on me, and didn't move. 'The man you brought here yourself. Dunlin.'

'Dunlin. *Rachiswater?* How?'

'He said we should all pull together ... He hates Insects. Oh no. Oh *shit*. Here she comes.'

'Wha—' I broke off as the ground began to tremble. I looked down and pebbles were shaking and jumping about on the ground. A long thin worm scurried between my feet. I jumped. Then all around me were worms, rushing together. Worms came out of the ground, disturbing the pebbles. In a five-metre radius they appeared, running in towards the centre, where they met in a writhing pile. Up sprouted a twisting column of worms, taller than me, it consolidated and reformed into the beautiful girl. She swayed, stood still, her hair was alive.

The gardener fled.

Keziah whined, 'Oh for Cretaceous' sake. We're doomed.'

'Jant,' the Vermiform said, her voice like harp chords, 'we told you not to return.'

'Yes, I know. It was an accident,' I said. 'I thought I'd try to save my friend, but as you see, there's very little left of—'

'You told him about His Majesty,' she accused Keziah.

'Not at all. He—'

'We're everywhere. We know.'

She held out her arms, and they elongated – worms ran down her shoulders and neck, adding to the ends. Her hair shortened and vanished. Her head shrank, melted like candle wax as worms left it, adding to her arms. The arms were like tapering roots; they came to points instead of hands and the points laid hold of Keziah. He roared in anguish. I took a step forward to help but he shook his scaly head, a sly gleam in his eye. He had an end to his protracted agony. I watched, wanting to run, but I wasn't going to leave him a second time.

The girl's shape thinned, her height decreased as worms poured down her writhing arms onto Keziah, where they crawled quickly all over him. She was just a thin column, then the column shrank; she was just arms, then the arms dwindled, shoulder, elbow, wrist, and all her worms were wrapped round Keziah.

Keziah couldn't shake them off. A moving net of worms surrounded his snout. They crept into his mouth, between his massive teeth, and down his throat. They emerged from his ragged-cut neck onto the trellis, red and sticky. Worms crawled into his eye socket and forced the eyeball out. They pushed between vertebrae and dropped in the bucket.

I had my hand over my mouth to stop screaming as I saw rivulets streaming into his nostrils, eyes and earholes. Keziah's head hung down. He stopped breathing, and the membrane flashed across his eye socket one last time. I guess enough of the worms had reached his brain and mashed it up. They gushed from his open mouth, and in mid-air reformed into the beautiful woman whose shape took a little adjustment as her feet hit the floor. She picked a lone bloodied worm from the bucket tenderly and stuck it back on herself.

She said, 'Never come back to the Shift, Jant.'

I said, 'No, my lady.'

If she approached me I would run, but I had seen that her worms moved like quicksilver.

'Then goodbye.' Worms at her feet began to dissociate.

'My lady! Wait! I want to meet Dunlin again.'

'He said he doesn't want to see you. Epsilon is at war.'

'Why?'

'You stupid creature! If I see you again I'll eat you from the inside out.' The Vermiform raked one hand across her chest, taking a fistful of worms. She moulded them like a snowball, mouthed, 'Catch!' and threw it. Worms splattered against my face. I squealed and spat, brushing them off – they ran down the folds in my clothes to the floor. When I could see again she was gone, the slightest tremble of gold soil showing her path underground.

There was a reorientation, and I woke. I woke in a familiar room, feeling a familiar feeling. I felt like death. I'd passed out with my eyes open, and they were so desiccated the lids got stuck when I tried to blink. I groaned, remembering the thornstick pain, metal through flesh.

Tern appeared, being comforting, holding my hand. I leant over the bed and threw up. Then I started crying.

'What's the matter? What's the matter?' she asked. It's nothing. It's just the reaction of the drug.

'I'm a useless, stupid Rhydanne,' I explained. Tern climbed in bed with me. Her legs were so smooth.

'Sh! Jant, it's about time you quit.'

'I can't,' I said, before I could stop myself. But Tern didn't see any hidden meaning behind my words. We listened to the sound of heavy rain drumming on the shutters. She stroked my wing for a while and then stopped, a typical woman – they don't expend any effort to help you if there's nothing in it for them. I ran my hand up under her skirt and got lost somewhere between crinolines, petticoats and unidentifiable lacy straps. I was a foiled lover, completely at the mercy of too many layers of clothes. Slowly I gained control and stopped sobbing. Tern doesn't believe in the Shift; nobody does. Poor Tern, she can't understand why her pathetic husband is killing himself.

177

I hugged her, saying, 'I just need to Shift once more and then I'll quit.'

'Why?'

'I'll quit forever, I swear it.'

'You've said that before.'

'I mean it. Aches to move. Don't want to do it again.' I rubbed my eyes and only succeeded in making the burning sensation worse.

'Then *why* bloody do it again?'

'I have to. Honestly, Tern. Trust me. Help me. Please?'

She shook her head, gazing in disbelief. I rubbed a hand over her stocking tops, hooked a finger under the suspender and ran it up to the belt at her waist, swept my other hand down her back, undoing hooks and eyes. Tern made an impatient noise and wriggled out of my grasp. 'You're taking me for granted,' she said.

'That's not the case. I ...'

'You simply don't care that Insects have reached Wrought! It's under attack!'

She slid from the bed and stormed out of the room, the open back of her dress flapping, her little black wings and narrow shoulder blades sticking out. Her footsteps diminished down the spiral stairs.

I lay back, pressed on purple-shadowed eyelids and said 'fuck' in every language I could think of. I used to find Tern's selfishness attractive, and I used to believe that with immortality she would learn patience. I'm losing her again, I thought; if she complains about my conduct to the Emperor that will be the end of both of us.

I started to shiver, hearing the rain and the low moan of the wind cutting around the tower. At length I got up and pulled myself across the tilting floor to the dressing table, which was a mess of perfume bottles, makeup and paper flowers, feather scissors and pens and one slim ornate syringe. I clutched it. Safe now. I fixed myself and lost consciousness lying on a bearskin rug, in front of the fireplace. I went looking for Dunlin again.

I felt much healthier in the Shift, which proved how sick I must be in the Fourlands. I'm sorry, Tern, I thought. When the Fourlands needs me, when Tern wants me, I'm lying, twitching, dying of overdose, alone in my room in the Castle. I knew I was treading the edge of death to take so much cat twice in close succession. Older Eszai would be feeling the Circle strain to keep me alive.

How much poison would break the Circle? How deeply damaged was too fucked to save? What would fail first? Respiratory depression, suffocation, heart failure, permanently Shifted; with maggot-girl trailing me.

With the Vermiform in mind, I began my search for His Majesty in places where I knew the floor was solid, where I would presumably be able to see her coming from a distance, rather than suddenly feeling worm-strands wrap around my legs and pull me down through the soil.

In the market place there seemed to be fewer Tine. After questioning people in bars and coffee shops I found that Dunlin was giving them good positions in his guard.

I raised a toast to Dunlin Rachiswater in the Bullock's Bollocks bar, and everyone there responded. Either they were loyal, or they were too afraid to differ. I learned from them that he had taken up residence in Sliverkey Palace; that I would find him there if the flag was flying, and if not, on any battleground with all the inhabitants of Epsilon pitted against the Insects. The punters toasted him again. Shift creatures had never united before; usually they gruffly ignored each other, or were cheery but vague. Only the Equinnes seemed capable of battle, but they had discovered athletics instead. Now they were so fanatically patriotic and bloodthirsty they seemed to be becoming Awian.

I left the bar intending to walk to Sliverkey, but I had not gone further than the market when I was sidetracked by a stall selling maps. Another amazing development – I had never seen maps in Epsilon before. The Shift changes so rapidly it's difficult to plan. Enchanted, I realised that each was a hand-drawn copy of the chart I had given Dunlin four months ago in Keziah's pub. And now they were available to everyone! I bent over for a closer look and got both buttocks pinched at once. I whirled round, drawing my sword fluidly – found myself face to face with Felicitia Aver-Falconet.

Felicitia froze with a squeak, both hands over his face. He lowered them tentatively. 'Lose the bleached hair and white jeans, my chimerical boy. They make you look like a ghost.'

'Felicitia! Just the man I need!'

'Oh, my tardy lad! I've waited so long to hear you say that.'

'I mean, I need you to come to the Palace at Sliverkey ... God, what happened to you?' His arm was bandaged elbow to shoulder, hanging in a sling of lined magnolia satin. The sling matched the rest of his tight suit, which left none of his small toned body to the imagination. He was leaning on a crutch, which pushed his other shoulder up to his ears, from which marcasite rings dangled. His skin shone like soap, and ingenuous eyes brimmed like ink blots. He swung on the crutch, blushing terribly. 'I was—'

'Oi, what're you doing talking to a tourist in the middle of the market?' At an angry shout I put a hand to my sword hilt again, but Felicitia slapped me.

'*Will* you stop doing that? It's not diplomatic. Over here, love,' he added, raising his voice, and a well muscled man with long red hair slipped to his side. The man was tall, tanned and completely naked apart from a furry headband.

179

'This,' said Felicitia proudly, 'is an Equinne gunner. My guess is he could even fight Tornado and win.'

I ignored the friendly hand, bulging with health, which was offered me. 'I'm not a tourist,' I said.

'Leigh, this is Comet Jant Shira. Less pigment than spaghetti at the moment but don't underestimate him. He can outrun racehorses, he's a Deathless—'

'Looks already dead,' the muscled man observed with cheerful careless-ness.

'Jant, this is Lieutenant Leigh Delamere from Osseous, who's come to help us fight Insects.'

'At yer service, Immortal.'

Questions buzzed in my mind. I couldn't believe that Felicitia – camp as a row of tents – would want to fight at all. Perhaps it was testimony to Dunlin's charisma. I couldn't believe that the Horse People would join Dunlin either. If their Shift land of Osseous had been in the Fourlands, rivalry between Awians and Equinnes would far surpass the Insect War.

'Pleased to meet you. The Castle Circle is at your service and that of Osseous.' Which was safe to say because no Eszai apart from me would ever visit Osseous. 'I would be glad to offer assistance against the Insects in any world.'

'He's the Castle Messenger,' Felicitia said.

Delamere grinned with a chummy politeness that left me quite cold. 'I must ask,' I said. 'Why are Equinnes always naked?'

Delamere looked aghast, ran big hands over his groin and thighs. 'I'm not naked.'

'Excuse me,' I said, 'But I can see your -'

'This is one-hundred-per-cent impossum fur. Invisible marsupials. It took tons of them to make this suit.' He offered me a brawny arm. I stretched out a hand, aware of Felicitia giggling, and stopped a centimetre from Delamere's skin, my hand sinking into warm invisible fur.

'That's amazing,' I breathed.

'Cheers. They're bastards to hunt, though. Have to walk around until you fall over them.'

Felicitia tottered on his carved crutch, wincing in agony. He asked if we could start towards Sliverkey straight away, as his broken leg was too much to bear in the heat and market crowds. 'Those Insects are tough,' he said.

Delamere took him under one arm, where he fitted perfectly. He clicked his fingers at a passing quandry, which slewed to a halt beside us. 'Can you take us to the mansion at Sliverkey?'

'Well, I dunno, darling,' said the leading whorse, licking lipstick smooth around its muzzle. 'Is the price right?'

'I have money,' I said, making Felicitia giggle again.

'God save us, a rich Rhydanne; nothing's changed at all, has it? Has it, my affluent lad?'

Delamere shoved Felicitia up into the open carriage where he sat swaying in girlish laughter. The lieutenant said a few short words to the leading whorse, in a different language; the beast pawed the ground and tossed her head. 'If you please, love,' she whinnied. 'If you promise to give Dunlin our regards, this ride is free.'

'All your rides are free,' nagged the whorse shackled behind it.

'Oh, listen to the girl, she's such a bitch!'

'Mare!'

The quandry set off at a brisk canter, scattering shoppers and Jeopards, and a couple of stalls. We turned right at the City Hall and, as town thinned, increased in speed until we were racing at a gallop along country lanes, all the signs pointing to Dunlin's Palace.

Every time the colourful coach zigged or zagged or jarred Felicitia was thrown against me on the amber leather seat, and I was pushed uncomfortably up against Delamere's fur. First we passed the Aureate, vast twin gilded domes of the Breasts on the skyline. Then we rushed through open country, over a vivid green plain where manila antelopes took fright and jumped away from the coach, white tails showing. Groups of giraffiti stretched their long necks to watch us, their bodies and lengthy legs a criss-cross of brown lettering on yellow hair. Herds grazed in the calm middle-distance. The quandry dodged away from snorting terribulls, which attacked to protect their herds, lowering their heads and gouging with gigantic horns.

After an hour the plain gave way to a bright blue lake, covered with lily pads, where fiery flocks of pink flameingos stalked on their matchstick legs. The air was crystal clear and sweet as melt-water; Delamere's hair streamed back like crimson silk.

In the distance I saw a grey line, like a low cliff, threatening as a bank of fog, which I recognised as we ricocheted towards it in the heat-haze – an Insect Wall. It loomed, silent; seemed to leach colour from the vibrant plains.

'Did Insects come from here to attack Epsilon?' I asked.

Felicitia said, 'Yes. Do you remember we used to call them Paperlands?'

'Back home we still do.'

'That Insect nest is empty now,' Felicitia said. 'Dunlin and I cleaned them all out. Didn't we, Leigh?'

'Yeh.'

'That was how I got my arm broken. I was right in the middle of the fight! Just like Hacilith! Well, maybe not. We drove all the Insects back behind that

Wall and there were so many they were stacked up on top of one another, running around.'

'So there are no Insects left in Epsilon at all?'

'There's a few pockets of Insects left. There's quite a few behind the Wall at Osseous. Dunlin wants to attack next week and destroy them all, my sweet tatterdemalion. We're positive of success.'

'There are too many Insects to hold in the Fourlands now.'

'You Eszai are always saying that. You don't fool me, my pretty propagandist.'

'It's true. Rachiswater's overrun, Lowespass is ten metres under paper, Wrought manor's infested. Insects have been seen in Micawater.'

'Even! You need Dunlin back. See, here's where we camped; the Equinnes had such good fun.'

'Yeh.' Delamere smirked. 'Bit slow, though. Prime your muskets and bide your time, the Captain of the Guard said.'

'I could tell the Insects didn't like being all squashed up together because they built a bridge to escape. It's there – do you see?'

I did see. Half a bridge reared into the brilliant sky and stopped abruptly at the zenith of its arch. The bridge was identical to the one in Lowespass.

'They built tunnels too,' Felicitia chattered. 'Then they ran down the tunnels or up the bridge and disappeared. Can you believe? Dunlin was hopping mad because he said they were escaping.'

'That half,' I said slowly, 'is the same bridge as our half.'

Felicitia didn't understand. 'There are lots of bridges.'

'You don't know where they go to?'

'Well, no, my outré one. Do they have to go anywhere? Dunlin climbed it, you know. He is *so brave*. He threw things off the end but they didn't vanish like the Insects did. They just fell down. Didn't they, Leigh?'

'Yeh.'

I started to feel strange. Invisible hands were pulling me back to my body in the Castle. Typical. Damn it, damn it, damn it. I fought hard, towing the line, pulling against the pull, a supple hook in my guts. My longest Shift yet was wearing off rapidly. I grabbed Felicitia, who simpered. 'The Palace,' I shouted. 'It's important! I'll come back as soon as I can!'

'We'll be there,' Felicitia assured me.

'Tell Dunlin not to ride against the Insects again! Not until I talk to him! I— ah ...'

'But why?' Felicitia's hand went straight through me, to the amber leather. The bright plain was dimming, a fast dusk to a monochrome grey.

I looked imploringly at the now ghostly Equinne. He said, 'You know where those bridges go to, don't you?'

'Yeh.' And I was gone.

CHAPTER 18

I'm surprised I'm still alive. Awake and alive! The rush that knocked me out had faded, but the high remained, and it felt wonderful. I grinned, unstuck myself from the carpet and bounced over to the washstand where I drank a whole pitcher of water. From the burnt-down candles I supposed that I had been unconscious for four or five hours. I rubbed at the bruise in the crook of my arm. 'Don't do it again, Jant,' I told myself. 'You'll get hooked.'

Rain still whipped against the shutters, storm clouds were moving in herds across the sky. The land outside was dark and soaking. I took off my shirt because I'd vomited all over it, rolled it up in the rug and dumped them both in the bedroom.

I was descending the steps when I heard a hurried knock at the door. I was still utterly wired on cat and didn't stop to think who could be visiting in the middle of the night, during a hurricane. I bounded across the room and flung the door wide.

The figure dripping there gazed at me in horror. 'Messenger?'

'Mm?' I blinked. 'You're wet.'

'Yes. It's raining.'

'Yes. Well, I suppose you'd better come in then.' The tall man pushed past me and it was only then I realised who it was. 'Harrier?'

'Comet, this is terrible. I—'

'What the shining fuck are you doing here? What are you wearing?' The custodian of Micawater unbuttoned his saturated coat, wrung the rain from his ponytail. He carried a mighty bow, which I took from him and propped against the wall. He looked too upset to be bearing arms. I sat him down in a chair by the fire.

'Comet,' he said palely, 'I rode from Awia. I lived there all my life. I'm never going back. This is terrible.' He seemed ready to collapse.

I had not seen this aspect of Harrier for twenty years. Gone were the elegant suits and polished boots; the woodsman was dressed as he was the first time I saw him. I observed as I poured a heavy measure of whisky. His green coat and hood lay in a pool on the floor. Under his belt, peacock-feathered arrows were still bright and keen. He had a bracer on his arm and a sword and buckler at his side. On the other side hung a well mounted dagger. A horn with a green strap at his back and a silver medallion on his chest completed the ensemble. Harrier looked like this when he shot against Lightning in a Micawater tournament twenty years ago. Lightning won effortlessly but Harrier's skilful archery and impeccable conduct impressed him so much he offered the loyal young man the next stewardship of his estate.

Long time pining – through novels, librettos and benefactions, with visionary masquerades and testing tournaments, Lightning created a golden age of the time of his youth which modern Awians desperately want to defend. Harrier and his family had subscribed to the fantasy and sunk without trace.

'I can never go back,' Harrier repeated in dismay.

'Shut up.' I gave him the whisky; he slugged it down and then spluttered it all over the long-suffering carpet. He grimaced like someone weaned on expensive wine. 'I have to see Lightning. The Castle's like a tomb.'

He buried his head in his hands, and his shoulders shook. No, it couldn't wait till morning. Yes, it was urgent. No, he couldn't tell me. Yes, he could only tell Lightning. Yes, he was terrified. I took a deep breath. 'We're all Eszai! I can help! Now stop snivelling and tell me what's going on!'

'I rode without rest. I left my horse in Great Court, half dead. Night before last during the storms, at the Palace, there was a fight. I'm so sorry. Fifty men forced the Lake Gate and rode into the gardens. A child could force those gates. There were no lights. Torrential rain, clouds were down to the ground. We couldn't see in the gardens at all. My family hid. The guards are useless – it was mayhem. Call them guards? Decoration, more like! We were expecting Insects, not men to attack Micawater! Men rode right into the entrance hall. I was on the balcony. I shot at them. I shot at *people*. I can't believe it. I took ten of them down with the arrows that were on the walls, but I only had ten arrows. Lightning will be devastated. Maybe I should kill myself.'

Harrier appeared quite willing to do so; I tried to reassure him.

'I couldn't stop them! The men broke everything. The first floor is in pieces. Ceramics, glass. It will break his heart. They ran up the stairs. They knew the way. They took ... They took Cyan from her bedroom and they took her away. I'm sorry. She wasn't crying; she was white with shock.'

'You've lost Ata's kid?'

'Yes. I'm so sorry. We tried to give chase but the storm was too fierce. The entrance hall flooded, because the doors were smashed. At daybreak I sent out search parties but there was no sign. The roads are all churned up. And Insects! Insects all over the place! They ate everything in the gardens, including the gardeners. I had to deal with the townspeople, I told them to leave for Rachiswater.'

'Do you know who's taken the girl?'

'Yes. He had the Castle's crest on a shield on his back. I had chance of a shot, but I didn't dare. I didn't want to hit Cyan. Lightning could have done it. But I couldn't shoot an Eszai.'

'Mist?'

'Yes.'

'He's more stupid than I thought!'

'I think they took her to Peregrine. I went there yesterday morning. The manor is like a war camp. There's a thousand fyrd there. They have the Grass Island badge, but they look very shabby. They told me to piss off,' he added, in a hurt tone.

Where did Mist get a thousand soldiers? Oh. No. I know. It was my turn to founder; I sat down. I had thought that I'd tied up every loose end. Now I wished the world to swallow me whole. The Emperor and the Archer would be furious with me. I swore miserably in Scree while Harrier watched me shrewdly. 'You don't know anything about this, do you?'

'Of course I do. I'm an Eszai. I know everything,' I said. The immortal line. Appear to lose control and Challengers pop out of the woodwork like Vermiforms. I couldn't tell Harrier that I had relocated Ata's fyrd to Awndyn manor, to send them out of the way.

It could never be known that I delivered a letter from Shearwater Mist to Awndyn manor. And Awndyn was not far from Peregrine. That letter must have recalled them – Mist used Ata's men to abduct her child. 'I'm going to knock their heads together,' I muttered.

'I think we'd better let Lightning do that,' Harrier said. 'Comet, I don't understand. Why would the Sailor want to steal his child back? Does he want ransom for her? Is Ata so fond of her?' Just because Ata has had many children over the centuries doesn't mean she isn't fiercely protective of each one. 'Perhaps he's going to use her to force Ata to drop her Challenge for his place in the Circle. Don't look at me like that. Everybody at the coast knows now.'

'If that's his aim,' I said, 'he'll lose his place anyway because extortion is certainly against the law.'

Harrier seemed to have mostly dried out now, and was warmed by the unfamiliar drink. He was patting his chestnut hair flat and examining my eccentric apartment with complete distaste.

'We'll go tell the Archer,' I said. 'He will not be in a good temper – he's feeling guilty. He had to answer to the Emperor for lending Micawater Fyrd to Ata. He hasn't broken the rules, but they're bent completely out of shape.'

'The lady deserves to be supported. She's suffered so much!'

I was of the opinion that the lady should be bound and gagged and dumped in the deep blue sea.

I led Harrier down my muralled spiral staircase, along one of the wide corridors that connects the Castle's thick outer walls to the Palace inside. He scuttled along behind me, one hand on his sword hilt, blunt head down as if he was still moving against the storm. There was a sheen to his pale skin that was not rainwater. He looked like a dying man, more grey than pale; flashes of lightning from the glassless windows lit his face in angles, light grey left, dark grey right – the timeless grey of the Castle stone. 'Calm down!' I shouted over the sound of the storm.

'Slower!' he gasped.

'Don't die on me, Harrier,' I said nervously. I have never found it easy to judge how much pain Zascai can take. He stumbled at a left-hand turn, sharp change of direction, into the corridors of the Palace itself.

'Not yet, Comet,' he muttered.

It is a long run from my tower across the Castle to Lightning's rooms. We paused in an unlit doorway, the engraved portal open wide onto a little cobbled courtyard six centimetres deep in pocked water. Sheets of water were running off the roof and falling in a transparent wall in front of us. I pushed Harrier through it, ducked after him and sprinted across the sudden lake to a gateway at the other side. Harrier gasped as freezing water doused down his back. His shirt clung between the bumps of wings.

Now we were leaving wet footprints on a dove-grey carpet. Blue glass lamps had depleted hours ago and the narrow hallway was slick with the warm smell of oil smoke. A midnight-blue embroidered hanging ran along the wall, thin white hounds chasing like a pack of crescent moons after a brimstone-yellow stag with a crown around its neck. I ripped the hanging back on its brass rail and there was a double door behind it.

'Are you going to knock or shall I?' I asked. Harrier tried to hide behind me. I sighed and hammered on the blue doors. Nothing. I knocked again, again nothing.

'Let's go.' Harrier shivered. He could barely speak. From experience I knew this would take a while.

Lightning, unusually crumpled and haggard, opened the door and stuck his foot against it, leaning on the frame, his face just visible in the gap, said, 'What have the Insects done now?'

'Not Insects.'

'Then could you go away, please?'

'This is important!'

'Comet, do you know what time it is?'

'Yes. It's—'

'I don't care what you're high on or what you have to whine about. Leave it till morning when I have enough energy to kick you back to Scree for waking me up!'

Harrier surfaced in front of me, and smiled like a ghost at his master. Lightning's demeanour changed completely. He ran a hand through tousled hair.

'What is it?' he said. 'No. Wait, don't tell me, come in.'

He dashed back into the room and started lighting candles in a candelabra on a low walnut table, fumbling with a tinderbox until I threw him a box of matches. Harrier walked into the room like a man into a new country, taking everything in. Polished floorboards reflected candlelight at the edges of the room, emerging from under a rug, iodine purple and potash grey. An albino bearskin stretched in front of the cold fireplace. Invisible rain battered the sash windows.

I closed the tall double doors, brass handles with copper-blue enamelling, and waited there like a guard watching immortalised raindrops glitter near the stucco ceiling – the chandelier.

Harrier knelt at the edge of the carpet. I found myself looking at the top of his head. 'You don't need to do that,' I said, confused. He ignored me.

Lightning picked up a bow that was leaning against a bookshelf. He braced it against his bare foot and strung it expertly, then sank onto a grey velvet chaise longue with the bow across his knee. He thought: nobody can hurt me while I have this. An unlaced white shirt fell down over one shoulder; he had struggled into black trousers that were part of a dress suit. The first thing that had come to hand. 'Comet. The harbinger of disaster,' he said. 'What is it?'

I motioned for Harrier to give the news. He did so, with an apology every second word. When he finished there should have been silence, hopelessly routed by the storm outside. Waves of rain tore against the windows, gales howled past around the corner of the building. The Archer was staring into a private world a metre in front of his face. 'I see,' he said, in a quiet voice. 'I don't believe you.'

'My lord.' The woodsman hung his head, overcome with shame.

'This ... doesn't happen to me. To the Palace. My home. What am I going to do?'

'Steady, Saker,' I said.

'What am I going to do? I'll kill him. I'm going to kill him!' Muscles bulged in both arms as he clenched his fists. 'We're leaving, right now.' He took a gulping breath.

'Steady!'

'Nobody. Has. *Ever* touched Micawater. For fifteen *hundred* years. One *thousand* five *hundred* years ... What am I going to do? What about Cyan? Is she hurt? Is she dead?' Lightning looked around wildly for something to break. Harrier had shrunk so deeply into himself that he was taking up no space at all.

He said nothing. He said, 'I have to do something.' Then, 'What will the Emperor do?'

'Saker, sit down and calm down. To San it's just another manorship.' I said it again in seventh-century Awian and he stopped, perplexed, the big hand went over his eyes like a visor.

'Please don't,' he said.

'That is no way to comport oneself,' I continued. 'Would your father have acted thus? Would Peregrine?'

He struggled with his reverences. 'Yes, they may well have,' he said.

'Is this what they taught you? Or do you betray Awia by behaving like a Plainslander? What would Teale Micawater say if she witnessed this?'

It seemed to work. Lightning placed the bow on his chair and pulled Harrier to his feet, taking his hand. Ashen-white, Harrier was totally bewildered at the fact we were suddenly speaking a dead language. 'I am so sorry,' he kept repeating. 'So sorry, my lord.'

'No. No, Harrier, you did well. Your name will be remembered and your family will be rewarded for this service. I wish you to remain as steward in the Palace, if you feel you possibly could.'

'It would be a great pleasure, Lord Governor, but I'm hardly worthy.'

'On the contrary; you are the most loyal servant I have ever had, and a very talented archer.'

I coughed. 'Do I have to listen to this all night?'

The Archer turned to me. 'How long will it take us to ride to the coast?'

'In this weather? A coach would take forty-eight hours; I could ride there in twenty-six hours if there are no floods. But I'm not going to Peregrine. None of us are.' I drew the knife that I carry, Hacilith-style, in my boot, shaking with cat-comedown. 'We should leave Mist and Ata to fight their battle. The Emperor's word. You have to stop the Insects in Awia.'

'Insects! What about Cyan?'

'San's word!'

'I don't care...' He was intent on rescuing the girl, a casualty of Ata's Challenge and not really our business at all.

'Oh, for god's sake leave her. How can we help the kid now?'

Lightning eyed me brandishing the knife. 'I am going to the coast,' he said coolly. 'You cannot stop me.'

'I can't stop you,' I agreed, 'but I could slow you down a bit.' I flattened myself against the door, the panelling pressing between my shoulder blades. We gazed at each other, animals of different species in the same cage. 'It's for your own good! What will San say?'

Lightning shrugged, retreated to the bedroom for a few minutes, leaving me alone with Harrier. The woodsman was too exhausted to stand, but too respectful to touch any of the furniture without permission. He drew strength from the fact that Lightning was satisfied with him, and maintained his sagging poise with gritted teeth.

'The moon had a golden ring last night; tonight there's no moon at all,'

I said. 'A tremendous storm is coming. I've lived and flown in Darkling so I know.'

'Worse than this?'

'Yes.'

Lightning returned with the shirt laced and tucked in, his red embroidered riding coat, boots, a shield slung over his left shoulder and an arrow at string on a longbow.

'Jant, put the knife down. Thank you. Please write a letter to the Emperor, tell him that we have gone to find Shearwater—'

'Spare me the bullshit, Your Majesty. He'll dismiss you from the Circle.'

'And ready my carriage? I know you don't understand ... You probably *can't* understand ... But this is something I should do.'

I went to the servant's quarters and woke them all up, half past two a.m. I chose the best of them to be the driver for the first leg of the journey, and sent riders ahead. I left a letter for San explaining everything, and then went out to the courtyard.

The rain fell through lines of torchlight. Six horses struck sparks from wet cobbles with their hooves as they stirred uneasily, water running in streams down their broad necks. The coach had gleaming trim and the Castle's sun yellow and red on the back. Micawater's crest was on both doors, and in miniature on the horse brasses and the hubs of the wheels.

Memo
To: Kitten
From: Me
Tern, darling, sorry I missed you. I have to go to Peregrine. Someone has to keep an eye on Lightning. He might be the best archer of all time but he's also a bloody idiot. Love you, Jant

We drove throughout the rest of the night, and the following day, changing horses at Eske, the Cygnet Inn in the dense forest, Laburnum House on the escarpment. There were no lights in Shivel; the town had fallen to the Insects. Altergate town was empty, and the people of Sheldrake had long gone. We pressed on through torrential rain, that at least would slow the Insects down. We changed horses at Salter's Stable, forded the floodland at dusk where Dace River had broken its banks, and then we were on the coast road. Before the first stop our coachman got hypothermia, so guess who had to drive the rest of the way?

After nightfall we arrived at Awndyn-on-the-Strand; the sandy track pulled at the wheels. I halted the coach in front of a little stable, a thatched outhouse with half-timber and brickwork.

189

The manor looked as if its buildings had clustered together for comfort. Wet ivy scaled the pairs of tall chimneys, which were dark red, slick with rain blowing between them. A yellow glow backlit the lead-glazed windows; they were grouped in fours and eights, and beaded with rain. Awndyn's small archway opened under a coat of arms in deep relief, and an iron-caged lamp shone there, invitingly.

CHAPTER 19

Creased and aching, Harrier, Lightning and I hurried through the archway as if pushed by the storm. They were damp from their dash from coach to porch, and I was drenched to the skin. Swallow's aged servant kept us waiting in an oak-panelled corridor. Lightning sent me a worried glance. He was still seething with fury, he was as powerful as I felt sickly.

I had no time to dwell on my sickness, couldn't think of an explanation or excuse.

'Why the delay?' he enquired petulantly.

'I imagine she wasn't expecting company.'

'Swallow has never been known to dress for visitors.'

Eventually the servant returned and we were shown through to the little hall. Swallow was there.

Swallow wore a green silk skirt. She was playing the violin. Her head was tilted away from us and a shadow hid under her jaw; she was thinner than last time I had seen her. She lowered the instrument and smiled. 'It is you! At last! I thought Pipit had been at the brandy. Did you get my letter? Have you come to hold the Insects off?'

Lightning simply stared, but fortunately I had more presence of mind. I bowed. 'Governor Awndyn, I'm sorry, but no – at least, not yet. We need a change of horses on the way to Peregrine.' I explained all, while Lightning's clenched fists dug fingernails into his palms in fury, and Harrier just stood behind him and looked peaky.

'Have you seen my town?' she asked.

'We came in along the coast.'

'That was inadvisable, Jant. The waves will be over the seawall tonight and up on the main road. I closed the road because of Insects. Did you see the lights of the town? No? That's because I've had to evacuate it! The *disgusting* Insects have eaten everything in the warehouses and in all the shops on the quay. I have the harbour-men crowded in their friends' houses at the top of the cliff. Thank god for the cliff houses – that's all I have left! Those men put their lives on the line defending the canal basin against Ata. She's a traitor, Jant; I hope her daughter drowns.'

'No, Swallow ...'

Swallow picked up her stick from where it was leaning against a slender music stand, and leaning on it, limped towards me, her skirt flowing. 'I'll help you, Eszai,' she said, 'because I owe you a thousand favours, and because of this fool here.' She stretched up on tiptoe and gave Lightning a light kiss on the cheek.

Lightning asked for permission, seized her agile hands and covered them in kisses.

'You can have my ships,' she said. 'I can't spare any Awndyn men. I'll co-operate on one condition, that you make your plans here in this hall. Awndyn is the most powerful manor on the coast, if we can hold out, because now only Awndyn and Moren have harbours intact.'

'Yes,' Lightning said quietly.

Harrier gave a great sigh. She looked at him shrewdly. 'You need food. Pipit! Fetch brandy! Bring bread and salmon, and stoke up the fire here.'

Once into the refuge Lightning forgot the storm completely. Our coats were left on the hot tiles surrounding the central fire where they slowly steamed dry. We ate at a trestle in the warm dim hall, Harrier and Pipit at the same table, dipping into the same platters of roast chestnuts and baked potatoes. I couldn't be soothed; I was overwhelmed by sea-terror. I did my best to hide it, but I hated the salt wind howling down the vent, under the manor annexe thatch. Thunder pounded with the waves on the long beach.

The cosy hall muted most of the noise; outside we would be deafened by the tremendous waves slamming into the harbour wall and hissing back, rain pelting into the ocean, blurring the sea's surface with the sky. I flinched with the impact of every wave, thinking that the ocean was eating its way closer over the dunes to the manor house. Waves will rear up and crash down on the roof like a wall of black water. How could the house keep standing against that weight of water? Any minute now we would be washed away!

'It's good brandy,' said Lightning.

'Jant?' said Swallow. 'Jant, are you all right? I've been offering you some for ten minutes and—'

'He's—'

'I don't like the sea,' I explained.

Swallow experimented with a version of the first smile. 'If you want to go upstairs please feel free. You need rest as well as repast; the storm will make it a hard ride to Peregrine tomorrow.'

Swallow didn't know half the problem. I needed rest and I craved cat. I had to know more about Dunlin.

And Swallow was confusing me as well. What was she doing? From where had she suddenly found femininity? Why was she acting like a beautiful woman instead of a spoilt brat? Clearly Lightning loved it; he couldn't relate to the wounded girl, but Swallow in calm command of her manor was more to his taste and she seemed to reciprocate. Was she simply recovering her spirit, or had she realised how wrong she had been to turn him down? 'Will you repeat your claim to the Circle?' I asked.

'I may,' she said. 'Now every morning I ride to town and we clear out the Insect carcasses, and we break down their walls, and we spend all the daylight hours killing as many as we can. And still we're losing ground! I'm not leaving my town to them!'

Lightning readily agreed, and I left them. Harrier took his cue from me and also left, treading lightly up the stairs to one of the linenfold-panelled rooms above the hall, hung with Awian tapestries and antler trophies.

I dawdled at the foot of the draughty stairs, where a little window with leaded diamond panes looked out over the strand. I could see only blackness, but sensed turmoil and movement, the roar of surf and flicker of lightning on flat cloud bases far out to sea. Violet flashes displayed the beach. In an instant I saw Insect carcasses jumbled above the tide line, spiny and angular.

By the stairs, a door led to the manor's church, which I knew was a calm, safe place to think and compose myself. Inside, the room was less than three metres square, and unadorned. Churches were more or less the same throughout the Fourlands.

An arrow of lightning illuminated a table set against the far wall, the only furniture. It was covered with a cloth embroidered with script that read: *Why are we waiting?*

These rooms are set aside to remind us of the absence of god. They call to mind the fact that the Castle was founded to protect the Fourlands while god is away from its creation, and that at some point in the future, god will return. Eszai and Zascai alike look forward to that happening, and the prolonged wait is another reason to want to join the Circle. People find it comfortable to have such a reminder, even if they can ill-afford the space. It's because they feel they have fulfilled their obligation to our departed god, and can forget about it.

I sat on the table and thought about Dunlin Rachiswater. Insects were coming to the Fourlands from the Shift – the world I could reach by drugs, the world that only I knew, no one but me believed.

How could I prove it? Head in hands and in deep despair I racked my brains trying to think of a way to explain it to the Emperor – 'My lord, Staniel's dead brother is chasing hordes of Insects into Awia from a land where blue monsters worship entrails.' I would be locked up permanently.

Maybe I *am* mad. Pressure from the Emperor's insistent commands and so much scolopendium has cracked my mind and I haven't even noticed. Or perhaps the Emperor has planned the whole situation so he can dismiss me as insane.

The only Fourlanders I have met in the Shift are Dunlin and Felicitia, people I already knew from the real world, so there is no way even to prove to myself that the Shift exists. The first time I visited the Shift, I excitedly recounted my experiences to Lightning, and his solemn countenance told me I had gone too far. He said, 'It's just a junkie hallucination. Don't waste my time.' It's just a hallucination. Are Insects coming out of my hallucinations and poisoning the world?

A Messenger should be pragmatic. With no way to prove the existence of the Shift, all I could do was trust my intuition. Was I too scared to take a chance to save the Fourlands? No! I would go back to the Shift ... even if it kills me.

Death from overdose was too dishonourable. What would stories tell of me five hundred years from now?

A shaft of light appeared, increased across my face as the door opened, and Swallow came into the little room. 'Jant? I followed you from the hall. I have to ask you something.'

Not now, please, Swallow. 'What?'

'Where did you find my ring, and can I have it back please?'

'What ring? Oh. This?' I wriggled Cyan's copper ring from my finger and Swallow held out a hand for it. 'Yes,' she said. 'It's mine.'

'I don't think that's possible.'

'The dolphin is my standard, as you know. Where did you find it?'

'I ...'

'I gave that ring to the Archer last year because he insisted on having some token.'

'Oh,' I said. 'That explains it. Well, yes, I found this in the Castle stables; it was lying on the floor and I thought it was pretty.'

'Lightning must have lost it. Excellent way to treat a token.'

Lightning? No. There is *no chance* Lightning could be Cyan's father ... He *couldn't* ... 'Mmm. Yes. I was thinking of giving it to Cyan.' I passed her the ring.

'Who's Cyan?'

'Ata's daughter, remember?'

Thank you, Cyan. Now I know. Why did I feel so sick? I didn't understand. The world had turned to dirt, heavy with disappointment. Anticipating the anger that would come later, I felt the warmth of gathering dread. 'I swear I'll never trust anyone from now on!'

'Jant?'

Why was Swallow changing yet again, becoming ladylike and persuasive? It might be the result of her trauma – I once knew a lord who was wounded by Insects and spent the rest of his life thinking that he was turning into one, that black spines kept growing out of his legs.

I thought, Swallow may look reasonably healthy, but the body heals faster than the mind, and sometimes the mind can't heal at all. We all have our private echo of the battlefield.

Mortals change immensely over their lifetimes, but rarely in the space of a few months. Women change incomprehensibly from day to day, but they keep the same themes. Neither mortality nor womanhood would explain what had happened to Swallow. 'What's your game, Awndyn? What the fuck are you playing at?' She backed off. I suppose she had a different opinion of me, too. How could she view me in the same light when she knows I've seen every bit of her, inside and out, stitches and all?

I followed her out of the gloomy church. 'First you're a restless ambitious bitch, then you decide to be content as a Zascai, and now you're acting sly as Tern with frocks and kisses. I'm sorry, but this is confusing the *fuck* out of me.'

Swallow tapped her stick on the floorboards. 'I'll explain later.'

'Explain *now*.'

'Now Awndyn is attacked! My home, where I grew up! I need a place in the Circle! I'm so scared, I can't save Awndyn. With immortality and Lightning's help I might reclaim it. I have recuperated, I've had time to think. Something inside me pushes me on, but since the battle I feel worn out. I have no energy to try like I used to for a place. Now I have to fight and I can't; I'm lame. I know the Circle won't give me any more strength than I already have, and my lameness will never be cured, but Lightning will help me. I received a letter from Mist. In fact, you delivered it yourself.'

'Yes.'

'Mist explained why Lightning loves me. I never considered it before. Mist said the reason was because I look like Lightning's cousin, whom he loved so many centuries ago when his family ruled Awia. He has never forgotten her image – and I happen to look the same! She was called Martyn Micawater; apparently she was a hunter, and a daring warrior. And she had auburn hair. He thought she was perfect.' Swallow glanced down to the folds of her green skirt pooling on the floor. 'And she wore silk,' she added.

'Having rejected Saker, you're trying to snare him again.'

'Well yes, I suppose I am.'

'Damn it, Swallow, hasn't it occurred to you we have more important things to worry about? Vireo and Tawny are marooned in Lowespass! Staniel is making no impact! Eske is at arms! You're holding Insects at bay every day yourself! Has it crossed your mind that Awndyn is the last manor before Hacilith, and if Insects reach the city what the fuck will happen? And what are you doing? Chasing feather. You selfish tart—'

'Don't speak to her like that,' Lightning interrupted, lounging in the hall doorway, one arrogant hand on his sword hilt.

I was betrayed, like a kicked dog. None of the Eszai were worthy; my confidant, teacher, creditor, was as flawed as I am. How do we manage to maintain the sublime image of the Circle to which Zascai aspire? I felt more estranged than ever before, even in the bleak mountains.

I pointed at him. 'I just found out this is all your doing! How could you sleep with Ata?'

'Oh. No! I—'

'No excuses!' I ran up the stairs and locked the guest-room door.

I sat down on a plain bed and stripped off my shirt, looked at my track-marked skin. When the world around me is falling to pieces and I am powerless in the wake of catastrophes there is still one thing over which I have firm control, my body. Here is a solution for all my troubles: I began to prepare a shot of cat.

Calmly looking at my arms I thought, there isn't any point trying to hook there. Once, probing deeply, I hit an artery, which was an experience I had no desire to repeat.

Swallow tapped on the door and called my name softly, but I told her to go bugger off. I opened a wing, resting it on the white sheets, feeling the sinewy muscles relax. The base where it connects to the hollow of my back is as broad as a thigh.

Lightning has let me down.

I felt between the black tetrice feathers on the inside, bristle-hard and thumbnail-sized. Parting them, I saw the delicate, pale skin beneath, showing the pleats of powerful muscle, hollow bone and healthy veins. I thought, Jant, if you do this you stand a very high chance of never flying again and then you will be nothing but a fated mortal. If the overdose itself doesn't kill me, that is.

How could he?

There's no such thing as honour. Chivalry isn't real. The walls are crumbling.

I didn't have anything to put in a will. Wrought manor belongs to Tern, Rayne could have my books, and Lascanne would keep the Filigree Spider. Goodbye, Tern. I began with nothing, and soon I will be nothing again, but now as the Emperor's Messenger, my highest achievement, I know it's worth the risk for the Fourlands' sake.

Where are we now?

I sat with the needle poised, hating the drug, hating myself, then pushed it in slowly. The skin was sensitive and it hurt so much I had to stop, blinking away tears, but then I found a vein and blood climbed up into the barrel.

I don't want to die. I don't want to do this. Tern, bring your cocoa voice here and murmur me to sleep.

I pushed the plunger down and it started hitting instantaneously. I just had time to pull the needle out – a smear of my blood in the glass – and dropped it as my co-ordination packed up completely. A streak of warmth gushed into my back, spreading rapidly down my legs to my feet, and burst in my head like a dark explosion. I lay back, wings open, struggling for breath, and I closed my eyes and fell without end, into the darkness, into myself.

Something moved. A sound. The sound moved in a dance, pale blue curlicues against a blazing white silence. I tried to speak and moaned a row of grey dots. The blue wisp got broader and darker, like a strip of cloth. It filled my field of sound, and tinted rapidly from sky-blue to a hue that was nearly black.

'Mmm,' I agreed in resonant rouge.

'Do I *have* to *shout*?' Pale blue, black, pale blue, black – Felicitia's voice. I woke to find myself lying on something green against a hard black surface under a glaringly bright sky.

'He made it,' said Felicitia, bluely.

'Yeh.'

'It's a hard ride. Take it from me,' Felicitia added.

A powerful hand raised me to my feet. I tottered about and fell over. I got up under my own power, rubbed my eyes and looked around. We were on a grassy lawn a hundred metres long, between two immense but graceful black obsidian walls that stretched straight up without blemish into the sky. The windowless walls had no decoration, and no steps were visible on the outside. They curved away, and I could see that at the furthest extent they swelled into round towers, with tall spires piercing the air. The walls were too smooth for even Genya to climb, the soaring pinnacles more slender than anything the Fourlands could sustain. I recognised Sliverkey Palace.

Felicitia on one side, Delamere on the other, walked me over the yielding grass until I remembered how to use my legs. I said, 'Is Dunlin here?'

'Let us go see, my persistent lad.'

'What about the Vermiform?'

'The Captain of the Guard? They're somewhere around. You have your sword?'

I checked my sword but without much hope for the efficacy of a blade against a million carnivorous worms. We walked around the corner of the building onto more lush lawns, covered with glossy Insects, brown and dark purple with a brassy sheen. Insect bodies were poised immobile on the grass, or frozen chasing in a tidal-wave onslaught on the gatehouse. I caught my breath and hauled at my sword. Felicitia giggled, and I recognised that of course real Insects would not stay still so long.

'The Tine brought those back from the battle,' Felicitia informed me, 'and they made sculptures out of them, see? They're modelling the battles in Insect shells so that Epsilon will always remember.'

We walked to the great entrance, a black archway in the inner wall, and up the stone steps which led through it. On the top step a stripy furry mass lay stretched out. At first I thought it was a rug, perhaps another of the Tine's trophies, but as we approached I saw its massive haunches and shoulder blades, over which rich orange and black fur rolled with the huge tiger's breathing. Its liquid eyes were shut, one paw hung over the top step, its tail was tucked underneath its great bulk.

'Step over him,' Felicitia whispered, and as I raised a foot to do so the great beast shot upright, fur on end, and roared, showing a rough pink tongue and a fringe of long white teeth made of string. The tiger was taller than me; as it sat on its haunches, it could look Delamere straight in the eye.

'Who'th there?' it snarled, blinking yellow eyes. 'Who approacheth the Palath?'

'If you please,' said Felicitia, 'tell His Majesty that Aver-Falconet has brought a delegate from Epsilon to speak with him.'

The tiger eyed me, its whiskers twitching. 'I thall. But thay here till I weturn.' It flicked its tail and bounded away noiselessly on soft paws as big as carthorse hooves.

'What was that?' Leigh asked.

'Fibre-toothed tiger. He can't bite you, it's like being mauled by fluff, but I've seen him pounce the length of the courtroom.'

I waited, fretting and trying to think what I could say to Dunlin, until the tiger gambolled back and slid to a halt. 'Come in! Come in! Fortunate favourite of Hith Majethty.'

We followed the tiger, who padded between obsidian columns, its stripy back at the level of my chest and its huge head moving from side to side. I searched the walls to see if Dunlin had added heraldry but there was simply the spotless stone which gleamed as if wet. The passage was so vast I couldn't see the edges; it was like a hall carved from black ice, the floor so well polished that we could see our reflections in it. The tiger's image moved like an orange cloud, the Equinne's bare feet held better on the cold floor than my boots did, but Leigh seemed uncertain of the tiger and hung back behind Felicitia.

At length the Fibre-tooth came to another arch, and sat down outside it. Felicitia raised a hand to its deep fur withers and the beast shook itself. 'You may pasth thwew,' it said.

Through the arch I could hear lively talk and flurries of laughter. I thanked the tiger and paced in at once, Felicitia and Delamere behind, to Dunlin's court.

Hundreds of creatures looked up as we entered. Tigers and Jeopards lounged on tasselled cushions by the wall, some with velvet collars. They turned their heads as I passed, mesmerised by the flaunting feathers in my ponytail, tempted like kittens to bat them with their enormous paws. Long-haired, well-hung Equinnes stood in a group; they bowed muscularly to Delamere. The Equinnes wore little, impossum-fur cloaks trimmed with platinumpus. They proudly carried their tubular weapons at rest on their shoulders.

Tine with lustrous shells stood in the corners of the room, their scimitars razor-sharp, the hilts wound with tendons. There were women I didn't recognise, with war-painted faces, and blue resin armour.

Leaning against the columns, and round the edge of the stone table, were human soldiers, in mottled green and brown livery. They stopped their chatting as we pushed through, and I was aware of how many were gazing, puzzled, at my wings. A girl with fin-crests fringing her tail, and silver skin like an eel leaned to her friend and whispered; they foundered in bubbly laughter. A gap in the crowd indicated the presence of an invisible creature, a Drogulus. There was a representative of the Sharks, a shabby group of waster-adventurers from Plennish, and eight or nine Market Analysts from the Triskele Corporation.

On the other side of the room were Polyps and some Nasnas – abhorrent beings that look like a man severed longitudinally, and a Hide-Behind, which I can't describe (of course).

An ebony-skinned Fruiting Body of the Chloryll wore a ball gown made of living leaves. She curtsied as we passed, her dress crackling, underwear of fresh flowers visible beneath. An Equinne delegate winked at her.

Flying animals drifted or hovered in the roof vaults. A motionless creature with stiff metal wings surveyed us with one bulbous glass eye. Dirigibles clustered like toy balloons, paper messages tied to their outgrown legs. Problemmings bounced and jostled against the ceiling, their black eyes like beads peering down. These rodents were lighter than air – they gathered in hordes, threw themselves off the edges of cliffs, and floated up into the sky.

The shaved women in Insect-bitten lacquer armour were the last to make way. I already felt the pressure of the curious crowd thronging close behind me. When they saluted and stepped aside, I saw my emerald-ink map spread on the table. Dunlin was seated behind it, on a solid obsidian throne. I bowed. Delamere bowed. Felicitia curtsied.

'Rhydanne,' Dunlin addressed me, 'you know I have no wish to speak to you.' He sat with chin resting on one hand, folds of a mantle pinned at the shoulder, an attitude that reminded me of the Emperor, except for his chain mail and the girth of his arms. A crested helmet sat on top of the throne; a cloth bearing his azure emblem hung there too, its eagle's wing folded over the armrest.

'I've come a long way with an important message,' I said.

'From the Fourlands? Is it a long distance away? Or is it as close as one dying breath?'

'I'm sorry, Your Majesty, but—'

'Jant, I find it hard to speak to the person who stranded me here. Although I cannot deny I'm enjoying life in Sliverkey.' He raised his voice to the crowd, which rumbled approval.

'You have done very well,' I admitted. I had left Sliverkey an empty edifice, and Dunlin's court was now held where my days of dancing and debauchery had been.

'Jant, look closely. I haven't copied the Circle, or instigated a rule anywhere near as absolute as that I held in Awia. All I have done is ask these people to help me, and each realised they could make more impact against the Insects by fighting together than alone. We have saved the city of Epsilon!' he said energetically, to a susurration of agreement from the crowd and a cheer from the ardent Equinnes. 'Aver-Falconet, take the weight off that broken leg. Come and sit here.' Dunlin indicated an onyx chair at his left side which Felicitia slid onto, smiling broadly. The chair at Dunlin's right was unoccupied. 'Give me your message, Comet, and then leave us.'

'I have a report from the Fourlands,' I said, thinking quickly. 'Your Majesty may think of it as a land you've left behind, but Insects run from the Shift to the Fourlands, and maybe between any other world as well!'

'How?'

'I'm not sure, Your Majesty. Instinctively. Like I can go any direction in the air when I fly, Insects scurry between worlds without being restricted by their boundaries. They don't see the difference between them – to Insects, all worlds are one.'

'Via the bridges?' Dunlin said.

One of the resin-clad women banged her ugly spear on the ground.

'You can speak at any time, Mimosa,' Dunlin told her. 'You don't have to ask permission.'

'Sir. I saw a bridge at Vista Marchan, before my city fell.'

'So, the Insects that I am clearing out from Epsilon are simply running somewhere else. To the Fourlands, is that it? And the Castle is taking good care of them there?'

'He says the Circle's overwhelmed,' Felicitia chipped in.

'I do not exaggerate. The Empire will soon be lost. We will be another part of the Paperlands. Thousands have died, Lowespass is finished. Your people in Awia and the Plains manorships are fighting on, but it's a losing battle. The Castle is divided and Insects are running unhindered as far south as Hacilith. So I have come to ask for your help.'

'Sent by whom?' Dunlin demanded.

'I come of my own accord.'

'Thought so.' He closed his eyes, reflecting on the news that his homeland was torn apart, and that he was the root cause. Dunlin tried to let no emotion show, but I glimpsed a second of despair before he masked it. 'How *can* I help you? There is no way!'

'I ask you to relieve the pressure on the Fourlands by letting Insects come back into Epsilon.'

The crowd gasped and hissed. Dunlin said, 'I believe I am speaking for all here present when I say we have struggled hard these past few months to clear the city and savannah, and the citizens of Epsilon don't want Insects back. These people neither know nor care of the Fourlands, Rhydanne; the world we come from is not so important in their eyes.'

'You remember Rachiswater?'

'Of course I remember the Palace.'

'The gardens are trenches now. Governor Awndyn was nearly killed there.'

'The musician? What drove her to fight?' Dunlin halted as he realised his court might interpret the love of his homeland for a weakness that would put them all at risk.

'If you let Insects back onto the savannah and were ready for them there, you could destroy them before they became a serious threat.' No answer. 'Dunlin, I rescued you from the battlefield. I gave you this place. You have to help us.'

'My brother is now King of Awia?' Dunlin asked, with the tone of one who expects the worst.

'Yes, although Staniel is surrounded, powerless in Rachiswater in much the same way as Tornado is in Lowespass. The front runs through his town and by the boundary of Eske, and our troops are spread too thinly along it. Staniel is called "weakling".'

Mimosa said, 'Sir. Time is precious. We have other matters to discuss.'

Dunlin raised a hand to calm her. 'Please attend in the spirit of this court, or Vista is on its own. I listened to your incantations and they didn't work, now let us momentarily concentrate on this Messenger's plea. Jant, tell me how my manor is faring and whether my brother is well.'

I described Tanager's flight to Rachis Town, and the wreckage of Micawater. I finished by saying, 'One way or another Staniel will not last long. Awia only has days.'

'Yes,' Dunlin mused. 'How will I find out? It's too dangerous to have regular contact between the Fourlands and Sliverkey ... People risk death every time they Shift through. As did I ... Jant, where am I in the Fourlands now?'

'Already the stuff of legend,' I said smoothly.

'I mean, you took my body back to Rachiswater? I lie in the Lake Mausoleum with the rest of my family and where Staniel will someday join me? Staniel ordered flowers and drapes to be spread on my tomb?'

I said, 'Sacrifices have to be made in times of conflict.'

Dunlin sprang to his feet, 'We will leave this court for half an hour! Please discuss your petitions amongst yourselves and I promise they will be heard when we reconvene. Aver-Falconet, come with us!' He grabbed the edge of my wing, so that I was forced to follow in an undignified manner, and Felicitia limped behind me, back through the mass of Shift creatures and strangely dressed humans, to the grassy Inner Ward, under the soar-clear sky.

Dunlin sat down on the glassy steps where the tiger had been. 'There are no seasons here,' he said. 'The weirdest thing is I miss winter most.'

'Your Majesty.'

'You don't have to use titles, Jant. The Tine are in awe of the "Deathless" and I am beginning to see their point. Tell me why I am not at rest in my own domain ... *Staniel's* kingdom.'

I explained about Staniel's flight from the funeral procession. I said that we knew where the coffin was, but we had no chance of retrieving it when Lowespass was teeming. Dunlin listened bleakly to all this, with his assured attention I remembered from when I ran messages between him and the Emperor.

He was silent for some time, then asked, 'If there were fewer Insects, would you be prepared to redeem this casket ... This ... I'm sorry, Jant, I am more inflexible than you, and this is a peculiar thing to say.'

'It's all right.'

'Let me say it: this casket containing the mortal remains of Dunlin Rachiswater. And will you convey the same to the Awian capital, to be entombed as it should?'

'It will be the first thing on your poor brother's mind,' I assured him.

'Make sure Staniel has a good advisor,' he said astutely. 'He must have talented counsellors if you are to defeat the Insects.'

'Brute force is more important at the moment.'

'I was coming to that. I agree with what you say. Time and Insects are the only things common to the Shift and the Fourlands. So, here is my answer: I will discontinue my campaign here for four weeks. During that time it falls to you to muster the Fourlands' warriors and launch their force against the Insects. If you push the Insects back I will be ready for them here. We'll exterminate them if we can, but if not I will allow them to dwell here on the savannah for four weeks only – and not cross the bridge, and not build more bridges! I'll tell Mimosa's Bacchantes that we need time for consolidation, but I doubt I can contain the exuberance of the Equinnes for more than a month.'

'We need more time,' I said.

'No, Jant. One month. If all you've told me is true, you have the hardest work of your long life ahead.'

202

Dunlin got to his feet, the bright armour plates on his legs sliding over each other soundlessly. He scratched his head, saying, 'Remember, this respite is solely so Staniel can retrieve my coffin. I would appreciate it if you would tell me when Dunlin's remains are safe in the Lake Mausoleum. When you do return to the Shift, Messenger – and I wish you wouldn't, for the sake of the Empire – but I know you and can't trust you, then come and tell me of the legend of Dunlin Rachiswater. There'll always be a welcome for you here in my Palace.'

'Once my Palace,' I couldn't resist pointing out.

His eyes sparkled. 'Yes. Never trust rich Rhydanne, thin cooks and fat soldiers. Isn't that what you used to say in Hacilith?'

Felicitia grinned widely, and nodded. 'Jant *writes* the legends,' he said.

'I will make sure you are remembered as the finest champion,' I told him.

'We have a deal,' he said. He embraced me briefly but strongly; I could feel the steel roundels on his armour dig into my biceps. 'Farewell.'

'Goodbye, Rachiswater.'

Dunlin walked back into the hall, and for long after I lost sight of him, I could hear his spurs clicking on the flagstones. I sighed.

'Well?'

'See you, Felicitia.'

Felicitia stamped his stiletto heel in the grass. 'Typical! I've been waiting for you for two hundred years! I help you, I bring you to the Palace and, well, you simply ignore me!'

I was preoccupied, looking within myself to try and sense the pull back to the Fourlands. It was beginning, slowly growing. 'You're jealous,' I told him.

'I *may* be jealous, oh promiscuous youth.'

'Felicitia, I'll never forgive you for the way I was treated in Hacilith, back when I didn't have the confidence to escape. So don't hold out hope, Felicitia; you're one of the reasons why I started using cat in the first place.'

'If I hadn't died of a flaming overdose I would have won you round, my lissom lad. I know I could. Or I could have had you shot.' Felicitia's lips pursed, then he spat, 'Shit. The Captain of the Guard.'

Worms were pouring in a thick, flesh-coloured mass down the stairs, taking the form of the steps as they slid over them. When they reached the lawn they pooled and coalesced, legs, torso, shoulders, head; and then again to create not one Vermiform, but two, at half the size. The beautiful woman was joined by a male body. For a second his form aped mine, then mimicked Felicitia, and then became neutral. Both occasionally showed gaps that opened and filled with the worms' fluid movement. They spoke simultaneously with the perfect timing of a choir, but no real emotion: 'We see you reached the court at last.'

'Despite intimidation!'

'We sit at Dunlin's right hand. We know he doesn't trust you,' the lethal creature chorused. 'In court today we found how important you are. How useful you may be.'

'You weren't in court just now,' I said, and for answer the female Vermiform dug her hand into her neck, where it sank up to the wrist, she rooted around and drew out a little worm that looked no different from the rest, dangling from her changeful fingers.

'I see. It just takes one worm.'

'That's why they're such a brilliant spy,' Felicitia observed distastefully.

The male and female figures wound their arms around each other, and worms crawled from one to the other along the length of their arms, their hair threshed and lashed. 'Jant,' said the male half, 'our world is one of the places where the Insects breed—'

'Think the Fourlands has problems?' the female part added in her myriad voices.

'You should see them swarm—'

'—in mating flights—'

'—above our dying somatopolis—'

'Their eggs are—'

'—Hungry. And Insect Larvae—'

'—ravenous—'

'More than we could deal with—'

'—so we came to Epsilon,' concluded the Vermiform that looked female. I had a feeling that something was expected of me, so I thanked them for their information.

'You must defeat the Insects,' said the male Vermiform.

'Good luck,' simultaneously from the female one. I shivered.

'For the sake of worlds not yet infested. Insects will reach fresh places from the Fourlands if your world—'

'—is overwhelmed.'

'We do not want that to happen.'

'So stay out of the Shift,' they said together. The female form raised a hand. 'You're needed in Awndyn.' Their bodies flowed together.

Felicitia and I watched them unravel and corkscrew down into the grass. They dug into the soil as easy as piss into granular snow. Their faces were the last to merge, the worms behind their faces leaving, their hair sliding off and their faces following, then gone; leaving just the traceless grass.

'I hate that thing.' Felicitia bit his lip and glanced up. 'Oh, Jant. You're not going as well?'

I felt the pull grow stronger and the black walls of Sliverkey ward began to dim, ever so slightly, and then fading faster and faster out of focus. Felicitia's purple satin and the blazing sky lost their brilliance. I was slack with relief. I wasn't going to die. I wasn't staying in the Shift. I was going home.

'No! Don't leave me!' He ran towards me and I went with the pull.

'Sorry.'

'Give my love to the Emperor!' He blew a hasty kiss.

'Goodbye.'

'Goodbye.'

'Goodbye? What? Jant! Did you hear that, Saker, he said "Goodbye".'

'Good.'

Immortals close to death will panic – I can't die now! Can't lose eternity! I fought frantically from the warm depths but only fully gained consciousness when Swallow slapped my face. I sat up in tangled sheets, tried to close my wings but they were too relaxed to obey. Lightning stood by the mullion window, looking out, hands in deep pockets. I realised that was where my syringe and wrap had disappeared to.

Well, let him; he could have them. I moaned and Swallow shook me, which cat blurred into a fucking unpleasant sensation.

'Jant? You stopped breathing then! Are you awake?'

'Yes ... In a few hours.'

'We are leaving *now*,' said Lightning grimly. I groaned and begged to be left alone, but I think the Archer, appalled, thought it a fit punishment for me to be dragged out into the raging storm.

'It's nearly dawn,' he said. 'There's enough light to see by.' Lightning was tenacious as a hound close to the kill. He was intent on reaching Peregrine as soon as possible, and from experience I knew his anger would not abate.

Swallow was wearing mail, with a leaf-green felt lambrequin tucked into the neck. With Lightning, she took me down to the stables, at the back of the manor house, where Harrier was waiting with Awndyn horses.

I was propped in a high-backed saddle and my wings shoved into my belt, as they kept concertinaing out and dragging on the floor. Lightning put my sunburst shield at my back for cover and I felt the chill metal through my flimsy shirt. I wound the reins in one limp hand, disturbed by my weakness. My horse followed behind Harrier's on a leash, although Lightning's servant said nothing.

My broadsword in its scabbard seemed weightier than before, and I wished for my ice axe.

Lightning unbuckled the Insect-limb quiver from his back and made it fast to the saddle so that his arrows were at hand. Swallow raised her face to him; he reached down from horseback and gave her a fleeting kiss.

A terrible wind blew from the sea, propelling salt spray and the whistling sleet to the speed of arrows. Spray struck and stung our right sides as we rode north along the coast. Our horses slipped in the mud and their course tended inland, but Harrier kept to the road, guiding my horse along.

Sea-breakers hurled halfway up the cliffs. Wind-blown foam drifted off and stuck to the grass, which was also blown in waves. The salt water wanted to climb onto the land and it roared with the strength of the fyrd at the failure of each wave to engulf us.

Seen from the sea we were three silhouettes – Lightning carrying his technologically perfect longbow in one hand, Harrier with a scarf wrapped around his ears and a strung self-bow resting on his knees. Me – shoulders bowed from the shield's weight, wishing I could just puke and get the nausea over and done with. My horse pranced, panicking when Insects reared up in front, scurrying in groups from the ruins of Sheldrake. Lightning and the Zascai shot the Insects till their arrows were diminished and then they rode with drawn swords.

I hated the sea air but the pale grey stormy morning was good for me. The bracing wind revived me; the freezing gale cut a smile on my face.

We sped past a kilometre-stone: *Awndyn 19 km. Awia, Peregrine 11.5 km.* From there the path dipped downhill, as the height of the cliffs decreased, and I heard the surf on a stony beach. We rode down the incline and plunged into damp woodland. The wind cut off, though I could still taste a tang of salt.

Our horses picked their way more carefully. The soft black path was strewn with blown-down branches and they were uncertain of their footing.

Lightning waited for my horse to catch up. He indicated the track. 'What do you make of this?'

'Mm?'

'Forget it.'

By the time we reached the Peregrine woods I had begun to take some interest in my surroundings.

By the time we arrived at Mist's manor house, which squatted among the untidy foliage, I had fully remembered who I was, where I was, and the reason for our ride. Gradually I stopped lolling and sat straight in the saddle.

The path had been widened by the passage of a hundred or so men, the leaf-litter was a mash of footprints. The men had walked in the opposite direction, a little time before, since a crumbly, peaty smell still emanated from the broken ground. They had been followed by several packhorses, which must have been well laden; their hoof prints had sunk deep.

Harrier muttered, 'We should have lanterns.' It was only early evening, but the short days of winter are either dawn or dusk, and nothing in between.

'Were there Insects on the cliff top?' I asked.

'Yes,' said Harrier, brusquely.

I rubbed an eye. 'I'm sorry, gentlemen.'

'Jant dozes happily through an Insect attack and the driving bloody snow and then he apologises!' Lightning informed the forest.

'I am sorry, Saker. But if you only knew—'

'I *do* only know. I know what you are.'

We joined the cobbled road, passed through the iron-railing gate, which flaked black paint and rust, up into the shadow of the cream-white mansion.

Lightning dismounted, gave the reins to Harrier, and strolled up to the house. He knocked on the door.

'There's nobody here.'

'God's holiday, Harrier, you do have an eye for the obvious.'

'Sorry, my lord.'

A bird flew up from the white turret, startling us. Lightning's hand twitched, as if he wanted to shoot it down. He turned back to the studded door and hammered on it again. 'Is there anybody there?' Silence. 'Is there *anybody* there?'

'There isn't,' I said. I dismounted gracelessly, my legs numb from the drug, from being pounded on horseback and sodden to the skin. I let the fretful beast feed among long grass and ferns of forest-overgrown gardens.

The Archer stepped back and looked up to a single great window above the archway. A heavy slab of white marble formed the sill; the balcony was deserted, the dirty windows, empty. 'Where has everybody gone?' he asked, perplexed.

'My lord, there were a thousand people here,' called Harrier. Looked like it, from the state of the muddy, rutted paths, litter and trampled grass; but Peregrine manor was now a deserted shell. Lightning, hands in frock-coat pockets, wandered around the porch, searching for a way in, and muttering how despicable it was that he couldn't get into his own house.

'This is so strange.'

'Allow me,' I said, and he stepped out of the way, remembering my suspicious lock-picking skill. Instead, I produced a key, fitted it to the lock, where it turned easily, and I pushed the doors wide onto an echoing hall. I presented Lightning with the key. 'From Mist's room in the Castle.'

He paused on the threshold. 'I haven't been inside for over four hundred years.'

'May I?'

'Be my guest.'

Harrier followed us in; our footsteps resounded in a mansion newly stripped clean. Marble blocks were the pedestals for vanished vases and busts, polished shelves were free of silverware, and brighter squares could be seen on the walls where paintings had been. We walked through to a main hall, a cold black and white, where two staircases converged at the far end. Between the staircases a blue flag draped, hanging on wires from the ceiling. A massive table in the centre of the room stood on a blue carpet, the same motif of a caravel in full sail.

Mist and his little band had gone, that much was obvious, and it seemed clear that he did not plan to return. Lightning walked up and down the cold vestibule as if measuring it, gazing at the places where treasure had been. He was looking inward, remembering past scenes when Peregrine was lighted, newly built, vibrant with movement and music. He brought haunting to Peregrine, images of his friends after hunting trips, telling stories over sumptuous feasts. He was remembering the dimensions of the mansion. Whether it seemed larger or smaller in memory, I knew that in reality the manor had changed little since his family owned it – apart from slowly falling into dilapidation. Mist had concentrated on building ships rather than palaces.

While the Archer paced the hall and wandered up and down empty steps to the rooms above, Harrier and I discovered the kitchens. The kitchens were deserted as if abandoned a second before; only the valuables had been taken and we found plenty of food that would just attract Insects. We lit lanterns and brought them through to the table in the hall.

Lightning snapped out of his trance and slammed his fist down on the solid table.

'No, no,' he exclaimed. 'This shouldn't be here!'

Harrier and I glanced at each other. Lightning threw off his coat and started pushing the table with a great show of effort, but for all his strength he couldn't move it a centimetre. 'I'll *kill* Shearwater!'

'Yes, if we can catch him,' I said. All the way from the Castle I had been anticipating a duel here in Peregrine and the bird was flown. Lightning had gained the mansion without the satisfaction of a killing and I knew he wouldn't give up the chase. Lightning's kin-worship annoyed me; it was a ridiculous waste of time. I alone knew we only had a month to push the Insects back into the Shift. 'Insects are moving south constantly, Saker. We should let Mist go; we haven't enough time.'

'Time ... Ha! Don't ... talk to me about time,' the Archer panted vaguely.

Harrier had realised that nothing was going to happen until Lightning had finished whatever he was trying to do, and so he set to helping.

'You're both mad!'

'Jant, shut up and help.'

The three of us heaved and shoved at the table until we had moved it onto the stone floor. Lightning dropped to his knees and rolled the carpet back. It was filthy but he dragged it, threw it aside. Under the carpet was another grimy patch of stone. He rubbed it with the side of his fist, and then with his shirtsleeve, and because that wasn't enough crumpled his brocade

208

coat into a ball and cleaned the stone with it. Harrier leaned close with a lantern and its yellow glow revealed the tomb.

It was a stone slab, three metres long, and it bore the deep relief carving of a square-faced man aged about fifty, broad in shoulder, his feet resting on an attendant hound. He was sculpted in full armour of ancient design, a horizontal-strip cuirass, a helmet with a horsehair plume; he lay on a round shield. I recognised the style of two thousand years ago, before Awians began to use scale armour and before the Morenzians invented plate. A seventh-century inscription edged the slab, punctuated by quatrefoils:

Peregrine of the royal dynasty of Micawater lies here at rest, King of Awia 629-687. This manor he founded will always remember. Those he loved and guided will never forget. Lightning Saker caused me to be made.

We waited respectfully. The silence grew, and Lightning still knelt there, his hands on the deepest engravings, in which fragments of gilt remained.

Harrier drew me aside with an anxious glance over his shoulder and whispered, 'What shall we do?'

'I think we should leave him alone.'

'Can we help?'

'There's nothing we can do. Come away.'

It looked like a mid-life crisis to me. I took one of the lanterns and left Lightning kneeling by his brother's grave.

In the kitchens Harrier set out wine in tarred leather cups and bread on scarred platters, and we ate in silence. I tried to enliven the woodsman – if he knew the truth he would realise I'm hardly worthy of reverence. But his ingrained respect and new astonishment got the better of him, and, 'I'm so glad I'm not an Eszai,' was all he would say.

'We should look for Mist at the quayside next,' I said. 'That's where the footprints were leading.'

'I really want to find my family in Hacilith,' Harrier confided. 'My wife and son are refugees now. I hate to think what Insects have done to the Palace.'

I wondered if Harrier would make a good Eszai; his open, honest face was a true indicator of his tractable nature. How different an Archer he would have been, had he beaten Lightning. I drew Harrier out by asking after his family; he began to talk more readily. I found apples and a block of marzipan to divide between us with more wine. Cat in my bloodstream eagerly welcomed the food, unlocked all its energy and gave me a second high. I decided to curb my exhilaration when Harrier gave me a strange look. I may have been speaking a little too fast.

That was why, when the moment came, I thought it was to do with the drugs. I was just raising the cup when it hit. It almost knocked me from the chair. A terrible feeling: dislocation. A million windows blew wide and an ice gale tore through me. I seized the edge of the table. I cried out.

Harrier's eyes were wide. 'What's the matter?'

I don't know. I really don't know. Cat has never done this to me before. Shift is not like this. For a second I felt cracked open and all the stuff inside me flooded out. I spread on a plane through the whole world in view of everything. It was like looking for too long at the spaces between the stars falling faster and faster up into them a mad sensation of space pulled me out in all directions paper-thin translucent-thin.

It snapped shut.

It was gone.

I sat there, blinking, surprised to look completely normal. The fire was crackling in the corner, the taste of marzipan in my mouth.

'What is it? Comet?' There was an edge of fear in Harrier's voice. I realised that I had dropped the cup and wine was spreading out on the table. The impression of infinity had taken a second. 'Shit ...' I said. 'Wow ... It's *vast.*'

Lightning appeared in the doorway, personification of intense panic. 'Jant! There you are!'

'You felt that too?' I asked.

He nodded. 'Of course.'

'Felt *what*?' Harrier demanded.

'The Circle broke,' said Lightning. 'One of us is gone. I mean – dead. One of the Eszai ... For a second I thought it was ... Thought it was you. Should have known better.' He rubbed his eyes, wiping grime all over his face. He looked grey and sick. He had more experience than me. He'd felt it before.

'Tern?' I got to my feet. Damn it, I should never have left Tern. I should be by her side all the time.

Lightning looked distant for a second, sensing the rest of the Circle. He felt for the presence of the other Eszai and our shared time, keeping us all alive. I don't have that ability, it takes centuries of practice.

'It's not Tern. Why should it be Tern?' he said slowly. 'Come on, Harrier. Let's go!' He pinched an apple from the table and strode out.

I thought of Tornado fighting to the last of his strength in dark Lowespass, overwhelmed by Insects. I thought of him baited by thousands, the last of his men long fallen, cut to shreds, borne down at last and with his last breath still bellowing defiance at them.

The sensation paralysed me but Lightning was stung into action. 'Jant, you Rhydanne failure. Your help is now *essential.*'

'Yes, yes,' I said testily, unable to drop the feeling that a part of me had died. I felt lonely, at a loss. I felt like a mortal again, now I knew the sensation of the Circle failing me.

'This will all change!' Lightning promised the mansion, with a glance at Peregrine's sarcophagus, then: 'I must take Mist's banner down.' He plucked one of his long arrows from the quiver, nocked it to string and flexed both arms, bending the bow. He looked to the flag with instinctive aim, and loosed. The arrow cracked into the wall. The ship flag swung slowly sideways, rippling, until it was hanging like a rag from its remaining wire. Lightning selected another arrow and shot through that wire too. The rich flag fluttered to the floor, draping the white double staircase in dark blue and golden folds.

'Now Peregrine is mine,' Lightning said briskly, buckling the nearly empty quiver to his hip. 'I hope we meet no Insects on our way to the quay.'

The quay was the last place I wanted to be, in reach of those mighty waves. I still thought of the ocean as a gigantic beast, its bulk grey-green, its rabid mouth white with foam. The water had a mind of its own, ever-changing, sometimes lying low, always ready to pounce. I understood the rules of the air and knew its moods, but I couldn't predict what the sea was plotting. With my feathers waterlogged and my acrobat's strength useless in the surf, I would surely drown. The wind was too strong, the ocean too alien. I was averse to horses, lacking an ice axe and I wanted the chance to fly. I had no chance to use my talent here and I was reduced to being hauled along unwillingly by Saker as if I was his flunky rather than an Eszai. Not the best assignment for the Emperor's Messenger and the only being in the Fourlands who knows the truth about the Insects.

I followed Lightning dourly, the horse hooves cracking on cobbles and through panes of ice that were forming in mud ruts on the path. I searched for a way to stop his stupid pursuit but could think of nothing; at least, not while he still had arrows left. I decided that I would stay long enough to find out his next move, of which I could inform the Emperor. I would see Lightning and Harrier to the quayside and leave them there – they could find their own damn way out of the sea's clutches.

The wind was waiting for us when we left the forest, as intense as before. It sped the dissonant seagull cries and the relentless boom and suck of surf on the pebble beach. Insect shells turned over and over on the tide-line. There were fragments of broken wood there, too, and stinking clumps of seaweed. Some horses, free of tack, stood on the path. We rode to the manorship's harbour, and there was no one there. The log-built boathouses, stores and offices were deserted.

'The tenders have all gone,' Lightning said.

He took his horse up along the harbour wall and onto the main pier, demanding that Harrier and I follow. Impossible. The planks were running with water, doused by waves that licked underneath and covered the horses' hooves. Kelp and limpets encrusted the stacks; the wind blew the water into an opaque expanse of ripples. I kept my eyes on my horse's black mane, and let my mount find her own footing to the end of the pier. It seemed to take hours.

'Look up, Jant.'

'Saker, you bastard!'

'Not in front of Harrier.' He smiled. His voice was light with triumph. 'The sea is for Peregrine!'

Puzzled, I glanced at the grey horizon, and the spectacle held my gaze: a wreck, transfixed prow to stern on the Grass Isle rocks.

CHAPTER 20

'*Honeybuzzard*,' I said, remembering the green copper-clad hull. The windows at the stern were ruined holes, the figurehead facing away – the ship had smashed sideways onto the clustered rocks. A tangle of broken spars and snarled rigging washed on her port side, buffeted by the waves. A rent down the other side held her keeling fast to the Grass Isle reef, the deck tilted away from us. Two of the three masts remained, but the first was trailing with the rigging, leaving a splintered stump.

Clear of the water, the caravel seemed the size of a manor house. And silent as the grave. The wind blew the deafening roar of wave after wave crashing onto Grass Isle's shore to us across the strait. It was wild out there, beyond the shelter of the harbour.

'The girl,' the Archer said cautiously. 'Cyan. Cyan Dei. She will be on the ship.' The tone of triumph fell to horror in a second.

'I'm sorry, Lightning.'

'Cyan ...'

'Nothing on that wreck is alive, Lightning. We felt the Circle break; Mist is dead. You must have guessed—'

'I felt it could be him. And I thought Mist would try to run. Wind too strong. Couldn't ... I suppose he couldn't make it round the headland. Lighthouse or not. But look, Jant, they have been there for hours. How else could the ship be so broken up? So, she's gone ... I thought I'd find her.'

'I have to tell the Emperor.'

'No. We will still follow my plan. Fly out to the wreck and see if Cyan is there. See if there are any survivors.'

The concept was ludicrous. Lightning took my look of hatred. He saw me take a deep breath and he motioned to Harrier, who goaded his horse round and rode out of earshot to the land. 'You take him for granted,' I said. 'Unlike him I'm no servant, Saker.'

'Fly out to the ship,' he said quietly.

'How could you be an adulterer? How could you have a daughter? You had an affair with Ata and kept it secret though Cyan herself found a way of telling me and now you're willing to put all the Fourlands at risk for her, not to mention my bloody life if it hasn't crossed your mind I'm terrified of drowning and the worst thing is I looked up to you, but now I hate you, you seemed to be in love with Swallow so earnestly all this time and now it turns out you were only pretending!'

'No. Not pretending. I am. I always will be. Fly out to the ship.'

'You rarely speak to Ata. You've never acknowledged the girl. Fuck it, I'm not hazarding my life for an illegitimate brat.'

'I had to keep the secret. I have watched Cyan. Fly out to the ship.'

'It's a secret I want to know. I thought you had a blameless past, so giving Ata grounds for blackmail was a doubly stupid thing to do.'

'Jant, please. I'll tell you of it later.'

'Seduce you, did she?'

'Damn it, stop it. What's got into you? This is not easy for me.' A wave of remorse broke in his voice; he sounded bitter. We watched the ship continue its slow disintegration under the force of the waves. 'Yes, if you want to put it like that I was seduced. We only had one night together—'

'A *pleasure* cruise.'

'Enough! Please. She said it was safe but now I regret it. How I regret it! Eight years is no time at all and I never thought the confidence would become known so soon. That beautiful bitch. I don't know how to cope with her. I have to know what's there on the wreck. Jant, please help me. Fly out.'

'Swear that you'll give up Swallow and Ata and any other women for a year, while we turn the tide to obliterate the Insects.'

'I swear it!' the Archer declared.

'All right.' I clambered from my horse, fighting down a bout of hysteria as the salt water wet my boots. I held my wings open. 'Give me some space.'

'Thank you, Jant.' I heard his horse's hooves backing. The needle-wheal stung on my numb left wing. I will never take cat again.

The gale was so strong I simply had to hold my wings open against it to feel light on my feet. I kicked off and the bay spread out beneath me, the pier shrinking rapidly. A frightening speed of ascent. I leant forward, pushing all my weight ahead, otherwise the gale would start to blow me backwards.

The coast fell behind quickly and I was over clear water. I tried to attend to the shape of the air, but I kept looking down to judge my height from the surface. I didn't want a gust to dump me into the water. My rapid forward flight meant I lost height quickly too, but every time I came within the waves' snatching distance I angled my wings and hurtled up vertically. I faced gusts head on, uplifting and falling between them like waves.

The sea seemed flat dark grey, laced with lines of foam, and it was only when I neared it at the end of each short glide that I saw how broken it was.

Wings knifed the air but my body dragged, aching my prominent carpal bones. It was hard to keep the four long fingers of each wing open against that unpredictable wind. Even the Darkling snowfields have refuges, but the sea is all death. I fought upwards desperately as the waves prolonged into crests and grabbing foam fingers. I flew frantically as a drowning swimmer thrashes.

214

I took a low altitude approach to the sloping hulk, aware that if I over-shot I would have to turn with the squall behind me, which would make my flight unstable. I pushed the air down with fingers, wrists, elbows; the whole six-metre wing span, steered with my legs and skilfully came up to the *Honeybuzzard*'s railing.

Flapping energetically, I made it over the railing and touched down. It should have been a beautiful landing.

My legs slipped from under me, I fell heavily on my backside and slid ten metres across the deck before crashing into the railings on the other side. Winded, I dug my fingernails in. I stood up and looked around. I was standing on a film of white ice-rime, like powdered glass. The deck tilted at an angle of thirty degrees.

Ropes hung from the splintered masts at head height and the rigging and wooden toggles swung and splashed against the seaward side. The side near-est the land was lower, water swirling among massive rocks. I looked over to see jagged black rocks scattered with fragments of planks, impaling the gash in the hull, twenty metres long and ten metres high. Water boomed deeply as it circulated inside the ship. Seeing the high-water mark on the Grass Isle shore, I realised that we were low on the rocks and, come high tide, all this would change. I didn't know enough to tell whether *Honeybuzzard* would be pushed upright, or if it would sink altogether.

A cable from the masthead snaked and cracked. Timbers rasped as waves forced the wreck further onto the rocks. Quickly I began to walk sternwards, keeping one hand on the railings and looking up to the port side. The deck was washed clean of anything not made fast, and I guessed the people, too, had been swept overboard. I searched the land for survivors, but saw no ragged figures, no movement, no signals. Out of Mist's two hundred crew, I saw one body, floating face down just inside the hull. An Awian man, his wet coat had trapped air that kept the corpse afloat, his sleeves rolled back, skin pale and abraded. His long hair and dark brown wings spread on the surface of the water. I looked for others and saw ripped cloth snagged up on the rocks, which could have been corpses or just cargo.

Everything Mist had taken from Peregrine manor had gone. I couldn't see anything but foam and spray smashing against the headland.

'Where were you taking it?' I said aloud. Then I caught my breath because I saw him.

The body stood against the helm, held upright by a rope passing under its arms and around its waist. Its head rested on the compass glass. Long grey and white rat-tails of hair were frozen onto the glass and stuck, glittering with ice and salt crystals, onto his shoulders. I slipped closer across the tilt-ing deck. The compass had frozen pointing east-southeast where north was supposed to be.

Shearwater Mist's stocky body hung in the restraining ropes. His arms had dropped to his sides. The skin on his hands was white-blistered and torn. His eyes were open and glassy; he was coated in ice.

Hard skin blue-grey, the skin under fingernails dark purple, folds in his clothes stiff with ice. The hair on his arms was frost-white; the bandages still bound tightly round his ribs and wings. His dagger was hanging on a red lanyard under one arm, ready for use. An ivory shirt was moulded over his torso's frozen muscles like a second skin.

It was true to say there had been no Awian hardier than Mist, but why would he take his ship into a storm with only a tricot shirt and denim slacks for protection? I scanned the deck, seeing that his cloak was piled at the foot of the main mast.

In the eerie quiet of this dead little world it began peacefully to snow. The flakes hissed and vanished when they hit the brine.

Shearwater had bundled up his cloak and roped it to the mast. Why? I examined it closely. Cyan's face was peering out of the bundle. I hunkered down and pressed the back of my hand to her blue-grey lips. A little warmth – she was still breathing.

'Cyan? Cyan, darling. You remember me. Can you hear?' I held both hands around her cheeks to warm her, a pointless endeavour because by now my skin was probably as cold as Mist's. I carried on a constant stream of encouraging chatter while sawing through the twisted cable with my sword.

'My dear, everything will be all right. Hold on a little longer, and I'll take you back to dry land.' But before we set foot on land there's a short excursion through thin air. I lifted the child; she was far too heavy.

I sat down cross-legged on the ice and proceeded to unwrap Cyan. Mist had tucked his thick sailor's cloak carefully about her, and under that was a shredded sail, then her coat. The girl's dress was cornflower blue. She had gained a belt with peacock-feather tassels. Her feet, though, were bare and dirty.

I unclipped my scabbard so that I could use my belt to buckle the child to my chest. I held her securely against me. Then I wrapped her beaded belt around us as well. I slipped my sword, in its scabbard, under the bindings at my back.

I have never carried a pack as heavy as this eight-year-old. A handful of letters is my usual load. This is hopeless. Not to panic is key. The down-drag will be incredible. If I battle against it I will run out of energy. So I will fly with long, strong beats. I will ignore the pain and stay on a straight path with a solid approach. I'll avoid the fucking pier and set down in the village; Peregrine harbour seemed an immortal's lifetime away.

'We're going to go home. To see your parents and to get some hot drink. Can you open your eyes?' She stirred and moaned. Good. 'I know you feel cold,' I told her, wildly understating. 'Soon we'll be safe and in the warm. But before that it's going to get very much colder and I want you to hold on. You must not go to sleep. Sing if you can – sing to yourself.'

I slid up to the highest point at the stern, and faced Grass Isle. The sea churned and bubbled. I was tense in anticipation of the shock when I, and Cyan, plunge into it. The freezing water will drench my hair and gush stinging salt into my throat. Don't give yourself time to think, Jant. Just go.

'Cyan, don't move. You must stay still.' Then I ran into the wind until my feet left the deck, turned towards the shore.

I struggled, confused – I was falling straight down! What a weight! I stretched and beat twice as fast. I maintained an unbalanced flight a metre from the licking waves and then slowly, slowly gained height feeling my muscles tearing. I kept my arms wrapped around Cyan, but I couldn't breathe with her weight on my chest. She pulled me down head first.

This pain is too much; just drop her. I kept my eyes on the land, wishing it nearer and nearer, larger and larger. The wind pushed me north so I was at the top end of the village when I eventually scraped in at roof level.

I lost height, turned into wind to land, was blown back up again, pulled my wings shut in desperation and came down with a smack that jarred every bone in my body.

Lightning and Harrier ran from the harbour. Breathless, I gestured for Harrier to cut through the bindings. I lay down in a wide splay of feathers, cradling Cyan in my arms.

The girl's eyes were still closed, her lips blue-grey and her cheeks ruddy with windburn. Harrier leant over and carefully brushed light blonde hairs from her forehead.

'Well done,' he said, so impressed that he forgot I was an Eszai.

I wheezed, 'Oh, my god. Oh, my *back*.'

'Is she dead?'

'No. Thank Mist. Saved her. Look.'

Harrier put his hand to her lips the same way I had done; he smiled, his guilt relieved. But Cyan was still in danger. Mortals never allow themselves to think how close to oblivion they or their friends could be, and Harrier was no exception.

I said, 'Cyan's very cold. I've seen people killed by cold in the mountains and they look all pale, like this.'

Lightning was standing some distance away, with a stony expression, hands clasped behind his back. 'What of Shearwater?' he asked.

'I saw him; he's still on the wreck.' I described what I had seen, the Sailor frozen to death, the ghost vessel and its shroud of ice.

'He cared for Cyan,' Lightning said. 'At what cost, I don't yet know. We'll have to bring him back.'

My Rhydanne immunity to all but the most severe cold meant I could not warm the girl; she was growing rainbow-coloured from exposure and bruises. I passed her dead weight to Harrier. 'Give her a hug and warm her up. There are some things I can't do.'

Lightning stirred. 'No. Give her to me.' He scooped his daughter from my grasp and held her close, face down to her face. He gathered the fur-trimmed riding coat into folds and wrapped her so that she was covered completely in brocade, the grey check lining and soft fur.

Harrier still thought the child was Mist's, but not for long. I watched realisation slowly dawn on him.

'What are you smiling at?' Lightning demanded.

'I'm happy to see Cyan alive.'

'My daughter,' he explained, and then said it again, more confidently. He kissed her forehead. 'My favourite.'

'Please allow me to offer congratulations, Lord Micawater,' Harrier said, amazingly calmly.

I rubbed my wings to stop the muscles stiffening. 'I have to report to the Emperor,' I said. I retrieved my sword, dug in my pocket for the sorry remains of the block of marzipan, which I stuffed into my mouth for energy food. Harrier offered a leather bottle of tan-tainted water. 'San must know about this,' I added.

Lightning broke off murmuring to the awakening girl. 'You're right, Jant. Harrier and I will ride to Awndyn. It's the nearest haven for Cyan, and Swallow needs us – if we can find her. I hope she's still there – she only had five hundred men, and this place is infested.'

'It will be dark soon,' said Harrier. He had once listened to me complain at length about the labour of flying at night.

'I can go one-twenty k an hour in this wind,' I assured him, spidering to my feet and stretching my long legs against the tight leather, extending my wings and arching my back like a cat. I was getting used to the freezing gale; it reminded me of the mountains.

Lightning sent Harrier to fetch the horses before saying, 'Offer my apologies to the Emperor. I beg his forgiveness, and I hope I am not too late ... Beware of Ata; she is dangerous, especially now time is passing for her again. If you have to negotiate with her, mark every word; I've known the lady longer than you have.'

'I haven't known her at all,' I remarked involuntarily.

'Cease the spite, Messenger; it's dishonourable. I have watched Tern and yourself happily married for a hundred years without showing any of the envy I feel for your happiness.'

'But—'

'Go carefully. Go *fast*.' He struggled into the unadorned saddle of the larger horse and fussed about, inexpertly securing Cyan in front of him so that he could still pull a bowstring back.

'You could put her in the saddle bag,' I suggested. When I was a child Eilean transported me in a papoose. The Archer looked scandalised. 'I am going to *carry* her,' he said proudly. 'When we meet Insects Harrier will just have to fight twice as hard.'

I watched them speed away, and then I ran back to the shore. I had to leave the cluster of boathouses that broke up the airflow, creating lees and bewildering down-currents. Then I sprinted faster, again jumped into the air.

I rejoiced in the lightness; compared to my last flight I was infinitely agile and manoeuvrable. The sea was there below me and couldn't harm me. I beat the gusts and rode upon their backs, long-winged.

There are some advantages to flying over the sea. Unlike the land there are no people below so it is safe to piss from a height if you are desperate, which I was.

CHAPTER 21

The lights of the Plainslands villages I used to navigate by – like stars on the ground – had gone out. Diw township was deserted, and Eske town was keeping a blackout in the knowledge that lights attracted Insects.

I aligned my flight west by the constellation called the Mad Sow's Litter, and skimmed close to the forest canopy. I flew all night to the Castle, and arrived in the grey dawn. I loped up the worn stone steps and through the great gate, desperately trying to order my thoughts.

Hundreds of people packed the Throne Room benches. Mortals, governors, fyrd captains and townsfolk. The screen had been rolled back, so the Emperor's gold sunburst dais was in full view from all parts of the hall. I didn't know the screen could be moved, and I had never seen such a crowd of mortals here.

I strode down the aisle and knelt before the Emperor, my hands on the platform's bottom step, salty wings chilled by airflow tense against my back.

The Emperor studied me carefully. 'We have been waiting.'

His forehead was furrowed, his cheeks were pinched – tiny changes imperceptible in anyone else were significant with the Emperor because in my experience he had always looked the same. Alarmed, I realised they were signs of stress that, even with his powerful will, San could not disguise.

The Emperor began: 'The first thing you should know is that Staniel Rachiswater is no longer King of Awia.'

'My lord! Has the King been killed?'

San smiled flatly, and I thought he looked tired. 'No, indeed. He is a prisoner in his own Palace. Lady Eleonora Tanager seized control last night. She has eighteen thousand men, and Rachiswater's lancers defected to join her coup.'

'I only knew she had fled her manor.' And she had taken the capital. Eleonora's reputation was fearsome; I had met her once before, in a cocktail party, but she was as good a huntress there as she is in the forest.

'I await my lord's command,' I said. King Staniel a prisoner in Rachiswater? Perhaps that's what he always wanted: to be safe.

The Emperor waved his hand, as if dismissing Eleonora's coup as the natural flow of things. 'The Princess is defending Awia. Her countrymen rally behind her, and I dispatched Plainslands Fyrd to her. I have sent some immortals and promised the help of the rest. Leave the whys and wherefores until the war is won—' He surveyed the mass of people behind me as he left unsaid – if any Awians survive.

I turned half-away from the podium and examined the rows of Zascai warriors and civilians. San tapped his age-speckled fingers on the armrest of the throne. 'I have made changes. I need their reports; and in return I am giving them reassurance, and hope.'

I said, 'There are no immortals here.'

'They are all in the field. Hayl and Sleat with the Artillerist; Rayne and the fyrd from Carniss are helping Eleonora hold Rachiswater. The Swordsman and thirty other immortals are holding the front within view of Hacilith city walls. The Architect, Treasurer, Polearms Master and ten more are seeking a way to defend the Plainslands. They lost Altergate yesterday, and Laburnum the day before that.'

Maybe I was projecting my exhaustion onto him. Another glance told me that was a vain hope.

San said, 'I suggest you give me your news now and your worries later.'

I took a deep breath and told him about the Sailor's death. The mortals behind me leant closer to hear, but after two minutes San cut me short. 'I know this – of course! I recovered the Circle! What can you add? About Insects! How close have they come? Cobalt manor?'

I bowed my head. 'No. All that is left in Cobalt are corpses. Diw is empty – Bittern evacuated her people to Grass Isle.'

'So Awndyn is next. So Lightning is in Awndyn when I needed him in Rachiswater, where half his archers are, the other half on the island! He will answer for this debacle!'

'He asked me to plead forgiveness.'

'Comet, what would you do with Peregrine manor? I know, you would give it to Lightning, who regards himself as the rightful owner. So then Lightning would keep indefinitely two of the six manors of Awia. He is breaking a primary rule of the Circle!'

I understood. If Eszai accumulated lands and were able to raise their own fyrd, they could dispute with Zascai Governors or Kings. And with time they might even be able to challenge the Emperor's authority ...

'I allowed Lightning to keep Micawater, his birthright. But no new lands. I think he and Ata will choose immortality over property.'

'Then who will inherit Peregrine, my lord?'

'Cyan Dei.'

'Cyan? She's just a child!'

The Emperor nodded, white hair brushing his thin shoulders. 'Yes, Cyan Dei is presently a child of eight. So, tell Governor Swallow Awndyn to protect her and her manor until she comes of age. As regental governor, Swallow has ten years to make Peregrine as productive as it should be, whilst equitably teaching Cyan the Empire's ways. Tell Lightning to salvage Peregrine manorship for Cyan. And he should *listen* to the child as well.'

I shut my mouth, because my jaw was dropping. At a stroke the Emperor had brought Lightning and Swallow together. He had burdened Swallow with so much to oversee that she would find it hard to pursue her claim for immortality. And if Peregrine manor could eventually return over twenty thousand men to the fyrd, Cyan would gain the title of Lady Governor.

'Peregrine manor will stay in Lightning's family, which is what he always wanted, Cyan the latest descendant of a long-dead dynasty. He will think it an excellent idea.'

'And Ata? She will be furious.'

'Tell her to direct her fury at the Insects!' I flinched, but the Emperor continued: 'The fleet needs maintenance. Tell Ata that if she is successful, I will bestow point eight million pounds from the Castle's Treasury to that end.'

'Yes, my lord Emperor,' I said, dazed.

San said, 'We must deliver Tornado, or none of this will come to pass ...' He became lost in thought; I waited, and there was neither motion nor murmur from the rows of battle-worn behind me, although a Sheldrake soldier was weeping silently, clutching his broad-brimmed hat.

Incense smoke rose in thin coils to the vaulted mosaics, the columns behind the throne glittered. Shafts of morning light from the high windows streamed across the hall, illuminating the ancient frescos of Insect battles and the Castle's founding.

'The fyrd need Tornado,' San said eventually. 'He is a great symbol of the Empire's might.'

I understood. Tornado was the most powerful fighter, the third oldest Eszai, the strongest man in the world in a millennium. The fyrd would rally behind him, if only because it was safer there.

'Comet, you and Ata must liberate Tornado from Lowespass Fortress. What intelligence do you have on Lowespass?'

It was time to tell him. However he reacts, whatever happens to me. I readied myself for the shock of being dropped from the Circle. Dislocated in denial of my own voice speaking I said, 'The bridge—'

San looked up sharply.

'That's where the Insects are coming from.'

San stood abruptly, called, 'Close the screen!' We waited as the ornate partition swung back into place. Now the crowd could not hear us; above the dais, the cupola's architecture damped our voices.

'Tell me,' demanded the Emperor.

I hunched up into a ball at the base of the steps. 'I resign.'

Please render me mortal, so I don't have to tell how I broke the world, and that I don't know how to put the pieces together again. This was like my confession to San and the Eszai in the ceremony when I joined the Circle –

easier to die than drag out the details of my past. What was I doing, trying to hide secrets from god's custodian?

'Comet, that is only the easy way. Tell me. Once, then never again to anybody, living – or dead. Do you understand?'

'Y-es. Yes, I do ... My lord Emperor, there are many other worlds: the Shift. I have been there. Insects cross between them by bridges and they lay worlds waste. They might travel by the tunnels too, if we consider how they first reached the Empire. Insects sense a place where the boundary between two worlds is thin. Then they build a bridge or a tunnel to reach it. They can see a passage through, but to anyone else, the bridge just stops in the air. Insects breed in some worlds; in others, seek food, and the Empire is at the very edge ...'

'Go on.'

'Dunlin Rachiswater, the last King, is still alive – in the Shift.'

The Emperor raised a hand, about to ask how this could possibly be. He studied me intently, and read the answer. 'I understand,' he said. 'Go on.'

'Dunlin fights Insects there. They escaped across the bridge to Lowespass ... But I found him! He agreed to restrain Epsilon City's prodigious host for the space of a month. If we push now, we can send the Insects back.'

Now I had told the Emperor, I was light and empty. San needed this knowledge; he would know what to do!

The Emperor's face was unreadable. Didn't he believe me? Did he think this was a madman's insane rambling? I pulled my wings tight to my waist.

'If we had the strength to make a push,' San said at last. 'Hear me, Messenger. Go to Sute and instruct Ata. When she clears Lowespass of Insects she can come to the Castle and join the Circle. I shall give her Mist's title when her campaign is complete, and not before. Now fetch me paper.'

I wanted to ask the Emperor how life was, back when god walked the earth. What did it really look like? Sound like? What did it mean to live when everybody knew everything? While San wrote, the pen scratching, I tried to imagine existence with god nearby, enjoying its creation, when there were no Insects, no Castle – this two-thousand-year-old stone, just lush grass. The Fourlands does not really belong to us – it is god's playground; god gave us responsibility for its creation, which we have failed to defend.

As ever, San read my mind. Almost imperceptibly, he said, 'Once there was peace.'

I folded the letter, melted the sealing wax, and impressed it with Castle's sunburst.

'Remember my orders. Now go.'

I stood and bowed, wings down in a flare of iridescent feathers, then backed and left the Throne Room, watched by the archers on the balcony.

As I passed the screen it was opened slowly, and the Emperor called people forward to hear their reports.

Outside, I seized the guard's shoulder. 'Lanner's son?'

'Yes, Messenger.'

I pointed through the arched arcade to the black sarsen twists of the Northwest Tower. 'See my standard? Lady Tern Wrought lives there,' I said. 'Find her, and tell her ... Tell her that I love her. Tell her *not* to journey outside the Castle. She is not to leave the Castle no matter what she hears. No matter what she feels.'

'I'll tell her, Comet.' Shocked by my candour he added, 'But won't you be back?'

I masked fear with a swaggering smile, put a finger to my lips and shook my head. 'For her sake I'll try not to get myself killed.' I desperately wanted Tern, the centre of eternity, and if I saw her now, nothing would induce me to leave her again. I stifled the thought; I had to go. Spreading my wings, I vaulted the balcony, fell two floors, righted myself in the air, sped up and over the Castle roof.

I lay horizontally in the air, found my pace for five hundred kilometres. Wings touched tips above and beneath me with each beat; the sun setting with a flash, below into the gentle hills of the Awian downland. A band of refugees emerged along the coast road, with fifty covered wagons and laden piebald ponies, they faltered their way south towards Hacilith from Wrought. I passed over the Peregrine cliffs, the land dropped away and there was the coastline.

I flew over the wreck of the *Honeybuzzard* in all its shades of grey and white. Its shattered figurehead reared on my left, a wild-haired sea woman jutting up from the slimy rocks where her wooden dress's cream folds scratched and grated. I shuddered, remembering the corpse helmsman; Mist, stocky and solid, was more terrible than a ghost.

I turned along the coast to the Sute Towers. Men stood on their crenellated tops acting as lookouts. The towers seemed unreal, illusory, frosted yellow gritstone forelit by the winter sunset shining under the edge of the clouds.

I reached the end of the serrated reef, the sea boiling around it. There was the lighthouse, a round stone tower built in the same pragmatic fashion as Ata's towers but with a stone platform and metal roof.

For every night as far back as I could remember, a huge fire was built in an iron cage on the platform to warn ships off the reef. Every morning the flames were allowed to burn down and the ash cleared out. The lighthouse's mechanism had been Shearwater's invention, and the procedure of running it kept several of the island's families in employment.

The lighthouse was useful; I navigated by its blaze at night and the stacks of seagulls carousing its rising air by day. Even now I could get some welcome lift from it. I flew over the conical black roof, curving slightly to circle into the thermal. Nothing happened. Strange, I thought, and tried it again; nothing happened. I glided lower and tried it a third time but the lighthouse was quite cold. All the missing answers dropped into place. Of course! I somersaulted in the air and hastened inland.

The Sute Tower named August was the only one flying a pennant. The banner was plain white and wind-torn with no insignia, a badge of Ata's self-sufficiency. Lookouts on the battlements scurried down a hatch as I approached. Some wore little bodhrans and wooden flageolets, laced to their belts, which Morenzian men play when on watch duty.

The Sute Towers have no entrances at ground level; their doors are half-way up, with wooden gantries for access. Stealth was not an option, and I could do little in the way of force. Ata frightened me. She caused the Sailor's death, would she have qualms about killing me before she knew my mission? Oh shit. The towers were a web in which Ata sat spider-like waiting for the fly to appear.

I whipped round, located the highest window, a glass-less, shutter-less square. I backed with every scrap of strength; even so, it took two laps to slow down and the drag nearly pulled my wings from my back. The window had no sill. I closed wings, drew my legs up and dropped through it without touching the frame, hit the floor and jogged to a halt.

A round room lined with people – men standing against the walls, perhaps fifty pairs of eyes. Click. Click. Click. Click. What? Then I saw four crossbows, in the extremities of the room, braced in the brawny arms of four intense-looking men. Their strings were spanned and the catches off. I spread my hands downward, showing that I had no desire to draw my sword.

'For the sake of the Empire.' Ata could dump my body off September Tower pier and sincerely maintain that the sea had claimed me. The unwavering crossbow bolts were sharp, I would scarcely feel the blow; they would rip straight through me. Like a damn fool Rhydanne I had swept in to where Ata was indisputably sovereign of her island and stronger than I had ever imagined.

Ata Dei stood at the far side of the ring of guards, behind a simple table. She had a nearly translucent dress that matched her long white hair, and she seemed most unlike a warrior. She smiled broadly, which made her all the more frightening.

An officious-looking woman was behind her, of similar age and build, with a scraped-back grey ponytail and a hatchet nose. She wore a soldier's coat over her red brigandine and carried a crossbow. A bracing hook hung on her belt and from her assured stance I could see she well knew how to handle it.

'Welcome,' Ata pronounced. Her tone was kindly but I didn't trust her. I hated the way the men were staring at me, awe mixed with a greater loyalty to her. There was no way I could reach the window if they took aim. 'You must excuse this treatment,' she continued. 'I don't yet know the reason for your visit.'

'Here is a letter from our supreme Emperor,' I said, keeping my voice low. 'And as an impartial Messenger I am at your service.'

'Give me your sword.'

I unbuckled my belt and laid it, with sword and misericord, on the bare floor, then took my knife from my boot, and dropped that too. Now I had no defence save a silver tongue. One of her guard took the weapons to her desk.

'I think we must stop threatening the Emperor's Messenger,' she said, in Morenzian, and the men removed the bolts from the runnels and lowered their crossbows. 'You can leave us now, but wait in the lower room and come quickly if I call. I have much to discuss with Comet, so let there be no interruptions.'

The men filed out, creaking the floorboards and with many curious glances over their shoulders. I realised what a weird figure I must appear to them. Apart from my exquisite good looks, I was by now more sharp-set and unshaven, with my damp flight-knotted hair and cat-eyes. The Hacilith men wouldn't wear a silk shirt in the middle of winter. They were two hundred years too late to understand my pewter Wheel brooch but they recognised what was previously a gang patch as Comet's standard. Even the corvine lady behind Ata looked apprehensive, as if she thought that a man capable of flight was capable of any feat. I bowed to her.

'I had better introduce you,' said Ata. 'This is Carmine Dei, the harbour-master of Hacilith Moren, and my daughter. Before the storm she brought Hacilith's ships to the island, the soldiers San sent her, and several hundred men we employed in the city. The Governor is unaware of the thugs missing from his streets. So our new fyrd are not as finely drilled as the Awians but they do know which end of a crossbow faces outwards.'

'I see you have a veritable host here,' I said.

'Aye, at present. Carmine, you'll have heard of Jant Shira: mad, bad and a pain in the neck.'

'Delighted to make your acquaintance,' said the human, resting her heavy crossbow at her hip. I understood that nothing would end her support of Ata, but I wondered whether her loyalty was freely given.

Ata dragged a chair away from the wall so I could rest. She took her seat, and her phlegmatic daughter guarded the window. I twisted the chair to see her; being shot from behind without warning was for some reason worse. Ata lit two oil lamps on the table, which gave a comforting yellow glow. 'We could hear you flying,' Ata said. 'Your wings make an awful din.'

'Thought it was too dark to hear me,' I muttered.

'Start from the beginning,' she said.

'You're mortal now, Ata Dei.'

'Start at the start and tell me something I *don't* know!'

'San decrees that you will be the next Sailor. You will rejoin the Circle when your campaign is complete.' I passed her the correspondence; she sliced the seal and read it.

'No. This must be wrong ... Jant, the Emperor wants to kill me! I must become Eszai *first*.'

'You can't possibly make it to the Castle! There's thousands of Insects in the way!'

Frustrated, Ata examined the letter. 'This is practically a death warrant. Fight Insects as a Zascai? Without the Circle to support me if I'm wounded, Jant? Succumb to little cuts and bruises when so much is at stake?'

This woman, adulteress, murderess, was jealous with her own life. I had an idea that San wanted Ata to face Insects on a par with the mortals whose lives she played with so dispassionately.

'Jant, you wouldn't be in the first line if you were a Zascai. You'd run away!'

'Insects bite immortal flesh too.' I hid my resentment with a shrug. 'Remember the last Hayl was ripped apart at Slake Cross? The Circle was no protection then! If you want immortality, you have to accept San's rule.'

Ata collapsed into her chair. 'And fight for his favour. Yes, I must ... I will. A risk of death to gain immortality ... Eternity is worth it. Do you have any other news?'

I described the wreck of the flagship, her husband's body preserved at the wheel, and the cross trees sparkling and dripping with nitid ice.

Ata's forehead wrinkled with astonishment. 'I knew *Honeybuzzard* had foundered on the rocks,' she exclaimed. 'I just sent Diw's men to search for salvage! No doubt they'll bring him back ... Shearwater was from Diw, you know, originally; not from Peregrine at all.'

The room was gloomy now, the seascape outside impervious black. Knowing Ata to be callous, I was not surprised when she showed no grief, though it made me hate her. When every other woman I've known would break down and cry, Ata became calm, with steel fortitude. Ice eyes bade me continue, her strong arms folded across her commodious chest. She showed no sign of joy when she heard about Cyan, and guarded her expression when I spoke of Lightning, too. Her eyes were emotionless; though there was some strong feeling behind them I could not tell what.

'I felt the Circle strain to hold Shearwater,' she said. 'I felt it break and I felt him die. I was right here, in this tower, and I knew what I was looking at. It was just the same as when Hayl Eske died, only this time it felt *good*.

'And the clock's ticking for me now. So I'm Zascai, but not for long, either way; I'll be killed, or you will be calling me Mist. I don't like this weight of time, Messenger; maybe you'll have the nasty experience yourself one day.'

'I want to know what really happened to Mist.' I braced myself for the tearing impact of a crossbow bolt – none came, but Carmine Dei was holding the bow steady.

Ata still let no emotion betray her. Her smile and her sigh were an excellent contrivance. 'Jant, you said you were impartial.'

'I am impartial, but I do know the truth and I need tell it to no one else if we beat the Insects.'

'You're out of your depth, as the seahorse said to the jockey.' She smiled. 'What in Empire could this accusation be?'

I walked to and fro across the room. Movement might untangle my jumbled thoughts. It helped me to put Carmine's crossbow out of mind and hopefully made it harder for her to aim.

Moreover, the level of cat in my bloodstream was dropping and I was starting to miss it. Withdrawal doesn't come on immediately but the calm before the storm is a confused paranoia: something is missing, something is not quite right, something awful will happen. Which it will if I don't soon take a fix. In the dullness of encroaching illness I can't think properly. I tried to concentrate, swallowing to clear my hearing. Ata realised that if debate grew difficult all she had to do was stall for time and I would turn into a suffering ruin, glad to agree to anything so I could get out of there.

I said, 'Mist wouldn't sail to Lowespass. That's what started all this. There was no excuse for Mist's violence and of course he was to blame, but we assumed you were innocent. No one asked *why* he hit you. I think it was because you told him about your affair with Lightning, and Cyan's origins. A man like Mist wouldn't know what to do, and maybe he felt that violence would make the problem go away. Instead, you asked Lightning for help. He agreed, because you trapped him eight years ago by seduction. Lightning's now full of remorse and a desperate admiration – it isn't love – and he's losing his nerve when the Empire most needs him. Is all this true?'

Ata shrugged. The lamplight coloured her white hair and dress a soft yellow, and gave a pleasing roundness to her face. When she shook her head, every hair was illuminated separately so her appearance changed from young lady to mature woman in a second. Then she gestured to Carmine. 'Darling, leave your bow, it's making Jant shaky.' Carmine complied and, relieved, I continued, convinced by her reaction that I was right.

I sniffed. 'You sent Cyan to Micawater, knowing that Mist would attempt to abduct her, as Cyan was now a wonderful tool to use against you. In doing so, he brought Lightning further into the fight. Damn him, he's so predictable ...'

'As you are.'

'Ata, killing me will not seal your secret while Lightning lives. You may not have planned Mist's getaway into the terrible storm but he played into your hands there, as well. To escape from Peregrine harbour he had to sail through the strait. And Grass Isle has a tail of rock ... He was a brave man to make such a move and he didn't deserve what happened to him.'

'Shearwater's ship was blown off course and there's an end to it. Many boats come to grief on that coast. The islanders have been picking wood and bounty from it since time began.'

'Yeah. So Mist had the lighthouse built and I don't doubt it saved many lives. But the fire wasn't lit, and you are the only person who could have ordered such an omission. I know because I flew over the lighthouse and it was cold.'

'It's been a cold day,' she said.

'On these dark mornings the fire's always stoked; it *never* cools down.'

'Oh, Jant,' she said, expressionlessly. The lamplight made her body a compact dark shape within the diaphanous dress. I ripped my attention away from the curve of her breasts. How confusing can the world be, when murderesses have great breasts?

'So you caused Mist's death. You extinguished the lighthouse and he ran into the reef.

'And I'm disgusted and repelled by the way you've treated Cyan. How can you plot eight years ahead? You planned her entire existence! The purpose of her life was for you to use Lightning to fight Mist. I suppose you let Lightning watch her grow, to secure his love for her. Now she's fulfilled her purpose and useless to you, what will you do?' I sought Ata's gaze and held it. 'Was every one of your children bred for a reason?'

'Jant ...'

'Don't involve me in these schemes any longer! I only wanted to fly errands and fight Insects!'

'There's a change from your usual anomie.' Ata smiled. 'But if you report such infamy in the Castle it will be your word against mine, and is San likely to believe the word of a junkie?'

I looked away. 'Don't use that expression. San believes the reports I bring in every single day.'

'They're facts, whereas your tale cannot be proven. Aye, most of the Circle knows Jant is a junkie. Think how it would look splashed all over the front page of the *Wrought Standard*. You would be facing Challengers every day for years! I marvel at your ability to keep the knowledge from mortals. Except Carmine; she knows now, sorry.'

I risked a glance at the harridan, who leant by the window with a mordacious smirk on her face. As an efficient harbourmaster she would be well aware of the trafficking that goes on in the Moren docks and I felt a twist of guilt even though I don't do that kind of thing any more. I tried to reassure myself but Ata knew she had hit a nerve. In fact, all my nerves were beginning to jangle.

'You want your drug now, don't you?' she enquired, guilelessly.

'No. I'm fine.' This will get you nowhere, Ata. I tapped my foot on the floor in a pointless attempt to alleviate the mounting tension. I felt as if all my muscles were starting to compress like springs.

'Go stick a needle in yourself. I can tell you want to. What's that jolt like?'

It's the answer to everything, Ata. The Shift, it's where the Insects are coming from. But of course I didn't tell her that. 'Why are you doing this to me?' I asked plaintively.

Ata glanced meaningfully at Carmine, and changed language to Awian. 'Because it's the first reason why you will tell no one your strange idea that I caused Mist's death.'

'The second reason?'

'Genya Dara.'

'What do you know about Genya Dara?'

'I know what you did to her. Rape.'

I folded arms, wings, legs tightly and perched on the chair staring at my jiggling foot. Fuck it, fuck it. I was so stupid! How could I have been so possessed? I didn't understand why the mountain girl should turn up now. She had nothing to do with this. Desolate, I said, 'I'm not like my father. I'm not. I do love her.'

Ata's eyes narrowed in interest.

'It wasn't rape. Rhydanne sex might seem like rape to a flatlander. It was only a short pursuit; we're both to blame for the affair. In the Scree culture things are very different,' I added.

'That won't matter, if Awia learns of it. For all I know, in the mountains you bizarre Rhydanne might chase down girls like deer every day. But people here will not be as understanding. I might just tell Lightning, you know how he puts women on a pedestal. And I will tell your jealous wife; imagine how she would react. With the gates of Micawater and Wrought closed to you – at least for the next couple of hundred years – your life will be more than miserable. Jant, if you slur my name and try to bar me from the Circle I'll bring you down too. In this situation the Emperor would make examples of us both.'

'How did you find out about ... Genya?'

'I just asked her. Men can be so blind. If we get through this you should find her and treat her well as she deserves; see if she doesn't come to you as promptly as a trained hawk.'

'Yes, Ata.'

'Isn't it strange that Rhydanne will soon be the only people left, even though they have never joined the fight against the Insects? Your kind will discover Insects scaling the Darkling massif only when the last Awian is extinct and the last human in Hacilith is bitten in two.'

'Yes, Ata,' I said, knowing no one could make Rhydanne co-operate long enough to fight. It was all too clear I had to take the only path left open, and become her accomplice.

Ata extended her calloused hand and we both promised to keep silent. I would have to live beside this lady forever, and I worried about how long our mutual secrets might last.

'I will be Mist Ata Dei. Immortal again, for good.' She stood up briskly. I sneezed three times in close succession. The tendons were burning in the backs of my hands.

'Let's end our discussion,' she said, returning to Morenzian vernacular. 'It's late, and I perceive you're unwell.'

'There's nothing wrong with me.'

'Jant, you're smoother when you're lying than when you're straight! Listen, I have eighty carracks, and eleven thousand men. You were on the deck of the *Honeybuzzard* when Shearwater ran my ambush, so you saw what I saw. He made a castle of his ship. He barricaded the railings and blocked my arrows. Shame, but I learnt from that – how ships carrying soldiers can be as sound as a fortress afloat. Ah, look at you! What's the use in talking?'

I wiped my watering eyes with a sleeve. I was having trouble concentrating; *I need a shot* kept drifting into my mind. I leant and rubbed my thighs and shins, trying to stop them aching, but tension made them stone-hard.

'What about Swallow?' Swallow had ten well-guarded caravels, and her fyrd could sail them. Swallow also had charge of Cyan. It was essential to know what Ata thought.

'The savante's music is breathtaking. What else?' I could tell from her hooded tone that if she had any plans concerning Swallow I would certainly not hear them.

'She's proved herself in battle ... I think ... and she will still try for a place in the Circle; I know she won't ever give up.'

'Jant, you're inexperienced. I'll be free of the Zascai in less than sixty years. She's a genius in music only—'

'The Circle is *based* on merit!' What am I, god's sake, but a specialist?

'Supposed to be,' Ata said wryly. 'Lightning, the eternal bachelor, will realise one day that what he pursues in all these wild young redhead girls is something he should find in himself. He tries to marry freedom rather than learn it. He should realise he doesn't need their carefree cheer to replace what he's long forgotten, and has to rediscover.'

'And Awia?'

'Flags and boundaries mean nothing to me; if we live I'll help the decadent kingdom. But perhaps we'll set the balance right in favour of Morenzia for once.' Carmine Dei began to smile.

'Now, Jant, I can tell you're worse now than you were when we started, all curled up like that, so let me give you a bed and see you in the morning.' An unintentional lightening of her tone crept in, reminding me again of her hundred children. I was desperately tired and longing, longing to lie down, but I refused her offer. I knew better than to give her the chance to cut my throat. I demanded to stay in the tower room, close to the window, and alone.

From behind her desk, Ata scrutinised me, intrigued, although her manner still appeared kindly; then she called her daughter and they left. The sound of the waves slipped back. Soon I thought it would wear my nerves away.

I lay by the window, on the floorboards like *Honeybuzzard*'s deck, and wrapped myself in the soldier's coat. I began trembling violently, which was nothing to do with the cold. I lay awake all night, sore-eyed with visions of the needle, Insects and ice.

CHAPTER 22

I relived my first meeting with the girl from the roof of the world. In winter, Scree pueblo nestled roof-deep into the snow, tiny fire-lit windows by the edge of a sheer gorge. I found the pass and sailed rapidly above the arête, down over a sharp rock buttress. The mountains sped by too fast for breathing. I flew below the level of the peaks, vast black splinters cutting a clear sprinkled sky. I navigated by Polaris and the scent of peat smoke, and I came home to Darkling, to stay in the Filigree Spider for a few days of rest.

A harsh, intensely cold wind blew down from the high peaks, Mhadaidh and Bhachnadich, straight off the glaciers. It dried the skin tight to the bones of my face. I rode that wind in, ice forming on my wings' leading edges. I landed in powdery snow, knee-deep on the pueblo's low roof, slid off in a minor avalanche and hammered on the door of the Spider.

Lascanne opened the top half, and grinned. 'You're late.'

'I'm *never* late.'

'Oh ... We've already started.'

'Free drinks?' I could smell warm whisky.

'In your honour, Jant.'

God, it was good to be back.

There were about twenty people in the little pub, flickered by firelight, quite drunk on gut-wrenching spirits, eating rye bread and smoked goat. Tern bought the Spider as my wedding present because I always used to say I was born in the bar in Scree; the only place where Rhydanne co-operate.

Unlike a human or Awian pub, there is very little conversation, and no music; Rhydanne society is a contradiction in terms. They are not gregarious creatures, each is used to a solitary, independent existence, and so even in the bar they were aloof, keeping distance from each other, and concentrating on drinking. I occasionally told stories, five-minute-long fables – as five minutes heavily stretches a Rhydanne attention span.

The second day was a solid and relentless blizzard, and few people visited. I must have taken too much cat because I stayed awake all night, buzzing with vitality. I checked the Spider's accounts, finding them very out of date. Hollow-cheeked Lascanne couldn't write; he kept all the numbers in his head. Nobody could fault him, he had the best memory for who owed a goat for their jug of whisky.

Lascanne was tall and stick-thin, with hair cut very short and spiked. The bones of his skull could be seen through it, knobbly and asymmetrical. His long fingers moved in self-deprecating gestures. Lascanne was scared rigid of me.

In the early hours of the morning he was still serving the Spider's patrons, in a lazy, relaxed atmosphere, safe from the snow. A peat fire had burnt down to sheaves of white ash, creeping orange sparks. The kilim-covered floor was warm, the room pine-scented.

Gradually I found my attention drawn to a figure sitting at a table, on a rough wood bench by the door. It was strange because people usually tried to sit close to the hearth. Female, although it was difficult to tell. She had her back to me and was drinking vodka steadily, making a pyramid of the pottery cups after downing each shot. I counted thirteen of them. Her very fine black hair brushed off her shoulders and hung to her waist. Her face was away from me and as I watched no one acknowledged her presence. They left her well alone.

Like me she had pale skin, Rhydanne eyes with vertical oval pupils that cut out snow-glare. A very rapid flicker-fusion speed in our vision gives us faster reactions – which a flatlander would call overreactions. Her arms and legs were collections of long muscles, sinewy and toned. Wearing? A black vest, loose and discoloured by a thousand stonewashings, pushed out by her tiny pointed tits – I strained to see – and a short skirt, no, a very short skirt, from the same valuable black cotton traded up from Awia. She had leather pumps with string grips, and that was all. As I stared quite openly taking all this in, she kept drowning herself in the house's best vodka.

'Lascanne,' I called. 'Come over here a minute.' He strode across, wiping a horn tumbler.

I pointed at the skinny girl. 'Who is that?' He shrugged and turned away but I leant over the bar and grabbed his elbow.

'Oh ... just some bitch,' he said.

'The name of the bitch?' I prompted.

'Jant, keep away from her. She's not all ... Well, she's a bit strange.' He smiled nervously, with thin lips.

'You're bloody weird yourself, Lascanne, and I do not need your advice. If you don't tell me I'm going to get angry. Three ... Two ...'

'Genya Dara!'

I released him and he rubbed his bony elbow. 'She's a Dara ...' he asserted. 'She's Labhra's daughter, so ... my half-sister.'

'I didn't know Labhra had a daughter!'

'He didn't want you to know, Jant.'

Curiosity momentarily stole my attention from the narrow-shouldered girl. 'What happened to Labhra in the end?' I queried.

Lascanne shrugged, a gesture he was built for. 'Oh ... his wife killed him,' he said.

I helped myself to a quaich of whisky, sinking back onto the bar stool. I felt like I walked on a feather's edge. When fate throws something as delicious as this my way I find it hard to believe I have not strayed into someone else's life. The bar seemed slightly unreal and I was shivering with delight. Lascanne saw the decision set hard in my eyes after a few moments' thought. 'Oh, no, you don't,' he said softly, with the lilting Darkling accent I so often miss.

'Why haven't I seen her before?'

'Jant, I— Oh. All right. She doesn't come down much ... She only visits in when the weather's too harsh up on the peaks; the rest of the time she's out on Chir or Greaderich.'

'Is she, indeed? And what does she do there?' The thin ice of Lascanne's patience cracked and he told me perhaps I should ask her myself. 'She's a lone wolf bitch, that's all I know,' he said bitterly. He could tell how much I wanted her, I was charged with need. I had thought I would never have another chance since Dellin rejected me. And here she was, my other chance. My last chance. I had to have her.

'She's taller than Dellin,' I murmured, thinking aloud. The barman caught the comment, and smiled.

'Yes,' he said. 'I know what happened back then.'

'Mortals can't remember that!'

'Jant, your thorough failure with Shira Dellin is legendary up here.'

That was a hundred years ago. This is here and now. 'What sort of man does this one like?' I asked, levelling a finger at Genya Dara's scrawny shape.

The bitterness in Lascanne's voice took on a strain of self-pity. 'I don't know,' he admitted. 'She won't let me near her.'

Over the next day and night, I put in some hard work. All my efforts were in vain; Genya refused to notice me. Eventually I couldn't decide whether Genya's world was too untranslatable even for me, whether she was just obstinate, engaged, or simply bloody stupid. Two things were clear: she was as beautiful as she was intractable and she was a very dedicated alcoholic.

When in a drug haze I called her Dellin by mistake she simply smiled, showing teeth white as snow. I bought her whisky and she drank it (as fast as I could bring it) but she never thanked me. I ran through my repertoire to no avail – which only made my desire for her worse. She declined to dance. Cards? She didn't know how to play. Stories of other lands? She was less than interested. Would Genya like me to accompany her home? This caused a flurry of icy laughter, which set in little drifts around my feet.

The Rhydanne girl had a mannish face, although still with high cheekbones and a graceful jaw. She always wore the same clothes, thin vest or a polonaise. She was too leggy, starved and muscular to resemble petite Dellin, but my anger at Dellin, preserved over the years, was now directed at her.

When I lay awake and the rest of the house was sleeping, I thought of her. I was eaten alive by thoughts of her, which I tried to salve with scolopendium. But desire pooled in me like melt water. So much desire. I had to have her. A gram of cantharides would have done the trick in an Awian court, but nothing's aphrodisiac above the snowline.

I wanted to fuck her. What a chase she would give me! I would catch her. Bring her down among the ice formations.

Or I would screw her in a warm bed while snow plumes fell past the window. I wanted her to ride me, muscles appearing and disappearing in those long legs. I was erect again. I was so hard I felt my heart beat blunt in my groin. Genya made me like this. It's what she has to answer for. Lying on the pallet, I cup and caress my balls with one hand, rub my hard cock. My cock is narrow but average long, the tip is smooth. These painted nails are hers. The fist around my cock is hers, tightening on the upstroke. Her body is stretched out underneath me. Little tits, chalky with cold. Cat-eyes, shining with pleasure. When I come, I spurt into her mouth. I sigh. It's just lust, Shira. It's never been 'love them and leave them' so much as 'fuck them and flee'.

On the last night I was at my wits' end. I was expected at the Castle next day and was preparing for a long and uncomfortable flight. My habit was serious, I had run out of money and had no success at all with Genya Dara.

'You've failed, Comet,' said Lascanne happily.

'Not yet, struidhear. Not yet, damn it.'

'Ha! Try again in a hundred years' time. What do you want the sullen bitch for, anyway?'

Because she's a piece of the mountains, a potential memory. Because she's Rhydanne, quick and feral. Because she looks just like me, Lascanne; she's our kind. I'm a rape child, so is Lascanne Shira; I pity his mother when Labhra pounced on her. The mountain people considered illegitimacy to be a curse – a curse you can pass on.

I hogged the bar, feeling faint, my movements blurred, and forgot about Genya until she pushed past. She usually avoided contact but wanted to know why the drinks had dried up. She had come in from outside, where people go round the back of the pub to piss in the snow, and her skin was cold although she looked flushed and panicky. I saw her brush her hand down the front of her skirt. 'Let me do that?' I suggested. Silence. 'Sweet vixen,' I said, 'I'll probably never see you again.'

Dara came close for me to grasp her round the waist, thin enough to encircle with one arm. She didn't pull away.

'I want you,' I told her, in all honesty.

'Then chase me!' she said, and ran.

236

She sprang over a bench, over a pile of skis, and was out of the door before my next breath. Lascanne whined behind me. He looked like he was going to vault the bar and follow her. I slipped off my sword belt, threw it at him. 'Stay!' I ordered. And I was gone. Running.

Freezing night air burnt my lungs. I sipped at the air, spit gathering in the back of my throat. The road was snow; Genya's footprints led up a little rise. I followed, long-legged. I trod in her footprints, shallow with speed. Genya was nowhere. She had completely vanished. God, she's fast. Without the weight of wings to carry, she was my equal. I hoped she would tire easily.

I ran up the rise and onto a narrow plateau above Scree. She kept close to the cornice. I swept doubt from my mind and concentrated on running. Fast. One foot in front of the other, for hours. My heart thundering on cat and whisky. Genya slipping always ahead of me like a black ghost. Watch my own thin legs. Desire is a splinter of ice in my mind. Shadows spindly on snow, the frost-twisted trees. She led me between them and I thought she would stop there. She had no intention of surrendering. She was leading to a better place. I wanted to bite her, fast and hard.

We went up a stone chute between sharp rock pillars. Quartz is rock snow, granite froth. We ran on, flight in her mind, fucking in mine. We ran up to the edge of the Klannich glacier, a rearing white wall. Ice crackled as she high-stepped through a frozen stream.

My cock was so hard I could hardly run. I could see her, in the distance, starting the climb of a massive crag. I closed the distance as she gained altitude. At the foot of the cliff, I looked up and she was way above me. I put a hand to the frost-shattered rock. Cold. Detailed in grey. See – this is not a dream. I'm going to fuck that bitch, I thought, as I paused for breath and bent over, coughing and spitting.

Genya had made a mistake. We had run the length of the corrie, into the heart of the mountains. She outpaced me, but she had led to a sheer escarpment, where the hanging valley ended. It stretched up onto a knife-sharp ridge. She climbed with a quick, sure grace, stabbing the hard, pointed nails on her long fingers into every crack. But she didn't have wings and so she had to take care. Falling is nothing to me. I took little heed and climbed faster still. Meagre handholds offered themselves. I flowed my weight each to each and climbed. Fast. I overtook her halfway up that wall of rock, reached the ledge first and gave her a hand over the top.

Wide clear sky. Vertigo view – peaks linked by ridges marching out for kilometres. The mountains were stark, ice-spattered. Their slopes were fir-lined and patched with black shadows.

I clasped her wrist hard enough to bruise and dragged her over the edge. In that vast empty sky I touched her.

She cut at me with her free hand. I twisted her arm behind her back and made her kneel. I would have taken her like that, on her knees, grabbing her flat tits. She kicked me. I didn't slap her; I wrestled her onto her back. She smelt of stone, she was shivering.

That isn't right. She shouldn't be shivering. It isn't cold enough yet. I put my weight on top of her, forearms on her shoulders, forced her to lie prone. She squirmed. I struggled with a cold button and shoved my buck-skin trousers down. My cock was so hard it ached. I rubbed a hand over it, in the chill air. Lying between her legs I was already flicking my hips against her. I felt my feathers rustle. My tongue was dry from gulping the cold air but I licked at her neck, holding one hand entwined in dark hair to stop her biting me. So I could look into her eyes. I was desperate for orgasm. I ripped her thin panties, she seized my arm and licked it.

'Is this good?' I said.

'Deyn.'

'What do you mean, you don't know?'

She was quite dry. Strange, I thought, and then I realised why. I realised why she was shivering. It wasn't with cold, it was with fear. She hadn't done it before. Suddenly disgusted, I sat back on my haunches, hard-muscled belly and prick stuck up in front, larger than ever before. She focused on it, awed.

I rubbed her with the tip of my thumb, and slowly eased two fingers in together, feeling the membrane tear stickily. Her strong struggling gave way to whimpers. She became slick with blood. I wiped a red fingertip over her pale mouth. She spat.

I could feel her heat. I was dizzy with it. Stark with impatience I held my cock and tried to ease in. Bony bitch. I wriggled my hips. Just inside her. Soft, warm. In a hard cold world. One hard thrust and I was as deep in as I could reach. A gasp of pleasure from me, a scream from her. Lust overcame my annoyance and I started fucking her as hard as I could.

I was propped up on stiff arms, looking down onto her sharp-featured face, using her body to rub my cock. I was shoving her body backwards on the rocky ground. She was very tight and very hot, lubricated by blood. Her nipples were small and pointed, dragging faded cloth like a ridge between them. She felt better than I had ever imagined. I was elated, had a cat-eyed girl at last. Sex is scrambled with flatlanders.

I spread my wings, to angle my hips better, but Genya wouldn't run her fingers between the feathers tented over her. She put one hand on my arse, to pull me in further.

I threw my fuck into her, scooping with my hips. I felt a point of heat at the base of my cock. I gasped. She tried to throw me off. That made me more excited. I meant to pull out, but she was too delicious. I emptied myself into her. Fast, and the next few thrusts were slick and squeezed. Her body went limp.

238

Possession slackened its hold on me. I pulled out and stood up, already guilty. My muscles were aching from the exertion of the chase. I shoved my damp prick back into leggings and buttoned my trousers.

Gradually Genya stood up, pallid, and contemplated the cliff edge.

'You're leaving now, aren't you?' she said.

'Yes.'

That's Rhydanne sex.

Genya watched me lift my wingtips from the ground, a look of utter dismay on her face. There was a smear of my come and her blood on her thigh.

I found my bearings; we were on the slope of Stravaig. Mhor Darkling's triple peak was just visible behind its white summit, a sight I had not seen for a hundred years. I lost interest in Dara, remembering my long-lost life in Darkling valley.

Genya set off at a sprint along the ridge – the spur formed a track leading to Basteir sheiling. She hit a snow patch and slithered dangerously, regained her balance and increased her speed until she was almost flying, running above nothingness. I took a slow glide back to Scree.

Now, in August Tower, as the sickness came on, I spent all night dwelling on my deficiencies. And on Genya.

CHAPTER 23

Ata returned an hour before dawn, in a heavy woollen shawl. She was wearing her husband's 1851 Sword, that he had so greatly prized. The lacquer scabbard described an arc at her side; rayskin-covered ivory and black silk accents on the hilt. The blade was forged from a charcoal-hardened steel sheet folded one thousand and one times; its weighting was immaculate. Wrought steel is the finest produced anywhere. The sword had never been used; as keen as the day it was honed, it could bisect an Insect without slowing. I lusted after it. It would perfect every fighting move I knew; just wearing it would bring respect and brawlers would steer clear. It was the apex of Awian craft, made for their Great Exhibition, and then presented by the King to Peregrine manor, where it remained in pride of place. Mist kept the 1851 Sword in a glass cabinet. Ata had smashed the cabinet and buckled the sword at her waist.

Ata began to take measurements on a map of Lowespass Fortress Crag. Out of the window I could see the tapering mainland, which looked as if it was hanging in the air; the sky and the sea were the same pale blue and I could not distinguish between them. The wind had dropped, now blowing from the land out to sea. Where there had been foam-capped breakers, the water rippled silver like a tray of mercury. I watched the mainland, waiting for the sun to rise.

Instead, a star appeared on the mainland, shining at the water's edge. I could see the star's reflection in the sea; it was a pallid, flickering yellow point of light. I squinted at it but couldn't figure out what it was, and the concentration made my headache worse.

'Mortal,' I called, 'come and look at this.'

'Ah, it does speak,' Ata countered. 'Thought it just slumped there and shivered.' She gathered her thick shawl and joined me at the window. I pointed out the bright, unsteady light. 'Do you know what that is?'

'Of course. It's the Awndyn lighthouse.'

'We can see that far?' Awndyn was thirty kilometres straight flight away. The storm had washed the air clear.

'Aye. It's at the end of the harbour wall. Strange Swallow should light it by day, eccentric lass.'

'It's not strange. It's a signal! Lightning, you're a genius!'

'That's as maybe, but it's not a good sign – it's a steady light. I think they're in trouble; we have to go *now*. Jant, can you fight?'

'Fight? I can't even stand up!'

Ata ran to the stairs and called down, 'Carmine, what's ready?'

The hatchet-faced hoyden appeared in the doorway. 'Everything. The twenty Great Ships are packed with Hacilith Fyrd. Horses and wagons are on the *Ortolan*; the third-raters and pinnaces are to carry supplies. The *Tragopan's* still loading, but we can't all leave the harbour on the same tide anyway.'

'Then we will take the *Stormy Petrel*.'

Carmine bowed her head.

'You take charge of the *Tragopan*, my dear, and the other seventy-eight to follow. Meet us at six tonight ten degrees north of Sheldrake Point.'

Carmine nodded and ducked back down the stairs.

Ata pressed my sword into my grasp. 'Jant, you can do better than this!'

I scrambled to my feet. 'Have you got any cat?'

'Cat? You mean scolopendium? No, and I doubt there's any available anywhere in the world now.'

'I only have a couple of hours left, I don't want to go—'

She beckoned, sternly, and I followed her down the stone spiral staircase, out onto the wooden gantry and down to the flat rocks at September Tower harbour. I screwed my eyes up against the sunshine. My pupils were so dilated everything was glaring white or deep black shadow. The ocean was just a huge, painfully bright hole. Ata's white slacks and flaxen hair dazzled in the light.

The cobbled quayside bustled with thousands of men, talking loudly. It was a crush, polearms soldiers and sarissai, bands of crossbowmen with the Red Fist blazon of Hacilith on their buff coats, and at least two divisions of Awian Select longbowmen looking worn out, stressed and unpreened.

Stevedores were loading the *Tragopan* with three weighted hoists. Men were pushing dockside carts on their iron rails, full of barrels, pitch casks, piles of arrow sheaves. Chains of people passed along sharpened staves, sacks of anti-Insect salt, creels of food – they were stowed in the holds until the brightly painted caravel sat low in the water.

The harbour wall hugged all the ships in an angular embrace, concrete shining slick with slime. The ships' masts were so close together they looked tangled, and wires clattered against them as the wind blew through rigging.

Hacilith men caught sight of Ata and I from the deck of the *Stormy Petrel*. They yelled, 'Look!' to their comrades, pointing excitedly to the quayside. Ata waved demurely, and they erupted in a cheer. I wondered if any would see their city again.

Ata prodded me across the narrow plank over the gap between September Tower harbour and the *Stormy Petrel's* deck. I hung onto the railings as a whistle called the crew to attention and Ata ordered the sails set.

The *Stormy Petrel* pulled elegantly away from its mooring. I gazed at the harbour wall sliding past.

'Are you still alert, degenerate Rhydanne?'

'I need—'

'Don't say it! Don't talk about drugs – I don't like it!'

'Neither do I.'

'Thousands of people are dying in Awia, and we are going to stop that happening.'

The *Stormy Petrel* scudded swiftly across the thirty-kilometre-wide strait to Awndyn strand. The square burgundy mainsails bellied out like clouds. Slipstream poured off the lateen rig behind; it ruffled my feathers, making me gag. The sea has definite advantages. You can puke in it if you are very ill, which I was. I retched over the side, for hours until only bile came up; it tasted like Insect blood.

At the wheel, Ata muttered to her ship all the time, 'Faster, you bastard.' The katana in its black scabbard hung loose at her thigh.

Awndyn harbour looked deserted. Streams of pale grey smoke rose from the lighthouse, the only movement. But along the seven-kilometre sweep of sand tiny figures milled and churned.

About five hundred soldiers in Awndyn green were fighting in a tightening ring of Insects.

Insects appeared from the town's façade. They darted along the harbour wall and down sea-wrack stone steps, up from the shallow river bed. Insects the size of ponies ran over the grassy machair, jumping onto the sand. They picked their way between the headstones of Awndyn Cemetery, plunged down among the yellow dunes.

Further back, Insects were nibbling spilt blood on the marram grass. They followed the scent trail down to the beach. I could just make out patches of sand stuck to their gore-spattered chitin.

Some reared on saw-edged back legs, feelers flickering as they closed in. The Awndyn men were being pushed together, losing ground. They retreated towards the sea. The gap between them and the Insects was narrowing all the time.

Adrenaline roused me. 'There's a division's worth of men!' I called.

'I hoped for many more,' said Ata.

'I can see the Archer!'

It was impossible to miss Lightning. His gold scale armour glittered in the early sun. Bareheaded, and with bindings unwrapping from his greaves, he was waving the soldiers round into a circle, and pushing someone back behind him with the other hand.

Swallow. It was Swallow Awndyn, propped on her spear, and she had Cyan under her arm.

242

Harrier was shoulder to shoulder with Lightning; he faltered back on the wet sand then flexed his bow again.

Long dawn light cast their footprints as jumbled blue shadows on the yellow sand. The air was very clear, faint shouts carried to us; Lightning trying to keep their formation but men kept breaking away, chancing a run to the sea.

Ata steered starboard, as close in as she could, and *Stormy Petrel* careened parallel to Awndyn strand, almost at right angles to the wind, and lost speed until we stopped opposite the mass of Insects and struggling men.

'This crate is so unresponsive,' said Ata. 'If I go any nearer, leeway will beach the bastard.'

The Insects closed in. Lightning shot straight into them. He was loosing arrows the fastest I had ever seen. The quiver on his right hip was empty, and he was pulling arrows from the quiver on his back. Insects ran straight at him; he shot them down. He kept a distance of thirty metres, twenty metres, ten metres.

I could hear Cyan crying.

'We only have a minute!' I said.

Ata strode onto the lower deck. 'We'll have to pick them up.'

She shouted the length of the deck, and I heard the thick anchor chain rattle out from the bow. The *Stormy Petrel* drifted completely round before the anchor caught, and the stern anchor was released. Ata's crew began to lower boats in rope cradles, three from each side, into the water.

The boats splashed down simultaneously. Six sailors to each descended neat cord-and-lath ladders and unshipped the oars.

Ata turned to me. 'Messenger, wait here.' She caught a ladder and lowered herself over the side.

The *Stormy Petrel*'s massive flanks dwarfed the six landing craft. I watched them buck and toss over the waves, oars like Insect legs leaving white tracks in the water.

Most of the Awndyn Fyrd were already waist-deep in the sea. Around fifty archers were standing in the waves, bows held above their heads, swords drawn in their free hands. Insects followed them into the surf, holding their abdomens high and gnashing mandibles.

Ata stood in the prow of her boat impassively, while it dipped and heeled, and the oarsmen struggled. The six boats approached the cluster of archers – and nearly capsized as men grabbed the sides and tipped the boats in their haste to get aboard.

Grasping and spluttering, they ignored Ata's cries for order. They surged forward, up to the neck, throwing bows away. The oarsmen reached down, heaved them, belts, wings and armpits, and hoisted them over the gunwales.

As the boats neared shore, they reached men still in their depth, and boathooked them aboard, arses in the air. Laden boat hulls grated against the sand.

Lightning said something to Swallow, who kicked off her leg-armour and plunged in, wisely making for a boat which didn't have Ata in it. Harrier carried Cyan. Lightning removed the silk string from his great bow, held it up and stepped into the surf, the last Awndyn men behind him.

The six boats were so crammed with soldiers – about seventy in each – everyone was standing. The rowers held their oars up out of the locks, Ghallain-style. They fought to turn their boats prow-on-against the waves, and began to paddle back towards me.

The coast was left to the Insects.

The landing crafts' return journey took ages. I watched Insects pick over bodies on the sand. An Insect buried its head under a corpse and flicked it over. Two of them took an arm each, and, walking backwards, tore a man apart.

I was shaking.

Lightning might give me my syringe back. A soldier might have some medicine – I mean cat – to arrest my decline. I told myself, Jant, don't be so fucking ridiculous. I stopped trying to control the shivering, relaxed and it took over completely.

I helped Swallow as she appeared from the top of the rope ladder, panting, onto the deck. She had a leaf-green mantle around her throat, and a rondel dagger stuck down her bodice lacings.

I embraced her. 'What happened to Awndyn manor?' I asked.

'Awndyn manor!' She burst into tears. 'It's *swarming*! God's moult! The Insects have taken the whole Empire, and we'll have to stay at sea forever to escape them!'

'Rachis, Hacilith and the Plainslands are still holding out,' I said. 'Have courage.' With an arm round her, I tried to console her by explaining the Emperor's message, while soldier after soldier climbed the ladder and emerged, dripping, onto the deck.

Lightning was leaning over the prow, picking off Insects on the beach that were beyond any other archer's range. He didn't stop shooting until Ata ordered full sail, and the infested shore shrank out of view.

He turned. 'Bring us closer,' he commanded.

Ata was banging the compass housing with her fist and swearing. She spared him a glance. 'Save your arrows.'

'If I can't reach Micawater, I'll die there on the beach!'

'Oh, shut up. You'll have your chance when we get to Lowespass.'

'Lowespass? Ata—'

'I want to be Mist Ata. Eighty ships are awaiting a rendezvous at nightfall, full of warriors eager to improve their ranks with the addition of Tornado, the Castle's champion.'

Lightning gestured at the rabble behind him. 'These are the thirteenth division of the Awndyn Fyrd. They're all Select infantry, though there's nothing Select about them now. Do you have the Micawater archers I sent you? Enough to cover the Hacilith men? Their crossbows have no range at all.'

'Yes, and I have ten thousand soldiers gathered from Morenzia, counted with those from the island and the coast, who thought wrongly that my island would be the best place to seek sanctuary.'

'I see ...'

'Lightning Saker, you owe me.'

He looked at her with undisguised loathing, then mastered it and described a formal bow. 'Yes,' he said grimly, 'I do.'

Cyan did not let go of Swallow; cold and terrified, the girl clutched to Swallow's good leg and did not say a word. Swallow hunkered down next to me, wiping tears from her eyes and drips from her nose onto her wet auburn wings. She stroked the back of my hand. I forced a smile and squeezed her arm.

'What's wrong with you?' she asked. She was used to me looking gaunt, but not this defeated.

'He's sick,' said Ata. 'Will all you armour-clad bastards bugger off away from this compass?'

'Has he been bitten?'

'Not by anything you know about, my lady.'

I turned my head away. If I wasn't so fucking weak I could have gone to score. The Circle had not broken again, so the rest of the Eszai must still be alive, with the Swordsman holding Hacilith. I thought of the city's Rowel Alley, Needle Park, East Bank Docks, all the pure quality cat the knife-packing youths sell and cut-down cat in foil wraps the matelots deal between themselves. Zascai low voices, silhouettes at street corners, or a pickable lock on a field hospital coffer full of medical-grade phials. *Anything* to ease the pain.

'Catscratched,' Ata said.

The Archer looked back to the land.

Ata stared at me as if I was beneath contempt – just above derision, on about the same level as scorn. She continued to herself, 'I thought death was the worst evil, because if it were good then Eszai would be content to die. Didn't consider that some of them had chosen a living death.'

That was too much for my pride. What did she know? I tried to stand and only managed to kneel. I heaved a breath, struggled in a suffocating ocean. Tried to stay afloat.

Ata said, 'The Messenger's gone to pieces, Lightning. Hope you can keep your edge.'

Slid into the depths.

I lay on a bunk, shivered and convulsed. My long fingers brushed the floorboards with each twitch. Swallow did not find me an easy patient; she put up with being screamed at in ten languages:

'I can't go through this shit! There isn't enough time!'

'Hush, Jant.'

'We only have three weeks!'

'You're delirious ... He was close to Mist, wasn't he?'

'Yes.' – Lightning's voice – 'And it was another bad shock for him to discover that Eszai *do* die.'

'Well, I can't understand a word he's saying.'

I woke up at a lull point; the cabin was dark. I gripped my hands between my knees, lay with one wing half-spread, rigid with stress, shaking with accelerated heartbeat.

I felt the ocean boiling like tar, its surface paved with thousands of faces. A line of blue-grey elephants on cranefly legs whickered across the pillow. I plucked one from its perspective tightrope, and it stalked like an insect in my palm.

'Can't believe the sun will rise again,' said a voice.

I squirmed round to see, feeling the crustiness where they had mopped vomit away from my mouth. An Awian soldier I didn't recognise sat cross-legged on the floor, his face hollowed by shadows. Harrier, in his long, dark blue waxed coat, stood staring out of the porthole like a sleepwalker.

The soldier was spiral-binding goose feather fletchings to arrow shafts. His splitter-arrows had bodkin-sharp points designed to penetrate Insect shell, and heavy barbs along the length of the shaft to crack the shell open.

The cabin planks creaked. A lantern hanging on a chain from the low ceiling swung with its pattern of shadows. Its light merged with a horrible hallucinatory red glow radiating through the port.

Harrier said, 'When god reappears from its break it's going to have a shock.' Grisly humour twisted his voice.

'If it comes back tomorrow it just might save us.'

'Perhaps it will. Perhaps it will. They say it cares for the Fourlands, holidays notwithstanding. Maybe this is the Return the immortals are waiting for.'

'God's supposed to bring ultimate peace and prosperity. Doesn't seem very bloody peaceful to me.'

They wished for god's arrival, so they didn't trust in the Castle. I crushed handfuls of the blanket in agony and rage. For millennia the Castle held Insects at bay, kept a stalemate to make the Circle indispensable. Now the balance was tipped, Insects were everywhere, and it was all my fault.

'I doubt even the Emperor knows what to do. Maybe he will leave us.'

'Fuck sake, Bateleur! You heard Captain Dei and my lord say that the Circle is strong.'

The soldier glanced at me. I feigned coma, which was easy. He looked to Harrier as if to say if that's the strength of the Eszai, we're doomed.

'Did Lightning offer any other revelations?'

Harrier bit his lip. 'Have some respect.'

'Oh, I'm brimming with respect. Lightning was there at the beginning of the world—'

'Of the Circle.'

'Right. Of the Circle. So he might have some idea how it will end.'

Harrier began sliding the completed arrows into the spacer holes of his leather quiver. 'I'm not my lord's confidant,' he said. 'I don't hear them discussing the Castle's mysteries. Insects have never caused such devastation south of Lowespass in the Circle's time – Cariama Eske said that they're reaching her manor. If the immortals can't stop Insects in Eske and Shivel, the Castle itself is threatened.'

'Will San call the Eszai back?'

'The Emperor San is *not* like Staniel Rachiswater! Damn!' Genuinely upset, Harrier pinched the bridge of his nose and shook his head.

The fletcher named Bateleur continued, 'The Emperor founded the Circle, though, and shared the immortality god gave him because Insects defeated his mortal legions. If the Circle is overcome, I wonder what he'll set up next?'

'Daydream all you like.'

'Ask Lightning.'

'I may not ask my lord anything!'

I pulled myself up against the wall. 'Ask me,' I said.

'Oh— by god! I'm sorry!'

Bateleur's eyes were like saucers; the soldier was petrified. Weakly, I said, 'I have driven myself into the ground for the Empire, and to save your lives, and all you do is speculate. I am sick with exhaustion, and all I hear is blasphemy.'

'I'm sorry!'

'The Emperor is in the Castle, and all will be well. San tells us no one knows when god will return, but I can assure you this is no way to prepare.'

'We didn't mean anything by it, Messenger!'

I gave him a challenging look. 'Will I see you in the ranks of bowmen?'

'Of course!'

'Good. Then pour me some water and get out of here!'

The room stank sharply of vomit. I was fully dressed, my black shirt stained, open to my hairless chest, jeans and bare feet. I doubled my wings up onto the bunk, bones grating, wiped beads of sweat off the Wheel scarification on my shoulder.

Lurid shades dappled Harrier's face and coat; they looked like bruises, but as he stirred the bruises did not move. They were only shadows cast by the sickly red light, through water drops on the porthole glass.

My body shuddered. Pain wrenched; I groaned. Every muscle ached. Was the next wave coming on already? I needed some respite!

Harrier said, 'Lightning did entrust me with the real cause of your condition.'

'Cold turkey.'

'Well, rest assured I will keep the secret.'

I told him, 'You've seen inside the Circle. I'm nearly well now.'

'Yes, you're making sense for a change.'

I raised a shaky toast to him with a horn cup of water, sipped it carefully, feeling my innards deciding whether to accept it or not. I was pouring with sweat, my hair plastered to my back. I disentangled it from my earrings.

'Did we make the rendezvous with the fleet?'

'Yes. Four days ago. Comet, I apologize on the fletcher's behalf, but you should know there's a lot of real dissent among the Awian soldiers. They know that Eleonora Tanager is our Queen now, and they want to join forces with her.' Harrier smiled; I could tell he supported Eleonora too.

'Has no one cried treason?'

'Eleonora is not an usurper. They call her the Emperor's friend ... I don't know about Staniel. Communications are flashing back and forth between the ships that I can't understand. Ata told us: "Wait, and you can send Tornado the Circle's Strongman to Rachiswater, and four thousand Lowespass warriors." That made them think.'

'I bet. What *is* that red light?' Harrier hesitated, peered through the porthole again and lost his chance to answer when Ata came in through the low cabin door.

'Ah, the physical freak's recovered,' she said. She passed me a wooden bowl full of soggy pasta. I started guzzling handfuls – I was ravenous.

'If San ever decided to make an Eszai best in the world at being feverish and puking all over the place, it would be you. Lying in a pool of your own vomit ...'

Well, it's better than lying in a pool of someone else's. An amazing feeling of accomplishment was dawning on me. I'm kicking it. I really am. I'm really going to be *free*.

'And you rave about some very interesting things, Jant Shira.'

'What's the red light?' I said through a mouthful.

'We are sailing along the coast of Wrought.'

'Wrought? Oh, no – Insects?'

'I think you should come above and see for yourself.'

I ate, washed, and followed her up to the deck, awash with the terrible light. I joined Lightning and Harrier at the stern. The brick-red glow stretched into the sky on the western horizon. It hung in a gigantic arc, one single body of rising air, like a red bubble.

The town of Wrought, Tern's gothic manor house and Sleat's Armourer's Society Hall were out of sight, below the horizon. All I could see was the flat black landmass. I rubbed my dry eyes and just made out two thin black pylons in the centre of the glow. The steelworks was burning.

One of the massive coal stores overheated and exploded. We ducked instinctively as a dull rumble like thunder toppled over the marshland.

In an untended steelworks it would only take one spark – or a furnace left burning when workers flee from the Insect assault – and now it was utterly out of control. No building could survive the conditions in that inferno.

Around the mad glow, the sky lit dark blue. Everywhere else was completely black. Blue, red and black, the colours of Wrought.

'What are we going to do, with no armoury?' asked Harrier.

'We'll have to rely on Morenzia.'

I moaned. No scolopendium to stroke me, I only thought of Tern. Everything she owned was in that manor house. She had to be safe, within the Castle's walls. I didn't want Tern to face this; too much for her to manage, it would change her forever and her voice would lose its softness.

Lightning traced his scar compulsively. 'I watched that town being built. I witnessed Awia's achievements over fifteen hundred years. It *cannot* stop now ... Insects are eating their way to the core of my country and, by god, I will kill every last one of them.'

I watched Tern's manor. My responsibility, the town I knew so well.

'The Chatelaine Diamond. Esmerillion's crown ...'

All the people. All the people's homes.

'The glass sculpture by Jaeger ...'

I hope our steward has made it safe to Rachiswater.

'Conure's poetry. Wrought katanas...' came the voice from the golden age.

At least the children were evacuated.

'Donaise wine. The Pentice Towers. Micawater Bridge ...'

Ata said, 'Saker? Saker! Snap out of it.'

Ata took the wheel and adjusted the horizon glass of her sextant; she looked impassive and ethereal. Harrier's long brown hair was tangled, he had sunken eyes. And me, a pale blur. And faces lined the port side of every deck of eighty ships. I never knew eleven thousand men could make so much silence. Nobody spoke. Nobody slept. We all just stood there watching Wrought go up in flames.

CHAPTER 24

The fleet sailed in a crescent formation up the coast to Summerday bay. There, the great caravels and little pinnaces entered the mouth of Oriole River.

Immediately, a knot of six pinnaces got stuck on a sandbar. Ata could do nothing to dislodge them; we offloaded the soldiers and supplies, and left the boats.

A clock still running in abandoned Summerday town chimed five in the morning as we passed through the ruins. I saw burnt thatched roofs above the town wall, a snapped rooftree shedding stone tiles, an unstable weather-vane teetering on flaking charcoal timbers. Crows flapped above derelict shop courtyards.

Half an hour later, another clock chimed five, and bitter laughter rippled over the troops. The Hacilith soldiers wore baggy trousers tucked into half-length boots, daggers on chains looped at their hips, and their hair cropped short. Most looked even younger than me, at fifteen or twenty, although a few among them had grim experience. Their polearms and armour were mass produced, but painted, scrawled with slogans – personalised – so that the city fyrd gave me more to look at than the Awians in all their plumy panoply.

Grey-green estuary water became clearer as we sailed upstream. Through Midelspass the eddying river was broad, the tide was on the flow, and we made good progress.

A team on every caravel dropped lines, taking depth measurements.

'Fifteen metres. Twelve metres. Seven. Five metres.'

'A sandbar!' said Ata, and swung the wheel round hard. The keel scraped through the mud. I held my breath. Ata found a deeper channel, and we sailed on.

'The river's not tidal from here, the passage's too narrow. If one ship gets beached none of the ones behind it will be able to sail round. We'll have to leave them, only have half an army, and never escape.'

'The wind won't be with us on the way back,' Harrier pointed out.

'It blows offshore at night,' I said.

'We can drift back downstream,' Ata explained. 'For god's sake trust me.'

Our ships slipped into the Paperlands.

'It's so quiet,' said Swallow.

White paper buildings covered the ground, as far as I could see from the river banks up to the tops of the valley sides. Insect tunnel arches, scaly paper passages, the roofs of cells. No green fields were left, no trees. The river bank mud was dark with decomposing matter; its putrescent stench wafted over the ships.

I imagined Insect mating flights twisting up above the Crag. I thought of fat, pupa-pale maggots large as a man but soft-bodied on stubby legs, lying in damp nests glowing with decay, belching silent chemical demands for food. I shuddered; I blame my father for my Awian imagination.

My Rhydanne instinct, on the other hand, was telling me to quit now and go get drunk. 'God, this place is totally flyblown.'

'It's another world,' Swallow whispered, not aware how close to the truth she was.

The bridge loomed.

'The river winds between its legs,' said Ata.

'We're going *underneath*?'

'Aye. Soon,' she said shortly. It was getting harder for her to steer.

The *Tragopan* misjudged a bend in the river and smacked into the mud.

Ata yelled, 'Concentrate, Carmine!'

The caravel ran along the bank and veered off into the centre of the river, with mud smeared up to its railings.

An Insect was drinking from the river. Its abdomen pulsed; it stood on the tips of its claws, mandibles opening and closing underwater. A second Insect joined it, glistening light gold brown with darker dorsal stripes. It stretched up; they stroked their antennae together; four front legs rasped against thoraxes. They lowered their heads to drink.

Cyan pointed. 'Look! They don't even care we're here!'

'This is their land now,' Swallow said.

'I'm not scared,' said Cyan. 'Imnotscaredimnotscaredimnotscared—'

Swallow spread her wing around the girl.

Oriole River looped round and led under the bridge's white legs. The spindly, impossible construction reared higher than the Crag. It leapt at the sky like a frozen fountain; swept up and vanished cleanly at its height. Its long shadow cast on the Paperlands cut off too.

'It's so vast!'

'Look up!' I said. The bridge's shadow fell over us. Small as nutshells, Ata's great ships threaded beneath it.

Ata shivered. 'How do brainless bloody Insects build something like this?'

'They start at the top and work down.'

Ata grimaced when she saw I was serious.

Maybe these animals aren't so mindless; Vireo said that they organise themselves, speaking in gestures or scents. Infuriated, I thought: a language I don't know, in a medium I can't even perceive. I felt the weight of two centuries more keenly as I thought no matter how long I study them, the way they communicate with each other and the way they see the world are far too alien for us to understand.

The men pointed, muttered, looked up. They rubbed aching necks and gaped up to see the walkway's underside, a hundred metres above the topmost reach of our masts. The bridge's legs shouldn't be able to take that weight; they're only as thick as the masts. Closer, pale grey laminations showed on the surface. It looked like a wasp's nest, with striated curves, brittle but amazingly strong. The walkway was wider than the Grand Place. It hung from thousands of Insect spit cables, liquid set hard. Some fine strands trailed out on the wind.

I could soar through and around it, fly between the cables, explore the structure in three dimensions, see it fall past me, survey its depth—

'No Insects on the bridge,' Lightning said.

Without thinking I said, 'There probably aren't any more to come through.'

'What?'

'We have to destroy it.'

Lightning said, 'That's beyond our capability.'

'We have to!'

Ata put in: 'Jant, shoot some cat and look at this from your usual level of consciousness. While you were being impressively sick, Lightning and I worked out our plan of attack. I rallied the men until I had no brave words left.'

'The bridge is key! No matter what we do, if the bridge stays the Insects swarm in!' I demanded, 'What will burn? What can we sacrifice?'

Ata gestured to the flotilla behind us. 'There are wagons. Barrels of tar we prepared to heat-crack Insect walls.'

'Then to work!'

On twenty pinnaces I had men cutting spare sail into strips and packing all the cloth they could find around tar barrels, transferring them to the *Ortolan* and lashing them tight to the wagons with ropes.

I clipped my tertiary feathers shorter, the ones nearest my body; sculpting my wings sharp to manoeuvre like a falcon. Soaring would be difficult, but it was worth it for the fine control and gain in speed. I buckled my sword to my back, and long cuisses and poleynes to my legs, customised to my shape, the only armour I could carry.

As we sailed we drew Insects from every part of the valley to the river bank. They ran alongside us, on the mud and claw-deep in the water.

Five Insects snipped branches off a felled tree, dragged them to where others crouched, building up a passageway. They cemented the chewed pulp onto the end of the tube. Insects infested ruined villages; as the ship carried me past I saw the wall of a burnt-out cottage collapse, rust-brown claws thrashing under the rubble.

The Crag came into view. Solid Insect spit veiled the grey stone fortress; it jutted from rings of white walls. I could construct Tawny and Vireo's struggles from the concentric walls, holding out and falling back, until Insects sealed them in. White paper structures washed over Lowespass' outer defences, but the Inner Ward looked clear.

'They're in there.'

'It's like a maze,' said Lightning.

I spread my wings. 'I can direct you.'

From the sailors' noisy swearing and despairing it was clear they thought the terrain mountainous. Humans choose to live shoulder-width apart in the crowded capital of their flat country. The deserted Paperlands affected them – they tried to fill it with sound. Shouting stridently to each other, boasting, encouraging, captains organised the fyrd divisions on the main decks. Lightning made them check and recheck their equipment, keeping their minds occupied as much as possible, to lessen their fear.

The Circle broke. Faster than with Mist. For a split second I filled infinity, fell to nothing. The Circle reformed.

'No!' Lightning cried out.

I picked myself off the deck. 'Who's gone? Who's killed?'

Lightning paused momentarily, grey gaze on the surface of the water without seeing it, concentrating on the faintest external feeling. 'The Blacksmith, I think.'

'In Rachiswater! What the fuck is going on back there?'

'Two Eszai dead, forty-eight to go.' Lightning turned away.

Perhaps it's a good thing I'm too inexperienced to feel the Circle. I don't want to know just how much my drug abuse had been stretching it.

As the ships slowed, a hundred more Insects sprinted to the swarm on both banks, packing in around the ships, hungry, desperate to get to us.

'Steady yourselves,' called Ata. 'Here we go.'

The depth-finders at the prow were hollering, 'Ten metres! Eight metres! Five! Three!'

Stormy Petrel shuddered along her length as she ran aground. The caravel behind us nearly ran on to our stern.

Ata yelled, '*Tragopan!* Steady! Steady ... We need you to get away.' *Tragopan* dropped anchor and slid back in the current. I could hear the river trickling past the hull, pooling up as so many ships blocked the flow.

The landscape came alive. Insects teemed down from Fortress Crag, two kilometres away. Watching them, I didn't trust my strength to fly up there.

I saw myself falling onto thousands of razor-jaws. Hitting the ground and breaking my legs. Faceted eyes plunging towards my face, whip-like feelers whirling.

Lightning approached Swallow, and lingered to compose himself. 'Stay here, stay on the ship. Some of us will return. I ... If I do not ... ah ... you will take good care of Cyan, won't you?'

'Yes,' Swallow said. Cyan toyed with an arrow. Insects massed on the shore.

'If I survive, will you join me in the Circle?'

'Repeat to fade,' Swallow murmured.

'I can still offer you immortality. Will you marry me?'

Worn down, lamed, overwhelmed, Swallow's glorious ambition just buckled. 'Yes,' she said.

Lightning swept an elegant bow, gold-blond wings spread; he received Swallow's hand and touched his lips to it. 'Kiss?' he said hopefully.

'No. I think under the circumstances ...'

Insects waded into the river's edge and scraped mandibles on the ships' sides.

'Under the circumstances it would make me feel much better.'

Swallow threw her arms around him, fastened her lips to his, and gave him a really deep, long kiss that seemed to go on forever. Lightning reciprocated, burying his powerful hands in her red hair.

'The longer we wait the more arrive,' said Ata; she drew her Wrought sword.

'There's *hundreds* of thousands!' I shouted.

'*Hurry!*'

Each ship lowered a gangway, splashing down in shallow water. For a second, every fyrd captain waited for another to make the first move. Archers, pikemen and those leading the horses, all delayed.

'*Go!*'

Lightning said, 'Ata, raise flags to tell them I will shoot anyone who refuses to leave the ships.' He nocked an arrow to string and stood on the steps in view of all.

Ata agreed. 'Comet, do something useful! Into the fortress and speak to Tornado. If he can, ask him to start breaking through. It'll save time when we reach them.' She pointed up to the Crag.

I hesitated, and Lightning levelled his bow at me. All right! For Wrought. For Tern.

I went from standing to top speed in three strides. Launched from the deck, fell till I gained windspeed. Hurtled low over the Insects' heads.

They jumped up, jaws snapping.

Can't catch me!

Insects appeared from every crevice, streaming down into the colourless valley. Their red-brown bodies scrunched into one great mass around the ships.

I found no lift in the bumpy, dead air. I beat my wings fast, keeping just above the festering swarm.

I worked my way low up the profile of the hill to the summit. Lowespass Fortress, like a model, spun below me. A trace of green – some grass still in the Outer Ward. I swung round low over the tower tops. Concentrating on flying, I was surprised at my agility. I stretched, feeling braver, glided in with my wings held below me. I leant right, tipped the skyline crazily, and dropped into the fortress.

Faces peered out from arrow-ports in the grey bastions. There were more people than I expected, their packs dotted all over the ground. The filthy soldiers looked sullen, sitting in their curved square shields. I spotted Tornado looking up, surprised.

I flared wings, hit the grass, dropped to my armoured knees and slid to a halt; flicked sickle wings closed.

Tornado seized my jacket and shook me, bellowing, 'You should have come earlier!'

I struggled for breath. 'We had a lot of trouble at the coast.'

Tornado's shaved head was bristly. He stank of sour sweat; he was covered in cuts, his canvas trousers slashed. Fragments of chain mail strung on his belt hung round his loins and buttocks. Armpit hair stuck through his over-large leather waistcoat, open at the sides with criss-cross binding.

I said, 'I want you to break through the wall. Here ... to here,' pointing out a space where the Insects' defences were one wall deep.

Tawny raised his arms and a division of five hundred fyrd clattered to their feet. They wrapped scarves around their faces as protection from splinters. They fetched picks, mattocks and trench-spades and started to chip at the wall. Its surface began to shatter like porcelain; it broke away in lumps from the objects suspended within. Bones, petrified branches, dented armour all emerged and broke off as the Lowespass men hacked.

'Many more survivors than I thought ...' I said.

'There's nine thousand six hundred of us,' he answered. 'Fighters sought refuge here from, like, every town north of Awia.'

'Get them armed. Saker and Ata are here; we brought food. We brought *ships*. They have eleven thousand fyrd – but I don't know how many will make it up the hill.'

'Then who died?'

I realised Tornado had felt the Circle break as well, and how terrible it must have been for him, incarcerated here without any news.

'Sleat the Blacksmith. And Shearwater Mist – in a storm.'

'It was an accident?'

I nodded.

'Eszai don't die in accidents,' he said bluntly. 'Mist was Plainslands, and he could look after himself. Jant, I tried to fight my way out of here, people were dying round me all the time. Vireo said better to sit and wait if there's a chance we could save them.'

'Do any of the big catapults work?'

'We ran out of ammunition a long time ago. Just about the time I ate the last horse.' He raised his voice: 'Vireo! Vireo! All of you – prepare to fight!'

Vireo ran from the spur-buttressed gatehouse. Her armour was styled to look like an Insect – big eye bulges on the sallet, a keeled breastplate like a thorax. She carried a spiked warhammer on a metre-long pole.

'Is this it?' she asked. 'Comet, we had given up on you!'

'What did I tell you?' Tawny berated her. Then the muscle-bound maniac actually grinned. He was truly gigantic, living proof that Plainslanders fuck oxen.

Wondering how Tawny could have any men fit to do battle, I looked about and noticed a great heap of burnt shell stacked by the stables. The shells were smashed, reddened, pale inside. It resembled the remains of a massive seafood feast.

'You've been eating *Insects*?'

'Little one, I don't want to talk about it.'

But Insects eat people! 'Aren't they poisonous?'

'I said I don't want to talk about it!'

Back at the caravels, archers were pouring arrows in almost solid arcs onto the Insects, and akontistai on the decks hurled javelins. Under this cover, fyrd divisions in tight formation left the decks together, marched down the gangways onto the river bank, where they joined ranks with men from ships on left and right.

First out were spearmen, with their backups carrying bundles of spare spears, and pikemen with square shields beside them. With the bombardment from the vessels, they made space on the shore.

Their spears became clogged with skewered, contorting Insects, yellow fluid running down the shafts. They dropped their spears and were passed new ones. Then followed untrained polearms men with axes, pole-cleavers and gisarmes. They wore helmets with aventail and latten plate armour over padded shirts. The crossbowmen had discarded their brigandines for cuirasses, and to their scale armour the Awians had added plate protection on their limbs. All were behind the heavy wall of square shields, the spears bristling like a Shift creature's spines.

Ata left the gangway on her steel-clad courser. Too aware of her mortality, she kept three ranks of axemen in front of her, and I recognised one of her sons on either side of her chestnut horse. She was head-to-foot in polished, fluted plate with no crests, but its shine marked her out; she flourished the Wrought sword's phenomenal blade.

With everything Ata knows about me I hope she doesn't survive; in a battle any accident might happen, and it will if I get a chance to pick up a crossbow. But Ata was keenly aware what I'm capable of, and I thought her sons were here not to protect her from Insects, but from me.

I drew my sword, searched for a space in this defensive phalanx, landed next to her. 'Hear Tornado breaking the wall?' I shouted.

She gave a brief salute. 'How many Insects?'

'Can't count them! Thousands! Swarms!'

Ata could not see what I saw. It was like being in an anthill. Insects drained out of the whole valley towards us. They sped down the valley sides, out of the tunnels. Ata's men were a knot of colour surrounded for a quarter-k by a vast red-brown Insect tide.

I said, 'It'll be tight through the walls; follow me.'

A dark red Insect clawed at my face. I sliced its foot off.

The Hacilith men set up a howl, cut forward twenty metres; Ata made good use of the advance and directed the archers out from their positions on deck.

I flew up to see Harrier's archers on the left, Lightning on the far right. Lightning was mounted on a heavily armoured hunter-clip white stallion, the one other horse. He only looked ahead; he had a dint in his cheek where the arrow nocks had pressed. The archers shot twelve flights a minute. How long could they keep up that rate of bombardment? There were more Insects than we had arrows!

Insects fell, cut apart, Insects ran madly away, arrows sticking out of them, but more crammed into the space they left.

Under cover of the archers fyrd surged forwards and left the river bank. It took an hour to gain the foot of the hill.

Ata kept her men in one wide column, surrounded by shields in two staggered ranks. Then polearms men, chopping at Insects that got through. The sarissai's spears were used up by now. Archers shot from the column centre, but Lightning and Harrier's divisions cleared space out in front. The crossbowmen were shooting to the rear. All attacked the climb full of energy, but were out of breath after the first few hundred metres. Breathing heavily, shouting less as the gradient increased, they ploughed up, slashing at Insects.

A river of Insects descending the crag charged headlong, antennae waving.

258

Lightning's archers loosed, a hundred Insects dropped and the rest came on. I plummeted down, only thinking that I should aid the Zascai.

I landed by a Hacilith soldier, who had a black bandanna under his helmet and broken-off mandibles embedded in his round shield. He brandished his poleaxe out at arm's length, keeping two Insects at bay. The smaller one pounced at his throat; he swiped and cut through a feeler. The damp white nerve strand that ran down inside the antenna flopped out over its eye. It stumbled, scraping over his armour. The second Insect stabbed its jaws under his breastplate, between his ribs. It braced itself with six legs and pulled, dragging him forward.

I reached him as it tried to open its mandibles inside him. I smashed my sword into the globular knee-joint of a middle leg, shattering it. As the Insect shifted its weight onto the other five, I leant back and with one long overhand swipe took its head off.

The soldier panicked when he recognised me. I took his hand; he coughed and tried to fend me away. His jagged chest wound sucked as he breathed in, then an artery ruptured. A blood cascade erupted from his mouth, gushing over breastplate, dead Insects, the ground. It frothed from his nose. With a look of terror, he mouthed through the bright red gouts. He fell to the ground and that was it – he bled to death in ten seconds, blood filling his lungs.

Twenty Insects scented the blood and closed in, clustered over him, heads moving, munching. I spread my wings and got out of there. After witnessing that, I will never take hallucinogens again.

Our host spread out to either side, spanning the hill. The vanguard was a mass of struggling, falling people. The rearguard bunched up away from the river. The column continued to advance, leaving spiky arrays of dead Insects and severed human limbs. Insects pounded down from every lair in the landscape, eager to feed.

'Ata!' I shouted. 'Go left here, around the edge of this wall. Go along the wall. Then right. Climb up to where you see a gap.'

Ata urged her horse on.

I said, 'For god's sake don't let them move apart. The gap is very narrow.'

I watched as the columns passed between low, broken Insect walls. Teams of men between the columns planted sharp stakes in the ground, until every breach bristled with staves. The first charging Insects impaled themselves, the rest had to slow to pick their way through.

Harrier's archers on the left dropped their rate of shooting to ten per minute, then to six. Insects gained ground on them and started preying on their line.

'Go see Harrier!' Ata shouted to me.

'You want me to be everywhere!'

'Yes! *Be everywhere!*'

Volleys of arrows flew up, tilted at their zenith, dropped onto the Insects. Another cloud of arrows buzzed beneath me, and another.

Harrier raised a hand, fingers spread. 'Comet! Five minutes! Five minutes' worth of arrows left! That's all! Help me!'

I turned back, found the captain of the Hacilith crossbowmen behind in the column, and directed the whole crossbow division through Harrier's ranks, to spread out in front of them, 'Make way! Move down – let them through!'

'Out of arrows!'

'Out of arrows!' Harrier's voice.

Harrier's five hundred men simultaneously dropped their bows behind them and drew their swords.

Insects slammed into their ranks. The archers' solid line flexed, then Insects intermeshed into their edge like into a forest. The ranks disintegrated, Insects moving through and over them. Men were shoved together; the line dissolved into single men against Insects. Archers were struggling, disappearing. The crossbowmen started up.

I heard cracking as the Insects fractured archers' bones. Awians have hollow limb bones, which are tough, but cracked with a higher tone than human bones and splintered to shards in arms, legs and wings.

An Insect pulled the man next to Harrier out of the line, ripping his cheek open to bone and teeth. It raised a sharp claw, and unzipped his stomach from hip to chest. The archer screamed, wrapped both arms around his waist, his long coat slick with blood. Harrier slashed the Insect's abdomen to gluey yellow ruin; it lunged at him, quivered and collapsed.

The crossbowmen found their pace. The first line shot, stepped back, kicked their bows down to span and reload. The next two lines came forward and loosed, sending a barrage of bolts against the swarm.

Harrier looked, bewildered, to the scattered dead, the surviving longbowmen, then up at me. 'Thank you,' he said.

The Awndyn Fyrd at the rear were under a lot of strain from Insects running uphill, and they didn't stand it long. I know what their blank faces meant. Suddenly Insects are the size of god. They have god's power. Fighting is not an option. 'They're not invincible!' I shouted desperately. 'Don't run!'

I stooped and soldiers ran straight on underneath. A handful reached the river bank, and disappeared into a villagers' pitfall trap that was already full of Insects.

'Shit.'

I reached Ata. 'We've lost the Awndyn division!'

'They'll draw Insects away. Order a crossbow division back; I don't want the rear to degenerate into skirmishes. Keep going up!' Ata called for the troops to stay together as the slope became rocky. Vireo's archers inside the keep were shooting from the towers' wide windows high over our heads, thinning out the Insects reaching us.

I led the column up onto the saddle of the hill. It narrowed as the men marched between two low walls, which swept round in a long curve. The outer wall ended in rubble, leaving the inner wall an unbroken white surface. Tawny's men were hewing a hollow out of the far side.

I circled, wings beating furiously. 'Break through here.'

The front of the column milled around, calling over the wall. Shouts answered from the other side:

'Hello?'

'Yo! Hello!'

'We're nearly through!'

'I don't think they can hear us.'

'Hello! Hello, hello, hello!'

'Are you from Rachis?'

'From Hacilith! How many is there?'

'All of fucking Lowespass, mate.'

'Lightning is here. Eszai are here.'

'Watch out for Insects they come up the ditch!'

'Get back in your *places*!' Ata screamed. 'Keep the shield line!'

Lightning ordered his archers to the peripheries of Ata's wall-breakers. Her crossbowmen formed a semicircle around them, two hundred metres wide, facing outwards with their backs to the wall. I spiralled up, directly above.

A mighty crash – the wall-breakers burst through – the wall began to collapse. Men shouted – hands appeared from the other side and grabbed Ata's hands frantically. They started to widen the breach.

Ata left her horse and pushed her head into the gap. 'Make space! Come through here! Spread out on the hill! Fall in; we'll start back to the ships straight away.'

Part of Tornado was visible through the breach. 'No,' he said. 'Not yet.'

'But? We're here to get you out!'

I landed by him. 'What are you planning?'

His Lowespass Fyrd emerged in a long thick chain, carrying arrow-sheaves out of the breach. Those inside chucked sheaves over the wall to distribute among Lightning's fyrd. Tornado and Vireo squeezed through, surveyed Ata's host excitedly as the fortress troops jostled out to join them. 'Look at all these warriors! Just think what we can do with so many, Vireo!'

'Who's the leader?' Vireo asked.

'I am,' said Ata.

Vireo regarded Ata as a fellow mortal. 'We won't forget your courage. But Tornado's in charge now.'

'You can't do that!' Then Ata saw Tawny and I agreeing, and she let the giant take over without another word.

The fyrd, a sagging crowd, all heard Tawny bellow, 'Now you'll see what it's like to have a real leader!' They looked at each other, and they stood a little more proudly.

'My god,' I said, awestruck.

'You have a few minutes' rest,' Tornado announced. 'Any more time, and the Insects start their wall-building. We don't want them to build between us and the boats! I need a few more hours' work from you this evening. Drink water from the well. Let Comet see the wounded; those too injured to fight can stay here.'

Vireo turned to me. 'We have some too faint from hunger – the ones that refused to eat Lowespass Lobster. Pass them into the ward and instruct a captain to look after them while Tawny regroups the host, and we'll leave some archers here to protect them.'

Twilight was growing rapidly, the afternoon becoming evening. I was low on energy from so much non-glide flying, but I attended to the maimed, traumatised and starving. There were fewer badly wounded men than I expected; they fell behind on the march and Insects don't spare them. Still, I had my work cut out in the keep, while Tornado marshalled the troops up behind the shield wall in preparation to march out en masse. 'How many have we lost?' he asked me.

'Above fifteen hundred in all, I think,' I said.

Ata said, 'We've gained eight thousand, then.'

'They're knackered, what did you put them through down there? Well, I suppose they're ready as they'll ever be.'

Vireo raised her crow's beak hammer. 'Tawny, you're the best weapon the Emperor has!'

'Love you!'

'For Lowespass!' she howled. The Morenzians and Lowespass Fyrd swarmed to her.

Ata shook her curved sword. 'For the Empire!' she cried. 'For Sute! To me, Islanders!'

'For something!' yelled Tawny as he pounded past me.

'Survival,' I explained. I outpaced him, took off.

They charged down the hill, and the fortress fyrd followed. Tornado's two-handed axe decimated Insects at each stroke.

Lightning had not set foot inside the fortress wall. He had spread his archers along the crag summit, behind linked pavises brought out from the keep. Two divisions each toiled for thirty minutes, shooting non-stop, sending ten thousand arrows per minute down into the valley. I had never seen such desperate effort; Lightning kept them working at utmost strain. His hair was wet with sweat, he was bare to the waist but for the bracer on his left arm. His horse's white neck was covered in bloody prints from the blisters even on his hardened hands. As Ata went past Lightning stopped the shooting, then spurred after her, furiously protesting. 'I *said* we can only cover three hundred metres!'

'Tawny won't go out of range. Look! They're going to sweep round the hill.'

'Crazy! It will be too dark soon to see that far!'

'I'm going after them!' Ata leapt her horse down rocky outcrops. Her men peeled off in a long, formless line behind her.

I circled the archers. 'Look! Insects are crossing back over the bridge!'

Groups of Insects, and then a whole horde, began to run from Tornado. Other Insects wavered antennae, sensed the panic, and joined them. They bit at men they passed, tussled with halberds. The bridge teemed with them scurrying from Tornado's scything attack.

'Keep ranks,' I shouted, but a great wordless euphoria broke over the tired troops. Carried away, they began to chase Insects to the bridge, Tawny and Vireo marching ahead of the shield wall.

Now scarcely pausing to bite, Insects swarmed up to the apex and vanished into the air. They departed in a flood. Going back into the Shift; taking the line of least resistance – fleeing to safety. They think they're safe. But Dunlin Rachiswater is waiting, worlds away at the other end.

I shouted, 'They're going!'

Vireo beat Insects back before her. Tornado was on her left, towering above the normal-sized men, nineteen thousand warriors fighting behind him. Vireo put a foot on the white walkway, strode up onto the bridge itself.

A gigantic black Insect turned from the stream to face her, Insects running past it on both sides. Head down, jaws gaping, it struck forward. She embedded her hammer between its multifaceted eyes. With an agonised movement it swept its claw into her shins and knocked her over. She cracked her head on the edge of the walkway and lay still, face down.

I swooped over. Vireo was unconscious. 'Tawny!'

The big Insect crouched and brushed its antennae over Vireo's compound-eye helmet and metal-covered shoulders, trying to figure out what she was. Then it raised its sharp foreleg and jabbed it neatly into the nape of her neck.

'Tawny!' I yelled. 'Here! Can't you see?'

Tornado realised what was happening as Insects started to tear at Vireo's armour. He roared. He ran to her, picked up the black Insect bodily, and threw it through the air. Writhing, it crashed onto the swarm, fell between rounded backs and disappeared under their claws.

He shook her gently. Her face was calm; blood was pooling on the rough grey paper. He put her over one shoulder and began to fight back down off the bridge. He hewed Insects as he strode, casting their shell carcasses aside. The shields parted to let him through at the bridge's base, while the stampede kept on around them. The Insect crush became a river, a trickle, and after an hour complete silence.

I touched down heavily onto the scarred ground behind him. 'She's dead, Tawny.'

'No ... I just have to get her to Rayne.'

'She's dead!'

Tornado bounded to his feet and took a menacing step towards me. I fanned my wings out hastily.

'I won't leave her!' He picked Vireo's body up onto his shoulders. 'Rayne can save her!'

The hooves of Ata's mare boomed, her armour reflecting darkness and the wide, empty land. She spoke quietly, full of respect: 'Tornado, will you order the fyrd back to the ships? Sun's setting, tide's turning, and no one should remain in the Paperlands after dark.'

The ships got underway at nightfall, caravels and pinnaces packed with fyrd. We abandoned the *Stormy Petrel*; it was lodged upright even-keel in the gravelly river bed. Ata took command of the *Ortolan*. Tornado, standing at its stern, still carried Vireo's corpse; no one dared approach him.

Swallow and Harrier helped me with the wounded. Men sat on the steps between decks, hammocks were hung in the hold where arrow-sacks had been. Cabins stank of human grease, muddy river water and wet feathers. Food was passed around: bread, smoked cod and samphire broth, black coffee and flasks of water. Men and women laid their packs on the decks and slept there.

I brought a bowl of chips up to the stern, and Tawny told me to get lost. 'You can't avenge against Insects,' he said. Vireo's blood was dried across his back, her hair hung down, twisted around a quill.

'Come help me build a pyre,' I said. Vireo was Lowespass, I knew their tradition. Unlike Awians, the practical Plainslanders do not want to take up space forever in opulent tombs. 'Tawny, I will ask the Emperor to raise a memorial for her, where the bridge was.'

'Where the bridge *was*?'

'That's the idea.'

While the line of ships passed in the darkness under the bridge, I began sorting and laying out pieces of tubular steel scaffolding, elastic straps, piles of nuts and bolts on the stern deck of the *Ortolan*, to rebuild one of the Lowespass catapults.

'That contraption is far too dangerous,' Ata protested. 'I won't allow you to play with it on my ship.'

'Lightning – leave Swallow alone! Remember your promise. Will you help me with the trebuchet?'

'I think Jant's right.' Lightning strode up to us, hiding his fatigue with willpower, clear voice and upright bearing. 'We should be able to shoot safely from the stern.'

'I liked Jant better when he was on the drug salad,' Ata said.

Lookouts kept watch for Insects, as Tornado and I led an armed expedition to shore, with horses drawing wagons full of pitch barrels. We piled fifty barrels in pyramid-shaped stacks around each of the bridge's four nearest legs.

I hunkered down and touched a match to the sailcloth on one of the stacks, and called to my captains to do the same. We stepped back and watched flame lick up around the barrels. The fire took hold quickly, barrels bursting open and the pitch seeping out.

Tawny walked into the flames, shrugged Vireo's body from his shoulders and laid it down.

'Goodbye, love,' he said.

We watched the flames wrap round, until roils of thick smoke covered her shape. Intense heat drove us back little by little as the bridge's legs began to burn.

'Let's go,' I said. We returned along the river bank, through the alien scenery. Although I was still wary of Insects, their absence was dramatic – quick as blowing out a candle, they had fled and we were actually walking without attack in their noiseless landscape.

'There'll never be another like her,' Tawny said gloomily, as we reached the *Ortolan*.

'In all immortality there might be.'

'Vireo. Vireo … I should've made her Eszai. God knows why I always hang on until it's too late.'

We heard Lightning's clear voice instructing the catapult crew with an authority he must have been taught at an early age. The catapult loosed. A burning barrel of pitch arced high over our heads, crashed onto the bridge's walkway, dropping gobs of flame. Trust Lightning to get the trajectory right first time. Two more followed, spread throughout the walkway, and the bridge caught fire along its length.

From end to end of the ships' procession, men were cheering. They waved swords, helmets, cups in the air. The uproar grew as the bridge lit the night, Swallow's voice leading the applause, until men were gasping for air to cheer with.

The bridge blossomed bright yellow. Its nearest legs split open from the ground into the sky. They unfurled along their length in sheets of flame, and the whole thing started to collapse. Cables snapped, the walkway crumpled. It went down slowly, sinuously; debris raining down, ash flecks twirling into the air.

I thought of the citizens besieged in Rachis Town, and molten glass creaking as it set in the cooling ruins of Wrought. 'That'll show them,' I said to myself.

I watched the Paperlands lit flickering amber and black, seguing into empty fields and the Summerday town wall. Dunlin's coffin was buried somewhere in that mess; would I ever be able to find it? I determined to send search parties when soldiers began to smash the cells, fill in tunnels, and rebuild the town. Staniel knew the exact location where the metal coffin lay; I would drag him out here to give us directions, and examine every centimetre of ground. I would recover the King's remains and, no matter what happened, I would find a way to report the truth to Dunlin, as I promised and as he deserved. Now I'm clean, addiction's prison seemed distant, and it was strange to think that the Shift still exists, and Dunlin is alive.

'I must search for Dunlin.' I turned to Lightning. 'The King's bier has to be retrieved.'

Lightning nodded, as if this matched his thoughts. 'It will be built into a wall. When we destroy them, we'll find it.'

'Insects or no, it will take months to break up the Paperlands,' said Swallow. Cyan was quiet at her side; she still did not stand close to Lightning.

'Yes, but it can be done,' the Archer told her.

Tornado said nothing, his face was lined with grief. I didn't want to give him time to dwell on it. I said, 'Tawny, we need you in Rachiswater. There are still Insects to clear out; Eleonora Tanager needs help.'

'Eleonora's revolution,' Ata said, leaning on the ship's wheel.

'And her coronation,' said Lightning graciously.

I sighed. 'It never ends, does it?'

'Consider yourself lucky that it doesn't, Messenger.'

Lightning understood. He clapped my shoulder, face radiant. 'Don't worry, Jant,' he said. 'Times will pass, and we'll survive. We'll live long enough for all these trials to become satisfying memories and the best tales.'

Huge thanks above all to Simon Spanton. Thank you to my Eszai-good agents, Mic Cheetham and Simon Kavanagh, for their vital help. My gratitude to Ben Jeapes for his excellent advice. Thanks and love to Brian, immovable object of my unstoppable force.

NO PRESENT
LIKE TIME

✦

TO BRIAN

They change their clime, not their frame of mind,
that rush across the sea

HORACE

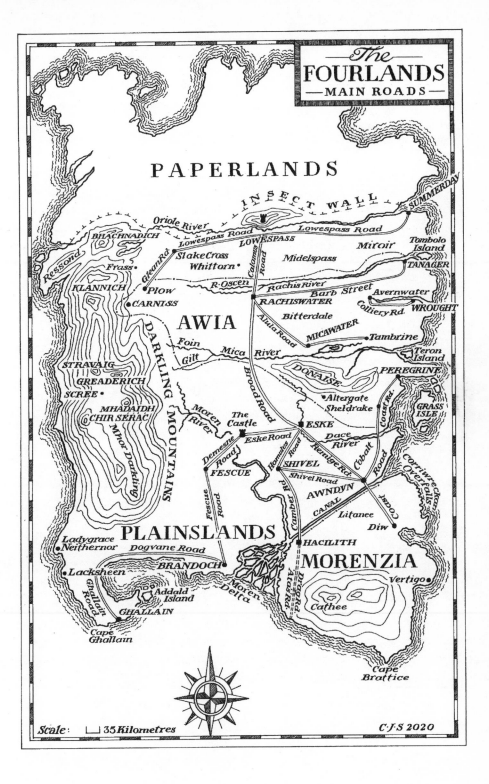

CHAPTER I

January 2020

On this soft night I followed the Moren River valley, flying back to the Castle, hearing the chimes of clock towers in the Plainslands villages as I passed high above.

The night air was shapeless. I couldn't sense any current. I concentrated, flapping steadily on, marking distance by time, marking time by going through all the songs I know. I lay horizontally, looking down around me, cruising with stiff, shallow beats. I felt the air rushing between my feathers on the upstroke. Then I pulled my wings down again, the feathers flattened, the tight muscles moved around my waist.

Thermals were dissipating as the sun set. I was dropping altitude to find them and the work was getting harder. Fog was forming, low in the pasture and along the river bank. The tops of the valley sides were dark shapes rising from the mist like islands. Beyond, I could see parallel hills all the way out to the beginning of Donaise. Hedges and drystone walls looked like black seams separating fields of clean, lapping white mist. There was no sound, just the skeleton zip of my wings peeling back the air.

I spotted a point of light in the distance, like a city, and checked my compass – bearings dead on for the Castle and hopefully there would be some supper left. The speck resolved into a cluster of lights, then each cluster separated again, and distances between them seemed to grow as I got closer. Lights slipped from the horizon down towards me, until I was over Demesne village. Street lights shone up, picking the mist out in flat beams. Denser wisps blew past, curling, and the fog began to take on a shape of its own.

The fog changed everything. Fog covered the river's reflective surface, meandered to the water meadows. Fog poured between the cultivar yew plantations and spiky poplar coppices where tomorrow's bows and arrows were painstakingly being grown. Fog drifted over the roofs of the village where most of the Castle's staff live. It pooled on the carp ponds, stole into the tax barns and settled on the market's thatched roof. It cloaked the watermill, the aqueduct's dark arches, Hobson's stable and the Blacksmith's yard. Fog overran the Castle's outermost boundaries. It advanced through the archery fields, lay in the tilting lists, rolled over the tennis courts. It muffled the concert hall and the bathhouse complex.

One of the Castle's spires was silhouetted against a white light, which suffused into the mist in an immense grisaille sphere. The floodlights were on in the amphitheatre. They only illuminated the sharp Northeast Tower, its black sarsen stone striking in the whiteout. Features became visible as I closed the distance. The Castle's vast bulk was obscured. Occasionally angular roofs and the crenellated tops of walls appeared, fragmentary, through the mist. The square base of the round tower was submerged two metres deep into a sea of fog. I flew through thicker patches – then it looked as if it was receding on the plains. On a whim, three hundred years ago, the Architect had encrusted her studio in the turret with sculptures. Eagles, storks and eels loomed out of the mist, with her company's logo and the tools of her trade in stonework blackened by kitchen smoke. The windows bristled with deep, tangled marble ivy so realistic that birds were nesting in it.

Fog cold in my eyes and throat like clouds. A smell from the kitchens of wood smoke, roast beef and dishwater had caught in it. A faint scent of lavender from the laundry house tainted it. Burnt whale oil from the floodlights saturated it, turning the fog into smog.

Storeys and gable roofs and towers rose behind towers. The spaces under the buttresses were filled with tracery. The Carillon Courtyard had a lawn mowed in wide stripes and a roof that had been covered in scaffolding for eight decades. On the steeplejack's walkway was a wooden treadmill twice as tall as a man, used to raise loads of Ladygrace stone. Its basket hung from the rope wound on its axle.

Two centuries ago, I thought the North Façade was a cliff face formed by the power of nature. I had tilted my head until I thought I would fall over backwards, but I still couldn't see the top of its spire. I had crouched on the hard grass a few hundred metres away, looked up and realised – all the crevices are carvings. The cliff ledges are parapets. Statues of idealised immortals, pinnaform spires embroidered with vertical lace. The glory of the Emperor, god's governor of the Fourlands. It had made my neck ache.

I flew an assured path around walls flaking masonry, mottled with moss. I passed pinnacles decorated with ball flowers. The Finials, a memorial sculpture, was a row of scalloped arches resting on free-standing black marble shafts. It carried the signatures of Eszai, people who through their peerless talents have won immortality, a place in the Circle, and reside here. Graffiti scarred the arches, the names of immortals past and present; I had incised *CJS & TW 1892* in a love heart on the highest topstone.

Now invisible in the mist, the gravel courtyard at the foot of the Finials encircled a statue of Dunlin, recently the King of Awia. I had ordered it to be placed there with the statues of other great warriors so that he would always be remembered.

The tall Aigret Tower seemed to drift in the mist and I sheared through it. It was the Slake Cross Battle cenotaph, square openwork, completely hollowed out to a lantern of air. At every level its pillars were thicker at the top than at the bottom, so they looked like they were dripping down – melting. It had no walls, its pillars were backed by those of a second and third tower nested inside; through its worn bird-boned latticework I flew without breaking pace.

Small, indistinct groups of people were heading along the avenue in the direction of the duelling ground. Some carried oil lamps; their golden light-points bounced away into the distance. Next to the floodlights' white glare, a whole crowd of lanterns was gathering. I must take a look and see what's happening. Standing on one wing I bent my knees and turned. The ground tilted sharply as I dropped onto the Castle's roof-forest, like a wasp into a very ornate flower. I swept in so low over the barbican that my wingtips touched, made a sharp right, narrowly missing the lightning rod. Airstream roared in my ears as I dived towards the duelling ground, wondering if I could see well enough to land safely.

Fog drifted with me over the low roof of the adjoining gymnasium, and a second later poured from the open mouths of a dozen gargoyles carved in the shape of serene kings like chess pieces, which leaned out, face down, over ornamental gardens. I flew through one of the streams, taking a shower in the damp fog. As I glided in on fixed wings, vortices curled off my wingtips so I left two spiral trails.

The duelling ground is inside a large amphitheatre with high, half-timbered walls topped by flagpoles. The fog had not yet smothered them but it rose up the outside like water climbing around a sinking ship – the oval building looked as if it was sliding down into the invisible earth.

Four floodlights stood at the edges of the amphitheatre, on ten-metre-high iron scaffolds. I circled the nearest floodlight, feet dangling, and settled onto its metal housing. I shook wisps of fog from my wings and pulled them around me, stood cloaked in long feathers.

The shade was very hot. I shuffled to the front and perched on the edge. The only noise was the oil lamps' hissing. Above and around, all was dark – but the pitch below was bathed in light. Two figures in the centre were swiping at each other with rapier and dagger.

There was Gio Serein, the Circle's Swordsman. When I was growing up in Hacilith, he was the immortal with the biggest fan club. Every child who wielded a stick pretended to be Serein and plenty of teenagers had aspirations to fight him. This could only be a Challenge. I peered closer to see who could possibly go a round with him. It was a young Awian lad, who kept his stubby dark wings folded so as not to present a target. His flight feathers were clipped in zigzags, the current fashion, making them lighter. Short brown hair was shaved at the sides and stuck up in sweaty spikes on top. For agility, he wore only a shirt and breeches. His sweat-patched shirt was fyrd-issue, dark blue of the Tanager Select infantry. He wore a glove on his left hand, grasping the rapier hilt. He moved as if he was made of springs.

Serein had his knuckles upwards and thumb on his rapier blade to make strong wrist blows. The stranger caught one on his dagger, thrust it wide, went in underneath with dagger and rapier. Serein struck back, low, with a cry.

The newcomer swept it aside, made a feint to the face, jabbing twice, and again Serein gave ground, keenly aware of his body's position. Then he ran in and scuffed up some sawdust with his leather pump. The Awian was wise to that trick; he parried the thrust. Metal slid over metal with a grinding swish.

I glanced up and the size of the crowd held my attention. The twenty-tier-high banked stands were crammed to capacity and more people arrived every minute, blowing out their lanterns, shoving a path down the walkways to sit on the steps and lean against the posts. Gazing around, I couldn't see any space where I could join them.

Directly opposite was a canopied box with the best view of the ground. The Emperor San was seated on a chair in the centre, watching the two fighters impassively and completely without expression. One thin hand rested on his knees, the other was curled on the armrest. His face was shadowed by the gold awning, thin magisterial features framed by white hair that hung loose to his shoulders. If San was out of the Throne Room this must be really important. I folded my wings neatly so the tips crossed at my back, and bowed my head in case he was watching.

On the Emperor's left, Tornado, the Castle's Strongman, was so big he filled that side of the box. He peered out from under the awning that bulged over his head. On his right, Mist, the Sailor, stood with a great big grin on her face, her hands on wide hips under a white cashmere jumper. Rayne, the Doctor, sat with her assistants on a bench at the side of the ground, ready to intervene if anything went wrong. I recognised many of my fellow immortals scattered through the crowd, all intent on the duellists. Well, I thought, it wouldn't be a new year if Serein didn't have another Challenger, but usually his supporters in the crowd bellowed and cheered and hissed. This time there was a breathlessness in the air.

The duellists walked in a circle, marshalling their strength. Watching tensely. Both had their sword-tips horizontal in third guard, daggers in their right hands held out straight to the right side. Footprints turned the sand dark in a ring where they trod. They must have been at it for ages; their clothes were wet and the sand was damp with sweat.

Serein thrust, knees flexed. The Awian traversed sideways and Serein's swept hilt nearly caught on his tightly taped sleeve. They never lost eye contact; I knew what that was like. Head up and body in balance, keep all the moves in your peripheral vision no matter how bright the steel is, cutting round your head.

Serein made his slicing arc too wide. The Awian jabbed at his stomach. Serein was forced back. The Awian jumped forward, thrust sword arm and leg out, aimed for the hamstring behind Serein's knee. Serein parried but his blade sloped. The Awian's rapier glanced off, he directed it to Serein's calf. Serein moved away fast. Top move! Yes! Eat your heart out, Serein! I bounced up and down on the floodlight housing until the whole thing shuddered.

Sorry.

They set to circling again, obviously exhausted but trying to see what chinks might open in each other's guard. They tried to spot any recurring foibles, to predict and use them. They were perfectly synchronised, reading the timing from each other's eyes. Seeing through the feints. Every time Serein sought a way to break out, the newcomer was with him, close like a shadow through every strategy.

Serein shifted into second guard, spun the dagger so the blade was below his hand, took a swipe across the Awian's face. Crash, crash! They moved apart. Serein has spent his life studying the art of killing. Why hasn't he won yet? His footprints on the sand traced out one of his geometrical charts. He was using every trick he knew and he was getting nowhere.

Some people climbed up on the roof and lit the last floodlight. If the duellists registered the white glare intensify, they didn't react. They concentrated on thrust and parry, leant in with both hands at once, dagger blocking rapier. A spray of sweat drops flew from Serein's fair hair as he flicked it back.

My floodlight was a good vantage point. Moreover, being half Rhydanne I could see movements faster than the flatlanders can, so I saw Serein's cuts; to the other spectators they must be a blur. This was Serein slowed by fatigue. I knew how impossibly fast he moves when fresh, because he's beaten me black and blue with a buttoned rapier before now.

Serein was two metres tall, his substantial arms were hard with tired muscle. He bared teeth in a snarl as he screamed at himself inwardly: concentrate! Even at this distance I could read the frustration in his pale eyes: why won't you yield? Why can't I hit you? He kept turning hatred into big, angry slashes that his opponent just leafed aside with dagger, his rapier in front narrowing the angle of attack. They were both as good as it was physically possible to be. The outcome depended on who would slip up first, or simply stop, ground down by exhaustion. Perhaps Serein was slightly more cautious than the boy, because he had more to lose.

Serein made two crown cuts to the boy's head, lunged for his feet. The boy tried to catch the blade in his dagger quillions, missed.

This kid has been around, I decided. He fights like an immortal. I had been flying on my own for days and my whole body was alert to their moves. I had been in remote Darkling, which made me conscious of the crowd.

There was the Archer. Lightning stood closest to the duellists, leaning on the crush barrier staring raptly at them. A wide Micawater-blue scarf was draped around his shoulders and a quiver of white-flighted arrows at his hip. He has the physique of a cast-bronze statue. The willpower of one, too, and to be honest their sense of humour as well. This century he is less glacial than usual, because he has been enlivened by another hopeless love affair. It was easy to see him; the surrounding crowd kept a respectful distance. Though they all stood shoulder-to-shoulder, Lightning was on his own.

I swept off my perch with my wings held right back, down to the edge of the pitch and landed neatly next to him. 'Who's the Challenger?'

Lightning smiled without turning. 'Welcome back, Jant. How was the road from Scree?'

'Very foggy. Who is he?'

'That young man is Wrenn, a career soldier from Summerday. He left the Queen's guard and made his formal Challenge to Serein last week.'

'Is that why the Emperor called me back?'

Lightning looked at me for the first time. 'No. Don't mention it in public – San has work for us. I was also recalled, and I am not at all happy about it, since I had to leave my betrothèd's side.'

(Lightning is the only person I know who still puts the è in betrothèd.)

'Wrenn looks like a fyrd captain.'

'He is. He made a name for himself in the town. He's working his way up through the ranks, and I think being such a fantastic swordsman has made him quite unpopular. Courtiers scent rumours and seek him out to prove themselves, but Wrenn refuses to know when to lose. He gave Veery Carniss more of a flaying than a duelling scar. If he was nobility, he could have been promoted higher. It's a shame; I suppose he was frustrated by the cut-glass ceiling which is why he's trying a Challenge.'

'They both look tired.'

'Jant, they started at six o'clock.'

'Shit!'

Lightning gestured at the crowd, 'Long enough for the Eszai and the whole of Demesne village to join us. Hush now. He's such a short boy, I don't know how he keeps going.'

There was no blood on the sawdust. 'Four hours and they haven't touched each other?'

'They've broken a sword each, though. Sh!'

Wrenn had obviously trained in broadsword techniques as well as the ideal figures of fencing. An overhead blow down to the face, a thrust to the belly, adapted to the rapier – duellist's weapons designed by humans for settling disputes between themselves in their city.

Winning is all. The Castle's constitution is simple: two men on a field and by the end of the day one of them will be immortal, and the other may as well be down among the dead men.

They used identical rapiers, damask steel blades with the same length and heft, issued by the Castle to ensure the Challenge is fair. The Challenger is allowed to set the time of the competition, but the Challenged immortal decrees the type of contest. Serein was formerly a fencing master; he had popularised the art across the Plainslands and Morenzia. Four centuries ago, he won his place in the Circle by broadsword combat but since then he has usually stipulated that Challengers use his accustomed rapier and poniard. Wrenn was so thickset that I could tell the long blade hadn't been chosen to favour him, but he had no problems wielding it. He cut straight at Serein's chest.

Serein flung both hands up and bounded back. He landed in high guard, with both blades pointing at Wrenn's face. Wrenn ducked below them to attack – he flattened himself to the floor, one leg out behind, lunged forward with the rapier at arm's length.

Serein got low to thrust, but Wrenn was quick to his feet. Serein stood still, parried with dagger, thrust with sword. Wrenn pulled his cut to keep out of distance. He thrust under Serein's arm.

'That's three from the left,' muttered Lightning. 'He'll change now.'

That's what Wrenn wanted us to think. He attacked from the left. He traversed to the opposite leg and changed dagger grip, so the blade was down. He leant in, back straight, made a wide sweep, but too close and almost ran onto Serein's rapier. The crowd inhaled, expecting a double kill, but Wrenn, off balance, gave ground and the two began to circle again.

Wrenn launched a heavy cut to Serein's shoulder.

If this was me, I would—

Serein jumped and stopped it with just his dagger before it gained momentum.

Well, I wouldn't do that.

Then he tried to kick Wrenn in the balls.

Wrenn leapt away, threw his weight back and returned a reverse thrust at the same time.

I gasped. I'd never seen a fencer move that accurately before.

Serein couldn't turn inside the thrust, and retreated, face sallow. He allowed his rapier point to drop from guard for the first time. It gave Wrenn time to rally; he tried a cleaving blow. Serein beat it aside, turned his sword and cut at Wrenn's exposed hand. Wrenn backed off just fast enough to keep his hand. He parried, the dagger coming up beneath his rapier for support. He lifted Serein's blade, but Serein snatched it free. Wrenn faced Serein squarely, his whole body curved into a hollow, his middle held away and his left foot down securely.

They found new strength, remembering that they're fighting for immortality. San forbids his immortals to kill their Challengers, although genuine accidents happen now and again. Serein looked furious at how long this was taking, he was channelling all his brilliance at getting first blood from the young man.

Of course, no money Serein's novices could offer him would lead him to reveal his finest moves. He never taught his students enough for them to Challenge him. But it seemed that Wrenn had reinvented all Serein's techniques from scratch, and added his own innovations.

Serein deliberately made an out-of-distance attack, trying to draw Wrenn in. Wrenn was having none of it, he kept his body well away. Serein tried a better angle, this time Wrenn's dagger parried low. Serein's rapier drove straight at it. The blades shunted together. Serein punched his swept hilt at Wrenn's fist. The dagger shot from Wrenn's stunned hand like a dart.

Wrenn did not look for it but changed his rapier to his right hand, wringing his fingers. He was at a serious disadvantage. Serein's eyes tracked Wrenn's expression as he deigned a smile.

'It's only a matter of time ...' Lightning said.

Wrenn knocked Serein's rapier up with his sword's forte, sliced. Serein kept out of the way. His confidence peaked; he could just wait.

'Serein will stick him like a pig.'

Wrenn made a straight thrust in *quarte*, Serein turned it easily. Everyone watched Serein beating Wrenn back across the releager, step by step until they were right underneath the Emperor's box. Wrenn was beginning to look from Serein's rapier to dagger, and I could see his mouth was open.

Serein was lining up a way to end this. He feinted with the dagger, swung his rapier round in an outside moulinet for force, straight down at Wrenn's head.

And Wrenn stepped into the blow.

He caught the inside of Serein's hand on the grip with his own wrist, forced it aside. His rapier arrested Serein's dagger and he stretched that arm fully to the other side. He tilted his blade; the tip lowered to Serein's throat. Serein struggled, stopped. Face to face they were so close their chests nearly touched. Wrenn looked Serein straight in the eyes, made an almost imperceptible movement of the point and a red trickle ran down below the Swordsman's larynx, between his collar bones into the front of his shirt. First blood.

Wrenn punched both arms into the air. 'Yes!' he yelled. 'I did it! I really fucking did it!'

For a second there was silence, and I could tell the same thought was running through every mind in the throng: how brave have you got to be to step *into* a cut in prime? Wrenn was prepared to die if his trick failed. Knowing he has to die sometime, he risked it for the ultimate reward. Serein had lost that mortal determination – well, all us Eszai are living on borrowed time.

The crowd erupted. A lady next to me put her hands over her ears, the cheering was so loud.

'What timing,' Lightning breathed. 'What bloody timing.' He vaulted the low wall and sprinted across the pitch. I got to the duellists first, saw Lightning throw a brotherly arm around Wrenn's shoulders. Wrenn lowered his rapier, swayed on his feet. He was about to faint.

I was suddenly at the focal point, and almost deafened by the crowds. Outside the lit ground the stands were invisible but the applause was like a wall of sound. A chant caught like city-fire and spread through the stands: 'Wrenn for Serein! Wrenn for Serein!' Fyrd swordsmen stamped their feet on the wooden benches; the thunder went on and on. Soldiers in civvies began to spill out onto the pitch. I clapped my hands until the palms stung.

'Yes!' yelled Tornado, with one fist in the air. He stuck two fingers in his mouth and gave a long whistle.

'Well done!' Lightning exclaimed. 'Well done, my friend!' He turned Wrenn to the yelling crowd and raised Wrenn's shaking arm. 'The victor!'

Serein, beaten, opened his hands and let his dagger and rapier fall to the trodden sand. They smelt weakly of disinfectant. He looked around for a place to lie, knelt down, then curled up from humiliation and sheer exhaustion with his hands over his head.

Wrenn seemed frightened. He looked more terrified the more he realised how many people were out there. His face had a lustre from the grease smeared on his forehead to stop sweat running into his eyes. He was beyond the limits of mental and physical endurance; he stumbled. Lightning walked him towards the Doctor's bench, but the crowd swallowed them in and then hoisted up Wrenn in the centre, hands on his legs and backside like a crowd-surfer. They carried him high above their heads, into the square passageway and rapidly out of the fencing ground. The floodlights highlighted tousled wings and assorted backs as they ebbed away from us. Serein and I were left alone.

The sea of fog breached the far wall and poured down, slipping towards us at ground level.

'That's it,' the Swordsman murmured. 'Is that it? Am I out?'

He gradually got to his feet, shoulders bowed, head lowered.

'Serein,' I said. 'It comes to us all in the end.'

He looked at me resentfully, but I couldn't tell whether he was sighing from overexertion or bitterness. 'Once I've left the Circle I won't want to see you again,' he admitted. 'Don't visit me, Jant – I don't want you to see me grow old.' He put a hand to his throat, rubbed it, and gazed at his red palm. The blood flow had practically stopped, but he was sticky with it chin to waist.

He looked up to the hulking empty stands. 'It's the fear that takes it out of you.' He rested his hand on my shoulder for a second. Then he picked up his rapier, broke it over his knee, and walked off the field.

CHAPTER 2

I climbed the spiral staircase to my tower room. The murals on its walls became more lurid and grotesque towards the top. I don't remember painting them; I must have been really stoned.

'Hello, lover,' I said, emerging from the doorway.

Tern was waiting in the lower part of the round split-level room, her hands on her hips. Anger spiced her voice. 'Look at you! All windswept! God, you look like a juggler from the Hacilith festival! Out of those flea-bitten mountain clothes and into a suit ... Here, wear this one; it's elegant.' She gave me a light and unusually demure kiss on the cheek. I looked around our untidy apartment that my wife had colonised with architectural drawings, cosmetics, rolls of fabric and an enormous wardrobe inside which I am sure a Rhydanne couple could live quite happily.

My carefully stacked letters slid into each other under Tern's discarded dresses. All my specific piles of correspondence had formed one mass like the Paperlands and reeked of her expensive perfume. She saw my look of horror and said, 'I tidied up your mess.'

'That was my filing system! The letters I've read go on the table, noteworthy letters on the floor under the desk. The ones I haven't read are on the fireplace next to the pine cones ... Where have they gone?'

My alphabetised books were spattered with used matches and sealing wax. Shed feathers littered my collection of old broadsheets. Tern's gowns covered the chaise longue where I like to lounge; dress patterns were taped on the posts of our bed. Her underclothes were scattered in mounds. She had even disturbed the dusty table on which stood my precious distilling apparatus, although I had reassembled the glass retorts and condenser solely for the production of barley sugars.

Tern wore a bustier of chartreuse-green satin; its pleated sleeves wreathed her small black wings. At her throat, her wide jet heirloom necklace looked like a collar. 'This is all the rage,' she purred. 'Well, I say it is.'

'How do I unfasten it?' Her bare shoulders made her all the more tempting. I tried to undo her hair but her usual loose dark waves were pulled back into a complicated chignon.

My wife's town was reduced to brick shards and ashy rubble by the Great Fire of 2015. Of her black stone manor house only one single outside wall still stood. Slug-trail slicks of molten glass hardened from its pointed arched windows; lead roofs lay in solidified pools. The stumps of scrubby trees in her woodland were burnt flat to the ground. Every building and foundry in Wrought was destroyed, none of her possessions escaped the flames. Wrought was her birthplace and the scene of our honeymoon; Tern now aspired to rebuild it completely. Luckily, her designer fashions sold well on the Hacilith catwalks and as far as she was concerned Wrenn joining the Circle was a opportunity for trend-setting. She caressed my wings as I peeled off my tight trousers and changed clothes. Long wings are considered the most attractive, and as feathers need a lot of preening, Awians look after their high-maintenance bodies with care.

'I didn't see the duel,' Tern said. 'I needed the time to get ready. I heard from Rayne that the Challenger gave Serein a good nick to remember him by.'

'It was a first-blood duel,' I said. 'Those were the rules, so Wrenn had to.'

'I hear that Wrenn is scrumptious,' she commented. I shrugged. I seated myself in front of the mirror and let her brush my black hair that reaches to my waist, removing all the tangles caused by flying. It was agony. When she finished I crossed feathers through it like windmill sails and underlined my eyes.

'Listen.' Tern raised a finger at the clatter of coaches vying for space in the courtyard far below. 'I hear some ladies inviting themselves to his reception. Those can't be reporters or they would never have managed to sneak past Tawny at the gate.'

'We have an hour. I've been on my own in Scree for weeks. I want you.'

Tern pulled away – so as not to ruin the painstaking work of art she has made of herself. I gave her the full benefit of my cat-eyed look that she found so exotic. 'We should clear a space to sit down ... Perhaps lie down.'

'Come and join the clamour,' she said.

Tern, you and your diamond self-sufficiency.

Unlike the stately homes of Awia, the Castle's sarsen outer bastions were thick, sturdy and unassailable. The Castle's purpose was defence of the entire Fourlands; it protected every manor, growing gatehouses and curtain walls while they bloomed balconies and arched dance halls, ornate turrets and painted bartizans.

The ground around the Castle was thrown into immense earthworks to ward off Insects. A channel of the Moren River was directed into a double moat around its man-made hill. The twin exterior walls that ran round the Castle's eight sides were strengthened by huge cylindrical smooth stone-faced towers decorated with crenellations and with shallow pointed roofs. Along the walls flags rustled and furled; the heraldry of the Fourlands' current sixteen manors and two townships. Fifty pennants flew under the Castle's sun, each with the sign that an Eszai had chosen for his or her position.

The Emperor's palace fitted inside the Castle like the flesh in a nutshell.

Its marble towers stretched up from inside the impenetrable curtain wall. The Throne Room spire was the tallest; farmers who worked the demesne saw the sun glint on its pinnacle and they knew the Emperor occupied his throne beneath.

As Tern and I walked from our austere tower we saw only glimpses through the cold fog; its attendant hush muted every sound, drawing all the lustre from the palace. We saw lights shining behind sash windows and the oculus ovals made to look like portholes of the Mare's Run wing where Mist had her rooms. A stone-balustraded balcony ran along the length of its top floor, like the gallery on a ship. The Mare's Run was built between the outer walls and the palace five hundred years ago; it filled some of the space where gardens used to be. Several other buildings were shaped to fit into the western side of the gap: the dining hall and a theatre with its scalloped bronze dome topped by a white wood lantern-turret.

I did not take the rooms owing to me as Messenger in the palace's Carillon Court when I joined the Circle. I preferred to move into the unused apartment at the top of the Northwest Tower on the outer wall because I found it easy to launch myself from its height. My window gave a view for a hundred kilometres of the river, the playing fields and white goalposts; red dock stalks sticking up from the green rough ground of Binnard meadow. Tern has never persuaded me to move back into the palace.

Tern shivered and I reached out with a wing to give her a pat on the shoulder. Tern's wings are much smaller than mine, as are those of all Awians, because although they are the only winged people, they are flight-less. I am the sole person ever to be able to fly. As I am half Rhydanne my light, long-limbed build and mountainlander's fitness, when added to Awian ancestry on my father's side, gave me my ability.

Hand in hand Tern and I walked down an enclosed passage over a flying buttress that spanned from the outside wall to the palace. It was a narrow, vertiginous bridge that soared over the roof of the Great Hall, stretching thin and tenuous in the air. Below us, we could only see the glow of lamps in niches outside the hall and on four stone steps that rose to double doors with opulent panelling. The deeply carved decoration inside its triangular pediment was even more ornate: two flamboyant white Awian eagles flanked the Castle's sun emblem.

Our buttress walkway crossed above the head of the marble statue that topped the pediment, a slender woman bearing a sword and shield, her luxuriously feathered wings outstretched. Sometimes I land on the roof, providing a sudden perspective – she is twice my size. The hall was built by architects from Micawater, and Lightning is the only Eszai who would remember what the statue actually symbolises. It could be anything: free-dom, justice, the wet dreams of a hundred generations of Awian adolescents.

As I walked with Tern I thought the whole building seemed smug, as if it had soaked up the atmosphere of too many whispered indiscretions at formal parties and was simply waiting for the next.

We descended to a small cloister. A colonnaded corridor ran round the misty lawn; we walked along two sides. Outside the Throne Room its stone ceiling was elaborately carved with fan vaulting; bosses hung down like leafy stalactites. Instead of curtains the drapes that framed the Throne Room portal were sculpted from amber.

The Throne Room seemed even more massive after the narrow narthex. Tern and I walked in down the long aisle past the screen and bowed to the Emperor. The Emperor San was first to be present, according to his custom. This was an important occasion, so he wore the tall spired platinum crown that Awia presented to him when the First Circle was formed. San normally wore no crown at all. We settled on one of the front benches, because they were closest to the sunburst throne and I wanted to hear what Wrenn had to say.

On this side of the screen, the benches faced each other and were gently stepped as in an auditorium. I watched in silence as the other Eszai walked in and gradually filled the seats. Most of the women gazed at Lightning, but some looked at me. I doubt that I cut a fine figure at court, since the fashion's long gone for looking pale and dishevelled, but there's no denying the effect I have on them. I may not command the battlefield but I can put the best spin on the outcome. I might not be a keen huntsman but I can gut a weekend newspaper. At sparring, I prefer words to swords, and I used to shoot drugs not arrows, but I'm free of all that now.

Wrenn entered the far end of the Throne Room, tiny below the huge rose window. It was symbolically important that he came in alone. He looked all around nervously and jumped as the doors closed behind him with an enormous crash. Then he began to walk, stiffly and obviously aching all over, towards us down the length of the scarlet carpet that was far more terrifying than any fencing piste. The Imperial Fyrd archers on the gallery with their pulley compound bows watched him carefully.

'That's the new Swordsman,' I whispered to Tern. 'This ordeal will be worse for him than the duel.' My initiation was an awful trial. 'Before this is over, he may well wish he'd died out there.'

She leaned forward to watch him. 'It depends how much he has to hide.'

Wrenn passed us slowly, giving the curious eyes of all the Eszai time to take him in. His short hair was wet from the bath or the steam room. His clothes were clean, but the same dull blue with thread holes on his sleeve where his fyrd patch used to be. He only looked straight ahead to the Emperor's dais – though not, of course, to the Emperor himself. He reached the platform's lowest step and knelt.

'My lord Emperor,' he announced. His voice gave way. He tried again: 'I humbly petition to join the Circle and I claim the title Serein, having beaten Gio Ami Serein in a fair Challenge.' He thought for a second, eyes aside like an actor trying to remember his lines – but also because it meant he didn't look at San. 'I intend to serve you and the Fourlands every minute of my life.'

San regarded Wrenn and the members of the Circle in silence. Even at this distance I felt the scrutiny of his incredibly clear and intelligent gaze. San always wore white – a tabard with panels of colourless jewels over a plain robe that reached to the floor. The pointed toes of his flat white shoes projected from under them. The style of San's clothes had remained the same since the year he created the former Circle, four hundred years after god left. His whole body was covered except for his thin and ringless hands.

The sunburst throne also remained a symbol of permanence. An ancient broadsword and circular shield hung from its back. They were a keen reminder that if us Eszai finally fail him in the Fourlands' struggle against the Insects, San will again direct the battle himself. In the Castle's stables a destrier is always reserved for him, never ridden, never used.

San rose and approached the front of the dais. 'You have selected yourself for the Circle. You have humbly placed your talents at the world's disposal. I thank you. Every successful Challenger must complete one last observance to become immortal. You must tell me everything about your life so far. Relate all that you think is significant from your earliest memory to the events that brought you here. You will not lie. My Circle will hear your testimony but they will neither interrupt nor judge. Nothing you reveal will ever be repeated. Only a refusal to speak will jeopardise your entrance into the Circle, not what you say. You have already won.

'The ceremony continues with your reception afterwards: for one hour the other members of my Circle may question you as they wish. You will always reply with the truth; they will neither criticise nor condemn. They are not permitted to repeat your words at any time or place. If anyone ever reveals what he or she learns, he or she will be rejected from the Circle. During the following hour you can question the other immortals about themselves. Likewise they are obliged to tell the truth and you must never disclose what they say.'

It's the only chance you'll ever have, I added to myself.

San looked expectant. Wrenn hesitated. He suffered in the intense silence, and so began, 'My name is Wrenn Culmish. I'm ... I am from Summerday bastide town. Insects killed my mother when I was an infant and my father brought me up. He was a fyrd soldier given land for his service, and he taught me to fence ... I surpassed him in skill when I was fifteen ... But he proudly organised bouts with the other townsmen. I learnt from them and soon I always won. So I had a faint dream of trying for the Circle.

'The year after, a soldier turned highwayman picked a duel with my father, who knew his identity. The robber waited on the road for him on the way back from the pub. My father did not return. I searched for him – I never stopped – but three days later the river washed his damaged and dirty body onto the sandy bank right in front of the governor's house. It was so badly beaten that we could not tell how he died.

'I borrowed some rich clothes to disguise myself and I went looking for the highwayman. I rode up and down the Lowespass Road until he held me up. I disarmed the swine in a minute and he knelt, begging for mercy. Before I handed him over to the magistrate – he was hanged – I ... I cut him ... I took him apart. Until he told what he had done to my poor father.

'The first night he buried the body in the woods outside town. He could only scrape a shallow hole because tree roots blocked the soil. The following day he fretted that a passer-by might find the grave and unearth his crime. So the second night, in raw weather, he dug it up, carried the body to the Miroir moor and buried it in a deep hole. But then the idea tormented him that the moorland peat would preserve it forever and the disturbed grass would reveal the grave. So the following night he dug it up again. He threw it into the river from the top of a rocky outcrop. The river's flow brought the broken remains straight to Governor Merganser's door ... I am sorry for what I did to the highwayman ...'

San made no comment, so Wrenn continued. 'Anyway ... when I knew that I was alone, I decided to travel south. If I had stayed in Summerday I would still be there now, gradually forgetting everything I dreamed of. I went to Tanager and joined the ranks of the Select Fyrd. I helped clear Insects from Rachiswater and the land around the River Oscen. I conducted myself well, I'm proud to say, and when Skua was killed I was made division captain. Then I saw the future stretching out, always the same. I was thwarted. I sparred with all-comers. I gave the gentry scratches but they came back wanting more, unable to believe they had lost to a smallholder's son. In the end I beat them all. Well, yes, I resent them ... But that doesn't matter now, does it? I've done something they could never do.

'My dreams of the Circle returned. Thank god, my skill rather than my background is what matters to the Castle, I reckoned; there's a way out of this circus. For five years solid I spent all my off-duty time training. I was full of doubt and hope. I thought I was a dupe and a wretch to consider fighting the Swordsman. I nursed the idea for years and did nothing about it, then one night on a mad impulse I sent a letter to him. He chose to fight using rapier and dagger, which is my forte ... Um ...' Wrenn's speech filled the hall and it seemed to him that his voice droned on. 'I am twenty-five years old,' he whispered, looking at the backs of his hands. He stuttered and fell quiet. He realised that in a few minutes he would be twenty-five for ever and their appearance would never change.

'Answer my questions,' said the Emperor. 'Have you ever fought Insects alone?'

'Yes, my lord. I've killed Insects one at a time in the Rachiswater amphitheatre and hunted a couple found lurking by the town.'

'Have you ever felt fear?'

Wrenn hesitated, wondering what the best answer was. I knew that doubt well; in my initiation I had to confess all kinds of crimes to the whole Circle. I saw from his panicked expression that we seemed more forbidding and the Throne Room door looked tempting. I thought he was going to make a dash for it.

'Yes ...' he said eventually. 'I have never been as frightened as I am right now. But I master my fear.'

San asked, 'Do you have a partner to bring into the Circle?'

Wrenn shook his head. He tried to smooth over his exhaustion with confidence but it could still be seen like the shape of wings under velvet. 'I've made no time in my life for girlfriends.'

There is no way you can lie with the Emperor's gaze on you; it's impossible to hide anything. Wrenn squirmed uncertainly and stared at the floor. 'You want me to tell? I spent my nights in the brothels instead. Well, it's easier. I've been planning this Challenge for years; I couldn't afford the time to have relationships.'

We all privately remembered how terrible it is to speak alone in that vast space and felt sympathetic. I had witnessed the ceremony as an Eszai three times before, firstly when Tern joined at my wedding, and most recently when Ata Dei became Mist. I glanced at Mist; she looked shifty, probably recalling how during her initiation she tried to lie but instead found herself confessing that she murdered her husband for his place in the Circle.

San stated, 'You swear to serve me, in my service to the Fourlands, in god's name, for as long as I give you life.'

'I swear,' said Wrenn, forcefully.

The Emperor raised his right hand, bony fingers and prominent joints. 'Come forward.'

Wrenn climbed the dais steps, wondering at the great transformation about to take place. I could virtually hear him thinking: *this is it*. He braced himself for immortality as if it would burn through him. It's nothing like that. It doesn't hurt, in fact when it happened to me I could feel no sensation.

The Emperor extended his hand to Wrenn. Wrenn grasped and pressed his lips to it for a second. The Circle took him in.

Wrenn looked up finally to the Emperor's eyes. San announced, 'Now you are the Swordsman. Your name is Serein.'

A smile broke slowly over Serein's face. He dropped to his knees at San's feet, in silence. Then as if he could not bear such close proximity to the Emperor and aware that the rite was over, Serein quietly backed down from the dais, turned and passed the benches. We all stood as he passed. Lightning and Rayne glanced at each other; they had felt the ripple in the Circle as San made the exchange: one out, one in. After the transfer they'd feel Wrenn's presence as slightly different from Gio's, like a new person joining an inhabited room. Serein walked down the aisle, seeming to diminish in size, and left the Throne Room by himself. Lightning would join him outside; he made it his responsibility to greet new immortals and give them some much-needed advice. One by one we bowed to the Emperor, who was always last to leave the court, and followed Serein. As I passed through the door I grabbed two pocketfuls of confetti and glitter, swept up my hands and threw it over our heads.

A babble of a hundred conversations hung in the air of the Great Hall. I wanted to climb up to my rafter where I customarily sit, legs dangling, to watch the party. But I couldn't do that with my arm around Tern. I led her through a dozen conversations.

'Is he here yet? I want to meet the boy. I've questions to ask him ...'

'He's twenty-five, bless. How rare it is to be so adept so young.'

'Try the smoked venison, it's excellent.'

'Eleonora? Busy revitalising the kingdom. She's good, by god, I only hear praise.'

'But the court's full of scandal. What she does with chambermaids, I—'

'"For an Eszai everything is easy." Ha! How can they think that?'

'Look! There's Comet. He's back! *Hais-gelet*, Jant?'

The Emperor was seated at the high table on a raised stage. He did not touch the feast before him. Tern swayed her skirt a little to the music – a young lad slammed away at the piano, lissom women in jasper red played fiddle reels.

Confetti on the carpet, candelabra; people leant on the oak panelling, kissed under the arches. Frost was building a cantilevered bridge out of forks and salt cellars. Rayne and Hayl played chess with marzipan pieces on an enormous pink and yellow cake shaped like a chess board.

What platters and plates and bowls of food! There were sugared almonds, edible stars, spiced wine, iced wine, spring water, wheat beer and cream liqueur. There were flambéed swordfish, sliced lengthways on silver trenchers.

There were packets of Cobalt cigarillos on the table for those who wanted them. Boar pies – speciality of Cathee, charcoal-roast mushrooms, fat onions, saffron rice from Litanee, steak that juices-up your mouth. There

294

was peppered asparagus and kale from the Fescue fields; squash, tomatoes, baked potatoes cracked and oozing butter, Shivel cheeses like crumbly drums with fat blue veins. There was fruit: glazed, glacé, covered in cream.

There were warm loaves, soft inside and smelling sensual, lobster claws pickled from the Peregrine coast, poached pike from the river. Northern exotics like pinnacle rabbits spirited in from Carniss, eels from Brandoch, Awndyn salmon and sundry seafood.

East into Awia, the spices were wilder – fenugreek and turmeric dhal, moist cake with nutmeg and cinnamon sultanas. The best coffee from Micawater, prime grapes plump with juice, olives like slick jewels, floury chorizo sausages in net bags, artichokes you had to be Awian to understand, pizza, prosciutto, ciabatta and more olives.

Tanager crispy duck, all kinds of little birds, larks in pastry, magglepies, dumstruks and starlings caught on lime and cooked on the branch because Awians consider falconry insulting. There were peacocks couchant looking haughty with their skin and fan-tails replaced. There were crackling hogs with grafted wings and bemused expressions. Bustards were stuffed with turkeys stuffed with pheasant stuffed with partridge stuffed with quails stuffed with chestnut – cutting into it revealed layers of meat like tree rings and was more than I can face. A swan glided up the high table, by gingerbread with silver metallic icing that the Emperor quite ignored.

Eat, eat, eat. Immortality in gluttony. Watch out for checkmate on the marzipan cake!

Lightning noticed us and remarked to Serein, who was gorging sliced beef and fruit sauce in a wood bowl. His chest was broad and his arms well-defined muscle. He held himself tensely, trying not to dissipate under the tide of strange things, expressive people. Serein's regime of training had not prepared him for the duel's aftermath – he was the centre of attention but he still felt alone. If he wished himself back in Summerday now, he would feel much worse when he bore the responsibility of command on the battlefield.

Aside from his skill in archery Lightning has cultivated many social talents. It was said of him that if he was in the building no woman would ever have to open a door. He was dapper in black tie and a raised-and-slashed celadon silk shirt, his wings sticking out the back. Some people say that wings have become smaller over millennia because they can't be used and as Awians, especially non-aristocratic ones, intermarry with humans. Whatever the truth, Lightning's wings were distinctly larger than Wrenn's.

'Serein Wrenn,' Lightning said, 'may I introduce you to our Messenger and Lady Tern? Comet can fly; I think that's because he takes things too lightly. He will carry your letters anywhere in the Fourlands, and will help if you need translations, so don't hesitate to ask.'

The frontier boy bowed, steering back his sword hanger with his left hand and staring at me. I tolerated the usual scrutiny. People don't notice the subtleties straight away but they find my leggy proportions jarring. I shook his hand. 'I'm impressed – nobody can be taught to fight like that.'

'Comet Jant Shira. Lady Tern. It's an honour to meet you,' he said, looking as if he meant every word of it. His eyes were so wide I could see all the whites round the blue irises. He was wired on anxiety. He could not put a foot outside the narrow sphere of etiquette for fear that he would say or do something dreadful and be rejected from his hard-won place in the Circle, without ever knowing why. His fear was unfounded because only another Challenger could replace him, but he was almost frozen by the manners he imposed on himself.

A servant passed by, carrying a salver of champagne flutes. I took the whole tray from her, balanced it on one hand. I swept it low in front of Serein. 'Take a drink.'

He declined, uncomfortably.

'Go on,' said Tern.

'I don't drink,' he said, reddening.

'No, really? Tonight of all nights!' I pushed the tray towards him. 'One glass of champers to celebrate?'

'Sorry, no, Shira – I'm not used to it. If I took a drink now, I could never rise at six to practise.'

After a duel like that, who would anyway? 'Sleep till midday,' I said. 'Your first day as an Eszai. That's what I did. I sprayed champagne everywhere; I love being soaked to the skin in it.'

Lightning was enjoying this. 'The Swordsman doesn't drink alcohol, so leave him alone.'

'Shira, if I slip up and lose my edge a Challenger will get the better of me.'

Every time he said 'Shira' I bit my teeth together and they were starting to hurt. I said, 'Call me Jant. The name Shira really signifies I belong in the lower caste among the Rhydanne. It means "Born out of wedlock" – I can't translate it better than that.' Well actually I can, because it means 'bastard', but I'm not putting ideas in his head.

Wrenn had caused offence already and he was appalled. His face moved awkwardly; he was over-aware of its every feature. 'I'm sorry.'

'Worry not.' I waved a hand. I make my body language expressive to compensate for the difficulty most people have in reading my cat eyes.

Wrenn shuffled his feet as if they took up too much space on the carpet. I wanted to tell him, I understand how daunting this is, but lighten up, you won't be out on the street tomorrow. You'll still be here, immortal, staring at the backs of your hands like a fool.

He was frantically searching for something to say. Every word sounded loud and momentous to him; he picked them carefully, knowing they would be permanently impressed on his memory. I remember when I was in his position, in my reception when I was surrounded by Eszai – I had heard of every single one before through tales or monuments to their work. They were all here, in one place, and they talked to each other! I had been a novelty to them. I tried to get to know them all in one night, but the Eszai I most wanted to speak to was the Comet I had displaced. I practically pinned Rayne against a column and gabbled to her excitedly about chemistry and the latest research into Insect behaviour. I told her far too much about my past, without realising she understood, and that in describing the slums of Hacilith I had reminded her too much of hers.

I could offer Wrenn advice and he might bring something new and interesting to the Castle. I began to understand why Lightning took newcomers rapidly under his wing. I said, 'Serein is your stage name; you'll be grateful for it. You can make Serein whoever you want and Wrenn, your real self, will be safe.'

Serein glanced across the hall and suddenly gaped at a gossipy cluster of extremely beautiful girls. They saw him watching and wafted their plumed fans, parading themselves. They were mortals – Zascai – only fleeting names; they stood on the outside smiling, craving to be chosen and drawn in. Tern eyed them stonily. 'That's just the beginning. Next time, when word gets round, there'll be crowds.'

'Look,' said Lightning urgently. 'Be careful of those ladies. You need to learn how to discourage them.'

'Have fun,' I said vaguely. He could choose a different gold-digger every night; no need for whores.

Tern snorted. 'Seduction's their job, Wrenn,' she warned. 'They've studied it. If you give them an opportunity they'll eat you alive. They will try anything to marry into the Circle.'

'They only want immortality,' Lightning added. 'Don't wed the first one you meet just because she shows interest in you. You should wait for one who loves you for yourself.'

The eldest girl was about twenty and she had a driven look that no make-up could mask. She was hungry for the chance to peel away from her rivals and address Wrenn alone; a social climber eager to find footholds in the flaws of his character. An expert seductress, Eszai-good, if there had been a place in the Circle for seduction. She had started young and become an expert in her teens. Well, that kind of dedication was necessary to win the ultimate prize.

Tern wagged her finger at the Swordsman. 'For god's sake don't tell them anything. You'll be reading it in the gossip columns for the next six months.' She smiled and I pulled her closer. She instinctively knows how to flirt with anyone. The problem with having a trophy wife is that you have to keep re-winning the trophy.

'There is Tornado,' Lightning said. 'Wrenn, come and let me introduce you to the Circle's Strongman.' Wrenn found himself shepherded expertly between the dancers, who turned to glimpse him at every step, so he was always the centre of a space surrounded with people, all smiles and for the most part slightly taller than him.

'That golden boy is going to get his orange juice spiked if he's not careful,' I muttered.

Tern giggled and curtsied. 'May I have this dance?'

We danced. Her hand draped on my whipcord upper arm. My hand clasped below her shoulder blade on the silk, basque-wired like a lampshade. My lace shirt cuffs hid my fingerless gloves. She followed my steps in quick time like a snappy reflection. We had practised this; we felt good. I felt great, only Tern can keep up with me when I go so swiftly. And underneath all her clothes she's naked. She was giddy already from the room spinning about us. All those faces. Our bodies together, shoulders apart; my hips rubbed just above her waist. 'I'll lead, you can spin.'

'Easy!' Her skirt twirled; she was laughing.

The music ended; Tern leant forward, hands on knees, little cleavage in danger of escaping. 'Oh, Jant,' she said breathlessly in her carnal voice. I rubbed my cheek on her cheek and kissed her eyelids. I kissed her lips, and deeply her mouth.

We were still snogging when Mist Ata appeared and nodded curtly. She carried a candle in a holder and her forehead was creased with worry. 'Jant, come with me.'

'Later, Mist,' I murmured.

'This can't wait any longer.'

I disentangled myself from Tern and placed a finger on her nose. 'Soon,' I promised.

'Soon,' she repeated, as if from a distance.

I followed the Sailor. 'You were brave to ask San for leave,' she said. 'Mind you, I could tell you needed a holiday.'

'I was improving my flying. And besides, no one else ever goes to Darkling so I bring back news for the Emperor.'

'Yeah, right. Lucky, lucky; I haven't had any leave for five hundred years.'

At the quiet end of the hall Lightning waited by the camera obscura, leaning against the door with his big arms folded. Mist beckoned us inside.

'Oh, so you found a hiding place to avoid Wrenn's questions?' I said.

Mist replied, 'Jant, you don't even know the *type* of reason why you're here.'

The camera obscura was a tiny, black-painted room with a pinhole in the door that shone a circular image of the hall onto the far wall. The entire party was pictured inverted there – minutely detailed figures crossing the lit screen. I examined it. There was the tiny piano and musicians upside down. Miniature people waltzed past a section of the long trestle table. A blurred servant trudged behind them with a leather blackjack jug. I squinted to see the Emperor below the sun shield in the centre. I spotted Tern; she was talking animatedly to someone whose image stepped forward onto the screen. I contorted trying to view them the right way up. It was Tornado, an unmistakable giant of a man. Tern put her hands up to his chest. He bent down; she kissed him lightly on the cheek. His hands embraced her hips, far too closely in my opinion, and together they danced off the edge of the projection.

Oh, no. I wanted to run straight to Tern, but Mist blocked the doorway, setting her candle on the floor. Her shadow hid the screen.

'Can we get this over with?' I said, annoyed. I craned to see the figures now dancing on Mist's blouse and face. My wife was out there, chasséing with a man who had enough muscle in one bicep to make three warriors.

Lightning said, 'At least choose a more comfortable lair for your conspiracies.'

Mist said, 'Jant, what would you say if a land existed far out in the sea about which the Empire knows nothing?'

'I'd say that if you want philosophical debate in a stuffy cupboard you can ask another Eszai. It's not like me to miss a party. Especially important parties.'

Mist delved in her shoulder bag and brought out a thick book with crinkled pages. Her hands were pockmarked from her pre-Castle life as a milkmaid and butcher's delivery girl on Grass Isle, rowing her skiff every day to deliver cuts of beef to the islanders and cutting remarks to the sailors who wolf-whistled.

She gave me the book. 'This is the log of the *Stormy Petrel*. I have discovered an island, named Tris, reached three months out of Awndyn harbour on an east-south-east bearing.'

I said, 'Where? Three months? No, that's not possible; nothing's that far away.' I glanced at Lightning. 'You're being very quiet.'

'I'm not going with you, Ata,' he said.

'Going where?' I exclaimed.

Mist said, 'The Emperor requests that you and Lightning sail with me to the Island of Tris.'

'No! ... Look, slow down, this is a lot to take in. San knows of this island?'

'Yes. I returned from my voyage last month. I kept it very confidential though I wanted to sail in triumph into port. I told San everything and he has ordered a second expedition that you two must join.'

'But … I don't believe you. My duty's here; I have lots of work to do in Wrought. You won't need a messenger on a caravel; yes, I could be of more use working for you here. I—'

'You hate ships, we know. Tough.'

'Ships are fine as long as I don't have to be aboard them.' I caught a glimpse of the projection, on which numerous Eszai by the long table were asking Wrenn questions, but I couldn't see Tern. I was sure that I was being made the butt of a practical joke. I tried to give the impression that I was amused but was willing to see how far I could push Mist's invention. 'So what's it like on this island?'

Mist handed me the notebook. It began with the co-ordinates of the Awndyn coastline, the edge of the chart off which she had sailed. Her round feminine handwriting encircled a sketch map: 'The Island named Tris by its inhabitants,' I read, and: 'The town drawn from the harbour. The natives say "Capharnaum", this must be the town's name? Another settlement due south, name unknown. Triangulated height of mountain approx. 3000m.'

'Natives?' I said. 'You mean the island is populated?'

'Aye.'

'Who by? Plainslanders?'

'Some are human, some are winged people, living together in the town. As far as I could see there is no Insect infestation whatsoever.'

The island was shaped roughly like the head of an Insect, being rounded with short, spiny peninsulae. Mist had recorded the inlets and promontories with customary precision. The land rose up a gentle concave slope, poured off a sizeable river, and then soared into a massive peak. No details were marked, and the east coast was just a dotted line. 'I didn't sail that far, it's only an estimate,' she explained. 'I was interested in the natives. I couldn't understand their language; that's why I need you, Jant. I wrote some of the words down, see?'

'Can I study this?' I said enthusiastically. I would soon learn if it was a practical joke or not.

'That's just what I want you to do! If the knowledge alone doesn't satisfy you, there's more than enough rum to wash it down with. Their accent gave me quite a shock. I think the corsairs used some of those words, who infested the Moren delta when I was a girl.'

I leafed through the logbook. Mist's entries for each day were brief: '5 June. Distance travelled, 240 kilometres, lat. 29°S long. 129°E. Fresh gales and cloudy, good visibility. Sounding 100m, black sand with small shells. Ate a number of flying fish.'

'Flying fish?'

'Yes. And I have seen a place where oysters grow on the branches of trees.'

I shrugged. Well, why not? 'You left *Stormy Petrel* stuck in Oriole River.'

'Aye. Frost's company raised her. I spent last year refitting her for a deep sea voyage.'

Lightning spoke: 'There have been explorations before. They found nothing.'

'Saker, the ocean is a big place.'

'It's not possible,' I said finally. 'I don't believe it.'

'Where the fuck do you think I've been for the last six months?'

'Keeping your head down and escaping embarrassment!'

Mist gave me a candid look, which was a sure sign not to trust her. 'I have but recently rejoined the Circle, and this venture will prove my worth to those who would Challenge me or mutiny. This is not just another Grass Isle project seeking Shearwater's Treasure. I'm serious! There's nothing for me on the mainland, is there, since I lost Peregrine?'

Lightning looked at her mildly without replying. He opened the door a chink because we were all starting to suffocate, and muted music seeped in from the party outside. I lowered my voice. 'How did you know which direction to sail?'

Mist said, 'By chance. Yes. Well, there might be many—'

'No, there are not!' Lightning was quietly furious. 'God founded the Castle to protect the world. If the Castle doesn't know about this island then how could we fulfil our purpose? Insects might run rampant over it and we'd be none the wiser.'

'It might not fit with your ideology but all the same it's there.'

I thought, maybe the Fourlands isn't the only land and maybe we're not the only guardians god left behind. I examined the scale. It was big – four hundred kilometres in circumference. 'It isn't an island like Grass Isle at all, more like a chunk of Darkling out in the ocean. Tell us, what's in the town?'

'I don't know. I didn't leave *Petrel*.'

'Convenient.'

'I wanted more than anything to put ashore! We had weathered storms with ten-metre-high waves. *Petrel* lost half her caulking and cladding because Awndyn's shipbuilders are so shoddy. You would not believe the trouble I've had with the unions. Her sails were torn, the rudder splintered. Most of my men were sick, some with scurvy, and we were desperate for fresh water. I took on supplies from the natives' canoes but I didn't land because the governors of the town didn't permit me. They have many governors.'

'What?'

'I'm telling you it's true. People came out in big canoes and surrounded us. I sketched them, there.' *Stormy Petrel* dwarfed the canoes, looking like a goose with her goslings, and none of the vessels had details since Mist was a poor artist.

I crouched down in the cramped space on the parquet floor by Mist's feet.

The sea was not my element; boats bring on a phobia that I can never rid myself of completely. My fear was reasonable because if I ever tried to swim, the weight of waterlogged feathers would drown me. I also had a sneaking idea that everybody was acting and deeper lies were readily being believed. 'I'm not going. I might be the only Eszai who can crack this language but you can choose mortals from the university who have just as good a chance.'

'Don't mistake me; I hardly want you there, Jant. The last thing I need is dead weight and winged liabilities on my ship. If I had my way, I'd be doing this on my own! But San picked you two from the whole Circle to accompany me and we're obliged to obey. Here's his written command.' She passed Lightning and I small envelopes with the familiar crimson insignia. 'If you want to appeal, go ahead,' she added.

'I will,' said Lightning grimly. 'I would love to see the result of my invest-ment and your method of operation. I would like to be the first from the Fourlands to trade with Tris, but I am repairing Micawater and I should be there.'

'You knew? Damn,' I moaned, beginning to have the feeling that the conspiracy was against me.

'Yes, although I wish otherwise. The *Melowne*, the supply ship to be taken on this voyage, belongs to me. I have the Queen's permission to send it so that *Stormy Petrel*'s crew will not suffer hunger again. And in return I have a quarter-share in whatever goods we bring back. But that doesn't mean I must accompany the expedition, Mist. I will be a passenger on your ship if the Emperor decrees it. No more, no less.'

Lightning was rebuilding Micawater to look exactly the same as it did before the Insects damaged it five years ago. He obsessed about every detail in the restoration of his palace outside the town, believing it an inviolable duty to his family. He wanted to fulfil the trust they had placed in him to conserve the palace: he matched masonry, sourced silks, kept both its wings as symmetrical as the day it was first completed. I thought the fact he was tinkering with it and not helping Tornado and Queen Eleonora clear the remaining Paperlands that the Insects had built in northern Awia showed he had time to spare.

Mist addressed him: 'You can't sulk for a whole generation. Do you want your world view to become obsolete and eccentric like the portraits that hang in your house? Jant, listen to this: Lightning's family portraits have been repainted many times, about every two hundred years once they start to fade. The artists try to be accurate but scarcely perceptible changes creep in accidentally, flattering trends to the ideal of the era. Next time, those alterations are copied along with the rest and new ones are made. His por-traits are as idealised as his memories. Saker, how can you tell what's real and what isn't when you rely on the past? If you don't want to know of new

302

discoveries, how long will you last as an Eszai? Suppose the island has better bows than Awia? A better type of wood?'

'Without Insects to inspire them, I doubt it. Let them come with their Challenges.'

The camera obscura was growing even stuffier and I was gasping for air. I nudged the door wide, looking for my chance to escape. Serein Wrenn caught sight of us and strolled over with a limber gait. I wondered what he thought, seeing three Eszai in an alcove. When everything else at his party was so perfect, we stood out as a great anomaly. 'What are you talking about?'

'We beg your pardon,' said Lightning. 'This is a private discussion.'

Wrenn bowed and was about to leave us to it, but Mist sized him up. 'No, wait ... What time is it? We have to tell the truth for an hour.' I could practically hear her mind calculating. She took in his shirt buttoned down the left side showing his strong torso off to the best advantage, his small round stand-up collar and sharp-styled hair, the worn cherry-red leather thigh-boots with the tops folded over his knees.

Out came her travel-worn notebook again. 'You need experience. You'll find this interesting,' she said, and set her plans on him like wolves.

The others blocked my view of the party, so I turned again to the pinhole image. The beam angled by the half-open door illuminated the wall next to me, unfocused and with washed-out contrast. Fuzzy figures rippled over the uneven surface, so small that their activities looked quaint but nonetheless unsettling. I checked them one by one: Gayle exchanging a few words with the Emperor, Frost crammed into a ball gown and wearing steel-toed boots. I couldn't see Tern. Where was she? Why wouldn't Mist let me out? I tried to edge away from the stifling corner but Mist stood firm, talking hotly into my face, toes pressing against my toes, only the logbook between me and her ample breasts. Tern's figure must be in my shadow, but though I inched forward I couldn't see her waltzing on the wall. The perfume on Mist's long white hair tickled my sinuses; there was also the pong of Wrenn's gravy breath. His shoulder was up against mine and the bright love of adventure in his eyes would enthuse the entire fyrd. It was even worse to think I would be on the ship with him.

'... so the Empire must explore Tris,' Mist concluded eventually. Lightning glared; he rightly thought that we were making unnecessary problems for ourselves.

'Are you worried?' she asked Wrenn.

'Nothing worries me,' he said.

'Nothing!' I said. 'Poor lad, there's quite a lot of it out there.'

He stared at me. 'I haven't even unpacked my rucksack. I'm ready to go.'

'Aye, thought so. Gentlemen, you will be discreet and keep this a secret.

You must go out into the party with knowledge that no one else in the whole world has. Smile; you'll find it hard. I will see you at Awndyn by the end of the week; the *Stormy Petrel* is ready to sail.'

Lightning beckoned a butler and said, 'Go down to the cellars and bring me a bottle of Micawater wine. The oldest you can find.'

The party sashayed and shone around me. I walked through it, dead to the heart and scarcely seeing Tern in a clumsy two-step with the Strongman.

I ran out to the balcony and jumped to the balustrade, threw myself off. Beating hard and yelling with fury I reached eighty k.p.h. between two spires, just brushing stone with my wingtips. I zigzagged close to tightly packed walls near-missing by a centimetre on every familiar turn. I exploded out of the fog, still climbing to the clear starry sky. The tallest towers poked though the mist's cotton blanket like black sea stacks; lights flickered deep among them. I reached the top of my trajectory, for a second hung there. Somersaulted. Fell, head first, masonry soaring past, the mist's surface undulating.

I splashed through it, silently.

I flew circuits of the Castle until I slowed down and my anger wore off, turning into hopelessness. I landed on the sill of the Northwest Tower, bounded down into my room, sprang onto the four-poster bed and ripped its curtains together. In its gloomy, ivy-entwined brocade cave I sat and thought. Drugs, that's what I need. Drugs.

CHAPTER 3

Next morning I decided to seek an audience with the Emperor and appeal against the terrible orders that he had given me. I left Tern sleeping in the four-poster bed; I had pretended to be asleep when she came in late. I dressed, ate breakfast and shut the door as the Starglass struck ten. I ran down the frescoed spiral steps three at a time, at a speed that may well be the death of me one day. I ignored the thick rope that serves as a handrail and opened my wings for balance as far as was possible on the dizzying staircase. I hurtled round the last corner and crashed into Lightning, who was climbing up. 'Huh? Get out of my way, Micawater.'

'Jant! I have to talk to you. The Emperor's just asked me to put Gio out of the Castle!'

'Who?'

'Gio Ami. The Swordsman for four hundred years until last night.'

Gio was from Ghallain, a bleak town on the tip of an inhospitable cape. His wealth and acumen were entirely self-made. Three-letter names were often used among the coastal Plainslanders, a tradition dating back as far as the Emperor's birth. Like Awian names, they're not gender-specific. I thought, Gio really belongs in sixteen thirty-nine. What the fuck is he going to do out there, in the twenty-first century?

We walked towards the Simurgh Passage on the extreme eastern side of the palace, and along past Lightning's rooms where pale watercolour paintings covered the walls completely, their frames touching. The Archer said, 'Gio refuses to leave. I have sometimes seen defeated Eszai act this way. He has lived a long time in the Castle; he may fear the outside world although he'll never admit it. It has changed since he was last mortal.'

I remembered Gio's arrogance and said, 'More like he can't accept that anyone could beat him.'

'Yes, I agree.'

'Well, I hope he isn't armed.'

'Oh, of course he is armed. That's why I need your help to evict him.'

We walked up a flight of steps to the attic of the passage and the quarters traditionally appointed to Serein. Bucklers were displayed on the walls outside his doorway, with dusty bullfighting cloaks and wood-and-leather dusack swords for practice. Broadswords and falchions were arranged in circles and fans, next to sail-hilted daggers and Wrought katanas with naked blued steel. There were ceremonial two-handed swords with curlicued quillions and flamberge blades inlaid with gold wire, and several portraits of

Gio. Servants passed us, carrying boxes and suitcases down to the ground floor. One wore a sallet helmet and the others had shirts wrapped around their heads.

Lightning and I peered into the awkwardly shaped room, which had a sloping ceiling. It looked like the den of a sports-obsessed teenager. It smelt of rubber-soled shoes, canvas ingrained with sweat, the wooden grips of polearms smoothed and varnish worn away with use. Twinned rapiers in cases and practice foils in holdalls were stacked along the wall, under a shabby dartboard with a fistful of darts jammed into the bullseye. A beautiful schiavona cut-and-thrust sword with a basket hilt and a sharkskin grip hung in pride of place on the opposite wall.

In a big glass tank at the far end of the room enormous yellow koi carp cruised back and forth, their mirror scales glinting like plate armour. Two servants were indiscriminately stuffing the clutter into boxes and moving it out.

Gio Ami was sitting on the divan, slouched against the wall with despair. A foil with a round guard lay across his knees. His long, old-gold-coloured hair hung in twists to his shoulders, he had a single ring in one ear. His face was somewhat lined and worn, hollow cheeks offset by a broad chin, which now had fair stubble. His bare chest and taut belly showed under his unfastened frock coat. It was of Awian manufacture because it had wide slits up the back that were empty and looked peculiar without wings. His pale blue breeches matched, but laces trailed from his open boots. A number of Diw Harbour Gin bottles lay discarded on the floor.

Gio still had the quality of those who are great at what they do, an intense concentration unknown to most people. His coat's rich embroidery was testament to his affluence, gained through running his fencing *salles d'armes* since the turn of the seventeenth century. Branches of the Ghallain School had been opened in Hacilith and the majority of Plainslands manorships.

Gio had taken the dressing off the wound at his throat, which gaped a little, pink and clean. He must be trying to make it scar. He noticed us standing in the doorway, 'What do we have here? A lonely aristo and a gangland killer.' He looked from Lightning to me. 'Neither high looks of authority nor smart words will make me leave.'

Lightning sighed. 'Gio, if you don't go now, Jant and I will put you out of the Castle bodily.'

Gio spun the hilt of the foil, making the sword roll up and down his thigh. I watched it, well aware that he was still the second-best fencer in the world. His voice slurred slightly. 'Don't call me Gio. I am still Serein.'

'You were outmatched.'

'I have just said goodbye to the Sailor, the Cook and the Master of Horse. All my former friends are abandoning me.' He gestured at the servants. 'And the new Serein will have my rooms, as well as my title and my immortality.'

'We're not deserting you,' I said.

'All immortality belongs to the Emperor,' said Lightning.

Gio gave him a dirty look. 'Yes, you nobles are great at knowing who owns what. None of you will stand by me now I've fallen from grace. Why should I be cast out? It wasn't a fair fight!'

The oldest servant began to pack Gio's combat manuals. 'Bugger off,' said Gio, and threw *The Academy of Defence* accurately at his head. 'The flood-lights in the amphitheatre are useless. I demand a retrial.'

I thought for a while. 'You can Challenge him in a year's time, that's a rule of the Castle.'

'Challenge him as a mortal? Try to regain *my* title from *him?* Damn! I still don't understand the move he made. He tricked me with an unorthodox caper,' Gio spat contemptuously. 'No one will want to be instructed in my method now, the techniques I spent my life recording. My school will empty like the court of Rachiswater and then what will I do for a living?'

'Having been in the Circle will bring you fame enough,' I said in a concili-atory tone.

'Fame as a has-been.' Gio pointed the foil, working himself up. 'Why did I ever aspire to such a corrupt little world? Wrenn killed me in that duel! All right – so I might die forty years from now of old age, but he has killed me. Ruined by a non-fraternity fighter, opportunist, someone who never studied! A coarse recruit from a frontier town who wasn't even listed in the top five hundred swordsmen. He never competed in the annual tourna-ments. I hadn't even heard of the insane kid before he turned up!'

Gio did not realise how hidebound he had become over four centuries. He had systematised the art of fencing and relied so much on his perfect know-ledge that Wrenn's irrational move confused him completely. Immortals who are afraid to risk their lives are as useless against the Insects as those who become lazy or overconfident, solitary or debauched. San's rules for the Circle are wise; fresh blood will take our place if long life causes us to lose our edge.

'You've gained a year and you can try again.'

'A year for what? A year to practise?' He gestured at a wall-chart of foot-prints coding positions for rapier exercises. 'To shape up, lose weight, gain stamina?' He bent a sinewy arm until the long muscles knotted.

I took Gio's point that clearly he was in the best fitness and still got beaten, but none of us could know what effect the following year of renown and a six-month sea voyage might have on Wrenn's condition. The Castle has lost all Gio's knowledge now, replacing him with someone who is expert but inexperienced. It struck me as wasteful; I wished they could all be saved. I wondered why the Emperor refused to widen the Circle to accommodate more warriors; we would never pose a threat to San because we would never accumulate enough experience to be as wise as him.

I said, 'Gio, the Empire needs you too. We don't want to lose you.'

'The Castle's already rejected me. Though I devoted my entire life to its service ... I defended Hacilith in the last swarm.' His voice was drained of its usual energy. He would take days to recover from such an intense fight. 'I felt the Circle dropping me. I knelt down and couldn't get up. You bastards. But now I don't feel much different, I suppose because I'm only twelve hours older. I think mortals feel like they're twenty-one years old all their life, though their body gets slower and then they die. I'll provoke a few duels before I die, though. I'm going to send a few of them ahead of me.'

Gio picked up his predecessor's book, *Treatise on the Art of Fencing*, and weighed it thoughtfully in his hand. 'What happened to the Serein before me? When I displaced him from the Circle he went mad and hung himself.' A downward twist of his lips showed what he thought of a Swordsman committing suicide. He spun the book through the air and swore when a servant ducked and it hardly clipped him.

Lightning said, 'We are nowhere near restoring Awia and people already gripe about the necessary austerity. We need your imagination, not to mention your leadership.'

'Saker Micawater, what the rich fuck do I care about Awia now?'

Serein Wrenn, in his fyrd fatigues, hurried into view down the corridor. He made as if to enter the room but Lightning spread his blond wings across the doorway. The youth blinked at him, bewildered.

At the sight of Wrenn, Gio leapt to his feet, the foil loose in his right hand. Wrenn swept his rapier from its scabbard. Great. Now I was trapped between the best and second-best swordsmen in the world.

'No!' said Lightning. 'You may not fight.'

I took the knife from my boot and pressed the button for the blade.

Gio eyed me. 'Nice. A Rhydanne with a flick-knife.'

Lightning said, 'Put it away, Jant.'

'If you think I'm afraid to keep duelling, you're wrong,' Wrenn called.

'Every single year until one of us is dead,' Gio spat.

'You were wide open with that moulinet. You bloody deserved it!'

Lightning repeated, 'You may meet in twelve months. You may not fight now.'

'Step aside, Archer.'

Lightning stared at Gio, arms folded and wings spread.

Wrenn stretched out in a broad ward stance, an action that seemed to say: come on, stab me in the chest.

Gio shook with fury. 'I swear, Archer, get out of my way! Or I'll cut every tendon in your bow arm! I'll have my title back within an hour!'

308

'Honour demands a respite.'

'I'm mortal, I'm going to die anyway! Where's the honour in that? I've nothing to lose!'

Wrenn watched guardedly through the gap between Lightning and myself. He was calm, in control, just as I am aware of every centimetre of my body when I prepare to fly.

Gio flourished the foil. 'I'll die famous by running you both through!'

'Jant,' Lightning said eventually. 'It looks like we need Tornado's help to close this situation. Go to his room and fetch him; quickly, please.'

I hesitated.

'I can skewer you all on one blade!'

I nodded, ducked past and sprinted away. Gio watched until I reached the stairs and then he threw his foil aside. He pushed past Lightning and Wrenn, head up and haughty eyes averted. I stepped out of his way; he descended the staircase and walked out swinging his arms, across the wet grass of the quadrangle towards the Dace Gate and the Castle's stables.

Lightning exhaled and rubbed his forehead. 'God,' he said. 'Such a worthy adversary.'

Memo

To: Tern

From: Jant. You know, your husband. Tall, cheekbones, black wings ... Yes, that one.

Tern, darling

Where are you? I wanted to say goodbye. The *Stormy Petrel* sails Friday – Mist has ordered us straight to Awndyn and I doubt I will be coming back. It is bound to sink, and I shall drown. Or be lost, becalmed, and starve. Besides, the sea nourishes monsters far worse than Insects. If you feel the Circle break, think of me, and open the letter I left with Rayne.

NB I borrowed a thousand pounds from the Wrought Restoration Fund. Hope you don't mind. If we return in six months' time, I'll make enough money to pay it back with curios from 'Ata's Island'. Love you. Goodbye.

Jant.

CHAPTER 4

A shower of sleet fell at dawn, covering the stable courtyard with lumpy, slushy ice. Shallow puddles in its gutters looked grey as laundry water. Darker clouds smeared in the overcast sky above the large square forecourt. The sparrows that infested the eaves and stalls shouted out a dawn chorus. Warm air steamed from three pairs of thoroughbred horses harnessed to a gleaming coach. Lightning's carriage was waiting to carry him and Wrenn to Awndyn. It would take them three days to reach the coast, so they had planned to spend the first night at Eske manor, enjoying the hospitality of Cariama Eske.

There was a clock tower on an arch above the main gate. I landed in front of its peacock-blue dial, which showed eight a.m., and watched Wrenn and Lightning sheltering from the rain inside the nearest stable while their belongings were loaded onto the coach. Mist had said we could bring no more than one sea chest each, but my rucksack and Wrenn's small knapsack were so meagre – since I travel light and Wrenn was poor – that Lightning allowed himself more luggage.

The coachman stooped to check the bits in the mouths of the dapple grey mares and ran the reins through brass rings on the centre bar. His scarf and thick buttoned coat made him look portly. He held the coach door open; Wrenn jumped up and struggled inside. Wrenn obviously didn't know about the steps, which Lightning kicked out from under the polished splashboard. Wrenn settled himself on the seat and removed his woolly liripipe hat. He was obviously feeling self-conscious; I doubted that he had ever been in a coach before. He had changed his clothes – the ones he wore in the ceremony were discarded to show his entrance to a new life. The coachman slammed the door and pulled a leather strap to lower the window. He leaned in, exchanged some words with Lightning, then climbed up to his bench, took the whip in his left hand and flicked the reins. 'Hoh!'

The whole heavy rig rolled forward with the clop of clean hooves, a hiss of water from the wheels. The mares with braided manes shook their heads trying to see round their blinkers. They walked to the gates; I saw their six broad backs, then the dark red shining lacquer of the coach's roof loaded with wooden chests pass beneath me under the arch. The wheels sucked up sleet from the ground, spraying it into the air above them, leaving two tracks of paving clear from slush.

*

Wrenn twisted round to stare at me through the back window, one elbow on the tan leather. I wished that I could hear their conversation on the journey. Lightning paid Wrenn more attention than he paid me, offering the same time-refined advice. But I wanted to reach Awndyn before the coach did. I jumped off the clock tower.

My wings' muscular biceps, as thick as thighs bunched together, creasing the middle of my back, then separated as I pulled my wings down in the laborious effort of sustained beating. My long wings are pointed and fairly narrow, good for gliding but taking off is as hard as sprinting. I can usually settle into a rhythm that uses less energy but it's still like running a marathon.

I love long-distance journeys; I can stretch out along the route. I relaxed and leaned into the first of the long kilometres. The coach-and-six sounded hollow over the stable's wide drawbridge across the second moat and out of the Castle's complex. They passed the paddocks with steaming dung heaps and soggy ploughed fields, joined the Eske Road and entered the oak forest that comprised most of that manor.

I flexed my wings in and rolled once, twice, risked a third although I fell fifty metres each time. I opened my wings hard against the rushing air. High above the coach I rolled wing over wing, watching the even horizon turn a full three hundred and sixty degrees.

Then I set out for the coast. Diagonal lines of sunlight slanted down, patchily highlighting the level, loamy fields of the plains around the Moren. When flying from manor to manor I find it useful to follow one of the straight military roads that the Castle commanded to be built between towns for the movement of troops. But to fly cross-country I pick a point on the horizon, a notch or a hummock, and head directly towards it. The notches become vales, the hummocks turn into hillsides. When I become tired I fly a more convoluted route to find and climb onto thermals to rest.

At a height of two hundred metres I don't see individual tree tops, just a mass of twigs and pine needles. The slate roofs of the towns are scaly patches that look flat among the forest's green-brown froth. The houses built from local stone were camouflaged in the landscape, and I passed over hunting lodges without seeing them. Towns all seemed the same from the air; I hardly distinguished between them. My travels have taught me that people everywhere are intrinsically the same: well-disposed to me as Comet.

The same would not be true for Tris. I considered the events of the last two days as I flew. No one could predict what the Trisian people would make of us; I hoped that I could communicate with them. I was terrified of the hated uncharted ocean. The things that swam and slapped suckers on ships' sides beggared any description – behemoth serpents and sentient giants amassed from the rotting bodies of drowned sailors.

I wondered what to do about Tern. At this very moment she could be stroking Tornado's wingless back, hewn muscles, shorn head, and I had to leave on some damn godforgotten ship! I imagined her sitting on the palm of his hand and he lifts her up to kiss her. Away at sea I was powerless to stop this latest outbreak of her infidelity; it might deepen and then what would I find on my return? Tern married into the Circle through Tornado, myself divorced and having to live next door to my beautiful ex-wife for all eternity?

I knew every landmark – the white fences along the 'racehorse valley' race-tracks that Eske is famous for, their stables where destriers are bred. A line of tall poplars by Dace River; further on in the forest smoke straggled from a charcoal burner's shack. I concentrated on keeping the horizon level to fly straight, but in the evening I was grounded by a heavy hailstorm and, annoyingly, had to spend the night in the Plover Inn on the Remige Road. If this was a routine journey I would sleep in the woods because, since I'm Rhydanne, temperatures have to be much below freezing before I start to feel cold.

By the following afternoon I could see the faintly lilac-grey Awndyn downs in the distance. Cobalt manor's hops fields and oast houses dotted the downs; a bowl-shaped pass resolved into the coast road. Finally I crested the last hill – and there was the sea. The grey strip of ocean looked as if it was standing up above the land, ready to crash down onto it.

Every window in Awndyn-on-the-Strand was brassy with the setting sun. The town's roofs slanted in every crazy direction. The manor house stood on a grassed-over rock-and-sand spit jutting out into the sea. It had tiny clustered windows and tall thin octagonal chimneys with diagonal and cross-hatched red brickwork. I glided down through another sleet shower so strong I had to close my eyes against it, and landed on the roof of a fish-and-chip takeaway. I waited till the squall stopped spitting wet snow, then climbed down from the chip shop and walked into town, crossing the shallow, pebbled stream on a mossy humpbacked bridge. The Hacilith-Awndyn canal ran beside it into an enormous system of locks and basins packed with barges.

A creative cosmopolitan atmosphere hung over Awndyn, with a smell of cedarwood shavings and stale scrumpy. It was the only Plainslands town to prosper after the last Insect swarm, profiting from the merchant barges that paid tolls to navigate the locks and carracks with full coffers anchoring in the port. It was well positioned to make use of all their raw materials. Swallow, the musician governor, had encouraged a bohemian community; artists and craftsmen were welcome in the tiny crumbling houses and ivy-shaded galleries. Artisans' slow and friendly workshops overhung the shambling alleys; glass-blowing and marquetry, cloisonné and ceramics, leatherwork, woodturning and lapidary, musical instruments and elegant furniture were crafted there.

I was prospecting for drugs, just as a gold miner follows rules to find deposits. Scolopendium is illegal everywhere except the Plainslands – in Awia the laws have been tight for fifty years and counting; in Hacilith's deprived streets the problem is at its most serious; and at the Lowespass trenches its use is tackled very severely. But centipede fern grows wild in Ladygrace, the sparsely populated foothills of southern Darkling. The governor of Hacilith tried to pay the Neithernor villagers to burn the moorland hillsides and destroy the plants but thankfully they never succumbed to the offer. Scolopendium extracted from the fern fronds flows out of Ladygrace together with more well-known drugs, and addicts' money is sucked back in along the same routes. The ban is almost impossible to enforce.

To find scolopendium in a town look for boundaries, for example the edge between rich and poor districts, or between streets of different trades – where houses begin at the edge of the market or where at night people empty from cafés into clubs. The prospector should investigate places where newly arrived travellers are lingering. Longshoremen with cargoes from Hacilith are the most promising, because a handful of cat hidden in a cabin is worth twice as much as a richly stocked hold. When I was a dealer I witnessed even the most scrupulous merchants give in to greed. I determined not to buy from the pushers at the dockside, but they would only be a couple of links down the chain from one of the more powerful traffickers I know.

Buildings give clues: dirty windows and peeling paint in a rich district, or a tidy house in the middle of a slum. This is because they are houses where business is done. When I'm hooked, I read the signs subconsciously; a sixth sense guides me to a fix.

I walked past clustered half-timbered buildings with warm red brick in herringbone designs. Stonecrop grew out of the walls that were topped with triangular cerulean-blue tiles and bearded with long, grey lichen. The town looked like a grounded sunset.

Following my rules brought me to the quayside. Awndyn harbour was a mass of boats. At low tide they all beached, propped up against each other, and fishermen walked across their wooden decks from harbour wall to sand spit. At full tide they all sailed together, a flotilla of bottle green and white, Awndyn's dolphin insignia leaping on prows and mastheads. As dusk fell, I watched them unloading, passing metres of loose netting in human chains to the jetty, where boys rocked wooden carts on iron wheels back and forth to get them moving on the rails. The boys were paid a penny a half day to shunt the heavy carts to a warehouse where fisherwives unloaded the catch into crates of salt and sawdust.

After dark it began to drizzle sleet. The road was plastered in a thin layer of wet brown mud. I walked along the seafront and passed the Teredo Mill, a tall cider mill with peeling rose-pink window frames, dove-holes in diamond shapes in its ochre-coloured walls. It was roofed with white squares cut from sections of Insect paper. Last harvest's apples had been pressed so the intense sweet smell that hung around the mill in autumn was replaced by the heady reek of fermentation.

A group of young apprentice brewers were sheltering in the underpass where a path ran under the waterwheel's cobbled sluice. The wheel was raised from its millstream and clean water flowed along the conduit above their heads. They were smoking cigarettes after a day's work. One of the promenade street lamps cast my shadow long across the road. The brewers regarded me curiously. The youngest had dyed purple hair, baggy chequered trousers and a black coat that reached the floor. I checked him out for the marks of an addict, drew a blank. Well, I haven't hit gold but I'm very close. We fell into the quiet of mutual examination, until he nudged his friend and bowed. He walked over the road to me. 'Comet?'

'Yes?'

'It is ... it is you?' He looked back to his friends, who all made 'Go on' motions.

I didn't want their presence to scare away the sort of character I was really looking for. I was about to tell him to get lost but something of my Hacilith self was reflected in him. He didn't know what to say – there was awe in his eyes like tears. His co-workers crowded round with eager expressions. They were a little too well-heeled to be true rebels. 'So you've met the Emperor's Messenger,' I said. 'How can I help you?'

'Did you see the duel between Gio and Wrenn?'

'What's the new Serein like?'

'Tell us the tactic he used!'

'Tell us if he's married,' a girl said. Her lanky body had a passing resemblance to a Rhydanne woman and momentarily I had to control myself.

'I just flew here ...' I said.

'Is it true there's never been a Swordsman as good as Wrenn?'

I tried, 'I've just returned from Darkling. Let me tell you—'

'I don't believe Wrenn taught himself. He must be a genius!'

'My name's Dunnock,' said the boy with purple hair. 'I study music – in the governor's arty set – but she demands a lot of her circle.'

Wonderful, I thought; other Eszai have the Fourlands' best vying to be trained by them in the Select Fyrd; I attract gangs of disaffected youth. I tried a simple approach. 'Actually the Governor sent me to find a man called Cinna Bawtere. I've been ordered to arrest him. Have you heard of him?'

'What if we have?'

'Why do you want to arrest him?'

I rounded on Dunnock. 'Show me where his lair is these days.'

The brewers, now quiet, ushered me through the underpass. My leather-soled boots squeaked on the tiling; then we turned left on Seething Lane away from the sea, past the puppet-maker's shop and into the artists' quarter.

Shop signs projected above doorways: CROSSBOW CLOCKWORK LTD and FYRD RECRUITMENT LOWESPASS VICTORY HOUSE. APPLEJACK AND FINE TEREDO CALVADOS. Bleak graffiti sporadically decorated the walls between them, declaring, 'Ban the Ballista' and 'Featherbacks go home!'

The local resentment of Awian refugees was worse than I thought. It made me angry – they weren't to blame for being made homeless by the Insect swarm. In fact, I thought guiltily, the swarm had largely been my fault. I knew that Tern was trying to persuade the Wrought armourers back to continue their vital tradition in her manor. Her blacksmiths worked extremely hard wherever they had been forced to settle.

The Swindlestock Bar was dead centre of the artists' quarter. It was built inside the mouth of a gigantic Insect tunnel, like a grey hood with a rough, deeply-shadowed papier-mâché texture. The tunnel had been cut from the Paperlands and shipped south for building material; the nightclub's front projected from its opening, with two storeys of green-glazed bricks and black beams. Paper curved down to the ground, looking like a huge worm cast. Windows had been cut in it. Outside the door, a sloughed Insect skin hung in an iron gibbet, its six spiked legs sticking out. It was transparent brown and gnarled; it revolved slowly, a dead weight in the sea breeze.

I know some clubs in Awndyn that could be described as meat markets. This was more of a delicatessen. Green light so pale it was almost grey reflected on the water pooled between the cobbles. The vague and eerie light came from cylindrical glass jars by the club's open door – larvae lamps – lanterns full of glow-worm larvae. The doorman picked one up and shook it to make it brighter.

The brewers nodded at the doorman and walked straight in. Inside, the floor was malachite-coloured tiles, the decor ebony with a matt shine. In a deep fireplace sea-driftwood burnt with copper-green sparks. A lone musician up on the stage was salivating into a saxophone. He played exceptionally; he must have been one of Swallow's students. The larvae lamps emphasised his sallow face as he leant across their shifting light. He paused, recognising me, and his eyebrows sprang right into his hairline, then he started up another low, sexy drone, playing his very best as if I was a talent spotter.

The brewers vanished into the press of bodies around the stage. Dunnock turned to me and pointed at the ceiling. 'Check upstairs. They ask to see track marks,' he added, agitated. 'You're not wearing a sword.'

I raised a hand to calm him. 'I don't need a sword to arrest the likes of Bawtere.'

'Wow. They're never going to believe this back at the vats.'

'Keep it a secret!' I said. I elbowed through the dancers' slow jazz wave to the stairs. They creaked as I climbed them. At the top, a bullseye lantern swung in front of my face, startling me, and a voice rasped, 'Oo's that? One for Cinna?'

'Yes,' I said.

'Oo is it?'

'His boss.' I deliberately looked straight at the lantern because I know that my Rhydanne eyes reflect. Cinna's flunky must have seen them shine as two flat gold discs. His chuckle stopped abruptly.

'All right, Comet,' he whispered. 'You want t'see Cinna?'

'Of course,' I said.

'Just ... wait a minute, please ... Shit, a fucking immortal ... He's a fucking immortal ...' The voice trailed off, and then returned. 'Come through, Comet.'

He beckoned me along the dingy corridor, then through a beautiful door inset with opal to a big black and white room. In the middle of the square chamber stood a vast carved table. Its rectilinear designs were echoed on printed six-panel paper screens that folded like concertinas along the dim walls.

Cinna Bawtere had no friends, only collaborators. He was fat but suave, with a receding hairline and flabby, incandescently red lips like a couple of cod fish lying in the bottom of a boat. He had a duelling scar like a dimple by his mouth, suggesting that long ago his skin hadn't been pasty, his belly protruding and his chin double. But these days Cinna could get out of breath playing dominoes. People worked for him now, and his big hands had lost all the cuts and calluses they had when he was a sailor. He was a tactless, feckless, reckless individual with an ego the size of Awia and a conscience the size of a boiled sweet. Cinna's extras included a cutting-edge understanding of chemistry as it applied to narcotics, and of the law and how to break it. His wings were speckled; every fifth feather had been bleached. He wore new blue jeans and a patterned cherry silk dressing gown. Like so many ugly men, he was fond of good clothes.

I sat in an engraved chair and hooked my wings over the low back. 'How great a sense of hearing do the walls have?'

'It's all right. We're totally alone.' Cinna gave me a hard stare from the other side of the table. Eventually he said, 'You haven't visited for a long time, Comet.'

'Four years isn't a long time to me.'

He creased into his chair. 'By god, and you look Just The Same as you did when I first saw you, twenty years back.' He gave a little smile. 'I thought you'd forgotten me, because I hadn't heard any word since the Battle Of Awndyn.'

'So how is business?'

Cinna raised his hands to indicate the shadowy room. 'As good as you see it.'

'Cinna, I'm here to tell you that I won't turn a blind eye to your dealing any longer.'

His round shoulders sagged. He scooped a packet of cigarettes from the table, poked one out and lit it. 'I'd been expecting this. So it's finished? The game's over?'

'If you continue and you're caught, you can't invoke my name; I won't help you. If you keep selling contraband to Mist's sailors and she complains to me, the next time you see an Eszai he'll be with a fyrd guard to seize you.'

'Now, Jant, how disappointing after all this time!'

I shrugged. 'I want you to go back to legitimate trade. Why not?'

Cinna placed both hands flat on his polished table. 'Because it's Not That Easy! This latest "paper tax" from the Castle caused an uproar in Hacilith. You should hear the merchants muttering. All the money's sent to Awia.'

'You know there's a worthwhile cause. We need to break down the Insects' Paperlands there.'

'Well, why can't that kingdom look after itself?'

'For god's sake, they're doing all they can. Awia will repay its debts in full; you mortals just can't see the long term.'

'Oh, I understand,' said Cinna. 'But I hope Eszai realise how quickly Plainslanders forget Insects once the immediate threat cools off.'

'Look, you have to stop dealing. In Hacilith now, the punishment for pushing cat is death. I've seen dealers broken on the wheel. In Awia they just jail them for life.'

He nodded. 'Well, ergot pastilles are all the kids want these days. They have no taste.' He wallowed over to a side table where there was a decanter of port and some crystal glasses. He poured one for me.

'To the Emperor,' I said, and drank.

He topped up my glass. 'And another toast. To all the kids who ever sang protest songs against the old king's draft.'

I put the glass down. 'It's the Empire's war,' I said evenly. 'Let's talk business, not nostalgia. I know how you feel about the past but I have to obey the Emperor's command.'

'You singled me out and saved me because I was an Independent, Deregulated Pharmaceutical Retailer,' he said. It was true; I wanted a dealer and I found Cinna trustworthy, who owed me his life and his livelihood. Once I got my fingers round the edges of his ego, he was a business partner more loyal than a fyrd captain. 'Do you know it's twenty years ago almost to the day, when you appeared with a handful of draft notices,' he continued. Worry lines on his forehead came and went as he talked. 'Nailed on the lifeboat house door – lists of families to contribute to Tornado's division. My mother wanted to hide us but I knew how relentless you were. She showed us a trapdoor to the coal cellar, but, god-who-left-us, what use is that against someone who knows every Trick In The Book?'

I swirled beeswing in the glass, embarrassed on his behalf that he would rather hide than fight.

'You took my brother. He was killed at Lowespass. All they could find of him to bury was a handful of feathers; the Insects cemented the rest into their Wall.'

'Many people die in Lowespass.'

Cinna grimaced and picked at one of the spots around his mouth. 'Jant, I remember we had to line up in the courtyard – you were there checking names off on a list. You looked younger than me and I hated you, the way schoolkids hate swots. You looked as calm as a merchant checking sacks of corn, a buyer at a livestock market—'

'As if I'd done it a thousand times before.'

'Yeah. It made me want to strangle you, and you looked so frail I was sure I could. My brother knew what I was thinking; he elbowed me in the ribs and said Comet's Two Hundred Years Old! Knowing that I wouldn't stand a chance. Then he climbed onto the cart bench with the rest of the stevedores and that was the last I ever saw of him. Taken away to the General Fyrd. Every one of the five hundred men in his morai were slaughtered.

'Well now I've witnessed Insects flatten Awndyn I can understand why we need to keep the Front – but back then I'd never seen one and it took me fifteen years to recover. Your frozen age is so misleading, it makes us mortals underestimate you. You can run faster than a deer, but you just looked like a Bloody College Kid.

'We know the effect scolopendium has on the people who trade it, let alone the users. I haven't sought friendship or lovers – just money – thinking that at any second the governor's fyrd could snatch me away.'

I glanced up from the mediocre port. Cinna was not known to be a man of great imagination. 'What are your plans?' I asked. I knew he would find it hard to relinquish his beautiful suite. He had become too much of a *bon viveur*. He was too fat to return to life as a sailor, honest or otherwise. 'Are you holding any now?'

'I've a quarter kilo of Galt White to sell, and that will be The Last Deal. Maybe.'

'Let me take it off your hands.'

318

'Oh ho!' He pointed a finger over the top of his wine glass. 'I thought there was another reason for this visit! Once an addict, always an addict!'

'That's not true, Cinna. Besides, it's not for my use.'

'Well, I don't know anybody else who buys in quarter-k quantities. Not even Lady Lanare when she's poisoning her whole family.'

'Are you selling or not?'

Cinna chortled.

'It'll be the last time I ever buy cat.'

Cinna chortled with wicked glee.

He unlocked a panel in the wall and scooped out a large white paper envelope. He gave it a shake to settle its contents, then pushed it to me across the table.

I rubbed it, feeling the fine powder inside. 'Go first,' I said.

He held his palms up. 'You know I don't do that. I can't stand the hallucinations.'

'This time you do.'

He dipped his finger in it. 'Damn you, Eszai.'

I knew that my tolerance would have decreased, so I took just the edge of a fingernail full and licked it. It spread on my tongue, tasted numb, slightly grassy with a crystalline metal-salt edge. This was snap-condensed. Fuck, it was good. I closed my eyes in shame as I realised what I'd done. It was five long years since I last tasted scolopendium.

'You look like the Archer tasting fine wines. It's Pure As Darkling Snow,' he assured me, hands wide in a ham actor's gesture. 'We make it using your technique, no one else can match the quality.'

'Yes, this will help. At least until we reach the island,' I said. Cinna gave me an odd look. I explained rapidly, 'No, not Grass Isle, I mean Tris. Mist told us a strange tale of a new island three months' east of Awndyn. She tells of a fascinating culture and mouth-watering fruit like, like apples that look like pine cones. Six months' leave from the Castle! Unless it's some kind of mirage caused by sailors drinking their own piss. Think what it means, and not just for bored Eszai, for everyone! ... But, knowing Ata, we won't make it out of the bay before something awful happens.'

I huffed out a breath and stood up. The weight of the envelope seemed correct. I had a feel for it, like a long-time card sharp knows by touch how many cards are in a deck. I dropped it into my satchel and reached for Cinna's packet of cigarettes, slid them towards me and pocketed them too. 'Thanks. Now may I have a lantern? I'm needed back at the manor house.'

'Ah-ah. That's a thousand pounds please, Comet. And unfortunately cheques drawn on the defunct Bank of Wrought are not welcome at Bawtere Unlimited Imports.'

I haggled down this outrageous price, that would only be right for

Lowespass, to a more reasonable eight hundred and eighty pounds. I counted out nine hundred from my wallet and Cinna swept the money away.

I noticed that, out of the pound coins he gave me for change, the majority were Awian, embossed with Tanager's swan. From the other three of the Fourlands' mints, there was only one each with the Summerday scallop shell and Hacilith fist, and a couple of the Eske mint's 'daffodils'. Currency was supposed to be produced at the same rate throughout the Fourlands, as advised by the Castle. I hoped that Awia hadn't responded to its adversity by minting more money. It would be a typical Zascai way of thinking, a short-term solution that would just drag Awia further into the mire.

Cinna's bristle-chinned henchman returned with the bullseye lantern, muttering, 'Thought Rhydanne could see in t' dark.'

Cinna is one of the few dealers I know who has not ended up using. They take to it because drug-dealing is so wrong and they find that scolopendium is a very tempting, potent salve for all misdemeanours and open emotional wounds. However, Cinna had always stayed at the money-worshipping stage, a bit like myself when I lived in Hacilith. He was from one of the Morenzian villages and had worked hard to escape. I didn't blame him; the Morenzian industries, law courts and markets were all in the city. The intellect of the country was leached by Hacilith's University and its Moren Grand Theatre monopolised the fame, leaving the surrounding villages lacklustre and dull.

Cinna knew that everything he is or owns he has built himself on a precarious base. He is always waiting for the tiny push from an Eszai or governor that will send the whole card tower tumbling back into the dirt. 'Taking cat is a waste of all-too-precious time,' he said. He held the door open for me and added, 'But I have thought what immortality truly means, Jant. I'd do drugs too.'

I left the nightclub, crossed Seething Lane and went down a couple of slippery steps onto the hard expanse of the beach. The breeze blew stronger and colder here than in the sheltered town. I left no prints on the rippled wet sand. I won't get addicted again, I told myself; this is just casual use. The empty ocean was a sucking black space; there were no lights out there. I swung my lantern but it only just illuminated the lapping water's edge.

Far beyond the harbour mouth an obscure profile merged with the night, a motionless hulk like a premonition. It must be the *Stormy Petrel*. By god it was a huge ship.

I passed the quay, the only part of town that the governor bothered to maintain properly. Small vessels were roped together across the harbour mouth, each one bore a swinging lamp. Their yellow arc reflected in the gentle ripples; they made a silent blockade. A succession of boats was rowing out towards the *Stormy Petrel* from the quay. I dimly saw a man in each, straining at the oars. Every boat was stacked with barrels; the last stocks of fresh water were being loaded. Mist's night workers on the jetty stooped and rolled kegs, muttering in a smuggler's undertone. The first rowing boat blurred into darkness but I still heard with dread the rhythmic splashes of its oars distorted by the breeze. The rower gave a shout; at his familiar voice a passage opened through the blockade.

Mist had spread the word that this voyage of discovery was no different from the others she had attempted, but if you compared the current level of secrecy to the previous expeditions you would draw a very different conclusion.

CHAPTER 5

The following day, the subculture of Awndyn was invisible in the bright winter sunlight. The black and amber crosstrees and crow's-nests of fishing cogs anchored in the harbour protruded above the houses as if the rooftops had masts. The harbour master's office had sculptures of caravels in shining bronze on its tower tops, complete with wire rigging.

I met Lightning and Serein Wrenn at the quayside. They were watching the procession of boats still plying out to a deep channel called Carrack's Reach where the tall ships were anchored. A crowd had gathered on the promenade. The air was cold but a glorious sun beat down, flattening the waves to translucent ripples that lapped up inside the harbour wall, hardly moving its heavy sheaves of green-brown bladderwrack.

Wrenn and the Archer descended to a rowing boat that was stowed with our belongings. Wrenn sat upright on the plank bench with his scabbarded rapier and sword belt gripped between his knees. Lightning leant on the gunwale, trailing his fingers in the water, with a distant smile on his wood-cut face. He carried a bow and a quiver of exquisite arrows, and the circlet around his short hair glinted in a most annoying way.

I sprinted along the jetty, wings half-open to build up airspeed. I ran faster and faster still, towards the lighthouse at the end. I passed it, reached top speed; the jetty ended, I jumped off into the air. My wings met below me, I swept them up till the primary feather tips touched.

I flew over the waterfront that was lined with several hundred people. Some ducked, swearing. They had a glimpse of my boot soles and ice axe buckled across my waist. I heard their murmur of envy ripple like waves.

I leant with my wings held up in a V-shape to circle tightly, and began to rise on a weak thermal above the chaotic roofs. I reached the height of the buff sandstone cliffs and soared above, seeing their grassy tops. Then I turned out towards the ships; the sea's surface sped beneath me. I would miss Awndyn's homeliness. I had taken a pinch of scolopendium with breakfast and as a result I was less afraid of the ocean. When you're intoxicated, the balance changes between all the facets of your personality, making a different character. I was eager for Tris.

A group of people proceeded along the rough stone jetty. From high above I mostly saw their heads. The woman with a walking stick had long red hair over a green shawl held tightly closed; it was Governor Swallow, surrounded by her attendants. They stopped at the foot of the lighthouse and looked out to sea. Swallow began to sing. She keened, she swelled the dirge with all the force of her opera voice. The wind gusted the melody up to me; clear and high, it slid over eerie minor notes that prickled my skin. Her melancholy lament rose past the crowded quay, past the rowing boats to the caravels. The rowers heard it. Lightning heard it and looked back. The breeze blew it to Tris. I didn't know why she sang a dirge, but it seemed apt.

Outside the harbour, the boats began to churn from side to side. At least I don't have to sit in one of those little tubs. Colourful caravels lay at anchor, scattered some distance apart. As I gained height and my viewpoint widened I saw around thirty – like brightly painted models, some with windmills on deck to wind winches, some drab and barnacled, some with men sitting in the complicated cat's cradles of their rigging, all lashed to buoys with flags atop, and streamed out in the same direction by the flowing tide.

The fleet was a sober reminder of Mist Ata's talent. Her patience and will power could conquer the world. In the fifteenth century, caravels were developed from ungainly merchants' carracks, although since that time they have undergone many improvements. San recognised their use for bringing supplies and troops to the Insect Front, so he made a place in the Circle for a Sailor and held a competition that Ata's predecessor won. The first Sailor immediately tried to deter Challenges by forbidding any Zascai company to build caravels. It was a plan that the Emperor certainly didn't condone. Ata knew it, and ignored the ban. For her first Challenge in fourteen-fifteen she made caravels in sections, in Hacilith where the Sailor couldn't observe them. She had them dragged overland on a road she commissioned to be built, to a secret assembly yard made for the purpose at the coast. She sailed her new ships cockily around Grass Isle – their sudden appearance frightened her predecessor. That's the kind of determination Ata has, and joining the Circle had not affected her admirable ambition. She planted vast forests to grow elm and oak for future ships.

The *Stormy Petrel* was by far the largest caravel, sixty metres in length. No surface was left undecorated. At her rear was a high aft castle, painted red and spiralled with gold curlicues. The forecastle at her bow was slightly smaller, and between them was a low deck with the largest of her four masts. The black hull was very rounded, its sides slanted in steeply, giving her a teardrop shape when seen end-on. *Stormy Petrel*'s figurehead was a muscular young man with a folded breechclout. Above him projected a square prow, heavily decorated with scarlet zigzags and the Castle's sun. A varnished spar jutted from it like a tusk, and at the waterline five metres below the prow a taut anchor cable ran from its port. The foremost part of the deck was a sort of promontory with cross-planking through which I saw the waves.

The Sailor must seriously want to impress the islanders with the Empire's ingenuity and riches. *Stormy Petrel* inspired confidence in me, too: Mist was pragmatic, so if she had spent money on decoration, the rest of the ship must be sound and formidable. She would be as trustworthy as the best Sailor in the world could make her.

A narrow balcony ran the *Petrel*'s length on both sides, three metres above the waterline. Baroque woodcarving clustered around the stern, picked out in the Castle's colours, red and yellow. The vertical dimensions of the fixed lanterns were tilted to the rear, and the entire top of the aft castle slanted backwards, so the *Petrel* looked like she was racing along even when she was sitting still. The diamond-leaded stern windows were adorned with ruby-stained glass sunbursts. The sun-in-splendour formed a sumptuous centrepiece below them, covered in dazzling gold foil. It scintillated with sunlight reflected from the waves.

Banners twined from the masthead, spinning on their cords like kites. Mist's plain white pennant was the longest. I also recognised the argent swan of Queen Tanager, and Cyan Peregrine's sleeping falcon. There was the black plough insignia of Eske manor, Shivel's silver star, and Fescue manor's crest of three sausages on a spike. Carniss manor must have sent funding too, because its flag was there, a black crescent pierced by an arrow. One hundred years ago I told a Rhydanne girl called Shira Dellin that she had just as much chance of driving the Awian settlers from the lower slopes of Darkling as she had of hitting the moon with an arrow. The settlers founded the manor of Carniss and they immediately took that image for their badge, which made it even more painful when they proved me right.

I made a controlled descent between the first mast and mainmast, and dropped with a hollow thud onto the deck. I settled my wings and folded them. Cinna's scolopendium was so good I couldn't feel them ache at all.

Lightning and Wrenn climbed aboard and joined Mist by the wheel. Wrenn grinned uncontrollably. He was brimming with excitement. Sailors began to stow the flags. Mist called, 'Make sail! Half-deck hands below for the capstan. Brace full the foresails! Send order, if you please, to Master Fulmer on the *Melowne*; we shall be underway ... Welcome to the ocean, Serein,' she added.

With the *Melowne* behind us, we slipped past the ships in Carrack's Reach, black barrel buoys on our left side. An Awian racing yacht called the *Swift Shag* ran close to escort us; her bell rang in salute. 'They're wishing us luck!' I waved. I was completely high on the fact I wasn't afraid.

Ata leant on the wheel. 'How are you, Jant?'

'Yeah. Uh-huh.' I was staring at the carved mascle emblem on the bow of our sister ship. The *Melowne* was painted in the colours of Micawater, dark blue and white lozenges; she carried so much ornament she looked as if she had been decorated with the fittings from a bankrupt brothel.

'Tell me, what day is it today?' Ata asked.

'Mmm.'

'Let me see your eyes.'

I took off my sunglasses and looked at her. 'Well, OK,' she said eventually, but with some doubt.

The *Melowne* flew all the canvas she could, to match our pace, and kept behind us on the right. Lightning didn't greet me, being deep in conversation with the Swordsman. He pointed to the great blue wedding cake of a caravel. 'She's named after my sister. Little Melowne ...'

'Yeah,' I said. I leant over the railing and noticed that no two wave peaks were ever the same shape.

'She was the youngest of my family,' Lightning began. 'The youngest of nine. She died when she was only six years old.'

'That's a great shame,' Wrenn said.

'Oh, I'm all right. I got over it around the turn of the first millennium,' Lightning said staunchly. I heard that in the year one thousand, through the use of many economic pressures, he eventually managed to run the Avernwater dynasty into the ground and turn their manor back into parkland.

'It was a long time ago, you understand,' he said quietly. 'Melowne was the youngest of my family; she was full of life, happy all the time. My third-eldest brother, Gyr, was exceptionally fond of her. He tended to be morose and she brought out the life in him.

'They were playing, one morning in midsummer, while we prepared to celebrate godsloss day. A flowery parade headed by the July Queen came towards us down the avenue and the young maiden playing queen was about to pass in front of the palace. People lined the streets to cheer her. Inside the palace we wanted a good view, so all us children ran up to the top floor. I found a roof window. Melowne and Gyr were just below me, out on the parapet. Melowne had daisy chains around her head and in the buckles of her shoes. She leaned right out over the balustrade as the procession passed below and he held the back of her dress. She was laughing with delight, pointing at the chariots and kicking her feet. She kicked Gyr under the chin accidentally and, in shock, he dropped her. I just saw her vanish.'
Lightning pointed down over the railing.

'That's terrible.'

He nodded slowly. 'My little sister's death caused an uproar. Nothing was the same after that. My brothers hated Gyr ... and I did too. He became enraged and silent; eventually he left us to found a new manor at Avern. I don't think I ever forgave him.'

I paced across to Mist in the hope of less sentimental talk. She watched the supply ship carefully before relinquishing the wheel to her second-in-command. I think she had appointed her sons and daughters to all the officers' positions. 'Gentlemen,' she said, 'let me show you your cabins.'

Mist explained that the *Stormy Petrel* had five levels, including the open-air decks and topcastle. The hold was the largest, where pinnace boats for exploration were carried in a dismantled state, and at the stern, an animal pen full of ruddy, bright-eyed chickens. We climbed down the hatch to the living deck, which was above the waterline and had small, sunburst-painted shutters from bow to stern. Every sailor had just forty centimetres by two metres' length to sling his or her hammock. I marvelled that Awians could force themselves into such a claustrophobic space. Rather than their leafy towns that nestled in countryside, and their small families in roomy houses, here featherback men were crammed together without enough space to spread a wing. Mist's cabin cut into their quarters at the stern and extended into the deck above; I could almost stand upright in it. She had a bedroom and a study that doubled as a dining room, with a polished mahogany table quite incongruous on the ship. It seemed that she intended the *Petrel* to be her manor house.

Back above, she said, 'Jant, you have the cabin under the poop deck.' She opened a door onto an empty compartment with a sloping floor, one metre wide by two long, and a metre high. One hinged shelf was folded back against the wall above a hook for a hammock. Was I expected to fit in there?

'It's a fucking closet,' I said.

'I swear, it's the most luxurious passenger accommodation we have! Well, if you want to sleep outside, feel free ... Come on, Lightning, let me show you the fo'c'sle.'

At least my cabin was furthest from the waves. I could lean out of the porthole and judge the level of water against the planks of the hull to determine how fast we were sinking. It had the best view, fresh air, and I could fly from the deck above. The motion of the waves swayed my cabin the most but that didn't bother me. I was anxious to be rid of Mist's smiling face so I folded myself into the tiny wooden box. What the fuck was I doing here?

Once noticed, the ship's movement was relentless. I could still fly home, but then I would have to face the Emperor. I was stranded between two terrible eventualities. I sat cross-legged, elbows on knees, head in hands, fingers through my black hair like a waterfall.

Footsteps boomed up and down the tilted ladders between decks and above me. Timbers creaked. On second thoughts, *Petrel* seemed extremely flimsy. The sailors adjusted something, the floor righted and, even-keel, she began to gather speed.

I shuffled further into the cabin, bolted the door and opened my razor. I started to divide up my quarter-kilo hoard of cat. I tipped out the powder on a book cover, cut it and made paper wraps of roughly a gram apiece. Why did I buy so much scolopendium? So that Cinna couldn't sell it to his victims? No, because I need enough to stay high for the whole voyage. With an ex-addict's ingenuity I hid the paper wraps in every possible niche, wherever they were concealed from view. I wedged them in the ceiling joists and between the floorboards. I taped them to the underside of the shelf, packed them into the lantern and the squat candlestick. I concealed wraps between the pages of books, in the whetstone pocket of my knife scabbard. I even sewed them into my coat lining.

An hour later I still had two hundred grams left in the envelope, enough to poison the entire crew of both caravels. I tipped a fingernail-full of cat into a beaker of white wine. It touched and dissolved like melting snow. I cut a line on the book cover and snorted it. My jaw sparkled. I threw the porthole open and threw up, monumentally, down the *Petrel*'s side.

Then I returned to the poop deck, dazzled by brightness. The fresh wind made me shudder. The mainland was ridiculously small and featureless – I could see the entire Cobalt coast, a pale green line edge-to-edge of the horizon, already turning blue. The Awndyn cliffs were a faint smudge less than half a centimetre high. In every other direction spread the indistinguishable ocean. I didn't want to look at it. 'It's as if we can see the whole east coast,' I said to Mist.

She laughed and shook her head. 'Say goodbye to it, Jant.'

I could fly back even now. I leant over the stern and stretched my wings to feel the wind under them.

'This is something you've never seen before?' the Archer asked calmly.

'It's horrible.' I hissed a breath. 'It's a travesty.' I always have to work in their world. Lightning has visited the mountains on adventurous expeditions and once when I needed help; but I defy any of them to trek to the high plateaux. I cross boundaries more vertiginous and worlds far more precarious than this, I told myself, but I didn't feel at all reassured. 'Are we in water deep enough to be attacked by sea monsters?'

Mist tutted. 'Jant, there is no such thing as a sea monster. I have circumnavigated the Fourlands. I have sailed past this longitude for six hundred years, so you can absolutely take my word for it. Monsters are just the tales of drunk, braggart harpooners. You might see a whale spouting in the distance, but that's about all.'

I sipped my doctored wine and watched the *Stormy Petrel*'s green wake curve out like lace from a loom. The horizon receded; I expected a clap of thunder or something when it merged with the haze and vanished. I stared in that direction for long after, memorising the position. In an hour's time *Petrel* would carry me too far to fly home.

I turned away from the railing. I had been looking out to sea for so long the size and bustle of the ship surprised me. My hands were weak, my glass was empty. I took a step and the deck tilted. Shit, if the others see my condition they are definitely going to know. I must reach my cabin, lock door, sleep it off. I edged along the railing to the top of the ladder, and felt about with one foot for the rungs. I can step down, it isn't so far.

I crashed heavily onto the half deck, shook my wings and arms to locate them. Yes, of course the floor is bloody tipping, I told myself; we're on a sodding ship. I clawed the cabin open, threw my coat down but it slid towards the door. I have taken too much. But it feels so good, oh god it feels good. The buzz and dislocation comes on slow when I drink cat. So I forget to be careful and I always drink too fucking much. It'll peak soon, I hope. I was clever to return to the cabin while I still could. Now there's no coast only sea no land to land on only sea. We must trust our memories that the Empire still exists.

I've taken too much. I lay on my quilt, curled up, eyes closed – can't observe the outside world any more, too much going on out there. Thoughts rush round my mind and cat begins to break them down to their constituent cycles. Consciousness is circular. Thoughts come in cycles. There are big, slow, infrequent cycles and fast rings repeat inside them. Words are made when sound cycles click the right combination. Consciousness is circular; thoughts come in cycles. There are big— It's happening to me! I think I'm dying. Don't worry, I won't die; this has happened before. I hate it when this happens. I'm probably going to Shift. And I haven't been to Epsilon for years. Epsilon. Words are made when sound cycles click the right combination. Oh, no, it's starting to happen – am I dying? Don't worry, I won't die; this has happened before. God, I hate it when this happens. I'm probably going to Shift. And I haven't been to Epsilon for years. Probably going to Shift. Last time, I almost died. Rayne said I was dying. Don't worry, I won't die. This has happened before. I hate it when this happens (it's happening to me; it's happening to me). I'm going to Shift. And I haven't been to Epsilon for years. Consciousness is circular; thoughts come in cycles. Haven't I just thought this? Words are made when sound cycles click the right combination (—to me, it's happening to me, it's happening to—) What is? This feeling of dying. Don't worry, I won't die, this has happened before. Words are made when sound cycles. God, I hate it when this happens. I'm probably going to Shift. And I haven't been to Epsilon for years (—me, it's happening to me, it's happ—) I think I just thought that (—ening to me, it's happening to me, it's happening to—) oo to me ahp ap hap happening oo fu tu to me see words are made when words are made words worr dd hut hur lur wur wor words are ay ma may dde words are made words are made ugh dug dur wer wur words arr are geh neh ney ay made words are made ur err are arr ... ar ... r

Shouts assailed from all sides and before me were market stalls running into stalls out to where the horizon met the orange sky. Constant Shoppers hustled and bustled, a little boy selling postcards of Epsilon darted through the crowd. I recognised the Squantum Plaza bazaar.

I sat on the pavement cross-legged and concentrated, changing my appearance from just a pencil sketch of Jant to something more solid that looked like me, with a few improvements.

Having brightened myself up, I staggered to my feet. I swore I would never come back here and now I've broken my promise again. A small grey cloud appeared above my head and began to rain on me. 'All right,' I told it, waving my hands. 'All right! I'm not that depressed!' The cloud showered a few more desultory drops and dissipated.

There were market stalls of mildewed books, cloth and raffia, cakes and beer. Horse brasses, porcelain, thousands of gemstones spilled on velvet. Flat green grief toads sang mournfully in glass tanks. Stalls sold ancient sea-krait scales, barometz root – looks like a sheep but tastes like turnip – trained falcons apparently 'the best hunters in the Scarlet Steppe' and confused stacks of bamboo crates full of finches that cheeped and fluttered.

There were bonsai ents – little gnarled trees with root-legs stumbling around on a polished tray. A marsh gibbon capered on a stall's canopy. It had pale green silky fur and round intelligent eyes; its back legs ended in duck feet. I couldn't help laughing at it. The monkey pulled its top lip back in a bubblegum-pink grimace.

Now that I was trapped here for an uncertain length of time, I decided to enjoy myself. I went looking for the pair of golden shears that was the sign of the Bullock's Bollocks bar. It was no easy task because Epsilon changes constantly.

A crowd of nasnas with tour guides wended their way between the tables. Nasnas are men with one arm and one leg each. The two nearest me were heavy-set columns of flesh, and they supported each other, hopping along in a pair. The arm of each man projected from the middle of his chest, waving like a trunk. I studied their faces and caught my breath. Each had a big, single eye directly above his nose, all his features in a vertical line, a wide mouth and rough skin. The men turned their great round eyes on me as they passed. Their guide announced, 'This is the edge of the Tine's Quarter. Take special care on the road please . . . And if you see any Tine, *run*. Well, hop *quickly*.'

Behind the nearest stall sat a big, bear-like animal. Its fur was pure black and white splodges. Backward-pointing spines grew round its neck and down its back. The beast shook itself and its quills clattered. Its head was bowed; it looked so hunched and miserable that I stopped, intending to buy it and set it free. The stall holder was a greasy man with a glass eye. A parrodi perched on his shoulder, with colourful ruffled feathers. It rolled its eyes and copied his every gesture.

The stall holder saw that I was a tourist and delightedly shook the bear's chain. 'A porcupanda, sir! A highly prized delicacy. Not five hundred pounds, not four hundred pounds. Three hundred pounds to you only, sir!'

'To you only, sir,' drawled the parrodi.

I concentrated and imagined the right amount of money in the pocket of my suit. I paid the stall holder and freed the porcupanda. When I patted its head, it licked my hand then bounded away.

I walked on, to the central fountain built with stinguish technology out of solidified water. White cement could be seen between the transparent blocks. It made a wonderful three-dimensional matrix with beams of sunlight dancing through, cast by the liquid water lapping inside the fountain. A couple of wet thylacines barked and played in the great jets that fell like diamonds.

A bouquet of chloryll courtesans lounged beside the pool. The chloryll co-cultivate this quarter of the city. Their extreme beauty reminded me of Tern, slight and exquisite; their skin was ebony black. One had tiny fruits growing in her shining hair, piled on top of her head. Her floor-length dress rustled, it was made of living foliage; here and there tiny pink roses budded among the leaves. Vines wrapped around her arms like long net gloves. Behind her hung a trail of coiling tendrils, fronds and variegated ferns. These fruiting bodies were great to sleep with, but instead I wanted to have a good look around Epsilon after so long away.

The market continued into the Tine's Quarter, where a wide road paved with eighteen-carat gold formed one side of the market square. A shiny building with smooth pillars housed four tall rectangular machines that emitted a low vibration. The salt-copper, watery-rotten smell of the Tine's red liquid was thick in the air. A sign hung above the machines read:

TINE AUTOMOBILES, THE HEART OF MOTORING
Driving the arteries of Epsilon, you can't beat the Carotid Café.
All tastes catered for: blood, beer, coffee. Next: ten miles.

A girl sat in a low carriage underneath the sign. It was made of gold, so it must be of Tine manufacture. It was moulded in feminine curves, with bulging panels over its small, spoked wheels, doors as in a roofless coach but an upright glass window fixed at the front. It had no shaft for horses.

I vaguely recognised the girl inside. She waved. 'Hey, winged boy! Jant! Remember me from court? I was the Shark!'

'Tarragon!'

'Come over. Don't worry about the Tine.' A Tine was attending to her car. He was a carnivore like all his species, three metres tall, bursting with muscle. He was naked except for a loincloth, his sky-blue skin scarred and tattooed. His blank eyes were pupil-less, uniform blue. His eyebrows were two pierced rows of steel rings: the Superciliary Sect. I thought that he could live for a week on the meat stuck between his sail-needle teeth. His taloned hands held a black rubber tube which snaked down and disappeared under the ground. He was pumping the red liquid into Tarragon's gold automobile.

The whole floor hummed. I trod carefully, ready to sprint at any time. I kept Tarragon between myself and the growling attendant, but Tarragon was a Shark, or rather the Shift projection of a Shark, and she was just as dangerous.

Tarragon grinned with sharp teeth. Fins emerged from the middle of her back and the sides of her body. With a look of concentration she mastered her shape transformation so they retracted and her skin smoothed. She briefly became a beautiful woman rather than a Shark.

'Do you like my shape?' she said. 'I find that air-breathers are nicer and more obliging to pretty young girls.' Then, lost in thought, the changes gradually reasserted themselves, so that I was confronted with the difficult challenge of talking to a frothy blonde teenager in a strapless dress and stiletto heels, with three rows of triangular teeth. Parallel slashes appeared in her neck; deep gills like black ribbons. They widened, inhaled, and vanished.

She concentrated on improving the shiny crimson dress wrapped round her body. A furry phlogista stole draped her shoulders. Phlogistas are rare and expensive; they're long, like mink, but dark red in colour with deep, sumptuous fur. It had a little lion's head, but instead of a mane its face was framed by a ring of fleshy petals. This feline flower-face formed the clasp of her stole, and its yellow glass eyes glittered. Phlogistas are resistant to fire; to clean a fur you place it in flames.

I offered Tarragon my hand, but she looked at it as if it was her favourite sandwich. 'You can touch the car, you know,' she said.

I surveyed the vehicle. 'It's not alive?'

'No, Jant. It's not alive ... *Parts* of it are alive.'

It was made of a thin sheet of pure gold, and the complicated fittings inside were gold, too: a wheel where Tarragon rested her delicate hands, and a dial that looked like a clock face but wasn't.

'The car won't hurt you,' she said carefully. 'But keep clear of the Tine. They invented these sports cars to do their hunting and to make religious sacrifices, injuring victims in interesting ways for the purpose of their worship. They're keen on fast, fast cars, the faster the better, like this rocket; the best that meat can buy. To build speedy cars they need good athletes. You are an athlete, aren't you?'

I nodded.

'Tine will do anything to lay their hands on a runner as excellent as you. If they knew about Rhydanne you would already be dead. They need athletes, that's what makes these babies go,' she said, tapping a flipper lovingly on the steering wheel. 'Take a look.'

She pressed a button and a trapdoor popped open at the front of the vehicle. I sloped round and peered inside.

Lying under the bonnet, a mass of green-purple guts quivered and heaved. Clear rubber tubes ran red liquid round them. They stank of ripe meat. Diagonally across the centre were six big hearts, doubled up in a line. Solid red-brown muscle pumped in unison. I had an impression of the mighty strength they produced to drive the spoked wheels.

At the top two pale pink lungs inflated and deflated of their own accord like bellows. They were joined to the depths of the engine by a windpipe ringed with cartilage. Dark clots lay slickly around it. Nearest me was a blood-smeared glass tank of water; gleaming veins ducted it out to cool the hearts. I saw about twenty red-brown kidneys attached by a network of ligaments to a porous gold pipe that led towards the rear of the car. As I watched, hot yellow liquid spattered out of the pipe onto the forecourt making a steaming puddle; the car relieved itself.

'Ugh.' I shrank back. 'God, it's disgusting!'

'I bought it to help me in my search,' Tarragon said. 'I'm looking for a way to save the sea kraits. That's why I'm here in Epsilon instead of at home studying, basking and eating tuna.'

Sea kraits were the largest animal I had ever heard of, but I had thought they'd all died out centuries earlier in the worst disaster Insects ever caused. 'I don't understand. Why are you bothered about sea snakes? And anyway, aren't you a bit late? Their ocean dried up a long time ago – and good riddance.'

'Yes, but I have ways to talk to them. Sea kraits are intelligent animals with a sophisticated knowledge all their own. I think it's a great pity they died out. All their learning was lost, Jant; don't you care? I saw you free the porcupanda just now.'

'There's a difference between a porcupanda and a kilometre-long sea snake! The Shift's better off without foul, slimy sea creatures!'

'So says the Rhydanne. Take care you're not threatened with extinction yourself. The Tine will want to make sports-coupés out of you. Wait! Don't run away! Be a nice Rhydanne and look after my car for a minute while I pay.' Tarragon hefted a slab of succulent steak, which was lying on the spare seat. She jumped down from the running board and turned her shark's waddle into a very sexy walk as she strode into the kiosk.

I leant on the car's curved side, staring all round for approaching Tine. If Tarragon was right they would be waving cleavers and bent on my demise. She had called this vehicle a sports car, but I have never seen one play sports, and if you ask me it is quite unsporting, sitting in a car when one is expected to run.

Tarragon reappeared, unwrapping a chunk of the Tine's red water frozen to a flat wooden stick. She gave it a big lick, then offered it to me.

'No way!'

'Suit yourself. Weird air-breather. You shouldn't visit Epsilon, Jant; you don't belong here. It makes me so sad to see you poisoning yourself. I hoped you had given up drugs.'

'Well, I'm having a bit of a relapse.' I explained the island, my fear of the sea and my current predicament on board *Stormy Petrel*.

Patches of grey sandpaper skin blotched her body and faded. 'A voyage of discovery!' she said enthusiastically. 'Well, in that case I'll help. I fancy taking a look at your vessels. I'll follow them at depth for a while so you don't have to fear the sea. If anything untoward happens to your ship while I'm in the vicinity you should be relatively safe.'

'Thank you. Thank you, Tarragon. What can I do in return?'

'Learning motivates us Sharks. An edifying experience is reward enough. And although I'm cruising distant waters right now, it shouldn't take me too long to swim to you ...'

I frowned.

'All the seas are connected. Actually all the oceans in every world are one ocean. The sea finds its own level across the worlds; you can reach anywhere if you swim far enough. As long as the water is to our taste, what matters it what sea we breathe?' She continued, 'I wish I could see the ocean from the outside – an immense orb of water hanging in vacuum, so my school tells me. That's one Shift I can't make.'

I thought about this for a while. The same sea that is surging into Capharnaum harbour laps on the beach at Awndyn, backs up the sparkling Mica River at high tide – brackishly flows into Epsilon market, glistens in Vista Marchan two thousand years ago, and is swept the next minute by Tarragon's fins in the deep abyss. The land changes, but the ocean is a still pool, a pool like a sphere, hanging in the universe.

I decided that Tarragon was making fun of me so I giggled and she gave me a contemptuous look. 'It's true. You don't think angler fish and manta rays originated in your world?'

I shrugged, not knowing the animals to which she referred.

The Shark sighed. 'Jant, call yourself a scholar? No real student would mess with their mind the way you do. Why destroy yourself? Do you want to be found lying dead, a stiff corpse with a needle in its arm? What's cool about that? I get here through study and you get here through pleasure. I can smell it on you. Pleasure is actually bad where I come from.'

'And what is good where you come from?'

'Little bits of fish.'

'I'm sorry, Tarragon. I Shifted by accident. I'm only here because the ocean unnerves me and I OD'd.'

'There are other methods to achieve enough disconnection to Shift.' She smiled triangularly. 'By pain, or the way us Sharks do it – by thought. Promise you won't do drugs again and I'll teach you! You may eventually be able to Shift at will, just as I can – but probably not as well, because air-breathers aren't very intelligent. For example you would never be able to Shift as far as my world. The degree of dislocation would certainly kill you. You must be near death to get this far.'

'Shift at *will*? How?'

'You can will yourself to wake up from a nightmare, right? This is no different. Your body's not here; you're a tourist, a projection same as me. If you must travel to Epsilon, do it by meditation – you need a relaxed state of mind to project yourself. Of course, it's easier to leave the Shift than it is to arrive so you can either meditate or force yourself back home. All I do is wake from my trance and I return to my sea.'

It never occurred to me that I could find a different way to Shift. I had thought travelling to Epsilon city was a side effect of scolopendium, and that I could only wake when the drug wore off. 'I don't think I can.'

'Oh yes. You can travel along what, let's face it, is a well-trodden path. It just takes patience – and concentration. I'll show you!'

She leant over the car's low door, grabbed my belt and shirt front, and pulled me into the car. Her strength was incredible. I sprawled onto the passenger seat, into the footwell. My long legs waved in the air as I thrashed about trying to find purchase to jump out.

Tarragon held me down effortlessly with one little hand on my chest. She pressed a pedal to the floor, released a lever. The car lunged forward with such power I was thrown back against the seat. 'Let me out! Let me out! Help!' I struggled. 'Tarragon, you bitch!'

'I'll teach you a lesson, Shark-style!' Her pert breasts heaved with laughter. She blew a wordless human scream on the car's larynx horn.

It moved faster than a racehorse, rushed at my flight speed along the ground. Tarragon talked loudly as she steered: 'Let me tell you the safe method to Shift – you should lie still and empty your mind, relax and think your way here. It might take a few years to perfect but you immortals have time to practise. Try now – think your way back to the Fourlands.'

I refused. I wouldn't risk returning to a drugged sleep. My consciousness must be kicked out to the Shift for a reason; perhaps to stop it being damaged by the scolopendium I keep pumping into myself. What if I returned to a body lying in a coma? I'd be rejected from the Circle, could age and die without regaining awareness.

Tarragon saw me shudder and exclaimed, 'You can do it! Let me show you!' She spun the wheel, swung the car round and accelerated down the Coeliac Trunk Road, into the Tine's Quarter.

The sky was dark, and lights on either side of the Aureate's road gave a golden glow; a chill mist made a diffuse halo around them. Skin-worshipping Tine worked by the roadside. Their arms were flayed to the elbows. Tattoos covered their skin and the shells on their backs were painted with spirals. Their muscular blue haunches were cut with lettering like graffiti in old tree trunks. They had the broken noses of heavyweight boxers and the thick arms of fishermen. They carried other bits of victims' bodies too that I couldn't identify.

An immense spoked wheel four metres in diameter turned unhurriedly and a needle rose and fell. Tine fed skin backed with yellow fat under the needle; it hung over the edge of the sewing machine's serrated gold platform. 'Is that Tine skin?' I asked.

'Oh, they're just embroidering it. They'll put it back on later.'

They snarled as we passed.

'Don't look,' said Tarragon. 'It gets worse from here on.' But she knew I would look, because curiosity motivates not only Sharks but me as well.

Shattered glass ground under our wheels. I turned my head with a disconnected feeling. We passed burnt-out vehicles at the roadside, smashed and overturned. Blackened Tine bodies lay between them, marking their experiments with engines. Long lines of automobiles had impacted so hard that they were all joined together. Metal crumpled back on itself. Tine assembled around them, carrying hoses, wielding axes. Water sprayed above them; in a flashing yellow light the drops seemed to fall slowly. Nightmare slow motion as water and blood pooled onto the road. Curtains of bloodied skin hung out of broken windows. One muscle tissue axle throbbed in pain.

We passed a gorgeous woman that the Tine had welded into her car. Her body was set into the seat as smoothly as a jewel in a bevel. Only the front could be seen; her face and neck, breasts and belly. Wreaths of gold tubes ran out of the seat into the sides of her body, completely obscuring her ribs and the sides of her slender thighs. Her hands had vanished; bulges at the ends of her arms were seamlessly attached to the steering wheel. Her long hair became a stylised immovable gold curve sweeping back to form the headrest. Her feet merged with the floor; its solid gold seemed to lap up her slender legs. She was part of the car.

'If the Tine catch us, that's what they'll do,' said Tarragon. 'Make this car grow through us. Would you like to be a passenger forever?'

'Let me go!'

'Think yourself home.'

Something terrible is happening down there. Something vast in the heart of the Aureate is pumping viscous liquid around the drains and dykes bridged with connective tissue. 'Let me go!' I shouted. 'I want out!'

'Think yourself home, I'm not stopping you.'

'But I don't know how!'

'If I call out that you're a gymnast, Rhydanne, you'd be spending the rest of your life as a car. Well, your guts will. The rest of you will make a good roadsighn. Look, there's one.'

The roadsighn whispered, 'i trespassed in the aureate, look at me, save yourselves, go home, save yourself, tarragon, where are you going, tarragon?'

His legs twined together were planted in the verge, and a membrane road sign grew from between his outstretched arms. In the mist he was just a spindly écorché silhouette murmuring, 'oh tarragon, what have you brought us?'

As we passed I saw his sticky dark pink colour, stripped to pus and muscle, his face locked in a wide *risus sardonicus* leer; 'tarragon, who is that? where are you going?'

'We're going deeper,' she said to me. 'The Spleen is on your right. On your left you will see—'

'Am I a sacrifice? Let me out!'

Gold buildings loomed smooth and rounded, lobed against each other like internal organs. They were horribly organic, studded with empty ulcerous portals – foramina and fistulae. The Ribs were flying buttresses with nowhere to land. We skirted the Labyrinths of the Ileum and in the distance the Cult of the Oedemic Prepuce had erected a tall gold wrinkled spire with an onion dome. We drove down a rubber subway that stretched and sagged. We emerged from beneath dripping red stalactites through a puckered textured sphincter onto the shore of—

A lake. Against the black sky I could just make out its dark red liquid and hear the lapping as rare ripples ran over its stinking surface. Gold ducts of varying bores, hollow femurs and arrays of tubules sucked liquid from it and ran underground. Glomeruli like fleshy cups fountained in occasional bursts so the automobile wheels sank in ground made spongy by gastric juices. On the far side, spotlights picked out and roved over the highly polished gold shell of the Western Kidney. I tried all the time to wish myself back to the Fourlands.

'Tine are a most religious and honest people ...' said Tarragon. Tine crowded the shore. It must be a feast day because hundreds had gathered. Most were Duodenal Sect; their intestines had been pulled out of a hemmed hole in their stomachs and wrapped around their waists, and I could see waves of peristalsis going round them. One was a Novice of the Flectere Doctrine, who snap all their joints to bend the opposite way. His bare feet lifted in front of him because his knees were bent backwards like a bird's. His pale blue palms were on the backs of his hands, his fingers curled outwards. 'You have to admire their devotion.'

A gold paddleboat that ran on striated muscle fibres and catechism ferried between the Islets of Langerhans in the distance. 'We're going deeper,' said Tarragon. 'Soon we'll reach the Heart and Lungs, and we'll drive the length of the backbone processional. The Heart! I want to show you the Heart of the Aureate.'

'No!'

'Then think yourself home!'

'I can't!'

'Or the brain, deep beneath the Transgressor's Forest. In the brain there's a temple where any creature drawn on the wall comes to life. Don't draw stick men, they have enough of those. It's sickening to see them, limping towards you dragging their misshapen limbs and squeaking.'

I couldn't feel the pull. It would be at least an hour before my overdose wore off and woke me. I tried to be calm, pictured my cabin on the *Stormy Petrel* and imagined myself back there.

'That's a good boy!' Tarragon exclaimed. 'I know you can do it!'

She gave me a Shark's grin but I didn't give it back. We drove along the lakeside and I screamed when I realised what was pinging out from under our wheels and rattling off the chassis: a gravel beach of kidney stones.

Tarragon called to a whole congregation of Tine kneeling on the shore, 'Hey, see my passenger? He runs marathons! He can sprint as fast as a car!'

The Tine paused and stared. They gestured to each other, howled and ran directly at us. 'Hurry!' I yelled. 'Hurry up!'

Tarragon stopped the car. 'Will yourself home.'

Through rising panic I forced myself to stay calm and yearned, forced, demanded myself back to my body. Tarragon tapped a finger on her forehead and repeated the dictum, 'Shift by meditation. Not sensation!'

The Tine were almost upon us.

The dark shore twitched in and out of focus, then a wave of distortion rolled through it. Tarragon's face and the gold vehicle belched into disturbing shapes. They dissolved to grey. To black.

My stomach creased with fear; I closed my eyes. And when I opened them again, slowly and stickily, I was back in my cabin, lying on the floor.

CHAPTER 6

I woke with the green taste of bile in my mouth, curled up so tightly I ached. Shit, I almost got eviscerated. I clenched my fists. Tarragon almost had me killed.

I rolled onto my back and contemplated the too-close ceiling. A gentle sighing must be the wind on the mainsail, and that constant slap and hiss will be the prow cutting small waves. There were no other sounds, so it was probably night-time. These deductions left me feeling rather proud but I sensed that the cabin had become a little bit narrower. It had changed shape – it was also longer. There was not enough room to open even the tips of my wings. What the fuck was going on?

I lit a candle and held it up. The walls were painted blue, not black, the portholes were square with white borders. It was a different cabin. Could I have Shifted back to the wrong place? Panicking, I ran my fingernails between the planks, brushed my hand along the shelves: nothing. Where were my wraps? Where were all my fucking wraps? I saw my rucksack, seized it and rummaged through it. The fat envelope containing scolopendium had gone. 'Damn you, Ata!' I shouted. 'Damn you, damn you, damn you!'

There was a knock on the cabin door. 'Go away!' I yelled.

I rubbed the hem of my coat and felt nine hard paper squares still sewn in. Thank god, they had missed some!

Cold air gusted into the cabin as a stocky figure pushed the door open with his shoulder. I saw Serein's silhouette, a round head with spiky hair. Behind him, dull blue inky dawn clouds packed the vast sky. He sat in the doorway, legs out onto the half deck, huddling in his greatcoat. 'Comet,' he said. 'You weren't well.'

'Is that understatement a new type of sarcasm you're experimenting with?'

'For god's sake, Comet. You look like you've been dragged through a battlefield backwards. Mind you, I've been seasick. The sailors started laying bets on the number of times I would puke over the taffrail. Mist told me you don't get seasick. She explained about scolopendium.'

'I see.' I took a swig of water from my leather bottle. 'I suspect that I am on the *Melowne*?'

The Swordsman nodded. 'We rowed you across from *Petrel*. You were out cold.'

'What! A rowing boat? So close to the waves? What if it had capsized?' Drowning while unconscious was too awful to contemplate.

'Ata said you could have this berth because you filled the other one up with drugs. Drugs aren't an answer, Jant. What are you doing that for when you're an Eszai?'

'What happened to my wraps and the envelope?' I said threateningly.

'We threw them overboard.'

'Shit.'

The Swordsman sounded both disgusted and surprised that an Eszai would knowingly use cat. 'How much did you take?'

'As much as I could.' I wriggled out of the constrictive cabin and pulled myself up, water bottle in hand. I scraped a match, lit one of the cigarettes I had stolen from Cinna and sipped at it. I blew the smoke out of my nose and coughed. I was never going to be any bloody good at smoking. It doesn't agree with Rhydanne as they are accustomed to thin air. I only do it rarely, when I'm under extreme duress, because if I ever got hooked it would destroy my ability to fly.

Wrenn joined me at the rail, standing upwind of the smoke. 'Are you all right? Apart from being dark and moody, I mean.'

I said, 'I loathe this bloody floating coffin of a boat.'

'It's a ship.'

'*She's* a ship. Apparently it's female. I hope all her masts don't break off when they fuck in the shallows.'

The Swordsman fell quiet, looking at the midnight-blue water. The waves swept up into points, lapping and side-stepping. Their ridges looked like cirques of the Darkling Mountains. Apart from a sailor manning the wheel and a watchman at the prow, all was quiet. Only knavish sailors, rakish swordsmen and drug-addled Rhydanne are about at this hour.

'The *Stormy Petrel*'s close by,' he said, pointing forward at two faint lights, one red, one white, which rose and fell gently. The dawn clouds were gradually becoming paler, but the *Petrel*'s sails and hull were blurred, a drifting perse-grey shape. The ships creaked continually, and when they weren't creaking they groaned and flapped and sighed. They were like animals talking to each other.

'Hm. I'm surprised Lightning and Mist can bear being on the same boat.'

'Can you see who's at the helm?'

I glanced at him. 'Rhydanne can't see in the dark, Wrenn; that's just a story. In fact I have crap night vision. Rhydanne eyes reflect to cut out snow glare so I don't get blinded. It's not much of an advantage at sea level ...'

'Really?'

'Yeah. While I'm putting to rest myths about Rhydanne, you should know that they don't turn into lynxes on their birthdays. They can't survive being frozen solid and thawed out again. And they're not cannibals, whatever Carniss may say.' I lit another cigarette with the stub of the first. 'As for the bit about shitting in little pebbles like goats do, I reserve comment.'

'I didn't mean to be nosy. I'm sorry.'

'You should be. I stay smooth-skinned, mind. It would take me weeks to grow as much stubble as you.'

Wrenn rubbed his chin. I turned back to the cabin thinking that I needed more time to recover. From behind me Wrenn said, 'What's it like up there? In Darkling, I mean. Is it true Rhydanne don't talk to each other at all?'

Much as I wanted a few hours alone, that made me smile. I said slowly, 'Oh, they say all they need to. But that's not much compared with flat-landers, for sure. Even Scree village was only built by accident – it started out as a cairn. There was a tradition that every traveller puts a stone on the pile when he goes past. So it grew, very gradually, into a pueblo with rooms and an inn. Rhydanne come to the village every winter, when any person can occupy any room. They all get snowed in and drink themselves legless. In summer, they leave the rooms empty. The conditions make Rhydanne very self-reliant; they can't act in large groups. When an avalanche destroyed my shieling I couldn't find anyone to help me ... The cornices were hanging waiting for the slightest shock. Eilean was crushed by the barrage and the whole valley changed shape.'

I hung onto a rowan tree's upturned roots as the mountainside liquefied and tabular ice thundered down. The air filled with powder snow. The next day saw me scrabbling at the granite debris until my fingers split, trying to dig her out.

I smirked. 'She's still up there under tons of rock, flat as a waffle.'

'That's terrible. I'm so sorry.'

I huffed and tapped ash off the cigarette. 'I hated them. I grew up too slowly for Rhydanne and in the end I'd no love of their way of life. But Darkling paled into insignificance when I went to Hacilith and fell in with the Wheel. They were named from their habit of nailing enemies to the waterwheels of the city. The weird thing was that I was happy as a chemist's apprentice and I didn't need a gang's protection until I joined them. The longer you live, the more scars you gather, see?' I traced my fingertip over the deep scarification on my right shoulder, a circle with six spokes, the initiation to the gang.

'Shit, Jant. That's terrible ...'

Felicitia pulled apart the hilt and suede sheath of a hunting knife until its long steel emerged. It was unbelievably sharp: Felicitia had a lot of time to spare. His hands shook and he fumbled as he traced the lines drawn on with lipstick. My washed-out feeling of suspense tipped into agony. Unlike tattoos it was not superficial; it was deep. It could not be dealt with lightly. I swear the first cut went straight to the bone. My hands were bound behind me to a cast iron chair in a beer garden. I struggled, and when I started screaming they gagged me.

I stumbled home, leaving a trail of blood that rats scented, scurrying out from refuse piled on street corners. I dressed the wound myself, though my fingers slipped into and through the lacerated flesh.

'It didn't hurt as much as Slake in 'twenty-five though,' I said, pushing my T-shirt up so he could see the remains of an Insect bite, a sixty-stitch-long scar that curved into the left side of my belly, ending in a puckered mark where its mandible hit my lowest rib. 'I held my guts in with one arm. I crawled a metre, collapsed and started to drown in the mud.'

'God. Slake Cross Battle. I heard stories ...'

'Well, I took all the cavalry but none of them had mounts. Every man was sliced to bits. That's why we introduced testing the ground with poles for Insect tunnels before we camp. The Doctor knew I was still living but god knows how she found me because she said I was nearly buried. She pushed all my innards back in and stacked my stretcher on the cart. Because the Circle holds us, we can gain consciousness with life-threatening wounds and no desire to witness them. That got me back on scolopendium again but it also won Tern's attention. I was in hospital for a year; I kept turning up the drip's dial and passing out until Rayne threatened to take me off painkillers. While convalescing I began to panic that I had lost the ability to fly. I tried to glide out of the hospital window and ripped all my stitches ... Zascai were queuing up to Challenge me but, true to the rules, San held them off until I had recovered. Lucky you, Wrenn; Insect battles to look forward to.'

'I get it. You're scarred by living an adventurous life. The same will happen to me ... You're brave, Jant.'

I am? 'Well, not so brave as to duel with Gio,' I said, and we stood for a while in an uncertain quiet. I found talking like this reassuring – I had almost forgotten about the Aureate.

I lit a third cigarette but simply held it. I wondered how long it would take for me to fill the entire sky with smoke. When immortals think those things we are not being entirely whimsical. 'Couldn't you sleep?' I asked. I was fully aware that Wrenn had been left here to keep an eye on me.

'No. I keep thinking about this island. Then I got too excited and had to come up here to cool down. I can't wait to see Tris.'

'Personally I think it's Mist's plan to take all her enemies on one ship and scuttle it. I warn you, she's very dangerous.'

'But gorgeous.'

I glanced at him. 'So Ata has her hooks in you already? She's certainly beautiful; it's all the more reason to be wary. Even Lightning was taken in by her deceit, her callous human inventiveness and her beauty. She probably put you here on *Melowne* so he can't advise you, or to preserve her mystique. She plans centuries ahead; you haven't been alive long enough to think on our timescale.'

341

I ground the cigarette into a flurry of sparks on the rail and flicked it into the sea. 'Do you want to explore this boat?'

'Oh, yes!'

I raised the grating and trotted down the open-plank steps, looking around. Wrenn followed with his lantern. The *Melowne*'s hundred sailors were asleep. They mumbled and stirred in white canvas hammocks that hung three deep on the left and right of the deck, leaving a clear walkway down the centre. Some of the Plainslanders were snoring. Awians sleep on their fronts or their sides so they hardly ever snore. The deck stank of sweat, damp linen and the brown-sugar smell of cheap beet rum; a bowl full of laurel leaves intended as air freshener just added its own scent to the reek. Five porthole shutters on each wall were bolted shut.

'Don't disturb them,' I whispered. 'Let's go down a level.' I tried to move, and couldn't. Wrenn was standing on my feathers, bending the quills over the edge of the steps.

'Oops, sorry.' He shuffled back. I put a finger to my lips and descended through the second hatchway. This level was pitch dark but the air smelt better, heavy with camphorwood, pine sap, oak sawdust and quality leather. I investigated some kegs stencilled 'Grass Isle', and Wrenn reclined on a pile of sacks of dried beans and rice, swinging his lantern about. The deck was packed floor to ceiling with well-stowed sacks and oil flasks, as far as the light could reach. 'We're under the waterline here,' he said.

'Don't.' I shuddered, thinking how the sea's pressure might cave in the hull, squashing it like an eggshell.

'Mist says this is the orlop deck, for stores and dunnage. The hold's below us; that's the lowest level.'

'What the fuck is dunnage?'

Wrenn shrugged. I levered a lid plank off the nearest cask. 'Wine, Wrenn, look at all this wine! Half of Lightning's cellar must be in here.'

He picked up a chunk of cheese covered in wax paper. 'Breakfast!'

'This one's rum.' I dipped a rationing cup in another barrel.

'I've found salted meat, oranges, a barrel of sauerkraut. What's "portable soup"?'

We forced our way between the racks. I climbed on top of the hogsheads and walked along, hunched over, brushing the ceiling, but the deck was so crammed we couldn't go more than a few metres. Wrenn sat back on the ladder, I leaned on the wooden pump pipe next to it, and we nibbled handfuls of booty – me with chocolate and rum; Wrenn with dried fruit, bread and water.

'There's another grid,' I said. 'Let's go down again.'

'It's locked, see?' Wrenn crouched and turned over a padlock.

'I should be able to crack that,' I said, wanting to impress the Swordsman, although I was not sure why. I put a hand to the small of my back, selected one of the smallest secondaries, gripped it and pulled. Flight feathers are very strongly attached so I had to give it a hard wrench to pull it out, teeth gritted because it hurt. It dragged the flesh, just like pulling a fistful of hair. It came out leaving a hollow funnel of skin from which another pinfeather would grow in a couple of months.

The quill was old and did not bleed. I flattened its translucent-cream point, and jiggled it about in the lock, turning clockwise and pressing hard to poke the tumblers round. I remarked, 'People say I had a misspent youth, but no other Messenger has so many useful talents to place at the Emperor's service.'

I felt the mechanism give in the lock; it clicked open and we hefted the hatchway cover. Wrenn stepped down first with his guttering lantern. 'Check it out, it follows the shape of the hull.'

The hold's walls curved up on both sides, like being in a wooden bowl. The ship's ribs were clearly visible. The ceiling was two metres above and I could stand up straight for the first time. *Melowne*'s side-to-side rolling was not so obvious here; we were standing directly above the keel and the ship felt stable. More equipment had been carefully stowed between the ribs and lashed to each of the knees supporting the deck above.

The timbers for the pinnaces had instructions printed on them like model kits. There was an enormous amount of folded canvas and all sorts of tackle. There were metal buckets full of solid tar like warm black ice, chains, cord on reels, copper nails and many times the ship's length in coiled hemp cables.

'This is all spare rigging,' Wrenn said, as he kicked the shaft of an anchor twice my height and as thick as my thigh. He clicked a latch on a long oilskin-lined casket. He let the lid fall. 'Oh, my god.'

'What's that?'

'Arrows. Look!' About one hundred arrows with very sharp broadhead points filled the box, laid in leather spacers to keep their flights apart. Wrenn dug his fingers between them and they rattled. I looked up and realised I was staring at a wall of similar boxes. Wordlessly, we counted them and made a quick calculation, 'Ten thousand arrows?'

'At *least*.'

'If there's shafts there must be—'

'Bow staves,' I said, breaking the seal on a larger coffer. It was full of heavy longbows, all with fresh strings and the bowyer's mark stamped two-thirds along their length where the arrow was intended to be placed. 'A couple of hundred bows, one for every man on the ship.'

'Look, there are halberds,' said Wrenn. 'And shields!' They were stacked along the hull walls, covered with sailcloth. He unbuckled the straps of a huge sea chest with joyful abandon. 'I wonder if there are any swords? Oh, yes, look!'

The chest was full of fyrd-issue swords with double-edged blades and brown mass-produced leather scabbards. Their pristine hilts flashed in the light as he swept the lantern over. 'I'd like to test one. Here we are—'

'Put it back! Wrenn, the grid was locked for a reason! Mist doesn't want us to know what's down here!'

But Wrenn, happily ignorant of Mist's cruel streak, was not afraid of her. He selected a seventy-five-centimetre blade and stuck it in his belt.

'By god, what does Mist expect us to do to Tris?' I said.

'Maybe the islanders are fierce.'

'Don't be a fool. Mist said Tris has no Insects; they've nothing to be violent about.'

We went forward, seeing more of the same; the *Melowne*'s hold was a ship's chandlery and well-stocked armoury. I hesitated. 'Can you smell something?'

'What?'

A sharp metallic scent like spilt blood or cut leaves lay very faint beneath the hot greased-iron smell of Wrenn's lantern. 'Nothing. Forget it.'

At the bow a huge black tarpaulin hung floor to ceiling like a curtain. A skittering sound came from behind it, as of something metal not made fast. Wrenn took a handful and swept it aside.

A massive Insect launched itself at us.

I ducked. Wrenn yelled. The Insect crashed into the bars of its cage and drew back on six legs. Its antennae whipped round in frantic circles.

Its back legs slipped on the steel floor, scraping bright scratches. Its mandibles opened, a smaller set gaped inside and it jumped again, into the bars. An enormous knife-sharp foreleg stabbed out at us. It clicked and snapped; the bars boomed as it hurled itself against them. Wrenn went for his sword and dropped the lantern. Suddenly we were in total darkness with the red spots of the flare-out dancing before our eyes.

Wrenn and I thought the same thing at the same time. We bent down and pawed frantically around on the floor for the lantern, but we only felt each other's hands.

'Where's the— Ow! Damn it!' I burnt my fingers on the hot oil leaking out. I stood back, seething with frustration as Wrenn picked it up. 'Is it broken?'

'I don't think so.'

'Are you sure? There's all that bloody rum up there!'

'There's a sodding great Insect right here!'

Wrenn struck a match and his shaking hand rattled inside the lantern as he lit it.

344

I shouted, 'For fuck's sake! Give me it, you daft fucking featherweight!'

He hauled his new sword from its scabbard; with the blade balanced in his hand his composure returned.

The Insect raked the bars with its foreclaws. It chewed them, mandibles clicking like shears. Strands of drool hung down and wrapped round its feet; glutinous bubbles stuck to the floor. The Insect rubbed its back pair of legs together; it turned round and round furiously in its four-metre-deep cage. Its body hung from long legs jointed above like a spider's. It was one of the biggest Insects I had seen, the size and strength of a warhorse; it battered the bars in absolute desperation to reach us.

It tilted its head and tried to push through, but the bulbous brassy eyes wouldn't fit. It pressed against the bars until its stippled thorax creaked, reached out its mandibles and gnashed. The mottled brown jaws met and overbit; they were the length and shape of scythe blades, chitin-hard and so powerful they could bite a body in two. A foreclaw swept the air. Wrenn and I backed off. He said, 'What's it doing here?'

'I don't know. I mean to find out.'

The cage's sliding door was secured by another big padlock. Its roof was a dented metal sheet. Wrenn pointed to some scattered meat bones that the Insect had voraciously scraped clean. It had macerated some into a sticky white paste and dropped it into the space between the cage and hull wall. 'They make short work of marrow bones!'

I grimaced. 'I thought I could smell the magnificent beast.' I thrust the lantern at Wrenn, dashed aft to the ladder and pulled myself up much faster than he could climb. He struggled behind me, probably realising for the first time what I can do. I swung my knees between the rungs and bent them to hang on, leant backwards upside-down, face to face with Wrenn. I prodded his chest. 'Mist will regret her latest trick.'

I flexed back upright and swarmed to the orlop deck. I scrambled onto the companionway and emerged from the hatch onto the main deck. All the sailors were eating their breakfast and rolling up their hammocks. Mouths full of porridge hung open in astonishment as I bounded past.

'Comet!' Wrenn shouted. 'Eszai are all equal! Stop and—'

'Kiss it,' I said. I jumped off and flapped across to the *Stormy Petrel*.

Mist is, of course, an early riser; she was already in her office eating ginger biscuits from a toast rack and walking a pair of brass compasses across an expansive chart draped over the table. I touched down outside next to the red hurricane lamp. I pounced into her cabin, right onto her, bearing her to the floor, my knees on her belly. The biscuits and a cafetière went flying. Mist was in control of herself; she saw my expression and screamed, 'Saker!'

'No more deceit!' I spat.

'Jant,' she said. 'Uppers make you manic. Why don't you calm down, before I have you locked in the brig?'

Her long white hair spread out, finer than silk. Her right hand edged behind the table's baluster leg, reaching for a paperknife. I snatched it and clattered it away against the bulkhead. 'An Insect!' I said. 'All those boxes of halberds! Why is there a live Insect on the *Melowne*?'

Mist's fair skin turned paler, her amethyst eyes wide. 'An Insect?'

'In a fucking cage!'

She caught her breath. 'Please get off me.'

I didn't want to let her move. I could only see one course of action. 'We must sail back to Awndyn. Fulmer will turn these over-ornamented crates around and take us home. In the Emperor's name, with god's will and the Circle's protection, you can consider yourself under arrest. I'll bring you before San, at knife-point if need be!'

'Comet ...' she said calmly.

'The only good thing about being at sea is we won't be eaten by Insects. And you bring one along! A huge one! I'll throw it overboard ...'

She saw there was no point in dissembling. 'Aye, I thought you would pry into everything like a starved rat. Let me up and I'll explain.'

As I disentangled her cloak folds from round us, Lightning glowered into the cabin with a cursing eye. The sea wind ripped his fur-lined coat into billows. He grabbed me and pushed me away from Mist. I hit the wall hard and sprawled down in a winded pile by the joist. 'Damn it, are you fucking trying to break my wings?'

'*What* is going on?'

Mist held her upper arm as if I had hurt her. She conjured an expression of gratitude for the Archer and sobbed experimentally but it had no effect on him. 'Jant is such a junkie.' She shrugged. 'He's so screwed up I am tempted to Challenge him myself.'

'No! This is nothing to do with cat!' I can't escape my one failing; my fellow Eszai use the label to taint *everything* I do, even when I'm clean. With always the same friends, I can't move on and begin anew, my mistakes stagnate around me. I smacked my fist against the joist, to take the heat out of my frustration. 'Don't tell me it's a hallucination, because Serein saw it too! There's an Insect, hundreds of cut-and-thrusters, a hundred caissons of arrows.'

Lightning listened carefully and at the latter he held up his hand. 'I know about them. Of course, Jant, think about it. Stop flouncing around and sit still. Would you travel to an unfamiliar country without armaments? Our ships are our only means of returning home so they're worth more than the Empire to us now. We have to protect them.'

'Mist said the island was peaceful,' I said sullenly.

'On the other hand, shipping Insects sounds sinister in the extreme. What is it for?'

Mist kicked open her folding chair and regarded the coffee soaking into her sea chart. 'I have a licence. No, not the usual showground licence. A warrant you'll respect.' She unlocked a tortoiseshell casket and removed a paper with the Emperor's seal.

She passed it to me and I read aloud: '"Every item of cargo carried by Mist on her journey is required and permitted in my name. It will benefit the Fourlands at the present time and in the future. San, god's guardian of Awia, Morenzia, Plainslands and Darkling, 19 January 2020."'

'That's all it says. It's the Emperor's signature all right. But does he know we have a live cargo?'

'Comet, I'm surprised at you, suggesting that I could keep information from the Emperor,' Ata said mildly. 'Aye, listen gentlemen. Tris has no Insects. Imagine their surprise, interest and fascination when I exhibit one. I will tell them: the Circle protects the world from these maneaters – see our benevolence. Even the fact that I have brought it such a distance alive will right well impress them. The governors of Tris can have the Insect for a zoo or a circus, or make soup out of it for all I care. I'll present it to them with all our Darkling silver and Donaise wine.'

'Bullshit,' I said and glared at her as only Rhydanne can.

Lightning said, 'I think Mist is telling the truth.'

'I'm going to hang her off the thingy mast on the doojah until she confesses and Fulmer can take us back to dock.'

Lightning said, 'We can't wrest command of the fleet from Mist. Anyway, Fulmer is not just captain of the *Melowne* but Awia's representative to Tris. Queen Eleonora's spy, in other words. If we turn back he'll make her a dismal report.'

The wind changed direction, the ship heaved, we lurched and Lightning shifted position woodenly, his coat hanging in limp folds to the floor.

Ata smiled and shook her head. She tied her platinum hair into a ponytail, making her strong-boned face look even more martial. She smoothed down her waistcoat with its frogging and brass-domed buttons. 'Don't worry. We won't risk enraging Eleonora. God, Lightning; I try to show you more of the world, but you just bring your own world with you.'

I was struck by a thought. If I was Wrenn, sincere and uncertain, or a sailor who witnessed my rapid departure from the *Melowne*, I would row across and try to eavesdrop on this conversation. I listened for any sounds outside the cabin and called, 'I can hear you; there's no need to bloody hide!'

Wrenn pushed open the glass-paned door and appeared, abashed. His shirtsleeves were wet with spray; water squeezed out of his soaked boot seams at every step.

I said, 'Great, why don't we invite the rest of the Circle in here and then we can have a party?'

'You could really hear me?'

'Not at all, but I thought it best to check.'

'Oh. Clever,' he said, downcast. He glanced around, taking in the leaded bay windows that gave a view over the stern, Mist's cot with its embroidered canopy, a stand of scrolled charts, the navigational instruments laid out on her ledger and ginger biscuits all over the floor. With a fencer's grace he had adapted well to the ship's dimensions and he was short enough to stand without stooping, whereas Lightning rested his head on his hand pressing the beam.

Wrenn was well aware of Lightning's one-night stand with Ata. It was common knowledge that one night Lightning comforted her a little too assiduously and now they have a daughter. Wrenn folded his wings submissively, their elbows at his backside and the wrist-joints just visible from the front, clasping his shoulders. He picked his way with care: 'My lord. Um. Lightning. I respect your experience but this is my first assignment as an Eszai. You know that's important. I don't want to return empty-handed only a couple of days after setting out. I'm dependent on Mist for success and I'm sure you don't want me to fail. Anyhow, we left with such pomp that all the matelots in Awndyn will laugh fit to piss if we sneak back.'

He slid his fingers into his rapier's swept guards and grasped the grip worn to the shape of his hand. 'When I was in the ranks Lightning's honourable ideas sort of filtered down. None of us ever deserted. Well, I think it's dishonourable to turn back.'

I scowled. Wrenn bit his lip but continued, 'I agree that ambassadors shouldn't carry weapons. "Weighted down with iron, weighted down with fear", the saying goes. If Mist intends to use the Insect against the islanders I'll kill it myself. But she has set her heart on exploring Tris. Jant, if you threaten her you will cross swords with me. One sword keeps another in its sheath, so maybe if I support Mist there will be peace. You should be ashamed of yourself for intimidating a lady.'

I said, 'She's scarcely a lady.'

Lightning eyed us pensively. He stroked the scar on his right palm and eventually said, 'Very well; we press on.'

'But—'

'Enough!'

Ata relaxed. 'Jant, you clown. Stir a mutiny again and I'll have you towed behind in a barrel.'

I said, 'I need some fresh air.' I walked out to the main deck, slammed the cabin door with my drooping wing. I climbed the whatever ropes to the top of the mainmast and sat up there for hours on the something spar, face into the wind, and let the sea air fan my anger.

CHAPTER 7

Wrenn's Diary

29 February 2020

Comet suggested that I keep a diary to record my exploits on this voyage. This morning I woke at six a.m. (bell eighteen), and did two hours of rapier-and-dagger exercises on the deck. I improved my time by a second or so on the 'wild boar' sequence. I have to be ruthless with myself in practice because a Challenger wouldn't spare me. Then jogged up and down the keelson in the hold until Fulmer asked me to stop. I would like to practise sparring but no one here is even half as good as they need to be to test my arm.

Lightning is the best fencer among them, I'll ask him for a bout and in return he might teach me some archery. He puts target butts forward on the foredeck and shoots at them from the half deck. His arrows fly the length of the *Petrel*. It's great to watch when we run alongside, but Mist only lets him have a quarter-hour a day rather than the four hours he needs. It's amazing to meet Lord Micawater in person – and he treats me like an equal! I've always wanted to be like him. I wish Dad could see me now.

So even though we have been aboard for a month, we are as fit as we can hope to be. Comet is either holed up with his books or away flying. Every morning he slings a water bottle on his shoulder, takes off and flaps up into the sky until he is just a speck and I worry that Lightning might mistake him for a seagull and shoot him. I still can't get used to a man gliding. He must feel so free. It must be odd to see people from above. He can always tell who they are, I suppose he has got used to it. I wish I could fly – think of the fencing moves I could use!

I can't wait to fight Insects. As soon as I get back from Tris, I'm going to the Front. I have loads of ideas to rid Lowespass of Insects completely – such as filling the river with salt, so they can't drink it. But Lightning tells me they tried that back in 1170. When we return, I'll be surrounded by foxy girls and, by god, I need it. Who knows, Lightning might be pushed off the most eligible bachelor top spot for the first time in fifteen hundred years.

It's a shame Mist swept me away from my moment of triumph. I wish I could be back with all those girls who were longing for me. But Mist said my absence will make them keener. She's grateful that the best Swordsman in the Fourlands is at her side. Any time.

1 March 2020

The weather is lovely, very bright and a lively wind clips us along. Comet
refuses to leave his cabin. I think he is ashamed. He is drinking doped wine
every day now. I reported to Mist, but she says let him be, the remains of
his cache that escaped confiscation won't last much longer. Why doesn't
she punish him for bringing scolopendium on board? In the fyrd it's the
most serious offence to be caught with drugs, especially if you deal them to
other soldiers. Scolopendium is pretty mysterious and old-fashioned stuff. I
don't know anything about it but, god, I can't accept that an Eszai uses it. I
suppose since Comet can fly, in good weather anyway, he takes his success
for granted.

Mist said that people like Comet were the most useful, just as crooked
wood is handy to the shipbuilder because odd shapes can be made into parts
that hold the rest together. I don't get that, really. I thought the Circle was
of one purpose.

Rain showers make the boards slippery. The tars say they're chancing their
lives every time they go to the latrine planks at the prow to have a crap.
Great waves break over the beakhead so they chance to get washed off, or
slip and fall five metres like a turd into the sea where the ship will sail over
them. Being valued passengers, our latrine is a tiny cubicle with a hole in
the seat, on a private balcony at the stern. If you get the angle right you can
piss against the rudder. The whole gallery smells of Captain Fulmer's poseur
aftershave. Fulmer took one look at Lightning's frock coat and said, 'Good
grief. This isn't the eighteenth century.'

I went to Comet's cabin and disturbed his work. I lost money at cards as
we chatted. Those flat-chested mountain girls are so wild their love-bites need
stitches, he says. We talked about rapiers and the new spring-loaded daggers
whose blades split open into three points to trap swords. They impressed
Comet but I told him they are just for show and would be dangerous in a
real fight. I said, if you see a man wielding one you know he is a braggadocio.

I slipped Wrenn's diary back under his bunk and returned to my cabin.
I worked there during the day with my notebooks that are so pleasant to
begin and to dent the neat paper with a fountain pen. Contrary to what
Wrenn thinks, neither flying nor languages is instinctive. I have learned
the shapes of the air; I have to think carefully about my moves when aloft
and sometimes I make mistakes. And if I make a gaffe in jotting down a
translation, it's just as dangerous as a botched landing.

Mist had noted Trisian words from her first expedition, although without
phonetics or even context. I figured out most of the unknown words from
their roots, working back from modern equivalents. A few remained tantalis-
ing. The Trisians appeared to speak a form of Old Morenzian, pre-dating the

first millennium. Nothing of that language survives recorded, apart from dusty learned works in a weird thirty-letter alphabet, ten letters more than I was used to. It dated from before the time of the First Circle when the fricative Low Awian language became the common tongue of the Fourlands. At around the same time, to be fair in the standardisations, San advised that the Fourlands' currency should be based on Morenzia's system, which was far simpler than Awia's.

I knew that the Trisians would be expecting us. The canoeists and governors that Mist dealt with will have spread the news across the island. They'll know it's human nature for us to return prepared to a great discovery, to tease out every detail. When our sails appear on their horizon, whatever plans they have made will be set in action. The Trisians will scurry to receive us, but I could not predict how.

I will just keep working and if I do too much cat and collapse, the others might realise how much torment my constant thoughts of Tern are causing me. I doubt she's dwelling on me this much, back in the Castle with her lover.

'Damn it!' I said aloud. 'Just stop the waves for one hour and let me think!' I wished myself back in Darkling, where I would still be drinking happily in the Filigree Spider if Ata's message hadn't got through. I reverted to thinking in Scree, a good language to be misanthropic in, as it has no words for groups of people and no plural verbs. Best of all it lacks a word for ocean. The Rhydanne word for climb is the same as the word for run, and there are plenty of words to describe the various types of drunk.

The only pub in Darkling is in the centre of Scree pueblo, where the bare rock buildings merge shapelessly on both sides of the raised single track. The pueblo has a shallow, all-enveloping roof with a hatch for each room, to prevent winter snows sealing people in completely. The Filigree Spider was busy, as it was the height of the freeze season. The herders had arrived, bringing their goats down from the high pasture. A few hunters visited to rest; they were nomadic and they pleased themselves. Many were afternoon-drunk (drinking becomes moreish and you write off the day).

I sat on one of the benches by the low bar and ate bread with rancid butter and salted llama's cheese. A row of freeze-dried rabbits hung tacked up by their ears behind the bar – Lascanne catches them by hand. I pushed my cup across the counter again; he slopped more whisky into it with an exaggerated gesture. 'It is snowing and drifting,' he said, as if that was news. 'Want a pinnacle rabbit?'

'No, thanks.'

Lascanne was alone-drunk (everything seems vaguely amusing). I suppose I was slightly daytime-drunk (no matter how much you drink it doesn't seem to have any effect).

The walls and most of the slate floor were covered with bright flat-woven kilims with warm red and indigo geometrical designs. A big hearth was on my right, its chimney shared with the distillery. A hunter lay on the furs beside it, very occasionally murmuring. She was drunk (dead-drunk); her sharp face rested on her folded hands. A family of four slept piled together nearby.

Three or four howffs were stacked against the wall. Howffs are tents of thin leather attached to rucksac frames. They could be rolled out and propped up by the frames to form triangular shelters. There was the ladder up to the Filigree Spider's unfurnished second floor, where many people were lodging until the thaw season. Square, dark openings were the entrances of small passageways that lead to other parts of the pueblo, again to escape heavy snows. The pub smelt of peat smoke and stew.

The door crashed open and two hunters struggled through manhandling a heavy bundle between them. At first I thought it was a rolled-up rug. The hunters, Leanne and Ciabhar, dropped the bundle in front of the hearth and turned it over. It was an unconscious body.

Leanne Shira saw me. She paused with one foot in the air before placing it down slowly. 'Jant! Look what Ciabhar found ... We would have left him but we thought you might be interested.' She darted over and bit me gently on the shoulder, for a kiss. I think she was working-drunk (just a light haze on your life that lasts for days). Her face was cold to the touch. I watched her sleek narrow body, hard muscle flowering under pale skin at every movement. Fast movement, a melting of potential, she was gracile but strong. Her rubbery sprinter's midriff showed between her crop top and short black skirt. She had two pairs of snowshoes tied on her belt, one on each hip for herself and her lover.

'Bring some whisky,' Ciabhar suggested.

'No alcohol!' I cried.

'Idiot! You're supposed to give them hot water,' said Leanne.

'What about whisky and water?'

Curious punters clustered round, making helpful suggestions: 'Take his coat off.'

'Put him in a hot bath.'

'Or under the snow.'

'He looks weird; I don't like it. I'm off.'

Now that they had accomplished dragging him in, their effort fell apart into the typical Rhydanne unit of organisation – one. Ciabhar Dara stood back and stared. He was tall and so lithe I could see the muscle fibres through his tight skin and the hollows where they joined the bone. His black hair was wrapped in a ponytail. The nails on his long fingers came to hard points. His trousers were worn buckskin; bright ribbons criss-cross bound his woven shirt's loose sleeves close to his arms. A heavy three-stone bolas was wrapped around his waist – a bolas is the best weapon for mountain conditions, and Ciabhar was a very skilled and patient hunter. He blinked cat-eyes. 'This man is really ill,' he said lucidly.

I pushed through. 'Let me see.'

The handsome stranger's skin was so waxen he looked like a statue carved from tallow. His lips and nail beds were blue; his breathing crackled. 'Oh, god,' I said, feeling snow-wet hands and an ice-cold forehead. He was severely hypothermic, but the Rhydanne wouldn't know that. Leanne flickered to my side and tried to pour hot water into his open, frost-blistered mouth.

'I watched him for ages,' Ciabhar said. 'On the Turbary Track. Walking on, walking up, without crampons. He wasn't a featherback so I left him in peace. He was searching around but he never saw me. At the top of Bealach Pass his pony lay down and died.'

Leanne gave him a look meaning, 'Breakfast is sorted.' She sped out, leaving the door open. She ran without pause over the bridge across Scree gorge that was just a single tightrope with two handrail cords, then lengthened her stride and disappeared, sliding, down the gritty path. She ran over the crystalline swathes of erosion between the naked rocks. Distant peaks looked as if ice had been poured down from their pointed summits and sharp boulders thrown sporadically up their slopes.

I said, 'I can't do anything for him here! Stupid! You should have descended. Down-slope – towards Carniss.'

Ciabhar shrugged.

'It's the *altitude* that's killing him. You just made it worse.'

I thumbed open an eye, the iris brown, pupils dilated. The lids were dark and swollen. I handled him gently as I took his pulse, which was slow. He stopped making the effort to shiver, as there was no warmth to gain by shivering. His breathing rate was dropping back to normal – too exhausted to keep the rapid pace. He coughed once, dryly, and a bubbling noise began in his lungs as he breathed.

'We're at eight thousand metres here. When did you last see a flatlander in the Spider?'

'They don't come to the plateau,' Ciabhar mused.

'That's because they can't breathe! They can't get sustenance from thin air; even I take days to acclimatise. And they freeze easily. Ciabhar, you know nothing. Help me carry him down to Tolastadh.'

I wrapped more rugs around the man's jacket, and noticed a small ink-blue tattoo of Cobalt manor's fishing bear on his wrist. 'A sailor?'

'What?'

'He's travelled a long way.'

As we hefted him his body convulsed once, froth ran from the corners of his mouth, and he died. Ciabhar dropped him, gave up cooperating and sloped away. Some more (cheery-drunk, boisterous-drunk, and totally pissed) hunters appeared and eagerly began stripping the corpse's clothes but I chased them off.

I checked his pockets, finding a damp paper bag containing sugar-cake, a wet box of matches and a very damp and fragile envelope. It wilted and started to disintegrate in my hands. I flipped it over, seeing a crimson seal. Behind me Lascanne dragged the body out, intending to drop it over the edge of Scree gorge. Outside in the mountains, the dead are left where they fall. No Rhydanne cares about the dead in Darkling, where the living have so much to contend with.

I went back to the bar and slapped the letter down on its stone slab. Chamois-fat candles guttered in their horn holders. The script read: 'To be delivered to the hand of Comet Jant Shira. From Mist, Sailor and Captain of the Fleet. Send to the Filigree Spider, Scree. Please note – this envelope does NOT contain any money!!!'

'Oh, bugger!'

Just a few degrees colder, or another half-hour out in the drifts, and Mist's courier wouldn't have reached me, and I wouldn't be sitting here in a hot, weltering caravel.

I perched on the ladder between poop deck and half-deck, watching a severely freckled Serein do stretches below in the main area. In order to impress Mist, he had learnt the names and actions of every part of the ship. He thrust his rapier through imaginary combatants who obviously didn't stand a chance.

He took a break and trotted over, swinging the rapier. 'Hello, Jant. You look a bit spaced out. What are you daydreaming about?'

'Darkling,' I said. 'And Tern.'

'Don't blame you. I'd miss her too.'

'Oh, yes?'

'Yeah. You're very lucky. In fact one of my mates in the fyrd had her picture as a pin-up. Just a tatty etching, of course, on the barracks wall. Tern is much, much more beautiful in real life. She's stunning. I wish my mate knew that I'd met her … Jant, are you all right?'

'I will be, if you don't ever speak to me again.'

CHAPTER 8

'Very well,' Lightning said to Wrenn. 'I will spar with you. But I am only ranked sixth best with the rapier in the world, so a duel won't last long before you win. Give me a few hours to organise these men' – he gestured at the main deck where the *Petrel*'s sailors were hard at work – 'to make a more interesting game for you. After all, Insects don't play fair.'

'Agreed!' said Wrenn. He drew his sword and eagerly poked the point into the Insect-paper caulking between the deck planks.

Mist looked up from her ledger. 'Good, Lightning. That's better than you and Jant spending another night getting pissed on Micawater port in my office.'

'I blame Wrenn for not drinking ... We had to finish the open bottles.'

'Ha. I have to leave you boys to it every midnight to check navigational readings against the stars; when I come back in you're still carousing and reminiscing. Well, entertain my deck hands by all means, they need some leisure time, but you had better not injure any.'

Lightning leant on the rail and nodded. He was enjoying the novelty. 'Then here are the tournament rules: I'll do my best to hit you. We'll use buttoned rapiers and flat of the blade only. Every sailor you touch will play dead. Mist will arbitrate. The whole of *Petrel* is the arena.'

'And the *Melowne*,' said Mist. 'I'll bring her alongside and rope her to *Petrel* to make a gam. Then I can spare up to one hundred sailors. How many do you want?'

'All of them, of course.'

That afternoon, I circled above the lashed-together caravels. The sails were furled on all but the rearmost masts, which Mist said were mizzen masts with lateen sails set to keep the ships' prows into the waves. I took her word for it. My shadow flitted over as everyone on the *Melowne* crowded at the railings and clambered into the rigging to watch the *Petrel*'s main deck.

Wrenn and Lightning faced each other in the most spacious area by the foot of the mainmast. They raised their swords in salute, turned to honour the audience and Mist. Then they began to circle warily, watching each other with deliberation. Wrenn trod cautiously but didn't strike.

'Don't be afraid, shorty,' Lightning taunted. 'Besides, call that a haircut? Allow me to improve it.'

Wrenn tested Lightning with a pass; Lightning deflected it. Wrenn realised that Lightning was good, very good. He ran straight in with a diagonal attack. Lightning parried, let Wrenn run past him, turned – thrust – missed.

They circled. Lightning stabbed at Wrenn's chest, a killing blow had it landed. Wrenn regained the initiative, made a prolonged attack but Saker forcefully parried the blows.

Lightning gave a shout. At the signal, sailors rushed from the edges of the deck and open hatchways, straight at Wrenn from every direction. They all brandished the new broadswords. Some held them two-handed. Wrenn gasped – ran to back himself against the ship's side. Men clustered close, their mint-condition swords gleamed but Wrenn's rapier danced around them with agility. He parried every single one on his rapier's forte to protect his lighter blade.

I wanted a better view. I glided down to the crosstrees, curled my bare toes around the thick wood spar and then settled on it, legs dangling. Ten metres directly below me Awians and Plainslanders churned about, pushing Wrenn back against the gunwale. He jumped to the top of the railing, grasped a rope with his free hand, swept his rapier, clashing off all their raised staves and blades. He touched the padded knee of a woman's breeches. She backed away to the forecastle where she sat down. A cheer went up from the eager audience on the *Melowne*: 'You got Sanderling! Get Lightning! Go on!'

The sailors moved back on one side as Lightning pulled himself up to face Wrenn on the railing. The sailors cut off Wrenn's retreat. He held his rapier over his sturdy shoulder and climbed with his free hand, up the rope netting towards me. Lightning tested his foot on the lowest taut ratline. He stretched up and slashed with his point but Wrenn reached his rapier down and spun circles around it.

Wrenn hauled himself onto the crosstrees. I slipped into the air out of his way and glided over the ship as he ran lightly along the spar and climbed down the shrouds at the other side. He swung himself down to the half-deck leaving the sailors behind but Lightning dashed sternwards, scaled the half-deck ladder and confronted him there. He attacked Wrenn with a cut to the left shoulder. Wrenn retreated behind the helm to catch his breath. Mist was standing at the wheel but she didn't flinch or move a muscle. Behind her back, Lightning lunged, Wrenn gave more ground and came up against a rack of fire buckets.

Lightning made strong cuts to Wrenn's head; every time Wrenn parried his sword blurred with vibration. The furious clangs rang out over the ocean.

Wrenn caught a blow on his rapier's tip close to the round leather button. He twisted, almost disarmed Lightning. Lightning stamped his foot to distract him, rushed in with a flèche aimed at the solar plexus but Wrenn dodged.

Sailors started to climb the ladder from the main deck. Wrenn struck the first one at the top; the man jumped down. Wrenn 'killed' the next two and the third became uncertain how to attack. Three men on either side of the main deck spread out, anticipating Wrenn's escape route. They braced themselves by holding the sail lines above their heads.

Lightning called, 'Hey!' Five men jumped down off the topcastle, two burst out of my original cabin underneath. Wrenn ducked behind the helm. They charged at him; he touched them dead in seven seconds, his blade moving too fast to follow. Wrenn whipped round, rapier arm at full stretch, and arrested Lightning's blade mid-thrust.

Mist grew exasperated with ten men cutting round her and the helm. She yelled at the sister ship, 'Fulmer! To starboard!'

At the *Melowne*'s helm, Fulmer jumped. He spun his wheel simultaneously with Mist. The sails on the mizzen masts swivelled, all their air spilled out. *Petrel* and *Melowne* lurched, braked and tilted left.

Wrenn and Lightning lost their footing and slid on their backsides across the deck into the gunwale. Wrenn scrabbled to his feet first, fled down the ladder, and poised in first guard by the mainmast. Lightning gave Mist an angry glance, then sped after him. They started fencing enthusiastically. The sailors who maintained their balance quickly clustered round. Their mates picked themselves up out of the wet gutters and scuppers, and joined to restrict Wrenn's retreat from Lightning's attacks. Wrenn pressed back at them; he deflected every blow and kept his balance with clever footwork. Lightning never slowed but Wrenn still found chance to kill ten of the nearest sailors, alternately striking them between parrying Lightning.

The caravels righted themselves with a crash. But, bound together, they idled in the water, sails limp. They drifted side-on to the waves, which hit *Petrel*'s right hull and threw spray onto the main deck.

I flew closer, lost sight of the duellists while I landed on the poop deck, tricky because the ships were drifting slowly round. Everyone watched Wrenn.

Wrenn almost touched Lightning. Lightning fell back and let his team of sailors surge forward. He pulled a silk handkerchief from inside his shirt and wiped his face with it. Sweat ran freely down Wrenn's face.

Wrenn touched two more sailors; they flopped down at his feet. He avoided a huge Awian hefting a capstan bar, darted under and prodded him on the belly. The burly salt refused to die. He tried to trap Wrenn with the bar against the railings. He bounced on his feet like a boxer.

Melowne tars booed and started shouting, 'You're dead, Smew! You old bastard, get down! Stop being a bad loser! Finish him off, Serein!'

Wrenn jumped rat-fast onto the covered water butt and gave Smew a resounding slap on his bald pate. The big man must have been mindful of his audience, because he died theatrically.

On top of the barrel, Wrenn lunged and touched two more sailors. His right, middle, left; three more fell. His rapier was everywhere. I was dying to join in. I picked up a broadsword. Wrenn was obviously a head case; the most berserk of the crew members didn't perturb him. I wanted to cut him down to size.

Lightning glanced at me and made a covert spiral gesture with one hand. I recognised the gesture – a strategy we arranged long ago for the occasions we fight Insects in the amphitheatre. Lightning engaged Wrenn while I ran silently down to the main deck and crept up behind him. All I have to do is touch his back.

Wrenn read from his opponents' body language that I was there; either that or he can see behind him like an Insect. He stepped back sharply to keep us both in sight, swooped a parry past Lightning and onto me.

I immediately hacked throat to waist, making the most of my long reach. Wrenn took a bound backwards as if he could fly. He landed and slipped on the wet deck. He steadied himself, stubby wings spread, looked for eye contact.

I stabbed straight for his nipple; he fended my blade far out to the side in prime, his hand down. He riposted back in sixte to my chest, got nowhere near – my fast sixte counter-riposte batted it away. Surprise flitted across Wrenn's eyes. No time to think in words but I felt satisfied. Don't under-estimate me.

Wrenn beat my blade aside to the right, parried Lightning, then back to attack over my blade to my shoulder. As his rapier rose, I dodged and sliced across his stomach. He turned his blade down and stopped my cut.

Again with his blade flat he smacked Lightning's cut away and made a return blow to me. The sailors had no room to attack with Lightning and I working as a pair. We fell into step but I couldn't pre-empt Wrenn because he kept cutting away to Lightning on my left.

My speed worried Wrenn. He twisted left, bound and locked Lightning's blade. He shouted and freed his sword in a motion that left Lightning con-fused, stepped away and concentrated on me. He blocked my slices with a short economical movement, parried down and outwards, jabbed under my guard. I moved reflexively, almost on automatic.

He attacked to my face. I brushed it aside with a weak cut from the wrist. It was a feint. Wrenn pulled the blow, punched past my hilt. I felt a sudden sting on my knuckles. The grip slipped out of my grasp and my broadsword looped pommel over foible, over the ship's side into the water.

Wrenn breathed through open mouth; his gaze slipped away as he switched his full attention back to Lightning.

Being disarmed and out of the game, I retreated to the steps and watched the fight continue. Wrenn was tiring, but eighty out of the hundred men were down.

Lightning hallooed again: 'Hey!'

The last of the crew rushed out of Ata's cabin. Wrenn made as if to dash back but instead ran to the gunwale. He vaulted *Petrel*'s side and landed on the main deck of the *Melowne*. The audience there drew back with surprised cries.

Wrenn hurtled past them and up the forecastle ladder. *Petrel*'s crew followed him, climbing or leaping over the perilous narrow gap and the log fenders between the ships. Wrenn defended the lofty ladder so well he killed ten more before they forced their way to his level.

A sailor made a lunge so long he overbalanced. Lightning ran in on the advantage but Wrenn parried coolly. Dead combatants sat down dotting the little triangular deck. Lightning made a concerted effort but Wrenn with his back to the foremast was invincible. The last two crewmen fell on Lightning's left and right. Only he remained.

Lightning feinted once, twice, thrust at Wrenn's sword arm. Wrenn had anticipated it and bound Lightning's blade. They grated together with a sound like knives sharpened on a steel.

Wrenn angled his blade and thrust down; his rapier point bounced off Lightning's thigh. Lightning knelt but before he hit the deck the round padded button was under his chin. Lightning spread his arms wide, his sword loose in his right hand.

Wrenn froze. His blue Summerday FC shirt had turned black with sweat; his face was crimson. He looked at Lightning straight and whispered, 'You're dead.'

Bodies in white shirts sprawled all over the ships. A gust buffeted *Petrel* and *Melowne*; water sloshed under their bows. There was complete silence.

Lightning brought his hands together in applause. Wrenn saluted him with his rapier on which new scrapes and scratches shone bright.

Everyone began to cheer. The beaten sailors got to their feet, brushing down their clothes, grinning at each other and staring with envy and respect in Wrenn's direction. The Swordsman concentrated on stretching his back and robust limbs in his customary sequence. His rapier stuck upright between the planks.

I vaulted to the *Melowne*, climbed to the forecastle and shook his hand. 'You're amazing.'

Wrenn bowed to me, and the audience; drops of sweat fell from his hair to the deck. Lightning shook and flexed his sword arm. It must have felt like lead from the strain and vibration.

Mist clapped her hands briskly; her high voice carried over the ships. 'On your feet, crew, and to your stations. Double rations tonight of rum and beer if you drink to the health and genius of Serein Wrenn.'

Wrenn turned to Lightning and said effusively, 'Thank you. That was a great idea. Thanks for letting me show the Zascai my flair.'

'Indeed. I admit I've never fought on a ship before, but one thousand years ago I saw the then Swordsman take on *three* hundred men in the Castle's dining hall. Not just sailors, either; six lamai sections of a Select Fyrd division.'

Wrenn's smile faded instantly, his pride deflated. However I saw a teasing gleam in Lightning's eye; I think he was making it up.

Into the second month every sailor and passenger on the *Stormy Petrel* and *Melowne* started to become possessive about their property. I knew with detailed intimacy the few items I had brought on board; I mended and cared for them jealously. I put a keen edge on my axe. I polished my mirror. I kept my wings preened and oiled in perfect condition. The ocean yielded nothing so the neatness of my cabin and the conservation of materials took on a great importance. I protected my private space thoroughly; we all became territorial. Lightning acted as if he had condensed his entire palace into a ship's berth. He spent too much time talking to Wrenn and seemed not to have noticed that I was taking cat again.

As a passenger I felt powerless and incarcerated. There were few chances to be of use but Mist employed me to carry messages between the ships. Every morning I tried to instruct her in Old Morenzian but she wasn't comfortable with formal study.

Something about the precise figures in Mist's ledger, her neatly complicated compasses and the vermeil astrolabe fascinated me almost as much as the glassware and herbs in the chemist's shop where I once worked. She had a quadrant made of incised ivory, a shining brass sextant and a very accurate sea clock in a cushioned casket. For all Mist's expertise she couldn't see from the air as I could, so every afternoon I checked the coastlines of her portolan charts. The sheer distance we were sailing frightened me, but there was no way I could bring her to confess the danger we were in.

Every dusk I went below deck to check on the Insect. Immediately it saw me it attacked, crashing into the bars of its cage. I crouched behind my axe, enjoying the adrenaline surge, and watched until it tired itself out. Everybody knows that Insects can't be trained; if it had been any other wild animal I would have dedicated the voyage to bringing it under control. It didn't understand my signals. It only sensed me as food. It raged and starved.

One evening I managed to loop a leather strap around the Insect's foreleg, but it tore off the tether and ate it. It chewed bones and layered them onto the smelly hard white paste spread round the edges of its cage. The concretion grew thicker over days and weeks. When it reached six centimetres high, I realised that the Insect was building a wall. I think it wanted to find other Insects, after all they are animals that work together. Since it found it was inexplicably alone and trapped, it began walling itself into a cell in which it presumably felt more at home.

I hoped that the Insect didn't have the ability to call others through, from whatever Shift world it hatched in. I imagined thousands of Insects popping into the hold, the ship gradually lowering in the water with their weight. Or our Insect finding a path to vanish back into the Shift, leaving an empty cage. That would raise some questions.

Each night, I stayed inside my cabin with the door bolted. I tried to meditate into the Shift, but every time I was unsuccessful and extremely frustrated. I tried to relax and empty my mind but I couldn't concentrate for more than a couple of minutes before I started on another line of thought, for example Tern's infidelity. After a week, I gave up.

I put red and yellow wraps in my hair and threaded fat jade beads onto my dreadlocks. I swigged rum. I masturbated myself sore. I lived immersed in sensation for weeks on end until the scolopendium stashed in my paper wraps ran out. I tried to ration it but that just made the craving worse. Since I've been addicted in the past, my body recognises cat and knows how to use it. I knew I could become quickly hooked again and had to be careful, but it was the only thing that stopped me thinking of Tern.

I slid down the scrollwork to the orlop deck and started searching among the supplies. The strength of the craving is difficult to describe to someone who has never been an addict. It is like an intense hunger, the same deep, terrible need a starving man has for food. It gnaws all the time, from the moment of waking through to the night, a tiny whisper or a cold gale that will push you into the most bizarre behaviours. It made me creep down here to the lazaretto lockers at the stern. Most of my will power was spent on coping with the constant fear of floating in the middle of the ocean; I no longer had the strength to stand against my yearning for cat.

The ship's medical supplies were in a wooden trunk. Unable to pick the lock, I took my axe to it. I sorted through all the various pieces of equipment, steamed-clean scalpels, folded bandages and ointment jars, and came across a cardboard box with struts separating corked glass ampoules. I ran my hand over them and they rattled. I pulled one out and looked at the label. A little skylark logo; *scolopendium. 3% aqueous solution. Do not exceed the dose prescribed. Export interdicted.*

Skylarks. I counted across a row and down a column; there were fifty tubes, a great deal too much for this ship to be carrying. I was convinced that the Sailor must expect a fight on Tris. There were also a number of slender glass syringes in clean paper packets. I tore the end off one and shook it out. It's a better rush than I've had so far. No! God, honestly, Jant, you have no self-control. I put it down, feeling as if I wasn't in my body, with denial so great I wondered if I were actually here at all.

I have a choice. I'll just use it once and then throw all these ampoules overboard. I gave in – yes, I'll do it – and a flush of relaxation spread through me, a warm feeling of relief as if I had taken the shot already. I hadn't even noticed how on edge I was, how tightly I had been holding myself.

I hurried back to my cabin, braced myself in the lowest corner with my sinewy arm across my knees and looked at the inside of my elbow. I was in great shape and didn't have to tie up, my veins were hard like cables under the skin.

I felt guilty, then rebelled. Why feel remorse? If any other man aboard knew, the skylarks would be long gone. On the street in Hacilith us kids skilfully used guilt to hold each other back. Like little Eszai, we tried for any opportunity with all we had. But those few who succeeded were brought down by guilt, because they knew their friends were still in the gutter. I'm doing this because I can. Who would say no to such intense pleasure?

The timbers creaked and I jumped. Every time a wave gulped under the hull I was sure it was about to split and spill us all into raging water. Mist told me that the boards are meant to yield slightly to make the ship flexible. In my mind's eye the planks buckled, leaks sprayed between them. Frothing water races from the bilges into the hold, erupts through the hatchways; the ship tilts and sinks dreamily intact down to the seabed.

My mouth was dry with anticipation and I concentrated so hard on measuring the dose that nothing else existed – no ship, no other immortals, none of the sailors in the rigging feeling the breeze through their open wings. I know what I'm doing is wrong. But just once, to get it over with, and that will be the last injection I ever take.

When I'm hooked, which I'm not, I try to keep a little scolopendium in my body all the time. Drinking it is fine, to keep the level constant, but if it runs out and I dip below the basic amount, then I'm more likely to panic and ... do this:

I pushed the tip of the bright needle into my skin, which separated as the point sank in delicately; deeper. Dark red blood shot up into the barrel and started to diffuse. *I want that back*, I thought, and pressed the plunger down as quickly as I dared. I lay back with the needle in my arm. My hands spasmed. A wave of contortion passed over me – the ecstasy was almost unbearable.

We travelled on. The days became indistinguishable. The days smeared into each other. And the sun rose over and over again.

CHAPTER 9

I woke up horrified to find myself still on the ship, and another whore of a day stretching out in front of me exactly like the last. I reached under the pillow for another phial and with the help of scolopendium managed to stall its inevitable onslaught for a few more hours.

April. Needle scars were making a calendar on my arm. I kept my long-sleeved T-shirt on to cover them. An occasional shower refreshed us and filled the barrels, but overall the heat was oppressive and all the deck hands worked barefoot and stripped to the waist. Our clothes were faded by the sun and mine were patched. I was slightly more shadowy around the eyes, but not so anyone would notice. It suited me, anyway, and cat kept my weight down. The first thing any drug abuse removes is the part of your mind that gives a damn about your health. And there's an advantage to addiction – cat was a protection. All my anxiety was concentrated on one problem so I dealt with the rest of the world without concern.

I went to lounge on the foredeck, seeing the ocean plunge away in all directions the same. Wrenn and I watched *Stormy Petrel* sailing as close to the wind as possible, canted with all canvas out, three hundred metres ahead of us on the right side. Lightning climbed up to her aft castle and waved to us from the rail. He was tanned, and the sunlight had bleached his fair hair.

He strung a gold-banded compound bow and flexed it, loosing an arrow that looped high into the air. Wrenn ducked and shouted, 'Look out!'

The arrow plummeted straight at me and appeared sticking out of the deck plank not ten centimetres away from my left hand. I sprang up. 'Saker! What do you think you're doing?'

He couldn't hear me. He waved cheerfully and pointed at us, then at the horizon.

'What is that flash bastard on about?' The arrow had a letter tied to it. I broke the thread and unspooled the paper that Lightning had wrapped tightly around its shaft.

Comet
By Mist's calculations you should be able to see the Island of Tris now, if you
fly to a height four times the main mast and stay close to the ships. Look due
east. Come and tell us if you see anything.
LSM

While I read it, Lightning, who now had Wrenn's attention, proceeded to show off. He shot an arrow skywards and Wrenn watched it describe a high parabola while Lightning rapidly took another arrow and sent it after the first, shooting straight out in a flat trajectory. As his first arrow came down the second one hit it, spinning it head over flights. A second later we faintly heard the crack they had made as they collided. Lightning did this again to prove the first time wasn't a fluke.

'He can hit an arrow in the air!' Wrenn said.

'Yeah.' Lightning had been passing the last couple of weeks by sitting on the crosstrees and shooting at albatrosses. He halved their feathers to make more arrows. Only the dwindling numbers of seabirds slowed him down. 'You should see his trick with an arrow in a cork and a wine bottle.'

I gave Wrenn the letter, spread my wings and arced up from the stern. I climbed steeply, forcing my fifty-eight kilos into the air. I sensed every ripple in the breeze *Melowne* distorted with her massive cream sails.

The ships diminished quickly. I was terrified of losing sight of them in such a vast expanse. I tried to stay above the mainmast of the *Petrel*, although there was no lift at all. I could easily outpace them, and then I would be crossing and recrossing the same area of ocean, trying in vain to find them, until I fell from exhaustion and drowned.

I searched ahead, and saw nothing but more water, so I flew higher until the ornate *Petrel* was the length of my index finger, trailing rainbows in her bow wave. The ships' wakes were two Vs around their prows and white veils stretching behind them for hundreds of metres. I glided into a shallow spiral to rest. Either Mist's calculations are incorrect, or the island does not exist at all.

I chandelled up, higher still, and looked out east. On the horizon, raised on haze, a dark green patch seemed to float. A mountain! A mountain in the sea! I kept climbing, aware that I was the second immortal ever to set eyes on Tris. The island emerged, summit first. I felt a firm companionship with it, as if it had been set there especially for me. Fluffy white clouds hung over it, and I could just see their shadows on the smooth mountainside. The crest was pale grey with distance.

There were some crags around the shoreline. Maybe they were cliffs, I couldn't tell. I stared until my eyes watered. The haze began to dissipate, the perspective suddenly clicked, and I realised I was looking at a town. The white buildings resembled a slope of scree, tumbling from the mountainside down to the coast and perching on what must be lower buttresses of the peak. It was incredibly beautiful, so wonderful I found myself laughing. I whooped, somersaulted in the air and dived down to *Stormy Petrel*.

'Oh, my god. Oh god, Mist, you're completely right! You're a genius, Mist. I take back all I've ever slandered. It's there, where you said it'd be, and it's magnificent. Magnificent! I mean, even Awia never had anything like this—'

'Can you see it?' asked Lightning.

'He can see it,' said Mist, hanging on the wheel.

I aligned myself in the wind flow, beside the railings, facing towards her. 'I've never seen anything like it! It's so pretty it's just not true. Like ...' Like a piece of the Shift in the Fourlands. I paused, and described it more calmly. A scout is useless unless he gives sensible reports. At sea level, the heat was stronger; it annoyingly slowed my thinking. 'I can see the town, though at the moment it's just a speck. I can see the island's whole west face – actually Tris is a huge mountain growing up out of the sea!'

Mist carefully noted a compass reading in her ledger with a pencil stub, and snapped her telescope out from its case. This was utterly fantastic – a new part of the Empire we—

A gust nearly sent me into the waves. I was losing too much height. I gestured to Lightning, 'Chuck me that ... and that,' pointing to a water bottle and a hunk of bread. He threw them from the back railing one at a time. I dived and caught them. 'I can't wait to scale the summit. I'm going for a closer look.'

'No!'

Try and stop me. I said, 'Don't worry, I'll be back before your heart beats twice.'

I half-folded my wings for strength, pulled them down through the air resistance. Mist had said the town was called Capharnaum. I repeated that word aloud as I cruised, the only wholly Trisian word I knew. I couldn't wait to speak to the islanders in their ancient language. That is, if they didn't run away at the sight of me. I was used to flatlanders staring, or their outright hostility. Once in a Hacilith café the waiter put a bowl of milk and a fish skeleton on the floor for me when I ordered beer and a sandwich. My gang returned the following night and burnt the café to the ground.

Nowadays I give Zascai something to stare at; I dress up to the role. But surely no Trisian would have heard of a Rhydanne before. I was very tempted to scare them on purpose. I'd have an eager audience, no doubt about that! They will just have to take me as I am, I concluded. After all, they're part of the Empire and I'm their Messenger as well.

Over an hour, the island grew larger and details appeared. Dark green bushes on the mountainside became twisted trees, an olive grove. A rugged shape in the centre of the town became an outcrop, and on its summit, fifty metres higher than the town's rooftops, a bright white complex resolved into a series of elegant, airy buildings with fluted columns, much bigger than I expected. It could be the manor house. The outcrop seemed to move across my field of vision faster than the mountainside behind it, so I could tell that it was a pinnacle standing out alone.

Black flecks on the sea became big canoes with five to ten men paddling in each, riding the surf with great dexterity. They even drew their paddles in and went flying down the funnels of the waves. A white strip underlining the town was a harbour wall of admirable workmanship, nearly three times larger than the lighthouse quay at Awndyn. Rolling surf broke and peeled along it. Elsewhere on the coast, cypress trees extended right down to high-water mark, where the rocks were yellow with lichen and stained black by the sea. The trees were small and gnarled; the Trisians had no chance of ever building a caravel. Breakers boomed on the shingle, deep-water rollers thundered in parallel lines. Above their reach, an amber band of seaweed and a white band of shellfish striped the boulders.

Capharnaum was like a model. Closer now, and the model came alive, men and women in the streets. A winged lad in a straw hat cast a fishing line, and paid no attention as my shadow sped over him. I soared up, and marvelled.

A warm, delicious breeze blew constantly in from the sea, like the updraught from the hypocaust rooms in an Awian bathhouse. It's certainly difficult to find lift this good on the mainland. I was flying automatically, so occupied in staring around that I hadn't realised how little effort I was putting in. I rode the same current with several gulls, who watched with an attitude that said: You can't be serious. We whirled round each other, but they were the better gliders and they gained height. I peeled out of the thermal to look at the town.

I glided as slowly as I could without stalling and constantly made tiny adjustments with my legs acting as a forked tail, counteracting the air currents that now came from all directions. Even so I flew too rapidly to see much detail and I could only look down on the roofs.

Two main streets intersected in the centre of Capharnaum. They were surrounded by smaller roads that ran in a neat criss-cross pattern, like a grid. The houses were spaced very regularly; it was bizarre, completely different from Hacilith's sprawl and unlike the graceful curves in which Awians build. Cypresses flanked empty avenues leading north and south into the countryside. Roughly at five-kilometre intervals along the roadside there were tall black and white posts like gibbets, with short planks nailed at right angles to them. Probably some kind of flagpole.

At the edges the street grid lost coherence and the houses were jumbled together. Trees invaded between them. All the villas were exactly the same size, square and whitewashed, dazzling and clean. The terracotta tiles on their shallow roofs looked like overlapping feathers. Their square windows had alabaster screens instead of glass; their shutters were open. They had porticos surrounding square peristyle lawns or dark green gardens, some with statues. They faced out to sea. It was quiet, unlike Hacilith, it was tranquil. I could see no poor section of town, no slums, no kids standing on street corners. It did not resemble any town in the Fourlands, but maybe when Micawater was founded it looked like this. If I flew any lower I risked being seen. With an acute sense of unreality I wheeled above the town. It's a dream, I assured myself. It's all a damn dream.

Here the warm wind smelt of sage and thyme, herbs growing wild. Shrubs among the boulders bore yellow flowers. At the far north and south extremes of the island, on the gentle slope before the mountainside became steep maquis, there were two other towns, smaller than Capharnaum. Both seemed connected with the sea, but pale green terraced hillsides stepped above them.

Thin air at last, I thought. I had a brief glimpse of the mountain top – my god – is that snow on the summit? I wanted more than anything to investigate the white gleams and see if they were snow patches, and roll in them if they were, but Mist would not receive my report kindly if it focused on conditions at the peak rather than in the towns.

The mountain top was not a sheer arête as in Darkling – it didn't come to a point. It was a smooth, arid ridge that leant over into a big bowl-shaped hollow not visible from sea level. It was veiled with chutes of small grey stones. Clouds formed on the edge of the bowl and blew eastward.

That side of the island looked uninhabited, although it was too far to see any detail. Decaying cracks split the sheer sea cliffs, a drop of at least three hundred metres around which white birds swirled and dived. The black, denticulate reefs below them were like a half-submerged wolf's jawbone; churning water smashed over the narrow serrated molars and canine points. I determined to warn Mist. But calm and remote, far off in the eastern ocean, two other peaks of smaller islets emerged in a line.

Tris was fresh, quiet and, it seemed to me, content. My duty to bring news of the Empire to the island will probably be the most important task I will ever have as Messenger.

I winged back to the ships, which were still scudding stoically towards Tris. The weak wind did not affect the enormous rollers they rode. *Petrel*'s deck rose up to my feet as I landed next to Mist. 'Tris is an archipelago,' I said. 'I flew right over; there are more islands on the other side.'

'Did anyone see you?' she demanded.

'No. I saw ladies in smocks selling food from the porches of townhouses and boys drying green fishing nets on the harbour wall, but not one of the Capharnai saw me,' I said with dignity, coining an Awian word.

'When we arrive you must *not* fly. I don't want them to know; I mean, you'll only frighten them. Did you see any vessels other than canoes?'

'Don't think so ...'

'What about signs of Insects? Any Walls? Paperlands?'

'No.'

'Fortresses?' Lightning asked. 'Bastions? Châteaux?'

'It's too big,' I said defensively. 'You have to see for yourself. There are plantations, vineyards, and goats on the mountainside.'

'Typical Jant, always thinking about sex,' Mist smiled, looking into the distance. A crosswind tangled her fine hair. The waves were reflected on the ships' sides as a moving mesh of light.

I returned to the *Melowne* in time to hear Fulmer complaining. The billows tossed the caravel every direction but forward. She ran headlong down a steep wave and pitched into the next rising roller. Puffs of spray burst off her keel and splattered back. We went up and down, up and down vertically on an irregular see-saw. Wrenn and I retreated to the poop deck.

Fulmer leant against the wheel's kicks. He was having a lot of trouble steering. *Melowne* jerked sideways every time she struck and wrenched the wheel from his hands. The broad ship had a massive drag; he couldn't keep her from sliding aslant into the troughs of the swell. 'Damn it,' he wheezed. 'Mist will just have to slow down for us, yes? Shit, she makes it look effortless. Get the flying sails in. Sea anchor back there and see if I can keep her prow half as straight as *Petrel*.'

From the poop deck we could see the back of Fulmer's head. Not a brown hair was out of place. As usual, and against all the odds, he looked pristine, still a court dandy three thousand, eight hundred kilometres from Queen Eleonora's entourage. Fulmer's genteel manner impressed me until I remembered that he had known about the Insect even before we set sail, and it was he who had been feeding it bones all this time.

Wrenn scrutinised the horizon. 'I can see it! I can see a tiny island!'

'In the next couple of hours you'll find it is huge.'

Up to the deck came barrels of wine, and bar silver was stacked in quadrilaterals. A forest of colourful pennants unfurled. As Tris filled our vision, the evergreen and pumice shore proceeding past, unbridled excitement overcame the crews. Mist and Fulmer found it difficult to keep the sailors working; men stared and pointed at houses, vineyards, the palace on the crag. They waved at tanned Capharnai fishermen in the first canoes.

Mist brought the ships in. She yelled commands to her crew, keeping them moving. I heard her from the *Melowne* three ship-lengths behind; the tension in her voice made me nervous. In contrast, Fulmer gave his orders in a quiet, assured style, politely addressing the hands. They copied every movement of the *Petrel*'s men, furling the sails in completely synchronised manoeuvres. Fulmer's ship sailed slick as fiddly clockwork in the *Stormy Petrel*'s wake.

The harbour walls pincered together on our left and right and formed a strait about five hundred metres wide. Dead centre of the channel was a flat-topped rock with a lighthouse on it. It towered above us, one hundred metres high, built on a square base half the *Petrel*'s length. As we glided past, the sailors became even more frantic. At first I assumed they were shocked by the lighthouse's great height, which was certainly surprising considering that the Trisians only have canoes. Then I realised they were pointing at the fire reflector: it was made of polished gold. The fittings of the beacon were all solid gold.

Fulmer called, 'Jant, do you see?'

'Yes, I do!'

'It's the most glorious thing I've ever seen.'

I muttered to Wrenn, 'What I don't like is the fact Mist never mentioned it before.'

I wore my purple scarf wrapped around my waist as a cummerbund, stripy black and white leggings under cut-off denim shorts. A black kerchief kept back all my locks and albatross feathers. The swell was making Wrenn look green but he was determined to watch the tumult on the main deck. He clung onto a network of ropes. 'It's all right to lean on the deadeyes. Sailors before the mast are going to reef the mainsail now, look.'

'Fascinating ...'

'And lower it on parr—'

'Oh, shut up!'

He stared forward at the bow, which pointed like a pike at the town. 'Do you think there are ladies in Capharnaum?' he asked.

I glanced at him. 'Well, obviously.'

'No. Whores, I mean.'

'Oh. That kind of lady. They're human, well, they look it to me,' I regarded my fingernails in a secretarial gesture. 'So they'll have wine, women and song.'

CHAPTER 10

As we crossed the harbour our ships fell under the lee of the mountain. The lagoon's surface was mirror-still; it reflected *Petrel* and *Melowne*'s images from waterline to masthead. Their sails went slack and they coasted in very slowly indeed, on the last of their momentum. Fulmer ordered the last sails furled and I looked up to see clear blue sky between the masts for the first time in three months.

Trisian men, women and children poured out of the town's façade and rushed to form a crowd on the sea wall and all along the corniche. The men's clothes looked quite plain – white or beige linen or silk tunics with coloured borders, and loose trousers underneath. Some of the girls wore pastel-dyed stoles over their double-layer dresses but none of their garments looked embroidered or rich.

Men pushed out dark wood canoes and jumped in, paddling towards us. The canoes had outriggers; blue and white eyes were painted on their prows. They moved very swiftly and were soon clustered around our hull. The Trisians shouted and pointed, held up all kinds of food and objects. Dozens of hands reached to the portholes, waving spiny fruit, enormous seeds, stoppered jars, dead fish on skewers, silver flasks. Our sailors hung over the railings eagerly offering anything to hand on the deck. They passed or threw down belaying pins, hatchets and belt buckles, the plumb line from the bow.

Fulmer's composure broke. He yelled, 'No trading! Stop it, fools, before you give them your vests and pants! No barter, till Mist gives the word! Hacilith law and punishment applies from now on.'

He glanced at me. 'The rash bastards will swap anything for curios. They'd pull the nails from the futtocks and even trade our instruments away if I don't watch them. We must beware of thieves, yes/no? Even a fishhook from Tris is a novelty that will fetch money in the Fourlands now. Still, at least Capharnai are friendly.'

The *Petrel*, in front of us, glided through the reflections of Capharnaum's first houses, came alongside the harbour wall and docked. Our ship's salt-stained prow stopped just a metre behind the ornate windows of *Petrel*'s stern. Then two gangways slipped down and simultaneously locked into place. Wrenn immediately ran to the quay, where he stood smiling and waving, the first of our company to set foot on Tris. Native men and women approached him, asking questions that of course he couldn't understand so he just kept nodding in cheerful agreement.

There were no mooring loops on the wharf so Mist made her crew unload the stern and bow anchors of both ships and place them on the pavement with the ropes drawn taut.

Mist and Fulmer descended the gangways of their respective ships and met on the quayside. They shook hands politely in front of the astonished townspeople. 'We did it!' she said.

'I had every confidence in you, Eszai,' said Fulmer. He smoothed a couple of invisible wrinkles out of his suit sleeve with a spotless hand. The breeze opened his jacket and I saw a dagger swinging from his belt.

I descended to dry land at the same time as Lightning disembarked from the *Petrel*. He carried his strung longbow over his shoulder; arrow nocks protruded from the quiver at his waist. He glanced at the windows of every villa fronting the quay.

Wrenn bounded to a halt, panted, 'Have you noticed that none of the Capharnai have any weapons? Some of the fishermen have knives in their sashes but they look a bit odd.'

'It's true,' said Lightning. 'Jant, do you see?'

I said, 'I think the blades are bronze.'

Lightning said, 'But obviously there's no reason for Capharnai to know of swords. The Fourlands had no swords before the Insects arrived.'

'And then they were invented pretty quickly!' I grinned. I was loving the attention.

Mist gave me an expectant look. 'Make your introductions, Jant.'

I spread my arms and began to address the townspeople with a speech I had carefully prepared: 'Governors, ladies and gentlemen, thank you for receiving us from the Fourlands. We have brought some gifts as a sign of goodwill: casks of wine and silver ingots—'

The large crowd of people giggled as if I was mad. Mist and I glanced at each other. 'Keep going,' she said.

'We would like to meet the governors of Capharnaum to tell them of the Em—'

The crowd parted to let a man through. He walked forward until he faced us alone. I assumed he was the Capharnai's own representative. He was a tall old man, every aspect of his comportment upright and efficient. His eyes were the same dark brown as beer-bottle glass, hair every shade of grey, once so windblown it would never lie flat. He was dry as a ship's rib. His face was pinched; his mouth slotted in under his cheekbones. It looked like he was smiling wryly all the time, with a wicked grin that enticed me to smile with him, like a collaborator.

He wore a short cloak over a tunic with a deep hem border. His laced boots with open toes were so unusual Fulmer especially couldn't stop staring at them. No doubt Fulmer was wondering if he could start a fashion in the Fourlands for toeless boots.

The Trisian spoke slowly, giving me time to translate. The terms that I could not decipher, I left as he gave them. 'My name is Vendace. I was a fisherman, now elected to the Senate. They have sent me to thank you for coming here. Are you the same as the boat that appeared nine months ago?'

'Yes, from the Fourlands. Call me Jant. I can speak Trisian but please talk slowly; I don't know many words. My friends can't speak it at all; I'll translate for them.'

'What's he saying?' asked Mist, who was becoming very frustrated.

'He's welcoming us,' I said in Awian.

'Tell him I'm in charge and ask him to give his word that my ships will be safe here tonight,' said Mist.

I told Vendace, and added, 'We're here on peaceful terms.'

Vendace said, 'We saw your sails this morning – the Senate has convened in an emergency session to discuss our course of action. The Senate is still in progress and they have asked me to bring you to the House. Our constitution warns against contact with another land; our constitution is important to us.'

Mist tugged my arm. 'What's he saying?'

'I've no idea. He seems to be going on about their fitness.' I paused for a second to stop my mind whirling. 'He's offered to take us to the governors' house.'

Mist said, 'Well, at least ask a guarantee for our safety on land. I see some victuals being brought out. Thank him for giving me the opportunity to buy provisions and offer to pay with the bar silver.'

I stumbled over a translation to Vendace. The Trisians surrounding us all began laughing again. Even the fisherman couldn't keep a straight face – he smirked.

'Why are they sniggering?' Lightning enquired.

Mist asked, 'Are you actually saying what I tell you to say?'

I wished that she would stop hassling me. I hadn't had any chance to practise. I pinched the bridge of my nose. 'Well, I think so! Or I could have asked him to serve us a warm dog.'

Lightning said, 'They laugh when you speak of – of what?'

'The wine and silver,' I said.

Lightning said, 'Hmm. I should think they have wine of their own. And more than enough gold, if you remember the priceless lighthouse mirrors.'

I looked more closely at the crowd. 'You know, none of the Capharnai are wearing jewellery. But gold's available here; in fact it's abundant. Do you think it could be that Capharnai don't care for it?'

Lightning indicated a small girl who was sucking her thumb. A gold band held back her dark hair. 'That puts us on a level with their children. And I will wager that her crown is pure, refined gold.' He removed the circlet from his head.

Mist rubbed her eyes. 'But ... Well, if precious metals are worthless we've no valuables to trade with. This island seems to lack nothing; what do we have that they could possibly want?'

'Steel,' said Wrenn.

Fulmer said, 'You clever, clever man! Yes, we can give them nails, tacks and chain links. Knife blades and hatchets were in demand; I saw the canoeists admiring them. How about halberds from the *Melowne*? The Trisians must use axes so they'll recognise halberds that are superior to bronze. They should be willing to accept what is better, yes?'

'It's possible,' Mist said guardedly.

Vendace remained unflappable but kept glancing at my eyes. He showed us a stone cistern on the quayside and Mist organised two squads of sailors to fill barrels with fresh water. She arranged another team to buy fruit, meat and vegetables from Capharnai merchants who were already approaching us out of the town, but she forbade them to barter for any other goods, or to buy items for their own keeping. Then she turned to her second-in-command. 'Viridian, tell *Melowne*'s bosun to obey my orders and follow them yourselves if you love me and your place in my fleet. Don't leave the ships unprotected. Move them only if you're threatened ... And if we don't come back tonight, you know what to do.'

'Certainly, Mist,' she said. 'And good luck, Mum.'

Mist was dissatisfied with Vendace's appearance. She said, 'The Circle doesn't need a fisherman.'

'I was unaware we have the authority to recruit for the Circle,' Lightning commented.

Mist gave him a venomous look. I suppose she was right; it would be a stroke of luck if a leader of Tris excelled at some occupation and could join the Circle. She said quietly, 'This man is elderly enough to be very grateful for immortality.'

'Wisdom comes with age,' said Wrenn, vaguely.

'Maybe it does, here,' said Lightning.

'Aye, well no matter what venerable age he has reached, he's still a baby compared to us.'

Vendace had listened to their exchange without understanding a word. He smiled and pointed a direction through the crowd; we followed him.

The heat was like a barrier, and every rare midday gust of wind just blew hot air at us, into our skin, and offered no relief. It seemed to come in waves, each more stifling and cloying than the last. I unlaced my shirtsleeves, slipped them off and tucked them in my belt. The heat made the five of us walk slowly, with smooth, languid movements.

Fulmer said, 'I could quite happily live here. See the promenade, it's splendid, yes?'

'Yeah,' said Wrenn. 'I've never seen such sexy girls. Check out that honey with the short skirt.'

Fulmer selected a cigarette from a whale's-tooth ivory case and screwed it into a holder. He rubbed his short beard. 'I plan to come back and never leave at all, at all. I have no ties and our huntress Queen will gladly grant me permission. This is much better than Awia, which copies the Castle. We turn everything into a bloody competition, from maths to pottery, and we wear ourselves out. Here no one's the best and no one cares. See how happy they are?'

We were led from the harbour into a long, straight main boulevard bordered by white marble columns. Steles stood at regular intervals, topped with statues of men and women draped in cloth. I counted them, and noticed that after every ten statues an archway spanned the street. Smaller alleys led into the road-grid on either side of us, between the two-storey buildings. Small shops opened onto the pavement, with striped canvas porticoes: a confectioner selling pasties and pastries; sausages hung above smoked viands and a mess of octopus in a butcher's; a barber swept his shop.

Everybody was pointing things out and bursting with questions, far too many for me to translate. 'Look at the vines,' Mist said, enthralled. They twined up a trellis on the last quayside house, heavy with black grapes, tendrils reaching to the terracotta chimney.

I surreptitiously peered over the green window boxes as we passed, seeing that the furniture in the lower room was slight and elegant. A small dog lay curled on a chair cushion. The cool walls were painted with a stylised frieze of pearl divers in an underwater garden. Trisian art seemed to cover everyday items rather than being framed.

'The knives,' Wrenn said. 'Ask him about the bronze daggers.'

'I certainly will not!'

Fulmer indicated a workshop where a canoe was being carved. Vendace said, 'We travel for hundreds of kilometres around Tris and the unoccupied islands.'

'Hundreds?' I asked.

Vendace nodded with enthusiasm for his profession. 'Easily, past the Motley Isles into the open ocean! Why do you question it? I'll speak slower if you want.'

Next we saw a large paved piazza surrounded by colonnades. Mist said, 'This must be a marketplace. Isn't it cute?'

A restaurant occupied the open, airy ground floor of the nearest block.

374

About twenty Capharnai tumbled out and joined those lining the street to stare at us. A stout café proprietor wore a loose tunic, a single piece of material gathered at the waist by a sash. He beckoned. 'Come in, come and dine.'

Vendace raised his brown hands apologetically. 'Excuse me, Derbio, I must take our visitors to the Amarot.'

The round man giggled. 'Of course, but they're invited to drink tea with us afterwards.'

I was thrilled that I could understand a dialogue between two native speakers; my ear for the language was improving. I said, 'It would be a pleasure. What's tea?'

He seemed staggered. 'By Alyss, you are in for a treat!'

I listened to my friends' conversation. Mist was enthusing, 'The shops are so clean. No smoke, no grime ...'

'No litter,' said Fulmer approvingly. 'You don't get that in Hacilith.'

I agreed: 'I thought something was wrong. No one's standing at street corners or porches. When I lived in Hacilith I never wanted to walk past threatening groups of lads.'

I translated for Vendace, who said, 'Youths don't wish to loiter. They are occupied learning the trade of their choice.'

'Not all the time, surely.'

Vendace said, 'In the evenings they discourse in the tea shops.'

'Wow. Tea must be powerful stuff. Doesn't Capharnaum have any crime at all?'

There was a hint of smugness in Vendace's voice. 'Of course there is, occasionally, but why should people break the law when they all decide on the laws?'

Wrenn whispered, 'That waiter was wearing a tablecloth.'

Lightning said laconically, 'What's odd about that? It's much more practical than the clothes we have now; you can put your wings through the back.'

'How do you know?'

'My mortal years were not so long ago that I don't remember them, Serein.'

As we walked through town, I noticed that the houses really were similar; apart from superficial variations in paint and plaster their furnishings were all equal. I wondered aloud, 'No one is poor.'

I elaborated for Vendace, who didn't understand me. He said, 'Our currency is based on labour. Every trade is paid the same, in days and hours. You can get more if you work longer, but people tend to work the same length of time. Time is the most valuable thing that exists, surely?' He unfolded some banknotes from his purse and showed us. 'That one is five hours. This one's the smallest – thirty minutes. What do you have?'

'Coins. Notes are small change for us. See here? Where we come from is similar because everyone in the Castle's given the same yearly handout – just a pittance. We can only ask for more money for appropriate projects.' I thought, if we give the Capharnai steel, it would be worth hundreds and hundreds of hours in their currency, as precious as months of lifetime.

Mist pressed me with more questions to translate. I waved my hands and glanced at the sky, trying to find words quickly, but Vendace stopped me: 'Please save your queries for the Senate. Then we can all hear and you won't have to repeat yourself.'

In the centre of town the road passed through a rotunda. The surfaces of its columns were covered with gaudy mosaics, squares of gold, blue sapphire and deep garnet; illustrated panels decorated the edges of its conical roof.

We approached the crag, and the street began to ascend a slope. The gradient became steeper with a series of long steps. We were heading for the columned halls high above. I pointed up to them. 'Lightning, aren't the buildings beautiful? Your pad looks a bit like that.'

He scanned them eagerly. 'The Tealean north front of my house emulates the style. It was a fashionable revival in the latter half of the sixth century.'

'A *revival*! Then how old could this be?'

'Sometime in the early four hundreds the Insects put an end to the people who originally built like this. That was before my time, but I'm sure I recollect my history lessons.'

Mist glanced at us. 'Yes, but we don't need one now! We are making history, gentlemen. Will you pay attention, please?'

Vendace led us along the magnificent boulevard, between the shuttered dwellings. Suddenly we emerged from the town, the red riot of roofs below us. The panorama extended to the ocean beyond the massive harbour walls which enclosed the lagoon and narrowed together either side of the beacon islet. The Trisians' canoes sheltered within it, secure from the breaking surf. Here and there between the sharp corners of the buildings I caught glimpses of a clean narrow river glittering until it merged with the ocean just south of the harbour.

'The Architect must see this,' I said.

Mist combed her pearly hair out with her fingers, pulled at the front of her strappy T-shirt and stared at the incredible view. 'We could easily get trapped up here,' she said. I was an unarmed emissary, but Lightning and Serein carried their customary bow and broadsword as respective signs of their status. Mist walked between them, knowing that with Lightning's lethality at a distance and Wrenn's invincibility at close quarters she was as safe as in a fortress.

I was wilting badly; I wasn't born for a temperature of forty degrees.

376

My clothes clung to the backs of my knees, my armpits, chest. I was more uncomfortable even than Fulmer in his designer suit; I was desperate to stretch my wings. Mist had decreed that their strength would raise too many questions among the Trisians. I had folded them under my baggy shirt, which gave me an unattractive hump running the length of my back. The wings' elbows brushed behind my thighs and the wrists hugged at the level of my shoulders. My wings' leading edges were damp; from the wrist of each one to the small of my back the feathery patagium webbing cleaved together with sweat. The flight feathers stuck out from under my shirt.

'Don't spread,' Mist muttered.

'You don't know what this is like. I'm boiling!'

'Come now, it's no hotter than a Micawater summer,' Lightning said cheerfully.

The crowd of Trisians were not at all bothered by the sun. They kept pace with our party at a respectful distance and chattered together inquisitively, with curious and affable expressions. Children ran among them, peering from behind their parents' legs. A flock of white doves burst from a roof, wings whistling. I strained for refreshment from the faintest breeze, and I envied them. They didn't have to hide their ability to fly.

The street started to zigzag up, its steps closer together; it turned hairpin bends as the gradient steepened. It was immaculate with low walls on either side beyond which was open ground strewn with boulders under craggy outcrops. Blooms of butterflies rose and fell on lavender, wavered over planted hibiscus, lemon trees and bougainvillea, honey-drunk.

Then we reached the flat hilltop and entered the open courtyard of two dazzling white granite buildings. At the far end was the massive columned square edifice we had seen from the quayside, set edge-on to the sheer side of the crag's cliff. A second, longer hall of the same two-storey height adjoined it on our left. It had pilasters with scroll capitols set flat against its walls, a roof made of red pantiles. I was awestruck by the vibrant buildings; they were only the size of the Throne Room but somehow as impressive as the entire Castle.

The crowd trotted in behind us, and when we stopped they gathered round, watching Fulmer exhale smoke and stub out his cigarette in its amber holder.

'This is the Amarot,' Vendace proclaimed. 'From here, the Senate cares for Tris. Please follow me ...'

'It's the hall of the governors,' I said in Awian. 'Come on.'

We crossed the courtyard that was one hundred metres square, paved with mosaics in copper, blue glass and black ceramic. Geometrical designs ran round its edge, and in its four quarters there were pictures: galleys, a weighing scales, a dolphin and Insects. *Insects?*

The mosaic showed a young woman with brown flowing hair, standing in a swarm of Insect heads and huge ant-like bodies. She held a wine-coloured pennant that streamed out behind her and the folds of her dress moulded closely around her breasts and thighs. She had flowers in her hair and an expression that looked more pained than noble.

Lightning recognised it at once; his eyes opened wide. 'I'm right,' he said. 'It's Alyss of the Pentadrica.'

'It must be a coincidence. How in the Empire could they know that story?'

'I don't know, Jant. I really don't know.'

Vendace led us through an open door into the long building. The air was cool and still, and we all stood blinking for a second until our eyes adjusted.

'If this is a church,' said Wrenn, 'then thank god's coffee break.'

Vendace said, 'This connects with the Senate House. I will show you the way. It is the library of Tris. A quarter of a million books have been collected here. Danio is the Senate member who takes special charge of it.'

'It's a library,' I translated.

'Then thank the librarians!' Fulmer took a cambric kerchief from his pocket and dabbed his forehead with it.

A library! I trailed my fingers along the cedar shelves as we passed, and my heart beat faster than in the Moren double marathon. A quarter of a million books! It may not be as extensive as the royal collection in Rachiswater, or the archives of Hacilith University, but I had been through most of those.

Vendace saw my rapt expression and chuckled. Every single book was unknown to the Empire and brimful with new information I could spend the next century piecing together. Some of the larger tomes were attached to their shelves with brass chains. They were bound in leather and their pages were paper or vellum. There were coffers full of codices and square baskets packed with papers.

The lower stacks were divided into pigeonholes storing scroll cylinders made of bronze. Some were green with verdigris and others polished by use. There were ledgers of loose leaves; slim volumes bound in boards, in violet and dark red buckram. There were folded maps and plans of every town on the island.

A few books lay open on a table where a reader had left them. One was actually hand-copied and beautifully illustrated with coloured ink. The rest were woodcut-block-printed, which again showed how far behind the times Tris was.

We passed bay after bay; each shelf had yellowing posters listing its contents but Vendace was leading too quickly for me to translate. All the same, I was beside myself with joy; I had found my treasure.

As we were led through the long room I began to grasp the enormous extent of the repository – it was floor-to-ceiling full of recorded knowledge. A few solitary scholars occupied chairs and tables in the bays. Fluid music drifted in from outside, a stringed instrument, but the windows were too high for me to see who was playing.

I tried to glimpse words on the covers and I lingered until I was trailing behind the group. Wrenn and Fulmer gave the books not one glance. Fulmer swung his walking stick as if he was taking a lunchtime stroll in Rachiswater Grand Place. Wrenn's astonished gaze scanned everything without perceiving it. Mist was trying to communicate with Vendace and took no notice of the books. Lightning, however, had the gleam of fascination in his eye.

'It's wonderful, isn't it?' I said.

He nodded with the ardour of a collector. 'What an excellent discovery! I must have copies made and shipped back to my library. Of course it won't generate the profit Awia so badly needs, but the knowledge might help us. I think I can afford the payload-room for one or two shelves.'

I wondered if Lightning could see any work of beauty without wanting to own it. Sculptors and painters in the Fourlands vied for his patronage, knowing he would preserve their creations and provide the means to support them for life. 'We must curate this for the Empire,' he continued.

'It looks like the Trisians have done a good job of that already.'

'Jant,' Mist called back over her shoulder. 'Stop dawdling. Are you under the influence? Shall we maroon you here and pick you up in a couple of hundred years?'

The books on the nearest shelf seemed to be works of philosophy and natural science: *The Germ Theory of Medicine*, *Manifesto of Equality*, *Optics and the Behaviour of Light*, *The Atomic Nature of Matter and other theories by Pompano of Gallimaufry*, *Zander of Pasticcio's 'The Explication of Dreams'*, *An Enquiry into the Uses of Saltpetre*, *Worlds Beyond Worlds: Transformed Consciousness*, *Some Descriptions of the Afterlife*, *Tris Istorio – A History of Tris*.

Superb. I whipped *Tris Istorio* from the shelf and behind my back. I shoved the little book under my wings into my waistband and pulled my shirt down over it. No one had seen me. Vendace was still talking to Mist.

We went along an open corridor that joined the library to the taller square building. Its entrance was an alabaster arch with an inscription engraved above it. Mist stretched up and swept her finger over the words. 'What does this say?'

I considered it. 'You're reading it the wrong way. They write left to right. Um ... It says, "All men are the same."'

'You bet they are,' said Mist.

We found ourselves in a semicircular open area like a floor-level stage. In front and stretching up above us were rows of stepped seats on which around fifteen men and women sat, watching us. Some were young, some elderly. To our left, the columns were open to the air, the sheer side of the crag. The hall seemed to extend into space. We stood on the proscenium and felt the weight of the audience's scrutiny.

'What is this arrangement?' Lightning frowned.

I asked Vendace, who said, 'This is the Senate. Elected democratically—'

I waved a hand to slow him. 'I don't know that word.'

Vendace stopped and stared at me.

Mist said, 'What did he say?'

I struggled: 'There's no Awian analogue. It's – it's like the voting that takes place for mayors in Diw and Vertigo townships in Morenzia, or to choose a governor for Hacilith. But not just between influential families, for everybody. Um ... rule by the people ... That's what Vendace said.'

Lightning unslung his longbow and unstrung it. He bowed and whispered to me, 'This will do nothing but fray tempers and affect our judgement. We're depending on you to loose words as swiftly as arrows. Who's in charge of this court?'

'I think they all are,' I said.

Lightning concentrated on Vendace. For all the old man's gravity, he looked unsettled under Lightning's grey assured gaze. By now my throat was so dry it was sore. 'Can I have a drink?' I asked Vendace. After a while I was handed a green glass of water, cool and so pure it tasted of nothing.

A boy with a tray provided us all with glasses while Vendace continued to tell the Senate about our ships. I listened but was dimly aware of Wrenn sneaking out behind me, the way we had come, towards the library. I didn't know where he was going; I was concentrating too hard to worry about him. Our prestigious arrival was not proceeding the way I had hoped.

Vendace said, 'We are debating if we should let you stay, and whether or not we assent to any contact with the Fourlands. Our constitution advises against it, because we do not want your culture to damage ours, of which we are proud. Ours is a perfect society built on reason. There are myths that tell of others, very undesirable in comparison.

'The Senate is obliged to discuss every issue for three days before voting. So matters are considered thoroughly and no spurious motions are ever raised. We will let you know our decision in two days' time.'

I translated word for word. Fulmer almost laughed. 'Really, three days, the sluggards,' he spluttered. 'Imagine if on the battlefield you had to wait that long!'

'It sounds inefficient,' Lightning agreed. 'If we followed such a tradition the Insects would overrun us all the way to Cape Brattice before we made up our minds to fight.'

I grinned. 'Look, you two, be quiet!'

The senators murmured with curiosity, trying to figure out what we were saying. Mist hushed us, angered by her dependence on me. I marshalled my scanty knowledge of Trisian and introduced our company, ending with myself: 'Comet Jant Shira, the Emperor's Messenger, and you can call me Jant. We've come to tell you the fortunate news: you all have the chance to join the Circle and have eternal life, as we do. Time does not age us … Although I can't really prove it unless we sit here for ten years … Anyway, we want to remind Tris of its place in the Empire; we've come at the behest of the Emperor San, that your island and the mainland may no longer be adrift but firm allies—' I halted because at the mention of San the senators leant to each other and started talking.

Vendace turned to the fifteen men and women; they conferred together, speaking in complicated terms at a natural speed, much faster than I could hope to follow. They came to a consensus and informed Vendace, who motioned for me to continue.

'San makes us, and will make the best of you, immortal. We fight the Insects, but—' Another buzz passed between them, and I knew I had hit a chord. 'Insects, yes, like the picture in your courtyard.'

A young lady rose from the centre of the audience. She wore a short dress and a patterned stole wrapped around her body. Her sandal thongs criss-crossed her slender legs to the knee. Her features were light, her hair close-cropped. Unlike Vendace, she had wings; they were small, brunette and very pert. 'Danio, Bibliophylax,' Vendace announced. The library's keeper, if I understood him correctly.

Danio said, 'Insects are just a story; there's no evidence whatsoever. And how can people be eternal? You've taken old tales and you expect us to believe them? The threat of death defines humanity; nothing is as unnatural as an immortal.'

I translated, saying, 'Mist, they don't believe in Insects. I think it's your turn now.'

Through me, Mist spoke to Vendace, but everyone in the Senate assumed her words were also addressed to them. 'Sir, we brought an Insect to show you Capharnai – I mean Trisians. It's imprisoned on our ship, so if you come to the harbour I'll give you a tour of the caravels.'

Vendace said, 'What do you think, Professor?'

Danio paused, reluctant, then answered smoothly, 'Our visitors' colossal boats themselves suggest this isn't a hoax. Yes, this is truly a historic occasion. If they really have an Insect and if the myths I've spent my life discrediting are true, I want to see it.' She stepped down over the stone benches to the stage, approached me closely and looked at my face. A bitten-nailed finger brushed over my Wheel scar and then down to rest on my feathers, questioningly. We gazed at each other. She leant forward; humour danced in her strikingly intelligent hazel eyes.

Mist announced, 'Jant, tell them that anyone who desires can return with us to see the Castle. I'll show them the glory of the Fourlands; give them a great welcome and lavish ambassadorial treatment.'

Danio roused herself and turned away from me. Damn.

I closely translated Mist's offer but none of the Senate seemed impressed. Much of the island's adventurous spirit must be lost, because the few individuals who possess it in abundance could not be frozen forever at their optimum age. I resumed my speech: 'You don't understand. The Empire's hundreds of times larger than Tris. Our city of Hacilith could swallow Capharnaum ten times. Our fyrd's half a million men, our fleet of caravels like those two in the harbour is—'

Vendace cut me short: 'We are not interested. The Senate must consider for no less than three days, and you can not influence our debate because you are not an inhabitant of Tris.'

I ran a hand over my hair in exasperation.

From the corner of my eye I saw Wrenn scuttle out under the archway, holding a shiny object in both hands. He dashed rudely over to me and tapped me on the wing, 'Jant!'

I could stand no more. 'That's Comet to you! Can't you be quiet? This is a crucial moment, our first meeting with the Senate and you interrupt me! What do you think you're ... ? Oh, what are you carrying?'

For a second I thought it was a Tine artefact and my reality slipped; I felt dizzy and disconnected. Wrenn held a chamber pot. It was identical to every other chamber pot in the Fourlands, except that it was shining metal: gold. It must have been very heavy.

Wrenn showed me. 'All the fittings in their privies are gold!'

'Bring it here,' I said. But the senator's stunned silence was breaking into embarrassed or inquisitive chuckles. Wrenn looked around at them and pointed to it, 'Have you any idea what this is *worth*?' he said in Awian, loudly and slowly.

The Senate may have worried that we were dangerous, or that we expected to be treated with obeisance. Instead, they saw we were amazed by a simple chamber pot brought for some reason out of their bathroom. They thought we looked ridiculous. All the senators started laughing, and the tension in the air completely lifted. The ladies in cotton smocks or robes put aside their paper fans. The gentlemen unclasped their cloaks and craned forward to see us. Genial hilarity echoed around the spacious auditorium.

Wrenn thrust it at me, 'I can't believe it. Can *you* believe it? It's worth a caravel and it's a piss-pot of all things!'

'Put it down!' I said. 'Bringing the privy into the governors' hall! You're making us look really stupid!'

'Why are you interested in that?' said Danio.

I said coolly, 'Oh, it's nothing. I've seen pots before. We have them in our culture too. We are civilised, not simple ... Oh, god.' I tapped it, and wisely understated, 'But we like this metal; we can use it. We would quite like to buy more.'

'Well,' Danio said. 'Jant, tell your delegation: if you love this ... object so much, if you want this base material, please take it. It can be a gift from Tris, our first offering of goodwill.' Applause broke out from the senators on the stepped benches; appreciative exclamations supported her words. Danio laughed and offered the chamber pot to Wrenn.

'They're giving it to you as a present,' I explained.

Wrenn took it gratefully and said in awe, 'Shouldn't I give something in return? Oh, obviously.' He unbuckled the fyrd-issue broadsword and scabbard from his belt. He held it flat in both hands and presented it to Danio.

'Thank you,' she said. She accepted the sword and pulled the scabbard to bare a little of the blade, which she examined closely.

'Please be careful,' I said. 'It's extremely sharp.'

She gazed minutely at me again and asked the inevitable question, 'What are you, anyway?'

I shuffled one wing out of my shirt and opened it. *Duck you suckers* was painted in red on the inside but, shrewd as she was, Danio couldn't transliterate. 'I'm winged, see, just like you, well nearly.' I pointed to my face and took a sheaf of thick hair in the other hand. 'My mother was Rhydanne; they're a mountain people who look like this. I know that's new and strange but please don't worry – I'm not dangerous. My long limbs are from my Rhydanne side too. My good looks, I get from both sides.'

All fifteen senators accompanied us to the harbour with a surprising lack of pomp and ceremony. They walked without any attendants and just chatted to each other, waved at the townspeople with a familiarity that was nothing like Fourlands governors. The senators were dressed as plainly as the folk in the piazza and tea shops; they did not seem to be very far removed from them.

The Sailor conducted the senators onto the *Melowne*. I held the hatchway open and helped the ladies descend to the hold. I didn't see their expressions, but I heard their shrieks, and from Danio I learnt a whole ream of Trisian words that I won't be putting in any guidebook.

We tried to hide the state of the crews from the senators. The sailors had clearly contravened Mist's orders and discipline on board *Petrel* and *Melowne* had started to crumble. They had traded and squirrelled away every Trisian commodity they could lay their hands on, especially agate statuettes and the gold beads, chaplets and tiaras that the children wore. Only a few halberds were left unsold and the men had broken open the caskets of broadswords and started trading them. Every single man was completely drunk, some so legless they lolled as they sat dribbling the juice of exotic fruits, sloshing wine into cups or crunching on overcooked sardines. The carpenter retched and farted as Mist's boatswain sons dragged him down to be locked in the brig. He prattled, 'Capharnai might not want us – but their kids have made me rich!'

A bottle rolled round in the scuppers and bumped against my foot. I picked it up and sniffed it. 'Brandy, or something similar. The merchants are selling spirits to our men!'

'This is dangerous,' Fulmer confided. 'I must keep discipline. Lightning and Mist will stow a fortune in *Melowne*, under the noses of all our deck-hands. I doubt I'll reach home without a mutiny.'

Throughout the second day, Mist and Lightning employed me to translate their deals with the merchants who waited in long queues. Capharnai carried books in their pockets and either read or stood in groups debating rarefied philosophical points. I yearned to spend the rest of our landfall in the library but the Sailor and Archer kept me hard at work with filthy lucre. My fluency improved, and I made friends with Danio, who taught me many new expressions before she was called away to the Senate, where they discussed us non-stop.

In return for the broadswords the Capharnai filled the *Melowne* with bales of cloves, tea leaves, sacks of peppercorns; we bought a cask of ambergris and one of frankincense. Our sister ship became a spice ship – I could smell it on the other side of town.

'Gold for steel, weight for weight,' Mist said smugly, examining the pale metal chamber pot. 'But that last silversmith – manufacturer of children's toys – kept the location of the mines a secret.'

Lightning said, 'No matter. I have gained a return of seven hundred per cent on the initial investment. This tea is too watery for my taste but, seeing as it will inevitably come to the Fourlands, it might as well come with me. And I've also discovered some excellent brandy.'

Wrenn used me to question every islander he met about sword fight-ing, and although I kept telling him it wasn't a Trisian tradition he was astounded to find that no one knew anything about the art.

'It seems to me they fight by talking,' I said.

Wrenn huffed. 'Yeah. But if Capharnaum becomes a manor the Castle will ask for its quota of fyrd for the Front. I'll be given hundreds of people to train from bloody scratch and I've a sneaking feeling they're not going to like it.' He disappeared into town with a party of midshipmen who were searching for a wine shop. The Senate permitted our men to leave the harbour only in small groups under the charge of Eszai. They didn't want the boulevard to be swamped with hell-raising sailors.

By evening I was sick of translating; confused with words swarming round my head until they lost their meanings. I was exhausted, but all in all it had been a fantastic day. As the sun set over the horizon where the Fourlands lay, Trisian canoes paddled in through the strait. After dusk the Capharnai entrepreneurs began to disperse and supper was served on board. The Senate retired and Danio came aboard to make notes and sketch the Insect. She was hypnotised by it, loitering in the hold, flinching every time it threw itself against the bars. When at ten p.m. Mist asked her to leave the ship, she stood on the quayside and stared as if insane at the exterior of the hull.

I told Mist that I intended to sleep on the mountainside. I walked out of sight of dainty Danio, who insisted on keeping vigil till tomorrow when Mist would let her back aboard. I took off and flew up, nap-of-the-earth in the pitch-black night, just a few metres above the mountain's contour. The lower slopes were olive groves, then dim rocky ground streaked along beneath me. I found a low cliff with an overhang and sheltered under it on the rough bare stone.

By lamplight, the *Stormy Petrel*'s crew lowered a spare mainsail and lashed the edges to two poles projecting from the portholes. The sail drooped into the warm water, which filled it, and the men started swimming in it. Men stood on the railing and dived in. I was too far to hear the splashes but I saw spray fly up in the flickering light of the yellow lanterns as *Petrel* rocked at her mooring.

Everything was delightful, and I lay alone. I have rarely been so happy. The air was cooler than at sea level; the rock conducted warmth away from my skin. It was a close night, so hot and humid that your balls stick to the inside of your thigh.

A light breeze cut through the cocoon of heat that moulded round me. It blew the smells of salt and peppermint into the rock shelter and carried occasional sounds from the town. Lamps were lit in the windows of Capharnaum's bizarre houses. I loved this scented island. I smiled and snuggled against the stone. I could think clearly now, for the first time in weeks. I no longer worried about the caravels, or Mist who wanted a hold on Tris that she could never be allowed to have.

I knew every road and air current of the Fourlands; now Tris was mine to explore. I could learn to discover like a mortal again and not a jaded Eszai. My sense of wonder was as strong as the first time I saw Hacilith city, when I was a foundling from Darkling with aching wings. In my first decade of life

I had seen a total of just ten people, all Rhydanne. The city pulsed humans around its streets in a stream that terrified me. I could fly no further so I hid, amazed, among the mayhem for a year.

I suddenly realised that I hadn't been thinking about scolopendium. If I was on the ship, my body would be crying out for it by now. I laughed with surprise and relief. If I could spend a few more nights alone on the mountain, in the tranquil rock shelter, I could do withdrawal. If I could spend a few more days in this serene and secure place, I contemplated, my mind would never turn to scolopendium again. No more sliding down the OD ravine. No more cat. No need for coffee, ephedrine or myristica. Or whisky, papaver, harmine, veronal or datura. Thujone, digitalis or psilocybin; not any more.

I breathed the island deeply into myself. I wanted to take it in, inhale it, drink it, the whole island, until it became part of me. I felt organised and in control. Alone on the mountain I lost all sense of self, and the troubles that drove me to use cat went too. The Castle was an ocean away. How brilliant, I was still immortal with none of the risks. I wanted to stay alone on the mountainside forever, until eventually with no self left and no thoughts at all I would merge with the landscape. In my haven there was no need for language or communication. For a few hours I was free from the sickly need to identify, classify and name with words every single thing.

CHAPTER II

I returned to the *Melowne* very early next morning and had a wash with sponge and pitcher. I decided to go back to sleep until the call should come from Lightning or Mist to engage me in another day's frantic business with spice merchants and jewellers, and with the host of fishermen-turned-salesmen. They seemed determined to swap everything they owned for our damask steel or a handful of arrows.

I was woken by loud yells and battering on the cabin door. 'Comet! Help! *Quickly!*'

From the tone of Fulmer's snappy voice, I knew something terrible had happened. 'What? If it's a mutiny I'm on your side!' I stooped and wound a sheet around my waist like a sarong, then opened the door.

Fulmer stood on the half-deck, wearing only his trousers. Over his shoulder I saw the cloudless sky, the façade of Capharnaum's white villas, green shutters and balconies, the merchants waiting on the quay in a stunned silence, the lower deck. It appeared to be covered in tar.

Fulmer pointed. The Insect was poised on the gangplank. Between it and the quayside stood Wrenn. The Insect reared and struck, antennae whirling. Wrenn raised his rapier and dagger.

I dived back into the cabin and picked up my ice axe. Then I shoved past Fulmer to the rack of equipment beside my door. I snatched a long boathook and hefted it, at the same time yelling to Fulmer, 'Run down the other walkway! Go to *Petrel*. Wake Lightning and tell him to shoot it! You must knock *very loudly*. Quick!'

Fulmer slid down the ladder and slipped across the main deck. I saw bodies lying at unnatural angles and tightened my grip on the boathook as I realised the thick, dully reflective slick was congealing blood.

With a cold self-awareness I spread my wings, wiggled my ice axe into the folded top of my impromptu sarong, and found the right words to shout at the thirty or forty Capharnai: 'Run away! Go home! It will bite you!'

Holding the boathook shaft across my body like a weightlifter, I vaulted the railings. I plummeted straight down past the blue porthole shutters, reached flying speed and hurtled once round the ship's hull to build up momentum. I skimmed the figurehead and up over the forecastle deck for a straight run at the Insect. I jinked to miss the foremast, by pulling in my right wing and spinning right.

I swept over the Insect. I reached out with the boathook and put my full strength behind it as I swung.

The Insect's gold-brown compound eyes wrapped round its head and joined at the top with bristly margins. It could see in all directions. It saw me passing above and bent its six knees to squat down. It flattened its body flush against the gangplank, beaded antennae wavering and brushing the wood.

I missed and struggled to lift the hook as it glided towards Wrenn's head. I snarled, 'Fuck!' I turned downwind, dropping height and holding the pole out to the side, not upwards to tangle with my feathers. I flew over the merchants' heads so low my downdraught ruffled their hair. They all dropped to the ground in a wide swathe along my path. A few quick beats, and I veered round the stern of the *Petrel*, intending to circle the two ships and come in over *Melowne* for another swoop. There was no sign of Lightning in the frantic commotion on *Petrel*'s deck.

Wrenn had bare feet. He was naked but for shorts, the drawstring hanging down. The Insect stood higher on the gangplank, claws tightly gripping the edges. Wrenn blocked the route to the land, to its food. It struck at him. He stopped its mandible with his rapier and deflected its head aside. It swept its antennae back into their gutters, bore its weight on its hind limbs and slashed with its front legs.

Its hooked claws stabbed at Wrenn, who batted them aside. Its jaws closed on, then slid off, the rapier blade. Wrenn parried the tarsi feet in a sequence so rapid it was a blur. He had lost none of his skill – he was too focused to feel fear. But he couldn't predict the Insect's actions.

He followed the moves of its four claws and mandibles all at once, every cut the Insect scrabbled at him. But his totally inadequate rapier clicked and slid over its cuticle – it wasn't heavy enough to bite into the shell.

He thrust his blade past the base of one antenna, then drew it back, slicing through the feeler. It severed and fell between the Insect's feet. A drop of yellow liquid like pus oozed from the hollow cut end and dropped on its eye, running over the curved surface. The Insect recoiled. Wrenn feinted, and its left claw swept the air trying to catch his blade. Wrenn lunged explosively and hit its thorax squarely, under its mandibles. His rapier tip pierced the chitin.

The Insect took a step towards him and the blade slid into its body. Fluid the colour and consistency of cream welled up around the blade and trickled down its shell but the Insect did not react. It crawled towards Wrenn, spitting itself on his rapier.

The sword point burst from its back, pushing out a length of cream-streaked steel. It forced itself down the blade until the hilt was flush against its thorax. It stooped to bite Wrenn's arm. Wrenn shook his hand free of the swept guards and jumped backwards, leaving his thin sword embedded through the Insect.

388

I cleared the height of the foredeck, came in fast.

Wrenn's face set in a grim expression. He cut with his dagger left to right, scratching the Insect's eye, but the blade skittered off, only etching a thin line over one hexagonal lens. It struck; he slammed the dagger into its mandible. The dagger blade shattered from tip to ricasso so violently that two long glittering steel splinters spun away from the gangplank in different directions. Wrenn was left holding the grip.

My wings shadowed his head. 'Here!' I dangled the pole from its very end. He had enough sense to drop his hilt and jump for the brass hook speeding towards him. I let go and passed it to him.

Our contact caused a drag that slowed me down too much and slewed me to the left. The quayside rushed up; I saw the pavement cracks. Too big, too close! I was going to crash! I leant right and beat down – my wingtips smacked a crate of oranges. The shock transmitted through my feather shafts and hurt my fingers. I pulled out of my dive; the crate tops scraped my knees and feet. I flapped, stubbing my wings. I banked up steeply, groaning with effort, my feathers rasping the air.

I glanced at Wrenn and saw him teetering, the pole held out for balance. He recovered, pointed the boathook at the Insect. It crouched, lowered its head and pounced at Wrenn, forcing him sideways. He swung the boathook and clubbed it weakly as it pushed past him. The spines fringing its legs lacerated his skin.

Its barrelling bulk threw Wrenn off balance. His boathook flourished in the air; he toppled off the gangplank and fell head first, spreadeagled. The soles of his feet vanished below the level of the harbour wall, into the strip of deep water. A second later I heard the splash.

I glanced at the crowd; their faces were full of doubt and disbelief. The Insect was real; this was no drama laid on for entertainment. It was coming down the gangplank. About half of them trotted backwards, still staring, then turned and fled for the streets. The rest seemed frozen. Those not gaping at the Insect were gawking at me.

'Go!' I yelled. A couple more people responded to the urgency in my voice.

The Insect landed on all six legs on the harbour pavement. At first it moved unevenly, angularly; it leapt and hobbled. It quickly became accustomed to freedom and the sailors' blood it had lapped up helped the hydraulics of its legs function properly. It ran as smoothly as it had done in the Paperlands and the people scattered before it.

They fled with screams, leaving one woman sitting alone. I recognised Danio instantly; at the water's edge near *Melowne*'s hull, in exactly the same place as I had left her last night, her bare legs dangling over the harbour wall. She remained transfixed a second too long, not knowing what to do.

389

She pulled herself to kneel, then sprang up, all the while watching the Insect with a mixture of fascination and fear. She sprinted, arms outstretched, very fleet of foot. But she was too slow.

The Insect bounded after her. Its claws in the small of her back brought her down, face to the paving. She started screaming, high-pitched, struggling to turn round and beat it off.

The Insect dipped, sheared Danio's leg off at the knee and picked it up with its middle pair of arms. Its external mouthparts stripped the calf muscle from the severed limb. It held the dripping muscle with two sets of palps, which hung down like black sticky fingers. The maxillae behind its jaws guillotined up and down as well as left and right, masticating it into paste. Danio kept screeching until the Insect grabbed her round the hips, mandibles sinking deep, and tossed her into the air. She crashed full-length on the paving. The Insect jumped on her body and decapitated her with one powerful bite.

I flew low over them, frantically looking for a space to land. The Insect paused as my movement caught its attention. Its single elbowed antenna waved; the stub of the other one was covered with a yellow crust. Now all the Capharnai had gone from the harbour but a merchant in a tunic had stopped at a distance to look back at the abandoned goods, his chubby face white and eyes bulging.

Danio! I thought. It's killed Danio; what have we done? I found a clear gap between the baskets and boxes, but I was moving so fast I was in danger of breaking my legs. I stretched my wings back fully and flared off some speed. Gasping at the strain in my stomach muscles I swung my legs ahead and hit the ground braced, knees bent. I put my hands down and somersaulted over and over, till I crashed into a crate of cinnamon bark.

Winded, I picked my axe from the ground and crawled to my feet. The Insect had reached the entrance to the boulevard. It had slaughtered the corpulent man and was standing on his body with front and middle legs. It ducked its head, its lamellar segmented abdomen high in the air. It closed its jaws until they clicked, cutting across the fat man's belly. It backed, claws skidding on the blood. It pulled taut a length of blue-green intestine, then ate it all the way back down into the man's body cavity. His sightless eyes and pale mouth were stretched open, rigid; I could see the inside wall of his ribs.

I thought, I must distract it till Lightning shoots it. Breathing painfully, I dashed across. As I ran, avoiding the discarded cloaks and piles of produce, I curved to approach from behind, thinking that the Insect would take a second to turn round and I could chop at its rear. But the Insect did not wait to be attacked. I don't know whether it recognised me or understood I was armed, but it crawled swiftly from the fat man's cadaver and leaped towards

390

the boulevard. I swerved between it and the town and headed it off. I chased it. I lengthened my stride to sprint with Rhydanne instinct as if it was a stag. I closed in on the darting legs and aimed a blow at a hind femur, driving it to change direction.

The Insect slowed as it sensed a group of boatmen who, trapped against a villa's portico, prepared to use their paddles as maces. I made it switch towards the ships where Lightning should be, but it slashed a mandible at the last man, a thin teenager who fell clutching his thigh.

The Insect still carried Wrenn's sword through its thorax, the hilt like a silver badge. It had stopped bleeding. Its legs swept repeatedly fore to rear along its body. I aimed between them at a suture line that crossed its back like a joint in armour. I tore the glassy tips of its immovable little wings that projected from the middle segment, pressed close to its glossy shell. I tilted over and hit, but the blow nearly ripped the shaft from my hand, wrecked my running rhythm. I pushed hard at the ground to accelerate, change direction; to control the Insect.

My resounding strikes had more effect than Wrenn's clearly articulated technique. The Insect limped, but still ran rapidly on the bristly black pads under its slightly raised claws. I swung at the three small round eyes that formed a triangle between its compound eyes. But at this angle the plate of its forehead was too thick to crack.

The slabs cool beneath my bare feet; my ankles ached from the pounding. I panted the air. The Insect put on a burst and reached racehorse speed trying to escape. I sprang forward and kept pace with it although my leg muscles burned. I was exhilarated, keyed up with my own vigour. I sped my swiftest, desperate to snatch one more chance – I'll hook my ice pick into the copper striped abdomen and I'll bring it down.

I forced the Insect's route nearer to the glittering sea as we raced the length of Capharnaum's harbour. The last building had a blank stone wall. At its base was a semicircular drain opening as tall as my shoulder, edged with blocks. A shallow stream of dirty water flowed out of it into a channel, then over the side of the harbour wall. It was stained dark green and fuscous with flaking algae. The Insect sheered, rattled down into the sloping conduit and splashed straight into the black archway. I lost sight of it instantly in the darkness. I scrambled to a halt, scraping my heels on the verge.

The Insect had gone; no way was I going to follow it into the drain. In the confined space it would rip my throat out before I could even see it. I waited, on guard, feeling my pulse pounding in my neck. It quickly returned to normal but my temples hurt. I coughed a mouthful of frothy spit into the grey water and watched it flow into the sea.

Insects are at home underground and are not disadvantaged by the dark. When culling them in the Paperlands, the least popular operation is the task of channelling river water into their tunnels in order to collapse the deep, honeycombed structures. Fires are also lit on platforms at the tunnel mouths to draw air out and suffocate them, but Insects between the sizes of men and carthorses still burst forth to attack at full speed. I hated natural caves let alone Insect burrows and slimy sewers. If I went in there I would never come out. With terrible images playing in my mind, I loped back to the *Stormy Petrel*, past the merchant's bloated, half-eaten body with its ripped-open smock and Danio, headless, lying in a congealed red spray.

Lightning looked down from the *Petrel*'s highest deck, the back of the stern castle, an arrow at string, and wearing only trousers. Fulmer clutched the rope rail beside him. Mist's face peered out of an open window in the array directly beneath his feet.

The surviving sailors on the *Melowne* clung to her rigging. Wrenn was a tiny figure down at the waterline, steadily climbing a ladder of metal brackets up the rounded hull. His short hair was flattened; water dripped from his bedraggled wings. His feathers were completely tattered, split and peeled back to the shaft. His arse crack and leg hairs showed through his soaked white shorts.

'What happened?' Lightning shouted at me. He leant over so far that I thought the arrows would slip out of the quiver on his back. 'Was that our Insect? Where's Serein? Damn him, damn you! What were you bloody doing, perforating it?'

Mist yelled, 'Did it just get those three Trisians? How many of mine?'

Fulmer gabbled, 'Serein woke me up. I saw it massacre the sailors on the orlop. Master Mariner, I'm sorry. Serein said he would hold it off and took his rapier but it's no good against shell.'

Mist turned away abruptly and hurried out of view. A moment later she strode onto the main deck, staring around at the devastation on the quay. The wounded teenager had stopped crawling; I hoped he was just unconscious, rather than slain. The traders' goods were abandoned. The quayside was deserted by the living, but three or four faces crowded every open window and behind the bronze palings of all the waterfront houses, watching us with shock and outright terror.

'You didn't kill it!' Lightning raved.

I retied my sarong. 'I should have caught it, but it plunged down a drain. I wounded it and so did Serein, with his rapier. Stupid town swords. Fucking constables' swords. The idiot didn't have the right gear. It carried his rapier away! You— We must get archers to the tunnel as soon as possible. I need to know if it's trapped, so you can shoot it.'

'And if it's escaped to the town?' Fulmer whispered.

Mist shouted, 'Captain, to your ship! Why were all the grids open? I'll want to know! We can't discuss this outside,' she added *sotto voce* to me.

'Jant, speak to the Capharnai. Don't let them carry off their dead without an explanation. As soon as you can, meet us in the *Melowne*'s hold.'

Typically, I had the most difficult job. While I waited on the corniche to be confronted by furious islanders, the other Eszai disappeared into the hold, and from their exclamations I learnt that it was also strewn with carnage. I was very aware how alien I looked, wearing a sheet and with my long wings uncovered.

On the *Melowne*'s main deck the dismembered remains of six or seven men lay scattered, their limbs snipped at the joints and bodies gutted. The quartermaster's body drooped through the hatchway. Following Mist's orders, the sailors carried them to the land and lined them up by the anchor ready for burial because in a few hours' time the morning heat would be appalling.

Step by step, a group of Capharnai merchants approached me, finding courage in numbers. I spread my hands down in the peace gesture and they seemed to understand. The first one, with an expression of awe and distrust, opened his arms like wings. I explained why I was the only man ever to fly, and told them it was nothing to be superstitious about. I repeated apologies as best I could and instructed them to wait in their homes and keep their children inside. Over the hiss of indrawn breath I continued – they should wait for word from the Senate that the Insect was dead. I asked them to bring down one or two goats for me to tether outside the sewer entrance and tempt the Insect out, but I suspected it was too replete for the trick to work.

I found myself talking over the wails and reproaches of families who had come to claim the Trisian merchant, the fainting teenager and Danio. I repeated that it was an accident and I clasped my hands and knelt, begging them to treat us kindly. When they saw that I couldn't meet their eyes, they understood my sincerity but they were chary. News spread up the town, causing a commotion and banging on doors, until it reached the Amarot and a deliberative silence descended.

Frightened, I retreated to the *Melowne*'s hold. 'I did my best,' I said.

'We believe you,' said Lightning. 'This disaster makes us all feel inadequate; it's far from the work we're accustomed to. Please attend to Serein and we'll consider what to do.'

Lightning had found a young Trisian man lying halfway down the ship, his lower face torn off. He returned to inspecting the victim. Behind us the buckled door of the empty Insect cage creaked as Mist opened and shut it again and again.

Wrenn sat on a packing case that now held cardamom seeds instead of arrows. I cleaned his grazes. I slapped on some comfrey ointment and tied gauze around his shoulder. His crenated wings slipped open like damp fans; his adrenaline high was fading. His shorts stuck to his stocky thighs and blood had dried on his bicep; he was peeling it off in tiny flakes. Grim determination was vicious in his face. 'Is this mine?' he said muzzily. 'It's all right. I don't think it's mine.'

I said, 'Yes, it is, but your scratches are superficial. Keep them clean and go easy for a few days. We can succumb to infection and serious disease as readily as mortals. In fact I can tell you quite a few examples of Eszai who've died from dusty wounds.'

'No, thanks.'

'Unfortunately it won't heal any faster, but the Circle will catch you and stop you being killed outright by little lesions and contusions.'

'Hey – what an advantage for fencing.'

I looked at him sternly. 'The only Eszai who survive centuries are those who know they're not indestructible. Zascai are relying on you not to get cut up.'

Wrenn lowered his gaze. 'I know; I was just keeping it at bay.'

'No one can slay Insects with a rapier,' I admonished. 'How many years has the Castle spent trying to develop the perfect weapon and now you try to use a *duelling foil*?'

Wrenn winced. 'I managed it once in the amphitheatre. My rapier was all I had to hand – Mist's sold every single broadsword on the ship and I gave mine to Danio. But you didn't do any better with your skier's axe. Ouch! Jant, have a care! I know I need experience. It was the biggest, toughest fucking Insect I've ever faced. And I failed; I'm sorry.'

'I'm sorry I didn't catch it,' I said.

Mist slammed the cage door. 'Jant, you showed the whole town that you can fly. We agreed to keep it a secret.'

'Did you expect me to let your pet devour Serein?'

'I can defend myself,' said Wrenn sulkily.

Lightning picked up a bronze Trisian trident that was lying next to the youth's body, and a purse made of soft leather. He approached us gravely. 'It seems as if our midshipmen were accepting bribes from curious Capharnai to look at the Insect. See?' He tipped the purse and a knot of fine gold chains snaked out into his palm.

'It must have broken out of its own accord,' Mist concluded. 'In response to them goading it. I wish I had commissioned a tougher cage.'

Lightning and I looked at her. She was well aware that we no longer believed a word she said. Lightning gestured at the cage. 'The Capharnai just regarded this as a freak show.'

'That's how they thought of us all,' I said.

Mist snapped at Wrenn suspiciously, 'Why were you up at five a.m.?'

He glanced around, admitted, 'I'd just got back. I spent the night in town with a local girl.'

'Oh, really?'

'I think she was called Pollan. At any rate, she kept saying "Pollan". She had world-class tits, I mean; you could get lost in there. Given last night's performance she could be selected for the national team, but any more mushy stuff and I'll relegate her to the second division—' Mist cuffed the back of his head. 'Ow!'

Wrenn ran a hand over his feathers, knitting their barbs together. Missing vanes spoiled his zig-zag style. He was quite hirsute with feathers; a couple were growing on his back between his wings, since he had not been near a barber's in months. The pinfeathers were still wrapped in their transparent covering, like paintbrushes. Where the sheath peeled back and crumbled, the brown brush tip emerged.

Mist called, 'Fulmer?'

The dandy's shocked face appeared in the overhead hatchway. 'Yes, Master Mariner?'

'Help Lightning carry this body up to the quayside. We have to return him to his relatives and try to find some way of atoning for this incident. Comet, sally out to the Amarot and request the presence of Vendace, with companions if he wishes. The Senate might have finished their three-day debate about us and we need to know the outcome. *Fly* there, and tell Vendace to meet us at his convenience, all together in my cabin.'

She looked at Lightning, who was naked from the waist up with dishevelled hair; me in a sheet skirt and needle scars; and Wrenn, caked in gore with semi-transparent shorts. 'Not as you are.'

I flew slowly to the Amarot, taking no pleasure in seeing the citizens staring up. I grieved for Danio; of course I'd only known her for two days but she was the Trisian I had spoken to most, and with untold depths of wit and humanity she had shown the greatest interest in the Fourlands.

I stood alone in front of the Senate and explained everything. I offered our services to catch the Insect but they interrupted me with outraged cries. They seemed to surmise that the Insect was a ploy for us to stay longer at Capharnaum. The Senate agreed that Vendace should accompany me to the *Stormy Petrel*, to announce their decision to all us travellers at once. I waited as he gathered an escort of townsmen on the mosaic, but as we walked down the boulevard more men joined us from the houses, almost spontaneously, following closely without a word. They were armed with harpoons, their knives in their belts; one or two carried the halberds we had sold them. They were quiet, giving me space, but still I knew they were watching my every move. It was nerve-racking. I acted as amicably as possible, trying to alleviate the atmosphere. When we passed the piazza I saw the man in the tunic working in his restaurant. I smiled openly but he gave me a cold look and pulled the shutters closed.

I reached *Petrel* with relief, but Mist, after some negotiation, invited all Vendace's supporters aboard. The caravel's size daunted them, but twenty or so filed up to the main deck, where Mist and I convinced Senator Vendace to leave them and enter her office alone.

The long shade of the mountain had fallen over the harbour, and Mist's cabin was so dark she had lit candles. The smell of tallow combined with brass polish, tar and black coffee made Vendace even more uneasy. He surveyed the Sailor's gloomy office: the waxed panelling fixed between tough, roughly adze-marked timbers, the door with long flamboyant hinges across it, and the cassone in which Ata kept her clothes. The table bore a cafetière and a plate of yesterday's bread rolls. Its turned legs were bolted to the floor. In the corner was a basket full of Trisian bric-a-brac and wine cups. This ornate room was at odds with the rest of the ship and the sound of uneasy crewmen scrubbing bloodied footprints off the foredeck.

Vendace did not sit down until I begged, and then only reluctantly. Mist pushed a lidded glass of coffee towards him but he did not give it so much as a glance. He watched his companions waiting on the main deck through the small panes surrounding the door. He announced, 'The Senate has voted. Tris will reject all contact with the Fourlands' Empire. We've heeded the advice of the constitution of Capharnaum. Everyone voted that you must leave, with the exception of well-loved Professor Danio, who wanted to learn more. We agreed this morning even before your messenger informed us of the tragedy. We do not want you here. The slaughter of Capharnaum citizens, including her, simply reinforced their decision. We know that your boats are restocked. Take them home immediately and never come back.'

I translated for the others. I was leaning against the wall at the back of the cabin, one knee bent and the boot sole against the wood, head bowed, listening. I let them speak directly to each other, facilitating their conversation without interrupting it, whatever words were said. I took no side, simply letting my translation flow from the shadow, echoing their words and rejoinders in the correct languages: Awian to Trisian, Trisian to Low Awian.

Wrenn said, 'But Tris is part of the Empire too!'

'No, we are not. One man should not rule five lands. The Senate was shocked to find that one man has so much power. You have already tainted Capharnaum.'

Mist said, 'Senator, let us—'

Vendace pointed at her. 'On the occasion of your arrival last year, the Senate discussed the likelihood of more visits from your island. We gave you the benefit of the doubt but now we accept that we were wrong and the stories were correct. Although I personally have no idea what to do about the Insect, the Senate are making plans.'

The black moniliform antenna lay on Mist's desk beside her cafetière. Vendace pushed it around with his finger as he spoke. 'You say there are thousands of Insects?'

I said, 'Hundreds of thousands infest the north of our continent. We're sorry we lost this one. The tunnel was empty when I returned with bowmen and – um – harpooners.'

Vendace said, 'Jant, you can actually fly, and you can run ... The merchants reported the speed you were flying!'

'I'm the fastest thing in the world,' I said. 'That's the only evidence I can give to prove that we're immortal.'

Vendace sighed. 'Some of the Senate believe you, but it makes no difference to us. Tris should be left alone by mortals and immortals alike. If you ask me, being able to fly is wonderful pleasure enough without heaping accolade and immortality on you as well.' He toyed with the antenna, asked plaintively, 'Why did you set an Insect on us?'

Mist said, 'We didn't. It was an accident and we're profoundly sorry. Please accept our apologies; mishaps like this will never happen again. The Insect escaped; we should have taken more care.'

'We'll hunt it down,' Lightning said solidly. His face had a bleak impassive expression. He stood by the door, occasionally checking Vendace's entourage. 'We're good at that; it's what we do. I will meet any proposal of compensation. At least allow us to give you advice and recompense for your people.'

'I'll go after it,' Wrenn volunteered.

'*Yes, we know; be quiet,*' I said.

Vendace said, 'The librarians are looking for charts. They've told me that the sewer drains the forum and branches throughout Capharnaum for six hundred metres. So you brought a legendary maneater as an object of wonder, and loosed it into the system under our town. I am astounded.'

'I can't translate this quickly,' I complained.

Mist asked the senator, 'If Tris communicates with the Castle even once again, we need a spokesman; a governor, you see. Tell me what you want.'

'The Senate wants you to leave.'

'No. Tell me what *you* want.'

Vendace turned pale, controlling his anger. He spread his dry palms like a scarecrow playing an accordion and said, 'I have learned some words of Awian: *Goodbye.*' He pushed his chair back and turned to leave.

Mist said, 'No, wait!'

She touched the chair asking him to sit down, though he looked very uncomfortable. She sighed and refilled her coffee glass. Without looking at me, she said, 'Comet, give us the benefit of your clever mind.'

'I say we stop insulting them. We should report to San and follow his instructions. I don't know about this town, but we're San's servants. I think he should make the whole Senate the governor; they seem to take decisions with one voice.'

'Don't interpret this,' Mist said. 'Forget the stubborn, overbearing Senate. The common man of Capharnaum will want something. I don't understand the desire that drives him.' She paced to the stern windows and looked out. 'Every people I have met want more than they can supply for themselves. In fact, every single person's greed is for more than he needs.'

'Not Rhydanne,' I said.

'Aye, a case to prove my point. Rhydanne are never drunk enough.' She nudged me as she paced back and nodded surreptitiously towards the casement. I peered through to see a crowd, mostly men, gathering on the quayside. Tridents glinted in their hands, with nets and the swords we had sold them. They stood in a passive silence that I found incredibly intimidating.

'Lightning, come here and take a look at this.'

Lightning muttered, 'They think the Empire is another little island.'

Mist said, 'Vendace, immortality's the most important offer your people could possibly have. The very opportunity will make you idle Zascai feel alive! Tris is so stagnant I feel smothered. We can tell that it hasn't changed for hundreds of years. You won't reject the Empire once you've seen its treasures – the sky-worshipping spires of Awia, mills of Hacilith! Everybody wants to be Eszai! Why turn the proposal down? Don't you wish to excel? Don't you want to know what the world will be like five centuries from now?'

Vendace was silent for a time, then he murmured something that had the rhythm of a quotation and sounded thoroughly resigned. He shot me an envious glance. 'It may be that we will not gain immortality, and we'll never be able to *fly*, but we all want to stay equal. We'll keep peace and our own pace. You have already threatened to upset the balance by coming here.'

'Give us a few more days,' Mist tried. 'We can buy another crate of gold. Serein will find the Insect.'

'The Senate's decision can neither be rescinded nor altered without a seven-day discussion. You must leave today.'

'I need to lay on enough water for the journey,' Mist countered. 'We'll leave tomorrow.'

'Yes, you will.' Vendace pulled his short cloak to his body, stood and left the cabin. Lightning stepped aside to let him go.

Mist gave a little scream and clenched her fists. 'Ah! Damn! Jant, I've one more chance,' she said in Plainslands. 'Follow him.'

'What did you say?' Lightning demanded. 'Don't exclude Wrenn!'

'It's private,' she spat.

On the main deck, Vendace's friends surrounded him. He looked reassured as they patted him on the back, and they began to file down the gangplank, Vendace shepherding them in front.

Mist caught the edge of his green-bordered cloak. The ex-fisherman tweaked it away and glared at her. She said, 'Jant, tell him this: I can give him eternal life. It doesn't matter whether we feel affection or not.'

She unnerved me. We must certainly be in trouble if Mist was prepared to play her last card. 'Do you mean ...?' I said doubtfully.

Her voice cleared of any vagueness, 'Aye! I mean marriage! A link through me to the Circle. Time is their currency, so immortality is my most priceless offer to one man.'

'I don't think that's a good idea.'

'Tell him, damn you – we don't have three days to mull it over!'

I repeated her words for Senator Vendace.

He was quiet, studying her for a long moment. His mouth twisted in disgust. 'No. How dare you bribe me to breach the Senate's resolution? To betray them! Just go! And never, *ever* return!' He strode down the gangplank without a backwards glance.

Over the next hour, the Capharnai melted away from the quay leaving an air of animosity. I watched the streets for the Insect through Mist's telescope, while the ships bustled with preparation to sail home.

'Well,' I said, embarrassed. 'You blew that, Ata Dei.'

She muttered, 'Next morning we'll set our backs and rudders to this bloody insular town.'

Nobody was present to watch us leave. As our sails filled and our figure-heads pointed towards the open sea, I felt my trepidation mounting. I did not want to go out there again so soon. I contemplated that the Trisians may never raise their sights or be forced into contest by a Challenger or by ambition as unquenchable as Mist's. Who here cared about the Castle's self-imposed trials? Half a minute's difference in racing time in a Challenge could literally be my downfall. A millimetre's distance on an archery target means life or death to Lightning. The Trisians will never know our accuracy or stamina but then they would never wear themselves out for a cause. By god, I liked them.

I sat at the stern, played a Rhydanne game of cat's cradle, and watched Tris shrink into the distance. The wind battered the clouds down to a thick bank on the skyline around it. Our caravels trailed a path back to Capharnaum harbour, but the waves distorted then covered our wakes as if the sea was determined to hide the trail we had blazed. I hoped that the spectacular failure of Mist's diplomacy would pass. I wished that Tris would eventually become a region like Darkling, which is part of the Empire but nobody expects it to get involved. The Rhydanne know vaguely that the Empire exists but really don't care; unfortunately the island of Tris has more to offer than Darkling.

That night I could see the lights of Capharnaum but not the land, so I became convinced the town was floating on the ocean. The next morning Tris had diminished so much on the horizon that I could put my thumb over it. By supper it was a speck; by the following day it had gone.

CHAPTER 12

When we lost sight of the island on the evening of 10 May, I had nothing to do but cross the sea as an idle passenger. *Melowne* and *Stormy Petrel* sailed across the longitudes. We were two ships standing out proud on the ocean.

I settled into my sleeping bag on my cabin floor, with a jug of coffee and cat, and some liquorice root to chew. I filled my silver fountain pen, carefully propped the book on my sharp knees and began to read. I transcribed the first chapter of the small volume I had stolen from the library, *A History of Tris*, by Sillago of Capharnaum.

In the year 416 – a date that every schoolchild knows – galleys from the mainland arrived at our then uninhabited island, and anchored in the mouth of Olio River. During the following day, the settlement of Capharnaum was founded on the northern bank and the mighty galleys were brought upriver and set aflame, a remarkable symbolic act that marked the dawn of our present society.

Why did this flotilla of galleys leave the mainland and put their hope in the creation of a new country? In this book I will argue that it was due to the ingress into the mainland of a swarm of Insects. According to the only manuscript surviving from the Pentadrica, Capelin's account of the second decade of the fifth century, I maintain that Insects truly existed and were not the symbolic creatures that recently fashionable theories would have us believe. Moreover, they must have been rather larger than the ants of our island. My esteemed colleague Vadigo of Salmagundi has on numerous occasions criticised my belief in Insects. However, my research draws heavily on the precious Capelin manuscript housed in the Amarot library with which, perhaps as it is such a distance from Salmagundi, my colleague does not trouble himself.

The Queen of Pentadrica, Alyss, travelled with her court – a rudimentary senate – from her liberal and enlightened country known as the jewel of the Fivelands, to satisfy her curiosity about reports of the problematic Insects. Capelin, a scrivener at the Pentadrican court, relates that five Insects had appeared suddenly in the vale of north-east Awia and were the subject of much curiosity. Apparently of their own volition the Insects confined themselves in a small area behind a wall. The nearby Awians were observing and throwing logs into the enclosure when hundreds more manifested so suddenly they had to flee for their lives. When Alyss drew close to the boundary the creatures burst out, devouring the Queen and her entire entourage. Insects laid the fields waste, eating the crops and building as vigorously as our own ants. Capelin recorded that more Insects emerged than could ever have fitted inside, but this may be an understandable exaggeration or poetic flourish.

An envoy brought the news of Alyss' death to her palace and to the King of Morenzia in Litanee. Various of the Morenzian nobility immediately laid claim to the leadership of Pentadrica – that is, the throne.

The crude southern horsemen, the Plainslanders, realised that they could also gain land. We do not know, unfortunately, what a horseman would look like. The Morenzian humans and the horsemen fought over Pentadrican land and many of the Morenzian nobility were killed. One suspects the Pentadricans defending their towns and hamlets could do little against forays from the barbarians beyond their southern borders. Capelin's harrowing description of the destruction of Strip Linchit village forms the appendix to this book.

The kingdom of Awia tried to organise resistance to the Insects – presumably gathering young men whose hunting parties were now asked to net the maneaters. We know for certain that thousands of Awians were displaced southwards and determined to settle the north of Pentadrica. Historians following Vadigo have stated that from this point the story seems credible, but have given no criteria for their method of determining between reality and allegory.

Awians and Pentadricans both appealed to San for help. This mythological figure was supposed to have been given eternal life by god before it left the world; to advise the world on god's behalf. San seems to have been an itinerant sage who objectively advised all the courts of the five countries involved and was respected by them. Capelin assumes his reader knows the identity of San and gives no evidence to support immortality. It was probably a rumour arising around an extremely adroit and possibly aged wise man as it is not possible to credit the idea that he was wandering the world for four hundred years before the Insects appeared.

Some theoreticians postulate that San was god in a different guise; some hold that the appearance of Insects marked the return of god, or that god intended Insects to triumph over people and form the next phase of creation. The argument that there is a god at all is beyond the scope of this book.

It is self-evident that San realised the Insects were the greatest threat since he attempted to organise bands to hunt them. If Insects were some sort of metaphor for decadence and never intended to be understood literally as animals, how are we to explain the decision of San as recorded in Capelin's document? It is the best evidence available that Insects, whatever they were, were tangible. San blamed the Morenzian nobles for the civil war and, although some accompanied him into Awia, fighting continued in the Pentadrica. The Pentadrica collapsed completely in the year 415.

The intensity of the skirmishes seems far-fetched to our imagination, but it is important to remember that in and around the fifth century all the land was owned by individuals dependent upon it for their survival. The pre-Senate times were indeed difficult. A further reason why the settlers founded a senate was simple horror at the fact that all this confusion resulted from the death of one woman, the beautiful Alyss.

To bring peace, San divided up the Pentadrica. From being the centre of the Fivelands, its territories were distributed between Awia, the Plainslands and the new republic of Morenzia. Those three expanded countries were united and hostilities ceased. San proposed to lead volunteers from them against the Insects. In return, the several leaders met in Alyss' empty palace and agreed to bequeath the building to San and proclaim him Emperor.

Now we come to the most exciting part of Capelin's record. From all countries came a host of people who were appalled by the thought of one man, however wise, holding sway over the world. They met at the coast and numbered about one thousand. Awian refugees collaborated readily with men and women loyal to the Pentadrica who could not accept being subjected to the rule of savage horsemen and the greedy nobles who had so recently ravaged their land. They agreed to leave for an island well known to the Pentadricans. Under cover of the summer night, they escaped the mainland in a flotilla of galleys.

Today, if one strolls along the sandy bank of the Olio, it takes little imagination to envisage the travel-scarred galleys rowing upriver, their single square sails hanging stained and torn from the tribulations of the long crossing. Indeed, the site of their landing is numinous and sacrosanct, as if after their long voyage the ghosts of those tired but eager fugitives still frequent the beach.

Their outstanding achievements in founding the Senate and the colony of Capharnaum brought us to where we are today. Under the wisdom of a senatorial government, the colony thrived. Capharnaum grew rapidly and in the following century was embellished to its present radiance which, with the particulars of the naissance of Farrago community, will be the subject of my next chapter.

I turned the page, and almost dropped the book in astonishment. There was a portrait of the Emperor San. I recognised him instantly in the full-page illustration, although he was not in the Throne Room, seated on his dais in front of the electrum sunburst. He was sitting on a rock, and he wore breeches. A black and white cloak around his shoulders was secured with annular brooches. Across his knees, his ridged and wiry hands held a boar spear. The backdrop was a verdant plain of fields and, dotted into the distance, towns that were tiny collections of beautiful domes and stepped-gable houses. They reminded me of the broken domes of old Awia that project from the Paperlands; Awia has not built domes for nearly two thousand years. When Insects forced their country southwards, Awians deliberately changed the style of their architecture to symbolise a new start and express their defiance.

San did not look stern and forbidding. He was smiling. He looked like a fyrd captain; he looked like one of us. The caption read: *San, from Haclyth village, proclaimed Emperor in 415 on the dissolution of the Pentadrica.*

I thought, this is what San looked like when he was the only immortal man; counsellor turned warrior when, in another world, Insect eggs hatched, imagos amassed, and the swarm broke through into peaceful Awia. One would gain great wisdom by living through such times, witnessing incredible events – Litanee raiders sucked into the space Alyss left, riding at each other through standing crops and the smoke of burning thatch. Maybe the nomadic Plainslanders settled down somewhat once they'd gained Pentadrican farmland. So that, some sixteen centuries later, the Plainslands sprawls with twice the range, merchant families rule Morenzia and, in the city of San's birth, waterwheels spin in industry.

Some of Sillago's story fitted with what I already knew. I was keen to show Lightning my translation, because he had told me that his manor was created from land that was originally Pentadrican, where they prospered from the Donaise hills vineyards. In 549 wealth gained from the Gilt River gold rush brought his family to the throne. The Murrelet dynasty ended, and Esmerillion Micawater made her town the capital of Awia.

San has kept his position as Emperor for sixteen centuries, I thought. The current Circle is only his most recent system. If he had not founded the Circle, he may not still be Emperor. He must have come very close to being deposed in 619 when the First Circle was defeated. Our immortality seemed dangerously transient and unstable compared to San's long life. If he found a better system and no longer needed us, I wondered what would happen.

I stopped transcribing and simply read until my eyes ached. Candlelight shadowed the texture of the page. Sillago's prose tested my comprehension of old Morenzian but I read on, absorbed. In the Amarot library this was just a flawed textbook, but to the Fourlands it was a priceless artefact.

As I came down from my high, for the first time I felt the waves' motion as lulling rather than threatening. Outside, the whistle blew for the three a.m. watch. With a warm feeling of achievement I nodded asleep, curled protectively over the book, the pages kept open with one loving hand.

*

I woke with a quick intake of breath. I lay listening, afraid to look round, feeling that something was standing over me. I was used to the wide sky and the enduring size of the Castle – the *Melowne* was a claustrophobic floating wooden box. I forced myself to ease the cabin door open and look out at the empty night. I thought: shit, someone's stolen half the moon. But it was only clouds, I think. I must be more careful what I drink. Thin purple cirrus whipped past under the stars. There was no one about. Just a bad dream, I told myself. Go out and have a breath of fresh air.

I climbed down to the gallery and looked at the water. The open ocean was a wasteland. From edge to edge of its black expanse there was no visible life. But its endless sound and movement made the ocean itself seem like an animal. The whole febrile sea was horribly alive in a way that the static mountains could never be. A cold feeling lapped over me again. Something was wrong. What *was* that? Running alongside *Melowne*, about ten metres out from the hull, was a hollow in the inky water, silvery with the reflection of *Melowne*'s lamps. Is the hollow real? It must be, a trick of the light wouldn't persist for so long. I thought I knew all the sea phenomena by now. I shrank back; was something sentient there? I glanced up to the lookout in the crow's-nest but he stared straight out ahead. Either he hadn't noticed, or he thought nothing wrong. The wind was directly behind us. The indentation in the water was pointed at the front and rounded inside. I could see the far side of the wall of water inside, about two metres deep. The waves broke around it but didn't fall into the hole. It was as if something pressed down on the brine, like it was being displaced by the hull of a non-existent ship.

The indentation overtook us and veered away, gradually dissipating as it went. The hollow filled, leaving the surface smooth. I stared at the sea for a few minutes. Had I imagined it? Then a fin broke surface. I struggled with the perspective as the black triangle rose. Its wet tip came up to *Melowne*'s gallery, then passed it to the height of the deck. I could have touched it. It was fully five metres high. At its base, the rough back of a shark emerged, a thinner, more elongated shape than the ship. Way behind our stern, the tips of its tail flukes projected like a second dorsal fin, moving back and forth in the water. I froze. The shark was the same length as *Melowne*. It was fifty metres long. There *were* monsters out there. A flick of its tail would turn us to floating splinters.

The shark swam alongside. I suddenly wondered why the lookout hadn't seen it. I leaned over the gallery. 'Tarragon?' I called. 'Tarragon? Tarragon!' The dorsal fin rolled away from the ship, bringing the pectoral fin to the surface. The shark's silver fish eye, as big as a buckler, stared straight up at me for a second. Water washed through open gill slits like loose metre-long wounds. It rolled back. Water rose up around the wave-cutting dorsal fin as its body sank to the level of our keel.

'Tarragon...?' The shark gave a slow wriggle, left-right along its length. Its immense power sped the fin past me, then its long arched back, the vertical tail flukes. It was gone, deep under the ship.

I became aware of panic on the main deck above. Pale, frightened faces appeared at the rails. Shouts in three languages stopped abruptly when Fulmer's voice bellowed something.

Tarragon said she would watch over us. Was it her down there? I thought she was a cute fish; I expected her to be girl-sized. I didn't know she was a hundred-ton leviathan.

Fulmer slid down the ladder and confronted me with an intent look. 'Are you awake, Jant? There's nothing there.'

'Whatever it was,' I whispered, 'she's gone.'

For the sake of my reality, I was relieved I couldn't see where Tarragon had gone, or what she could see underwater with her cold, filmed eyes.

Wrenn's Diary

1 June 2020

Today Mist and Fulmer had a blazing row and one of the sailors was put to death. He had been caught stealing a gold boot-scraper from a chest in the *Melowne*'s forecastle. He was one of the sailors who didn't go ashore because we left before it was his turn. The men who missed their chance to see Capharnaum are very restless. Fulmer insisted discipline had to be kept, and for stealing cargo while under way the sentence is death. All seagoing vessels operate under Morenzian law. It is harsher than Awian justice – I think because Awia is in more danger of being wiped out by the Insects, we know better than to harm our own people. But Fulmer says that ruthlessness is needed at sea to stop mutinies happening.

This ship in Fulmer's charge is worth a dynasty's fortune. It's so crammed that I have to sleep sitting upright between sacks of allspice. Fulmer said that if the men before the mast can thieve as they wish there'll be nothing left by the time he reaches Tanager.

Mist Ata yelled, 'I forbid you! After all the losses to the Insect I'm not losing another crewman. Just put him in the hold and lock the hatch. Take your "I must make an example" and stuff it!'

Fulmer yelled, 'I'm sick of interfering Eszai! You're no better than anyone else just because you can handle a tiller or sword!'

I learned that at sea a captain is like a governor; on a matter of law Eszai can only advise him, not overrule. Fulmer was adamant and he had the law on his side.

Mist piled extra sail on the *Petrel* and swept ahead as if she was abandoning us. Fulmer said, 'Never trust a woman who has a point to prove. Yes? All hands to witness punishment!'

Jant refused to attend; he said it was stupid and brutal. He said that only Zascai exercise power so crudely and severely, but then only Zascai need to. He's been acting even more weirdly than usual, he keeps saying how vulnerable our cobbled-together hollow ships would be, should any sea monsters actually exist.

The thief was bound, wrists and ankles. He begged and struggled all the time. He was thin as a lath, a weather-beaten man from Addald Island off the Ghallain Cape. I was sorry his life had to end this way when he had seen so much, navigated the storms of Cape Brattice on the southern tip of Morenzia, Tombolo and Teron Islands off Awia, the reef of Grass Isle, and the wild seas around the empty coast of the Neither Bight. He was brave enough even to have anchored in the rending whirlpools of the Awndyn Corriwreckan.

Two of Fulmer's sailors passed a rope across the bow and paid out line until the loop dragged in the water. They each held it at their waists and walked the loop down under the ship to the main deck.

One end was made into a noose and the man's ankles fitted through it. He kicked, both legs together, and screamed for mercy so horribly every man on the *Melowne* was chilled to the bone.

They picked him up and threw him over the side like a parcel. He splashed in, curled foetally. The loose rope snaked about him in the water. He bobbed to the surface, waggling his head and gasped, screamed.

Fulmer gave the order and a team pulled the other end of the rope that ran under the hull. The Plainslander's yells cut short as it tightened and he sank under. His body was drawn down a long way, still thrashing and bubbles rising all around. He disappeared from view.

I heard knocks as his body scraped over the rough, barnacled hull. Blood swirled up, it looked black. I hoped that he had exhaled the air from his lungs and breathed brine in before the scraping started.

The wet rope coiled onto the deck, water ran from the hands of the men pulling it in. Behind them a team of men paid the dry rope out. Halfway through, Fulmer wanted to stop the teams and offer each man a tot of rum, leaving the body under the boat while they drank Queen Eleonora's health. But the rope snapped. It went slack. Fulmer said, 'Lads, reel him in, yes?'

The men pulled the rope up fast, hand over hand. They dragged a pale pink and shredded mass to the surface. The cable hadn't broken, his body had. His arms were worn through, nothing was left of them. The noose had protected his ankles and feet but his legs were bare to the bone. Tiny waterlogged pieces of muscle tissue floated off, into the depths as fish food.

I saw his face had gone, just eyeballs in a fleshy cranium. His back teeth showed in the gums. Tufts of wet grey hair still stuck to the skull. His back was flayed.

This wet skull on a spinal column dropped to the deck. Fulmer made sure every man of his crew saw it before they washed it overboard.

Mist is still furious, and rightly so. I hope I live till god-comes-back, but if I die, I swear it will be by steel or chitin, and not by Morenzian law.

I was in my cabin, putting the finishing touches to *A History of Tris*, when the *Petrel* raised a series of flags. Mist was asking Wrenn and I to come across for a meeting. I found Wrenn talking uneasily to Fulmer. We were all three thinking of the mess she had made of diplomacy with Tris, although only I had witnessed the worst of it. Fulmer said, subdued, 'She's making preparations for landing. We want to avoid pirate vessels as we cross the trade routes, yes?'

I flew and reached the *Petrel* long before Wrenn's boat rowed over the gently purling water. 'It's July the tenth,' Mist said. 'I'm confident that sometime today we'll have sight of the Fourlands. Watch for the coast, it's heart-warming to see it appearing. It feels like the first time a newborn babe is placed in your arms.'

I sipped water that was faintly brackish, owing to the habit of refilling seawater ballast casks with drinking water. Mist watched the big, gimballed compass in the binnacle dipping as if it was dowsing for land. The morning sky was a slightly powdery pale blue that meant it was going to be a hot day. The haze had burnt off by mid-morning and the temperature was so intolerable that I climbed the rigging and clung there, a black-clad starfish in a giant net, with my wings spread as a shade. When I opened my eyes the bright world was tainted blue.

Thick white salt dried on the stern carvings, encrusting them like the lumps of salt that fyrd throw into trapping ponds to immobilise Insects. It smelt as dirty as flotsam; I could practically hear it crystallising.

Whale fins gnomoned all over the ocean. Seagulls trapezed in the sky. We came in slow. The lookout in the *Petrel*'s crow's-nest used his own feather as a plectrum to strum his guitar. He gave a false shout of 'Land!' twice and Mist snarled that if he did it again she would slice his tongue out and fly it as a pennant. There were tiny glossy plaques of severe suntan on her shoulders. A sweat sheen covered the golden-brown skin above her breasts, startling with her cream clothes. She had cut her platinum hair short and ruffled like dandelion fluff. She squinted at the sun-glare and when she relaxed the folds at the edges of her eyes showed white.

Evening set in, and dry, porous ship's biscuits were dealt out among the crew. Heat was radiating back out of my sunburnt skin to fill the cool air. A thin black line began to rise on the horizon, becoming a part of the night sky where there were no stars, but nobody dared say anything until Wrenn strolled over and said, 'I might have heatstroke, or is that land?'

'Aye, that is land.' Mist admitted, tiredly. She raised her voice. 'Land, ho! We're home, boys! Send a signal to Master Fulmer.'

The *Melowne*'s sailors read the series of flags. They took up the shout and jubilation broke out all over the ship, in the topgallants and below in the galley. From the *Petrel*'s half-deck I heard them shouting and cheering Mist. We had been on our own so far from anywhere that sighting the Cobalt coast was like seeing an old friend. We surveyed it with unbridled joy but, because we had been self-sufficient for three months, with slight trepidation.

'Drinks all round,' I said.

'Order!' Mist snapped. 'We return as we left. Clear the decks shipshape and Sute fashion. Wait till you have your feet on dry land before howling with your hounds' tongues, or by god I'll separate them from you now.'

I was obsessively trying to judge the distance to the coast – the moment that I could safely fly back. I wanted to travel under my own power, at last! More importantly, I had to catch up on six months' worth of news. I was desperate to know the latest, and even more keen – as a Messenger should be – to give San my report of Tris. I was also determined to face Tern and demand the truth from her about Tornado.

Mist observed me hopping from foot to foot at the prow. She collapsed her telescope back into its casing with a snap. 'You want to fly?' she asked.

'I need to know the news.'

'Please don't leave us. I need you to deliver my account of Tris to San. I've just finished writing it.'

'I intend to give my own; it's Comet's duty.'

Mist scratched her fluffy head. 'Since when were you objective, Shira? You and your stupid eyeshadow.'

'It's not eyeshadow it's late nights. Look, Ata, I'll come straight back. I only want to buy a newspaper.'

She looked at me closely. 'If you go to land, promise not to breathe a word about what happened on Tris. Aye, god knows I can't stop you, but I'm trying to contain this discovery and you can see how important it is not to blab.'

'I'll just bring you the news, I promise.'

'Then off you go. And buy me a couple of bars of chocolate, as well.'

I landed on the dark strand, and jogged up the beach from the hard wet sand to the dry sand, then climbed some steps to the promenade. I looked back and laughed to see my footprints appear from nowhere at the point where I touched down. The days were already getting shorter; I somehow felt cheated. It was ten p.m. and the Artists' Quarter, that reputedly never sleeps, was just beginning to wake up. One seafront kiosk was open. A grey, hircine old man chortled when he saw me. I asked why, and he pointed to the headlines.

I said, 'Oh, fuck,' and bought a copy of every newspaper he had. I jammed them into my satchel. I gave the man a handful of pound coins and for my fifty-pence change he used a pair of clippers to cut the last one along the line stamped on it. He returned half the coin.

As instructed, I also picked up some chocolate but I had eaten most of it by the time I reached the *Petrel*. I called Mist, Lightning and Serein to Mist's office and spread the newspapers on her table:

Rebellion Poised to Strike the Castle

Troops raised by Gio Ami are proceeding towards the Castle itself. Lady Governor Eske has, of her own accord, given over the first four divisions of General infantry and more than thirty Select Fyrd to his cause.

Gio Ami has also commandeered Insect-wall-breaking machines from Eske. They include two battering rams and seven catapults, probably mid-sized trebuchets although it is difficult to specify the exact type. At the time of going to press, the engines are en route along the Eske Road.

Gio Ami's volunteer force and non-combatant supporters are extremely varied in background and opinion but are strongly united by their discontent at the Castle's role in the slow recovery of the Empire from Insect damage. Gio Ami will address them in his second meeting, to be held at midnight on Thursday at the Ghallain Fencing Academy in Eske.

In response, the Castle has received command of four thousand General, one thousand Select Fyrd from Fescue and Shivel, placed under the control of Tornado and Hayl. The internal guard of the Castle, the Imperial Select, are on alert.

Sporadic clashes occurred today on the Dogvane Road from Ghallain between demobilised soldiers loyal to the Castle and rebels attempting to join Gio.

Kestrel Altergate
10.07.20

'How can Gio dare?' Wrenn said. 'This is all on its head! We're their guardians!'

'Many things are happening recently that have never occurred before,' Lightning said quietly, as if adrift.

'There's an embargo on ships,' I read.

Mist pressed her hand on her belly, growled, 'What kind of stupidity? Where does it say that?'

410

'Look, here. It says Gio's men have occupied Awndyn and nothing can enter or leave the harbour, including your caravels.'

'Oh, for god's sake. If I'd been here things would never have gone this far.'

I translated the Plainslands article aloud to make it easier for Lightning, and then I picked up the broadsheet he had been reading. He pointed out an editorial at the bottom of the page. 'The Grand Tour just got longer,' he said.

Race is on to the Island of Delight

As Gio Ami's uprising confounds the Plainslands, news spreads about the Island of Tris. It has caused a stir in Lakeland Awia. Our correspondent at the court writes that Queen Eleonora Tanager yesterday summoned to Rachiswater Palace one of the mariners of the 2019 expedition. The Court was entertained to hear, at first hand, the bizarre travellers' tales currently filling the penny dreadfuls.

The *Wrought Standard* remains sceptical of the details, yet accepts that an island has been discovered since the flagship *Stormy Petrel* departed on another journey not one month after returning from the first. Mist's statement that she returned empty-handed is now regarded as a half-truth at best. The Castle must have planned her venture because *Stormy Petrel* was careened and resupplied within a month; the Castle is invited to reply to allegations that it has been economical with the truth.

No place is perfect, but Tris comes close. The islanders are both winged and wingless people. The climate is good, and the soil on the slopes of the central mountain is as fertile as Plow's black earth wheat fields. The sailor said their food was succulent fruit he had never seen before, and fish with sweet, rich flesh. The culture seems sophisticated, but sailors' tales are not wholly to be trusted. They also tell of having seen men with paddles for hands and mountains that emit smoke like chimneys.

The island is mostly in a wild and natural state. There are no settlements in the interior; the natives travel around their rocky coast by canoe.

Queen Eleonora has expressed interest in mounting her own expedition, as has Lord Governor Brandoch. Tris offers opportunities to trade, and a place of settlement that can be offered to our displaced countrymen sadly suffering the lot of refugees. The race is on to construct or engage craft worthy of making this long sea voyage.

I was interrupted by a cry from Wrenn, who had turned straight to the sports pages. He pointed out a paragraph:

Gio Ami's admirable life's work was shattered in one flukish move by Wrenn, all reporters present at that immortal duel agreed. Wrenn proved that there are no universal laws in the Art; now, characteristically, the master of the Ghallain School seems determined to take unpredictability to extremes. His rebellion could not be foreseen by those of us who knew his cool fencing style. His aggression in the game used to be well controlled, he always kept some tricks back. Now he gains followers like swarms of Insects, determined to deal the Circle a mortal blow.

As Gio Ami told us, 'Serein Wrenn is away, maybe lost at sea. If Eszai can't give one hundred percent for the Empire, they should not be Eszai at all.'

D. Tir, Editor, Secret Cut Fencing Times

'So,' said Mist. 'Gio Ami doesn't know when to leave.' We were all silent, thinking of the man's gall.

Lightning said, 'There must be some mistake. It's unthinkable! What does he imagine he can achieve?'

Wrenn tore the paper up and cast the shreds on the floor. 'I'll meet him for you.' He glared round at us. 'I'll take him back to the amphitheatre and run him through!'

'It's his followers I worry about,' said Lightning.

'They won't stay with him,' I conjectured.

Mist slammed her hand on the table. 'Gentlemen, a council to decide our course because we don't know what we'll find.'

'We should hasten to the Castle as quickly as possible,' Lightning said simply.

'Aye, but I won't put in to Awndyn and risk a clash with any of Gio's followers.'

Lightning said, 'I will answer for Swallow Awndyn.'

'No, no, don't be so unwise. We can't trust any Zascai. Especially the allegiance of Swallow, whom San won't allow into the Circle. I will not chance the safety of my ships. I'll hide *Stormy Petrel* and leave an armed guard on her. You know in the past the most precarious times for the Castle are those when we've managed to beat back the Insects.'

Lightning nodded and said, 'Well, Serein wanted a chance to prove himself.'

The next day the mainland was nearer. At first it was a pale grey silhouette, and at ten kilometres out I saw the exact instant when it became green. Colours on the coastline differentiated as we sailed nearer. The water had a blindingly bright mirror glare, as moving ripples reflected the sun. It was so calm it looked solid, almost as if I could walk on it.

At five kilometres out the sea was busy with traffic of various vessels coming and going, small sails in the distance. Ships turned left on sight, out of each other's way; they hailed each other when gathering to approach the port. We were at the depth and bearings of the main north-south route along the coast, which the sailors called Carrack Roads. We anchored and all the *Petrel's* crates of precious cargo were transported to the *Melowne*.

The *Melowne* sat lower in the water, a target for corsairs, so Mist ordered all her Castle pennants to be furled one by one until she only flew Tanager's ensign. The *Melowne* then parted from us and Fulmer steered her northwards, heading for Tanager harbour, where he and Mist had decided that the precious cargo would be most secure.

Grey dolphins packed our bow wave, jumping and snorting; their hard bodies slicked through the water. They rolled, breaking the surface and half-somersaulting as if they were spinning on a wheel. I wondered what Tarragon thought of them – snack food, probably.

'We'll anchor in a sheltered bay I know well,' Mist said. But we headed for a blank chalk cliff with none of the cleavages where harbours lie. I didn't much like it, so I climbed on the back railing, spread my wings and let the ship slip out from under me. I sailed up on a current, seeing the white chalk and lines of black flint speed past, till I was above the cliff. I looked down on the grassy top and realised that what I had thought was a continuous wall was an enormous flat, rugged stack hiding the narrow mouth of a cove. I soared along the cliff edge, hanging suspended in the wind which blew in from the sea and was driven vertically up its face.

Stormy Petrel tacked once, so close to the rock that the gallery at her waist scraped it. Mist and her bosun spun the wheel between them, and *Petrel* slipped through the passage behind the stack with only a couple of metres on either side. I turned again into the wind and glided back along the cliff top towards the inlet.

Stormy Petrel anchored herself fore and aft. She was hidden, but only from the sea. Anyone on the grass could look down two hundred metres to see the ship calmly bobbing in the dark quiet water crosshatched with ripples. Every wavelet made her dance; there was nothing in her hold but ballast and bilge water. The walls of the deep circular pool were sheer but there was a floating jetty constructed from barrels. From this landing stage a series of uneven steps hacked into the chalk led up to a cave entrance above the high-water line – a smugglers' hideout. Though since Mist knew about it their contraband would be long gone.

Petrel lowered her landing craft and spewed out a procession of tattered sailors who climbed the steps into the cave, where they vanished, and more men behind them tramped into the grotto that surely couldn't hold such numbers. It was like a conjuring trick. Half an hour later, the first man emerged onto the cliff top through a pothole I had not previously noticed. Another head-torso-legs followed, until all the sailors were sitting on the grass, scraping chalk sludge off their boots. Lightning and Wrenn climbed out last, absorbed in an intense conversation, but I couldn't hear what they were talking about. I was having too much trouble defending myself from fluttering little songbirds. My big cross-shaped silhouette pinned in the sky on motionless wings reminded them of an eagle. They could out-fly me; they orbited and dived on my head. I tried batting them away, but their tiny beaks were very sharp.

Mist paid her crew and told them when to muster at the Puff Inn in Awndyn-on-the-Strand to gain a cut of the profit from the spice ship. She briefed them to hold their tongues about Tris with a promise of future employment, and dismissed them.

I flew into Awndyn feeling that the atmosphere had changed; people were looking up at me suspiciously. I visited the offices of the Black Coach, the postal system of stagecoaches that uses the stables and hostels of coaching inns. It was set up by my predecessors who were reliant on horses. Its mail network was nominally answerable to me as Comet, and despite their palpable disquiet the Awndyn branch seemed to be coping just as well as the last time I visited six years ago. I procured horses from their yard for Mist, Lightning and the Swordsman, and had to sign in triplicate for a carriage-and-pair for our luggage. I joined the others on the main road and directed them to the Remige Road in the direction of Eske manor and the Castle.

The sensation of the waves' movement still lasted from the ship. I felt as if I was rising and falling although I had both feet on dry land. It was a pleasant feeling that lulled and confused my senses; coupled with the warmth of scolopendium it sent me into a condition of bliss.

CHAPTER 13

The Remige Road was one of the main routes built by the Castle for the movement of fyrd to and from the Front. It was wide, for two wagons abreast, and it had worn a deep cutting into the chalk on the downs west of Awndyn where it had not been cobbled. Lightning, Mist and Serein led the coach-and-pair inland across a broom and gorse heath, under a sky of the vivid blue that is the field of the Awian flag. They rode alongside an oak plantation belonging to Mist, then an orchard. Sunlight shone on the horses' well-groomed flanks. Light reflected from the metal panels on my boots and darted bright patches on the path.

Flying is the most selfish pastime in the world. It's all I ever want to do. Flying is being alone but not lonely, swept up on the exhaust of the world; my wings and the ground two magnets pushing each other apart. The sky is more gentle than the touch of any lover, and gliding on a hot day is as effortless as sleep. I hold out my wings, supported on rounded air, and change direction with a tiny movement. I travelled at an altitude too great to be seen from the patchwork farmland and toy cottages. I urged myself higher, trying to cram more miniature moated granges and dwindling trees into my field of vision. I sang, 'Oh, we met in the Frozen Hound hotel, down on Turbary Road.'

Lightning and Mist seemed to be arguing. I dropped height and circled above them, my backswept sickle wings beating quickly with the wrist joint bent gracefully as a falcon's. I risked spooking the horses but I wanted to hear the Archer.

'This is far worse than the year fifteen-oh-nine,' he rebuked Mist angrily. 'Gio Ami is much more desperate than Eske was then.'

Mist said, 'Well, I agree, but the Castle will weather another such revolution, especially when you and I can negotiate.'

'Let us send Comet ahead.'

'No. I want to be present when he gives his report.'

'What was the year fifteen-oh-nine, anyway?' asked Wrenn.

'Oh, don't get Lightning started or he won't shut up till nightfall.'

'Your charm never falters. Wrenn, I'll tell you. Five hundred years ago we pushed the Insects further out of Lowespass than their Wall had been for centuries. The Insects were less of a threat, so the southern manors decided they were safe. They thought they no longer needed the Castle, so they refused to pay our dues. The governor of Eske manor led the way, and the whole Plainslands followed within the year.'

Mist sniggered. 'When the taxes dried up, many Eszai thought their power was being eroded and they panicked; it split the Circle half and half. The Sailor – my predecessor – led those who wanted to use violence, and San nearly expelled him from the Castle. But Lightning's diplomacy won, as it will again.'

'Oh, yes,' said Wrenn admiringly. He drew nearer to Mist.

Lightning continued: 'The wisdom of our Emperor resolved the situation. We're only his servants, whatever Ata may say. You see, San offered Eske's only son a place in the Circle. He was a damn good horseman and deserved to be Hayl. Lord Governor Eske died of old age fifteen years later, taxes unpaid. His immortal son inherited the manor and the uprising simply collapsed.'

They reached the edge of the escarpment and looked down; the land fell away like the inside of a bowl, to the flat – or at most gently undulating – Plainslands. From the curved grassy ridge that formed Awndyn's border they could see to the serrated horizon of Eske forest.

The square fields on the hillside were white with chalk soil; they looked like they were covered in snow. Yellow patches of barley with straggly orange poppies between them contrasted with the sky and hallucinogenic-green grass of the downs. Awndyn was a beautiful manorship.

Eske and Awndyn were the only two Plainslands manors owned by families who originated, centuries ago, in Awia. The Plainslands manors might seem weak and old-fashioned, incessantly bickering over their boundaries, but because the land was decentralised, its cultures were stable, tolerant and as varied as the Plainslands landscapes – peoples of forests, heath, Brandoch marsh and Ghallain pampas.

At the foot of the hill the coach and riders forded the pure water of a trout stream. Dust clouds and chaff blew across the road from a tariff barn where schoolchildren, who holiday at harvest-time, were brushing the paved floor in readiness to store next month's crop. They peered out from under the barn's thatched fringe. The older ones bowed their heads when they saw our sunburst insignia – while the teenage girls turned to each other and shrieked with passion.

I descended and said to Lightning, 'There are fewer farmers here than usual. If they've gone to Gio, more people are involved than I thought.'

'Great. With a shortage of labour and food the last thing we need is the farmers joining a rebellion.'

The air brushing the pits of my wings and the paler silky feathers under them was so erotic I started thinking of Tern again. How she giggled when I pushed my cold face down her bodice lacings. How her touch was so gentle I screamed but she kept stroking. I remembered Tern walking slowly in the snow, a parasol over her shoulder. My flitting footsteps crunch as I sprint round the corner of the black manor house. My body collides with hers. 'Caught you!' We fall embraced into the snow, laughing and kissing. She would bend my flight feathers to give me a sensation of speed, and I would encircle her whole body with them. Her wondering face looked up at my smile. And all the time she carried on her affair in secret. I snarled and spat down into a corn field.

I borrowed the horses just over ten hours ago. It had been one hour since we descended from Awndyn heath and entered the arable land. It should take another thirty hours' travel to reach the Castle. In five hours it will be sunset. One hour after that we will reach the Cygnet Ring Coach Inn in the dense part of the forest. In eight hours I would need another fix.

It was four p.m. when we entered the forest. The road cut through it cleanly; the spaces were open and bright sunlight permeated between the trees and threw moving highlights on the ground. Bracken and angelica sprouted among piles of bleached-white timber. In the tussocky clearings luscious purple foxgloves stood like racks of lingerie. I saw the road clearly from the air – two tracks from the wagon wheels with a grassy strip between them.

The air above the road shimmered; it looked wet and glassy. In every hollow of the dry track there was a mirage of a silver puddle that peeled away as we got nearer, and repeated further up the road in the hot air rising from it.

We passed a cleared area beside the road intended for a fyrd division muster point. About every forty kilometres we passed a coach inn. These pubs and stables were semi-fortified with high walls. Travellers, hunters and workers of the surrounding farms could seek refuge there if Insects set upon them. Luckily, there had been no attacks this far south for twelve months. I considered the forest to be free from Insects; we had spent the last five years hunting them down.

Wrenn dozed on the back of his palfrey. The Swordsman had no horsemanship whatsoever and sat like a sack of spuds, his chin on his chest, nodding forwards and jerking awake so I thought he was going to fall under the hooves of Ata's mare. Ata reclined in thought, under a denim cap. Her legs braced in the stirrups pulled her leather trousers tight over well-defined muscles. She stared at the backside of Lightning's stallion.

Lightning knew the forest well, and he loved it. He rested his bow horizontally on his knee and an arrow across it, nocked to the string. Holding a weapon changes your perception of the surrounding world. The very act of carrying a bow tunes your awareness to find the quarry. Lightning listened to every rustle in the undergrowth, or breaking twigs in the canopy. He noticed the 'coc-coc' of pheasants, the sound of grasshoppers switched on by the heat. He noticed the subtle odour of deer and differentiated it from the stink of the horses, wild garlic and ditch water. His senses were heightened – in the country, after an hour smell and hearing became as important as sight. A less experienced hunter would jump at any play of shadows and snatch up his arrows, but Lightning was confident. He knew that you always have more time to draw and loose a bow than you think.

I noticed a commotion further along the road. The highway ascended a slight hill; near the top it was blocked completely with people. At this distance I could only see splodges of colour, brown or black clothing, some pikes or flagpoles moving about, and an occasional bright flash in the centre of the milling crowd that was either a mirror or polished steel. I narrowed my eyes. This could be Gio's work.

I wheeled over my colleagues and called, 'Lightning?'

'Yes?'

'There's something strange ahead. I want to find out what it is.'

'A den for you to sleep in, perhaps.'

I clacked my wings together impatiently. 'It looks unusual ... Just because I'm hooked doesn't mean I can't function,' I added, muttering. I pulled on the air and surged up. I was only between one and two on the room-spinning scale. I should be treated the same as when I'm clean, especially if I have a good supply; it takes very careful examination to tell the difference.

A company of about one hundred men was walking slowly up the hill behind a double ox team that pulled ... At first it looked like a massive farm dray, but with an enormous wooden beam across it. At the front the square-sectioned beam was attached to a horizontal capstan whose great spiked handles projected like an unfinished cart wheel. A hawser made of twisted sinew joined a leather sling half a metre wide. It was a trebuchet, a thing of horrible potential.

The tops of heads, like dots, became pink as men turned their faces up to see me. The drover slapped the oxen's snouts, and when the trebuchet team ground to a halt he slipped wooden wedges under its solid wheels.

On the hilltop was another circular, grassed-over clearing maintained for a fyrd camp. Tents packed the earth, some small triangular shelters around a spacious cream canvas pavilion. Most were threadbare, stained with dirt, grease and wine, but some were from brand-new supplies. There were awnings and lean-tos, but I had no time to take it in because people on the ground spotted me and started shouting. Men dashed from all over the encampment to the centre where a huge bonfire smouldered. They stoked it, poked it, and threw on new logs and green boughs.

A thick column of dark grey smoke rose up. I saw it coming and a second later I was completely enveloped. Smoke burnt my eyes and nose. I breathed in a lungful and started coughing violently. Acrid smoke seared my throat. My sinuses were full of it; my inflamed eyes ran with tears.

418

Black flecks and sparks swirled past me. Leaves and lichen burning round the edges stuck to my shirt. I beat my palms on my stomach. I tumbled out of the billowing smoke, blinded and disorientated. I started to fall. Air whipped past me. Treetops hurtled up from where the sky was supposed to be. The sky was underneath me. I rubbed my face vigorously, tore out of my spin. I found myself above the road again, very low.

The hard-faced men by the ox team drew their longbows with disorganised timing and loosed. A hundred arrows flew straight up; I banked away hard. Long shafts passed in the air on my right. Flights whistled as they reached their zenith, turned round and plunged back. A breeze brushed my face from the nearest one. Spent arrows thumped on the upper surface of my wings. Shafts slipped between my fingered feathers. I straightened my flight path and beat madly away over the forest.

This could not be a case of mistaken identity.

Hot with panic I yelped, 'In San's name, stop!' Arrows poured around me like solid raindrops. 'In the name of ... San Emperor, for the will of god ...' But I was coughing too much.

I flew out of range but they kept shooting for five seconds to make their point. The arrows' broad heads crackled down behind me onto the topmost branches.

I winged back to the coach, furious. What's it like to be hit? To have a solid wooden rod impaled through my whole body – would I be able to feel it with my insides?

I landed next to Lightning and Mist. 'Did you see that?'

'Yes,' said Lightning.

'They aimed straight at me. Me! The Emperor's Messenger!' My clothes stank of smoke. I blew my nose and flicked mucus off my fingers. 'Bastards! Bastards! It's a wonder they didn't hit. If it wasn't for my agility ... They wouldn't even stop for "the will of god and the protection of the Circle"!'

'Aye,' said Mist. 'You shouldn't have gone ahead. Now they know we're here, and soon they'll tell Gio.'

'Me! An Eszai!' I was smart enough to know I am not universally loved, but I never thought I was hated.

Mist said, 'There must be something in that camp they don't want us to see.'

'Probably another bloody big trebuchet like the one they're dragging up the hill! I didn't see its serial number.'

I described the ox team and Mist listened with a faint smile, either admiring Gio's ingenuity or passionate for a good chase. She said, 'Why's the trebuchet this side of Eske, if he's taking it to the Castle? Has Swallow given it to him? Or has he stolen it? There, Lightning; you see that Awndyn's as treacherous as the other Plainslands manors.'

Wrenn's eyes were wide in disbelief. He ventured, 'Stop here and see if they come down to us.'

'In range of the trebuchet? Why not carry a target and make it their sport? We could offer foreign gold as prizes!' Lightning had a clearer idea of Gio's character.

'They must be very confident,' said Mist.

'They shot at me!' I said.

'Jant, quit wringing your hands and tell us – you know these roads – how can we reach the Castle without pushing past them?'

I said, 'We're about halfway to Eske. This is the only coach route, unless we go back into Awndyn and join Shivel Road. It'll take a couple more days because it'd put us two hundred kilometres out of our way. And it's probably packed with mangonels.'

Mist took off her cap and ruffled her hair, which was damp with sweat. Her face betrayed the stress she was under, some puffiness around her disturbing indigo eyes. 'Into the woods and outflank them, then. I'm carrying important information that I don't want them to capture.'

Wrenn found this ignominious. 'We can fight if necessary!'

'Unfortunately, Serein, I think they'd shoot you, too.'

I ordered my driver to take the carriage back to the last coach inn, the Culver Inn, and wait there for instructions. If he received none after three days, I told him, he should return to Awndyn. I didn't want to lose my possessions. Lightning, Mist and Serein dismounted and led their horses off the road into the forest undergrowth. At first the going was hard; brambles hooked in my trousers and tore them. The pungent smell of bracken was up round our noses. Further from the track, less light penetrated the canopy and fewer plants grew between the trunks. Tinder-dry oak and beech leaf litter crunched under our feet and the hooves. 'I hope Gio's rebels don't torch this,' I said.

Mist said, 'God, now he thinks of it! Scout ahead and tell us how far we have to walk before we can rejoin the road.'

I shrugged off my water bottle that glugged at every step, and hung it on Wrenn's saddle. I dashed away. It was impossible to move without sound in the forest; stories that tell of my predecessors doing so are just flattering lies. But I have lively reactions and I can run so swiftly through the tangle that no one registers the sound as human. I ducked under branches, leapt over fallen brushwood and sprinted with long strides. I sped up the rise and doubled back to the road. It seemed clear beyond the camp. I hid behind a tree, peered out and withdrew immediately. Another band of men strutted past with their pikes on their shoulders.

I ran on again, enjoying myself, but every kilometre I spotted more groups, so I returned to my friends, nimbly through the spaces between snarled undergrowth. Hot saliva was gushing into my mouth; I felt real once more. 'This isn't good – they're all along the road! We …' I lowered my voice. 'We could walk in the forest all the way to Eske but there's a hundred and twenty kilometres to go, so it would take you days. I say we keep going until nightfall and then try to rejoin the road further on, when the rebels should be encamped or indoors. I'll scout ahead again.'

Mist said, 'Lead on then, smoky creature.'

'Somewhere around here is the Cygnet Ring Inn ratskeller. Foresters drink there so we should pick up a track eventually.'

'Damn, you move so fast I can't even see your footholds,' Wrenn grumbled. 'There's no path here.'

'Then we make a path.'

We walked, leading the horses, over the copper-coloured floor, under the stippled green ceiling for the next few hours, some distance from the road so we wouldn't be heard. The light began to fade and the dusk became darker by degrees. The ground could not be seen clearly; tree-boles seemed to float towards us, distanceless. I felt as if something sentient and silent was watching us. I couldn't decide whether it was large and invincible, or small and instinctive.

On the road with their mounts, the others had been slow, but now negotiating trees and bramble thickets they slowed still further until they didn't seem to make any headway at all. I burned with frustration. I kept urging them on until Mist lashed out, 'I'm going as fast as I can! I can hardly see. I keep stumbling over things and so does this stupid nag. I *hate* this; we're in the middle of nowhere and the Empire's suddenly crawling with people who despise us.'

Lightning intervened. 'Look, Jant, let's rest here, have a few hours' sleep and then check if the road is safe. The newspapers said Eske is full of unrest and I don't want to be exhausted when I travel through town.'

'You're all so unbelievably tardy,' I said, but I flopped down immediately and made myself comfortable on the leaf litter. The others, who were not as practised at bivouacking or as careless as a Rhydanne, looked about for a patch of grass or a landmark to camp next to.

Wrenn threw his pack on the ground and sat on a stump that was so rotten he bounced off it and it fell to pieces. He brushed moss from his arse and began to unlace his boots.

Lightning paced about. 'I think that the town will be safe without Gio to stir up the Zascai. The ingrates don't understand how hard we have been working for them all this time …' He tripped over a tree root and kicked it angrily. 'Creeping about in the dark like highwaymen!'

The post-coach jumps the news from manor to manor. I imagined every governor realising that the Castle is only protected by tradition and their own beliefs. I almost heard them thinking: what could be in this for us? 'Half the Plainslands has supported Gio for six months. We don't know what we're heading into.'

Mist said, 'I only know we must make haste to reach San.' She made a small hearth, unrolled her blanket and shared out some Trisian *pan forte* and a flask of red wine. 'I think Gio wants to cause us as much pain as possible before we inevitably catch him. I can tell he must have little hope because his methods are so desperate ...' She fell into a reverie and did not speak again. We heard people passing by at the road's nearest approach. I felt satisfied that I could lie hidden and observe them, and they wouldn't know I was listening.

Lightning took out one of his books. He was writing his three-hundredth romantic novel, which would probably be much the same as the other two hundred and ninety-nine, but maybe this time with a nautical theme. Their popularity was a constant source of wonder to me. He usually pays me to translate his unimaginative but ardent scribblings, but he always has my translations checked. Lightning looked wistful, a powerful emotion he had practised over centuries, which he now fell into easily. He had adopted it when it was fashionable, although it didn't suit him. 'Swallow is never here when I love her,' he said. 'I wish I could speak to her. In times of trouble, she finds an inner strength. Maybe it's because she lives in pain and is hardened to it.' He sighed, and went back to writing, with the practicality of a lover who has sought the same character in different women over fifteen hundred years.

For the past hour I had thought of nothing but scolopendium. My mouth watered for it and my joints ached. I couldn't hold out much longer before my need began to show. It's just a weakness of my body, I thought; it isn't really *me*. I opened a knotwork painted tobacco tin containing my stash and a syringe. I acted casually to protect me from the others; underneath I bubbled with excitement and blame. 'Don't mind if I hook up?'

'Oh, go ahead.' Mist shook her head in disgust, though I could tell she was taking notes.

'Thanks. You don't know how much I ...'

'I'm beginning to guess,' said Wrenn.

'So one day it'll kill me. Want some?'

'Certainly not!' he said contemptuously. He walked to the edge of the clearing and stood with his back to us to have a piss. Then he returned and lay down on his coat with his rapier to hand. He watched me covertly, pretending to be asleep.

I hunched over and mantled wings round a candle stub. I licked my needle more or less clean, ran it through the flame and filled it from a skylark phial. I tied a tourniquet around my upper arm, and made the injection. I flushed the syringe out with my own blood and pulled the spike from my arm. Then

I keeled over, into the leaves. An aching nausea filled my empty stomach and dispersed as my rush came on. Gradually and gratefully I gave up on thinking about anything at all.

The tops of the oak trees were pushed by a wind that didn't touch us below. Each gust churned the topmost boughs in the distance, then shook the branches above us as it passed.

A crunch sounded somewhere deep in the forest. Lightning glanced up from his book and stood up silently. He bent his longbow against his boot and strung it. He kicked the fire out, then hauled me to my feet by the scruff of my neck and simultaneously gave Wrenn a hefty kick on the bum. The Swordsman woke with a start and Lightning raised a finger to his lips. 'Footsteps,' he whispered.

'Insects?' Wrenn's eyes widened.

Lightning shook his head. After the first few trees the ground was obscure. I listened. The footfalls extended deep into the woods from our left to right. As they came closer, we could tell they were made by men. There were at least five directly ahead of us, but the noise seemed to stretch out far on both sides.

'How many?' Ata mouthed.

Lightning held up his free hand with the fingers extended, clenched his fist, then opened the fingers again.

Wrenn sprang to his feet, crossed his arms over his waist and drew his rapier and dagger at the same time. Mist pawed uneasily for the 1851 Wrought sword that she carried buckled to her pack.

The footsteps resolved; the people making them walked about two metres apart. I peered into the gnarly gloom but I couldn't glimpse anybody. We should be able to see them by now. I smelt hot oil. The crunching continued; they were almost on us. They stopped. There was silence.

Wrenn went into guard.

A yellow glare turned our camp bright as day. Black jumped to colours, disorientating us. They had been carrying covered lanterns and with one accord they raised their shutters.

I was less blinded than the others. I turned as a man jumped from the forest behind us. Dagger in hand, he ran past Lightning and cut the bow-string with a neat slice. Lightning's powerful longbow sprang back straight.

It gave a dry crack. Splits opened along the bow's limbs from the tips to the grip. It snapped its eighty-kilo draw weight back into his arm. Lightning jerked away so the string didn't gash his face. The shivered wood creaked. He dropped it and the arrow, and grabbed his left arm. 'Damn you, Gio Ami! Traitor and sneak!' He drew his sword with an efficient gesture but his wrenched arm seemed awkward.

The horses neighed and reared, frightened. They pulled out their tether pegs and scattered.

I can't take off. The branches are too dense for me to push up between them. I'd be scratched to bits and never break through into the clear air. Fuck it, there isn't even enough room between the trees for me to open my wings, let alone run with them spread.

Gio sauntered towards Wrenn, gazing fixedly at him.

'Revenge isn't worth it,' I said quietly.

'Comet, aren't you fast?' Gio sneered. 'Is fame worth it? I walked through Wrenn's party and no one spoke to me. When I entered the hall, the Eszai all fell quiet and turned their backs. *You* didn't even *notice* me!'

He pointed his rapier at Wrenn. Gio still wore the blue frock coat, open to his naked chest. His dusty trousers were the same, tucked into scuffed boots with stirrup guards. He had probably been riding between manors, raising his rabble, for weeks. His fair hair was dirty; strands escaped his ponytail and hung round his face. His lip raised in loathing, hatred contorted his features; it burned in his eyes as he stared at Lightning. I thought: This is not the Gio I once knew. I must be careful until I know what he's become. I said, 'What do you really want?'

'I want to fight the *novice*.'

Wrenn's whole body language was a swagger. He spun his poniard like a drumstick. 'I'm Serein. I get to live till god comes back. What's it like to be older, Gio?'

Gio kept his rapier levelled at Wrenn. He motioned with his dagger and the twenty or so men behind him placed their lamps on the ground and advanced.

Lightning stepped across in front of Mist. His gallantry annoyed Gio so much that he turned from Wrenn and made a thrust low under Lightning's sword. Lightning evaded it expertly. Gio's rapier was blacked with boot polish; the point was difficult to see. He stabbed in again. Up went his other hand to ward off an overhead blow from Wrenn.

'Oh, shit,' said Mist. She slid her Wrought sword from its scabbard.

'Keep a clear head!' I shouted to her. 'They're nothing but Insects – defend yourself!'

My old gangland fury seeped through my high. If these guys are attacking me it's their funeral! A man squared up to me, tall and very broad. Everything was dark and indistinct but I glimpsed the purple ribbon of Ghallain Fencing School wound round his swept hilt. Bugger. There's no way I can stand against one of Gio's fencing instructors. The man smiled, his teeth incandescent white in his shadowed face. He watched me like a cat with a mouse many times its size. He strutted and said, 'Comet?'

A fencing master wouldn't use such bluster, only a poser apprentice. To bolster their own self-esteem town-boys have to believe they can fight. Heat rose into my head. I yelled, 'What?'

I ducked under his blade, came up well in distance, kneed him in the balls and as he fell sank my ice axe in his throat. The pick emerged from the back of his neck, shining, covered in blood.

I didn't see Gio's next moves because I pounced onto the man's body, both feet on his chest, to pull my pick free. I rolled and slammed it through the nearest foot with so much force that I fastened it to the earth. The foot belonged to the man Mist was fighting. He howled. He jerked his leg, tripped over the handle, which jolted the pick from his shoe. He reeled away.

It seemed that Gio was now the one prepared to die in the struggle for immortality. Wrenn stamped the ground and thrust at Gio. He blocked it halfway. His rapier and dagger moved fast as an Insect's feelers, keeping Wrenn at bay. Wrenn failed to engage his sword and Gio reached right to cut at Lightning.

None of the Zascai were prepared to help Gio take on Lightning or Serein. They concentrated on me instead, stepping forward warily, trying to time their attack together. I backed against a tree and motioned for Mist to do the same. She never stopped swearing as she raised her katana with both hands. A gleam ran along its perfect edge, daunting the rebels.

Gio circled Lightning's short sword with his rapier blade and then hit it hard under the forte. He flowed the move on with grace, beat away the straight thrust Wrenn made at his chest. He kicked a foot at Wrenn's hips, shoving him off balance. Wrenn bounded back, spread his wings.

The man fighting me turned and ran. I looked to Mist; she was shaking, white hands wrapped around her hilt and an expression of disbelief on her face. Blood peeled off the blade's razor edge. Her adversary lay on the ground in two pieces. For one beat, blood pumped out slickly around his solid guts. His lips moved, then set.

'Shit,' I said. 'It went straight through him!' I hadn't seen before what a blade designed for cleaving Insects could do to a human.

Mist said nothing, trying to think her way out of the horror.

Gio spun on the ball of his foot and lunged at Lightning. Lightning missed his parry but instinctively turned away from the point. It ripped through the left side of his shirt at the waist and into his back.

Gio whipped out the black blade, thirty centimetres slick with blood.

Lightning fell to his knees, heavily. Gio turned to Wrenn.

The Zascai stopped and looked at Lightning. He lay on his side with his body arched, knees bent, his wounded side raised from the ground. His eyes clenched shut with agony; he drew deep breaths through his open mouth.

The thugs shrank back, their broadswords loose in their hands. Gio's charisma had worn off and they were themselves again, every terrified individual. I shouted, 'See what you've done? Killed the Archer!' I made no attempt to hide the panic in my voice. '*Lord* Micawater. The oldest man in the world after the Emperor himself! Put your weapons *down*!'

Their blades dropped to the earth. They turned tail and fled, in ones and twos, every direction into the forest. I yelled after them, 'San will bring you to justice! I'll see you all hang!'

Gio and Wrenn were still duelling to kill fifty metres away. Gio forced Wrenn to retreat against a broad oak trunk; he was in danger of tripping over its roots. The last of Gio's allies raced past. A look passed between them – the terrified man urged Gio to run. Gio glanced back, realised his friends had split and his chance had gone. He jumped out of Wrenn's reach, shouted something I couldn't catch, then disappeared between the trees.

'What did he say?' said Wrenn. 'Jant, chase him!'

'No such thing – look at Lightning!'

'Hurry!' Mist snapped. 'Help me with Saker! Saker, you're going to be all right.'

Lightning's square face was pallid as clay; sweat broke out on his forehead. His body was rigid. 'Leave me alone,' he said faintly. He tried to fend me off and pull himself into a sitting position, so Wrenn and I supported him, me on the left and Wrenn on the right, and eased him against a tree trunk. We propped him upright and I rucked up his shirt to see the damage.

The rapier had passed through the forearm of his left wing, between its two long bones; radius and ulna, and then out and through the wing's bicep before gouging deep into his side. So his folded wing had been stuck through twice, leaving two entrance holes and two exit holes, but it had protected his side from receiving the length of the blade.

Lightning tried to spread his wing but couldn't. 'It's only a scratch,' he said, vaguely and inaccurately. I took its wrist, held together its three elongated fingers and pulled it open with a grating sound deep within the lacerated gristle. Blood flowed in strong pulses from the upper limb and soaked it. Normally broad with splayed feathers like a hawk, it looked thin with the wet golden plumage plastered down to the skin.

'Water. Hot water.' I rounded on Wrenn. 'You can do that, can't you?'

Wrenn fetched a canteen from the fire Ata had built and began to pour water through Lightning's wing. I whispered, 'He can live without a pinion. The stab in his side's more serious. Here, cut away the shirt.'

Lightning tried to tug his wing out of my hand. He would rather die of blood loss than be in such an improper position. 'I'm sorry, Saker,' I said aloud. 'We have to treat it.'

We mopped away the blood on his back, leaving a red-brown map of his skin's tiny pores and lines. The skin around the puncture hole was spongy and inflamed. Lightning was growing too confused to be rid of our administrations. 'Better luck next time,' he said to Wrenn, then rested his head on his knees. 'Ah ... it *bloody* ... hurts.'

I applied my tourniquet to his wing for a minute while I cut strips from his shirt to make a field dressing. It was impossible to tell how deep the wound was. I saw that it was more than four centimetres, but I had been taught not to probe them. I couldn't do anything about internal bleeding. I couldn't prevent infection; I didn't have sutures, nothing even as basic as a mould plaster or a clean bandage. Lightning looked so weak that all I felt was shame. I had never seen him like this before, and I should never have to. It wasn't the right way round: as at Slake Cross, I should be the injured one and Lightning should be helping me. He's the second-oldest Eszai, the richest immortal. He is the centre of Awia; he taught me its language, etiquette, martial arts. His money drip-feeds Wrought. What will happen without him? 'My god, what are we going to do?'

Mist said, 'Finish the job.'

Wrenn said meekly, 'How can I help?'

I yelled, 'Look after your own sorry hide! Gio had a system for fighting two men that you didn't know!'

Mist spat, 'Shira, keep working. Wrenn, get rid of those dead bodies then go and fetch the horses.'

Wrenn plunged about in the forest, falling over, cracking branches and making an awful noise. When he returned holding the reins of our three mounts Mist took two from him and left him with his palfrey. 'Ride back to the Culver Inn, find our coach and summon the driver. I'll build the fire up so you can see where we are.'

The Swordsman was only capable of a canter rather than a gallop; he led his horse to the road and we heard its hooves resound loud in the night then steadily fade. Mist said, 'I wish you weren't tripping so hard.'

'Ha! I saved you.'

She looked surprised. 'Well, a second later I saved *you*! That man I cut apart, he ... Oh, forget it ...'

A quick fix would steady me and help me think clearly. Or I could take my whole supply; unconsciousness was very appealing. I pushed the inappropriate thought away and said, 'He can't reach the Castle. In fact, I don't want him to lie in a coach even as far as Eske.'

Lightning forced himself to recover a little. Calmly but muzzily he said, 'San needs us. I'll be there. Gio broke my bow ... Pass me my bow; I want it.' He was blanking out the pain, which I admired because I have tried to do that more than once and failed. 'I *hate* rapiers. A *murderer's* sword. Worse than ...'

'You haven't been hurt before in my memory,' said Mist.

'Long ago,' Lightning sighed.

'There's something I can give you,' I offered, gesturing for Mist to fetch the splintered longbow and my pack. 'Everything will look a little strange for a while but you'll be too relaxed to care. Don't worry and let yourself—'

Lightning seized my hand and clenched it so tightly I winced. 'No drugs. Promise?'

He spoke with such certainty that I nodded. 'I promise.'

He huffed in great breaths, chest heaving like the sides of a tent in a gale. Then he lay down carefully and in a couple of gasps was unconscious. Mist dragged across his opulent gold and pale yellow coat, its grey fur lining collecting beechmast and broken twigs. We draped it over him.

Then I sat down beside him on a tree root. I ignored the blood soaking through my trousers and tried to sense the Circle. The Doctor once told me how, but she had more practice than me. She had taught herself to feel when the threads of our lifelines are strained. She can sense if someone is close to death because they pull on the Circle and it tries to hold them. Like a spider with her fingers on invisible filaments, it's possible that she already knows Lightning is injured. The Emperor would feel it; after all, he makes the links, sharing our time and preventing us from dying.

I watched the rise and fall of Lightning's shallow, in-shock breathing. If it stopped, I wanted to be prepared for the terrible sensation, the very moment when he rips through the Circle. No, I mustn't think that.

Mist stalked up to the fire and turned to me, her expression livid. 'Zascai shouldn't be *able* to murder Eszai. Immortals can't be struck down this way! Saker *can't* die. He'll wake up. I'll kill Gio Ami. I will – the bastard – how could he dare?'

'Ata—'

Her white hair tousled as she beat her fists on her thighs. 'Gio Ami. When I've finished with him there won't be enough left for a dog to roll in!'

'Look,' I said loudly. 'The thrust hit his wing and didn't go deep in his back. If dust doesn't infect it, the wound may not be fatal. But if we stay here, I won't bet on it. Return to Awndyn, and his so-called lover can nurse him.'

Mist's eyes glittered; their shine in the darkness looked halfway insane. 'No – on to the Castle.'

'You landed us here. For once plan for someone other than yourself.'

'I can't believe a Rhydanne has the gall to say that!'

'Only half—'

She interrupted, 'If we retreat we give Gio the advantage.'

'As if we have the advantage now!' I glared at her. 'Wrenn's illegal vendetta against Gio is bad enough without you joining in. He'll duel with Gio's followers all together or one at a time. Now *you* are trying hatred on for size.'

'You're right,' she said softly.

'Eszai are supposed to work together; let's earn our immortality. Damn it, Mist, god will show up, coffee mug in hand, before you bother cooperating. Go back to Awndyn, where I'll bring you San's directions as I should have done in the first place.'

Hours passed and Wrenn did not return. I watched over the Archer, straining to see by the insipid moonlight. Mist said little but glowered more and more until sometime in the early hours she burst out, 'I should have gone instead!'

'Serein is a poor rider but *nominally* the best Swordsman,' I said shortly.

'Well, where has he got to? Has he been captured?'

'I hope not. Lightning's condition is deteriorating, thankfully slowly because he's strong. It's imperative we get him out of this wilderness.'

Mist stomped around the clearing, cracking twigs underfoot and kicking dry leaves onto the hearth. I hissed, 'Keep quiet! And keep listening; Gio might return. You islanders don't realise how far your noise carries.'

Lightning woke up but only stayed conscious, unmoving, for a few minutes. I tried everything except scolopendium but I couldn't bring him back.

I sighed. 'Gio's wrecked his chances of regaining the Circle, that's for sure. He could have – one of my predecessors was displaced then rejoined it.'

Ata shook her head. 'There was such a fast turnover of Messengers that they had a good attitude; they saw it as a temporary prize and a few more years of life. I remember one man, three or four Messengers back, who when he lost his Challenge joined the Imperial Fyrd. We saw him grow old. But most people who leave the Circle are too broken to try again.'

If I was displaced from the Castle as a Messenger, I would try to convince San to make me a new place in the Circle – an Eszai for reconnaissance. Somebody might one day be able to outpace me, but they would never manage a bird's-eye view. It is theoretically possible for someone to hold two titles in the Circle but it has never happened because it's so difficult to keep hold of even one title. Anyway, seeing as every Eszai has to be beaten on his own terms, I would change the requirements of my Challenge to favour my strengths no matter who I'm up against.

All I really fear is the advent of another hybrid like me who has taught himself to fly and appears out of the blue with a Challenge. As far as I know I am unique and I'm careful not to have any children. In mortal living memory, relations between the countries of Darkling and Awia have become appalling; Rhydanne and Awians are active enemies, at least in the Carniss area. I only know of one marriage between them, when Jay 'Dara', a fyrd captain from Rachiswater and man of rare tastes, climbed to Scree to find himself a wife.

Jay was my best soldier and after Pasquin's Tower Battle nearly thirty years ago, when the governor of Lowespass was killed, I placed Jay and his wife Genya as governors in Lowespass fortress. I knew that I could check on them there, and especially on any of their offspring that might have both a sprinter's speed and long wings. But unfortunately for Jay running Lowespass fortress is a hazardous job, and twenty-one years later he died childless when Insects ambushed him by the Wall.

Gradually the sky paled; the darkness shrank away into the long shadows of the trees across the whole forest. The dawn chorus broke out; roosting birds roused and called from the branches above us. Mist listened to them with extreme suspicion as she chewed the last of the *pan forte*.

She paused, hearing the clop of hooves and the heavy whirring of iron-bound coach wheels from the direction of the road. Between the trees a light glowed, faded. The din ceased. Wrenn's voice called, 'Comet? Hey!'

I raised my voice: 'Hey, Serein! Over here!'

'Good morning. I'm sorry I took ages. It was a long way and there were rebels everywhere.' The young man's voice swung towards us, obscured by the sound of hacking as he cut his way through dewy briars. He emerged from a thicket, grinned and pointed his rapier at the road. 'But they've all passed by now.'

I motioned for Wrenn to help me lift the Archer. He said, 'I feel as if I shouldn't touch Lightning.'

'I understand. You heard tales of his exploits in history when you were a boy, right? Well, you take his legs and I'll lift his arms.'

We struggled to carry Lightning out of the forest, over the uneven ground. He seemed even bigger limp and lifeless, and was a dead weight, although his bones were hollow. Wrenn climbed into the coach, reached down to grasp him under the arms and pull him up.

'It's not as elegant a carriage as he might have wished,' Mist remarked dryly, but with obvious relief.

I laid Lightning on his side, on the floor because the seats were occupied by our sea chests. The wound in his back started bleeding again, dark and clotted blood. Mist staunched its sluggish flow with the last of the cloth. 'What am I supposed to do?' she snapped. 'I don't have the faintest idea how to care for casualties. Jant, come with us to Awndyn. Tris is three thousand kilometres away, and at the moment your report is hardly San's vital priority!'

'But I have to help San muster fyrd against Gio.'

Wrenn said, 'You can't stop Gio; you're just a messenger ... Shit, I'm sorry, Jant.'

I said, 'Don't you *dare* go after Gio! Sit up there with the driver.' Wrenn

430

hopped onto the bench with the nervous obedience of a captain receiving direct orders. I took the opportunity to whisper, 'I'll accompany you to Awndyn and we won't stop en route. But when I leave you, don't trust Mist. She doesn't fancy you, Wrenn; it's all bluff. Ignore her seductive words and low-cut tops if you know what's best. Without Lightning, you and I have little protection from her schemes. And – I never thought I'd say this, but – beware of Zascai. Too many are Gio's devotees.'

'Jant, this is overcautious.'

'No. Do as I say. When I return with San's orders I want to find you alive.' I climbed into the coach and thumped the ceiling. The driver cracked his reins, and we gathered speed down the straight road. The forest formed a block on both sides, a palisade of trees. The Remige Road was so silent that I found it hard to believe our desperate fight had actually occurred.

We reached the manor house after five hours and I ransacked it for medicines. I explained everything to Swallow Awndyn, who made sure that the Archer was given a clean bed. The manor's resident sawbones was a sensible man, but seemed to be completely out of his depth.

I wrote a letter for Swallow's courier to deliver post-haste to the Doctor at Hacilith University: 'For the hand of Ella Rayne only. Follow the bearer to Awndyn manor where Lightning lies in a serious condition from rapier wounds. A single thrust pierced his wing twice and made a puncture lesion in his back near the kidneys which pours blood at the slightest provocation. Rapid pulse and dyspnoea; the rapier blade was dirty. C.J.S.'

I caught a few hours of sleep but it was late on Monday evening, a full twenty-four hours after we were ambushed, when I felt able to leave Lightning and set out for the Castle.

I flew in a strikingly clear sky. A full moon gibbered over the forest. Above me, stars between stars; the familiar constellations could scarcely be distinguished among the litter of faint points of light. The immensity of what had happened began to weigh on me. 'Saker,' I said aloud. Lightning was hurt. But why now? He had survived so long. I had never known him injured by Insects; he could only be hurt by people, now that the Empire was turning on itself. I flew, chilled by extreme loneliness. Tern has abandoned me and now Lightning was gone. I need to take a bit more scolopendium, I thought, and was suddenly terrified that I might. I was vastly more afraid of scolopendium now that I was alone.

Strange. I beat my wings, finding their strength reassuring. I can rely on no one. Whatever I am going to do is up to me now and I have to stay alert. We must trust the Emperor. My wingtips brushed the forest canopy as I flew low, throughout the night, back to the Castle.

CHAPTER 14

I followed the Eske Road in, a grey line ruled through the woods. If I had to rely on my compass, then the crosswind, gentle as it was, would have pushed me northwards kilometres off course.

By dawn, the Castle was a dark smudge on the horizon. Even at this distance I could sense the tension: something was wrong. Dozens of tiny fires were scattered just inside the forest's fringe where it ended at the clear grass of the demesne surrounding the Castle.

Hundreds of specks fanned out from under the trees – running men who purposefully converged on a few sites and set to work. I approached watching timber being felled, ranks formed out of thronging mobs. They abandoned carts to choke the final approach of the road, and at the forest's edge they were winding back the huge wooden arms of trebuchets. I counted six machines of the largest class. Men with shovels were rapidly topping up their counterweight boxes with earth, while another team systematically dismantled the last watchtower on the Eske Road, carting blocks back and distributing them, stacking a pile beside each catapult.

Just forward from the trebuchet line, Gio's rebels drew up into a long ragged crescent in front of the Castle's east wall, centred on the Dace Gate. Facing them across the open ground, with their backs to the Castle and the outer moat, was a much smaller formation, the Castle's defence.

They were framed between the Northeast and Southeast towers: Fescue Select, Shivel Select in front of Fescue General, Shivel General – the full fyrd of two Plainslands manors, but only two. Either the rebellion was very widespread or the manors could not marshal men in time. Their banners cracked in the breeze, a sound that always filled me with dread. The centre was a solid block of heavily armoured hastai – veteran Select infantry – and a figure so huge that as I angled over them I easily recognised Tornado. To either side ranked pikemen raised a forest of jostling pikes. Cavalry pawed restlessly at the flanks, Hayl's white horse pennant above the larger group. All the loyal fyrd were unusually well equipped and their armour shone – they were offering a deliberate contrast to the ragged rebels.

Hundreds of helmets glinted as they looked up to see me flying over. I waved my arms in acknowledgement. Don't look at me, I thought; watch the rebels! I passed above the curtain wall, reassured by its bulk. Along the east wall, longbowmen of the Imperial Fyrd were stationed between the crenellations – I suddenly realised that the toothed tops of the towers were not just for decoration; the defenders on the parapet could shelter from missiles behind each merlon tooth. But the Castle was the only fortress to have crenellations – the Insect forts, like Lowespass, didn't have or need them. The Castle was a fortress designed for protection against people as well as against Insects. 'Shit,' I said aloud in astonishment. 'How long ago had San anticipated this?'

The two forces faced each other, hearing the clacking as six trebuchet arms wound tight and still tighter. Each side waited for the other to move first. I banked around the Southeast Tower thinking that I couldn't tell Tawny anything that he couldn't see from the ground, so I circled up two hundred metres in the dawn air, wary of more arrows.

Archers detached from the main crescent of rebels and advanced slowly, their line like a loose screen. Tornado's infantry responded by locking their hooked square shields together into an unbroken wall. A second later the ranks raised their shields over their heads, forming a makeshift roof against the arrows. The odd formation was unlike anything I had seen before, but I admired Tawny's ingenuity.

With a crash of counterweights, the arms of all six trebuchets jerked up. I was far above them and saw, in plan, six stones arc out. One smashed down just in front of the machine – the stone had been too light; the middle two fell short, ripping up turf swathes; a fourth crunched through the canopy of the furthest plane tree in the paddock and dropped into the moat in a white water spout. Two rocks seemed to grow in size as they came up under me, shrank on their descending trajectories and struck the crenellations. Bowmen dived out of the way as chips flew off the facing stone.

A distant roar of exultation burst from the woods, tinged with fear at their own audacity. Teams of men hauled on the capstans to rack the trebuchet arms down; then others staggered forward and rolled a stone into each sling.

Appalled, I thought, isn't Tawny going to *do* anything? People are actually damaging the Castle itself. Zascai are really attacking *us*. What have we done to make them hate us so much they want us dead? Do they want to harm the Emperor and annihilate the Circle? If Gio gets inside he knows the way to the Throne Room. My mind whirled at what would happen if every Eszai at once found himself suddenly returned to mortality.

In less than a minute the trebuchets were ready to launch again – their crews were obviously Eske's trained fyrd. Their accuracy improved: only one block fell short, in front of the Yett Gate on the southeast wall. One went wide and bounced along the paddock fence, smashing it into matchwood; the remaining four thudded into the curtain wall. The Castle bled more rubble into its inner moat. I noticed that the wooden bridge to the Dace Gate had been removed.

Now the rebel archers started to send volleys towards the loyal fyrd.

Arrows stuck in the shell of shields protecting the infantry. They found their marks in horseflesh spreading disorder and agitation throughout the cavalry.

Hayl Rosinante had had enough. He waved his horsemen forward, and they surged and gathered speed, spreading into a thin line, raising their lances. The archers immediately turned and raced back towards the safety of their own spearmen. From my vantage point I saw they wouldn't make it. Swift as Insects, Hayl's men ran them down. Ridged lance points devised to crack shell drove straight through the soft bodies of Awians and humans. Half the riders abandoned their lances in their impaled victims and drew swords, continuing their charge towards the rebel line.

I was ... I had never expected to see mortals fighting immortals, and here of all places. In front of the Castle with Eszai leading troops against the Zascai we were sworn to protect! I wheeled round, sick with disgust, and sped towards the Throne Room.

As the breeze propelled me sideways, I kicked away from the pinnacle tops and lead sheet roofs coming up under my feet. Another horrible crash sounded from the direction of the Dace Gate.

The Throne Room spire sprang like a frozen fountain three hundred metres into the air. Its shadow swept round an enormous sundial on the Berm Lawns. The spire was built on Pentadrica Palace, which settled to accept it, ninety centimetres into the ground. The pressure caused little splits in the beams, cracks in the plaster. Its base was a harder stone, to stop the spire's weight crushing the blocks.

The end of the Throne Room was pierced by stained-glass windows in primary colours. The rose window crowned it, twenty metres across. One of its multifoil panes was propped open. I could fit through there. I pulled my wings to my body and folded them up as I felt the feathers brush the mullions. The arcuate sill passed below me; I slipped through.

The dim, silent hall was five hundred metres long, its cross-vaulted ceiling thirty metres high. At the far end was the black screen; way below me was the tiled floor with its scarlet carpet. People no taller than a centimetre looked up as I appeared in front of the rose window, my wings stretched in silhouette against its red and blue light.

I flew at the height of the diaphanous gallery adorned with different colours of marble. Above me were smaller lancet windows, the great bays divided by pointed arches below. Every window gave a fragmentary view of another part of the Castle.

My body rose and fell with wing-beats. With every beat I passed an arch – with columns like bundles of thin tubes, supporting ribs interlacing the ceiling. I was in perfect rhythm with the arcades' march down the Throne Room. They met at the vanishing point, where the Emperor sits.

The capstone bosses were larger than life – a double-headed axe, oak leaves, turtles, cascading cornucopias, flowers complex as chrysanthemums. The walls were bright with daylight. The sun shone on the east side and cast the shadow of the pointed windows all the way down the west vault. San watches these shadows tilt, shorten and reappear on the east vault every day. Above him, the ceiling vanishes up into the octagonal spire; behind him shines the sunburst.

The scent of incense thickened. The marksmen on the balcony looked distressed; then the carved ebony screen filled my vision. I swung my legs down, alighted gently on the carpet before it, and trotted through the portal, pulling my wings in and folding them. I knelt fluidly before the dais.

'My lord Emperor, I have returned from Tris and await your command.'

A crash, scarcely muted by the pierced walls, echoed through the hall. I winced. 'What's happening out there? How can I help?'

San said, 'The guards will inform me of the situation outside. Am I right that you can add little news about the rebellion?'

'Lightning is wounded. I left him at Awndyn manor.' I outlined the ambush, the spice ship, and *Stormy Petrel* hidden in a fissure. I paused at every clash or an outburst of shouting, wondering if they were coming nearer. I could only hear the loudest shouts, chaotic and disjointed. I fretted – why didn't San send me outside to watch them? The rocks were smashing the outside wall and destroying the buildings in the gap. Can they reach as far as the Palace? If Tornado doesn't keep them out of range Gio will aim for the spire.

The Emperor listened impassively and at length said, 'Be calm, Comet. The Archer's injuries are to be regretted, yes, but he is not the whole Circle. There are other ways to defeat Gio. Tell me about Tris – everything concerning the island.'

'I have Mist's written account.' I took the scuffed stack of papers from my satchel, climbed the four steps to the rostrum and passed it to San. His pinched, wolfish face watched me keenly. Under his ivory cloak, his sleeves were loose to the elbow. His fine white hair hung down to curl on narrow shoulders.

A breathless guard ran past the screen then prostrated himself on the floor, his sense of etiquette battling with the need for urgency. 'My lord,' he panted, 'Hayl's cavalry have been turned back by the rebel pikemen but casualties are light. Tornado says he must break the rebel lines in a melee if he's to stop the trebuchets.'

San nodded. 'Tell Tornado I have full trust in his judgement. However, remind him that there must be no pursuit once he has broken the resistance.'

The guard stumbled to his feet, bowed, and left.

'My lord,' I said. 'Perhaps I should go and help the Strongman. We're heavily outnumbered.'

The Emperor gave a grim smile. 'This situation is not unforeseen. Last month Queen Eleonora offered half her fyrd to guard the walls. I declined as the involvement of Awia in any such engagement would increase discord. Instead the Plainslands manors have shown their loyalty, and the weakness of Gio's support.'

Two more crashes, only a second apart; falling slates then silence. I looked tentatively at San, unable to hide my doubt.

'Comet, remember that the Circle is composed of the unsurpassed. The strongest warrior and finest horseman in the world defend us. These walls were built by a succession of the world's pre-eminent architects. Gio Ami may be the *second*-greatest swordsman ever but he cannot be everywhere. His followers have disloyal natures or they would not have joined him, and once the battle turns against them he will be unable to hold them for long.'

'My lord.'

'Now, report on Tris.'

I began to describe everything that had happened on our voyage, in chronological order. I took pleasure in doing my job well. San listened to me talk, and act, as I paced back and forth on the carpet before the dais, in a red patch of light cast by the stained glass windows.

Another crash resounded, and the noise of shattering glass – the telescopes and sundials in the Starglass Quadrangle. The Emperor frowned and sent a guard to check on the damage. The Starglass Quadrangle was full of accurate instruments that set the time for the entire Fourlands. In fact, the Fourlands' prime meridian runs through it; the north axis that crosses the east axis at zero degrees through the Emperor's throne.

Another soldier sped in. I stepped aside while he flung himself on his knees in front of the throne and spieled out the latest news seen from his vantage point on the Skein Gate tower. 'The Select Fyrds have engaged the rebel centre. The cavalry are regrouping on the flanks.'

'Very well, return to your post.'

I thought of the picture of San in *Tris Istorio*. He was acting like a fyrd captain once more. I resumed speaking but was interrupted every fifteen minutes by news of the battle. There were longer waits between the trebuchet impacts now and the shouts were further away. Tornado and Hayl are driving the rebels back, I thought with relief.

I spoke for so long that we had to break the court session to give me a meal. The four hundred kilometres I had just covered were taking their toll. By the time I finished it was early evening, and the bombardment had ceased some time ago. Nervous servants came in to light the torchères and wind lamps down on chains from the ceiling to fill them. I was exhausted from sleep deprivation and practically flayed by San's questions.

I stared at the four gemstone columns in the niche behind the throne: blue azurite for Awia, purple porphyry for Morenzia, green jade for the Plainslands, silver-grey haematite for Darkling. For the first time I noticed that although there was equal distance between them, the four columns did not span the apse symmetrically. There was room for another pillar on the far right, just by where some small steps descended to an arched and iron-studded door that led to the Emperor's private rooms. There was a gap where a column used to be – for the Pentadrica.

An Imperial Fyrd guardsman entered, bowing to give his final message without meeting the Emperor's eyes. 'Tornado reports that the rebels have been routed. Gio Ami didn't dare face him in combat and his body is not among the fallen.'

'Very well. Tell Tornado and Hayl to bring their reports as soon as they are able.'

The guard left and San returned his gaze to me. 'So you even left the Insect running loose?'

I picked at the unravelling seam of a fingerless glove. At this very minute the Insect was probably dining on the Capharnai. 'Yes, my lord. We respect-ed the Trisians' wishes. It'll be difficult enough to deal with them in future; we didn't want to exacerbate the crisis still further. Vendace found it easy to reject Mist's offer, because to the Senate immortality is just a nebulous concept. Half of them don't believe in it.'

'I see. You failed to convince them. In fact you have given them one more reason to mistrust us. The situation must be healed, and quickly. Comet, you have worked hard so far. Can you do better?'

I bowed. During my meal in the empty guardroom San had written a missive that now lay on the marble arm of his throne, neatly sealed with the crimson sunburst. He regarded me carefully, as if he could read all my private thoughts from my face. He resumed: 'Gio's followers hold up our stagecoaches at every point between here and Cobalt. Gio himself is not easily found, except when he wants to be, it seems. This letter' – he picked up the small envelope – 'must be delivered to Mist urgently. Do you have someone you can trust to do it?'

That was a poor precedent: a mortal asked to do my work. I said, 'Messages are only truly secure if delivered by my hand.'

San's pale thin lips turned up slightly. 'I don't doubt it, Comet. But I have other work for you. Following his defeat, Gio Ami will attempt to regroup. I know that he will be holding a meeting in two days' time in Eske, in a *salle d'armes* hall that is a branch of his school.'

'Yes,' I said. 'I've been there often.'

'I want you to go and listen to what he has to say, and then come back and inform me.'

'Your wish.' Obviously I wouldn't be able to walk straight in, but I would relish finding a way to spy on Gio. He had once given me fencing lessons and I knew he was an excellent teacher; when in front of an audience he was a born performer. I said, 'I'll send the letter with a fast, dependable rider who should be able to slip past Gio. Mist should receive it late on Wednesday night.'

'Very well. In the meantime, if Tornado needs your assistance as a lookout or envoy do as he asks.'

Help the man who was fucking my beautiful wife? But San gave me no time for introspection: 'Comet, what do *you* think of Tris?'

Danio was immediately brought to mind; I shied away from the memory of her drumming feet, and recollected the Amarot library. 'The islanders love debate and casuistry that's misguided compared to our practicality. It's great that Tris now knows of the Fourlands. If we can make allies with them, if they become willing to communicate with us, their theories added to the Empire's will increase our inventiveness a hundredfold.'

'What is your opinion of the riches of Tris?'

'My lord, I think they're very dangerous. They'll cause avarice, not to mention inflation.'

'And the people?'

I sighed. 'On Tris, everything works, but that's because it's a tiny island. I think they have sorted out their problems – a very long time ago, perhaps – and they've not changed since. On Tris, a thief can become a honest governor ...' In our case, it's usually the other way round. 'But I find it strange that the citizens of Capharnaum don't want to cooperate with the Empire, like Rhydanne, and they hide themselves away when they clearly do care about the world and want to improve it, like Awians ... It'll probably do Tris good to learn of the real world. Maybe they're in shock. I hope that when they understand us the whole Empire will benefit.'

San watched me carefully, sitting straight in the throne without stirring. He was satisfied that I was telling the truth. 'Make sure that letter is sent to Mist swiftly and with the highest security,' he said.

'Yes, my lord.'

'Go now and rest, but return on Friday and tell me exactly what Gio says in Eske.'

San gave me the Top Secret sealed letter. I made obeisance, taking a few steps back before turning and passing the screen. As I left the Throne Room I called, 'Immortals and fyrd, bring any letters for Eske to my room before midnight. Any questions about Tris, keep them.'

*

438

Walking down the corridor I caught sight of a flicker of movement on the opposite wall and went back to investigate. It was my reflection, pickled in a tall mirror speckled with tarnish. An expression of horror crossed its face – even in the half-light I don't look as good as I did this time last year. Still the same age of course, but my eyes were ringed with deep shadow; my cut-off T-shirt was the grey texture of clothes washed hundreds of times.

I called at the stables and watched my courier race away with San's letter. Enormous plane trees grew in the wrecked paddock outside. I walked past the one that I had sheltered underneath, two hundred years ago. Suddenly I saw a vivid image of my tattered self back then, leaning against the tree trunk. If I had known that any Challenger was welcome to walk into the Castle at any time, I would not have spent three days sitting under this very tree, wondering how to present myself. On our way from Hacilith, highwaymen had murdered my girlfriend and stolen the money I'd gained by blackmailing the city's governor. I owned nothing but my crossbow and a switchblade.

On the third day under the plane tree I felt a presence watching me – a man, all his colours subdued and outline unfocused as if seen through gauze. I felt a chill and didn't dare move. I stared at him and he looked back, so strange, full of confidence and concerns larger and more frightening than I could comprehend. An adult world, seen by a young man terrified for an instant by the inkling that he will join it and have heavy responsibilities every day.

I didn't know in eighteen-eighteen that I was looking through thinned layers of time, at myself. But now I realised that I was the ghost that my younger self saw. I wanted to tell him that everything would work out fine, that he would win his Challenge and two hundred years later he would still be twenty-three. I couldn't speak to him, but I smiled – and I remember receiving that warm compassion, because when I sat with my back against the plane tree's bark, I wondered at the manifestation but felt heartened and at ease.

Two centuries ago, what happened next was that at nightfall some immortals returned from the Front. I rushed to hold the reins of a horse carrying a well-built man with stripy grey and white hair, and the Castle's sunburst on a big round shield. His horse's withers were smeared with yellow blood.

I don't know why I expected Eszai to look different. A sparkle of the Circle about him was simply my excited imagination. He said, 'You're no groom.'

'I want to be Eszai.'

He must have wondered at what in the Empire I could possibly excel. 'Then come in, waif.' He kicked the horse's ribs and it cantered forward. Its hooves boomed over the wooden bridge and echoed between the weighty towers of the massive barbican.

I picked up some more steak sandwiches; I expend so much energy flying that I have to eat vast amounts. I walked from the kitchens through the ground-floor corridor of the Mare's Run, the inner west wing, past Hayl's apartments. I passed the Southwest Tower, where Tawny's well-lit room was located, full of indiscriminately chosen prizes: Insect legs, bear pelts and jousters' helmets. Then I climbed the three hundred and thirty steps of my tower, leaning on the wall all the way up, past the myrtle-green storeroom and the bathroom on its first floor that smelt as musty as hessian. I could lie on the bed for a while and fantasise about Tern – although I am more in a mood for a Rhydanne. Or I could, and I know I will, be distracted by the obvious alternative.

Wind-thrown rain began to scour the shutters. Tern had not been in for months; my room was dark and bundles of letters overflowed the shelves, piled everywhere. My valuable pendulum clock had stopped; I wound and set it to the right time and date. Masquerade masks hung around the mirror, beside a hookah as tall as I am, its fuzzy orange tube coiled around its brass pipe like a python. I spun the oval mirror around on its stand, face to the wall.

Faded posters taped to the round ceiling advertised music festivals, marathons, and Challenges when I wiped the floor with the mortals who wanted to contest me. I'm usually Challenged in winter when conditions for flying are at their worst, and I set the same test that won me my immortality – a race from the Emperor's Throne Room to the throne room of Rachiswater and back.

There was a vase of dried flowers, the only plants that withstand Tern's immortal forgetfulness. There were a few neglected old projects: my guitar, tennis racquets and a crossbow, all equally broken. There was my bike on which I lavish much attention, wrapped in its red rope that I use to lower it out of the window. Hanging on the wall above it was a series of obsessively concentrated little pen-and-ink sketches by Frost of jousting tournaments. The mantelpiece was cluttered with some wax seals in their skippet boxes; a souvenir from Hacilith – a spider's web preserved between two sheets of glass; and a lump of solidified Insect paper with a coin pressed into it. By the window stood 'Butterfly' my Insect trophy wearing a sailor costume, and my suit of armour stuck fast to the wall with decades of rust. An array of kettles, toast forks and dirty plates filled the hearth. On the dusty table beside my still's retorts and condenser was a note covered in Tern's dying-spider handwriting. I screwed it up and threw it in the cold fireplace. Looks as if the temptation of Tornado was more than the pretty lady could stand, I thought, fishing in my satchel for my syringe.

Once I start to feel the need I can go downhill very rapidly, and the room seemed suddenly very warm. I have to shoot some, I found myself thinking. No, I don't need it. Oh, yes, I bloody do; I don't want to be sick. Maybe when Tern sees how badly her adultery affects me she'll come back. The trouble is that we spend so long apart that when we do meet we are still self-sufficient, which is a barrier to becoming really close.

I sat down at my desk, reached behind me to pull down one wing, unfolded it in front and held it between my knees. I preened fingers through feathers like a harp, hearing them rasp, and felt the thin skin ridged over my quills. Here are veins I haven't used and they looked tempting. But if I made a slip and something went wrong, or if I damaged it and was paralysed, that would be the end of me. I have only shot up in a wing once before when I was desperate. This was sacred. Sighing but pleased at some show of will power at least, I untied the pendant thong from round my neck, looped it over my right arm and licked the ends up between my teeth. I flexed my fingers, impatiently tried to raise a vein. Don't poison yourself, Jant. Meditate your way to Epsilon. Yeah, right. Why did Tarragon think I wanted to go to Epsilon? The Shift was an unwanted side-effect when I only needed the drug to make me forget my pain. Why walk through worlds if you're immigrant in each?

I sat with the needle poised, feeling a last blast of guilty defiance, then pushed it in neatly. In the space of a heartbeat it hit like a coach-and-four. Feeling like a god, if a rather incapable one, I located the chaise longue under my maps and lay down. This was like flying into a wall.

My thoughts played out in the air above me, but they were rudely curtailed by the door unlatching. A graceful and chic figure entered, and seemed to flow over to me. Tern looked at me closely. Her body was a fair; there were dances there. Her spine a snake, voice like icing on cakes—

'Oh, typical,' she said crossly. She touched up her lipstick in a mirror above my head.

'Where have you been?' I asked suspiciously.

Tern glanced down and must have realised from my expression that subterfuge was pointless. 'At Tawny's apartment ... I had a good time.'

'What, all of it?'

'Tornado single-handedly held Gio off from attacking our home. He said if Gio came nearer I should run to the Throne Room. I have been encouraging him ... Is it OK for you to enjoy yourself but not me? I've heard that Tris is a perfect land. You sailed off and left me here.' Tern slipped out of her dress and searched around for her silk dressing gown, clad only in a white bra and underskirt. I was too stoned to be angry. I found it hard to care about anything, not even if the strongest man in the world came in and bent her over in front of me. I gave her my orphan look: please take me home and put me in your bed.

'Wipe that off,' she said. 'Are you going to lie there all night with your hand dangling? We had a pact, Jant. You're not being sophisticated, just sedated.'

Yes, we had a pact, which we began after the span of a mortal lifetime had lapsed. We promised that it is acceptable to have affairs because we will still love each other the most, and we will always return to each other. Actually, sleeping around should be refreshing because we have to spend the rest of eternity together without becoming bored.

I propped myself up on the velvet cushions. 'Tern, why Tornado? *Amre*, he's stupid; *demre*, he can't converse worth shit; *shanre*, he's bald; *larore*, he's ugly; *keem* he's poor! Is that the kind of man you really like, so you don't love me any more? Was your pride among the possessions you lost in the fire? *Keemam*, is he better in bed than me or, *keemdem*, are you so worried that I might be beaten in a Challenge that you're prepared to shag the whole Circle?'

Tern said, 'Why did you steal my money? Can I have it back, please, or have you mainlined it all?'

I ignored this transparent attempt to change the subject. I kept pleading: 'Remember when I proposed, how I brought you the filigree spider? We could go down to the Hall and dance without music, the way we did back in 'ninety-five. Come on! Wear your brooch – it can be our seventh honeymoon.'

'Ten minutes and you'll simply collapse.'

'Come to bed then.'

'That's not the point! Shira, you're never here yourself!'

'I'm the Messenger! The point of my existence is to bugger off and bring back news! It's my job!'

Tern drew the curtain across our room. I lay and watched the details of its velvet folds; they looked like letters of the alphabet.

She wiped her eyes and said quietly, 'All your holidays are spent in Scree. Fighting Insects nearly burnt you out – so off you go to the mountains. Do you have any women there? Even when you're here, you're unconscious! I knew your cycle would come round again. You can't stay off cat – you can't stand to be sober for more than five years. You're not thinking about us; you are thinking about that *fucking* drug.'

Tern knew how to hurt me. She had observed it well over the last century and her infidelity had pushed me into addiction before. If she was not adulterous I would not be a junkie. 'I took cat because I'm scared of the ships,' I said. 'Everybody knows that but Ata still forced me to sail. Besides, I would rather not use cat at all than bother you with it. It's under control.'

'That's not always apparent.'

Well, it wasn't always true.

Tern kept going. 'Oh, for god's sake! If I upset you, you suddenly start to notice – but you don't think how your actions affect anyone else! I should never have married a Rhydanne.'

'Where did *that* come from?' I blinked.

'I don't mean your appearance! Some things you just can't grasp, no matter how hard you try. It doesn't occur to you to think of anybody else, like you're still living alone in a hovel in the mountains. When you're away on errands do you ever think of me?'

'Yes. Yes, all the time! That whole Rhydanne thing is just bullshit. Don't lay it on me as well now.'

'The pact—'

'Sod the pact! It's all right in theory but neither of us can actually stand it!' In a lull between the waves of chemical pleasure I sprang to my feet and stalked around the room. I ran my hands down the embossed spines of the books on the shelves. I ended up leaning on the stone mantelpiece looking at outdated invitations to dances. Our marriage rings were smoke rings and they soon dispersed. 'I'm still Eszai,' I said.

'Shira ...' said she, and then fell quiet as she remembered what my name meant.

I kicked a neat hole in the bottom of the wardrobe door, then sat down cross-legged on the bearskin rug. 'Yes! See how important fidelity is to Rhydanne. If you're going to make all these unfair comparisons! I'm mostly Awian anyway!'

Tern said nothing; she had not seen me this angry for years. I stared at the ceiling, the only part of the room that didn't spin. I understood affairs; Tern wanted the same intensity of feeling now that she had when she was young. We might have young bodies, but we have had so much experience that we can't be young again. Tern should face it: she's one hundred and twenty-one. She would be dead by now if it wasn't for me, the ungrateful bitch.

'Do you drop your underwear on Tornado's floor as well?'

'At least I don't vomit on the floor!'

'Where do you think I've been? Tris and back! This is the first rest I've had in months; I'm serving the whole Fourlands, not just Wrought! You can't see further than your own nose! Having been through all that – *ocean* – don't I deserve some affection from my wife? Well, I can speak a patois that Tornado will understand. I will challenge him to a duel.'

Tern laughed. 'Don't be ridiculous.'

'I'll throw down the gauntlet and fight him. When I have a clear year to recover from being hospitalised. Of course he'll rip my wings off but it's worth it to get through to him.'

'You mad bastard,' Tern said, with something of her original admiration.

'Yes, I am. And remember, none of the mortals were. Not Sutler Laysan—'

'I didn't—'

'Or Aster—'

'That—'

'Or Sacret Aver—'

'No!'

It was the fact that her latest affair was with an Eszai, not a mortal, that angered me so much. I would outlive the mortals and my talent reassured me; I knew that Tern would always come back. Now for the first time she had a choice. 'Are you going to divorce me and marry the Strongman?'

'Jant, don't ask such questions … I'm going now. I'll come back when you've straightened out. When you can return the money you stole.'

'Money has nothing to do with this!'

'It does. Oh, it does indeed.' Her pure, sparkling voice instantly froze. She picked up the most expensive beaker from the still, turned it over and put it down thoughtfully. 'I can't keep up repayments on Wrought's debts. I can't afford to rebuild the foundries. With no workers in the colliery or armouries, my manor is sunk.'

But I knew all that; I had always tried to help Tern. I was suddenly uncertain how to answer because I had been listening more to her voice than her words. 'What are you saying?'

'Wrought will have to be leased. I considered selling but I don't want to lose my title, so I have managed to find a tenant. A coal-quarrying, canal-building nouveau-riche Hacilith businessman. I have no idea what Lightning will think of that. But who cares? Micawater itself is not in a position to help us financially any more.'

'But that's terrible! How will we live?'

'Soberly. The rent will pay my creditors – thankfully credit rates for immortals are good – but there will be little left over, and I will have to live *here*. The man from Hacilith and his family will help me reconstruct the manor house. Until my fortune improves, he'll reside there and also take the revenue from the armouries. He's keen to work with Eszai.'

'I bet he is. I'm sorry. I do love you, Tern.'

Tern came and placed manicured hands around my cheeks. 'You look awful,' she observed, and laughed red-wine fumes into my face. She lightly kissed my cheek and I smelt her powdered skin; the scent went straight to my groin. I swept one wing across my body to hide an erection that swelled so large I thought it was trying to climb into my belly button. I might get some sex tonight, after all. 'What would you say to a quick fuck?'

'Don't push your luck, quick fuck.' And she left, bound for Tawny's rooms.

I yelled after her, 'Don't ever come back! You're not that important to me anyway!' I picked my needle off the floor and threw it at the dressing table. 'Cat makes me feel better than you ever did!'

I felt as if I had a hole in the middle of my chest, and everything I am and everything I had been was draining through it until there was nothing left. I was hollowed out, utterly emptied. No smile or kindly deed I will ever perform will be rooted in myself; it will be carried out from duty rather than love. The world's conflicts carry on, oblivious, elsewhere and unreal; from now on there was no way to connect with them. I was animated only by that sick sense of duty, because all the love had been washed away.

I retrieved my needle and staggered up the steps to the four-poster bed with a feeling of desolation and a strange desire to get down and walk on all fours like a dog.

I drew the curtains; the dark brocade bed became a ship spinning on a whirlpool's rim. Its sails would not fill. Cold fish push up under my feet, fall flapping from beneath the bolsters of this bed and everywhere I'll ever sleep. In the tiny phial eels seethe and bite. I wanted to sink out of the world. I tapped up a vein running over my biceps and slid the needle in deep with a practised hand. Then I huddled against the ivy-covered headboard, sighed, and bubbles rose around me. Scolopendium pulsed through me, so good, to my toes and fingertips. A solid blow hit my heart and I squeezed a fistful of shirt tightly. I can ride the rush. But there's nothing to hold on to on this ride, because the ride's yourself. I gasped ice water into my lungs and then was nothing. It kicked me heavily out of my body and into the Shift.

Into Epsilon, the place you find when you take a wrong turning and decide to keep going. There is no easy way in.

I walked down the street. It's a one-way street; from the other end it looks like a mirror. Litter blew past, in the opposite direction to the breeze. Some of the Constant Shoppers were already arranging their wares, buying from each other with a muted morning energy. Tine made their stalls of smooth, living bone. They shaped a grainy bone gel with their hands and it set in sculptural sweeps. They exhibited framed emotigraphs, pictures faint with age or new and piquant, that recorded the subject's emotion and emanated it for the viewer to experience. A wedding picture radiated every feeling from rapture to secret jealousy. A picture of an autumn forest evoked nibbling nostalgia: lighting up a stolen cigarette, smell of leaf litter and first-night stand sweat.

Traders at a pet stall were herding some pygmy house-mammoths, the size of dogs, into an enclosure. An indigo-feathered archaeopteryx on a perch rattled its scaly plumage and twisted its head down to bite at its toes. The strawberries on a nearby fruit stall chatted between themselves of whatever strawberries talk about.

I walked to the edge of Epsilon city, along the bank of the river that runs mazily in right angles and often uphill. The market clustered round, infesting both banks. It seeped out of the town's perimeter, down to the estuary and towards the open plain, a lush grassland dotted with tiny isolated hermite mounds.

Out on the savannah, in the distance the skeletal white city of Vista Marchan tilted in the air, hanging like an enormous moon in daylight. Flocks of birds flew through its insubstantial mirage towers. Single-humped dronedaries grazed the long grass. They wandered, complaining, without even glancing at the ghostly streets around them. An Insect bridge arched up from the green plain, became transparent at its apex, then descended into the centre of Vista Marchan. The bridge was so old that cracks showed in its silver-grey patina like weathered teak.

Vista Marchan is a city that crashed through in the wake of an Insect invasion. The entire world of Vista was undermined by the Insects and collapsed into the Shift, where it is now visible from Epsilon. Its sandy wasteland seemed to emerge from the ground and extended at an incline to high in the sky. The dead towers of its capital city leant at forty-five degrees through the Epsilon plain, listing so that their tops hung over the Insect bridge. Their basements looked to be embedded in the ground, but actually they neither entered nor overlaid it, and they shimmered slightly in a heat that the savannah did not feel.

Nothing survived the Insects in Vista Marchan, but since they destroyed the boundary between the worlds so completely, people could walk there now, over their bridge.

One Insect tunnel bored into Vista's deep sea abyss, causing a kilometre-high waterspout in another world, through which the entire ocean drained away. No good came of this apart from the fact that it killed god knows how many millions of Insects, and there is now a peaceful saltwater sea in downtown Somatopolis.

I wondered if the Insects would eventually reach Tris of their own accord; some time millennia from now the Trisians might truly need Eszai to defend them. I wondered if the Insects burrowing down and piercing through the worlds would in the far future infest them all – the last worlds forming the outer layers of their teeming nest. Were they imperceptibly surrounding the Fourlands on all sides? Were we at the centre, near the Insects' long-overrun world of origin, or were we on the outer reaches, one of the last to fall?

Tarragon said she wanted to view the ocean's sphere from the outside. I wanted to strip away the worlds and look at the complex extensions, apertures and twisted continuous shapes of the Insects' domain.

*

Lost in contemplation I wandered through the market's fresh clothing region and the designer food district, to the edge where the Constant Shoppers' rickety shacks were dotted around between the stalls. The poorest Shoppers had to walk hours to reach the Squantum Plaza, heart of the market. They are a collection of all species but habitually a breed apart. They are either creatures of Epsilon, or Shift tourists like myself, so overwhelmed by Epsilon's bazaar they never escape.

'They buy things all the time,' Tarragon had said. 'Compulsively. I mean, that's their only pastime. They trade morning to night, and then all night in the southern souks. It's fashionable to spend money. Some of them are terminally addicted, which is as terrible as your habit.'

'These Constant Shoppers, what do they do when they run out of funds?'

'They set up their portable stalls on the other side of the Plaza and sell everything they've bought. Then, with that money, they start shopping again.'

I explored towards the river mouth. The market did not end at the waterline; the rows of stalls kept going, unbroken, straight into the estuary and along the sea floor.

Out here in the periphery Epsilon market extended into the air as well. Tall metal struts supported stalls on platforms thirty metres high. Creatures on top flitted, squawked and chirruped, eager to buy and sell. Marsh gibbons swung hand over hand along ropes strung between the poles; vertebrate spiders with metre-long fangs spun webs across them to catch flying machines.

Seldom ripples came in on the limp Epsilon sea. The water was as clear as air. At first half-submerged, the market continued down to great depths, where it faded from view in the poor light. Jellyfish hung motionless above it. Things with long, intricate shell legs waded between the stalls and reached down to select bargains. In comparison with the aerial stalls, the underwater market moved slowly and gracefully; columns of kelp swayed like trees. Temblador eels glowing eerie white swam at a sedate pace in shoals through the passageways. Nicors with ivory tusks and whiskery faces flapped along with lazy fins. Saurians snacked on pre-Cambrian sushi, tasty bundles of seaweed and writhing worm junk food. They haggled over jewels – green glass beads on silver rings. Anorkas clustered with geeky excitement round a shell stall and frales – very small whales – cruised picking up crumbs just as dogs, rats and trice do on land.

There were red octopi with pale undersides and eight shopping baskets. Rays with sinister ripped-off goods under their cloaks avoided the pikemen patrolling the aisles.

The market surrounded a large, translucent hall that the stinguish had constructed out of solidified water. Their building materials were monumental, colourless pyramids of spring water atop black water slabs from the lightless abyss, and grey speckled blocks from the deep silt where soft carcasses degrade to their elements. Their edifice was decorated with bricks coloured bright blue from the brine captured in sea caves, and rare aquamarine from the surface water that flares green when the last ray of the setting sun flashes through it.

A mirth of female stinguish looked up from the forecourt of their hall, through the surface tension. I waved to them; they turned to each other and giggled, long silver fingers over their lipless mouths in girly gestures.

Stinguish are a light-hearted people who live in groups called mirths. They communicate by laughter that carries underwater for thousands of kilometres, so any two individuals can chatter to each other through a network of mirths, anywhere in the vast ocean. According to Tarragon, chatter is exactly what they do; their flaky airhead nonsense pervades every cubic metre of the sea. Stinguish mirths migrate fifteen hundred kilometres twice a year, dive two thousand metres down to chasms, or lounge on the beaches in the tidal zone and breathe air. No stinguish was ever solitary. They had even more camaraderie than Plainslanders did. If you kicked a football along the streets of Rachiswater, an Awian would either tell you to keep the noise down, or point at the KEEP OFF THE GRASS signs. If you kicked a football about in the wrong side of Hacilith, someone would knife you and steal it. In Eske, Plainslanders start fifty-a-side matches that last for a week. But stinguish never stopped playing. How they managed to swim vast distances and remain cheerful is one of the great mysteries of nature.

My boots crunched on the pebbles. I passed a refreshment stall under which crouched a pair of brown, scaly tea dragons. Their innocent yellow eyes tracked me. Tea dragons breathe streams of hot, black tea. They were being used as caddies; I approached carefully because I didn't want to be sprayed with it. The stall holder was a polyp, a teacup held in each tentacle and its wet skin shining in the sun. 'What's it like being a polyp?' I asked.

'It's awful. Bits of me keep budding off and becoming accountants.'

The polyp sold tea to a flabberghast who bought a whole armful of ghostly doughnuts. I didn't see the flabberghast in time and accidentally walked straight through his corpulent, overhanging belly.

'Hey!' he exclaimed. 'Look where you're going, skinny boy!'

'Sorry, sorry.' I backed down to the water's edge, my hands raised.

Immediately a stinguish girl shot out of the wavelets. She grabbed my ankle with fingers as bony as a bird's feet.

I shook my leg. 'Get off! What are you doing?'

'Can you spare some change, please?'

The stinguish was young, with circular silver eyes, not much of a nose at all, and an ample mouth side-to-side of her round smooth head. Her mouth turned up at the corners like a dolphin's and was full of small pointed teeth. Her thin arms grew down into long, bony claws, her chest was flat and lacking nipples, and her body ended in a broad tail like an eel's – thick in the middle, edged with a fringe of fin that came to a point. She coughed up some water, shuddered and quailed as she took a lungful of air, as if she didn't like it at all. Water drained out of the gills that lay shaped over her ribs. The stinguish's smooth silver skin was extraordinary; every imaginable pastel colour shone on her iridescent metallic hide. I could see the herringbone arrangement of muscle in her tail. Her ribs were like ripples in platinum sand; she looked malnourished.

Oddly, she was alone and she hadn't laughed once. She was not behaving like a stinguish at all. She waved her tapering tail exhaustedly and pleaded with big lidless eyes. 'Please. I need to buy things.'

I crouched down and peeled her pointed, nail-less fingers from around my ankle. 'Hello, little urchin,' I said.

'I'm not an urchin. Urchins are prickly.'

'No, they're not all bad-tempered. I was one once.'

The stinguish shook her head and an expression of confusion appeared in her medallion eyes. 'What are you going on about? Can you spare any change, or not?'

I wondered what a cheerful, giggling, stupid stinguish wanted with money. 'Why aren't you with your mirth?'

'I don't have the time for this. I have to go and buy more things. Look at it all,' she said, distraught. She turned her face left and right taking in the vast market. She was desperate to be out there, beachcombing among the stalls.

'Listen. There's a stinguish representative in Epsilon's court. I can introduce you to her if you're lost. She's called Far-Distant. I'll—'

'I'm not called that any more. My name is Summer-Sale.'

'Far-Distant? Is it you? You've grown very thin! Don't you remember me?'

She bubbled distractedly. 'All the things on the stalls look really pretty and exotic when they're arranged together, but if I buy one and take it away, it's not the same. It seems to turn into tacky crap. I just want them all. I spent all my money on clothes, slime and jewellery, and now I've no money left. Please ... I'm missing the music and the lights, and the stall holders talk so friendly.'

Far-Distant had evidently become a Constant Shopper. 'No, my sister. I won't give you anything. No one you meet in the market will be as friendly as your mirth. I think you should go back to them.'

The stinguish started wailing. I understood why, because I know the torment of addiction, and the effects of all addictions feel similar. Far-Distant would have to do withdrawal from shopping, and whatever world she must return to will seem very cold and unforgiving. I stroked her head but hundreds of tiny circular transparent scales rubbed off and stuck to my hand. Her mackerel skin shone.

She tried to shake me by my ankle. 'I need money; I'm so unhappy.'

'There's much to be happy about. If it had seasons, the ocean would be beautiful at this time of year.'

She looked for a way to escape me. 'I'd rather go hungry than trouble you further ...'

'No! Come back! OK, I'll give you some cash,' I said soothingly. 'You're just a bit lost. Why not call for your mirth, they'll help you.'

'You don't understand,' she said bitterly. 'All stinguish are lost and they always have been. All of us! We don't belong here. Insects keep destroying our homes.'

'You mean Epsilon isn't your home?'

'No. Up there.' Far-Distant dragged her arm out of the water and pointed vaguely away from the sea, across the open grassland.

'In the sky?'

'No, silly. Vista.'

Vista's pale wasteland seemed to focus as I stared at it. For all its immense size, it looked weightless, part of the air. 'I know that the Insects bored through from Vista to Epsilon so thoroughly that Vista slipped down the path they made.'

'All the sea fell into the Somatopolis,' said Far-Distant. 'And the water carried us through, too. Ha! Not us exactly; our ancestors – it happened a million tides ago. But Insects ate the Somatopolis so we swam on again, and we ended up here. We're very lucky to survive; the sea kraits and so on all became extinct. Everyone who was too big to fit down the waterspout died, left high and dry. The bad old snakes squirmed around in the ooze, too heavy to support their own weight in the air, and they were crushed. The ones trapped in pools starved when the food ran out. All of us stinguish rejoiced. The kraits used to eat us, but we escaped and they didn't, ha ha. But that's why stinguish are very lost. No wonder I feel lonely and have to go shopping to cheer myself up ... Now can I have some change?'

'Well, all right.' I dug in my pocket for coins. 'But tell me first; it's just a myth, isn't it, that stinguish can chat underwater?'

'We can! For two thousand kilometres.'

I shook my head. 'I hardly believe it. I'm a messenger and if it was possible to shout that far I'd be redundant. But I'm not worried by those tales; I know water's thicker than air and probably just muffles the sound.'

'It's true!' she said indignantly.

I shrugged.

'Look! It's true! Watch!' She ducked under and gave out her signature laugh. Bubbles rose from her gaping mouth and burst, releasing her wonderful inflective giggles. 'Ha ha ha ha!' the bubbles chuckled. 'Ha! ha!'

She listened for a second, then surfaced, blowing out spray. 'I called "Hi." The littoral mirth is passing it on.'

Stinguish began to swim in from all directions. They all looked the same but different sizes. Naked and grinning they wriggled between the market stalls or glided effortlessly above them. Their tadpole-like tails waved in sinuous ripples, their long arms trailed, heads raised, watching the surface tension. Their swimming reminded me of flying; the grace of both belies the strength it takes. I appreciated their sturdiness, but I didn't envy them the cold water.

The first stinguish thrust his hands against the estuary bed and burst upwards, in a shower of spray. He gave a smile so wide I thought he would drink the ocean. 'Far-Distant! I haven't seen you for tides and tides.'

'Way-Farer!' shouted Far-Distant.

He batted her with his tail. 'Have you recovered from your latest spending spree?'

'I think so,' she said uncertainly.

'Ho ho! So come back to us! We won't lose you again, Far-Distant. We'll surf the warm current over the reefs while fish shoals scatter before us. We'll echo the sonar laughter rising from the benthic mirth five hundred fathoms down!'

Her mirth all broke surface at once; a hundred rounded backs rolled on the wave. The sea was silver with their bodies; chuckles and gasps wet the air. They surrounded Far-Distant, guffawing and tittering. Their round heads bobbed up, some leapt from the water and somersaulted back, flicking their gleaming tails. The nearest ones beached themselves on the pebbles, propped up on their spindly arms. They pointed at me in my 'Club 18-∞' T-shirt and black wings, and collapsed in helpless belly laughter.

Far-Distant looked up at me. 'It's my mirth. Mine! They want me back. Thanks for your help; I'll always remember. Um? Bye!'

'Wait!' I called. 'I want to know about the sea kraits. If they're extinct, how can Tarragon save them?'

'Tarragon?' cried Way-Farer. 'Where? A shark! A shark!' He submersed and laughed an alarm call through the water.

'A shark?'

'Worse – a megalodon! Swim for your lives!'

Their heads bobbed down and their fleshy tails fluked up. Bubbles trickled between them. They whipped the sea into froth which the next wave brought ashore. The tight crowd of stinguish glided towards deep water, vanishing into the gloom. I shouted, 'Far-Distant! Come back, you annoying amphibian!' But her mirth had gone, leaving just the occasional giggle swept back on the wind.

I felt the unusual warm glow of having done something right. I lingered and observed the aquatic commerce in the soaked souk. Far-Distant was an addict, and I managed to help her; maybe there was some hope for me. I couldn't tell if her cure was temporary, or what strains drove a carefree stinguish to class-A shopping. For me, it was my past, and now Tern's infidelity was eating me alive. But every Shift I start to die, and that's the trip. I wished that someone in the Fourlands would save me the way I have saved Far-Distant. I needed someone strong and forthright to barge in and force me to stop.

The attraction to my body began to drag me back. I concentrated and redoubled the rate at which the vivid marketplace faded to grey. To black.

To black. to black toblack oblac obla bla la a was e was f ge was fu nge was fulinge was full ringe was full yringe was full syringe was full syringe was full of blood. The syringe was full of blood.

Blood was trickling out of the back of the barrel. It had soaked into the sheet and mattress in a patch around my elbow. The syringe looked like a red glass feather growing out of place on my arm. Fuck it. I sat up and wiped at a warm trickle that had been running out of my nose and horizontally across my cheek. I stared at my hand – it was smeared with red.

Shit, I thought; what time is it? I glanced at the clock – six p.m.! And it's Thursday! How could I have slept for two days? Oh, by god – Gio's meeting! I'm late! I pulled myself out of bed, feeling weak and sick, viscid with self-recrimination and resentment. Shira, you stupid bastard; you really can't leave it alone, you can't control it. Ninety years in and out of scolopendium; you should have learned by now. I snarled, 'You don't fucking deserve to be an Eszai at all!'

Evening was now invisible through storm clouds clustered over the Castle. The rally starts in three hours; at full speed I might be able to make it in time. Torrential rain had seeped in through a broken shutter and my satchel was lying in a shallow pool. I couldn't stand the thought of putting my hand in cold water, so I kicked it to a less saturated part of the floor.

I looked for any sign of Tern, but she had spent the day away. Catching myself shaking, I suddenly flooded with anger. Nothing rules me; what the fuck have I *become*? My syringe lay on the floor under the bed and just the sight of it overwhelmed me with lust and despair. I picked it up and, holding it like a dagger, I smashed it down onto the slate top of our dressing table until fury deserted me in a wave and I was left looking rather cynically at the bent object. You are really going to regret doing that in a few days, Shira.

Can't waste the rest, anyhow, I vindicated. I stalked down to the lower room, where I diluted my last phial of cat and decanted the preparation into a little hip flask so I could take sips while travelling. A drift of letters had piled up against my door and when I opened it they fell into the room. I ignored them and pinned up a withered note that read, 'I'm not in but you needed the exercise.' I spread my wings, wriggled through a slit window and jumped off bound for Eske.

CHAPTER 15

My wings skirred in the wet air. I flew fast, but the faint trace of Tern's perfume on my clothes kept distracting me. I pulled the neck of my T-shirt over my nose and sniffed her rich and peppery scent. She smelt the same as she did the first time I saw her. I met Tern when, on a Messenger's errand, Lightning gave me a missive to deliver to his neighbour, the Governor of Wrought. The letter was a blank piece of paper and Lightning is an accomplished matchmaker, but I didn't discover that till decades later. I think that Lightning, being a connoisseur of exquisite things, appreciated Tern's beauty and hoped that I would preserve it forever in the Circle. I sought an audience with Tern in her stateroom. She was untouchable, as self-contained as a cushion cat, small and dark-haired, infinitely more refined than a Rhydanne. Her white dress clung to her body all the way down to the floor. I adored her voice the instant she spoke; it was like being dipped in warm caramel. I wanted to offer her books to read aloud.

In the following year, 1892, Tern decided to marry. She put out word that she would welcome challengers for her hand and organised a series of formal balls and dinners for her suitors, who arrived in droves and began to decant gold into the vaults of Wrought. The competition was much tougher than I had imagined; they all had titles and most of them had manors. I had nothing to offer her except my kiss, which bestowed immortality, but I thought she could not possibly want someone like me.

I had lost my virginity with three girls together in Wellbelove's *petite maison* – a whorehouse in Hacilith that I had rented one night for my own use, and I was a drug dealer so I could afford it. I knew never to pick a skinny whore: Rosie Brosia, Titmouse Slow and a girl called Anything Once threw themselves on me and taught me well and good.

When I first visited Awia I was just as wild; I swept through the country like a swarm. In Peregrine and Tambrine I partied till four of the morning. I frequented the theatre each night in Micawater and strayed from pavement cafés to bars, meeting artists and dollymops in the narrow streets of that pristine town. In Rachiswater I took advantage of the local girls and long walks by the lakeside. In Sheldrake I stayed, finding the sea air analeptic, and at Sarcelle's palace they set fifteen tables of feast for us each night.

From there I rode the Black Coach to Tanager, and dropped meringue and absinthe on the patched bedspreads of the Corogon School Whorehouse. Enclosed by bowers and founded by schoolgirls, its roof garden was rampant if the weather was fine. It slouched across the adjoining roofs of a whole

454

street, warmed by the hot, stale shops below. I fucked the girls and drank their homebrew while cries drifted out from the inmates in the lunatic asylum; the girls knew them all by name.

I never believed that love existed. I wanted to smash it all up into shards and cut myself with the sharpest. But Shira Dellin changed me. Then came Tern, who transformed me a little more. I loved her, the colour of her skin, shapely legs and plumage; I wanted to fill my senses with her.

Tern's unattainable demeanour was an aphrodisiac and a barrier. I didn't want to join her noble class but I dreaded that her chocolate voice would laugh and reject me. Her suitors sensed my insecurity and uttered barbed comments to convince me; she wouldn't want to marry a freak. When I met Shira Dellin I had been surprised to discover that I found Rhydanne girls captivating, but she had turned me down spectacularly. I flew to see Lightning, who instantly understood the cause of my haggard, insomniac appearance. I desperately begged him for advice. After all, he was the expert and I was so bewildered I was prepared to follow any instruction. He suggested, 'Lady Wrought would love to receive gifts.'

I gave her a live kestrel that I caught in the air, its wings bound to its body with embroidery thread. 'Comet,' she said, 'what am I going to do with this?'

Next day I stole in, offering her edelweiss from a mountain that no one can climb. 'Get out!' she said. 'I'll only see you at dinner with the rest of the suitors!' I backed off, stepped up to the velvet window seat and, horrendously, found that my boots were still filthy from the stables. She pointed sternly at the casement through which she had released the kestrel. 'Your turn to fly away!'

In despair and fatigue, I started to use scolopendium. One night, because I was unaccustomed to it, I overdosed and discovered the Shift. I slowly had a palace built there, Sliverkey, in order to give me confidence to court Tern, but in my homeland I owned nothing, no lineage, barely a pot to piss in.

'No, no!' Lightning admonished, amused. 'She's not a hungry Rhydanne. It's important to give her beautiful presents, ones that will last, to remind her of you when you're absent. You must make her feel wanted and special – I suppose you could always offer her stories. Ladies love tales and you seem to have an inexhaustible supply.'

I flew from the Castle to see Tern when my duties were done. I perched by the bedroom window and told her stories. She was very eager to know about the Castle; she urged me to tell the things I took for granted – what's behind the Throne Room screen? What does the Emperor look like? How does one talk with him? Few of my exploits genuinely held Tern's wandering attention, but she liked me to describe a ruined ancient Awian citadel far north in the Paperlands.

The unreachable chateau had interested me since the first time I saw it, from the sickle summit of Bhachnadich. The Paperlands surrounded northern Darkling like an ocean, an unbroken surface of grey Insect constructions that lapped into points and fell away into shallow valleys. In perfect conditions, a ruin was seen on the horizon, rising through the paper crust. It appeared to be a massive square edifice topped by a stone dome. Sunlight flickered on its peeling leaves of gilt as they fluttered in the wind.

Tern's interest spurred me to the idea that if I dared travel to the ruins I might touch down on the dome and return alive. I trialled a distance flight without landing once, I then climbed Bhachnadich and launched myself from its thousand-metre rock face. I picked up the katabatic Ressond gale and sped over the Insects' territory.

A long lion-gold winter light lay across the Paperlands. Far below among the rigid cells I saw Insects scurrying, going about their instinctive lives. If I crashed, thousands would dart out of their tunnels and tear me apart. If I don't crash, Tern will love this story.

I glided to rest and then flew on. After hours of alternately gliding and flapping I became exhausted. Burning and stiffening in my wings and back distracted me from Tern and punished me for being so stupid as to fall in love. When it became too much to bear I took tiny sips of the wonderful panacea painkiller I had bought; the agony melted away.

As evening advanced the Ressond wind declined in strength. I shed all unnecessary weight in mid-air; unlaced and dropped my boots and bits of clothing until I was just wearing a shirt and shorts. After sunset I flew by a hunter's moon and as I drew closer to the derelict building I realised how truly gigantic it was. The Paperlands broke around it. Ridges of paper adhered to it like buttresses and thinner web-strands reached up and anchored to the base of the dome.

The tops of adjoining walls were still visible, kept upright by Insect cells, but the roofs had fallen away. Insects had eaten the timber rafters and the entire structure was unstable.

The broken dome loomed beneath me, rounded and silvered with moonlight. I landed on its cold stone apex and looked back towards the jagged Darkling peaks, while I ate some honey sandwiches and glugged the last drop of water, then threw my pack away. I was utterly exhausted and my wings ached so much I couldn't close them. The landscape was dead; no birdsong, the silence pressed me like deep water. For hundreds of kilometres, nothing was alive but Insects. I was the alien here.

I dozed until I felt some energy returning, but all the time I listened for Insects. I lay on the dome and looked through the lightless hole. I couldn't hear any beneath me so I dropped through, landing awkwardly on a slope of rubble and roof blocks that had collapsed onto a travertine-tiled floor. I only had seconds before the Insects smelt me – some new food in the Paperlands they had chewed bare – and they would amass around the building, race up the echoing steps.

Moonlight lit the angular corners of fallen masonry blue-grey. I could see just a small part of the circular room but it was empty. Insect mandibles had scoured the fabric off the walls leaving grooves like chisel marks.

Perhaps it was a municipal building rather than a royal residence after all. I curled my toes around a carved cornice block. I dared not leave the circle of moonlight directly under the hole; the room was in shadow. As my eyes became accustomed to the dark, I saw a dull shine among the furthest blocks. I picked my way over them and reached down. It was a bronze castor from a table leg, and three more were scattered nearby. Presumably they were left by the Insects when they ate a wooden table. Anything inorganic left on the table would still be buried. I hefted a couple of the smaller bricks aside – and uncovered the lair of a spider as big as my hand.

I fled to the top of the cone of debris, glanced back. The spider did not move. Its ovoid abdomen glittered darkly. I approached with great caution and prodded it; it skidded over the stone dust with a tinkling sound. I lifted it carefully. It was a brooch made from two flawless emeralds fixed in peculiar curlicues of silver wire, a reticulate casing ingeniously twisted into eight jointed legs. I pinned the spider to my shirt and was about to dig around between the blocks in the hope of uncovering more jewels when there was a clattering noise outside.

My pulse soared so fast blood rushed in my ears. Feelers waved in the doorway and an Insect charged into the room. I scrabbled up the rubble. I jumped, grabbed the edge of the roof and pulled myself onto the dome. Claws thrust out of the hole and snatched at the air. The open ground around the building bristled and seethed with Insects. I watched them erupt from the tunnels, like red-brown droplets racing towards a simmering sea.

The ache of the flight and the anxiety of proposing to Tern are all too easy to remember now I am speeding towards Gio's meeting in Eske. I recall that it took me a fortnight to recover my strength, muster my courage and present myself decorously at Wrought manor. I dropped the filigree spider, the priceless gem of old Awia, into Tern's comely hand and her sloe-eyes lit with admiration.

I said softly, 'A talented jeweller must have crafted it before the Insects invaded. It held some wonderful meaning for a lady in antiquity, maybe one of your ancestors.' I looked down. 'I want you to wear the spider when you kiss the Emperor's hand.'

'You mad bastard,' Tern pronounced. 'You could have got killed.'

'The aim is to give *you* eternal life.'

She examined the emerald spider that sparkled in the light from twenty candelabra. 'You mad, crafty bastard.'

I had turned away, wondering if this was a compliment or slight. She poked a finger under my chin and lifted it. She kissed me; we kissed for hours.

Tern dismissed her suitors from the mezzanine where they queued with their plumed hats in their hands. A gust of wind through the tall sash windows swirled out white gossamer curtains and the dust covers on the furniture in her nearly empty bedroom. Outside, snow clouds passed over a crescent moon. Wrought's twisted river roared in spate through sparse black woodland. Beyond the doorway three cats postured in the long hall where the shadows of spindly trees moved on the polished floorboards.

She undressed me and dropped my clothes to the floor one by one. Her small hands fumbled the front of my trousers, pushed them down and unhooked my pants from my hard cock. Her fingers traced the grooves on my hips that lead down to it; she took a good look. She touched the tip; it swelled under her fingers. I moaned and she said, 'Hush. You chanced your life to impress me, Eszai. Don't you want me?'

She walked to the four-poster bed and sat on the counterpane. The spider brooch squatted on the pillow. I approached her slowly; she was five years older than my physical age and confident in her extreme beauty. I did not know how to have loving sex; I had only ever fucked whores and the ambitious. I had a horrible feeling that I was being tested but all I could do was surrender and follow Tern's lead. She stroked my wing and encouraged me to slip under the covers.

She undressed elegantly, leaving her stiffened silk bodice, with white suspender straps to her stocking tops. The bodice covered her breasts to her belly; her panties had somehow gone with the dress. She lay on her side as Awian ladies do, but unlike the others I'd slept with, she did not avert her gaze. She was uninhibited, too proud to follow fashionable repression. I lay behind her on my left, my body fitted close to her. The smooth hollow between her shoulder blades was snug against my chest, my scarred shoulder high above her. Her warm wings were tight between us, tucked up in the small of her back. Her satin feathers rustled and rubbed, driving me mad with lust. She trapped my hard cock between her thighs. I moved my hips, pulling it over her silk stockings. I was not sure what to do. She made no move to help me so I pressed and only felt soft flesh. She leant her whole body backwards and opened her legs slightly. I pushed upwards carefully and felt flesh part. She enveloped the tip of my cock.

She opened her eyes and looked back over her shoulder. 'Oh, please ...'

'My lady.' I propped myself on my left elbow and made quick flicks but not very deep. I couldn't penetrate far, the angle was wrong. Just the head of my cock rubbed slickly in and out of her. I felt her cunt yield and stretch, hot and wet.

'Keep going,' she ordered quietly. 'Harder. Fuck me harder.' She began to whisper filth. I was shocked to hear her murmur, calling up wisps and bodies in twos and threesomes that populated the dark room with ethereal fucking. She was not delicate; she kept straining to see my chest. She raised a knee, backed into me trying to impale herself deeper. Her thighs were becoming very wet. I wiped a hand over her outline, pausing in the softer reprieve between ribs and hips. I wriggled my left arm under her waist to angle her higher, all the while hoping that my best performance was good enough.

'You'll do,' she said with wonder. 'You'll do ... you'll do, you'll do, you'll do. *Don't* scratch.'

She firmly pushed my hand between her bodice lacings and flattened it against a small breast, encouraging me to rub it in circles. No other girl I've slept with has ever done that. Her brown nipple was hard against my palm. Her locks coiled on the pillow. A braid hung down from my hair and brushed her neck.

I pumped and struggled. I changed my stroke, long and slow. I could see my cock going in and out of her. Amazed, I thought: It's actually happening. This is really happening to me. Her small rounded buttocks pushed me back every time she rolled against me. I bent my arm that was underneath her and easily lifted her body up. I rubbed my stomach on her black glossy wings and felt the tips of her flight feathers bristle into my crotch.

I brushed my hand down to her front and wiry pubic hairs. I found her left hand already working away there; her fingertips traced wet circles. She took shallow breaths through parted lips. She pushed my hand away. Low, under the skin of her back, her wing joints moved as if she wanted to flex them.

'Open them around me.'

She spread, either side of my waist. Her black wings shuddered with every thrust I gave her, and brushed my skin. I almost came helplessly into her. I paused, held myself still.

'Look at me,' she said.

I was right on the edge. Another thrust and I'd come. I paused to gain control; Tern moaned her displeasure. She shook her body on my cock.

'I can't,' I gasped. 'I have to wait.'

She looked into my eyes and came. Her body thrashed and whiplashed. Her uppermost wing fluttered. She breathed deeply and cried out, 'Now harder!' She almost slid off me but I gripped her hips and laid into her, thrusting as hard as I could. I leaned over, twisting her top half down, breasts to the sheet, my chest pushing above her back. My hips slapped against her bottom. I forgot her status. I pumped as hard and selfishly as with a whore. I felt the flutter in my groin. Her cunt pulsed, squeezed like a fist and drew my come out of me in quick hot spurts. I thrust slower and stopped, panting.

I couldn't tell if she was giggling or crying. She pulled my arms around to hug her. Relief filled me; I had done well. 'Stay here tonight, Jant "long-nails",' she said warmly. 'My legs are tingling.'

We cuddled close and listened to the river. I wondered how many other men she had slept with before me and I hated them. The stiff sheets crackled under the white brocade coverlet; a draught stirred lace hangings on the heavy four-poster bed. After a while Tern murmured, 'Mmm ... I want chocolate ...' Then she fell asleep.

I held her for months and years and decades. I took her like poison through the skin. I knew her salt taste like sea bruises, stretched nets of sinews in her neck and waves of ribs. I loved her body as she twisted like a hooked fish, kicked like prey. I was dog to her: I laid my open mouth over her throat.

I thought of the many times when I have been asleep or drugged and gradually wakened to find her touching me, my cock already hard under her hand. I wanted Tern. It took a trial as harsh as a sea voyage for me to feel the first pangs of loneliness and realise how much I need her. I was wrong to neglect her. I must apologise. I'll win her back.

CHAPTER 16

After midnight, people were gathering at the fencing school in Eske. I landed on the tiled roof, well-concealed by a chimney stack, looking down at the wet streets. Below the dripping thatch of the last houses in the town, I could see dark coats underneath bobbing umbrellas. Men carried lanterns hung from hooks on their shields. Some drunken kids on tired nags clattered past on the Hamulus Road from the direction of Hacilith, slowing and relaxing as they travelled the opposite way from the city's magnetic pull. I perched on the roof, out of sight and watched through the rain.

A cold front was coming in. The clouds scudded across to merge in one mass in the eastern half of the sky. Lightning flickered in the fingers of the bare forest. The rain fell with more intensity and the pitch of its noise increased. I really didn't think it could rain any harder. The constant hiss of the wind in the trees was indistinguishable from the rain hissing on the roof. Drops pattered on the sagging willow leaves along the river bank.

Dace River wound through the south side of town close to Gio's hall. I could still see the river but the surrounding countryside was too dark to make out detail. Silver snakes slithered over the river's surface. I watched them resignedly; Tern had put me in a melancholy mood. I had run out of people to shout at, and was rather regretting storming off in disgust with the world because it was evident by now that the world had no intention of going away and leaving me alone.

Some of the snakes are actually part of the river. Fascinating. I tried to disentangle the snakes' silver bodies and the reflection on stirred water, before I realised that the whole thing was simply a hallucination. Only take me a couple of weeks to quit. Shouldn't be any problem. Theoretically. I shrugged, sending all the water that had gathered on my broad-brimmed hat down my back. I swore silently, taking my hat off and wringing out the rain.

I don't even know if fucking her will be the same now Tawny's had his big cock in her. I pulled the hip flask out of the top of my thigh boot and took a satisfying swig. It tasted green, like cut-grass smells. I felt lighter and tighter every second. Under my long coat, my wings were warm. To cope with the gusts I had had to fly constantly flexing them open and closed at the elbow, and now they were aching.

The fencing school's steep roof was a sheen of water reflecting the lanterns of people arriving. Rainwater was running in wide rivulets over the tiles, dripping off the guttering. Yellow lamplight beamed out of a high square window just below me. At the far corner of the whitewashed hall Gio's watchman swung a lantern, illuminating the empty road. He saw there was no one else to come and banged the door closed. I flicked my wings out from the slits in my coat and bounced along the ridge. A couple of slates gave way. I scrabbled madly, slid with them down the roof. I hit the gutter, heels in the trough, my pointed toes over the edge. The tiles shot off, fell and broke on the road ten metres below. I lay with my back against the slope and listened. There was no response from the hall.

I grasped the lead gutter, swung myself over in a controlled drop onto the window ledge. I pressed against the frame, pulled myself into the smallest area possible, inhabiting space slyly as if stealing it, with the concentrated acrobat grace of a Rhydanne. I peered through the window.

Gio's fencing academy was packed. About eight hundred people were taking off their coats and settling down on the folding chairs. Some were seated on the floor; between them on the floorboards I saw white diagrams painted to teach fencing exercises.

A small stage directly below me was decorated with the coats of arms of Gio's past pupils from the nobility. The walls were hung with charts and geometrical figures, the rear wall was covered with a mirror. Padded gloves and chain mail gauntlets hung on racks, with rapiers and their corresponding diamond-sectioned daggers, round leather target shields and lead-soled shoes – which Gio used for training lightness of foot. A pendulum clock with a large, clear ceramic dial had run down and stopped, showing the wrong time. Beside it in a polished glass case awards were displayed in tiers – engraved silver cups and plates, tiny posed figurines of swordsmen on black plinths, and hundreds and hundreds of satin rosettes.

Gio stood by the stage, looking at his audience. He was as relaxed and confident as always, perhaps more so now that the anger of being dropped from the Circle had caused him to lose his respect for people.

Veteran Awian soldiers grouped at the back of the hall, probably fresh from fighting Tornado. They carried their reflex longbows in waxed cotton bags on their shoulders, arrows in lidded quivers. The edges of their dark blue cloaks were cut to look like feathers, drawn across each man's body and pinned at the shoulder with enamelled or billon badges. The shell-edged armour on their legs was damp with condensation. Their worn, damp lorica had some chrome scales missing. Their expressions were as grim as the weather; they only spoke amongst themselves. I guessed they were men disbanded from the General Fyrd who, upon finding their homes and crops destroyed by the Insects, had a very valid reason to harbour grievance against the Castle.

The same was not true for the excited, fractious Hacilith kids, in tooled leather jackets, loose jeans and chain-link belts. Some seamen in ox-blood check or orange shirts laced at the neck tucked their wet oilskins under the chairs. Unshaven highwaymen brushed down the arms of their greatcoats that were silvered with rain. They undid the spurs on their side-laced boots and let them hang loose. Gio had no coherent force. He had gathered deserters, poachers, outlaws, smugglers and fugitives.

Twenty fencing masters leant against the walls, with wryly amused expressions at the defiant party taking place within their hall. They were Gio's accomplices now, not potential Challengers. They had the swagger of swordsmen who knew the brilliance of their skill.

The cold Insect-wing window was steamed up inside and droplets ran down, channelled along by the black veins. No one could see me at this angle and the hubbub was so loud I was quite safe. I was so intrigued, I became unaware of the chill seeping into my body from the stone. I seized up, wedged into position in the corner of the window with my legs out along the ledge.

A limber young man wearing a beautiful rapier tiptoed to the stage and held up his hands for silence. He was shaking so hard he practically blurred. The crowd fell quiet in patches, and Gio picked out one or two individuals at the back to stare at until the hall was completely silent. I strained to hear the young man introduce his master: 'Gio Ami, rightfully Serein.'

Gio nodded, stepped forward, and immediately a hundred voices vied with each other, shouting out questions. A frown line appeared between his eyebrows. He walked beneath my window, so I could no longer see his expression. He still wore the same coat, still open to a bare chest, but he wore the light purple Ghallain armiger ribbon in his buttonhole as if it was a manorship badge. His lank hair was pulled into a little ponytail.

Gio looked at the stage floor as if thinking the elevated position didn't suit him. He sat down on the edge, with his legs dangling over. He began to talk to the crowd rather than at them. He was a teacher and he knew how to make his voice carry.

'Put up, put up,' he said loudly and then, 'All right, I will answer one or two questions. What is it, Cinna?'

A very fat man seated at the front wallowed to his feet. I was astonished to see it was Cinna Bawtere. His cheeks wobbled as he shouted, 'You *never* said we would attack the Castle! You *said* we would speak to the Emperor. Why is there fighting between the fencing masters and the Circle itself? It's a simple matter for San to send Tornado to Crush Us All!'

Gio took a deep breath, 'I have no argument with the Emperor. I think San knows that—'

'Or we'd be behind bars already!' Cinna's riposte raised a susurration of agreement from the crowd. They seemed to be thinking in similar fashion – they had trusted Gio to air their grievances with the Emperor, and he had lead them into conflict instead, with the Eszai who had always been their protectors. For an instant I thought that the crowd might turn on him.

'The problem lies not with Emperor San but with his deputies, the Eszai, who are corrupt and mislead him. You all know the Emperor doesn't leave the Castle. To understand and rule the world fairly he needs his immortals, but their own interests are embroiled in what they tell him.'

The crowd fell silent; this was what they wanted to hear. A chill wind stuck my soaked clothes to my skin; the gale whined, high-pitched, through the eaves. I pressed my ear to the pane to hear Gio's words.

'There is no present like time. San gives the immortals lifetime in return for their service, but few of them deserve such a priceless gift.

'We are lucky to be alive at this point in time. Times are hard for us all, I grant you, but the opportunities are better than any period I have lived through in the last four hundred years. I truly remember the past, and I know that the only cure for despair is action.

'Since I left the Circle I have realised how little the immoral immortals understand us Zascai. They're all too slow and spoilt by luxury to see the advantage of this great opportunity we have: Tris. It's up to us to make the most of it.

'None of you worthy people will be able to join the Circle. Cinna, although you're a good sailor; Mauvein, although you're an excellent jeweller, the Circle's too corrupt for either of you to enter in an honest Challenge. And I, the greatest swordsman of all time, am forced to give way to a newcomer because I speak too much truth. The prospect of immortality they hold up is nothing but an illusion to lull you. The Circle would never accept a man who really recognises the need for change.

'Awia can't feed itself – they tell us – so they ask us to send our money to what is the richest country in the world. The shortage of workers is caused by bad management. Five hundred men are employed just to clean the Castle, to scrape lichen off its walls and polish its sumptuous treasure when every last drop's squeezed out of the Plainslands to nurse Awia. Food is short all over the Fourlands except in the Castle because immortals must have their strength. Isn't that so?'

He looked to the winged soldiers at the back of the hall. 'Awians are angry because you feel you're making the most effort against Insects. It's your kingdom that disappears under the Paperlands each time they advance. You feel threatened. I can understand why you think that help from Morenzia is not forthcoming. You're right, but for the wrong reasons.'

Gio glanced at Cinna and the city ruffians on the rows of chairs. 'Morenzians and Plainslanders are angry because you're overtaxed and fed up to the back teeth with money being sucked out of Hacilith. You're right to feel discontented, but for the wrong reasons. Last time the Insects attacked, the Castle just followed the downright craven policy of the Awian king and it failed to control them. They fed so well on the plenty of Awia that they almost reached the banks of the Moren.

'I have lived in the Castle and been part of the Circle. I have felt San hold time still for me. If I were yet Eszai at least my voice would be heard. I could try to make things better. San is keen to hear us – if Tornado was not bloodthirstily blocking the way we would be standing in the Throne Room now. San would open the Castle's treasury to aid us. But in respect of your fears I have called my men to retreat. Now I'm mortal again, same as you, I'm free to tell you how the Circle is a web of deceit. San would benefit greatly to be free of the lies of his ministers.'

The crowd sensed his conviction and gave their faith to his terrible mendacity. By god, I thought; he's not acting, he believes it.

Gio stood and stretched then sat down again, swinging his legs to tap the folded-down bucket tops of his boots against the planks. He swept a hand over his hair, which slipped out of its ponytail and hung around his shoulders. The crowd watched, some uncomfortably, although I imagined Cinna alert for the promise of scandal. Gio did the public speaking equivalent of swapping hands in a fencing match: 'Your suffering is the fault of the duplicitous Eszai. Mist Ata Dei's one of the worst. Ask yourselves how she could be allowed to be immortal at all.'

Gio paced across the stage, around the lowered wrought iron candelabrum and back, his coat tails flowing out behind him. He wore the 1969 Sword, a faultless rapier custom-made for him, and the jewels on its scabbard scattered lamplight as only diamonds can. Their adamantine lustre threw moving spectra on the walls.

'Zascai don't know half of what this monster has done, because of course the confessions of new Eszai are customarily kept secret. You already know that Mist once razed your harbours, raided the coast and sank the fleet – out and out piracy from which the coast has hardly recovered! Would we be in such a poor state now if this arch-bitch hadn't wreaked carnage? How many lives were lost? Well, we don't know because Comet never told us.'

I tensed at the mention of my name. How was I supposed to know? I had other pressing matters to attend to back then, like Insects besieging Lowespass. But the mortals followed Gio's every word.

'Ata was a wife who brought her husband down. The Emperor let her Challenge stand legitimately. Why did he make the decision to let her run riot at such a vital time? Was Comet informing San properly? What was going on between the Sailor and the Messenger that that layabout ladykiller should support Ata so much?

'And while Comet misleads the Emperor – either deliberately or through laziness – his wife spends her time living lavishly. Every other governor leads their fyrd. How many parties and fashion shows have been thrown by Tern while Wrought is still smoking rubble?

'And while we consider the misgovernance of manors by those Eszai lucky enough to own land, consider the most corrupt of the Circle whom you may have thought of as the most capable because you are accustomed to lies. Lightning Micawater is the best Archer ever. Nobody can deny that. Of course he is – his family could afford the best tutors in the distant past when he was a student, and he makes sure the skill of archery hasn't changed since then. What an unfortunate mishap that he chanced to inherit the manor on the glittering river. Lightning embellishes his palace even as your farms and towns lie in ruins. What happened to Awian artisans anyway – those of you who aren't here?'

A chuckle went round the hall.

'They're all competing for work in other countries. Lightning the romantic archaist does not spend his money rightly but spends his time having affairs with married women – how chivalrous can you get? He was involved in the destruction of the harbours with his lover, Ata, and when the greedy blue-blood bagged Peregrine manorship in the spoils of war he gave it to his illegitimate daughter!

'The newfound Island of Tris is part of Lightning's kingdom too, now he's just returned from playing at explorers with his pirate queen and their drunken lackey.'

Drunken lackey? Who's that? I puzzled. Oh, no, he means me, doesn't he?

'Lightning is not venerable but obsolete. He was young in spirit when the world was young but times have moved on. He's a thing of the past; he holds us back. It's time we took control and it's an exciting moment for Awians to make their own decisions and live without him.

'Frost and her River Works Company profiteer from the rebuilding process. Hayl and his immortal husband are both reckless men. Only yesterday, they attacked us without provocation and Tornado joined them soon after with a division of your own brothers in the fyrd. Now I believe that too many people are being drafted. Since Tornado lost his girlfriend five years ago, he's taken his fury out on the Insects and the draft continues while fields lie unplanted. The Circle should preserve lives but the Messenger flies in to the Plainslands to tear families apart.

'Comet is fond of the bottle. The truth isn't widely known because he really indulges in the Castle – out of the public eye. I've seen him staggering drunk in the Great Hall. He often isn't spotted for days at a stretch – during which time it's known he hasn't left his room. Why does the Emperor keep him when I felt the Circle twitch every time he binges? I don't know if the alcohol affects his *reliability* – but is it any wonder there are rumours that his wife sleeps with another man?'

466

Gio waved his hand against the crowd's torrent of wicked laughter.

'No, no,' he said. 'I go back on that. Far be it from me to slander anyone. Tern manages it very well herself. The rumours are unsupported – just like her!'

How dare he call me a filthy drunk! I nearly flew down and told him – scolopendium is a much better type of substance abuse. And I'm good at it; I have it under control! But at least alcohol is legal. The crowd believed Gio because it matched their caricature of a Rhydanne, and that hurt even more.

I ground my teeth and the blood rushed, red hot, to my face. Oh, Tern, why did you do this to me? In private it's bad enough, when my prowess in bed is the only reputation I have – but I don't think I can stand being the capricious and irresistible Messenger cuckolded in front of the world.

Gio strode up and down, his hand resting on his sword hilt. He mused, 'The worst thing about these corrupt members of the Circle is that they'll never die.

'I can offer you a way to live outside their rule. Better still, it comes with riches, a chance to shape your future free of kings, governors and fyrd captains too. Anyone who follows me will be set up for life. I can give you Tris.'

The crowd was silent. Gio saw this and didn't pause for long. 'I've spoken to some of the mariners who saw Capharnaum. They say the tiles on the roofs of the houses are embedded with turquoise and tourmaline. Even Trisian infants wear crowns. They esteem gold because of its beauty, not because of its rarity – they think less of it than we do of spelter or brass. They use it for household objects: mangles, boot scrapes and – you'll love this – chamber pots.'

Gio scanned the aisles of sceptical faces. 'You clearly don't believe me. Well, look; I have one here.' As he spoke, he trotted to the back of the stage and unpacked several items from a canvas bag. He held up the very chamber pot that Danio had given to Wrenn. He had polished it to a brilliance and it dazzled.

Everybody in the hall began to laugh, and Gio smiled too. He was scarcely audible over the tumult. 'Mauvein is a practically Eszai-good jeweller. Verify this for me.' He slipped down off the stage and gave the pot to a portly man whom I recognised as one of Ata's sons – although by now he was much older than his mother.

The gleaming chamber pot was turned round under his big fingers and then he nodded. 'It's enough bullion for a manorship to buy out of providing fyrd for two years. I could find better things to do with this than piss in it.'

'Well, you can't have it … yet.' Gio flourished it. 'You see that Trisians have so much wealth the meanest utensils are solid gold. Yet Mist's clique are determined to keep it for themselves. I have bought the caravel *Pavonine*. At this very moment my allies in Awndyn are stocking her, and other ships. From Hacilith University I've found it easy to hire a pair of crusty scholars well versed in Old Morenzian inscriptions. They are optimistic of being able to interpret the basics of Trisian for us. The journey will be a challenge, I grant you, but not so difficult now a trail is blazed. There's safety in a convoy – if you want to commandeer berths in other caravels who'll stop you?

'I earned wealth enough from the Ghallain School to pay the crews and create an ideal life in Capharnaum without being constantly tested by the Circle. Who knows, in a couple of years, consolidated and stronger, we might return.'

A swordsman called something I couldn't hear.

'Ah, Tirrick. I'm just skating all over the floor on those pearls of wisdom,' Gio answered sarcastically. He put the chamber pot down, fished in his inside coat pocket and held up a thick notebook that I recognised immediately. 'This is Mist's own rutter. My agents stole it when they took the chamber pot. Here are the coordinates of the island, and a comprehensive description of the route. "Twenty-nine degrees south, one hundred and twenty-nine degrees east",' he read in a respectful tone. 'Nearly on line with the Awndyn northing, I'm given to understand. So, how many of you will join me?'

Two or three hundred hands went up immediately; these men had nothing to lose. Gio pushed the priceless piss-pot with his toe. The Awian soldiers conferred among themselves, weighing the risks of the voyage against the rewards. Having fought in Lowespass, they were accustomed to frontiers. They raised their hands.

In fencing, it is very important to be able to change the direction of your thrust the instant you see that it's going to miss its target. Gio knew now that he could never be strong enough to destroy the Castle, so he turned the thrust to Tris. He was prepared to exile himself to survive.

My lamp-lit window was the only source of light and sound in the whole pitch-black landscape. Everything that existed was in this hall – Eske Forest was a void. Gio raised his voice above the roar as again the rain swelled to a cloudburst. Drops bounced off the brim of my leather hat. Forked lightning bit colour into the forest for an instant. Gio paused as a ten-second-long thunder crash rolled around the hollow of the little town. It hypnotised everyone in the hall. Gio stood right foot forward, held the rapier scabbard and drew the 1969 Sword with his right hand. He swung it casually, feeling its balance.

'We start for Awndyn tomorrow morning. By Sunday I'll be in the harbourmaster's house to meet you adventurers. We will sail next week.' He held the rapier up above the crowd ostentatiously. 'The Eszai have outlived morality. I won't lie back and think of the Fourlands while the Castle screws us, time and again. Come with me!' he exclaimed. 'To seek this new world – for gold and brandy!'

Gio ended, and the crowd began to applaud. They stood up, clapped and cheered him. The ovation went on and on. Gio glanced up at the windows; I turned my white face away and shrank back against the frame. Gio bounded off the stage and his friends shook his hand and slapped him on the back all the way down the hall. His eyes were hectic bright and his cheeks were flushed. The doors were thrown wide – light and people spilled out. I looked with hatred. Kill him, god, if I only had my crossbow! Kill him, I'll jump straight on his head! If he wasn't surrounded by swordsmen.

Gio's voice was too low for me to hear as his knot of well-wishers bustled him out of town along the woodland path. Some men fetched their horses, others dawdled in the doorway fiddling with their lanterns.

Gio is impugning my virility and I can do absolutely nothing about it. I banged the heel of my hand against my forehead. Be calm! There will be time for revenge later. I'm not very good at later; I wanted him to suffer *now*.

God, I was livid. I was going to take this out on someone, and since I couldn't beat Gio, Cinna Bawtere would have to do. I dived off the roof and flew in very turbulent air just under the low storm cloud's base. I risked being sucked up into it. A gull battled along underneath me, vivid white against the dark iron-grey. The hurricane tussled my hair and coat out behind me. My clothes were light even when waterlogged. My wings cleaved the gale, driving rainwater off their oiled surfaces, but the covert feathers were becoming damp and thinning; I was beating harder to stay up.

I followed Cinna out of Eske along the dark forest track, straining to see him. He was hidden beneath his black umbrella, sploshing towards the nearby Slaughterbridge village pub. Air roared over my wings as I slid down the sky. I struggled to slow my ground speed and manoeuvred directly above him. I folded my wings back with a jolt and fell on him.

I hit Cinna with the soles of both boots between his shoulder blades, bowling him over and over into a puddle. I absorbed the impact into my legs and landed in a crouch. Cinna rolled around on his back, knees pulled up, winded. I burst out laughing; falcons must feel this exhilarated when they hit prey. 'I take my hat off to you, Mister Bawtere! Never knew you had an acrobatic streak!' He kicked like a struck rabbit. A dagger appeared in his hand. He crawled out of the chalky, rain-pitted puddle and collapsed in a milk-white wet heap on the path. 'The gallows waits in Eske; it's a much shorter drop! I can take my pick of felonies in your catalogue of crimes. You're as good as dead!'

I did want to kill him. I wanted to feel the life go out of him under my hands. He saw my cruel expression – comprised of Tern's rejection, Gio's slander and six hours in a rainstorm – and he curled up, sobbing. Cinna's predictability was consoling – I had thought I was losing the ability to read people. They seemed to be becoming gradually more incomprehensible.

'Ah …' Cinna panted. 'Please don't hurt me. Please … I …'

'How did Gio acquire the logbook?'

'I don't know! … Ah … I swear! He's a clever man; he has many agents. Ah … I respect you, Comet. You're Eszai. You're a legend in Hacilith.'

'Put the dagger down, then.'

Cinna did no such thing. I kicked his hand and the knife flew out of it. *'Put it down!'*

Cinna huddled under the remnants of his broken umbrella.

'How did Gio know of Tris?'

'I informed him. I'm sorry! You never said it was a secret!'

I suddenly realised that I had told Cinna everything, six months ago, under the influence of a fingernail full of scolopendium. Shit. It began to dawn on me that this appalling turn of events could be all my fault – caused by my big, stupid mouth.

I bated forward with my wings spread, made as if to kick and he cowered. 'Are you sailing with Gio?'

'Yes … Yes, what of it? I am My Own Man.' He huffed in a breath. 'I'm to be captain of the *Pavonine*. Yes, Comet, I was a sailor by trade; had you forgotten? I'm returning to that trade now. It's legal!'

'I see.' I drew my sword from under my coat skirts. 'Do you believe all that bullshit Gio was spouting in there?'

Cinna knelt up, several acres of ghastly fawn brocade, and started prodding his saggy chest to check for broken ribs. His blond pin curls were plastered to his skull, his fat cheeks were ruddy. The pathetic specimen looked at me carefully through the pouring rain. 'No, of course not … Though there's a seed of truth in everything he said … He thinks you're an alcoholic.' A knowing, assertive look appeared in his eyes. 'I have a reliable source for decent cat, by the way.'

'Blackmail now, is it? That's just one more reason to kill you!' I snarled, though his words set my mouth watering.

'Come on, Comet. Just because you're illegitimate doesn't give you free licence to be a bastard. I haven't told Gio about your love of scolopendium. Why should I? It'd bring me no benefit, and I'm a savvy businessman … Of course I don't believe that the island is full to bursting with precious metals for the natives to bestow on us. However, I do know that Gio's As Rich As Rachiswater. He's paying me five times a merchant captain's wage. He's packing coin, plate and banknotes – he has chests full of it! He wants to set himself up on Tris. I've just finished conveying it all to Awndyn myself.

Look, I still have the letter he gave me. I'll show you, here.' Cinna fished inside his coat for a crumpled envelope with a broken seal, Ghallain manor's whale emblem. I took the letter from his gnawed fingertips and raised a wing to shelter it from the rain, whilst I read:

To: Sitella Grackle, First Bank of Hacilith
I hereby instruct you to immediately liquidate all my assets currently in your care and to dispatch the monies to myself at the harbourmaster's office, Awndyn. They are, to whit: i) the proceeds collected to date from the sale of my academies, ii) all ordinary stocks held in the Hacilith bourse, iii) gold and silver plate held in the bank's safe. The bearer of this letter, Cinna Bawtere, holds my full confidence in this matter and is to be trusted as the guardian of the money.

Gio Ami

Money, lots of money, I deliberated while I refolded the letter. Cinna was smiling, showing textured teeth. 'Comet, are you envious? You know you'll never be free to escape to Tris yourself. You have to fly around the Fourlands until the inevitable happens – a goddamn Insect eviscerates you – and I don't mean like at Slake Cross, I mean fatally. You're cast off the Emperor's fist like a hawk, to spy, and he lures you back and tethers you with the promise of eternal life.'

I took a squelching step towards him. 'But, Bawtere, it's jail for you! Make haste! We'll see how far Gio sails without a captain.' I gestured with the sword and Cinna staggered to his feet, protesting and quaking. 'Into town, Cariama Eske's guard will look after you ... They'll throw you in a freezing cell, lock you in fetters and you can fuck your mother for all I care.'

'She's dead.'

'Should make it easy for you, then. Hurry! I've a lot to do tonight. I'm busy because I have to find someone who will keep an eye on Gio and accurately report his plans to me when, for example, I land on the *Pavonine*'s gallery at dusk.'

Cinna had begun to snivel. 'OK,' he said, miserably; 'I'll do it.'

I said, 'Oh, good. Then the noose can wait; tell me a little more about Gio.

Cinna said: He knows that the Trisians distrust the Castle. He has a silver tongue, that man.

I said: Even if it was gold he couldn't Challenge me.

Cinna said: Gio's failed and he knows it. He might have got away with insurrection, but he tried to murder an Eszai. Oh yes, I heard from his own lips how he stabbed Lightning!

Me: He's running?

Cinna: Yes. He can't storm the Castle and skewer every Eszai much as he wants to. So he's making his mark – leaving his name on history is immortality of a sort, seeing as he can't have The Real Thing. If he holes up at Ghallain or hides out on Addald Isle it'd only be a matter of time before he's betrayed and captured. But on Tris ...

Me: Never!

Cinna: He wants to win over the Trisians. And San would have to leave him there, the King of Tris, because the Castle's purpose is fighting the Insects. San could never fight people or invade islands.

Me: I'm glad you trust San.

Cinna: Yes, but I'm fed up of being kept in the dark. He keeps everyone hooded like falcons, whether callow Zascai or haggard old Eszai. You don't know what San's real quarry is, even though you're one of his spies, and you will just go back and tell him my every word.

Me: Um ... Cinna said that, not me.

San: Yes.

I skipped a few pages in my report, and resumed: 'Then I said to Cinna, "If I fail to stop Gio setting sail, I will meet you again on the ship." I followed him to the tavern, stole – I mean, requisitioned – a fast horse and rode here directly, my lord. I sent a courier to lock every stable at every coaching inn between Eske and Awndyn. That'll slow the main part of their force down by a couple of hours, and as it takes five days to walk to Awndyn those without horses might miss the *Pavonine*.'

Drops of rain ran down the shafts of the wet feathers in my hair and dropped off their curled tips behind me onto the carpet. I shook my head, flicking water from the backward-pointing quills. I had ridden out of the storm; my skin was singing. I was covered in the stringy mud thrown from the horse's hooves. My svelte boots were sheathed in white liquid mud up to the thigh. I smelt of clouds and the thin air. My heart beat hard; cat made me feel too fast and bracing, thermalling on a strange energy burst that I knew I was going to pay for later but really needed now.

CHAPTER 17

San said, 'Good. The majority of Gio's followers deserted him during the battle. The only people prepared to flee with him are those who have no option and no dreams other than those he concocts. So his last act of defiance is to stop Tris joining the Empire ...'

I knelt on the damp carpet. 'My lord, why should they listen to him?'

San continued as if he hadn't heard me. 'Whether Gio means to build his own stronghold or – more likely – take the Senate I cannot tell; but we must not let him impose any rule on Tris. Mist has sold swords to the Trisians, now Gio can train them. He is a teacher, is he not? He can perform several deeds to ingratiate himself with the Senate: he can hunt down the Insect that you so carelessly set free! Assuming a Trisian has not caught it already. And if a man has, he is more worthy of immortality than all of you!'

'My lord.' I closed my hot and bloodshot eyes for a second, ran my hands over the bangles on my left arm – my pointed nails in a variety of chipped colours. I squeezed water out of a handful of hair and managed to ask, 'What will you do?'

San began again in a brisk tone of voice: 'Before Gio became the Swordsman, that place in the Circle was for broadsword fighting, not fencing. But my current Swordsman has clearly demonstrated what everybody knows. Rapiers are ineffective against Insects, so immortals should not use them. From now on, Challenges for Serein's position must be with broadswords or Wrought swords or, taking future improvements into consideration, the most effective blade to kill Insects. Tell Serein that.'

'Yes, my lord.' With a single edict, the Emperor had put an end to the Ghallain School and all its flamboyant sparring. Few people would practise rapier combat if it was not a key to enter the Circle and if there were no successful Eszai to inspire mortals to take up the art. The Morenzian and Plainslands fashion for duelling and wearing rapiers would decline.

San stated, 'Now to deal with Gio himself. When he leaves harbour, the Sailor must pursue him. But if Gio arrives at Capharnaum, he will wreak havoc as he prepares for her.'

'I'll go and tell her.' I stood up, tucking strands of wet hair behind my ears. San must want Mist to catch Gio at sea and deal with him out of sight of land, where there would be no witnesses, he would have no reinforcements, and the sea would cover the remains.

'You will travel *with* her.'

'My lord ...' The last thing I wanted was to be involved in a sea battle.

'The Castle protects the Fourlands against aggressors, Comet. Thankfully Tris is free from most of them, but Gio is certainly an aggressor, and one of our own making; our duty is to stop him. If he succeeds in reaching Tris you will deliver Capharnaum from both him and the Insect. I hope that if that eventuality occurs, the Senate will be inclined to communicate with us. You could tell them: "Our Emperor has sent us to protect you from Gio Ami and his criminals." And, only if the situation is right, tactfully restate my offer to join the Empire.'

San perceived the doubt in my eyes, and added, 'With the help of Mist and Lightning you will be able to do it, I am sure.'

'My lord, have you heard news or can you feel ... Would you tell me how Lightning is doing?'

'He lives, Comet. Walk with me.' San rose from the throne that had been worn over time to the exact shape of his body. He paced down the dais steps; his stiff white satin cloak trailed over them.

Amazed, I followed slightly behind him. We walked between the piers of a tall ogive arch into the west vault, up some worn steps and through a side door that led to a long outside terrace five metres above the lawns. Next to us, the arched windows of the Throne Room triforium ran the length of the building. Last night's downpour had stopped, and a quite hot sun was sending all this travel-sick water skywards again.

I had never accompanied San outside the Throne Room before and had never seen him out on the terrace. I felt very awkward. I had some conception that I should kneel, but when I abased myself San just sighed and motioned for me to rise. So I stood next to him, looking towards the Dace Gate, and I felt like the most honoured immortal until I followed the Emperor's gaze and saw, for the first time in daylight, the destruction that Gio had wrought.

The Dace Gate was completely destroyed. Its tower was smashed open to the sky. Holes half a metre across shattered the top of the east curtain wall for fifty metres to our left, and chipped stone blocks lay all over the rutted lawns.

Northwards, in the gap between the palace and the Castle's outer walls, the trebuchet stones had obliterated the Aigret Tower's top arches; their uprights remained like broken stalagmites. Cylindrical marble blocks lay among the statues in the monument square beneath and, peering through the skeletal tower, I saw that several of the Finials had fallen. Two whole trefoil arches on supporting pillars lay full length on the ground. I could see the signatures that covered them, like tiny cracks in eggshell. Gio had no right to attack the cenotaph, bring down the statues of mortals or wipe out the names of Eszai more ancient than him.

*

Tornado emerged from the Dace Gate barbican and ran heavily across the grass. He looked outsized even without any other men for comparison. He threw himself on his knees and looked up to our balcony, showing a round chin covered in stubble and enormous pectorals. His thick leather trousers and steel-toed boots were smeared with mud and I was satisfied to notice a bandage wound around his huge left shoulder, under a chain mail waistcoat that was mended with pieces of twisted wire. Hooked in his belt was a soup ladle, because whenever Tornado was not fighting, eating or drinking, he was cooking sumptuous meals. He smiled so hard his eyes disappeared. He boomed, 'My lord, the clean-up's going well; we're just dismantling the last trebuchet.'

San nodded. 'Good. Tornado, Gio will certainly not return. He is in the safe hands of the Sailor.'

The Strongman said, 'I can march the fyrd towards Eske to trawl for any stragglers but – like – I need outriders or we might get ambushed in the forest.'

Tornado was ten times smarter than people gave him credit for. He glanced at me; I glared back daggers and he looked a bit puzzled. He was easy-going and probably thought that Tern wasn't worth fighting over. It's a shame to break such a long friendship but he's doing the breaking, not me. I will fight him. I dropped my gaze only when I realised how closely the Emperor was studying us both.

'There is no need,' San said. 'Take your Select Fyrd to the Front where the governor of Lowespass is calling for help. Please take the dismantled trebuchets with you; you may well need them.'

Tawny ran a big hand over his shaved head and the thick corrugations of fat and muscle at the back of his neck. He stood, bowed in a gainly manner, and walked back into the ruins.

The Emperor said quietly, 'No one has attacked the Castle before. Whatever precedent it sets for the future, the governors are now abashed. They are already competing to demonstrate their loyalty by repairing this damage. They are sending their best architects, money and materials. A particularly generous quota is expected from Ghallain and Eske.'

'My lord, I can fly a circuit round the Plainslands and—'

San's voice was unexpectedly sympathetic and warm. 'I know you do not want to go back to Tris. You feel forsaken; you do not trust Tern and you want to be with her. But listen, your wife will not stay with Tornado.'

Then San stepped back into the Throne Room and was gone, leaving me on the balcony. The Emperor had mystified me again, this time with kindness. The warmth of his reassurance sank into my very core; I was over-come with gratitude. He touched me with a word and inflamed me with his energy. I felt like a great Eszai once more.

Long ago, Lightning told me how Tornado joined the Circle. In the year 885, Tornado strode into the Throne Room while court was in full session. The guards at the gate tried to stop him but Tornado just carried them along. Everybody fell silent as the giant stranger deposited two guardsmen in front of the throne. He leant on his axe and said loudly, 'I'm a Lowespass mercenary. I have no idea who to Challenge but I'll fight any one of you!'

The silence continued; everyone stared at the nameless fighter. The Circle members looked perturbed while the Emperor regarded them expectantly. 'I didn't answer him.' Lightning shrugged. 'I'm a bowman, not a brawler.'

The Emperor listened to the shuffling of feet before he broke the silence: 'Very well. Warrior, tell me about yourself.'

Tornado came from the area where Frass town is now, a ravaged landscape since strengthened by the chain of peel towers built by Pasquin, the previous Frost. He led a company of mercenaries who were paid by the farms in proximity to the Wall to protect them from Insects. Back then, the bounty was a pound per Insect head, and his troop made enough money to survive. Tornado loved his itinerant life until his wife died from food poisoning – a dodgy beef curry killed her when a thousand Insect battles couldn't.

The day after he arrived at the Castle, Tornado was taken to the amphitheatre and the Eszai loosed Insects against him. He chopped Insects into pieces all day until San, satisfied, created a new place in the Circle for the Strongman. Tornado remains the world's strongest man in eleven hundred and thirty-five years. He owns no lands nor houses, nothing but a shelf of Lightning's novels and seven-eighths of the Fescue Brewery – from which he takes his dividends in kind.

My buoyant mood stayed with me all day, as for fourteen hours I rode a convenient south-easterly to Awndyn. It was cold and rather damp, and the clouds gathered at nightfall, hindering my navigation. I gained altitude and flew above them.

The flat cloud cover ended above the last extremity of the land, precisely following the coastline. As I descended through the clear space in the cloud surface I felt as if I was diving to an underwater Awndyn far below. The full moon gave a much better illumination than the autumn evening daylight; the roads looked smooth as glass. I imagined the news of Gio's conspiracy flashing in along them from Eske and Sheldrake.

The promontory at the head of the strand was covered with grass the colour of rabbit fur and, with patches of bracken, it looked like aged velvet that was losing its nap. The beach was a peaceful collage; bottle-green waves soughed and sucked back through the sand. It could not be more different from yesterday's hurricane, which had spun windmill vanes around so rapidly that across the plains three hundred were still burning.

I landed and ran to the squat manor buildings, finding them dark and silent. The dewy grass around the annexe was criss-crossed with smudged footprints. Sometimes it could all just be one of my fever dreams. A glow radiated from one window on the ground floor. Cyan Peregrine was sitting on majolica-orange cushions on the window seat behind a pair of curtains that separated the window alcove from the rest of the room, to make a cosy den. Cyan's head was bowed; she was reading intently from a large book by lamplight. Her straggling blonde hair escaped its ribbons; the sleeves of her dress were puffed like cream cakes.

I tapped on the glass with a pound coin. Cyan jumped and looked all around, saw me beaming at her. She grinned and reached up to raise the latch and swing the window out. 'Jant!'

I gave her a hug but she pulled away from my cold skin. 'Sorry to scare you, little sister.'

'I'm not scared. Are you looking for Daddy?'

'Yes. Where is Lightning? Where is everyone?'

'They went out to the boat. Mist's red carnival. Caravel. She sailed it into the bay ... I saw it. I wanted to go on it but Daddy wouldn't let me. He's ill.' Cyan sat back on her heels, hazel eyes wide.

'He's awake? How is he?'

'That old woman said he'd be OK. I don't remember her name.'

'Rayne?'

'Yeah.' Cyan reached for my feathers and I gave her a wing to stroke. She often pestered me to fly carrying her, although at twelve years old she was far too big. 'Governor Swallow told me about the battle at the Castle and there are loads of men coming into town who don't like Eszai ...' Cyan made an effort to remember. She forgot the book of natural history that lay open on her knee but her finger still pointed, holding down a page with a grey watercolour of seals reclining on a shingle beach. 'Swallow said she ... Um, she "couldn't guarantee their safety" so Mist took them aboard. Are you going to fly after them? You're not going to stay?' She sounded resigned.

'Where is Swallow?'

Cyan sighed. 'Governor Fatbottom is trying to get rid of the men who don't like Eszai. She wants them out of Awndyn. She says they're trouble-makers. I was supposed to go to bed, but I didn't want to, so I hid.'

'Fatbottom?' I giggled.

There was a wicked gleam in Cyan's eyes. 'I keep thinking you're the same as the rest, but you aren't.'

'I can't be.'

Cyan complained, 'Swallow tries to teach me the harpsichello. The piccoloboe. Loads of instruments ... I hate them. She says, "You think you're good because you're Saker's kid." I feel like I've always done something wrong. I don't belong here.'

That sounded like me at her age. 'You don't have to do what Swallow says! You'll be a governor when you're twenty-one.'

'When I grow up. Yeah, yeah.'

'It's not a long time to wait. Take it from me; I'm twenty-three.'

'Hmm. That's reallllly ooooold,' she said thoughtfully.

'Isn't it?' Cyan had everything she could possibly want, but her fortune was just a spacious cage, as Lightning had planned out her life. Swallow, her guardian, knew of nothing apart from music and she found the child an obstruction to her obsession. Swallow may well never succeed in joining the Circle but she was determined to spend her whole life trying. I thought that if the bitterness set in, she wouldn't stand a chance. 'Remember that you can do anything you want.'

'I want to grow wings – it's like having four arms. And to fly like you.'

'Within the bounds of possibility. Cyan, lots of people who live in Awia don't have wings. The Emperor doesn't, either; it's not important that you take after your mother.'

She gave the concept serious consideration. 'I like it when Daddy teaches me archery. I wish he was here more, but he's very busy and now he's hurt. Everything's collapidated again. I like talking to him – he brings me presents – but he says I should do what Swallow tells me.'

I waved my hands emphatically. 'You don't have to believe anyone, no matter who they are – not Lord Daddy and not Diva Fatbottom. Think things through for yourself instead. Swallow isn't teaching you the right subjects, for a powerful governor-to-be, so you will have to observe and question. Remember, brother Jant is at your command; all the Eszai are. Governors don't seem to realise their power, and we need you to keep us in check with Zascai reality. That's what's been going wrong recently.'

She scowled, slightly resembling Lightning. Her tattered socks were rucked round her ankles and her shoes were scuffed with the grey-green mould found on tree trunks. She clenched her jaw to stop her teeth chattering; her breath hung in the cold night air.

'Goodbye, Cyan; look after yourself.'

'Are you going to fly? Why can't I fly?'

'Because you're normal.'

'Why can't I see this island?'

'Soon you will, sister. Soon everybody will.' I ran on the wet grass and took off, bound for the harbour.

*

Many humans envy wings. A few years ago, a serial killer murdered only Awians, chopped their wings off and wore them. But it doesn't matter whether one has wings or not when none of them can get off the ground. Cyan was more perspicacious; she envied flight. I worried about her as I remembered the Carniss saying: Wolves track lonely people.

When I was her age, in 1807, I was solitary too. No child wants to be left alone, but Rhydanne children grow up quickly. When they fall, they don't cry; when abandoned, they're independent.

My childhood in Darkling came to an abrupt end in my fifteenth year. Eilean insisted we remain every winter in our scanty summer dwellings in the high peaks. She said it was for my own protection that we did not go down to Scree pueblo with the other herders, although winter storms brewed and raged in the cirque every night.

Eilean Dara, my grandmother, was forty years old. She was a good runner; she had only ever let herself be caught by one man, who married her and treated her gently, but he died shortly after their daughter was born – my mother inherited a very fast speed indeed. I never understood how my rapist father could have caught her and Eilean wouldn't say.

My presence forced Eilean to change from her beloved hunting way of life to herding. She built our shieling herself, although it looked as if it had grown, part of the uncompromising mountains; an antlered hillock with moss on the roof that the goats ate in summer when the ice thawed. The shieling was a one-room box with bedding on the floor. Every wooden surface was covered in pokerwork designs, my grandmother's pastime in our desolate world. She burnt board games into the low table top – a chequered square for solitaire and trapper's luck, brown teeth for backgammon, and rectangular patches where packs of cards were placed for telling fortunes. When hunters visited they played games that were fast and simple compared to those I learned later at the Castle.

I discovered the rules of flight from trial-and-error; no child was ever as covered in cuts and bruises. Eilean made me look after our eight goats; I was good with a sling but I was never taught the bolas so when hunters came to poach them, I had to call her for help.

I left the goats tethered while I improved my gliding, soaring too far to hear their bleats and bells clacking. A pack of white wolves attacked the herd. The goats panicked, leapt high and strained at their ropes but the wolves devoured them in a leisurely fashion. When I landed hours later I found a pile of bones, tethers and bells. I hid from Eilean for days before she gave up trying to throttle me. She then steadily reverted to her previous life, chasing ibex and swigging whisky to forget the strain of my existence.

I sat cross-legged in front of the hearth and stared at the flames. After a while the door was nosed open and two massive tame wolves slipped through, padding solemnly. I relinquished my space on the mat for them; they lay down and sighed simultaneously. Compacted snow sticking to their pelts became translucent as it melted and dripped. Thunder tumbled down Darkling valley; there was a great sense of waiting in the air. Eilean Dara kicked the door back on its leather hinges and strode in. She hung up her bolas, reclined on the rugs, resting an elbow on the table, and looked around vaguely for me. 'Look at you, Jant; why are you still here? You should have left home by now. Have you no sense of shame whatsoever? I think you're determined to slow me down like powder snow. First, I can't even marry you off because how do I find someone who wants a deformed Shira as a husband? Second, you remind me of what those vile Awians did to the daughter I loved. Third, then you killed her, with your chunky body and wings trapped in her belly. We had to cut you out with an axe.'

I gathered her plate from the fireplace, pine nut crackers and meat stew cooked for so long it was a stringy paste. Eilean continued: 'A full seven-month pregnancy and you were still tiny. I fed you goat milk and raised you despite the fact that of course your birth wasn't timed and you arrived in the middle of the freeze season. So now you're grown, the way you show gratitude is by feeding my vicuna to the wolves.'

She reached out and I flinched. 'Have you caught anything?'

She carved a chunk off the stew, stuck her fingers in it and licked them. 'Nothing,' she taunted. 'Not faun not fowl not fuck.'

'Do I go bring them in?'

'Not green sludge in a dead deer's gut, not frozen milk in a dead girl's tit. There's no game this side of Chir Serac any more. I think we all starve.'

I peered at the whited-out valley. The temperature was plummeting and the sky was fantastically clear. There were more stars above the Darkling Mountains than anywhere else in the Fourlands, because they liked the clear air. Stars gathered there and fell as snow.

Two grouse were strung up on the shack's wall, their feathers harassed by the wind, purple in the impure light. A llama from Mhadaidh shieling still had a bolas wound round its legs, and a light covering of snow settled on the black antlers of a buck chamois. Its slack tongue was freezing to the ground; it looked at me with yellow teeth.

Eilean's fingers chased the last shreds of meat around her bowl. 'Oh, you are always under my feet. I need some space. Get out! Out!' She shoved a couple of thin skewers into the embers, knocking out sparks onto steamy wolf fur.

There was nowhere to go but the empty goat shed high on the rocks, built around the twisted trunk of a rowan tree that spidered up the cliff as if trying to creep away from me. I had believed Eilean's gibes that if I ran down to Scree the other Rhydanne would pull my wings off.

I wrapped a blanket around my shoulders and nestled in the bothy among the heather hay. Thick cornices hung over the vast black splintered cliffs, looming dark against the snow clouds. Eilean shouted, 'And don't come back in tonight!' She slammed the door, cutting off the firelight abruptly.

I listened, motionless, as from far up on Mhor Darkling, the highest spire of the range, an ominous creaking echoed down the valley. Tabular layers of snow began to slide.

My head was full of its white roar as I flared my wings and landed on the deck of the *Stormy Petrel*. I shook my head to silence the resounding smashes and splitting, buckling rock. For two centuries the avalanche has echoed in my ears.

I ducked into Mist's cabin and she immediately leapt up, dashed across and flattened a piece of paper against my chest. She yelled, 'What is the meaning of this? What's going on?'

'Huh?' I tried to pick at the note but her palm pressed it tightly to my shirt.

'What have you done, Jant?' she demanded, clapping the paper to emphasise every word. I recognised it as the Emperor's letter that I had sent to Awndyn with a loyal rider four days ago. My handwriting covered the back of the envelope.

'Hey, hey ... Don't blame the Messenger. San sealed this, not me. I haven't read it.'

Mist threw up her hands in complete exasperation, 'Then read it!'

Deliver to the hand of Mist only
Gio Ami shows interest in Tris. Be informed that his spies will try to discover the coordinates and the means to reach the island. You will make it easy for them to learn this information. With discretion, leave your charts or records where they may be readily accessed. Comet will tell you my further orders.
San, Emperor of the Fourlands, 13 July 2020

I threw a cushion to the floor and sat down. Through the stern windows the panorama changed as *Stormy Petrel* turned on her anchor. The lamps of homes and pubs on the seafront, the lighthouse on the harbour wall, the notched tops of yew trees in Awndyn cemetery protruded above the land's dark profile. The ship swung back: yew trees, lighthouse, seafront.

'I don't know what this means,' I said weakly.

Serein Wrenn had his feet crossed on the table, honing his rapier's edge with a tiny silver whetstone and watching the barometer drop. He said, 'We hoped you would explain.'

I told him San's edict on rapier fighting and Mist listened intently as I described Gio's rally. I folded the letter and held it in a candle flame until it burnt completely back to my fingernails. I finished by saying, 'So, Wrenn, you have to relearn broadsword techniques quickly; and Mist, you gave Gio's spies that chamber pot and notebook.'

Mist tutted. 'Never! As ordered, I neglected to lock them in the safe, and they were stolen by a midshipman with confused allegiance. He thought he had performed a cunning heist ... But it makes me scream with frustration; after all last year's secrecy.'

'Gio has a very strong force around the *Pavonine*,' Wrenn added. 'And he's got three other carracks. It's not going to be easy to stop him leaving.'

'Damn. That explains the lights I saw on the quay.' Wrenn threw me a packet of ginger biscuits and I started munching them. I said to Mist, 'San said you have to take care of the rebels offshore. Can we follow him?'

Mist gave me an incredulous look. 'You have no idea, Rhydanne. Ninety per cent of Awndyn supports him. He recruited most of my old crews and he's cleaning out the harbour stores. Gio's more ravening than Insects! May dogs shit on his grave. I need to send to Grass Isle to hire sailors loyal to me – mobilise some Awndyn Fyrd – call in old favours. He'll be long gone before we can raise the troops. So I must find food and ... blood and foam! That's without counting recaulking, fumigation, repairs! It'll take at least a fortnight! San *knows* that!'

'Tell him I'll certainly follow Gio – *Petrel* is faster than those Plainslands crates. We have stun sails, bilge keel; we're stable while they corkscrew, pitch and roll. I have tricks up my sleeve. If I catch them I'll sink them all right, but I might not gain more than a couple of days on their tail.'

She ruffled her hair vigorously. 'This is not like the Emperor. San knows very well it takes me two weeks to get this ship prepared. He doesn't make mistakes. Gio's Awndyn carracks are tough second-class merchantmen designed to round the cape. Ships Taken Up From Trade. In the right hands they could reach Tris. So now we're all STUFT.'

'I heard that Tornado already had the dissidents under control,' Wrenn said. 'San's given Gio a means of escape. Why in the Empire does he want to do that?'

Mist said, 'He usually asks a lot of me, but this ...'

Wrenn slid a scabbard over the rapier lying across his knees. 'Perhaps San thinks Gio will sink, then he'll be rid of the little plucker and two whole boatloads of bastards.'

Mist said, 'No. He never leaves anything to chance. Sometimes I think even god coming back is just a story he invented to suckle us.'

Nausea rolled over low in my stomach. I wanted scolopendium and my hands were beginning to shake. 'San can't be allowing Gio to reach Tris. Tris is so peaceful. Gio intends to ruin it.'

'True, but if we save the island from Gio, it's more likely to become part of the Empire,' said Mist. 'What does Tris mean to San?'

'I don't know. It must be more important to him than Gio's rebellion is ...' Then I figured it, and in a moment I saw time as San sees it. Its profound length funnelled out before me. I stared into a black well, as linkages and patterns suddenly lit up across centuries. Even Eszai can't see them; the Emperor plans them.

Of course I had no proof, but I was convinced that I was right. It was a feeling of falling as terrible as when the Circle breaks. One life was a second, a spark. No human can think back and forth over such an immense span. 'Oh, my god! I'm absolutely certain ... Gio is acting as the Emperor's cat's paw.'

Mist gave Wrenn a smile. 'I know inspiration when I see it. Jant, what's the real meaning of San's command?'

'He's sending Gio to Tris!' I jumped to my feet and pointed at her. 'You didn't discover Tris *by chance*, did you?'

She blanched, but stood her ground. 'Comet, let's work tog—'

'*Did you*? How stupid I am! One little island – the vast ocean! What are the odds on that? *Petrel* should have sailed straight past on either side! You weren't just lucky; San gave you the location, didn't he? He *sent* you to find Tris. San must have wanted to find the Trisians ever since they left the Empire in the first place!'

'What?' said Wrenn.

Mist said, 'I don't understand. What do you mean, "in the first place"?'

'Ata, what were your orders? Why did you do it – to prove yourself? No wonder you even played the marriage card. San wants Tris back in the Empire at any cost.'

Mist admitted, 'Yes, Comet. All he gave me were the rough coordinates and I tacked east until I came upon Tris.'

'The *rough* coordinates? You must have itched to ask him how he knew!'

'Yes,' she said softly. 'But I can't question the Emperor, and I practise self-control.' Her eyes were expressionless.

'Everybody knew, back then,' I said, awestruck. 'Two thousand years ago, the whole Four – Fivelands knew there was an island in the eastern ocean. San wanted us to rediscover Tris.'

'But why give it to Gio?'

'Because every new problem is a solution to an old problem,' I ranted. 'San has sent Gio to invade the island instead of us!'

Mist said, 'Oh. Because he can't be seen to do it himself?'

'Yes. Listen; San ordered me to tell the Senate, "Our Emperor has sent us to protect you from Gio Ami." He makes Gio sound like a formidable enemy, so that he has an excuse to send us!'

'Gio *is* a formidable enemy,' Wrenn pointed out. 'I'm determined to prevent him and his scumbag highwaymen from destroying Capharnaum.'

My hand on the door handle. 'Well, at last San has the means to reach the Trisians, to catch up. Tris is a loose end that must have bothered him for two thousand years! He gave you money to rebuild the fleet after the last Insect swarm, didn't he, Mist? How does it feel to be one of his instruments? And Serein, what's it like to be his Swordsman executioner? No better than Gio, who thinks he's rebelling but he's just San's pawn. San wants the descendants of the fifth-century rebels returned to the fold; wouldn't you? Oh, I really need a fix.'

'Come back!' said Mist. 'Tell us how you know all this. Where are you getting it from?'

'*A History of Tris*. It's ...' I faltered. 'I could do with some cat.' I ran to the hatch and down the ladder, heading for the sickbay.

The book I stole from the library recorded that a group of radicals left the Pentadrica to found Capharnaum. San must have known. I was sure that he wanted their reintroduction to the Empire, and Gio provided the means. I knew that we had to stop Gio. I also knew that I had just flown an awful, demanding itinerary all over the Plainslands and that being back on a caravel was not helping the fact I badly needed cat.

I ducked along under the low beams. Smells of gravy and hot flour rose from below. The ship creaked; the deck was gloomy. I paused and listened at the sickbay door lit by a single swinging lanthorn because a compassionate voice emanated from inside. It was the Doctor. I thought she was addressing Lightning, but no other voice answered or interrupted her. The old woman was talking to herself.

'Over time, Eszai are supposed t' get worn out and replaced. You're no' supposed t' live for ever, really.' I heard her bustling about. 'My dear, you like stories? Of course you do, you're a romantic. Hard t' believe once I was a lit'le girl with brown plaits and a patched skirt tha' spun ou' when I twirled. I was walking down the cobbled back streets in a Hacilith summer, and I heard music. That were before you were born, Saker, a long time ago. Such music! It were a shawm an' sackbut, though there could've bin a hundred of each, the way they wove t' most tempting tunes. T' music were coming from behind a high wall, with an arched green gate in it. I tried t' gate but i' were locked. I shouted to t' musicians, but nobody answered. I sat down on t' cobbles and began to cry.

'Then along the road there came this crowd of people, dressed in t' most beau'iful costumes, with plum-coloured feathers and foil masks. They caugh' me up in their masquerade, an' I slipped in behind them when the green gate opened t' le' them through. From then on, I were lost among t' drunken guests of an outlandish party, and I, only a lit'le girl with a calico skirt, became their amusement. They whirled tall and grotesque around me, an' I stared in fright. When I tired of t' constant noise and mysterious innuendo, I tried t' run away. I tried t' ge' out of t' ornate garden, but t' high wall trapped me in. Ladies and servants bat'ed me away, their sharp heels ripped my skirt. Eventually I crawled under a bush covered with these massive waxy flowers and I fell asleep. When I woke up I found myself out in the stree' again. I had been cleared up and put ou' with all the refuse from t' party.

'Saker,' she said tiredly, 'I heard how men break wild horses; tie their back legs, and when they attemp' t' run, they fall. That's how i' was for me before the Circle. You saved me then and we've been friends since. I'm saving you now. I can't do withou' you. Simply, if you leave me, I shall be alone forever.'

The voice stopped and all was quiet behind the door. I pushed it and slipped inside. The Doctor was sitting beside Lightning, playing a game of solitaire with glass beads. She put her wrinkled finger to her lips.

Lightning lay on his side on a cot that was attached head and foot to the ceiling and swung slightly with the ship's motion. His wings were open, one thoroughly bandaged, the other spread to stop him moving on the mattress. The feathers had been cut down in accordance with Rayne's theory of cleanliness. He was asleep. The blanket rose and fell with uneven breathing but in the indistinct light he looked like a tombstone effigy.

Rayne followed my gaze to a half-empty brandy bottle on the floor. 'Tha's the strongest narco'ic I can get him t' drink,' she said. 'He's feverish and t' wound's infec'ed bu' he refuses t' take painkillers. He's afraid of them, I think, having seen what drugs have done t' his friend.'

I hugged her; her face only came up to my chest. Wrinkles beneath her eyes overlapped like an oyster shell. Her plain cotton frock smelt of wintergreen oil and steam. In the small cabin she stood tall whereas I had to stoop.

'How is he?'

'In a serious condition. T' wound won' close. I' will take a long time, stabs have t' heal from t' base up and this one's deep. He los' a lo' of blood. He's weak, but a' least he's eating. A blood transfusion is t' las' resor'. I told him, "Lie still or i' will trouble you for a century." I'm treating his sprained arm as well. What about you? You look like you're dependen' again.'

'Yes ... I'm ... I'm back on the needle. Is there any way I can help Lightning?'

She seized my wrist firmly and pushed my loose sleeve back. 'Shi', Jant. T' pet cat you're keeping has been scratching your arms again. What a mess. Thought you'd beaten i' las' time. More fool me.'

I crouched down against one of the ribs that supported the deck above.

If you use drugs, in time you grow unusually familiar with the corners of rooms. My own predictability sickened me: 'Do you have any cat?'

'Yes. I had t' bring new supplies' cause *someone* made off with t' ship's complement of skylarks. No pity this time, Jant. You use your habi' t' bask in sympathy, soaking i' up like a sponge.' Rayne shuffled to prop her ample bottom on the work surface, obscuring her medicine case. 'T' chest stays locked. I can shou' for Wrenn. He's easy strong enough t' chuck you in t' brig.'

'I'm not violent,' I said, aghast.

'I know. Bu' in a few hours you'll be desperate.'

I wanted to get away. 'Look, I don't want to take cat any more but I don't have the will power to stop. In the last week I've had three nights without sleep and small shots give me the energy to keep going. I am trying, Rayne.'

'You certainly are. Wha's your dosage?'

'Five grains every two days.'

'Shi'. A Zascai wouldn't live long a' tha' rate. I thought I felt t' Circle strain t' hold you.'

Slumped against the hull and starting to shiver, I wretchedly submitted to her examination. She cleaned down my track marks and peered at my tongue and red-rimmed eyes. Macabre old woman. 'If you don't qui' soon ca' will kill you. You have one bugger of a problem.'

'What problem – Gio determined to ravage the Fourlands' only idyll, or Tern's adultery that I dwell on for hours at a time?'

'Silly boy. Tern's infideli'y is her way of coping with your drug habi'.'

'It's the other way round,' I said. 'I use cat because I can't bear to think of her affairs.'

'Pull yourself together! You and Tern blackmail each other ... but she's more likely t' enjoy i', whereas you hurt yourself t' ge' her attention. You're addic'ed t' sympathy – from Tern, from me and even Saker. Well, i's run out bu' you're still dying. Stop get'ing guilt kicks from asking for help and then rebuffing i'. Stop saving all your pain till later, live in t' real world. I know i's harsh but i's no' as bad as t' damage you wreak on yourself trying t' escape. If you don' break t' vicious circle, you'll wreck both your lives.'

'Tern left me first ... She doesn't care about me any more,' I complained.

'Don' argue,' Rayne snapped.

'I'm not arguing. I agree with what I'm saying!'

Lightning stirred and Rayne continued quietly. She turned her back on me and began to sort through phials. I didn't want to listen but I had no option. 'I find tha' selfishness is t' worst chronic disease of Eszai. Tern also suffers from t' condition. She loves you as a daredevil, how you used to be – flying t' Ressond gale, climbing t' cliffs a' Vertigo. Admi' that you're a lo' less beau'iful lying on t' floor staring a' t' ceiling. An' after ninety years t' res' of t' Circle's bored and sick of you collapsing all t' time… Sometimes I think t' greatest strain on San is restoring everyone's livers. Tornado challenges ten men to a drinking contes', Frost sups enough coffee for ten men, and you do both stimulants and narco'ics.'

I wished that people could see and believe my exploits in the Shift. I folded my arms tightly; my sharp fingernails dug into my biceps. I rocked forward. 'It hurts, it hurts. I don't want to do the fast cure … I can't kick now. The Empire needs me.'

'You mus' have some now because you're going into shock. I don' wan' two Eszai in life-threa'ening states. Then I ration you, one dose a day, oral no' intravenous, until I have chance to straigh'en you ou'. I can guess a' t' difficulty of injec'ing on a moving ship in a tempes'.'

I nodded, relieved to submit to Rayne's regime. She would look after me. 'It's a deal.'

She held out a hand for my nearly empty hip flask. The whorls on her fingertips were worn smooth through age and she had cured the warts, leaving small brown circles. I forced myself to open my fist a finger at a time and drop the bottle.

'Well done, Jant,' she said approvingly.

Hopelessness washed through me; dread filled me. I gave her a look that would have been puppy-dog if my eyes hadn't been so wildcat. A few minutes later I was rewarded with Rayne's confident grip on my bare arm, and a flick of her finger as she pushed the needle into the crook of my elbow. I felt no pain; Rayne was good. Unlike me she left no time for a red wisp of blood to spring into the syringe and dissipate, be sucked back with the drug. She just pushed the plunger down efficiently. So I got half of the ritual that I so badly craved. She shook her head, shaking her wattles like a bantam. I lost focus of her concerned face. I may look ill but it's beautiful in here. I breathed a week of strife out in one sigh; sleep at last.

I spent the next four days delivering communications. Governor Swallow could only find fifty Select Fyrd whom she could vouch had no sympathy with the rebels, and double that number of reliable General Fyrd. Mist employed a crew but could only find basic supplies, poor quality and meagre quantity: salt fish, three hundred barrels of flour bulked out with ground peas.

Mist came to the deck where I was supervising the fyrd carrying baskets of crossbow bolts up the gangplank. She said, 'Make them work faster. Gio's ships left during the night and they're already out of sight.'

'How many ships?' I asked.

'Three. Well, he took four carracks. Three of them, *Pavonine*, *Cuculine* and *Stramash*, sailed right out through the overfalls at slack water. I don't know the lead skipper, but he's a capable navigator. Gio's braving heavy seas – force-ten gales! But no one will follow him since the *Demoiselle Crane* capsized. I altered the harbour coordinates in the logbook before I so carelessly let a deckhand steal it.' She laughed with asperity. 'The *Demoiselle Crane* hit the Corriwreckan overfalls at flood tide, one a.m. exactly.'

Her thin-lipped expression was unsettling. I shuddered, as an echo of my sea-fear returned.

The loading continued night and day under Mist's impatient gaze, but it took a week before the stevedores' footsteps stopped resounding up and down *Petrel's* ladders and in the hold. The gale-force wind filled the sails and hauled us forward, and we began to crash through the storming seas outside the harbour. I retreated below to tell Lightning the news.

I took the first turn to watch over Lightning. When awake, he refused to allow the pain to affect him and was as courteous lying in the sickbay as in his palace. I wished that I had his self-assurance, but I don't have the security that comes from never questioning my place in the world. Rhydanne always see my wings and flatlanders see my cat eyes.

Because wolves track lonely boys, I was hunted out of Darkling in the melt season of the year I later calculated to be eighteen-ten. I was unaware that the high airstreams would carry me to the biggest city of hungry rats, bewildering to a mountain child, and proving nearly impossible to escape. Until I joined the Circle I was always pushed on, only ever seeking to get away from the places in which I was trapped. I became so used to defending myself that in the Hacilith chemist's shop, when I began to feel I belonged, my behaviour left me ruined and homeless again.

After the avalanche I ran down from the devastated valley keeping Mhor Darkling's colossal crags on my right, onto the plateau and warily towards the pueblo. I sneaked into the storeroom of the distillery, desperate to find food, filthy and tottering from exhaustion. I had not run such a long distance on my own before.

I descended a gravel and damp matting slope into the dark cellar and splashed onto a stone floor. It was covered with a good six centimetres of standing water. Drops ran down the dank walls and fell from the ceiling, plinking rhythmically. This was so wrong. Did anyone know the store was flooded?

It was like creeping into a cave. The cellar was stifling with the smell of pounded meat; the freeze-dried pemmican had become a sodden, slimy mass. But I had grown up with the smells of pelts drying and antler soaked in urine to soften it for carving, brown fat spitting on a cooking fire of burning bones, the reek of split long bones boiling to make grease.

I reached up and pulled down one of the baskets of dried berries that were stacked in piles of five. Rhydanne count in base five because it is warmer to keep one hand in a mitten. Besides, five of anything is a lot in the mountains. I ate an entire basketful of bilberries and cloudberries. Then I scooped water from the floor and lapped it out of my cupped hands until I was satiated.

Throughout my childhood in Darkling, I mainly ate meat. So when I reached the city I lived by stealing sizzling burgers from market stalls, which was as near to meat as I could find. When I figured out what fruit was, and how to peel it, I changed to pilfering apples and oranges, loving the intense sweetness, although to start with they gave me indigestion. The first words of Morenzian I learnt were the tradesmen's cries and curses.

I crept back to the distilling room and checked that it was deserted. I dashed out of the stone doorway, left the pueblo and jogged onto the plateau, while biting grit from under my nails. The dull sun shone a white pathway in the overcast sky. A skinning wind blew from the direction of Scree gorge, carrying the roar of the meltwater torrent and bobbing the sparse heather patches. Thick snow lay in hummocks everywhere, receding from dashes of black rock. Muddy blots in the distance were chamois, wandering along the vast plateau. Above them ancient glacier scratches scored the distant cliffs, as if in desperation.

Two Rhydanne sprang out in front of me. I dodged with a cry but they blocked my path. They were adults, I was as tall as them but not as strong. I didn't know the man's name but I knew his reputation. Being the area's fastest runner, he had caught a lot of women and lorded it over the other men. He had married and keenly defended a very desirable fellow hunter, who stood beside him.

A handful of condor feathers quivered in her long matted hair; it was dried back with ochre paste and red daubs stained the hair roots on her forehead. She had a pierced bear-canine necklace, and wolverine claws strung on the babiche lacings of her tasselled puma-beige breeches. She looked old, perhaps thirty-five. They both had knives on their belts and armfuls of plain bangles, prized possessions that confirmed their status. As the mountains grow, earthquakes and erosion sometimes uncover veins of Darkling silver that Rhydanne beat into jewellery.

These hunters were out of their territory, which I knew to be on the other side of the aiguille-lined ridge called the Raikes. They were not at all impressed by the farouche shock-headed boy who, having summed them up, was trying to flee. They strode around me. I couldn't dash between them; I was trapped.

'What is this?' she said with curiosity. Her eyes drilled into me like pale shards of bone.

'He's an Awian. Stocky as he is, he's young.'

'Alone?'

They looked around. 'If he is an Awian he's not old enough to be here by himself, I do declare. An orphan, then.'

The woman spoke slowly, 'Are you an orphan? Or abandoned?'

I said nothing.

'What are you doing here?' the man asked.

With overwhelming isolation I thought, I do two things: I can keep people company or I can leave them alone.

The woman shot out a wind-burnt hand and started pinching my feathers. Her husband gave a laugh and pick, pick, picked at the other wing. I yelped and sprinted away. Why were they doing this to me?

The cold wind lifted my dirty hair. My soaked feet were freezing; my three layers of fur socks had been shredded when I scrambled among the landslide rock shards.

I ran frantically over low outcrops, knocking stones from their frost-shattered surface. The Rhydanne kept pace without quickening their breath and all the time they laughed and plucked my feathers, leaving a trail of the ones they managed to detach. The woman poked me and I staggered; the man shoved me back towards her. I made a break but she leapt and pushed me; I fell over and broke the ice on a snow patch. I got to my feet whimpering with frustration and the numb pain from last night. The woman teasingly flicked my head and tore the hood from my alpaca wool jacket. The man pulled all the horn buttons off and the belt that kept it closed, since I had long outgrown it. They packed snow down my back. If they stripped all my clothes off, I would die of exposure. I thought that was their intent.

I wish I had realised then that my ability to fly would awe all Rhydanne, because it was faster than they could ever run. If I'd known that I would have armfuls of bangles; if I'd known that I would own the Spider, and remind them of the fact with free drinks every year, then I wouldn't have sobbed and darted about in vain attempts to escape, tears rolling down my face.

I wrenched free and ran as fast as I could. The man gave a double whistle. The woman whistled once to show she understood and they spread out on either side of me. They're hunting me, I thought with horror.

I swerved away from her and ran straight. Her mate narrowed the gap and forced me towards her with a laugh of pure joy. The ice inside my collar rubbed my skin raw and was seeping down my neck; the cold air seared my throat.

They easily followed their hunting system and mercilessly passed me between them. For them it was a leisurely pace but I was trembling and close to pissing myself with fear.

The third time around a stack of antlers marking a meat store scraped in the frozen ground I realised that they were deliberately making me run in large circles. I yearned to jump far away from Scree – to leave every one of the Daras and hunters. Blind with tears I swerved abruptly and headed straight for the gorge. They chased me, grinning. The lip of the crevasse loomed far too close. They halted, called, 'Stop!' I heard concern in their voices but I wasn't falling for any tricks.

I spread my wings and glided over the gorge. The ground fell away and I was suddenly one hundred metres in the air above lashing milk-white water.

The Rhydanne clutched each other, their mouths agape. Apart from Eilean, they were the first to see me fly. But I remember terror rather than triumph as I watched their figures shrink into dots. A powerful air current grabbed and hurled me up. The Pentitentes Ridge of Chir Serac lengthened, covered in cone-shaped ice-formations. Mhor Darkling's highest white peak pulled down past my wings; the entire mighty, beautiful massif spread out beneath me.

Above my world, a steady broad slipstream of wind blew to the south-east. I fought for breath in the thinnest air and talked myself calm. 'Then that's the way I'll go. Wherever I land has to be better than this.' I turned with the wind stream and let it speed me away.

'Jant?' Lightning's voice sounded amused. 'Jant, wake up! Are you all right?'

I sighed. 'Yes. Don't worry about me; how are you?'

'Bearing up. Burning, weak. Snatches of music keep going round and round in my head. You look dazed too.'

'I was just thinking,' I said. 'Reminiscing about my childhood.'

The dingy cabin creaked and lurched. The Archer nodded approvingly and said, 'Please tell me about it. It must have been wonderful, living in the mountains and being free.'

CHAPTER 18

The ocean was a choppy swell laced with lines of foam, a breathing shape over the back of which the *Petrel* rolled. The mastheads were beginning to glow, freezing spray cracked from taut sails, and she listed hard to starboard as she slid rather than sailed down into another trough.

A passing squall blew the surface of the waves opaque and slated rain horizontally onto the gleaming deck. Water dripped off the strips of lead nailed over Mist's cabin door. White rain screamed down so strongly I couldn't see through it. It pounded the waves flat.

I slid the forecastle hatchway open on its runners and peered down into the sickbay. Lightning's figure was just visible in the gloom. The bed had been hooked to the padded leather wall and he sat propped up, a glass of brandy cradled in his big hands. He pressed his back to the wall in an attempt to relieve the pain that still immobilised him. I teetered uncertainly on the creaking threshold until he beckoned me down. 'Come in. It's so tedious lying here for weeks. I've either been talking to Rayne or listening to my own heartbeat in the pillow. Close the hatch, please; the chill seems to nip into my wound.'

I dangled off the ladder as the ship lurched unexpectedly, and dropped onto a spare sleeping bag by the opposite bulkhead. 'I was just on deck getting some fresh air – if you can describe sea air as fresh. We keep sliding down the waves sideways, they're like black pyramids. Mist's furious; in the teeth of the storm we're getting nowhere and Gio is increasing his lead. Wrenn hasn't stopped being sick yet. Where's the Doctor?'

'Collecting clean water from the stove. I am in good hands.'

The ship rolled and molten wax poured off the candles in the lantern. The flames jumped up high on their long wicks. Lightning blinked. He winnowed out his uninjured wing to scratch between the contour feathers, then folded it up by hand and tucked it under his voluminous surtout coat. The creamy candlelight cast his face into pallor. He was clean-shaven and, through long practice, fastidiously neat. Living on a ship for three months is like camping at the Front and Lightning knew how boredom, bad conditions and long waiting cause men's discipline and ultimately their behaviour to degenerate. The bandages under his barn-owl-yellow coat were fresh and crisp.

He said, 'I worry about Cyan; I need to see her more. I only have a short opportunity to raise her and I can't depend on Swallow to do it properly. This is such appalling timing; last century the Emperor could have done without me for a decade. Poor Cyan, she always looks delighted when I visit, though she's different every time, she grows so fast. Jant, one day you might find that you rely on prominent features to recognise people from one decade to the next.'

He veered from Low to High Awian, an outrageously complicated language in which every noun has a case, a tense, one of three genders and one of two social classes. Most of the verbs are irregular, and the least slip in the forms of address can cause offence. I am not sure whether High Awian became so intense through its long evolution in their aristocracy or deliberately to discourage aspiring farmers, tenants and Morenzians.

'This is the longest time I have failed to practise. I'll be in a sadly Challengeable state when we reach Tris, but it is my responsibility to catch Gio. This hurts, Jant; it certainly hurts. I can still feel the steel piercing my side – cold and inflexible. Have some brandy. I'm not drinking much, it would be disastrous for my aim, but it really is better than ours.'

'It's the only decent drink on board,' I said. 'Mist left in such a hurry that we've taken Gio's leftovers for rations. My guts are shrinking; I've had nothing but soup and juice all week. Can I bring you any?'

'No, stay awhile and talk. I have a Messenger's errand for you ...'

'What is it?'

'It is somewhat unusual.' Lightning stared into the centre of the cabin. It was easy to underestimate how debilitated he was, with those overdeveloped shoulders. I waited patiently; perhaps he was rambling. The warm round smell of wax pervaded the berth, making it rather cosy. The rain smelt green; the ship's oakum soaked it up and stank like a wet dog. Thankfully it was difficult to envisage the breakers tearing over the main deck; above us the shredded topsail cracked and plaited. The driving waves caught red dusk like smallpox as sunset flashed under a suffocating sky, transforming the sailors' frantic activity into a series of stills.

Lightning breathed, 'It is autumn again ... her birthday. I should be with Martyn. Since the Circle was founded I have never missed the date, my long-kept secret. If I could order *Petrel* around and sail for Awndyn, I would.'

'Count me in!'

He gave a bitter smile. 'I knew that at some point I would fail Martyn. It matters not, when Gio is persuading mortals to massacre us. But although my tradition is just a whim, I find breaking it makes me uncomfortable and I fancy she will miss me.' He looked away. 'I suppose you are eager to know what has been eating me up for one and a half thousand years ...'

Lightning stared into space for a long while. He judged the time was right and suddenly said, 'Jant, I want you to carry a message to a dead woman. If I am killed fighting the rebels, you must visit the mausoleum and speak to her about the circumstances of my end. Explain why I can no longer come to see her.'

493

He feigned interest in his brandy. 'My cousin's body lies in an aventurine casket near the tombs of generations of my family, in a high-ceilinged sepulchre. You will find it amongst the trees on the man-made island in Micawater lake, in the palace grounds. I visit her once a year; I should be there today. I always leave the door ajar so that a shaft of light falls across Martyn's tomb. She loved the lake, you see. She used to trail her hand in the water, for the suspended mineral flecks that reflect the sunlight.

'You will see one clear track that my steps have made through the dust that lies thickly over every surface, from the entrance to the head of her vault. I sit beside the inscription that I keep free of dust. For the space of a few hours I tell her all the events of the previous year. I say that I visit as promised, because I still love her.

'I always bring balsam flowers. I store them in the underground bow room, which you have not seen. It is near the ice house, a beehive-shaped cellar, a cool, homeostatic store where the bows hang horizontally on stands. The flowers must be white because they set off her magnificent deep red hair so well. They must be balsam, as in the rhyme that no one even remembers any more: balsam for lovers, willows for brides, briar for maidens, lilies for wives.

'When I have finished telling her the news I leave the balsam, gather up the dried remains of last year's bouquet and row back across the lake.'

Lightning rubbed his forehead and sipped at the brandy. In his mind's eye he stroked the glistening green stone, sitting on the plinth while maple leaves fell past the mausoleum portal and doves cooed in the baroque cote.

'Martyn and I were struck with pure and sincere love,' he said very sourly. I was startled, but I suppose nothing causes bitterness so much as a downfall from ecstasy. 'I don't know why. Maids of honour packed my mother's entourage. There were ballrooms full of girls, all very pretty and accomplished, but not one of them was real.

'As a child Martyn was often at the palace. Then one banquet night we noticed each other and everything changed. We fell through into a panorama of hidden possibilities. We stared at each other across the laden table; nothing else existed. Without a word we rose together and left the hall. She was nineteen years old, I was twenty-nine. My conscience made me hesitate; she took my wing and led me to the antechamber, where she pushed me into the cloaks hanging on the wall and allowed me to kiss her.

'We rushed to the stables at midnight. "Don't you want to escape?" Martyn said. She was wild, she didn't care. She charged her white hunter at hedges and ditches, taking the jumps at a mad speed and I galloped beside her.'

An unruly smirk that I had never seen before appeared on Lightning's face. He looked almost boyish. '"Don't you want to escape?" We escaped a lot after that – every opportunity we had.' He held his index fingers ten centimetres apart. 'I was this far from quitting the court, marrying her and exiling ourselves. We were this far, one fistmele, from escaping properly. I wish I had had the courage; she would still be alive today. She would be here *now*.

'I sometimes fought Insects but my lineage shielded me. Martyn and I spent most days in a world of our own. My family never mentioned it but they knew. Oh yes, they knew. The court thrived on Mother's blissful love for Garganey, but my love for her sister's daughter was taboo.

'We talked for hours and rode great distances, far from the palace to converse in the forest. All those long conversations, words came so easily. At dinners we were careful to sit apart. In dances she was serene and unperturbed while I tried hard not to look.

'Martyn was a peerless rider. I remember her perfume, her sepia and sage silk, her strong limbs, pale skin, and her auburn wings that she would spread like an excitable girl. She had seen so many forests the green of them stayed in her eyes.'

I felt like a voyeur in the undergrowth next to Lightning's cousin as she pressed herself against him and lay between the roots of an oak tree. She pulled up her tunic, her necklace's fine links pooled in the hollow of her throat. I peered to see a young Saker kiss her neck and full breasts and repeat her name tenderly and urgently. Her red curls spread on the crisp leaves as Saker mumbled, 'We mustn't do this,' desperately down the front of her blouse.

I felt uncomfortable because I had always considered Lightning to be sexless and celibate; the thought of him shagging Martyn was strange and a bit disgusting.

His tired voice continued: 'I see her again and again. Sometimes a woman's beauty reminds me of Martyn, but she doesn't act the same. Anyway, even the most breathtaking beauty only approximates to Martyn's. If I wait long enough ... well ... the types of characters are not endless, and with time they recur. She looked very much like Swallow, but taller, and she resembled Savory too – remember her?'

I nodded cagily. Lightning sent me to deliver his love letters to a fyrd captain called Savory, and she let me fuck her after she read them. I was single, individualistic and hedonistic, so I took it as proof of how wrong Lightning was about women. I now keep the burden of guilt to myself, because for his peace of mind and my own safety he must never know.

He continued without noticing. 'Martyn was as close to perfection as it's possible to be. A happiness so intense can't last long; it's always the case that the arrows we shoot up to the stars fall back on our own heads. The Insects swarmed ever closer, decimating the First Circle, and in the year six-twenty San announced the Games. Martyn watched me win through the hundred rounds in the archery tournament but she did not travel with me to the Castle, where he made us victors immortal. I whispered to her afterwards how nobody in the Circle felt immortal and we hardly believed the Emperor. I established myself, organised my lodging in the Castle, and next thing I knew, San sent us to the Front. The Wall ran on the north bank of Rachis River and we struggled very hard – they stretched the Empire to breaking point. I had no sleep for a week, I fought to the last of my strength. It took years to push the vermin back into Lowespass. It was a harder struggle than that of twenty-fifteen.

'Then San gave me leave. I visited my family, and everything looked different. They were all older.'

Lightning pulled his knees up under the blanket and wrapped his arms around them. The informal gesture made him seem shockingly smaller; I suddenly saw the boy in a man I had thought too old and awesome to contain one.

'The gentry and my brothers gave sidelong glances from the periphery of the courtroom as I knelt before Teale. She raised me to my feet, pinched my cheeks and turned my head. "By god, it's true," she said, with both pride and envy. Their bodies changed with time, mine didn't. The world had seen nothing like Eszai before. I seemed to be a threat although I had no power to intimidate them; I couldn't even age. The stilted politeness of the quality crowd barely covered their distrust. I was keeping their wealthy world safe from Insects but because the Circle was successful the courtiers lost the concept of danger. They took my sacrifice for granted. They drifted, I fought.

'I proposed to Martyn but she could not deny the will of our Queen. She would not leave the court and the country. Although it would have been easy, at the time we couldn't see how. What happened to the carefree rowdy girl in those years I was away? Martyn didn't ... Now she was older I don't think she trusted what I'd become. I think I frightened her. I wasn't strong enough to take her from the court, and she wasn't as strong as I thought she was ... or maybe I appeared stranger to the world than I realised. In the blink of an eye she was married, raised a family of beautiful children, was an old woman; she died. She was always very changeable. I admired her ability and loved her all the more. I adored and guarded her until the end, but I never spoke to her.

'Life seems to be more about the choices you don't make. San decreed that I could be Eszai or King of Awia, not both. The throne passed to Avernwater. I threw myself into my work again. Eventually I saw Martyn's own line die out. The bustle and crowds had gone from the palace and I lived there on my own. Hardly anything happened for two hundred years. I had a lot of Challenges because, after all, archery is the national sport. Next time I looked up, I barely recognised the kingdom.'

Lightning realised he was staring at nothing and seemed surprised. He gave me a sharp look and said harshly, 'Never mind. I had expected to out-live you, Comet, but these are not Insects we're fighting now. Will you carry the message to Martyn?'

His confidence overwhelmed me. 'I'll do better than that. I'll bring her balsam blooms and chat to her on your behalf this day every year for the rest of my life, and then, if I can, I'll pass the duty on to another willing Eszai when I die.'

'God, Jant; so generous. I am indebted. Thank you very much ...' He sighed; he was too exhausted to continue. The silence that followed purged the air. We both knew that we would never mention Martyn again.

I looked at us there: a young and old immortal. The lanky Rhydanne one curled up, safe in his own self-interest, had a bright pride in his eyes because he had the chance to watch over and listen to a prince aged four-teen hundred and thirty-something, talking in a tired attempt to unpick his past. You could peel away shell after shell and still never understand Lightning, because you only get a little of him with each shell. In response I told him everything about Tern's affair, and I asked for advice. 'When Tern's in Tornado's rooms I'm too scared to confront them, because it's his territory, you know.'

Lightning scowled, then surprised me by saying, 'But from the start she was so keen to marry you! I can have a word with her if you like. I can explain how you feel, to show my gratitude for the favour you have promised. I once told Rayne about my cousin, but no one else. You will keep the secret?'

'Yes, of course.'

'You are a good friend.' He lay down, propped on one elbow, and said, 'Leave me for the night. I have to sleep.'

Next morning I waited till the rain dwindled, then ran out of my cabin along the slick bowed deck past the wheelhouse that Mist had constructed around the helm. She had also lashed a copper rod to the mainmast like a lance. Two sailors clinging to the wheel muttered, envying my sense of balance and the way I can relax into the cold.

Stormy Petrel barrelled along furiously under full sail, an arrow shot towards an as yet invisible target. The knife-sharp waves scooped up water and rushed forward, all the water slipped off, then up went the peak again, further on.

Every time the *Petrel* bucked up she went 'whoosh', then slammed down 'splash'. This whoosh-splash wound my muscles tight; I was sure it would tear the ship to pieces. When she pitched forward the bowsprit dipped and touched the waves. I waited for it to break off. Water sprayed over the prow, rushed down the deck, sluiced off between railings and down drain holes.

I thought we were going to do a headstand on the figurehead all the way to the sea floor. Next second the bowsprit pointed straight at the sky like a flagpole. It described an enormous curve as it crunched down again. The masthead drew a wide circle in the sky as *Petrel* rolled.

Worse, the five-metre waves pushed by the hurricane started overtaking us, and pushed *Petrel* forward a little in time with each tip-up. With each tip-down the bow slammed in the waves and braked the ship, so a stop-start jolting added to the vertical lift and fall.

In Mist's cabin my entrance was met with a nod. She was busy with her charts, while her navigational instruments hurtled from one edge of the table to the other with every whoosh-splash.

'It's been one hundred days,' I said. I wedged myself in the corner. 'When will this stop? You said we should be able to see Tris by now.'

'If there was no sea-fret we could,' Mist muttered. 'How's the Archer?'

'Variable. He can walk but his wound keeps catching.'

Wrenn's voice interrupted me: 'Fret, she says! It's not a fret, it's a hurricane.' He lay abjectly on the bench by the stern windows. His angular Adam's apple pointed at the ceiling. His short chestnut-coloured wings folded neatly to fit under the curve of his spine, so he could lie flat on his back. His face had a greenish pallor; sweat bristled his hair and stubbly razor-cut sideburns. I noticed a tiny lip of fat over the waistband where he used to be trim. The sea crossing was taking its toll. Happily, I thought, I'm better company for Lightning now he's injured. Lightning wouldn't have told Wrenn his secret.

The whole room see-sawed up and free-fell down. I winced at the crash. The Swordsman moaned, 'After I puke I feel better until fifteen minutes later I have to puke again. My nose is full of it. The teeth ache in my gums. When we lift my stomach is left up there. I plunge with a hole in my middle – on the next rise I meet it and god knows what other internal organs.'

'Try flying,' I said merrily.

'Oh, god ...'

The salt-smeared panes behind him gave onto the pockmarked water. *Stormy Petrel* trailed a green wake. Air bubbles deep inside the waves jiggled and struggled to rise, broke as froth.

The violet rings under Mist's eyes were the same colour as her irises; with her pale hair and fading bronze skin she looked unearthly. She pushed a wooden rule back and forth along the raised rim of the tabletop. 'Patience,' she snapped. 'I can't help that we're hindered by dirty weather, or that *Pavonine* missed it by days. I can't control the seasons! I need to know what Gio is doing. I hope to predict him ... Against this gale every manoeuvre I make is as pointless as a Circle masquerade.' Her lips cracked as she smiled. She bent over her chart again, preoccupied. 'It's simply chance. I thought I'd find him! I can't run him down with the wind in my face no matter how much sail I fly. The *Pavonine's* skipper isn't better than me. He's just a lucky fucker.'

Wrenn and I remained quiet. The thought that Mist was failing filled the cabin with despondency. She stretched her arm across the table and neatly caught a brass protractor as it slid past. 'Can Lightning draw a bow?'

'He says so.'

'Can you fly in this weather?'

'If I can get above the clouds. Otherwise the rain—'

'Good.' She beckoned me to the chart and stroked her finger along some ruled pencil lines. 'Here's your direction from our current position and we are making just over a kilometre an hour so we'll be at *this* point by the time you return. If Gio reached Capharnaum at the rate I watched him leave Awndyn, he'll have been on Tris a fortnight. We'll have to catch him there.' She sighed and continued almost in a daydream, 'When Gio was Serein, I liked the man, I can't pretend otherwise. We were friends for three hundred years of campaigning. He plays to his strengths so he'll stay ashore. Aye, I recognise that Zascai extreme desperation; they drive themselves so far and so pitilessly they can't survive. There but for San's favour go I. Right. I admit I don't want to deal with Gio on dry land, but I have no choice. I'll let Lightning and Serein take their turn.

'We're coming up on Tris in the next day or so. See? Scout around, Comet, and bring us some intelligence.'

I memorised the calculation and said to Wrenn, 'Don't worry, there's only one day left.'

'Aye, go back to training,' Mist gibed him. 'I want you as keen as a harpooner when I set you on Gio. This surf will break straight onto the rocks. I'm lucky that the Capharnai built such an imposing harbour wall for their piffling little canoes.'

The sky and sea were so overcast that the very light was grey. Cloud lowered to liquefy and make the ocean. The *Petrel* was always the centre of a dull opaque sphere, half-filled with thrashing water. Great spirals of spitty white foam went round and round on the sea's surface.

Waves thumped on the bow and resonated through the whole ship, playing her like a drum. She crashed down, the displaced water spurted up over the figurehead and pattered on the foredeck. Half a metre of white spray stood solid on top of the waves, where raindrops were bouncing back off. Their power smoothed the waves, filled the troughs – the sea was white as a snow field. Spume blew off the wave tops. I was inhaling it; the air was full of salt.

I shrugged my leather coat on over three layers of T-shirts, and shoved my hair down the collar. I drank a mug of hot reconstituted soup with stale biscuit broken into it. Then I set off and climbed unevenly, beating painfully against gusts that came from every direction. Behind me rain fell as a slanting grey strip from a single patch of cloud onto the heeling caravel.

Flickering lightning illuminated the clouds from within. I zig-zagged up, terrified of it. I beat a path with great difficulty through the wind, already waterlogged by raindrops as big as snowflakes.

I disappeared into the cloud base and continued climbing calmly to avoid disorientation. Rain streamed down my coat and cold wisps whipped past my face.

I emerged, pulling up shreds of cloud, into a most perfect, tranquil world – with a population of one. The sky above was a uniform winter blue, a bright sun shone on complete cloud cover beneath me like a second, motionless ocean. Its wan surface was hollowed and carded into static points like a blanket of wool. The light was so brilliant it reminded me of the glare on the Darkling glaciers.

I breathed deeply in the thin air. Directly ahead cumulo-stratus lapped around the summit of Tris's mountain, its charcoal and olive colours muted with distance. Further away the silhouette tip of the second island in the archipelago poked through the cloud. They were like islands in the sky.

I held my wings out in a long shallow glide. On the ground I never had freedom from responsibility, from people, freedom from drugs. This was the ultimate release. Only the dull and earthbound sit in hulking carracks, the humid forest. They will never understand my world because I am the Messenger and I have all this air.

The clouds' surface sped away under me. While *Stormy Petrel* and Capharnaum town laboured under the storm, the setting sun cast the colours of northern lights over my private sea. Meringue cloud turned opalescent blue, pale orange and rose pink; the mountain's shadow lengthened. I loved the uninhabited mountain. The splendour of Tris from my unique perspective filled me with elation, but I wished that I could show it to Tern. I would paint it in words for her if we were ever snug in bed together again.

I reached the mountain's slope after nightfall. The gale concealed my wings' noise, so I descended through the clouds to Capharnaum and circled at height trying to discern detail. It hadn't rained on Tris; the main boulevard and its rotunda were lit but the surrounding streets were completely dark. A few people stood by the crossroads. A group of men walked towards them, carrying lanterns and some sort of polearm. The loiterers started up, slouched downhill towards the harbour and filed into a wine shop, leaving the paved street empty. From the foot of the Amarot crag, a bell pealed ten strokes, and all was silent.

I sailed over the Amarot, seeing its walls lit flame-yellow. About a thousand men were bivouacking on the mosaic between the Senate House and the library. They were Gio's rebels and they had lit a cooking fire right on Alyss's face. The aroma of goose fat rose up to me. Real food! God, I wanted some of that meat.

Shadows ten times life-size reared and lunged on the Senate House columns as they dipped tin mugs and tarred horn cups into an enormous keg of rum and passed them around. Dirty faces reddened by the firelight jeered and laughed. Thousands of hours of effort had been poured into constructing the mosaic, and now Gio's thugs were trashing it.

The night seemed to jump darker by degrees, making me blink; my eyes were adjusting all the time. I made out a small building perched on the cliff edge behind the Senate House. A shape as fat as Cinna waddled out of the dark entrance, buttoning his fly. I bent back my wings to descend. Yes, it was Cinna, appearing like a coagulation of all the lard in the Fourlands.

He sauntered, his hands deep in his pockets. I swung into a standing position and dropped to the ground behind him. Cinna halted in his tracks and turned around very slowly. He said, 'I'm not wanking. I'm just keeping my hands warm.'

'Huh? Shut up and follow me.'

I ran, hugging close against the library wall, to the unlit colonnade that joined the library to the Senate House. I slunk inside and beckoned to Cinna. He reeled; his peacoat was spotted with rum. I grabbed his lapels and positioned him squarely behind one of the columns where he stood less chance of being seen, although he overlapped it on both sides. His red nose was darker than his shocked white expression. Drops of sweat detached from his shiny forehead and rolled down puffed-out cheeks.

I drew the ice axe from the back of my belt and whispered, 'If you cry out I'll kill you.' Cinna gave me a beseeching look, wiped his palms on his knees and pointed at the ground. I let him sit down and lean against the column. I hunkered down too, in shadow and well out of sight.

'What's going on?' I asked. 'Quickly. Why is Capharnaum so dark? The streets are deserted and a bell was tolling. I saw men loitering; there was nothing threatening about Capharnaum before. What's Gio done to them?'

Cinna's frightened whisper was so low I scarcely heard it. 'You saw that, Messenger? Yes, the patrol just called for the next watch. They're not fyrd – the Senate appointed men to maintain the curfew and guard the houses.'

'Curfew? There's a curfew? Why?'

'Because of an Insect that's loose. It's killed eighty people so far. The Senate and Gio have divided the town into sectors and they're searching systematically, even sewers and attics, but they can't find it. One Insect is causing more trouble than all the swarms of Lowespass. See those posters over there? They warn people to stay indoors.' He nodded towards some sheets of paper pasted on a board at the end of the library. 'They carry a picture of the latest victim. But the fact that Capharnai have discovered The Joy Of Insects isn't the only reason for the curfew. Thieves are roaming the streets. Gangs.'

'Gio's men are desperadoes,' I agreed.

Cinna belched quietly and chuckled. 'Not us. Them. The citizens.'

'But Tris had no crime six months ago.'

Across the square the rabble's voices rose in a raucous cheer and Cinna took advantage of the noise to say, 'It's your fault!'

'Sh!'

'Mist Ata bought up all the spices, didn't she? Now they've nothing to preserve food. So a lot of the Capharnai's stores have gone rotten, it's winter soon and some food supplies are running low. Prices are steep – The Price Of Spice is like scolopendium, Messenger. The Senate have unconditionally banned trade with the Fourlands and they're endeavouring to ration everything except bread and fish. Well, all I know is they're muttering because Gio's nine hundred men have to eat and they've no choice but to feed us. Those drunks you saw Being Moved On have made themselves a nuisance here all day.'

'I didn't know Capharnaum had drunks.'

'It does now. Those men were the merchants Mist paid. I know, because they hassled me for rum as we were rolling the kegs up here. I don't know how I'm supposed to look like a pusher or a captain if I have to sleep in the outdoors ...'

'Keep to the point.'

'Well, Mist gave them so many riches they don't have to work any more. Their money is time, and she gave them years of time so now they're idle. I hope she profited from those peppercorns and pickles, the Entrepreneur Of Misrule, like myself.' He rubbed his plump hands together. 'They're not used to rum but they've found a taste for it. They drink it like wine. Because they're armed, they're Creating Trouble. It just goes to show that the only Truly International Language is drugs.'

I began to understand. I prompted, 'They're armed? They'll be armed with the swords and halberds we sold them?'

Cinna nodded. 'Yes, I think so. I was told that the Senate tried to buy up all the weapons from the townspeople to give to their patrols but they clearly didn't get them all because I hear there were armed robberies – at storehouses and the market. Also, young men keep soliciting to buy swords from us. It seems they've become quite a status symbol. Capharnai have never seen quality steel before; it's worth its weight in gold. And of course men have to protect themselves from the Insect.'

'Shit.'

'The Senate are discussing imposing taxes to pay the patrols.' Cinna appraised the Wheel brooch on my patched coat. 'Gio is waiting for you and Serein. Gio wondered if *Stormy Petrel* had gone down in the storm. Of course, he reckoned without Mist's marvellous seamanship. He was thinking about his next move. He told Senator Vendace that we would leave Capharnaum, but he doesn't really mean to. He's safe here; the Senate is In His Pocket.'

Cinna put a special emphasis on Gio's name. He was obviously firmly under the fencing master's influence. Nine hundred men following Gio, I thought. They outnumber us more than three to one. Still, that's better odds than against the Insects. 'If I have to stain my hands with blood, I must admit this rabble is less daunting than the swarms.'

Cinna gaped. 'You think it's just Gio? No, Comet. God, sometimes I believe all you have to do to be immortal is out-arrogance each other.'

'Spit it out.'

'Gio has won over the Senate and he's prepared to lead all Capharnaum against you when you land.' He went on, 'Everyone here hates you, and Gio has been planning. When *Petrel* sails into harbour she'll be surrounded, you'll be seized. There are twenty thousand people in this town.

'Vendace was wary because of the disastrous effects of your visit. But Gio's rhetoric quite convinced him. You should've tried making long speeches in the Senate.' Cinna smirked. 'Gio's here for the same reasons and on the same terms as the original settlers – to leave the Empire and San. Vendace thought he had found a Kindred Spirit. Gio offered to help hunt the Insect and being desperate they welcomed him with open arms. His interpreters are at home with their old lingo. The Senate didn't like the look of us tars as much. They've been discussing it for three days but they haven't made a decision yet.'

I wished for another stint in the Senate. If Gio can sway their opinion simply by talking to them, I thought how much better I could be when it was my turn. Gio may have had two weeks to work on their hearts and minds, but I'd love a verbal battle with him.

Cinna sniggered. 'They are so naïve. Myself and three colleagues could control this town in a year without drawing a sword or promising immor- tality— Ulp!' I pressed my ice pick to his throat. He gulped: I expected his eyes to pop in like a frog's. I couldn't bear the thought that he could turn Capharnaum into a slum worse than East Bank Hacilith. I hissed, 'You bastard, if you ever bring drugs to Tris, if you even *think* of peddling here, I swear I'll kill you. If you hide your tracks I'll trace them, because I know every link in a larger world than you could ever comprehend. You'll beg to be sent to the Front. You will beg for the wheel. I will have you keelhauled from bow to stern of the *Petrel*—'

'No!'

'You could do with losing some weight. The same goes for if you tell Gio I've been here.'

Cinna wiggled his shoulders, trying to pull away from the pick dimpling his neck. 'Please, Comet. I'm a businessman and San's humble servant. I shall always give a truthful account and say nothing to Gio. In the meantime I've arranged to stay on board *Pavonine* ... It's the safest place to be.'

'Coward,' I mouthed. I licked salt off my lips.

'Look at you grin. You're enjoying this! Mad Eszai. If *Petrel* lands, Gio will kill you. If you turn tail and run home, you'll starve on the journey. I wonder what San will think when his Circle breaks for Four Immortals At Once? Bet that'd give him a headache.'

I prodded him with the axe. 'Where's Gio now? Does he stay on *Pavonine*?'

Cinna shook his head; the blond hairs on his chin wagged. He pointed up, across the mosaic, to a concertina-shuttered lit window above the Senate House. 'See the end room? Right on the corner past the last column? That's the bedroom of the apartment that Vendace gave him. All the senators have rooms up there. It's very plush,' he added, with a quiet admiration of Gio's achievement. 'Now tell me, Messenger, isn't that a useful piece of information?'

'It certainly is.'

Cinna glanced at the firelight and the rebels singing drunkenly. He pressed a note into my hand. 'Please let me go. I respect Mist. I'd like to help her, the little I can. It's tough to find a way through the surf. I wrote down the details of our approach to the beacon and the position and condition of *Pavonine*. Please give it to her.'

CHAPTER 19

Midnight on the open sea. The attendant hush of an imminent downpour. I flew circuits over the correct position but couldn't sight *Stormy Petrel* through the rain clouds. A weak glow backlit them; I homed in on it and descended. Mist had festooned every surface, cable and yard with lanterns showing me where to land. *Petrel*'s lights blazed on a yellow ring of water in the impenetrable night. She looked like a party yacht, but she yawed and rolled madly.

Lights attached to the main deck railings marked two parallel lines. I had touched down safely between them. Now, sitting at the table in Mist's quiet cabin, Lightning and I watched her sailors disassembling the lanthorns and hurricane lamps. They were extinguished one by one, until the office and wheelhouse were the only cabins lit.

'Take a good look,' said Mist. 'Tomorrow night we burn no lantern. The wind is dropping and our approach is good, thanks to Jant's spy. You will have the pleasure of sneaking to Capharnaum in complete darkness, through the narrow strait by their beacon islet. You must trust me.'

'Yes, but for god's sake don't trust Cinna. He's a craven liar, he only worships money. Thankfully Gio doesn't know what to ask, or Cinna would tell him everything.'

'Just how did you come to know Cinna, anyway?' Mist asked.

'Let's not go into that,' I said dismissively. I poured myself a quantity of Lightning's brandy and rested my head on my arms.

'Why is Wrenn not present?' Lightning demanded.

'He is too young,' said Mist demurely.

Lightning raised his eyebrows. 'Why isn't Rayne here?'

'She is too old.'

'Simply that they would disagree with your methods,' Lightning said.

'Wrenn is impetuous and idealistic. The Doctor's not a warrior and can bring little to the table. Please let me outline my plans for you clear-headed gentlemen first.'

Lightning said, 'It is the same as when I tried to eradicate Insects from the streets of Micawater. How do we get rid of Gio and his vicious followers without damaging the town?'

'Or making the Senate detest us more than they already do?' I added.

Mist said, 'San gave me the task; I *will* fulfil it. The way ahead is clear. Listen! Lightning, if you were to remove the leader, the rebellion would collapse. Your skill with the longbow makes you best suited to try.'

In the short silence Lightning gazed at his rummer glass. He said amiably, 'You're asking me to capture Gio? Or assassinate him?'

'Saker, think—'

'No.' He looked at her directly. 'No, Ata; I won't do that.'

Mist folded her arms. 'Saker, I'm surprised that you don't want to regain your honour and take revenge on Gio for stabbing you in the back.'

'It would be less worthy still to become an assassin,' Lightning explained. 'I have never killed a man, and if I were simply to hide and shoot him, I don't know if I could live with myself afterwards. I do not want to spend the next few centuries troubled by guilt and introspection. In addition to the fact that it would lose me my esteem.'

'No one on the mainland will ever know. None of your sentiments apply to us in this plight. We're far from home. There are no ingrained traditions, carved beasts carrying pennants, heraldic old charters to say who we are. We're understocked and badly prepared. The Capharnai don't know us and Gio has stacked the odds against us. Eliminating him is the only way.'

'Why?'

'Because it'll save Trisian lives! They're innocent; I don't want to harm them. If we remove Gio, the Capharnai will be peaceable without him. If we set foot in Capharnaum while Gio controls it, we're dead. I think that Gio's lust to rejoin the Circle is driving him insane. You know the saying: Pure ambition seeks one goal only. Don't you think Gio's deeds are a mad panic, rather than a Challenge?'

'I think mad people want to see the madness in everyone,' I commented.

The Sailor ignored me. 'Saker, you *must* stop him. Can you think of a better idea?'

Lightning slowly replied, 'No. Nonetheless, you have my answer. I will not shoot Gio. I do not want it on my conscience for the rest of my life.' He undid the buttons at his collar and pulled the silk down so that we could see a small circular scar pierced front and back through his shoulder. 'See this? An arrow shaft. Eight hundred years ago I beat a Challenger and he turned round and shot me. Fortunately he had a terrible aim and failed to take my life. He spent the rest of his days in the Sturge Prison on Teron Island. There is nothing honourable about assassins; I don't want to be one ... Anyway, it would look pretty obvious if Gio is found with an arrow in his chest. It is not for me ...' He trailed off, thoughtfully, and stroked the scar on his right hand.

'Jant—' Mist began.

'Ha! Just because I'm not Lord Micawater you think I have no morals! Besides, Gio's the most dangerous man in the world. Lightning is more capable of dealing with him than I am.'

'But the bastard wounded him. Lightning, your good friend ...'

'Yes, and the bastard would run me through if he had the chance.'

'Remember all the awful slander you said Gio lambasted us with in his rally? You said you were ready to shoot him.'

I thought privately of how he slurred Tern's reputation and my manhood and dependability. Yes, I had been prepared to kill him.

Mist smiled eerily and prompted, 'Gio attacked the Castle, Jant. There's no doubt but he deserves what he gets. A few drops of the drug you keep injecting yourself with should do the trick.'

I looked at Lightning, who shrugged. I said reluctantly, 'All right, I'll do it.'

'Good!' said Mist. Her leather trousers creaked as she stood up. She turned to her cot and began to delve around energetically inside it. 'If you make it look like he was addicted and took an overdose, we can discredit him in the Fourlands.'

I gave her a flat stare. 'And make the climate dangerous for other people who happen to be users? Thank you, but no. Besides, I need all my supply.'

If an Eszai commits a crime and is caught, the Castle has no power to try him, nor may the Emperor intercede on his behalf. Instead, he is handed over to the court of the country in which the crime took place, to be tried and sentenced there. I couldn't guess how a Trisian court might work, or how severe the penalty may be. Or if I could successfully talk myself out of it.

Likewise, there is only one circumstance in which the Castle may interfere in a country's business – if an Eszai has been attacked or murdered, the assailant must be handed over to the Castle to be tried according to the law of his homeland, as happened with Lightning's erstwhile assassin eight centuries ago. If the murderer is protected by his country, San would forbid entrance to the Circle for anyone from that land, undeniably a terrible threat.

Mist's cot was a box-like bed with a drape of thick ivory lace. It swung as she pulled up the meagre mattress and extracted a bulky white packet – the envelope of scolopendium that Cinna had originally sold me. She tossed it onto the table. 'An additional supply. Use a pinch of powder.'

'But, Ata,' I said, startled, 'you said you'd thrown it in the sea! Wrenn told me you had. You led him to believe ...'

'I never discard useful assets.'

I stared at her wondering if she had *wanted* me to become addicted. My stash in the coat hem she had overlooked, all the needles and phials on the *Melowne* – I had been surprised there were so many – had she intended me to find them and get hooked so that I would be helpless and corruptible, under her control? And now she bribed me with the drugs I bought myself!

I knew how crazy that sounded, so I said nothing. Without proof, I did not dare to accuse her. I was as lost and confused as in an Awian maze. 'Oh, in San's name, what choice do I have?'

I pulled the envelope towards me gingerly, aware of Lightning's disapproval. The last thing I wanted was Gio materialising in Epsilon. I needed a poison that would kill him outright and quickly, so as not to give him a chance to reach a Shift world. I said, 'Gio might detect scolopendium; it has a distinctive taste. If you're devoted to this course, I can propose a less risky, more efficient substance.' I slipped my wedding band off my fourth finger, and the broader ring that I wore below it – a black star sapphire set in silver. I pushed the stone with my thumbnail; it depressed then popped open. Inside were two very small white tablets. I passed the ring to Ata.

'What are they?'

'Atropine. Extracted from belladonna root.'

'Deadly nightshade! For god's sake – what are you carrying that for?' She returned them carefully.

'I always keep them there. Atropine is effective in treating scolopendium overdose. One tablet would counteract the toxin, although I've rarely been able to take it. Two tablets are lethal. They're soluble and tasteless.'

Lightning made a decision. 'I think I should accompany you, unless you fear I will slow you down. I'll never murder but I will shoot to defend us.'

'Please,' I said gratefully. With Lightning to back me up, I felt I could do anything. Archer and Messenger, we'd share Gio between us. I picked his bottle from its holder clipped to the table. 'I'll decant for Gio a full-bodied draught. Unlike you I don't care enough for it to leave a bitter aftertaste. I know that he won't savour a lingering finish, because atropine will rapidly cause fever, a dry thirst balanced with the aroma of delirium, a sparkling racing pulse, a blend of spicy burning sensations, confusion, convulsions, coma and death. That's what I call a rich vintage.' I swirled the bottle and took a long pull.

'You are a sick man, Jant Shira.'

Mist shrugged. 'So we are decided. We approach tomorrow night at this time. *Petrel* will stay out of sight and I'll row you two to the harbour. I'll wait at the end of the quay. *Petrel* is safe under Viridian's command. I will arrange for her to bring the ship in to retrieve us two hours before dawn. Our hundred sailors and our hundred and fifty fyrd led by Serein will be ready on board if we need them. Lightning, what arms do you advise?'

The Archer pondered. 'Crossbows are better than longbows for fighting in a town, much as I don't like them. I don't want to cause casualties among the Capharnai, and you can take crossbows anywhere, even down tunnels.'

'Good. When Gio's body is discovered, the Senate will have little choice but to talk with us.'

'I hope it works.' Lightning sighed. 'Goodnight, co-conspirators.'

I was about to follow him out of the cabin when the ship slewed. Canvas flapped wildly as the wind changed direction, whistling around the main-mast. Ata shoved past me, stuck her head out of the door and yelled, 'Bring her about! She luffs, you lazy sods! Are you asleep in there? Make use of this wind!'

Cinna's envelope lay forgotten on the table. My mouth dried up. I never have enough cat, I always want more. I couldn't stop myself. I sneaked the envelope inside my coat and slipped out past Ata. "Bye, Jant ...' she muttered. 'Faster, *Petrel*. Faster, my love. Gio has nowhere left to flee.'

CHAPTER 20

I let Mist and Lightning descend the rope ladder first into the tiny rowing boat. It needed testing. I waited till they were settled before climbing down and gingerly feeling with my feet for the planks. The boat bucked. It was ready to roll right over, giving me no chance to fly off. I shuffled as quickly as possible to the middle of the bench-plank at the stern. Ata hefted her oars into the rowlocks.

I advised her, 'Sit still. You're rocking it!'

'Move your legs,' she said. 'You're in the way.'

'I'd rather not.'

'I'll climb over, then.'

'No!' I did not like being so near the water. My feet were actually *under* the level of the scooping waves, which was obviously wrong and shouldn't be allowed. Ata pulled the oars and the dangerous vessel leapt prow to stern. I concentrated on the floor.

'Are you all right?' Lightning asked.

'Of course. But this craft is clearly unstable. A single wave could swamp it.'

'He hates them,' Ata said.

'I'm just being careful.'

She dipped oars, pulled on, leant from side to side and the boat swayed alarmingly. 'You're tipping it deliberately!'

Ata said dryly, 'As if I would. She's hugely overloaded anyway.'

'Stop fooling about. It's not funny.' The rowing boat was completely different from the high-sided caravels to which I had become reconciled. They were designed not to turn turtle but this boat wallowed as Ata rowed. I felt the weight of my two centuries ever more clearly as I searched the extremely close water for Tarragon's fin, but all the wavelets looked like fins. 'Why can't I just fly there?'

'Act your age. Now the storm has died down, the rebels will hear your wing beats,' Ata breathed between strokes.

'I'll glide.'

'And see your silhouette ... Oh, in San's name!' she exclaimed in terror.

'What?'

'Jant, I forgot the rope. Can you help me? Lend a hand!' She passed me the end of a cable that ran over the side into the water and had been catching on the waves. 'Pull on this line. It's vital! The way she's built, the planks aren't safe unless you keep it taut.'

'Really?'

'Yes – if you let it slack for a minute she'll split into more segments than an orange!'

'I knew this was a death trap! How can you go to sea in a flimsy half-built boat? Shit!' I snatched up the damp rope and hauled on it until drops pinged off.

Ata nodded. 'Good. Now keep it tight or we'll all be in the drink.' Water ran from the blades as she feathered the oars. *Stormy Petrel*'s copper-clad hulk was a vague black shape in the distance. Lights on the three levels of decks were snuffed by the crew, and she vanished.

Lightning talked to the Sailor quietly. 'Eszai are not supposed to sneak around like this. Gio's forcing us to be murderers. I wish I was at the Front fighting Insects.' He had refused to blacken his sword blade even though I offered to do it for him. His concession to stealth had been to remove his signet ring and wrap a black mantle over his dark blue shirt. He held one arm around his new recurve longbow as if it was a lover.

'When the job's done return directly to the quay,' said Ata.

'I'm concerned about Cyan. I hope none of this dishonour rubs off on her.'

'Oh, don't worry. I find that daughters look after themselves.'

'And we have no back-up plot,' he said. 'None of us knows enough to predict the Capharnai.'

'We have our talents. Gio must be frightened of you, Archer. When his followers show their true colours, his lies will become manifest. The Senate will realise we're doing the best for Tris.'

Lightning and Ata fell silent as we came up to the beacon. Its uneven light did not illuminate the whole wide harbour mouth – the furthest point of the marina wall was in shadow. Ata rowed close to it, as quietly as possible. Slimy basalt blocks dwarfed us; thick kelp fronds stirred deep beneath us. I had been straining at the rope for thirty minutes, preoccupied with images of drowning, but I saw the rafts of empty Trisian canoes tied to their floating pontoons, undulating on the waves. In the distance they looked like needles on pine branches. *Pavonine*, *Cuculine* and *Stramash* were monstrous in comparison. At the waterfront, their unembellished sterns faced us, sails furled on skeletal spars, no flags flying. Lights flickered on *Pavonine*'s living deck. Their three tall masts, thinned by the darkness, were only occasionally visible against the night sky. Still, I sensed their bulk and heard the wavelets that slipped in and splashed back between the carracks and the harbour wall. They were rising on their moorings on an incoming tide.

Behind the harbour, Capharnaum's streets interlaced up the dark mountainside. Tris seemed far from fragile but, now we had touched it, it was starting to destruct. What if across the immense sea is an even stronger

Empire, more pervasive still, that will do the same to us? San would be furious if he knew that thought. God has not left anything other than us on this world and, since it nominated San to protect the world, San and his orders are right. I will one day announce contests for Capharnai to join the Circle. I will fly over the town carrying their pennant, letting it stream out behind me, and Ata will ride her white horse up the boulevard. Trisian travellers would eventually visit the Fourlands; I could hardly wait to show them the sights.

The harbour lamps reflected in the water. The end of the wall was in shadow, with some canoes upside-down outside a small square building. Ata manoeuvred us towards it past the last pontoon. Lightning whispered, 'I see no guards, but have a care. The wall's very near.'

She braked the oars. Lightning reached both arms over the side and fended us off. He pulled the boat around, long side to the wall. We all looked up to the top, two metres above. 'I don't see anyone.' He stood on the gunwale, palms on the flagstones, and pulled himself up. The boat bobbed and scraped the wall. His face appeared over the edge. 'Pass me my bow.'

'Sh! You should let me go first,' I said, nettled.

'Stop hanging on to the painter, please.' Ata took the rope from me, and gave me a leg up. I scrabbled to the promenade, lay flat on my stomach and peered over. Ata picked the rope from the water, running it the boat's length, then unwound it from the bow post. She threw it up to Lightning, who coiled it on the ground.

I gaped. 'Oh. It wasn't attached to anything?'

She sniggered. 'No. I just needed some way of shutting you up.'

'You—'

'Hush!' said Lightning.

Ata arranged knotted-cord fenders around the boat's hull, then she raised her hands to us. I turned my back, but Lightning took her hands and heaved her up, with a rasp of metal on stone. Her hair showed in a white flash under the hood of her black shawl – so different from the dazzling armour she wore in battle. She whispered, 'I'll hide by this depot. Lightning, follow Jant; he's done this kind of thing before. Jant, for god's sake stop sulking. Remember; return at five a.m., Starglass time. Good luck.'

I set off a few paces, found myself alone, turned to see Ata and Lightning still looking at each other. She gazed at him straight, and a whole spectrum of unsaid things passed between them. Then Lightning gave a little shake of his head, and stepped away to join me.

The façade of houses along the harbour was dangerously exposed because lamps on posts every fifty or so metres cast light on the paving. They were so bright I couldn't see the stars. We had to dash across the yellow pools and pause in the very narrow slices of shadow.

I reached one of the puzzling black and white posts that had a wooden cross-arm and dangling wires. I crouched behind it. 'Saker, we must keep silence from now on. I know you don't like this and I don't blame you. But, just once, please follow my lead.'

The Archer nodded. He carried his strung bow over his right shoulder, leaving his arms free. His mantle covered the quiver on his back, giving his shoulders a spiky crest, and was pleated into his belt. Nocks and fletchings of fifty arrows projected from the quiver on his left hip, crammed in so tightly they hardly rustled. He hunched awkwardly, trying to hide his broad frame. With an Eszai's determination, he was trying to be a sneak. I said, 'Let's go.'

Oil lamps on the shopfronts lit the entire boulevard. But the grid-streets of Capharnaum were perfect for us assassins; we stole down the adjacent parallel street. I kept near the wall and walked rapidly, ducked into a door-way, waited for Lightning to catch up. The main street glowed on our left every side alley we passed. A statue on a plinth. Sculpin's wine shop; Opah's seafood; Ling and Zingel, grocers, the shutters closed. I ran across the road and continued up on the other side. Lightning piled into the shop doorway behind me. He was favouring his wound. I waved him back into shadow while I took a look around.

Time to change streets. I sped right across an intersection, away from the boulevard and left uphill again. The junctions were sharp right angles, since Trisians don't have coaches. We heard a bell chime, the Senate's patrol call-ing for the next watch. This street was darker – the buildings were all homes. We dashed past open colonnades and hugged house corners.

If Capharnaum was scruffier and a lot more disorganised, then slinking through it in the early hours would be just like Hacilith: hiding at a corner, giving the constables the slip. Doubling back to be rid of the rival Bowyers gang.

I beckoned the Archer close as we approached a lighted house and together we strode confidently past their front door. When people are at rest in their homes, a furtive movement can alert them, but they don't look twice if they think you're a watchman.

The houses were all of equal size and gave no cover; we walked swiftly. The boulevard's light shone out of the side streets; we sneaked along close to the muralled walls. Behind me, Lightning trailed my movements sound-lessly. I value faithfulness among friends. If you have not honoured every childhood oath of allegiance to the gangs that changed every minute; adventuring among the rambling rose, the margins of ponds and darkened streets, you have not been true to yourself. I still have the Wheel scar on my shoulder. I have honoured those intense oaths of friendship, and as a result I am still a child.

The streets came to an end in darkness at the foot of the Amarot crag. Only the lit boulevard continued, climbing it in a zigzag path. A group of Trisians was descending the ten-metre-wide pavement from the Amarot into town. They wore cloaks over loose white shirts and wide trousers; they carried lamps and weapons. If they saw us they would recognise our outlandish Fourlands clothes immediately. We would have to pretend to be two of Gio's brigands, which would be the worst way to meet him. I urged Lightning back with a wave, and we lurked behind the corner of the last house.

The curfew meant that Gio's men were not wandering in the town. Unfortunately they were all corralled on the mosaic at the top of the crag – nothing between us and them but the Senate House itself. We watched the patrol pass by two streets away and descend into Capharnaum.

Lightning said, 'They're going the other way.' I seized his cloak and pulled him back as the previous patrol emerged. They exchanged a few words in a low tone with their colleagues and proceeded up the boulevard. We waited for what seemed like hours until they were thumbnail-sized at the top of the outcrop.

I mouthed, 'Our turn. Ready? Keep a good look round, your eyesight's keener than mine. Remember that bloody Insect. We can't see as well as it can scent us. It can certainly outpace you; it's very well fed.'

For the first few hundred metres, the crag's white boulders were conspicuous. Then we found ourselves stumbling up the escarpments, over the scrubland. I feared there was a scorpion under every rock. A woody smell rose from the damp thyme shrubs, and spiny bushes scraped my shins. Lightning struggled behind me kicking them.

At the lip of the crag there was no cover at all. The stony soil crunched under our boots and a gentle wind gusted down from the mountain above us. I lay flat on the hillside and after a dignified pause Lightning copied me. We listened. Gio's men were obviously on the rum again. They all seemed to be gathered around the roasting fire, lounging and enjoying themselves. Good.

Lightning touched my arm and pointed behind us. Capharnaum was spread out below; the boulevard gleamed like an amber river. Lights shone in the quadrangles of villas, picking out tiny green gardens, lit red-tiled roofs that were otherwise grey, highlighted smudges of colour on the frescoes. The harbour beacon blazed continually in a black strip, a single star under the lowest constellations. I found it hard to believe that, far beyond it, *Stormy Petrel* skulked up and down. Capharnaum was beautiful, but the curfew did not explain a sense of foreboding, an expectant hush. The town waited, but I doubted if any citizen knew why.

The tall outline of the Senate House blotted out the stars. Lightning and I glanced at each other. I tucked my coat back over my sword hilt; he nocked an arrow to string. We climbed as quietly as possible over the edge of the crag and onto its flat summit, into the Senate House's shade, beside the first of twelve columns with square podia that were arrayed along its length. Wind blew the rebels' cooking smoke over the roof ridge. Gio's room was above and round the other side.

Lightning steadied himself with a hand against the stone and looked up. The building towered over us; its columns were fifteen metres high, their edges wavered in the gloom. Lightning patted a smooth corner block, whispered, 'Can you climb it?'

'You do say some bloody ridiculous things sometimes. Look at it.'

'Damn. I hoped our scheme—'

'Well, of course I can.' I grinned. 'This reminds me of when, before I left Hacilith to come to the Castle, I climbed the governor's palace and left a blackmail note on Aver-Falconet's own pillow. It was easy.'

Lightning's volatile sense of morality flared. 'What? I don't remember you divulging that to the Circle!'

'Sh! It's a long story; forget it.'

I had asked for a whole one thousand pounds and I was amazed when Aver-Falconet paid up. I thought it was a fortune; how little I knew. Still, I bought horses and new kit, and kept enough change to make it worth the highwaymen's while when they robbed me of everything not ten hours later on the Camber Road.

'Stand here in the shadow until I return. Don't move. Apart from if the shadow moves, of course.' I took a firm grasp of the stonework with both hands, found a toehold with my leg fully bent and kicked off with the other. Hugging my body close to the stone, my rangy reach gained another handhold and toe. I was fully above Lightning. He kept his arrow nocked and waited flanked by a column. The darkness gave grainy texture to his severe face.

I strained to make out cracks in the mortar. Tiny white pinpoints prickled in my night vision. I folded my wings tight because their weight pulled me away from the wall. I stabbed my strong, pointed nails into the gaps, my fingers clawed. I jammed my boot in, straightened my leg. I raised my weight and stretched out for the next hold. I undercut the grip, cheek to the chill stone, stepped up.

The wind was stronger here. It blew around the exposed corner and cooled off my sweat. I hung on with one hand and both feet, stood up straight and took a break. I exhaled a long breath of admiration at the view: hundreds of houses and twenty thousand lives that Gio had snatched as a stake in his game. Well, now he is dealing with Comet who learnt to climb in the precipitous ice-split chimneys of Darkling's cliffs.

Above me was a narrow ledge. I reached up and felt about in the seagull shit. I secured a good foothold, bent my knees, sprang gracefully onto the cornice. I ran lightly along it, rounded the corner to the side of the building facing the mosaic. I flattened myself against the architrave of Gio's window. The brigands' camp was below, at the other side of the square. If any of them glanced up, they would see me plainly against this white stone. I quickly pushed the shutter open and peered into the room. No one inside, so I hopped over the sill and landed in a crouch, silently on the mint-green tiled floor.

Gio's apartment was enormous. A square bed stood in the centre, no curtains as in the Fourlands, just a taupe silk coverlet. The walls were covered in a *trompe l'oeil* scene of a sumptuous feast. Elegant diners in Trisian robes poised with grapes halfway to their mouths or in the act of raising goblets. Their eyes seemed to follow me across the room as I skirted a wooden screen and approached an alabaster side table on which burned one of the open-flame lamps.

Beside it was a glass half-full of clear liquid and a bottle with a familiar label: Diw Harbour Gin, Gio's tipple of choice. I released the lid of my ring and dropped both aconitum tablets into the glass. They dissolved instantly. I swirled the glass and set it down beside the lamp. The oil lamp was pure gold, in the shape of a breaching dolphin. Irregular coral in claw fittings and priceless pearl clusters encrusted its base. It entranced me—

'Yeah, right ...' a voice came from just outside the door, 'which I need like Mica Town needs more coffee shops! Goodnight, Tirrick.'

'Goodnight, Gio.'

Gio! I sprinted back across the room. Gio's foot appeared at the door. I couldn't reach the window. I jumped behind the screen. I was five clear metres from the window. Shit.

Poised to move, I peered carefully though the fine fretwork at the top of the folding partition. Gio slipped his coat off and threw it on the bed. He was wearing the same clothes as when he left the Castle, and though washed they smelt of ingrained mud and brine. He had still not bothered to find a shirt and wore the 1969 Sword slung on a double red belt across the waistband of his blue breeches. His bare ribs and hips were sinewy furrows.

Gio's obsession for revenge might be just another form of despair, but it had kept him disciplined if not hygienic. The scar Wrenn had given him showed as a pale pink incision at the base of his throat.

I wondered feverishly what to do. I was fast enough to escape but Gio would certainly see me and he wouldn't drink the gin; he would send his swordsmen against *Stormy Petrel* and Ata's plan would fail. I kept still. I could stay here until Gio was either asleep or dead.

Beside the bed and ranged against the wall I saw six steel coffers. If they were full, Gio was undoubtedly a millionaire. Stacked on top of the strong boxes were three ormolu jewellery caskets with more primitive locks, because like many Awian mechanisms form is valued over function.

In front of my eyes, the paintings on the screen panels depicted domed buildings, nothing like those of the island. That they were ancient Awian palaces could not have escaped Gio's notice.

He drew his rapier and practised two or three sequences back and forth. He didn't seem satisfied. I watched, excruciating pins and needles prickling my legs. My tight grip on my sword hilt was embossing an image of twisted metal wire into my palm.

Gio held his rapier over his shoulder, pounced to the side table and gulped down his glass of gin. Nothing happened. Gio returned to a cool first guard, began to spar with his shadow, leaving white dints in the plaster. I quietly stretched to see. He should be writhing in paroxysms by now, on the floor, in agony. He should be quickly asphyxiating, tongue too swollen to scream.

I could not for the eternal life of me think what had gone wrong. The poison was having no effect at all. In a few minutes Gio finished his exercises and, looking perfectly healthy, strode towards me. He was coming to close the shutters; I would be trapped inside. As soon as he passes the screen he'll see me. He was just one step away.

I sprang out and made a dive for the window but it was too far. I landed in front of it, facing Gio.

His face was grotesque with astonishment. *'Jant?'* He snatched himself into guard, with me at sword point. His rapier's bright tip hovered a centimetre away from my chest. I shuffled back until my calves pressed the window ledge, the night air behind me. I kept my hands down, in surrender. Gio's crazed eyes were wide, amazement stayed his hand. He checked the doorway – if I was here, the other Eszai might be closing in. 'Where's Wrenn? What were you doing?'

He saw my glance flick to the empty gin glass. I was so confused, I couldn't help but look. No man should stand upright after imbibing that much belladonna. 'Poison?' he whispered; he knew my history. His face went white with fury. 'You cowardly bastard! I'll pour it down your throat! How long before it takes effect? Answer, damn you!' Fear high-pitched his voice. 'What have I drunk? *What is it?'*

I said nothing out of sheer bewilderment; Gio should be very dead by now. My coat leather split at the breast under the pressure of his rapier point. He shouted, 'Tirrick! Help! I've been poisoned! Assassin! Quickly!'

Voices on the mezzanine took up the shout: 'Gio's been poisoned!' 'I knew the Trisians would try something!'

Gio leant forward with a deep, earnest look. 'Comet, do you blame me? Rejected from the Circle, you'd do the same.' He urged me to answer with a manic little nod. I made no move. He suddenly growled with hatred and drew his arm back for the thrust.

I dived backwards out of the window. I fell, back-flipped, spun into a full somersault, fighting to free my wings. Firelight stretched into a blur. Stars below me, white granite above. I forced my wings open. The left one bruised hard against a column. I flapped frantically to get air under them and banked breathlessly over the square. The rebels were all yelling but I couldn't see them. I tried to get my bearings.

I fought desperately upwards to the level of the Senate House ledge. Gio leant out of the window, staring in mute horror. I pedalled my legs, pumped my wings and skimmed the roof above him, kicked off the ridge and glided out over the cliff.

I yelled to Lightning, 'Run!'

Lightning said, 'Oh, no. Hush.'

'Run! We must! Follow me.'

He had no choice; the rebels were staggering to their feet and reaching for weapons. They looked at each other, finding the nerve to cross the mosaic and attack. Lightning dashed round the corner, straight in front of them to the only conspicuous door – the library.

Below me I heard Gio swearing. 'Get me water! Get me the ship's surgeon!'

Was the aconitum belatedly taking effect? I called to Lightning, 'The second floor is defensible. I'll meet you up there!'

Lightning rammed the door open with his shoulder and turned in the entrance to face the men. 'I am' – he loosed an arrow and the nearest one dropped his rapier and grabbed his hand, turned and fled trailing drops of blood – 'Lightning. The immortal Archer.' He let another arrow fly at the largest man in the middle. It went straight through his hand that held an axe shaft. He jumped up with a howl and shook the arrowhead from the skin between his fingers. They all backed off. 'You will find the stairs hazardous.' Lightning nocked another arrow to string. 'I recommend caution, mob. Stay out.' He disappeared into the dark library.

I think he just made it worse. Five uninjured men clustered in. One kicked the door jamb. 'Fuck him!'

He looked up at me; a birthmark half-covered his baggy face, grey in the dim light. Another was ex-fyrd, with Brandoch's white trident badge on his tatty jacket. He called to bring more people round – a big hispid man whose jumper hood hung over his greatcoat; a burly woman, although in the darkness I couldn't be sure.

I went over them low and swept up to the window to bleed off speed. I flared my wings, braked hard, bending my flight feathers right back. My air speed dropped to nothing; I fell. I hit the window's louvre shutters with the soles of both boots. The shutters flew apart. I dropped through and landed squarely on my backside on the floor with my wings jammed in the window.

This storey was pitch-black but I smelt the serious scent of paper and venerable patinated wood. I scraped a match and held it up, seeing that the well-stacked shelves lined a single central aisle obstructed with crates of papers. Lightning ascended the railed stairwell, whirled round with his back to me. 'Comet? Where are you?'

By striking matches and peering through their weak light, I made my way along the aisle. He took deep breaths like a baited bear, stood statue-still, listening to the voices rising from the stairs.

'They're both trapped. You go first.'

'Are you kidding? That's Lord Micawater. *The* Archer. He'll shoot me in the eye as soon as—'

'Lord la-di-da. Rush them.'

'Both eyes, probably ...'

Lightning snorted.

'They're *immortals.*'

'Then they can wait,' came the woman's voice.

Lightning lowered his bow slightly and sat on a table. I said, 'We're safe here for the moment.'

'Oh, we're safe, are we? Splendid. Shall I just make you a cup of coffee, then? This is *your fault*, Jant! We could have stayed unobserved. I was hidden. I was prepared to steal back to *Stormy Petrel*, whilst you could fly. But no; you cry out "Run!" Now the mob know we're here – and I'm cornered!' He shook a fist under my nose. His face was indistinct in the darkness but I could see he was pouch-eyed from lack of sleep. 'You irresponsible, foundling, Rhydanne—'

'Please don't use "Rhydanne" as an insult.'

'Drug addict. *Well!*'

'Well what? If you'd stayed by the columns they would have caught you. Gio saw me, then everything happened too fast to think.'

'Thinking is *supposed* to be your strong point. So, has he perished?'

Gio was far from dead. I protested, 'I don't understand it. Tolerance to that amount of belladonna isn't possible; there are no recorded cases of recovery.'

Lightning drummed his powerful fingers on the table, sounding like a small horse race. He held his great longbow in the other hand, finger over the arrow shaft across its grip. I lit an almond-shaped lamp and paced to the window. The outlaws milled about below.

I felt queasy knowing that the aconitum was useless. I might have needed it myself at any time. I have never actually used it because scolopendium is such a fast-acting drug that on the rare occasions I overdose I am not in a condition to remember it or operate the ring. I have carried aconitum since

I first learned of its effects, fifty years ago. Ah, damn. I haven't replaced the tablets for – how long? Twenty years? And how many rainstorms have I flown through since then; how many long soaks in the bathhouse hot tub? It was a mistake that only an immortal could make. I said, 'The tablets have been in my ring too long. The potency must have degraded. Gio isn't suffering the full effect, if any at all.'

'You have never learned to be an Eszai,' Lightning said quietly, which was worse than his shouting. 'Let me take stock. Item: Gio will be determined to repay our attempt on his life. Item: it is four a.m., so we have a full hour before *Petrel* arrives. Item: I only have one hundred arrows. Item: I am in considerable pain, and I will not be able to run for a sustained time.'

'What?'

For answer Lightning wormed his hand under the bandages around his waist. He held it up, red with blood, and wiped his fingers over the old scar on his palm. I hadn't seen the stain on his shirt. 'The exercise agitated my wound; it has not closed completely. I didn't want to mention it, but it'll hinder me so you must know. Damn it, don't look so taken aback; just go and watch the mob.'

Shrunken by guilt, I turned to the nearest window, swung one shutter open. Lightning said, 'Do you see any of my fyrd?'

'No. There aren't many Lakeland or coast Awians rebelling; they know they need the Castle.'

'Good. I'm grateful for that at least.'

A mass of people filled the plaza between us and the Senate House, red-lit by the bonfire. Their noise was incredible: a tumult of gossip, jabbering fragments of conversation and false rumours – I could use those. I looked down on their heads; hoods, caps and woolly hats. I spotted the mesomorphic woman elbowing her way to the top of the boulevard. There was a general slow flow in that direction, like the start of a landslide. The air thrived with anxiety and excitement. I listened carefully, trying to separate phrases from the chaos: 'Let's go. No point in staying now Gio's snuffed it, is there? You heard what that prat Tirrick said.'

'I would if I could see a bloody thing. If there's two Eszai there'll be more, see? The whole Circle might be here.'

'Gio's *not* dead! His orders are to stay put.'

'I gave up all that order crap last year. Come on, think what we can pick up on our way to the ship.'

Gio Ami emerged from the Senate House hefting a large rectangular shield which had a metal bracket to hold and a big padded hook for his upper arm to bear the weight while carrying it. He immediately sheltered behind a pillar, sword drawn. He seemed dazed and was hangover-pale; I could not decide whether the poison was working on him with reduced efficacy, or whether he was sick with tension. He bent nearly double to yell, 'I'm here! I'm well. Look!'

'Shoot him,' I told Lightning.

Lightning dipped his head, trying to see Gio. I leant out and shouted at the crowd, 'Tornado's coming. Mist is sailing half the Castle's fleet into harbour! Thirty caravels full of fyrd and an Eszai on each ship!'

Gio's adherents drew towards him but the woman beckoned people to join her. 'Come on, we must reach the boats before Tornado arrives.' They surged towards the boulevard.

Gio tried again: 'Come back! Listen, they'll hang you as pirates! I'll pay you an equal share of everything in this town! There are no more ships! Alone, you've no chance against Mist!'

I stuck my head out. 'Tornado's fyrd will arrest anyone who stays with Gio! He'll be brought to justice!' I withdrew rapidly as an axe smashed into the window frame and fell onto the people beneath. I remarked to Lightning, 'Gio can't stop them leaving. I've managed to split them up.'

'Good.' He sighed.

A young swordsman gestured up at my window and babbled something vehemently. Gio shook his head but his friend continued to remonstrate. Gio pointed his rapier. 'No, Tirrick!'

Tirrick looked at Gio, seeing a dirty and dishevelled figure, and he must have realised at the same time as I did that Gio was not poisoned; it was his paranoia making him act as cautiously as if he was really feeling symptoms. I said, 'I think Ata's right – Gio is mad.'

Lightning said, 'Maybe, but fortunately Wrenn is even madder.'

Tirrick glanced at the guards standing by the library entrance, and then ran past Gio into the Senate House.

'Now the fencing masters are arguing between themselves.'

Lightning bit his lips together. 'I have always disliked Gio Ami because he professes to be a man of honour but he only lives by the codes that suit him – like his damn Ghallain traditions. He was married once, you know; if he still was then perhaps we would be spared this. But he feigned respect for the peninsula custom. They receive a candle as a gift on their wedding day. If they argue in the following years, they must light the candle and leave it burning for a time corresponding to the length of the argument. So, when it is burnt down completely, the couple are automatically considered divorced. It happened to Gio. He called his wife a troublemaker, separated her from the Circle, and home she rode to find her friends aged and infirm, or dead and buried. Poor lady.'

I strained to see further down the boulevard. White puffs of smoke like cotton bolls were rising from the base of the hill, where the harbour wall was hidden behind lines of houses. 'I think Mist's signalling. She must have figured that it's all gone wrong. I bet she's burning canoes ... I just don't know if the signal is for me or the *Petrel*.'

Lightning watched the stairwell sourly. He said, 'Like amateurs we chose a stronger bow than we could manage and missed the mark. If I don't survive, Jant, will you remember to take my message?'

I nodded, dumbstruck. I had never heard a fatalistic word from Lightning before.

The sky above the Senate was pale grey now; I was able to distinguish the features of the people below. A dark coat became burgundy red, drab showed as light blue, a boy's hair was highlighted with henna. Dawn permeated a pallid, cloudless winter day.

I looked to the sea again and gave a yelp. The beacon islet was now dimly discernible, the surf breaking on its seaward shore. Heeling round it with four masts in full sail was a ship tiny with distance. She headed into harbour at a great rate of knots, her long pennants snaking. 'The *Petrel*! See, the *Petrel*'s coming in!'

Lightning sighed with relief. A few minutes later, some lads in padded jackets hurtled up the boulevard, pushed eagerly to Gio. Gio listened, then waved them aside and called out, 'This is it! We must meet the Castle's flagship. I tell you, there's only one caravel. There are two Eszai aboard and we'll overwhelm them. Let me have the satisfaction of dealing with Wrenn – and your prize is the *Stormy Petrel*!'

The crowd yelled. Gio lifted his shield and hastened across the square, shouting his rabble into a formation akin to a fyrd division. The Ghallain swordsmen he arranged at the front, then the biggest, roughest men, the Hacilith boys and a couple of harridan girls at the rear.

But the swordsmen at the library door refused to move and glowered when Gio beckoned to them. His authority had gone but he pretended that it didn't matter, gave up and returned to the thick column.

Lightning thought aloud: 'I can improve the odds for Wrenn and Ata.' He instantly flexed his bow and loosed. A man at the head of the column reeled with a scream and fell, the arrow through his thigh. Lightning selected another shaft from the quiver at his hip, let fly and the astonished lad behind the first man yowled and squatted to the ground. I could barely see the arrow projecting from his leg above the knee. Lightning started counting backwards from thirty, 'Twenty-eight, twenty-seven ...' as he lamed each of the men along the nearest edge of the formation, who were arranged like targets in a gallery.

Hearing their screams, the column flashed shields along its length. It surged away from us, bending and abandoning the wounded men, leaving around twenty sprawling and crawling on the mosaic. One man cried loudly as he snapped the fletchings off the arrow and pulled the shaft out through his thigh.

Gio, invisible behind his shield, led his file to the boulevard. They emptied very quickly out of the square, hurried between the slender stone walls and snaked around the hairpin bends. They left the battered mosaic empty; Alyss and the Insects were carious with missing tesserae. Litter was stacked up in the corners against the library and ash blew out of the cooling bonfire into the colonnade. Lightning cleanly and methodically shot down the rearmost rebels in the column, hitting the left thigh of each man. 'You, four; and you, three ... two ... one. There. That's all the arrows I dare to spend. Is this not disagreeable work?'

Some footsteps scuttled on the floor below us. Lightning called, 'Join our gathering, by all means. But please introduce yourselves so I know who I'm shooting.'

A movement at the Senate House caught our attention. A swordsman began to back out, lugging one of Gio's heavy coffers between himself and his friend. Another followed, and a fourth, until all the chests and ornate boxes containing Gio's fortune were lined up on the mosaic.

Lightning asked, 'What are those?' but I hardly heard him because I was seething with anger. Tirrick, the goateed little creep, was stealing the treasure and I could do nothing about it.

The senators were next to stumble out of the door at the foot of the pillars. A frightened youth in a pale tunic, then a dumpy old man were corralled by the swordsmen. Vendace came out last, reluctantly, being goaded by Tirrick behind him. The tall, wiry Trisian leant his head at a strange angle because Tirrick held a dagger across his throat. Tirrick shoved him out onto the mosaic, and looked straight up at our window with a bold smile.

CHAPTER 21

'They're parading the senators where we can see them,' I said.

'Tirrick,' said Lightning. 'I know the type. Privileged but strident and embittered, the youngest son of a minor noble.' He licked his fingers and held them out of the window to judge the breeze. Then his fingertips rasped over the arrow fletchings and settled on the string. Tirrick angled his dagger across Vendace's scrawny neck and called, 'We'll kill one of these for every shot you loose!'

Vendace rolled his eyes and stamped his foot. His brown arms were rigid by his sides.

I said, 'The boxes are full of money. I think the swordsmen will take it to the ship, with the senators as hostages to shield themselves. It's our chance to escape. Oh fuck, no it isn't ...'

Around twenty swordsmen ran out of the colonnade, carrying lamps and oil jugs with spouts. Lightning drew on them but saw Tirrick's blade bite against Vendace's skin, and didn't loose. The guards around the library door let them speed through. Crashes came up from below, smashing pottery, rustling and tearing.

A heavy thump shook the floor as the men pulled a bookshelf over. I heard them kicking the scrolls into heaps. 'They're going to burn the library!' I darted to the stairs and called down, 'Stop! In the name of San and the will of god. How *dare* you?'

A voice shrugged, 'Come out and be executed or stay there and char.'

But these are books – all the books of Tris. 'You *must* not,' I yelled desperately.

A blue-grey twist rose from the stairwell like cigarette smoke. Within seconds it widened to fill the whole well. From the window I saw the swordsmen pouring out onto the mosaic, shoving the guards back in their haste to escape. 'The fire's caught! Ready yourselves, they have to surrender. It's going up!'

Smoke billowed past me in a thick stream and drifted along the ceiling. Lightning released the tension on his bowstring. 'We have to break out. There are a dozen fencing masters. We can deal with them, but the senators will die.'

'The books!' I wailed. 'I can't leave—'

'Don't be stupid!'

'Maybe there's another way down.' Grey wreaths shrouded the rafters completely and were descending extremely quickly to fill the room. I fumbled through a stack of leather-bound books on the table and slipped them into my coat pockets. I picked up the lantern. 'Wait here. I'll check the far end.'

Lightning began coughing loudly. I called, 'Stoop low. Slouch down under it.' I had been in a burning building before and, as far as I knew, he had not. But my lungs hurt as I sucked smoke and I started choking more than him.

I had to save the books, as many as I could carry. I strode down the aisle snatching them from the shelves. I stuffed one in my waistband, another in my belt. I had no time to translate the titles; I couldn't see with the smoke stinging my eyes. I didn't know what I was snatching. I piled them frantically in the crook of my left arm, discarded a heavy tome, selected two more haphazardly. I thought, I'm rescuing a handful of volumes at random to represent the total knowledge of an entire culture. Which were most worthwhile? Were these engineering, cookery or poetry? Or even bloody fiction? I had no way of judging. I spat out the cloying smoke and the stack buckled in my arms. I reached the end of the library – which was just a blank wall – and I dropped all the books with a series of thuds.

Recognisable but horribly out of place, grey mottled, fibrous drapes strung between the last two bookcases: Insect paper. They looked folded but were as hard as concrete. They curved up from the shelves and blurred into the smoke creeping down from the beams.

Two long, brown forelegs emerged from the nest. The Insect's black spiny foot clicked down onto the floor between my boots, and its three claws articulated shut. I backed into the opposite bay.

The Insect ducked its triangular head and slipped out from between the bookcases. Its eyes' tessellations reflected the lamp-lit swirling smoke. It brushed a fringe on its front right leg over them. It must have pulled out Wrenn's rapier, because the hole through its thorax was now a deep concavity filled with smooth new shell. It had sloughed its skin and was even bigger than I remembered. The high joints of its back legs loomed out of the smoke.

Two club-shaped black palps shuffled like a pair of hands rubbing together. They retracted and the scissor jaws opened and shut. It lifted a foreleg and cleaned its single crooked antenna through filaments inside its knee.

Lightning flexed his bow and spoke with his lips to the string, 'Step aside.' Through the smoke he was just a silhouette blurred by the tears streaming from my eyes. I pressed my coat cuff to my nose and mouth. In another thirty seconds the room would be full and I could hear crackling from below.

'Wait!' The Insect stood still, close enough for me to see the scars and impressions I had made with my axe. A row of black spines four-wide supported the upper surface of its striped abdomen. The pale underside pulsed as it curled its abdomen under itself, pumping air through its spiracles which were wide open.

'Wait. It doesn't like the smoke.'

Its antenna flicked forward, sensing for the clean air. It jolted into an involuntary crouch. 'It's going to run – let it pass!'

The Insect leapt. It hurtled past Lightning, stretched its full length and reached over the handrail, down into the stairwell. Its back sword-shaped femurs kicked and claws scrabbled on the blistering varnish, then it disappeared into the gusting smoke. I ran after it instantly; Lightning seemed bewildered so I grasped his arm and urged him to the steps.

We took deep breaths and plunged down. I patted my hair – it felt so hot I thought it was alight. Lightning held his hand over his mouth and the tip of his bow rattled off the ceiling. The steep steps were opaque with smoke. Perspiration and tears trickled down my face.

We stumbled to the ground floor, onto ten centimetres of fallen books. They slid over each other, making the floor slippery. I led Lightning around the tall shapes of leaning shelves. We crushed scorching scrolls underfoot with a sound like old Insect shell. Even now I was torn with the desire to rake them up. The fire's crackling built into a steady sibilance and its raw orange light leapt behind the smoke, illuminating the surfaces of the billowing wreaths.

Lines of yellow flame spread between the parquet blocks. By the windows, flames began to lengthen and bend as air flow sucked them out of the shutters.

'Can't breathe,' I said weakly. 'Where's ... the fucking door?' The unbearable heat singed my feathers, my reddened skin stung. The pages of open books on the floor around us were curling and turning brown spontaneously. I saw one burst into flame.

I pointed to the rectangle of pale morning light; we rushed through without readying our weapons. Getting out of the smoke was all that mattered.

The men who had been guarding the door were spilt on the mosaic in a fan of visceral blood. We crossed the threshold with smoke pouring out above us. One had died quickly, eyes open, from a horrible gash that opened his belly to the sternum. Another crumpled in a red pool so thick the Insect must have severed an artery, though I couldn't see the wound. The arm of a third man lay beside a rapier some way off.

The Insect did not pause to clean its mandibles. It was confused by the scents and invigorated by the fresh air. Its six feet left prints, its knee joints bunched and separated as it dashed towards the senators and swordsmen. Their white clothes reflected in its directionless eyes. Their mouths were round in astonishment. Every one of the swordsmen bolted, including Tirrick, leaving the senators in the Insect's path.

Lightning leant into his bow and bent it fully with the strength of his shoulders. The broadhead point drew back to the grip. Across the square the Insect reared up before Vendace. Lightning straightened his fingers, released the string with a crack and the arrow whistled past me.

The Insect's foreclaws lashed the air in front of Vendace, then it fell sideways. It curled on its right side, the arched plates of its abdomen sliding over each other as it coiled and throbbed. A spasm went through it that flexed all its joints and pulled its limbs in, like the legs of a dead crab. They steepled angularly together, its feet drawn up to the six semi-translucent ball joints under its thorax. By the sunken ring at the base of its feeler, Lightning's arrow shaft made a second antenna. The shell gaped around it, an open crack showing an organ of dark brown gel deep inside.

The senators gazed at it, and at the library. All the erudition of Tris was rising with the fire. I faced the intolerable furnace as if it was a punishment and spread my wings to accept and be consumed by it. Rolls of heat belched out, shelves split with creaks and thuds. Tremendous flames raged through the library I respected so much; I felt sick in the pit of my stomach.

'Shira!' Lightning called. 'Come here, why are you standing so close? It's falling apart!'

'No. The books are burning … What has Gio *done*?'

'Get a grip! Speak to the senators.'

I was numbly aware of Lightning ushering the Trisian leaders to the boulevard. Behind us, the coffers lay forgotten. I thought, if I live through this I'll claim them. The Trisians would disregard the treasure as dross, so I relinquished it for the time being, avoided the dead Insect and stepped over three or four agonised rebels with arrows in their thighs, and ran to catch up with them. They were hurrying down the path with appalled backward glances.

Vendace was holding one of the senators tightly, a young lady. She was kicking and biting, frenziedly struggling and pulling in the direction of the library. I ran to help but Vendace snapped at me, 'She's Danio's successor. Don't let her go; she'll run in to the fire. Every time you come here, you put an end to our librarians!'

We tried to calm the hysterical girl. I explained to Lightning, who said candidly, 'I know how she feels. People pass away, there are always more, but the books are irreplaceable. They're the immortal part of Zascai – how many lifetimes are burning to cinders in there?'

I said to Vendace, 'You saw how Gio's men treated you. They're causing this catastrophe, not us. We'll deliver you from them before they destroy the rest of town. Lightning shot the Insect dead. We were sent to protect you from it and from Gio; he's a wanted criminal in the Fourlands.'

Vendace, mystified, turned his pinched, resilient face from myself to the

Archer. The Senate had prized Gio's rhetoric so highly that they found it hard to trust our actions. As I walked quickly they pressed close, trying to hear over the sound of the blaze. With an ear-splitting screech and crash, the library roof caved in at its mid-point. Timbers dangled like fingers from both sides. Glowing tiles slid into the fissure, adding to the noise; the rumble grew to a roar. Sparks whirled up and fell on the roof of the Senate House. It was hypnotic.

Lightning said, 'Jant, tell them that I'll see them to a safe place, then I'll clear looters from the avenue as far as the rear of Gio's column.'

I asked, 'Are you well enough?'

'I believe so.'

'Then I'll fly over Mist and Serein, and join you on the main road.'

An elderly senator with a rookery voice coughed. '*What* is going on? Where's Gio?'

I changed language and said, 'He's causing the mayhem – I'm going to find out. Lightning will help you, if you please lead him to a place of refuge. I'm sorry, I am really sorry.'

Vendace pointed a shaking finger at the Amarot. Flames were now lapping on the Senate House roof. Driven to incandescence by the wind, the fire spread to the apartments on its upper storey and began to engulf them. 'No amount of apologising will ever repair that sacrilege!'

When we reached the base of the crag, Vendace directed Lightning towards a road called First Street. I left them, and as soon as I carved into the air I found myself battling against the wind being sucked into the inferno. It whipped round the crag in one-hundred-kilometre-per-hour gusts, causing a swirling column of vertical flame to rise eighty metres above the devastated library.

Smoke layered and drifted out at the height of the Amarot. It completely blocked the sunrise and shadowed the town. Burning embers were falling into the gardens of the villas below. The whitewashed walls looked grey and the boulevard was littered with spoil and broken furniture dragged out by the rebels; here and there lay the bodies of the Trisians who had tried to stop them.

Sleepy residents stumbled into the street, looking up at the crag and trying to understand. At the edge of town, people panicked and began moving towards the harbour. I saw Capharnai of all ages responding to a call to make a bucket chain. About two hundred people filled pails, pans and bowls from cisterns and carried them up the winding road to the Amarot, but the air was unbreathable; the rising heat and wind stopped them before they reached the mosaic. A few of the lamed rebels who were still lying among the boxes of money, writhed as they inhaled smoke. Their clothes and hair caught fire spontaneously.

I soared higher, because I was alarming the Capharnai and they were wasting their time watching me. I lost sight of the peach-coloured sky beyond the edges of the smoke pall. Flocks of pigeons sped round the tiny rooftops, grouping to roost, confused by the eerie eclipse light. Dawn would not end; the light was dim, as if it was still seven a.m.

The looters were fanning out through the top of town, kicking in doors and pulling shutters off their hinges, leaving a wake of debris, barking dogs and half-eaten food.

Pages and whole blackened pamphlets, scroll fragments burnt thin, jostled up in the smoke then fell on the town as hot ash. The residue of hundreds of thousands of books was raining over Capharnaum. The gloaming light and the roar of the library added to the rebels' edginess. It was much louder than the sound of the wind on my wings.

Gio's rabble now packed the lower half of the main street, blocking the wide road as they progressed down the slope towards the harbour. Gio walked ahead of them with his rapier drawn. His column was twice the size of Mist's tight ranks.

Mist's fyrd was marching up the street from the *Stormy Petrel*. The boat-swains were drumming; their beats got louder as I dropped height and passed over them. I spotted Mist leading by Wrenn's side; she looked up and raised her hand. She had tied her shawl around her waist, revealing a cuirass and backplate. Wrenn wasn't wearing armour; he was in his fyrd fatigues. He was looking for Gio, dissatisfied with their disputable duel in the forest. He was determined to beat Gio on equal terms and leave no doubt that he deserved to be immortal.

Mist was surrounded on all sides by crossbowmen and a bodyguard of her strongest sailors, all in half-armour. After that came one hundred and fifty Awndyn men carrying halberds and spears; no space to wield pikes. They wore dark green brigandines; their helmets shone like globular mirrors.

As I watched, the rear of Ata's column stopped at the quay and the rest separated and continued up the street. She had left about fifty men, a fyrd lamai unit, to protect *Stormy Petrel* moored a hundred metres behind Gio's ships. From *Petrel*'s forecastle and poop deck, archers looked out. Both her gangplanks were down but coloured shields lined her railings. The longbow-men were tense, watching the rebel defectors who ran, laden with loot, out of the ends of the parallel streets. They raced up the *Pavonine*'s gangway to a deck that seethed with drawn weapons; white faces ugly with fear stared up at me. They had turned pirate; they were prepared to defend their carrack to the death.

*

When Gio's rabble caught sight of Mist's vanguard, rebels in ones and twos began to melt away from his column, down the alleys and into the streets of the grid. They turned left and right along the intersecting roads like counters in a board game. I decided that their movements were too random to be tactical, even before I saw them start smashing shop shutters and grabbing whatever was inside.

Mist's fyrd and Gio's horde stopped with twenty metres between them. There was a second's silence in which Gio, shield on his arm, walked forward of his line and scanned the people opposing him, looking for Wrenn.

The Awndyn Fyrd captain called, 'Crossbowmen! Span. Latch. Loose!' They shot straight into the rebel front at short range, aiming at the fencing masters, knowing they were the most dangerous. The metal Insect-killing bolts cut past shop canopies and statues, burying themselves in men's faces, chests and bellies. I saw black bolt points project from their backs.

The crossbowmen's partners stepped forward with a shout, raised and slammed their green and white shields into a wall, hustling into position across the road. Behind the shields, the crossbowmen began to reload.

Gio's men waited in horror for the next barrage. Heads bobbed up and down as some men split off down the side streets but most were trapped in the centre.

The shields were lowered, crossbows levelled. 'Latch! Loose!' Another barrage flew at Gio's front line. The last of the fencing masters fell, lifeless or mortally wounded. Gio peered from behind his shield; swung his arm. 'Forward! Break the wall! Bear down the shields!'

A wave of three hundred men together started running. The front of the column seemed to flake off, as faster and faster they closed the gap. They jumped high, crashed into the shields at full tilt, hitting them with their shoulders and forcing them down. Their swords thrust over the tops, into the necks and faces of the bearers.

The crossbowmen slung their bows into holsters on their backs, drew their swords and surged forward against the rebels. The confused mass began to shove up and down the street.

I saw that Ata's spearmen were trapped towards the rear of her host. Surely that was a mistake – wouldn't they be better than the crossbows? Crossbowmen had served Ata well five years ago; now she was relying on them too much. The shield wall was perfect but it should be backed by spears. The fyrd are simply following their usual procedure: Insect-fighting tactics. They're wrong but even Ata hasn't noticed the discrepancy.

Both the fyrd and the insurgents tried to outflank each other. From above I watched the side streets filling. As the melee widened, the columns in the boulevard shortened, with Wrenn and Gio in the exact centre.

I called to the fyrd who were exploring the alleys, and led them down the right routes to ambush the rebels, who were more used to fighting in side streets. I landed and directed a group; we surprised five of Gio's men before they could rejoin the main column, and killed them all.

I returned to the air, where I could easily distinguish Mist's bodyguards. I occasionally glimpsed her face but she no longer had time to look up at me. The press was so intense, she held her curved Wrought sword with the convex arc uppermost to thrust rather than slice. Her voice carried – she screamed commands to surround Gio and disarm him. Whenever he could, Gio yelled at his rebels to close in on Mist.

In Lowespass, women soldiers have always successfully fought Insects. The culls follow procedures; the women help each other and men sometimes back them up. The difference in strength was not important when six or seven infantry recruits can tackle an Insect together, or women can join the cavalry and ride destriers. But in this crush they were fighting one-on-one against men, and I gravely feared for them.

Capharnai families peeked from the windows of their houses above the shops all along the street. They were stranded in their homes, witnessing a scene they couldn't hope to understand. They saw the heads of men wrestling and stabbing along the centre line, and behind them, filling the street above and below, a pack of foreigners in strange clothes facing each other, putting pressure on the breathless crush. The strangers were so eager to push forward to the fight that they trampled dead bodies. At the end of the street, flames piled up from the civic centre and smoke boiled like spit in lamp oil. The Capharnai neighbours looked helpless, not knowing what to do. I shouted, 'Stay inside! Don't get involved – they fight each other, not Trisians!'

They saw their own shops vandalised below them. Their faces disappeared from the windows as they began barricading themselves into their upper rooms.

I glanced back; the library was now a roofless shell, the floors were falling through and just the façade was left. Flames leapt in the windows surrounded by blackened stonework – it looked like an animated skeleton.

Coruscating sparks and dull fragile ash dropped on us. I beat my wings to dislodge flakes from the feathers, thinking: the town is being covered in burnt knowledge.

Gio was looking for Wrenn, carving his own men aside. I landed on the nearest roof to watch, searching the alleys below for a crossbow to pick up. Gio, wild-eyed, saw Mist's bodyguards and Wrenn beside them in an area of calm because no fighter would engage with him.

Gio raised his rapier and saluted. 'Well, look if it isn't the *novice*.'

'Good morning,' smiled Wrenn.

Gio snarled, 'You could have chosen better last words.'

First-blood fencing in the amphitheatre was just an entertainment; no rules apply in a duel to the death. They watched each other with cool anticipation; Capharnaum didn't exist for them. They were in a world of two people, challenger and challenged.

There are no words in that world. I know, because I have been there.

Gio swept his rapier down in the rage cut. 'You stole my name,' he said. 'I'll be Serein again. I am good enough. I Challenge you, Serein Wrenn.'

Wrenn levelled his blade. 'Just run onto this and save me the effort.'

I took off and climbed above them through the deafening battle's noise.

They dropped the pretence of faking other styles to conceal their own. They flew at each other eager for blood. Gio rushed to chop at Wrenn; at the same time a bystander tried to catch him but Wrenn smashed his teeth with the rapier pommel.

Wrenn lunged at Gio, reprised. Gio swiped it aside with a blow that would have shattered a lesser blade than the 1969 Sword. I thought: How long can they keep this up? But I knew the answer – at least four hours.

Gio pointed his rapier, its lanyard loose around his wrist. He lunged to Wrenn's dagger side. Wrenn swept his rapier across – clash! – disengaged and cut down aiming for the sensitive bone of Gio's shin.

Gio jumped on the spot then attacked. Wrenn parried, riposted, enveloped Gio's blade in quatre, made as if to beat him on the arm and tried to stab him in the forehead. Gio spun away in a move that took me two years to learn. His thigh boots slipped on the pavement. He was trying to predict Wrenn's actions four or five moves in advance.

In a split second Wrenn slid his rapier tip through Gio's swept hilt, sliced the skin off his knuckles, withdrew the blade. Gio's grip became slippery on the freely-running blood. He hid his sword hand with his dagger, so Wrenn couldn't see to predict the direction of the next blow.

Their motions were wide; their heads ducked to avoid being cut in the eyes, watching with the faster speed of their peripheral vision. Their flexed sword arms were close to the body for strength. They hacked at the nearest enemies whenever they had a chance and the melee backed away from them, leaving them in a clear space. The fighting was spreading up and down the street and fragmenting. Tussling groups of men dispersed down the side alleys. The densest part of the fighting eddied around Ata's bodyguard; spearmen behind, rebels ahead. Five sailors linked arms, trying to preserve a space around her so she could breathe.

*

I'm doing no good here, entranced by the duel. I need a firebrand to drop on Gio.

I flew back to find Lightning. It was easy, because he was the only person in Fourlands clothes walking down the middle of the broad street. Behind him, the road rose up the hillside backed by the incredible blaze. He was oblivious to the Capharnai around him, with their crying children, bucket chains and packs of belongings. He sniped unerringly at the small groups of rebels-turned-pirates who were all busy with different intents. Some scavenged like wolves; a man pulled down a gold street-lamp bracket; two lechers were held at bay by a Trisian man defending his daughter.

Lightning limped on his left side, moving slowly. Conserving his energy, he held his mighty bow horizontally with the arrow on top, drawing back the heel of his hand to fit in the hollow of his cheek. He used short-distance arrows, colour-coded with white flights, and let fly at the looters. Anyone who touched a shop shutter or ran from a house with an armful of gold was sent reeling with an arrow through bicep or thigh.

I glided over and called. I landed and ran to a halt beside him. 'Gio and Wrenn are duelling! Ata's caught in the crush – we have to help her.'

I drew my sword and we continued downhill towards the rotunda at the road's mid-point. Lightning never missed a shot, counting under his breath, 'Fifty-five. Fifty-four. Three ... Two ...'

I scanned the windows for any movement that might end with a knife in my back. Beyond the forum we passed a precinct of narrow streets. We looked down the nearest and saw a gang of rebels heaving at a solid door. The first was a weasly man with baggy, low-crotched jeans. He had his shoulder to the cracking panels and the others all added their weight. They noticed Lightning and I but renewed their assault on the building. Inside, women were screaming in Trisian so rapid and full of dialect I couldn't understand. From the first-floor window an elegant lady with ringletted hair, a white chiton dress and red nails hurled terracotta dishes down on the besiegers. They angled their arms over their heads and kept pushing.

'Hey!' yelled Lightning. 'Away from that door! Jant, what are they shouting? What is this place?'

I read a tiny inscription on a stone block set into the wall: *Salema's Imbroglio.*

'It's an imbroglio; in Trisian, I mean. A brothel.'

The Archer raised his eyebrows. 'I see. Then we must save the honour of these ladies – regardless of whether they have any honour or no.' He loosed at the thin-faced Awian. The arrow rammed straight through the man's leg and into the wood. Its shaft made a high-pitched crunch of gristle, dimpling his jeans' fabric into his knee, locking it out straight. He tried to step forward but was fastened to the door. He screamed and hammered his fists and free leg against it.

'Are you all right?' said his friend, being slow on the uptake.

He screamed, 'Pull it out!'

'You can't, it's barbed.' Lightning spanned his bow. 'And if you try, I'll kill you both.'

The gang sloped off, then broke up and ran towards the forum. Lightning called to the whores, 'I promise you'll come to no harm.'

'I'm sorry,' the would-be rapist pleaded, leaning forward with both hands over his knee.

'You will be,' Lightning commented, without moving the arrow trained on him.

'Saker, what are you doing?' I said, disturbed by this change.

The rapist's eyes bulged. His left leg kicked, shoe sole scraping the step. He stuttered, 'No, no! I'll—'

'You'll do what, exactly?' Lightning said, driven to fury by the man's Donaise accent. He loosed the arrow; it pinned the rapist's left leg to a panel. It met some resistance at the kneecap but drove easily between the articulated surfaces of the joint behind and split the wood. Its arrowhead was a shiny stud in his flattened and mushy knee.

Lightning selected another arrow. 'My card. Seeing as you need reminding who we are.' He shot again, pinning the man's right elbow to the door. A wedge of broken bone clicked away from the metal point pushing past it.

The rapist howled and sobbed, 'Why? Oh god, help ... What-have-I-*done*?' He turned his head and vomited onto the top step.

'You know who we are!' Lightning shouted. 'But still you have to plead, you have to ask! You think Tris is beyond the reach of the Castle! You take advantage of this gentle town!'

Before I could stop Lightning he whipped out a fourth arrow. He couldn't be enjoying this. I dashed in front of him. 'Stop! Are you mad?'

Stony-faced, he aimed over my shoulder. 'The lout has an elbow left ...'

'Leave him!' I shouted.

'Rape is the worst of crimes,' Lightning muttered. He shook himself and looked up to where the beautiful whores were leaning out watching, some timidly, some brazenly. 'Interpret for me, Jant,' he said, and called, 'All right, girls. Do with him what you will.'

We walked away from the man's beast noise. With his whole shocking strength he made every breath a scream.

The Capharnai watched in horror from their doorways. They couldn't distinguish Lightning and I from the rebels. A young lad, his trousers spattered with somebody else's blood, ran from the piazza and confronted us.

He glared and brandished one of our broadswords, holding it like a tennis racquet. Lightning hesitated. I flicked my dreadlocks back, spread my double-jointed hands and wings and roared, 'Raaaah!'

The boy yelled and fled. Lightning looked impressed.

At the next intersection stood one of the unidentifiable poles topped by a right-angled black and white bar. A man stood beside it, manipulating levers that pulled wires to make the plank swing in well-defined motions, somewhat like a flag. He looked up the street to another pole at the foot of the smoke-obscured Amarot and operated the levers to follow its movements. A third device distant at the edge of the town replicated his signals a second later. I realised these were not standards at all; it was a system of communication, and quicker than anything I could provide. Even in the midst of the chaos I thought, I'll make this innovation my own. I'll put this system on the Lowespass peel towers instead of the beacons to monitor Insect advances lest someone else beats me to it.

We reached the rotunda that stood over the main crossroads, a domed folly no bigger than a room. It had round columns supporting arches taking in the boulevard and the north-south road. Someone had hacked great chunks of plaster off the interior walls surfaced with blue gems.

A woman wearing a fyrd greatcoat with the collar up was energetically prising squares of sapphire out of the mosaic. Seeing Lightning's arrowhead levelled at her, she shrank back, tossed up her knife and caught it by the point, made as if to throw it at him.

Lightning swung slightly left and shot at the edge of the nearest pillar. The arrow hit it obliquely, glanced off into the shade inside and she felt the breeze as it zipped past her face. She burst from the northern arch, away between the empty pavement tea shops, her coat streaming behind her. Lightning bowed – he could even bow sarcastically.

The rear of Gio's column was two hundred metres below us on the road. We could see the backs of heads, sallet points or bandanna knots at the napes of their necks. Two men in the last line noticed us, nudged their friends and the motion rippled out until everyone at the rear turned round. They were only inclined to watch us until one man, with a look of hatred, pulled a bolt from his bandolier, cocked his crossbow and raised it to his shoulder. Nine or ten others followed suit; I dodged inside the rotunda but Lightning stood still, in disbelief. I urged, 'Come on!'

Lightning shook his head as the men pulled their triggers and a barrage of bolts flew at us. Out of range, they dropped and struck the pavement, and the broken pieces skidded, stopping two metres from Lightning's feet. He stepped forward and kicked them, as if to check they were real and he wasn't imagining it. He sounded aggrieved. 'What have I done to warrant all this?

They think they can outshoot me. I'll attempt to confer with them.'

'*Talk* to them?' I stopped because Lightning took a handful of distance arrows, long thin shafts with stiff triangular red and yellow fletchings. He held them together with his bow grip, and shot rapidly along the line. 'Twenty, nineteen, eighteen.' Another handful. 'Seventeen, sixteen, fifteen.' The rebels ran like their arses were on fire, but they all ended up lying on the ground moaning or yelling. People in the next line pointed us out then made a break for it, forced to run towards us to reach the side streets' empty entrances.

The horn tips of Lightning's longbow shook. He lowered it, breathing deeply, gazing downhill to the churning front of the fray where Gio and Wrenn appeared and disappeared. His legs were trembling and he was pale with pain.

I watched the Sailor's bodyguards, in dark blue and steel, hacking at the rebels with Ata close behind. From the midst of Gio's rabble a spear looped up, fell steeply onto them. It hit Ata, impacting on her breastplate. She staggered, unhurt but knocked off balance. The mob surged forward and she fell under their feet, out of view. Her bodyguards lurched back, tried to stay upright by grabbing each other and the soldiers around, but simply pulled people down together, opening a hole in the crowd.

'Get up,' I said. 'Quick, Saker; shoot!'

Lightning now shot to kill, aiming at the rebels standing over Ata, in the most accurate volley I had ever seen: an arrow every two seconds.

'Get up! Get *up*!' he muttered.

The rebels fell around the place where Ata had gone down. He picked them off in the solid crush, no space between them. They couldn't even raise their shields. The arrows started to hit the same men again and again; dead bodies kept upright in the crush were filling with them, their heads and shoulders pinned with the bicolour flights, but Ata and the men stabbing her were underneath. We couldn't see her.

The bodyguards tried to shove forward, stabbing the rebels facing them in chests and stomachs. They shouted and tugged at the clothes of the men to either side, urging them to push ahead.

Lightning hissed in exasperation, 'I can't get a clear line of sight. Nine. Eight. Seven. Move out the way!'

His quiver was nearly empty. The ends of his bow vibrated; rapidly his right hand reached down for the short nocks, pulled one up and fitted it to string. Hooked the string with three bent fingers. Drew it past his ear, swinging his shoulder back for a couple of extra centimetres.

He shot with unflagging speed but dimples appeared around his pursed lips. 'Five, four. Jant, brace yourself; the Circle's going to break.'

Zascai are slaughtering Mist. And there's nothing I can do. I tried to feel it starting – couldn't – and it hit me. Time rushed past us; I felt torn across the middle. My awareness raced out, expanding in all directions. It stretched, flattened, spread thinner and infinitely thinner until my own identity and individuality vanished. I lost consciousness of my surroundings. I ceased to exist. The Circle reformed with a snap. I woke and blinked around at the battered shopfronts and blue domed ceiling overhead.

It happened so quickly I was still on my feet but I had dropped my sword. I felt cold, very aware of my body and the battle's noise.

'Three, two...' Lightning stopped with an arrow at string. 'I ... I am still here,' he said deliriously. We looked at each other.

'Killed by Zascai,' he whispered.

At the battlefront crush, Serein Wrenn staggered. New to the Circle, he didn't understand what had happened. Gio, on the other hand, had known it well. He took advantage and cut at Wrenn's forehead, drawing a red line across his temple to blind him with blood.

Wrenn came to and tried to defend himself but, concentration lost, all he could do was retreat. Gio pushed him back, slashing at his face to further unnerve him.

'Serein!' Lightning raised his bow again, arced an arrow up high over the entire rebels' column.

I just had time to see that someone had grabbed Wrenn from behind. Wrenn, still confused, struggled to free himself. The arrow came straight down into the top of the assailant's head; he crumpled up.

'One.' Lightning fitted his penultimate arrow to the binding on his bow-string. Behind Wrenn a man in a painted leather jacket brandishing a curved falchion leapt at him. Lightning drew and loosed; the arrow pierced the man's forehead and his body fell, knocking Wrenn. The crowd realised that anyone who closed with Wrenn received an arrow between the eyes. They left the duellists alone.

The Archer gasped, 'Serein is an Eszai and must win his own duel. But I made it an even fight; there won't be two Eszai murdered today.'

His shirt hem was soaked with blood; it was spreading to the tops of his trousers.

At the place where Mist's dismembered body was being trodden underfoot, someone raised a halberd, her head on the spike. I could only tell by the short white hair, because it was crushed and gashed. The pole turned and the head jigged round to face us. Its indigo eyes were turned up, its mouth open, its nose flattened and bloody.

Lightning's legs buckled. He staggered back to the rotunda wall, sat down against it, then collapsed sideways leaving a smear of blood. I helped him sit upright with the bow across his knees. He pulled the leather tab off his right hand with his teeth and dropped it. His face was ashen. 'The animals. How could they do that – tear her apart? An Eszai, and Cyan's mother ... Immortality's pointless in the crush. We're too used to Insects. They don't throw spears. Damn, don't you feel like you've died? I hate feeling someone else's death and the years I've cheated catching up with me. You know ... we all become a second older before San mends the Circle.' He bowed his head. 'You know that with me it adds up to minutes ...'

Lightning hugged arms around his waist and squeezed his eyes shut in agony. I crouched and laid a hand on his shoulder, trying to bring him round because he was drifting and talking to himself. 'They killed her. Her schemes were useless ... I don't know what they'll do next.'

He could not fight in this condition, and the rotunda gave sparse cover. Lightning knew this and made a tremendous effort. He nocked his last arrow and eased his short sword loose in its scabbard though it took all his mettle to lift it.

'Wait and gather your strength,' I said.

He nodded. 'Yes. I'll try to make my way back to Rayne ... I'll meet you at the *Petrel*.' He sighed, chin on his chest. He was thinking about Mist; the reality hitting him was as incapacitating as the wound. 'You and Serein must persevere. Kill Gio, for Ata ... for me. You are Eszai and that is your purpose.'

He looked so ill that I didn't want him to tangle with any more rebels. 'Don't stay here, those bastards will come up. Go all the way to the end of Fifth Street before you turn down to the harbour. The roads are quieter at the edge of town. Saker, I really think—'

He spoke through gritted teeth. '"Saker, I really think" nothing. Into the air and *stop this fight!*'

He watched me pick up two jewel-encrusted pieces of plaster, one in each hand. I ran to take off.

I dived at Gio and dumped both bricks on him. They hit him, one on his tow-head, one on his forearm, and he reeled. Wrenn jumped forward and thrust.

Gio's neat last-minute parry saved him – the rapiers clanged hilt to hilt. Their blades bound, they wrestled. Gio kicked Wrenn's shin. The muscle fluttered in Wrenn's calf but he threw the taller man back and wiped blood from his eyes.

'Shoot him!' Gio bellowed at a crossbowman. 'Shoot him, someone, why don't you?'

In return Wrenn spat at Gio and swiped low behind his knees to sever the hamstring. Gio pivoted on the ball of his foot and let the soft thrust go past.

A bruiser of a man offered his rapier to Gio. Gio fluidly slipped his dagger into his belt and snatched the sword from the man's fist. He levelled both rapiers at Wrenn. They must have had different hefts but I couldn't tell from the way he handled them.

Instantly at a disadvantage, Wrenn hit at the new rapier's side. Gio parried and at the same time attacked. Wrenn stood his ground. A sailor tried to pass his sword to Wrenn, but Gio severed his hand still clutching the hilt. Numbly, the sailor bent to retrieve his sword but he had no hand to pick it up with.

I circled above Wrenn, calling encouragement. He looked desperate; blood flowed down his face. He searched out the last of his strength and stood tall as if he had found hope, but I thought he was acting because Gio didn't respond. Wrenn feinted. Gio attacked with a move like a sneer. Wrenn evaded, left his dagger arm exposed, too low. Gio's rapier penetrated between his fingers, slid through his hand and up his arm under the skin. The point issued from his elbow in a patter of blood. Wrenn's hand opened, his dagger fell.

It's over, I thought; but Wrenn had trapped Gio's sword. Wrenn's rapier forced Gio's other blade far to the left, disengaged and thrust. His hilt slammed into Gio's chest.

Gio hunched; about a metre of bright steel projected from his back. A red patch darkened his coat around it. Wrenn pulled the hilt down, tearing his lungs. Gio staggered, blood spitting from his mouth. Wrenn couldn't hold Gio's weight on the blade and dropped it, leaving him sprawling transfixed by the rapier. Gio's blade snagged in Wrenn's arm tore out through the muscle making a gaping wound.

Gio lay curled up. He coughed around the blade. Blood sprang from his mouth onto the pavement, dribbled from his lips. He didn't breathe in again. Died.

Awndyn soldiers rushed to Wrenn and supported him. His fingers scrabbled, trying to stick the edges of the gash back together. Blood ran down into his mouth and he smiled. He had deliberately caught Gio's blade in his arm, in a furious variation of the same attack that had won him immortality a year ago.

Wrenn struck out with his fists at the soldiers trying to calm him. He fainted, so they picked him up and I led them to the *Stormy Petrel*.

I picked up a sheaf of arrows and a bottle of water, and my horn that I sound to give commands on the battlefield. I flew back to Fifth Street and landed near Lightning. He looked exhausted but grateful as I sprinted past, called, 'Gio's dead!', dumped the ammunition and bottle while still running, took off.

I swept low over the rebels and shouted, 'Gio has fallen; give yourselves up!'

The whole front of the column who had seen the duel, and several more, especially the girls, surrendered to the Awndyn Fyrd. The rear dissolved, rebels becoming looters or fugitives. Many became disorientated and I saw them running further into the meshed streets. But the leaderless centre of the column and the men who had killed Mist knew they were doomed. A new sort of aggression flared among them, affected by desperation, the strangeness of Capharnaum and the rum they had drunk.

There was a tangible atmosphere of possibility and menace. Instantly the five hundred rebels in the main street acted as if they were a single being, powerful, euphoric with it, and mad. I sensed their vigour and my pulse raced. Anything could happen; everything was happening – the riot obeyed no laws at all. The youths were at home with it; it was their atmosphere. They ran in large ragged groups. They all thought: why not take the wealth that surrounds us, in an abundance we've never been allowed before? The strength of individuals was nothing compared with the violence of the crowd – they tore the shopfronts apart. They were bent on spending everything in the town in one hysterical surge. They brought out bakers' trolleys and smashed them into caryatid statues. They infected each other to screaming pitch rejoicing at their own bodies' force, their freedom and their sudden riches. No future prospects Capharnaum could offer them were as good as the fun they could have trashing it. From the air I saw a mass of people sweeping away from the boulevard. They spiralled around ransacked shops like the eye of a storm.

The burning crag's jumping unnatural light lit the quay. Gio's men were now just pirates, plundering the surrounding houses. They dragged out tables, threw lamps into sheets and bundled them up. Fights broke out between them: men stabbed and punched each other over any precious-looking metal. They broke furniture and hefted the pieces as clubs.

Bricks were hurled against the houses' upper windows, and when a Capharnai man leant out and shouted, they threw bricks at his face. The pirates gathered cutlery and amphorae but discarded them when gold gleamed. So much gold, it was like the Castle's treasury. They hastily lashed together enormous packs of objects with their belts. When each had plundered all he could carry, he set off to the *Pavonine* leaving wailing and raging Capharnai families behind them.

Some Capharnai defended themselves. A group of fishermen threw a huge weighted net over thieves escaping from a house. As they struggled under it, the fishermen stabbed them with marlinspikes and tridents that sloughed dried white scales.

540

A group of Trisian lads came out of one house carrying sacks to loot food, kicking the door of a restaurant. Thick olive-oil smoke ribboned from its cellar grating. Little fires had been kindled at irregular intervals on the boulevard. The rioters set alight waste bins and chairs; I could see no reason why, apart from the lust to cause as much havoc as possible. I yelled, 'Stop destroying this wonderful town!' The ones that heard me started laughing.

There was no hope of catching the rioters without abandoning our own wounded men. I ordered the fyrd to pull back to the *Petrel*. At the foot of the gangplank the Awndyn unit had formed a barricade. They levelled pikes above a shield wall. Some fyrd regrouped there, but in equal numbers those who spied the gold were unlinking their shields and deserting to join the looters. Archers on the *Petrel*'s fore- and rear-castles sent sporadic volleys down at the pirates crossing the quay, who had no choice but to run through the hail of arrows to the *Pavonine*.

Thieves poured up the *Pavonine*'s gangways carrying their prizes or dragging their wounded friends. I flew over the *Stramash* and *Cuculine*, puzzled; their decks were on the same level as the water. They had been scuttled; they sat empty and perfectly upright, their keels on the sea bed. Their main decks were swamped with lapping waves, from which their castles projected like four square islands.

The crews of all three ships were at work unfurling and setting the *Pavonine*'s sails. Others, yelling, waved their friends aboard. Poleaxes and spears looked like metal hackles standing up on the ship's back.

I glided above *Pavonine*'s deck and saw Tirrick, and Cinna. Tirrick had Cinna Bawtere at rapier point, forcing him to steer the ship. Cinna clung to the wheel, shaking visibly, his porcine face set in a grimace. Tirrick, however, smiled rapaciously. He shouted, 'Climb aboard! We'll sink the *Petrel*, then pack provisions and sail for Awndyn! I'll be the next Serein and fatty will be the next Mist!'

Cinna glanced up at me and scowled. He had a length of chain around his middle, worn by fearful sailors so if they fell overboard their suffering would have a quick end.

I shouted, 'Cinna, don't you dare leave!'

He told me to go and do something unspeakable with a goat.

Sailors on the harbour cast *Pavonine*'s mooring ropes loose and swarmed up. The ship grated along the quayside with looters still chucking bags onto the deck and catching lines to haul themselves up.

Those left behind turned their attention to the *Petrel*. Small groups of rebels gathered out of range on the villa verandas; they began to coalesce, ready to attack the *Petrel*'s gangway in a desperate bid to hijack her. I thought of Rayne; I would not let anyone hurt the Doctor. She was my adviser,

Lightning's confidante and devoted friend. Lightning would be even more shattered than he already is, if anything happened to Rayne.

I have seen Mist die and Serein badly wounded. I have left Lightning faltering his way through the outskirts of town. The only books to escape the firestorm are in my pocket. I don't know how many Trisians have succumbed but their houses, their shops and the harbour are despoiled. Cinna was sailing off with their belongings, surrounded by pirates and protected by Tirrick. The remnants of Gio's men were completely beyond control. Our forces were disheartened and either retreating or deserting.

I needed everyone in the riot to listen to me, to stop and look up so I could shatter the hysteria that gripped them. I must attract their attention with a gesture more powerful than Gio's last stand. But how? None of my battlefield horn signals mean anything now. I couldn't drop rocks accurately onto *Pavonine* from above the archers' range.

I shouted, swooped acrobatically and landed on the main street, but although the rebels heard me they paid no attention and simply ran away. What was I to do – pursue them one by one? Infuriated by our failure, realising that we were stranded, I felt my scolopendium clock running down. A cold shiver washed over me; the long muscles twitched in my arms. Oh god, not *now*. If Tarragon surfaced she could soon put an end to the *Pavonine*, but that wouldn't stop the fighting on land that second by second was becoming bloodier. I needed Tarragon, her car or a congregation of Tine, a sea krait ... A sea krait! Did I dare speak to the kraits? I thought: I can *use* the Shift to stop the sacking of Capharnaum!

I flew to *Petrel* and landed on the half-deck. Rayne had transformed the main area below me into a field hospital, and she was extremely busy. Wounded men were being brought in and laid on camp beds between the masts and hatchways. Rayne bent over one, whose blood pooled in the brown stretcher. Her assistant struggled with the breastplate strap, having to pull tighter in order to release it through the buckle. Rayne said, 'No! Tha' sucking wound – ignore the res'.' She slipped a gauze pad under the edge of his armour and pressed on a jagged gash in his ribs. The soldier struggled. Rayne grasped his hand firmly and he lay still. Then his hand relaxed out of hers.

I watched as I retrieved my envelope of cat from my cabin, and I saw it all. Rayne looked into his eyes as he died. She often did that with the mortals for whom, no matter how hard she tried, she could not prevent death. She wants to glimpse the change as their eyes set. I once thought her obsession was compassion, now I think it's just her insatiable curiosity. She wants to see what they're seeing, she wants to know all that they suddenly know. It's understandable because people are always inquisitive about what they can't do. Or maybe, and although it's morbid I wouldn't rule it out,

Rayne is fond of being the last thing a man sees as he quits the world. One day her curious face might fill my field of vision, through a blood-red filter.

I ducked into Ata's office; the bottle of brandy stood on her table. Through the stern windows I saw the *Pavonine*, nearly stationary against an onshore breeze. Her sailors swarmed on the high aft castle, adjusting some timbers – the long beam of a trebuchet. I said aloud, 'Bloody fuck, not another catapult.' It could even be the one we saw being dragged along the Remige Road. It had two large wooden treadmills set upright on either side. A sailor crawled into each wheel and walked them around; others on the outside pushed to winch the arm back. It was so long it overhung the poop deck steps. Another pair of men lowered a ball into the sling. Tirrick gave a shout, the arm kicked up to one side of the mizzen mast, and the stone flew through the air.

It overshot *Petrel* and crashed into the roof of one of the harbour villas. Cinna's sailors busily set about winding a windlass to decrease the trebuchet's throw. Shit, if we ever needed Lightning's professional opinion it was now.

I dashed out of the cabin and called to Rayne, 'They're taking potshots at us! Move down below – and stay there till I bring reinforcements. Don't abandon ship unless they hole the hull. If you must go to land, ask the officer of the Awndyn Fyrd lamai to give you some cover.'

I heard Rayne ordering that her patients be taken to the living deck; I did not have much time. I tipped a fistful of cat out of the envelope. It ran like fine sugar between my fingers as I sifted it into the brandy glass. I tapped my hand on top to knock the powder out of the damp lines on my palm. Then I uncorked the brandy and sloshed it in. The crystals eddied and spun. I drank it down right to the dregs of undissolved powder where the brandy had not penetrated between the dry grains. I put the glass down with a click.

That was a massive overdose. Through the windows broadsword fighters battled at the junction of the boulevard. Pikes held the gangplank secure but only one line of fyrd remained behind them.

The metal clashes muted suddenly, as if at a distance; the bustle of the surgery shrank to background. My own breaths boomed loud and blood pressure rumbled in my ears. It is coming on.

Pavonine turned her slender stern to me and the flat towers of her soot-spotted sails. Her reflection vanished. The image of the quay wall and houses ripped away. The sea moved, silver but featureless. It wasn't reflecting; it should be mirroring the sky.

The waves slowed to the consistency of treacle. *Pavonine* lifted and fell again hours later. Another round shot slowed until it was almost floating; it tracked a lingering trajectory through the air and disappeared at the water's surface in front of the window.

I'm going under. I slipped to my knees, trailing my fingers down the dirty panes. If I concentrate on breathing I'll never remember how to. I could no longer kneel. I lay down, one arm extended. The bracelets on the other wrist pressed into my cheek, my sword belt dug into my hips.

Black haze filled my vision from the edges to the centre. I thought with a sudden flush of panic: I haven't taken anywhere near enough. This will never work. I need more—

CHAPTER 22

I set off flying over Epsilon's savannah towards Vista Marchan and the old Insect bridge. Hundreds of metres below, Tarragon's gold car left the edge of the market and followed, accelerating until it was directly below me. The car kept pace, a tiny shining rectangle on the immense plains, leaving a straight dark green track as it flattened the grass. I could see Tarragon in her short red dress glancing up at me.

I slowed, let the car race ahead and then swooped down, speeding faster as I lost height, and catching up with it from behind. I swept over it, lifting my legs so my dangling feet didn't hit the headrest, and then lowered my pointed boot toes onto the front seat next to Tarragon. She looked ahead, keeping the car speeding straight. I crouched and pulled my wings in unevenly, wiggled to sit down. I pointed at the grey Insect bridge. '*Go!*'

Tarragon clenched the wheel, rocked her body forward and slammed her foot to the floor.

The towers of Vista Marchan shimmered and cohabited the space where only the flourishing grassland was supposed to be. A warm wind blew directly from them, drying my eyes. Nowhere in the Fourlands has such a parched, relentless wind. Tarragon glanced at me, complaining, 'I've been looking everywhere. What's happening, Jant? I swam into harbour and saw stones falling through the water around the hull of your boat.'

'We're under attack. The other ship's throwing them. Rayne's on the *Petrel* – and so am I.'

Tarragon gnashed her Shark's teeth angrily. Her shape flickered violently between being a prissy lady and a vicious fish. 'What a waste of scholarship! I will flip their boat into flotsam!'

'It's even worse: the library's on fire – one thousand years of wisdom lost forever. We'll never know what essential works are gone for good. Mist Ata's dead. Oh – was that gargantuan shark you?'

'Yes. I followed a schooner that I sent to sail alongside your ship on a Shift sea. You asked me for help so I chartered it as a guard.'

'God, Tarragon; you're big.'

'Big-ish. Do you want me to bite your enemies' keel out from under them?'

'Even if you do, the pirates ashore will keep fighting and they're killing the islanders. The Trisians will still resist the Castle after this. No amount of talking will bring them round because after Gio's lies they're never going to believe any Fourlander again. We can't win. The only way I can think to take control of this riot is to stage a spectacle so incredible that both sides forget their differences. Sea kraits live far from land, don't they?'

Tarragon said, 'Yes. They wouldn't eat humans, not worth the energy. They live in the deep ocean; when they slough their skins they scratch themselves on the continent's roots shelving up from the abyss.'

'Well, I want a sea krait.'

'You want to save them! Are you sure?'

'Only if they agree to the deal. The stinguish told me their ocean dried up, and you said they needed a safe haven. Kraits can come to live in the Fourlands' sea on the condition that they obey me.'

I braced myself as we rushed onto the wide bridge. Our wheels hummed as they sped over the irregular surface. I could see the striations where individual Insects had added their masticated wood pulp. The bridge's stringy supports of hardened spit whooshed by on both sides. Looking between them I saw the savannah drop below us as we laboured up to the apex.

We crested the summit buffeted by Vista's breeze that blows across worlds, and for one glorious moment I could see the whole of the sprawling market.

Then it had gone; we were in the world of Vista. The wind howled through the top of the bridge. Below us, it blew the top layer of flaking sand across the wasteland as fine crystal dust, drifting onto high dunes against the base of the sea wall.

Many white tracks converged on Vista Marchan city; from up here they resembled the rays of a star. Its cluster of pale blocky towers appeared suspended in mirages and pooled in bent light across the entire wasteland.

I had not seen any place like this before. We descended past the towers that I realised were higher than the Throne Room spire. I was overawed and shaking as we rolled to a halt on top of Vista's great sea wall. On either side of us were empty, sand-choked dockyards and piers with long, dry barnacled ladders that stopped short of the ground.

I looked out over the salt flats, to see Epsilon as a translucent illusion, a lush plain and thriving market lying at forty-five degrees through the white wasteland.

Tarragon said, 'Aren't Insects fascinating creatures? That's the Vista desert. It used to be the ocean floor.' Her car's wheels pulled the grit into tracks as we drove along the top of the immense wall. The salt-bleached streets were devoid of movement. The only living things in Vista were myself and Tarragon; her fin annoyingly brushed my thigh as she operated the controls. Paper Insect cells meshed between and hung like grey lace around the worn concrete buildings.

546

'I'm sorry to bring you so far,' she added. 'Your trip home will cause you substantial distress.'

Rust stains ran down the dock wall from flaking iron rings bolted into the top. Sea-level markers and fading numerals were stencilled in a script twice my height. We stopped and stared out at the vanished ocean. The white sky and sand stretched away as far as I could see: two parallel planes meeting at the horizon. Occasional patches discoloured the dunes' glaring surface, chemicals and oil seeping up from below. A stagecoach that must have belonged to a recent tourist lay derelict and half-full of sand. The tops of its spoked wheels showed through the surface of a hard-packed ridge.

Behind us was the city, faceless towers and blanched walls abraded with centuries of wind-blown sand. Spiral steps emerged like spinal columns from their broken shells. Rusted girders jutted out of the fortieth floors – metal thinned to perforated wafers. There was no sound but the breeze skipping salt crystals over the dry ocean floor and concrete promenade. It was completely outside my experience. I said, 'It's not beautiful. It's ...'

'A desert, Jant. Lots of sand.'

'Tarragon,' I said impatiently. 'Capharnaum is burning!'

She tutted but moved quickly, taking a gold pocket watch from a box that was part of the car's fascia. She clicked its glass case open and I saw that it wasn't a watch at all. Inside was a gold mechanism and a wire gauze that securely held down a fat black fly, twice the size of a bluebottle. It buzzed energetically, sounding as if it was trying to drill through its gold cage. Tarragon said, 'It's amazing what you can purchase from the Tine in Epsilon market if you have enough meat.'

'What is it?'

'It's a Time Fly. They have a way of avoiding being squashed or eaten. They can jump a split second back in time, up to the point at which they emerged from the pupa. This Time Fly hatched in Vista Marchan and has been imprisoned here ever since. I'm taking you back there; we will turn back time until the tide comes in. Wind it for me, will you?'

I turned the contraption's little gold key, just like a watch, and the gauze began to put pressure on the trapped insect. It felt threatened and tried its method of escape, but because the mechanism snared it, it carried its threat along. It took us, too, and it went *fast*. Really fast.

For a few minutes, nothing changed. I twisted round and looked behind at the town. The buildings could be a little less grey, less dilapidated.

There was a blurring at street level around the car, as if I could see coloured air swirling. Tarragon said, 'They're city people, in their everyday lives or fighting Insects, moving back in time too fast to see.'

She patted my arm and pointed to the horizon. Prodigious steel ships began to rise from the areas of oily discoloured sands. Sand dusted away from

547

them, revealing masts and wheelhouses then unearthed long hulls lying on their sides. The sand's surface darkened to pale grey and began to glisten. Then shallow blue pools appeared in the lowest linear sand ripples, where I had not noticed hollows before. The long pools swelled and coalesced, turning the summits of the sand ripples into islands and building up around the dunes. Water ran together around them, darker blue as it deepened.

The ripples were all covered, the sea level climbed, the dunes were dispersed islands. Just a few islands left; then the sea covered the final dune. The ocean kept rising, closer to the bottom rungs of the ladders, bearing upright the drab metal ships.

Colour poured into the sky. From monochrome it became pale, then bright blue. The automobile's highly polished gold chassis reflected it. The Time Fly in the watch whined with effort. It was now a young imago, its wings crumpled and damp, as it had been when someone imprisoned it. Its six thin legs scraped against the watch's shiny inside surface.

Suddenly the Insect bridge vanished. Fresh paper, it disappeared in jerky stages from the foot of the arch to its zenith. Waves hit the harbour wall and climbed its sea-level gauge, higher and higher. The steel ships disappeared instantly; instead the ocean spat out white boats that bobbed at anchor. The rings in the dock wall were glossy; Vista Marchan's towers were complete and spotless, glass walls reflecting the sun. The buzzing in the watch stopped abruptly, and everything was clear and still. It was a beautiful day. Men and women in orange tabards and yellow helmets went about their business at the docks, blissfully unaware of the annihilation that will happen when the Insects' bridge crashes through.

Tarragon showed me the watch; it was empty. She said, 'In a factory in Vista, the Time Fly's just been hatched.'

An almighty wave reared from the middle of the ocean and cascaded into harbour, diminishing every second, until it lapped at the wall as a gentle ripple. A vast green and blue striped snake's head and upper body erupted from the ocean, spattering us with spray and blotting out the sun. Its head was four times bigger than a caravel, the solid muscle trunk of its monstrous body as thick as one of the towers behind me.

The glossy snake lowered its flat, pointed head onto the promenade. The harbour workers seemed annoyed but were too polite to say anything. Tarragon and I climbed out of her car. 'God-who-left-us,' I gasped.

'No, it's just a snake.'

'Shit ... How many are there?'

'Sh!' Tarragon chided. 'Their population numbers less than a thousand.'

The sea krait's bulk stretched into the distance. It meandered in colossal hundred-metre curves like the Moren River. A ship steered away from its side, panicking and belching smoke. Around half a kilometre from shore, the krait dipped underwater and the same distance further away a striped conical island trailed back and forth in the frothing sea – the flattened tip of its tail.

We stood in front of the snake's slightly domed yellow eye. Its vertical slit pupil was the height and width of my body. Its head was covered in bright scales the size of a table-top. Black skin showed between them, looking like stitching around the square scales on its closed lips. A deeply forked black tongue darted out of the tip of its snout and flickered around us. It didn't touch me but I sensed the motion of the air a centimetre away from my face and I felt its moisture. The snake darted its tongue back into the hole in its top lip, which was big enough for me to have crawled through.

Tarragon said, 'Jant, may I introduce you to the king of the sea kraits?' She addressed the beast: 'Your Heinouss, this is a messenger from the Emperor of the Fourlands who could soon be your Emperor too, if you agree to his terms … Jant, talk to him; he can hear you with his tongue.'

The snake turned its enormous head on one side like a keeling carrack, and rubbed its closed mouth on the promenade. With the grating of a thousand millstones, it scraped great grooves into the cement and uprooted the iron mooring posts on either side. Its eye moved back and forth, appraising me.

I declared, 'Tarragon will show you the direction to the Fourlands' ocean. You and your people can live there if you promise me three things. First, destroy the ship called *Pavonine* afloat in the centre of the harbour, that Tarragon will show you. Second, after that don't damage any other vessels or harm any people. Live in the depths and stay away from the shoreline, so you'll be less likely to cause accidents. Third, our world is threatened by the Insects too; that makes us allies and in the future I might call on you for help again, via Tarragon.'

All the time, the krait's pennant-tongue flicked in and out of its long colubrine smile, picking up vibrations in the air. It was tasting my words. It twisted its head looking for Tarragon and slithered dangerously close to crushing her car before she ran round in front of its eye. It hissed, and I felt its hot, fishy, miasmic breath blow from the arched hole in its lip.

'What is it saying?' I asked.

Tarragon said, 'He wants to know if your sea is of sufficient size. I don't think the Fourlands' ocean is roomy enough to hold every one of the sea kraits. I will tell him that there's only space to allow a few of them through. That way at least some will escape the disaster and their species will survive.'

The snake's glistening body writhed along its whole visible length. Tarragon gave me an encouraging look. 'The King accepts. He is convinced of your honesty; he says he can taste it.'

'How do I know whether to trust a sea snake?'

549

Tarragon laughed. 'You have a Shark's word that you can.'

The meanders of the krait's kilometre-long body drew tighter and closer together as it pulled its head back and smoothly submerged under the water. I stared at it, open-mouthed.

'You will see him once more,' said the Shark. 'Goodbye, Jant. I have to act as their guide and we have rather a long way to swim in this delicious water. Still, we've plenty of time.' Her red dress turned grey, and stippled to continuous sharkskin all over her body. She walked to the very edge of the massive wall, hooked her bare toes over and raised her shagreen hands above her head.

'Don't leave me here!' I cried. I was not only in a completely unknown, alien world, but somewhere in its past.

She turned a shark's cold eye on me. 'Have you not been practising? You should be able to will your way back by now! I advised you to study and I expected you to learn. Well, this is an excellent opportunity to try.' She leant forward, gave a little jump, and fell through the air in a perfect dive. She splashed into the crystal-clear water and did not rise again.

I might have to stay here forever, I thought in panic. I might have to *live* here. Berating myself, I examined the stinking abandoned car but it was already beginning to rot. I kicked it. The dock workers had left when we were talking to the King krait, and I was alone. I sat down and for about an hour, though I had no way of measuring time, I tried to copy the feeling of my return Shifts. I imagined the pull – a plausible path to the Fourlands – growing stronger, solidifying. I grasped it, and dragged myself through.

I lay somewhere that smelt of feathers. Darkness surrounded me. I felt nothing. My body was paralysed; I couldn't move. 'Because you're dead,' a heavy voice pronounced in my ear. I screamed with no sound. This is the wrong world; I've no body to return to. I struggled and thrashed and forced myself awake.

I came to lying on the worn carpet in Ata's cabin, by the linenfold panelled walls and brocade bench on which Rayne sat in front of the stern windows. 'Well done,' she enthused. 'You saved us!' The windows behind her were completely black. 'Shame i' killed you, though.' She smiled and her mouth widened on both sides. She smiled and smiled and smiled. I'm still not home. I'm still not awake!

I squeezed my eyes shut and fought desperately. I then saw a louring landscape with ruined bridges, fortresses, windmills all benighted backlit with raging fire, vast buildings with stone stairways running in every direction. I did not set down there. Someone's fingers were on my face, probing like worms in my mouth; they forced my jaw open and rammed down my throat. I simultaneously woke up and vomited helplessly.

*

I opened my eyelids to two slivers of glazed-green iris but lay otherwise inert. Rayne's pair of bloodstained pumps and Lightning's thick-soled buckled boots stood in front of my face. God, I hate it when I wake up lying in the recovery position.

'He's no' responding,' said Rayne. I felt her thumb my eyelid.

'I am,' I said, but it came out as a breath.

Lightning's voice sounded very weak. 'Well, bloody *make* him respond.'

Rayne made a sound like a shrug and slapped my face. 'His pupils are so thin they're like threads. Can you feel t' Circle working t' hold him?'

'Yes, damn him.'

Rayne slapped my face again and I gasped and spat.

Lightning said, 'Ah, Jant. Everyone fights to survive but you wipe yourself out! You couldn't poison Gio but you do a bloody good job of poisoning yourself! We need you to fly above and drop missiles on the trebuchet team. I know you prefer to be comatose under heavy bombardment; are you hoping to be revived by the cold water when we sink?'

I rolled into a kneeling position and blinked at him. He half-lay on a chair, still shaking with pain. Instead of his longbow he held a smaller bow with pulleys that could be kept drawn effortlessly.

Rayne said, 'Lightning, don' make him feel bad or you'll give him an excuse t' take another dose.'

'The gamin wretch! I'll—'

I whispered, 'You're wrong. You told me to stop the riot and that's exactly what I am doing.'

A ripple jolted *Petrel* hard against the harbour wall, throwing Rayne off balance. The snakes have arrived. I swallowed dryly, then I stumbled to my feet and out of the cabin. Rayne hurried and Lightning struggled after me, up the ladder to the poop deck where I gazed from the rail. The quayside was littered with bodies; its pavement was cracked and the walls of houses demolished where *Pavonine*'s shot had struck. Our figurehead and forecastle had been smashed into a mass of splintered wood. I took it all in with one glance, not knowing if I had really woken. The sky was dark – was this Fourlands or still Shift?

Looking down to the lower level through an open hatch I saw Wrenn sitting on a rope coil, drinking a canteen of water voraciously. Rayne's assistant was sewing the gash that was open to the bone in his arm. The sight brought me back to earth. He knew that Eszai can take wounds – although *not* wounds as serious as that. He must have badly misunderstood what I told him about the Circle.

The *Pavonine* continued her bombardment. Cinna spun the wheel, keeping the ship's stern towards us, rudder at full lock. Tirrick commanded the sweating pirates scurrying inside the treadwheels to ratchet the catapult back. They stacked its sling with slimy rocks from the ship's own ballast.

The *Pavonine* jolted. An unnatural ripple circled her. The water on either side of her hull began to churn and bubble; waves lapped in every direction. Behind her, between her and the beacon island, a long black ridge surfaced. It was domed like a whale's back but it rose higher and higher out of the water, passing the height of the *Pavonine*'s rail. It was the King krait's top lip.

Lightning and Rayne stared, stunned. The men on the *Pavonine* ran about in confused terror as the ridge continued to rise. Two curved sharp fangs emerged parallel with the waves. Longer than pikes they projected from the black arch on the far left and right. The sea krait's jaw showed its green and blue stripes and the water seething as it emerged glowed with phosphorescence.

A hundred metres away from the top lip, in the water between us and the *Pavonine*, the slick lower lip crested up. Men by the catapult shrieked and pointed; on the main deck they ran from one side to the other, unable to fathom what the arches on either side of them could be. The krait's open mouth ascended, its teeth curved towards the *Pavonine*. The ridged black skin of its upper palate faced us, twice the size of the mainsail and glistening like tar. Water sluiced off its smooth bony head.

The smoke-filled sky resonated with the pirates' screams as far as the town. I had the impression that the whole sea bed was ascending. Water thundered out of both sides of the krait's open mouth; in the rocketing froth between its upper and lower jaws the *Pavonine* danced and spun like an eggshell in boiling brine. The cocked catapult went off, hurling shot vertically into the air.

I heard Cinna screeching. The snake's lance-long teeth reached the height of *Pavonine*'s foremast, curving above the ship and caging it in. *Pavonine* canted over so far the crow's-nest on its mainmast slapped the water, now on the port side, now the starboard, throwing off men. The krait's bottom jaw obscured the ship. Its yellow eye emerged, surrounded with wet black skin, waves battering against it.

For an instant the water inside its mouth was carried higher than the harbour water. The snake reared out of the sea, bearing the *Pavonine* up. Sailors clung onto the ropes, dropped off with raucous screams.

Foaming brine spurted out both sides. The sea krait closed its mouth, with one sickening crunch.

In the sudden silence, the bitten-off masthead of the *Pavonine* tumbled to the surf. It floated, no bigger than a matchstick, beside the diamond-shaped snake's head projecting straight up from the waves. Its body rose to the surface, blocking the harbour entrance, and the length of it extended to the horizon. The King krait lowered its head and turned to look at us.

Lightning scrabbled for an arrow, stammering, 'What is that ... ?' He flexed his bow, aiming directly for its yellow eye.

'No!' I put my jittery hand over the arrowhead and forced it down. 'Don't shoot!'

Lightning gaped at me, striving to understand. 'Why not? Its carcass won't block us in. The sun will rot it. It will rot away.' He yelled at the sea krait, '*What are you?*'

The snake's long mouth stayed closed but the black tongue whipped out like a pennant at the summit of its snout, curling down to our railings, licking slickly in front of me. I assumed the krait was tasting the air for my scent. I actually admired its beauty and overwhelming incalculable strength. I waved my arms to it, grinning madly with gratitude. 'Thank you! Thank you in the name of the Emperor – now go find a home!'

It tilted its head to the side, but as it sank it scanned the *Stormy Petrel*'s deck with its great amber eye. The sea rushed back with a noise like rolling boulders, closing over the snake's eye, upturned mouth, pointed nose; the nostrils last to submerge. An enormous V-shaped ripple formed where, underwater, it began to haul its massive body and retract its head from the harbour.

I swear there was a gust of wind as everybody on the *Stormy Petrel* exhaled. The quay was silent for a second – it *was* silent, the fighting had stopped. I heard weapons fall and clanking as bags of loot dropped to the ground.

Pandemonium broke out as, shoulder to shoulder, some soldiers and pirates moved closer to the waterfront to stare at the floating topmast, the broken pieces of canoes and pontoons where the krait had been. The rest, especially the Trisians, tried to run as far from the sea as possible, back into town. The rioting on the quayside and all the way up the boulevard had completely ceased; everybody was watching the ocean.

'Did ... ?' Lightning stammered. 'In the name of ... god's arse ... I can't believe I just saw that.' He turned on me. 'Why do you keep stopping me from shooting monsters?'

'It saved us, Saker; it's a friend.'

On my other side Rayne spoke calmly. 'You were in too deep, Jant, if you reached Vista Marchan.'

I goggled at her, but she simply smiled.

'How did you know that *thing* was going to appear?' Lightning demanded.

I seated myself on the deck; I was too nauseous to question Rayne. I moaned, 'Oh, please let me lie down. They've stopped fighting. I halted the riot; we've won.'

'We los' so much, Jant, tha' I doubt you could call i' winning.'

Lightning nudged me with his boot. 'I see Vendace and the senators approaching the gangway. At the moment I don't think relations between Capharnaum and the Castle could be any worse. Can you address them?'

Rayne said, 'Jant is very disorienta'ed; I don'—'

I nodded. 'Yes. I will speak for the Castle.'

Scavenger smoke rifled across the sky. The moisture of the sea breeze condensed on the library's fumes to form a thick cloud descending over the crag; we gradually lost sight of the blackened, burnt-out Amarot. The air was filthy and muggy, unfamiliar to the senators. They stood huddled together, coughing. The sea krait had rendered them speechless and their eyes were downcast; they were in mortal fear. Lightning and I walked unsteadily down the gangplank to the corniche which was littered with debris. Vendace's tunic and unruly grey hair were soot-stained. He looked at the blood on Lightning's shirt, the puke on mine and the ash on us both. He faltered, 'We saw the serpent. Can you communicate with it?'

'I just did,' I said.

They conferred between themselves; they all had a tone of defeat. Vendace said, 'This is so much worse than legendary Insects coming to life. We had no idea that such a serpent existed. How did you summon it?'

'What are they asking—?' Lightning began.

'One minute!' I said to him. I gathered my thoughts and addressed the senators. 'Yes, I summoned the snake to stop the battle and save your homes. I don't want to call up any more but the Archer is furious and unmerciful. You heard us arguing on the ship; he wants to show you what we can do. I'm trying to make him agree not to encircle the island with giant snakes.' I turned to Lightning and addressed him gravely in high Awian. 'We must look like we're conferring. I'm bluffing, but the senators will appreciate the Empire after this. Pretend to be angry and speak to me; quote theatre or something.'

Lightning was quick to understand. He shook his head and said in a stern tone, 'Well, in that case – balsam for lovers.'

I enquired, 'Willows for brides?'

'Briars for the maidens,' Lightning retorted. 'Look, you will explain this afterwards, please?'

I patted his shoulder as if in agreement, 'Oh yes, but I'm positive you won't like it. And to wives we give lilies. Right.' I switched back to Trisian and said, 'My friend and I have decided not to summon the snakes, and to let them abide in the deepest ocean where they will be no threat to your country again.' I extended my hand to Vendace. 'There are many more wonderful things in the Fourlands. We're your allies; please join us.'

Vendace and the others seemed doubtful. His lean shoulders were sagging. 'If all the trials to face Tris from now on will be this arduous, then we cannot resist them alone. We'll give you a message for' – he paused and blanched – 'for San, now he has done to us what he did to the Pentadrica.'

'What?' I said.

Vendace looked at his associates for support, shrugged. 'Everybody knows that centuries ago San let the Pentadrica be destroyed so he could seize power. He deliberately contrived that unfortunate Alyss be slain, and now he's done the same to us.'

I shook my head. 'No, no. San was only an adviser. He would have told Alyss not to visit the Insects' enclave and she must have ignored him.'

Vendace glanced at the murk covering the Amarot, through which glimpses of the blackened library walls came and went. 'That is not what Capelin wrote. I have read the manuscript, many of us have, but now ... how do we prove it? It is ash with the rest.'

I didn't know what to say or who to believe. I searched around for more evidence of our goodwill, took the books from my pockets and gave them to Danio's successor, who was still choking back sobs. 'Here ...'

'Oh, thanks,' she said sarcastically, looking at the titles.

'The Castle's Doctor is here; she'll help your doctors with the wounded Capharnai. Her knowledge and supplies will be useful. We'll repair the damage that has been done, as far as we can. If you need grain ships I shall send them. The Circle is at your command; whatever you think about the Emperor's history and motives, I promise you we will work day and night.'

I thought, we have brought them misrule. Our presence has made Tris grow out of childhood to delinquent adolescence. But scolopendium was still hitting me in waves of sickness and bliss. I was simply glad to be alive, one of the lives remaining.

Our soldiers, seeing Lightning on the quayside, approached him. But he was feverish, so he simply sat down and left me to give the commands while Rayne tended to him. I told the Awndyn Fyrd captain to round up the rebels and put them in the hold. Then came Viridian, Ata's daughter, who had collected the gory pieces of her mother's body. She insisted that Mist Ata Dei be buried at sea, with the respect that was due to a famous explorer and the Circle's Sailor.

I said, 'It's terrible that Mist can never know how Tris turns out.'

Lightning glanced over the broken paving stones, the trebuchet shot and abandoned gold loot on the harbour pavement. His gaze loitered on the sea that splintered the dawn light. He was now as suspicious of the ocean as I used to be, and I loved it because it was not the same sea now the kraits swam in its depths. 'Yes, it is, Comet. And I wonder if the Empire will ever regain a vestige of normality.'

CHAPTER 23

The Castle, January 2021

The paths under the Finials' arches were slippery with snow that had partially melted and then frozen again. The translucent footprints preserved the detailed marks of boot treads and hobnails. Frost rime edged the stone leaves on the Architect's Tower, and icicles so long you could spit Insects with them hung from the Bridge of Size, which took the cobbled Eske Road across the Moren River. On the lawns between the Simurgh Wing and outer wall, two centimetres of snow were sealed beneath a centimetre of sparkling ice, blue in the early morning light.

I waited outside the Throne Room in the small cloister, staring out of one of its pointed glassless windows. I was contemplating the fact that if you put the world's finest – athletically or intellectually – into one Castle and let it stew for a thousand years, the results will not always be palatable.

Looking south between the outer wall and palace, the roof had been rebuilt on the Harcourt Barracks, where the Imperial Fyrd are based. Men were repairing the Dace Gate barbican, and all along the curtain wall flags flew at half mast.

Next to me, on the spandrels between the little arched windows, were green-men carvings, dead faces with branches growing out of their loose decaying mouths. Their sole purpose was to remind us that one day we will die and be nothing but plant food. It is a thought that spurs Eszai to keep their places in the Circle and mortals to do great deeds and join them, or be remembered for their great deeds alone.

Tris would take years to recover from the damage Gio caused. Lightning, Wrenn, Rayne, Viridian and I had left the island one month after the riot. I last saw it diminishing in the distance under a sunset pink from the amount of soot and burnt book dust high in the air. 'Ata's sunsets,' the Capharnai have come to call them.

Lightning was staying at Awndyn convalescing, and with Wrenn's help he was arranging for a monument to be built on Grass Isle in honour of Ata. Thousands of her extended family had gathered there; I found the way her whole network had clung together rather alarming. But most of all I felt sympathy for Lightning because he also had to find some way of explaining it to Cyan.

I had spent yesterday relating the battle to San, the ensuing riot and the debt we owe to the fifth land: Tris, manorship of Capharnaum. I was now to answer for giving the sea kraits a lodging in our world.

I looked up as Rayne emerged from the Throne Room. 'Now i's your turn,' she said. 'I told San everything I witnessed.'

'You told him about Vista Marchan?'

'Yes, but I couldn' tell if he was surprised.'

I said, 'It's hard to believe I'm not the only Eszai who knows about the Shift. And to find out that *you* have taken cat.'

Rayne grinned like a crack in a walnut, showing mottled gums. 'When I were a girl. I was a lass once, Jant; isn't tha' amazing? Rumours were rife a' t' university about i's effects. I only experimen'ed once, in a spiri' of scientific enquiry; I didn' like t' hallucinations because they were extremely intense. When I saw t' snake I though' i' were like t' krai' I saw when I dreamed I was walking in Vista. Then I though': hmm, that was under the influence of t' fern scolopendium too. Jant, I *wanted* t' go t' Tris. I wanted t' keep abreas' of new discoveries. But t' mos' interes'ing thing I learned wasn' Trisian; I have reconsidered my hypothesis.'

I sighed. 'People can learn to meditate their way through the Shift worlds. I doubt I'll ever be successful at it, but you might be able to – you're good enough to feel the Circle.'

We looked at each other, wondering if the Emperor himself might have visited the Shift. For all we knew, he might walk there nightly, observing the Insect hordes preparing to burst through into different parts of the Fourlands.

'I have no desire to go back to the Shift, Rayne. Ever since seeing the King krait, how powerful he was, the beauty of his striking colours, and how content and happy the stinguish are, I feel freed from my craving. I'm ready to straighten out. When I'm through withdrawal and recovered from the trauma, I'm going to spend Gio's treasure on Wrought.'

'For t' stability of Awia.'

'To win Tern back.'

'You know, Tern felt t' Circle break. She said tha' she worried herself sick with t' though' tha' i' was you. She asked t' Emperor if you had died and if she was aging, bu' he wouldn' tell her.'

I was aware that San was waiting. I pointed to the Throne Room door. 'Come with me. I don't want to walk in there by myself.'

We progressed down the scarlet carpet and through the portal in the screen like a couple about to be married: Rayne in her shawl that had seen better days at the turn of the millennium and me in a new shirt and waist-coat, with a long velvet scarf, fine black eyeliner and my hair cut so short it was cruel to my sharp-boned face.

Rayne curtsied and seated herself on the bench and I knelt before the dais. The shining sunburst behind the Emperor's throne reflected light in all the zestful colours of the stained-glass windows.

'Comet,' San said. 'You brought serpents from the Shift to infest our ocean. I cannot think of anything more dangerous and irresponsible than your playing with the boundaries and indigenes of worlds.'

I bowed my head. 'Tris is part of the Fourlands; the Fourlands is part of the Shift. They've always affected each other. As far as Insects, maritime creatures and ... and myself are concerned, it's a continuum.'

'The snakes will pose as big a problem in the sea as Insects do on land!'

'My lord, I assure you they won't attack us. They only eat the huge whales that never come near land.'

'And do we not need the whales and shoals? Furthermore the sudden appearance of a sea serpent will threaten people's very perception of reality.'

I was still desolated that Capharnaum library and its precious manuscripts had been lost. I looked up to let the Emperor perceive my anger. He couldn't expel me from the Circle so soon after Gio's rebellion. Although there was much less unrest in the Fourlands now, a bibliophile Messenger can be just as dangerous as a vengeful Swordsman. The Emperor needed me, a Trisian scholar known to the Senate and the sea beasts, and, though unwilling, his loyal servant all year. He sent us out to deal with battles and infernos and he offered no reward, just the measly Castle grant and yet more lifetime. I wondered again about his motivations, but no matter how much I cared I could do nothing. If I angered San he would make me mortal, and without him the Fourlands would be swamped by Insects.

I thought of the picture in the history book, showing San as an unassuming sage-turned-soldier. I spoke with determination: 'I know that my decision was best. It saved us and Capharnaum. We stopped Gio, and the Senate will be governors of Tris. You gave me to understand that we should use whatever means necessary, and calling the kraits was the right thing to do ...' My voice crawled slower and slower and dried up like a snail on a dirt track.

'You sound unrepentant, Comet.'

'My lord.' I fixed my gaze on the apse where the fifth land's column should be.

The Emperor understood and regarded me for a long time. 'Whatever happens, we can do little about sea kraits at the moment. If mariners and whalers sight them, hopefully they will believe that kraits have continually inhabited our sea. There have always been legends of monsters.' He paused. 'Comet, you will not tell anyone of the Shift.'

'I promise.'

'I doubt a debauchee such as yourself can keep his word! How many times has the Circle brought you back from the Shift when you would otherwise have died? Immortality was not meant for that purpose, Comet. Next time I am afraid the Circle will not be able to hold you. One more fatal overdose will indeed be fatal.'

The rest of the world would believe that scolopendium had at last killed me. I fiddled with my earring, thinking that anyway my private playground was somehow spoiled, now that I knew other Eszai had visited it. The meaning of Epsilon had changed and I no longer had a yearning to go there, especially after my experience trying to Shift home. I didn't think I was going to miss it.

I said, 'I can do without it. I don't want to be addicted any more; I want to be cured. The last thing Mist said to me was, "Stop sulking, Jant."'

Rayne stepped in on my behalf: 'I'll look after him and treat t' condition. I don' think he will go back to scolopendium again. T' prognosis is excellen'.'

The Emperor said with a warm tone, 'Well, I thank you, Comet. Despite your injudicious decision with the sea kraits, your service to the Fourlands has been invaluable. Now go with Rayne, and in the fullness of time you will invite the Trisians to compete in a games for the Sailor's position. You will send mortal emissaries who weren't involved to talk at length with the Senate, to invite them here and reduce tensions in Capharnaum.'

I bowed and took my leave. I paced past the screen and the first of the Zascai benches. San's voice called from behind me, 'What of Gio Ami's fortune?'

I stopped dead. *Damn.* I turned round slowly and slunk back, as the Emperor continued, 'That which you salvaged from the Senate House square? Rayne told me that she saw you leading a retinue of servants dragging metal coffers up to your apartments.'

Was there nothing San didn't know? I imagined my hard-won plunder disappearing into the Castle's vaults, or being divided up into projects that I would never see. I sighed, resigned. 'My lord, what do you want me to do with Gio's treasure? I intended it for Wrought.'

'In that case, Messenger, I believe it would be best if you keep it.'

CHAPTER 24

Tern walked through the ruined square, the walls of which are now just shapes of drifts. Snow piled up ever higher by the Northwest Tower. She climbed its staircase, cased in ice. The door of my apartment closed and she let her long coat fall to the floor. I lay naked in bed and watched her. I have plenty still to fight for but also plenty to celebrate.

I had arranged Gio's treasure around the room. Gold chains hung from the mirror, silver plates gleamed on the mantelpiece. Stacks of bar silver armoured the fireplace, constellations of coins glittered on the rug. I had draped the four-poster bed entirely in jewellery. Tern came to examine the riches; she stroked them and she began to smile.

Her fingers on my skin left delicious tracks of sensation, like sparks. I told her she was beautiful. She ducked under the sheet, tented it over her shapely shoulders. I threw my head back and howled.

A little while later, someone rattled the door handle, but it was locked.

Thank you to Simon Spanton and Diana Gill. I am incredibly grateful to my agent Mic Cheetham for her help and support. Many thanks to M. John Harrison and to Richard Morgan for giving me time. Thank you to Stuart Huntley of The Schoole of Defence for some of the moves in the Chapter 1 duel. Thank you to Chris Jackson and the crew of MV *Chalice* for minke whales and sea eagles. Thanks to Lynn Bojtos, Cath Price and Gillian Redfearn for hanging out at the Castle. Love and thanks to Brian for everything – touché!

THE
MODERN
WORLD

✦

TO BRIAN

He let go by the things of yesterday
And took the modern world's more spacious way.

CHAUCER, *The Canterbury Tales*

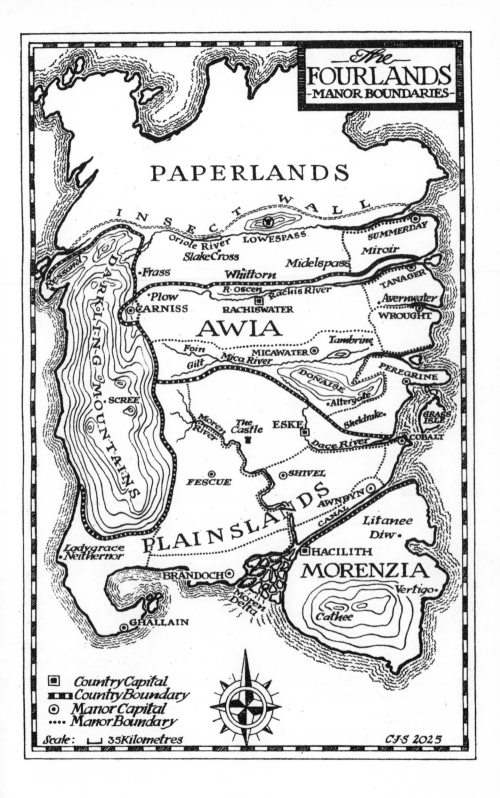

I wake, and lie motionless on my camp bed in the dark tent, listening. The wind roars down the gaps between my pavilion and the next, hisses over the guy ropes. Outside, heavy canvas cracks and flaps. The lantern outside my tent door vibrates on its iron stake and sets up a loud humming. When the gust dies back it unmasks the din that woke me. Soldiers are screaming. Men are shouting to each other in the absolute darkness outside. The gale gusts again so loud I can't distinguish anything at all. I can have been asleep for only a couple of hours; it must be one or two in the morning.

I throw my blankets aside and leap off the bed. As my bare feet touch the damp grass the ground shakes so violently I fall to my knees. My bed and the low cane table next to it collapse, spilling my letters and clothes onto the sparse grass. Is it an earthquake?

The tremor surges strongly, a guy rope snaps and in the gloom I see the poles of my fyrd-issue pavilion start to lean to the right. The walls begin to droop, gathering creases.

There is a constant banging, the lantern flame wavers. Its light blows out: suddenly everything is totally black. Its pole hits the ground with a thump.

Wind puffs out the walls then sucks them hollow, drawing in the far-off sound of a desperate, unearthly shrieking, urgent hammering and splintering wood. That isn't human. What's going on? What's happening? I fumble around trying to find my matches, before I realise what it is. Animals are making that noise. Horses. What the fuck would make them scream like that? They're in their stalls at the top of camp; the smashing is their hooves beating the gates where they're trapped. Their noise is solid panic but I can't hear anything else. In a second the power of their agony winds me so tightly on edge that I whimper. I grab my combat trousers off the grass, hop about on a bare foot shoving one leg into them, then the other, pull them up to my waist, button them.

The gale swells and punches the tent walls. The horses' screams die out, one by one. Now I can hear men and women yelling, their shouts come from both sides and from the row of pavilions in front of mine.

'Help!' A man's cry fragments in the wind. Footsteps thump on the duckboard track outside, resounding in both directions. People are running to and from the centre of camp; I can't tell what they're trying to do. Lamps flare outside, far on the other side of the pavilion lines, towards the gate. Their light shines through my walls as yellow dots with fuzzy haloes, outlining the ridges of the surrounding tents.

I thrust my toes without socks into clammy leather boots, shoving them right down to the hard sole and drawing the bucket tops over my knees. I pick up my scale-mail hauberk, hold it up, jangling, over my head and struggle into it as if it is a jumper, leaving the bottom straps loose. Its freezing scales slap against my bare skin but I have no time to put on the undershirt.

I fumble my left arm into my round shield's leather loops. I can't see anything but blackness at ground level. I feel for my ice axe, snatch it up and wriggle its webbing strap over my hand, around my wrist. The canvas ceiling sags down to my head. Its rear wall billows in on a cold blast, carrying the smell of tough grass and wet moss. The ropes stretch to breaking strain, then yank thick pegs out of the ground.

I dart to the entrance, unlacing the flaps from each other with my long, white fingers up in front of my face. A silhouette stumbles past outside, running for its life, then back again in the direction it came. He falters one way then the other, incapable of making a decision, swiping at the air with a broadsword clutched in one muddy hand.

I scrabble out under the cloudy starless sky, onto the planks that serve row fifty-one. I tread on something lumpy and yielding, and look down. It is a severed right hand. I lift my boot toe off its palm and its curled fingers relax slightly.

Abruptly a tremendous noise like a tree trunk breaking crashes through the gale, followed by a running series of snaps starting deep in the night in front of me. It sounds like sailcloth ripping, or a hunter stripping the ribs off a carcass. It approaches louder and closer, peels past me on my right, and ends far behind me with a ear-splitting crack. I crouch wondering what the fuck it was. The wind exalts with twice the strength and splatters water drops from the tent canvas across my face. The palisade must have gone down. Three sides of our square encampment are wide open. The wind roars straight from the high moor with no shelter to break it up and searches out the tiny gaps in my mail shirt. I have a sudden impression of the vast, empty hills. It is five kilometres to our reinforcements at Slake Cross, three to the nearest fortified farm.

This must really be an earthquake if it's strong enough to rip down the palisade. The ground shakes in short spasms. Behind me my whole pavilion collapses with a sigh, blowing air past me. The wind tugs at it, twisting it into a rustling, living form. Torn strips flap past, writhing as they ascend. They fly like flags from the tent next to mine; it has been shredded. Tangled bloodstained clothes roll and wrap themselves around the base of its pole. To my right, towards the centre of camp, the neighbouring tents in the line lie collapsed in the same direction, like trees in a blasted forest. There are more lamps along the track but the ones that aren't dead gutter feebly. I stare into the roaring night but I can't see any further.

572

A dark-haired man sprints along the duckboard, clutching his crumpled, padded undershirt to his naked chest, the greaves on his otherwise bare legs flashing.

'Stop! What's out there?'

He just disappears against the moors' lightless bulk.

I sense rather than see movement on my right towards the fallen palisade. Maybe men, heading away from the tents. They seem to thin out, are gone. I hear clicking and swing round with a breath to my left. Did something scuttle behind the canvas wreckage? My hand is so tight around my axe haft I feel its tally notches pressing into my palm. I bring it up into guard.

A soldier is squatting to shit in front of the next tent. The tent's walls are patched with blood and it emits a warm cloying smell of viscera. The soldier is looking away from me, so terrified that his bowels let go and he's getting it over with as fast as possible.

Another man runs past, wearing nothing but a coat and pants, his pony-tail whisking. I don't know how to stop them fleeing so I yell the rallying cry, 'To me! To me! Minsourai! ... Wake up! ... Wake ...' But there is no one to wake. I can't see inside the laced tents and even if I could I don't want to. I back away; I might be safer at a distance from them.

These are the advance guard, only five thousand men but still too many to rally. Where's Hayl? These pavilions are for his minsourai, mounted scouts who reconnoitre and find routes for the fyrd, locate and mark positions to camp.

I begin to pick my way in the opposite direction towards the centre and the Castle's field headquarters. If we can possibly regroup, the Sun Pavilion will be the best place.

I follow the duckboard raised above the grass that's bruised and pasted down into the mud. The mud is becoming more slimy with blood. Under the boards I see a boot with a lower leg protruding. No sign of the rest of the body. Further on, dismembered limbs scatter the tussocks and track.

The wind batters against me and, somewhere within it, I catch the rasp of an Insect's leg against its shell. I shrink back and stare around. I can't see anything!

Behind me, something the size of a pony but with thin long legs skitters across the track. I glimpse a flash of red-brown shell. They're everywhere! My scalp tingles: at any moment one will lunge out of the night and grab me before I even see it.

Far on the other side of camp, lights are clustering and moving away. I'll try to reach them. If I can trust what I've heard, the palisade's still upright over there.

The wind gusts from every direction carrying the brief sound of mandibles chopping closed, like a whetstone on a scythe blade. Closer to the centre now, the tents on either side are nothing but shreds. Inside one, I hear the sound of bone splintering. In each pavilion, ten men are dispatched by bites before they wake up, their bodies twisted into different postures. Ten men fused together into a slaughterhouse heap so unrecognisable I'll have to use their dog tags to identify them.

The next tent stores the armour consignment that arrived yesterday. I hear crashes as clawed feet skid over the steel, knocking against piles of plate, jostling sheaves of pikes. I smell whiffs and hear scraping from the latrine shack. Insects are in there too, turning over the earth and eating the shit.

The path begins to zigzag. The earthquake has shaken some of its joined sections apart. Then I see it folded into peaks; the boards are still connected but standing on their ends.

Grey eye facets glitter. I glimpse an Insect face-on. It pulls back into the darkness between two pavilions. Its triangular antlike head moves up and down; it is tangled among crossed tent ropes, severing them with bites. Pieces of paper and torn pennons fly through the night, brushing the ground and catching against buckled ridge poles.

I see angular shapes of Insects standing, feeding on the corpses. A brush of air, something rears. Instantly I see jaws like stag beetle mandibles, then it crashes into the shield. Its jaws slide off the curved edge. I yell and swing my axe, feel it connect. I free the axe and bring it down again. It's dead. It's dead! Calm down! Short breaths rush in and out as I feel not think – how many more? I have to get away. I plunge down the track, running blindly. I'm on the verge of completely losing control, then I stop.

The track has ended. There are no more planks.

At the same moment a heavy gust blusters against my face carrying the unmistakable firm burnt copper scent of Insects. When as a child I lost my milk teeth, pulling at a tooth and turning it rushed a salty blood taste into my mouth, and I had a strange sore pleasure from turning a tooth on a flesh thread or biting down the sharp underside onto my gum. That's what Insects smell like, and it's so intense there must be hundreds. How have they appeared inside the camp? My jaw prickles as if I'm about to vomit. I gulp down saliva and I let out a scream to release the fear.

'Jant!' a voice answers, faint on the wind. It is Tornado, bellowing but I think I hear an edge to it as if he's in pain. 'Jant, where are you? Hayl, is that you?'

'Tornado!' I yell with all my strength.

'Jant! Jant!' Tornado sounds desperate. 'Fuck—'

The wind's noise rises higher and higher. If I open my wings, it will smash me into the ground.

Something whizzes past my face, with the gale, and thuds into the duckboard behind me. I crouch down to investigate. An arrow is sticking in the plank at a steep angle, its bodkin point embedded deeply. Its shaft and white fletchings are still quivering. I start to hear, but not see, more arrows hissing down. They pelt from the sky, from somewhere ahead of me, not spent, striking with force.

I raise my shield in front of my face and feel it jar. Arrows come down like hailstones sweeping across the track, thudding into the corpses, into the soldiers who are still alive but wounded, lying on the ground sweating and twitching. All the ground I can see is filling with arrows. Our archers must be a couple of hundred metres away. Why are they shooting at us?

I yell into the night, 'Stop!' and the wind tatters my voice.

Invisible arrows strike the board in front of my toes; one deflects off my shield and drops at my side. They catch in tent fabric. I hear them tap on an Insect shell and the clicking of articulated claws as it scuffles under fallen canvas.

The arrows buzz in well-timed flights, but I can't hear any voice ordering the loosing. Who's out there? Lightning – if it is Lightning – must have concluded that everybody is dead or beyond help. The archers will be terrified. They're protecting themselves and they're never going to stop. I hurry away from them, stumble over a shaft embedded in the track, and break it.

I catch a glimpse of a single flickering light ahead. It illuminates a white tent from inside. All around is dark so the tent, rectangular because it's side-on to me, looks as if it is hanging in the air. The light moves slowly, in jerks, along at floor level. It inches towards the entrance; closer and closer. A sense of dread weighs on me because I know what I am going to witness next will be even worse. Whatever comes out of that tent is the last thing alive this side of camp and I don't want to see it. I don't want to have to deal with wounds so awful. It will be mutilated and driven so insane by agony it won't even be human any more. I fervently hope that it dies before it emerges.

A lean hand clutching a lantern pushes out from the flap and Laverock crawls out on his hands and knees – head, shoulders, chest. I know him as a minsourai captain, a local with vital knowledge of Lowespass. Digging ramparts made him sinewy, with shorn hair and a face like a weathered leather bag. He was raised with the constant pressures of the Insect threat and Awian ambition.

An arrow snicks into the grass beside him, its flights upright.

'Laverock!' I cry.

He looks in my direction, not recognising me. As he draws his legs from the tent flap I see he doesn't have feet. His feet have been bitten off above the ankle, though not cleanly because sharp tubes of white bone stick out from the severed ends: they look like uncooked macaroni.

Insect antennae flicker after him. Bulbous, faceted eyes follow and the thing strikes forward. Laverock's eyes widen in terror. He pushes himself upright and tries to run on the stumps but his bones sink into the ground like hollow pegs. The Insect seizes his hips low down; its jaws saw over his belly. Laverock knows this is his last second. He snarls in fury as he falls and swings round the iron lantern dangling from his hand. He smashes it over the Insect's head. Yellow-flaming liquid spreads over its brown carapace. I smell scorching chitin, then Laverock's shirt and wings catch fire. His long primary feathers drip and shrink as they burn, as if they're drawing back into his wings. The Insect bites through his body and with a shake of its head throws the top half towards me. The Insect and Laverock's remains sink to the ground, welded together in the fire, vivid against the line of wrecked tents.

By their light I can suddenly see I'm standing at the edge of a vast pit. The flames jump up and shadow its far side, twenty metres away. I stare at it, uncomprehending: this should be the centre of camp. The conical hole gradually, steadily, widens. Turf breaks off under my feet and rolls into it. I step back, seeing that the slope is covered with debris. On the other side, the Sun Pavilion, collapsed down the incline, lies plastered to it like a gigantic wet sheet, trailing ropes still attached at their ends to dirty uprooted pegs. The brass sun bosses that top its main poles glint among its folds. Dead men are splayed out around and underneath it, pale and naked or half-dressed, some still in sleeping bags. As soil rolls down, they slide towards the base of the cone. Their limbs shift position with jerky marionette motions – they look as if they're waving. Swords and broken camp bed frames rattle off stones in the soil as they slide; kitbags spill their contents.

Tornado's voice peals out again, 'Jant!' I look up to see the giant man standing on the far bank beset by seven Insects, five on the slope in front of him and one on his either side. Yet more Insects are running up out of the crater. Tornado backs himself against an empty ambulance cart. It has 1st DIVISION LOWESPASS SELECT roughly stencilled on the side, and its spoked wheels have curved boards nailed to the rims, to widen them and prevent them sinking in the mud.

Tornado's breeches are slashed and blood wells up from red cuts underneath. It flows down his leg from a deep wound in his thigh. His denim shirt is unbuttoned; his big hands curl around the shaft of his double-headed axe. Every second he is taking wounds that would kill me outright.

An Insect below him darts forward but Tornado swings the axe under its mandibles with such force that he decapitates it. He hews down the ones on left and right with a fluid movement. At his feet a mound of carcasses bleeds thick pale yellow haemolymph down the widening pit. Two more Insects run up the slope and over its rim. He deals one a massive blow, cleaving its thorax through. The other seems to brush past him with a movement of its head but it opens a huge streaming gash in the roll of fat over his unfastened belt buckle. Tornado bellows.

He starts to droop forward. He clutches at the cart for support; it rocks on its curved boards. His knees sag and his skin is pallid. He kneels, one knee then the other, head bowed. I can't see his face.

I watch as an Insect climbs the cart from behind, crests the top, appears above Tornado's head as a spiked silhouette, with actions like a jointed puppet. It reaches down to Tornado's rounded shoulders. It starts to feed.

Under their weight, the edge of the pit gives way and they tumble. Tornado rolls, unconscious and arms loose, down the slope. He hits the edge of the mass of debris and lies still, near the bottom. Soil continues to crumble away; the cart's front wheels jolt over the edge. It teeters and then runs straight down the slope. Its wheels' boards slap and leave footprints, its dragging hafts plough furrows. It runs over Tornado's outstretched arm and fractures it, impacts into the duckboards and broken tents, and comes to rest upright on top of him, its four wheels caging him in.

Tornado's down. What chance do I have? The oil is burning off Laverock's Insect and its light is dying down. The shadows shift and I see the base of the pit, where soil has been swept aside from the pale grey bedrock. It has been brushed clean. A wide crack runs across it, separating it into two slabs like deeply buried gravestones. The gap transfixes me – it is pure black – so black that as an illusion it seems to jump and shimmer. I stare at it as arrows still whicker and thud around my feet.

A flash of movement on my left, and an Insect's head with open mandibles lunges at my waist. My elbow's levered up, and before I can stop it, the head is under my shield. I flinch away inside its jaws, with a fast reaction but I can't dodge far enough: it turns and plunges its open left mandible into my stomach like a dagger. I go rigid with the shock of it penetrating. It tosses its head like a bull goring and I feel the razor mandible gouge upwards. My skin parts before it. My loose hauberk rucks up over its head with a metallic rasp. Its cold jaw slits all the way up and hooks under my lowest rib. It tries to continue its carving slice and pulls me onto the tips of my toes. By luck, I stumble backwards and slip off the point.

With my hand clawed I rake over the bastard thing's eye but my nails have no effect and I hate myself for reverting to act like a Rhydanne and scratching, while my ice axe drags on the ground.

My strength fails quickly. I raise the axe and bring it down between its eyes, into its forehead plate studded with three smaller eyes and dimpled antennae sockets. The frons plate cracks across like a nutshell and one side lifts up: I glimpse the base of its compound eye rooted in a damp membrane underneath.

577

The Insect rears up and shoves me. I topple backwards and fall. I brace myself but I'm surprised to find I'm still falling. My wings open instinctively. The pit's edge tilts up into the sky above me. I hit the slope hard with my left wing under me and – crack! – its bone breaks.

This isn't my camp bed. Where the fuck—? No: I'm lying on my back on the slope with my wing buckled underneath me and I had better not faint again. My right arm is outstretched, the strap around my wrist is holding me attached to the axe pick still embedded in the Insect's head.

It lies flat; its head moving left and right in its death throes tugs at my arm. Its mandibles open and close. Its flattened forelegs kick back and forth, scooping soil off the top of the slope. Turf chunks and grainy dirt sift down on top of me, covering me lightly all over.

I clutch one hand instinctively across my stomach but the gash is too long to hold together and my fingers sink under the edge of the flap of skin. It is warm and very slick. I feel a loop of gut spill out over my arm. I look down and see it adhering to the ground, picking up pieces of soil and grass blades. Unable to stop it, I watch it uncoil out of my midriff from under the mail shirt. The guts slither over each other; they are different shades of grey and firm to the touch.

All I can see of my wing is the bicep and a sharp shard of broken bone sticking out of the muscle close to my body between the black feathers. As I breathe out, air rushes out of the hollow bone. The air sac inside it inflates slightly out of its pointed end. It is a very thin, moist and silvery membrane. I know that Awians have two air sacs deep in their backs and in their limbs' long bones nearest the body; humerus and femur, but I'd never seen one balloon out before. I breathe in, dizzy from shock and lack of air, and it inflates. I exhale and it flutters where it's ruptured and the air flutes out. Under the feathery skin around it, a blister starts to grow as escaping air is trapped there. Oh, fuck. That's me fucked then if I'm breathing through the bone.

The ground shakes but I don't roll further down the slope because I'm anchored to the dead Insect at the top. I can't muster the energy to turn myself over and crawl. I can't move. I'm going to die here. I have to do something, anything, not just give up. The wind gets under my broken wing and blows it around, grinding as it twirls on the bone. Between gusts it settles down slowly on top of me, then the wind picks it up again. I take my hand from my ripped stomach and reach out to flatten it against the ground but the feather tips still curl up.

The agony begins. It is fiery and sharp, a white-hot blade the length of my side. I lie with my cheek in the cold, uneven soil like a toad's back and scream. Mud grains get into my mouth and coat the back of my tongue. I grit my teeth and they grate against the surfaces. I feel soil filling my nostrils,

I retch with the earthworm smell of loam and cut roots. I scream wordlessly with all my strength, trying to relieve the pain. A human or Awian would scream for help, but Rhydanne don't because Rhydanne know there is no help to be had.

I can feel the sweat trickling out of my hairline and a stream of blood running freely out of my side, into the ground. I didn't know I had this much blood.

The uneven piles of dirt close beside me, that I know are tiny, now seem as impassable as mountain ranges, and dark with the organic matter of rotting soldiers ... whom I will soon join.

The black sky rains arrows. The wind's noise is a great distance above me; it doesn't affect me any more. I feel a warm patch spreading between my legs: I have wet myself. I begin to suffer from an overbearing sense of shame. What will people say when they find out I've wet myself and my trousers are sticking to my crotch? But I will be long dead by the time they find me, if they find me at all.

I take another mouthful of dirt and scream again, petrified by the thought of leaving the world for ever. I'm twenty-three; I don't want to die. I'm one hundred and thirty years old, I don't want to die. I can't feel my toes or fingers, then feet or hands, then legs or arms. The cold clings to my skin like wet cloth. It permeates my bones and my muscles ache with tension. I can't curl up against it. I am shivering from the freezing air in the wound, it reaches inside my body until I feel as if I am more naked than naked.

I quickly run out of energy and lie exhausted, with my throat raw. The damp ground at last feels comfortable against my cheek. I am as cold as the soil, throughout my body, as if I am already part of it. I start to forget how to breathe. How still I am. I can hear an Insect's claws scraping underground as it pulls itself through the crevice in the rock.

I sink into fatigue and start slipping into warm sleep despite the pain. I am dimly aware of my body shutting down. I fight to stay awake, in furious denial, but why bother ? No one is left to help me. Sleep tempts me. I scream at myself – if you sleep you die! Stay awake! The numbness seeps deeper and I have no choice. It steals up inside my core. While my consciousness fights fiercely to stay awake, a part of my mind falls asleep, then another, blocking it in. I can't revive my memory. I can't wake my sense of hearing ... touch ... vision ... I am surrounded by sleeping mind; I die.

CHAPTER I

I woke. I tried to sit up and banged my head hard on a wooden plank above me. Shit, had they put me in a coffin already?

I was curled up tightly in a tiny space, tense with suppressed panic. I calmed down, relaxed and remembered where I was. It isn't 1925, it is the year 2025, and we are six kilometres south of the Wall in Slake Cross town. I had been sleeping folded up on the lowest shelf of an enormous bookcase. My wings extended, half-spread, taking up metres of the paved stone floor.

Frost, the Architect and owner of the bookcase, was sitting behind her table a few metres away. She glanced down. 'It's nearly nine o'clock, Jant. We only have an hour until the meeting, remember?'

I unpacked my long legs, stood and stretched, attempting to tie my hair back so I could see her.

Frost sounded curious: 'Did you have bad dreams again? Was it the nineteen twenty-five massacre?'

'Yes. I have flashbacks every time I come here. God, I hate this place.'

'I'm not surprised you have bad dreams if you sleep on a shelf. Sometimes I forget you're a Rhydanne but then you do something really bizarre. Tornado and Lightning haven't been bothered by nightmares.'

'They weren't eviscerated, and besides, they remember worse disasters.' I hooked my thumb in the pocket of my jeans and pulled the waistband down to show the old knotty scar that curved up the left side of my stomach.

'Yeuch. Still, you should have got over it by now. Have you been under the influence?'

'No.' Not since that last handful of mushrooms anyway, and whatever I'd washed them down with. 'I'm clean.'

'Well, being "clean" seems to have done wonders for your vanity.'

I had unfolded a little mirror to check the kohl around my eyes. My irises were dark green like bottle glass, the pupils vertical like a cat's, backed with a light-reflecting membrane. It's a Rhydanne trait. So are my silver bangles and a brightly coloured serape shawl wound around my waist, its indigo tassels hanging down. But I am half Awian and at the moment my clothes are too; well-tailored boot-cut riding trousers. The faience beads and broken buzzard feathers in my black hair. Then there was the natty slashed shirt I picked up in Wrought, through which I was windburnt, so now with the sleeves rolled, my arms were brindled and spotted. I had spent the last six months carrying messages for Frost and constant flying had honed me down to bone and muscle. I feel so much better these days and everyone can see how much better I look.

I stretched my wings and Frost watched the workings of the joints, unfortunately not with the eye of a woman who finds them attractive, but as a fascinated engineer. Frost, through and through a Plainslander, was a human without wings. She looked to where the limbs, as thick as thighs, joined to me above the small of my back. The muscles around my sides, attached to the tops of my hips, drive them.

I folded them both neatly so the quills lined up, like organ pipes emerging from delicate, corrugated skin. The limey Lowespass water had dulled my feathers.

Frost sat behind a rough table in the middle of the hall, with a large brass coffee pot at hand. Propped up against it was her small and extremely threadbare soft toy rabbit with one eye. It had been a present from her husband more than three hundred years before. The coffee pot and the rabbit weighted down a stack of papers, a mound of dog-eared textbooks and notes, all in Frost's handwriting but some of the paper was ancient. An enormous chart of the Oriole River valley curled off the table at either end. Fiendish equations were pencilled across it; underscoring, memos and neat, blocky doodles. Her genius calculations were written in lines; tiny numbers and letters. There were all sorts of little triangles there too. I appreciated the little triangles.

Frost presided over this orderly mess, a double-handled glazed mug cradled in her square palms. Her round face was slightly blotchy without any trace of make-up and her nose was red. Dryness lines bunched together around her eyes and two vertical creases between them made her look fearsome, but they were caused by peering into windswept trenches, not by scowling. She had a bulky brown ponytail with a few grey hairs twisted and tethered behind her head with a clip. Wiry strands fizzed out of it, around her broad forehead and the pencil wedged behind her ear.

The arms of Frost's chunky cardigan were rolled back into bunches above her elbows. Its wool was pilled and marred with snags. She had knotted a kerchief around her neck and her big thighs in comfortable trousers fitted into the seat of her camp chair. Frost was not concerned with the niceties of dress and she only ever wore black. Her feet, in thick socks and steel-toed boots, rested alongside a stack of architectural plans on graph paper taped to drawing boards.

The hall was thirty metres long, echoing and austere; its half-round ceiling arched above us like the inside of a barrel. Since Frost had begun to use it as her office, she had covered its trestle tables with samples of masonry; keystones, voussoirs and coping stones milled into interesting shapes. There were metal boxes – dumpy levels for surveying, pattress plates for strengthening brickwork, a basket of red-painted corks to measure water flow and an intricate scale model of the dam. The oil lamps hanging from the brick vault had just been lit as evening was wearing on and, against April's chill, a fire was set in the hearth. Frost's assistants were pulling some benches into rows. I reflected that her world is rather more practical than mine.

She said, 'Lightning and the Queen are out walking on the dam. They've been there since dawn; they said it was the best vantage point to decide how to position the fyrd. Can you fly over there and ask them to join us?'

I mimicked the Queen's decadent voice, 'Oh, my darling, *must* I?'

Frost's mouth twitched. A smile only escaped her when her guard was down. 'You've got her beautifully. Yes, you must. I mean she must. She probably finds it as tiresome as I do.'

'Have you seen any reporters yet?'

'God, no. Most of them are waiting in the Primrose. You know I don't like talking to them. They twist everything I say and I can tell they're not really interested. They wouldn't get even the most basic facts wrong if they were. I don't know why I bother holding press conferences. Everybody apart from journalists finds the dam self-evident, and their waffling questions always lead me away from the point.'

'I'll make sure it goes smoothly.'

She pulled her oversized cardigan closed and sipped her coffee. 'This is the culmination of years of work since I unveiled the model. The dam has occupied my every waking hour ... and my sleep too. But I doubt the reporters care. They look for other stupid stories and then concentrate on the wrong one. They'll chase off after any scandal no matter how momentous the occasion.'

I said, 'It's all right. Don't worry, just leave them to me. I'm used to keeping them in check. If they ask me a question I can't answer, I'll bring you in.' I waved my hand in the air and Frost stared at it. I dug it into my pocket. 'I'll find a quick flight refreshing. The dam breaks up the air in interesting ways. It is a masterpiece.'

'Oh, yes! It really is the most efficient structure! There's never been a dam with the functional strength of this one, there's never been a lake so capacious!' Keen enthusiasm lit her face. She had been boring people on the subject of river engineering for three hundred and fifty years and this was her greatest project. 'It makes Micawater Bridge look like an apprentice piece! Every engineer said I was being overambitious, but the figures were sound. So is the actualisation! They said it was impossible. They said, "You might hold the model in your hands but you'll never raise the biggest construction of all time right on the Insects' doorstep." Three years later, I took them for a tour! Since the Wrought blast furnaces are operational again I've had iron for the rack and pinion cast in segments and assembled here, an elegant solution, you must admit, and you should look out for the way I've bridged the walkway above the overflow conduit so—'

'Frost, please . . .'

'I thought you liked it.'

'I do, but you've just asked me to call in Lightning and Eleonora.'

'Oh yes,' she said, chastened. 'So I did.'

I blew her a kiss with both hands that became a mock bow. 'See you in an hour, OK?'

I walked out to the cobbled central courtyard, enclosed on its three other sides by the cookhouse, mess room and tavern. Each was built of limestone blocks and roofed with lauze; thick, heavy slabs that looked shaggy, like the boughs of a fir tree.

The buildings were pierced with arched alleys, three in each side, just wide enough for one man at a time. They were designed to stop all but the smallest Insects reaching this square, a final refuge if the town's outer defences were ever penetrated.

The plain hall had fulfilled many purposes over the years: a hospital, a headquarters for immortals, and it was now Queen Eleonora Tanager's temporary residence and Frost's office. Frost's orange banner ran along the length of the roof: 'Riverworks Company Est. 1692' in bold black letters. Beside it flew Tanager's swan pennant, Micawater's argent mascle on an azure field, and the Awian white eagle on sky blue.

Soldiers had gathered outside the Primrose Tavern opposite. They sat on stools made from barrels to watch two immortals sparring in the middle of the square. The Swordsman, Serein Wrenn, was fighting the Polearms Master, Lourie Hurricane. They had an Eszai competitive edge to their play; they both knew that if they weren't training, somewhere a potential Challenger was.

Lourie Hurricane was a quiet perfectionist, a tall man from Plow who used to be a vavasour cart-driver before he became immortal. Serein Wrenn, on the other hand, was short and stocky and had the silliest haircut of all the Eszai – waxed up into short spikes with bleached tips. His narrow sideburns tapered into a little chinstrap beard.

Wrenn had come forward and beaten the previous Serein in a fair Challenge, according to the Castle's rules, only five years ago. Many still said that his predecessor was the more steadfast fighter, but Wrenn was quick with the desperate gambit. He had frequently been Challenged until word of his flair spread. He had latched on to Lourie; I think he admired Lourie's ascetic, taciturn poise. In the depths of his aplomb Lourie might have been grateful; it is always the case that Eszai lose friends but gain sparring partners.

These two were often seen together arguing monomaniacally as to whether glaives or broadswords were the better weapons.

There were both objects of great amusement to the other immortals seated nearby watching them fight: Tornado the Strongman, the Sapper, the Artillerist, and Gayle Holthen the Castle's Lawyer who also acted as provost for the fyrd. She was a smart, cosmopolitan woman who had joined the Circle after a full career as a judge.

Lourie swept his glaive in balletic circling moves, not one millimetre out of the perfect sequence. He dipped the two-metre pole, swept the pointed blade under Wrenn's feet. Wrenn jumped it. Its hook caught behind his shin as he landed. Lourie tugged the pole with a grace that belied his strength. Wrenn hopped and let the hook slip out under his foot.

Gayle laughed and clapped her hands, bringing the Cook out of the tavern to watch.

All fifty immortals were arriving. I had been calling them up one by one, either from the Castle or wherever they'd been pursuing their interests else-where. Those involved in advance planning had been here for a month but all would be assembled by the end of the week.

Immortals, called Eszai in the low Awian language, are people proven to be the best in the world at their chosen profession. We all play our parts in the battle, because the Emperor San joins us to the Circle and shares his immortality with us as long as we lead the war. Here at the front we have overall authority, even over governors and the Queen; but elsewhere, or in issues not connected with the war we can do no more than advise them. Likewise, San's word is advice to the world but to us it is law.

Wrenn deflected Lourie's blade. Lourie pulled it back, grinding its rebated edge, and thrust the metal-clad base of the pole. Wrenn parried it with a full-strength clash. The mortals watching gasped, but we Eszai knew Lourie's great skill; we'd seen it a hundred times before.

The Castle saves the very best and improves on it gradually, incremen-tally; little is ever lost. I've been Comet for two hundred years, the fastest Messenger of all time. I'm a freak, yes, but it means I get to live forever.

I turned to the wall behind me, took a grip on the rough stone and pulled myself up. I climbed swiftly past the doorway and the plaque above it; the only decoration in the town. Its sgraffito red plaster, incised through to the white layer underneath, depicted the Castle's sun-in-splendour standard, surrounded by an inscription: 'In memory of the battle at Slake crossroads, one night in the ongoing war. 4981 Plainslanders, Awians and Morenzians died on the 12th of April 1925.'

As if we need to be reminded, I thought as I pulled myself over the gutter-ing and scrabbled up to the apex of the roof. Balancing there, I looked down on the mortal soldiers outside the pub and I suddenly realised they did need to be reminded. The massacre was three generations in the past, long out of their living memory. It meant nothing to them but a date in a schoolbook. I stepped lightly along the ridge, thinking for the first time that I had more in common with the other Eszai than with the mortals, the Zascai, who had no idea what it was like to stumble through the middle of a massacre. I contemplated with dread that no matter how much effort I put in to knowing every up-to-date trend in Zascai fashion and the developments in their business, the gap between us was steadily widening. Well, I decided, it isn't inevitable that I will become as out of touch as Frost or Lightning. I must simply try harder; it's my profession after all.

From the rooftop I saw the series of concentric squares in which the town was laid out. The buildings around the courtyard formed the first of three rings. Behind them ran a wide road, then another ring comprising the smithy, workshops, food, livery and ammunition stores, since Slake Cross is the supply base for all of western Lowespass. Every junction was staggered to prevent any Insects that might get in running straight to the heart of the town.

The smell of hot iron rose from the blacksmith's shop, mingling with the yellow-hay stink of horse turds on the road and the washy smell of potatoes boiling in the cookhouse adjoining the hall.

Below, the innkeeper thwacked a brass tap with a mallet to drive it into an enormous keg of beer. His blows rang around the square together with the wail of the innkeeper's squab and its mother shushing as she tried to calm it. She held it inside her cream shawl, against her breasts. It flailed one naked pinion with three pointed fingers like the wing of a plucked chicken. 'Squab' is Morenzian slang for Awian babies before they are fledged, and it was probably crying from the itching as its pinfeathers were starting to push through.

The long buildings of the third ring were barracks to billet ten thousand troops. I could see the stone cisterns on the shower blocks' roofs, replenished by recent rainstorms. The Awian soldiers had added a sauna and a talcum bath: conditions are bad enough at the front without suffering from lice in your wings.

Then came the stables and allotments, in shadow at the foot of the curtain wall. Mangy apple and hazelnut trees bowed over cramped, tilled plots with green shoots – hardy runner beans and turnips. The soldiers supplemented their diet by growing vegetables but they were only permitted to do so inside the walls because any kind of plant attracts Insects.

A few metal cages beside them each contained an Insect the size of a warhorse. Their jaws and antennae were bound with wire; they were soon to be sold and carted south to the Rachiswater amphitheatre. Their scent set mastiffs barking on the far side of town.

Towers reinforced the exterior curtain wall at intervals along its length and at all four corners. It was tall, height being more important against the Insects than thickness, and it extended below ground to stop them undermining it. Roofed wooden walkways overhung the tops of the walls along their lengths. The single gate faced north towards the Paperlands. A guard with a jaunty crest on her helmet stared out of the large, square windows in the gatehouse tower.

These military towns – Slake Cross, Frass and Whittorn – had been designed by Frost soon after her initiation to the Circle. She became a great favourite with the troops who no longer had to construct open air camps. Each town was in essence a fort, with a shifting population of fyrd and the people who supply them: quartermasters, fletchers, sutlers and male and female prostitutes.

Slake Cross gave me a sinking feeling like the cold trepidation you feel on returning to a place you knew long ago. All your friends have moved on; their houses have strangers in them now. Even the routes you used to walk have changed, because the pubs you knew have been boarded up and cafés opened where they shouldn't be. The last time I was here I was completely screwed up, living on drug time, time measured by needles and veins, not real time at all, and I scarcely noticed how bleak and utilitarian the place was.

I concentrated on the far end of the roof, breathing calmly like a gymnast on the high bar, arms out for balance. I started running, opened my wings and their fingers spread automatically. They dragged, pulling me back, and I pushed at the tiles to find more speed. I lengthened my stride, faster still. I reached the end of the roof, sprang into the air, pulled my legs up and swept my wings down powerfully.

When I begin to fall I always – because I have the same instinct as everyone – expect to hit the ground immediately as if I've merely tripped. But I keep falling, feeling nothing under my feet but more thin air.

Two more desperate beats, and I strained my body upwards in a graceful curve. My wingtips came together in front of my face, then I pushed away and I was no longer falling. I stretched out my legs, lying horizontally.

The people below saw the soft inside surface of my black sickle wings, the sun shining through their trailing edges. I felt air spilling off every flight feather. Their hard and sharp leading edges rasped louder as I beat harder and gained height. I scraped over the tavern's ridge, pushed off with my palms and started laughing ecstatically as I flapped over the road, the barrack ring, the curtain wall and out of town.

*

The Lowespass Road ran straight as a rule. Its cobbled, slightly convex surface was crispy with hoof prints in reddish clay mud. Water filled its drains; since the completion of the dam the whole countryside was like a puddle and pools had begun to appear all over the place.

From the air, Slake Cross looked like a square grey archery target lying on the contours of the pale green valley side. I looked back to the gatehouse. The gate, twice my height, was crisscrossed with deep iron strips. Shallow troughs scarred between them where Insect mandibles had reached through to scrape the old timber. On my right stretched the Lowespass Road and ahead the reservoir glimmered, flat and silver. I was heading towards the Insects' Paperlands covering the entire north bank of the river and as far as I could see into the distance, like a white sheet drawn over the land.

Strong gusts kept me flying low, no more than twenty metres from the ground where I could follow a direct path with the minimum effort. I flew over the crossroads with the smaller Glean Road along which troops arrive from western Awia. The Slake Cross monument, a smooth obelisk, stood there on grass scattered with yellow primroses – fragile blooms transplanted from the river bank before the flooding process began. Ointment made from them is a sovereign salve for wounds, and they had become a symbol of the massacre.

The uncompromising hills were always striding along the horizon, their stony summits rose to mid-sky and framed Lowespass valley. Further east at Miroir there were exposed tracts of moorland covered in peat bogs. Pondskaters V-rippled over black gullies of acidic stagnant water and mosquitoes whined over patches of spongy sphagnum moss among the heather. At this end of the valley the soil was thin. Thistles and ragwort sprouted in the clints and grikes of the limestone pavements. Caves riddled the valley floor. For thousands of years the rainwater has been carving faults in the rock into fathomless potholes and massive chambers, where drops precipitate strange and magnificent formations like the Throne Room columns. The Insects' own tunnels join the system; it does no good to think about it.

Slake Cross town itself is built over a resurgence of an underground stream, so it never lacks fresh water. Frost has used dye to investigate the routes of the system. She started messing about with the water table and everyone watched, unnerved, as the level in the deep well rose to its very brim.

The road crossed uneven ground, slicing through the outcrops, and a larger quarry had scarred the side of a big knoll. I glided over its levelled area where carts were parked, completely covered with hardened white lime dust.

I passed some lime kilns in the side of a cutting; room-sized stone ovens

587

with ragged chimneys, now cold and empty, with charcoal heaps growing damp outside their mouths. Frost had constructed them and employed the stokers; as soon as she knew she had enough cement she had moved them to work on the dam itself. A high wall protected a stand of pine trees, which grew relatively quickly and Frost used for building material.

On the north side of the road was the first of a series of static catapults called petraries, set into a concrete platform slick with pools of green algae. Its waxed wooden beam and sturdy foundations glistened, beaded with rain water. Its cable had been removed and the counterweight box was empty. Barbed wire rolls stacked haphazardly beside its pyramid of ammunition stones. Far off I could just see the nearest peel tower, a link in the chain stretching from Frass to Summerday to monitor Insect activity.

At the river I altered my course, heading upstream to the dam. Bulrushes bowed to the water's creased surface as the wind ruffled through reed beds on the south bank. Its other bank was nothing but mud mashed with three-clawed footprints: Insects had stripped the vegetation bare.

Frost's workings began and the ground changed abruptly. Her company had done nothing less than remodel the valley. Cart tracks criss-crossed the bank; water in their ruts reflected the sky. Broken shovels, dirty string and red striped ranging rods littered the ground, with abandoned workmen's huts, empty burlap bags, splays of spilt gravel.

The overturned earth was glutted with beige specks – calcined bone fragments – some recognisable as ribs or skulls; the remains of generations of men and women. There were pieces of archaic armour and broken Insect shells, which don't easily decay but weather to porous shards. The Insects have been creeping or swarming southward over fifteen hundred years. In response, we constantly move men and supplies to the front to stop them, on such a massive scale that I fancy all the Fourlands will eventually erode and end up here as a series of hills.

The river banks straightened, reinforced by walls of metal mesh boxes full of rubble. The river flowed more slowly but its level had hardly dropped. Frost couldn't allow it to dry up because, since Insects can't swim, the Oriole River was our main defence.

I approached the dam from the front, its stone face a gigantic sloping wall. The ends tapered down and curved towards me like horns. The outflow hole at its base looked like a giant blank eye. A fortified winch tower stood on the crest above it, holding the mechanism to raise the gate. The walkway ran through the tower, blocked with formidable portcullises on entry and exit, so Insects could not cross from the Paperlands.

Lightning and Eleonora were two tiny figures beside it, looking down from behind the split-timber fence. The wind's speed was increasing over the smooth outflow platform. Air hit the wall and hurtled up its slanting surface. I lay with my wings outstretched and let it carry me – square blocks and mortar streaked down past my eyes – I could have filed my nails on them.

Along the whole length of the dam the wind went rocketing up the incline faster and faster until it burst vertically from the edge of the walkway around Lightning and Eleonora and up into the sky.

I soared rapidly past them, hearing the last exchange of their conversation, '—This could be the answer.'

'Perhaps. I just wish that we'd thought of it before.'

I found the right balance to hang motionless above their heads. My shadow fell over them and my boot toes dangled at the level of their faces. They drew back and shaded their eyes, seeing me suspended in the middle of six metres of glorious wingspan.

The enormous lake formed from the backed-up Oriole River spread out behind the dam. On its north bank the water lapped and merged into the mazes of Insects' paper cells; irregular, many-sided boxes ranging from the size of a cupboard to that of a house. Passages wound between them, some covered with pointed roofs, the rest open to the air. They looked like ceramic fungi, or geometric papier-mâché termite mounds.

The lake stood cold and mirror-reflective in the fresh morning light. A swathe of ripples dimpled across its middle, broken by white, angular peaks projecting from the surface: the tops of flooded Insect buildings.

Insects had built and abandoned walls five times as the water level rose. Their tops contoured the irregular lake margin like tree rings. Our old camp and the shakehole that destroyed it were somewhere on the lakebed, completely papered over.

I could just see the Insects' new wall on dry ground ten kilometres distant, beyond the marshes. They had instinctively joined the new stretch to the immense Wall that seals them in, protecting their Paperlands from coast to coast of the entire continent.

I let the wind blow me backwards over the walkway. Little by little I flexed my wings closed and descended. I bent my knees, absorbed the shock, and landed in a crouch with my stiff feathers brushing the paved track on my either side.

I stood and bowed to Queen Eleonora Tanager. She kissed me on both cheeks and studied my face at leisure. 'How are you, darling? Oh, Jant, flying makes you so cold.'

Her attar of roses perfume enveloped me, calling to mind the rose-scented letters that she used to send. They were always crinkled and salty, having been written on her most recent lover's sweaty back. Eleonora was arguably the world's most powerful mortal, but she was shod with scandal; she was no good at delicacy and even worse at tact.

I stepped away and looked at the reservoir's breathtaking expanse. 'It's incredible,' I said. 'I admit I had my doubts. But from up here you can see the extent of Frost's vision. I feel privileged to be part of it.'

Lightning, the Castle's Archer, said seriously, 'Well, I hope it is not just the latest of the thousand plans we have tried and had to put aside.'

Eleonora shivered. She was wearing Lightning's long, fur-lined overcoat and, statuesque as she was, it nearly fit her. Her scale armour glittered underneath. Awians sometimes wear full plate, but prefer their traditional scale mail and I can understand why because plate is horribly restrictive.

She had tipped her helmet back from her head and it hung upside down from a strap showing its green satin lining. It had eye holes and a nosepiece in the Awian style. Its copper-pink horsehair crest rustled against her back and nearly touched the ground. Her chain mail coif and scale shirt were copper-coloured too, and damascened with a raised pattern of feathers matching her greaves and vambraces. She had pulled out her satin undershirt a little between each joint.

Eleonora had a wide, prominent face with a delicate, tip-tilted nose. I should say she was good-looking but she had a sly and filthy smile. Her ecru wings were naturally a different colour than her close-cropped dark hair, a phenomenon so rare I had never seen it before.

I said, 'Queen Eleonora, I don't know if you realise the time but you're already late for the press conference and Frost sent me to call you back.'

'Oh, I suppose we must attend,' she said huskily. She set off along the walkway, between the sheer drop on one side and the lapping water on the other. She strode with a slow, shapely-legged pace; from the deliberate way she carried herself it was clear she was used to being looked at.

She continued to enthuse as we joined her. 'If this works we have a way of destroying the Paperlands completely. The effect's there, right before our eyes! The Insects move out of the flooded area, make a new Wall and retreat behind it. Of their own accord, without any resistance!'

'Then we drain the area and in we go!' I said.

'Let us concentrate on clearing this patch first,' said Lightning.

Eleonora smiled. 'It all depends on infantry. We'll position them while Frost empties the lake. Isn't that right?'

'Yes.' Lightning indicated the town squatting in the mid-distance. A constant queue of mules and baggage carts plodded towards it, bringing provisions and tackle in preparation to set up the camp that would soon be surrounding it. Outriders protected the convoy, riding in formation at specified distances from the road as soon as they entered Lowespass. We had not yet mustered the main body of the cavalry, because they consume

590

a tremendous amount of fodder. In the other direction a tumbrel cart of manure was setting out from the stables towards the pine plantation. 'We will position twenty battalions of Select, wielding axes, there ... and there.'

I said, 'It'll be very muddy once they start to march.'

Lightning said, 'That is an understatement. Think what it'll be like for the battalions in the rear after the first ten thousand have walked over it in front of them. We will need a whole division to lay duckboards as they go. We will progress slowly across the drained lakebed, keeping in line, chopping down the Insects' buildings. Without ...' He savoured the words: 'Without any expectation of casualties at all.'

'I've never been in an Insect cell before,' Eleonora said thoughtfully. 'But they're too close together to take horses through.'

Lightning said, 'When we reach the new Wall, we will secure the area, continue to dismantle the cells and bring up some trebuchets. The Queen's lancers will patrol and act as rearguard.'

The wind was ruffling Lightning's dark blond feathers and making them stand upright. Irritated, he shook his wings out and folded them tightly. I can't believe he gave Eleonora his coat. Doesn't he know her reputation? I looked at him carefully, thinking that even he must be aware of the ribald rumours. Eleonora was the only child of Lord Governor Osprey Tanager, who was killed by Insects twenty years ago, the last of that family. When she was not at the front she held court in Rachiswater Palace, but as soon as she had rebuilt her family's manor house she intended to restore the capital of Awia to Tanager, as it was in 1812 before the Rachiswaters took the throne.

The lake reflected the banded mackerel sky, with thin clouds the grey-purple colour of an artist's paintbrush water. Trochanter, the morning star, was growing fainter. Below, the surface of the river winding east towards Lowespass Fortress had an oily, rainbow scum of old poison washing out from the Wall.

We crossed a bridge over the dry overspill chute and descended to the shore. The two soldiers guarding the access to the walkway uncrossed their spears promptly and we passed between them.

A beacon basket full of twigs and hay stood next to a large bell on a pole and my semaphore device set at neutral. Their metal stands prevented Insects eating them. Eleonora's bodyguard of four Tanager Select lancers sat obediently at attention on their warhorses. She appraised them out of habit: their embossed armour, the woollen cloaks hanging to their stirrups, their helmets with blue and white striped horsehair crests and fluttering muslin streamers. They love ornamentation, do Awians.

Eleonora's horse waited between them. The silver inlaid armour on his head was richer than anything I owned. The chafron plate beaked over his nose came to a point; the crinet covering his neck was steel openwork, scallop-edged like batwings. Lightning's horse was drab in comparison. Eleonora greeted them enthusiastically, 'Hello, Perlino! Hello Balzan!'

Perlino looked skittish at my scent. He put his ears back and flared his nostrils imperiously. 'I don't like you, either,' I told him.

Eleonora patted his neck and he nuzzled her hand.

I said, 'It isn't my fault most horses are afraid that Rhydanne want to chase them down and eat them.'

'Maybe I should take Perlino to Darkling and give him a sniff of pure Rhydanne for comparison. Then he'd appreciate you.' She fitted her toe into a stirrup, swung herself onto the horse. She sat straight, holding the reins loosely. Perlino high-stepped with his strong front legs, in rein-back, then Eleonora made him pirouette.

She leaned from the saddle and prodded my chest, 'Race you!' She tapped Perlino's flank and was away down the track. Her bodyguard looked at each other and followed suit, standing on their stirrups, their lances tilting backwards in their saddle rests.

Lightning hesitated, surprised, then stepped up astride Balzan, drew his reins left, turned and sped after her. They picked up the pace from a gallop to a charge; I watched them disdainfully until they were just dots above clouds of spray. Then I sighed, shook my wings open and ran to take off.

CHAPTER 2

Frost had given me days to prepare a speech but as usual I hadn't bothered; I'm used to speaking ad lib. I stood outside the hall listening to the low hubbub and expectant atmosphere. It reminded me of court.

Everybody looked up as I entered and silence descended over the benches filled with journalists and their assistants, saddle-sore in crumpled clothes.

Frost was sitting on a bench by the front wall, facing them. She fiddled with her river pearl wedding ring, her only jewellery, but she looked meditative rather than nervous; she was probably passing time by working out equations in her head.

A number of architects and engineers sat on the furthest benches. Many were women, watching their role model with expressions of adulation, fountain pens poised to scribble on sheaves of paper on their knees. I scanned the room for familiar faces, thinking: I'll watch out for the Morenzians, they tend to be the least respectful – but I spotted Kestrel Altergate, the exception to the rule.

Frost had taped a schematic drawing of the dam to the chimney breast. I stood in front of it and addressed the audience. 'Good morning, everybody. Welcome to Slake Cross, representatives of the governors and of the press. I know you've made many days' journey and I apologise that the lodgings we have to offer are of necessity fairly basic.

'Tonight is the centenary of the battle of Slake Cross. On this very night, one hundred years ago, thousands of Insects emerged from the cave system under the river, into the middle of a vanguard camp of five battalions. Only thirty mortals survived, all archers who showed incredible courage.

'I was there, and can never forget, but even for those who were not, the date is charged with meaning. We were forced to retreat in this part of the valley. Here and only here, for the first time since the foundations of Lowespass Fortress were laid in the year ten-oh-nine, the Insects extended their Wall on the south side of Oriole River. It is our vulnerable spot. For exactly a century the Castle has been striving to push the Wall back and reclaim our land. A hundred years and – by god – it seems like a long time!'

I waited until the journalists' polite laughter had subsided and then I opened my wing towards Frost. 'The Circle's Architect has taken five years to design and build the dam, the largest construction ever. It is truly the wonder of the modern world.

'Insects may be instinctive architects but they had to run when the river began to expand. I watched from the air, I saw them drowning, curling and twisting. Now, next week we will drain the lake and you are all invited to witness the prodigious sight. It'll be the biggest waterfall you can possibly imagine.'

My enthusiasm made them sit up. I was very excited at the prospect of seeing millions of tonnes of water spurting into the river. 'As the lake level drops, the Insect buildings will gradually emerge, slick and slimy.

'All the immortals will lead the fyrd to secure two hundred square kilometres of land and the north bank of the river. We have battalions already drawn up from coastal Awia – that is to say, the manors of Tanager, Peregrine and Wrought – and Lakeland Awia, the manors of Micawater and Rachiswater. I have also requested battalions from Hacilith and Eske, so you see the Empire's other capitals are participating with good will.'

Kestrel Altergate, on the first row, tried to interrupt me, 'Comet—'

I raised a hand, 'Please wait and I'll take questions at the end. I'd like to hand you over to Frost, who will give some more details of her magnificent achievement.'

I waved her up extravagantly and went to sit down. As we passed each other I clapped her shoulder and leant to mutter in her ear, 'Don't bog them down with technicalities.'

Frost stood behind her table, using it as a barrier between her and the audience, speaking over the top of her papers. She smiled, and a lifetime of looking uptight disappeared from her face. She held her hands apart and expanded the distance between them as she expounded her thoughts. 'I have built the dam where the Insect Wall crossed the river. Its wall is two kilometres long and thirty metres high. It holds back a lake twenty kilometres in length. The dam is an embankment, an earth mound with a core of rubble, faced with protective stone. It is an economical construction – the fyrd are used to building earthworks for our defences and this is no different. It is constructed around piers set into the former river bed.'

Oh god, I thought; here she goes.

'The headwaters – I mean, the lake – is intended to be wide rather than deep to flood the largest possible area. You see, the valley is shallow so the lake spreads out.

'A team of horses will be harnessed to wind a capstan and hoist up the sluice gate. It is so heavy I have used ship's rope for the winch rather than chain, or else the horses won't be able to lift it. However, rope doesn't last for ever in the damp environment and will need to be replaced, so a maintenance shaft accesses the top of the gate.

'The capstan's gears are a new invention and they're fascinating, you see—'

I caught Frost's eye. She dropped her notes, picked them up and shuffled them. 'Um. Well ... Two hundred million cubic metres of water will be released at a hundred and ten kilometres an hour. The waterfall into the stilling basin and the gabionned and canalised reaches of the river will indeed be impressive.'

I let her drone on while I appraised Kestrel. He was the son of the reeve of Altergate. Kestrel always managed to be the first reporter on the scene of any trouble and he was far too astute a commentator for my liking.

I kept half an ear on Frost's speech but I had heard it all before and my attention began to drift. I speak every one of the Fourlands' six current and seven dead languages but I will never be fluent in Frost's engineering jargon. She once tempted me to learn mathematics by telling me it was a language, but I soon found it was only used to describe things that were really dull. Frost was losing the rest of the audience too. Reporters don't thank you for too much information because newspapers are never more than three printed sheets.

I thought about my place on the Castle's tennis ladder. About ways to avoid Eleonora as much as possible. And about the fact that Frost could actually be rather attractive if she made the effort.

Eleonora strode in, waking me from my reverie. The brassy firelight starred her shoulder and waist. Lightning was close behind her, scraping his boots. I leapt to my feet and called, 'Please stand for the Queen of Awia!'

She seated herself on the bench beside me, placed her helm on the floor and tucked her 1910 Sword behind her on the seat. She sat with her hand on the fabulous opal hilt of that finely-tempered blade.

Frost waited for the audience to settle, then continued, 'I believe at long last we have a means of winning the war. I am determined not to stop here. The dam will allow us to control the river for decades to come. We can flood adjoining sectors, from which the Insects will also retreat. I can redirect the river and use additional dams to inundate more and more land. Canals will keep Insects out of cleared areas. Over the next half-millennium we can push them further and further back, until we reclaim the entire Paperlands ... Then my work, and the work of the Castle, will be complete ... Um ... I've finished, I think.'

I said, 'Thank you, Frost. Are there any questions?'

Kestrel raised his hand and shouted over half a dozen other reporters, 'Comet!'

'Yes, Kestrel ?'

'A hundred years ago the ground gave way. Am I right?'

'Yes,' I said quietly.

'Why can't it happen again?'

I gestured, allowing Frost to answer. She said, 'No, no. That's not possible. I tested the ground thoroughly and it's solid. The lake has flooded the Insect warren, and the bedding planes and phreatic passages in the karst bedrock – I mean, the caves – are completely full. Slake Master Cave swallowed twice as much water as I first estimated. I admit the tunnels are big. Really big – with a breadth the size of the Throne Room – but there are no Insects left underneath us; foam is pouring out of the resurgence to prove it.'

I said, 'They pose no danger to the advancing troops, wouldn't you say, Lightning?'

Lightning stood up. 'The only difficulty I foresee is an attack from further down the valley. Insects have been pressed back into the Paperlands where there is nothing edible left, so they will be ravenous. But with archers and lancers at all sides, I assure you no Insects will infiltrate our defences nor live to lay a scent trail for the rest.'

Kestrel nodded, and I pointed at another man who had his hand up.

'Smatchet, *Hacilith Post*,' he said. 'Is it true the Trisians are causing difficulties for the Sailor?'

I said, 'We're not discussing Tris now. We're talking about the dam.'

'I hear Trisians are striking because they don't want to be fyrd or sailors.'

'It must have been days since you ran a story on Mist Fulmer,' I said sarcastically. He was beloved of the gutter press, finding as he did a whore in every port and a port in every whore, and only half of them women.

'Is it true there's a garrison in Capharnaum?'

Kestrel turned to Smatchet and said, 'The Trisians have put a chain across the whole harbour mouth to prevent ships entering.'

'Really?'

'Absolutely.'

I glared eloquently at both of them. 'The Senate has asked the Castle for assistance in restoring order and we're complying with Governor Vendace, nothing more. OK?'

Smatchet backed down: 'OK.'

'Any more? Yes, Kestrel?'

'Will draining the dam be safe?'

Frost said, 'Oh, yes. I agree these are immense hydrostatic forces. To novices the interactions between fluctuating pressures would certainly appear frightening. But I will raise the gate very slowly and control the outflow. It will take five days to release a year's accumulation of water. I wish I could be more accurate but I can't, of course, because the reservoir and tunnels are an irregular shape, so we have conditions of flow under varying head. To put it in context ...' She rummaged through the papers on her table and emerged with a sheet covered in a complicated sum. She held it up, then looked frustrated as she realised few people in the room would understand. 'Come and see me afterwards and I'll explain ... Well, I'll try to. You can watch the event from a safe distance. It'll be great – air entrainment and bulking—'

'White water,' I said.

'Whatever.' Frost shrugged.

I said, 'Not only will it be safe, it'll be a sight you can tell the grandchildren about. Are there any more questions? Yes, Smatchet?'

The *Hacilith Post* reporter addressed Lightning, 'My lord, our readers would like to know if you are ready to announce a date for your wedding with Governor Swallow Awndyn?'

'That's not our topic!' I said, exasperated.

Lightning answered mildly, 'I think our engagement needs a little more time.'

I said, 'Well, there's your answer. Any more *relevant* questions?'

Kestrel crossed his legs and nudged his assistant to keep writing. He said, 'With respect, Comet, is Queen Eleonora making the same mistake as King Dunlin?'

Frost panicked but Eleonora stood up and looked at Kestrel impassively. I said, 'I don't understand. What do you mean?'

'Well, ten years ago the campaign of King Dunlin Rachiswater tried to breach the Wall and for our pains all we had was the worst swarm of Insects for centuries and a horrendous death toll. Altergate lost every man in its conscriptable generation, so that now the Castle has exempted it from the draft. Tambrine is also exempt from fyrdinge. Awndyn manor is in the enviable position of being able to use its Trisian trade profits to pay scutage rather than raise fyrd. Lowespass and Summerday are the only two manors where the Castle can appoint a governor, and both have been given to the Queen's lance captains. Their garrisons have been increased because the threat still remains—'

'Kestrel—' I said.

'—But you are proposing to advance into the Paperlands *again*. What did we gain last time? Nothing! The Wall is still in the same place. Many people think it should be left alone. Don't mess with it. Is your campaign military necessity, or are you rushing ahead too fast?'

Eleonora took a breath. 'Comet, I will answer the man. The offensive of Dunlin Rachiswater was poorly thought out. His was a campaign of muscle not the mind. The Insects' bodies are so much stronger than ours, we can only beat them with our skills and our brains. Dunlin responded to them rather than outwitting them and it was the downfall of his dynasty. Our current attack in no way compares. We're using our knowledge of the Insects' behaviour rather than our soldiers' lives. We will take ten times more land than he did. Our fresh approach uses the Castle's latest innovations – which are, dare I say, watertight? – and the might of my well-trained and experienced Select. The Emperor approves it.'

She hooked her thumb in her sword belt. 'Insects from here devastated the western reaches of my kingdom; I must protect Plow's precious fields. I will not allow Insects to make paper from Awian feathers and bones.

'I am simply first among the governors of Awia. In a time of emergency I took special care of my people and now that things are returning to normal I have made sure of my governors' support' – Lightning nodded in agreement – 'Awia has always had a stoic attitude. The Tanagers never accept defeat. I have fielded all my Select Fyrd because I know this will improve their families' lives.

'Let me tell you that if we are successful we will no longer need to call up the General Fyrd. There will no longer be a need for a general levy of the whole of the people. I know they resent their sixty days' unpaid service per year, and we are aware of desertions during the harvest and midwinter. Well, from now on they may remain at their proper work.

'There is good news for the Select Fyrd too. Their monthly payments will be raised to five pounds a week and an equipment allowance of twenty pounds a year. Commissions will be renewed as usual on godsloss day. I expect that the advance will be over by then. At last we have the means to win the war! In future we will look back on this as a momentous date, not because of nineteen twenty-five but twenty twenty-five, when we at last halted the onslaught and took the first step that led to the death of every last Insect!'

Eleonora gave her grand smile. Kestrel and the other journalists were hunched over, scribbling rapidly. None of them, therefore, was free to meet her eye. Their finished pages dropped, leafed down and slipped under the benches.

I said, 'Are there any more questions ... No? ... Very well. Then on behalf of the Castle I draw this meeting to a close, may it please Your Highness, ladies and gentlemen.' And added informally to the reporters, 'You can get lunch in the pub.'

They still took ten minutes to finish and gather their belongings. The benches scraped on the flagstones and they left the hall. It suddenly seemed very spacious. I rested my backside on the table edge, leant back, arms straight and stretched my legs.

The Architect had disappeared in a crowd of excited students in thick fustian jackets. They were asking her questions and surrounded the table to watch while she sketched an answer to one. She extricated herself by giving them as many figures and equations as they could take in and then we all watched them trickle out of the hall with their minds reeling.

CHAPTER 3

'I think that was successful, if I do say so myself.'

'Red or white?'

'No thanks. I had too much yesterday and I'm still recovering.'

Lightning was now on his second glass. 'The vintage is not as good as the previous year, but still ...'

'Well, a splash of red then, thank you.'

Frost, Eleonora, Lightning and me were celebrating with lunch in the hall. We were together at the head of the table so we could hear the hubbub of the other immortals further down and occasional voices from the tavern across the square as the journalists entertained themselves. Frost rested her notebook on the table beside her. Woe betide anybody who gets between her and its pages when she has an idea.

She neatened her bone-handled cutlery with precision and began to rub a little butter into her chapped hands. 'Thank you, Jant,' she said. 'I couldn't have done it on my own.'

'No more should you. It is Jant's office and I am glad he is pulling his weight for once.'

'Hey, Archer, what are you drinking? That's not like you.' I grinned at him.

Lightning scowled back. 'At least your Messenger service has become more reliable recently.'

Eleonora, at the head of the table, leant to the side as a boy served trout cooked in verjuice. She said, 'Cloud has surpassed himself, don't you think?'

'It is all right for the front,' said Lightning, who tended to bring good food and a cellar's worth of wine with him. It was his only show of wealth because his clothes were understated, if expensive. You wouldn't know from looking at him that he has millions a year.

Each of Lightning's features taken separately would also seem normal rather than striking, but even if I didn't know he was noble he would impress me as such; he has that confidence that casts a glow and makes a man the centre of attention, because he knows he ought to be. Give his plain grey eyes an imperious look but make them often prone to be cloaked. Dimple his chin, make his mouth firm, used to command but with a twist of sarcasm. Mark that he not only alternates between being ardent and brooding but sometimes manages to be both at once.

Constant training is the only thing that will make men stick fast in a shield wall, and Lightning drills the fyrd until they are less terrified of the Insects than they are of his anger. Since he is the Lord Governor of Micawater manor, as well as an Eszai, he boldly shapes the world but he still welcomes the yearly cycle of harvests, hunting seasons and accounts. He takes the world seriously, because he has no imagination. Because he has no imagination, he is a popular novelist.

The Lowespass wind blustered across the square and howled through the alleys. It never seemed to stop. The Riverworks banner fissled and slapped on the roof.

Frost glanced at me. 'The wind's getting up again.'

I shuddered. I had a sudden vivid image of the soil crumbling over my clothes. I could taste it. I said, 'We're supposed to be celebrating your accomplishment. Don't remind me of the state I was in a hundred years ago.'

Lightning said, 'You survived. Simply take more care next time.'

'*Next* time?'

'Most of us have been bitten. Tornado has been bitten more times than he can count.'

'Do you remember being picked up?' Eleonora asked me.

'Ha! Of course not.'

'He was in a coma,' Lightning said.

'I was moribund.'

'He lay unconscious for fourteen weeks in the field hospital at Whittorn. Rayne moved him to Rachiswater Infirmary, then to her hospital in the Castle. He stayed there for a year.'

I wrapped a strip of fish around my two-pronged fork. 'It was terrible. I'm far too impatient to convalesce in hospital for day after day, with nothing to do but the occasional haemorrhage.'

I had a collapsed lung and pneumonia – which injured Awians are prone to – and a bloody great hole in my side. Sepsis led to organ failure but Rayne knew to let me lie dormant until my body recovered itself. When I came round I screamed solidly, high and eerie like a sick infant until she pumped me full of painkillers. I was in shock; it cocooned and isolated me from reality. I knew I was very badly hurt but could only lie still and trust her. The thought I might never fly again constantly distressed me; if that broken wing had grounded me permanently I would have been vulnerable to Challengers so I made sure Rayne paid it careful attention. I also suffered from a great sense of failure because the mortals who looked to me to lead them had all been killed. I desperately needed to talk but I kept my silence. It was like being in a dark tunnel that very gradually widened and I began to realise what had actually happened to me. I relived it again and again and I grew to understand it. Then I began to talk about it and I healed more quickly.

'He harried us for all the news,' Lightning told Eleonora.

'Four months were missing from my life!' I said.

Eleonora asked Lightning, 'Where were you in that battle? Why weren't you hurt like Jant?'

He shrugged modestly.

'Go on,' she teased. 'Tell me.'

Lightning never needs much encouragement to recount a story. 'In the preceding weeks,' he began, 'everyone seemed tired, overworked and irritable. Little things kept going wrong. We couldn't know then that it was because something so momentous, so awful, was going to happen that it sent ripples back down the flow of time, to disturb us and disrupt our attention.

'I was in the Sun Pavilion, writing. You know the story where an Eszai is Challenged, but he sends an assassin to murder the Challenger before they meet, so San throws him out of the Circle?'

'No,' said Eleonora.

'Doesn't matter,' said Lightning. 'But this is proof that romantic novels can save your life. The ground began to shake and, one by one, the candles guttered out. I could see nothing, not the back of my hand, not the page in front of me. I couldn't grasp what was happening.

'I called the captain and together we walked along the line of tents summoning the archers, getting them kitted up and reassuring them. By the time we had one hundred men the rest had gone. They had fled. The ground was falling away under our feet so fast it brought down the palisade.'

Lightning was staring intently, watching the memory. He subconsciously dropped a hand to his sword hilt. With eyes bright and the other hand spread, he leant over the table, talking directly to Eleonora. 'You should never meet Insects on open ground. Use fortifications whenever possible. I knew that, but what did we have? Two companies of archers and a handful of arrows.

'We retreated along the stockade until we came to the only corner where it was still upright. I ordered them to form up inside with the fence at their backs. They were breaking down with fear but I made them pull a fallen section in front of us and shoot for all they were worth. We shot straight out over the top, in relays, all night long.'

'For the whole night?' asked Eleonora.

'If we slowed we would die, I knew that full well.' He swept his hand out over the table. *Fss! Fss!* Went the arrows. Every time we paused, stragglers were coming in, some no more than naked, and we lifted them over the defence. Insects scaled it and I had teams to chop them down as they reached the top. After the first hour men started giving up, falling from exhaustion and hypothermia. I dragged them to the back and I kept the rest going. We could see nothing. We knew we were hitting people out there, but they were already lost to the Insects. I could not help them. I did what every Eszai should do in a disaster: cut your losses and save your fyrd.

'When we ran out of ammunition I sent fifty men to bring more. Only ten returned. It was a suicide mission. We had no way of knowing what was happening beyond our palisade. We just kept shooting, holding out against the instant we would be annihilated. I felt the Circle break and I knew Hayl Eske was dead, but I didn't tell the men.' He glanced at me. 'I was waiting for the Circle to break for Comet and Tornado. It was not the first time I have had to leave the battlefield on my own.

'After that first hour I knew everything out there still moving was an Insect. I kept up volleys in pulses for six consecutive hours, until dawn began to resolve.

'The light came up slowly, pale grey, and through the murk we could at last see the utter devastation. The ground in front of us sloped straight into the pit. The middle of the camp had vanished. Only the tents at the far end were left standing, leaning inwards. Around us, the corrugated stockade sagged and twisted like a ribbon. Insects were everywhere, feeding on the bodies. We were helpless, stranded in our corner and tired to death. My vision was dark at the edges with exhaustion but I wrapped my wings around me and I persevered.

'Then came the sound of thunder along the road. Heavy cavalry were riding in. They were armoured head to foot and they poured into the camp with their lances levelled, riding the Insects down. Do you know who was leading them? Rayne. The Doctor. Bundled up in her old cloak on the back of a destrier.

'She had felt the Circle break. She had been here in Slake with the rear-guard and at first light she gathered all the cavalry left and set out to find us. We climbed the palisade and hailed her.

'She brought her horse around the lip of the crater. "Bracing morning you have for it, Saker," said she. "Where are the other two?"

'"I don't know," I said. They were both pulling on the Circle, we could tell that much.

'She said, "You have exposure. Go back to town."

'I did not return to town. I picked my way over the subsiding ground with her, looking for Comet and Tornado. She spotted the sunburst on his shield—' He gestured at me '—through the scattered soil and set her soldiers to dig him out. Finding Tornado was more difficult. She had to bring in some of her trained dogs. But of Hayl Eske we never found a single piece ... Long, drawn-out ordeals are the ones that change us. For me it was just one night. But what a night!'

I said, 'It was my biggest battle.'

'Falling down the hole was not the best thing to do under the circumstances,' Lightning assured me.

'At least I wasn't as useless as Hayl.'

Frost said, 'Everybody remembers where they were when they heard the news.'

Lightning nodded. His face was flushed. He unlaced the strings at the neck of his shirt, downed the dregs of his wine and called, 'Bring some more claret. No, no ... that old bottle ... You'll like this one, Eleonora. I had to sell a house for it.' A servant gave him the bottle and he clinked his intaglio ring against its glass. 'We shall toast Frost's dam with this. There are only six bottles left in the world ... Well, five. But you only live once.'

I made my excuses, left the table and walked out to the washroom block to have a piss. I was just buttoning my fly when a figure loomed behind me. I glanced over my shoulder and saw Eleonora at the doorway. She looked left and right with a pervert's smile. 'Hmm. Interesting in here. Why is it such a mess?'

'Why are you following me?' I asked.

'You have a pert backside.'

'Oh, bugger,' I muttered.

'Don't give me ideas!'

'Eleonora ... *no.*'

She laughed. I was begging and that was good enough for her. She said, 'No, anyway. I want to talk to you about the Archer.'

'What about him?'

'Not here.' She beckoned. 'Come into the church, out of this terrible wind.'

We walked past the stores, stepping over the rail tracks that carry fodder to the stables, through the alleyway and into the church beside the hall.

It was a quiet, white room with beanbags on the floor. Churches are only single rooms but they are often built and funded by governors and sometimes as a display of the sponsor's wealth can be quite ornate. They employ no officials, except a caretaker to look after the building, and they are places in which to think and relax, and reflect on the absence of god. People sit, or walk around admiring the decoration. Travellers are welcome to shelter there for the night. They are for people, not god, since god has left the world on an extended break and has had no impact on anybody's life since the calendar began.

The church was empty so Eleonora spoke openly. 'Do you know what's bothering Lightning?'

'Is something bothering him?'

She blinked in disbelief. 'Yes! Men – you never notice anything, do you? Have you ever seen him so tipsy before?'

I considered it. 'No, not for a long time. Is it his fiancée?'

'Swallow!' Eleonora said contemptuously. 'No. He wouldn't mention it to you, because it isn't connected with the dam. I know how Eszai hide their weaknesses. He told me and, since the weight of responsibility for the advance is on you immortals, I thought I should let you know what has shaken him.'

'He told *you*? What? What did he tell you?'

'Do you remember Cyan, his daughter?'

'Of course I remember Cyan.'

'She has gone missing.' Eleonora paused, dramatically.

I said, 'What, again?'

'Pardon?'

'She was kidnapped once,' I explained. 'While you were busy wresting the throne from Staniel Rachiswater and exiling the poor fool.'

Eleonora tipped her foot and thoughtfully rolled her rowel spur up and down on the floorboards, leaving a line of dents. 'Oh, I see. Well, that explains Lightning's extreme reaction. He jumped to the conclusion that Cyan has been snatched. She is, after all, the future governor of Peregrine and the daughter of Governor Micawater, so she's a target for kidnappers. They know he would give his manor for her safety.'

'Where did she go missing? Awndyn?'

'Hacilith. In the city.'

'Why? What was she doing there?'

'I don't know. I was hoping you'd sort it out. Eszai should bloody well tell each other if something goes wrong instead of moping around and drinking.'

I nodded. 'Maybe I can help.'

I was much more familiar with Hacilith than Lightning was. In fact, I know it like the veins in my arms. I could put the word around and if any hotelier or spa owner had spotted a girl as glitteringly important as Cyan the city would be buzzing.

Eleonora followed me out of the church – and pinched my arse hard as we passed through the door. I sped up to get away from her and returned to the hall.

A servant was moving around the table placidly, collecting plates and glasses, and pouring yet more claret for Lightning. He was talking to Frost but I barged in on their conversation. 'I can't believe you didn't tell me that Cyan's gone missing!'

Lightning looked confused for a second, then narrowed his eyes at Eleonora. 'I ... Well, I admit I have been a little preoccupied.'

'You can hardly concentrate,' Eleonora told him.

'On the contrary, the planning is taking my mind off the problem.' He took a sip of wine. 'But I can't stand the fact that Cyan's life may be at risk.'

'What are you talking about?' asked Frost.

Lightning sighed. 'I suppose I should tell you. My daughter has contrived to get herself lost while on the Grand Tour. It is an Awian tradition, Frost. I received a letter yesterday morning from my steward, Harrier. He was accompanying her. They'd toured Awia and were stopping once in Morenzia to see the sights of the city. That morning they had visited the Agrimony Campanile, the church at the place where the Emperor was born, and the great bronze façade of Aver-Falconet's palace. Harrier went to sign into the Costrel Hotel and when he turned his back, she vanished.'

'I would, too, with an itinerary that dull,' I said.

Lightning gave me a look with the force of every minute of his fourteen hundred and forty years. He was older than everything in this reclaimed valley, even Lowespass Fortress that you would have thought immutable. I shivered.

'It is not easy to give Harrier Disante the slip. He could have traced her anywhere but in Hacilith.'

'Did he see any kidnappers?' I asked.

'No. When she started the tour I thought it was essential tutoring for her to see the world, but now I am afraid she is learning too much. I would do anything for Cyan, buy her any present, let her travel anywhere except she must not be alone in the city.'

'I can put your mind at rest,' I said. 'I'll go to Hacilith and see if I can discover news. If I can find Cyan, I'll bring her back.'

Frost stared at me with incredulity. 'You're joking, aren't you?'

'No.'

'On the eve of the advance? Certainly not.'

'It's only four days' flight there and back,' I said blithely. 'You'll scarcely notice I've gone.'

'Of course I will!' Frost snatched her notebook off the table and held it pressed to her chest, her arms folded across it and her eyes round. 'Honestly, Jant. Another of your picaroon ideas! Just because it's Lightning's daughter. Just because it's him! Quite frankly I think all those beads you wear are cutting off the blood supply to your brain. The Emperor asked thee to work for me this year. Thou knowest I need thy help. I need communication and logistics more than anything else!'

I can tell Frost is distraught when she starts to pepper her speech with the remains of her old Brandoch accent. Nobody, not even in the Plainslands, has spoken like that since the seventeenth century.

I said, 'I've already sent out my dispatches. The troops are on their way and no matter how much I chivvy them, they won't march any faster. I want to see you raise the gate as much as the journalists do, but it's eight days from now. Even if I don't find Cyan, I can easily make it back in that time.'

Eleonora said, 'How like an Eszai to take too much on!'

Lightning said, 'Frost is right. When Cyan was kidnapped before, I deserted my duty and went looking for her even though Insects were swarming. The Emperor was unforgiving – and rightly so – because there are still bite marks in the gates of Shivel manor house and paper stains in the parlour of Tanager Hall. San only gave me one more chance and his decrees are set in stone. I do not want to have to crawl to him like that again. He went so far as to say that every one of those thousands of people killed had been worth as much as Cyan.'

'You're afraid of the Emperor.'

'Yes, I am. For myself and for you.'

Frost said, 'How old is this Cyan, anyway?'

'Seventeen,' said Lightning, refilling his glass.

'Seventeen!' Frost exclaimed.

Seventeen ... I thought, and confirmed my decision to go and find her. Mortals seem to age very fast these days. I had been thinking of her as a child but now she must have a mind of her own, and a body too. Her father was born with the silver spoon and could afford to believe the best of human nature. Her mother, who died at Tris five years ago, was a schemer convinced of humanity's worst. How had these traits mixed in Cyan? How had she turned out?

Frost said, 'She's probably just enjoying herself and she'll come back when she's ready. Don't you remember what it was like to be seventeen?'

'Yes. Why do you think I'm worried ? I did a lot of stupid things when I was that age ... There was that incident with my father's chariot and the lake ... Anyway, we had a sense of propriety and Cyan, I fear, has none. It is strange. Why should she run away? She can't be angry with me or I would definitely know about it, otherwise she would have wasted the effort. Either she has been untruthful for some time or this was a temporary aberration. I imagine her coming to her senses again and realising she's lost.'

'She's smart enough to get herself found,' I said. 'She hasn't exactly led a sheltered existence.'

Lightning twiddled his glass and gazed at the stationary surface of the wine inside it. 'She has not visited the city before ... Meanwhile I'm supposed to be drilling these archers who seem to think they're here for a stroll by the water stair.'

I thought Lightning was wrong. He had always said Cyan could do what she wanted, but now she chose to exercise that freedom he was up in arms. If she had only just discovered freedom, of course she'd want to know how much she could use it without losing it. She would just drink too much and spew in the street at three in the morning. She'd have gut-rot and a hangover, recover and feel ashamed. Then she would find the sheets rough in the coach house and bedbugs too; cold water in the pitcher and no soap in the bowl. I said, 'Lightning, she'll come home wiser in the ways of the world, with her tail between her legs, and vow not to leave the palace for a long time.'

Lightning passed a hand over his forehead. 'Oh god. You don't understand. Cyan has the blood of a thousand-year-old dynasty. She is the new heir of the house of Micawater ... Why does nobody have the slightest inkling what that means to me?'

I said, 'Blood doesn't matter any more.'

'It matters. It matters to me. Oh, I know what you're thinking. That I'm some sort of relic of the seventh century. Well, let me tell you, it was the golden age of Awia – hic! – (excuse me). The genealogies of every other family twisted and turned and snuffed out. But Micawater comes straight down through the centuries: me. And now Cyan. She is the heir to Esmerillion's crown. And she's also my daughter and I love her and I want to see her safe.'

'The old money of the country even then,' Eleonora murmured.

I said, 'All this past is just like a millstone around your neck. Can't you forget about it for once?'

Lightning said, 'That would be forgetting history.'

'I do forget history.'

'You would. You're a Rhydanne. But the history of my family is the history of my country, and even if Insects take our land they won't take what we are.'

'Hear, hear!' said Eleonora.

Lightning nodded, warming to his subject. 'When in four-fifteen the Insects first appeared in Awia, the chaos they caused led to the collapse of the governments in every country. The Insects extended their Paperlands and Awian families began moving south to escape them. Everyone knows that account, but my ancestors were among them. Our records don't stretch back that far; we were not notable then. We were unplanned settlers but we had courage and intelligence. We settled Pentadrican land. They were in anarchy and grateful for the order we brought. We also brought the knowledge of how to fight Insects. We lived in harmony with the Pentadricans who remained. Soon King Murrelet made a decision to shift the boundaries of Awia south. All the land from the rivers Moren to Rachis was Pentadrican land back then. If you know what you're looking for, Eleonora, you can still see vestiges of the Pentadrica today – the Dace River, that was one of their fish names, like the Trisians still use. Awia stretched from the Rachis river to the north coast of the continent, all under paper now.

'My family staked a claim on bountiful land in Mica River valley. We founded the manor and took the river's name for our family name. Then gold was discovered in Gilt River, my family started to mine it and we flourished. We married into the Sheldrake family and gained all the land south of the river mouth. Our rise in influence seemed unstoppable.'

'Look,' I said. 'We know all this.'

Eleonora said, 'Shut up, Jant. He's talking to me'

She gave Lightning an encouraging nod and he continued, unfortunately: 'The Murrelets held the throne for centuries. They had claimed the Rachis Valley, but they died out in five four nine and we inherited the throne. Queen Esmerillion was the first of our dynasty – her charm was legendary. She moved the capital from Murrelet to Micawater town. She built the palace, away from the best land, obviously, but she gave it the best vista.

'Ninety years passed. Then my grandfather, King Gadwall, married Minivet Donaise and we gained her manor – the whole of the Donaise hills were added to Micawater. Gadwall and Minivet had two daughters, the firstborn being Teale. Teale Micawater married a warrior called Garganey Planisher and, though their children – my siblings and me – numbered nine, we were the last generation ... until Cyan was born.' Lightning sighed and folded his arms.

I drained my glass noisily and declared, 'God, I needed that.'

'I understand, even if Jant doesn't,' said Eleonora. 'We live forever through our descendants.'

'I prefer to live forever through being the fastest messenger in the world,' I said. 'Lightning, do you want some more wine?'

'Thank you. But, you know, I was only fourth in line for the throne and I was never expected to inherit so I was not brought up knowing how to run the manor as were my brothers Peregrine, Gyr and Shryke. I made many mistakes in the first few years.

'Peregrine knew he was dying of cancer. He speculated that I would live longer than a whole mortal dynasty so he placed the manor in my hands, but Gyr should have inherited. Gyr was the last of my brothers left alive but he was the black sheep of the family; he had been embittered by the death of his sister decades before. We quarrelled ... I handled it badly. You see, the Castle had made me a soldier not a statesman. I beat him around the Great Hall and I threw him out. Every harsh word is still burnt into me.

'That was in the year six eighty-seven and it was the end of our dynasty. Gyr wanted to put some distance between us, so he married bloody Korhaan Allerion. He wanted to change his name but the process was the same then as now; the name of the wealthier parents' family was passed on to the children. The Allerions could never be wealthier than the Micawaters, so Gyr changed his name completely. He called his dynasty after the river that

flowed through the lands he carved off from my manor. His lack of original-
ity was the final insult.

'Eventually the Avernwaters yielded the throne to the Piculets and I knew
there was not a drop of my family's blood left in the world, apart from
me ...' His forehead creased, then he shrugged and sipped claret.

'I try to trace my line as far as the Rachiswaters, but I am only fooling
myself,' he added. 'So, when I say the seventh century was our golden age,
I mean it. I have managed to keep my manor preserved at the peak of my
dynasty's expansion and achievement. We brought stability to our manor,
then the whole of Awia, and we stopped the Insects coming further southward. I have always thought that's the reason why San let me keep the land
when I became Eszai. It also meant that Awia couldn't expand its borders
any further into the Plainslands. Adventurous dynasties like the Tanagers
beat north against the Insects instead, and the Rachiswaters pushed west.'

Frost had been talking to Gayle on her other side, but she caught a frag-
ment of our conversation and smiled. 'No one can better Lightning on the
ebb and flow of featherback dynasties. He remembers them all.'

Lightning raised a finger shrewdly and drunkenly. 'I knowed ... I mean
... I knew them all.'

'We realise. Why don't you have some of this?' I said, offering him a slice
of fudge cake which would be well-nigh impossible to talk through.

Lightning refused it for the chance to show Eleonora his knowledge. 'Our
court was in power from five forty-nine until six eighty-seven. My mother
held the throne at the time of the Games. The Avernwaters followed, from
six eighty-seven to the year one thousand; they held out a long time but
their town is now only a Tanager muster. The Piculets rose in power, from
the year one thousand until ten eighty-one. Then the Pardalotes were very
successful, ten eighty-one to thirteen twenty-six, when Insects killed the
last. The Piculets returned from thirteen twenty-six to thirteen ninety-eight.
I liked them, but I didn't think much of the Fulvetta dynasty (thirteen
ninety-eight to fifteen sixteen), very debauched in the fifteenth century.
The exhilarating times of new Awia had long gone. They used to tell me,
"Be decadent while you still can. The Insects will destroy us too." Well,
the last one, Lanare Fulvetta, poisoned her family and was imprisoned for
patricide. Then rose the Scoters (fifteen sixteen to fifteen thirty-six) until a
flu epidemic put an end to them and tens of thousands more. They were
followed by an interregnum and I was champing at the bit then, let me tell
you. The Falconets were merchant arrivistes – with sporadic insanity – who
filled the vacuum from fifteen thirty-eight to sixteen forty-one. I had to sit
through that; they were all quite mad. There was a schism in the family
and poor Petronia Falconet went to Hacilith, but his son did well as the first
Aver-Falconet. Then the Tanagers appeared, a famous warrior family—' He

smiled at Eleonora '—and succeeded to the throne. They restored some of the wonderful original vigour from sixteen fifteen until eighteen twelve ...'

'Financial problems,' put in Eleonora graciously.

'Financial problems,' Lightning concurred. 'The Rachiswaters rose to power (eighteen twelve to twenty fifteen). They founded Carniss but an Insect swarm ended them, and back came the Tanagers ... twenty fifteen until who knows when?'

Eleonora said, 'That's the way you see mortals, isn't it? Just offshoots of family lines, just the latest kings or servants or soldiers.'

Lightning prodded a finger at the table top. 'That is a very involved question. So in simplest yes and no terms, let me just say, perhaps.'

'I expect you think there's no point in getting to know them personally.'

The smile spread over his face again. 'You, Eleonora, are an *excellent* personification of the Tanagers.'

'We may have been good warriors but we weren't so successful in peaceful times. My forebears didn't care as much about money as yours must have done.'

Lightning said, 'Nevertheless, I think you'll last. Pass the wine, please.'

'You've drunk enough.'

'I ... have drunk enough claret in my life to fill Micawater lake. 'S true. I worked it out. A whole damn lake of calret. Claret.'

'Only Awia has such royal splendour,' Eleonora continued. 'I feel sorry for the other countries.'

I felt sorry for Lightning's daughter. He seemed to want her to begin his dynasty once more, so this time he could watch over it properly, but evidently he couldn't even look after her. I said, 'If I find Cyan, I'll explain all this to her. Besides, I've been at the front for a long time; I'd welcome a change of scene.'

'You all have your priorities wrong!' Frost wailed.

Lightning said to her, 'I wouldn't let Jant go if I didn't think he could do it. Cyan knows and likes him. She listens to him.'

'I know the underworld, too,' I said.

'Oh, god ... Good luck.'

'What do you want me to do if I find her ?'

Lightning propped his head on his hand. 'Hmm. Send her to the palace. No, on second thoughts, bring her here. I can keep an eye on her. Otherwise she might run away again. Harrier may be growing too long in the tooth to keep up with her.'

'She can watch us drawing up the troops,' Eleonora suggested.

'Yes. It might do the uncouth young lady good to see the fyrd in action. She needs a firm hand. She calls herself Cyan Peregrine, as she should, because she will inherit the manor when she's twenty-one. I am glad she accepts it, but everything else she does these days seems designed to cause me pain. If ... If the worst has happened and you need constables, or horses, ask Aver-Falconet. Cyan was supposed to be meeting him anyway ... Harrier had to make all kinds of excuses.'

Frost shook her head and clasped her hands around her coffee cup. 'I don't like it. I'm busy with my speciality as San wants us to be. I don't branch out. I don't have pastimes; I work all the time. But, Lightning, when you're not playing geopolitics you're playing family history!'

He asked her, 'Will you be able to work without Jant?'

She bristled. 'Yes, of course! I coped for hundreds of years before *he* flew in!'

'Use my couriers,' I said.

'Typical. Everything to be done at the pace of a nag rather than the pace of an eagle.'

Lightning said, 'Give him six days, Frost. You never give anybody enough time off. Including yourself, I suspect.'

'How else would I have built the dam?' she asked, then turned to Eleonora. 'Your Highness, be my witness that I object to this ridiculous errand.'

Eleonora shrugged. 'As you wish, but we're at the front so I can't intervene in an argument between Eszai.'

Frost could see she was outnumbered and I felt a twist of guilt because the advance is supposed to be our priority. However, I can manage both and she's probably just annoyed that I'm more busy than her. She said, 'Jant, when you return, report straight to me. I'll have a stack of letters for you by then.'

I picked my jacket off the back of the chair, leant over the table and gathered some cheese rolls.

Lightning said, 'Wait a minute.' He struggled to his feet and threw an arm around my shoulders. He was taller than my one metre eighty-five and nearly twice as broad as I am. He accompanied me to the door with a confidential air, saying, 'Jant, you must know that ... Um ... I have my own doubts. Um ... Oh, god knows I have always tried to show you the right way but you are far too easily tempted ...'

'What?'

'Cyan is a very attractive girl.'

'Good,' I said.

He rubbed the tips of his fingers over the scar on his right hand. 'I'm not sure if ... if she pretty how knows she is. Knows how pretty she is. It might have an effect on certain men ... On certain men who have volunteered to find her.'

'What!' I said indignantly. 'I promise I won't touch her!'

'You never know what you are going to do, Jant, so don't bother promising. I wish for once you would plan ahead rather than living in the instant and rushing into things. I remember how you were when you first joined the Circle, eagerly looking for ways to destroy yourself. You still pride yourself on being dangerous.'

It took him some time to say this and I waited patiently. 'Lightning, you have old-fashioned ideas.'

'With time you'll learn they're the safest. If you ... If you take advantage of Cyan I'll have your guts for bowstring. I will do you more damage than that battle did ... I'll break every one of your weird-looking fingers.'

'God. You really know how to get through to a Rhydanne. There's no need to worry, trust me; I told Cyan to think of me as her brother.'

He nodded, mollified. 'Well, my town house and hunting lodges are at your disposal, as usual. Oh, and Jant, if you can't find her in the six days, you must return. Don't let your tremendous energy tempt you to ridiculous feats. The Emperor would dismiss us both.'

CHAPTER 4

I found my pace and the wind was with me; I flew over the convoys coming in to Slake Cross. I was glad to be flying in the opposite direction, against the flow, at right angles to society. I was enjoying myself; I live for flight. I felt light and ethereal.

The wind buffeted my wings. I exerted my strength and held them steady, like struts. I respect the winds, because at a touch some gales could snap my bones and tear my muscle, so to be weather-wise I study the clouds.

Flying long distances is a very fulfilling challenge, because it has taken me all my life to learn the rules of the sky. It is always laid out like a chessboard halfway through a game, a confusion of risks and potentials. Flying puts the minutiae of life into perspective – I was concentrating so hard playing out the moves, I didn't dwell on any of the daily worries.

I looked for the small, fluffy white clouds that sit on top of thermals. They had been forming all morning and were drifting with the wind to make an archipelago, each cloud a signpost in a corridor of updraughts that would carry me south.

I entered the first thermal and felt a jolt of lift. I turned and circled close to its centre, the tips of my wings spread wide to catch the rising air. The moorland spun under me as I rose smoothly, and all the time I was looking around, trying to predict the next source of lift. After a few minutes the warm air bubble faded and no longer bore me up, but I had already gained so much height I could glide out towards the next one.

This is the best way of flying. From birds I learnt the trick is not to flap all the time but glide as much as possible to save effort. It's a game of wits for me, though. When I was on drugs, I took the overfamiliar countryside for granted; flying around in a daze, delivering letters or failing to. No longer – I was seeing it with new eyes, full of gladness that I'm clean at last. The excitement of the real world made me high – the sky was more vivid than a trip – how could I have forgotten the scenery's intense beauty when in love with all the Shift worlds to which cat could take me? The Fourlands was so much better.

I pulled my little round sunglasses down from my forehead and looked out far in advance. The shape and colour of the ground influences the wind currents and spots where thermals form.

As I left Lowespass the lines of trenches fell behind, but pillboxes and platform towers dotted the border of Awia – places to seek refuge from Insects. I could tell I had crossed into northwest Awia when I went over the Rachis River, a thin silver thread shining like flax unspooling through flower-spotted water meadows.

I was flying over the upper Rachis valley, patchwork farmland thickly and evenly spangled with villages. This was the muster of Plow. All manors are divided into musters of roughly equal population, with the original purpose of marshalling fyrd. Each muster is administered by a reeve who is appointed by the manor lord. The reeve's family change their surname to match the muster, a system created in the distant past, probably to make it easier for us immortals to remember them.

I caressed the air over Plow, the largest town in its muster, but still not much more than the reeve's moated farm around which gathered stone granges with red-tiled roofs and courtyards. They belonged to the tenant farmers who work the land under the reeve, and the vavasours who sub-rent from the tenant farmers.

All the barns were empty of hay and the cattle turned out into the fields. Men and women looked up and pointed me out, pausing from their work bent double pulling up weeds from between shoots of wheat and barley. I waved and motion flourished all over the fields as hundreds of people simultaneously waved back.

No wonder Plow muster is called 'the bread basket of Awia'. Rock dust ground by glaciers in the mountains blows down in the high air streams and settles across the area, where the rivers add loam and make the most fertile land in the Empire. Awia is fortunate that the country is so fruitful; it would otherwise soon be ruined since it bears the brunt of the Insect incursion while the rest of the Fourlands can prosper free of any fighting.

I passed over Toft town, built of ivy-clad marble tracery salvaged from old palaces. It was once famous for being the seat of the Fulvetta dynasty, and now famous for nothing but its ruins.

The land started to bump up into grassy slopes. The last thermal failed me and I had to ascend by flapping. I beat strongly, breathing deeply to quell the pain in my wings and stomach muscles. When I fly long distance I try to dissociate from the pain by counting off the landmarks and seeing how soon I can pass them. It's just like running a marathon; it gets harder and harder until a certain point. If I can break past that point I feel I can go on for ever.

I crested Irksdale, the heather grouse moor, into Micawater manor. The land dropped steeply in limestone bands and escarpments, leaving me gliding high above fresh beech and old oak woods. This was no wild wood but Lightning's carefully managed purlieu, a hunting ground popular for the revels of ladies and gentlemen. They come up from the Awian palaces and the summer homes of Hacilith businessmen further down the valley. Every time I fly over it brings home to me how rich Lightning is, with all these thousands of people paying rent to him. His manor alone was probably worth half the Plainslands. Long accustomed to immortality, he plans far ahead and his people profit from his vast experience. He looks after them well; in fact, nobody lives as a cottar in Micawater.

Lightning would be even richer now his investment in Trisian trade is starting to pay off. But I'm not envious. What would I do with all that cash, hey? I have twenty primary feathers and the blue dome of the sky!

A herd of fallow deer caught sight of me and panicked. They were so far below, they looked to be the size of hares; they bounded beneath the trees, white tails flashing. I could only see them occasionally, grey-brown backs and the stags' antlers in velvet, but I drove them along in front with glee. They reached the edge of the woods and waded out into the shallow Foin River, where I left them standing in the fast current. The Foin is fordable along its length, giving rise to the proverb, 'When there are two bridges over the Foin'; that is, never.

I looked directly down and found myself staring into the ground – a rocky chasm. I was over the fuming torrent of the Gilt River in a breath and above the trees again. The Gilt cascades down from Darkling where it rises in the mountains' black granite and schist, from which it abrades tiny translucent flakes. They sparkle in the water all the way downstream and embed themselves in the plashers of waterwheels from Kettleholes to Micawater town that glitter as they turn.

The shadows were lengthening and already the evening was drawing in. It was better to cut my journey short today and enjoy Lightning's hospitality, than to press on, gain a few more kilometres but have to spend the night in a grim Fescue coaching inn. I leant my weight and swung left, to follow the river down to the next village, Chalybeate. A long skein of geese straggled into view, a few hundred metres below me. Their honking and whirring wings awoke my ingrained hunting lust. I let them pass under me, then swung into a standing position, folded my wings and fell, feet first. I hit the last bird in the line with the soles of my boots and knocked it stone dead. It dropped out of the air and crashed through the branches.

I landed, picked it up then ran to find the path, kicking up clouds of spores from puffball fungi. The stalks of bluebells on the bank were invisible; their flowers hung in the air like fine eye-shadow dust. Silky beech leaves were unfolding like fans from the buds, ferns uncurled like green question marks, up from the ground covering of dog's mercury and herb robyn.

I knocked on the door of Chalybeate Chase, one of Lightning's picturesque and immaculate hunting lodges. I have a delightful privilege as Messenger: I can ask for lodging anywhere. It always amuses me to see great lords scrambling to give their best suites to a junkie ex-street kid. The care-taker's surprised face appeared in the doorway.

I held up the goose and he broke into a grin.

Every centimetre of Chalybeate Chase's inside walls was crammed with hunting trophies. The table, where I was sitting to eat my roast goose dinner, was a glass-fronted cabinet containing a display of stuffed wildfowl. Hundreds of deer heads surrounded me, mounted looking left and right to fit their antlers into every available space. Pink and orange paper chains draped all over them – the debris left by Lightning's last party hadn't been cleared up yet. He has a habit of announcing that it is his birthday at random intervals. Sometimes he has two or three in a year, sometimes none for a decade. The first time he asked me to deliver invitations I thought it really was his birthday until Rayne explained it was nothing but an excuse for a party and no one knows when his real birthday is. According to Lightning, immortals' birthdays don't count.

Next morning I headed out of Awia, flying south and watching the Plainslands expand. It was fantastic, so refreshing! If one day I crash and die flying, then it will all be worth it. Look at me, the Emperor's Messenger! I hold all the rights of passage. My strength, my speed, the scars of Slake Cross Battle seemed to burn in my flesh. God, but it was good to be alive, in the chill exhilarating air!

I waved my arms from sheer exuberance but that didn't seem to help dissipate it. All I need now is my old guitar, so I can coax 'The Frozen Hound Hotel' out of it while I ride.

I glanced up to another layer of fine, thin cloud thousands of metres above. I have tried, but it's impossible to fly that high. I can't breathe up there and I come down covered in ice. I usually travel long-distance at about one and a half thousand metres and never higher than five thousand, much lower than the valley where I once lived in Darkling.

In such fine conditions I can glide a hundred kilometres without flapping once, but I could no longer see much detail. Navigation was easy; all I had to do now was follow the Moren to Hacilith. The river was speckled with barges sailing upstream to the mining villages. Their sails were angled and they had white mounds on their decks, probably sacks of coal being shipped in from the collieries of Avernwater and Fusain muster in Wrought. As the terrain flattened, the Moren began to meander lazily back and forth. Fescue manor continued on its south side, all poor sandy heath interlaced with dirt-track drove roads. Little more than gorse grew in central Fescue.

*

By early afternoon I passed over the Castle itself. From this altitude the grey octagonal walls, corner towers and the Emperor's palace fitted inside looked as if they could sit on the palm of my hand. I couldn't distinguish the elaborate buildings but I saw sunlight reflecting with a flash on the gold sun finial topping the Throne Room spire. A spur from the river fed the gleaming double moat. On the smooth glacis lawn grass I recognized various outbuildings; the oval amphitheatre adjoining the square gymnasium and the stables' courtyard. The archery fields and jousting lists looked like green tiles.

It was strange to think the Emperor was sitting on his throne directly beneath me, not knowing I was gliding thousands of metres above his head. I unpacked my sandwiches and let the paper fall. It tumbled away and dropped behind me amazingly quickly, suddenly giving me something to judge my speed against. I hoped the Emperor was standing on his balcony and it fluttered down onto his head.

The Castle's curtain wall dwarfed Demesne village just west of it, past the series of mirror-like fishponds. The Castle's servants live in Demesne village and it is the only land the Castle has ever owned. The land on which it and the Castle stands is independent of any manor but much smaller than any muster. Its fields can only sustain the village itself and not the Castle, which is dependent on the good will of the Empire; San's deliberate wish, to symbolise that the Castle is the Empire's servant.

Pinchbeck town crowded into a bend in the river. Open, blunt-prowed barges no bigger than apple pips nosed onto its jetties. Timber-framed cranes were swinging sacks onto their decks. Here was the first sign of the city – Hacilith sucks in a vast amount of produce – the whole Plainslands and the rest of Morenzia can't match the quantities its markets buy and sell. My excitement began to grow – even out here in Shivel you can feel the pull of Hacilith.

Heavier barges sat low in the water, carrying millstones and masonry from the Heshcam quarries. Felled logs butted among them, floating in huge rope corrals, to be drifted downstream to the hungry capital.

Pinchbeck diminished and I flashed by plain farmland; all beehives, tariff barns, cow sheds, pigsties, duck ponds, threshing sheds, oil-presses. Before me, Shivel, the second-largest Plainslands town, spread out from the river, flat over the land like lichen.

Shivel manor house was just outside the town on the main road. I contemplated how unlike most Awian manor houses that was. They're usually at a distance from town in their own parkland, but the Plainslands governors live near their citizens. That may encourage their people, but I'm dubious, because for all their physical proximity the Plainslands aristocracies are even more distant from their tenants than are those of Awia – and the corrupt oligarchy of Hacilith, living in the same streets as their citizens, may as well be in a different world.

Further on, I passed over a scatter of reed-thatched, run-down hovels, the dwellings of cottars who scrape their existence by hiring themselves to the tenant farmers at sowing and harvest, at little more than subsistence levels. In the months between, they labour at any odd job available – women were pegging linen on lines to dry. All the men seemed to be busy building another hovel from clay cob. Kids ran about barefoot and chickens scratched around under their ladders; the cottars let their scrawny livestock live in their own houses.

I lifted my wings a touch from the horizontal to glide efficiently. They cut the air; it forced over their hard, smooth upper surfaces with a swish like sword blades. I was having to fly faster now, to get enough lift, and I had neck ache from keeping my head up and looking forwards.

A squad of archers were marching along the road, just dots with long shadows stretching before them – probably a patrol returning from the downs – all governors use them to keep the main roads clear of highwaymen. The horse jumps in the next field looked no bigger than matchsticks and dainty trotting palfreys were like models. I felt I could reach down and move them about.

The land began to look crumpled, like a sheet that had been shaken and left rucked and folded. I was rising up over the tail of the Awndyn Downs. I went over Coutille town in its muster, all uncobbled roads and self-consciously traditional half-timbered homes. The walls of the oldest buckled outwards so they looked as if they were about to collapse and concertina down in a pile of thick thatch.

More signs of the city dotted the south Awndyn Downs: the handsome private houses of Hacilith industrialists or lawyers; litigious and venal merchants, shipmen, and businessmen. They were not interested in owning land because it's more respectable to be a merchant in Hacilith, but they were eager to display their wealth.

All along the horizon white figures cut into the chalk hills were turning pink in the twilight. They were miniscule in the distance but just distinguishable as the badges of the adjoining manors, the dolphin of Awndyn, Eske plough, Hacilith fist and Shivel star, cut and maintained by their fyrds.

Hacilith cast an upwards glow on low cloud base; the pale yellow of cannel coal fires in thousands of homes. I could smell the coal tar already. Closer, and the larger buildings loomed into familiarity; I could name every one. The field of vision narrowed, the roofs increased in size, and the suburban tatter of the Pityme district opened out beneath me. It extended in a ribbon

618

along both canal banks and for a shorter distance up the Camber Road as if stuck to it.

I cruised at the rate of two beats a minute, my legs straight and pressed together in quick accipitrine flight, above the road as it ran across the single, flint-faced span of Pityme Bridge, the oldest on the canal, carrying the Camber Road into the city of Hacilith and the republic of Morenzia.

The Moren River was silted and sluggish, seemingly a solid bulk. It reflected dully, as if shellac varnished, the lights glimmering on its far bank – the Marenna Dock piers and waterfront way over in Brandoch manor.

The Moren is tidal as far as Hacilith and its banks are brackish. I saw a dismal grazier wandering on the marsh, looking after emaciated sheep. Then the huge iron lock gates at the end of the Hacilith–Awndyn canal hove into view and the marsh ended in a continuous stretch of wharves.

This immense canal was Frost's grand waterway; it took her fifty years to complete and it ensured the rise to prominence of the Wrought armouries. The canal made Awndyn's fortune too, but it turned Diw harbour into a ghost town, as ships no longer needed to risk rounding Cape Brattice.

Below me, the rough Galt district docks sprawled along the whole east bank of the Moren, surrounded by refuse tips and the shacks of 'mudlarks' who scrape an existence by beachcombing the mudflats. The paddletrams had been decommissioned decades ago, and their waterwheels had been dismantled, but the decaying supports reared like spires out of the river.

Fat chimneys, squat chimneys of pottery and slate. All the mucky house backs with alleys hung with washing and piled with so much refuse it was turning into soil.

I made very sharp turns and fell steeply with my wings fanned out and my legs dangling. My descent and angle of vision became more acute: the shop fronts too sheer to see, just lines and lines of roofs running in the same direction. I seemed to be going faster the lower I dropped, because I could measure my speed against every ridge and gutter. Landing is the most hazardous time and I concentrated completely on finding a safe place. It was impossible. I couldn't glide down any of the roads without hitting a shop front.

I turned and the exclusive Fiennafor district tilted into view ahead. The tall eighteenth-century town houses were regimented in quarter-circle curved terraces. Aver-Falconet's bronze-clad palace front glowed dully in the street lights. Puddles glinted among the cobbles on its wide parade.

Here was the arc closest to the palace, all double sash windows, Neo-Tealean white fronts with plain columns flat against the walls. The gates in their iron railings gave onto the parade, around an immaculate oval lawn with a spreading plane tree. It was The Crescent, and Lightning's house was number one.

I descended in front of it. I thrust my wings forward and the feathers spread flat automatically to stop me stalling. Wings' fingers open, legs down: my boot toes skimmed over the surface of a puddle leaving two long ripples. I stepped down out of the air and began walking without a pause, folding my wings behind me.

The yellow wheels of a glossy coach rolled past an arm's length away. I let it pass, crossed the road and walked up the steps to the black painted door.

The door knocker was so highly polished it looked unreal. I rapped it and looked around as I waited for the major-domo to answer. The sky was heavy with more rain and the evening still.

The major-domo showed me a room. She laid out a dressing gown of the best Awian silk and took my clothes to be cleaned and pressed. She spread the table with hot coffee and pancakes. When I had eaten I stripped all the covers off the bed and slept on the floor.

CHAPTER 5

I began searching for Cyan and thought it best to try the fashionable district first. I walked around Fiennafor and looked in Aver-Falconet's palace, then Lorimer Street with The Moren Grand Theatre, The Bourse and The Old Almshouse Café. I found no sign of Lightning's daughter anywhere.

I hired a carriage and drove east to Moren Wells, a very upmarket spa town recently swallowed by the fringe of the city. I searched for Cyan in the Sinter Spa and Calandra Park, but no one there had heard any news.

The next morning I wondered what to do. I only had one day left and I doubted I could find her. I decided to work my way south through Galt into Old Town. That way I could visit Rayne at the university before leaving. I made sure my wallet was safe, buttoned my coat pockets tight, and submerged myself in Galt, the largest of the five districts.

The further I walked, the more I realised that I would never find Cyan but, ever hopeful, I walked slowly and looked around carefully, especially at the girls, as I passed the:

Scuttlebutt Casino
Cockfighting pits
Prize-fighters' boxing booths
Clutchfut Vintners
Inglenook Hostel
The bull ring
The paper mill
The brass hammer mill
The denim mill
The cartwheel lathes
The markets:
The cattle market
The hides and skins' market
The broadcloth Furbelows Market
The woodwork Treen Market
The glass and pots Frit Market
The fish and salt Gabelle Market
The Meal Market, where shiploads of corn change hands
The Meat Market, its drains running with blood
The Mop Market, where job seekers sell their own services
The Crimp Market for mountains of coal

The Whispering Market for perfumes and objets d'art – a covered arcade where the stalls are packed so closely together that business is done at a whisper in case anybody hears the deals

Past the butterstone at the markets' end
Past the Cooper's yard
Past the Atilliator's yard
Past the rope walk
Past East Sea Customs House
Past the dry dock, where ships were repaired
To the wet dock where goods were being unloaded.

I paused there and looked out over the river, a solid mass of inshore galleys, barges, tugs and flyboats; waiting to load, register, enter the canal or extricate themselves from the chaos. Upriver, a single armed caravel watched the teeming industry with a constable's eye.

The incredible number of wagons, drovers' turkeys with pitch on their feet, grain storehouses full to the roof, the stink of coal tar and the hubbub of the markets reminded me of the queues coming into the battlefront. I didn't stand any chance of finding Cyan if she was lost in these crowds.

I bought a kebab on a stick, and a copy of *Lammergeier* fashion magazine to see what my wife, Tern Wrought, was doing this season. I scanned her column, called 'Ageless Taste', but it had nothing about me. I had not seen Tern this happy since last century; she had paid off most of her debts with the booty from Tris and was supervising the rebuilding and redecorating of her manor house. Wrought isn't called the fashion capital of Awia for nothing; Tern was working hard, from party to party, trailing people without noticing them, except for when they itched.

It began to drizzle and the damp Hacilith chill sank into everything. I turned away from the river and walked deeper into Galt, heading towards Old Town. The houses here were all back-to-backs with alleys between them; no yards but one outside toilet shared by each alley. Rainwater chuckled along the gutter, washing over some rotting pamphlets from the recent elections.

The poverty was obvious here; many lived in the streets. Everyone wore hats, endless designs of cloth caps and liripipes. A beggar was shouting, 'Fists and daffodils! Swans and shells!' I riffled through my wallet and dropped him a couple of ten-penny notes with the Summerday shell.

I glanced over to the shield factory's covered courtyard. Boys from the workhouse were laying out unpainted shields for their glue to dry. I could just see onto the factory floor where craftsmen were making them by hand.

I stopped and looked around. I knew I was still heading towards Old Town because the university's tower, with turrets at each of its four corners, projected above the shambling roofs. I was deep in Galt now but I felt weirdly disorientated. I had expected to recognise my old haunt, but it bore no resemblance to the Galt I knew. There was no ground plan left of the streets, no trace whatsoever of the old docks. It's been two hundred years, Jant, I told myself; what do you expect? It was unfamiliar ... no, so *nearly* familiar, that it was giving me the creeps.

A cart laden with rubbish went past; the whiskery driver bellowing, 'Raag and Bo-one! Raag and Bo-one!'

What was that about? Where were all the wharves? All this used to be open ground – it seemed impossible – how could so many houses have been fitted into it?

I was sure I should have passed the Bird in the Hand Awian strip joint, but there were just more houses. Either I was completely in the wrong place or the very roads had changed. Well, I thought, the chemist's shop where I used to work would have been over there. I'll walk down and see if I'm right.

When I lived here, the city way of thinking trapped me, narrowing my horizons just as the factories block out the sky. I didn't even want to leave. I put all my energy into misguided actions and negative reactions until I couldn't pull myself from the mire. Back then, the roads out of Galt led in two directions. To the left, the streets thinned out and one road wound over Pityme Bridge into the beginning of grassy hills in the distance. I could have taken that road and escaped, but I never did; not until I was forced out. That road may as well have not existed. Every night I went right, down the other alley to the strip joint with a sign promising 'Great Tits!' in the window. I convinced myself that I'd had enough of travelling, should stay in the shop and read books, and visit whores. It never even crossed my mind that the Castle would want my talent, until my life in Hacilith was in ruins.

I had liked working in Dotterel's chemist shop, it was dim and quiet; the gang's fear of employment made it a safe refuge. With the shutters down, every customer who entered saw me, a boy slouching on the counter who had already looked them over, a freak perhaps, tall and skinny even for adolescence, but a perfect confidant.

My time looking for Cyan was nearly up. It's hopeless, I thought – I'll go and see Rayne instead, if she hasn't already left for Slake, and then I'll head back. At least I'll be able to tell the others when Rayne should be arriving.

I reached an open plaza and stopped. This should be Cinder Street. Maybe ... that row of shops was along the same line. I looked around. If this was Cinder Street, then the Kentledge pub would have been at the far end ... And my chemist's shop would have been ... there. And the Campion Vaudeville! That should be on the next street over! I ran quickly towards it, remembering the peeling playbills fluttering on its boards, the shards of glass that topped the walls around it, the masks and scrolls around the windows in its leaking mansard roof.

The street ended at an empty plaza with a row of smart boutiques and some sort of trendy wine bar. The Campion Vaudeville had totally gone.

They've redeveloped my street! How dare they? Yes, it had been run down but I had liked it! There was no trace of the second-hand shops full of individual texture I had loved so much. That corner was where I busked with Babbitt – and now it had all been swept away.

The new shops had no character; time hadn't given them any unique pattern of wear. They blocked my view of the canal towpath, pressed up tall and narrow against each other as if someone had put a hand at each end of the plaza and squeezed them together. Their colour-washed fronts were rose pink, yellow, pale blue, chalky green and grey. They proudly announced they'd passed inspection, with firemark, ratmark and lousemark tin badges tacked to their walls.

I walked along the row, half whited-out by drizzle. Streams of water dripped from the sign of the horrendous new bar at the far end and pattered into concentric rings on the paving stones. That bar would be more or less on the place where the Kentledge pub used to be, where our gang leader carved the Wheel scar into my shoulder. The power of the memory made me shudder: I outlast whole *streets*, and now Cinder Street and everything I remembered was no more.

This must have been exactly where Dotterel the chemist picked me up; when he made me his apprentice. I stood and stared at the row of shops until I could call up an image of the Campion two hundred years ago. It seemed larger in memory, closer and brighter than the shops it overlaid. Its smoke-stained stone had flaked off here and there showing clean, biscuity spots.

I heard a whir, a paddletram! – It sounded like it could be ... but it wasn't. Simply flocks of starlings screaming and swirling in to roost.

A vision of my younger self jumped down from the Campion's portico and ran past me, soundlessly though his footsteps should have splashed. He vanishes. He reappears again in the alley by the Kentledge; transparent – then solid – a lanky fifteen-year-old in a filthy parka. He ducks his head and wipes his nose on his sleeve.

Lines of coaches are waiting outside the Campion Vaudeville, and wisps of smog are curling through and around their wheels. Oil lamps are guttering out with gin-blue flames since it is three in the morning and the late show is just ending. The act closes to half-hearted acclaim and people begin to stagger out into the street. Linkboys hang around in a curious cloud, their tapers scribbling lines of smoke into the air above them. The Rhydanne boy hates them, because they understand each other. They know how to buy bustard burgers and tablet fudge. They swagger with the all-encompassing importance of their job.

From the end of the street there are raised voices, lads shouting to each other about the can-can dancers. Paddletrams groan past in the background, grinding cabbage leaves and hawked-up chewing tobacco into a black sludge between the rails. The boy is faster than sight; he pauses to draw breath and ducks behind the frame of a waiting coach. The nearest human moves on and the boy relaxes.

He moves in quick bursts, waiting behind lamp post and coach wheel, doorway and alley. He crooks his elbow and tears the Insect wing windows of all the coaches along the line.

'I saw you!' calls a voice from somewhere in the fog. Quick as a rat the boy leaps onto the top of the carriage, which hardly rocks at all on its flat springs. He crouches, nose streaming, piercing eyes in a grimy face.

An old man emerges from the porch of the Campion. His head is bowed and his face is in shadow. This is a trick the boy very much admires. The man looks up; his face is padded, deeply wrinkled and his nose veined cranberry red. Wisps of hair too white for Galt adhere to his bald head. He is wearing a long, grey coat and carrying a cane with a silver handle, which he points at the boy. The boy simply crouches further on thin haunches and spreads his wings.

The man knows that if he takes a step or even stares too hard, the boy will run. Very querulously he says, 'Who are you?' but he says it in Scree.

'You speak Scree? How? At last! What is this place? Er ... I haven't spoken to anyone since last melt season. I'm ill all the time. I've never been this ill before. I have to hunt for myself! And I c-can't make any one understand! No one—'

'Sh! Slower, boy; don't gabble. You're alone?'

'You're observant!'

'Why did you break the windows?'

The boy shrugged. What else could he do to show his anger or make his presence felt? He sat cross-legged on the coach roof, reached a hand down through the torn window and brought out an apple. He began to examine it with the delicacy of mime.

'They don't belong to you, Dara.'

'I'm a Shira. That could be the reason why I am finding it so entertaining to break them.'

'You're quick,' said the old man, smiling.

'I'm the quickest,' said the boy.

The man took a tight grip on his cane and tapped the cobbles for a while in thought. The boy, seeing this, threw down his apple which rolled under the folds of the man's long coat. Enthralled, the boy watched it, head on one side. His instincts were to bolt, but this man was the first person he had spoken to in a year. Indecision rooted him to the spot. He swore in Scree, but all those insults about goats didn't seem too relevant in Hacilith.

The man gave a rustle of coughing laughter. 'Well, I need an assistant, but I never thought I would have to tame one ... I will turn now and walk away,' he continued slowly. 'You can follow me if you want. No one will hurt you. No one will force you, but it will be best for you if you come.'

The man walked on and did not look back, and gradually disappeared into the smog. He did not seem to be a threat; indeed, he could be a saviour. The boy watched from his precarious perch, then fluttered down and sauntered after him, still prepared to run.

Dotterel and the boy walked through the wall of the bar and disappeared. I sighed. Any Rhydanne would have been naïve in the city, but I had been naïve even by Rhydanne standards. I was quite the little foreigner; it's a wonder I survived at all.

I need a drink after seeing that, and besides, the rain was running down my neck. I investigated the bar, plated with brushed and burnished bronze along its whole front. Smooth almost featureless metal statues with folded arms and stylised wings like blades stood with heavy elegance on either side of its doorway. It was done up to look like Aver-Falconet's square palace, in the new Decorative Art. Its sign said: The Jacamar Club. An Awian pub, then, the sort popular with the few tourists who came out this way from Fiennafor. As if to prove my thought, some frightful shrieking laughter resounded from inside. I have never understood why travellers and expats feel the need to go to a pub mocked up with all the features of a bar of their homeland to drink wine at ten times the price. There were any number of Morenzian inns nearby where they could drink beer, eat boar pie and hear the citizens speaking their own language.

I went inside, flapping my half-closed wings to dry them and flicking drops everywhere. A couple of students at a nearby table yelled, but when they looked up and saw me, they shut up abruptly.

The pub's fittings were the most up-to-date design but the floor was sticky with spilt drinks. Square columns were bolted to the walls, all painted black but with gold lightning flashes and pointed feathers on the tops. A strikingly graceful fresco of a deer chased by hundreds of hounds fled along the walls. All the way to the rear wall the hind ran with the hounds ever at her throat and, below her outstretched legs, on a leather sofa stained with nicotine, sat Cyan.

CHAPTER 6

Oh, no. I could hear Cyan's voice from the doorway. She was too conspicuous, blissfully unaware she could be attracting every thief and rapist in Galt. She was recounting an anecdote at the top of her voice to a group of students and she hadn't noticed me, so I approached slowly, watching.

Cyan was no longer a child. Her blonde hair hung perfectly straight to the level of her bodice top. Its straps and laces showed and so did her armpit hair. Her short skirt kept riding up and she kept pulling it down. Her stockings plunged into huge black boots. She didn't have wings, she took after her mother, and she was willowy; slighter and more hourglass-shaped than an Awian woman.

At her hip hung a dagger, tied into its scabbard as city law dictated, and the most impressive little compound bow I have ever seen hung off the chair arm in a lacquer holster. Under the table a waxed cotton quiver held enough arrows to depopulate the whole bar. Didn't she know it was illegal to carry a bow openly in the city?

I hadn't seen Cyan since her mother's funeral. Her very poise seemed to have changed; a vehemence had taken root in her previously innocent adventurousness. This was the girl I used to tickle until she was helpless with giggling. This was the girl I picked up off the shipwreck years ago – but of course she wouldn't remember. I watched covertly, feeling special, slightly dizzy having flown such a great distance and having walked into the city-dwellers' trivial little world. There was no way they could understand or even acknowledge my effort. To them I just appear.

As she talked animatedly an enormous ruby pendant on a gold chain rolled back and forth above her flattened breasts. Fortunately some of the other women's glass costume jewellery was just as ostentatious, but you didn't have to look closely to tell that Cyan's ruby was real.

She was surrounded by lots of girls, who must mistakenly think she could arrange a rendezvous with Lightning. They started to notice me and one by one slunk or darted back to their tables. She didn't look up until I was directly opposite her and the last of her court sloughed away leaving just one rugged-looking fyrdsman.

Cyan jumped nearly clear of the cushions in surprise. 'Jant! Come here, come here and sit down! Why have you come all this way? Never mind; the coolest Eszai will make my night complete!'

I sank into an armchair on the other side of the table. Everyone's eyes were prickling from the corners of the room. Cyan was overjoyed. 'Let me introduce you. Rawney, this is *the* Comet Jant Shira. He flies in from the Castle to see me. Sometimes he carries ice down from Darkling for our drinks … Jant, this is Rawney.'

'Rawney what?'

'No. Rawney Carron.'

'Very Morenzian. Pleased to meet you.' Rawney Carron ignored the hand I offered him and glowered at me. He seemed to have claimed ownership of Cyan. He was not tall so I guessed he was city born and bred. He wore fyrd fatigues with the murrey fist blazon of Hacilith sewn on the breast and he also had it tattooed on his arm. He had a weightlifter's build and he clearly fancied himself.

'He's a corporal,' said Cyan. 'And this … er … that *was* Sharny. He seems to have gone. Well, never mind. What are you doing here? Did Daddy send you? And why do you have soot on your eyes? Oh, it's make-up.'

Rawney sniggered.

'Shut it,' I told him. I was not prepared to take any cheek from a fyrds-man. 'Cyan, this time I'm here to bring you home.'

'She wants to stay,' said Rawney.

'Go and join the rest of your squad,' I told him.

'I haven't got one yet. I have to press a General Fyrd squad tonight.'

'Are you going to the front?'

'Yes. I'm looking forward to it. It's better than working in the docks. It's an adventure.'

'Good.' I gave him a grin.

Only the musters of Hacilith pressgang fyrd, and I knew Rawney must be professional Select Fyrd because only Select can be officers of any rank in either fyrd. He leant back on the couch and put his arm behind Cyan. I shuffled forward, as if to protect her.

'Did Daddy send you?' she repeated.

'As a matter of fact I suggested it to him. Are you all right?'

'I'm having a great time!'

'Do you have lodgings?'

'Yes.'

'And money?'

'Yes, of course. Daddy gave me pocket money for the tour, and I can always draw on my account. He fills it up now and again. He's loaded.'

'In that case I'll have a double whisky,' I said.

'Fine.' Cyan shook a five-pound coin from her purse.

'Ask him to fetch them.' I nodded and smiled at Rawney, and pushed the coin towards him.

'Rawney, go and bring some whisky, another wallop for me and get yourself a jug of beer. They don't take orders at your table here,' she added to me. 'It isn't that Awian.'

Rawney lumbered off to the bar. I called after him, 'And a couple of baskets of chips!'

'I wonder where you put it all, you're so thin.'

'I fly,' I said shortly. 'Cyan, why did you run away? Lightning's worried sick. And don't you know it's illegal to carry bows in the city?' I took it off the chair arm and slipped it under the couch. 'What are you doing here? You have to come home.'

She looked me over. 'There's no such thing as "have to". I am not going back to Micawater or Awndyn. Not ever. No way. You can't make me.'

'Yes, I can, actually. What are you doing with that hulk?'

'Rawney? He's gorgeous.'

'He's dim. Lightning wants you to come to the front. We're about to advance at Frost's lake.'

'That old eel-eater. I don't want to go to the damn dam. I want to stay here.'

'You're not lodging with that Morenzian meathead, are you?'

'That's none of your business! Hmm ... I don't think I'll tell you, because you'll just flutter off back to Daddy and spill the beans. I know what I'm doing.'

'Do you really?'

'I was fed up with dull old Awndyn.' She sighed. 'I had to get away. Away from obligation! I want to stay here and live it up for a few months. I have a freedom here I never had with Swallow, with Daddy; they're all living in a dream world. They have no idea how the real world works. This is the real world—' Her gesture took in the bar and what little of East Bank was visible through the window '—This is where the real people are.' She lit a cigarette and narrowed her eyes against the smoke. 'I know I'm lucky and I can do anything, but I just haven't made my mind up yet.'

'Please come back.'

'Don't be crap, goat-breath. You do what you want, you always told me that. Why shouldn't I?'

I was frustrated that I had to spell this out: 'Hacilith is dangerous.'

'Yeah!'

'You can't be Rawney's girlfriend. You might pretend but you'll never really understand him.'

She smiled sweetly. 'I can play him along for kicks. He worships the ground I walk on.'

I hissed, 'No. You might think that, but he reckons you're his girl. If you try to leave him, he might hurt you.'

'Whatever gave you that idea?' she said, shocked.

'Oh, Cyan. Please be careful. You might find it hard to get rid of the likes of him. He knows he can't really have you, so instead he could try to make your life misery. He could blame you for the fact that he's Insect fodder and you're glittering with rubies.'

'I don't think so.'

'Oh, yes. Worse still, if he believes you're something you're not, he could chase you unto the last of his energy and be prepared to die for what his imagination makes you into. He'd love to marry the heir to Peregrine.'

I glanced over to the bar but fortunately Rawney was taking a long time. He was chatting with a skinny, wasted-looking guy. I took a sip of Cyan's 'wallop' – ginger beer that was more beer than it was ginger – and went on; 'You'll never understand what Hacilith is like under the surface. It's impossible, but try to grasp that I'm telling you this from my own experience. My image isn't just an image, Cyan; I witnessed the last days of the East Bank gangs.' I pushed my coat off my shoulder so she could see the circle with six spokes that our gang leader had carved there. 'The other gang, the Bowyers, had arrowheads scarred on their forearms. We used to flay them off and stick them to the door of our warehouse.'

'Wow.'

'Yes. Well, I suppose I should never have tried to encroach on their patch. When they caught any of us, they dumped us in the canal lock. When we caught any of them, we nailed them to the struts of a waterwheel. Hence the Wheel.' I took her hand and traced the furrows of my scar with her finger.

'I can feel it.'

'That's right.'

She didn't know whether to believe me or not. 'Didn't the constables do anything?'

'Oh, I always tipped off the constables. But they left them revolving round and round for a few hours before they took them down ... The Bowyers eventually traced where I lived. I came home one night and found my shop on fire. I ran in, trying to find my master ...' I continued sadly as I put my coat back on. 'He was called Dotterel. I tried to run upstairs but the steps were burning through. I expect – I hope – he died of smoke suffocation long before the flames reached the second floor ...'

Cyan said, 'I'm sorry.'

'I couldn't feel grief back then, only despair. It was the next inevitable avalanche to happen to me. What sort of life was Hacilith, anyway? My girlfriend pulled me out of the shop as it rose in flames about me and, right then, we determined to leave Galt. We took the road that went left over Pityme Bridge and we realised that even the Castle was possible.'

I never tell Zascai that I used to be a drug dealer, but I let them know my unfortunate adventures. It makes me seem so much more talented for having escaped them.

Cyan said, 'Hacilith must have changed.'

'Yes, it's different now. The underworld is more inconspicuous and a damn sight more complicated, but it hasn't gone away.'

She took a sip of her drink and rolled her eyes. 'Oh god. If that's your advice, I don't need it. I don't want Daddy's advice either, and I certainly don't want Swallow the mad diva's homespun instruction. I thought better of you. Let me make my own mistakes!'

'You don't want Lightning's advice? Fourteen hundred years of it?'

'Fourteen hundred years of boredom, more like!'

'You'll inherit Peregrine when you're twenty-one,' I said.

'That's what I'm running away from! My true place in life, huh. How can I be an Awian lady when I don't feel Awian at all? Not that being wingless matters; Awians will accept me and anyway, they don't have a choice. But I don't feel I belong anywhere. Daddy gave me this—' She hooked her fingers under the chain of her ruby pendant as if she was about to rip it off and throw it away. 'He says it's an heirloom. But I don't belong in Micawater either. "Come home," you tell me, but just where home is, I can't say. Morenzia is the only country that's free.'

'Don't say that in front of Lightning.'

'Just five families in Awia own eighty per cent of the land. Morenzians don't have such a silly aristocracy. They don't have to bow and scrape. You don't know what it's like to be a girl stuck in Awndyn.'

I nodded. That much was true.

'Hacilith is so big! There are so many people my age! I never had friends in Awndyn. But, god, Jant, what does that mean to you? You're bloody ancient. The Castle protects you, just like Daddy.'

'You should have seen me at Slake Cross trying to hold my guts in with one hand.'

'Oh, yeah. Sorry.' She pinched her cheek and wiggled it. 'You think you see a girl but looking out of these eyes is a very experienced woman, in experience terms at least as old as you are. Well, nearly. I've travelled all over the place.'

'Did you go or were you taken?'

Her eyebrows drew together. I continued, 'You haven't been south of Awndyn before and you haven't been north of Micawater.'

'I'm here of my own accord *now*. So don't misunderestimate me. Take Rawney, I only met him four days ago and he says he will do anything for me. He can get anything for me, even jook. He helped me move onto the Tumblehome.'

'Is that where you're staying?'

'Oh … Yeah, it is, actually. So let me express myself. I'm not going to be cooped up in Awndyn with the mad diva.'

Rawney returned with the drinks but without any food. He didn't give Cyan her change either but she didn't notice. He put a whole bottle of cheap whisky down in front of me. 'There! Get your talons round that!'

'I don't have talons,' I said indignantly, but he continued to stare rudely while I poured a glass. I stared back, and he looked away.

People naturally resent anybody who gives them orders and Zascai are especially resentful of good-looking immortals who can fly. Rawney was trying to find something to feel superior about and, as usual for such people, he was concentrating on my Rhydanne heritage. There is not much in my appearance and bearing for Morenzians to identify with; all that is human in me, I have learnt. They characterise Rhydanne as a bunch of hopeless drunks; the fact that one might flap down from the mountains and start giving them commands is a further affront to their dignity. Also, if he is like most Zascai, he will think of me as the voice of the Emperor and be doubly afraid. Mortals often assume that because I have the Emperor's ear I am somehow closer to him than other immortals. That isn't true, and anyway why would San send me to spy on someone like Rawney?

Cyan gave an embarrassed giggle. 'It's so strange to be talking to one of Daddy's workmates.'

I said, 'As the future Governor of Peregrine, you'll get used to it.'

'How many times have I got to tell you? I don't want to be governor! I hate feeling the weight of Daddy's expectations on me all the time! It's all right for you, flying around and never counting the cost. I'm not impressed with his plans for me. I have different plans. How dare he assume my tastes are the same as his? He doesn't even know me!'

'But you used to love hunting in Peregrine,' I said.

'Yes, I know. Weird, isn't it? It became overfamiliar, I suppose. It disappointed me. I don't want to see all those same faces again.' She turned to Rawney. 'Jant used to frustrate the fuck out of me with all his exciting plans I wasn't allowed to realise. I loved his tales of faraway places. Now I'm in one!'

That made me smile. 'Lightning would be furious if he knew you were sitting in a bar.'

'Huh. Him. He doesn't understand what's real in life. He's stuck with his sense of honour. I think we should feel first and act on our feelings instead. I wanted someone to know my mind, Jant. No one in Awndyn could, so it's me who has to change. I thought: if I don't change, I'll die. But now the future has opened up wide!'

I poured more whisky. Every spoilt teenager talks like this, and Cyan was in full flow. 'I've got my enthusiasm back. I used to feel dormant, as if I was waiting to start my own life. I was breathless and apprehensive, but I was ready and now things are starting to happen! My hatred of Awndyn wound me up like a spring and shot me out to Hacilith. I'm not stopping now.'

I said, 'You might find the front just as refreshing. Have you ever seen a live Insect? No? Well, I can show you things even more exciting than Hacilith.'

She glanced at Rawney. 'Bring him, too,' I said. 'Lightning will love him.'

She said slowly, 'Hacilith is more cleansing. I can get lost here. Nobody knows who I am.'

'I think they do!'

'Bollocks, Jant. Bollocks. Listen. There are three sorts of people: the ones in Awndyn or Micawater don't have to ask who one's father is, because they know and they take it for granted. Then I travelled a bit and met the sort, like in Aver-Falconet's household, who do think it's important to ask who one's father is. They're surprised and a bit scared when I tell them, because they don't really know what to say. They think they should treat me with kid gloves. I hate them. Then there are the real people, like these Morenzians. It never occurs to them to ask; as far as they're concerned it's a meaningless question. They treat me the same as any other girl.'

'That's the problem.'

Rawney said nothing but became gradually redder and redder in the face until he burst. 'You know fuck all, immortal! You left this town! You hit the big time. Yeah, you went away and won immortality and married money. So what are you doing here? Why have you come here? Go fuck off back to the Castle. Go on – get out! You don't belong here with your fucking smart comments and your weird old-fashioned clothes!'

I tilted my head and gave him a good look with my cheekbones. If he wanted a fight I could shove my axe up his arse in three moves. 'I swear,' I said softly. 'If we didn't send the people of Hacilith to fight Insects, they'd be fighting each other.'

Rawney flinched, glanced at Cyan and rallied. 'Look, babe, we're talking to a madman. A real creep. He's two hundred years old and he's not going to die so he must be mad compared to us mortals. He has nothing to do with us.'

Cyan pursed her lips. 'It *is* off-putting that he always looks the same. It reminds me of when I was small.'

I sighed, sick of invective. 'Please, Cyan. I don't want to leave you here. I can't tell Lightning this.'

'I can't believe you're on Daddy's side!'

'I'm not. I agree that you shouldn't sweetly follow the life he's planned for you. Forget the governorship, if you want. That's fine by me. But I think you're a bit vulnerable and—'

'I can look after myself!' She grabbed the bow from under the sofa and before I could stop her, she slid it out of its holster.

The bar suddenly went very quiet. Every face turned towards us, but Rawney stood up and called, 'Do you want to see another trick?'

To my astonishment they all began to applaud. Nobody slipped out to call the constables. Cyan acknowledged them with a wave. She held her bow across her knee and ran her hands over it to warm it, then carefully bent its limbs back and strung it. They were tapered, surprisingly whippy for a reflex bow. She slipped a horn ring on her thumb and pulled two arrows, shorter than fyrd standard arrows, from the quiver. She pressed ginger beer bottle corks onto their sharp bodkin points, saying, 'I'll show you my trick.'

'I've seen this. It's one of Lightning's stunts.'

'No, it's *my* trick.' She lost none of the emphasis the second time round, so I decided to let her win. 'Go on, then.'

She did not bother to stand up. She nocked an arrow and drew it to her cheek with a pinch grip. She aimed and let fly.

A bottle on the furthest table jumped into the air, clattered down and started spinning round, flashing its empty neck and base.

Cyan shot the second arrow and it recorked the spinning bottle. The force of its impact sent it off the edge of the table. It skidded across the floor bounced off a young man's foot. He held it up, the cork firmly fixed and the arrow protruding.

Cyan's impromptu audience gave her another round of applause. She stretched up her arm and raised her three middle fingers, her thumb holding her little finger down. It was the archers' salute, long ago, and now it's a very filthy gesture.

'See!' she said to me. 'All these new friends!' And louder: 'Let's show Comet a good time. All the drinks are on me!'

There was a cheer and the sound of a general rush to the bar. Much impressed, I said, 'You're very accurate. And that's a glorious bow.'

'Thanks. It's one of Daddy's own designs.'

'Don't ever use it in Hacilith again when I'm not here! Why don't you come to the front, if you're keen on shooting? You can practise on Insects every day.'

'I am *not* going to Daddy. There'll be two bridges over the Foin before I do! The Emperor will leave the Castle, god will return and the world will end before I talk to him!'

'He did his best. He brought you up as well as he could.' I indicated the bow as an example of Lightning's largesse.

'Huh. It was his fault my mother was killed. He could have saved her but he let her die.'

I put the bottle down. 'What? Who told you that?'

'Carmine Dei. One of my stepsisters.'

'She's lying. Lightning did all he could to save your mother. I know; I was there.' Cyan's stepsister was as big a bitch as their mother, Ata, had been. After she died, some of her huge family remained in contact, a large clandestine organisation, and these days Carmine has the whole suspect network well under her hand. She was the city's harbourmaster; she had failed in the last competition for Sailor, and being Sailor manqué had made her even more poisonous.

I said, 'You mustn't listen to anything Carmine says. Are you staying with her?'

'No. Not quite. Carmine told me a lot of Daddy's secrets and I know some of them must be true. After all he abandoned me with Governor Swallow Fatarse. She made me learn silly musical instruments I wasn't the slightest bit interested in. Once, when I was little, I pretended to be an Insect under her dumb piano and I accidentally scratched it. She went totally crazy. After that being an Insect was out of the question. Silly cow. And she plays Daddy better then she plays any instrument! I visit Micawater now and then, but he doesn't realise how long the gaps are between visits. What is he doing that's so damn important I had to fend for myself?'

Cyan has never had to fend for herself. Everywhere she goes, servants hover to accommodate her every whim. I tilted the glass back and swilled whisky. I didn't want any more hassle. Cyan had used up my quota of patience and I had far too much on my mind. I wasn't sure if I was becoming wise with age, or simply exhausted; but then, if wisdom is a more prudent use of one's time, maybe it's exhaustion that forces us to be wise.

I shook my head. 'Whatever. Oh, what it is to be seventeen and open to rumour. Believe what you like. I won't tell Lightning that I found you. But when you tire of gallivanting around the city, join us at the front, all right?'

'Great!' She lit another cigarette and offered me one, leaning forward to light it with her own.

Rawney glanced at her jealously, but he slopped some more whisky into my glass. Maybe he wasn't so bad after all. He shook the bottle, then looked at me oddly. 'Damn. All the tales I've heard about Rhydanne are true.'

'Another cretinous comment from you and I'll post you to Ressond. Anyway, Rhydanne live above five thousand metres. We need to drink alcohol so our blood doesn't freeze.'

'Oh, yeah,' he said sarcastically.

'All true,' I said. 'No word of a lie. Would I lie to you? No. We have to drink alcohol constantly. And it takes Rhydanne minds off their awful food. There's no time for cuisine between the hunting and the hangovers; I think they only bother to cook because they can't eat it raw.'

Cyan said, 'It can't be true you're the only mix of Awian and Rhydanne.'

I shrugged. 'I'm sure there were others, and there will be others in future, for as long as Awians keep trying to conquer peaks ... I keep pulling their stupid flags off and sending them back. Some Awian–Rhydanne children might have been unviable and didn't survive. Maybe some never made it out of Darkling or weren't able to fly, either not strong or not clever enough to learn. It took me ten years, after all. I should imagine most half-breed babies were thrown over cliffs. I would have been if it wasn't for Eilean. A Rhydanne single mother will kill an unwanted baby that slows her down.'

Rawney said, 'That's brutal. Animals.'

'No. It's a matter of her own survival. And anyway, look who's talking.' I turned to Cyan. 'Maybe we are similar. I've left my heritage behind me and you're trying to.'

'Rubbish,' she teased. 'You love being different. You keep turning your head so your eyes reflect.'

'I do not!'

'You do. And you read fortune cards. You carry them around everywhere.'

'Only for a party trick.' I dug in my inside jacket pocket for the battered sheaf of twenty-five squares of leather and, with a flick of one hand, spread them out. I offered them to her and she leant forward to pick one. She examined it closely, turning it over. 'Look, Rawney. Jant has these Rhydanne fortune cards.'

'Give me a break,' he said. 'Come on, babe, we ought to be going.'

'I keep telling you to stop calling me "babe"!'

He grasped her wrist and I tensed, but Cyan twisted herself free. I saw her blood rise and for the first time I could actually believe I was talking to Lightning's daughter. She made the most of her accent: 'If you do that again, fyrdsman, I will leave with Comet.' Then she said to me, as if to cover up, 'Will you read the cards for me, Jant?'

'All right.' I wiped whisky off the tabletop with my sleeve. I tapped the pack to neaten them and arranged them face down.

'How does it work?'

'The cards ...' I swigged my drink. 'The cards don't tell the future. How could they? The future isn't set. These cards tell you about yourself in the present. All you need to know, to predict the future as accurately as possible ... all you *can* ever know, is yourself right now. Most people don't know their own character well and these cards help you reflect. Then for the future, you extrapolate. Go ahead and make the future up – your character will be the main factor.'

'They're cards for the *present*?'

'Rhydanne live in the present. They don't think ahead to the future much; it's just another present to them. You have to do the reading yourself. You're best placed to interpret your own character.'

'But I don't know what the pictures mean!'

I waved my cigarette around. 'They're just pictures. They don't have defined meanings. They mean whatever you think they mean. That's how it works.'

Cyan looked daunted. 'I think I'm too drunk for this.'

'There are five suits: ice, rock, alcohol, goats and eagles.' I turned over the lowest in the ice suit, the snow hole shelter. 'That one, for example, can mean: remember to maintain your equipment or you'll starve. This one, the goat's kid, can mean: don't chase a woman you're not married to. Or don't marry some slow-running slut whose children are all Shiras. It depends on your circumstances, you see. Pick five cards ...'

Cyan did so. She set them precisely in line and turned over the first. 'Boulders,' I said.

'I beg your pardon?'

'That's from the rock suit: grit, pebbles, boulders, cliffs and mountains. Make of it what you like.'

She pondered the square of hide. 'It means something that blocks your way, doesn't it? An insurmountable problem. Like Daddy. You know his palace? Did you know that all the keyholes in the doors along the Long Corridor line up so well you can look down them from one end of the palace to the other? That's how infuriating it is. It's so finicky and stultifying it makes me sick. Every time I visited I was terrified of breaking something. I think I scare him, because he's been trying hard to cultivate a friendly fatherly image. I hate Micawater. Boulders all right; it's so heavy and stagnant.'

She turned the next card, and exclaimed, 'What in the Empire is that?'

I peered at it. 'It's the dead goat. From the goat suit: dead goat, pastured goat, randy goat, mother goat, kid.'

'You have got to be joking.' She looked from the card to me. 'It's to do with mortality. These cards really do work, don't they? I'm mortal and Daddy isn't ... Everyone knows that at some time in the future their parents will die. They wonder how it'll happen. What will it be like to hear the news? How will they bury him? If they're the eldest, they can't help but think about the inheritance. I don't have that. I can't speculate. That's one of the things I can't stand – Daddy will always be there, exactly the same. In fact, I know that the day he buries me in a tomb on his stupid island, he'll look just the same as he does now. The palace will be no different. I'll never be rid of him! It makes me feel heavy ... I think it's dread.'

She opened another bottle of beer. She had not inherited Lightning's connoisseurship but she had his ability to discourse at length. Beer begets beer, as you know, but she wasn't as drunk as I was. I sipped the whisky appreciatively. 'This was shit at the beginning but it's all right now ... All the nice whisky must sink to the bottom.'

Cyan turned the next card, the soaring eagle. 'Well, that's easy. That's me escaping, trying to fly free of the flock and find some clear air, trying to do something different. It's a wild animal, symbolic of freedom like my name. I'm glad I didn't bring any belongings. I've stranded myself here deliberately with no past, nothing to prove I exist. I have myself, that's all; I'm content with that ...'

I waited, indulgently.

'... I feel awkward in the city, big and clumsy. I pull at doors I'm supposed to push, push at doors that open by pulling. But I'll get used to the city soon. I'm alone, scattered in the multitude – just as I want.'

'To be scattered in the multitude, hey?'

She glowered at me and flicked over another card. 'What's this one?'

'The nesting eagle.'

'A nesting eagle ... That must stand for domesticity, marriage. Marriage ... oh, yuk, did I tell you about all the men Daddy introduced me to? They're horrible.'

Rawney smirked. 'Don't the suitors suit you?'

'They're so superficial! They make all these unfounded assumptions!' Cyan slipped into High Awian, which was good for talking of art, society and its insults, but not much else. 'This is their repertoire: "You are Lightning's daughter, really? When do you come of age?" "Oh, are you acquainted with Cyan Peregrine? Such a well-groomed blonde." I grew up with all that small talk, it's maddening. Their conversations revolve around themselves, they never talk about anything outside their own heads. I hated every last battalion warden of them. I didn't bother to convey myself, I let them slip through my fingers – and I don't care that they've gone.'

She looked at the window, now a mirror backed by darkness. 'In the palace the days seemed to last forever. I went to bed an entirely different person from when I woke up. I rattled around inside that bloody great building like a piddock in a rock.'

'Like a what?'

'Sorry. Awndyn slang. I tried to continue from habit but I couldn't attend to my tutor. An inertia came over me. I kept excusing myself from the dinners and going to my room. I lay on my bed and wondered why I felt such confused dislike. I goaded and rebuked myself. I turned my thoughts over until they were a thick, boiling mass. I needed someone to talk to or I would have cracked. Swallow puts a dampener on everything and she's happy to be of no use whatsoever. So I ran.'

I folded my arms on the table and put my head down. I was at the point of drunkenness where any further drink tasted like puke. I felt my brain shrinking and my thoughts drying up.

Rawney put his big, hairy arm around Cyan's shoulders and whispered in her ear. She nodded, preoccupied with the cards. 'I keep toying with ideas of the future. What will happen to me? I keep imagining myself in future scenarios but I can't see myself as Governor of Peregrine no matter how hard I try.'

'I'm not shurprised you're afraid of telling Saker,' I slurred.

'Saker ? Who? Oh, you mean Daddy.' She giggled. 'Weird ... I never think of his real name ... Yes. He's been alive forever. It's scary to argue with him. Maybe I am conceited to disagree with him. He has an answer for everything, tried and tested, and he's always right! He knows everything and he never gets angry, he's so bloody patient. He just gives me more boring answers! It's so infuriating! I want to try something new, even if it's wrong!'

She turned the last card in the line.

'That one ... thatsh the jug of beer.'

Rawney said, 'Well, that has to be a lucky card for Rhydanne.'

'Mm.'

'So everything will turn out well,' Cyan exclaimed, getting carried away. 'I'll be successful in making my own way in the world. It's beer not Micawater wine!'

'There isn't a card for wine,' I murmured.

'I'll learn who I am. If it really did depend on blood, Lightning would know me better, wouldn't he? I might have inherited one or two family traits, but I'll rediscover them myself!'

So you should, I thought. My mind's sky had thoroughly clouded over. I closed my eyes.

Cyan leant and whispered in my ear, 'I'm living my own life from now on, where and how I choose to. Tell Daddy to forget about me. In a couple of hundred years, he will. It's the only way.'

I woke up. The pub was unlit and deserted. An uneasy lamplight shining under the landlord's door illuminated the shapes of chairs placed on the tables and textured lines drawn by the broom in the stickier patches on the floor. Towels hung over the pump handles.

Shit. I am absolutely pissed ... and I've lost Cyan. She's given me the slip. Oh, shit, I had her, and I ... she ... Rawney got me drunk! The bastard, and I fell for it!

I staggered over to the bar and stuck my head under a tap, pumped water into my face. The landlord must have left me sleeping there while he closed up the bar around me. Of course, he wouldn't have dared to wake an Eszai.

I wrestled with the door bolts. Outside, the misty drizzle gave everything a slick sheen. I turned my coat collar up, but it soaked through the denim, wetting me as effectively as pouring rain.

Galt was very dark, none of the lamps were lit and the shops' upper stories had closed their shutters. All I had to see by were occasional chinks of light between them.

Now I was back to playing hide and seek with the little cow across the entire city.

CHAPTER 7

All the oil lamps stood disused, their glasses fly-spotted and filthy. Whale oil was scarce these days, reserved for lighting homes, not streets. It had soared in price since some enormous sea snakes had taken up residency in the ocean. Their main source of food seemed to be whales.

The paving of the plaza outside the bar was covered in a sheen of water, mixed with mud trekked in from the towpath. I looked down, at the palimpsest of footprints spreading out from the door. Could it be possible to track Cyan? I searched around and found the fine mud drawn into a distinctive print of a thick-soled boot, too small for a man. Those are Cyan's expensive boots. I followed them slowly, careful not to miss any. They were few and far between, but if they were hers she seemed to have walked along the towpath.

I carried on, beside the dark canal, shunning the varicose hookers and their crisp pimps revealed by the night. The mud squashed under my boot soles. I was heading east towards Old Town, but I wasn't out of Galt yet, and horrible sights loomed in alleys and alcoves. I passed quickly by a whore with bare breasts and ragged shorts, her razor ribs showing through the stretch marks on her sides.

I lost the trail under furrowed bike ruts and glanced all around, overly aware of how Rhydanne I looked. I learnt how to track on visits to the mountains. Veering towards the canal, a smooth leather imprint with a firm, mannish step could be Rawney's. Yes, there was one partially obscuring Cyan's smudged trace. I continued, thinking; I really tried not to be like a Rhydanne in Hacilith but other people's expectations kept throwing me back on it. I often found myself playing out the solitary self-centred flightiness they expected. But what the fuck, it meant they gave me leeway. They might be patronising but they also didn't expect too much, and they left me free to do what I liked.

There was a strong smell of fried food grease, as if every citizen had scoffed a newspaper-full of chips, then belched simultaneously. I passed out of Galt into Old Town. The canal basin has obliterated most of it, but the remaining buildings, replaced many times over, are still so close together there isn't room to fit one more between them. Awian towns are sometimes destroyed by Insects and rebuilt in one go, but here old buildings persist, with a mishmash of modern styles between them. New houses spring up in the wake of fires and the residents continually improve their city so much of Old Town was quite new. I ran under the merchants' tall houses. Their baroque gables sprouted pulleys and platforms to bring in goods they store in their own attics. I walked by the mooring of the River Bus that shuttles to Marenna Dock on the west bank. I passed a roast chestnut stand littered with paper bags and dripping with rain. I cut past Inhock Stables, making the rum-sellers' pannier donkeys bray uneasily. Horses were tethered here, since they weren't allowed in Old Town's narrow streets.

I passed the wharfinger's office and came to a deserted part of the navigation, heading towards a footbridge. I swore as I walked; the whisky was smearing all my thoughts together and the rain was getting worse. All storms arrive first in Hacilith from the sea, all seasons seemed to start here too, and the spring rain fell with a vengeance.

The gutters drained into the soupy canal basin where timber narrow boats were moored. Some were impossibly shiny, others rotting hulks. Several were a full thirty metres, others no more than boxes. Their curtains were closed and they were silent. The darkness muted their paint to different shades of grey.

I went under the bridge, lit by the lamps of a narrow boat moored on its own. The tracks ran into a mass of scuffed ground, so many other prints I couldn't tell what had happened at all. Some led back towards Galt; Rawney's was among them but Cyan's weren't. She had stopped here – or the men had carried her.

I searched for her tracks further away, my task made easier by the lights on the boat. In fact, the rotund lamps at its prow and stern were glowing as brightly as if there was a party on board, but it was quiet. Who would desert a boat and leave its lamps burning?

The small barge was bottle green with red panels and brass trim. Its tiller was polished with use and wound with ribbons, and by it hung a bell to sound instructions to the locksmen. I casually looked down to its bow, just above the level of the quayside paving stones. Red and white diamonds like sweets decorated the top of its transom, either side of the nameplate that read: *Tumblehome*. Underneath in small white capitals: CARMINE DEI. REGISTERED: OLD TOWN.

I crouched down to the leaded windows. A rug had been tacked over them on the inside. I tapped the glass and called, 'Cyan! Hey, Cyan? Rawney?' Silence.

I listened, aware of all the sounds of the night – at a distance the noise of Old Town had merged into a low murmur. Ducklings were cheeping, somewhere in the undergrowth on the far bank. I called, questioningly, cheerfully, politely, and finally with a firm demand, but it only produced more silence.

I'm the Emperor's Messenger and I'm not standing for this! I grabbed the rail on its roof and jumped onto the flat ledge running all the way round the boat. It bobbed slightly and I felt its keel bump off the fetid slime of the canal bed. I really cannot stand boats. I could all too easily imagine it turning turtle, pitching me into the black water. I edged towards the stern, feeling my boots grip on the grit embedded in its paint.

I stepped down onto the stern deck, ducked under the tiller, and pushed open the varnished, cupboard-like doors. I wedged into the little entrance. The air inside was warm and stuffy.

I looked down into a long rectangular room. A draught of wind blew in past me and started tinkling some capiz shell mobiles. Discs of coloured glass clattered against the windows. A hanging lantern with moons and stars cut out of its sides sent their projections spinning round the walls.

From a futon, which was a piled mess of quilts and sheepskins, projected a slender blue-white arm, and a limp hand hanging down. I gasped. Cyan!

She sat upright among cushions, her head lolled back and away from me, her legs apart and her skirt rucked up. A thin man lay on the floor at her feet, head back and foam dried into a crust around his mouth. He was stone dead.

OK. This is nothing to do with me.

Yes, it is. She's *Lightning's daughter*!

I stretched a leg down the steps and shuffled in on my backside. The dead man was lying wedged between the wall and the futon. He must have had a fit and thrashed around because he'd kicked a potbellied stove free of its tin flue. It stood at an angle on its platform. I turned him over; he was so stiff that when I propped him on his side, his arm stuck up in the air. His blank eyes no longer stared at the ceiling but at me instead. I checked his dog tag – his name was Sharny. As I did so, something fell to the floor and rolled across the rag-rug. I leant down and felt around until my fingers closed on a glass hypodermic. Sharny's sleeves were unbuttoned; I pushed one up. His arm was covered in red pinpoints, packed so densely his veins had collapsed, looking like they were open to the air. The skin inside his elbow was juicy with infection.

Shit, shit, shit. Not *cat*, surely? Not *Cyan*? When I use, I try to space out the tracks so that they can't be seen when I'm at the podium, to keep the veins fat and easy to hit. Sharny, on the other hand, had sunk lower than the dregs.

I turned Cyan's face towards me gently. Her eyes were rolled back, only showing white slivers under half-closed lids. Her lips were blue, she was hardly breathing; just a little sigh every so often. Two sips of the air, another ragged sigh with a high-pitched whistling sound. From elbow to shoulder her right arm was a solid bruise. I loosened the tourniquet above her elbow, hooked my thumbnail in it and pushed it down. I could only see one needle mark in the crook of her arm but that didn't necessarily mean this was her first time.

643

I tried to ignore the thought of her fast dropping into unconsciousness, helplessly watching Sharny's avid experimentation with the needle in the back of his cold hand.

I pressed my finger inside her fingers, waiting for a grasp response but nothing happened. 'Cyan, can you hear me? Breathe. Breathe in. And out. Again. Keep going. Can you squeeze my finger ? No? OK ...'

I must get her outside, into fresh air. I lifted her; she folded like silk, gave every impression of being dead. I laid her completely relaxed body on the bedspread and wrapped it around her.

A table beside the stove caught my attention. It carried a decanter of water, a spoon, a razor and an unfolded paper of fine white powder standing in a peak. Some had been nicked away.

I recognised it immediately. It called me like a lover and the next second I was down on my hands and knees. Don't look at it! I thought; steady! Turn away. If I so much as touch it I'll be hooked again. I'll be hooked before I know it! Where did Cyan get cat? Where the fuck did she get so *much*? I felt sick and giddy. I knew I was going to pick it up. I moved with no volition of my own; the drug there on the table had more control over my limbs than I did.

Let me explain what craving is. Craving is when your friend manages to talk you out of the corner and gets you to put the knife down. Craving is when you ask to be locked in, because otherwise you'd fly all night from the court to score. Craving is when you wear your fingernails to bloody stumps trying to pick the lock.

What was she doing, playing with cat? But they hadn't called it cat or scolopendium. What was their word? Jook? *Jook, don't you know, it's the latest thing, all the rage.* If I just take a little bit no one will mind. The Emperor won't be able to tell. Shut up and help Cyan. I realised I had been holding my breath for so long my ribs were hurting. I swallowed hard, then stood up. Very slowly and judiciously I refolded the fat wrap of cat and dropped it into my pocket, where it burned.

I bundled Cyan out of the double door, hoisted her onto my shoulder and jumped onto the bank in a bound that set the pool of lamplight lapping up and down. It slid up the inside of the bridge's brick arch, then quickly down to the mooring loops. Viscid water sloshed around the *Tumblehome's* ridged hull.

I lay her on the ground and checked her. She had stopped breathing. Her eyes had receded into round hollows as if her skull was rising to the surface. Shit. This isn't just a dead faint, it's respiratory failure. I tilted her head back, fingered her mouth open, pinched her nose and blew into her mouth. Her chest rose. I rocked back on my heels watching it fall gently, then blew again.

Her lips were soft, but her mouth was rank with beer, smoke and the metallic taste of death. I had to blow hard to overcome the resistance from the air inside her; my cheeks prickled and my jaw started aching. Her hair brushed my cheek every time I put my head down, but it stank of stale cigarettes. She was only a child, just as when I saved her from the shipwreck. Her chest rose, I looked sideways down the length of her body, between her breasts falling back from the bodice collar as she exhaled.

She twitched, but it must have been nerves, because she definitely wasn't anywhere near consciousness. She gasped and began to breathe for herself again. Thank fuck. 'Well done, girl,' I said as I wrapped her up. 'Keep breathing.'

I had been working so hard keeping her alive that I hadn't been aware of my surroundings. Footsteps were running over the bridge. A boot ground on the path in front of me. I realised I'd seem like a mugger hunched over his victim, so I looked up – into the baby-blue eyes of Rawney Carron.

Two men I hadn't seen before stood either side of him. Movement at the edges of my vision told me three more had closed in behind me. They held naked broadswords, their hair was tied back into tarred pigtails. They couldn't be sailors, because sailors, doctors and armourers are professions safe from the draft. Ex-dock workers, then, and probably owlers, a very dedicated breed of nocturnal smuggler.

'Is this your fyrd squad ?' I asked Rawney, calmly keeping anger out of my voice. 'Were you coming back to check on her or to collect your payment?'

Rawney spat, 'Comet, don't you just know everything?'

'Let me go, quick – she's dying!'

'We won't let you arrest us.'

'Look. I don't care if you're dealing. I won't report you. Even though you've done this.'

Rawney shook his head. They knew that to be caught in Morenzia would be their end. One by one they'd be carted to the scaffold, bound to a cart wheel and every bone in their body, ending with their skulls, systematically broken by blows from a mace. What they don't know is I never turn dealers in. The only time I confiscate cat from soldiers is when I'm in short supply myself.

I stood up, palming the flick knife from my boot. 'This is an emergency!'

'No!'

Exasperated, I said, 'I know two cartels that run "Ladygrace Fine" in from Brandoch. I know Emmer Rye fences everything coming into Galt. I don't know you, so you must be kids.'

'Fuck you. You're one man against six. And you're not much of a man anyway!'

'Don't mess about.'

The legs of one soldier were starting to bend with fear. He never thought he'd see an Eszai so close in his lifetime, let alone face one with drawn sword. I could see Rawney trying to balance this against the fact I was obviously drunk and apparently unarmed. He jerked his head and said, 'Kill him.'

I whooshed my wings open, yelled, 'In San's name, with god's will – get out of my way!'

The man on Rawney's left and the three behind me turned and ran.

Rawney snarled and drew his dagger. I flicked my knife. The big man next to him chopped with his sword but I was already inside his reach and up against him. I hugged my arm round him, pulled him close and drove my knife deep into his heart. Blood forced thickly up the runnel, like rising mercury.

Before it reached the handle he became a dead weight. I stepped back and let him crumple.

Rawney was running, putting ground between us as fast as he could. I sprang over the dead soldier. I pounced – caught a fistful of Rawney's hair at the nape of his neck. He cried out. I dragged his head back and pushed my knife's point alongside his windpipe. He stumbled to his knees and I followed him down, my arm tense against his snatching hands, careful not to sever the artery. When the knife was in deep enough I levered it to the horizontal and pulled it towards me. I cut neatly through his windpipe from behind.

Rawney worked his mouth but had no air to scream. He put his hands to his throat, ducked his chin. Blood sprang out like red lips. The ends of the tube snicked as they rubbed together. He drew his next breath through the cut and it whistled.

I booted him in the solar plexus and he doubled up. He turned his head away and the stretched skin parted, laying bare more of the cords in his neck, slick gleam of a vein and the rings of cartilage above and below his severed windpipe.

I hissed, 'You're to blame! You fucking killed Cyan! You can't be her boyfriend. You're scum. Like me. See? Eszai don't do this ...' I crouched and leant onto him, weighting him down. With four quick slashes I drew a square around his fyrd tattoo. I sunk my fingernails under one edge, peeled the skin off, and I stuck it to the ground in front of his frantic eyes. 'But gangsters do. *Never push cat on my turf!*'

Rawney bubbled. His lungs were filling with blood. Huge amounts of bright pink aerated foam frothed between his fingers clutching his throat, and bearded him down to the waist.

I lifted Cyan and jumped up fluidly into a sprint down the towpath. Behind me I heard the strangled liquid gargle, gargle, gargle, of Rawney try-ing to breathe through his slit throat.

I ran. I ran along the slippery pavements, over the open drains. Above the roofs the moon gave a sick light through the clouds. I swear, anyone who ever bared his teeth at me has had them kicked in, and anyone who ever bared his neck to me has had his throat bitten out.

I sped south, away from the canal, passing a sign pointing to the Church of the Emperor's Birthplace. I ran beside the tiny portion of the original town wall that still remains – because no one had yet built over it. I passed through Watchersgate, the one surviving town gate, useless in its broken piece of north wall, with grooves where its portcullis had been. Life-sized statues with raised arms stood on top. They once held spears as if defending the town, but the spears were removed a hundred years ago after one fell off and, dropping twenty metres, transfixed both the Awian ambassador and his horse.

The venerable astrolabe clock high in Watchersgate's tower was called 'The Waites'. Its iron rods started to grind as I passed and it querulously struck two. The damn thing was attached to a mechanical organ that played automatically at dawn to wake the town's workers. If they didn't pay their taxes it was left tinkling continually to remind them. It only had one hand, because back when Hacilith was a walled town, the hour was all you needed to know.

Cyan was still locked off deep in a tiny, animal part of her brain. I didn't know if she would ever come out, or if what crept back out would still be Cyan. I was terrified for her – and for myself – how the fuck was I going to explain this to Lightning?

'Cyan, scolopendium is powerful shit. Nobody knows better than me on this subject, nobody! When I overdosed the Circle always bailed me out. I based my life round that cycle of "feel good, feel bad". But you can't shrug it off like I can. I've seen what it does to Zascai who don't respect it. I've seen too many die. Stupid girl! What did you do it for? You've got to be already screwed up if you're taking to drugs. Some people need it but what pain could you have?

'Oh, god, oh god. Don't worry, Cyan, I won't let you die. I'm the one who's good at becoming addicted, not you. I'm the one who leaves used needles around the place. I wake up junk sick. I punish myself for taking it by taking more. I'm the one who shoots enough to kill a destrier, not you. You'll be fine ... Nearly there ... keep breathing ... please keep breathing ... Oh, god. Why did you come here in the first place? The city is a cess pool, where the same shit goes round and round and round!'

I continued blethering in low and high Awian, then in Morenzian and its old and middle forms, Plainslands and its Ghallain and Ressond dialects, ancient pre-vowel-shift Awian, Trisian and Scree. I could tell I was closing in on the university, because the number of brothels was increasing.

Five minutes and eleven languages later I reached the south end of Old Town, and the curlicued gates of Hacilith University, the oldest university in the world.

The university's gates were always open, just as the Castle's gates are always open. Its red oriflamme pennant flew from a pole beside them, representing the light of knowledge. I sped through the gates, ignoring the porters shouting behind me.

I flitted into the shadow of a residential hall and quietly along the path, leaning sideways to counteract Cyan's weight. Her stockinged feet jutted out in front from the end of the bedspread roll.

The university buildings were older as I neared its centre. Joss stick smoke caught at the back of my throat. Student poverty everywhere smells of cheap incense and burnt toast. Light diffused from oilcloth windows, each of which gave onto a different student's room. They were silent – not tranquil – ominously dead quiet so I feverishly envisioned every undergraduate inside had been murdered in a different way. But worse still – they were cramming for exams. My imagination removed the outer wall, so each square room was suddenly visible in a cutaway like pigeonholes. Each room has a lamp, a book-laden table, a chair, a scholar sitting pen in hand. One lies on the bed, one sits on the floor. Each one works by himself, no one talks to another. Hundreds of individual student's lives are separated in tiny rooms in a huge building; they reminded me of polyps in a coral.

I clattered through a courtyard, past a marble statue of the founder, so ancient it wore a doublet and hose. An old professor stood in its shadow with two prostitutes, male and female, on the plinth in front of him. They were stroking his bald head and I heard their silky voices, 'You're sexy ... you're so sexy ...' The don was shaking but I couldn't tell whether it was from fear or excitement. They didn't look up as I hurtled past.

Now in the very centre of the university I came to an unsurfaced track. I slowed my pace in awe, feeling as if I had walked back in time. Stony and yellow in the lamplight the track ran for a few hundred metres and stopped at the perimeter fence. It did not join nor bear any resemblance to any road in the modern Hacilith street plan. The city I knew had been built around it and the university's buildings now hemmed it in. It was sixteen hundred years old – a road when Old Town was all of Hacilith, the only town in Morenzia, and the country was ruled by a king from a palace god-knows-where in Litanee. The wattle-and-daub houses along the track had decayed over a millennium ago, but the College of Surgeons survived.

I walked across and jumped the remains of a deep stone gutter. It once drained stinking effluent from the boilers that had reduced cadavers of paupers and rarities to skeletons for teaching aids. I hammered with my free hand at a nail-studded door. 'Rayne! Rayne! Help!'

Cyan's body convulsed and she vomited down my back. 'Oh, god! Well, better out than in, I suppose ... Ella Rayne! Open up!'

Rayne's squat, square tower was once the College of Surgeons. Other faculties, refectories and dorms had gradually aggregated around its revered centre of learning – the university formed in much the same way as flowstone in a Lowespass cave. It was officially founded in the fifteenth century, only because it was no longer convenient for the faculties to ignore each other.

The tower's sixteen hundred years gave it a serious gravity. The newer buildings would have overshadowed it if the university had not built them at a respectful distance. Small bifora windows let meagre light into its upper level where a three-tiered lecture hall, now disused, once doubled as a dissecting room and operating theatre. Its roof was flat and its walls unmasoned stone, apart from the deep arch around the door decorated with several bands of zigzag carving. Ironically, given Rayne's origins, the university had presented the building to her, and when she was not at the Castle or the front she lived here among her cabinet of curiosities.

A shutter slid open and Rayne peered out through its iron grille. 'Comet!' She clanged the shutter and creaked the door open. 'Wha' are you doing here?'

'Thank fuck!' I pushed past her into the room, seeing stacks of chests and medicine boxes packed ready for removal.

Rayne said, 'You're supposed t' be a' th' dam. My carriage is on i's way. Wha'— you're covered in blood!'

She grasped her brown skirts and hurried after me, as I loped through the museum and a doorway leading to her bedroom. Her pudgy, purplish feet bulged out between her sandal straps. She had been seventy-eight for fourteen hundred and five years, the oldest Eszai, and the oldest person in the world apart from the Emperor himself.

I strode to her box-bed, set into a deep niche in the wall hidden by a curtain. I laid Cyan down gently inside it, on the crochet blanket, and unwrapped her. Rayne saw a patient and immediately hastened to examine her with quick, expert movements, while she bombarded me with questions: 'She's no' bleeding. Whose blood is i' then? Wha's happened t' th' lass?'

'She's Lightning's daughter,' I said, swaying.

Rayne stopped and looked up at me. 'Cyan Dei?'

'Cyan Peregrine.'

'Has she been mugged? No. There's no concussion. I's drugs, isn' i', Jant?'

'Cat.'

She knelt and turned Cyan on her side to prevent her swallowing her tongue. She observed the girl's violet-grey face, her clicking, shallow breathing. She pressed her dimpled fingers against Cyan's neck for her pulse. 'Obstruc'ed air passages. Bradycardia. Classic scolopendium poisoning. Wha' have you done t' her?'

'It's not my fault.'

'Yes, i' is. Of course i' is! How did you give her i'?'

'It wasn't me!'

'You're a born liar! You're tot'ring, yourself! Oh, Jant, I hoped you wouldn' take i' again. I hoped you'd learned your lesson. You can' be bored, you should be occupied wi' t' dam.'

'I haven't touched cat for five years!'

'You haven' made t' decade. You're no' truly cured.'

'Please,' I begged Rayne. 'Don't jump to conclusions.' The appeal to objectivity quietened her long enough for me to shoehorn a word in. 'Cyan did it to herself. I wasn't there. She bought it from a Zascai, cocktailed with alcohol and god knows what else. A knackered old junkie showed her how to shoot it and for all I know they shared a needle. At any rate, it was backflushed. I found her already under. I gave her the kiss of life and I'm still trying to get her taste out of my mouth! I killed the dealer—' I tugged my shirt demonstratively, pulling the material, hard with clotting blood, from where it had stuck to my chest.

'You murdered a Zascai ?'

'I never murdered a Zascai who wasn't the better for it.'

'Shi'. If t' Emperor finds ou', he'll ...'

'Nobody is going to find anything out. Are they?'

'I—'

'*Are* they, Rayne?'

'No.'

'He was a corporal and he'd turned his whole squad into a gang. They probably were, before they were recruited. Fuck ... Select Fyrd pressganging street scum. If I catch any of them again I'll pump them full of twenty poisons ... Anyway, they didn't know that I'm twice as fast as a human. Well, nearly, 'cause I *am* the worse for drink but I'm not stoned.'

'No. You're replacing one drug with another.' Rayne had her back to me but I saw her expression reflected in the mirror by the bed. She was preoccupied with Cyan.

In Rayne's white bedroom, the eye slid along arrangements of objects as smoothly as a scale of music. Models used for teaching stood on the mantelpiece; large anatomical figures of a man and woman, accurate and to scale. There were painted clastic models of torsos with removable organs like a jigsaw, and a 'wound man' demonstrating various injuries.

Mice were carved seamlessly onto the furniture, scurrying up the chair legs and nibbling the table edge. But netting held the far wall together: ancient goat hair and wood laths showed through the flaking plaster. A bookcase dominated the corner – the books she had written – and it was buckling under the sheer weight of paper.

Cyan wants experience. She'll run headlong into ordeals like this and each one will chop a bit off her teenage enthusiasm until it's down to adult size. I looked at her slack face and burned with fury. 'Is this what you bloody want? Tell me, does it make your party go with a swing? People like Rawney don't want you. He wants to be *like* you! I know, I always did! Did you think it was funny? Well, it's really fucking hilarious. Look at me; I'm laughing!'

'Jant ...' Rayne said.

'It's fine to be an outsider by choice, but if you get addicted you'll be an outsider by necessity! Then you'll be the loneliest posh minx in the world!'

'Calm down! OK, Jant, you're no' t' blame. I believe you.'

I pulled up a three-legged stool and sat down heavily, legs apart, wings splayed to the floor. I stripped my vomit-covered shirt off and scratched at the bald spots in the pits of my wings. 'Can you bring her round ?'

'We may jus' have t' wai'.' Rayne rang a small hand bell. She asked her servant to go across to the medical faculty and bring atropine, and some clean clothes for me.

'I'll do it,' I offered. 'I'm faster.'

'She knows her way through t' complex. And I don' trus' you wi' th' key t' th' vaul's.' Rayne filled a glass of water, took a dropper from the drawer and began to drip water onto Cyan's lips. 'I used t' do this for you, when you had i' bad.'

I huffed. The last time I fell asleep under the influence, Wrenn and Tornado shaved my head and painted me blue. I woke up shackled to the prow railings of the Sute Ferry. I haven't taken cat since. You can face down death, by choosing the harder alternative. Not that I'm overly brave or more than usually lucky; I simply never believed death was an option so I never took it. 'You can't begrudge me a little escape now and again. I'm immortal, I need to lose track of time.'

'You risk losing too much.'

'Yeah, well, the only excitement in immortality is a possibility of loss.' Rayne grunted vaguely.

I indicated the anatomical male carving. 'He's well-endowed, isn't he?'

She looked up. 'No, tha's t' average size.'

I was never any good at waiting. I paced through to the museum and stood blinking until my eyes adjusted. Rayne's museum, representing her workshop through the ages, was a vast collection so tightly packed together it overwhelmed. Candlelight reflected on the curved surfaces of glass jars, thousands of different sizes, and on the sliding door of a *materia medica* cabinet with tiny square drawers for herbs. What to look at first? Here and there I noticed an object because of its special rarity: a two-headed foetus floating in a jar; or its great size: a broken sea krait tooth; or its beauty: a baby vanished to nothing but a three-dimensional plexus of red and blue veins and arteries to show the dissector's skill; or its ghastliness: the preserved face of a child who died of smallpox. Some objects caught my eye because they were illustrated in the etched plates of books I'd read.

I stepped back, trying to perceive an order to the collection. In the centre a grey stone fireplace housed a copper alembic with a spout, resting on a little earthenware furnace with a bellows handle projecting. It was for fraction-distilling aromatic oils. The lintel above it bore the deeply incised and gilded legend: 'Observe nature, your only teacher.'

I looked at the anatomical preparations: dense white shapes in jars, organs folded, wrinkled or bulging, or feathery and delicate like branching lungs. Alcohol preserved specimens like paperweights, of this or that organ in sagittal or cross section. Living with these, Rayne must see people as machines, nothing but arrangements of tissues and liquids, interesting puzzles to solve. She also knows that individuality is mostly skin-deep because, inside, people are all the same. Rayne and Frost, I reflected, had many traits in common.

Her reference collection was ordered by pathology. Some samples were hundreds of years old – the only immortality available to Zascai by virtue of their interesting ailments. The sufferers usually readily agree to be preserved; it's all one to them whether their useless remains are placed in the ground or in a jar. The only exception are Awians, who prefer to be interred in tombs as florid as they can afford, as if they want to take up space forever.

A glass case housed a collection of surgical instruments past and present – steel bone saws and silver catheters, water baths for small dissections. Rayne kept some – like cylindrical saw-edged trepanning drills and equipment for cupping and blood letting – to remind the world of the doctors' disgusting practices to which she put an end when she joined the Circle.

A six-fingered hand, a flaky syphilitic skull. A hydrocephalic one five times normal size, and the skeleton of a man with four wings growing out of his chest.

Rayne uses me in demonstrations when I'm available. I pose at the front of the auditorium while she lectures the students on how weird I am, or on her great achievement in healing my Slake Cross injuries. One day my skeleton might stand here to be prodded by subsequent generations, my strong, gracile fingers adapted for climbing, my curve-boned wings articulated to stretch full length to their pointed phalanges.

Beside the door I'd come in by stood a large showcase of chipped stone arrowheads, which Rayne had arranged into an attractive pattern. She buys them for a few pence each from boys who pick them up on the Awndyn Downs. There was also a 'piece of iron that fell from the sky onto Shivel'. On the other side of the door a skeleton inhabited a tall cabinet; its label said: 'Ancient Awian, from a cave in Brobuxen, Ressond'.

Over two thousand years the grey smell of old bone and neat alcohol had saturated the tower's very fabric. It was a haze of carbolic and formalin. Spicy volatile notes of orange and clove must be the essential oils Rayne had most recently prepared.

I examined the labelled majolica jars: oenomel, rodomel and hippocras; storax, orchis and sumac. Patent medicines crusted or deliquesced in slipware pots. Their names skipped off the tongue like a schoolyard rhyme: Coucal's Carminiative Embrocation; Popinjay Pills for Pale People; Ms Twite's Soothing Syrup; Cornstock Electuary; Emulsion Lung Tonic; World-Famed Blood Mixture; Dr Whinchat of Brandoch's Swamp-root Kidney Cure; Fruit Salt; Spa Mud; Abortion Lotion; Concentrated Essence of Cinnamon for Toothache; Confection of Cod Livers; Balsamic Elixir for Inflamed Nipples; Bezon & Bro. Best Beet Juice. A pot with a spout: Goosander Lewin's Improved Inhaler. Preparation of Bone Marrow: an Ideal Fat Food for Children and Invalids; Odiferous Macassar for Embellishing the Feathers and Preventing Them Falling Out.

'I' doesn' work,' Rayne said.

'What, any of it?' I asked, but I turned and saw she was referring to the atropine, which her servant had brought, and she had mixed a miniscule amount with the water drops she was squeezing into Cyan's mouth. 'This should work. Why doesn' i'?' she said, annoyed. 'I' brings you round, on t' times I try i' wi' you. I daren' give her more than this. Do you know how much she took?'

'No ...' I suddenly remembered I had the wrap in my pocket. I stopped moping around the museum and joined her in the bedroom. 'But I can assay it. I picked up her scolopendium from the barge.'

'Of course, you would.'

I sighed. 'Just don't let me put my fingers in my mouth.' I cautiously brought out the wrap – the sight of it triggered my craving and damp sprang up on the palms of my hands. Truly we are nothing but chemicals.

'Don' give in,' said Rayne, over her shoulder.

I pinched the bridge of my nose. 'I ... I can't ...'

'So you'll give in? Think of t' disadvantages – look a' her! Remember how bad you feel for six months after kicking. You're doing well now; each time you ge' clean i's for slightly longer. The balance has tipped.'

I calmed myself, thinking; no one is asking me to do without it permanently. I said, 'It's cooked at source somewhere in Ladygrace. But is it cut?'

653

The rounded hills of Ladygrace, where scolopendium fern grows, have that name because as you approach from a distance their profile looks like a voluptuous woman lying on her back with her knees in the air. The most difficult part of the route is shipping the finished product across the Moren estuary. It never occurred to me, when I was ripping off Dotterel's shop and selling at the wharves, how much more money I could have made smuggling by air.

I poured water into another glass and delicately shook the paper over it. Grains fell out and dissolved on impact with the surface, leaving no residue. Even the largest had gone before it fell half a centimetre through the water column.

'Shit, it's pure. Maybe eighty to ninety per cent ... If I hadn't used for a while I wouldn't shoot this.'

Rayne said, 'If Cyan was buying, I think she could prob'ly afford pure.'

'That's what killed Sharny. He wouldn't have been used to it. He didn't even have time to take the tourniquet off ...' I imagined him thinking – some bastard's cut this – then the fact it isn't cut hits with full strength. His hands clench, he struggles for breath but it's clear there won't be a next one.

Feeling suddenly nauseous I dumped it in the fire and wiped my hands. 'It'd lay *me* out.'

'For how long?'

'A day and a half. Is she likely to die?'

'I can' tell. But if she does i's no' my faul'.'

'I'm fucked. What will Saker do when I tell him his only daughter is in a coma from a massive overdose? I'm the only junkie he knows. He'll shoot me!'

'Mmm.'

'When I first saw her I drooled like a dog on a feast day. I thought she was feek! She was a mink!' I ran out of slang and just scooped a feminine body out of the air with a couple of hand movements. 'But now she looks like a corpse! They called it jook, not cat, or I would have known!'

We called the stuff cat because it makes you act like one, roaming all night on the buzz at first, then languid and prone to lying around.

'Did you jus' throw i' *all* away?'

'Yes.'

The night wore on, mercilessly. I put on the clothes the servant had found for me, though they were not svelte enough to fit – I have to have clothes made to measure – and the shirt was red. Red is not my colour at all. I ate some bread, but it didn't cure my hangover. The liquor settled in my gut, leaching water from my body and diluting it. The water I drank turned straight into piss and I was still so dehydrated my tongue clacked on the roof of my mouth like a leather strap. I felt as if my skin was drying; my fingertips were wrinkled and a headache like a steel band tightened round my temples. My heartbeat shook my whole body, and I scarcely knew what to do with my hands.

Pit.

I looked up. 'What's that noise?'

'I don' hear any noise,' Rayne said.

'That noise like water drops?'

'Look around,' she said. 'My collections are valuable.'

I did so and noticed a movement on the first turn of the spiral steps where the staircase rose into the gloom. A worm was crawling there. As I watched, another one fell from the upper floor. It wriggled to the edge of the step, tumbled over and dropped onto the step below. *Pit.* Another one fell. *Pit.* The worms began descending the steps with a determination I could only attribute to one thing. They were dropping faster now, like the first giant drops of a rainstorm. *Pitpitpitplopplopplopplopplop*, in ones and twos, linked together. The austere steps began to disappear under their pink flesh.

Rayne yelled, 'Worms? Where are they coming from? An infesta' ion?'

'It's worse than that,' I said.

'I had t' theatre cleaned this morning!' She glanced from them to her patient.

I said, 'It's from the Shift. It's called the Vermiform.'

'Is i' safe?'

'No ...' I giggled. 'It's not safe.'

With a sound like flesh tearing, a curtain of worms appeared over the top of the spiral stair. It started to tatter as individuals fell from it. Large holes appeared, a rent, the curtain swung sideways and fell with a slap onto the steps then began to undulate as it slithered down them.

A flake of plaster fell off the wall, leaving a round hole. Something that looked like the end of a twined rope spewed out, then all of a sudden swelled to the thickness of an arm, and a mouth formed on the end. Under the plaster, flesh seemed to continue in all directions. The mouth bobbed closer to me, then back, as the mass undulated. It said, 'Go to the door.'

'Go to the door!'

A crack ran from the hole and raced splintering along the wall, then forced out another flake of plaster. A thin cord, rolled like a butterfly's tongue, unspooled from the hole and hung, dangling, a mouth on a flesh tube. 'Go to the door.'

It touched the floor and dissociated into long worms that went crawling out in all directions. More mouths started sprouting from the bases of beams, the corners of the room, 'Go to the door! Go to the door!'

Rayne's face was set with fear but she didn't back off. She went to the grate and picked up the coal shovel. 'Wha' is i'?'

'Don't bother. Even if you hit it you can't harm it. It's a colony of worms and it's sentient.'

The Doctor nodded sagely. 'I'll le' you handle i'.' She went to stand next to Cyan, still holding the shovel. As far as she was concerned, her most important task was to protect her patient.

The handle of the outside door turned. Rayne and I glanced at each other. The door burst open and the Vermiform woman flowed in. Ten arms appeared from all over her, waved at me, then sucked back into her. She was much larger than last time I saw her; her worms must have bred, and though her shape and features were pretty her skin was a padded, pulsating mass. Added to the pink tide toppling down the stairs and falling from the ceiling the Vermiform must be huge, and this time I could hear it. Its worms made a rasping noise as they stretched, contracted, slid, with invisibly small bristles. They seethed and pressed like maggots and gave off a stink like urine-ridden sawdust, like old piss.

Through the open door I saw that the statue of the university's founder had gone. That was even more horrific – I couldn't stand the thought of the statue wandering around out there. I stared at the empty plinth until I realised that must have been the place where the Vermiform Shifted through and it had crumbled the marble into rubble.

More worms were pouring through the plaster as if Rayne's room was moving. They twitched out of the ceiling and wound down the wall. They knocked her models onto their sides, and swept them off the mantelpiece. From her shelves a stack of tiles on which pills were made fell and shattered. A flask smashed, spilling heavy mercury. Its curved shards rocked like giant fingernails. A jar tipped over and ovate white pills cascaded onto the floor.

Rayne flinched. 'Hey! Stop destroying my house!'

The worm-woman created two more beautiful female heads on stalks from somewhere in its belly and raised them to the level of the first one. It moved them about in front of my face. I couldn't choose which to focus on and I felt myself going cross-eyed.

'Are you the same Vermiform as before?' I asked it.

'We are always the same.'

'Well, you've grown.'

'We were asked to find you, Comet, although we do not appreciate being a Messenger's messenger. Cyan is in Osseous – for the moment. She is in deadly danger. She is trapped in the Gabbleratchet.'

The Vermiform paused, as if it expected me to know what the fuck it was talking about. Its surface covering the walls smoothed and stilled, lowering slightly as the worms packed closer together. It became denser and more solid, and the shapes of the furniture buried under it bulged out more clearly. I had the impression it was deeply afraid.

Rayne asked, 'Gabbleratche'? Wha's tha'?'

'Why are you frightened?' I added.

The layers of worms blistered as individuals stretched up indignantly. They looked like fibres fraying from a flesh-coloured tapestry. The necks bent and the heads swayed. Their lips moved simultaneously, and its voice chorused like thousands of people speaking at once: 'The eternal hunt. It is travelling through Osseous at the moment. We must try to intercept it before it veers into another world carrying Cyan away for good. We cannot predict it. No one can pursue it. Time is of the essence.' The worms around my feet reached up thin strands and spun around my legs.

I tried to wipe them off. 'What do you mean, "we"? I can't Shift. If I take an overdose the Emperor would feel it. He promised he would cut my link to the Circle and let me die.'

At the other end of the room the worm tentacles were picking Rayne's clothes out of the wardrobe, filling them, and making them dance about. Rayne folded her arms. 'Tell us more.'

This vexed the Vermiform. 'Dunlin asked me to fetch Comet, not an old woman.'

'An old woman! Do you know ...! Dunlin? ... Jant, why is i' talking abou' Dunlin? Does i' mean t' former King?'

'Yes. He's still alive, in the Shift.'

'*Jant!* Wha' have you done?'

'I'll tell you later.' I addressed the Vermiform: 'Did Dunlin see Cyan?'

'Yes. He saw the Gabbleratchet snatch her. Dunlin was advising Membury, the Equinne's leader, how to wage war against the Insects when the hunt appeared. We saw it cut a swathe through the Equinne troops. Those who survived have taken shelter in their barns.'

'Can't Dunlin command these eternal hunters?'

'No. The Gabbleratchet is unfixed in time and space. It was ancient even before the Somatopolis achieved consciousness. We do not pretend to understand it. It never separates and nothing controls it. It eats what it rides down. Cyan mounted a horse when the hunt was still and it ran with her. Like the others it has abducted she will fly until she dies of starvation.'

'*Fly?*'

'Yes. Be careful the instant you arrive. We are easy prey. If it catches us, it will tear us apart.' The Vermiform's three heads on long necks danced about on the surface of the worm quilt like droplets of water on a hot stove. 'We will take you through bodily, without causing a separation of mind and body. It will not strain the circle that suspends time for you, so none of your co-immortals will feel the effect of it labouring to keep you together.'

I shook my head. 'I don't like the sound of this. So I won't be a tourist in the Shift but actually there in the flesh? So this 'Ratchet thing can eat me? No way, it's too dangerous.'

The Vermiform washed up around my legs and bound them together. 'Make haste. Be ready.'

I wasn't ready at all! The room started shrinking: the ceiling was lowering. It drooped in the middle, sagged down, brushed my head. The corners of the walls and the right angles where they met the ceiling smoothed into curves, making the room an oval. I saw Rayne protecting Cyan with her coal shovel raised, then the walls pressed in and obliterated my view. They came closer and closer, dimming the light.

From the box-bed Rayne must have seen worms hanging down from the ceiling, bulging out from the walls, passing her; closing in and leaving the furniture clear until they tightened around me in a flesh-coloured cocoon.

I struggled but the Vermiform held my legs tight. The meshed worms masked my face. I closed my eyes but I felt them squirming against the lids. They let me take a deep breath, then pressed firmly over my lips. Worms closed tightly around my head, all over my body, seething upon my bare skin. I pushed against its firm surface but had no effect. It was like one great muscle.

I couldn't move, panicked. I was bundled tight! Hard worms gagged me. My chest was hurting, every muscle between every rib was screaming to exhale. I was light-headed and dizzy. I lost the sensation in my fingers, my arms. The curved muscle under my lungs burned. I held my breath, knowing there was nothing to inhale but worms.

I couldn't stand it any more. I gulped the stale air back into my mouth and exhaled it all at once. I sucked on the worms and my lungs stayed small, no air to fill them. I started panting tiny breaths. My legs were weak, my whole body felt light. I started blacking out.

The next breath, the worms peeled away and cold fresh air rushed into my lungs. I collapsed to my knees, coughing. The Vermiform extended grotesque tendrils and hauled me upright.

CHAPTER 8

I was standing on the cold Osseous steppe, where the horse people come from. It was twilight and silent; the sky darkening blue with few stars. Around me stretched a flat jadeite plain of featureless grass. A marsh with dwarf willow trees surrounded a shallow river; deep clumps of moss soaking with murky water and haunted by midges. Far on the other side of the river a silhouette line of hazy, scarcely visible hills marked the end of the plain.

In the distance I saw a village of the Equinnes' black and red corrugated metal barns, looking like plain blocks. Between them was one of their large communal barbecues, a stand on a blackened patch of earth where they roast vegetables. A freezing mist oozed out between the barns to lie low over the grassy tundra.

I couldn't see any Equinnes, ominously because they spend most of their time outdoors and only sleep in their barns. They're so friendly they normally race to greet strangers.

The Vermiform had reassembled – she stood a head taller than me. She said, 'We told Membury and the Equinnes that even when the Gabbleratchet vanishes they must not come out for a few hours.'

'Where is it now?' I asked. The Vermiform pointed up to the sky above the hills. I strained to make out a faint grey fleck, moving under the stars at great speed. It turned and seemed to lengthen into a column. I gasped, seeing creatures chasing wildly through the air, weaving around each other.

'It has already seen us,' the Vermiform chorused. Worms began to slough off her randomly and burrow into the grass. 'When I say run, run. It won't be able to stop. Don't run too soon or it will change course. Be swift. Nothing survives it. If it catches you we won't find one drop of blood left. Beware, it also draws people in.'

'What do you mean?'

'Don't look at it for too long. It will mesmerise you.'

It was an indistinguishable, broiling crowd, a long train of specks racing along, weaving stitches in and out of the sky. Their movement was absolutely chaotic. They vanished, reappeared a few kilometres on, for the length of three hundred or so metres, and vanished again. I blinked, thinking my eyes were tricking me.

'It is Shifting between here and some other world,' said the Vermiform, whose lower worms were increasingly questing about in the grass.

The hunt turned towards us in a curve; its trail receded into the distance. Closer, at its fore, individual dots resolved as jet-black horses and hounds.

The horses were larger than the greatest destriers and between, around, in front of their flying hooves ran hounds bigger than wolves. Black manes and tails streamed and tattered, unnaturally long. The dogs' eyes burned, reflecting starlight, the horses' coats shone. There were countless animals – or what looked like animals – acting as one being, possessed of only one sense: to kill. Hooves scraped the air, claws raked as they flew. They reared like the froth on a wave, and behind them the arc of identical horses and hounds stretched in their wake.

They were shrieking like a myriad newborn babies. Dulled by distance it sounded almost plaintive. Closer, their size grew, their screaming swelled. As I stared at them, they changed. Yellow-white flickers showed here and there in the tight pack. All at different rates but quickly, their hides were rotting and peeling away. Some were already skeletons, empty ribs and bone legs. The hounds' slobbering mouths decayed to black void maws and sharp teeth curving back to the ears. Above them, the horses transformed between articulated skeletons and full-fleshed beasts. Their skulls nodded on vertebral columns as they ran. Closer, their high, empty eyesockets drew me in. As I watched, the skeleton rebuilt to a stallion – rotten white eyes; glazed recently dead eyes; aware and living eyes rolled to focus on us.

The horse's flanks dulled and festered; strips dropped off its forelegs and vanished. Bones galloped, then sinews appeared binding them, muscle plumped, veins sprang forth, branching over them. Skin regrew; it was whole again, red-stained hooves gleaming. The hounds' tongues lolled, their ears flapped as they rushed through hissing displaced air. All cycled randomly from flesh to bone. Tails lashed like whips, the wind whistled through their rib cages, claws flexed on paw bones like dice. Then fur patched them over and the loose skin under their bellies again rippled in the slipstream. Horses' tails billowed. Their skulls' empty gaps between front and back teeth turned blindly in the air. The Gabbleratchet charged headlong.

I shouted, 'They're rotting into skeletons and back!'

'We *said* they're not stable in time!'

'Fucking— what are they? What are they doing?'

'We wish we knew.' The Vermiform sank down into the ground until just her head was visible, like a toadstool, and then only the top half of her head, her eyes turned up to the sky. Her worms were grubbing between the icy soil grains and leaving me. They kept talking, but their voices were fewer, so faint I could scarcely hear. 'The Gabbleratchet was old before the first brick was laid in Epsilon, or Vista or even Hacilith; aeons ago when Rhydanne were human and Awian precursors could fly—'

'Stop! Please! I don't understand! You've seen it before, haven't you?'

'Our first glimpse of the Gabbleratchet was as long before the dawn of life on your world as the dawn of life on your world is before the present moment.'

Never dying, never tiring, gorged with bloodlust, chasing day and night. The Gabbleratchet surged on, faster than anything I had ever seen. 'How do you think I can outrun *that*?'

'You can't. But you are more nimble; you must outmanoeuvre it.'

I saw Cyan on one of the leading horses! She rode its broad back, decaying ribs. Her blonde hair tussled. Her fingers clutched the prongs of its vertebrae, her arms stiff. She looked sick and worn with terror and exhilaration. I tried to focus on her horse; its withers were straps of dark pink muscle and its globe eyes set tight in pitted flesh. The hounds jumped and jostled each other running around its plunging hooves.

On the backs of many other horses rode skeletons human and non-human, and corpses of various ages. They were long dead of fear or hunger but still riding, held astride by their wind-dried hands. Some horses had many sets of finger-bones entwined in their manes; some carried arms bumping from tangled hands, but the rest of the body had fallen away. They had abducted hundreds over the millennia.

The Gabbleratchet arced straight above me and plunged down vertically. White flashes in the seething storm were the teeth of those in the lead. The moonlight caught eyes and hooves in tiny pulses of reflection.

I had never seen anything fly vertically downward. It shouldn't be able to. It wasn't obeying any physical rules.

Cyan clung on. I wondered if she was still sane.

'Run!' shouted the Vermiform.

The Gabbleratchet's wild joy seized me. I wanted to chase and catch. I wanted the bursting pride of success, the thrill of killing! Their power transfixed me. I loved them! I hated them! I wanted to be one! I tasted blood in my mouth and I accepted it eagerly. My open smile became a snarl.

The dogs' muzzles salivated and their baying tongues curled. They were just above my head. I saw the undersides of the hooves striking down.

'Run!' screamed the Vermiform.

I jumped forward, sprinting at full pelt. The hunt's howling burst the air. Its gale blew my hair over my eyes and I glanced back, into the wind to clear it.

The lead beasts plunged into the ground behind me, and *through* it. The air and ground surface distorted out around them in a double ripple, as if it was gelatinous. The whole hunt trammelled straight down into the earth and forked sparks leapt up around it, crackling out among the grass. It was a solid crush of animal bodies and bone. I saw flashes of detail: fur between paw pads, dirty scapulae, suppurating viscera. The corpses the horses were carrying hit the ground and stayed on top. They broke up, some fell to dust

661

and the creatures following went through them too. Cyan's horse was next; it plunged headfirst into the earth, throwing her against the ground hard. She lay lifeless. The stampede of manes and buttocks continued through her. The column shrank; the last few plummeted at the ground and disappeared into it. Two final violet sparks sidewound across the plain, ceased. All was eerily quiet.

The Vermiform emerged beside me but its voices were awed. 'It'll take a minute to turn around. Quick!'

I ran to the area the Gabbleratchet had passed through, expecting to see a dent in the frozen soil but not one of the grass blades had been bent; the only marks were my own footprints. The hairs on my arms stood up and the air smelt chemical, the same as when I once visited a peel tower that had been struck by lightning. There was no reek of corruption or animals, just the tang of spark-split air.

I turned Cyan over carefully. She had been flung against the ground at high speed – faster than I could fly – and I thought she was dead, but she was breathing.

'I can't see any broken bones. Not that it matters if that thing's driven her mad.'

'Pick her up,' said the Vermiform.

I did so and she jolted awake, gasped, open-mouthed. 'Jant? What are you doing here?'

'Just keep still.' The Vermiform sprang up from under my feet and wrapped around us. More worms appeared, adding to the thread, beginning at my ankles then up to my waist, binding us tightly together.

Cyan waggled her head at the deserted tundra. She screamed, 'Do you have to follow me everywhere? Even into my nightmares?'

The worms nearest her face grouped together into a hand and slapped her.

Cyan spluttered, 'How dare—!'

The hand slapped her again, harder.

'Thanks,' I said.

A horse burst from the ground, bent forelegs first. It pawed the grass without touching it. Its enormous rear hooves paced apart. Long hair feathered over them; its fetlock bones swayed as it put its weight on them and reared.

Cyan wailed, 'What does it want?'

Its fore hooves gouged the air, its long head turned from side to side. It couldn't understand what we were. It sensed us, with whatever senses it had, and it shrieked at us. It could not know its own power nor regulate its voice to our level. It gave us its full unearthly scream, right into my face.

The Vermiform tightened around my legs.

Its tongue curled, its jaw widened, it was bone; no tongue but the jaw dotted with holes for blood vessels and peaks for ligament connections. Its incisors clamped together, the veins appeared running into the bone, the muscles flowered and rotting horseflesh became a whole beast again. It turned its mad, rolling eye on me. Sparks crackled over us, tingling. Hounds and horses began springing up around us. No soil stuck to them; they had treated the earth as if it was another form of air.

The horse arched its neck. I looked up into the convoluted rolled cartilage in its nasal passages. Its jutting nose bones thrust towards me, its jaw wide to bite my face. Slab teeth in living gums came down—

—The Vermiform snatched us away—

Its coils withdrew and dropped me on a hard surface. I sat up and crowed like a cock, 'Hoo-hoo! That was a neat move, Worm-fest!'

Beside me Cyan crawled and spat. I helped her up: 'Are you all right?'

'Jant, what are you *doing* here?'

'I've come to rescue you.'

'*Rescue* me? Sod off! What just happened ? Did you see those horse things? ... Argh! Worms! ... What the fuck are these worms?'

'Allow me to introduce you to the Vermiform,' I said. It was writhing around my feet in a shapeless mass. If it had been human, it would have been panting.

'We must keep going,' it chorused.

Cyan said, 'A horse was lying down and it seemed friendly. I climbed on its back. I didn't know *that* was going to happen ... Oh, god, what *is* this place?'

A water drop landed on my head. Good question. I looked around and realised we were in a gigantic cavern, so vast I could not clearly see the other side.

The sound of a bustling market broke all around us. The stone walls rucked and soared up a hundred metres in the gloom, latticed with ledges from which bats dangled like plums. I gazed up to the roof, into vaults and rifts and wedding-cake tumbles of flowstone arching into darkness. The ceiling dazzled with circular gold and purple jewels, so lambent I was tempted to climb up and collect them until I realised they weren't gems embedded in the stone but water droplets hanging from it. They reflected the cool, blue light from the bulbous tails of Neon Bugs clinging to great trunks of suspended stalactites, bathing the whole chamber in their glow.

Market stalls were laid out in disorderly lines on the uneven floor, filling the cave, and up into a circular tunnel climbing slowly to the surface. Slake Cross town in all its entirety would fit into that passage. Stalls tangled along both sides of it like a thread of commerce linking the cave to Epsilon city's immense market a kilometre or more above us.

'It's Epsilon bazaar!' I said. I'd known it extended underground but I had always turned down invitations to visit. I envisaged a dirty crawl with my head caught and pressed between two planes of rock, my feathers wet and muddied, and my knees popped from kneeling on stony nubs in a stinking stream passage all the way. But this was wonderful!

At the distant end of the tunnel its entrance shone with white sunlight like a disc. Shafts of light angled in, picking out a faint haze in the air. Reflections arced the tunnel walls, showing their smooth and even bore.

I began, 'Well, Cyan, this—'

The Vermiform seethed urgently. 'Explain when we have more time! The Gabbleratchet could be here any second!'

'What?'

'It could be chasing us. If it can still sense us, it will pursue us.'

Cyan said, 'This is weird. In dreams you're not normally able to choose what you say.' She crawled to her feet and wandered off between the stalls.

The Vermiform heaved limply. 'Come back!'

Cyan was looking at the gley men browsing in the aisles. Gley men are completely blind, just a plate of smooth bone where their eyes should be. They feel their way with very long, thin fingers like antennae, touching, touching, searching. They are naked and hairless with milky, translucent, waterproof skin; but underneath it is another skin covered with thick fur, to keep them warm in the deep abyss. You can see through their upper skin to the fur layer pressing and wiping against it.

Cyan didn't seem as repelled by them as I was. She seemed entranced. One of them, by a refreshment stand, was picking cave ferns off the wall and putting them in sandwiches. He had beer bottles, brown and frothy, labelled 'sump water'. He sold white mousse made from the twiggy foam that clings to the roofs of flooded passages. He had boxes of immature stalagmite bumps that looked like fried eggs, breccia cake, talus cones, and crunchy tufa toffee.

Cyan paused at a jewellery stall and examined the cave pearls for sale. She put on a necklace made from broken straw stalactites and looked at her reflection in the mirror-polished shell of a moleusk – one of the metre-long shellfish that burrow far underground.

She didn't know that, as a visitor to the Shift, she could project herself as any image she wanted, so she appeared the way she imagined herself. Like most female Shift tourists Cyan's self-image was nothing like her real body. She was a bit taller, more muscular and plumper, and she wore casual clothes. She looked like a young, unattached fyrd recruit spending her day off in any Hacilith bar. She was slightly less pretty here than in the Fourlands; I suppose that meant she lacked confidence in her looks.

For once, I couldn't alter my appearance. I was here in the body and I planned to take it home intact.

Some stalls sold stencils and crayons for cave paintings. Some displayed everyday objects that 'petrifying water' had turned into stone. Mice with three legs (called trice) ran under the rows and cats very good at catching trice (called trousers) ran after them.

Neon Bugs illuminated beautiful constructions of silk. Replete Spiders hung from the ceiling on spindly, hairless legs, their huge, round abdomens full of treacly slime. It dripped, now and then, on the awnings of the stalls and the tops of our heads. The noisome things lived suspended all the time, and other bugs and centipedes as long as my arm swarmed over the cave walls to bring them morsels and feed them in return for the taste of the sweet gunge they exuded.

The smell of wet pebbles rose from the cavern floor, which descended in a series of dented ripplestone steps to a pool so neatly circular it looked like a hand basin. A waterfall cascaded down a slippery chute, gushing into it. Its roar echoed to us across the immense chamber as a quiet susurration.

Naked gley children were sliding down the chute and splashing into the water where Living Fossil fish swam; the play of their luminous eyes lit up the pool. It was screened by thick, lumpy tallow-yellow stalactites so long they reached the ground and were creeping out over it like wax over a candleholder. Between them chambers and passages led off, descending in different directions into the depths. Most were natural but some were like mine shafts, with timber props and iron rails.

Tortuoise with huge shells crawled frustratingly slowly up and down between the stalls, towing baskets on wheels. There were Silvans, child-shaped shadows who live only in the shade of cave mouths and tree-throws in the forest. At the furthest end of the cavern, where the subterranean denizens who prefer to stay away from the light shop and sell their wares, hibernating Cave Elephants had worn hollows in the velvet sediment.

'Call her back!' the Vermiform chorused. 'The Gabbleratchet could be here any second!'

I glanced at the cave mouth.

The Vermiform said, 'It doesn't need an entrance. It can go anywhere! It can go places you can't, where the atmosphere is poisonous: hydrogen, phosphorus, baked beans. You saw that solid rock is nothing to it. It can run straight through a planet without noticing.'

A big, lumpen Vadose was standing by a stall. Cyan realised that the man was made of clay. She sank her fingers into his thigh, pulled out a handful and started moulding it into a ball. The Vadose turned round. 'Excuse me, would you return that, please?'

665

'It's my dream and I can do what I want!'

'Dream?' articulated the Vadose. 'I assure you, poppet, this is no oneiric episode.'

The ball of clay in Cyan's hands puffed up into a tiny version of the Vadose – it tittered and waved at her. She yelped and dropped it. It ran on little feet to one of the Vadose's thick legs and merged smoothly with it. Cyan slapped his round belly, leaving a palm imprint.

He cried out bashfully and caught the attention of a Doggerel guard stalking past. It was a big bloodhound, bipedal on its hock-kneed back legs, wearing a constable's coat and the helmet of a market guard, black with a gold spike on top. The chin strap was lost in its drooping jowls. It rhymed:

'Shall I remove this silly lass

Who seems to be doing no sort of good?

In fact, you seem in some impasse.'

The Vadose said, 'Yes, if you would.'

It placed its paw on Cyan's shoulder but she wasn't perturbed. She gave it a kick. Its hackles raised; it picked her up, tucked her under one arm and carried her to us. It set Cyan down in front of me:

'Here is your rowdy friend,

Please keep her close.

Otherwise she may offend

One more dangerous than Vadose.'

'Thanks,' I said.

'Talk in rhyme

All the time,' insisted the Doggerel.

'First we are chased, then we are irritated,' the Vermiform complained.

'No, wait,' I said. 'I can do it ... Thanks for being so lenient

For my friend is no deviant

She's a tourist here for the first time

From now on she'll behave just fine.'

The Doggerel sniggered. 'Only a tourist and she looks so boring?

I'll leave in case she has me snoring.' It strode away with dignity, sturdy tail waving.

Cyan said, 'If this is a jook dream I'm going to do it all the time.' She set off towards the pool but the Vermiform snared her round the waist. She beat her fists at the worms reeling her in. 'Hey! Get off me!'

A small black puppy was trailing her. When she stopped, it sat down on its haunches and looked at her intently. It had pointed ears and alert, intelligent eyes. 'It's following me,' she said. 'It's cute. Makes a change from everything else in here.'

'It's just a Yirn Hound,' the Vermiform said dismissively and pushed it out of the way. It took a couple of steps to the side, resumed staring at Cyan.

'Can I pick it up?' she asked, and as she was speaking another dog padded towards her from under the nearest stall. It sat down and regarded her. She looked puzzled. Another two followed it, clustered close and stared up plaintively. Three more materialised from behind the corner of the next row and joined them.

The Vermiform's surface rippled in a sigh. 'They're desire made manifest. For every want or desire that a young woman has, a Yirn Hound pops into existence. If you stay in this world you won't be able to get rid of them. They will follow you around forever, watching you. Most girls grow accustomed to them, but otherwise Yirn Hounds drive them mad, because until you grow old they'll do nothing but stare at you. You could kill them, but more will appear to fill the space.'

At least twenty little terriers had arrived while the Vermiform was talking. They sat in a rough circle around Cyan's feet and continued to regard her.

'Well, I like them,' she said, bent down to the nearest one and caressed its ears. It allowed itself to be stroked and waggled its head with pleasure. Their crowd thickened, but I couldn't tell where they were coming from – just trotting in from nowhere and taking their places at the edge of the pack.

Their inevitable steady increase repulsed me. I said, 'God, girl, you have a lot of wants.'

'Compared to you? I bet you'd be buried in a pile by now!'

Sparks began to crackle in the tunnels at the far end. I caught a glimpse of the Gabbleratchet thundering in their depths. It more than filled every passage and morphing beasts charged half-in, half-out of the bedrock. Their backs and the tips of their ears projected from the floors: for them, the rock didn't exist. Skeleton horses, rotting horses, horses glowing with rude health reached the tunnel mouths. Paws and pasterns projected from the wall – they burst out! The front of the screeching column came down the cavern in a red and black wave.

'The 'Ratchet!'

I couldn't look away. Their screaming was so deafening Cyan and I clamped our hands to our ears. They tore everybody in their path to shreds – obliterated the Neon Bugs on the walls as they passed, and the lights went out.

The Vermiform wrenched us backwards—

—Bright sunlight burst upon us. I squeezed my eyes shut, blinked, and tasted clean, fresh air. A warm breeze buffed my skin ... We were on a beach. Cyan yelled, disorientated.

'Precambria!' said the Vermiform. We tumbled out of its grasp onto the yielding sand.

'Good Shift,' I said.

'The Gabbleratchet *is* chasing us!' It quivered. 'We doubt we have thrown it off. We will take you on again.' It pooled down around us, its worms moving fitfully, trying to summon up the energy.

A barren spit curved away into the distance. The aquamarine sea washed on the outside edge, moulding the compact sand into corrugations. Low, green stromatolite mounds made a marsh all along its inside. Behind us, on an expanse of featureless dunes, nothing grew at all. I looked down the spit, out to sea.

A splashing started within its curve. The water began to froth as if it was boiling. Creatures like lobsters were jumping out and falling back, lobes along their sides flapping. They had huge black eyes like doorknobs. One flipped up, and in an instant I saw ranked gills and an iris-diaphragm mouth whisk open and gnash shut.

Hundreds of crab-things scuttled out of the waters' edge; their pointed feet stepping from under blue-grey shells with arthropod finesse. There were long, spiny worms too, undulating on seven pairs of tentacle-legs.

'Something's chasing them,' said the Vermiform. 'Oh no. No! *It's* here already!'

The patch of frothing water surged closer. Cyan and I stared but the Vermiform started knitting itself around us frantically. Different parts of it were gabbling different things at once: 'Eat the damn trilobites – hallucigenia – eat the anomalocaris – but LEAVE US ALONE!'

Straight out of the froth the Gabbleratchet rode, without disturbing the water's surface by so much as a ripple. Dry hooves flying, the stream of hunters arced up against the sun. Red eyes and empty sockets turned to us—

—Endless salt flats. The vast ruins of a city stood on the horizon, its precarious tower blocks and sand-choked streets little more than rearing rock formations in the crusted desert that was once the ocean bed.

'I've been here before,' I said. 'It's Vista.'

'What's that in the distance?' Cyan said, pointing at a bright flash.

'Probably a Bacchante tribe.'

'They're coming closer.'

'They doubtless want to know what the fuck we are.'

After Vista Marchan fell to the Insects, its society transformed again and again and eventually collapsed completely. At first the people inhabited the city's ruins, but little by little they left in search of food, surviving as nomads in the desert. Bacchante tribes are either all male or all female and they meet together only once a year in a great festivity. The desert can't sustain them and their numbers are dwindling, but they roam in and out of Epsilon over the great Insect bridge to survive.

I remembered the only Bacchante I had met. 'Is Mimosa still fighting the Insects?'

'Yes, with Dunlin,' The Vermiform concurred.

'*King* Dunlin,' I said.

The Vermiform produced its woman's head, and shook it.

'No. Just Dunlin. He has renounced being king. He now presents himself as simply a travelling wise man. He advises many worlds in their struggle against the Insects.'

'Oh.'

'It seems to be a phase he's going through. He is growing very sagacious, but he hasn't yet realised the true extent of his power.'

'Their horses are *shiny*,' said Cyan.

The Bacchantes galloped closer. The four polished legs of each mount flickered, moving much faster than destriers with a chillingly smooth movement and no noise but a distant hum.

'They're horse-shaped machines,' I said. 'They don't have real heads, and no tails at all. They're made of metal.'

'They're made of solar panels,' the Vermiform said.

High over the ruined city, the Gabbleratchet burst through.

The Bacchantes halted in confusion. The black hunters were so much worse against the bright sky. They cast no shadow. Dull, cream-yellow jaws gaped, sewn with white molars. The Bacchantes stared, hypnotised.

The Vermiform screamed at the riders, 'Run!'

The Gabbleratchet plunged down and—

—Splash! Splash!

Freezing muddy water swirled up around me. I sank in a chaos of bubbles. Something tugged me and I broke the surface, spluttering. Up came Cyan, and the Vermiform held us above the algae of a stinking, misty swamp.

The sky was monochrome grey, filled with cloud and a hazy halo where the sun was trying to break through.

'Infusoria Swamp.'

Cyan wiped slime off her face and hair. 'Hey! This is my dream and I want to go somewhere nice!'

'Shut up!' The Vermiform seethed in fury. 'All for you, little girl! We don't see why we have to do this and now we're being chased! We don't know how to get rid of it. We don't know where to go next that won't kill you!'

She shrieked in frustration, grabbed handfuls of worms and tried to squash them but they forced her fists open and crawled out.

'Shifting is sapping our strength,' said the worms.

'Come on!' I shouted at it. 'Let's go.'

'It's my dream so get off me!'

'Stop squeezing us.'

'Piss off and keep pissing off, piss-worms!'

A colossal blob of gel flowed towards us on the water's surface. Flecks and granules churned inside it as if it was a denser portion of the swamp; it extended pseudopodia and started to wrap around the outlying worms.

'What's that?' said Cyan.

'Amoeba.' The Vermiform pulled its worms out and hoisted us up higher with a sucking noise.

'Isn't it rather large?'

'We're very small here.'

'Look at the sky!' said Cyan.

The bright patch was growing in size. Violet forks of lightning cracked the sky in two, leapt to the swamp, hissed and jumped between the reeds. The Gabbleratchet arced out.

The Vermiform gave one completely inhuman scream with all its strength and jerked us out—

—A hot plain with cycads and a volcano on the horizon. Giant lizards were stalking, two-legged, across it towards a huge empty sea urchin shell with a sign saying 'The Echinodome – Sauria's Best Bars'.

A flash of green on the scorched sands before us. The Gabbleratchet burst towards—

—Cyan screamed and we both fell onto a cold floor, knocking the breath out of us. We were in an enclosed space; we Shifted so fast my eyes didn't have time to focus.

The Vermiform parted from us in one great curtain. Its exhausted worms crawled around with Sauria sand and Infusoria gel trickling from between them. I stamped my feet, feeling water squeeze out of my boot lacings.

'We must have thrown it by now,' the worms moaned. 'We must have … We think …'

Cyan and I looked up and down the corridor. It was unpainted metal and very dull. 'That's more steel than a whole fyrd of lancers.'

The Vermiform started sending thin runners around the curve of the corridor. 'We're above Plennish,' it said.

'Wow,' said Cyan. 'What an imagination I have.'

I found a tiny, steel-framed window. I stood on tiptoe and tried to peer through the thick glass. 'It must be night time. Look at all the stars.' There certainly were an awful lot of stars out there, filling the whole sky and – the ground! 'Cyan, look at this – there's no ground! There's nothing under us but stars!' I looked up. 'Oh … wow …'

'Let me see,' she said.

I refused to let her take my place at the little window. I pressed my face to the glass, gazing intently. 'The grey moon fills the whole sky!'

'It isn't a moon,' said the Vermiform. 'It's Plennish. It's grey because it's completely covered in Insect paper.'

'Ah ... shit ... All that is Paperlands?'

'Yes.' It sighed. 'The Freezers once tried to bomb it. Now radioactive Insects come from there to infest many other worlds.'

'I'd like to fly around outside. There's so much space.' I looked down again – or up – to the stars. A little one was racing along in relation to the rest, travelling smoothly towards us. It was so faint it was difficult to see. I said, 'A star is moving. It's coming closer fast. Shift us out of here.'

A shiver of apprehension flowed over the Vermiform. 'We can't keep going. We're exhausted.'

'You have to!'

'We can't ... We can't! Anyway, this is a refuelling dock. If any ship tries to land without the protocol the Triskele Corporation will blow it to cinders.'

I glanced out the window, and saw them from above. Horse skulls like beaks, pinched withers falling to bone. Their long backs carried no corpses now. Sparks crawled around them, flicked up to the window glass; they ploughed straight into and through the metal wall.

'It's the Gabbleratchet!'

Human screams broke out directly underneath us. The Vermiform threw a net of worms around Cyan and myself. Sparks crackled out of the floor beside us. The muzzle of a hound appeared—

Rushing air. I was falling. I turned over, once, and the black bulk of the ground swung up into the sky. The air was very thin, hard to breathe. I fell faster, faster every second.

I forced open my wings, brought them up and buffered as hard as possible against the rushing air. I slowed down instantly, swung out in a curve and suddenly I was flying forwards. I rocketed over the dark landscape. Where was I? And why the fuck had the Vermiform dropped me in the air?

And where was Cyan? Had it separated us? I looked down and searched for her – saw a tiny speck plummeting far below me, shrinking with distance. I folded my wings back, beat hard and dived. She was falling as fast as I could fly. She was spinning head over arse, so all I could see was a tangle of arms and legs, with a flash of white panties every two seconds and nowhere to grab hold of her.

'Stretch out!' I yelled. 'Stretch your arms out!'

No answer – she was semi-conscious. She wouldn't be able to breathe at this altitude. I reached out and grabbed her arm. The speed she was falling dragged it away from me.

She rotated again and I seized a handful of her jumper. I started flapping twice the speed, panting and cursing, the strain in my back and my wings too much. Too much! We were still falling, but slower. My wings shuddered with every great desperate sweep down – and when I raised them for the next beat, we started falling at full speed again.

'Can't you lift her?' said a surprised voice, faint in the slipstream. A wide scarf wafted in front of my face, its ends streaming up above me. It was the Vermiform: it had knitted some worms around my neck!

'Of course I can't!' I yelled. 'I can barely hold my own weight!'

'Oh.'

The scarf began spinning around us, binding us together. More worms appeared and its bulk thickened, sheltering Cyan but her head bobbled against my chest.

We fell for so long we reached a steady speed. I half-closed my eyes, trying to see what sort of land was below us. I could barely distinguish between the ground and the scarcely fainter sky. There were miniscule stars and, low against the far horizon, two sallow moons glossed the tilting flat mountain-tops of a mesa landscape with a pallid light.

The ends of the scarf swept in front of my face as they searched the ground. 'I'll lower you.'

It shot out a thick tentacle towards the table-topped mountain. The tentacle dived faster than we were falling, worms unspooling from us and adding to it. It reached the crunchy rubble and anchored there. We slowed; the wind ceased. It began lowering us smoothly, millions of individual worms drawing over each other and taking the strain. They coiled in a pile on the ground. We came down gently on top of them and toppled over in a heap.

The Vermiform uncoiled and stood us on the very edge of an escarpment that fell away sheer to a level lake. Other plateaux cut the clear night sky. In places, their edges had eroded and slipped down into stepped, crumbling cliffs. Deep gorges carved dry and lifeless valleys between them. They gave onto a vast plain cracked across with sheer-sided canyons. The bottom of each, if they had floors at all, were as far below the surface as we were above it.

A series of lakes were so still, without any ripples, they looked heavy and ominous, somehow fake. It was difficult to believe they were water at all, but the stars reflected in their murky depths. The landscape looked as if it was nothing but a thin black sheet punched out with hollow-sided mountains, with great rents torn in it, through which I was looking to starry space beneath. There were no plants, no buildings; the grit lay evenly untouched by any wind.

The Vermiform threw out expansive tendrils. 'How do you like our own world?'

'Is this the Somatopolis?' I said. 'It's empty.'

'It is long dead. We were the Somatopolis, when we lived here. Once our flesh city was the whole world. We covered it up to twice the height of these mountains. We filled those chasms. Now it's bare. We are all that is left of the Somatopolis.'

The pinkish-white moonlight shone on the desolate escarpments. I imagined the whole landscape covered in nothing but worms, kilometres deep. Their surface constantly writhed, filled and reformed. I imagined them sending up meshed towers topped with high parapets loosely tangled together. Their bulk would pull out from continents into isthmuses, into islands; then contract back together, throwing up entire annelid mountain ranges. Caverns would yawn deep in the mass as worms separated, dripping worm stalactites, then would close up again with the horribly meaty pressure of their weight.

'Let's go,' I said. 'The Gabbleratchet will appear any second.'

'Wait until it does,' said the Vermiform. 'We are bringing it here deliberately. We have an idea.'

'The air's so stale,' said Cyan.

'It is used up. The Insects took our world.'

I said, 'Look, Cyan; this is what happens to a world that loses against the Insects.'

The Vermiform raised a tentacle that transformed into a hand, pointing to a plain of familiar grey roofs – the beginning of the Insects' Paperlands. Their raised front arced towards us like a stationary tidal wave and their full extent was lost to view over the unnervingly distant horizon. The cells were cracked and weathered – they were extremely old. They were darker in colour than the Paperlands in our world, but patched with pale regions where Insects had reworked them hundreds of times.

'They bring in material from other places to build with,' said the Vermiform. 'There is nothing left for them to use on my entire planet.'

As we grew accustomed to the distance, we began to distinguish them: tiny specks scurrying over the plain, around the lakes and along the summits. It was like looking down into an enormous ant's nest. I stared, forgetting this was a whole world, and imagined the mountains as tiny undulations in the soil and the Insects the size of ants, busy among them. There were single Insects, groups of a few or crowds of several thousands, questing over the grit from which everything organic had been leached. They swarmed in and out of their hooded tunnels.

The Paperlands bulged up in one or two places and paper bridges emerged, rose up and vanished at their apex. In other places the continuous surface of the roofs sank into deep pits with enormous tunnel openings; places where Insects had found ways through to other worlds. They were carrying food through – a bizarre variety of pieces of plants and animals: legosaurs, Brick Bats, humans, marzipalms. Countless millions bustled down there, pausing to stroke antennae together or layering spit onto the edges of the Paperlands with an endless industry and a contented mien. Their sheer numbers dumbfounded and depressed me. I said, 'We'll never be able to beat them.'

'We could have defeated them,' the Vermiform choired. 'We were winning our war. We fought them for hundreds of years. We forced inside their shells, we wrapped around their legs and pulled them apart. We even brought parasites and diseases in from other worlds and infected them, but the Insects chewed the mites off each other and evolved immunity to the diseases, as they eventually do in all the worlds of their range.'

'They're tough,' I said.

'They become so, over many worlds, yes. We turned the battle when lack of air started to slow them down. We gained ground. We forced them back to their original tunnel and they built a final wall. One more strike and we could have driven them through and sealed their route. But then Vista's world collapsed and its colossal ocean drained through. See those lakes? It was their larvae that did for us.'

'Their young?' I asked.

'Once the Insects started to breed in their millions. Their growing larvae are far more ravenous than adults. They scooped up mandibles-full of worms and ate the city.'

Cyan shrieked, 'Look out! There's one coming!'

Twirling antennae appeared over the escarpment edge and an Insect charged towards us. Cyan and I turned to run but the Vermiform shot out two tentacles and grabbed the Insect around its thorax, jerking it to a halt.

The tentacles snaked around the Insect, forced its mandibles wide – then its serrated mouthparts. The Insect ducked its head and tried to back off, but a third stream of worms began to pour into its mouth, keeping the mandibles open all the time. Worms streamed up from the ground and vanished down its throat.

The rest of the Vermiform still pooled at our feet waited. For a couple of seconds, nothing happened. Then the Insect exploded. Its carapace burst open and flew apart. Its innards splattered against us. Its plates fell in a metre radius leaving six legs and a head lying with a huge knot of worms in the middle where its body had been. They moved like a monstrous ball of string, covered in haemolymph, and reformed into the beautiful woman. The worms of her face moved into a smile. 'We love doing that. Wish they would line up so we can burst them one by one.'

'Ugh,' said Cyan.

I said to her, 'Keep watching for more Insects.'

Cyan said, 'I hate this place. I want to go. I want to see the cave.'

674

'The market was destroyed.'

'No. This is my dream and I say it wasn't. Take me back; there are too many bugs here.'

'Why do you think I dropped you in the air?' the Vermiform said bitterly.

It was easier to speak to the worm-woman than the amorphous bunch of annelids. I asked her, 'What has the collapse of Vista got to do with you losing the war? Did Vista's sea drown you, or something?'

'It drowned billions of us.' She pointed down to the lake. 'The Somatopolis was dry before that, very hot and arid. That is how we like it; in fact we brought you here during the night because otherwise the sun would roast you. The waterspout surged from an Insect tunnel beneath us and forced up between us. It erupted a kilometre high and Vista's whole ocean thundered out. We fled – how could we cope with running water? Still, it was salt water and we might have survived ... But the ocean began to evaporate, clouds began to form and, for the first time ever in the Somatopolis, we had rain.'

The worm-woman indicated the pools. 'Freshwater lakes formed deep among us. We recoiled from the water and erroneously left it open to the air. And the Insects began to breed. We tried to stop them. We kept fighting but, as our numbers diminished, we found it harder to cover the ground. Generations after generations of larvae decimated us, so we sought shelter under the surface. From there we Shifted to find a new world to colonise ... as many worlds as possible from the construction of the Insect's nest.'

The Vermiform woman dissolved into a snake and slithered to rejoin the main mass. 'We hope the Gabbleratchet might destroy some Insects,' it added. 'Brace yourselves. We will try to shake it once and for all by retracing our steps.'

We looked around for the Gabbleratchet, in the cloudless sky, against the rounds of the moons, among the peaks of the Paperlands and directly down to the lake.

I thought I saw something moving in it! I blinked and stared. Something was swimming in its murky abyss. It became darker and clearer as it rose close to the surface. It moved with a quick straight jet, then turned head over tail along its length and disappeared into the depths.

'What the fuck? What was that?'

A flash of green on the sheer rock face below us. The Gabbleratchet hurtled straight out of it. Empty white pelvic girdles and scooping paws reflected in the lake.

Cyan screamed. The Gabbleratchet turned; it knew where we were.

'Now!' The Vermiform lifted us off our feet, through—

—Plennish—

—Infusoria Swamp—

—Sauria—
—Precambria—
—Epsilon Market—
—Somewhere dark ... ?

Somewhere dark! Cyan cried, 'Are you there?'

'I'm here, I'm here!' I felt for her hand. I opened my eyes wide, just to be sure, but there was not one shred of light. Then, seemingly in a vast remoteness I saw a faint glow, a thin vertical white beam seemed to ... *walk* past us. It stopped, turned around and began to hurry back again with the motion of a human being, though it was nothing but a single line.

'Where are we?' I demanded. 'You said we were going back to the Fourlands!'

'Stupid creature! This *is* your world. We want to hide for a while in case the Gabbleratchet comes.'

'But ...'

The Vermiform said, 'This is Rayne's room. That is Rayne.'

I think the Vermiform was pointing but I couldn't see anything.

'She is pacing back and forth. She's anxious; in fact, she's panicking. Can't you feel it?'

Curiously enough, I could. The intense emotions were radiating from the white ray and putting me on edge. 'But what's happened to her ? That's just a thin line!'

'Hush. If we see the Gabbleratchet's sparks, we will have to leave fast. This is the Fourlands, the fifth to the eighth dimensions. You occupy those as well as the ones you're familiar with, seeing as you've evolved in a world with ten. You can't see them with your usual senses, but you do operate in them. We are amazed that you never consciously realise it.'

Close by, Cyan shouted, 'It's talking crap! Tell it so, Jant.'

'Hey, it's interesting.'

The Vermiform harped on: 'Emotions impress on the fifth dimension, which is why you can sometimes sense a strong emotion or see an image of the person who suffered it, in the same place years later. What other examples can we give? Acupuncture works on the part of you that operates in the sixth dimension, so you'll never be able to understand how it works with the senses you have. And the seventh, if only you knew of that one—'

Cyan screamed, 'Take me home! Take me home *now*! Now! Now! Now!' I could hear her thrashing and kicking at the flaccid worms.

'Think of it as a shadow world,' I told her.

'You goatfucking son of a bastard's bastard's bastard!'

We waited for a long time. The Vermiform eventually said, 'I think we've thrown off the Gabbleratchet. Let's go.'

676

It gave us a small jolt and our worm-bonds dropped to the floor. Off balance I stumbled forward – into Rayne's bedroom.

CHAPTER 9

Rayne was staring at me, still holding the coal shovel, standing beside the bed where Cyan lay unconscious. I turned to see the cluster of worms behind me, like a tall mould – the back of my head and my folded wings were imprinted in it.

They tumbled to the floor in an inert, exhausted mass; then began to ebb away, slowly and fitfully. Their pool diminished in size as they invisibly poured back into the Shift. When it was about the size of my palm it split into three and dribbled away to the coal scuttle, under the door and between my feet under the rocking chair. I tilted the chair back, but they had gone.

Rayne, with a speed that belied her years, headed off the worms crawling towards the coal scuttle and shovelled them up. She took an empty jar from the shelf and tipped them into it. Then she pressed on the metal lid, held the jar to the light and shook it experimentally. The dollop of worms remained inert at the base.

'T' Vermiform, you say?' she asked.

'That's right.'

'This is a priceless sample. Are t' worms still sentien' when they're separa'ed?'

'I think so. At least, they act independently. I think they're just exhausted.'

She put the jar on the mantelpiece. The worms inside rose up in a wave and pushed against the glass. The jar tipped up, teetered on its edge and clattered back down. The worms collected themselves for another push, so Rayne picked up the jar and wedged it safely between the cushions on the rocking chair.

Cyan jolted awake with a gasp – fell back on the bed. Her eyes were glazed and confused, socketed with deep purple shadows. Her pale lips were set in a grimace, far from her nonchalant expression of earlier. She was still breathing more shallowly than a fish in the Shift and her limbs were enervated, motionless. She turned her head to one side and vomited over the pillow.

'Cat is addictive!' I shouted at her. 'Don't do it again!'

'Quie', Jant,' said Rayne.

'How could you have even wanted to try it? It's a cure-all for slum kids not stupid rich girls!'

'Quie'! Look, Jant, you can help me. Gelsemium and salicin for her aches. Henbane for her tremors. Hamamelis for her bruising. Go and fetch me all these, and some cotton t' dab in the ointmen'.'

I did, and when Rayne was concentrating on Cyan, I also slipped the jar of worms into the pocket of my new coat.

At length Rayne said, 'I think she will take days t' recover.'

'She can't stay here for days.'

'No.' Rayne glanced at a casement clock, then at the piles of packed equipment. 'Especially no' as my coach will be here within t' hour, and I mus' go t' Slake Cross.'

'Lightning did say to bring her to the front.'

'Wha', like tha'?' We looked at Cyan dubiously. She lay quite still, slowly testing her relaxed body, trying to wake up without throwing up. 'I wouldn' wan' t' move her ...'

'Think of it as another leg of the Grand Tour.'

'I'll "Grand Tour" you! Bloody Awians.'

If we left Cyan, she would go straight back to Galt with a story in her repertoire to add to her growing collection of cool credentials. Rayne seemed to realise this. 'All righ'. I'll take her.'

'Thanks.'

'She migh' benefi' from some advice on t' journey. I'll make sure she's well by t' time she meets Ligh'ning.'

'Don't tell him,' I said.

Rayne pursed her smooth lips. 'I can' promise tha'.'

A faint voice whispered from the direction of the box-bed. 'Help ...'

'Oh, so you've found your voice. You are by far the most stupid girl who ever crossed paths with mine. Jook! Is that what you call it? What did you do it for ? Did you think it was a laugh?'

With her eyes shut, she asked quietly, 'Is Sharny dead?'

'Maybe,' I said angrily.

'He is,' she said, resigned. 'He's dead.'

She turned over and slipped out of the bed onto weak legs, staggered, and I caught her. I knew she would be seeing the room as a single flat picture and the objects as shapes. She wouldn't be able to distinguish their depths and the light would create confusing patches of bright and shade that would seem more real and significant than the objects themselves. I delineated a chair for her from the other shapes and made her sit down.

Cyan slurred, 'That trip ...'

'It's over now.' I spoke slowly and calmly to reassure her, although I knew she'd hear a scrambled version of my words, if she could hear me at all over the roar of her own pulse and breathing.

'Pu' her back in t' bed,' Rayne said.

Cyan's eyes cleared briefly to an avid violent look. 'I had visions.'

'It was real,' I said.

'Now is no' t' time,' Rayne told me warningly.

'I dreamed about *you.*'

'I was there,' I found myself saying. 'I saw it too. Trust me; I used to live with this.'

'No!' She grabbed the nearest object on the dresser – a bamboo birdcage. Her thin fingers sank between the bars. She hefted the cage at an angle, spilling seed and water all over the floor, and the finches inside fluttered madly. She was about to throw it at me, but she gave a little sigh, her eyes rolled up and she toppled out of the chair in a faint, the birdcage still grasped in one hand.

Rayne looked at me with a horrified expression.

'I'll put her in the coach,' I said.

I watched Rayne leave at full speed in a smart coach-and-four. She would change horses at Wichert in Shivel, Shivel town, Slaughterbridge in Eske, Eske town, Carse, Clobest in Micawater, the Rachis valley coaching inns at Merebrigg village, Oscen town, Spraint, Floret and Plow.

I flew.

CHAPTER 10

On the second day I headed towards Awia, passing over the bleak hills of upper Fescue, where the Brome stream meets the Rill and the Foss and becomes the Moren River. Rayne should have reached the Shivel coach stop by now. I hoped Cyan still didn't look two days dead when she arrives at Slake Cross or Rayne is going to have a hard time explaining it to Lightning. I just hope he doesn't connect me with Cyan's condition.

The air was sluggish so I concentrated on its changing shapes as I flew past the quarries at Heshcam and Garron on the Brome stream. The Brome's peaty water, the colour of beer, tumbled out of ghylls between rounded hills topped with millstone grit crags like pie crusts.

Cyan needs to learn who she is. She's as confusing as a shot of pure cat in fourth-day withdrawal. I just hope her experience has taught her not to take the stuff again.

Tapering black chimneys poked up from a cleft between two hills. That's my next landmark – Marram mining town. I flapped towards it tiredly, noticing my shadow on the hillside far to my right.

Marram was tucked in a valley and the roofs and chimneys of the lead and stannary furnaces seemed to take up most of it. I came in very low over the surrounding grey-purple slag heaps. A massive lead crushing wheel turned slowly in an overshot sluice, around which spots of red and yellow were the woollen shawls, head scarves and wide trousers of women picking ore fragments from the machine's trays.

I flapped overhead and they all looked up, began shoving each other and pointing me out. The women seemed glad of a break; they started leering and catcalling. One or two had wings but most were human and they were all very raucous.

One spread her arms and yelled, 'Hey, Comet, where are you sleeping tonight?'

'Wherever they leave me, lover!'

They doubled up with laughter. God, I thought, I can tell this is Fescue.

I couldn't gain height and I flapped around low, making a complete fool of myself until I remembered the smelting furnaces. I circled the tall chimneys and went up like a kite on their updraught.

The roofs of Marram began to spin under me; the smoke-stained houses built in close terraces, the steep narrow roads with ridged cobbles so horses could find purchase. At the edge of town I went over the long, bronze-green roofs of the communal latrines which, by law, all the townspeople had to use. Marram villagers save everything; even barrels of urine for use in alum extraction and the nightsoil to spread as fertiliser on their sparse oat fields.

Higher on the rock face planks and girders shored up a five-metre-wide mine mouth. A dirty piebald pony walked round and round, tethered to a pump capstan at the pit head. The men were all underground already, rooting out copper, tin and lead. These Marram villagers were hollow-eyed and blue-toothed from shale dust and lead fumes, but they were wealthier than the farmers of the Plainslands. Everyone here could own his own house: Lord Governor Darne! Fescue keeps the trade for metals fair.

I was covering distance extremely quickly now, about a hundred kilometres an hour, and in a straight line. On the twisting dirt track roads below, people take a day to travel as far as I can in thirty minutes. I passed into Awia and over Cushat Cote village on Micawater manor's southern border. I flew past Cushat's 'naming court' house, a courtroom where an Awian marriage judiciary meet. They settle disputes as to which of the two married couples' families is the wealthier – a hot topic for status-obsessed featherbacks as the richest bequeaths its name to the children.

The Circle broke.

I blacked out – for a second – came to so quickly I was still gliding, fifty metres lower in a steep dive. The ground filled my vision. I straightened my flight, brought the horizon level, wondering what the fuck had happened.

It had been the Circle, surely? The Circle had just stopped. One of my colleagues had died – I couldn't tell which one. Or maybe – shit – maybe the Emperor has found out I've been in the Shift and that jolt was him dropping *me* from the Circle. Could I be mortal again?

I held my arms out and looked at my hands. Could time be passing for me? I had no way of telling. I can't feel the Circle like the most experienced Eszai sometimes do. I was shaking but I pulled on the air and began to ascend.

The Circle broke.

A second time. It reformed promptly and I spun out of my fall yet lower in the sky. I yelled, 'What's happening?'

The Circle broke.

With a slow sense of void so horribly vacant I screamed. I blanked out for a few seconds and found myself descending still lower. My wingtips touched treetops on each down beat.

I gained height, bracing myself in trepidation of it happening again. Three times! Who'd been killed ? Which of us – Lightning? Serein? Frost? The last one had died horribly slowly.

What could injure three Eszai in close succession so badly that the Circle couldn't hold them? In what circumstances could the skill and strength of three of my friends be useless? They were surrounded by troops and fortifications. Could it be a fyrd revolt?

Perhaps I was lucky not to be there. I found myself sobbing, feeling light and drifting. A second of time had passed for me, for all of us, before San reformed the connections. It felt awful, much like the shock on hearing the news that someone you love has died – which is not fair considering that few Eszai love anyone apart from their spouses.

I examined myself. Did I feel tired? Could anyone badly hurt be pulling on the Circle? I couldn't tell.

Shit, shit, shit. Another disaster at Slake Cross and I'm not there. The Emperor will have felt it and he'll be expecting me to come and tell him why – and I don't know! He'll find out I wasn't at the front!

I was cold with rising panic but I forced myself to concentrate. I'm in deep trouble – and so is Lightning – assuming he's still alive. I spoke aloud: 'There's no time to hesitate. I must reach Slake, find out what's happening, then race back to the Castle and take San the news. I'll have to outpace all the dispatch riders and reach the Castle before them, because if any beat me there and tell the Emperor I was absent, he'll have my balls.'

Where the fuck was I, anyway? I looked down on the valley. The oblique morning light cast a shadow of one valley side across the other and the stone buildings of Cushat Cote village at the bottom were still in darkness. The border of Awia. Having got my bearings, I turned sharply. I must steel myself to be prepared for anything. I beat my wings powerfully and flew my fastest towards Slake Cross.

CHAPTER II

I came upon the baggage train along the Glean Road. It was decimated – nothing was moving down there.

I descended and let the road stream along under me. It was solid with dismembered bodies of men and women, severed heads and limbs. Between the shafts of overturned carts lay the white or chestnut flanks of the hitched horses. Ragged green vegetables and leather-fletched crossbow bolts spilt from the barrels. Dead Insects lay among them, each two metres long. The devastation stretched into the distance along the road. If a swarm has reached this far, what's happening at Slake?

I skimmed over them – the horses and mules were no more than jumbles of bloody hide and entrails, a semi-digested green-shit stench. I could see no sign of the attack having come from any direction – the people lay in equal numbers on both verges as if they didn't know which way to flee. Few were armed. Horses had bolted dragging their carts off the road; they lay on the grass further off, their black hooves raised and rigid.

It didn't make any sense. Where were the live Insects? Once they were out of danger they would always stop and feed but few bodies showed any signs of damage beyond the wounds that had killed them. It was as if a great force had swept through and torn them apart instantaneously.

Here was one of the armoured wagons – steel plate riveted to its wooden sides – designed to be a temporary refuge in case of attack. The worst Insects could do was eat the wheels off and cause it to tumble to the ground. Its doors were firmly shut. As they had to be bolted from inside, somebody must be in there. I landed squarely beside it. On the ground the silence was terrifying. The pools of blood between the carts had dried to brown but the corpses still smelt salty, like fresh meat.

I looked all around, drew my ice axe and banged the haft on the door. I called through an air hole, 'Anyone in here?'

'Just me,' said a young man's voice.

'This is Comet. What happened ?'

'Comet!' The voice degenerated into sobs. 'Everything's gone.'

'Open the door. The Insects have left.'

'No!' screamed the man. 'I'm not coming out! Leave me! Leave me here!'

I peered through the air hole but could see only blackness. What would I do with one man crazy with terror in the middle of the Lowespass country-side? 'OK,' I said calmly, 'I'll fly to Slake and send lancers. They'll get you out; you'll be safe.'

'Fly? Safe?' The man started laughing with a horrible high-pitched tone.

I took off and flew as high as I could trying to catch a first glimpse of the town. Beneath me, both sides of the road were 'trap fields' where iron traps had been set. Yellow signposts warned travellers not to leave the highway. The pressure of an Insect's foot on the trigger plate will spring a trap shut and bite the claw off. Now I started to see them, maimed but still alive, moving slowly or spasming on the ground.

I went over the valley head and the moorland pass dropped away – reddish spots were Insects roaming randomly on the slopes. I hastened on, frightened for my friends. This reminded me far too much of 1925.

Slake Cross town sat in the distance, the lake beyond it. A massive misty funnel of black spots was rising high and thin in the air above the lake. It was drifting slightly with the breeze but twisting with a slowness unlike any whirlwind I'd seen. And there was scarcely a wind anyway. I couldn't tell what it was; I stared at it until my eyes hurt. The great spiral towered over the lake and specks cascaded from it like water drops or debris. They rose and fell like soot specks coming off a fire, but they must be huge if I could see them at this distance.

Below me another defence – a 'field of holes' – was full of struggling Insects. Pits had been dug close together over the whole valley floor. Each was two metres square and five deep, straight-sided, concrete-lined with sharp, tar-painted stakes fixed upright in the bottom. I looked directly down into them; some were half-full of Insects skewered on the stakes, in the base of others lone Insects raised their heads, convergent compound eyes glittering. They would try to dig their way out until they wore their claws to stubs.

Further still and I was over the zigzag trenches running parallel with the river. The trenches were square-based, cut in chevrons, so that trapped Insects could be more easily dispatched as they slowed down to scurry round the corners. The trenches trimmed across my field of vision and Insects looking no bigger than ants scuttled up and down them, bristling.

I approached, with a feeling of trepidation like facing the cold wind that precedes a storm. The swirling flurry in the sky was more than five hundred metres tall. The whole sky was mottled with specks bumbling around each other, some over the town, some now between it and me. I concentrated on these, and as I came nearer the space between them seemed to increase. From looking at lots of motes plastered against a blank grey sky I was soon aware of them as individuals hanging in the air. I picked one and closed in on it.

The dot resolved into a dark crescent moving at my altitude with both points facing downwards. Closer still, I could see the crescent had three segments. It was bulky, not streamlined like a bird and I couldn't understand what was keeping it up. Then it turned towards me and I saw its bulbous eyes. It was an Insect! An Insect flying!

I yelled, pulled my wings closed and fell below it just as it swept over my head. Its buzzing nearly deafened me even above the sudden roar of the air stream as I went into freefall. I forced open my wings, looked around, saw I hadn't fallen more than twenty metres, and performed a slow roll so I could look down the length of my body and see it behind me.

A *flying* Insect?

I couldn't believe it was real! It was heading away and starting to turn. I could see its ten bronze-brown abdomen plates, its tail curved and hooked under like a gigantic wasp. Its legs were bunched up under its body, the knee joints sticking out. Above its thorax was a continuous flickering – one, no, *two* pairs of long translucent wings, beating so fast they blurred! They protruded from under its thorax's first lamina, attached by a narrow joint that seemed flexible, like a hinge. What *were* these things?

Another one underneath me altered its path, rising up diagonally, but I jinked to one side and it missed. I looked forward, realising what the rising funnel above the reservoir was – a flight of Insects. Thousands upon thousands of winged Insects.

Their massed humming caused the sky to vibrate as if struck, resounding from all directions like the sound of flies on a corpse. It drowned out my own beats.

I have fought ground-bound Insects for so long I was bewildered; I couldn't believe they were doing something different. Are these the same animals? Insects have always had tiny wings. Where have they suddenly got long wings from? And why now? One struck my foot a glancing blow – I dived hastily.

Below me, normal Insects swarmed over the whole valley bottom. They floated dead in the moat, scurried on the road, tore tents down and dragged them over the heather. Trebuchets stood abandoned. Warning beacons blazed on all the peel towers but I could see no other sign of life. A convoy of wagons by the town wall had been chained together to form a laager but every soldier inside the enclosure was dead. The Insects were raining down from above, bypassing our defences, overwhelming everything on the ground.

Arrows pulsed out of the towers' overhanging belfries and irregularly from the covered walkways along the walls of Slake Cross. I thought of Lightning – surely he must be alive, directing the archers? I had to find out what was going on.

I passed over the town and towards the Insect flight. Like a single being, it threw off graceful wisps as myriads tumbled from the apex. Its base was russet with them ascending from their side of the lake.

686

Every sense was alive as I dodged past the Insects hurtling towards me. I flew low, dropping underneath the main concentrations. I would never see down through the flight if I went above it. I stared out towards the Wall and what I saw took my breath away. On the far side of the lake, against the panorama of the muddy valley bottom, thousands of Insects, no, tens of thousands, were crawling out from irregularly spaced breaches in the white Wall. They blanketed the ground, scuttling slowly and purposefully over the bare earth before the lake. Ranks and ranks of Insects were flowing out. Each had four transparent wings, so long that their wider rounded ends overlapped each one's abdomen and dragged on the ground behind it like a bride's train.

They stopped on the bank. I picked one and focused on it. Its elbowed antennae twirled, even more active than usual, and its head was raised, alertly tasting the air. It turned its head, separated its drooping wings with a mandible and a stretched back leg. It began to twist them up and down with beats. The wings beat faster into a blur and the Insect's back began to arch. It was being tugged up. I could see its feet shifting position and rising until just the tips of its claws touched the ground, then they lifted off and with a tremendous birring the Insect slowly took off from standing, rose into the air and joined lines, skeins, then great clouds of them spiralling up above the Wall.

Hundreds of metres above, the multitudes were converging. Insects clung together in clusters; enormous aggregations of chitin plates and thrumming wings. They were tussling to touch the tips of their abdomens together. They rolled as they fell, losing height rapidly and separating again. When their abdomens retracted I saw sticky strands of mucus stretched between them. They reminded me of ants in ... in a mating flight!

With this chill realisation I flew a circuit around the rising funnel, risking being attacked, but the insects paid me no attention at all, totally intent on each other. Their numbers seemed to increase and ebb in waves. Individuals in the spiral rose and fell, dropped height and struggled up again, as if with fatigue.

I glided and watched spent Insects tumble out of the spiral, still trailing strands of slime. They righted themselves and descended, drifting south with the wind, around the town and over it. They fell into the town, onto the wreck of canvas outside the walls, onto the glacis between the walls and moat. The moat was completely full of thrashing, hopelessly tangled brown legs and abdomens.

Some landed in the reservoir, or in the river, where they didn't resurface, and I saw the current turning them over and over as it swept them downstream.

Those that survived were suddenly free of their wings, running rapidly back towards the Wall. Whole wings were scattered all over the ground like glinting shards. The Insects trampled them heedlessly. I concentrated on one Insect alone on the river bank. It settled, took hold of its wings with its nearest pair of legs and pulled them off. They didn't leave a wound or a scar, or any sign of the enormous muscles that must surely be driving them.

When the newly grounded Insects reached the lake they joined thousands of others all along the south shore, gathered so densely they were clambering over each other. Many were turning around, dipping their abdomens into the water. What appeared to be streams of froth drifted away from them. All around the lake margin the Insects' tails were pushing out lines of white foam, which lazily tangled with other streams into an irregular lace, drifted towards the lake centre and became indistinct as it slowly sank in the depths.

I put some distance between myself and the chaos of the mating flight to gain a clearer picture of what was happening. Were these different Insects altogether?

The fresh perspective simply brought new questions. More Insects were swarming over the Wall and their saliva was melting the paper as if it was wax. They were working hard to pull out darker lumps from within the liquefying spit. I glided closer to see what was happening – then wished I hadn't. The lumps were cadavers, the remains of soldiers. Free of the spit that had formed the Wall and preserved them, some were so rotten that they began to fall apart. There were horse limbs and heads, whole sheep from Lowespass farms, the feral mastiffs of the forts, and some chunks of matter I couldn't recognise, all covered with the white paste.

The Insects carried them directly to the lake. All along its shores they were wading into the water as deep as their middle leg joint and dropping their burdens. They lowered their heads and nudged the ancient carcasses further in; I could see them bobbing, leaving ripples.

The reservoir edges were filling up with a putrid mass of sodden rotting meat. Chunks washing at the surface and at the water's edge were releasing a thick, dark brown and oily scum that started to resemble broth. They were turning the entire lake into a waterlogged charnel pit. The amount of matter being dumped was displacing the water and the dam's spillway glistened as shallow pulses ran down over its cobbles.

'Oh shit,' I said, for want of a better word. I had never seen Insects do something so complicated. What if they were sentient after all?

The rank smell of rotting fat and skin rose on the breeze, making me retch. I folded an arm over my face and gained height above it, but I knew it would stick in my sinuses for days. I took a last look at the gruesome mess and skimmed away from the lake. More Insects were beginning to build a new Wall around it.

They were ranging freely over the whole countryside, scurrying on the road, feeding on dead men and horses – and carrying fresh pieces, still dripping, back to join the corruption they had made of the lake.

I couldn't stay there, not so close to the stench. It seemed to cling to my feathers no matter how high I flew. I winged towards the town.

High above the gatehouse I saw an Insect buzz through the hail of arrows. They found their mark and it suddenly bloomed with white flights. Shafts stuck out all over it as it passed underneath me. It went into a steep descent, wings beating furiously, and crashed into the roof of the tavern buckling all its legs. Its wings flickered; the time between each vibration lengthened until it died.

I took this as a warning – the steel crossbows mounted on the ramparts have an awesome seven-hundred-metre range – so when I was about a kilometre away from town I climbed high and came in above them.

I looked down into complete confusion. The outermost road of the three concentric squares was totally infested. Soldiers were shooting Insects from the safety of the curtain wall, the large square shutters all hooked back. Archers stood on every available rampart, crossbowmen leant out of windows, rocks and boiling water issued through the machicolations of the hoardings, bombarding the Insects directly underneath. I even saw civilians hurling roof slates into the seething mass.

From the window in the first ring of barracks, spearmen jabbed frenziedly at any Insects getting too close.

In the inner two roads and the central square, smaller numbers of Insects ran at random, claws skittering on the cobbles. Bodies littered the streets. Most of the iron paling gates had been shut across the roads. Others were barricaded with heaps of furniture, anything men could lay their hands on in the panic. Slake Cross was designed so that if a road ring was taken, we could pull back to the next one, and so on, to the middle – but that design depended on Insects attacking on the ground, from outside. The Architect could never have envisaged them dropping in from the sky.

I banked, turning in a shallow glide towards the intense throng continuing to rise into the air above the lake. Their opaque buzzing made it difficult to think and the sweeping movements of the flight were so ultimate, so terrible, it drew my gaze and I watched, hypnotised.

A shout rose over the buzzing: 'Hahay!'

Surprised to hear an Awian hunting cry I glanced down towards the source and saw an Insect pacing me, only a hundred metres below. As I saw it, an arrow storm poured from the walkways. Enfilade shooting from the tower tops caught it in cross-volleys. It twisted in the air. Arrows slashed its wings to ribbons – it seemed to fold up and dropped like a stone, straight down, its abdomen writhing with a blind life of its own. The Insect hit the ground by the moat and splattered – great splits opened up in its carapace and its insides began to seep out, pooling yellow on the grass.

I slewed left and right in acknowledgement at the favour although in reality I was far more alarmed by the prospect of being riddled with arrows than being bitten by the Insect.

Time to show them I didn't need their help. From what I had seen of the Insects' manoeuvrability I was definitely the stronger flyer. I put my hand behind me, unfastened a stud and drew my ice axe from its holster fastened horizontally on my belt. I went into a glide and tapped its steel head thoughtfully against my palm as I circled the town.

I stripped off my bangles and shoved them into my coat, and buttoned my sunglasses into my inside pocket. I positioned myself above the nearest Insect, my shadow covering it. Its dragonfly-like head swivelled: it could see three hundred and sixty degrees around it. It saw me and tried to climb to my altitude, but I was far more agile. I stood on one wing and turned, soared directly over, and gave its rapidly beating wings a good solid kick as I passed. The Insect rocked, righted itself in the air and dived.

I whooped and dived after it. It wouldn't let me stay above its head. I saw dark patches on its compound eyes that looked almost like pupils, one pair on the top, another pair facing forwards. At first I thought they were reflections, then I realised they were areas of smaller facets, set closely together. Perhaps the eyes of these mating Insects are different too; it seemed to see well directly above it. I decided to attack by coming in fast and from the side. I swerved away, turned so steeply the ground and all its towers swung up to my left. I beat with my wings close to my body and bore down on it with full speed.

The Insect saw me too late, jinked, but I rammed into its thorax, grappling so it couldn't turn to grab me. We whirled together, losing height, and the wind stream roared up past us. The ground rotated and spun crazily. I didn't look down, I have a sense of how close I can fall, how big the buildings can grow before I seriously start to panic. I hefted my axe and chopped through its neck. The Insect's head detached and I let it fall but the body flew on thirty metres before tumbling to the ground.

I wheeled away, plastered in yellow blood, yelling in triumph. 'Get out of my sky! Back on the ground, you fuckers!'

I spotted another on the far side of town. I beat upwards, climbing to approach it, then swooped. Its wings whirred beneath me and their wind streamed out my ponytail. I hacked with the axe, missed and collided with its shell back, pushing it downwards in the air. My axe fell free, jerking on its lanyard. My hands were next to the bases of its front wings. They were moving so fast I didn't dare touch them. The great, glassy wings flicked back and forth on either side of me – dry black veins around clear cells – I saw the moorland distorted through their transparent surfaces. I matched its pace, hanging on to the top of it while I recovered my axe and chopped through the base of one wing. The Insect jerked away erratically. Spines on top of its abdomen grazed my hands. It began to fall. Its antennae with ends like strings of beads flicked frantically. Its other wing started beating twice as fast. It spun violently, spiralling tighter and tighter until it hit the road and exploded into a thousand shards.

'Great!' I shouted, and swung into a long turn looking around for more. One was buzzing in a straight path from the mating flight, at around seventy kilometres an hour. I can do twice that. I let it pass overhead, beat hard to come up behind it. Its very thin waist and haze of wings passed beneath me an arm's length away. I tilted, slowed down. The Insect beat faster and it knocked up underneath me, hitting me along the length of my body. I gasped a breath, frightened, then swung my axe and cut through a wing stem. It plummeted away, curling into a ball so tight the pointed tip of its abdomen was over its mandibles. It spun; the brown hunch of its thorax, smooth rounded abdomen, goggle compound eyes.

On the ground, I saw upturned faces and men pointing at me. I grinned and pressed the fingers of my wings together like paddles, pulled the air past me more strongly with the right than the left, rotated as I rose steeply showing them the soles of my boots. Then I fanned out my wings' fingers, came to a standstill for a second, levelled my flight and sped swiftly towards the next Insect, wondering if this is how a peregrine feels.

I ran rings around them. I had no real impact on their numbers but I was more effective than the arrows. I sparred with them for the next three hours until sunset. The swarm above the reservoir was starting to falter and disperse; fewer Insects were crawling out from the Wall. Below me, troops were being marched out of the buildings of the two outermost rings, in an attempt to clear the centre. Civilians packed the hall and church to capacity. I could still see clearly, my eyes had attuned to the dusk and the red-gold smudge of sunset over the hills in the distance. The town's floodlights were abandoned but lamps glowed along the concentric roads and the square. I was exhausted and losing concentration but a few Insects were bombilating in from the flight.

I cut the wings off one and swept on to the next. I soared over and tore a wing, stalled deliberately in front and cracked its head with my boot heels. I glided towards another and dealt it a blow that smashed both antennae roots, knocking it sideways. It turned over and I felt a strong tug above my belt. I looked down – the Insect's back right foot had caught my shirt, its claw had closed and now as it turned away from me it was winding the material around its foot. I pulled frantically at my shirt but I couldn't free it. I yelled and flapped madly – then we plummeted together.

The Insect kicked its extended leg, struggling frantically, and every movement just wound my shirt tighter into a knot around its three claws. I grabbed the hard ankle joint and pulled at it.

The Insect and I began to spin around each other, centripetal force pulling us away from each other the length of its leg. Airflow rushed past faster and faster. I flared my wings, desperately braking, but lying on my side I couldn't gain any purchase on the air. The Insect's underside faced me, the ball and socket joints of its legs under its thorax. Its five other legs razored past as it kicked and it bent at the waist bringing its tail close to my legs. The roaring airstream tore its wings along their length and the loose strips started fluttering around us.

Relative to the Insect I seemed to be stationary but the ground below us swept round faster and faster. I sipped at the rushing air through gritted teeth. The horizon climbed up the sky and the awful gusts buffeted us, blowing my ponytail upwards. The end of it tangled with the Insect's other back foot.

My axe dangled. I grasped its shaft back into my hand and swiped down at the leg projecting from my shirt. I missed. Tried again, and missed. Panicking, I reached down and tapped with little cuts but the angle was impossible. The narrow blade kept chipping past the smooth leg on both sides. I couldn't put any force behind it so even when I did strike the tubular chitin, flattened to barbs on the back, I couldn't sever it. Fuck, fuck, fuck, why do I never carry a sword?

The town blossomed up beneath me. The stone rings opened up; widened; then I lost sight of the outer wall and all beneath me were barracks roofs and the square. I've only got seconds.

I folded my wings in and bent my legs arching my back concave so my feet were almost behind my head. I scrabbled in my boot top for my flick knife. With less drag, we whirled round each other faster – the Insect pulled my shirt and the tight material cut into my waist, restricting me further. I flicked the blade and swept it behind my head, cutting the end of my ponytail free. Then with swift cuts I slashed through my stretched shirt feeling it open up around my sides and tear of its own accord over my stomach. The claw ripped free.

I snapped one wing closed, raised the other and stalled – slipped sideways away from the Insect.

It turned over in the air, legs uppermost, mandibles snapping and antennae whipping. A long bronze line of light reflected from the sunset along the length of its body.

I braked as hard as I could. I spread my feathers wide and flat, fighting against the airflow forcing them up. They hissed and jiggled, bending like bows. I splayed my legs trying to counteract the spin. The distance between me and the Insect increased. It shrank below me. I saw it, still rotating along its length, fall towards a messy impact with the barracks roof.

I did not have enough distance left to stop. I was braking as hard as I could but the spinning roofs were too large, too near. Well, this is it, I thought. This is how it ends. At least it'll be over quickly. I had an image of Tern in my mind like a portrait. I spun as I fell, every couple of seconds, trailing my foot in the corner of my vision. The barracks ring flashed away. I levelled with the towers; they shot above me. I glimpsed soldiers on the ground, their mouths round Os. Detail leapt out: the flags, the cracks between hall roof slabs, grit in the drainpipes. I hugged my arms and legs in tight. I closed my eyes and my mind was already dissociating, awaiting the impact.

Thumpf! I hit something elastic and jolted. I seemed to arc out in a slow trajectory. I almost stopped, then – *crack! crack!* – I tumbled head over feet straight down and hit the ground heavily, backside, wings, and my head jerked back and hit the stone.

Oof. I skidded to a halt feeling my skin burning. I opened my eyes and looked around. I was loosely wrapped in voluminous folds of canvas, through which the lamplights shone orange. The stuff around my face blew in and out with my panting. All right, I thought; I'm alive. I'm on the ground and alive. Ooh, my head. I pressed a hand to it with Eszai stoicism but nothing gave way. I rolled around, winded, and scrabbled at the material but I couldn't find an opening. I stabbed my axe into it, cut a rent and crawled out, onto the cobbles of the central square.

Acres of orange canvas seemed to curl away from me on both sides. I looked at it and saw the massive letters, backwards and upside down: 'Riverworks Company Est. 1692'. A glance up to the roof of the hall told me I had snapped the flagpoles holding Frost's banner. They hung down, trailing it between them.

I hugged my head, rolled over and moaned. My right arm and shoulder were skinned and bleeding profusely. Sliding on the cobbles had worn a hole in the banner, through my jeans' denim as if it was tissue, and blood was trickling down my right leg. My shirt was laddered and my axe scabbard reduced to leather shreds.

I rotated my shoulder, gasping at the pain.

A jangle of chain mail and the flash of plate armour – Tornado was running towards me out of the hall. The front of his helmet was featureless and forbidding. He hooked the visor back and I saw his shocked face. 'Jant, are you all right?'

'I think so … I mean, I'm bleeding … Shit, I'm bleeding!'

'You lucky bastard.' Tornado pointed at the broken banner. I shrugged lopsidedly at him.

He slipped his shield from his arm and stuck it upright with its spike between the cobbles. It had a printed street map and the horn blast codes pasted on the inside. He hung his axe on top.

Tornado, I'm so glad it's you. I would have wasted hours trying to explain my ordeal to someone with more imagination. Now the nightmare faded rapidly when faced with this bloodstained mail-coiffed frontiersman smiling like a maniac behind a blade I would have been unable to lift.

I said faintly, 'Who's dead? ... I felt the Circle break. Who did we lose?'

'The Lawyer.'

'Gayle? Damn ...'

'Thunder.'

'Thought so.'

'And Hayl.'

'Gayle, Hayl and Thunder ... That's one fuck of a storm ...'

Tornado wiped the edge of the padded hood drawn over his forehead and the thick stubble on his cheeks. 'Come inside.'

I took a couple of steps and stumbled, but he supported me. He said, 'When all this started Hayl rode out to the dam to close the winch tower portcullises. We didn't want Insects to crawl through. Then they started flying! He shut the gates but he, like, never made it back. Thunder was covering him with bombardment from the trebuchets, but the first Insects came down and swamped his crew. He didn't stand a chance, either. Gayle's men tried to stop the artillerists fleeing and she got killed with 'em. Lightning made everyone else stay inside. Flying Insects – I haven't, like, seen anything like this before. We need to tell San. We need Rayne too.'

'She's on her way.' I sighed. Concussion was greying-out my thinking, and I could do nothing more. Tornado walked me into the hall and we pressed through the crowd of civilians and armoured soldiers. Vowing to pretend it was only a hangover I climbed the stairs to my room, still feline but not in as much that cats walk in straight lines. I dressed my skinned arm and leg myself and collapsed on the bed.

CHAPTER 12

The clatter of hooves in the street roused me. I lay with a terrible pain in my arm and a stiff ache in my wings, feeling like death – fast-thawing like a corpse out of the Ilbhinn glacier. I wondered why I was always doing this to myself, until I remembered I came by this pain in the line of duty rather than pleasure.

The sound of hooves intensified, with the jingling of bells. There must be a whole company outside. I tried to get out of bed and gasped as the ache fired into a streak of agony. I slipped a T-shirt on and looked out of the window. It gave onto the second ring; the road below was full of horses, and lancers riding in full plate, holding their lances point down. Their line, two abreast, wound around the corner. The noise of bells on their bridles might reassure the horses, but it put my nerves on edge.

High over the barracks roof, a few Insects were twisting up into the air.

The lancers passed by and the street emptied. On the cobbles a dispersed smear of brown fur and pink bone was all that remained of the Eske fyrd's grizzly bear mascot. Behind it, a door to the barracks block was open and two soldiers with crossbow bandoliers stood on its step. One leant forward to light a cigarette, then straightened up and blew out smoke.

A quick movement caught my attention. An Insect ran round the corner and hurtled down the street. The smokers slammed their door shut. The Insect dashed beneath my window, then seemed to lose its footing with all six legs at once. It fell and bowled tail over forelegs with its own momentum, crashed into the wall and lay still, with a red-fledged arrow sticking out of it.

Lightning will be awake, then.

The door was ajar and I heard Tornado's voice counting to ten three times as he ascended the stairs. He reached the top and knocked so powerfully that the door swung wide.

I called, 'Yes!'

He continued knocking.

'It's bloody open; you can bloody come in if you bloody have to!'

He entered, still in filthy armour, and a scowl. 'You're looking good this morning.'

'The flight is starting again. What time is it?'

'Six a.m. There aren't as many, yet, but the ones that came down yesterday are still clogging the roads. Wrenn's clearing the middle road with a company of hastai, and I'm going to relieve him soon. Lightning says where are you? Lourie sent me because Lightning bawled at him to come and fetch you. He said, "Get that lanky Rhydanne git down here now!"'

'Lourie said that?'

'No. Lightning.'

'Ah.' I tried to comb my hair and gave up, made the mistake of consulting the mirror. Blood and iodine had seeped through the bandage on my shoulder and dried, sticking it to my skin.

Tornado bent to peer out of the window. 'I've never seen the like of Insects in the air. I bet it pisses featherbacks off to find that Insects can use their wings.'

I agreed. 'There we were, happily taking wings as trophies and using them to glaze windows, never thinking they could grow them and use them to fly.'

'I wouldn't have believed it.'

'They're heavy, graceless fliers. They seem glad when they touch down.'

Tornado shrugged. 'You were pretty impressive.'

'Up until the point I crashed. Look how badly skinned I am.' I glanced at my scale mail hauberk and gambeson, which I hang upright on crossed poles like a scarecrow. My helm sat angled on top, the rust-stained tail of its white horsehair crest hanging down.

'At least you're not mad.'

I paused in lacing my boots and blinked at him. 'Mad? Why should I be mad?'

'You should see Frost.'

We descended the stairs into the hall full of soldiers and townspeople, not crushed together like last night but running about in panic, shouting over the distant buzzing. Zascai came and went from the doorway, crowding around Lightning, who stood leaning against the doorjamb, scribbling a note. He had his bow on his shoulder and, standing at his heel, his favourite deerhound, Lymer the-two-hundred-and-tenth, watched the street attentively.

He folded the paper and handed it to a runner, who raced out of the hall. I pushed to his side but he didn't notice me.

Immediately a fyrdsman vied for my attention: 'Comet, what do I do if—'

'Wait,' I said.

'But how can they be *flying*?'

'Just wait!'

The same was happening to Tornado, who was dealing out orders for an infantry company. Eszai are equal in status and there is no hierarchy among us, meaning there is no final authority in a crisis and, if we have no pre-planned strategy, it causes problems. Lightning tended to dominate and I usually deferred to him, knowing he was the best of us at envisaging the whole battlefield. He could remember where every company was at any given time.

'Snow sent me, Lightning,' a woman said in pidgin Awian. 'He said the flamethrowers now are working.'

'At last. Have you any infantry to fend off Insects? No? I'll send for a squad. You – who are you?' He was pointing at an approaching longbow man.

'Warden of the first battalion Rachiswater archers.'

'You are? Since when? What happened to Cirl?'

'He's dead, my lord. We can't get into the barrack attics to shoot from the windows because people are hiding inside and they've locked the door.'

'Can you not reason with them?'

'They won't reason.'

'Break the door down, but make sure you guard them back to their houses. Ensure the houses are free of Insects and for god's sake make them stay there. Then take up your position.'

'Yes, my lord.'

'Lightning ...' I spoke up, but he was too harassed to hear.

A warden crowded into the doorframe. I guessed from his stainless accent that he was one of Eleonora's cousins appointed to her lancers. He said, 'I believe we should—'

Lightning interrupted, 'I asked you to tell me where Hayl's husband has gone.'

The captain said, 'He is bereaved. He is as furious as he is demented with grief. He has taken a company of lancers to rescue people from the armoured carts and peel towers.'

'Outside town?'

'Yes.'

'I told him not to!'

'He said it was his revenge on the Insects. He said he will ride them down, unless the flight intensifies. The horses are even more terrified of Insects above them, especially the noise, and they can't hear our orders. Becard only has one company from the third battalion Eske lancers.'

'I thought you said the first battalion?'

'Third, Lightning.'

'Third. Third. Well, take the first, then. Put your armour on and venture out. Give him support but order him back as soon as you can. Tell him I said so, in the Emperor's name.'

The hound's hackles prickled; it started barking furiously. Lightning peered out around the doorjamb, unslung his bow, drew and loosed. An Insect charging down the street skidded to a halt in front of us, in death throes. Lightning lowered his bow and noticed me. 'Jant, don't just stand there!'

The fyrdsmen crowded around us. Lightning looked from face to frightened face. 'You will all damn well wait while I speak with Comet ... Jant, what's happening? How can they fly? They never have, before. Never! Have you discovered anything?'

'I think it's a mating flight.'

'A what flight? It's chaos. Come and see Frost.' We turned away from the crowd and his dog padded after us. Lightning continued, 'We've lost seven hundred men and I would say twice that number are too afraid to leave the barracks. I need you to bring me more information. Tornado, please take over and by god tell the second Rachiswater archers to stop dropping stray arrows on the pyre crew.'

'I'm going to report to the Emperor,' I said.

'Yes, of course.'

I heard a soldier mutter to his mate, 'Fody said that Insects are carrying men off and drowning them in the lake. Picking them up and flying away with them!'

I rounded on him. 'That's false! Fyrdsman, don't spread rumours! Insects are weak fliers, and they can't lift anything. On the ground, they return to being normal Insects. Bear that in mind, all of you!'

As we crossed to Frost's table Lightning continued quietly, 'It's not true, is it? They are not normal.'

'No. Their behaviour has completely changed. The ones in the streets are trying to run back to the lake. They all return to the water, and I think they're laying eggs in it.'

'They're *what*?'

'They put their tails in and a sort of froth comes out. Then they range over the whole valley. They drag the people they've killed to the lake. They're dissolving the Wall and pulling all kinds of dead shit out.' I explained how they were making a splanchnic swamp of the lake and were agglutinating a wall to enclose it. It was as if they had claimed it as their own.

Lightning looked shocked. 'Take care how you speak to Frost.'

'Why?'

'She hasn't slept for three days. She is near breaking point. If she worsens I will send her to Whittorn, Eszai or not.'

'No, Lightning. Zascai stress casualties are kept at the front, so we should do the same for Eszai. People recover much faster with their dignity intact.'

'Well, she's having a bad effect on the Zascai.'

'We need her to work the dam.'

Frost had arranged four tables into a square, with no opening, and she was hidden by a high wall of folders, books and stacks of paper piled on top. We walked around two sides, seeing that when she had run out of books she had continued building with tool boxes. Only the far side was clear, facing away from the crowd, with her coffee pot and a pile of nuts and raisins on the surface. Frost was sitting, shoulders hunched, and her head on her hand. She swayed very slightly as she spoke to one of her engineers in emphatic, low tones. 'So Insects are flying again? I need to know.'

'Yes,' he said.

'Go and man the telescope. Watch the dam. If they start papering over any part of it, come and tell me.'

'Yes, Frost.'

'I want all the barrels of limestone-cutting acid under lock and key. I want fifty draught horses ready to ride to the dam at a second's notice. I want weather reports four times a day. If a drop of rain falls I want to know.'

'Yes.' The engineer glanced at me and rolled his eyes.

'Bring me the spillway capacity calculations. If they block the spillway, it's goodbye, Lowespass.'

Lightning cleared his throat. The foreman saw his chance to escape and dashed away.

Frost had dirt under her fingernails and white salt crusted at the edges of her eyes. Her hair, dry with neglect, was tied back but the ends straggled on her shoulders. She shoved her sleeves up her broad forearms with a gesture like a washerwoman, and said, 'Tell me the figures.'

'What figures?'

'How many men have died? How many injured? How many people have I killed?'

'It's not your fault,' Lightning said.

'Come on, Saker, what else can it be?' Her voice took on a hard edge. 'There's no record of Insects ever flying. Thou knowest that more than anyone, thou hast been around almost as long as they have. My lake is the only thing that's new. The Insects are reacting to my action. To my dam – to water.'

'Water?' Lightning said. 'There has always been a river.'

'Standing water.'

'It could be population pressures,' I suggested. 'Maybe they only swarm every two thousand years.'

'They are flying to reproduce,' Frost stated.

Lightning rubbed the scar on his palm. 'Don't be awkward ... If Insects reproduce in the air we would have seen it before. Besides, Rayne dissects them and she says they have no male and female forms.'

'They had no wings, either, before I built the dam.'

'They had very small wings,' Lightning said.

'Oh, yes. We thought their wings were vestigial, but it turns out they were just immature.'

I said, 'Having wings isn't enough. They've also somehow gained the instinct to fly. It isn't easy, it took me years to learn.' I pulled my T-shirt neck down so they could see my collar bones which had been broken so many times they were gnarled.

Frost murmured, 'Two, four, sixteen, two hundred and fifty-six ...' She grabbed papers and started screwing them up. 'It's my fault! I brought it on us! I renounce it!'

I said, 'Why not have some breakfast?'

'Eat? I've no time! The milk in my coffee is all the breakfast I need!'

I sat down on the edge of the table and she indicated her fortification of books and tool boxes. 'This is my office. I am in charge of the dam.'

'Of course,' I said soothingly.

'Even if everything else fails, my project won't!'

'Cool it.'

She put the handfuls of paper down slowly. 'Oh, Jant. Why are we engineers always hoist with our own blocks?'

'We need you. You're the smartest of us,' I said.

'It gets thee nowhere. Being smart just gets people killed.' She poured another coffee.

'Maybe you should stop drinking that,' I added.

'It's just a cup of coffee.'

'It's not a cup of coffee, it's a state of mind.'

Doubt masked Lightning's usually stately face. He said, 'I don't know why the Insects have changed ... Rayne once suggested that they bred underground or in cells behind the Wall. Why have we never seen a flight before?'

I said, 'I told you they were coming from the Shift.'

'Shut up about your drug fantasies!'

'Don't you remember the bridge?' I asked. 'Where do you think it led?'

Lightning blanked me out, and said, 'Maybe there are lakes out of view in the north.'

I sighed. 'If you want. But I circled their flight and I saw them coupling in a big, slimy orgy up there.'

Frost squeezed her eyes shut. Her body jerked upright, rigid in a long shudder. In a second she was back. 'A ... another white flash. It's the pressure. Bad tension. I – I didn't know this would happen. How could I?'

Lightning said, 'We can't be sure—'

'Oh yes,' I said. 'I'm sure.' The sights I had seen in the Somatopolis began to make sense: the obscure shape swimming in the pool, and how the water that had spouted through from Vista had triggered the Insects' instinct to breed.

700

I said, 'They're dropping food in the lake. The Wall is not just their means of protecting the Paperlands but also a way to store food.'

'Food?' Lightning grimaced. 'Why?'

'Because whatever comes out of those eggs will want to eat.'

Frost buried her head in her hands and started murmuring, 'I only wanted to be immortal because of Zaza ... Two hundred and fifty-six; two hundred and sixty-five thousand, five hundred and thirty-six; four billion, two hundred and ninety-four million—'

'Please stop doing that,' said Lightning.

I wondered how to help Frost. Asking her to relax would be like trying to convince a shark to stop swimming. If they stop, they drown, so I'm told. She habitually imposes so much stress on herself that this additional stress was more than she could cope with. The very qualities that had helped her gain immortality – remarkable self-discipline and a drive to work herself to the bone – were now impediments.

She is addicted to work and buries herself in it so deeply she's surprised when her actions affect anyone else. Let me give her a task, a purpose, another dose of work to calm her mind.

I picked up a scrap from the tide of paper on her desk, folded it into a glider and threw it past her. She looked up resentfully, selected another sheet and made a glider of far better design. She creased the edge of one wing and tossed it. It described a circle around me, turned on its side and flew back to her.

I said, 'Do you know that water is running down the spillway?'

'Ha! A little overtopping; I'd expect it to be displaced by all that detritus. The culvert is adequate.' She sobbed and wiped her nose.

Lightning sighed, looking at the mortals lingering just out of earshot awaiting our command. 'Try to put a better front on for the Zascai.'

'She's in shock,' I said.

'We're all in shock.' Lightning added, 'There are not so many today. The flight could be dying down of its own accord.'

'I hope so,' I said.

Frost began to stutter, 'D-don't you see? That's the point. My lake affected all the Insects in in in the area. When they've all ... mated ... the flight w-will stop. Then what? Then what?'

Now did not seem to be the right time to tell her and Lightning about the death of the Somatopolis. The Vermiform had implied that Insects don't lay eggs in sea water. I asked, 'Can we make the lake saline?'

Frost's arms tensed. 'W-we don't have enough s-salt here.'

'Well, order some up.'

Lightning shook his head. 'Not a hope. How would you take it to the lake? There are too many Insects running free outside. With thousands over such an open area, they would slaughter us even if we had three times the number of troops.'

A commotion in the doorway interrupted us. Wrenn entered the hall, in full armour, dragging an Insect by its two antennae bundled together in one gauntleted hand. He had hacked off all its legs at the first joint, leaving stumps. Its antlike body squirmed, bending at the neck and waist, and it rotated from side to side as he pulled it over the straw-strewn floor to us.

He had caught it before it detached its wings. The long, hyaline membranes surrounded it completely, shredded into ribbons on one side, rattling and clattering together. It reared up its front femurs threateningly and yellow paste oozed out of the severed joints.

Frost stood up. 'Serein Wrenn Culmish, that is absolutely disgusting. Take it outside!'

'Morning, all. Think of it as one less Insect. I want to show you something.' He let go of the antennae and the Insect rocked on its back until it rolled the right way up. It was constantly trying to get to its feet, regardless of the fact that it didn't have any. The loss of a leg or mandible isn't a serious injury for an Insect because it can regenerate them in subsequent moults. This one was missing all six legs but it was still wriggling. It squirmed around and grabbed Wrenn's ankle.

He drew his broadsword with a flourish. As its jaws closed on the greave plate he swept its head off, leaving it dangling from his leg.

Its body slowly stopped moving. Wrenn kicked his foot free, and the head rolled to rest, compound eyes downward. 'I picked this one up on the road. Do you see it's fatter than usual?' He poked its abdomen with the tip of his sword. Pressing with both hands on the hilt, he punctured the softer sclerites under its abdomen at the waist and sliced it open to the tail. He turned his blade to widen the cut and a mass of white capsules the size of my palm suspended in clear jelly splodged out.

'Eggs. Lots of them. Do you see?' He stirred them with his sword point, cutting their cuticles, whereupon they leaked a milky liquid.

I slipped my hand into the cold, gelatinous spawn, picked up one egg and squeezed it. It was the size of a tennis ball and very slimy, with a tough, sclerotic skin. It slipped between my fingers like a bar of soap, and bounced on the floor.

'Ugh,' said Frost.

'Sorry.'

'Thank you, Wrenn,' Lightning said. 'No less than your usual brilliance.'

'So why do they drop their wings off when they could keep flying and attacking us?'

'They're working on instinct,' I told him. 'They're interested in the lake. It's just coincidence that we're here at all.'

'But why fly? Why do they have to fly to shag?'

'Ask it,' I said.

Wrenn took the point. 'Fair enough.'

He sat down on a bench end, removed his helmet and padded cap and ruffled his flattened hair to make the spikes stick up. He called to Tornado, 'It's your shift, Tawny. I've been at it since five. Give me half an hour for breakfast then I'll come back out.'

Tornado picked up the Insect by the tip of its abdomen and dragged it, still dripping transparent gel, out of the hall.

Frost had knelt down and was counting the eggs, picking them up with gluey strands and piling them on one side. 'There are upwards of a hundred in here. Tens of thousands of Insects are laying. If they all hatch, there'll be millions of offspring in my lake ...'

She brushed her hair back, leaving a trail of slime stuck to it, sat on her heels and looked at us, wide-eyed. 'I have to drain the lake – as quickly as possible.'

'How long will it take?' I said.

'I expected it to take days. I can't just reel the gate wide open; it would flood everything from here to Summerday. The breakwave would be ... well, maximum outflow could easily wash the levee away, and then ... I don't like to speculate.'

'How fast can you open the gate safely? What do you need? Tell us, so we can make plans.'

She jumped up and dashed to her desk. She whipped a sheet of paper towards her, grabbed two pencils, shoved one behind her ear and poised the other. 'If Q is the flow rate and dt is the time ... Hum! Could the debris block the gate? No, its compressive stress is tissue to that force of water ... You there! Yes, you. Bring me some more coffee! Where's my foreman? Asleep? *Why?* We have work to do! Oh, if Zaza were here we could do this in a couple of days!'

Lightning and I backed off. 'Thank you,' he said gratefully.

'I'm just trying to keep her occupied. We don't have sufficient troops to reach the winch tower anyway.'

He nodded. 'I know. We're stranded here, Jant, for now. But at least we're stranded with the largest store of arrows in western Lowespass.'

I noticed Kestrel Altergate at the far end of the room, trying to help a field surgeon without actually touching his patient. 'Just make sure Frost sleeps at some point, and keep those bloody reporters away from her.'

*

One of Lightning's wardens called from the spiral stairs. Lightning raised a hand in acknowledgement and said, 'I have to organise the archers on the towers. Please bring us some instruction from the Emperor.'

'I will.'

'I hope San knows what to do, because I fear I don't ... Jant, did you find Cyan in Hacilith?'

'Er. Yes.'

'Wonderful! Well?' Lightning glanced to the Zascai clamouring for his attention. The bolder ones were beginning to approach. 'Is she safe?'

'She's safe now,' I said.

'Now? She wasn't safe before?'

'She was safe before and she's safe now.' But not during the time in between, I thought. Lightning gave me an urgent look, but I met his gaze. 'Rayne is bringing her here. They'll arrive in a couple of days.'

'Good. Thank you, Jant ...' I could see Lightning wanted to ask me more but the Zascai were waiting. He fidgeted with the scar on his palm, then he nodded and went back to issuing commands.

Wrenn beckoned to me. 'When you see the Emperor, tell him that all our fyrd are knackered and scared stiff. The Cook said that he'll try to resume the wagon train, with extra outriders for protection, or we'll soon run out of food. I don't want to have to chew gum and tighten my belt until new supplies arrive.'

Wrenn pressed the clips to release his plates with a click; gorget, breast-plate, faulds, and placed them on the floor. He was so hot his feathers stood up like needles on a pine branch, to let the heat escape. A few detached ones floated down. Wings don't perspire, but everywhere else his undershirt had brown tide marks and with the sweat of his latest exertion it stank.

He said, 'These clips don't last long. I have to keep threading on new ones. God, that's better. I feel much lighter now.'

His armour was state of the art, top of the range. I cast an envious eye over it. 'Nice gear.'

'Isn't it? Check out Sanguin.' He passed me his broadsword.

'Very nice.'

'You can see the temper line and everything.'

I tilted the blade to see its etched arabesques and the name in a flowing Awian script.

Wrenn took his helmet on his knee and picked at the lining, then undid the finger-screws that held its bedraggled crest in place. He slid the crest out of its runners and began to wipe mud off it with his sleeve. 'It's a quagmire out there. And my arms are covered in bruises from lugging those fucking shields.' He looked at my bandages. 'What happened to you?'

'I crash-landed.'

'Did you? Armour, Jant; get yourself some of this.'

'I can't fly in harness.'

'Wear something on your arms at least.' He grinned. 'What do you think you are, bloody immortal ?'

I picked up one of his mirror-finish arm plates from the floor and turned it over. Its canvas straps were hidden underneath it and woven through with steel wire resistant to Insect jaws. The straps had metal spring clips – they could be unfastened in a second if something did go wrong, and they were all easily reachable. Wrenn could don full harness in minutes.

He nodded at it. 'You should ask Sleat to make you some. It's much better than that old crap scale you wear.'

'Show me,' I said.

He took off a greave and ran his finger inside it. 'Well, it's lightweight. Feel that. My breast and back plates are thinner than the ones for my arms and legs. Chain mail strips sit under every joint – elbows, waist, knees – they don't add much weight but no claw is going to find its way in there. And see the little holes?' He ran his finger along a line of perforations. 'They make it lighter still, but they're to let the air breathe. It doesn't collect sweat and rust and I can wear it all day without overheating. Not like old lancers' armour.'

It was the highest-quality steel with the sunburst inlaid in orpiment yellow. I ran my thumb over the smooth embossing and Wrenn chuckled. 'Decoration won't save your life. Look here – all the plates are straight-edged and tapered. Mandibles won't find purchase on that. There's deep fluting along every plate – no jaws will be strong enough to crush that much reinforcement. Sleat's proved it in trials. Best of all, there are no small pieces for the bastards to grab – the elbow couters are attached to the vambraces and the besagews aren't discs hanging loose, they're part of the breastplate, see?'

'Is this Morenzian?' All human armour was adaptable to Awians these days but sometimes the added pieces were unreliable.

'Sleat extended the pauldrons for me and I tuck my wings under them. He can do the same for you. He took my measurements when I joined the Circle. He made exactly what I wanted.'

'Sleat custom-forges armour for every new Eszai,' I said.

'He made me a whole garniture suite.'

'Really?'

'Yes. All interchangeable plates, for all purposes and the decoration matches. I wear this to joust; I just change the breastplate for one with a lance stop, and I have a closed-visor bascinet with a crest instead of this light casque.'

'Clever.'

'Oh, and I have a matching surcoat too. I don't want to joust in bare Insect-fighting steel when there are ladies watching.'

'Frost is a keen jousting supporter,' I said. 'You should talk to her about it and help calm her a little. She remembers all Hayl's scores.'

'At the moment I'd rather not.' He began unhooking the leather spats stretched over his feet to prevent mud working in between the joints. 'These are the only thing I have a problem with. Leather never lasts long in a bout with an Insect – I might as well wrap myself in bacon.'

Lightning yelled from across the hall, 'Jant! Are you going to the Castle or are you going to wait until we've all been eaten?'

'Damn,' I said. 'I'd better go. See you in a few days.'

'Bye.' Wrenn attended to replacing the madder-red crest on his helmet. His plumes were an Awian symbol of bravery and he must have bought them at market, moulted by a girl whose feathers were so beautiful she could sell them. They couldn't have been keepsakes from lovers, because Wrenn was enjoying being single far too much. Only one clever lass has come close to snaring him; she was an ardent swordswoman and applied to be taught by him, but when their conversation never turned on anything but swordplay even her patience wore thin.

I walked out to the square and climbed up to the hall roof, dwelling enviously on Wrenn's armour. I wanted some. I thought, we have come a long way since the year 430 when Morenzians started sewing thick metal plates onto clothes. Insects' carapaces are the optimal natural armour and we have learnt from them how to give ourselves the best possible exoskeletons.

I stood on the ridge, watching Insects descending on the town. I ducked as one buzzed overhead, blotting out the rising sun, and waited for a clear space when it would be safe to take off.

In the square, Hurricane was forming up a company of shield lines; five lines deep, ten men in each, standing shoulder to shoulder. They wore thick gauntlets, and padding on their left arms.

Along their lines the heavy rectangular shields reached down to the ground with little space under them; their ground spikes had been unscrewed. Each had one flat edge and the other edge curved into a hook along its length, so they clipped together loosely into a flexible continuous wall without gaps or overlaps that an Insect claw can pin together.

At the far side of the square, under the direction of the Macer, squads of infantry were dispatching dying Insects with heavy lead mallets, their handles one and a half metres long. They looked as if they were breaking rocks or knocking in tent pegs, but I heard the awful cracking as Insect limbs and heads gave way.

*

706

Three men with shields, one at the front and two beside him on his either side formed a triangle, running towards the gatehouse tower. A young man, sheltering between them, dragged a tiny limber cart loaded with arrow sheaves. They ran as fast as they could, reminding me of servants under umbrellas dashing across the Castle's courtyards in heavy rain. An Insect descended towards them and the three shield men raised their shields into a roof.

The Insect landed squarely on the shields – which angled in different directions under its scrabbling feet. It slid off and the whole thing collapsed – the Insect came down in the middle, tangled in the cart and spilling arrows everywhere. Before it could right itself, the men crowded around and I saw their swords flashing as they rose and fell.

I looked down the road, seeing Tornado's shield lines coming around the corner. They were clearing Insects before them, pushing them forwards. Insects were bracing their powerful legs on the shields' rims, tearing at the spears, trying to crawl up the sides of the buildings, slipping over discarded wings and backing, backing, backing, as the shield wall advanced.

Tornado was walking in the gap between the first and second lines. His company was also five deep. Each line was of shield bearers and spearmen arranged alternately to thrust their spears over the tops of the shields. Those in the last line walked backwards to deal with Insects running up behind them.

Five lines isn't many. I've seen this formation twenty deep when we were clearing Insects from Awian towns.

Tornado's lines were approaching one of the radial roads. Tornado boomed, 'Cover right junction!'

The men who heard him repeated it at a shout. It made them focus, it bound them together and those at the back heard the concerted yell. They pulled their shields in and advanced towards the street corner. Tornado called, 'Line one, continue! Line two, stack to right!'

Behind the first line, line two began to dissolve their line across the road and instead queued up behind the right end of the first line. As they approached the junction, the men in the first line looked down the side road, saw it was crawling with Insects, and called, 'Ten Insects, right!'

The queue of shield bearers and spearmen together dashed out from behind the first line and ran across the side road, turning as they ran to face the Insects in it. They filled the side road wall-to-wall, spacing themselves out. They slammed their shields together. 'Ho!'

The Insects forced against the shield wall but the spearmen had them under control so quickly Tornado didn't have to detach another line to

707

stand behind them. He left them blocking the road and all the other lines marched across the junction.

The shield wall was left defending the junction, a vital position for the overall strategy. They shifted their weight from foot to foot, rubbed their bruised arms and hands and stared up at me. When more Insects hove into view they shouted to steady their nerves. Insects are deaf so our shouts mean nothing to them, but the men needed to reassure themselves over the unearthly buzzing.

A hiatus in the Insect storm, and I was aloft. I flew over the camp and saw the extent of the devastation. The tents outside the town wall were flattened, plastered in mud. Their drainage ditches had collapsed into brooks of sludge. Shining carapaces bobbed in the moat's coffee-coloured water.

Around twenty soldiers were constructing a pyre outside the gate. Bodies were laid side by side next to the woodpile to be cremated. No one buries corpses in Lowespass because Insects simply unearth them.

A squad of ten women were stripping armour, belts, boots and identification tags from the bodies, leaving only the clothes on. A girl crouched, entering the details in a ledger, because armour and weapons are reissued to new fyrd and she would send any money and jewellery to the family of the deceased.

Men were looping ropes around dead Insects and dragging them out of the gate, hefting them onto a pile beyond the pyre.

A fireman was unwinding the leather pipe from his flamethrower, a cart carrying a metal cylinder of neat alcohol and rape oil. He directed the nozzle while his mate pumped the handle. They sprayed liquid flame onto the Insect carcasses. Insects are supposed to be deterred by the smell of burning chitin but I've never seen any evidence of it.

I hastened south to the Castle for the rest of the day and all night, rehearsing in my head what I was going to say to the Emperor. I couldn't see the horizon, so I tried to keep the strain on both wings the same and maintained a straight line. I navigated south carefully, checking the sultry stars by my compass.

Their constellations reflected like scattered salt on my oiled wings. I have always been convinced that stars are an illusion, just like rainbows, because no matter how high I fly they never seem any nearer. The spaces between them mesmerised me and I flew on, composing my report to the Emperor in my head. I wondered what to do if Frost's madness worsened. I couldn't think of any way to ease the pressure on her, because she was the only one of us who really understood the dam.

I didn't know Frost's pre-Castle name but I have heard how she joined the Circle. She won her Challenge in 1703. She had lived all her life in Brandoch, where she founded the Riverworks Company in partnership with her husband.

Brandoch town is built on a little rise so low as to be almost indistinguishable from the rest of the drowned fenland. In Frost's day it flourished because it overlooked the only passage through the Moren Delta deep enough for carracks. Frost and her husband laboured in the manorship's tradition of reclaiming low-lying land from the sea which often flooded it: every one of its polder fields are man-made. They worked as a brilliant team, draining and shoring the marshy levels with dykes and long, raised roads.

Frost only sought the Castle when her husband fell ill with malaria. She realised that if she could make him immortal she had a chance of saving him. She is the most selfless of us all.

Her predecessor, Frost Pasquin, set her the Challenge of moving a fyrd division across the Oriole River using nothing but their own manpower and the materials to hand in Lowespass. Pasquin had been working at the front for too long and had lost touch with the rest of the world. He had not been aware of his Challenger's area of expertise and he was surprised at how gladly she accepted the competition.

Pasquin took eight days to build an ingenious pontoon bridge of pine and cowhide, with a load-bearing weight enough for the five hundred men. Then it was the Challenger's turn.

She moved the river. She surveyed it, dug a short channel and ran it into an old meander. Her husband lay on a stretcher and watched her silently, growing ever weaker while she worked day and night for five days solid. He was forbidden to help her by the Castle's rules even if he had been well enough. The river altered its course and flowed a little south of the camp of fyrdsmen. They didn't have to walk a step; Pasquin's bridge was left high and dry.

The Emperor asked Pasquin if he could return the river to its original course. But Pasquin couldn't, and had to admit he was beaten.

Frost's husband died the same night. She won her place in the Circle but all she would say was that she had failed to save him. She became locked in mourning and refused herself any pleasure.

The changes in people's characters cannot be divorced from the changes in their bodies. An adolescent is passionate and changeable because of his changing body, not just his lack of experience. An octogenarian is fatalistic since he can feel his body failing, and knows it prefigures his death, not solely because he has seen friends die. Middle-aged mortals change more slowly than the very young and very old, so their characters are more stable. And we Eszai never age at all, so aspects of our characters are also fixed.

Moreover, I doubt any Eszai really grows up while the Emperor San is our immortal father. They preserve their identities against the grind of long centuries, and by their quirks they distance themselves from the crowds. So, Frost still retains the attitude of mourning. She lives for her work but complains she can't achieve as much working alone. She leaves the fruits of genius scattered through the Fourlands, like the tidal mills of Marenna Dock, the Anga Shore breakwater on the Brandoch coast, and a hundred six-sailed wind pumps along Miredike and Atterdike that drain the malaria swamp.

Frost is, without doubt, a genius. The traits of genius often coincide with madness, but that isn't strange, because if genius is an infinite capacity for taking pains, then you tell me what madness is.

CHAPTER 13

I flew out of the dawn, into the Castle, my heart racing. I soared in over the curtain wall, bleeding off my downwind speed, and all the Castle's quadrangles opened up as I passed over. Hidden inside and between its buildings, they revealed themselves to me.

I ignored the confusing levels of the roofs slipping away under me; the shallow lead cones of the six Dace Gate towers ascending in size from the bastions in the moat to the enormous barbican. I focused on the spire of the Throne Room as I glided over the Berm Lawns. The spire filled my vision – I flared my wings, swept up close to its wall and landed on a gargoyle projecting from halfway up.

The wind gusted; I steadied myself against the stone, turned around on my narrow perch and braced myself with one foot either side of the drainage channel. It was blocked with moss, pigeon shit and the grit weathered out of the stone. I kicked it clear with my toe and the black water spattered down onto the Throne Room's sheet lead roof. I looked out down its length towards the North Façade; pinnacles and the tops of flying buttresses emerged at intervals around its edges.

Every gargoyle was different, arcing out to my left and right in a ring around the spire, with bulbous human faces and lolling tongues. The one I was standing on had a round, white pigeon's egg in a nest of twigs amassed in the joint of its wing swept back to the wall. I always felt as if their flamboyant features had been carved for me. It seems too much effort to craft such inventive expressions, when the only people who will ever see them are me and the steeplejacks. Still, if a stone mason with carte blanche can't have fun, who can?

I shook out my wings, hopped off the gargoyle and spiralled steeply down to the Berm Lawns.

The door at the end of the Simurgh Wing was locked. Typical. I can't be expected to carry keys to all of the damn doors. I hammered on it but no one was within corridors' distance.

I sprinted around the side of the building, on the grass between it and the Harcourt Barracks, past the armoury, the hospital and its herb garden. I sped onto the avenue bordered with tall poplars and ran down it, automatically avoiding the few uneven flagstones. The magnificent fronts of the Breckan and Simurgh Wings grew before me, with cool, modern open arches. I hastened through the space between them, taking the formal entrance through the Starglass Quadrangle.

I rushed past astronomical and horological instruments, on the main path between their large, square enclosures. The dew made the flint cobbles set in concrete at the edge of the path as shiny and slippery as ice.

The gleaming Starglass Clock struck ten as I passed. I counted its chimes almost subconsciously. The last one remained hovering in the air and seemed to grow louder, with a note of defiance, before fading.

Kings and governors and their retinues sometimes process along this route to the Throne Room when seeking the Emperor's counsel. I hurtled through the massive portal. Its deeply carved tympanum panel showed San entering the Castle to stay for all perpetuity. I crossed into the narrow passage around the Throne Room.

Two guards with halberds stood always by its entrance. They took one look at me, unshaven and panting manically, 'The Messenger!'

'The Messenger!'

'Let me through!' I cried.

They pushed the doors wide across their polished arcs of stone.

The Emperor was sitting in the sunburst throne, and all was quiet behind the screen. He has resided in the Castle, seeing no more of the outside world than is visible from the walls, for fifteen hundred years.

I paused for breath, insignificant in size beside the column of the first arch. I leant forward, hands on knees, to catch my breath, and I was still trying to formulate what to say.

Diagonal shafts of sunlight so bright they looked solid, shone down from the east wall's Gothic windows, high above the arcade of arches and the balcony where ten Imperial Fyrd bowmen stood in silence. Motes of dust and old incense in the air enjoyed brief fame, transformed to flecks of gold as they floated through the beams.

Without looking up or giving any indication that he had noticed my presence, the Emperor said, 'Come here, Comet.'

I shuddered. I strode down the scarlet carpet to the dais, so quickly through strips of light and shade that they flickered red in my eyes. I passed haughty Awian eagles, rearing Plainslands horses and Hacilith fists between the arches. All the Fourlands' heraldry was bold in the stained-glass windows behind the Emperor.

The sunburst, a solid electrum screen behind the marble throne, was polished to a mirror radiance and its rays haloed the throne for a metre on all sides. It rested on its lowest two points and, since the Emperor was sitting, his head was in the exact centre of the sun disc. Every beam extending out around him reflected me indistinctly as I approached.

'My lord Emperor!' I knelt at the foot of the dais, peppered with yellow light from the rose window. I was panting too much to continue.

712

The Emperor said calmly, 'The Circle broke. Hayl, Thunder and Gayle are dead. Do you know what killed them?'

'My lord, something awful's happening. They were all at Slake Cross – and Insects are *flying*!'

'Flying?'

'Yes, my lord. A gigantic mating flight, over the lake and the town.'

I looked up, but the light was in my eyes and I couldn't see the Emperor's face. He sat in the shade under an octagonal marble vault that stretched high above him into the traceried interior of the spire, like the inside of a gigantic lantern. The white marble throne was imposing, but not so big that it diminished his form. His ancient broadsword and shield hung on its back. I was very glad I couldn't read his expression.

His knurled hands, raised bone covered with ancient thin skin like batwings, uncurled from the scrolled armrests as he stood up. He came to the edge of the dais. 'Tell me all.'

I recounted everything, and ended, 'If the flight has stopped, the others will have cleared the town by now. There must be millions of Insect eggs in the lake ...' I hesitated, nervously. 'Have I made sense, my lord ? Have I been completely clear?'

'This is unprecedented,' the Emperor said.

I bowed my head, frightened. Could this be new even to San?

The Emperor said nothing. He stood in thought, tall and gaunt, with perfect stature, his hands clasped behind his back. His white hair hung straight to the level of his shoulders, his sarcenet robes hung straight to the floor. His clothes were the style of the time he founded the First Circle and was proclaimed Emperor. He wore no crown, never anything but plain white, apart from the robe's wide embroidered collar with panels of colourless jewels.

San looked up to the gallery and called, 'Summon the captain of the Imperial Fyrd!'

He unfastened his cloak at the shoulder, took it off and placed it on the cushion of the throne. He lifted the broadsword from the back of the throne and wrapped its belt around his waist.

I gasped – my hand covered my mouth – I couldn't believe I was seeing this. He had never so much as touched the sword before, and now he really was buckling it on. He tucked the strap end through and the sword hung at his side, in the folds of his robe.

The Imperial Fyrd captain ran in, down the side aisle. I waited in stunned silence, hearing his footsteps approach behind the piers of the arches. He knelt beside me. He was shaking, staring, and so pale I thought he was going to faint.

The Emperor took his round sunburst shield from the back of the throne and slipped his arm through it. He stood with the shield held fittingly. 'Is my horse ready?'

The captain was too terrified to speak, but he gave an obeisant nod.

The Emperor said, 'The people need my direction. Assemble all the Imperial Fyrd on the Berm Lawns. Fetch my armour and the locked chest from the treasury. Make haste! I will lead you to the front. Bring the fastest horses; for speed we will overnight at manor houses and we ride without pause. Comet?'

'My lord?' I managed, dry-mouthed.

'Call up the fyrds. All of them, from every manor. Every battalion, every division, every company, every squad. Signal Slake Cross to warn them of our arrival. Then you will meet us at the town.'

San stepped down from the dais, passed us, walked through the first arch to the small door to his private apartments. He shut the door behind him.

Noises began to resound from up on the balcony; a crash as one of the archers fainted. The others dropped their bows and turned to each other open-mouthed, seeking an explanation – as if they could ever begin to explain San's actions.

My insides seemed to liquefy. I risked a glance sideways; the captain's eyes were shut, his jowly face hung forwards. He whispered, 'San is leaving the Castle. It's the end of the world.'

Commotion on the balcony as the archers started gabbling hysterically, mouthing reassurances, anticipating the imminent arrival of god. They rattled down the turret stairs and sped out to spread the news.

I slowly rose to my feet. The captain turned dark blue eyes up to me. 'Why Slake Cross? Is that where god—?'

I was brusque, since I was just as scared. 'You have your orders. Put nonsensical myths out of your mind and do what the Emperor said.'

'Is it the end of the world?'

'We can't change what's happening. Do your job and I'll do mine; it's all we'll be remembered for.'

The Castle suddenly seemed very empty; the archers had gone and the Throne Room was deserted for the first time since the Pentadrica fell. I glanced at the five columns in the apse behind the throne: an azurite column for Awia, jade for the Plainslands, porphyry for Morenzia, haematite for Darkling, and a new, solid gold column for Tris.

I ran to Lisade, the Castle's library. It takes all the books and journals of the Fourlands – the Emperor is believed to read every one. I ran past the Lawyer's vacant rooms, up to the semaphore tower recently built for me on the roof. I had brought the idea of the semaphore back from Tris, figuring that if I didn't then someone else would Challenge me with it later. I had employed several Trisians to handle the network which is being installed across the Fourlands. Its instant communication posed no real threat to my position since the Messenger must be at least as much a diplomat as an errand runner.

I left my messages with the Trisian semaphore operator, and he began pulling the levers which would swing the white planks on their post to send the news out across the Empire. I sped to the other side of the Castle and grabbed some food from the kitchens, called in at the treasury in Carillon Court building and picked up a bag of coin.

The Starglass struck eleven as I sped out to the Berm Lawns, to take off. Had it only been an hour since I landed? The Castle had broken into a whirl-wind of activity. Servants raced from building to building, hollering the news before them. The gaudy-liveried Imperial Fyrd were lugging saddle bags out of Harcourt Barracks; halberds and armour gleamed as they were jostled out of the armoury behind it. Stable hands were leading horses in through the Dace Gate five at a time. A few grey-haired Imperial Fyrd guardsmen were piling up equipment between the Throne Room's buttresses.

The preparation gave me a vivid image of the Pentadrican Queen a millennium ago, leading her court to view the newly arrived Insects; a flower-decked procession out of the Throne Room's very building straight into their jaws.

A trainer dashed past, dashed back and valiantly tried to attract my attention. 'Messenger! I brought Alezane.' He indicated a flawless black warhorse. I cast an eye over its splendid tack. I had always seen Alezane kept in the stables or out exercising, always ready for the Emperor, but I never had the slightest inkling I would see San riding it.

The boy put a finger in his mouth. 'I saddled Alezane for the Emperor *himself*! Is he really leaving?'

I said, 'The Emperor isn't abandoning us. He's leading. To Slake Cross – where every one of us is going.'

The boy tried to fit all his fingers into his mouth. 'Is god coming back?'

'I don't know. But within the hour the Emperor will lead the Imperial Fyrd out of the Castle—' I pointed at the Dace Gate. I spoke with growing confidence and a sense of surprise at the back of my mind that I did not need to act. My own self-belief overcame me and gave my voice strength. The grooms began to gather around me, warming themselves on my reassurance. '—Help them to leave as fast as they can. Then all of you, follow on behind to Slake Cross. We'll need you at the other end.'

The semaphore doesn't yet extend to the outposts of the Empire, so I would have to fly to the most distant manors and to those with the most obstructive governors. Brandoch was my first stop. I clapped my hands briskly. 'Right! Let's be *organised* about this!'

I took to the air. As I flew I recalled San going through the nondescript little door of his private apartments. I itched to know what was in there. No one has ever been inside; no servants are allowed to enter. The Cook told me he brings the Emperor's meal to the door every night, after the closing of the Throne Room session. As far as we know, the Emperor only eats one simple meal a day.

Perhaps when San has departed, I could peek inside. No, I didn't dare; not unless I could put at least the length of the continent between him and me. I wouldn't mind trying the sunburst throne, though.

I rode the wind, lost in my thoughts. The Emperor remained an enigma to us all, even those Eszai who had known him longest. He was old before god stopped time affecting him, two thousand years ago in Hacilith. His centuries as sage to the ancient kings, then warrior against the Insects and finally as advisor for the Fourlands, have given him an understanding of people so profound it seems inhuman.

San leaving the Castle signifies the end of the world. Everyone knows that myth. It has been embedded in the Empire since the Circle was founded. But it didn't specify how the world was supposed to end, or the means of god's return.

There's no evidence, one side of me said; you've studied it long enough and you know it's no more than a fable. My other side replied: how long do we have? Days?

CHAPTER 14

I called the lancers of Rachiswater, the longbow men of Micawater, the swords of Peregrine. I called the famed cavalry of Eske. I called the Cathee axe men, the spears of Brandoch, the Litanee pikemen and Awndyn halberdiers. The brave Fescue shield fyrd I called, the Hacilith crossbow men, the horse archers of Ghallain. I called the General and Select Fyrd of every manor. The governors heard the emphasis in my voice and saw the panic in my eye, and took up their arms.

By the time I returned from Carniss, the Select of Awia was already packed on the roads, marching under the manors' colours. Ahead of them, great trebuchets and espringals were trundling from Lowespass Fortress, escorted by the hard-bitten troops of the garrison. The roads from the Avernwater workshops were clogged with flamethrower carts, and barrels of tar were en route from the Lacksheen tar pits. Every troop-carrying caravel in Diw and Cobalt weighed her anchor and stretched her sails.

It was a full mobilisation. Two people from each family, male or female, from the ages of sixteen to fifty, must answer the call. I spoke to the governors, who spoke to their stewards, who spoke to their reeves; who spoke to farmhands and cottars, so that by the day following my visit, everyone had heard my news.

In the city, desks were set up in factory halls and under awnings in the market place. People of every walk of life soaked from the streets towards them, frightened by the urgency of Aver-Falconet's announcements. He sent couriers galloping out across Morenzia to the townships at the coast.

As I glided over the Plains I saw queues of men mustering to the General Fyrd in manor hall courtyards, the porches of reeves' houses and the village greens. Every man realised there was nothing for it but to join the queue and, at the front, sign your name and pick up a shield and sword or pole-axe from the mounds unloaded from the carts from Wrought. Or if you're Select Fyrd, take down your heirloom breastplate and broadsword from the bedroom cupboard. A night's work with sand and oil will restore it to service.

The sheer number of people moving took my breath away. The storehouses of Wrought were turning out crates of weapons by the neat ten thousand into a seemingly endless coming-and-going of covered wagons. Horses and carts appeared singly from scattered farms, convened by the thousand to fill whole fields, then each rank decanted out onto the road. Anything could happen. Everything was happening! The scale of the effort astounded me.

Carnival girls turned entrepreneurs walked up and down the long queues of traffic dammed up outside Shivel, selling food and drink.

I have put all these people in motion myself! The power of my words filled me with exhilaration. I dropped from the sky onto a different manor each day, and people upwelled in my wake and channelled out to fill the highways all the way to Slake Cross.

CHAPTER 15

When I returned to Slake Cross, we gathered in the hall. The Insect flights had ceased but the valley was swarming with them. Rayne and Cyan had managed to ride through and had been here two weeks. I heard that Cyan was already antagonising her father and had offended nearly every Eszai.

Lightning crouched down and held a wooden taper in the hearth. Shielding it with his cupped hand he crossed to the table and touched the taper to the rope wick of an oil lamp. He turned down the wick until the smoky flame stopped fluttering, then stubbed out the taper and sat down next to Tornado and myself.

The yellow glow illuminated our faces and Tornado's front as he hunched over a pint of beer with a glum expression. Wrenn paced up and down in the darkness between the table and the fireplace, more restless than a rat on a stove, his hand on his sword hilt. Nobody spoke. Cyan was sitting on the hearth step, reading one of Rayne's books. She looked a lot healthier now. She was poking her thumb through a hole in her jumper, making a woollen glove, and paint was flaking from the designs on her riding boots.

A heavy, insistent hammering came from outside; the Sapper was keeping soldiers working long into the night, building palisades to enclose the canvas city growing outside the town.

The fire took some of the dampness out of the air. The first week of May had ended but the cold night rain still permeated everything. It flattened the grass on the moor and sent ripples down the dam's overflow chute. Pools in the mud along the Lowespass Road deepened and coalesced. Many carts mired to the tops of their wheels were abandoned haphazardly on the verges.

Frost had fallen asleep sitting at her table, her head down on a sheaf of calculations. Lightning went to her and put a hand under her rounded shoulder. He gently tipped her backwards, her head lolling. He caught her with his other hand in the small of her back, put his arm under her knees and lifted her up. He carried her to her camp bed and laid her down carefully.

'Is she all right?'

Lightning shook his head. 'She's been awake seventy-two hours. Every noise and shadow has her on her toes. She forgets that if you keep a bow strung all the time it will warp – and then when you need it, you won't be able to use it. She is tillering the string of her mind so taut I wonder it hasn't already snapped. Tell us the news, Comet.'

I said, 'The Imperial Fyrd are on their way and so are all the manors. I've never seen anything like it – a hundred and fifty thousand soldiers and nearly the same in auxiliaries. All the inns and camp clearings are full, they're filling churches with straw sacks to sleep on. They strip the depots clean as they pass. It's as if all the towns are moving – the roads are just like long, thin towns. When I tell the governors that San has left the Castle, they don't give me any problems raising fyrd. I haven't even had any resistance from Eske or Hacilith. I think that's why San is coming – to demonstrate how important this is.'

Tornado folded his arms. 'When will the Emperor arrive?'

'I saw his entourage this morning. They're passing the troops already coming in on the Calamus Road. It's taking them longer to get here than I expected because half of Awia and the Plainslands is ahead of them. At that rate they'll take a couple more days.'

Lightning said, 'I have ensured billeting for the Imperial Fyrd. The quartermasters and armourers are checking our stocks, and we're carting in more fodder as fast as we can.'

The sleeves of Tornado's leather jacket were pushed up to his elbows, so I could see the faded red sunburst tattoo under the hairs on his massive forearm. He said, 'I'll send troops to clear the way. There are too many Insects running around out there. I don't like it. I don't like it one bit. That Insect flight was not, like, natural. It creeps me out. We're the Emperor's bodyguard so I'll go and take charge of the Imperial Fyrd. Half of them hardly ever leave the demesne. They're like, only the Castle's guard.'

'They train very hard,' said Lightning.

'They only bloody parade! They never campaign together, at least not as a single division.'

Lightning said, 'Most of them are veteran Select. If they weren't good they wouldn't have got the job. But yes, I agree theirs is an honorary position and you should go out to meet San. He will have this hall as a centre of operations.'

'Where will his private quarters be?' I asked.

'Your room.'

'Oh, thanks.'

'Well, you weren't here and we thought you wouldn't mind ... After all, you can sleep on a bookshelf.'

I picked up a bottle and poured some wine, hoping it would ease my nerves. Wrenn paced around the table and said to the room in general, 'The boss is coming. What have we done wrong?'

'I wonder whose head is on the block first?'

Wrenn pressed me: 'Doesn't San leaving the Castle mean the end of the world? I was taught he would leave to prepare the way for god. Is god returning? What will it do?'

I had met with this question in every manor and it was really starting to annoy me. I said tiredly, 'Shut the fuck up about god.'

Lightning said, 'Don't swear in front of Cyan.'

I glanced across to Cyan, who smiled innocently.

Tornado spoke up: 'I hope god returns. It's what I've been waiting for all these years.'

I gave a frustrated shriek and waved my hands in the air. 'Hundreds of thousands of troops are coming and we have no space! Let's concentrate!'

Tornado ignored me and addressed Wrenn: 'I know I'm prepared for god. To me it's the whole point of being immortal – I get a ringside seat when it shows up. San knows everything I do is for the Castle so I'm damn sure he'll give me a good report.'

'God is an inhuman power,' Lightning said quietly.

'Still, I like to think it'll be refreshed and in a good mood.'

Lightning said, 'Please can we keep to the point?'

'This is the point!'

He shook his head. 'No, Tornado. In my experience stories are rarely as old as people say; and traditions are never as time-honoured as they like to believe. The idea that San never leaves the Castle originated about a hundred years after the Games. I don't remember him announcing that he would never leave. Many opinions sprang up around that time; they became stories and then the centuries twisted them into legends. Please do not be distracted by myths of the world ending because the truth is much worse. We all know the original version deep down. Cyan, Wrenn; when San leaves the Castle it logically means the end of the *Circle* not the end of the world. We have failed him and he needs to take command again himself. I think – I fear – that he will disband the Circle.'

'He took charge of the Imperial Fyrd just like a warrior,' I said with wonder.

'Yes. San the warrior is not so strange to me. I remember him leading the First Circle. I was introduced to him once, in the field at Murrelet, where Rachiswater is now. When I was a boy he would stop at the palace on his expeditions from the Castle to the front. Could we be redundant?'

'No,' I said quickly. 'San asked for every fighter we can field. Who'll lead them? He needs us more than ever.'

'I cannot begin to predict what he plans.'

Tornado said, 'I still think god might appear.'

'Well, you are from a more religious era,' Lightning said airily.

'And you're full of bullshit!'

'What will god look like?' Wrenn asked Tornado.

The giant man's voice sparked with interest. 'Dunno. I asked San to, like, describe it, but he wouldn't. San says god made us, so it's more powerful than us, so it can't be Awian or human. It wouldn't have made us anything like itself, either in looks or the extent of its power, because then we'd be able to rebel and of course god wouldn't chance that. That's why god is an "it". Most books I've read say it can look like whatever it wants to. It, like, creates stuff. That's what it does. So it can create forms for itself. If god was speaking to you, then I guess it might choose to look like an Awian.'

'You're making this worse,' I complained.

Wrenn glanced at Lightning for support. 'Do you believe in god?'

Lightning said, 'I see no reason not to, because San does not lie. No one has ever given me a more convincing alternative. Besides, we are immortal. God must be behind it somewhere, or how could San have immortality to share?'

Wrenn gave a great worried sigh. He unbuckled his belt and laid his sword on the table. He ran his fingers through his hair and set off pacing to the fireplace again.

I was suddenly furious. I couldn't believe we were talking about this crap! 'Tornado, you're wasting our time! Are we credulous Zascai? Are we Trisians, to be sitting here pontificating? Is this the Buncombe Beach Young Philosophers On The Brink Of Disaster Club?'

'Don't speak Plainslands,' said Lightning. 'I can't follow you if you go that fast.'

'Sorry. I'm just telling him that we're in this together and god is not going to help us. Nothing is going to come and save us. We have no one to run crying to, nothing to rely on. We must stand on our own two feet. Can we just grow up, please? Why do you think San told me to muster everyone from Frass to Vertigo? The strength and resources in each of us is all we have!'

'You used to believe,' Tornado said. 'I remember when you joined the Circle. You weren't so cynical then.'

I shrugged. When I was an apprentice in Hacilith I saw how seriously my seniors took the story. What other conclusion can a child draw from the sayings of adults? I grew more experienced and I realised that adults don't have all the answers, and in many cases they're even more credulous and confused than children. Then I saw the Shift, then I saw the Somatopolis, and I realised how truly alone we are – not only in this world, but in all of them.

'All right,' I said. 'I have no proof. But if we don't know whether god is real, we can't depend on it. If we can't prove anything either way, and if we'll never know the answer, we should shut up about it and do something more practical. Instead of talking we should save ourselves! God might return and make everyone immortal, or us mortal. It could alter and revoke the laws of physics at will and leave us with a terrifying disorder. God might already have come back – remember the posteventualist heresy? Maybe San is god, watching and chuckling to himself. Maybe the Insects are god; they appeared, didn't they? Or maybe god intended them to be the next phase of creation, more perfect and far hardier than us men.'

'Fuck that!' Tornado thundered. He stood up, so I did too, but I foolhardily kept going: 'San is coming to see something new to him, that's all.'

He patted me on the shoulders – and I sat down heavily on the bench.

'Please!' Lightning said.

Tornado said simply, 'If Jant picks holes in my belief, it will shine still brighter through them.'

I sighed. 'God coming back is nothing but a story. I've lived everywhere; I know a tale when I hear one. From Darkling to Hacilith to the Castle I've had to don and doff beliefs so many times I've realised stories are only ever about the people who make them up ...'

'Have you quite finished?' said Lightning coldly.

'I think he's crazy,' said Tornado.

'No, I'm not crazy. I've just been around. Let me show you what I mean. Tales of god from different countries would seem as outlandish to you, as yours would to them.'

'I have had my fill of outlandish countries,' Lightning remarked quietly, stroking the scar on his palm.

'You find Rhydanne strange, don't you?' I asked Tornado.

'I find you strange,' he said.

'Rhydanne think of god as looking like a Rhydanne.'

He sniggered.

I said, 'Listen to the Rhydanne version. God the hunter made the world, the mountains, the plains, the sky; but it was empty of animals. So god made an animal to chase, and the animal she made was enormous, as if every single creature of the Fourlands, dumb and rational, had been joined together in one giant form. It had feathers and scales, skin and fur, hands, claws, wings and tails. It had hundreds of heads and thousands of eyes. It was both male and female. The beast sat on Scree Plateau and used the Plainslands as its footstool. Its heads towered above the peaks in the highest mountain clouds.

'God chased the beast all over the Fourlands. She twirled her bolas, the stones of which were as large as the glacial boulders on the slopes of Tarneilear, tied to leather strings as long and as wide as the Turbary Track. Eventually the creature tired and god caught up with it. She cast her bolas and brought it down on the summit of Great Fheadain.

'God killed the beast and its blood flowed down the gullies of Fheadain and created the first waterfalls. Then god skinned it and carved up its flesh.

She kindled a fire and placed the cuts of meat on flat stones near the hearth. The warmth of the fire brought all the pieces of meat to life. They jumped up and ran off, all over the Fourlands and became the people and animals of the world.

'The Rhydanne were quickest; they ran away first, before the fire could cook them. The humans were closer to the fire, and got burnt, which is why they are not as pale as Rhydanne and they need a warmer climate. Some cuts of meat had stuck together – humans and eagles – so now we have Awians. The Rhydanne had already populated the mountains, so humans and Awians must perforce live in the lowlands. God saw this had happened accidentally and decided to get drunk. She drank and drank and eventually fell asleep. One day she will wake up, with the heaviest hangover of all time. Rhydanne live in dread of having to pacify her with more alcohol on that day, I can tell you—'

'Jant ...' Lightning cut me off with a calm voice.

Tornado said, 'That's the biggest load of rubbish I ever heard.'

'Eilean told me it when I was small, back when I assumed Darkling valley was the whole world.'

Cyan brushed her silky hair back with her jumper sleeve and turned up her face. Rather self-consciously, she said, 'If god is coming back, wouldn't San have told Jant?'

'Maybe even San doesn't know,' Tornado said.

'Why don't you ask him?'

Everybody looked at Tornado, who said, 'Um, no ... I can tell you haven't, like, met the Emperor, girl.'

I said, 'If San wants us to know, he'll tell us. But the Insects are a more pressing consideration.'

'You know what your problem is?' asked Tornado.

'No. But I know what you think my problem is.'

The veins stood out on his bull neck. 'Oh, I'm sick of your smartarse comments, you flying streak of piss! Why don't you step outside?'

I bridled. 'Gladly!'

Lightning said, 'Jant, wait until the Circle's disbanded before starting a new career as a quintain for Tornado.'

'If we don't know what will happen,' I repeated, 'it's sensible not to waste time arguing about it but continue with our plans.'

'Hear, hear!' Frost's crackly, desiccated voice came from the direction of her camp bed. My outburst had woken her and she lay propped on one elbow watching us. She said, 'I will use science to fix the problem that science has caused.'

She reclaimed the reeking coffee pot from her desk, poured herself a cup

724

and scooped powdered milk into it. 'Only scummy powder left, damn it ...
Can't Snow stop that hammering?'

Her voice was faint, as if coming from kilometres away. She rubbed a
bloodshot eye and watched wrinkled skin forming on the surface of her
coffee. She appeared less like herself and more like an actress adept at pretending to be Frost. She was like a deserted mill relentlessly grinding grain
because its mechanism can do nothing else, although nobody is inside to
tend it.

She fingered a raisin out of the pile on her desk and ate it. Then she
returned to her calculations.

'Now, as to the Imperial Fyrd,' said Lightning. 'I don't trust them if things
get tough—'

'Dad ...' Cyan interrupted. She was bored to be stranded here, while her
father talked with his workmates above her head. The fact she was a minor,
helpless in front of the world's best warriors, embarrassed her even more.

'Dad.'

'Eszai should provide San's bodyguard instead—'

'Dad ...'

'I'll do it,' said Tornado.

'Why not me?' said Wrenn.

'Because I'm the strongest. Officially, like.'

'Da-aad.'

'*What?*' said Lightning.

'Nothing. Can I go to the tavern?'

'No. Stay here where I can see you, young lady.'

'I have enough money.'

'I know you have. But there is nothing left in the tavern to buy.'

'I'm going, so tough!'

Tornado said, 'Lightning, will you keep your daughter under control ?'

'Oh, she won't be any trouble.' He gave her such a warm, conspiratorial
smile that it made the whole place seem homely; for a second it shrank the
room, but she did not return it. 'Come sit down by me,' he added.

Cyan scudded over and slumped onto the bench. She said, 'You're all
scared, aren't you? You are, you're all terrified, you just don't want to admit
it.'

'Hush,' said Lightning. 'We must simply let San see the overall strategy.
He will direct us.'

'God might,' said Tornado.

I pushed the heels of my hands into my closed eyes until grey-green patterns kaleidoscoped. I had only been back on the ground for two hours and
I was on edge already.

'Are you all right?' Wrenn asked me.

'Hmm? Yes. All it is, is ... I've been on drugs for a very long time and now I'm not and I'm finding it a bit difficult, that's all. Especially at night ...'

Wrenn looked as if he was going to make a remark, but decided against it. Stranded on the other side of the age gulf, all he could do was start pacing again. The lanterns were flickering outside in the square and darkness was trailing in, with the sound of the innkeeper's baby crying. 'You know,' he said. 'It wouldn't be so terrible if civilian women and children weren't trapped here too.'

Tornado stood up. 'Can you hear the watchman's bell? Someone's at the gates.'

'It's probably god!' I glared.

'I hope so,' he said casually. 'Only god can stop your nonsense.'

Lightning said, 'It must be another fyrd troop.'

A minute later the watchman sent a runner in, who stood open-mouthed until I beckoned him to the table. I recognised him as one of the Castle's servants; I know them all by name. 'Yes, Eider; what is it?'

'Carniss manor has arrived, Messenger. We opened the gates because Insects were harrying them – they've been fighting off Insects all the way from the mountains. The governor says he's recruited everybody he can; he has a whole battalion but they lost most of their mules. He requests orders to billet his men.'

Lightning said to me, 'I'll greet Carniss. I expect that manor holds unpleasant memories for you.'

'More likely those bastards will be uneasy taking orders from a Rhydanne.'

'Do they only have one battalion?' Wrenn asked. 'Well, I suppose every little helps.'

Lightning picked his coat off the back of the chair, thrust one arm into it and felt about for the other. He said, 'Carniss may be a small manor but their archers are superb marksmen. They earn their living hunting.'

I glanced at the ceiling. 'They're bastards to a man.'

'Jant, I know you don't like Carniss, but we're very crowded and strained here, so don't sow discord. Even their General Fyrd bring their own fine bows. We can give them horses; I know they fight better as skirmishers than in formation.'

Frost added, 'They have excellent master miners too, from the silver mines. They're tough and they work hard.'

Tornado nodded. 'I like Carniss. They have a decent attitude for feather-backs; they're very down-to-earth. Frontiersmen make good garrisons. They're used to danger, so they stay alert and observant, which is more than you can say for the city fyrds.'

I said, 'They're a lot of grubby unmanageable trappers who take deep revenge for slight offences.'

Cyan said, 'Cool. Can I come and see them?'

'No,' Lightning told her. 'Stay here. Jant, would you look after ... *No*, don't give her the wine! Bloody stop drinking! And, Wrenn, can you ... Oh, forget it. I can't believe what's happening to the Circle these days!' Lightning swung his quiver on his shoulder and stormed out after the servant.

Cyan looked up at me. 'I want to watch Governor Carniss's men come in.'

Wrenn said, 'Let's go, then.'

She glowered at him. 'Not with you! And don't look at me like that!'

'I wasn't looking at you like anything.'

'You've been staring at my tits all night, you syphilitic Miroir bog-trotter!'

Wrenn's face split in a grin. 'Well, they are nice tits. You must be very sporty. I've heard you can shoot straight.'

'Now you're leering!'

'I'm not leering. I'm smiling. Don't you want a smile from the world's best swordsman?'

'The only weapon you handle is your own dick ... mangy wanker.'

'I don't think she's feeling the fun of the day,' Wrenn said to me.

She stuck her nose in the air. 'No, because a short-arsed whoremonger keeps asking if I want to see his sword.'

'Come on, Cyan,' I said hastily.

Sheets of rain hissed down on us as we walked out to the gate. I cupped my tall wing around her to give her some shelter and I felt her warmth. We stood in the archway under the lanterns and watched a line of horses moving above their amorphous rain-pocked reflections. The men's heads bowed, greasy rivulets ran down their waxed cotton hoods and tent-like cloaks they had stretched over their saddles. Bow cases projected from bundles and panniers on their cruppers. The nearest horse's ankle flexed, its unshod hoof splashed down shattering the reflection.

Most men were on foot, carrying spears over their shoulders. They walked past wearily, in a worn and handed-down, or looted, assortment of armour; threadbare brigandines with steel scales showing through the rents. Their cuirasses were flecked orange with recent rust, fur scarves tucked into their metal necklines. Mud had rubbed up their boots between their legs to the thighs.

Their standard bearer dipped the Carniss crescent flag under the archway as he passed us. I thought the outpost's association with the rest of the kingdom was a thin veneer; the slightest battle tension scratched it and showed their harsh settlers' identity. Their greatest loyalty was to each other.

Cyan breathed, 'Wow. I haven't seen anything like this before. Awndyn fyrd never go anywhere.'

'Wait till the Eske heavy cavalry turn up. Then you'll have something to stare at. See the man who looks like his mare? That's Governor Veery Carniss.'

Veery was dismounting to greet Lightning. His teeth were so horsey his voice whinnied. His ears were like bracket fungus and, though he frowned, a duelling scar lifted one corner of his mouth, permanently changing his expression for the better.

Cyan said, 'Oh no, look at Daddy being bloody effusive.'

I wondered what to say to her. I wanted her to stop making Lightning's life so difficult, but on the other hand I didn't want her to end up stuck in a palace all her life, even more jaded than she already was.

I said, 'Lightning's torn between his duty to the Emperor and to you. Ten years ago he put his love for you first and it cost him severely. I know in the past he hasn't given you the attention you deserve. But he's incredibly busy now and your attention-seeking is distracting him. Have you told him about your brush with jook?'

'No.'

'Well, Rayne knows. If you took it again, she would definitely tell him.'

'God, no. I don't want to see those *things* again.'

'The Gabbleratchet?'

Cyan shot me a look. 'How did you know?'

'I was there.'

'It was just a dream. It wasn't real.'

'Oh, the Shift is real, all right. San ordered me to keep it secret from Zascai. I suppose he doesn't want mortals trying to reach it and dying in the process.'

Her quick temper ignited. 'You pansy boy! That's bullshit – all bullshit!'

'I was there, Cyan.'

'As a trick of my imagination!'

'The Gabbleratchet is not a trick of your imagination.'

'Gabbleratchet.' She rolled the name over her tongue and scowled. 'I once longed to fly like you can. I used to dream of the smell of clouds and the thin air, the way you smell. Now I have nightmares of rotting hounds. I woke up screaming last night. Daddy wanted to know what was the matter, but I told him that being lost in Hacilith had frightened me. You're not joking, are you?'

'No. There are more worlds than we visited but the distance to Shift would kill us. The Insects' own domain cuts through thousands of worlds; I meant it when I said they make us look inferior.'

'God might be in the Shift.'

I laughed. 'Oh, don't you start.'

'God is on a break. Why not in the Shift?'

'Sure,' I said sarcastically. 'San keeps it prisoner in Epsilon and feeds it chocolate biscuits.'

'Are you the only person to know?'

'No. Rayne has also been to Vista, when she was your age ...'

'What a scary thought.'

'Yes. She was young once ... so she says. Your father has seen a Shift creature but he wouldn't discuss it with me afterwards. He won't say a word about the Insect bridge too, even though he burned it down. It's too weird for him.'

'Typical of Daddy to ignore an adventure so important!'

'He's denied it, filed it away in the same part of his mind that he'd use if you told him you'd taken jook. He treats me with a bit more suspicion, though; as if I'm having a disordering effect on the world.'

'I think he blames me for a sea change too,' Cyan said. 'But if he can't deal with it, it isn't my fault.'

'Maybe in twenty years I'll drop the Shift into the conversation and see if he responds.'

The Carniss troops filed in past us. Those on horseback were mainly women, with crossbows slung on both sides of their saddles – two crossbows, to work in duo with their reloaders. They were pulling bolts from bandoliers around their bodies and slipping them point first into the depleted racks attached upright on their saddlebows.

The crossbow bolts' points gleamed – hard steel moulded to soft iron sockets, which cushion the shaft so it doesn't split on impact with Insect shell but drives straight through.

Cyan stared at the division captain, who wore a rain-darkened leather apron over her lap on which a hook from her pulley belt rested. She had been spanning her crossbow in the skirmishes. Insect mandibles had slashed her boots and the metal toecaps shone brightly through the cut leather. Her sallet helmet was not as shiny; it had a golden-brown patina from being polished with sheep fat every night.

She bowed her head to me as she passed. She trailed a leash from the saddle, attached to the muzzle of the division's mascot. It padded beside her on big paws like snowshoes, pasted with mud. Its deep, pure white fur was flattened by the rain, but its galena-grey eyes were keen.

'What's that?' said Cyan.

'A Darkling white wolf.'

Wrenn appeared beside us. 'Don't mind me standing here?' he asked, risking death by dirty look from Cyan. 'The others, they ... Well, I just feel better to be around you two.'

I understood. He's only thirty, and the average age of our colleagues in the hall was about eight hundred.

'It's good to see Veery again now I'm Eszai,' he said. 'I gave him that scar but he seems OK about it.'

'After all, you did turn out to be Eszai-good,' I said.

He hopped from foot to foot. 'The Emperor, coming here! We're in for it, aren't we?'

I nodded. We stood there for a while, watching the seemingly endless procession. Sporadic hammering still echoed in the background; rain drove through the spotlights around the palisade. The carpenters, proficient Peregrine shipbuilders drafted to the fyrd, were continuing through the night.

Eventually Cyan said, 'That captain was a woman.'

'Yes,' I said.

'Not much older than me.'

'That's right. Come inside.'

'I want to watch.' She stood, stubbornly, and descended into her thoughts again.

I drew my wing closer around her. I don't know about her, or Wrenn, but I wished I was a very, very long way from here, sitting in a bar.

OUR BRAVE BOYS ARRIVE SAFELY

The Hacilith General Fyrd began arriving at Slake Cross today. The pals from Galt and Old Town marched in with a smart step and big smiles, after 900 km by cart. The Captain of the Ninth Division, Connel, 22, said, 'We're raring to have a go at these flying bugs. The people have been great as we came through Awia. The Awians have a spotless record, but now the Hacilith lads are here those bugs haven't got a chance.'

They are the best that Morenzia has, strong, keen and selfless. We wish them the best!

Smatchet, with the troops at Slake Cross fort
Hacilith Post 27.05.25

731

CHAPTER 16

Lightning reluctantly agreed to let Cyan leave town. Since I was welcoming the governors and wardens while Lightning was holding Insects off from attacking the arriving troops, he asked me to look after her. I took her to the armoury and got her kitted up.

'Here's a brigandine jacket.' I passed it to her and she let it drop dramatically almost to the floor. 'It's heavy!'

I helped her buckle it on. 'It fits very well, though. Here are some greaves for your legs, made for a woman about your size.' I showed her how to fasten them. Even if she was strong enough, I thought it too risky to give her plate armour made for another person, which wouldn't fit properly or might have unseen deterioration. The fyrd who wear the mass-produced stuff that comes in three sizes only do so because they can't afford better. I found her an open-faced sallet helmet with a tapered tail to protect the nape of her neck.

Then we went to the stables but Cyan didn't want to go in. 'I don't know ...' she said. 'Since the ... since the Gabbleratchet ... I don't really like horses.'

It took me half an hour to convince her to enter the stables and she walked close behind me holding my hand. We passed the stalls of a hundred other mounts until I found her an exceptional piebald palfrey that in no way resembled the horses of the Gabbleratchet.

Cyan examined its hooves uncertainly. She still needed some coaxing. 'The eternal hunt won't come here,' I said. 'The Shift is so big that the chances of it reaching our world are minute. To be honest I've always got the impression we're a bit of a backwater. Besides, those things weren't horses. You know that, Cyan; you've been riding since you could walk.'

'I couldn't control that black horse. It was the only time I've never been able to manage one.'

'Because it wasn't one. The Gabbleratchet is just itself. It's inexplicable but we left it behind.'

The stable boy brought me my sleek racehorse. Pangare butted her buff, suedy muzzle into my hands and shook her head, flopping the neat knots of her short, hogged mane from side to side.

'What a peculiar animal,' Cyan said. 'I didn't know you had a horse.'

'Well, now you do.' I held Pangare's halter. 'These Ghallain duns have unbelievable stamina. She might not be a thoroughbred but she can outlast anything your Awian stables have to offer.'

It always takes me a long time to find a mount who can both tolerate carrying a Rhydanne and is fast enough for me. I had heard of Pangare, a seventeen hands high courser winning every race on the Ghallain pampas, and she had cost the Castle a fortune.

While the boy fitted Pangare's bridle and buckled the wide strap of the saddle under her taut belly, I corded my satchel to the cantle through rough-cut holes and clipped my crossbow to it. 'Come on, then.'

Cyan swung up into her saddle, ducking under the beams. 'I'm brave, aren't I? I got back on.'

'Yes, you are very brave.'

'Just like that fyrd captain? I'm as brave as she is.'

'Of course, you could be.'

We walked our horses out of the stable and rode slowly through the commotion of the growing camp. Smoke from cooking fires rose into a pall above the lines of cream tents.

We rode off the road – it was completely packed with carts, horses, and men marching quickly – now that town was in sight they wanted to reach it as soon as possible. It was a river of humanity, and lancer escorts formed other streams on either side.

Cyan leant forward, sped to a gallop and hurtled past me. I gave Pangare rein; she loped exuberantly, kicking out with her forelegs, and caught up with the girl at once. 'Hey! What are you doing?'

'I'm just glad to be outside,' she said, free for the moment of her usual ennui. 'I've been cooped up since Hacilith. I think without a doubt this is the worst place I've ever been dragged to.'

'I'm inclined to agree. Where would you rather be?'

'In the city, of course. All the places I've lived are dreadful compared to Old Town. Where would you rather be?'

'Up there.' I pointed to where, far behind the town, the cliff-topped hills stretched along the horizon.

'In the mountains?'

'Those are just the foothills,' I said. 'You should see the high summits – there are so many pinnacles and valleys that a hundred Rhydanne could live there for a hundred years and never meet each other.'

'Sounds awful.'

'Let me show you what Pangare can do. Come on!'

We galloped beside the road. In the fresh air, it was almost as fulfilling as flying. The sky was a uniform white, with blue-grey round the edges like milk in a dish. The sun, a burnished silver coin, blazed ineffectually at its zenith. An infuriating, unsettled breeze stirred the few grass stalks still upstanding between drying, churned-up clods of mud. Higher on the hillside, bunches of heather hooped and shivered, clustered around the white rocks that looked like the moors' uncovered bones.

Cyan kept looking down the road with a twinge of wanderlust. I would have to watch her carefully or she would try to escape again.

'How many thousands of people?' she asked emphatically. 'Their line goes on into the distance.'

I checked my notebook. 'This is just the Cobalt baggage train. The Peregrine archers should be next.'

'Peregrine?' she said. 'You mean – my manor ? I have fyrd?'

'Of course! When you come of age you'll have a fyrd of more than twenty thousand men. That's more than we can see to the horizon.'

'Like the Carniss men the other day?'

'Pah. Carniss only has one muster. Cobalt here, only has two: Cobalt and Grass Isle, and their governor is too old to lead them. You have four musters. The baggage train for Peregrine is twelve hundred wagons.'

'Can we see them?'

'If you want.'

We rode to the end of the Cobalt carts but there was still no sign of Peregrine's sleeping falcon standard. 'They're probably delayed by the traffic jam,' I said. 'We'll have to stop here. I don't want to take you too far from town.'

Cyan reined in her palfrey, halted and gazed at two standard bearers with vertical gonfalon pennants covered in knot-work. It was the Morenzian dexter red hand banner, rendered completely in interlaced lines. The standard bearers, riding wearing nothing but purple or grey singlets and breeches, were so covered in tattoos that their outlines looked blurred. The ingeniously entwined bands, alaunts biting their own legs, elongated horses and spiralling sea snakes in every colour covered them so confusingly that it was difficult to tell where their tattoos ended and their clothes and knot-work jewellery began. Old tattoos had been interlinked with new ones, storiated over their whole bodies apart from their faces.

The battalion they led marched to the beat of similarly decorated drums on their saddlebows. Thickly accented voices burred among them.

Cyan said, 'Wow. Who are they?'

'The first of the Litanee cavalry.'

'Such beautiful designs ... They're so weird.'

'You'll have seen their designs on the pottery and glass Litanee exports. The Plainslands esteems their work highly. Well, these are the richer craftsmen – most of Litanee's battalions are infantry and they'll be coming in by ship. Let's have a closer look.'

We cantered to meet the head of the column and I greeted the warden and took his name. He let Cyan look at his panoply, all covered in knotwork; stencilled on his brigandine from Hacilith, his helmet adorned with twisting, intertwining Insects. Tooled on his saddlebag and belt, painted on the sides of their carts; every surface was filled with interwoven designs.

'To us they're just pictures,' I told Cyan. 'But the Litanee can read them like biographies. They encode the stories of their lives. He's covered in his memories, so to speak; no one from the Litanee region is ever short of a topic of conversation.'

'I've crossed the canal into Morenzia but I never saw anyone like this.'

'You probably didn't go far south enough. See the pictures of grey wolves, beavers and boars? They're extinct everywhere but the Morenzian forest. And the dogs on their muster flags? Their hunting hounds are considered the best. Your father loves them. See – there's one.' A huge mastiff loped alongside one of the horses. 'Litanee brings them for guard dogs, but I've seen a pack take an Insect down.'

I was cut short by the rumble of hooves behind me. A shrill whistle made the nearest men stop abruptly, and those following stumbled into them. I looked around; a body of Awian lancers were bearing down on us. Metal strips like blunt fingers, riveted in splays to the backs of their saddles, screeched as they cut through the air.

The eagle banner unfurled above them; it was Queen Eleonora and her bodyguard.

The Litanee humans, most of whom had probably never seen such a behemoth of steel and horseflesh, slowed down to squint at the Awians' ostentatious armour.

The Queen raised her hand and the others, with their lances like sema-phore poles upright in their rests, slowed and spread out in a semicircle around us. She cantered up to us alone.

She had pulled the chrome tubes of her saddle back out of their housing and it projected higher than her shoulders, a padded support. The saddle's faring almost enclosed her legs; with her feet in long stirrups she was practi-cally standing up in it. It provided cushioning against the impact when the speed and weight of her horse drove her lance through an Insect. It was splashed with haemolymph.

She tilted her helmet to the back of her head. 'Comet? What are you doing on the ground? Enjoying a good ride?'

I made the introductions: 'Your Highness, I present Lightning's daughter, Cyan Peregrine ... Cyan, your Queen; Her Royal Highness Eleonora Tanager.'

'So this is Lightning's daughter. What a pretty girl.' She looked Cyan over, narrowed her eyes at me and said to her confidentially, 'I'd watch that one, if I were you. He moves faster than rumour in a morai.'

I said, 'Eleonora ...'

Cyan closed her mouth and gulped. All the etiquette she had been taught didn't seem to fit this situation. She tried, 'I am at your command.'

'Of course you are.' Eleonora made her horse high-step sideways. She spread her long, aristocratic wings and gave me and the Litanee men a flap. 'Don't let him be a bad Rhydanne now.'

She wore the 1910 Sword, one of the classic, bejewelled masterpieces made, about once a decade, by the Wrought blacksmiths. All the craftsmen must agree on whether a sword is good enough to be 'dated' and they sell at a very high price.

She put a hand on the hilt and tilted the sword back, pivoting where it hung at her waist, until the scabbard stuck up in front of her like an erect cock. She grasped the hilt and drew the sword little by little, and its soft scabbard flopped flaccidly from the tip downwards. All the lancers guffawed loudly.

'You wicked bitch,' I muttered.

'You wicked bitch, Your Highness,' she corrected with a smile.

She turned, and all the lancers fell in behind her, wheeling away over the open land towards the Wall to resume their patrol.

'What was that about?' Cyan gaped.

'Nothing,' I said, and in silence we watched the Litanee men go by.

I remember Eleonora's costume masquerade in 2017 at Rachiswater Palace. I recall it with extreme clarity; it still sends a shiver through me. I was sitting on the high balcony that curved around the exterior of the circular, spotless hall. Below me, a servant carried a tray of sparkling wine out to the geometrical gardens. All was quiet, compared to the riotous clamour of Eleonora's birthday ball.

She had only recently been crowned, and to emphasise her reign this lavish party had drawn in all the nobility. I had come as an Insect, having half-heartedly pierced holes in real sclerites and laced them over my usual clothes. I picked up my glass of wine and took a sip, sighed and lay back along the top of the balustrade. My wife had a few moments ago taken Tornado's arm and walked him out to the spiral maze for a 'breath of fresh air'.

Music slid luminescent from the hall; I looked down into its white drum filled with laughing, cotillion-ing figures.

Eleonora stepped out onto the balcony, her bronze mask in front of her face. She pulled her metallic silk skirts away from the threshold and shut the casement door. She tilted the mask away, raised her eyebrows and half-shrugged, meaning: What are we doing here, two sensible people like us?

I spidered a bow. 'Happy birthday, Your Highness. Looks like you've passed me at last.'

'Never ask a lady's age, Jant. I'm three years older now.'

'Your beauty increases.'

Eleonora strode towards me with hauteur. Her gloves covered her arms up to the shoulder and the level of her bulging breasts. Her voice was fleshy; 'It will look better if you join the party.'

'I like it out here.'

'Why do you always sit near sheer drops?'

'They attract me.'

She turned from the gardens and looked at the palace front. On both sides of us, its crescent wings curled forward, clasping the gardens' falcate terraces between them. 'It looks like a snail shell.'

'I think it's spectacular. The Rachiswaters had taste.'

My snub didn't bother her. 'Yes. They're almost legend already – but we're still here, making history.'

'You've achieved a lot.'

'Oh, there's still so much remaining.'

I drained my glass and picked another from the tray on the floor. The rumours about Eleonora had piqued my interest. (Why, oh why, did I drink so much that night?) I'd heard that she likes to watch maids tie each other up, that she spends afternoons arranging footmen in interesting patterns for her pleasure, or she calls up gladiators three at a time, two to hold her legs open and the most well-endowed to fuck her.

I'd have to sleep with her, of course; or at least try – the Queen of Awia would be the biggest notch on my bedpost.

She said, 'Did you receive my letter? I mentioned I always noticed you.'

I contrived to look nonplussed. 'I always noticed you, too.'

'You always notice everybody.'

'But I notice you more.'

She said, 'Jant – be careful or you'll appear desperate.'

'I thought I appeared like an Insect.'

She eyed my skew-whiff antennae. 'Where's your wife?'

'In the—' I gestured at the maze.

'Oh. With someone?' She suddenly sounded predatory. She leant over the balustrade and shouted down to the water terrace, 'Let it spray!'

A footman dressed as a ship's captain turned a silver wheel on a polished pipeline and all the fountains sprang up in the gardens. Shrieks from the maze as its water jets spurted. They latticed across its annular marble entrance, trapping everyone inside.

Eleonora laughed. 'Now, feline-with-feathers ...' She studied every part of my body, imperiously spinning her mask. 'Such long wings. Such a sculpted back. I bet you fuck so athletically ... you can make me come so hard I see gold flashes ... Can you?'

I didn't meet her eye. 'Eleonora, I'm the Messenger at your beck and call but I'm not your call boy.'

'Pity. Still, there are others. Merganser's here but he's not as good as you're said to be.' She turned away.

'No!' I said. 'Wait.'

She gave a sidelong glance. 'Go to the Onyx Room ... no, that's occupied. Go to the Topaz Room, remove your clothes and fold them on the chair. Then kneel on the bed. Await me there.' And she was gone, like a caravel in full sail back into the party.

Eszai have seen most things but I'd never encountered anyone like Eleonora before. (My curiosity will be the death of me.) Some Awians were starting to object to her hedonistic rule, for all that she saved them from the Insects two years before. If the previous King, now exiled in Summerday, living in a garret and writing bad poetry, ever had offspring who could claim the throne, then Eleonora would need to spend even more on guards and spies.

I turned a handstand and walked on my hands through the party, and I ran up to the room. A bottle of wine was already opened for me.

The warm summer evening backlit the curtains drawn over open windows. Eleonora kept me waiting. When she entered, she seemed pleased that I was kneeling. She swung the door shut behind her and fiddled with her skirt. It fell to the ground, revealing her bodice and some riding boots extending over her knees, tight to the shape of her legs.

I could only see her silhouette as she crossed in front of the curtains, tapping the stem of her mask on her gloved hand.

She started to lick my feathers; she ran them through her mouth and tongued between them until I was in ecstasy.

'Put your hands on the bedpost.'

'Why— hey!' She grabbed my balls.

'Put your hands on the bedpost!'

I followed her command. 'Why? Bloody let go!' Before I had finished protesting she whisked a cord around my wrists, tied an ingenious knot and bound my hands to the post.

I struggled, but I couldn't free them. I leant forward and bit the cord – but she was pulling another one from under the pillow. She looped it around my wings, leant back and pulled it tight.

I gasped, beginning to lose the feeling in my wings' fingers. 'What are you doing?'

'Now you can't cover your pretty backside with your wings, when I sodomise you with my riding crop.'

'*What?* – Ow!' She cracked me across the backside. It wasn't her mask – she was holding a whip! She passed it over my mouth and I tasted the leather, and felt the little gold ferrule on the end. Suddenly I was dangerously sober. 'Let me go!'

738

'Please let me go, *my lady.*'

'Ow! ... My lady.'

Eleonora smiled. 'You're a fast learner. Not so loud or they'll hear you downstairs. If you dare kick, I'll call for an audience.'

She tilted her head, appreciating her handiwork, studying me closely. She stroked the whip into my arse crack and ran it up and down. I pleaded, but it delighted her; no matter what I said she wouldn't let me free.

She bent her knee up between my thighs and pressed it on the inside of my legs. The sparse light picked out shiny creases in the leather. She pushed me flat and straddled my arse, riding my cheeks as if fucking me until my backside was wet with her juices. My cock stiffened despite myself as it rubbed against the sheets.

Her breathing quickened. I heard her sigh and felt her shudder.

Then— oh, but I won't go into it— she ... no, I can't say ... What am I telling you this for, anyway?

Finally she left me kneeling, my cock sore from her quick, expert tugs, because she didn't like the way I kept growing soft. She had flicked my come out of me and it was helplessly dripping off my chest. I felt as if I had been milked, and my arse was ... raw.

She said, 'I'll send word around the party to come up and view you.'

'No!'

'Yes. They would laugh to see the Messenger so ... compromised. Oh, and your wife's downstairs, isn't she?'

'Please, Eleonora.'

Smack!

'Ow! Please, my lady.'

She lowered her mask onto my face and pulled its string tight, restricting my vision to a few centimetres of rucked sheet and my breathing to a warm hiss. She sighed with a beautiful facsimile of sadness, 'Now you're used up. I'll have to leave you on your knees until you're ready again.'

'Again?' I whispered, muffled.

'I'm taking your clothes, so even if you bite yourself free you won't be able to leave the room. Unless you want to join the party naked, on a leash?'

'No!'

'I will leave the door unlocked. Anyone could come in ... I'll leave it to chance.'

She slipped out of the range of my vision. Music leaked in from the party, then the door clicked shut. Rays filtered through the curtains. Flies buzzed in the open window and landed on me. They puddled their sucker mouthparts on my skin. The tracks of their feet tickled me infuriatingly as they crawled, but I was too abandoned in my shame to shake them off. I felt squandered ... And I felt beaten ... I was tricked. Deceived. Eaten.

*

Hours later Eleonora returned, dropped my clothes on the floor, and untied me without a word.

CHAPTER 17

I flew reconnaissance flights over the seemingly never-ending procession of troops. Far below me, the Peregrine General Fyrd were marching into the gate. Behind their line came the Summerday Select Fyrd, clad in dirty brigandines that had once been saffron yellow. They were driving oxen pulling room-sized espringals on wheels, capable of shooting a vireton spear through the Insect Wall. The Summerday Select were excellent at demolishing Insect paper and they knew the whole front well.

Behind them came the Shivel Select, mustered weeks before for the advance. Their columns were in close order between the lines of outriders and, further off in the distance, another body of men whose colours I couldn't see. I winged closer and looked down to the road. After the leaf-green of Shivel rode the crimson column of the Imperial Fyrd.

The Emperor had kept cohesion in their formation and the five hundred men rode perfectly spaced. All the other fyrds had become one mass, trailing baggage carts tens of kilometres behind.

I glided lower and saw the Emperor. He was leading, on his black stallion, and the diffuse sunlight gave his figure an unnatural luminosity – he was wearing full plate. Two spearmen rode behind him on either side, each steadying with one hand his pennant in his saddle rest. Reflections darted from their helmets. Their banners with the Castle's red sun on yellow flickered forward above them.

I wheeled away and found Tornado with a division of horsemen patrolling the road's north verge. I half-folded my wings and came tearing down helter-skelter a hundred metres in a few seconds, rocking and side-slipping, legs dangling, to the ground.

Tornado looked down from his enormous, ivory-clad saddle. His worn armour had a raised design that replicated the stitches and hemming of denim.

I said, 'The Emperor's in sight.'

'How far?' he boomed.

'About five hours away.'

'You tell Lightning that I will go to escort him.'

'Of course.'

'The Imperial Fyrd will be looking to me for their lead.'

I heard the excitement in his voice; he was absolutely prepared for some unspecified apotheosis. 'You want to stay close to San in case he conjures up god, or something.'

Tornado smiled. 'My place is at his right hand, whatever happens. No Insect or madman will harm him in Lowespass, where I was born and bred. He'll be safe like he was inside the Castle's walls. And you, Comet; you'd better make sure everyone hears his words. And, like, acts on them.'

'Lightning and I will come out, too.'

'I'll be first to San's side ... I'll be certain to witness any revelation.'

'What revelation?'

'Any revelation!' His shire horse started forward.

Great, I thought. Now we begin to jockey for position in serving San. Nothing short of god returning would quench our bloody egos. I knew Lightning likes to see himself as San's second in command but now he was anxious that the Circle had failed, and Tornado's grim-faced but calm faith and certainty of his role gave him a rock-sure composure. He doesn't understand that it is often the beliefs we hold most adamantly that turn out to be wrong, because we never examine them.

I sped back to town. More sprinting along the streets, knocking on doors, a few breathless words at each one. Lightning, with Cyan unwillingly in tow, was at the top of the gatehouse.

The large square windows in its overhang were a good vantage point. Lightning and Cyan were watching Insects running among the straggling troops, dropping into quarries. They scurried, carried on their long legs over the uneven ground. They bit experimentally at abandoned carts. When the wind gusted in our direction, we could hear them crunching as they chewed up the wood's surface in long lines. They methodically gathered balls of grey pulp in the palps behind their jaws and then rushed away to plaster it along an edge of the Wall.

They tugged at bodies on the ground, cutting them up and carrying them to the lake. The lake glimmered brown as if the wet land had been scraped flat. Dark patches of carcasses and vegetation floated on its surface. On occasional gusts we smelt it; and it turned my stomach. The rotting, waterlogged corpses stank, a bloated, gutsy miasma as thick as gravy. Above the lake, the atmosphere was so solid with the smell you could slice it. It intruded into everything and was destroying our morale.

The wooden room at the tower top always smelled of tar. I leant on the windowsill as I told Lightning the news. He rubbed his eyes and said, 'Ask Wrenn and Lourie to increase guard on the road and I'll send them mounted archers. We'll go out to greet the Emperor.'

A stablehand brought our horses and we set off from town. The last of the Peregrine General Fyrd were coming into the gate. 'Those are my men,' Cyan said.

'Not yet, they aren't,' Lightning told her. 'I called them up with Micawater and I integrated them with my battalions.'

'Why are they all archers?'

'You will mainly field archers. Every man in Awia from eleven years old drills in archery every Sunday. I had that law passed centuries ago. Select longbow men train every day, shooting volleys together.'

'Awndyn doesn't,' Cyan said.

'Only Awia trains so thoroughly. The General Fyrd from Hacilith don't drill at all because Aver-Falconet doesn't want proficient soldiers in the city.'

Cyan's oval face was wind-burnt and coppery and, despite herself, she had an interested shine in her eyes which I found compelling. She kept watching the troops. A small gap and the next set started past, bleary-eyed from sleeping in camps, and with moustaches and beards, not like clean-shaven Awians. She peered at them. 'Who are these?'

Lightning said, 'Can't you see their standard?'

'Yes ... just. So?'

'So who is it?'

'Green, with a white splodge.'

'It is a silver star on a field vert. A green flag means it's Plainslands, and a silver star is ...'

Cyan swung her feet in her stirrups and bounced them off her horse's ribs.

'Shivel. By god, what has Swallow been teaching you?'

'The harpsichord, mostly. And the violin. She said I have no talent what-soever. She said even you're better at playing music than I am.'

'I daresay,' Lightning said, with a smile. 'I was unaware your education was inadequate. I did give Swallow funds to hire the best tutors for you.'

'She just brought in the old codger from school. I complained but you never checked ... because you can't abide the thought that she could do anything wrong.'

Lightning said nothing.

'Because you keep pretending you love her,' Cyan added.

'I do love her! With all my heart.' Lightning shifted his position in the saddle. 'She is the best musician the Fourlands has ever produced.'

Lord Governor Anelace Shivel greeted us as he passed. Then his Select cavalry vanguard followed on, all in green brigandines and small star badges stamped from pewter.

'Look at all these men!' Cyan gasped.

'Yes, and they've been in the Castle's pay ever since they left their manor boundary,' Lightning said. 'That will dent the treasury badly.'

'As if whether we can pay matters any more,' I said, and turned to Cyan. 'You haven't seen anything yet. This is only half of Shivel's Select, from

Coutille and Pinchbeck musters. Basilard and Spraint musters are a day or so behind – and all his General Fyrd are yet to come.'

Lightning added, 'Governor Shivel has the title "lord", so he is able to raise twenty thousand troops or more, and from the sight of these I would say this is the first occasion he has mobilised them all. You see, my dear? Your manor will easily raise enough for you to be *Lady* Governor.'

'Good incentive to look after your people,' I said. 'Encourage them to multiply and they might replace those we'll lose here. Pregnant women don't get drafted. If they have a large family they can choose who to send.'

'Hark at the cynic,' Lightning said.

'The villages are empty,' I told him. 'San will never do this twice.'

'I think I should lead my fyrd,' Cyan said thoughtfully.

I had thought she wanted to renounce her manorship. I glanced at her, seeing her expression resolving into determination; she was reconsidering her identity yet again.

'Certainly not,' Lightning said. 'You don't even know one standard from the next.'

She sat up straight in her saddle for the first time. 'Well, tell me. How do I organise them?'

'I can't believe she doesn't already know this,' I said.

Lightning sighed, 'I blame myself. I'll do something about it as soon as we get back. However, no reason not to start now. Mm ... let me see.' He hovered a hand at the weary men riding past in loose formation. 'These are Select troops. Select have the same ranks as the General Fyrd and they are also used as officers for the General Fyrd – except for the lowest ranks where you can make shift with veteran General Fyrd if you have to. All Selects are trained using the same methods so different manors can fight side by side.

'You will see, after that gap – that's supposed to be a gap – a new battalion starting. The fellow on the smart black courser is its warden. The warden leads a battalion of a thousand men. Beside him is the vice-warden, and behind him comes the captain of a division, that one on the stallion.

'The captain leads a division – that is, a morai – of five hundred men. The division is comprised of companies – or lamai – of fifty men apiece, and each company is led by a sergeant. A company is split into squads of five to ten men, depending on what you need them for – and squads are led by a corporal.'

'I know that one,' said Cyan.

'At least!' Lightning slapped the reins on his saddlebow in mock exasperation.

I said, 'The fyrd has more or less stayed the same since the time of the First Circle.'

'It's an ugly Morenzian word,' said Lightning. 'Each officer has a deputy;

you can see the vice-captain walking past us now. The one with the beard. Give him a nod.'

Cyan gave a cutesy nod, and the vice-captain grinned and nudged his mate.

'All right,' said Lightning. 'Don't get carried away. As a governor you can fine anyone, General or Select, who refuses the draft or goes absent without leave; and depending on the circumstances you can confiscate all their property. Your manor's bureaucracy takes care of that sort of thing.'

Cyan was watching, wide-eyed, realising what she had been missing all this time. 'I want to take part.'

Lightning shook his head. 'No, blood of mine. Not yet.'

'You try to stop me doing everything!'

'It is for your own good.'

'You want me to stay inside playing instruments!'

'No – I'm glad you want to fight. At last you've given me a clear clue as to what you want to do with your life. But you need experience before I give you command. We can't waste Zascai lives. You have no idea what to do, you don't even know the manoeuvre codes. You don't appreciate how terrible the confusion can be in the battle's heat.'

'Tell me and I'll remember.'

'You have no practice yet, my dear. If something changed or went wrong you wouldn't know how to improvise.'

'Of course I do. When you visit Awndyn, your work – battles and hunts – is all you talk about!'

'Have you ever seen an Insect close to?'

'Not closer than the ones we've just been watching.'

'And you want to lead men into battle? Everyone would be killed beside you! Our name would be reviled. When the push starts you must not leave town, do you hear me? Continue to learn archery and in a few short years you may lead your fyrd.'

Cyan spat, 'Archery! I'm sick of people foisting their obsessions on me. Every time you visited me all I had was hours of shooting lessons. You just assume I'm interested. Well, I'm not and I didn't want to take part in your tournaments – or Swallow's music. But this suits me—' she waved at the mounted soldiers '—I like this on my own terms, not just to please you. Why should I do archery or music when I'm not interested? I need to find something of my own. Something that's really *me*.'

Lightning sighed. 'You are proficient with the bow, and at riding, but you can't jump straight in.'

The soldiers were staring at Cyan now and she was heat-hazed with embarrassment, but even more determined to make her point. 'You don't know me at all. Even the presents you bring are the same as when I was a little girl. I liked them then, OK, but I'm grown up now. I'm not a kid! You won't let me fly.'

'What? Only Jant and Insects can fly.'

'I mean metaphorically! I want to be at the centre of things!'

Lightning nodded. 'That is your noble blood showing. Very well, but you must learn poise.'

'Must learn poise,' Cyan repeated, making fun of his deep voice. 'Typical. What about you, with that thing you keep doing with your hand?'

Lightning looked down and seemed surprised. His right hand was closed and he had been touching the scar across his palm. He snorted disparagingly, then pulled his gloves from under his belt and wiggled his fingers into them. He said, 'We might be redundant soon. I have more important things to think about.'

Cyan persisted: 'What is it with your hand?'

'A scar from my wedding.'

'Savory? All the poise in the world didn't save her.'

'Ah!' Lightning looked at Cyan sharply. 'You have no right! You know nothing of what happened!'

'Well, tell me.'

Lightning took a breath as if he was about to speak, but hesitated and drew into himself. 'Whenever I smell pine I remember her,' he said quietly.

I spoke up. 'Cyan's half-sister has filled her head with all kinds of lies.'

'I can speak to my sisters if I want.'

'Your half-sisters are envious,' Lightning said dismissively. 'They do not have your prospects and they must come to terms with Ata's unpopularity.'

Cyan and Lightning, like a peregrine and its prey, were trying to gain height on the other in the flight of the argument and it was an unsettling spectacle. I told him, 'Cyan's little more than a squab, but I can find her some work. Otherwise she'll just wander around insulting Eszai. If she was my daughter I'd find her something to do.'

He shook his head with a stony expression. 'Jant, if by some freak of nature you had a daughter, you would want to keep her safe. You saw what happened to Swallow. I've seen her lamed in battle – and Cyan's mother herself slain. The same will not happen to her.'

Cyan raised her three middle fingers at the troops watching her. She did remind me of her mother, who was more of a rebel than I could ever be, because she had been capable of seeing the whole system and knew how to put her immortality to use. I ameliorate myself to the system, with drugs, because I can only see my own small part, as a Rhydanne does who's used to hunting alone.

*

Yells broke our sullen silence. Pangare raised her head, ears forward. Riders were galloping up the line, passing by the queue and racing towards us at a mad speed. They were at one with their wild skewbald mounts. Their tack and clothes blazed with colour; their flowing black scarves and loose cotton trousers rippled. Red and green pompoms bounced on the bridles, the thick woollen tassels strung along their reins and the fringes over the horses' foreheads.

'Here's something different,' said Lightning, and twisted around to shout at Cyan. 'Look! The Ghallain gauchos!'

They sped past us and barged into Shivel's column at the gate. Annoyed shouts drifted back. More gauchos charged past. Their saddles were low and minimal, with gaudy numnah rugs underneath, and hoppers full of feathered javelins hanging on both sides. They had gathered transparent Insect wings and lashed them to their cruppers. They had tied on Insect heads by the antennae; and dragged the rest of the carcass behind them on lariats.

A man with a wide scarf around his face rode at their fore, his white trousers tucked into leather chaps. He pulled his horse round so tightly it reared. It pranced up to us sideways, spitting foam. It was so high-spirited it looked like it was about to fly.

'Vir Ghallain!' I shouted.

'Salutations, Comet. Lightning, long time no see.'

'Good to see you,' Lightning managed in Plainslands.

'And I you! And I you! Here are my cavalry, owing to San. Do with them what you will. If you can!'

I said, 'What about your infantry? Where are your draftees? They must be weeks behind!'

Governor Vir pulled his scarf fully down from his mouth and said in a singsong accent, 'They are! My steward, he leads them! Has Brandoch arrived yet?'

'Not by a long way,' I said.

Vir turned to an excitable man in a loose headscarf who turfed his horse to a halt beside us. 'Ull, you see, we beat Brandoch. That's fifty pounds you owe me.' He pointed back up the queue. 'San is here. For San to be here this must be the motherfucker of all battles, we said.' He jigged up and down in his worn saddle. 'We can't miss it. Let's see which of us lives!'

'You're a nutter, Vir Ghallain,' I said.

'Nutter enough to Challenge you one day! And put some clothes on. Hey! Hey!' This last to his horse, which bounded forward and he had his back to me before I could take my next breath. Yet more hurtled up the line, churning the muddy ground either side of the road.

'Incredible,' said Cyan.

'Ranchers,' I said.

'There are thousands.'

'Hundreds. He isn't a lord governor,' said Lightning.

I said, 'If you ask me, they're all little kings within the bounds of their manors. They—'

'Hush, Jant! Look!'

On the road, Shivel's green livery was thinning out, and behind them, all was scarlet.

'By god, the Emperor. In armour.'

'I can scarcely believe it.'

The last few lines of Shivel men kept glancing back. They saw the Emperor mounted on black Alezane, with the banners licking the air above him like forked tongues. Shivel men slowed down, walked their horses off the road and stood watching.

As they parted, the Imperial Fyrd rode through, and more of Shivel's infantry gave way before them. I glanced at Lightning; he nodded, and we urged our horses through the crowd.

The Emperor saw us and reined his horse in. Tornado, a step behind him on his right, the standard bearers, and the whole Imperial Fyrd slowed to a halt.

Lightning dismounted and threw himself at the Emperor's feet, on both knees. I heard his greaves grind on the cobbles. I stepped my leg over Pangare's saddle, hopped to the ground and knelt beside him. A couple of quick jingles behind me told me Cyan had done the same.

Seeing us, all the Shivel fyrd dismounted and knelt in a great swathe either side of the road.

Lightning and I looked up to San's face, clean-shaven and expression-less. He wore an open-faced sallet helmet that pushed his fine white hair close to his hollow cheeks, but the wind blew the ends that protruded from underneath.

Every plate of his armour was lustrous – enamelled white with no orna-ment but the fastenings of a billowing white silk cloak. Suns were damascened on the bare steel scabbard of his ancient broadsword which hung with his shield from the saddlebow.

I managed one glance and bowed my head again.

Peach-coloured shafts of sunlight shone between our horses' sinewy legs. Their musty, sweaty bellies and withers hemmed us in, their hair brushed against the grain in dark streaks, their hocks covered in drying mud. Their shadows were no more than small patches directly beneath them. Pangare flipped her docked tail and pawed the road too close to my head. I looked up to the underside of the Emperor's horse's long chin, as it chewed its bit imperiously.

The first company of the Imperial Fyrd raised a cheer, then the second company, then the third, and when all ten companies had cheered separately, the five hundred men cheered together; a great, deafening wordless roar that went on and on until San raised his free hand. The cheering straggled into silence.

'My lord,' said Lightning, so dry-mouthed I could hear his tongue clicking. 'I'm sorry – we are – that it's come to this. Please ... And we'll ... We will bring the Insects under control. We will mend our error.'

San rested his reins on his scrollwork saddlebow. 'Lightning, Comet, to your feet. Every second we stay the numbers in our rearguard diminish.'

San's long limbs were encased in armour and, once I'd recovered from the shock of seeing that he actually did have legs, I noticed how thin they were; no muscles on his shanks at all. He must be wearing the cloak to make himself look bigger. I risked a closer glance and saw beads of sweat on his neck. He must be feeling the exertion of wearing armour and riding after fourteen hundred years in the Castle, but it did not tell in his noble bearing. He showed no sign of strain on his face: his self-control was absolute. He conveyed the same majesty under the open skies as he did sitting at the focal point of the Throne Room.

The pennant-bearers behind him were whey-pale and poker-faced, their jaws clenched, their mouths firm lines. They were telling themselves this wasn't happening. Their set expressions were partly pride that such a role had fallen to them, part anxiety from riding for days in far too close proximity to the Emperor, but mostly the blank-eyed denial of men determined to carry out a job they really didn't want to do.

The Emperor asked Lightning, 'Have Insects flown again?'

'They flew every day for three days. There have been no more flights since.'

'Good. I must talk with Frost immediately.'

I stammered, 'Er, Frost has changed. She's ... well ... she's somewhat stressed.'

'Is she still the best architect?'

'Um ... I think so.'

'She will be the Architect until she loses a Challenge. I will make a new Lawyer, Artillerist and Master of Horse from the best in the town to complete the Circle. We will need them in the coming days, but when times are easier I will open their positions to worldwide competition.' San gestured for Lightning to ride on his left, level with Tornado. The Strongman was calm-faced and expressionless, looking straight ahead, his hands invisible under the circular vamplate on his axe haft.

Lightning beckoned to Cyan with a smile, asking her to join him, but she turned her face away. She seemed overwhelmed.

San said, 'Comet, ride ahead and announce our entry to the town.'

I don't remember climbing back onto Pangare but I must have done because the next instant I was on a level with the Emperor's face. I gave a quick nod and with shaking hands I unlaced my dented post horn from the saddle, where it shone like a New Year's decoration. I gave Pangare a single word and she leapt down the road.

Behind me the whole Imperial Fyrd and Shivel fyrd began to move again, with the jingle of tack and clop of hooves.

The Emperor San here! I thought as I rode. The Emperor San in armour! I had seen his white panoply before; it was displayed, by tradition, in the Castle's armoury but nobody ever thought he would actually wear it.

When a new Armourer joins the Circle it is always his first honour to make a perfect suit of armour for the Emperor to the highest specifications, copying the measurements of the last. Sleat had put so much effort into creating San's perfect armour that I am surprised he ever made anything again.

I heralded San's arrival into Slake Cross. People lined the roadside, leant out of windows, clustered in the hoardings, stood on the new earth ramparts. I slowed and cantered Pangare through the gatehouse arch, and hundreds of people dropped to their knees in a great swathe as I passed. I could get used to this.

CHAPTER 18

I rose before dawn and went to the washroom to have a powder bath. Those of us who have wings moult and re-grow flight feathers continuously, one or two at a time, but in the last few months I had lost six or seven, leaving me with great gaps in my wings. It made flying more laborious and I was at the stage of exhaustion when, no matter how much I ate, my meals didn't provide energy any more. San had asked me to sleep in a pavilion in the canvas city because he thought my presence might curtail the fyrd's drinking (ha!), the inter-manor rivalries, brawling and petty theft breaking out there.

As I rubbed handfuls of talcum powder between my feathers I reconsidered the problems of the last few days. I had been gathering information for the Emperor, everyone was bombarding me with questions, and I had to think one step ahead. The Rachiswater fyrd vied with Tanager, and the Carniss fyrd stole things from everybody. The Awndyn fyrd had been arriving all night, stomping past my tent. The carpenters had been hammering, by firelight, while the Emperor slept – presumably – in my bed. It was bloody bizarre. On the positive side, he had waived most of the formal courtesies, so I spent less time kneeling on the floor.

The powder relieved some of my itching. I took a shower, preened and oiled my feathers into a glossy iridescence. I tied back my hair in wet black rat-tails, lit a cigarette and returned to the hall feeling much more relaxed.

The hall had become a small, austere version of the Throne Room. Most of the Eszai were listening attentively as the Emperor, with Tornado and Frost beside him, discussed our situation.

Tornado was so huge that usually his very gravity pulled everyone's attention towards him, but now he managed to look humble and our concentration focused on San's gaunt figure. Nobody dared question the Strongman's self-styled role as San's bodyguard, testimony to his profound faith although I thought he was overdoing it.

Frost, on the other hand, looked cadaverous. She spoke clearly although much too fast: 'M-my lord – I have estimated the number of eggs in the lake. Given the parameters my approximation is, of necessity, rough. Rayne dissected an Insect and and and she thinks they're hermaphrodite. I have calculated the capacity of air w-which one Insect needs to fly, then figured the dimensions of the flight, and therefore the number of Insects in that volume of air, and what percentage reach the lake, and since they seem to contain between ninety-eight and one hundred and fifty eggs, assuming all eggs are v-v-viable, I—'

'Frost,' the Emperor said gently.

She bit at a crooked finger. 'Um ... between seven million, eight hundred and eleven thousand, six hundred and twenty-one, and—'

'I see,' said San. 'Seven million Insect spawn.'

'Nearly eight, yes.' She gave a quick nod and continued. 'I estimate three hundred thousand five hundred and twelve adult Insects in the v-vicinity of the lake. They defend it so vigorously that no lancer has m-managed to reach the shore. My only suggestion is that we open the d-dam gate and d-drain the lake.'

The Emperor said, 'Does anybody have an alternative proposal?'

Silence around the room. Most eyes were downcast, including mine. 'Very well,' the Emperor continued. 'We shall march to the dam. Frost, what do you need?'

'Twenty draft horses – to be harnessed in two teams of ten – and and and sufficient troops to clear the way.'

'Very well.'

Frost sat down again, muttering, 'Two, eight, five hundred and twelve, one hundred and thirty-four million—'

'Comet?' said San. It was my turn to rise. 'Yes, my lord?'

'What new troops do we have? What manor is currently arriving?'

'Fescue, my lord. Lord Governor Darnel Fescue came in last night with the musters of Fiorin and Melick, both Select and General. They're mostly infantry and shield fyrd, with a few thousand archers. I've put some on escort duty. Marram muster is coming in now and the others will be arriving all through today.'

'How many men?'

'Twenty-two thousand. Behind them, probably after dusk, will come a division of felons under guard from Hacilith's jails. I'm lodging them in Lowespass Fortress. We can discount some manors from our plans: Cathee takes six weeks to raise troops, and Brandoch's infantry will be coming in last, if at all. When I visited, the governor was away touring his musters for the biannual assizes. I had to go around all his reeves' halls till I found him. But I'm expecting the remnants tomorrow.'

'Is our provisioning adequate? Where is Cloud?'

Tre Cloud stood up, in the front row. He was an energetic, sinewy Grass Islander who never seemed to need any rest. He pulled his cloth cap from his crew-cut head and twisted it between his hands as he spoke. 'The rationing will have to continue. I have requested grain throughout the Fourlands. All our depots in Lowespass are empty and the bastle farms have mostly been ransacked. I've ordered all the goods being unloaded to be sealed so their scent doesn't attract Insects. The carts coming up from Rachiswater all have armed protection, and my agents are licensed so no one can defraud us or buy in our name.'

'What about lodging?'

The Cook shoved the cap into a pocket in his striped apron. 'We're extending the encampment. The barracks in Whittorn is full. I sent men there until the reeve sent letters back saying he couldn't accommodate any more. I'm glad it's unseasonably cold because the towns are overcrowding. We can't keep so many people together for much longer. Not to mention the lake, it's a potential pool of infection.'

He continued, very self-assured. After all, he had won his Challenge by provisioning these forts – with the world's best cassoulet which the troops much preferred to the previous Cook's pork stew.

While he was speaking, a movement on the steps caught my eye. Cyan had crept down from the upper storey. She peered around the stone newel post, but Lightning was the only one to acknowledge her. He swung his arms unfolded happily and gave her a smile. She straightened up, glided towards me, and settled beside me on the bench.

'We must determine the order of the advance,' the Emperor said. 'Tell me your suggestions.'

Tornado said, 'Infantry. Lots of infantry with axes and so on. That's our best bet.'

Wrenn said, 'I agree, but swords are lighter to wield for a day's march.'

'A swift cavalry charge,' said the new Master of Horse. 'That way we'll break through 'em.'

'No, no,' said Wrenn. 'If I only had the pick of the resources, I'm sure my approach would be best.'

'Well, you don't have the pick of the resources.'

Lightning rolled his eyes: here they all bloody go again.

Lourie Hurricane, the Polearms Master, spoke. Lourie was usually so silent that on the few occasions he opens his mouth everybody listens, knowing he will say something well thought out and worthwhile. 'The advance should be led by a pike phalanx as best adapted to open ground. We have ten thousand trained pikemen from Rachiswater, Litanee and Eske. My Lord Emperor, they will provide maximum protection to the rest of the host following.'

San asked Tornado, 'Do you agree with Hurricane's suggestion?'

Tornado considered it. 'Yes, my lord.' I could barely see his eyes, shadowed as they were in a deep mass of wrinkles. The rest of his round face was smooth with no wrinkles whatsoever – perhaps they gathered to make a determined assault on his eyes. He reminded me of one of the massive columnar stalagmites in the caves below the town. The signs of constant physical endurance had worn into his face just as surely as water carves clefts in rock; I could imagine him formed of living flowstone. By a slow, cold process, in a cavern stifled by darkness, water that looks clear but is saturated with dissolved rock drips to the ground and precipitates, building a sullen soldier from the feet up. Trickles run down the outside of the column depositing a trail of wet stone, that over millennia grows lumpen and irregular to form his paunch and buttocks. The hollows in the sides of his elbows and knees are smooth solution pockets. Random drips of hard water give him a physiognomy and knuckles. Then with a great heave he tears one foot and the other free of the bedrock and walks off to fight Insects. Tornado could be crystallised loyalty. With a beer gut.

'Lightning?' said the Emperor.

Lightning had been smiling at Cyan and he jumped. 'My lord?'

'Do you agree with Hurricane's proposition?'

'Yes.'

'What arrow-power can you supply?'

'Well ... We have forty thousand archers, ten thousand crossbow men. I will not use crossbows on the field because they cannot shoot indirectly. We will shoot blind over the pikemen's ranks and eliminate Insects immediately in front of the advance. I'm sure the Polearms Master and Javelin Master will agree. However, we need Tornado's infantry to flank us. We have long used this technique with sarissai, akontistai and hastai ... I mean, pikemen, javelin men and heavy infantry.'

Cyan was frustrated. She leant to me and asked, under her breath, 'What are the plans? What does he mean?'

I gave an irritated little gesture to quiet her.

'I want to take part,' she said. 'I'll lead my fyrd as a great governor should.'

'Well, listen and you might learn something.'

'Just what I'd expect from a glorified errand boy.'

Lightning said, 'The Armourer informs me we are holding nearly a million arrows and we can secure the same again. That includes two-thirds unmade arrows, and the off-duty fyrd are making them up.'

Cyan rocked from buttock to buttock. Lightning gave her a 'not now' look, and continued, 'The Lowespass, Carniss and Ghallain mounted archers will provide mobile support.'

Cyan cleared her throat and piped up, ''Scuse me?'

The Emperor looked straight at her. So did the rest of the Eszai.

Under San's gaze, Cyan had no choice but to rise to her feet. 'My lord ... um ... I would like to lead Peregrine's archers.'

Lightning sent her a sharp look. The silence of curiosity quickly became one of embarrassment. Everyone glanced at each other impatiently.

I tugged her jumper, hissed, 'Sit down!'

Lightning looked from Cyan to the Emperor and spoke calmly. 'My lord Emperor, this is my daughter Cyan Peregrine. She will soon inherit the manor but I am afraid she is a little premature in her ambitions.' To Cyan he said, 'That is impossible for now, my dear. Please sit down.'

'But—'

Lightning beamed around at everyone and spoke louder, for our benefit: 'I'm sure that some of us will be happy to listen to you after the meeting ... for a very reasonable fee.'

A ripple of nervous laughter discharged around the room. We darted quick smiles to and fro.

'But—'

'I will brook no more argument. You don't understand; this is a very important conference.'

The Emperor waited patiently but Tornado said, 'Get her out of here, Lightning.'

Cyan glowered at him. Lightning said, 'She's just trying to be noticed. Find yourself a sense of humour.'

'This is not, like, a cabaret.'

Lightning said to the room, 'See how ready she is to roll up her sleeves and lead the fyrd? Don't you wish she was your daughter ?'

We laughed more openly this time. Cyan did not take well to being discomfited in front of the Circle. 'Peregrine manor seems no more than one of Micawater's musters,' she said. 'If I mayn't lead my men, I'd like to win their trust as a captain perhaps.'

The Emperor looked at Lightning, clearly requesting him to end the interruption. I was about to chip in, myself, but Lightning, with his hands on his hips and an amused expression, seemed well in charge.

'No,' he said. 'You may not. You may watch our operations from the town walls.'

'I'm joining in, so tough! You can't stop me! When you're engaged, I'll ride out!'

He spoke to her only, with serene persuasion. 'You are being unreasonable, blood of mine. Unless you sit down I must find you new accommodation. Say, the upper chamber of a peel tower?'

Cyan hesitated, trying to figure this out. 'Are you threatening to lock me up? You can't do that!'

He sighed, exasperated. 'These men will escort you safely to your new apartment.' He gave a nod to the Micawater fyrdsmen standing with spears either side of the door. They began to walk towards Cyan.

She glanced with round eyes from them to her father. 'No! I only wanted to—' A guard took her arm but she booted him in the ankle and snatched herself free.

She pointed at Lightning. 'I Challenge you!'

An intake of breath around the room.

Lightning stood still, mouth downturned, transfixed. Emotions welled up one after another in his expression: profound hurt. Bafflement. Pride, too, and anger. The anger surfaced quickly and quenched all the rest. 'Do you?' he said, measuredly.

Cyan stuttered and recovered herself. 'I, C-Cyan Peregrine, Challenge you, Saker Micawater, for the position of Lightning within the Castle's Circle.'

I looked around at all the shocked faces. Even the Emperor had raised his eyebrows. Tornado turned his eyes up to the ceiling, his mouth in an amused twist.

San announced, 'I uphold the Challenge. After the current campaign.'

'Very well ...' Lightning managed a dry whisper to Cyan. 'Now get out of my sight.'

'But ...'

'But what? What do you mean, but? Haven't you done enough? Do you *know* what you've just said? Now the words are out, you can't take them back! I'll have to shoot against you now!' He took a step. 'How could you *do this to me*? After all I've done for you. You repay me by ... throwing it back in my face! Not a thought of what I've given you. I saved you, on the ship. I reached out! I keep reaching out!'

He spread both hands and shook them towards her. His face and neck flushed so red they were blotched with white. He yelled in fury, 'Think before you speak! How can you Challenge *me*? I *taught* you to bloody shoot! Any man here has a better chance than you do. Any Select archer is stronger than you. What do you want? My attention? Now of all times? You always had my fond attention – now you have my Lord Emperor's and Her Highness's and all the *bloody* journalists' attention as well!'

He took a breath, turned and punched the table. Punched it with the other hand, and leant his weight on it to breathe, leaning over the map, his head bowed and massive shoulders hunched like a lion's. Cyan was too petrified even to cry.

He continued, more quietly, 'Nothing I do is good enough. Is it? Nothing I can buy you. All those days I shirked target practice and spent with you. Look at yourself—' contempt turned in his voice '—cashmere and my sister's ruby pendant. You want for nothing, I made sure of that. You don't know how privileged you are. I protect the farmers grafting in your fields. I look after the ships lying in your harbour. In return, you interrupt me! You try to get yourself killed and borne off to the Wall! Fractious, captious, ungrateful, delusional child! You're just like your mother. She took advantage. She betrayed me, and now you do, too. Oh, you are no flesh and blood of mine!' He collapsed into his chair. ' ... Fyrdsmen, take her to tower ten.'

Their footsteps died away in silence.

'We will resume,' the Emperor stated. 'Tornado, what is the current casualty rate?'

Nobody listened to the Strongman. We were watching Lightning. He sat, chin on chest, staring at the floor, numbly unaware of his surroundings. Minutes went by and he seemed to have retracted totally into himself.

His shoulders were so taut they drew horizontal creases across his waistcoat's chest; under his shirt sleeves his forearms' pleated muscles were like iron. His hands dangled on the rests covered by his greatcoat, but all of a sudden he relaxed and the breath went out of him. He stood up, and muttered, 'I must have some fresh air.'

As if running on instinct he swept a deep bow to the Emperor and said glassily, 'My lord, will you excuse me?'

The Emperor inclined his head.

Lightning folded his arms because his hands were shaking, and left the hall.

His few enemies in the Circle looked smug; a couple leant to each other and whispered – the Archer humiliated by his impudent, imprudent daughter. I glanced around the room – most of the Eszai seemed determined to pretend it never happened. They never let someone else's misfortune affect them.

'Like mother, like daughter,' I said loudly.

'Shut up, Jant.' Eleonora crossed her legs with slow deliberation. But I had broken the tension and the meeting continued.

I remembered, ten years ago, the Emperor saying that Lightning should listen to the child. I wanted to dash out and offer him my sympathies, but I was obliged to attend to the battle plans. In the past, I would have gone after him regardless of the consequences, but that was many years ago, and I am so very different now. Maybe in one of your romantic novels, Saker, your daughter would have loyally complied with your wishes and fought by your side, but real life doesn't work like that. Real life doesn't work at all.

CHAPTER 19

LIGHTNING'S CHAPTER

My own daughter just Challenged me! In front of the Circle and the Emperor – and my lady Eleonora! I think I'm burning up. By god, by god. What has she turned into? With all I've done for her! Try as I might, rack my brains as I do, I can't think what I could have done better. Does she think I don't love her? – I would have changed the world for her! May the rivers Mica, Dace and Moren flood the world and drown it if she ever had cause for a fraction of one complaint.

I have failed, for her to turn out like this. I don't know how. Yes, I do. I have not spent enough time with her. First there was the swarm and then Tris and – why can't she be patient?

The girl is my just deserts for being a damn fool. I went against my nature with Ata; I didn't really love her. She sent for me and I found her sitting, sobbing at her table on the ship. Such a strong woman should never be driven to tears. I put an arm around her to comfort her ... fool that I am.

I must have spoilt Cyan. Yes. Yes, that's true. My pampering her desires must have led her to think she can demand the world ... How dare she? ... She doesn't realise that worlds are hard to come by.

By god, I haven't been this angry since ... since my family spilt. We all make errors, there's no need to keep castigating myself about that. Yes, the little mistakes made by princes are devastating on account of our power.

Who has she been talking to, to turn out so badly? It must be the effect of Hacilith and that rotten brood of Ata's. Cyan always seemed all right before, but now delinquency hangs around her like a cloud of perfume. I used to love her innocence. She might have been an accident, but she woke me up. A year feels like a year now, rather than ten minutes. I'm alive again – or becoming so – I'm experiencing more now in a year with her than I did in a century before. She invigorated me ... more, far more, than even Swallow could. Damn it, I even wished I could be like her.

Do I have to give up my own daughter like I've given up everyone else? No, wait. Take a breath. Step back from this – you know you can, there's been worse – and think. In a way she has played into my hands. I have a ... a legitimate way of dealing with her. She isn't familiar with the procedures of Challenges. I did the right thing; I'm free of her for the time being and I can talk to her later, at my convenience ... I am sure she will be very repentant.

The way she has turned out is not my fault. Events swept me along too quickly to make time for her ... I regret not having the pressure of time that mortals do. Promises are made; time passes and sometimes they are not properly kept. Reality intrudes on the best of intentions: doesn't every arrow that flies feel the pull of the earth? But, damn it, I have my duty; I can't neglect it. I knew she was growing quickly, but millions of things demanded my attention ... Swallow should have been more dutiful herself.

But no. When an archer misses the mark, he should turn and look for the fault within himself. A failure to hit the target is never the fault of the target.

The world is becoming too crass. Oh, that old refrain: everywhere is similar, and becoming more so. In the time that reared me the Grand Tour only took us around Awia, and it startled and inspired us. Now the Tour takes our sons and daughters thousands of kilometres and shows them four lands in the space of a year, and they return unimpressed.

I am fighting to protect the very ideals that Cyan is trying to change, and ... oh, what is the bloody point? I'm sure in the past I never had to justify my every move. There is an informality, these days, that causes uncertainty; nobody knows how to behave any more. It was easier when there were proper codes of behaviour ... I am too old and inflexible to bear this blow. Old armour splits; only soft jackets withstand sword blows.

Don't talk rubbish.

The world *is* changing, though. Changing radically, in ways I don't care to understand. And what will I be left with? A sense of nostalgia, for the rest of my life in long centuries to come. A terrible sense that I have missed the only thing worthwhile. Be steady, keep calm. Where are the nerves of steel I have when Insects are charging at me and I have to wait for my range?

I walked more slowly because a recent, mostly healed, rapier wound in my back was starting to catch. I passed into a deep shadow and looked about me, perturbed. I had come as far as the outer road. I must have paced across the square and three streets completely oblivious.

The tower of the gatehouse overshadowed the barrack blocks on my either side. Soldiers smoking outside on their steps were staring at me in surprise, curious at the sight of Lightning striding down the street in his shirt sleeves.

I passed them, then I stopped dead. The banner of Morenzia was flying above the barrack doorway. A red clenched fist. The red fist: the marriage rite. The Hacilith fyrd must have assembled, one part of my mind observed, but with the sight of the flag my other thoughts winged far away, to Savory. My Savory. Cyan was wrong to taunt me about her. If she knew what happened she wouldn't dare to mention Savory at all.

The wind gusted and the flag flapped, pulling its cord through its eye hole. It released me from my trance and I looked down, aware I was touching the scar across my right palm, rubbing it with my left thumb and forefinger. I turned and walked slowly back to my room. The civilised parts of Morenzia don't conduct the blood-red hand ceremony any more, only the people of Cathee still do, but the country has kept it as their device. I am so used to seeing it, it hardly registers, but occasionally when I am pensive I look a little deeper and the realisation of what it means takes me back to Savory. And again I am in the marriage hut, waiting for nightfall.

I was in the marriage hut, waiting for nightfall. The hut walls were wattle hurdles woven around living trees; I sat on the floor and looked up to the beams of the round roof, constructed in spirals like a spider's web. Through the smoke hole at the apex I watched folds in the clouds push against one another. The dusk sky was different shades of old gold like the mixture in a bottle of illuminator's ink.

After dark she will call me, if she hasn't had second thoughts, celebrating in the village all day with her friends and family. I heard their laughter as they dressed her up and drank to her, and asked her over and over, as is their custom, if she's *sure*, if she's really *sure*. Soon I will know if they have managed to sway her conviction; if I stay here well into the night and she fails to call me, then without a word I will go to the trader I had employed as a guide and leave the dense forest.

Outside was nothing but pine trees behind pine trees all the way up and over the fir-covered ridges of the vast mountain forest of Cathee. Cathee could not be more different from my hunting woods I loved so well; it was dark; it was trackless; it was wild. For hundreds of kilometres from Vertigo town to the Drag Road, from the clay paddy fields of Litanee to the cliffs of the cape there were only trees. Even at the edges where conifers segued into broadleaf forest it lost none of its impenetrability.

I had fasted in the marriage hut for twenty-four hours, alone, and I was expected to use that time to think about Savory and whether I wanted to marry her. I did with all my heart; Savory, when she called me, would never find the hut door swinging wide and her groom long gone.

Love filled me and uplifted me. I was intoxicated; I floated; I was full of love. After so long I was about to be married! Completed – as I had never felt complete before. I had always felt as if something was missing. I had always felt unfinished, but two people living together as one is to be complete. Savory did not have wings, so we would not be able to tangle our pinions together and I would not be able to bury my face in the warm, feather-scent in their pits, or stroke my fingers along their serried rows. They couple in a vulgar way, do humans, face to face rather than belly to back, but then my cousin Martyn and I used to throw ourselves on each other that way, when she had the key to the belvedere, or with excitement after the day's hunt.

The smell of deer blood, oiled armour, dry leaves, the perspiration of our eager flesh ... It would be strange at first to have a woman without wings, but then it would be strange, so strange, to have a companion at all.

The beauty of it – waiting outside in a far place, for my love to call me, while sunset dyed the sky strange colours and the light drained out of the forest. I wanted to tell her all my history – the past to be discussed in the future – we would have so much time!

I glanced up as the first wolf howls carried on the breeze. The Cathee grey wolves were dumb lanky beasts with dirty pelts and eyes glazed by starvation. They scavenged in large packs and scratched ancient things out of the villages' middens. The few villages sheltered from them behind circular palisades, but I had my new crossbow and I was not afraid. The worst they could do was give me fleas.

I could hear distant laughter from the village and I felt ostracised, but it would be worth it when they throw open their gates and Savory leads me in, when they accept me as one of their own.

I wondered what Mother would think of that. I found it easy to picture her face, even after all these centuries. *Son,* she would say, *do you know what you are doing? She has no fine blood whatsoever.*

That never mattered to me.

You just picked her out of the ranks!

I always knew I would meet my true love on the battlefield.

She is probably not even a virgin. Some fyrdsman or woodcutter will have taken her en passant.

Oh, let me marry whom I love.

Mother raises her eyebrows: *Ah, but is she your true love or your latest substitute?*

She is my true love, and besides, she has the strong will I admire and she is my equal in intelligence. I am immortal and I need someone of whom I will never tire.

Son, immortal or not, you vex me. What are you thinking of, participating in barbarous rituals?

True, I had always assumed I would be married our way, but Savory wanted this, and the way she explained the ritual seemed to be more deeply binding than anything invented in Awia and the Plains. Back home, bride and groom simply stand at the front of the audience and together proclaim, 'We are married.' To undo the union is just as simple a procedure, but there could be no separation when Savory and I are wed. This was to be her last visit to her homeland, and I agreed to the suggestion with delight, although later that night her face seemed strangely clouded. I would not have denied her anything. I was determined to know everything about her, and become familiar with her circumstances, the places that she had known and loved.

I wished I had met her earlier, and I knew too little about her and the Cathee, but I thought I could learn quickly through taking part. I fretted; where is she? Surely it's nightfall. Why hasn't she called me?

Powders for preening feathers were not imported this far south, so I felt rather unwashed. I fiddled with the red plaid cloak they had given me, because it kept slipping down. The rough wool was unbearably scratchy and I was not at all sure that I had folded it correctly.

I first saw Savory – the doyenne of hoydens – at the front, sitting on a bench outside a pavilion, waxing her bowstring. I was struck that moment by love's arrows, and they sank their barbs deep beneath my skin. The first arrow was her beauty; it entered through my eyes and from there to my heart, where nothing I could do would extract it. The second was her simplicity, her few belongings, her careless mode of life. Like all the Cathee she lived within her skin as if it was someone else's coat she may well have to pawn for her next meal. The third arrow was my own memory, of Martyn, because Savory had the same fox-red hair. Unbraided, it tumbled on her shoulders, pooled on her lap. Its tips brushed the backs of her knees as she sat with one leg over the other, massaging linseed oil into the risers of her bow. From that instant I was her willing servant; my heart belonged unreservedly to her.

Savory had seen the seasons, slept outdoors and laboured hard. Martyn, on the other hand, had skin as pale and clean as split sycamore wood. Martyn was taller than any forester and Savory did not have her upright bearing, but Savory's sparkling, little-girl lightness shone through her experience of harsh realities – like cultivated flowers in a garden grown wild.

Savory had left Morenzia owing to a blood feud between her family and another in the village. It had whittled down her family until she was the last. The forest had nothing wholesome to offer her, so she joined the fyrd and led a division of Cathee woodsmen, the best archers outside Awia. I pieced this together from her broken language, because I could not speak Morenzian. I yearned for a word that we could share, that might begin our courtship, and for agonising weeks I stayed silent and watched from afar.

She taught me her language over six months, though I remained hesitant and only Savory could fathom my accent. She had heard of Lightning in old legends, but they were rarely accurate and she only half-believed they were about me. I tried to impress upon her how different her life would be from now on but, having never seen my palace, how could she understand? She was strong enough to break through my reserve. After all, it had been a hundred years since I had ...

I loved her the more because she did not hang back, afraid. Her antics made me laugh. She was not so headstrong as to ignore my sincere advances.

Neither was she afraid of the depth of my devotion, retreating into reserve of her own. She reciprocated. I would have given her roses if we hadn't been stranded at the front. She would have found herself with half of my estate. So then, I asked her to marry me, as composedly as I was able, although I felt like froth inside, like bubbles in Stenasrai wine.

She hung on my arm and looked up, all smiles as she consented. She did love me as I loved her! If perfection blooms only once in a thousand years, that's enough, because I can pick that bloom and it will live the next thousand years too, and on into forever. Constancy is rewarded, I know that much.

'Saker!' Her voice broke the silence. It rang out with confidence above the rustle of roosting birds. 'Saker Micawater!' She called me to the stone. I rearranged the uncomfortable cloak one last time and hurried out.

Savory stood outside next to the cup-and-ring stone. She was an indistinct figure in the dusk, her hands and face pale patches. As I drew nearer I saw her face was painted with henna: red dots with concentric circles on both her cheeks. Her hair hung in long red braids either side of her face. A plaid cloak pinned at her shoulders reached the ground, and beneath, a short simple cambric dress with a girdle. On her forearms and lower legs she wore half-armour for me. The glittering vambraces and greaves showed her limbs' slender curves. The contrast between the hard, warm metal and her soft yielding skin made me desperate to touch her. All along her arms and legs she had daubed the double black stripes of Cathee war paint and her first two fingers were still stained from where she had dipped them and drawn them over her skin.

The dark and glossy smell of wet pine needles was all around, acidic and medicinal, almost like liquorice. The trees' straight boles stood close together as if at attention. Above them, a crescent moon hung like a cutlass in a sky so dark blue it appeared purple.

The cup-and-ring stone was as tall as my chest, a natural rock pushing up from the soil and penny-coloured fallen needles. It was rough-grained and uneven at the edges. The cup-and-ring had been carved on its sloping top many centuries ago, Savory had said, perhaps even before the Empire was established. Though privately I doubted that it could be so old.

In the centre was a shallow round cup, surrounded by five concentric rings, the pattern you see if you drop a pebble in the lake. The carvings had long since taken on the red rock's patina. From the cup in the centre a channel had been carved, deeper as it cut through the rings, to the edge of the rock. The cup was therefore a tiny basin with a drainage conduit.

I did not study it for long. I only had eyes for my painted warrior bride, and she smiled at me but we must not speak a word. My heart beat fast and I was suffused with warmth and exultation. I would take her from here to the Castle to kiss the Emperor's hand and then we would live together forever!

Savory drew her skinning knife from her belt scabbard. It had been polished and it gleamed. She raised her right hand, the fingers spread wide, the vulnerable palm showing. She pressed the point to the ball of her thumb and it slid under her skin. A dark stripe sprang up. Blood ran shining, down her wrist. Savory fisted her hand and dripped it into the hollow of the cup.

She passed the knife to me with a solemn nod. I did not take it: the occasion required a grander gesture. I drew my short sword and held it horizontally. Savory's eyes widened. Hastening to reassure her, I grasped the blade in front of me and slid my hand along it. I felt it bite. My signet ring zipped on the surface; my hand became warm and slick. A trail of blood shrank on the oiled metal into a thin line of crimson beads. I did not let the pain show on my face. I curled up my hand as she had done and let the drops fall into the cup until our blood, mixed together, breached the level, ran down the conduit and began dripping on the ground.

Quickly we held our wounded hands under the flow and felt drops patter on our cut palms.

Still separate, still without speaking, I yearned to hold her. The strength of my desire was close to desperation: *I couldn't go without touching her for any longer.* She produced some cloth and bandaged my hand tenderly, and I bound hers.

She nodded. 'Now we may speak.'

'I love you,' I said simply. I spread my wings completely around her. In our feathered sanctuary we found ourselves looking into each other's eyes, and were trapped there. I whispered, 'What would you have me do for you?'

She found it hard to say anything at all.

'Kiss me.'

She tilted her head upward and touched my lips with hers. I smiled and returned the gesture. She took two handfuls of my cloak and pulled me down to the bloodstained grass. We consummated our marriage there.

Savory stepped happily, leading me along the meagre track. Hatchet nicks on tree trunks marked the way. Among the scuffed fallen needles, the forest's myriad little white flowers had their petals closed.

We went through the gate and into the village. A huge bonfire was blazing in the middle of its clearing. The villagers rushed hand in hand in a boisterous, whirling dance around the fire, in and out of the houses in a long, crazed chain, wherever the maiden at the front chose to lead them. Their uncouth music flickered like a flame up and down an insensible scale; it seemed to have no timing, no beginning, no middle; it ended abruptly and started again. Seeing me staring, the guitarist grinned and plucked with his dirty fingers a most ideal arpeggio.

Some men were digging out a pit in which they'd roasted a wild boar. Five hours ago they had built a fire in a cobble-lined pit, let it burn to heat the stones, then put out the fire. They had laid in the carcass and buried it to cook. Now their spades scraped on hot cobbles, they thrust them underneath and lifted up the boar. They cheered and shovelled it out onto a trestle table. I caught a glimpse of golden crackling and flesh as brown and shining as mahogany. Whole branches of rosemary had been wrapped around it which had cooked onto the skin like fragile and blackened embroidery.

A delicious aroma drifted over. A shout went up, the chain of dancers broke and ran towards the roast pig. They crowded and shoved around the table.

Firelight pulsed and merged, making yellow and hollow beasts of their faces. They tore at the crunchy skin and ripped it away to the hot meat. Juices ran between their clawed fingers. They shoved it into their mouths – round black holes – and while they chewed, they flailed both hands to grab more. Boys and women turned away with fistfuls of stringy meat. Still more villagers arrived to join the frenzy. More and more came running and pressed themselves close around the table. Outside the circle of firelight the village lay empty. As the meat stripped away it became pinker, the white fat was bubbling. They dug their fingers into it, split the carcass apart. They dragged it up and down the table, opened it up. With a warm rip they detached a leg and they jostled into two clusters, a smaller group around the leg wiping it this way and that on the table top as they pulled off the shreds of flesh, holding them preciously until they had enough for a mouthful.

I felt awkward. I was ravenously hungry but was I expected to shoulder between them? I couldn't bring myself to. I didn't want to touch them.

The villagers drew back. They regarded the table: the bones lay stripped clean. Women shrugged and walked away, licking grease from their fingers. Such a show made me feel sick – they had taken less than five minutes to demolish the boar.

One man was so drunk he staggered towards the pit without seeing it in the darkness, a blacker rectangle on the shifting grey ground. He fell straight in. Then, finding the ashes still warm, he turned on his back looking satisfied up at the overcast sky and went to sleep.

A woodcutter at the table unbuckled his axe. He cracked open the bones with a few deft blows, and the villagers set to again on the marrow.

Savory jigged up to me, a succulent earthy smell of roast boar on her breath and an oily shine at the corners of her mouth. She had torn mouthfuls of it with her teeth. She looked surprised, then annoyed: 'Didn't you have any?'

'I couldn't get close.'

'Ay! What will they think, that you haven't tasted your own marriage feast?'

She lead me to the edge of the clearing, in front of their log cabins that all face inward. Some bear skins were spread on the damp grass in front of the reeve's cabin.

'Sit down there, my love; I'll go and bring you some. Smoked pig, baked spuds and pine beer! Isn't that a feast for an Awian lord?' She kissed my cheek and ran lightly towards the smokehouse.

I watched the party. A travelling troupe were enacting a raucous play. The villagers still paid me little heed and took it to be as much for their benefit as for the bride and groom's honour. That was of no consequence; I sat and watched happily. I couldn't understand a word, but I recognised it as a familiar play based on an incident I remembered well. Some five hundred years ago, the Castle's Master of Horse was beaten in a Challenge. He lost his place in the Circle but in the following years his devoted wife practised so much that she was able to beat the new incumbent and win immortality again for them both. Such is the strength of love.

In amongst the mummers, children kicked the embers for baked potatoes. I looked around at the few windowless log cabins, thatched with pine branches held down by netting. Big stone weights dangled from them, all carved in the shapes of animals: beavers, cockerels and squirrels. Every doorway had a beaming white plaster face mounted above it.

The reeve's house was behind me and, on either side of its door, bas-relief sculptures of naked women adjoined the wall. They were life-sized in smooth plaster, so white they seemed to glow.

By the woodpile a big cooking pot hung on a thick chain from a tripod. It was smeared with the remains of hide glue, in which boar nets had been dipped to make them stickier. The enormous twine nets were draped on A-frames. All Cathee villages trap wild boar and carry them to Vertigo to be salted, barrelled, and sold as salt pork to the caravels.

The play was ending and, as usual with dramas of that nature, my character turned up to sort everything out. I was smiling at the actor playing Lightning, when from the corner of my eye I saw two men at the far end of the clearing. They caught my attention because they were skulking at the edge of the firelight. They had a similarity; maybe a father and his grown son.

They began to walk purposefully towards the smokehouse. Was this part of the play? Their faces were masked with determination. As people noticed them, they fell silent and it stirred a sense of menace. I felt the crowd's expectation. Should I be doing something?

The men walked behind the bonfire; its rising heat rippled their figures, and where they passed, people turned aside and the party fell silent. The villagers near me watched, fearful eyes most white and nostrils flared. The two men reached the smokehouse, and axes appeared in their hands! They were wearing cuirasses!

The blood feud! I jumped up and dashed into the reeve's house. From the rack I grabbed my crossbow and a bandolier of bolts.

The backs of the axe men were disappearing through the smokehouse door. I frantically wound the cranequin, but my wound reopened and my hand shook badly. I raised the bow and shot at the father. The bolt snicked into the log wall; the man turned and looked at me, then ducked inside. I *missed*. I was struck stock-still in shock. I *don't* miss. I *never* miss. I can't remember the last time I missed!

I lost sight of him inside the smokehouse. There was no time to reload. I started to run to Savory, but a second later the men were out of the door. They tore across the clearing, eyes popping, fists punching in front of their chests. What had they done to her?

They passed some distance in front of me, their axes flashing in their hands. From their other hands dangled longbow strings. I had seen enough of the world to know they are used as garrottes.

I tried to spin the cranequin back but the strength had gone completely from my cut hand, as if it didn't belong to me. *Click-click, click-click* was all I could get out of the damned mechanism as it rocked back and forth on one ratchet. The men had reached the gate. A woman of their family pulled it open. They sped into the forest and it swallowed them.

I yelled and sprinted into the smokehouse. Where was Savory? Hanging hams swung at my touch as I felt my way between the drying racks. My wife's white dress was a spectral smudge. She lay face-down on the pressed earth floor. I knelt next to her. The back of her neck was cut across cleanly with one axe blow. There did not seem to be much blood.

I jumped up and dashed after the murderers. As I passed the bonfire I threw in the crossbow, in a flurry of yellow sparks. Who talked me into using that thing? If I had my longbow, I could have put seven arrows through them in the thirty seconds they took to cross my field of vision.

I dashed through the gate and into the prickly frustration of the forest's edge. Their fleeing footsteps crackled far in front of me, deep between the trees. The cold leather of my sword grip was damp in my hand.

I saw pale flashes heading downhill. By god, the bastards were signalling at me! But it was only the reflection of the bonfire on their back plates and it soon vanished.

I found myself surrounded by a wall of fretted branches, hard cones, bending needles. They clutched my clothes but I pushed further and further in. Shadows and twigs looked like they could be ... but they weren't, when

I got closer. I could hardly judge distances, over the nettles and around snarled brambles. Where the trees grew more densely packed, the ground was clear and springy with needles. I couldn't see in the low space under the branches; it was pitch-black.

I ducked down and hesitated, trying to catch my breath. All was silent. The murderers could be anywhere; without faithful Lymer I would never find them. They had gone to earth, and even if I flushed them the forest was their world and they might have picked up longbows. I was more lost than I have ever been. I listened carefully, but I only heard wolf howls muted in the far distance.

The village's bonfire backlit the trees. Numbly, I turned and stumbled to the palisade, to the clearing, and into the smokehouse, to Savory. Those craven murderers knew she could have beaten them, with her skinning knife and the desperation of self-defence, had they faced her. They had cut her down as she knelt to slice meat onto my plate.

As my dear wife fell she had upset a sack of kindling and there were pieces of bark all over her. I cleared them away and I turned her over. She was ghastly cold. I used my cloak for a pillow and closed her glazed hazel eyes gently. I kissed dear Savory.

The pointlessness of it unhinged me. I jumped up suddenly and ran out of the smokehouse, but the village was deserted. Everybody had bolted into their homes and wedged shut the boards serving as doors. 'Savory is slain!' I shouted. 'Help me find the murderers!'

From inside came small sounds that told me they were busy with other tasks. They were hinting that I should stop causing a disturbance, stop bawling and go away. I stared around the clearing: the bonfire burnt down to a red ember murmur; a clutch of boar ribs on the table; an overturned cup on the bruised grass. Nothing indicated that minutes ago this had been a lively party.

I ran from cabin to cabin banging on the blank doors. 'Help! Help me for god's sake!' But I could not speak the language properly; nor they mine. I hammered on the reeve's door. 'You know me, Asart! We must catch the murderers!' No answer from within. I clapped my hand flat over the sun brooch on my shoulder. 'In the Castle's name, I'm her husband! Tell me who the murderers are! I'll bring my fyrd! Damn you all – help me or I'll raze this village to the ground!'

What was I doing here? Here in the back of beyond? I should never have come to this filthy, tree-dark province at all. These folk had no inkling of my power. My palace where one of their daughters would have lived was no more than a tale to them. They valued their murderous traditions more highly than the distant Castle itself. Here I was the foreigner and how could they understand? With all the time in eternity I would not get through to them! I lost my mind and I curled up, faint, beside the fire.

At first light people emerged from their houses and went about their daily chores as if nothing had happened. I lay on my stomach on the wet grass watching abstractedly. They spoke not a word of Savory. They shut the events away and went on with tapping sap and lathing wood. How could they – when the world was shattered?

Years of blood feuds had bred in them a toleration like a collective sickness of the mind. They were quiet and cowed, but acted as if the random murder was fair and justified. She had been, after all, a Savory. Father Savory killed Pannage and was killed by Pannage's grandson. So it went on. So it still goes on today.

Day only truly dawned on the village when the sun rose above the trees and slanted its rays down into the little enclosure. The dew began to vanish, though it remained, grey and sparkling, in the cobwebs, the palisade's shadow and each hovel's woodpile.

Two men, their sleeves rolled back, went into the smokehouse and brought out Savory on a stretcher. She was naked. They had stripped her naked. I felt a jolt as if I had been punched. My legs went weak but I stumbled to her and tried to cover her body with the cloak. The men put their arms out and blocked me. She was a pale sculpture, she lay on her long hair like a pelt, as red as the hair on her legs and sex. I had last seen her naked when – I had kissed her thighs and breasts – their disrespect was too much for me. 'I'll take her back to Awia! I'll place her in my tomb!'

My pleas were cut short by the high squeal of a fiddle and a flute. The door of the nearest cabin flung open and the troupe of mummers tumbled out. They started dancing! They began to dance the old, false story where the King of Morenzia steals the King of Awia's wife and Awia raises its fyrd to bring her back. The dancers whirled furiously around Savory's stretcher, stamping either side as they acted out the battle. The King of Awia was mock-stabbed by the human king, and he fell. The dancers all jumped on the fallen actor, their hands scrambling under his clothes. They brought out real human bones, all dry and painted black, and began to dance with them, clacking them together.

What did it mean? I had no idea but the dishonour was too much. I drew my sword and was about to set among them and slay every last man, when the reeve came out of his house.

He was wearing a mask. It was a human visage, of heavy white plaster, as if his own face had been smeared with thick paste, but for its blind eye sockets, in which were placed cowry shells. Their pursed toothy grooves made blind black lines. In the mouth of the mask real human teeth were set. No, not set: the mask was the front of a real skull, sawn off and covered

769

in plaster. The rest of his clothes were normal and he came towards me walking confidently, as if he could see through some hidden contrivance in the mask.

Savory had introduced me to reeve Asart, the village leader, answerable to Lord Governor Aver-Falconet. He reports to Aver-Falconet's steward twice a year. Why was he part of this abhorrent dance? Did Hacilith know? Did the Castle know? Of course they must, I wrested from myself. I am the only one ignorant of the Cathee, because nothing like this is written in the books of Awia's libraries.

The rest of the village left their work or emerged from their cabins silently, as if at an agreed signal. The women in short shifts and rawhide aprons, the men in their plaids and breeches, they formed a silent queue behind the stretcher.

I stared around the log cabins, and now I could more clearly see their ornamentation. The heads above the doors were real skulls! They were covered in plaster, shells set in their eye sockets, and affixed with paste all around them to the surface of the logs. Their snaggling yellow teeth showed between carefully moulded lips.

I looked to the reeve's house. The sculptures that I had taken to be women were whole articulated skeletons re-fleshed with plaster. It had flaked off here and there; I saw brittle weathered bone underneath. Their curves and features had been shaped, but where the breasts swelled over some woman's ancient rib-cage, projecting instead of nipples from the plaster were the hooked and open beaks of vultures.

The reeve had by now left the gate and the rest were following. I stumbled behind, some distance from the rear of the procession. I had to see where they were taking Savory. The reeve, villagers and mummers still carrying bagpipes, flutes and bones pushed between the trees on a little-worn path, in complete silence.

We were walking uphill, but I could tell no more. All the forest looked the same to me and I could scarcely see it. My eyes were stinging, I was weeping freely, and trying to see through my tears as through an awash uneven glass. Savory was a white blur as the procession wound between the close phalanxes of dark green pines on either side. The twisting brambles at the trackside scratched me, held me back, and snatched loops of thread out of the damn plaid cloak.

At length we came to a clearing, and beyond the screen of trees I glimpsed a gigantic mound, grassed-over equally with the ground. It must be man-made because it was completely circular, some ten metres across and surrounded by flat black stones propped up against its circumference. Three huge undressed rocks at the front formed a portal, one resting horizontally on two uprights, from which a tunnel lined with slabs led into its lightless depths. A single stone, standing a metre in front of the entrance, obscured the passageway from my sight. I assumed this was their crude mausoleum, like my great family tomb, in which they would lay dear Savory, but the procession did not stop.

The villagers cast glances at the knoll as they passed by, with looks on their faces almost as if it reassured them – and even the reeve's skull mask turned towards it for an instant.

The forest was now alive with birds cawing and skitterings in the undergrowth. I took the arm of the last man in the procession, who carried his toddler son on his shoulders: 'What's going on? Tell me, man!'

He shook me away with an angry sneer.

A great cloud of birds burst up out of the trees ahead, cracking through twigs and branches. They separated out; kites and buzzards began to circle but the big glossy ravens dropped back down into the tree tops further on.

A terrible stench of corruption rose with them and hit me with such strength I gagged. It was the fatty smell of putrefying human flesh, which I have often encountered on the battlefield. The villagers showed no concern. I pulled my handkerchief from my trouser pocket and pressed it over my nose.

We came up to a high log palisade, but the silence and the smell told me this was not another village. Its gate had a woman's skeleton plastered to the centre. Its eye sockets shone dully with cowry shells and all its teeth were bared between open lips. Again, its breasts were sculpted with panting beaks instead of nipples.

The Cathee entered an enclosure where the short grass was free of saplings and in the centre a great wooden scaffold stood two metres high: a platform raised on six trunks stripped clean of bark. The top of the platform was not solid, it was a criss-cross of rough-hewn timbers. Shreds hung down between them. At first I thought the shreds were fabric but they did not move with the breeze. A large strip dangled through the grating, tasselled at the end – it was a human arm and hand.

They set down the stretcher next to the platform and gathered along it, standing in ragged fashion side by side. I remained in the shadow of the gate and watched.

The reeve stood by Savory's head. She looked so peaceful, as if she was asleep, were it not for the outrage of her nakedness. The reeve climbed a rough ladder of logs, up to the platform and appeared high above us against the sky. He crossed towards the villagers looking up, but as he did so he accidentally kicked the arm. It was mostly bone, it swung and fell off, and up stirred the rank smell of carrion. My gorge rose and I hunched over and

771

vomited. What were they doing to my wife? I fell to my knees and heaved again and again – till it hollowed me out.

They did not hand up the whole stretcher. There were no ropes nor pulley to raise it to the top of the platform with any sort of dignity. The two bearers just picked up Savory's body, one holding her ankles, the other her upper arms. He grappled with handfuls of her hair. Stiffness had set in and they had to turn her body as they lifted her. I saw in a flash the pink line of her sex between her legs. The masked reeve bent and seized her round the ribs, manhandled her onto the platform and laid her down.

And then he descended and walked underneath the scaffold, beckoning the villagers to join him. They huddled together, bent over, and began to pick bones and teeth from among the grass. The women folded their skirts and gathered them inside, the men cradled handfuls. Up and down they walked in methodical lines as if harvesting, and any man who found two bones still articulated, pulled them apart with a twist and a yank.

They piled all the bones on the stretcher, and in silent procession like before, they carried the stretcher out past me, though I was on my knees and coughing up bile. I shrank from them but I had to follow or in their stony blindness they would have barred me in with the dead. The first few heavy ravens were swooping down with guttural calls from the trees to feed.

I trailed some distance behind the procession to the mouth of the burial mound. They stopped by its portal, in a semi-circle. The reeve and stretcher-bearers slipped behind the stone screen and into the tunnel. They must have intended to deposit the bones in there.

I had seen enough. I spat and turned away, deranged. I ran back to the village, where I took a bow, a quiver-full of arrows and a spade. If any of the Cathee had tried to stop me I would have cleaved his head in two with it.

So they would take Savory, my Savory, and leave her to rot, feed her to vermin, then jumble her bones with everyone else's? So they wanted to obliterate her identity until no one could recognise her remains? So they were content to forget her unique, intriguing life? What did that mean? What sort of people scrub out the honour of their ancestors? Their disrespect tore at my heart, cracked open and bleeding inside me. Savory is still a person, still my love. What is she to the Cathee? An empty vessel? No longer a woman, just an object that's part of their past, that they will place with the rest and tidy away so life can go on? My life could not go on. My life had stopped. I thought of what we Awians do, with our glass carriages drawn by ebony-plumed horses. I thought of the vigil I kept over Mother's lying-in-state, a drawn sword in front of me and my wings spread. How we exhibited the old bat as if she could still feel, in satin on the catafalque strewn with lilac and lavender and rue.

I could not leave Savory there to rot. I was furious with myself, my jaw clenched so hard my head was pounding, my fingers rubbing over the dirty bandage around my palm. I *missed*. I missed my *target*. I fouled a shot with a crossbow. I went over and over it in my head, unable to comprehend how that could be. When blood began to seep through my bandage I welcomed it as a punishment and a reality.

She will not be crows' food up there on that *platform*. I kicked my way into the enclosure and scaled the ladder. Corpses were arranged lying on their backs all over the timber grid: naked old men and women, some babies, and a dried puddle of a foetus. Some were the maimed fragments of fellow warriors that the Cathee fyrd had managed to ship home from Insect battles. They were in various stages of decomposition and most had lost the small bones of their fingers and toes already through the grid. Some skulls lolled back, disconnected and eye sockets staring at the sky. One was bloated, but most were pecked to no more than skeletons pasted with dark red shreds of sinew and muscle. Green algae grew on the cups of their vertebrae. The ravens had started already on Savory's hazel eyes. I quickly picked her up and, hugging her to my chest, carried her down the ladder.

I bore her in my arms to the clearing with the marriage stone. *Savory, it will make shift for the only monument I can give you here. But you will have a monument, my hunting lady. You don't belong with those people any more.* I raised the spade and speared it into the earth with all my strength. *You are not one of them.* I turned over the tangled roots and soil.

I dug Savory a grave where we first made love. The cup-and-ring stone was her headstone, and I did cheat the villagers of their foul ritual. I covered her tenderly and then I lay down beside the grave and embraced my arm over the little mound of disturbed earth. I do not know how many days I lay there.

I do not remember leaving her side. I must have walked east through the forest for days to the coast. I must have lived on the game I shot, but whether or not I could still shoot I cannot recall. I was absent all that time. At Vertigo, the town built against the sheer walls of a deep chasm, someone gave me passage on a ship for Awia. I returned to my house at a gallop and ordered the gates locked and chained. I wrote no letters and spent no time on the archery field. I accepted no visitors and ignored the Messenger's frantic queries. I waited for my hand and a shredded heart to heal.

CHAPTER 20

Some time after Lightning left the meeting, it ended and the Eszai dispersed. Over the next five days I flew errands for them. Each evening I had piles of correspondence to digest and report to the Emperor; mostly badly spelled semaphore transcripts.

I returned to my desk in the corner of the hall. I started writing but I could hardly concentrate. I kept wondering about Cyan's Challenge and Lightning's strange behaviour. I stared at the piles of letters, under the glass jam-jar of worms I was using as a paperweight. The worms didn't seem to be moving very much. I leant forward and peered at them. They were all limp and flaccid, coating the bottom of the jar. I picked it up and shook it, and they put out a pink, braided-together tentacle and tapped on the glass.

The worms arced up in the middle and raised two perpendicular strands. A sagging worm swung across from one to the other and joined halfway up. It looked like the letter H. It collapsed back into the feebly writhing mass. Weakly they sent up another string from which three comb-like projections shot out: E. A single thread with a right angle of worms at the base: L; and it summoned its energies for a thick strand that curled round on itself at the top: P.

I picked up my paperknife and poked some holes in the lid. The worms sprang to life, stretched up eagerly forcing their tiny mouths against the underside. They pushed ineffectually at it, swaying like animated hair.

They dropped down and started swirling around the jar, in one direction like water going down a plughole. They became a whirlpool of worms, riding up the inside of the glass with an indentation in the middle. I thought they were trying to push the glass apart so I gave it a shake and they slumped again. They started throwing up angry tendrils so quickly I could scarcely make one letter out before it was replaced by the next. An L, an E and a T. Let. A U, an S and an O. What? A U and a T. Us Out. Let us out. Y-O-U-B-A-S-T-A-R-D.

'There's no need for that,' I said, and placed the jar back on top of my correspondence. The Vermiform furiously started cycling letters. As it warmed to its task it threw up whole tiny words, the letters made of one or two worms apiece.

L-E-T-U-S-O-U-T
L-E-T-U-S-O-U-T

I signed a missive, blew on the ink, folded the paper. I dropped some sealing wax on it and embossed it with the garnet sun emblem seal which I wear as a pendant.

L-E-T-U-S-O-U-T

LET! US! OUT!

PLEASE

'That's better,' I said, and was about to flip the jar's clips when I was struck by a thought. 'If I free you, promise you won't harm me?'

The worms paused.

'All right,' I said. 'You're staying in there.'

I looked up across the hall and saw Rayne approaching, carrying an envelope. I didn't want her to see that I had stolen her sample of Vermiform worms so I picked up the jar and slipped it into the big pocket of my coat folded under the table.

Rayne looked over my shoulder. 'You're transcribing code,' she observed.

'It's shorthand. What can I do for you?'

She offered me the letter in her clean, smooth palm. 'Could you take this t' Cyan?'

'Are you sure? It's nearly midnight.'

'Jant, think of wha' she mus' be going through up in t' peel tower. She knows she's made a fool of herself.'

'Well, I'm not sympathetic.'

Rayne nodded sagely. 'Neither am I, bu' I do like her. She's a smar' girl. When t' Circle broke three times, we were in t' coach between Slaugh'erbridge and Eske. Cyan consoled me. I'm grateful for tha'. We talked all nigh'. Can you take i' now? I'm up t' *here* with work in t' hospi'al.'

I stood up and gathered my coat. 'Of course.'

The full moon's light basted the surrounding moorland grey and smooth. Like a ball of butter, it rolled along the top of a platter of thick, opaque cloud and lit up the margins from behind with a creamy glow. Silver noctilucent clouds hung in the western sky over the foothills; the last light ebbing from their thin streaks gave enough illumination for me to see Insects hunting by scent in the valley.

Small bats were fluttering in circuits around the top of the peel tower. I could hear their squeaks as they passed me.

I have had planks nailed out from the window ledges of each peel tower's uppermost room. I swept up to this one and touched down on the end. The plank bent like a diving board. I shuffled up to the shutters of the bow windows in the hoarding. The shutters, as large as gates, were closed. I splayed both hands on the splintered and weathered wood, bent down and put my eye to the crack.

Cyan stomped past the slit, lit by a lantern outside my field of vision. She disappeared and then stamped back again. She was muttering to herself and biting the end of a pen.

I knocked on the shutters and she looked up. She rushed over and pushed them wide. They flew open and hit me in the face. A brief whirl of the sky; I flapped my wings powerfully, cart-wheeling my arms. I toppled off the plank, caught its edge with both hands, and dangled there for an instant before I kicked my legs, flexed my arms and drew myself up again.

'Careful!' I hissed. 'You nearly broke my nose!'

'Good!' said Cyan, and drew the shutters to. I pulled them wide and stepped down into the room.

The tower-top room was big, ten metres square. A single bed and side table by the fireplace were the only furnishings apart from empty crossbow bolt racks on the walls. It was ill-lit, no fire burning in the huge stone grate, but lamplight shone up through holes in the floor, through which arrow sheaves could be hoisted. Cyan's lantern gave a pool of colour on the table next to her silver plate and fork and a chessboard that seemed to have stalled halfway through a game.

Lightning's dog rushed up from the bed, barking, then recognised me and sat down by my feet. I closed my wings, the primaries sliding over each other like fans. 'I only have an hour.' I said. 'I shouldn't be here.'

'Well, I've been trying to write to you for hours,' Cyan retorted. 'Where have you been? What's going on? No one's visited me. I haven't spoken to anyone except the guards for five days!' She retreated to sit on the plain bed, leaning on a blanket roll against the wall, and gave me a baleful look. 'Will you let me out?'

'I'm sorry, Cyan; no. The least the Castle can do is save your life.'

'You could rescind Daddy's orders if you wanted, and the guards would release me. Why are you so afraid of him?'

'I'm not.'

Her forehead furrowed. 'After the guards dragged me out, what happened? What did Daddy say? ... No, don't tell me. I hate him. Old titwart. I can't believe he's done this to me!'

I stalked across the room, pushed my ice axe hanger behind me and sat down on the fireplace surround. I ached all over and I felt sick. The constant undercurrent of panic and sleep deprivation we were all living with was taking its toll. I said, 'I brought a letter from Rayne.'

'One letter in five days!'

'You don't know how hard-pressed we are—' I gestured at the window in the direction of the town. 'Everyone's terrified and San is driving us like pack horses. I've been sending dispatches to position battalions for the advance in two days. I spent the last hour fending off journalists and checking Lord

Governor Purlin Brandoch's cavalry slinking in on second-rate nags. In an hour's time I have to collect letters for your father—'

'Huh!' she cried.

'—Hand-deliver the important ones and collect replies. I think I'll report that you're still furious.'

'I'm fine,' she said, not looking it.

'Do you have a message for him?'

She glared at me defiantly. 'If the bastard is in a good mood, tell him I'm dying of melancholy. If he's feeling miserable, tell him I'm singing like a lark.'

'I can't fathom what mood he's in. He's bottled everything up, and he seems very detached, as if he isn't allowing himself to think about it.'

I pulled a sheaf of letters from my coat pocket and leafed through until I found Rayne's envelope. Cyan accepted it and scratched the seal off with her fingernails.

'Is Rayne the only person who's thought of me?' she asked.

'Don't be ridiculous. No. Hasn't Lightning given you his dog for company? He's been sending you the best food, otherwise you'd be eating biscuit and salt beef, like the rest of the Zascai.'

'So he hasn't forgotten me?'

'No. He's incredibly busy too.' I sighed, wondering how I could make her understand what was happening. 'This is the biggest advance of all time. When they start lining up in formation, you'll see what I mean.'

Cyan lay back on the bed. 'I tried to write to you but I couldn't concentrate. I made a complete arse of myself.'

'Yes, you did. I wish I'd—'

'Oh, I don't care what you'd have done. I wasn't Challenging you.' She put an arm across her eyes and said, 'Pissflaps. Will you let me free, Jant; please?'

'Look, Lightning put you in here for a reason. If I let you out, and you get killed, he would shoot me. If through your actions, you get someone else killed, I would be blamed. And I don't fancy that.'

'It's like being in prison!'

I stared at her. Her truculent tone was beginning to pique. 'Trust me, it's nothing like being in prison.'

'Oh, Jant's *angry*.'

'Stop that! Behaving like a ten-year-old is what landed you in here.'

'*Please* set me free. I'll reward you. I'll give you—'

'It won't happen, so don't try to tempt me.'

The deerhound leapt on the bed and Cyan took its head in her lap. 'Good dog, Lymer.'

I knew she had never really seriously considered joining the Circle.

Everybody harbours a secret wish to be immortal. Everyone, now and then, wonders what it would be like. But like most people Cyan had never genuinely entertained the thought, and I bet, in her head, she keeps repeating over and over what she did and imagines the Eszai laughing at her.

I knelt down with a cheerful air and began to build a fire in the grate, refusing to be overwhelmed by the awkward situation. Cyan watched me with animal antipathy.

I said, 'I recognise a spur-of-the-moment Challenge when I see it. All Eszai recognise bluster, too. We're often Challenged by people who know they're not capable of beating us but simply want the attention. By the Castle's rules we have to take each and every one seriously, and separately, because you never know when one is a true talent ...'

'I *don't* withdraw my Challenge, if that's what you're driving at.'

I gathered handfuls of the dried moor grass, heather sprigs and sprays of thyme strewn as a floor covering. I used them for kindling and lit some skilfully with the last of my matches. I swung the kettle spit above the flames and began to make some coffee.

'Rayne was recently Challenged,' I continued. 'By a healer, some Awian noblewoman. High Awian is a useless language for science, and Rachiswater university mainly teaches arts. They're not far behind Hacilith though. This woman believed in the properties of precious metals to cure diseases. She made gold mirrors and shone light into the patients' eyes. It was no laughing matter ... her bedside manner was so good many patients were cured by their own expectations. Rayne set her a Challenge at the front, and she learned that no shiny mirrors or soothing music can stuff a patient's guts back in.' I shrugged. 'Only three places in the Circle have never changed hands: Rayne's, Tornado's and your father's. Everybody who Challenges them makes a fool of himself. You're not the only one.'

'It was his fault,' she said. 'He pushed me to it. In front of the Emperor and everything.'

'Cyan, I've better things to do with my free hour than talk with a stroppy cow.'

'Please tell the guards to release me.'

'No. After seeing you make an exhibition of yourself and humiliate Lightning, even though I told you to sit down, I'm surprised I'm here at all.'

'I don't regret it,' she said.

'He's been the best archer for over fourteen hundred years!' I tried to make her understand that length of time. 'Awndyn didn't exist when he was mortal. Or Peregrine. They didn't have highways, they didn't even have coaches. They used to have ballistae and now we have espringals, thanks to the effort of San knows how many Artillerists. Lightning improved bows, from the early awful type they had before the Circle, to the shit-hot bows you use now. He's lived through all this, and been on top all the time! It's as much his day now as it was then. So it's bloody stupid to Challenge him.'

''Spose you're right.'

'He's seen the four corners of the world … Five, including Tris.'

'In the past, though. He lives in the past. And Swallow lives in the future – but I live in the present.' She got up and crouched in front of the fire, rubbing some warmth back into her hands. 'He hasn't been a father to me at all. He's been more of a father to you than to me.'

'Not really. I—'

'That's what he is, your substitute father. It makes me sick how you're blind to his faults.'

'Nonsense.'

'Yeah, well why are you defending him so much?'

'I don't need a father. I survived by myself for years in Hacilith. Worse than anything you've seen. And—' I swept a hand, rattling the bangles around my wrist '—for example, these peel towers. I won a battle myself at the furthest one, at Summerday in nineteen ninety-three. Yours truly and Shearwater Mist beat the Insects before Lightning had even ridden out of Awia. We were the only Eszai in command; the brains and the brawn.'

'Which one of you was the brains?'

'Me! Damn it.' I poured hot water into two cups of coffee. 'Mist was bitten through the shoulder and I had to look after him almost as much as the Zascai.'

'I wish I could be involved in something like that.'

I would have laughed if she had led with a trace of humour in her voice. 'You're not joking, are you?'

'No, I'm not … I want out.'

'Stay here, Cyan. Insects are running everywhere. These towers provide enough shelter to last a swarm. There are rainwater butts on the roof and enough stores in the cellar.'

She said, 'I've been watching the archers drill all afternoon. I can see everything from up here. Daddy was riding up and down in front of the ranks as if he'd forgotten me. There are two enormous women soldiers guarding me and all the money stored here. Not men, worse luck; "Bitchback and Nobless" from Midelspass.'

'Really?'

'Mm. They don't pass on my messages. They don't listen to me, even.'

'Wonder where Lightning got them from?'

'I don't know but they adore him. They're so desperate that if they knew a man was up here they'd strip-search you … And the lake reeks,' she went on. 'All day when the wind was gusting I could smell it.'

She pushed Lymer aside and lifted the chessboard onto her knees. 'Do you want a game?'

'Huh? No, I don't know how to play.'

'In all this time, you haven't learnt chess?'

'No. Can you fend off wolves using only a sling?'

'No.'

'Well then.'

'I'll teach you,' she said.

'It's a stupid game. I can't think of one good reason for it, and besides, my time's nearly up.'

'You mean you don't have the patience.'

I picked a lancer and offered it to her, but palmed it so Cyan found herself grasping at empty air. She giggled. I placed it back with a click on the board. 'Check! Now, why don't you read Rayne's letter ? She likes you.'

'Yeah, I like her too ... but I find her accent a bit impenetrable.'

'That's the seventh century for you.'

Cyan unfolded the letter. 'Rayne must be an amazing doctor to hold her title for as long as Daddy.'

'She is. As time goes on, it seems less likely that she'll ever lose a Challenge. The mortals' behaviour benefits her, I think.'

'Why?'

'Other doctors all stunt each other's growth. They never share their discoveries because they all want to Challenge her. Rayne's fond of saying that the branches of science wouldn't be so separate if scholars were less secretive.'

'I suppose, living in the university, she's the first to hear of anything new.'

'Yes. She loves it when novices notice something different. She encourages them. Otherwise they'd just follow her and ape her experiments.'

Cyan read the letter for a few minutes while I played with the chess pieces and sorted out my eyeliner, and then she passed me the letter. 'Why not have a look while I write a reply?' She pulled a pillow from the bed and sat down on the floor next to the low table, her long back rounded above it. She began to fiddle with the nib of her pen.

While she scrawled her reply, I perused Rayne's pages of neat, close writing.

Slake Cross Hospital

17th May

1.30 a.m.

To be delivered by the hand of Comet

Dear Cyan,

I know you are trapped and must be feeling miserable. Your father's rage seemed shocking, but I hope at some time in the future you will agree he may have saved your life and that life is indeed more precious than you currently hold it. Lightning loves you with all his heart but you simply refuse to understand how much strain he's under. He does not want to lose you and he must concentrate on reaching the dam. I didn't think he would do anything like this no matter how hard you pushed him, but San has never put us under this pressure before.

In the coach on the way from Hacilith I enjoyed our conversation. How agreeable it was, for an old lady who does not need much sleep, to talk through the night with a young lady who is too excited to sleep. And then when the Circle broke and you consoled me ... Please turn over in your mind the tales I told you of your father's life, and understand that in Hacilith you were fed a lot of slander. It shouldn't colour your opinion of him now.

Once you realise of how little consequence you are in the immensity of time, you gain a great power, a liberty and you can follow your own path in peace. Bide your time and learn.

You probably don't feel lucky, but let me tell you, you have been living in a time of such equality and freedom it almost seems to me that the people of this era act like spoilt children. People like myself have toiled over decades and centuries so that you may have such freedom. I expect you feel you have little choice in life but in times past you would have had even less. When I was mortal, girls could not be students and few people could read. I guided Hacilith University to develop in the image of the Castle, so it's run by merit, not by dodderers. These days an applicant to the university must have worked in the outside world for two years, so the prospective students are people who know how to put in a day's work and their mature approach recognises the great worth and luxury of study. You never needed for anything, Cyan, so you never needed to learn until now. I urge you to put your time to good use.

Watch your father from the window as he leads the battle. Would you be able to do what he does, so well? As a Challenger you seem to think you could do better. Lightning and the others who surround you are not simply faces, not simply there to grant your wish but every one has a long and complicated history to which his reactions pertain, just as much as they do to you. The road to becoming immortal is so uniquely steep and tortuous that every man travelling it has a story to tell. Your father is no exception.

Lightning and I discovered the privileges and tribulations of immortality at about the same time, though it meant different things to us both. During six nineteen, when the Emperor's First Circle was defeated, I was scrubbing out the washing coppers in Chattelhouse's laundry room. We were aware that San was losing Awia but the intense fighting was happening somewhere far off in the north. We could only keep going and wait until the Insects arrived at the walls of Hacilith. Every day the news came, the atmosphere grew more and more ominous and we lived under a constantly encroaching threat. How Lightning can call it a golden age I don't know.

Until I was about ten years old I lived on the street with no roof over my head, but I hung around the gates of the College of Surgeons as if drawn to them. I was sitting playing knucklebones on the track outside when I saw the cleaner being sacked. She hefted her bags and stomped away in a huff. The porter began to close the gates but I slipped between them and begged to be allowed to clean the floors. He rolled his eyes but he hired me and I became the most lowly servant to the Guild of Barber-Surgeons. Guilds disappeared before the close of the first millennium, but they were very influential when I was mortal.

I dreamed of being a subsizar, a scholar's assistant, but girls were not permitted and, besides, they would never employ an orphan with no clue as to her parentage.

After I turned thirteen, the gentlemen students sometimes offered to let me stay in the rooms they hired in town or in Chattelhouse, the wattle-and-stone residential hall. I'd move in, then be ejected back to be bullied in the deprived and unbearable servants' quarters, until I could find another Chattelhouse room. The boys never gave charity freely; they always pressed for sexual favours in return. Indeed, one of them suggested that I become a prostitute so he could make some money – but I all wanted was to talk about medicine with them!

Many's the time I tried to sleep on a boy's couch and late at night he would loom in the doorway, turn back the covers and slip in next to me, his hands on my breasts and his penis hard. One man in particular would strew his apartment with pornographic pamphlets as a hint, and every morning he would demand ... Well, Cyan, the things that happened were so awful I will not set them down on paper.

By the time I was thirty, Chattelhouse employed me as charwoman and cook in exchange for board. Some of the fourteen-year-old scholars grew to regard me as a mother far more approachable than the one who sent them away to study logic, rhetoric and grammar. One boy, whom I'll never forget, developed an infatuation and spent his afternoons teaching me to read. He stammered and blushed his way into finding me a better job. At long last I could mop the Surgeons' lecture theatre after lessons. The chalk scrawls left on the blackboard enthralled me. If I made myself scarce during the anatomy sessions I was allowed to lay out the instruments and clean them afterwards. Eventually I had my chance to attend! I placed the scalpels and saws on the bench, and then hid in the equipment cupboard and peered through its slats. If I had been discovered spying they would have cast me out, but I learnt exactly which implements to lay out for each lesson, so nobody had occasion to open the door.

Huddled in the dark with chinks of light shining on my face, I watched the dissections for years and years until I knew the procedures by heart – and here was the strange thing – they never changed. It was as if the professors couldn't add to their knowledge because they had mastered everything – which, I reasoned, could not be the case if patients still died.

The young men on the tiered seats either sat carving their names in the benches or lapped up the professor's witticisms. But I peered at the cadaver. Of course blood couldn't move through the septum of the heart, which had no holes. Of course ligation after amputation would reduce deaths from shock caused by dipping the stump in hot pitch. He told them that dead flesh spontaneously generated maggots, while flies buzzed round his head and laid eggs on the hanged felon's body right there on the bench.

He propounded the myth that Awian hearts are larger than those of humans because Awians have a higher sensibility for love, without considering for a minute that their wings might need a larger blood supply. He told them that Rhydanne children grow rapidly because they are savages, no better than animals. It never occurred to him to ask how else they would survive the mountain winters. It was clear to me that Rhydanne have short pregnancies and small babies because their mothers have narrow hips to make them better sprinters, a trait Rhydanne must needs inherit if their females choose to be caught by the fastest men.

It was unthinkable that a woman should set foot in the Barber-Surgeon's library. With hindsight I'm thankful that I wasn't filled with the books' received wisdom. I had no framework to force my observations into. But I was consumed by my interest in medicine; I *had* to find out more. It was what I was *for*. Cyan, sometimes in life you will have to admit that you are wrong and alter the way you think. Cherish that process. Why do you think I've lasted so long? The entire discipline of medicine we have today owes itself to my belief, then as now, that knowledge can only be recovered from nature by close observation and practice, not through revered manuscripts or bombastic speech.

My dear, I am remembering my aggravation and losing the thread of my story, so let me simply say that I wondered why their wisdom did not accord with my notes. I questioned whether the gentry really knew better than me. Suffice it to add that Chattelhouse's 'long room' latrines were over a cesspit so vastly deep that it was only emptied every two hundred years. And they wondered why they got plague.

Try to imagine me at the foot of a narrow spiral staircase to the dormitory, mopping the flagstones. It was evening so the tiny arched windows high on the walls gave no light whatsoever.

A student bounded down the stairs, making the rush lights gutter in their sconces. He tripped over my bucket and fell headlong measuring his considerable length on the floor. Dirty water slooshed down the corridor. The dice he had been tossing up and down in one hand rolled to a halt in the puddle at my feet and showed double six.

'You stupid beldam!' he howled, rubbing his knees. Although he was a vain Awian, he had adopted Morenzian clothes against the cold and damp – well, the style we wore in the year six twenty. He had a knee-length robe with the cape of his hood around his neck. His hood's pointed tippet end hung down his back. He'd rucked the robe up in his belt, from which a silk purse dangled, the only ornamentation in his drab garb. The tops of his woollen hose were tied somewhere up under the robe with strings, his ankle boots were soft leather, and now they were soaking.

Lightning was dazzling in comparison, the first time I saw him. He had a white tunic with a long toga wound around his waist and over one shoulder, the one pulled back to keep his bowstring drawn and— well, I am getting ahead of myself.

I offered the hearty boy a hand to pull him up but he ignored it. 'Look at my robe!' he said petulantly. 'It's ruined! This cost more than you'll ever see. Now I shall be late for the gaming table!' He squeezed water out of his curly hair. 'You seem to be amused. It's not bloody funny. I shall report you to the Housekeeper.'

I began to answer but he stopped me. 'I do not speak to servants. Obviously you don't know who I am, but—'

'You're from Awia.'

'I am the son of the Governor of Foin – third in line anyway. So you may—'

'Everyone in your country seems to give themselves a title, so I've read.' I righted my bucket and sloshed my mop about. The water was soaking through my shift and making my legs itch.

He retrieved his dice without answering. 'Something you read ... Hm? ... Servant? You can *read*?'

'Yes. Come with me and I'll dry your clothes. I'll make up some liniment for your knees as well. A bruised knee can swell badly since the body tries to cushion damaged joints.'

'You sound more like a prelector than a servitor,' he said carelessly. 'Would that you could write my essays as well.'

'Oh, but I can.'

That night, I did not sleep. I had explained all to Heron and my thoughts were in turmoil. I knew what to do, what I *must* do, and wondered if I dared. I heard the students clatter to the refectory. I opened the shutters and found it was already morning.

I began, behind the scenes, to do Master Heron Foin's homework. At last I could air all my observations, my theories! I wrote the methodologies of his experiments, delineated hypotheses in novel articles. Heron became suddenly famous, and he knew how to use it; he was a consummate self-publicist. He set himself up as the foremost student, the pride of the college. He brought me more books, though he could never fathom why I wanted to learn.

Far from suspecting the fraud, the Chancellor awarded him the acclaimed prizes in anatomy, physiology and penmanship. He was even recommended to succeed Professor Pratincole. Heron's conceit grew deeper. He loathed and resented the fact he was simply an actor, a mouthpiece for my work, while all and sundry told him he was a genius. They expressed surprise that he could pay so little attention to lectures, spend so much time on the playing fields and still make groundbreaking discoveries. He began to believe that he was doing the work, not me. He would throw me a half-remembered essay question. 'And it has to be done tonight! If you don't, I'll tell the Housekeeper how often you hid in that cupboard. Just bear in mind what you owe me, Ella. You're my servant, I raised you from "below stairs", and you'll have to go back there, anyway, because the damn freshmen are hinting at all kinds of relationships between us.'

Thank god I was grown too old for their sexual advances.

Then on the first of July the Emperor came to Hacilith. Governor Donacobius accompanied him into the town square. Everyone poured out and crowded around their caparisoned horses. I left my washing soaking in lye, dropped the shirt I was squeezing around a wringing post, and dashed to the window to listen. The Emperor himself proclaimed the Games. He announced that every man and woman regardless of age or background was welcome to compete in organised tournaments. San would share his immortality with the winners providing they were prepared to act as leaders in the war.

Many students left to try their skill at the Games, but as far as I could tell, they all came back in the following weeks, and very chastened. Life at the guild went on as normal.

Until, that is, Heron disappeared. On my morning visit I found his rooms vacated and I panicked. His landlord told me he'd gone to the front. Heron had been in communication with the Messenger and had suggested that the Circle needed a doctor. San agreed and asked him to come to Rachiswater to be tested by treating the casualties of the ongoing massacre. Everything I had worked for vanished instantaneously – what good was a rich student's famulus without the student? Devastated, I returned to darning socks.

Less than a month later a letter arrived from the front, from my 'grandson'. Its ink had run where Heron's tears had hit the page. He begged me to come and help him. He was completely out of his depth with the number of men slashed and disembowelled. We had never seen an Insect up close and the injuries they caused horrified him. He had never dirtied his hands in the operating theatre and hadn't the first idea how to organise a hospital. The assistants were afraid, he had lost his authority over them, and the Messenger was too busy to listen to his excuses.

Heron had included enough money in the scroll for me to bribe a fyrd captain to ride pillion on his cart when the next draft left town. So I came to the grimy field hospitals of Rachiswater and I soon had them under control. I know when a floor hasn't been cleaned properly and I was not above showing the assistants how to do it. I improved or made comfortable the majority of the patients, organised supply chains of medicine from the capital, and upbraided Heron as if I really was his grandmother.

San noticed the progress and visited the infirmary. Heron greeted him and showed him in, bowing low and explaining the enhancements he had made, whilst blocking San's view of me. The Emperor looked past him and saw me bloodied up to the elbows, trying to stabilise the condition of a maimed soldier. He came to question me and quickly understood that the improvements had coincided with my arrival so, as I worked, he joined me to the Circle and made me one of the immortals. It was my dream, what I was made for! At last I was in the right place!

That night, I was shown to a pavilion that would temporarily serve as my scriptorium. I sat down to write. Heron burst in, stinking of brandy.

He disentangled himself from the tent ropes and slurred, 'I know the rules, you old bag. I've always learned the rules so I can work the system.'

I said, 'Yes, and that's all you do.'

He sneered. 'San wants the best specialists. I suggested the Circle have a Doctor, and you walked in. That's not fair. Well, I'm the next best doctor, so if you were to die I'd take your place.' He drew his dagger and dived at me. I tried to dodge but his fist on the hilt caught my eye such a crack that I fell off the stool, onto my back on the grass.

In a trice he was on me. He raised the dagger above my throat. I had a vivid image of myself as a cadaver on the dissecting table. Female, aged seventy-eight, note cause of death; a single deep puncture. Carotid cut, thyroid and oesophagus pierced, sixth cervical vertebra shattered, spinal cord severed. I'd make a fine lesson! I braced myself to feel my blood spray.

The point arced down. A shout made Heron flinch. His dagger deflected and tore through my hood.

'Fuck!' he said, and glanced behind him. Then he turned as pale as if he'd been bleached.

The Castle's Archer was standing at the entrance, bow flexed and an arrow unerringly trained on Heron. He said, 'I only have to let go. And believe me, nothing would give me greater pleasure.'

Heron collapsed into a kneeling position.

Seeing his face, the Archer looked surprised, but only for a second. 'Heron Foin?'

'I'm sorry, my lord prince, I'm sorry.' To my astonishment Heron began to grovel at the Archer's feet. He changed to High Awian and wept apologies into the grass.

The Archer lowered his bow. 'I know of you, Heron Foin. I know your father. Go home to the backwater little manorship you crawled from. If you harm our genius surgeon or even show your face here again, my brothers and I will take your hall apart until it is nothing but a field with stones in. Do I make myself clear?'

'Yes! Yes!'

'Get yourself out of my tent.'

Heron kissed the ground, jumped up and sped out. I never saw him again. I unpinned myself from the grass and dabbed my black eye with a handkerchief. I had never before heard a voice with such natural authority; it made even the professors sound strained. The Archer helped me to my feet, then bowed low and kissed my hand. 'Now,' he said, 'I would be honoured if you would call me Saker. What is your name?'

So, Cyan, you see how much I owe your father. Imagine how overwhelming life must have been for him in the early days of the Circle. Before the Games, the First Circle were no more than boastful mortal warriors leading a mass of untrained fyrd with swords and spears. The First Circle had lasted for two hundred and five years since San first drew them from three countries, but they gradually gave ground to the Insects all that time and left northern Awia to the Paperlands.

There was no effective way of fighting Insects then. The nobility and peasant levies simply fed the hordes and although the First Circle fought, manor after manor fell. We thought we were doomed. Your tutor may have taught you this, but don't forget it really happened, and Lightning was there. A million corpses is not some story you tell children at bedtime!

The blizzard winter of six nineteen put an end to the First Circle. Those who weren't eaten died of starvation, disease and exposure in snow holes by the Rachis river. Deep drifts covered the ruins of Murrelet.

San realised that the First Circle's brave but stupid warriors weren't enough. He needed the best to train fyrds. He needed an infrastructure to keep supplies flowing – cooks and doctors; and to keep knowledge from being lost – agriculturalists and armourers. He needed an administration to take decisions on his behalf on many battlefields simultaneously. In short, he needed people who could think in the long term, as he did.

When San revealed he could make other people immortal, everyone suddenly saw him in a new light. Before, he had relied on the goodwill of the governors to raise and lead fyrds; now everyone clamoured to join the Circle.

San also knew that the celebrations and ceremony of the Games would raise our hopes. He let us see our own capabilities. Our fighting spirit soared.

San kept his personal symbol, the Imperial Sunburst, and extrapolated it to invent all our Eszai names. With the First Circle gone, the Castle's Breckan and Simurgh Wings stood empty, waiting for the victors of the Games. It was an exhilarating time. It threw us together, people from every stratum of society across the world and some with naught but the clothes they stood up in. I heard that Lightning arrived with a retinue of eight carriages of belongings and attendants, to discover that the rooms he was allocated by ballot were tiny compared with those he was used to. He divided his treasures among the new Eszai and filled all their rooms.

In the seventh century I discovered that sexism was not a glass ceiling but is present at all levels, in all classes. It was a glass web, and I threaded my way through it, cut by the strands I broke. San was the first to see my merit and your father was the first man truly to see me as an equal.

Since he has confided in me on many occasions, I suppose I am even more indebted to him for his friendship. It is impossible for you to understand a friendship of fourteen hundred years. You discover things about a person that you might not like, but it makes their virtues all the more admirable. I have the measure of Lightning and he has the measure of me.

I hope I have given you food for thought.

Send word with Comet if you need anything.

Love, Ella Rayne

That *is* food for thought. I folded the letter and placed it on the table. Cyan was putting the finishing touches to hers. 'Will you deliver this?' she asked. 'I don't have any sealing wax. Actually I don't have bloody anything here.'

'It's all right, just fold it. I can take it to Rayne unsealed.' I slipped her letter into my coat pocket and said, 'But she might be too busy to reply. I haven't seen anything like the crowds down there in my whole life before.'

'Will you be able to come back at least?'

'I'll try to.'

'You're the only person who's noticed me.'

I patted her shoulder but she shrugged away. She smelt of soap and birch bark chewing gum, reminding me how young she was for her years. Other seventeen-year-olds don't make idiots of themselves by Challenging Lightning.

I went to the window and opened the shutters. In the still night I could hear the clucking of the hens kept by the guards in their room downstairs. Very bass in the distance, the bass toll of the town's gatehouse bell rolled out over the moorland, thinning as it filled the expanse.

'Midnight. I have to go.'

Cyan tried again, 'This is a prison.'

'Honestly, it's for your own good. You should thank Lightning.'

'I'll kill him!'

'Shame. Thought cage birds sang more sweetly than that.'

'Well, if you won't free me, then bugger off!'

'I'll send you up some bread and water ha ha.'

I climbed onto the plank, ran along it and launched myself off. I flapped to the town with broad, uneven strokes, and landed on the hall's roof. I sat down on the ridge, wings drooping, and shook my hair down my back.

Below me the square was bustling with people. Around fifty of Rayne's orderlies with their white sashes were pulling tables out of the tavern and constructing beds. Fyrd squads were sitting on the tables, assembling arrows from piles of shafts and glittering points. The hall was packed with governors, wardens and captains as Lightning briefed them on the advance.

All the oil lamps and spotlights burned fiercely. The stars were dim in comparison, while the thick clouds at the edge of the sky seemed banked up above the town walls, hemming us in.

I unfolded Cyan's letter and read it.

Peel Tower Ten

Thursday

Dear Rayne,

Please will you help me get out of here? It's not fair that i'm locked up – it's just not fair. Daddy is cold & distant – like he always has been – and Jant says Daddy is like that most of the time. Will you ask him for me?

Apart from you and Jant everybody is ignoring me. I try to be independent, and i'm punished. Typical. Even Jant says i made a fool of myself. But i have put it behind me & i'm not thinking of it any more.

I don't want to be stranded in here during the battle – i'm not afraid of what may happen. I want to see the advance – i can come to help you at the infirmary. I'm sick of trying to be a good girl, i just want to be free – please, if you're really my friend, send a note to the guards and cancel Daddy's orders. Thank you for writing – please write again.

Yours,

Cyan xxx (Lady Governor Cyan Peregrine)

Slake Cross Hospital
18th May
2.30 a.m.

Dear Cyan,

I'm sorry but neither Jant nor myself can let you out of the peel tower, given what is happening down here at the moment. But please do not despair, my dear. Bear out your imprisonment patiently and in time the awful things that are happening will bring you wisdom.

You are intelligent but you are not yet wise. Do not blind yourself with opinions drawn from your own intelligence, because even the cleverest people can be wrong if they do not examine solid facts.

Wisdom never comes from staying at home and avoiding unhappiness. In order to become wise you must go out into the world and be tossed about in its storms, stripped bare by terrible experiences and confused by good ones. After a long time you learn to see and control the effect those circumstances have on yourself. Then it will never matter one bit where you find yourself in the world, because you will be able to cope with it. The top of a peel tower or a Hacilith bar will be all the same to you if you are comfortably at home with yourself.

Now you are a little uncomfortable you are crying out for help. But you are a Challenger! You can't be Eszai material at all if you are disturbed by a little inconvenience. Every Challenger is prepared to forgo pleasure and comfort in the pursuit of success. You are now a Challenger, so what are you complaining about? Hadn't you better prepare yourself for the competition instead? In a sense it's already underway, your father made the first move and now you are in check.

I thought you wanted to rebel, to put distance between yourself and Lightning. Then why on earth have you Challenged him as if you are yet another good archer? Everyone expects Lightning's daughter to have a modicum of archery. I thought you were trying to re-create yourself. You must know that if you follow the career of a great man like your father, you will have to accomplish twice as much to shine. You won't be able to shine in your own right if you're known as another archer, because everybody knows Lightning is the best archer.

I doubt you have even thought about it – but of course, you don't really want to compete with Lightning, you just want to escape from his shadow. Consider this – every Eszai and Challenger must submit to a much greater authority: that of the Emperor. None of us can escape San: not even Lightning. You rebel against your father and come under the power of a more authoritative man. Oh, Cyan, when you become wise you'll realise that freedom is a teenager's aspiration and illusion, and the world actually consists of varying degrees of compromise.

You say that Lightning is cold and distant. My dear, nothing could be further from the truth! He is passionate in the extreme! He must hide from his passions because they're so strong. I could give plenty of examples, but I only have time to tell one, a secret to which Lightning never refers, and the other Eszai are too polite – or afraid – to mention.

Eighteen nineteen was a year in which everything changed. It was the year after Jant joined the Circle. Lightning was married and widowed in the same night, and his grief for Savory threw him into an almost catatonic state.

There had been no letters from Micawater. I taught doctors in the university. I sat in my room and read books. I did my daily rounds of the general hospital and came home tired but only in body; I was wondering how Lightning was. He was missed in court and at the front, at the King's table and in the hunting stables. He had sequestered himself, to the exclusion of the real world. I am very much of the real world and, as his closest friend, I decided to pay him a visit.

Eighteen nineteen passed into eighteen twenty. On a freezing January night I arrived at your father's palace to find the Lake Gate locked. The stone winged hounds stood rampant on the gateposts, rain dripping from their paws. I peered through the fine drizzle, but saw no lights shining in the bulk of the palace beyond the river.

I left my coach and followed the estate wall in the dark, until I came to the tradesmen's little arched entrance. I hurried through and across the soaking lawns. I passed the grand staircase and instead knocked on the door of the kitchens in the basement.

Lightning's steward brought me in and gave me supper. As well as his white apron, he wore a black crepe armband. He gathered a candelabra from the dresser and took a taper from the stove, talking all the while. He bent close to light the candles and whispered, 'M'lord scares us. He sits alone for days, no meals, no sleep. He doesn't bother to open the curtains and we don't dare light the lamps in Main. Doctor, he's wound up in himself and the manor go hang. Thought it best to warn you.'

He guided me, up out of the Covey cellars and through the silent, unlit palace. I think even you would find it discouraging, the building so majestic I felt it extending on both sides of me as we ascended to the main floor. The steward pressed on, past the drawing rooms.

Mourning cloths covered all the statues in the niches, reducing them to featureless, barely human shapes. The portraits had been turned to the wall; their blank backs faced us. I wondered at them, when there had never been any changes in your father's house before; now I believe he wanted to rid himself of the mute, accusing glare of his ancestors.

The rooms leading off from the corridor were in impermeable darkness, but when light from the candelabra flickered in I glimpsed the furniture and objects of virtu standing in shades of grey. Dust sheets had been thrown over them, as when the servants expect Lightning to be absent for years on business. The chandeliers hung in thick wraps. Black linen masked the deep-framed mirror in the salon. The great gold clock had been deliberately stopped.

The ceilings may have been painted by the world's greatest masters, but we walked past like thieves without looking up. A glimmer of candlelight shone under the door to the dining hall. The steward hesitated and looked at me anxiously. I nodded to reassure him; he gave me the candelabra and showed me through, then bowed and made a hasty retreat.

Lightning sat at the very end of the long table, halfway down the hall. He was leaning forward with his head down, resting in the crook of his arm. His reflection was blurred in the polished marble.

He was not aware of my presence. He picked an orange desultorily out of a bowl with his free hand and rolled it down the table without looking up. It rolled through the small gap between the legs of the silver centrepiece, out the other side and on for another five metres until it dropped off the end of the table beside me.

I put the candelabra down but Lightning did not acknowledge me. He picked another orange and sent it trundling straight down the middle of the table, through the centrepiece.

He was wearing a silk dressing gown and, over it, a very dirty and bloodstained Cathee plaid. He had wound it around his waist and over one shoulder with an automatic gesture from back when he used to wear a toga.

The rear of the hall was invisible in the gloom. I looked past Lightning, and at the edge of the darkness stood his grand piano, wreathed in paper music. Its keys were smeared thickly with dried blood.

The centrepiece was the same then as now, the small statue of a girl reclining on a couch. Lightning rolled another orange between its legs with an accuracy that was both considerable talent and long, long practice. The orange fell off the end of the table and joined several others on the carpet.

'Talk to me,' I said, but the room was so sombre it came out as a murmur. I pulled up a chair and sat down. His breath misted the table top. I touched his arm. 'Come on, Saker. Speak to me.'

'That chair ... is two hundred years old.'

'I'm not going to break your chair.'

He said nothing else.

'What happened?'

'I was married ...'

'I can see that.'

'I was ...'

'Saker ...'

'... Married.'

'I really think—'

'Do you really? Leave me, Ella, please.'

He was still looking away from me. I put my hand to his cheek and turned his head. He complied, though his eyes were blank.

I said, 'I'm—'

'Going to leave me alone?'

'Saker, please tell me the matter.'

'Savory was killed. I tried to shoot the man but I ... I missed my shot ... I missed.'

'It's been three months,' I said gently.

'Three months is nothing. Nothing.'

'Long enough for Challengers to prick up their ears.'

'*Challengers*,' Lightning sighed. 'How you worry me. My heart is torn from my body and I'll never heal. Ever. No matter how long I live. I weep every day. Savory was real, she was strong. In an ugly, unworthy world I had seen a hundred thousand and found just one to love ... And everything I'd been through seemed worth it.'

His washed-out voice continued ' ... When I close my eyes I see images of her. Smiling in the village. Shooting at the butts. My mind flicks through still pictures shockingly quickly, as if I'm constantly waking from sleep ... It seems odd that I was really in Cathee.'

'Yes.'

'How could Savory have come from among such a people? They ... I should ... well, in a hundred years the birds will have eaten them every one ...'

For all my fourteen centuries I hadn't lived long enough to know what to say. I tried, 'You're missed at the Castle.'

'Already?' He looked away abjectly. 'I feel that if just one more thing goes wrong, everything will fall apart. Just one tiny thing and I'll go mad. There were hundreds of things I should have told her and never had the time.'

'I'm sure she already knew. Sentiments sound crude when voiced, precious when understood in silence.'

'Oh, Ella. She was perfect, and I'm such a fool.'

'You are no fool.'

'Maybe I have been ... but now I have some of her blood in me. I can carry it for the rest of immortality.' He began to stroke his palm.

'Let me see your cut.'

He extended his hand to me and opened it. I saw the wound shining, encrusted with dried blood. He had kept it open to the white fan of bone.

So, Cyan, you must see Lightning as a person, not just as your father. There is no point in thinking about death because no amount of thinking will arrive at an answer. He had to return to the Castle. He still has not properly recovered from Savory but the Circle needs him. The Kingdom of Awia needs him, too; who's to say that without Lightning's generosity and sense of order their aristocracy wouldn't have dissolved into something akin to the pack of wolves who run Morenzia.

Cyan, I must go now. I have been writing this letter in between giving orders to prepare for tomorrow's advance. I apologise for my deteriorating handwriting: it is about four a.m.

The Eszai and soldiers will be exhausted for days after this – I have seen men in full armour come in off the battlefield and sleep where they fall. For twenty-four hours straight they're even oblivious to the cries of the wounded and nothing rouses them except extreme physical danger. So, Cyan, if nothing seems to be happening directly the dam gates open, and if Jant doesn't visit you, be patient.

I shall give this letter to him now and go to check the preparations in the hospital.

Yours with love,

Rayne

I collected the letter from Rayne with a stack of last-minute dispatches. The rest I gave to my couriers to deliver.

Rayne's scale of organisation was incredible, and only one part of the preparations heaving the town into action. She had called all her surgeons and doctors drafted with the rest of the fyrd and given them their chain of command. Anyone else in the fyrd who had medical knowledge – first-aiders and nurses – reported to the doctors.

She was preparing to take over the hall as well as the hospital and tavern, because as soon as San is out of the hall tomorrow morning it will be the overspill for intensive care. The medical supplies had been divided into each site and guards kept a sharp eye on them.

Her hundreds of stretcher teams had received their orders. She was stocking the two enormous pavilions inside the canvas city's gate to be used as triage. Dressing stations were being set up on the road behind the troops, as the battalions were already starting to assemble. She had girls at every station to count the casualties coming in, or record dog tags and remove the dead.

The dawn air was cool and fresh. The first light of a new day rose pale gold on the horizon. A last word with the Emperor as the Imperial Fyrd were arming and I swept up into the air. One hundred and fifty thousand men were marching out of town to take up their positions.

I helped direct each battalion into the enormous formation. From the air, the ground filled with men like a fluid jigsaw, pouring into squares of colour. The battle array was one of our many familiar standard plans – Insects are predictable so we have honed the perfect ways to face them in different situations. But this was on a massive scale, taken to an extreme. We had never fielded anything like these numbers before. The front of the host was three kilometres long. It was incredible, just incredible.

I was busy keeping the multitudes in line, with some difficult flying between the enormous host, the town and the canvas city. While one battalion was being eased into place, the next was lining up behind it, then decanted up along the flank to fill their patch. I ordered, threatened and encouraged the wardens depending on their personality. I wove an aerial web linking the Eszai to one another. In the distance I could always see the lake and the dam. The lake was silted and filthy, coffee-coloured brown, with fuliginous shapes and rafts of detritus bobbing in it like broth.

Sirocco the Javelin Master's ranks were filling in behind Lourie's pikemen. The Javelin Master arranged his battalions with great expertise so, while the last ranks were aligning, the front didn't lose coherence. I had a spare second, so I swept away to the edge of the field, and Cyan's peel tower.

The shutters were hooked back wide. Cyan was leaning out, her bare shoulders high as she propped herself with straight arms on the ledge. She was watching the movement of people on the entire ground: from the fresh earth embankments of the canvas city into the extreme distance the road was solid with tight companies of lancers trotting past archers on foot, trailed by dogs pulling diminutive arrow carts, whole divisions of infantry sitting on the verge awaiting their turn to march.

I dropped down, feet together, onto the plank. The draught of my wings tangled Cyan's hair.

'What do you think?' I leant back, sweeping my arm at the colourful, clinquant steel expanse of troops behind me.

'It's exhilarating! The Empire's sheer might.'

I nodded. 'Here's a letter from Rayne.'

A gust of wind snatched it out of her hand, but I caught it. 'Don't drop it! And for god's sake don't let anyone else read it. If I were you, I'd burn it when I've finished with it.'

'How do you know?' asked Cyan.

I boinged up and down on the end of the plank. 'I just imagine it's full of Rayne's advice. You don't necessarily have to listen to her. Other people's advice is from their own experience and you won't reach your full potential following it.'

'Not more advice.' Cyan gave a mock grimace. She shrugged and her ruby pendant rolled down the cleft of her breasts in the bodice.

I pointed at the dam. 'Watch for the great wave when we open the gates!'

'Will you come back and tell me the news?'

'Your wish is my command!'

'I *wish* that was always the case.'

I grinned at her and raised my arms, bouncing on the end of the board. Two more jumps, higher, and I sprang up, arced out backwards, hugged in my legs and described two perfect somersaults.

Falling high above the road, I stretched out my arms in a swallow dive. I opened my wings and curved out over the soldiers' heads, gliding so fast I didn't have to beat my wings once.

CHAPTER 21

The five kilometres to the dam had never seemed so far, there were so many Insects scurrying about between us and the winch house. It would be hours before we could cut our way there and open the gates.

Our skirmishing cavalry had been out since first light, preventing the more adventurous Insects getting too close to the mustering troops. The Ghallain prickers' horses were skittish, being not used to Insects. The men were unruly, but disciplined by long experience working together. They dashed and wheeled in small charges, hurling javelins at attacking Insects. Those with the swiftest horses offered themselves as bait to break up larger groups, luring them in different directions, and their comrades swooped to surround them. Their seemingly effortless efficiency was a pleasure to watch. I swept over, hearing them calling scores to each other.

'Thirteen!'

'Fourteen! ... Hey, Jant, away! You Eszai will get your turn later!'

'You're crazy, Vir Ghallain! There's Insects enough for everyone here!'

He laughed. 'There won't be when I've shown Summerday and Lowespass how real men can ride!'

I shook my head and headed back to our lines, wondering how long he would wait before Challenging our new Hayl. The wind was beginning to shift to the south. Lightning would appreciate a good tailwind to add force to the arrows but it was also blowing our scent towards the swarm near the lake, stirring them up.

The main force was drawing up into two deep blocks of roughly equal size, one about ten metres behind the other. The first block would have to break through the Insects, with the reserve formation offering support and engaging if those in front started to waver. In such a large force the Select units were interspersed with the inexperienced General Fyrd to provide an example and keep them fighting.

The centre of the first body was a solid phalanx of pikemen led by Lourie, stationed astride the road to the dam. They stood sixteen deep and, once engaged, their lowered pikes would present an impenetrable forest of points to the Insects, who would simply impale themselves on the barbed shafts trying to get at the men. They wore greaves and breastplates but trusted in the six metres of ash and steel they wielded to fend off Insects better than any shield. Behind them came a triple rank of javelin-throwers commanded by the Javelin Master, in their front line. They would hurl their missiles over the heads of the spearmen should they be hard-pressed by Insects. They were unarmoured and when their ammunition was exhausted they would pull back to the munitions carts following the troops at a safe distance to rearm.

Guarding both flanks of the phalanx were thousands of heavy infantry: solid blocks dripping with chain mail and shining plates, with tall rectangular shields and spears. In addition each carried a mace, axe, or Wrought sword to destroy any Insects who broke through their shield wall. They were a patchwork of colours as they drew up by battalion, each with its standard flickering in the breeze, and within that by division and company. Each square seemed tiled with smaller squares, in five hundreds, and smaller patches still, in fifties. The commanding Eszai stood in their front lines: Tornado and Serein on the left flank nearest the reservoir, the Macer and Sapper on the east flank by Cyan's tower.

The second body of troops were lines of archers, predominantly Awian, and more shield men in reserve, mostly Morenzian. The archers were on foot, their captains and wardens mounted, with Lightning clearly visible on his white horse in their centre. Those on horseback directed the shot of the footmen, who would be loosing blind over the heads of the ranks in front. In the open, archers cannot be left to face Insects alone so they shot high and indirectly, relying on the sheer weight of arrows to impact into the Insects' backs. The Awian ranks were typically orderly, each soldier turned out in blue livery and gleaming helmet, but more spacious to allow each man sufficient room to draw his longbow. The Morenzians were a motley contrast; only their officers and the richer fyrd were armoured. But a sea of banners fluttered above them, proudly proclaiming the village or Hacilith district from which they'd been raised. Each man in their jostling ranks held a shield and spear provided by the Castle and wore a sword, from Wrought. The Armourer and the Blacksmith led this infantry reserve.

Slightly to the rear on each flank of the second block of infantry were the armoured lancers. Eleonora held the left with the Tanager and Rachiswater lancers; and Hayl held the right with detachments from Eske and Shivel. They rode in discrete wedges, ready to intervene quickly if Insects threatened to envelop the archers and infantry.

The aristocracies of Awia and the Plainslands found it increasingly fashionable to arm as lancers, but I thought it an unnecessarily hazardous way of fighting. I couldn't help but remember how the last mass cavalry charge I had witnessed at Lowespass turned out. Still, the casualties probably helped keep inbreeding amongst the nobility under control.

Finally, directly behind the reserve block, the Imperial Fyrd rode onto the field together: a bright red square. They took position in the exact centre of the line, and in the centre of that, the Emperor on his midnight black stallion. Above him flapped the Sunburst, the largest banner on the field.

798

Frost, mounted on an immense destrier, trotted to his right surrounded by the company of her bodyguard, Riverworks's foremen and navvies. She was to take command of operations when we reached the dam.

The whole host was centred on the metalled road leading to the dam's walkway, though only a few men in the deepest part of the mass were actually walking on it. It emerged from under the leading pikemen's feet, and stretched ahead of them, bisecting the expanse of ankle-deep mud that they would have to cross.

Occasionally tiny gaps opened in the battle lines, where a man was having a piss, and his fellows on either side were trying to shuffle out of the way of the splatter, because none were allowed to leave the line for any reason. I curved up, gaining height to about five hundred metres, until the whole host was arrayed in browns and splashes of colour below me; pennants, padded jacks and white armour bright against the mud. There were the many-shaded blue backgrounds and individual devices of Awian manors; the greens and devices of Plainslands manors; the red hand of Morenzia. All the fyrds of the Fourlands bar Cathee, Brandoch and Ghallain's infantry were represented.

Behind the fighting troops, auxiliaries of all kinds trailed through the canvas city back to Slake Cross, industrious as Insects. A constant pony cart relay brought up supplies of arrows and javelins to stockpiles behind the ranks. Wagons laden with stacks of stretchers swayed through the mud to the forward dressing stations, where orderlies fussed over them. Water-bearers staggered under dozens of canteens they would carry to the men once underway. Swarms of boys tried to sell apples from barrels to the stragglers. Whores were doing a roaring trade in the tents with young fyrdsmen who didn't want to die as virgins. A party of artillerists tried to lever a cart-mounted repeating ballista out of a ditch. Squads of Gayle's mounted provosts brandished their truncheons as they trotted between the pavilions and alongside the road, scaring skivers back to their units.

I heard Lightning's horn calling thinly into the sky. Each Eszai carries his or her own signal to call for the Messenger but it has taken me years of selective deafness to convince them that just because I can fly I can't answer them all at once. Now they have learnt only to use them in truly important cases. I wheeled back over the tumult.

Lightning had ordered his Select to bunch up, clearing a strip of ground for me to land on. It simply looked brown, but as I dropped closer it looked like someone had decided to plough a pond.

I came to earth in front of his horse, peeling off the top layer of mud in a sliding flurry of feathers, probably just as Lord Melodrama had planned. 'This had better be good! Even if I can get airborne from this muck, I'll be carrying half the field around with me all day.'

'Hush.' He looked around and then, sighing, dismounted to stand next to me. His riding boots squelched into the slurry and stopped being so damn clean. In a low voice he said, 'I do not want the fyrdsmen to hear. I am worried.'

I whispered back, 'Look, this is the strongest we've ever been. It looks glorious from the air. Half the Fourlands is here. The Insects can't even outnumber us by more than three to one.'

'Yes, that is exactly my concern. Nobody here has experience of handling a host this size. Forget the governors, even most of the Eszai have barely commanded a force bigger than a battalion in the last two hundred years, and then mostly on the defensive. The Emperor hasn't directed a battle for almost eight times as long.'

I shrugged, annoyed. Trust Lightning to be so perfectionist he finds fault where there is none. 'So?'

'Nobody has proper control over this field. A developing situation could get quickly out of hand. The mud will slow the dispatch riders. Most of these troops are untried and barely trained – we have many men but not many soldiers. Originally we just expected them to make a great show for the press and then spend the next month demolishing cells.'

'Look, all the Select is here. You know nearly all the Awians drill regularly. The entire Circle is here. The *Emperor* is here. The green troops will either be straining their best to impress or be terrified of us. Don't fret. Oh, and I checked on Cyan this morning; she'll be safe.'

He scowled. 'That wasn't what I was thinking about. Jant, you're the only one who can watch everything as it happens. If you see anything start to go wrong, tell me immediately.' He looked down the first line. 'Damn! Ata had a proper head for this, so had Dunlin. Or Sarcelle. And the last Hayl.'

I was shocked. Had he really so little confidence in us?

'What about San?'

'You must go to him if he summons you, of course. But remember that he is here to inspire and observe. He hasn't taken formal command from any of us. They are forgetting—' he waved an arm towards the front, in Tornado's general direction '—that San created the Circle to do this for him.'

I looked Saker full in the face. Behind his usual expression he had a weariness I wasn't used to seeing.

I nodded. I pulled my damp feet from the ooze, ran soggily, and leapt into the air. A whole division of Morenzians ducked as I flashed over their spear-points. When I looked behind me again, Saker was still standing where I had left him, patting his horse's neck abstractedly.

I could see my couriers converging on the Imperial Fyrd and its captain turning around in his saddle to speak to the Emperor. San raised his hand.

The standard bearers of the Imperial Fyrd sounded their horns and the buglers of every division responded, till the air vibrated with a single note. The advance began.

Lourie's phalanx started to elongate as the men in the front line began to march; then those towards the middle. The lines separated slightly and narrow gaps opened between them as those at the back, and the infantry behind them, waited for their space to move.

Their pikes jutted ahead, held straight out from the first few ranks, and directly upwards in the others. They looked like a hairbrush. I looked down into the spaces between the spears; they seemed to bristle as I soared over.

Hurricane's polished glaive was clear among them, a wider blade in the centre. He was setting the pace deliberately slowly, to prevent men stumbling in the adhesive mud or advancing too far ahead of the archers.

The prickers fell back as planned. Around the flanks, exhausted men headed their horses to the rear to rest. As they retreated, Insects began to venture forward. The strong south wind gusted, spreading a ripple of interest through the Insects gathered around the lake.

I watched the forward movement surge through the infantry and reach the archers. Over the roar of airflow and the rhythmic swoosh-and-batter of my wings I could hardly hear their horns but I saw thousands of men bend their bows in unison. Their shot arced high, arrows pausing at their zenith, turning and falling at a steeper angle, thicker than rain or snow, spraying out in front of the first spearmen.

Their barrage was so thick they were catching Insects in a broad strip in front of the host. Insects writhed and fell. The closest rushed powerfully up against the first pikes. Some were killed outright, others slowed down until the pike points buckled into and cracked their hard carapaces.

Hurricane let the arrow barrage come down some fifty metres ahead of the pikemen – he kept the distance with incredible skill.

The pace was so slow it was a quarter of an hour before the wave of movement reached the last ranks of the Imperial Fyrd. It was mid-morning already but we were only ten minutes behind schedule. It is absolutely impossible to keep men walking abreast in perfect rows, and they were stumbling and dragging in the mud. Every formation was warping slightly; growing thinner and longer. The archers' line bent forwards at the ends as the men there walked faster, spreading onto open ground where the infantry hadn't churned it up.

I stretched out in the air, way in front of the pikemen, with the storm of arrows coming down behind me. I was watching Insects charge in up the slope from the lake shore, where they were ranging all over the mud in great numbers, but nowhere so densely packed as to be a serious threat to the infantry.

I turned and flapped upwind in an ungainly fashion, resting now and then because the gusts were strong enough for me to lean against. All the spearmen could see me poised stationary like the figurehead of a ship.

Back towards the town I saw the dual lines of Thunder's immobile trebuchets drawn up in front of the walls. The machines weren't operating but were still manned, just in case – they seemed no bigger than my thumbnail and the crews no more than black dots.

Better go see if anyone needs me, I thought. I swept out wide and came in under the tunnel of arrows pouring up from Lightning's ranks. I flew down the tunnel and out of the end. Then I gained height so as not to frighten the horses, and cruised over the Imperial Fyrd, looking down on their sun banners. It was easy to see the Emperor's billowing white cloak against his horse's back.

I was worried that San was on the field. His presence was foremost in everyone's minds. We couldn't risk him getting hurt – if he was, none of us knew what would happen to the Circle. At least he's well protected in the rearguard.

Back on the other side of the arrow storm, Insects rushed towards the spearmen. The spears thrust out or down. Little dents formed in the first line where shield and spearmen had to stop and make sure an Insect was dispatched before walking round or clambering over it. Eleonora's and Hayl's lancers trotted forward to guard the archers' flanks.

The fyrds walked steadily for three hours, cutting a wide swathe through the Insects, with some attrition of the spearmen and heavy infantry, and horses as the cavalry fended off Insects coming round to our rear. The host trailed bodies like rag dolls, curled up and sinking in the shallow liquid mud.

We had reached the gradient leading down to the lake – the slope helped the men walking but was too faint to speed up the lines. Hordes of Insects were racing from the shore, skittering over the road and pouring towards us. The curling breeze carried the stench of the lake.

I was turning, intending to tell Lourie how many Insects were approaching, when an almighty shouting broke out from the spearmen. The front of the phalanx nearer the lake ground to a halt, but the rest kept going a few steps downhill, staring left at their fellows, wondering what was happening. They pulled the whole of the phalanx front out in a long concave curve.

The first pikes started rattling side-to-side and jabbing at the ground. The men in the second line were also trying futilely to bring their weapons to bear, stabbing the mud. A shout went up to call Sirocco's men into action. They started casting their javelins. Already? I thought. What's going on?

I pulled my wings in close and dropped steeply downwind, air screaming past me. I hit my top speed in seconds, blinked and tears forced out of the corners of my eyes. I swept my wings forward and up, either side of my face, and braked hard. I had to keep above the arrows. I circled, lying in the air, my wings beating quickly, and looked down through their storm.

The men in the first few lines were dropping their pikes. Throwing them down. Their long shafts lay all over and already men were tripping on them. Some had drawn swords and appeared to be digging them into the ground.

The men on the edges of the phalanx flung down their weapons and turned to run. The ones nearer the centre began to follow suit. Unable to force back through the tight ranks behind, they had to run the whole length of the line to get round the flanks. Some fell as they fled and didn't get up again. Bodies struggled and contorted in the mud but I couldn't see that they were fighting anything.

Men in the centre of the first ranks turned around completely and tried to beat their way back into the middle of the phalanx. They came face to face with men behind them who also turned to run but could go nowhere. Time seemed to slow down and I felt a rising nausea. Shit. They're going to rout. The fastest way to die in battle is to break formation in front of Insects.

'Lourie!' I shouted. I couldn't dive lower – I couldn't land. The air beneath me was thick with missiles. The wind took my words. I screamed at the top of my voice: 'Hold the line!'

I saw helmets moving into the centre of the phalanx then falling under the crush. The square's middle was thickening and the edges flaking off, men running back. Lourie and a body of soldiers around him were left isolated on the road out in front. He was bent double, shouting, but no volume could make his troops take the slightest bit of notice.

The javelin-throwers following had now also stopped, their front rank mingling with the last line of the phalanx. They couldn't see forward and were even jumping up to try to see over the pikemen's heads and find out what was happening. Fleeing pikemen began running into their ranks at the sides, pushing them towards the middle, making the crush worse. Sirocco blew his horn, then every Eszai with the infantry began to sound theirs. I glimpsed Tornado looking up to me and frantically waving, mouth moving in a silent bellow. Then I was past, over the vast formation grinding to a halt. Men crunched up together as they walked into each other; the flanks rode on by a few metres as the centre collapsed into itself. The reserve block realised that the men walking ahead had stopped and came to a halt themselves.

Lacking further instructions for the cause of the delay the archers, piece-meal, suspended their barrage. As the last arrows hissed to the ground the screams of the ever-worsening crush below seared up clearer than before.

Finally I could descend – and suddenly all the ground ahead of the pike-men seemed to be in motion. Tussocks and rocks poking through the thin layer of muddy water over the waterlogged soil were advancing of their own accord.

I had no idea what they were. Lower still, I could see shapes, seething in the mud, half-crawling, half-swimming. I judged the scale against the men – they were about half a metre long and mottled brown, very hard to see. They were moving close to the surface of the soil, like little Insects. I saw one lifted up on a man's spear, writhing. It had a longer, narrower abdomen than an Insect. I saw its legs opening and closing as they waved in the air. Its thorax and triangular head were flattened, but they had the same high-gloss goggle eyes.

I looked towards the lake and saw them emerging from the water, climbing up on the lake shore. They were scurrying, slower than Insects, but faster than a man could run. I couldn't see the ground between them on the shore; there was no end to them. They weren't Insects. I hadn't seen them before – they were monsters!

The waters' edge was slick with glistening wet carapaces. The tops of their eyes emerged first, then their leg joints, combing through the ripples. They crawled straight out, head, thorax and the strange long abdomen; rivulets running down between their hard segments.

Oh no ... These are the hatchlings. Young Insects. Insect *larvae*.

Lourie's troops had dissolved into a tussling, hopelessly entangled mob of men, crushed by their own confusion and swarmed over by the larvae. They were pressed so closely together they were suffocating. I saw armoured fists raised. Men used sword pommels to club each other out of the way. None of the infantry could see the lake. To them, the creatures were closing in from all sides equally, so thick on the ground that one man could do nothing. They had no idea what they were facing. The great length of pikes was useless against creatures close by and tight against the mud, and the small sword or misericord most carried was too short to be effective without bending down. The larvae were crawling up the legs of the armoured men, biting in between their plates, hanging off faulds, curling around men's necks. As they stabbed at one, another bit them. Men wrenched them off, leaving chitinous legs trapped between their armour's plates, but as they pulled one off, more swarmed up.

The heavy infantry by now were seriously worried, even though few had even seen the larvae yet. On the wings I could see their step beginning to waver and corporal looking to sergeant; sergeant to captain; captain to warden; warden to governor or Eszai, all wanting to know what to do.

Lourie and those with him – already no more than a company – were now nearly surrounded. Larvae flowed towards them like a tan wave. He knew it was safer to keep fighting than to run. Anyone who ran was borne down by clinging hatchlings, or tripped as several lunged at his feet, or he slipped in the mud and they overwhelmed him.

Lourie was spinning his glaive and stabbing larvae before and behind him. He was making his way steadily backwards but his path was blocked by the jostling crush – the remains of his own ranks. Bodies were beginning to pile up on the edges. The men in the middle were heaving their own dead out of the way to give themselves more room, but the armoured bodies only hemmed them in and gave the ravenous larvae a feast.

I chose a spot some distance from Lourie, slightly ahead of the front of the advancing larvae, and landed. 'Hurricane!' I yelled.

Lourie's sallow face turned towards me for an instant. His legs were muddied up to the hips. He had taken his helmet off and his cornrow-braided hair glistened with sweat.

I yelled, 'Run! There's a way out, here!'

Lourie ignored me. 'The Emperor,' he said loudly, looking down. 'I'm not running in front of the Emperor.'

'There's nothing you can do! Come on!'

Lourie said something derogatory about Rhydanne. He spun the glaive high and under his arm, accurately stabbing a crawling larva. He lifted it into the air. It flicked its tail under it, spattering mud.

They were sweeping towards me quickly, jetting water out of their tails to propel themselves through the liquid pooled over the churned earth, swarming on their short legs across the drier ground. Their hunger seemed even more desperate and insatiable than the adults'. I readied myself, trying to make out the nearest. It had a narrow, cylindrical shape and a long abdomen made up of segments that came to a point.

Familiar, but smaller, six jointed legs were bunched together under its thorax. The flattened head was hunched and joined to its body by a thick neck. It was dark brown with paler sandy and black spots along its sides. The crook-backed carapace was thinner, with many more joints and far more flexible than an Insect. Thick spines edged and topped its sinuous abdomen. Tiny wing-buds lay tight against its thorax like a backpack; much smaller than Insects' undeveloped wings but these were recognisably a different stage in the life-cycle of the same creature.

I had seen enough. I swung my ice axe at it, missed, and the pick passed close to its head. It reared up onto its two back legs, spread out its front legs and opened its jaws threateningly. Another made straight for my foot. Its jaws shot out and grabbed my ankle. Fucking shit! Its jaws shoot out! It bit straight through my boot and suddenly a pair of hooks twisted in my ankle. I slammed my axe down through its neck, with the speed of pain. It was impaled, but it didn't let go. It flexed the joint of its extendible jaw and pulled its body towards me by the fangs anchored in my boot. I levered them out with the axe pick. It curled up, convulsing – its mandible folded limply back underneath its head.

I took steps backwards, smashing the heads of larvae around me. Pleased with my prowess I looked up – the whole kilometre of ground from myself to the lake was swarming with them! I ran, limping, in the opposite direction and took off.

Dank though it was, the air had rarely felt so welcoming. Unfortunately I couldn't stay up here, I had to stop the rout spreading. I could feel my bitten foot bleeding into my boot. My flight path took me over the left flank; Tornado's halted formation. I'll tell him first.

I came down in front of the heavy infantry. Their nervous eyes peered from helmet slits. More mud splattered into my flight feathers as I slid to a halt. I couldn't keep doing this or I would soon be grounded. Tornado exploded out of the ranks before me, over two metres of confused belligerence in chain mail.

'Jant! What the fuck's going on?'

'Insects. Larvae, I think. Loads of them, coming this way.'

'What?'

I stopped, took a breath. 'It's a new type of Insect, coming from the lake. They're smaller but there's millions of them. Hard to see cos they keep very close to the ground. I killed a couple; they're softer than adults. But they're fast and they can swim. Lourie's cut off! Pikes are useless against them. His men are running.'

'No! No one runs! Not now!'

I had never seen him look so furious.

'Tornado, this is something new ...'

'What about spears? Are they any use?'

'Short ones might be, if you stab down with them. Long swords, maces, axes maybe. Their jaws are on a hinge, like an arm! They shoot out *this* far in front! One bit me in the ankle! I saw them reaching through gaps in armour.'

He called, 'Signal the advance! Fyrd! Follow me! Your Emperor is watching! Runners! Tell Serein to keep his men close to us – don't let any spaces open up!'

'What are you doing?'

'My job. These soldiers are the Select of the Plainslands and they're not trying to wield a pike like a tree-trunk. You can tell San that we're going to rescue Hurricane and then we're going to reach our objective. If you can kill them, so can we.' He spoke loudly, for the benefit of the front ranks. They cheered. He looked at me levelly, though without malice.

'Look—'

'That's all, Jant.' He turned away.

'Excuse me!' But the bastard didn't pay the slightest bit of attention. I muttered as I took off, 'I'll go find someone intelligent to talk to.'

Now with a better view I could see the central phalanx had disintegrated into a bloody shambles. Those who could were splashing away, shoving through the archers behind them, discarding weapons and armour. The captain of a Rachiswater division tried to halt them. She grabbed a man but he kept running with such force that he pulled her from her horse and they both fell struggling into the mud. The surrounding infantry began to form up into shield walls, whether out of fear of Insects or their own routers I couldn't know.

Sirocco was trying to stage a more orderly retreat with what remained of his command but he was now faced by solid ranks of shields and spears in the hands of panicking men.

Lourie's diminishing band were standing in a circle, completely surrounded as, hundreds of metres away, the left wing began to wheel ponderously towards him. Tornado's men were fighting already in fresh swarms of nymphs. The right wing was still halted in confusion, not yet in contact with the larvae: cavalry rode up and down trying to see what was going on even while the ranks nearest the slaughter were peeling away and breaking up. The ground was heaving as larvae, attracted by the blood, funnelled into our centre from the left, from the lake. The sky was alive with horns, shouts and screams. Shit. Shitshitshit! I glided low, heading for the Micawater standard, until I picked out Lightning.

I leant against the wind and soared lower and lower to horseback-level, then pulled my wings in and dropped to the ground. At that very moment the Circle broke.

Lightning gave a great cry of rage: 'Lourie!'

I furled the blades of my wings and staggered to my feet. The mud here was atrocious. Lightning's horse was smeared in it up to the breast.

'Hurricane is dead.' Lightning looked down from the saddle. 'What in San's name is happening out there? Do I shoot or advance?'

'I don't know for sure,' I said. 'The sarissai were attacked by Insect larvae. They routed and the akontistai are caught up in it ...'

'Insect *what*?'

I briefly described the new kind of Insects. 'Little, long Insects. So big—' I held my hands apart. 'But their jaws shoot out *this* far on a kind of jointed appendage. They're intent on eating. And they're going to keep coming because the ground from here to the lake is solid with them.'

Lightning looked to his steward, who was on a brown horse beside him, acting as a division captain. The warden of the first Micawater battalion was on horseback just beyond him. Lightning said, 'We don't know what these things can do. We haven't seen them before and they're not Insects; I don't know what it could mean. Abort the march. We will return to town.'

I said, 'Tornado and Wrenn are already advancing. They are – were – trying to relieve Hurricane. They're in amongst the larvae all up there—' I pointed towards the centre.

'What! Into my target zone?'

'Yes. The larvae look small and easy to kill but they don't know how many there are.'

'Why are they advancing independently? Why didn't you stop them?'

'Tawny wouldn't listen. He's been throwing his weight around ever since San arrived. But there are millions of larvae. They're bound to get cut off.'

Lightning rubbed his hand over his mouth and gazed at me. 'A battlefield is no place for heroics, Jant. The fate of the First Circle is all the proof we need. San's presence is causing us to act like fools.'

'What can we do?'

'I can't see Tornado's and Wrenn's positions. I can't cover them now without hitting them. And bloody Tornado's advance must have left all my archers following him exposed to attack from those *things*.'

'Yes.'

'Right ...' Lightning shook his head and focused properly on me. The crisis had revitalised him. His depression had lifted. He said, 'We're pulling out. We're not going to have a second massacre at Slake Cross.'

He called up four dispatch riders simply by pointing at them, said, '*You* go to Sleat. Tell him to get his fyrd to form a shield wall in front of the archers on the west flank. The archers must shoot at will to support them. *You*, go to the Sapper and Macer on the east flank. Tell them to sound the retreat and retire *in order*. Advise them we are facing a new type of Insect and they should avoid engagement. Tell them the Emperor commands this. *You* tell Hayl the same and then command the reserves on the east wing to follow the hastai as they pull out. *You* go to Thunder. Inform him that we will be retreating and ask that he prepare to cover us. Suggest that he tries flaming projectiles – they may scare these larvae. Then tell the Slake Cross garrison to man the walls.'

The dispatch riders galloped away, spraying muck over the front rank of archers. Lightning turned to his steward. 'Harrier, speak to the Blacksmith and organise the battalions here into a proper defensive position – because when the Insects finish off Hurricane's men they'll be up against us. We will retreat in unison with the west flank.'

'Yes, my lord.'

Lightning sighed, looked at his saddle pommel then up again. 'Harrier. Make sure the fyrd know that the Emperor is watching them and they must stand firm. But if anyone runs, they must be shot. Tell the wardens this. And have the provosts form up behind us. We can't afford another panic.'

'I understand, my lord.' He paused, nodded, then sped away.

'Jant, go to Eleonora. I mean the Queen. Say her lancers must charge straight up the flank and pick up as many of Tornado's and Wrenn's troops as they can, then retreat to camp.'

'Consider it done.' I prepared to take off.

'And you must inform the Emperor of what I have ordered.'

I stared at him. I had to tell San we were *retreating*? 'Yes, but ...'

'Do it. I will meet you at the Imperial Fyrd once I have finished here.'

Back in the air I could see the formations below beginning to reorganise themselves with glacial speed, drawing together more tightly. I shuddered at the thought of being land-bound, encased in metal, clumsy and slow in the face of the darting nymphs.

The Queen's cavalry were gleaming on the extreme west flank. As they were not treading in the infantry's tracks they had escaped the worst mud and, being upwind of the Insects, the horses were calm. At the point of their wedge I could see Eleonora's upturned face calmly watching as I circled down to land nearby.

She spread her wings in greeting, called, 'Why, Jant! You honour us with your presence!'

I approached her. She sat confidently astride her steel-clad thoroughbred, armoured in her usual mix of shining metal and self-assurance. She held her helmet beneath one arm and lance in the other hand, a pale blue pennon lazily waving from it. Her dark hair was immaculate and I even imagined I could detect a trace of rose perfume. An oval shield and a selection of weapons were slung from her saddle. She looked just as formidable on the battlefield as in her boudoir. 'Such a shame to bring you down here, when you look so ... graceful in the air.'

I had no time for Eleonora's crap. 'We're being attacked! 'Leon, there's a new kind of Insect coming out of the lake. Lightning has ordered a retreat. A total withdrawal! Tornado and Serein's hastai will soon be cut off at the front. Lightning commands you and your lancers to charge, rescue them, and carry as many as possible back to town.'

I described the larvae. Eleonora frowned, then changed to an overhand grip on her lance, pointing it at the ground like a spear.

'Tell Lightning I accept his command.' She turned, shouted, 'Lancers of Awia! Follow your Queen!' She glanced at me and pulled her helmet visor down over her smile. I staged my own tactical retreat.

I flew to the Emperor and tipped my wings to him. He raised a hand and the Imperial Fyrd walked their horses aside to let him through. As he did so, Frost on her dapple stallion emerged from behind the last riders on the corner of the square. She urged it into a trot and began to advance, even as the call to retreat was going up. Her bodyguard trailed her. I circled, trying to keep her in view. She's an experienced Eszai, she should realise how serious this is. What was she playing at?

I glanced down, acutely aware of San watching me. Frost could look after herself. I descended. The horses of the Imperial cavalry tossed their heads and held them high, their white-edged eyes watching my great wings beating. The horses were actually shaking as their riders struggled to still them.

The riders and mounts acted as a windbreak, and I had no current to balance on for the last few metres. I fell down heavily and landed in a crouch. My coat-tails flopped to the ground. There was a smash and tinkle of broken glass in my deep right pocket. Crouching in the hoof-printed mud I wondered what it could be. Shit. The jar with the Vermiform worms.

I hadn't thought about it at all up until this instant. I looked down, and worms were wriggling out of my pocket.

CHAPTER 22

Worms, bursting from my pocket, squirmed down my coat in rivulets and dropped off onto the ground. They scattered in all directions and began sinking into the mud, wriggling and twisting around my feet as they burrowed their way down. I scrabbled frantically with both hands, trying to catch hold of them, but they disappeared right under my fingers. I went after others, and the same thing happened. They were too quick; the ends of their tails vanished into the mud. In a few seconds, they had all gone.

I looked up at the Emperor, who was leaning forward over his horse's neck, watching me curiously. I said, 'Ah, my lord ...'

'Comet?'

I stood up. 'Lightning sent me to say he's halted the advance and is recalling the men to camp.'

'So I see. Why?'

'There are millions of little Insects with extendible jaws, coming out of the lake. They killed Hurricane; now Tornado and Wrenn are surrounded. Lightning's sending the Awian lancers to their aid.'

'Little Insects?' the Emperor queried.

I felt something tighten around my ankle. I looked down and so did the Emperor. A thick tentacle of worms was pushing from the soil like the fat stem of a vine. It had wrapped twice around my ankle and the tip was halfway round another loop.

The Emperor's eyes widened but he said nothing. Apologetically I tugged my leg. The tentacle paused, tugged back, then yanked me off my feet. Before I could hit the mud the tentacle shot out of it, a thick column, hoisting me up. I dangled helplessly from my ankle as it poured up, past the Emperor. It kept going, bursting from the ground like the trunk of a tree. Its surface had a linear texture; millions on millions of worms streaking into the air.

The Emperor and all the square of horses shrank quickly below. I could see the whole battlefield now. The Imperial Fyrd's faces looked up, pale and shocked. On all sides of the square they were turning their horses and taking flight. Those in the middle were stepping this way and that trying to push a way out. San, in complete control of Alezane, was looking up at me calmly.

Further off, the canvas city; the pavilions and interlaced ropes – I swung round and caught a glimpse of the clash of lancers and dazzling armour against the Insect larvae, and behind them the lake's brown mirror.

I yelled and yelled. My other leg flailed, knee bent, and my bitten foot was throbbing. My arms dangled, and my coat swished somewhere below my head like a slashed leather curtain. My letters dropped out of my pockets and started fluttering to the ground. My keys and hip flask plummeted after them.

The blood was rushing to my head. My wings slipped open and settled down past shoulder level, loosely spread. My ice axe bounced around, hanging in the space between them. I waved my arms about but couldn't find anything to grab on to. My ankle was agony – the worms were squeezing it tight and my leg was stretching.

I did a sit-up to see the thick snake of annelids wrapped around my ankle, a branch from the solid column stretching to the ground.

'Hey!' I yelled at the stem. 'Let me go, you fucking thing!'

I felt something give and I plummeted a metre. It went taut and held me again.

'No!'

It let me go ... caught me. The worms moving over and clinging to each other gave an elasticity, so I bounced slightly. My joints stretched to popping point. It let me go, caught me. I automatically flapped my wings, looking like a hawk hanging upside down in a snare. I wouldn't have time to turn and fly if it dropped me on my head.

'No! *Don't* let me go! Please don't drop me! Let's talk.'

It just shook me, furiously. My jaw clattered, my bangles jingled and my hair, streaming out under me, swept against my coat skirts.

I stomach-crunched up again and tried to grab the tendril but it just twirled me around. The mud and horse-backs streaked round and round beneath me.

'Aeee! No! Talk to me! Vermi—'

Three more branches spurted out of its stem; the tips pointed, quested towards me and coiled around my wrists and other foot, faster than I could move them. I felt my limbs gradually drawn out with a strength I couldn't resist, until I was spreadeagled like a starfish.

The Emperor's horse backed off until he checked it. He was still looking at me, emotionlessly.

The worms kept pulling me taut. My shoulder joints cracked. I screamed, 'Oh, god, no!'

They stopped pulling and suddenly whipped me the right way up. I was standing in the air, twenty metres above the battle. I had never been upright and stationary in the air before, and the chaos was going on all around me.

Among the rivers of soldiers streaming past in retreat, people were pausing, making a slower flow of steel helmets and heads looking up. Some had stopped completely to gawp and the flow went around them; there were collisions here and there. An enormous, clear space had formed where the trunk went into the ground. Nobody was prepared to approach it. God knows what they were making of a clearly recognisable Messenger stretched like a spider in a vast flesh vine.

Worms slid over worms, providing a greater strength by far than muscle fibres – another tentacle snaked out from the mass. Its tip came to within centimetres of my face and seemed to look about, then it flattened, turned upright and formed into a stylized female face, like a mask, with no eyes in the almond-shaped sockets. I could see down to the mud through them. The well-sculpted lips moved quickly but the Vermiform's polyphonous voice was not in synch; it harped out from both the mask and the main trunk: 'What have you done? How could you bring this on yourselves?'

Wonder and despair vied in its voices but I was panicking too much to care. 'I'm sorry I put your worms in a jar. It was wrong. I—'

The Vermiform pulled my limbs smoothly. Bands of shredding pain flamed up my back and across my chest from shoulder to shoulder. I shrieked. There was something experimental in the pull, as if it could haul much harder if it wanted to.

It said, 'Not that! The water ...' It swung me from side to side and pushed its mask close to my face. 'Where did the lake come from? You stupid, stupid people! You've made a hatching pool!'

'We built the dam to flood the Paperlands,' I said.

'You have caused the death of this entire world!' It sent out thread-thin but steel-rod-strong strands and jabbed me all over my body, which was as effective as a slap. 'You gave the Insects a place to breed! They lay their eggs in still water! Didn't the Somatopolis tell you anything?'

I looked to San; his face raised and eyes narrowed to see me against the bright sky. His horse was trembling and so dotted with sweat his cloak was sticking to it.

Lightning galloped in, standing in his stirrups, his reins tied down and an arrow at string on a longbow. He drew and loosed. The arrow passed clean through the trunk – the worms seethed aside making a hole, then resealed.

He came to the Emperor's side, nocked another arrow, his face white. His horse paced back and forth, stomping the mud, pawing and snorting, head lowered, but he wouldn't let it bolt. He kept beside the Emperor – his spurs drawing blood from its white flanks.

'The Emperor ...' I gasped.

'Where?'

'Down there.'

The Vermiform snapped its mask back into the trunk and started retracting. It carried me down, still stretched out – I saw the mud rushing up closer and closer. It brought me to the Emperor, though San didn't give me so much as a glance. It stopped, jerking me to a halt a metre off the ground.

The top of the curving trunk overhung San's head but the surface nearest him extruded its mask and brought it close to his face. He returned its gaze equably, without moving a muscle.

Lightning aimed at the mask and loosed. His arrow passed harmlessly through it – the worms parted again. The arrow whistled past me and through a sudden gap in the trunk. With the slightest ripple the holes closed and the mask regained its composure.

'Comet,' San said, without moving his gaze from the female visage. 'What is this?'

'It's the Vermiform. And arrows are no good against it.'

The Vermiform addressed the Emperor: 'So you are the one whom Dunlin has told us about?'

San tilted his head as if asking the Vermiform to continue. It said, 'Ourselves in the soil see that larvae are already coming out of the lake. Why? Why did you do it? Do you all have a suicide wish? Do you even *know* what you've done?'

'What have we done?' the Emperor said emotionlessly.

'Created a breeding pool for Insects in this world! Was there a mating flight? Do you know they lay a hundred eggs a minute? Have you any idea how many more are to come?'

The Emperor said nothing.

The Vermiform threshed, furious. 'Are you going to miss this warrior?' and slowly drew my bonds tighter and tighter. I tried to pull back but it was hopeless: agony flared straight through my shoulders – my arms and legs were riving out. I started screaming – I could feel the suck of the cup-joints in my hips stretched to the point of dislocation.

The pauldrons of San's armour moved infinitesimally, as if he shrugged. He did not look at me, only at the mask.

The Vermiform said, 'Dunlin is a better commander than you ever were, San. He is marshalling an army in several worlds that is much better than anything you've managed to establish here.'

San said, 'I thought that would happen.'

'Dunlin will be infuriated when he hears it's come to this.'

'That is the least of my concerns ... Could you put my Messenger down, please?' he added, although he said it as if my shrieking was irking him rather than if he cared that I was being torn limb from limb. I was released abruptly. I fell in a loose tangle, hit the ground heavily and curled up in the cold mud, hugging my shoulders.

'These are just the first nymphs emerging,' the worms choired. 'There will be hundreds more of these waves. Larvae are so ravenous that if they all hatched together they would devour each other for want of food. Countless worlds have fallen this way.'

814

The Emperor said, 'It is an extremely long time since I was last in the Shift.'

The Vermiform continued, 'The older larvae will shed their skins and become Insects, and begin dropping food in for the new larvae. Five moults later, those adult Insects will take flight too – and you'll have yet another generation of millions of larvae emerging. Once that started happening in the Somatopolis we didn't have a chance. You certainly don't have one, with the stupid pathetic weapons you still wield. We can taste saltpetre, aluminium, tungsten, uranium in the earth yet you still fight using wood and iron! You'll be overwhelmed. Every body of standing water in your whole continent will soon become a hatching pool. Every pond, every lake—'

Lightning nocked another arrow to string.

'Dunlin is more active than you are!' the worms said. 'He understands that Insects are a mortal threat, but you don't seem to!'

'We are doing all we can.'

'Even when Insects were building bridges here, you did not respond seriously enough. They have overrun our world completely, and many others we have seen. Worlds take thousands of millions of years to form and Insects can destroy them in a decade! But you ... it is as if you were deliberately trying to keep a stalemate with them. You never take an inch against them. We know why: without their outside threat, the Fourlands wouldn't need your Circle, your rule, or *you*. But your plan for keeping the Insects at a manageable level has all gone wrong. First there were swarms, then bridges, now they're breeding! The balance has tipped. You will never hold them in check now.'

The Emperor bridled at the accusation. 'We keep the front and push them back when we can. There are far too many to defeat. This is a stalemate of necessity, not intention.'

'No. Dunlin told me this was a world where a few Insects appeared at first. When that happens, the residents can easily exterminate them. Awia could simply have wiped them out. When they began to spread you could still have made a concerted effort and killed them all. But you let the situation get out of hand in order to get into power, didn't you? They needed you as a leader once the swarms started. And you kept them needing you ever since.'

San shook his head. 'False. We were all ignorant of war before the Insects arrived. We had no way to fight them. They are more difficult to kill than you say. We had no knowledge of their habits. We didn't know they were going to expand so quickly.'

'And when they did start spreading, you let them so the people would put you into power!'

For the first time ever, I saw the Emperor lose his temper. 'We fought tooth and nail! Yes, when Insects first began to proliferate, if we had made a concerted effort we might, *might*, have killed them all, but more were always following! We were embroiled in a civil war—'

Which you ended by dividing the Pentadrica as a prize, I thought.

'—It was all I could do to stop three countries tearing a fourth apart and then turning on each other. We had no proper weapons, no strategies; we had no idea how to kill Insects.'

The Vermiform fermented with fury. Eight thick worm-pillars thrust out of the ground in a two-metre circle around San's horse. Like the first trunk they tapered towards the top. As they rose, the main trunk thinned, worms disappearing into the earth to shoot up as the new pillars. They grew to its height, bending over San and his horse. They looked like gigantic octopus tentacles waving around a boat. His stallion reared, but he rode it.

The tentacles joined together above him, caging him in. The mask extended into thin strings and pushed towards San's face. Worms separated and flowed onto his skin, spreading to crawl all over him.

They snaked down his breastplate collar, under his helmet, into his hair, in the folds around his eyes, circled his lips and slithered into the wrinkles on his neck. The Emperor did not move as worms turmoiled out of his armour's joints at armpits and waist, from his wrists to slip between his fingers holding the reins. They wriggled under the plates on his thighs and shins to the shining laminae on his feet. Lines of worms formed a moving, living pink net all over him.

Lightning yelled. He spurred his horse over to me, dismounted and helped me from my Jant-shaped hole in the ooze. I poked around among my sodden letters, found my hip flask and took a long swig.

'What's happening?' Lightning said wildly. 'What are these maggots attacking San? What must we do?'

'It's the Vermiform. From the Shift.'

'How can I kill them?'

'You can't.'

The worms stopped writhing over the Emperor, poured up to his breast-plate and webbed its surface. From the centre, a rope of worms spouted out and dived at the ground. They pooled on the mud and gathered themselves into a semblance of a man, building from the feet up. All the worms peeled off the Emperor, and onto the man's shape. It gained height, thinned, worms represented hair hanging down to the shoulders, pinched cheeks, a thin nose, a body flanged or curved, closely portraying plate armour. It became a perfect imitation of San.

'We have tales of god coming back!' Lightning cried. 'And this thing appears!'

'It isn't god,' I said. 'It's a Shift creature.'

The effigy of San chorused, 'You told them what? You told them there's

816

a god? You ...' Its contempt knew no bounds. 'You gave them the idea of god?'

'There is always a god in the minds of men,' the Emperor said quietly.

The Vermiform said, 'Have you used that for your own ends too? No wonder this world is about to be lost to the Insects, if you are waiting for god to help you. Your people will all die as they wait!'

'We are not waiting,' San said. 'We are fighting.'

The mask bobbed. 'They're being slaughtered! Do they know of the Shift?'

Lightning muttered, 'Is this mountain of livebait saying there is no god but the Shift exists?'

'God isn't here but a Shift creature is,' I said.

The Vermiform said, 'San, your Fourlands are lost. Your Circle will break and your Castle will fall. I must warn Dunlin that this world does not have much time left, and I must arrange defences. The Insects here will soon build bridges to other worlds. We hope they will act with more intelligence than you did.'

'Leave the Empire, you foul thing,' said San calmly.

The eight tentacles that joined together above the Emperor, caging him in like the struts of a tent, sent out a thick strand into the air. We could see worms streaming up to its tip, which looked truncated; they were vanishing there. The thick rope was pouring into nowhere – an area as big as a buckler that looked the same as the rest of the sky.

The trunks thinned, the caricature of the Emperor dissolved as worms left it and joined them. The trunks shrank to strings, then their bases lifted up from the earth as if being reeled in. They looped into the hole in thin air, twisting together into a rope as they did so. The end of the rope vanished. The Vermiform had gone. I knew it would be appearing like a cable in another world.

The Emperor looked directly at me accusingly. So did Lightning – he had been gaping at the worm-arc, as had all the soldiers standing or on their knees in traumatised silence around us. Streams of retreating riders and men-at-arms coming off the flank were passing us, back to town. The Emperor looked at them and sighed.

Lightning said, 'That was a throng of earthworms, wasn't it?'

'Yes,' I said.

'Mmm. From the ...'

'From the Shift, yes.'

'Right. Uh-hum. It said flying Insects will lay eggs in every lake. Not in Micawater lake they won't.'

I accidentally put my weight on my bitten foot and yowled. Lightning shook himself. 'Are you injured?'

I honestly could not tell whether I was seriously hurt or not. I had my arms crossed, hands clasped desperately around my shoulders. I said, 'I'll go to Rayne.'

San began to turn his horse but Lightning ran across and grabbed its bridle. The horse, true to its training, stood still. San glared down at the Archer. Lightning, from force of habit, lowered his gaze, then rallied and looked the Emperor straight in the eye. 'My lord,' he said. 'Where are you *from?*'

I knew what he meant, and so did San, but he didn't deign to answer. The thought of a Shift world full of potential Emperors was enough to make me shiver worse than the horses.

'Where are you from?' Lightning repeated. 'Not from the ... from the ... You're not like that thing, are you?'

The Emperor closed his eyes and shook his head gently. 'I am from Hacilith ... From the place where Hacilith city now stands. I am a man. A man like any other Morenzian. Believe me, Archer.'

'My lord.' Lightning let the bridle go.

A thought occurred to me. '*When* are you from?'

The Emperor ignored me, but Lightning took up the question, frowning. 'Yes. That thing said millions.'

San gave the clear impression that he neither knew nor cared what the Vermiform said. He was regarding Lightning closely. He stated, 'No, I am not that old. Yes, I am older than you think.'

Lightning swallowed hard, pressed, 'Then how old?'

San was still scrutinising him. 'You must dine with me tonight, Archer.'

We were astounded. 'Yes, my lord,' Lightning mouthed. 'Yes – certainly.'

'Now you must return to your fyrd. You have my full authority to supervise the withdrawal.'

Lightning bowed, white-faced. San glanced at me. 'Messenger, put aside your pain. Find the Architect. We must discover a way to drain the lake. Everything depends on this now, it seems.' He looked slowly around him. 'Everything.'

I struggled into the air. My wing muscles were tender from the assault and the constant take-offs. If I kept using them now I knew I would be grounded for days. But I had to carry out San's request, and I was anxious to escape from the curious queries of the fyrdsmen still gawking at the air where the Vermiform had vanished.

I soared up above the devastation and circled, looking for Frost. The Imperial Fyrd were now toy soldiers beneath me. Lightning was tiny on horseback as he galloped away from them. The host's advance, seemingly so inexorable only an hour ago had stopped and it was ebbing away.

I searched in vain for Frost. I looked among the east wing that she would have to pass through. It was a wide stream of men in full retreat. If Frost was heading the other way, her small group would be battling against the current and I'd see the flow of men dividing round them like water cleaving around a rock. But they seemed in good order with no stragglers – Hayl's cavalry was carefully screening the withdrawal. From the lack of agitation in their ranks they seemed to be still ignorant of the larvae.

I climbed, widening my search. The reserve had formed into a solid shield wall with archers in tight-packed shooting positions behind them. Lightning's orders reached slow actualisation in the movements of tens of thousands on the field. The archers resumed shooting and arrow volleys sailed by below me, rippling the air. Already the rear echelons were beginning to form into columns, ready to pull out following the east wing. The real battleground was in front of the shield wall. But I didn't have time to look – I had to find Frost and, even in her recently *disturbed* state she wouldn't have been stupid enough to go that way, surely?

I circled again, and cast my gaze towards the periphery. A motion caught my attention, so fast I thought it had to be Insects. I angled towards it, and saw it was the orange Riverworks banner accompanying Frost. Her horsemen were out on the east flank, far beyond the retreating troops and moving at a full gallop, something I wasn't expecting in the mud soup. I dived towards them and saw they were heading rapidly towards the river bank, following a narrow supply road of quarry chippings. It was a causeway over the sodden ground, built at the same time as the plunge basin. Frost knew the valley like the back of her hand and was taking a quick detour around the chaos. I scanned the route ahead. Near the diminished river the track met the road, wide enough for wagons, that climbed the ramp to the dam and formed the walkway on top.

I shed height quickly and checked for larvae. Along the entire length of the lake margins they were crawling up the shallow slope, long bodies twisting from side to side. Their claws pushed trails in the gravel. Some turned on each other, and on the carcasses of Insects littering the lakeside.

Scores were emerging onto the dam's face where the lake lapped up against it. In ragged lines they climbed its nearly sheer wall, finding purchase where it would be too steep for an adult Insect. Ripples broke over them, but they hung off its cobbles, moving up with mindless persistence; six legs and hooked feet scrabbling slowly.

Nearly all headed directly to the carnage before them; downstream of the dam the shore was reasonably clear. The adult Insects were likewise occupied. Frost would only have to worry about stragglers as long as the shambles in front of her continued to offer an easy supply of food.

I bit my lip, realising I was thinking of Tornado's and Wrenn's battalions only as bait to draw Insects away from Frost. Guiltily, I decided to take a closer look.

Tornado's men had advanced barely a few hundred metres after I'd left them before becoming trapped. There was no end to the nymphs emerging from the lake. The infantry divisions were concentrating on chopping as many as possible, but they were already an island cut off and disappearing under a chitin tide. They had formed into isolated schiltroms, standing in circles of shields shoulder-to-shoulder, presenting their weapons in all directions. Larvae were chewing through shields, running up them and over the heads of men so I saw waggling larvae crossing the circles. Two larvae replaced every one dispatched. The circles were visibly shrinking; the air was heavy with screams. I picked out Wrenn, a Wrought sword in each hand, slashing and cutting the nymphs to shreds but there were too many. It was like trying to sever snowflakes in a blizzard.

The Queen's lancers were whipping their mounts through the swarm. Each rider stopped only to pull a desperate foot soldier up behind him before turning and spurring back. They stabbed with their lances but the best weapons they had were their horses' iron-shod hooves. The chargers' long barding frustrated larvae trying to climb it but they could crawl under and they shot their jaws into the horses' pasterns. Casualties were beginning to tell. Some mounts threw their riders in terror. I never saw any get up again.

I put the terrible sight behind me and turned back towards Frost. My course took me over where Lourie's soldiers had fallen. I was shocked to find myself staring at what looked like an ancient battlefield: skulls grinned under pot helmets, bones shone through the gaps in battered armour. Every last scrap of flesh had been consumed. The bone-mounds were covered in gnarled, motionless larvae sitting with heads looking up and long tails pressed to the ground. Their thin carapaces were translucent. Some were missing legs or heads. The back of every thorax was cracked and open.

Shit. They weren't dead larvae, they were empty shells. They were growing, shedding their carapaces within only a few hours of emerging. Five moults, the Vermiform had said. Surely all the moults couldn't take the same length of time? At this rate, by the end of the week we would be up against a swarm of Insects greater than any we had ever seen.

I found Frost leading her group, galloping flat-out up the curving road. Gaps appeared as the stronger mounts pulled away. She lashed her horse mercilessly, obsessed with reaching the dam. The horses were dripping sweat and wide-eyed with terror at the smell of Insects.

I waved. 'Come on! The way's clear if you're fast!'

They pounded on, only a couple of minutes from the dam. But as they drew closer, nearby larvae began to converge on them.

820

'Look out!'

Frost ignored my warning and carried straight onto the dam's crest, pushing her horse through the larvae as if they weren't there. The rest followed her. I could see larvae hanging on horses' legs by their jaws, working their way up the sides of the screaming animals. The riders flailed at them with swords, maces, gauntleted fists.

I saw the trailing horse eaten as she staggered; larvae swarmed up her legs and took her apart, stripped the skin from her side in great swathes until her guts fell out. Here and there, they laid her bare to the bone in seconds. She died squealing, trying to free her hooves from the close-packed spiny nymphs. The rider, flailing at the beasts working through his armour, threw himself over the parapet and plummeted to his death rather than being eaten alive.

With a terminal burst of speed, Frost reached her destination: the winch tower. She leapt off her horse, just short of the portcullis, shot the bolts of the iron maintenance door and disappeared inside the tower itself. The majority of her company were following. Abandoning their horses to occupy the larvae, they sprinted to safety, finally swinging the door shut behind them when it was clear there would be no more survivors. A minute later, the Riverworks Company banner jerked up the flag pole and unfurled in the breeze.

CHAPTER 23

I focused on the banner, soared round and set down on the roof of the winch tower. I slipped to the parapet, between its beacon and enormous warning bell. I looked around; the timber fence along the walkway had completely disappeared. Insects had chewed the stakes down to pulpy stumps.

I looked down the faces of the winch tower. Both its portcullises were down, blocking the walkway on both sides. Both tracks were covered with larvae; they clustered around the grating trying to get through, but it was thick metal mesh and the gaps were too small. Adult Insects on the side nearest the Paperlands were chewing the bars fruitlessly.

A rhythmic clanging echoed from inside the tower. I listened carefully; it was heavy and sharp, metal against stone, and muffled as if coming from a distance, which was strange because it was directly below me.

I shimmied over the parapet and kicked a louvre through. I swung one leg inside, ducked my head under the top lintel and sat straddling the ledge, hunched half in, half out of the tower. I looked down.

The tower had no floors – it was one great, hollow dark space filled with machinery. Some candle lights flickered far below me on the ground. The scale of the crowded shafts and cogs interlaced with each other completely took my breath away.

I soon distinguished the mechanisms. On the walls below my window and opposite were fixed those needed to work the two portcullises – spindles wound with the last couple of loops of rope, and greased metal runners. The larvae's short, whisker-like antennae poked between the bars of both gates and their jaws flashed out, tearing at the air.

The mechanism to raise the dam gate was even more impressive. Only Frost's dedication could have designed it, and only the effort it took to have drawn it together could have made her love it as much as she did. The shafts were painted black, but their naked steel working surfaces shone with oil. The inside of the tower looked like that of a windmill in which all the wheels and beams and pegs had turned to metal.

The square floor was paved and on either side were circular, stone-rimmed holes from which thick cables ran, like ship's ropes. They were tarred and very taut. They led up to a horizontal brass roller and were wrapped around it at both ends. It looked like the spindle used to raise water from a well, but on a massive scale. The roller was braced with girders attaching it to all four walls, secure at head height. Its vertical wheel meshed with a complicated system of gears onto a horizontal capstan carrying a chain. Lots of tackle to harness horses lay tangled, attached to the free end of the chain.

Frost was down there, dwarfed by the machinery. I could see her rounded shoulders and bandanna; she had taken her helmet off. I shouted down but she couldn't hear me. She was bent double, peering into a square hole in the floor. Its trapdoor was open and it was big enough for one man to fit down at a time. The clanking resounded from deep underground.

Several soldiers were distributing gear piled by the walls. A big man beside Frost held a rope around his waist with both hands. The end disappeared into the shaft, and he was lowering it.

I climbed down the rough wall and ran to her. 'Frost?'

'Jant!' She stood upright and stretched, her hands in the small of her back. Her face was streaked with dirt and her brigandine jacket hung open. She had stuffed her brown velvet rabbit under its fastening flap and its head nodded comically at her bosom.

'Jant, we lost our horses. We couldn't bring them in. We had to leave them outside and the Insect young just ripped them apart.'

'I saw it,' I said.

'We needed horses to raise the gate and open the dam. Now we can't.' Without looking she slapped her hand onto the weighty rope. 'See?'

'Shit!'

'Yes. Shit. But I think I've figured a solution.'

'What are you going to do?'

She pointed down the maintenance shaft. A line of brackets bolted to the wall formed a ladder leading into the depths. A murky flicker of lamplight came and went down there.

'Climb down and I'll show you.'

'I'd rather not.'

'Come on. There are ten men crammed in the gate chamber but you can hang on the ladder.'

'No, no. I don't have time. I have to get back to the Emperor and tell him what you're doing.'

The rope around the soldier's waist tugged twice, pulling his hand, and he began hauling something up. Frost said, 'Now we've made a start, I can rig a block-and-tackle to make raising the spoil easier. This is your last load doing it the hard way.'

'As you say.' He grinned at her. He seemed in good spirits.

'What are you doing?' I asked again.

She stamped her steel-toed boot on the paving stone. 'If you went down into the chamber, you'd see the top of the gate emerging from the floor, with the ropes attached to it. Millions of tonnes of water are pressing on the gate, keeping it shut. So we are digging down on either side of it.

'We are going to provide a new passage for the water over the top of the gate, then down into the original outlet pipe. Of course we're digging on the downstream side first to open up the passage to the face of the dam. Then I'll ask them to excavate the other side. Water will burst up, fill the chamber and drain away down the downstream side, out through the face of the dam, like it's supposed to. We will drain the lake, lads! You'll be heroes!'

The men broke out in optimistic smiles.

I said, 'Really? Won't the water gush back up the shaft?'

Frost's lips set thin. 'No.'

'But—'

'Sh!' she snapped. 'I'll put a lid on it, or something.' She took my sleeve and turned me away from the toiling fyrdsmen. 'Not in front of them. Don't ask any questions, just spread the news as to what I'm doing.'

I said, 'The downstream face is covered with larvae too. I expect some will have crawled up the passage.'

She stared at me, then nodded. 'Oh – when we break through? Yes, some might crawl into the chamber but we have our pickaxes. And the water will flush the rest out. I left a few stores here but we don't have many spades. Fly thyself to the town and bring us more supplies.'

'There's a limit to the weight I can carry.'

'Yes, of course. Bring what thou canst, thou wilt have to make a few trips. I want water, clean fresh water—' she gestured in the direction of the lake '—because my men can't drink that muck and this is thirsty work. They're afforst from the ride, and forspent already.'

'Frost, the first law of communication is to speak the same language as the person you're speaking to.'

'Sorry. You know what I bloody mean. Bring some more lanterns, another couple of spades because we don't have enough to go around, and some food.' She dithered. 'Oh, and can you bring me some coffee too?'

'Sure.'

'I can make it on the stove. It's going to be a long night and I think I'm going to need it. We'll keep digging until we make the breakthrough. The men have to remove all the cladding from the floor of the chamber with muscle power alone; there's no way we can use acid down there.'

I shook my head. 'You're mining out the core of your own dam?'

'No. I'm just making two little holes, one either side of the gate.'

'But whoever's trapped in the chamber will—'

'Will be able to climb to safety up the brackets,' she said firmly. 'Now, do you have a pen and paper? I need to write a message to the Emperor. Go and fetch the water bottles, and when you return I'll have it ready for him.'

I nodded to her, then quickly scaled the tower wall, slipped through the window and felt the pull as my wings took my weight. I flew back to Slake Cross.

824

The town was a collage of hideous sights. It was incredibly crowded; people were still coming in from the battlefield but they were also drawing back behind the town's walls out of the canvas city. We had no chance of holding the palisade and camp against the approaching larvae. They could climb, and they could swim, too, so the moat was useless. The tower tops bristled with soldiers ready to repulse them.

I ran towards the centre square and the water pumps, passing stretcher-bearers carrying horrifically injured men. They left trails of blood through the streets already slippery with mud and horse dung. Exhausted soldiers crowded the staircases and corners, trying to summon the last reserves of energy. Some were chewing handfuls of hazelnuts, their iron rations. The walking injured leant against walls waiting for their friends to bring them pannikins of stew. Soldiers bare to the waist were queuing endlessly outside the shower block. Its doors were wide – men too tired to undress were standing clothed under the flow of water.

More queues of thousands: up to the enormous cooking pots on a table under an awning. Under the Cook's cornucopia banner, his assistants were doling out tremendous quantities of bean stew to whoever was well enough to take it. Soldiers were waiting in line holding their bowls.

As I passed them, Tre Cloud darted out. 'The Swordsman's lost his leg!' he cried. 'Featherback lancers just carried him in.'

'Is he conscious?'

'I'd say. He's bawling blue filth.'

I set off sprinting to the hospital. I could hear the screaming from a street away. I skirted round wounded men laid side by side on stretchers in the street against its wall, and entered onto a floor slick with red. Gore was spattered up the walls to above head height. Doctors were concentrating on their immediate patients and yelling for assistance, dressings, fresh water. Nurses carrying pitchers or bandage rolls shouldered past each other, dashing through the maze of beds.

All around me men were lying, moaning, crying. One reached out and grabbed my belt. I looked down at him, and as I did so, he died.

I slipped on blood, distracted by the tremendous variety of injuries. There were lots of empty eye sockets, or men with bandages over their eyes, because larvae had pulled their eyes out. There were plenty of men with cloth wrapped around bloody stumps; adult Insects had lopped off arms and legs. There were wounds to the throat, to the groin, to joints that were less protected by plate. Along the walls slumped hundreds of men with extreme exhaustion and dehydration – every one being given litres and litres of salty water. One porter with a mop was ineffectually stirring the pools of glutinous blood on the flagstones. It reflected the camp beds along the wall.

Lying in a corner there was a man whose face had been chewed down to the bone on his forehead and cheeks – I could see into his mouth. And in another corner – something so terrible I quickly blotted it from memory.

I saw Wrenn – lying by the wall, on a stretcher bed extending towards the middle of the room. Three lancers in plate were holding him down, one on his either shoulder and one on his leg. His other leg was nothing but a bleeding stump, bitten off below the knee. He was kicking it in the air and drops of blood were spattering on the soldiers. He was yelling, his mouth a black oval, his cheeks stretched and eyes slitted. Where his shin should be, I saw the white ends of neatly severed bone.

They had stripped him down to his padded gambeson but he still had armour on his uninjured leg. He was covered in many smaller excruciating wounds, bleeding heavily through tears in the jacket. Most of them were deep punctures, where larvae's fangs had slid in like curved smooth thorns, but they were nothing compared to what had happened to his leg.

Rayne was resuscitating a man with a crunchy broken jaw and a mushy nose. She left him to her assistant and dashed over, leaving sticky footprints.

She gave Wrenn an injection into the crook of his arm, pressed a cotton pad on the place, withdrew the needle. She quickly dropped some clear liquid on a white tile, and mixed it with a drop of blood pricked from one of the three soldiers who looked most like him. The mixture did not go grainy but stayed smooth, so she patted the windowsill for the lad to sit up there, and she rigged up a waxed cotton tube that would transfer blood down from his arm into Wrenn's.

Wrenn was yelling all the time. 'No! Put me back on the field! Leave me there! I want to be left! Bitch!'

She grasped his hand and he tried to fend her off, but he calmed a little as the scolopendium took effect. 'Leave me! I can't be Eszai any more! Let me die!'

'Let him die unbeaten,' I said.

Wrenn glanced in the direction of my voice, with unfocused eyes, and smeared blood across his cheek with the back of his hand.

Rayne was furious, 'Ge' ou' of t' way, Jant!'

'He can't be the Swordsman now. He'll die anyway. Let him die without the indignity of being beaten by a Challenger.'

'There's more t' life than tha'!'

'I've never had pain like this before!' The fear was stronger than the agony in his voice. 'And ... and ... Oh, god, I'm so bloody cold.'

He turned his head and spoke to empty space: 'Skua? You can't be. You died … I lost Sanguin. I left it out there …' He stared, glazed-eyed, and then passed out.

Rayne pointed to a tourniquet on his thigh, and looked at the soldier on the window ledge. 'Did you pu' tha' on?'

'Yes.'

'Good. You did t' righ' thing.'

Wrenn's stump was bone surrounded by meaty pulp. The end of the artery dangled, swaying loosely and dribbling blood. Rayne pinched the end and expertly wound turns of silk thread around it – four, five, six times. She tied the thread and then smeared on an ointment of turpentine and phenol, with tansy extract. Then she bound a poultice loosely around it. The poultice, a pad of spongy elder pith wrapped in linen, had been steam-cleaned then infused with a lot of rose honey.

She stepped back and surveyed her work. 'I can feel him pulling on t' Circle. This could've killed any other Eszai bu' Wrenn. He's such a figh'er. Wha' are you doing here? Have you brough' a message?'

'No. I'm passing through. Do you have anything to tell Frost or San?'

She shook her head. She was untying the tourniquet from Wrenn's thigh. 'You're no' encouraging, Jant. Saying "leave him"! How dare you!'

'But how can he swordfight now?' I protested. 'Even if he survives, he'll lose his place in the Circle to the first Challenger who comes along.'

'I've deal' with maimed Eszai hundreds of times. I know I'm righ'.'

'I'd hate to be forced back to obscurity,' I said. 'Wrenn is the same. Do you expect him to win duels on a wooden leg?'

Rayne said, 'Stranger things have happened.'

I huffed. 'A Swordsman with one leg? How likely is that?'

Rayne said, 'Look. There are all kinds of freakish abilities in t' Circle. We even have a man who can fly. Tha's pret'y damn weird.'

I took her point. She continued, 'He migh' go on for a year or even more before get'ing bea'en. He may well have t' come t' terms wi' being mortal again. Bu' a' least he'll have more life. He can change his outlook. He can change from being t' Swordsman t' someone else. I am giving him time t' think. Once he thinks abou' i', he'll thank me for no' let'ing him die. They always do. As long as they can continue t' live wi' digni'y, and have the chance t' die peacefully in bed surrounded by grandchildren, i's bet'er than dying on the field. Isn' i'? Dying in shi' and confusion means nothing. You gain nothing. He'll prefer living and growing old t' dying in bat'le. If he wan's to die in bat'le he can do i' later. He needs time t' clear his mind. No ex-Eszai has ever told me any differen'.'

'He's gashed here as well.' I pointed to a deep, narrow cut above the knee of his severed leg. The black tip of a broken Insect mandible stuck out.

'T' poleyne plate mus' have come off his knee. Tell Sleat those clips don' work. A shard is still in there. I'm going t' take i' ou'. T' soldiers tried t' pull i' ou' and i' broke.'

Insect mandible shards are much worse than their leg spines. I know many people living with Insect spines embedded in their bodies. If Rayne can't extract them without causing further damage, she leaves them in. But jaws are highly septic, considering what Insects eat, and broken pieces will rankle in wounds and cause fatal septicaemia. I helped Rayne as she began to operate to extract the shard.

She eased the blood-hardened cloth away from his skin. Then she took a scalpel from the steamed-clean tray and made a cross-shaped incision at the point where the mandible had gone in, widening the cut. She squirted spirits of wine into the wound with a syringe, and grasped the end of the triangular shard with forceps. It had one very sharp edge, and to prevent it cutting Wrenn's flesh when she drew it out, she took a little hollow steel cylinder like a straw with an open slot along its length. She slid the tube onto the shard's sharp edge. Then she drew it out firmly and smoothly along its path of entry. In time with his heartbeat, blood welled up, overran the camp bed and pattered on the floor. Rayne rinsed out the wound and put a dressing on it.

Then she detached the tube from the arm of the soldier who was giving Wrenn his blood. He looked very pale and weak by this stage. She nodded to him. 'You can go. Take a sip of juice, over there ... Then go and ea' mea' and drink a lo' of water, and have a res'.'

The dazed soldier wandered off. Rayne crooked her thumb at Wrenn. 'Even if their blood is incompa'ible you can risk i' once, but a second time would be fatal.'

She felt his pulse with a couple of twiggy fingers on his neck. 'No' a' home.'

'When will he wake up?'

'Could be any time. Migh' not. But if I know Wrenn, he'll wake as soon as he can. Tha' one never gives up.'

'We'll see.'

'And i' makes a difference from having t' cure him of VD.' She smiled without any trace of humour. Invisible flies were buzzing around my head. I hunched my shoulders and an avid pain ran between my wings; I stretched them against the stiffness.

Rayne wiped her hands on a cloth. 'I have Tornado in here as well, you know.'

'What's wrong with him?'

'He lost an eye.' She pointed across the room to where Tornado was sitting on another stretcher bed, with his head in his hands. Bandages covered his eye. He was stripped to the waist – you could reconstruct the battles of eight centuries from the scars on his body.

'What! By a larva?' If they could wound even Tornado, the Vermiform was right; we were finished.

'No. In the crush someone's spear went into his eye. Don' talk t' him. He's very pissed off about i' – he's embarrassed, too.'

'I told him not to advance.'

'If you remind him of tha', he'll punch you. Fescue's jus' lef' here, dead. And Vir Ghallain has been mauled. From wha' I've seen, they've los' him too.'

'I'll speak to his Select.'

Rayne beckoned a doctor. 'Watch over Serein and remove his armour.' Then she turned to her next patient. She wouldn't be diverted until all that could be done had been done.

I set off towards the water pumps where containers were stacked. I filled as many as I could carry and slung them around my body on two crossed leather straps. As I left, the last of Tanager's lancers raced in. They didn't seem to be bringing many survivors – some injured men rode pillion, but others were little more than chewed parcels, slung over saddlebows.

I flew bottles of water, packets of food and enough coffee to keep Frost going out to the dam for the next two hours. I even managed a couple of spades for which Frost was even more grateful than the coffee. Each time, the spoil heap by the portcullis had grown. By the fifth or sixth time I climbed through the window of the winch tower, it had completely blocked the portcullis and was slumping through to the walkway. Inside, a chain of men were passing buckets along and the one at the end threw the dirt onto the mound.

I sat on the ledge and hooked the supplies on a winch that Frost had rigged up. One of the soldiers lowered them, hand-over-hand, while I climbed down the wall.

Soldiers stood around the machinery, leaning on it to eat the latest packet of bread. They had all kept their helmets on for protection underground, and they were filthy; their faces black with dirt and glossy with sweat. They were surprisingly cheerful, though; I took their measure as I approached Frost.

She was sitting on a pile of burlap sacks, intent on her writing. Her jaw was clenched so tightly she had dimples in her cheeks. Tears ran down both sides of her nose.

She had a climbing rope wrapped around her waist, through a metal loop and coiled on the floor. She had obviously found it easier to abseil down the shaft, and the soldiers looked as if they would be happy to belay her anywhere.

I touched her shoulder and she jumped. 'Jant? Wait, I'm finishing this letter. For the ... will of god ... and the ... pro-tect-ion of the Cir-cle,' she pronounced as she wrote, and signed it. 'Arch-it-ect for the Sovereign ... Emperor San ... and Chief Eng-in-eer of River-works Com-pa-ny.' She blew on the paper, then folded it and dripped candle wax along the fold.

I said, 'I brought more bread. It's all I can carry.'

She nodded, and bellowed down the maintenance shaft, 'Change of shift! Come up, the kettle's boiled!'

She tittered hysterically, hyperventilated a few breaths, and checked herself. Her teeth were edge-on-edge, her forehead furrowed.

I offered her a muddy loaf. She wiped the tears away with her brigandine cuff and shook her head contemptuously. 'No! No more time off!' She sat down on the sacks. 'Will you take the note to San?'

'Yes. Are you OK?'

'I'm fine. There's no problem. I don't know why you think there's a problem, because there isn't.' I could hear the steel in her voice. She was showing both her personalities at once. Her extreme stress had laid them bare in front of me and it was like talking to two different people. I didn't know whether to speak to the tearful, emotional woman or the single-minded engineer; whether to give her a comforting hug or a quadratic equation.

She took her bandanna off – her hair flowed loose, matted with mud. She blew her nose on the bandanna and stuffed it in her pocket. 'Right! Comet, we have broken through into the downstream passageway. We've made a big hole in the maintenance chamber floor that the water will drain through. Now we are digging on the other side of the gate where the tunnel's full of water. If we can keep up this rate, I expect to make a breakthrough sometime in the early hours of the morning ... and the lake will start to drain ...' She turned to the men preparing to take the place of the even grimier diggers climbing out of the shaft. 'Do ye hear that? The faster you shovel, boys, the more lives you will save! People out there are being savaged! Your fellow fyrdsmen are dying in whole battalions! Insect spawn are crawling all over the town and more of the ... *horrible things* ... are coming out of the lake every minute. Accept victory, and we will win. We will do what we set out to do!'

The men cheered.

She gave them a smile, then drew me aside to the spoil heap. Her eyes were bloodshot and brimming. 'My last p-project. Riverworks's final contract will be successful. The Emperor must then c-complete our plan and advance the t-troops over the lakebed ...' She caught a breath. '... And kill all the larvae we leave stranded in the mire. You must give him this—' She handed me the letter.

830

'Of course.'

She looked at me levelly, she seemed to have swung round to a calm phase. 'Describe to the Sapper exactly what I am doing. Tell him the Glean Road will be passable but the Lowespass Road will not. The waters will take two days to subside. Will you tell him that?'

'Of course.'

'I never – ah – oh, Jant, I never built the basin for a hydraulic jump this huge ... It's ...'

'*Are* you all right?'

'Yes, yes, I'm fine. You must also send a semaphore to Summerday ... Tell them to evacuate.'

'Most of the Summerday people are here,' I said. 'The governor has been fighting.'

'I know. But some are left in the town, and you must evacuate them.'

'Why?'

She glanced over to the wall, on the other side of which was the lake. She breathed out the breath she had been holding for a few seconds, and tittered. Then she panted another breath. 'When the lake drains, their ... streets might flood.'

'Might?' I had never known her to be so unspecific.

'Mm. Tell them to get out, immediately. And tell Mist to move the ships he has in the river mouth. I don't remember who Mist is at the moment; I mean, what his real name is ... So many come and go. But if he's the Sailor, he'll be able to do it.'

'I'll tell them.'

She nodded slowly. 'Then goodbye, Jant.'

'See you, Frost.'

I turned to go, but she clenched my hand. 'Goodbye. Goodbye, Comet.'

Tears rolled unnoticed down her cheeks. She bit on her bottom lip, then smiled at her workers gathered around the hearth. 'Oi! Shift B! Did I give you five minutes or five hours? Go back down there and *dig faster!*'

I climbed up the wall. As I slipped through the window, one leg in, one leg out, I looked down to see her sitting on the sandbags. She had taken the brown velvet rabbit from her lapel and was holding in both hands, looking at it as if in silent conversation.

Dusk was obscuring the gruesome remains. Larvae were crawling everywhere, covering the uneven ground sickeningly swiftly, and gathering in hordes around any flesh they could find.

I only saw adult Insects in the distance towards Plow – they were already moving on. I wondered why and then I saw larger larvae among the rest – the second moults. They moved nearly as fast as adults, eating their smaller brethren. Maybe the adults were leaving because they feared their own growing spawn turning on them.

I noticed one about to shed its skin and circled low, watching. It suddenly raised its head and froze. I could see through its shell; a slimy bulk was moving inside, pressing uneasily against the surface as if struggling to get out.

Its thorax split down the midline. A pale bulge pushed out through the crack and arched up: the new thorax. The nymph pulled back and withdrew its head from inside the head of the empty carapace. Its chitin was almost white; its legs looked soft as it clasped its empty shell, standing on top. It had a dented, unfilled look but it arched its back and pulled its abdomen free of the casing. As I watched, it began to harden, turning darker brown. The hollows in its abdomen filled out and rounded; its short antennae began to move.

I hastened to the town. The Emperor was sitting in the hall, surrounded by a crowd of people, giving out commands to Eszai and Zascai alike. I pushed through them and gave Frost's letter to him. He read it, then nodded gravely. 'Thank you for bringing this, Comet. There is no need for you to visit the dam again. You should have your wounds seen to now.'

I repeated Frost's words to the Sapper, who received them with his usual glum acceptance. I gave her message to the semaphore operator and watched him begin to pull the levers to move the semaphore arms that would send the order to evacuate, hundreds of kilometres down the valley to the governor's steward.

I returned to the hospital, where a doctor cleaned and bandaged my bitten foot, though it was so swollen he had to cut the boot off. He checked my wrenched limbs and said I would be all right if I looked after myself. Not a chance. I am growing experienced enough to realise that if you wait, the pain will go. Long life gives you an ability to weather anything.

I told the journalists that no news was to be given out in any form. Then for hours I did the rounds to see if anyone needed the Messenger. Rayne just shooed me away.

Tornado was too humiliated to speak to anyone. Lightning had been the last to leave the field and he was organising archers on the ramparts. That reminded me – what about his daughter? Nobody had taken Cyan any news. From her confinement in the peel tower she would have seen the whole battle taking place.

I missed a gust and had to wait for the next. Go! Now! I took off from the gatehouse and looked back once I had gained height. It was one a.m. and, through the pitch dark, hails of incendiary missiles poured from the towers. Larvae covered the walls. Men on the walkways were tussling with them.

832

The lamps on the curtain wall only illuminated a few metres of churned mud, the moat and the innermost fallen tents.

Cyan had put a light in her window to guide me in. I landed on the plank and stepped down into the room. Cyan bolted towards me and threw her arms around me, sobbing into my chest. 'Oh! Terrible ... it was terrible.'

'It still is,' I said, trying to disentangle myself.

'I saw everything.' She pointed out to the sea of mud. 'I watched it happen. I felt so powerless. I saw all those people dying – I tried to look away but I just kept watching!'

She thumped my chest. I caught her wrists gently. She looked up at me as if seeing me for the first time. She began to cry in earnest. 'The Insects ... they ... They would have killed me, too!'

'Yes. Hey, shush! Sh-sh, little sister. Crying doesn't suit you.'

She stepped back, wiped her eyes and glared at me. 'I'm Lady Peregrine. I can cope with it.'

'Remains to be seen.'

'Is Daddy all right?'

'I think so.'

'Not that I care, of course.'

'Oh no. Course not.'

'What's happening down there now?'

'Well, the larvae are growing. The Eszai are picking mandible shards out of each other. The mortals are shrieking and dying.' I told her what had happened to Wrenn, Tornado and Hurricane, and Frost trapped inside her dam, digging into its rubble core. Cyan grew more and more alarmed. I said, 'But this is the safest place to be. We've lost the canvas city already; the larvae are scaling the town walls. I don't know if they will crawl all the way up this tower but if they do, look – here's my axe – you can cut them off the walls as they come up to the window. Don't let them get close because their jaws pincer out.'

Cyan sat down, on the bedspread smudged with old sleep. 'Oh, god, Jant ... if I had been down there, I ...'

I sat beside her and spread my wing around her. 'You shouldn't have watched.'

She turned and hugged me, her face pressed to my throat. 'I don't need protecting,' she whispered, and I felt her lips move against my skin. She looked down at my trousers, ripped and scratched and plastered with mud, Insect and human blood.

'Oh god. What happened to your foot?'

'It's nothing. Don't worry.'

She kissed my neck and I smelt the hot, comforting scent of her little body. Her hair was so silky it was like putting my hand into a cool stream of water. She began to stroke my feathers. 'Is it all right now?'

'No, it isn't.'

'Can't you regroup and ...?'

'There are too many. We're totally fucked; I don't know what the Emperor can do.'

I knew I smelt overpoweringly of fresh sweat. That, or something else, was having a strange effect on her. The ache of my muscles and the stinging of all my little scratches began to feel triumphant. I was so tired I felt light; she started caressing me and her touch loosened the tired muscles in my back. The world closed down to this room; this bed and Cyan. Nothing else existed.

'Mmm ... mmm ... I need to do this ...'

'It's the crisis ... Mmm ... . think nothing of it ... Oh god; touch my wings.'

'Your body's so taut. You're like a racehorse ... With too many limbs ... Shit. I didn't mean to say that. Comet ...'

'Most girls call me Jant. It's useful to have two names.'

I felt my cock straining at my underwear. I shuffled to free it and it pointed straight up inside my trousers. Cyan saw the bulge and said, 'Oh. I ...'

We were both minded how much her father would hate us to do this, and that made us want to do it more. 'Do you want me?' I asked.

She wouldn't meet my eye. 'Yes ... but I'm inexperienced.'

I blinked. I hadn't expected her to be a virgin. I don't know why; I suppose because she had seemed so adventurous – she'd always been surrounded by admirers.

'I'll be careful ...'

'Yes, OK.'

'There's just this, here.' I guided her hand to my crotch and she felt the stiffness through the cotton. Her fingers moved up my cock as if she was trying to find an end to it. I took off my trousers and briefs and let her take it tentatively in her hands. 'It's smooth,' she said.

'Yes. Not like that; like this ... ah ...'

Her bodice lacings had come loose and her undershirt was open. Her breasts had fallen a little outward, pressing against the stiff panels, caged in by the criss-cross lacings. I could see their curves but their nipples were hidden.

'I'm good at giving pleasure. I'll make you feel amazing. You'll feel like you're floating.'

'Oh.' She remembered. 'It's not safe.'

'You're safe with me.'

I pushed her gently down until she was lying on her back. I put my head under her skirt, into the darkness between her thighs and kissed their soft skin. I licked the silk of her panties. I poked my tongue around them and started licking her. She gasped and flinched but I calmed her with whispers. I soon found out that she was on her period, a little string sticking out of her. That explained why her scent was so beguiling. Women are most sensual when it's their time of the month.

I pushed her skirt up, her panties down and kept licking. She wasn't used to it; she wriggled and whined and kept looking down at me, one arm across her face, biting her shirt sleeve. I must be giving her so much pleasure ... and soon it will be my turn.

The muscles in her legs tensed. Her thighs became more and more rigid, until they were like steel. She grunted and her body stiffened. She clamped her thighs around my head so tightly I nearly suffocated. Then she cried out and all her tension released at once.

I looked up, bedraggled with her juices. Cyan gasped, with an expression of wonder, pure bliss, and started laughing. Her face was open and unguarded for the first time; it was so wonderful I started laughing too. At that moment the chessboard beside the bed slid off its table with an almighty crash.

The chess pieces rolled all over the floor. The floor began to shake. No, the whole building was shaking; I could feel the vibrations. 'What's that?' Cyan shrieked.

The lamp on the window ledge flickered. 'What's happening?' She sat up and drew the blanket round her.

She said something else, but I wasn't listening. I was backing into the doorway of the staircase leading to the roof – the spiral steps wound up into their turret behind me. It's happening again. This is nineteen twenty-five all over again, and the ground's giving way. It was that night when—

I woke, and lay in my camp bed in the dark tent, listening.

'Jant!' Cyan was yelling at me. 'Jant! Don't go crazy! What are you doing?' Her voice took on a hysterical edge. 'Snap out of it!'

I snapped. I dashed across to the window and grabbed the lamp. If the earth really was falling in and we were locked in the tower I couldn't see how we could survive.

We both looked round as one of the vixen guardswomen appeared in the doorway. She threw something I couldn't see. It bounced off my foot and by the time I had located it on the floor she had disappeared. It was a key.

· The crashing roar grew and grew. It was composed of hundreds of other noises: a gravelly sliding crunch. A landslide ... I knew this had to be a landslide ... There was the din of rock cracking, thuds as individual stones tore loose and fell. The long hiss of earth shifting; the tremendous roar of water.

Through it we heard the bell on the top of the winch tower clanging; madly, unevenly. *Dang ... dong. Dang! Dong!* No one was ringing it – it was tolling of its own accord.

We strained to see. From far out in the darkness came a sense of motion, commotion; gigantic shapes moving. It was like listening to a ship in distress, beyond the mudflats, sinking in the dead of night.

The lights on the tower seemed to tilt, rush forward and down; then they vanished. The deafening roar of a mighty, mighty wave thundered towards us. We could see nothing.

The roar swept past us, obliterating all other noise. The churning of foam and swoosh of falling water resounded on every side.

'The dam!' I yelled. I felt crushed and hopeless – a sensation I recognised – the Circle was breaking. Frost – what is she *going through* out there? It started slowly creeping up – came on in a rush.

I felt the Circle go dead. Frost's link had gone and I was loose again. We were aging. I felt separate and lonely without the other Eszai to back me up. Mortals must feel like that all the time ... I had forgotten what it was like to feel mortal.

The Circle reformed, gently. I could almost feel the Emperor soothe it back into existence. Why had he left us falling apart into nothingness for so long, like beads slipping off a string? Had he been asleep? Was he deliberately reminding us of mortality?

I was kneeling on the floor. The shock had dropped me to my hands and knees and I was looking at a patch of floorboards covered in dried herbs. Their crispy leaves were sticking to my palms.

I had felt Frost dying. By god, what had happened to her ? I couldn't tell if the overwhelming, crushing sensation of darkness had been her experience, or if it was my imagination.

'Get up!' said Cyan.

The roar of the wave went on and on. It passed us and we heard it receding into the distance. Another noise followed, the same volume, still loud enough to shake the tower – the rush of water swirling in spate, out of control.

Cyan stepped squarely in front of me, shouting, 'Jant! What's wrong with you? Stand up!'

'The Circle broke,' I murmured.

'Daddy!' she screamed, and started crying in terror. 'What's happened to Daddy?'

'Sh! It wasn't Lightning. He's in town.'

'How do you know?'

'It was Frost. I knew what she was doing ... She broke the dam.'

I felt different, and I realised that I was actually feeling the Circle. It was the Circle that had changed. Its sensation was subtle, just background; then it had gone. No one can feel the Circle or distinguish individuals in it unless its equilibrium was disturbed. I realised I was so used to its ever-present sensation that I had taken it for granted, and now I was feeling its slightly altered shape. Frost's qualities had gone, and the combined effects of every-one else's, whether enhancing or cancelling each other out, had settled into a new equilibrium.

'Frost was in the Circle when I joined,' I said. 'I was always aware of her without knowing.'

'Look!' She pointed down. The spent flood waters, hissing and edged with foam like a wave running onto a beach, poured up to the base of the tower and broke around it. We watched the level start to nudge up the wall.

Our lamp reflected parts of the water's surface rushing past. It picked out eddying lines as flickers of silver and eel-like flashes. It was moving so fast it was backing up its own bulk into peaks and troughs of great, corrugated standing waves.

Continuous rapids hurtled over where I knew farms had been, now reduced to rubble. The rock outcrops were drowned metres deep. We looked out to Slake – the wide expanse of churning, crinkling flood waters between us and the town reflected its lights.

There was nothing left but water. Everything had been swept away. Everything in the path of the massive wave had vanished and we could hear nothing over its roar.

'"The waters will take two days to subside,"' I repeated.

'What?' said Cyan.

'That was Frost's message. She worked it all out.'

Cyan sought out my hand. She sighed, head bowed, looking at the gush-ing torrent. We stood next to each other, hand in hand in the warm night, and watched out of the window until the faintest light of dawn began to splinter onto the floodwaters.

CHAPTER 24

MODERATE INTELLIGENCER

TROOPS ADVANCE INTO DEVASTATED VALLEY
Exclusive special report by our own correspondent in Slake Cross

I stand on the observation platform of Tower 10, a sturdily built peel tower close to Slake Cross. Beside me stands a veteran artillerist of the Lowespass Select, calling out directions to his trebuchet team in their bombardment position – a makeshift construction of logs and sandbags providing a stable platform on the soggy ground. Another barrel of burning pitch jerks up into the sky, joining half a dozen more, as they crash down on a distant ridge of paper.

Two days have passed since the dam collapsed and the waters have now receded sufficiently to allow infantry to advance. I am further forward than any journalist has been so far. Only the cooperation of the enlightened artillerist has got me past the provosts, passed off as part of his battery. At such elevated points alone can any real picture of the situation be gained; the land is an otherwise flat quagmire, nearly devoid of vegetation and dotted with thousands of dirty pools. Divisions advance cautiously over this ground, pioneers laying brushwood tracks for the fyrd to follow.

A Plainslands unit clears the way north of us, their spears audibly 'popping' eggs that have been scattered by the dam collapse. To my left flamethrower crews are moving forward under the guidance of the Sapper. Occasional bursts of fire mark their encounter with a clutch of undeveloped Insect larvae still wriggling in a pool. The same scene is being re-enacted all the way along a twenty-kilometre front. It is strangely orderly because it is, with few alterations, the plan envisaged years ago.

The intention then, though, was to drain the lake gradually. The Castle has confirmed that Frost sacrificed herself deliberately to destroy her own creation. The gates could not be opened with Insects freely swarming over the dam. Frost's terrifying calculation was that only by engineering a collapse from inside the dam could the lake be emptied. In a single catastrophic torrent, adult Insects have been drowned, their eggs have been left to wither in the sun and their hideous young have been smashed by debris or washed into the sea's fatal salinity.

The mood of the troops, though, is sombre. This promised bloodless advance has proved to be anything but. Their mood stands in stark contrast to the optimistic banter when they, the largest force mustered in the Empire's history, prepared to attack three days ago. Many dwell on lost comrades, the casualties of the recent battle greatly exceeding those of the famous defeat one hundred years ago. Their exact numbers will not be known for weeks; the remains have been swept away by the inundation, complicating the sad task. The immortals have also suffered heavily, adding Hurricane and Frost to their losses, with Serein critically injured.

Still more wonder what the recent changes in the Insects portend. Whilst the horrific larvae are now lying dying or dead, many are openly sceptical of the Castle's assurances that the mating flights were caused by the dam. The Castle has abandoned plans for any such future constructions and claims there will be no future flights. So far it is too early to tell. Surely there deserves to be a full public inquiry as soon as possible?

Reports from the surrounding areas are still sketchy as the signalling network was badly damaged and large parts of the Lowespass Road have been washed away. Comet has flown reconnaissance missions as far as Summerday. He reports the town walls saved it from the force of the break wave but with the surrounding country it is inundated, with thirty centimetres of water in the streets. Thousands of farmsteads and fortifications along the entire valley have been destroyed and fatalities are high. Few casualties are reported in Summerday owing to the successful evacuation efforts.

Rayne, fearing outbreaks of disease, has requested that the inhabitants of the region do not return yet. Only fyrd are permitted into the devastated area; priority is being given to hunting surviving larvae, most of which have been spread over a wide area. In the meantime the civilians are facing a bleak existence, cast on to the charity of others.

Of the dam itself, nothing remains apart from two low mud hillocks scarcely a man's height. The sluice gate was discovered in the ruins of a peel tower forty kilometres further down the valley.

Tomorrow, the Emperor will lead a ceremonial advance to the drained lake bed, land lost to the Empire for a century. There he will formally reclaim the ground as far as the river and annex it to Lowespass manor. Two hundred square kilometers will be reclaimed from the Insects. Most General Fyrd units will remain for two months to secure the area and rebuild defences. Only then will standing garrisons take over and the fyrd be disbanded. If the land can be kept, and the Insects' aversion to running water raises the hope it can be, it is the first successful advance in over three centuries.

Perhaps this, then, is Frost's ultimate triumph. How reasonable was her brave notion that the Castle could defeat the Insects? For the second time in a decade a plan has met with a bloody check in the mandibles of our enemies. Frost, in her ambitions and her actions, had overstretched herself – but that is no more than the world expects its immortals to do.

Kestrel Altergate,
Eske, June 13th

*You are cordially invited to Micawater Palace for the Challenge of
Cyan Peregrine to Lord Governor Lightning Micawater,
which will be held in the palace grounds, on August 12th
this Year of Our War two thousand and twenty-five.*

The Challenge will be preceded by two days of events and feasting.

*All other Challengers for the position of Lightning this quarter-year may
submit their Challenges in advance so they may shoot in competition with
Lightning preceding the Challenge of Cyan Peregrine.*

RSVP to Lightning at Micawater Palace

CHAPTER 25

Two months later, I was standing on the roof of Lightning's palace, feasting my eyes on its fabulous vista. I slid down from its ridge to the balustrade, knocking off a couple of tiles. The groundsman, far below me on the terrace, waved his fist; so I gave him a cheerful salute. The view was so amazing, and the summer sun so hot, that I wanted to see Lightning's majestic tournament from above.

I leant against the slope of the pediment, in the shadow of the gold ball on its point. The tiles beneath my feet were hand-made to look like feathers; the chimneys behind me were collected in refined plain pillars.

Everybody who was anybody was here, and some people who were nobody at all. Coaches were arriving continually, through the Lucerne Gate and down the Grand Walk to the front of the palace. The Walk was wide enough for three coaches abreast to drive between the double rows of pollarded elms. In the middle each coach reached a marble statue on a plinth of Lightning's mother with a winged stag. They trotted around it on either side and parked next to each other on the vast gravel semicircle in front of the portico.

I walked along the balustrade, onto the end of the portico and peered over. I could just see Harrier on the front steps, welcoming in the latest batch of visitors. His age was showing; he had grey hair above his ears. He gave each guest a key on a ribbon and ushered them into the cool shadow of the exedra porch. They entered under the pediment, between its four fluted columns with drooping plume capitals, into the house.

The Austringer and Eyas Wings stretched out on both sides of me, perfectly symmetrical. I returned, along the top of the balustrade, to the back of the palace. Pavilions covered the whole lawn down to the lake.

The celebrations started yesterday, with archery competitions in the main ring adjoining the blue and white striped awning of the long stand. Notable archers shot at novelty targets like a dove tied to the top of a pole, or a hazel wand upright in the ground. There had been promenades and pleasure boats on the lake. Lightning had laid on no contemporary entertainments like jousting; instead he had had chariots made and a track built on the other side of the lake. He had stepped into one of these brass-clad contraptions, taken the reins of a pair of coursers and showed us how to race them. His youngest brother had been a champion charioteer. Tern and I had watched the races, very tentative at first but people quickly got the hang of how to drive them.

Then last night Lightning had held a ball. We had found costumes laid out in our rooms. The women looked beautiful in their draped gowns, and laughter echoed along the corridors as the men tried to figure out their togas. We were surprised but we took it as good entertainment. Everything, from the ancient harp music to the sickly mead, orgeat and boar roasts served in archaic style, was a reconstruction of his memory of the original Games. Lightning was beside himself with joy. He was home at last!

Down on the lawns everyone was scattered around the enormous stand along one side of the archery ground, roped off from the rest of the grass and outlined by hay bales. The other side was open, towards the lake and bridge. Beside it stood a cloth-of-gold pavilion for the Challengers and, on the other side, servants carrying trays of chilled Stenasrai wine came and went from a refreshment tent.

The pavilions were an ancient round design, not triangular, and the lines of bunting surrounding the archery ring were the same as those topping the walls of an amphitheatre. The whole scene belonged in the pages of a picture book: Lightning was indeed reliving the founding of the Circle.

A series of tall flagpoles flew long, dark blue banners with the Micawater mascle. My Wheel flag and Rayne's red oriflamme pennant were there too. We were acting as witnesses for the Challenge. At least two Eszai witness every Challenge; mortals are never used as witnesses because Eszai are less likely to be corrupted. We have a vested interest in keeping the Challenges fair and we would fiercely resist any less than the best being admitted as to do so would tarnish our own status.

I looked out into the distance. The avenue ran straight on the other side of the lake, between beech plantations to the crest of a low hill. A folly stood there, a scaled-down replica of the entire palace, placed exactly opposite it at the end of the vista. It was so ingeniously decreased in size that it skewed the perspective – making the avenue look longer than it was. Everyone who saw the folly for the first time believed it was a palace exactly the same size at a great distance. I knew it housed only a single ballroom, but its trick of the eye was so exact I imagined that I could see a tiny Jant leaning on the pediment looking back at me. I shuddered.

Lemon trees and spear-like cypress grew on the brow of the hill clear against the sky around the folly and, beyond it, livestock grazed on smooth-turfed grass like a carpet. I could just see the beginnings of the hills rising up to Donaise in the distance. Tiny, spidery vine frames climbed them, and their lower slopes were lines of immaculately planted grey-green olive groves and coffee plantations.

I suppose the landscaped garden isn't really designed to be seen from the roof. The guests on the terrace will have the best of it, or those strolling along the avenue, from which smaller pathways led and opened up new vistas. The perspective presented statues that seemed far off, suddenly near at hand. Gaps in the woodland revealed winter gardens, espaliers, great pillars, all meticulously landscaped for kilometres around.

Beyond the beech wood two smaller avenues crossed the main one in an asterisk, and of course Lightning had had time to watch over the trees as they grew and matured, so now centuries later, they were looking their best.

I stood on tiptoe and looked down the length of the Austringer Wing; over the roof of the Austringer building at the end. I could just see a dark green pattern of tall hedgerows – the labyrinth. It was enormous; lemon hedge on one side of the path and box on the other, so if you got lost you could smell your way around it to the great trellis and pergola in the centre. They are covered in vines drooping fat clusters of purple grapes. The tendrils hang down like a screen of falling water, and it is wonderful to push through them to the hideaway inside, where you can sit among statues in its shade.

Past the maze grew the long, unkempt grass of the 'wilderness' – nothing of the sort but a well-designed meadow where Lightning held garden parties. I'd rather have kept it natural than have it look so through artifice and expenditure. Beyond that rose the belvedere, once copied by the Rachiswaters in their circular style. I wondered why it was that the richer people became, the more sequacious?

At the end of the Eyas Wing, in the other direction, a slope went down to 'the farm' by the river, a few kilometres distant but the clutch of aslant roofs looked more like a small town. Most of the estate workers lived there, tending beehives, kitchen and herb gardens, a phasianery for peacocks and pheasants, a rabbit warren, brick kilns and a dovecot. Lightning calls the estate office 'The New House', although it is four hundred years old. The Alula Road passes through to Micawater town itself, which was disguised behind another well-placed copse. Lots of townsfolk were here, watching the festivities and loving it. They were the sort of Awian citizens who hold street parties on their lord's birthday.

People were converging on the archery stands. From up here, parasols over women's shoulders looked like little circles. I noticed a knot of people heading from the refreshment tent and in their midst I recognised Eleonora's confident stride. Beside her was my little, dark-haired, vivacious Tern. The Challenge is about to start. I had better go join them.

I stepped off the balustrade and tilted out in a long, slow glide. I swept over the terrace onto which the palace's doors opened; then the water gardens below them, a round central spring framed symmetrically by four limpid pools.

The ground dropped away and steps led down to a parterre, with the sky-blue roses of Awia in flower beds bordered by low hedges. More box hedges looked like embroidery, clipped into lacy flowing designs, scrolls and plumes against the rich, loamy earth. From that level stone hounds guarded a balustraded double staircase descending to the avenue. People walking on the paths between the flower beds looked up as my shadow sped over them.

I focused on Tern and Eleonora and the courtiers surrounding them, who were settling on the lowest seat of the stands nearest the archery ground, reserved for the Queen's use and covered with samite silk. I came in above the rounded end of the awning and veered wide to the arena's grass, flared wings and touched down. My landing drew a little tentative applause from the crowd.

I hopped over the ropes and Tern came forward to meet me. 'My love,' I said over her shoulder as we hugged. 'My dear, dear love.'

'Isn't this exciting?' Tern exclaimed. 'What a magnificent day!'

Eleonora nodded contentedly. 'It's a Lakeland summer all right. Three fine days and a thunderstorm. It's like clockwork.'

'Well, the sooner we get this over with and on to the party the better.' She passed me a glass of sparkling wine. 'I pestered Lightning to give us some real Stenasrai. "You must have had Stenasrai in six twenty," I told him. "It's better than that ridiculous mead." It's a wonder anyone in the seventh century had any teeth.'

I was enjoying the party but I still had a lot to do. Since the slaughter of the battle there had been more people hiding from the draft. There was a groundswell of sentiment against the war and criticism of the Emperor, which the Emperor was ignoring until it gradually subsided.

Eleonora had covered herself with glory and was full of pride. We hadn't regained so much land since the Miroir battles of the last Tanager dynasty. No wonder the Rachiswaters had been so keen to match them by making advances in Lowespass, but Eleonora had taken more than any of them. Our shared knowledge of how awful the battle had been brought us together in this warm sunlight, whereas Tern, who could never understand, just kept talking. 'I worried about you when the Circle broke,' she said. 'Although worry is quite an inadequate word for what I felt.'

'I was fine, my love. I saw the flood. I never want to go back to Slake Cross though. Every time we go there we get massacred.'

Tern said, 'Some people are talking about an odd phenomenon. My warden says god appeared to the Emperor on the battlefield.'

'Really?' I said casually. 'In what shape?'

'A very strange one. A tall column of smoke, and trees made of worms.'

'Mass hysteria.' I shrugged. 'People report all kinds of visions under battle stress. It's terror that causes it. Lowespass generates more folklore than it can use.'

'Well, I don't see why it should have to export it.'

I said, 'Some fyrdsmen say that you can still hear the winch tower bell, tolling underwater in the river. Fyrdsmen will tell you any old crap.'

I was interrupted by three flights of whistling arrows being loosed on the other side of the lake in honour of the victor of the chariot races. Eleonora shook herself. 'Lightning slept through the dam breaking,' she said. Tern and I laughed. It's a joke that Lightning is such a sound sleeper Insects could be eating him and he wouldn't wake up.

'You dare wake him, Jant,' said Tern. 'Why didn't you?'

'Um ... I was busy.'

'And the Emperor asked Lightning to have dinner with him. At least, I heard so ... Is it true?'

'Yes. That *is* true.'

'But it's unheard of! For Lightning, for anybody! Well, come on. Tell me. What did they talk about?'

'I asked Lightning, but he wouldn't say.'

'I would never have thought anything like a one-to-one conversation could ever happen.'

'It was in the hall at Slake,' I said. 'No one else was there.'

'Couldn't you have spied? No, stupid question.'

Eleonora spun the key to her suite around her finger on its ribbon. 'This place is quaint. I like the marble bathrooms. But it's not as big as Rachiswater. Or as grand as I've planned Tanager to be. It's odd to think it was the capital once.'

'It's not bad for five four nine!' Tern said.

'Lightning's town was even bigger than Hacilith back then,' I added. 'Hacilith took a hundred years to overtake it. He never wanted to extend it; he wanted to preserve it and the palace too.'

Eleonora spun and spun her key. 'What a shame. Lightning rattling around in the house alone for fourteen hundred years. One hundred and forty bedrooms and no woman to share any of them with. It's enough to turn a man's mind. Why hasn't he ever married? Does he bat for the other team, or what?'

Tern laughed. 'No-oo. He's just looking for the perfect match.'

'Well, we'll have to do something about that.' The two women looked at each other. 'He just needs to relax. Perhaps his Queen could ... command him to.'

'I think he wants some kind of red-haired huntress,' Tern said as we settled ourselves in the stands.

'Nonsense. He just needs the attentions of a woman *au fait* with her desires.'

From here was a much better view uphill to the palace. It was all warm, shortbread-coloured Donaise limestone, from the rusticated stonework on the lower storey to the rich carving in the great pediment; many strips of decorative mouldings surrounded a smooth bas-relief of the winged hounds bearing the lozenge coat of arms. Each column led up to a statue on the roof as if supporting it. Between the columns two levels of windows proclaimed how many rooms could house Lightning's guests. The Eyas and Austringer buildings at the ends of the two wings had enormous windows with round arches giving on to the ballroom and stateroom respectively. It was built in the most regular manner rare in the country today; Awia has gone straight from Micawater's classical to neoclassical, and now Rachiswater's art nouveau, without ever having been through a rustic phase like the Plainslands.

'It's all right for some,' I said.

'What do you mean?' said Tern.

'Well, Lightning walked straight in to the Circle. He never had to wander around the world the way I did, before I even found out the Castle existed. He didn't have to plot and scheme like an Awian prince, either, because he had the Castle and his immortality instead. No wonder he can pretend this noble liege fantasy.'

'It's how he had time to bring us together.' Tern laid her hand on my knee.

'I call that plotting and scheming,' said Eleonora.

Tern said, 'I paid him a routine visit and he mentioned I might be interested in Jant. I remember taking my coach to see Lightning one morning and I told him how Jant's courtship was progressing. "He came to see me last night – I love his appalling timing. And do you know – his boots were covered in manure!" How we laughed!'

I snorted unhappily. Travelling from the Castle to Wrought to court her had been the start of my drug-taking. I stayed awake for two, three nights at a time, driven to extreme exhaustion by a fear of inadequacy. And apparently Tern had already decided to marry me before I started and there was no reason for me to have used scolopendium at all.

She had flicked open a pamphlet. 'Ha!' she said. 'Lightning has a grotto. He never told me.'

'A what?'

'A grotto. How exciting. I've been coming here for nearly a hundred and twenty years and he never showed me. Listen.' She read from the book: '"Who would have thought that a cavern of such delightful artifice would lie at the end of the path? A passageway leads to a charming rocaille grotto with a small waterfall. Niches in the walls form shell-adorned seats, and above them is the inscription: *All time not spent in loving is lost.*" Ah, isn't he sweet?'

I said, 'The grotto's on the other side of the secret garden. We can visit it later. What's that?'

'It's a programme for the party and a tour of the grounds. All the sculptures and so forth.'

I let her chatter on, dwelling on how beautiful she was – the gentle contours of her face, her manicured hands. I thought how lucky I was that she found me equally wonderful.

Tern loved the summer sun, though her manor had a much more dismal climate. Wrought is in the rain shadow of Bitterdale; all the clouds that come in from the sea rise over the hills, drop their rain on her manor and leave the inland manors clear.

I looked down to the glistening lake. Far on our right towards its centre an artificial island was covered with trees. The pink marble pediment of the dynasty's mausoleum, its engraved frieze, and the pinnacles of other memorials showed between the tree tops.

The still water reflected them, but further off by the sluice gate bridge, the stirred-up water scintillated as its silica flecks reflected the sunlight. Many people were promenading along the bridge, and I don't blame them because Micawater Bridge is one of Frost's finest legacies.

It spanned a little man-made river flowing out of the tail-end of the almond-shaped lake, once natural but artificially enhanced since Esmerillion's time. The bridge carried the avenue through its roofed and arched arcade, and below it had square windows along its length above the span. Their shutters were closed; all were honey-coloured varnished wood to match the stone. From flagpoles along the length of the parapets, blue pennants draped down almost to the water.

There were rooms inside the bridge: all well-furnished and painted, and there was even a tiny theatre for music recitals. Lightning's friends sometimes use it as a summer house. From the windows they can look out over the lake to watch fleets of swans, dragonflies whizzing over the water's surface beneath them, and sometimes horse hooves clattered overhead along the avenue. So, over the centuries, Lightning has shaped the landscape much as Frost did, but for beauty and convenience. Whenever he had enlisted her help for a feat of engineering it was also a feat of elegance.

'Look!' said Eleonora. 'Here he is.'

Lightning emerged from the gold pavilion, carrying a compound bow so big it looked like a longbow. Cyan was behind him in a black T-shirt, waistcoat, quiver and a bracer on her arm. Lightning strolled up to us and bowed to the Queen. 'I hope you enjoy the tournament.'

'I will,' said Eleonora.

The Challenged Eszai always acts as his own master of ceremonies, conducting the Challenge himself according to his own style. It was a necessary part of the façade of unshakable confidence which is our most effective guard against Challengers. Lightning had asked his five reeves, from his musters of Micawater Town, Bitterdale, Altergate, Tambrine and Foin, to act as functionaries.

Lightning walked to the centre of the area and held out his hands to the crowd. 'This is my standard Challenge, which I set to show I can defeat a Challenger at all kinds of shooting. There will be three rounds. The first is for distance. There will be just one arrow each, unless the bow fails. I wish the Challenger, Cyan Peregrine, to shoot first in each round.'

Cyan stood behind a dark blue pennon on a cane. She looked small next to her father and seemed very aware of the inconsequential figure she cut, with the slivers of her legs and narrow squared shoulders. Her red compound bow looked like a toy in comparison with Lightning's. She took an arrow and nocked it to string and then, with the bow in her hands, she lost her uncertainty and became businesslike. She knew what to do, and I knew how good she was: I had witnessed her skill in the Jacamar Club.

The crowds waited. There was not a breath of wind. Cyan took the string in a pinch grip, the horn draw-ring on her thumb. She drew the string, tilted the bow high for a distance shot, and loosed. Her arrow looped high above the lake, seemed to pause at the top of its arc, turned and came down, easily clearing the grassy far bank. It clattered on the avenue.

One of the reeves went to place a flag where the arrow had fallen. The crowd gave a polite round of applause, which we joined in while Lightning stepped up to the pennon. He held the arrow across the grip, already nocked. He crafts his tournament arrows himself, for perfection; each has azure fletchings and a gold cresting band.

The crowd fell silent. It is an awesome thing to see Lightning shoot. He raised his bow and tipped it back, drew it fluidly full compass until it formed a perfect semicircle and the tang-less pile point drew back into a groove cut into the massive grip. His powerful shoulders and back muscles took the eighty-two-kilo strain. Eleonora looked avariciously at the angle of his shoulder blade.

He loosed – and the arrow sped from his bow, so high it disappeared. It started coming down way past the point where Cyan's arrow had fallen. It passed the avenue, the grass behind it, and fell silently into the beech woods. The crowd applauded and Lightning acknowledged them. Well, he made that look easy.

Minutes passed before the official result could be returned. The Bitterdale reeve came running and announced, 'Seven hundred and thirty metres! Three times the Challenger's distance!'

Cyan was pale. I wondered whether her intermittent self-control could stand such a test.

'Now,' Lightning said. 'We have the speed contest. One minute to shoot as many arrows as possible into these targets.' He gestured at some archery butts scarcely a hundred metres away. 'Reeve Tambrine will time the minute.'

He put his great compound bow on a rack and picked up a smaller one, much like Cyan's, faster to draw than a longbow. He stood beside her and they both pushed a row of arrows into the ground in front of them. The Tambrine reeve lowered his arm and Cyan started plucking up the arrows and shooting them as fast as she could.

Lightning dawdled. He picked an arrow, loosed it, looked in its direction, chose another and turned it over, fitted it to string.

There was a great hiss of indrawn breath from the crowd. We rose to our feet, staring at him. Tern touched my shoulder. 'What is he doing? Why is he doing that?'

'I don't know.'

When the minute was up, Cyan had shot fourteen arrows and Lightning had shot ten. Cyan was panting, then she looked at Lightning's target and her eyes and mouth went wide.

There was silence, then a sudden uproar as everyone turned to their neighbours and started asking what it meant. The reeve was looking, concerned and frightened, at his master but Lightning wasn't meeting anybody's eye. He turned to Cyan and said, 'The heft of that bow of yours warps left at a distance. See, your arrows are tending left on the target? You should shoot a little right for the next round.'

He came over to us and took a drink of water. I said, 'What are you playing at? You lost! Deliberately. Obviously deliberately!'

He smiled at me and the ladies. 'Don't worry. I needed to give Cyan some sop to her pride. There's one round left.'

'You're playing with your life!' Tern shrieked.

'I just don't want to show my daughter up too much. I know what I'm doing. I'm unbeatable at accuracy.' He didn't say it as a boast, it was a plain fact.

Lightning gave me the compound bow and took his customary longbow from the rack. He carried it as fluidly as if it was part of him, an extension of his body. An accuracy target was set up at two hundred metres' distance – a black ring on the outside, then white, blue and gold in the centre.

Lightning announced. 'We have five arrows each. Whoever scores most highly on the target will remain – I mean, gain – the title of Lightning. Cyan Peregrine will shoot first.'

Cyan came forward to stand on a stone slab set into the grass. She felt for the reassuring ends of the arrows in her quiver, selected one composedly. She sighted and loosed. The arrow appeared in the middle of the cross in the gold, the target's exact centre. She stepped aside and looked at her father defiantly.

Lightning stood on the flagstone. He was the target archer absolute. He made it seem so effortless. He faced the butt with a calm expression, confident and determined. His whole attitude was of command and power over the bow, the arrows and the target. He placed his feet apart with the weight equally on them, in a firm but springy stance. He was balanced and relaxed – a finger above the nock on the string, and two below. He used no marker, he knew it so well. He drew, and loosed sharply, the string free in an instant, and the arrow flew straight and sure.

There was a crack of wood. Lightning's longer arrow had split Cyan's in two. Its blue flights stood out from her white ones.

A roar from the audience. The reeves and servants sitting on the bales jumped up to applaud. Lightning acknowledged them but the noise seemed to daunt Cyan. She wasn't experienced enough to have expected it. She said nothing, just looking out to the target and down to her own gear. She pulled the string and extended her left arm in one movement, and the arrow point came up. She looked directly to the target.

Her arrow hit the edge of the gold. It was Lightning's turn to shoot. His arms were firm and unwavering, his attention never relaxed. Again he split Cyan's arrow perfectly.

The crowd's applause ceased immediately.

'What is he doing?' I said. 'He could have won then!'

Eleonora murmured, 'By god, he's brave.'

'What?'

'One day, immortal, in the far future you'll be able to say you saw this, and the rest of the world will look on you with awe. You will be able to say you were there at the beginning.'

'I don't understand.'

'Just watch.'

Tern edged closer to me and put her arm around my waist.

Cyan shot again, and again Lightning hit her arrow directly, splitting it in half.

She raised her arm and wiped her face on her sleeve. She was desperate, but she stood with an elasticity to resist the force and recoil of her twangy little bow. She was the timeless picture of grace as she drew it with a beautiful movement until it filled her whole frame. She hit the gold above the arrows – they were as snug together as a fistful of sticks, their flights entangled.

Lightning split her arrow.

This was the last one. Cyan was aware of every factor that might make a difference. She shrugged her waistcoat tighter, she adjusted her bracer. She dug a thumb behind her belt buckle. Her little movements were like the wriggles of a worm on a hook.

She raised her bow and shot. The arrow snicked in next to the others on the gold cross.

Lightning's turn: he drew. He loosed.

His arrow went wide – into the black outer ring.

Everyone in the stands was on their feet. He had lost.

He trembled as he lowered his bow. He gulped as if with a dry throat and tears came to his eyes, but with absolute mastery of himself, they weren't shed.

Cyan was walking in a small circle with an expression of confusion. He stopped her, and made her look at him. He kissed her and said something softly. Cyan blinked.

Louder, he added, 'Now I am out, and you are in. Enjoy it.'

He placed the end of his bow against the inside of his shoe, and unstrung it. He wound the string around his hand and slipped it in his pocket. Then he began to walk, past the stands and the dumbstruck audience, leaving Cyan behind. 'But ...' she said. 'But who's going to look after me?'

We stared, motionless. My head felt like it was full of cotton wool. I couldn't think: my mind wasn't allowing me to form any thoughts. There was nothing in my head but a wondering space. I felt light on my feet and nauseous, as if my body wasn't real. Black shadows began to gather at the periphery of my vision – I was about to faint. Everything was blurred. San only knows what Lightning must be feeling.

Tern sat down heavily. Her speech stumbled: 'W-What has he done?'

'I don't know.' I answered too quickly.

'Deliberately. He did it deliberately.'

The Queen's voice quivered at a higher pitch as she made an effort to control it. 'What a way to teach Cyan a lesson.'

There was a scuffle at the end of the stands and Rayne rushed out. She grabbed the back of Lightning's shirt and sank to her knees. She was hysterical; the ends of her open mouth were down in her jowls. Tears were running from her eyes channelled into the crevices between her cheeks and the sides of her nose. 'Saker!' Lightning tried to raise her to her feet but she had no strength; she just sank back.

'Saker, what have you done? Why? Tell me you won' leave! There's no need t' leave t' Circle! You aren', are you? Tell me you're jus' playing t' system. Tell me i's jus' a trick. You'll Challenge Cyan in a year's time and bea' her. Won' you? Or you'll bea' t' next man who's sure to bea' her ... Tell me tha's true! Or ... or you'll Challenge Wrenn and bea' him, and be t' next Swordsman. Oh yes, tha' must be i' – so you can be together wi' Cyan ...'

Lightning supported her at arm's length, his hands on her upper arms. Rayne kept screaming, 'Where will you end up? I's horrible t' be old. I know

– i's terrible! You don' want i'! Don' let i' happen! Don' le' time pass, Saker, you're a' your best! A few years and you'll never have security again! You'll die! ... After all this time, why? Why? I can' bear t' be alone. Don' leave me!' She collapsed to her knees, sobbing, and as she did so she pulled his shirt out of his belt. She pressed his shirt tails to her cheek.

'Come with me into the house, Ella.'

'You were my friend!' Her voice was ugly with distortion.

He turned her towards the palace and, speaking to her quietly, led her up the avenue towards the terrace.

I tried to hold Tern's hand but my palms were sweating and my hands had no strength to grip. Uncertain whether I could feel her or not, I pressed too powerfully and she winced.

'I just feel numb,' I said. 'I can't allow myself to think about it ...'

'You'll have plenty of time for that, immortal,' said Eleonora. Cyan crept into the gold pavilion to escape the crowd's disdain. Nobody congratulated her and nobody applauded. All eyes were watching Lightning and Rayne climb the monumental staircase onto the terrace and go through the tall open doors. They disappeared from view under the great elliptical ceiling of the dining hall.

CHAPTER 26

The feast, that evening, was a solemn affair. We were back to normal food and clothes; Lightning had moved on from needing his seventh-century nostalgia as well as from needing the Circle, but his guests were embarrassed and confused. They didn't know what to say nor how to phrase it. They didn't know how to react, so they made their excuses and drifted away.

Lightning, at the head of the table, tried to make us feel we should celebrate, although none of us could see any cause. We were all wondering at him and frightened on his behalf. So we gave up on the feast and retired to the library.

Lightning sat at his grand piano and played so calmly that Eleonora, Tern and I thought he must be planning to get back into the Circle.

The library's coffered ceiling had panels painted with pastoral and historic scenes. It was so lofty that a man on horseback could wield a lance in the room. The walls were covered completely with three tiers of bookshelves. Baroque wrought-iron steps could be pushed on rails along each level, leading to three rectangular balconies that stepped out, rising to the ceiling.

Eleonora was up on the first of these. She was examining the nearest shelves filled floor-to-ceiling with Lightning's diaries – maroon leather with the dates embossed in gold. A few were of paler hue when he couldn't find a colour to match exactly. She was flicking through one randomly; it would take years to read them all.

Tern was perched on the window seat, idly watching the stream of departing guests' coaches fall to a trickle then sputter to a stop as the great and good of the Fourlands hurried away. Rayne had already left, with Cyan in her care, both of them crying. In two days they would reach the Castle, where the Emperor would make Cyan immortal.

I studied the panels in the stucco ceiling, Mica valley landscapes rendered in oils, more mannered and pastel-toned than the dramatic colours of real life. The same iconic images over and over, and yet again in the ceramic and champlevé enamel vases on the delicate side tables – maybe that's the brake of Lightning's patronage. I picked at my chair's lavish cushioned seat, slowly creating and unravelling a loose thread. I marked imaginary lines in the rock crystal carafe of vintage port before me as I worked my way down it.

Over each lintel around the room were lunette paintings of Lightning's other properties. I could see through the nearest door, down a short corridor lined with small bronzes, toxophilous or booted and spurred for the charge, a sinuous ormolu clock, a walnut escritoire, and through to the Great Dining Hall.

Its doorway was crowned with his coat of arms in marble marquetry, plain, veined or flecked, each from a different part of the manor, surrounded by cipolin stone wreaths symbolising the Donaise Hills. Servants were clearing away the untouched feast from the huge table and, high above them at the end of the hall, portière curtains concealed a musicians' gallery.

I lost track of time; it certainly felt like we had been here for hours, exchanging only pleasantries, all tacitly waiting for some kind of explanation from Lightning while he pretended not to notice. I shifted position and flapped my wings open. I scuffed the carpet with my feet; I wanted to run and shout to break the tension. I considered going for a flight to blow away the fevered stuffiness of the room.

Lightning suddenly changed the music to an expansive waltz and looked at me steadily. 'No, I'm not disappointed with the world. I'm not tired, just bemused. I want to find out more and I need time to think.'

Finally! 'Is it to do with what the Emperor told you, when you had dinner with him?'

'Yes, tell us what he said. We all want to know,' said Eleonora, leaning forward on the balcony railing.

Lightning paused, then smiled. 'He said that you would certainly ask about it, and he would prefer it if I didn't tell you.'

'I'll ask him myself.'

'Comet, you know very well San keeps his past a secret.'

'He told you his past?'

'Yes. The Emperor explained it to me. He told me about the Shift as well. The things he said are just so incredible ... I need time to come to terms with them. He only told me because he realised, at that point on the battlefield, that I didn't need immortality any more. He realised I had grown out of it.'

Tern spoke up from the window seat, unable to keep the sour note from her voice: 'Did he know you would throw the competition?'

'I expect he considered it. He knew I was leaving.'

'Didn't he ask you not to?' she urged.

He laughed. 'San has known Rayne and I a long time, longer than anyone else in his life. He might only speak to us once a decade, but I suppose that's as close as he gets, to friends. He knows Ella and I well, and he didn't find this too hard to predict. San relies on people wanting to be immortal more than anything else in the world, but if one of us Eszai finds something he wants more than immortality, San can do nothing to keep him. Ten years ago, when Cyan was kidnapped by Shearwater and I set off to rescue her, I must have valued her more than immortality, subconsciously I suppose. I mean, I wasn't aware of it at the time. So, no ... I am free to change, now. I am free to understand your other worlds, feel the passing of time again.'

'Well, aren't you afraid of dying?' Tern demanded.

Lightning lapsed into silence again. He played a little more loudly for a while, until a crunch on the gravel drive outside interrupted him.

'A little coach is coming in!' Tern cried.

'Is it? What are its colours?'

'Green and grey.'

Lightning stopped playing. 'Green and grey is Awndyn.'

The coach slewed to a halt. In the light from the palace lamps we saw the two horses were frothing. A plump woman in a shapeless silk dress and long ginger hair, leaning on a stick and moving slowly, swayed out of the carriage, ascended the steps and disappeared into the portico.

We heard her footsteps resound loud on the Reception Hall's terrazzo floor, then soundless as she passed into the carpeted winter south wing, through the salon and study. The door flew open and Swallow Awndyn barged in. A servant was following worriedly, close behind her. She slammed the door on him and glared at us all.

Lightning stood up. 'Welcome!'

His fiancée took a fistful of her hair and pulled at it in fury. 'What happened – Lightning? Have I heard right? You lost a Challenge? To your vile squab?'

'So it seems.' He relaxed back onto the piano stool. 'I'm sorry you missed it, my love. I sent you an invitation.'

'*You stupid moron!*'

Lightning quoted mildly: 'I love my love with an S, because she suddenly shows a slanderous side. Her name is Swallow and she comes from the strand.'

'I came straight here when I heard!' She ground her walking stick into the carpet. 'I can't believe it! You *never* lose! I never thought I'd live to see it! I can't even imagine it!'

Lightning offered her a glass but she didn't register it. She was incredulous. 'I expected to see you dejected, and here you are slamming at the piano like ten madmen. Are you insane?'

'That is no way to speak to your betrothèd.'

'All my life I've been fighting to get into the Circle and you just throw it away! Like it's nothing! Throw your life to a stupid child like a bauble!'

'The surprise should improve your music. It has become a bit samey over the last few years.'

'You!' She was speechless, and she still wouldn't sit down. 'How dare you!'

'Answer me this first – do you still want to marry me?'

'But ... you're a loser. You lost.'

856

Lightning closed his eyes for a second. Swallow continued, 'You're going to become mortal. To get older!'

'So you don't want me now?'

She hesitated and Lightning continued artlessly, 'So you were interested in me for my immortality, rather than as a person?'

She looked to the books portrayed in the lush weave of the carpet and the cascades of fruit in the deep wood mouldings on the door jambs. She ground the heel of one hand into her eye. Her red wings opened slightly, pulling her gown tight across her front; she was as flat-chested as a narrow boat. Her face had become lined, and she had plucked her eyebrows into an expression of constant surprise.

Swallow was the best musician of all time, but the Emperor did not need a musician. He didn't need music to rally the fyrd when everyone agreed Insects must be fought. He didn't need music for propaganda when he was offering immortality. She hated the fact that the sole determiner of the value of anything was its usefulness in the Insect war. After fifteen years of the same ambitious refrain the pressure had made her diamond inside, but she wasn't sparkling, however emptily. She was cutting.

'I want to join the *Circle*,' she said. 'How can you help me now? I *am* a musician. It's *all* I do. Just like an Eszai.'

Lightning leant back, his elbow on the piano's music stand. 'Oh, Swallow,' he said. 'You never noticed for one second that I really adored you. But now I'm leaving the Circle you suddenly see me. For ten years I have been offering you a place in the Circle through my love and you were too proud to take it. Do you think I can't tell, after hundreds of years of fending off gold-diggers? You strung me along – with your pride you believed you could make it into the Circle on your own merit and I was your back-up plan. Even if you had become Eszai, you still wouldn't have married me, because deep down you don't want to. I was just as wrong to court you, but I didn't want to admit it, because I thought you were like Martyn—' He looked momentarily surprised at himself. 'But you are not. Now you are showing your true colours.'

'Ha! At least I still have feelings, not like you, always controlled, living in this fucking art gallery; you're so transparent.'

'On the contrary, you barely noticed I existed. I wondered what I had to do. If you had wanted Donaise you could have had it. I would have done anything. Now it's too late.'

She said, 'You're always deluding yourself. You with love, Jant with drugs; god knows what the rest of the immortals rely on. In a few years you won't be able to draw any of your wonderful bows any longer because you'll be *old* and *weak*.'

'I am sure it will be an interesting experience,' he said brightly. 'I never considered what I would look like when I'm forty. Or sixty. Well, now I'm going to find out.'

Swallow couldn't stand the fact that he was looking on it as an interesting experiment. 'You're a fool! And I've been looking after your nasty daughter all this time! I wish I'd known!'

'Be quiet about Cyan. I *have* just given my life for her. I only regret I didn't do it earlier, so I could have been with her as she grew up. I should have raised her instead of you.'

Swallow exploded with fresh anger. 'And now you're leaving me – where? Your bastard games will have wasted my talent! One day I'll be just a faded memory to you Eszai – worse still! – an old governor! And you won't hear my music any more.'

Lightning smiled and glanced away. He reached around with one hand and pressed a couple of keys, twiddling the first bars of a piece of music. Swallow stopped dead. 'Don't you *dare* play my aria.'

Lightning brought his other hand into play and expanded the music to its full glory.

'Stop it!'

He had turned back to the keyboard. 'What, this? You make your own immortality with every effortless opera. You are the greatest composer in the world, Swallow. What do you really want? Immortality might not give you what you really want. It didn't for me. Ask yourself, and be true to yourself. You already have fame. You have recognition. Your music brings a great response and many friends. But you harp on the same old tune of wanting the Circle. You don't appreciate the magnitude of your achievements, you only see the things you haven't done.'

'It isn't good enough, if I'm still mortal. I don't want to die.'

'Everybody dies except San. Eszai just take longer. Why should you be saved?'

'If I can make music forever, I'll be happy.'

'No, Swallow. Immortals are those who prize success and fame over happiness. They gain what little happiness they ever have from success. Their thirst for perfection and fear of being beaten drives them on. I no longer prize immortality in those terms, and neither should you. Learn from my example. Escape. You don't have to forgo an Eszai's single-mindedness. I won't let anything get in my way, even though the obstacle in my path was immortality itself.'

Swallow made a sound of disgust. She pulled off her engagement ring and flung it in rage. It hit the inside of the piano's upraised lid, dropped onto the strings and we heard it chime.

'I did love you, Swallow.'

'Liar!' she screamed. She turned to me. 'Jant, you'll help me, won't you?'

'All I can, but I doubt it'll do any good. It's up to you, now.'

'You said I was like a sister!'

'I can't change the Castle, Swallow.'

She bowed her head and sighed. 'I sometimes feel that I'm on the edge of some great truth. I get excited. I start scrawling the notes on the manuscript. I see the glow, the edge of the bright light where genius resides. I can never reach it completely. Maybe my excitement makes it ebb. The intense white light retreats, eludes me. I grow cold. I am left on the shore. No genius breakthrough tonight, just another symphony finished and my eyes are sore. It is happening more and more these days. I am getting older, and I no longer write from the heart. I'm getting older, Jant, and I will lose my genius. I'm still running the race; time is still burning down the bridges to things I could have achieved.' She burst into frightened tears.

'None of us can change the Castle,' I repeated.

'You immortals only exist because we allow you to,' she sobbed. 'If you're a ... barrier to me ... I'll make your life hard in the real world.'

Eleonora cut in, with a voice used to command battles and law courts. 'Spare us the vulgar threats, *Governor* Awndyn. There are not even a hundred immortals and you had one more chance to join them than the rest of us. You held out for yet another and lost both. Return to your music. We look forward to your next concert.'

Swallow swept the room with a look of pure hatred, took a step forward, hesitated, turned on her heel and stormed out. Her progress down the passageway was marked by a vase smashing every few metres. A little while later we heard the clop and crunch as her coach departed at a gallop. Silence returned.

Lightning sighed. 'I'd just had those replaced. The third time.'

I smiled. 'Well I'm sure you can afford to have them repaired. Or make some new replicas.'

'I don't think I'll bother this time. Time for a new look.'

'Lightning, are you sure?'

'Never more so. And you will all have to get used to calling me Saker.'

'I think people will still call you Lightning,' Eleonora said. 'And Lightning, I *do* want to escape.'

CHAPTER 27

Next morning I took breakfast in the Orangery. I sat at the round, polished table and pressed my toes into the soft moss that covered the ground like a carpet. An orange tree grew through a large hole in the centre of the table, over which its boughs hung low with fruit. The table was laden with all the foods that pass for breakfast in Awia, a variety far greater than I could actually eat. I had no appetite, I was thinking back to what happened the previous night. I still couldn't understand Lightning's volte-face. I felt an open rift in the centre of my being, as if he was already dead.

The sun shone through the glass wall which curved up to the panes of the ceiling. Black-painted wrought-iron flowers and tendrils spiralled from the curlicued frames, as if the struts of the glasshouse themselves were growing. More orange and lemon trees with smooth bark were rooted in the clean, deep moss all around me. The air was rich with scent.

An arcaded loggia passage connected the Orangery to the palace just behind me. In front, I looked out down the lawns to the shimmering lake. On the nearest end of the island the tops of tall monkey puzzle trees poked up from the dense woods extending to the shore, where a tiny jetty emerged.

The Queen of Awia appeared at the glass portal, kicked off her shoes and walked across the moss barefoot. As always she looked fantastic, elegant in cream suede, with her sword scabbard swapping the back of her legs. But beneath her soft feathers, her porcelain face and sepia eyes, I thought she was just another thick-skinned tart. She sat down beside me, so the orange tree didn't block her view of me. A servant appeared immediately and started loading her plate with kedgeree.

I said, 'The guests have gone. When are you leaving?'

'Me?' Eleonora laughed. 'Oh, no. I'm staying here for a while, Queen's prerogative. I'm going to do all I possibly can to impress him. And I'm well capable of that.'

I wondered how to warn him. I couldn't think how without incriminating myself. I said sarcastically, 'He'd be overwhelmingly impressed by dressage and the lash.'

'Do you think I can't change? If Lightning can, I can, of course. The Eleonora you saw won't be the one he sees. On the contrary, I intend to marry him.'

'What!'

She continued, 'But I won't hide all of my ... more wanton side. If I try

860

to act like a maiden, well, he might not like maidens, and that would be a great shame, wouldn't it?'

'Your talents lie elsewhere.'

She stifled a smile. 'You'd be surprised. It's difficult to break through his romantic pose but there's a real man under there. I've never met another with such a mix of strength, intelligence and perfect self-assurance. A real equal.'

'I don't want to know.'

'And he's better hung than you. You can tell from the crease of his trousers.'

'I *don't* want to know! I can't believe it! Imagine: sell all your antiques, Lightning, and redecorate with mirrors – Eleonora's moving in! All the servants must wear leather harnesses and nipple clips!'

She laughed. 'I'm not that bad.'

'Well, I don't *bloody* understand why he chose to lose the Challenge.'

'I think his leaving the Circle is a very clever move. When we marry, it will be the joining of the two greatest houses in Awia.'

'Oh, god ...' Realisation began to dawn.

'Think what he's doing. When Cyan becomes Eszai, she cannot inherit Peregrine manor, because the Emperor no longer allows immortals to own land. Lightning will keep Peregrine, so reuniting all the scattered lands of his original manor, which has always been his aim. When he marries me he'll regain Avernwater too, and we will possess all the manors of Awia except Carniss and Wrought. Lightning will not only have united his manor, but the whole of Awia. He will be King, as he should have been fourteen centuries ago. He can fulfil the role he had to relinquish when he joined the Circle, and bring the Micawater dynasty back to the throne, that has lain dormant with him so long. That's what he always wanted. It's a long time to wait. We will have a single great manor and Awia will have a degree of stability that has never been seen before. Never!'

'You're founding the first absolute monarchy in Awia.'

'Well done, Jant. You have figured out my aim, at least.'

It did not sound so good to me.

Eleonora added, 'The Emperor would be pleased.'

'Would he?'

'Of course. All the manors would be in Zascai hands.'

'Except Wrought.'

'Don't worry about Tern, I think that would suit San, too. He would like the Castle to keep some degree of control over the weaponsmiths. And with Lightning and I to lead the Awian fyrd, think of all the business they'll be getting! If Wrought is threatened by anything, it's the new industries in Hacilith.'

I felt nauseous, staring into the future of a new dynasty. The thought of Eleonora and *Lightning's* future generations, that I would have to watch, and to serve as an Eszai, for hundreds of years after them, terrified me.

'I feel time-sick,' I said. 'Who knows what will happen?'

'Whatever happens, you're shielded from it. Protected by the Castle's walls, you immortals experience the arrows of misfortune as nothing but a tickle, compared to us. You should even enjoy the experience, because you know you'll live long enough to see the wheel of fortune turn up once more. You might even see the system change yet again, from our dynasty – though I hope it won't.'

'What if Cyan is beaten and Lightning wants to rejoin the Circle?'

'He would bring me into the Circle too. We could stay together forever and I would be immortal as well. I've always fancied it.'

'But then you'd have to abdicate.'

'Yes, but we would crown Cyan Queen. Cyan, instead of us, would restart the Micawater dynasty. Lightning can't lose, really.'

'Providing Cyan complies with his wishes.'

'Oh, I think she will learn humility in the Circle. I think she would make a good Queen.'

'You can't tell what will happen, Eleonora.'

'No. But we welcome the uncertainty! Awia is free to change now. The role of Archer can change, too! Saker is no longer holding them back.' Eleonora took a forkful of kedgeree. 'And he has such a fantastic body.'

I looked at her, and her eyes were shining. It could be love, or it could be all that seafood.

Cyan was right; for all my show of independence, Lightning had been a father to me. Now with this sudden view of the future he daunted me even more. 'Where is he? I must speak to him,' I said, though without much relish.

'At the boathouse.' She pointed through the front windows. I put my boots on at the Orangery door and walked out.

On my way down to the lake, I threw up in a random corner of the ivy-clad stone staircase. Great, I thought; the vomit Comet is back.

The ground's spinning. Wow. It's been years since it did that. I felt amazing and I didn't care. I think I've come to terms with scolopendium. I've been drinking it for months without increasing the dose, so I was sure I could live this way.

This was the scolopendium I took from the barge – the drugs that Cyan bought. I've been taking a sip every day since I crash-landed; dissolved in wine in my hip flask. How else do you think I could keep going after the

Vermiform's assault? I know I told Rayne that I had thrown it in the fire, but I lied to her. I lied to you as well.

But that was my only lie. Trust me.

The glorious palace front was clear-cut against the sky. It looked as bizarre as a building from the Shift. But, I thought, ours was a Shift world as well, one of thousands in the continuum, and it was as strange and beautiful as the rest.

I looked for the window of our bedroom, on the second floor of the Eyas Wing, with its curtains drawn. I pictured Tern still asleep up there, her manicured hand brushing the coverlet.

Two floors below our window, Eleonora was eating breakfast alone, her feet on the cool, mossy ground. She suddenly feels indescribably happy. A beam of light sparkles on the lake, shines through the panes and dazzles the glasshouse. Her country! 'This place is great!' she says enthusiastically, puts down the coffee cup and decides to go for a ride.

On her way out she passes the bow store, where Harrier is sadly placing his master's bows back on their racks. His sense of disappointment has left him swirling with the current; Lightning's skill was a tenet of faith with him, because Harrier himself was a Challenger once. He pauses, then takes his own longbow from its case, holds it in both hands and presses it to his chest, thinking, why shouldn't I go and join the archers who'll soon be queuing up to Challenge Cyan? He starts to wipe the longbow down.

A hundred kilometres away, Cyan and Rayne in their coach are crossing out of Awia. Cyan is alternately crying and defiant. She is horrified by what she has done to her father, but she can see no way out. She would see it through to the conclusion. What else could she do? Ornate shadows lengthen behind the coach's intricate fretwork screens. 'Daddy lost deliberately,' she repeats.

'It crushes me, too.' Rayne bites her lip. 'But he gave you t' chance t' step ou' of his shadow and develop your own life. Establish your own name and identity. Isn' tha' wha' you wanted? Don' yield to preceden' and t' power of t' past. You'll forge' him, though I never will ... I'll think of him, sometime in t' far future.'

Rayne, when she arrives at the Castle, will visit Serein Wrenn, who is currently lying in the hospital mourning the loss of his foot and his friend. He glances up when Mist Fulmer comes in, bringing a tray of beer and cakes. Mist cheers him up by telling him he can still take the wheel of the caravel *Windhover*, on the bright ocean out of Tanager.

Mist walks back to his room via the Breckan Wing roof walk, looking out over the parapet across the plains. 'At least I'm still here,' he says. 'In this great place.'

In the chamber below his feet, those of Tornado are being massaged by his new girlfriend. Sleat in his room is busy polishing armour but looks up and sees them, tiny figures in the window of the opposite building. Tornado and his girlfriend disappear, rolling off the bed and pulling the covers with them.

'What was that thump?' thinks the Cook, looking up. Never mind. He checks his watch; he doesn't have much time. He takes his jacket and hastens out of the ground floor of Breckan, across to the kitchens. The clockwork of the Castle ticks steadily, it pushes years around; the slow hand – centuries.

The Cook hangs up his jacket and begins to prepare a fulsome feast for Cyan Lightning. His kitchens are shaded by the towering Throne Room. When Cyan is made immortal, the Eszai will convene inside, where for ever and ever, the Emperor San is sitting on his throne.

CHAPTER 28

Lightning, his shirt sleeves rolled up to the elbow, was pushing a flat-bottomed boat over the grass towards a slipway and landing stage jutting out into the lake. He saw me coming towards him, straightened up and wiped his hands. 'Good morning, Jant. Will you give me a hand with this punt?'

We pushed the boat to the top of the slipway, settling it onto the metal rollers. 'What are you doing?'

He slid a punt pole out from under its benches. 'I'm going to the island. To see Martyn, you know. I am going to visit her one last time and explain what has happened. I will say goodbye to her and take my leave. I do not think I will need to visit her again.' He smiled sadly.

'I must go back to the Castle, for the ceremony,' I said.

'Of course. In two days' time, when I feel the Circle drop me, I think it will be a fraught moment ... I will need to be alone.'

'Be careful of Eleonora. She ... well, she ...'

He raised an eyebrow.

'I think she ... you, er ... she said ...'

'I can handle her. She gave me cause for hope, when Swallow had not. I'd like to pretend I never noticed her while I was engaged to Swallow but time is now too precious for me to hide from myself.'

Could he really be capable of leaving his palace to chance and future generations, whether his offspring or not? I raised a hand to it. 'Imagine that ruined, all the treasures gone, the roof falling in. How can you tell they won't squander it?'

'I think Cyan will look after it. But if not ... Look, Jant; who knows what changes she'll make and what innovations subsequent Lightnings will come up with? Who knows what the discipline of archery will turn into? To think, your Vermiform even laughed at our weapons.'

I understood, though it frightened me. A future without the constraints of Lightning's authority will be uncertain, but it would be more free.

'I'm free to change, too.' His eyes sparkled. 'I have to adapt, and come to terms with these different times. I'm looking forward to the coming of the modern world.'

I pleaded, 'You could return to the Circle. If not as Archer, as Swordsman. Wrenn's been maimed and you're officially the second-best.'

'But I don't feel like Challenging my friend. I no longer feel the lure of the Castle. Isn't it fabulous!'

'I barely understand.'

A breeze gusted across the grounds, cooling my face; followed by the low rumble of thunder over Donaise. Saker looked out at the ruffled water. 'Jant, I remember when you joined the Circle. I was afraid of you.'

'No!'

'Yes. I was living here and I hadn't done anything new for a hundred years. I had settled into a rut. Rayne sent me a letter saying, "Come and look at the man who can fly!" But it's impossible for a man to fly. You stormed the Circle. I remember you standing on the spire to show us all what you can do. You dived off and we gasped. We thought you'd be killed for certain. But you swooped over the bonfire and vanished up into the sky. I was so shocked, so inspired! I thought I'd seen everything, but you reminded me there was yet more. There will always be more. Thank you, Jant. I hope I have opened your eyes in the same way.'

I nodded, speechless. I hoped being tongue-tied wasn't going to become a habit.

'Then I saw you become disenchanted, and we know what you're like now with the drugs. Try not to be disillusioned; it's a fate worse than death. You proved that all your other worlds exist. San knew all the time your drug-fantasies were real.' He shook his head in wonder.

'The Shift?' Yes, I wanted to talk to him about that. I said, 'Remember Dunlin?'

'The last of the Rachiswaters?'

'He is in the Shift. Don't ask me how, because it's a long story. But if you grow old, and at the very end of your life you don't want to die, then you can Shift. Take scolopendium – I'll make it for you – and you can go through and join Dunlin. And if you're mortally wounded while fighting the Insects, I can ask Rayne to give you enough scolopendium to Shift. That's more or less what happened to him.'

There was a long pause. Lightning said thoughtfully, 'Jant, do you know your power?'

'Huh?'

'Rhydanne are such a curious people. You have such a clever mind, yet you never see the bigger picture.'

'What? The Shift? They're just other worlds, a bit different from here.'

'No, I didn't mean that ... No wonder San doesn't want you cornered ... but don't you realise the Emperor is scared of the Shift? I can tell you that much. He knows about things which he really doesn't want you to bring back, even if they followed you accidentally.'

'What? The Gabbleratchet?'

Lightning shrugged. 'He didn't say. Besides, I know San doesn't want the truth to be widely known in case people start trying to go there themselves instead of staying here to fight the Insects.'

866

'There are Insects there as well. And worse.'

'Ah, so many new secrets I'm learning – it's a whole new world ... Will you do something for me, Jant?'

'Yes.'

'Will you look after Cyan? When she becomes immortal, will you guide her the way I have guided you? You've seen so much trouble yourself, you should know how to keep her out of it.'

'That's very clever. She's inheriting your place in the Circle.'

'Yes. When she is in the Circle she'll become part of the establishment and she won't be able to be rebellious any longer.'

I said, 'In fact, she's submitting to a much higher authority in order to escape yours.'

'Well, she hasn't realised it yet. Even if it's just for a short time, it'll do her good.'

In turn, Lightning had cast off the Emperor's authority. This was *his* teen-age rebellion, and San knew it was time to let him leave. He looked stronger and more confident than ever.

'All right,' I said. 'I'll look after Cyan.' He had saddled me with the girl, given me a wayward subordinate to look after. I can't sleep with her now, can I?

'Thank you, Jant.'

Incredibly, there had been nine new Eszai in the last ten years. I was one of the older ones now, having to give advice to the new immortals. I hated that, but with a tired resignation I didn't see that I could do anything about it. 'Now *I'm* becoming part of the establishment,' I said.

Lightning grinned. 'It is the inevitable process.'

'I never thought it would happen to me but it's happening at last. I'd never have the guts to leave. I barely understand it.'

'You can't. You're too young.' He stepped up onto the covered stern and I passed him the punt pole. 'When you put another thousand years between yourself and your past, you'll understand.'

'I'll never leave the Circle, Saker,' I said with conviction.

He smiled. 'Look after Cyan. She'll need it.'

'I will.'

He held the pole up and rocked his weight forward, enough to tip the boat onto the slipway. It ran down, spinning the rollers, and splashed into the lake, sending out a wave before it. A cloud of glittering specks rose up from the silt.

Lightning dug the pole in. Standing tall on the back of the boat, he pushed calmly away from the shore without a backward glance. I remained looking out in the direction of the island for a long time after, when he had gone.

A big thank you to all the people I used to go caving with. Thank you to CU Hang Gliding Club and Blooners 2000 Hot Air Balloon Company for helping me see the Yorkshire Dales and the Chiltern Hills from the air. Thanks to the Yorkshire Dales Falconry and Conservation Centre for days out hawking. Thank you to Dr Jo Cooper, curator at the Natural History Museum Bird Group at Tring, for letting me view the awe-inspiring collections, and to Alison Harding for letting me play with the Ornithology Library. Many thanks to Stella Swainston for details of PSU Riot Procedure, shield instruction and equipment, used in my fyrd shield walls. Thanks to Dr Marco de Boni for memorably explaining hand-to-hand combat in between mouthfuls of pizza. Thanks, John Berlyne. Thank you, Mac and Jenny. Above all, love and thanks to Brian, without whom none of this would have been possible.

Look out for the forthcoming prequel to the Castle series

ABOVE THE SNOWLINE

Coming in 2010 from Gollancz